THE COURTNEYS

The novels of Wilbur Smith

The Courtneys:
When the Lion Feeds
The Sound of Thunder
A Sparrow Falls

The Courtneys of Africa:
The Burning Shore
Power of the Sword
Rage
A Time to Die

The Ballantyne novels:
A Falcon Flies
Men of Men
The Angels Weep
The Leopard Hunts in Darkness

Also:
The Dark of the Sun
Shout at the Devil
Gold Mine
The Diamond Hunters
The Sunbird
Eagle in the Sky
The Eye of the Tiger
Cry Wolf
Hungry as the Sea
Wild Justice
Golden Fox
Elephant Song

The Courtneys

WILBUR SMITH

When the Lion Feeds
The Sound of Thunder
A Sparrow Falls

HEINEMANN : LONDON

When the Lion Feeds
First published 1964

The Sound of Thunder
First published 1966

A Sparrow Falls
First published 1977

Three novels first published as one volume in 1987
as *The Courtneys*
by William Heinemann Ltd
an imprint of Reed Consumer Books Ltd
Michelin House, 81 Fulham Road, London SW3 6RB
and Auckland, Melbourne, Singapore and Toronto

Reissued 1994

Copyright © Wilbur Smith 1964, 1966, 1977, 1987, 1994

A CIP catalogue record for this title
is available from the British Library

ISBN 0 434 00091 4

Printed in England by Clays Ltd, St Ives plc

When the Lion Feeds

This book is for
ELFREDA AND HERBERT JONES SMITH

I. NATAL

I

A single wild pheasant flew up the side of the hill almost brushing the tips of the grass in its flight. It drooped its wings and hung its legs as it reached the crest and then dropped into cover. Two boys and a dog followed it up from the valley: the dog led, with his tongue flopping pink from the corner of his mouth, and the twins ran shoulder to shoulder behind him. Both of them were sweating in dark patches through the khaki shirts, for the African sun still had heat although it stood half-mast down the sky.

The dog hit the scent of the bird and it stopped him quivering: for a second he stood sucking it up through his nostrils, and then he started to quarter. He worked fast, back and forth, swinging at the end of each tack, his head down and only his back and his busy tail showing above the dry brown grass. The twins came up behind him. They were gasping for breath, for it had been a hard pull up the curve of the hill.

'Keep out to the side, you'll get in my way,' Sean panted at his brother and Garrick moved to obey. Sean was his senior by four inches in height and twenty pounds in weight: this gave him the right to command. Sean transferred his attention back to the dog.

'Put him up, Tinker. Seek him up, boy.'

Tinker's tail acknowledged Sean's instructions, but he held his nose to the ground. The twins followed him, tensed for the bird to rise. They carried their throwing sticks ready and moved forward a stealthy pace at a time, fighting to control their breathing. Tinker found the bird crouched flat in the grass; he jumped forward giving tongue for the first time, and the bird rose. It came up fast on noisy wings, whirling out of the grass.

Sean threw; his kerrie whipped past it. The pheasant swung away from the stick, clawing at the air with frantic wings, and Garrick threw. His kerrie cartwheeled up, hissing, until it smacked into the pheasant's fat brown body. The bird toppled, feathers flurried from it and it fell. They went after it. The pheasant scurried broken-winged through the grass ahead of them, and they shouted with excitement as they chased it. Sean got a hand to it. He broke its neck and stood laughing, holding the warm brown body in his hands, and waited for Garrick to reach him.

'Ring-a-ding-a-doody, Garry, you sure gave that one a beauty!'

Tinker jumped up to smell the bird, and Sean stooped and held it so he could get his nose against it. Tinker snuffled it, then tried to take it in his mouth, but Sean pushed his head away and tossed the bird to Garrick. Garrick hung it with the others on his belt.

'How far do you reckon that was—fifty feet?' Garrick asked.

'Not as much as that,' Sean gave his opinion. 'More like thirty.'

'I reckon it was at least fifty. I reckon it was farther than any you've hit today.' Success had made Garrick bold. The smile faded from Sean's face.

'Yeah?' he asked.

'Yeah!' said Garrick. Sean pushed the hair off his forehead with the back of his hand, his hair was black and soft and it kept falling into his eyes.

'What about that one down by the river? That was twice as far.'

'Yeah?' asked Garrick.

'Yeah!' said Sean truculently.

'Well, if you're so good, how did you miss this one–hey? You threw first. How come you missed, hey?'

Sean's already flushed faced darkened and Garrick realized suddenly that he had gone too far. He took a step backwards.

'You'd like to bet?' demanded Sean. It was not quite clear to Garrick on what Sean wished to bet, but from past experience he knew that whatever it was the issue would be settled by single combat. Garrick seldom won bets from Sean.

'It's too late. We'd better be getting home. Pa will clobber us if we're late for dinner.' Sean hesitated and Garrick turned, ran back to pick up his kerrie then set off in the direction of home. Sean trotted after him, caught up with him and passed him. Sean always led. Having proved conclusively his superior prowess with the throwing sticks Sean was prepared to be forgiving. Over his shoulder he asked, 'What colour to you reckon Gypsy's foal will be?'

Garrick accepted the peace-offering with relief and they fell into a friendly discussion of this and a dozen other equally important subjects. They kept running: except for an hour, when they had stopped in a shady place by the river to roast and eat a couple of their pheasants, they had run all day.

Up here on the plateau it was grassland that rose and fell beneath them as they climbed the low round hills and dropped into the valleys. The grass around them moved with the wind: waist-high grass, soft dry grass the colour of ripe wheat. Behind them and on each side the grassland rolled away to the full range of the eye, but suddenly in front of them was the escarpment. The land cascaded down into it, steeply at first then gradually levelling out to become the Tugela flats. The Tugela river was twenty miles away across the flats, but today there was a haze in the air so they could not see that far. Beyond the river, stretched far to the north and a hundred miles east to the sea, was Zululand. The river was the border. The steep side of the escarpment was cut by vertical gulleys, and in the gulleys grew dense, olive-green bush.

Below them, two miles out on the flats, was the homestead of Theunis Kraal. The house was a big one, Dutch-gabled and smoothly thatched with combed grass. There were horses in the small paddock: many horses, for the twins' father was a wealthy man. Smoke from the cooking fires blued the air over the servants' quarters and the sound of someone chopping wood carried faintly up to them.

Sean stopped on the rim of the escarpment and sat down in the grass. He took hold of one of his grimy bare feet and twisted it up into his lap. There was a hole in the ball of his heel from which he had pulled a thorn earlier in the day and now it was plugged with dirt. Garrick sat down next to him.

'Man, is that going to hurt when Ma puts iodine on it!' gloated Garrick. 'She'll have to use a needle to get the dirt out. I bet you yell–I bet you yell your head off!'

Sean ignored him. He picked a stalk of grass and started probing it into the wound. Garrick watched with interest. Twins could scarcely have been less alike. Sean was already taking on the shape of a man: his shoulders were thickening, and there was hard muscle forming in his puppy fat. His colouring was vivid: black hair, skin brown from the sun, lips and cheeks that glowed with the fresh young blood beneath their surface, and blue eyes, the dark indigo-blue of cloud shadow on mountain lake.

Garrick was slim, with the wrists and ankles of a girl. His hair was an undecided brown that grew wispy down the back of his neck, his skin was freckled, his nose and the rims of his pale blue eyes were pink with persistent hayfever. He was fast losing interest in Sean's surgery. He reached across and fiddled with one of Tinker's pendulous ears, and this broke the rhythm of the dog's panting; he gulped twice and the saliva dripped from the end of his tongue. Garrick lifted his head and looked down the slope. A little below where they were sitting was the head of one of the bushy gullies. Garrick caught his breath.

'Sean, look there—next to the bush!' His whisper trembled with excitement.

'What's it?' Sean looked up startled. Then he saw it.

'Hold Tinker.' Garrick grabbed the dog's collar and pulled his head around to prevent him seeing and giving chase. 'He's the biggest old inkonka in the world,' breathed Garrick. Sean was too absorbed to answer.

The bushbuck was picking its way warily out of the thick cover. A big ram, black with age; the spots on his haunches were faded like old chalk marks. His ears pricked up and his spiral horns held high, big as a pony, but stepping daintily, he came out into the open. He stopped and swung his head from side to side, searching for danger, then he trotted diagonally down the hill and disappeared into another of the gullies. For a moment after he had gone the twins were still, then they burst out together.

'Did you see him, hey—did you see them horns?'

'So close to the house and we never knew he was there—'

They scrambled to their feet jabbering at each other, and Tinker was infected with their excitement. He barked around them in a circle. After the first few moments of confusion Sean took control simply by raising his voice above the opposition.

'I bet he hides up in the gulley every day. I bet he stays there all day and comes out only at night. Let's go and have a look.'

Sean led the way down the slope.

On the fringe of the bush, in a small cave of vegetation that was dark and cool and carpeted with dead leaves, they found the ram's hiding-place. The ground was trampled by his hooves and scattered with his droppings and there was the mark of his body where he had lain. A few loose hairs, tipped with grey, were left on the bed of leaves. Sean knelt down and picked one up.

'How are we going to get him?'

'We could dig a hole and put sharpened sticks in it,' suggested Garrick eagerly.

'Who's going to dig it—you?' Sean asked.

'You could help.'

'It would have to be a pretty big hole,' said Sean doubtfully. There was silence while both of them considered the amount of labour involved in digging a trap. Neither of them mentioned the idea again.

'We could get the other kids from town and have a drive with kerries,' said Sean.

'How many hunts have we been on with them? Must be hundreds by now, and we haven't even bagged one lousy duiker—let alone a bushbuck.' Garrick

hesitated and then went on. 'Besides, remember what that inkonka did to
Frank Van Essen, hey? When it finished sticking him they had to push all his
guts back into the hole in his stomach!'

'Are you scared?' asked Sean.

'I am not, so!' said Garrick indignantly, then quickly, 'Gee, it's almost dark.
We'd better run.'

They went down the valley.

2

Sean lay in the darkness and stared across the room at the grey oblong of the
window. There was a slice of moon in the sky outside. Sean could not sleep: he
was thinking about the bushbuck. He heard his parents pass the door of the
bedroom; his stepmother said something and his father laughed: Waite
Courteney had a laugh as deep as distant thunder.

Sean heard the door of their room close and he sat up in bed. 'Garry.' No
answer.

'Garry.' He picked up a boot and threw it; there was a grunt. 'Garry.'

'What you want?' Garrick's voice was sleepy and irritable.

'I was just thinking—tomorrow's Friday.'

'So?'

'Ma and Pa will be going into town. They'll be away all day. We could take
the shotgun and go lay for that old inkonka.'

Garrick's bed creaked with alarm.

'You're mad!' Garrick could not keep the shock out of his voice. 'Pa would
kill us if he caught us with the shotgun.' Even as he said it he knew he would
have to find a stronger argument than that to dissuade his brother. Sean
avoided punishment if possible, but a chance at a bushbuck ram was worth all
his father's right arm could give. Garrick lay rigid in his bed, searching for
words.

'Besides, Pa keeps the cartridges locked up.'

It was a good try, but Sean countered it.

'I know where there are two buckshots that he has forgotten about: they're
in the big vase in the dining-room. They've been there over a month.'

Garrick was sweating. He could almost feel the sjambok curling round his
buttocks, and hear his father counting the strokes: eight, nine, ten.

'Please, Sean, let's think of something else. . . .'

Across the room Sean settled back comfortably on his pillows. The decision
had been made.

3

Waite Courtney handed his wife up into the front seat of the buggy. He patted
her arm affectionately then walked around to the driver's side, pausing to
fondle the horses and settle his hat down over his bald head. He was a big man,
the buggy dipped under his weight as he climbed up into the seat. He gathered
up the reins, then he turned and his eyes laughed over his great hooked nose at

the twins standing together on the veranda.

'I would esteem it a favour if you two gentlemen could arrange to stay out of trouble for the few hours that your mother and I will be away.'

'Yes, Pa,' in dutiful chorus.

'Sean, if you get the urge to climb the big blue gum tree again then fight it, man, fight it.'

'All right, Pa.'

'Garrick, let us have no more experiments in the manufacture of gunpowder—agreed?'

'Yes, Pa.'

'And don't look so innocent. That really frightens the hell out of me!'

Waite touched the whip to the shiny round rumps in front of him and the buggy started forward, out along the road to Ladyburg.

'He didn't say anything about not taking the shotgun,' whispered Sean virtuously. 'Now you go and see if all the servants are out of the way—if they see us, they'll kick up a fuss. Then come round to the bedroom window and I'll pass it out to you.'

Sean and Garrick argued all the way to the foot of the escarpment. Sean was carrying the shotgun across one shoulder, hanging on to the butt with both hands.

'It was my idea, wasn't it?' he demanded.

'But I saw the inkonka first,' protested Garrick. Garrick was bold again: with every yard put between him and the house his fear of reprisal faded.

'That doesn't count,' Sean informed him. 'I thought of the shotgun, so I do the shooting.'

'How come you always have the fun?' asked Garrick, and Sean was outraged at the question.

'When you found the hawk's nest by the river, I let you climb for it. Didn't I? When you found the baby duiker, I let you feed it. Didn't I?' he demanded.

'All right. So I saw the inkonka first, why don't you let me take the shot?'

Sean was silent in the face of such stubbornness, but his grip on the butt of the shotgun tightened. In order to win the argument Garrick would have to get it away from him—this Garrick knew and he started to sulk. Sean stopped among the trees at the foot of the escarpment and looked over his shoulder at his brother.

'Are you going to help or must I do it alone?'

Garrick looked down at the ground and kicked at a twig. He sniffed wetly; his hayfever was always bad in the mornings.

'Well?' asked Sean.

'What do you want me to do?'

'Stay here and count to a thousand slowly. I'm going to circle up the slope and wait where the inkonka crossed yesterday. When you finish counting come up the gulley. Start shouting when you are about halfway up. The inkonka will break the same way as yesterday—all right?'

Garrick nodded reluctantly

'Did you bring Tinker's chain?'

Garrick pulled it from his pocket, and at the sight of it the dog backed away. Sean grabbed his collar, and Garrick slipped it on. Tinker laid his ears flat and looked at them reproachfully.

'Don't let him go. That old inkonka will rip him up. Now start counting,' said Sean and began climbing. He kept well out to the left of the gulley. The grass on the slope was slippery under his feet, the gun was heavy and there was sharp lumps of rock in the grass. He stubbed his toe and it started to bleed, but he kept on upwards. There was a dead tree on the edge of the bush that Sean had used to mark the bushbuck's hide. Sean climbed above it and stopped just below the crest of the slope where the moving grass would break up the silhouette of his head on the skyline. He was panting. He found a rock the size of a beer barrel to use as a rest for the gun, and he crouched behind it. He laid the stock of the gun on the rock, aimed back down the hill and traversed the barrels left and right to make sure his field of fire was clear. He imagined the bushbuck running in his sights and he felt excitement shiver along his forearms, across his shoulders and up to the back of his neck.

'I won't lead on him—he'll be moving fairly slowly, trotting most probably. I'll go straight at his shoulders,' he whispered.

He opened the gun, took the two cartridges out of his shirt pocket, slid them into the breeches and snapped the gun closed. It took all the strength of both his hands to pull back the big fancy hammers, but he managed it and the gun was double-loaded and cocked. He laid it on the rock in front of him again and stared down the slope. On his left the gulley was a dark-green smear on the hillside, directly below him was open grass where the bushbuck would cross. He pushed impatiently at the hair of his forehead: it was damp with sweat and stayed up out of his eyes.

The minutes drifted by.

'What the hell is Garry doing? He's so stupid sometimes!' Sean muttered and almost in answer he heard Garrick shout below him. It was a small sound, far down the slope and muffled by the bush. Tinker barked once without enthusiasm; he was also sulking, he didn't like the chain. Sean waited for his forefinger on one trigger, staring down at the edge of the bush. Garrick shouted again—and the bushbuck broke from cover.

It came fast into the open with its nose up and its long horns held flat against its back. Sean moved his body sideways swinging the gun with its run, riding the pip of the foresight on its black shoulder. He fired the left barrel and the recoil threw him off balance; his ears hummed with the shot and the burnt powder smoke blew back into his face. He struggled to his feet still holding the gun. The bushbuck was down in the grass, bleating like a lamb and kicking as it died.

'I got him,' screamed Sean. 'I got him first shot! Garry, Garry! I got him, I got him!'

Tinker came pelting out of the bush dragging Garry behind him by the chain and, still screaming, Sean ran down to join them. A stone rolled under his foot and he fell. The shotgun flew out of his hand and the second barrel fired. The sound of the explosion was very loud.

When Sean scrambled on to his feet again Garrick was sitting in the grass whimpering—whimpering and staring at his leg. The blast of the shotgun had smashed into it and churned the flesh below the knee into tatters—bursting it open so the bone chips showed white in the wood and the blood pumped dark and strong and thick as custard.

'I didn't mean it. . . . Oh God, Garry, I didn't mean it. I slipped. Honest, I slipped.' Sean was staring at the leg also. There was no colour in his face, his eyes were big and dark with horror. The blood pumped out on to the grass.

'Stop it bleeding! Sean, please stop it. Oh, it's sore! Oh! Sean, please stop it!'

Sean stumbled across to him. He wanted to vomit. He unbuckled his belt and strapped it round the leg, and the blood was warm and sticky on his hands. He used his sheathed knife to twist the belt tight. The pumping slowed and he twisted harder.

'Oh, Sean, it's sore! It's sore. . . .' Garrick's face was waxy-white and he was starting to shiver as the cold hand of shock closed on him.

'I'll get Joseph,' Sean stammered. 'We'll come back quickly as we can. Oh, God, I'm sorry!' Sean jumped up and ran. He fell, rolled to his feet and kept running.

They came within an hour. Sean was leading three of the Zulu servants. Joseph, the cook, had brought a blanket. He wrapped Garrick and lifted him and Garrick fainted as his leg swung loosely. As they started back down the hill Sean looked out across the flats: there was a little puff of dust on the Ladyburg road. One of the grooms was riding to fetch Waite Courtney.

They were waiting on the veranda of the homestead when Waite Courtney came back to Theunis Kraal. Garrick was conscious again. He lay on' the couch: his face was white and the blood had soaked through the blanket. There was blood on Joseph's uniform and blood had dried black on Sean's hands. Waite Courtney ran on to the veranda; he stooped over Garrick and drew back the blanket. For a second he stood staring at the leg and then very gently he covered it again.

Waite lifted Garrick and carried him down to the buggy. Joseph went with him and they settled Garrick on the back seat. Joseph held his body and Garrick's stepmother took the leg on her lap to stop it twisting. Waite Courtney climbed quickly into the driver's seat: he picked up the reins, then he turned his head and looked at Sean still standing on the veranda. He didn't speak, but his eyes were terrible—Sean could not meet them. Waite Courtney used the whip on the horses and drove them back along the road to Ladyburg: he drove furiously with the wind streaming his beard back from his face.

Sean watched them go. After they had disappeared among the trees he remained standing alone on the veranda; then suddenly he turned and ran back through the house. He ran out of the kitchen door and across the yard to the saddle-room, snatched a bridle down from the rack and ran to the paddock. He picked a bay mare and worked her into a corner of the fence until he could slip his arm around her neck. He forced the bit into her mouth, buckled the chin strap and swung up on to her bare back.

He kicked her into a run and put her to the gate, swaying back as her body heaved up under him and falling forward on her neck as she landed. He gathered himself and turned her head towards the Ladyburg road.

It was eight miles to town, and the buggy reached it before Sean. He found it outside Doctor Van Rooyen's surgery: the horses were blowing hard, and their bodies were dark with sweat. Sean slid down off the mare's back; he went up the steps to the surgery door and quietly pushed it open. There was the sweet reek of chloroform in the room. Garrick lay on the table, Waite and his wife stood on each side of him, and the doctor was washing his hands in an enamel basin against the far wall. Ada Courtney was crying silently, her face blurred with tears. They all looked at Sean standing in the doorway.

'Come here,' said Waite Courtney, his voice flat and expressionless. 'Come and stand here beside me. They're going to cut off your brother's leg and, by Christ, I'm going to make you watch every second of it!'

4

They brought Garrick back to Theunis Kraal in the night. Waite Courtney drove the buggy very slowly and carefully and Sean trailed a long way behind it. He was cold in his thin khaki shirt, and sick in the stomach with what he had seen. There were bruises on his upper arm where his father had held him and forced him to watch.

The servants had lanterns burning on the veranda. They were standing in the shadows, silent and anxious. As Waite carried the blanket-wrapped body up the front steps one of them called softly in the Zulu tongue. 'The leg?'

'It is gone,' Waite answered gruffly.

They sighed softly all together and the voice called again. 'He is well?'

'He is alive,' said Waite.

He carried Garrick through to the room that was set aside for guests and sickness. He stood in the centre of the floor holding the boy while his wife put fresh sheets on the bed; then he laid him down and covered him.

'Is there anything else we can do?' asked Ada.

'We can wait.'

Ada groped for her husband's hand. 'Please, God, let him live,' she whispered. 'He's so young.'

'It's Sean's fault!' Waite's anger flared up suddenly. 'Garry would never had done it on his own.' He tried to disengage Ada's hand.

'What are you going to do?' she asked.

'I'm going to beat him! I'm going to thrash the skin off him!'

'Don't, please don't.'

'What do you mean?'

'He's had enough. Didn't you see his face?'

Waite's shoulders sagged wearily and he sat down on the armchair beside the bed. Ada touched his cheek.

'I'll stay here with Garry. You go and try to get some sleep, my dear.'

'No,' Waite said. She sat down on the side of the chair and Waite put his arm around her waist. After a long while they slept, huddled together on the chair beside the bed.

5

The days that followed were bad. Garrick's mind escaped from the harness of sanity and ran wild into the hot land of delirium. He panted and twisted his fever-flushed face from side to side; he cried and whimpered in the big bed; the stump of his leg puffed up angrily and the stitches were drawn so tight it seemed they must tear out of the swollen flesh. The infection oozed yellow and foul-smelling on to the sheets.

Ada stayed by him all that time. She swabbed the sweat from his face and changed the dressings on his stump, she held the glass for him to drink and gentled him when he raved. Her eyes sunk darkly into their sockets with fatigue and worry, but she would not leave him. Waite could not bear it. He had the masculine dread of suffering that threatened to suffocate him if he stayed in the room: every half hour or so he came in and stood next to the bed and then he turned away and went back to his restless wandering around the house. Ada could hear his heavy tramp along the corridors.

Sean stayed in the house also: he sat in the kitchen or at the far end of the veranda. No one would speak to him, not even the servants; they chased him when he tried to sneak into the bedroom to see Garrick. He was lonely with the desolate loneliness of the guilty—for Garry was going to die, he knew it by the evil silence that hung over Theunis Kraal. There was no chatter nor pot-clatter from the kitchens, no rich deep laughter from his father: even the dogs were subdued. Death was at Theunis Kraal. He could smell it on the soiled sheets that were brought through to the kitchen from Garrick's room; it was a musky smell, the smell of an animal. Sometimes he could almost see it: even in bright daylight sitting on the veranda he sensed it crouched near him like a shadow on the edge of his vision. It had no form as yet. It was a darkness, a coldness that was gradually building up around the house, gathering its strength until it could take his brother.

On the third day Waite Courtney came roaring out of Garrick's room. He ran through the house and out into the stable yard. 'Karlie. Where are you? Get a saddle on to Rooiberg. Hurry, man, hurry—damn you. He's dying, do you hear me, he's dying.'

Sean did not move from where he sat against the wall next to the back door. His arm tightened around Tinker's neck and the dog touched his cheek with a cold nose; he watched his father jump up on to the stallion's back and ride. The hooves beat away towards Ladyburg and when they were gone he stood up and slipped into the house: he listened outside Garrick's door and then he opened it quietly and went in. Ada turned towards him, her face was tired. She looked much older than her thirty-five years, but her black hair was drawn back behind her head into a neat bun and her dress was fresh and clean. She was still a beautiful woman despite her exhaustion. There was a gentleness about her, a goodness that suffering and worry could not destroy. She held out her hand to Sean and he crossed and stood beside her chair and looked down at Garrick. Then he knew why his father had gone to fetch the doctor. Death was in the room—strong and icy cold hovered over the bed. Garrick lay very ill: his face was yellow, his eyes were closed and his lips were cracked and dry.

All the loneliness and the guilt came swelling up into Sean's throat and choked him into sobs, sobs that forced him to his knees and he put his face into Ada's lap and cried. He cried for the last time in his life, he cried as a man cries—painfully, each sob tearing something inside him.

Waite Courtney came back from Ladyburg with the doctor. Once more Sean was driven out and the door closed. All night he heard them working in Garrick's room, the murmuring of their voices and the scuff of feet on the yellow wood floor. In the morning it was over. The fever was broken and Garrick was alive. Only just alive—his eyes were sunk into dark holes like those of a skull. His body and his mind were never to recover completely from that brutal pruning.

It was slow a week before he was strong enough to feed himself. His first need was for his brother, before he was able to talk above a whisper it was, 'Where's Sean?'

And Sean, still chastened, sat with him for hours at a time. Then when Garrick slept Sean escaped from the room, and with a fishing-rod or his hunting sticks and Tinker barking behind him went into the veld. It was a measure of Sean's repentance that he allowed himself to be contained within the sick-room for such long periods. It chafed him like ropes on a young colt: no one would ever know what it cost him to sit quietly next to Garrick's bed while his body itched and burned with unexpended energy and his mind raced restlessly.

Then Sean had to go back to school. He left on a Monday morning while it was still dark. Garrick listened to the sounds of departure, the whicker of the horses outside on the driveway and Ada's voice reciting last minute instructions: 'I've put a bottle of cough mixture under your shirts, give it to Fraülein as soon as you unpack. Then she'll see that you take it at the first sign of a cold.'

'Yes, Ma.'

'There are six vests in the small case—use a new one every day.'

'Vests are sissy things.'

'You will do as you're told, young man.' Waite's voice, 'Hurry up with your porridge—we've got to get going if I'm to have you in town by seven o'clock.'

'Can I say goodbye to Garry?'

'You said goodbye last night—he'll still be asleep now.'

Garrick opened his mouth to call out, but he knew his voice would not carry. He lay quietly and listened to the chairs scraping back from the dining-room table, the procession of footsteps out on to the veranda, voices raised in farewells and at last the wheels of the buggy crunching gravel as they moved away down the drive. It was very quiet after Sean had left with his father.

After that the weekends were, for Garrick, the only bright spots in the colourless passage of time. He longed for them to come, and each one was an eternity after the last—time passes slowly for the young and the sick. Ada and Waite knew a little of how he felt. They moved the centre of the household to his room: they brought two of the fat leather armchairs from the lounge and put them on each side of his bed and they spent the evenings there. Waite with his pipe in his mouth and a glass of brandy at his elbow, whittling at the wooden leg he was making and laughing his deep laugh, Ada with her knitting and the two of them trying to reach him. Perhaps it was this conscious effort that was the cause of their failure, or perhaps it is impossible to reach back down the years to a small boy. There is always that reserve, the barrier between the adult and the secret world of youth. Garrick laughed with them and they talked together, but it was not the same as having Sean there. During the day Ada had the running of a large household and there were fifteen thousand acres of land and two thousand head of cattle that needed Waite's attention. That was the loneliest time for Garrick. If it had not been for the books, he might not have been able to bear it. He read everything that Ada brought to him: Stevenson, Swift, Defoe, Dickens and even Shakespeare. Much of it he didn't understand, but he read hungrily and the opium of the printed word helped him through the long days until Sean came home each Friday.

When Sean came home it was like a big wind blowing through the house. Doors slammed, dogs barked, servants scolded and feet clattered up and down the passages. Most of the noise was Sean's, but not all of it. There were Sean's followers: youngsters from his class at the village school. They accepted Sean's authority as willingly as did Garrick, and it was not only Sean's fists that won this acceptance but also the laughter and the sense of excitement that went with him. They came out to Theunis Kraal in droves that summer, sometimes as many as three oń one bare-backed pony: sitting like a row of sparrows on a fence rail. They came for the added attraction of Garry's stump. Sean was very proud of it.

'That's where the doc sewed it up,' pointing to the row of stitch marks along the pink fold of scar tissue.

'Can I touch it, man?'

'Not too hard or it'll burst open.' Garrick had never received attention like this in his life before. He beamed round the circle of solemn, wide-eyed faces.

'It feels funny—sort of hot.'

'Was it sore?'

'How did he chop the bone—with an axe?'

'No.' Sean was the only one in a position to answer technical questions of this nature. 'With a saw. Just like a piece of wood.' He made the motions with his open hand.

But even this fascinating subject couldn't hold them for long and presently there would be a restlessness among them.

'Hey, Sean, Karl and I know where there's a nest of squawkers—you wanta have a look?' or 'Let's go and catch frogs,' and Garrick would cut in desperately.

'You can have a look at my stamp collection if you like. It's in the cupboard there.'

'Naw, we saw it last week. Let's go.'

This was when Ada, who had been listening to the conversation through the open kitchen door, brought in the food. Koeksusters fried in honey, chocolate cakes with peppermint icing, watermelon konfyt and half a dozen other delicacies. She knew they wouldn't leave until it was finished and she knew also that there'd be upset stomachs when it was, but that was preferable to Garrick lying alone and listening to the others riding off into the hills.

The weekends were short, gone in a breathless blur. Another long week began for Garrick. There were eight of them, eight dreary weeks before Doctor Van Rooyen agreed to let him sit out on the veranda during the day. Then suddenly the prospect of being well again became a reality for Garrick. The leg that Waite was making was nearly finished: he shaped a leather bucket to take the stump and fitted it to the wood with flat-headed copper nails; he worked carefully, moulding the leather and adjusting the straps that would hold it in place. Meanwhile, Garrick exercised along the veranda, hopping beside Ada with an arm around her shoulder, his jaws clenched with concentration and the freckles very prominent on his face that had been without the sun for so long. Twice a day Ada sat on a cushion in front of Garrick's chair and massaged the stump with methylated spirits to toughen it for its first contact with the stiff leather bucket.

'I bet old Sean'll be surprised, hey? When he sees me walking around.'

'Everyone will,' Ada agreed. She looked up from his leg and smiled.

'Can't I try it now? Then I can go out fishing with him when he comes on Saturday.'

'You mustn't expect too much, Garry, it's not going to be easy at first You will have to learn to use it. Like riding a horse—you remember how often you fell off before you learned to ride.'

'But can I start now?'

Ada reached for the spirits bottle, poured a little into her cupped hand and spread it on the stump. 'We'll have to wait until Doctor Van Rooyen tells us you're ready. It won't be long now.'

It wasn't. After his next visit Doctor Van Rooyen spoke to Waite as they walked together to the doctor's trap.

'You can try him with the peg-leg–it'll give him something to work for. Don't let him overtire himself and watch the stump doesn't get rubbed raw. We don't want another infection.'

'Peg-leg.' Waite's mind echoed the ugly word as he watched the trap out of sight. 'Peg-leg': he clenched his fists at his sides, not wanting to turn and see the pathetically eager face behind him on the veranda.

6

'Are you sure that's comfortable?' Waite squatted in front of Garrick's chair adjusting the leg, and Ada stood next to him.

'Yes, yes, let me try it now. Gee, old Sean will be surprised, hey? I'll be able to go back with him on Monday, won't I?' Garrick was trembling with eagerness.

'We'll see,' Waite grunted non-committally. He stood up and moved round beside the chair.

'Ada, my dear, take his other arm. Now listen, Garry, I want you to get the feel of it first. We'll help you up and you can just stand on it and get your balance. Do you understand?'

Garrick nodded vigorously.

'All right, then up you come.'

Garrick drew the leg towards him and the tip scraped across the wooden floor. They lifted him and he put his weight on it.

'Look at me–I'm standing on it. Hey, look I'm standing on it.' His face glowed. 'Let me walk, come on! Let me walk.'

Ada glanced at her husband and he nodded. Together they led Garrick forward. He stumbled twice, but they held him. Klunk and klunk again the peg rang on the floor boards. Before they reached the end of the veranda Garrick had learned to lift the leg high as he swung it forward. They turned and he stumbled only once on the way back to the chair.

'That's fine, Garry, you're doing fine,' laughed Ada.

'You'll be on your own in no time,' Waite grinned with relief. He had hardly dared to hope it would be so easy, and Garrick fastened on his words. 'Let me stand on my own now.'

'Not this time, boy, you've done well enough for one day.'

'Oh, gee, Pa. Please. I won't try and walk, I'll just stand. You and Ma can be ready to catch me. Please, Pa, please.'

Waite hesitated and Ada added her entreaty. 'Let him, dear, he's done so well. It'll help build up his confidence.'

'Very well. But don't try to move,' Waite agreed. 'Are you ready, Garry? Let him go!' They took their hands off him cautiously. He teetered slightly and their hands darted back.

'I'm all right–leave me.' He grinned at them confidently and once more they released him. He stood straight and steady for a moment and then he looked down at the ground. The grin froze on his face. He was alone on a high mountain, his stomach turned giddily within him and he was afraid, desperately unreasonably afraid. He lurched violently and the first shriek tore from him before they could hold him. 'I'm falling. Take it off! Take it off!'

They sat him in the chair with one swift movement.

'Take it off! I'm going to fall!' The terrified screams racked Waite as he tore at the straps that held the leg.

'It's off, Garry, you're safe. I'm holding you.' Waite took him to his chest and held him, trying to quieten him with the strength of his arms and the security of his own big body, but Garrick's terrified struggling and his shrieks continued.

'Take him to the bedroom, get him inside.' Ada spoke urgently and Waite ran with him, still holding him against his chest.

Then for the first time Garrick found his hiding-place. At the moment when his terror became too great to bear he felt something move inside his head, fluttering behind his eyes like the wings of a moth. His vision greyed as though he was in a mist bank. The mist thickened and blotted out all sight and sound. It was warm in the mist—warm and safe. No one could touch him here, for it wrapped and protected him. He was safe.

'I think he's asleep,' Waite whispered to his wife, but there was a puzzled expression in his voice. He looked carefully at the boy's face and listened to his breathing.

'It happened so quickly though—it isn't natural. And yet—and yet he looks all right.'

'Do you think we should call the doctor?' Ada asked.

'No.' Waite shook his head. 'I'll just cover him up and stay with him until he wakes.'

He woke in the early evening, sat up and smiled at them as though nothing had happened. Relaxed and shyly cheerful, he ate a big supper and no one mentioned the leg. It was almost as though Garrick had forgotten about it.

7

Sean came home on the following Friday afternoon. He had a black eye—not a fresh one; it was already turning green round the edges of the bruise. Sean was very reticent on the subject of how he had obtained it. He brought with him also a clutch of fly-catchers' eggs which he gave to Garrick, a live red-lipped snake in a cardboard box which Ada immediately condemned to death despite Sean's impassioned speech in its defence, and a bow carved from M'senga wood which was, in Sean's opinion, the best wood for a bow.

His arrival wrought the usual change in the household of Theunis Kraal—more noise, more movement and more laughter.

There was a huge roast for dinner that evening, with potatoes baked in their jackets. These were Sean's favourite foods and he ate like a hungry python.

'Don't put so much in your mouth,' Waite remonstrated from the head of the table, but there was a fondness in his voice. It was hard not to show favouritism with his sons. Sean accepted the rebuke in the spirit it was given. 'Pa, Frikkie Oberholster's bitch had pups this week, six of them.'

'No,' said Ada firmly.

'Gee, Ma, just one.'

'You heard your mother, Sean.' Sean poured gravy over his meat, cut a potato in half and lifted one piece to his mouth. It had been worth a try. He hadn't really expected them to agree.

'What did you learn this week?' Ada asked. This was a nasty question. Sean had learned as much as was necessary to avoid trouble—no more.

'Oh, lots of things,' he replied airily and then to change the subject. 'Have you finished Garry's new leg yet, Pa?'

There was silence. Garrick's face was expressionless and he dropped his eyes to his plate. Sean put the other half of the potato in his mouth and spoke around it.

'If you have, me and Garry can go fishing up at the falls tomorrow.'

'Don't talk with your mouth full,' snapped Waite with unnecessary violence. 'You've got the manners of a pig.'

'Sorry, Pa,' Sean muttered. The rest of the meal passed in uneasy silence, and as soon as it finished, Sean escaped to the bedroom. Garry went with him, hopping along the passage with one hand on the wall to balance himself.

'What's Pa so mad about?' Sean demanded resentfully as soon as they were alone.

'I don't know.' Garrick sat on the bed. 'Sometimes he just gets mad for nothing—you know that.'

Sean pulled his shirt off over his head, screwed it into a ball and threw it against the far wall.

'You'd better pick it up, else there'll be trouble,' Garrick warned mildly. Sean dropped his pants and kicked them after the shirt. This show of defiance put him in a better mood. He walked across and stood naked in front of Garrick.

'Look,' he said with pride. 'Hairs!'

Garrick inspected them. Indisputably they were hairs.

'There aren't very many.' Garrick couldn't disguise the envy in his voice.

'Well, I bet I've got more than you have,' Sean challenged. 'Let's count them.'

But Garrick knew himself to be an outright loser; he slipped off the bed and hopped across the room. Steadying himself against the wall, he stooped and picked up Sean's discarded clothing, he brought it back and dropped it in the soiled-linen basket beside the door. Sean watched him and it reminded him of his unanswered question.

'Has Pa finished your leg yet, Garry?'

Garry turned slowly, he swallowed and nodded once, a quick jerky movement.

'What's it like? Have you tried it yet?'

The fear was on Garrick again. He twisted his face from side to side as though seeking an escape. There were footsteps in the passage outside the door. Sean dived at his bed and snatching up his nightgown pulled it over his head as he slid between the sheets. Garrick was still standing beside the clothes basket when Waite Courtney came into the room. 'Come on, Garry, what's holding you up?'

Garrick hurried across to his bed and Waite looked at Sean. Sean grinned at him with all the charm of his good looks and Waite's face softened into a grin also. 'Nice to have you home again, boy.' It was impossible to be angry with Sean for long.

He reached out and took a handful of Sean's thick black hair. 'Now I don't want to hear any talking in here after the lamp's out—do you understand?'

He tugged Sean's head from side to side gently, embarrassed by the strength of his feeling for his son.

8

The next morning Waite Courtney rode back to the homestead for his breakfast when the sun was high. One of the grooms took his horse and led it away to the paddock and Waite stood in front of the saddle-room and looked around him. He looked at the neat white posts of the paddock, at the well-swept yard, at his house filled with fine furniture. It was a good feeling to be rich—especially when you knew what it was like to be poor. Fifteen thousand acres of good grassland, as many cattle as the land would carry, gold in the bank. Waite smiled and started across the yard.

He heard Ada singing in the dairy.

> 'How rides the farmer
> Sit, sit, so
> Sit, sit, so—tra la
> The Capetown girls say
> Kiss me quick
> Kiss me quick—tra la.'

She had a clear sweet voice and Waite's smile broadened—it was a good feeling to be rich and to be in love. He stopped at the door of the dairy; because of the thick stone walls and heavy thatch it was cool and dark in the room. Ada stood with her back to the door, her body moving in time to the song and the turning of the butter churn. Waite watched her for a moment, then he walked up behind her and put his arms around her waist.

Startled, she turned within his arms and he kissed her on the mouth. 'Good morning, my pretty maid.'

She relaxed against him. 'Good morning, sir,' she said.

'What's for breakfast?'

'Ah, what a romantic fool I married!' She sighed. 'Come along, let's go and see.'

She took off her apron, hung it behind the door, patted her hair into place and held her hand out to him. They walked hand-in-hand across the yard and into the kitchen. Waite sniffed loudly.

'Smells all right. Where are the boys?'

Joseph understood English though he could not speak it. He looked up from the stove.

'Nkosi, they are on the front veranda.'

Joseph had the typical moon-round face of the Zulu, when he smiled his teeth were big and white against the black of his skin.

'They are playing with Nkosizana Garry's wooden leg.'

Waite's face flushed. 'How did they find it?'

'Nkosizana Sean asked me where it was and I told him you had put it in the linen cupboard.'

'You bloody fool!' roared Waite. He dropped Ada's hand and ran. As he reached the lounge he heard Sean shout and immediately there was the sound of someone falling heavily on the veranda. He stopped in the middle of the lounge floor; he couldn't bear to go out and face Garrick's terror. He felt sick with dread and with his anger at Sean.

Then he heard Sean laugh. 'Get off me, man, don't just lie there.'

And then, incredibly, Garrick's voice. 'Sorry, it caught in the floor boards.'

Waite walked across to the window and looked out on to the veranda. Sean and Garrick lay in a heap together near the far end. Sean was still laughing and on Garrick's face was a set nervous smile. Sean scrambled up. 'Come on. Get up.'

He gave Garrick his hand and dragged him to his feet. They stood clinging to each other, Garrick balancing precariously on his peg. 'I bet if it was me I could just walk easy as anything,' said Sean.

'I bet you couldn't, it's jolly difficult.'

Sean let go of him and stood back with his arms spread ready to catch him. 'Come on.'

Sean walked backwards in front of him and Garrick followed unsteadily, his arms flapping out sideways as he struggled to keep his balance, his face rigid with concentration. He reached the end of the veranda and caught on to the rail with both hands. This time he joined in Sean's laughter.

Waite became aware that Ada was standing beside him; he glanced sideways at her and her lips formed the words 'come away.' She took his arm.

9

At the end of June 1876 Garrick went back to school with Sean. It was almost four months since the shooting. Waite drove them. The road to Ladyburg was through open forest, two parallel tracks with the grass growing in between—it brushed the bottom of the buggy. The horses trotted in the tracks, their hooves silent on the thick powder dust. At the top of the first rise Waite slowed the horses and turned his seat to look back at the homestead. The early sun gave the whitewashed walls of Theunis Kraal an orange glow and the lawns around the house were brilliant green. Everywhere else the grass was dry in the early winter and the leaves of the trees were dry also. The sun was not yet high enough to rob the veld of its colour and light it only with the flat white glare of midday. The leaves were golden and russet and red-brown, the same red-brown as the bunches of Afrikander cattle that grazed among the trees. Behind it all was the back-drop of the escarpment, striped like a zebra with the green black bush that grew in its gullies.

'Look, there's a hoopoe, Sean.'

'Yeah, I saw it long ago. That's a male.'

The bird flew up from in front of the horses: chocolate and black and white wings, its head crested like an Etruscan helmet.

'How do you know?' challenged Garrick.

''Cause of the white in its wings.'

'They've all got white in their wings.'

'They haven't—only the males.'

'Well, all the ones I've seen got white in their wings,' said Garrick dubiously.

'Perhaps you've never seen a female. They're jolly rare. They don't come out of their nests much.'

Waite Courteney smiled and turned back in his seat. 'Garry's right, Sean, you can't tell the difference by their feathers. The male's a little bigger, that's all.'

'I told you,' said Garrick, brave under his father's protection.

'You know everything,' muttered Sean sarcastically. 'I suppose you read it in all those books, hey?'

Garrick smiled complacently. 'Look, there's the train.'

It was coming down the escarpment, dragging a long grey plume of smoke behind it. Waite started the horses into a trot. They went down to the concrete bridge over the Baboon Stroom.

'I saw a yellow fish.'

'It was a stick, I saw it too.'

The river was the boundary of Waite's land. They crossed the bridge and went up the other side. In front of them was Ladyburg. The train was running into the town past the cattle sale pens; it whistled and shot a puff of steam high into the air.

The town was spread out, each house padded around by its orchard and garden. A thirty-six ox team could turn in any of the wide streets. The houses were burnt brick or whitewashed, thatched or with corrugated-iron roofs painted green or dull red. The square was in the centre and the spire of the church was the hub of Ladyburg. The school was on the far side of town.

Waite trotted the horses along Main Street. There were a few people on the side walks; they moved with early morning stiffness beneath the flamboyant trees that lined the street and every one of them called a greeting to Waite. He waved his whip at the men and lifted his hat to the women, but not high enough to expose the bald dome of his head. In the centre of town the shops were open, and standing on long thin legs in front of his bank was David Pye. He was dressed in black like an undertaker.

'Morning, Waite.'

'Morning, David,' called Waite a little too heartily. It was not six months since he had paid off the last mortgage on Theunis Kraal and the memory of debt was too fresh in his mind; he felt as embarrassed as a newly released prisoner meeting the prison governor on the street.

'Can you come in and see me after you've dropped off your boys?'

'Have the coffee ready,' agreed Waite. It was well known that no one was ever offered coffee when they called on David Pye. They went on down the street, turned left at the far end of Church Square, passed the courthouse and down the dip to the school hostel.

There was half a dozen Scotch carts and four-wheelers standing in the yard. Small boys and girls swarmed over them unloading their luggage. Their fathers stood in a group at one end of the yard—brown-faced men, with carefully brushed beards, uncomfortable in their suits which still showed the creases of long hanging. These men lived too far out for the children to make the daily journey into school. Their land sprawled down to the banks of the Tugela or across the plateau halfway to Pietermaritzburg.

Waite stopped the buggy, climbed down and loosened the harness on his horses and Sean jumped from the outside seat to the ground and ran to the nearest bunch of boys. Waite walked across to the men; their ranks opened for him, they smiled their welcomes and in turn reached for his right hand. Garrick sat alone on the front seat of the buggy, his leg stuck out stiffly in front of him and his shoulders hunched as though he were trying to hide.

After a while Waite glanced back over his shoulder. He saw Garrick sitting alone and he made as if to go to him, but stopped immediately. His eyes quested among the swirl of small bodies until they found Sean. 'Sean.'

Sean paused in the middle of an animated discussion. 'Yes, Pa.'

'Give Garry a hand with the case.'

'Aw, gee, Pa–I'm talking.'

'Sean!' Waite scowled with both face and voice.

'All right, I'm going.' Sean hesitated a moment longer and then went to the buggy.

'Come on, Garry. Pass the cases down.'

Garrick roused himself and climbed awkwardly over the back of the seat. He handed the luggage down to Sean who stacked it beside the wheel, then turned to the group that had followed him across.

'Karl, you carry that. Dennis, take the brown bag. Don't drop it, man, it's got four bottles of jam in it.' Sean issued his instructions.

'Come on, Garry.'

They started off towards the hostel and Garrick climbed down from the buggy and limped quickly after them.

'You know what, Sean?' said Karl loudly. 'Pa let me start using his rifle.'

Sean stopped dead, and then more with hope than conviction, 'He did not!'

'He did,' Karl said happily. Garrick caught up with them and they all stared at Karl.

'How many shots did you have?' asked someone in an awed voice.

Karl nearly said, 'Six' but changed it quickly.

'Oh, lots–as many as I wanted.'

'You'll get gun-shy–my Pa says if you start too soon you'll never be a good shot.'

'I never missed once,' flashed Karl.

'Come on,' said Sean and started off once more–he had never been so jealous in his life. Karl hurried after him.

'I bet you've never shot with a rifle, Sean, I bet you haven't, hey?' Sean smiled mysteriously while he searched for some new topic; he could see that Karl was going to kick the subject to death.

From the veranda of the hostel a girl ran to meet him.

'It's Anna,' said Garrick.

She had long brown legs, skinny; her skirts fussed about them as she ran. Her hair was black, her face was small with a pointed chin. 'Hello, Sean.'

Sean grunted. She fell in beside him, skipping to keep pace with him.

'Did you have a nice holiday?'

Sean ignored her, always coming and trying to talk to him, even when his friends were watching.

'I've got a whole tin of shortbread, Sean. Would you like some?' There was a flash of interest in Sean's eyes; he half turned his head towards her, for Mrs Van Essen's shortbread was rightly famous throughout the district, but he caught himself and kept grimly on towards the hostel.

'Can I sit next to you in class this term, Sean?'

Sean turned furiously on her. 'No, you can't. Now go away–I'm busy.'

He went up the steps. Anna stood at the bottom; she looked as though she was going to cry and Garrick stopped shyly beside her.

'You can sit next to me if you like,' he said softly.

She glanced at him, looking down at his leg. The tears cleared and she giggled. She was pretty. She leaned towards him.

'Peg-leg,' she said and giggled again. Garrick blushed so vividly, and suddenly his eyes watered. Anna put both hands to her mouth and giggled through them, then she turned and ran to join her friends in front of the girls' section of the hostel. Still blushing, Garrick went up the steps after Sean; he steadied himself on the banisters.

Fraülein stood at the door of the boys' dormitory. Her steel-rimmed spectacles and the iron grey of her hair gave her face an exaggerated severity, but this was relieved by the smile with which she recognized Sean.

'Ah, my Sean, you have come.' What she actually said was, 'Ach, mein Sean, you haf gom.'

'Hello, Fraülein,' Sean gave her his number one very best smile.

'Again you have grown,' Fraülein measured him with her eyes. 'All the time you grow, already you are the biggest boy in the school.'

Sean watched her warily, ready to take evasive action if she attempted to embrace him as she did sometimes when she could no longer contain her feelings. Sean's blend of charm, good looks and arrogance had completely captured her Teutonic heart.

'Quickly, you must unpack. School is just now starting.' She turned her attention to her other charges and Sean, with relief, led his men through into the dormitory.

'Pa says that next weekend I can use his rifle for hunting, not just targets,' Karl steered the conversation back.

'Dennis, put Garry's case on his bed.' Sean pretended not to hear.

There were thirty beds arranged along the walls, each with a locker beside it. The room was as neat and cheerless as a prison or a school. At the far end a group of five or six boys sat talking. They looked up as Sean came in but no greetings were exchanged—they were the opposition.

Sean sat down on his bed and bounced experimentally, it was hard as a plank. Garrick's peg thumped as he walked down the dormitory and Ronny Pye, the leader of the opposition, whispered something to his friends and they all laughed, watching Garrick. Garrick blushed again and sat down quickly on his bed to hide his leg.

'I guess I'll shoot duiker first before Pa lets me shoot kudu or bushbuck,' Karl stated and Sean frowned.

'What's the new teacher like?' he asked.

'He looks all right,' one of the others answered. 'Jimmy and I saw him at the station yesterday.'

'He's thin and got a moustache.'

'He doesn't smile much.'

'I suppose next holiday Pa will take me shooting across the Tugela,' Karl said aggressively.

'I hope he's not too keen on spelling and things,' Sean declared. 'I hope he doesn't start all that decimal business again, like old Lizard did.'

There was a round of agreement and then Garrick made his first contribution. 'Decimals are easy.'

There was a silence while they all looked at him.

'I might even shoot a lion,' said Karl.

10

There was a single schoolroom to accommodate the youngest upwards of both sexes. Double desks; on the walls a few maps, a large set of multiplication tables and a picture of Queen Victoria. From this dais Mr Anthony Clark surveyed his new pupils. There was a hushed anticipation; one of the girls giggled nervously and Mr Clark's eyes sought the sound, but it stopped before he found it.

'It is my unfortunate duty to attempt your education,' he announced. He wasn't joking. Long ago his sense of vocation had been swamped by an intense dislike for the young: now he taught only for the salary.

'It is your no more pleasant duty to submit to this with all the fortitude you can muster,' he went on, looking with distaste at their shining faces.

'What's he saying?' whispered Sean without moving his lips.

'Shh,' said Garrick.

Mr Clark's eyes swivelled quickly and rested on Garrick. He walked slowly down the aisle between the desks and stopped beside him; he took a little of the hair that grew at Garrick's temple between his thumb and his forefinger and jerked it upwards. Garrick squeaked and Mr Clark returned slowly to his dais.

'We will now proceed. Standard Ones kindly open your spelling books at page one. Standard Twos turn to page fifteen. . . .' He went on allocating their work.

'Did he hurt you?' breathed Sean. Garrick nodded almost imperceptibly and Sean conceived an immediate and intense hatred for the man. He stared at him.

Mr Clark was a little over thirty years old—thin, and his tight three-piece suit emphasized this fact. He had a pale face made sad by his drooping moustache, and his nose was upturned to such a degree that his nostrils were exposed; they pointed out of his face like the muzzle of a double-barrelled shotgun. He lifted his head from the list he held in his hand and aimed his nostrils straight at Sean. For a second they stared at each other.

'Trouble,' thought Mr Clark; he could pick them unerringly. 'Break him before he gets out of control.'

'You, boy, what's your name?'

Sean turned elaborately and looked over his shoulder. When he turned back there was a little colour in Mr Clark's cheeks. 'Stand up.'

'Who, me?'

'Yes, you.'

Sean stood.

'What's your name?'

'Courtney.'

'Sir!'

'Courtney, sir.'

They looked at each other. Mr Clark waited for Sean to drop his eyes but he didn't.

'Big trouble, much bigger than I thought,' he decided and said aloud, 'All right, sit down.'

There was an almost audible relaxation of tension in the room. Sean could sense the respect of the others around him; they were proud of the way he had carried it off. He felt a touch on his shoulder. It was Anna, the seat behind him was as close as she could sit to him. Ordinarily her presumption would have annoyed him, but now that small touch on his shoulder added to his glow of self-satisfaction.

An hour passed slowly for Sean. He drew a picture of a rifle in the margin of his spelling book then rubbed it out carefully, he watched Garrick for a while until his brother's absorption with his work irritated him.

'Swot,' he whispered, but Garrick ignored him.

Sean was bored. He shifted restlessly in his seat and looked at the back of Karl's neck—there was a ripe pimple on it. He picked up his ruler to prod it. Before he could do so Karl lifted his hand as if to scratch his shoulder but there was a scrap of paper between his fingers. Sean put down the ruler and surreptitiously reached for the note. He held it on his lap, on it was written one word.

'Mosquitoes.'

Sean grinned. Sean's imitation of a mosquito was one of the many reasons why the previous schoolmaster had resigned. For six months old Lizard had believed that there were mosquitoes in the room—then for the next six months he had known there were not. He had tried every ruse he could think of to catch the culprit, and in the end it had got him. Every time the monotonous hum began the tic in the corner of his mouth became more noticeable.

Now Sean cleared his throat and started to hum. Instantly the room was tense with suppressed laughter. Every head, including Sean's, was bent studiously over a book. Mr Clark's hand hesitated in writing on the blackboard but then went on again evenly.

It was a clever imitation; by lowering and raising the volume Sean gave the effect of an insect moving about the room. A slight trembling at his throat was the only sign that he was responsible.

Mr Clark finished writing and turned to face the room. Sean did not make the mistake of stopping, he allowed the mosquito to fly a little longer before settling.

Mr Clark left his dais and walked down the row of desks furthest from Sean. Once or twice he paused to check the work of one of his pupils. He reached the back of the room and moved across to Sean's row. He stopped at Anna's desk.

'It is unnecessary to loop your L's like that,' he told her, 'Let me show you.' He took her pencil and wrote. 'You see what I mean. To show off when writing is as bad as showing off in your everyday behaviour.'

He handed her back her pencil and then pivoting on one foot he hit Sean a mighty crack across the side of the head with his open hand. Sean's head was knocked sideways and the sound of the blow was very loud in the quiet room.

'There was a mosquito sitting on your ear,' said Mr Clark.

I I

In the following two years Sean and Garrick made the change from child to young manhood. It was like riding a strong current, being swept with speed along the river of life.

There were parts of the river that flowed steadily:

Ada was one of these. Always understanding, with the ability to give her understanding expression, unchanging in her love for her husband and the family she had taken as her own.

Waite was another. A little more grey in his hair but big as ever in body, laugh and fortune.

There were parts of the river that ran faster:

Garrick's reliance on Sean. He needed him more strongly each month that passed, for Sean was his shield. If Sean was not there to protect him when he was threatened, then he used his final refuge: he crawled back into himself, into the warm dark mists of his mind.

They went to steal peaches: the twins, Karl, Dennis and two others. There was a thick hedge around Mr Pye's orchard and the peaches that grew on the other side of it were as big as a man's fist. They were sweet as honey but tasted even sweeter when taken on the plunder account. You reached the orchard through a plantation of wattle trees.

'Don't take too many off one tree!' Sean ordered. 'Old Pye will notice it as sure as anything.'

They came to the hedge and Sean found the hole.

'Garry, you stay here and keep cats for us. If anyone comes give a whistle.' Garrick tried not to show his relief, he had no stomach for the expedition.

Sean went on. 'We'll pass the peaches out to you—and don't eat any until we're finished.'

'Why doesn't he come with us?' asked Karl.

''Cause he can't run, that's why. If he gets caught they'll know who the rest of us are for sure and we'll all get it.'

Karl was satisfied. Sean went down on his hands and knees and crawled into the hole in the hedge and one at a time the others followed him until Garrick was left alone.

He stood close to the hedge, drawing comfort from its protecting bulk. The minutes dragged by and Garrick fidgeted nervously—they were taking an awfully long time.

Suddenly there were voices, someone was coming through the plantation towards him. Panic beat up inside him and he shrank back into the hedge, trying to hide; the idea of giving a warning never even entered his head.

The voices were closer and then through the trees he recognized Ronny Pye: with him were two of his friends. Each of them was armed with a slingshot and they walked with their heads thrown back, searching the trees for birds.

For a time it seemed they would not notice Garrick in the hedge; but then, when they had almost passed, Ronny turned his head and saw him. They stared at each other, ten paces apart, Garrick crouched against the hedge and

Ronny's expression of surprise slowly changed to one of cunning. He looked around quickly, to make sure that Sean was not there.

'It's old Hobble-dee-hoy,' he announced and his friends came back and stood on each side of him.

'What're you doing, Peg-leg?'

'Rats got your tongue, Peg-leg?'

'No, termites got his leg!'–laughter aimed to hurt.

'Talk to us, Peg-leg.' Ronny Pye had ears that stood out on each side of his head like a pair of fans. He was small for his age which made him vicious and his hair was ginger.

'Come on. Talk to us, Peg-leg.'

Garrick moistened his lips with his tongue, already there were tears in his eyes.

'Hey, Ronny, make him walk for us, like this.' One of the others gave a graphic imitation of Garrick's limp. Again laughter, louder now, more confident and they closed in on him. 'Show us how you walk.'

Garrick swung his head from side to side searching for an escape.

'Your brother's not here,' crowed Ronny. 'No good looking for him, Peg-leg.'

He caught a hold of Garrick's shirt and pulled him out of the hedge.

'Show us how you walk.'

Garrick plucked ineffectually at Ronny's hand.

'Leave me, I'll tell Sean. I'll tell Sean unless you leave me.'

'All right, I'll leave you,' agreed Ronny with both hands shoved him in the chest. 'Don't come my way–go that way!' Garrick stumbled backwards.

One of the others was ready for him. 'Don't come my way–go that way!' and pushed him in the back. They formed a ring around him and kept him staggering between them.

'Go that way!'

'Go that way!'

The tears were streaked down his cheeks now. 'Please, please stop.'

'Please, please,' they mimicked him.

Then, with a rush of relief, Garrick felt the fluttering start behind his eyes–their faces dimmed, he hardly felt their hands upon him. He fell and and his face hit the ground, but there was no pain. Two of them stooped over him to lift him, and there was dirt mixed with the tears on his cheeks.

Sean came through the hedge behind them; the front of his shirt bulged with peaches. For a second he crouched on his hands and knees while he took in what was happening, then he came out of his crouch at a run. Ronny heard him, dropped Garrick and turned.

'You've been pinching Pa's peaches,' he shouted. 'I'll tell–'

Sean's fist hit him on the nose and he sat down. Sean swung towards the other two but they were already running, he chased them a few paces and then came back for Ronny, but he was too late. Ronny was dodging away between the trees holding his face and his nose was bleeding on to his shirt.

'Are you all right, Garry?' Sean knelt beside him, trying to wipe the dirt off his face with a grubby handkerchief. Sean helped him to his feet, and Garrick stood swaying slightly with his eyes open but a remote and vacant smile on his lips.

There were landmarks along the course of the river. Some of them small as a pile of rocks in shallow water:

Waite Courtney looked as Sean across the breakfast table at Theunis Kraal. The fork-load of egg and grilled gammon stopped on the way to his mouth.

'Turn your face towards the window,' he commanded suspiciously. Sean obeyed. 'What the hell is that on your face?'

'What?' Sean ran his hand over his cheek.

'When did you last bath?'

'Don't be silly, my dear.' Ada touched his leg under the table. 'It isn't dirt—it's whiskers.'

'Whiskers, are they?' Waite peered closely at Sean and started to grin, he opened his mouth to speak and Ada knew instantly that he was going to make a joke—one of those ponderous jokes of his, as subtle as an enraged dinosaur, that would wound Sean deep in his half-formed manhood. Quickly she cut in, 'I think you should buy him a razor, don't you, Waite?'

Waite lost the thread of his joke, he grunted and put the egg into his mouth.

'I don't want to cut them,' said Sean and flushed scarlet.

'They'll grow quicker if you shave them a bit at first,' Ada told him.

Across the table from her Garrick fingered his jowls wistfully.

Some of the landmarks were big as headlands:

Waite fetched them from school at the beginning of the December holidays. In the confusion of loading their cases onto the buggy and shouting farewells to Fraülein and to their friends, some of whom they would not see for another six weeks, the twins did not notice that Waite was acting strangely.

It was only later when the horses were heading for home at twice their normal speed that Sean asked, 'What's the hurry, Pa?'

'You'll see,' said Waite, and both Garrick and Sean looked at him with sudden interest. It had been an idle question of Sean's but Waite's answer had them immediately intrigued. Waite grinned at the bombardment of questions but he kept his answers vague. He was enjoying himself. By the time they reached Theunis Kraal the twins were in a frenzy of curiosity.

Waite pulled the horses up in front of the house and one of the grooms ran to take the reins. Ada was waiting on the veranda and Sean jumped down and ran up the steps to her. He kissed her quickly. 'What's happening?' he pleaded. 'Pa won't tell us but we know it's something.'

Garrick hurried up the steps also. 'Go on, tell us.' He caught hold of her arm and tugged it.

'I don't know what you're talking about,' Ada laughed. 'You'd better ask your father again.'

Waite climbed up after them, put one arm around Ada's waist and squeezed her.

'I don't know where they got this idea from,' said Waite, 'but why not tell them to go and have a look in their bedroom? They might as well have their Christmas presents a bit earlier this year.'

Sean beat Garrick to the lounge and was far in the lead by the time he reached the door of their bedroom.

'Wait for me,' called Garrick desperately. 'Please wait for me.'

Sean stopped in the doorway.

'Jesus Christ,' he whispered—they were the strongest words he knew. Garrick came up behind him and together they started at the pair of leather cases that lay on the table in the middle of the room—long flat cases, heavy polished leather with the corners bound in brass.

'Rifles!' said Sean. He walked slowly to the table as though he were stalking the cases, expecting them at any moment to vanish.

'Look!' Sean reached out to touch with one finger the gold lettering stamped into the lid of the nearest case. 'Our names on them even.'

He sprung the locks and lifted the lid. In a nest of green baize, perfumed with gun oil, glistened a poem in steel and wood.

'Jesus Christ,' said Sean again. Then he looked over his shoulder at Garrick. 'Aren't you going to open yours?'

Garrick limped up to the table trying to hide his disappointment: he had wanted a set of Dickens so badly.

In the river there were whirlpools:

The last week of the Christmas holidays and Garrick was in bed with one of his colds. Waite Courtney had gone to Pietermaritzburg for a meeting of the Beef Growers' Association and there was very little work to do on the farm that day. After Sean had dosed the sick cattle in the sanatorium paddock and ridden an inspection around the south section he returned to the homestead and spent an hour talking to the stableboys, then he drifted up to the house. Garry was asleep and Ada was in the dairy making butter. He asked for and got an early lunch from Joseph and ate it standing in the kitchen. While he ate he thought over the problem of how to fill the afternoon. He weighed the alternatives carefully. Take the rifle and try for duiker along the edge of the escarpment or ride to the pools above the White Falls and fish for eels. He was still undecided after he had finished eating so he crossed the yard and looked into the cool dimness of the dairy.

Ada smiled at him across the churn. 'Hello, Sean, I suppose you want your lunch.'

'Joseph gave it to me already, thanks, Ma.'

'Joseph has already given it to me,' Ada corrected mildly. Sean repeated it after her and sniffed the dairy smell—he liked the cheesy warmth of new butter and the tang of the cow dung smeared on the earth floor.

'What are you going to do this afternoon?'

'I came to ask you if you wanted venison or eels—I don't know if I want to go fishing or shooting.'

'Eels would be nice—we could jelly them and have them for dinner tomorrow when your father comes home.'

'I'll get you a bucket full.'

He saddled the pony, hung his tin of worms on the saddle and with his pole over his shoulder rode towards Ladyburg. He crossed the Baboon Stroom bridge and turned off the road to follow the stream up to the falls. As he skirted the wattle plantation below the Van Essens' place he realized he had made a mistake in picking this route. Anna, with her skirts held up to her knees, came pelting out from among the trees. Sean kicked the pony into a trot and looked straight ahead.

'Sean—hey, Sean.'

She was ahead of him, running to intercept him; there was no chance of evading her so he stopped the pony.

'Hello, Sean.' She was panting and her face was flushed.

'Hello,' he gruffed.

'Where are you going?'

'There and back to see how far it is.'

'You're going fishing—may I come with you?' She smiled appealingly. Her teeth were small and white.

'No, you talk too much; you'll frighten the fish.'

He started the pony.

'Please, I'll be quiet; honest I will.' She was running next to him.

'No.' He flicked the reins and pulled away from her. He rode for a hundred yards then looked round and she was still following with her black hair streaming out behind her. He stopped the pony and she caught up with him.

'I knew you'd stop,' she told him through her gasps.

'Will you go home? I don't want you following me.'

'I'll be quiet as anything—honest I will.'

He knew she'd follow him right up to the top of the escarpment and he gave in. 'All right, but if you say a word, just one single word, I'll send you home.'

'I promise—help me up, please.'

He dragged her on to the pony's rump and she sat sideways with her arms round his waist. They climbed the escarpment. The path ran close beside the White Falls and they could feel the spray blowing off them fine as mist. Anna kept her promise until she was sure they'd gone too far for Sean to send her back alone. She started talking again. When she wanted an answer from him, which wasn't very often, she squeezed his waist and Sean grunted. Sean knee-haltered the pony and left him among the trees above the pools. He hid his saddle and bridle in an ant-bear hold and they walked down through the reeds to the water. Anna ran ahead of him and when he came out on to the sandbank she was throwing pebbles into the pool.

'Hey, stop that! You'll frighten the fish,' Sean shouted.

'Oh. I'm sorry. I forgot.'

She sat down and wriggled her bare toes into the sand. Sean baited his hook and lobbed it out into the green water—the current drifted his float in a wide circle under the far bank and they both watched it solemnly.

'It doesn't seem as though there are any fish here,' Anna said.

'You've got to be patient—you can't expect to catch one right away.'

Anna drew patterns in the sand with her toes and five minutes passed slowly. 'Sean—'

'Ssh!'

Another five minutes.

'Fishing's a silly old thing.'

'Nobody asked you to come,' Sean told her.

'It's hot here!' Sean didn't answer.

The high reed beds shut out any breeze and the white sand threw the sun's heat back at them. Anna stood up and wandered restlessly across the sand to the edge of the reeds. She picked a handful of the long spear-shaped leaves and plaited them together.

'I'm bored,' she announced.

'Well, go home then.'

'And I'm hot.'

Sean pulled his line in, inspected the worms and cast them out again. Anna stuck her tongue out at his back.

'Let's have a swim,' she suggested.

Sean ignored her. He stuck the butt of his rod into the sand, pulled his hat down to shield his eyes from the glare and leaned back on his elbows with his legs stretched out in front of him. He could hear the sand crunching as she moved and then there was another silence. He started to worry what she was doing, but if he looked around it would be a show of weakness.

'Girls!' he thought bitterly.

There was the sound of running feet just behind him. He sat up quickly and started to turn. Her white body flashed past him and hit the water, with a smack like a rising trout. Sean jumped up. 'Hey, what're you doing?'

'I'm swimming,' laughed Anna, waist-deep in green water, with her hair slicked wetly down her shoulders and over her breasts. Sean looked at those breasts, white as the flesh of an apple and nippled in dark pink, almost red. Anna dropped on to her back and kicked the water white.

'*Voet sak,* little fishes! Scat, little fishes,' she gurgled.

'Hey, you mustn't do that,' Sean said half-heartedly. He wanted her to stand up again, those breasts gave him a strange tight feeling in his stomach, but Anna knelt with the water up to her chin. He could see them through the water. He wanted her to stand up.

'It's lovely! Why don't you come in?' She rolled on her stomach and ducked her head under the water; the twin ovals of her bottom broke the surface and Sean's stomach tightened again.

'Are you coming in?' she demanded, rubbing the water out of her eyes with both hands. Sean stood bewildered—within a few seconds his feelings towards her had undergone a major revolution. He wanted very much to be in the water with all those mysterious white bulges—but he was shy.

'You're scared! Come on, I give you guts to come in.' She teased him. The challenge pricked him.

'I'm not scared.'

'Well, come on then.'

He hesitated a few seconds longer, then he threw off his hat and unbuttoned his shirt. He turned his back on her while he dropped his pants then spun round and dived into the pool, thankful for the cover it gave him. His head came out and Anna pushed it under again. He groped and caught her legs, straightened up and threw her on her back. He dragged her towards the shallows, where the water couldn't cover her. She was thrashing her arms to keep her head out and screaming delightedly. Sean's heels snagged a rock and he fell, letting go of her; before he could recover she had leapt on him and straddled his back. He could have thrown her off, but he liked the feel of her flesh on his—warm through the cool water, slippery with wetness. She picked up a handful of sand and rubbed it into his hair. Sean shrugged gently. She threw her arms round his neck and he could feel the whole length of her body along his back. The tightness of his stomach moved up into his chest and he wanted to hold her. He rolled over and reached for her but she twisted out of his hands and dived back into the deep again. Sean splashed after her but she kept out of his reach, laughing at him.

At last they faced each other, still chin deep, and Sean was getting angry. He wanted to hold her. She saw the change of his mood and she waded to the bank, walked to his clothes and picked up his shirt. She dried her face on it, standing naked and unashamed—she had too many brothers for modesty. Sean watched the way her breasts changed shape as she lifted her arms, he looked at the lines of her body and saw that her once skinny legs had filled out; her thighs touched each other all the way up to the base of her belly and there she wore the dark triangular badge of womanhood. She spread the shirt out on the sand and sat down upon it, then she looked at him.

'Are you coming out?'

He came out awkwardly, covering himself with his hands. Anna moved over on the shirt. 'You can sit down, if you like.'

He sat hurriedly and drew his knees up under his chin. He watched her from the corner of his eye. There were little goose-pimples round her nipples from the cold water. She was aware that he was watching her and she pulled back her shoulders, enjoying it. Sean felt bewildered again–she was so clearly in control now. Before she had been someone to growl at but now she was giving the orders and he was obeying.

'You've got hairs on your chest,' Anna said, turning to look at him. Sparse and silky though they were, Sean was glad that he had them. He straightened out his legs.

'And you're much bigger there than Frikkie.' Sean tried to pull up his knees again but she put her hand on his leg and stopped him.

'Can I touch you?'

Sean tried to speak but his throat had closed and no sound came through it. Anna did not wait for an answer.

'Oh, look! It's getting all cheeky–just like Caribou's.'

Caribou was Mr Van Essen's stallion.

'I always know when Pa is going to let Caribou service a mare, he tells me to go and visit Aunt Lettie. I just hide in the plantation. You can see the paddock jolly well from the plantation.'

Anna's hand was soft and restless, Sean could think of nothing else.

'Do you know that people service, just like horses do?' she asked.

Sean nodded, he had attended the biology classes conducted by Messrs Daffel and Company in the school latrines. They were quiet for a while, then Anna whispered.

'Sean, would you service me?'

'I don't know how,' croaked Sean.

'I bet horses don't either the first time, nor people for that matter,' Anna said. 'We could find out.'

They rode home in the early evening, Anna sitting up behind Sean, her arms tight round his waist and the side of her face pressed between his shoulders. He dropped her at the back of the plantation.

'I'll see you at school on Monday,' she said and turned to go.

'Anna–'

'Yes?'

'Is it still sore?'

'No,' and then, after a moment's thought, 'it feels nice.'

She turned and ran into the wattle trees.

Sean rode slowly home. He was empty inside; it was a sad feeling and it puzzled him.

'Where are the fish?' asked Ada.

'They weren't biting.'

'Not even one?'

Sean shook his head and crossed the kitchen.

'Sean.'

'Yes, Ma.'

'Is something wrong?'

'No'–quick denial–'No, I'm fine.' He slipped into the passage.

Garrick was sitting up in bed. The skin around his nostrils was inflamed and chapped; he lowered the book he was reading and smiled at Sean as he came into the room. Sean went to his own bed and sat on it.

'Where have you been?' Garrick's voice was thick with cold.

'Up at the pools above the falls.'

'Fishing?'

Sean didn't answer, he leaned forward on the bed with his elbows on his knees. 'I met Anna, she came with me.'

Garrick's interest quickened at the mention of her name and he watched Sean's face. Sean still had that slightly puzzled expression.

'Garry,' he hesitated; he had to talk about it. 'Garry, I screwed Anna.'

Garrick drew in his breath with a small hiss. He went very pale, only his nose was still red and sore-looking.

'I mean,' Sean spoke slowly as though he were trying to explain it to himself, 'I mean really screwed her, just like we've talked about. Just like. . . .' He made a helpless gesture with his hands, unable to find the words. Then he lay back on the bed.

'Did she let you?' Garrick's voice was almost a whisper.

'She asked me to,' Sean said. 'It was slippery—sort of warm and slippery.'

And then later, long after the lamp was out and they were both in bed, Sean heard Garrick's soft movements in the darkness. He listened for a while until he was certain.

'Garry!' He accused him loudly.

'I wasn't, I wasn't.'

'You know what Pa told us. Your teeth will fall out and you'll go mad.'

'I wasn't, I wasn't.' Garrick's voice was choked with his cold and his tears.

'I heard you,' said Sean.

'I was just scratching my leg. Honestly, honestly, I was.'

And at the end the river plunged over the last waterfall and swept them into the sea of manhood.

Mr Clark had not been able to break Sean. He had provoked instead a bitter contest in which he knew himself to be slowly losing ground, and now he was afraid of Sean. He no longer made Sean stand, for Sean was as tall as he was. The contest had been on for two years; they had explored each other's weaknesses and knew how to exploit them.

Mr Clark could not bear the sound of anyone sniffing; perhaps subconsciously he took it as mockery of his own deformed nose. Sean had a repertoire that varied from a barely audible connoisseur-testing-the-bouquet-of-brandy sniff to a loud hawking in the back of his throat.

'Sorry, sir, I can't help it. I've got a bit of a cold.'

But then, to even the score, Mr Clark had realized that Sean was vulnerable through Garrick. Hurt Garrick even a little and you were inflicting almost unbearable agony on Sean.

It had been a bad week for Mr Clark. His liver, weakened by persistent bouts of malaria, had been troubling him. He had suffered with a bilious headache for three days now; there had been unpleasantness with the Town Council about the terms on which his contract was to be renewed; Sean had been in good sniffing form the day before and Mr Clark had had about as much as he was prepared to take.

He came into the schoolroom and took his place on the dais; he let his eyes move slowly over his pupils until they came to Sean.

'Just let him start,' thought Mr Clark. 'Just let him start today and I'll kill him.'

The seating had been rearranged in the last two years. Sean and Garrick had been separated and Garrick was now at the front of the room where Mr Clark could reach him easily. Sean was near the back.

'English Readers,' said Mr Clark. 'Standard Ones turn to page five. Standard Twos turn to–'

Garrick sniffed wetly, hayfever again.

Mr Clark shut his book with a snap.

'Damn you!' he said softly, and then, his voice rising, 'Damn you!' Now he was shaking with rage, the edges of his nostrils were white and flared open.

He came down from the dais to Garrick's desk. 'Damn you! Damn you–you bloody little cripple,' he screamed and hit Garrick across the face with his open hand. Garrick cupped both hands over his cheek and stared at him.

'You dirty little swine,' Mr Clark mouthed at him. 'Now you're starting it too.'

He caught a handful of Garrick's hair and pulled his head down so that his forehead hit the top of the desk. 'I'll teach you. By God, I'll teach you.'

'I'll show you.' Bump.

'I'll teach you.' Bump.

It took Sean that long to reach them. He grabbed Mr Clark's arm and pulled him backwards. 'Leave him alone! He didn't do anything!'

Mr Clark saw Sean's face in front of him–he was past all reason–the face that had tormented him for two long years. He bunched his fist and lashed out at it.

Sean staggered back from the blow, the sting of it made his eyes water. For a second he lay sprawled across one of the desks, watching Clark and then he growled.

The sound sobered Clark, he backed away but only two paces before Sean was on him. Hitting with both hands, grunting with each punch, Sean drove him against the blackboard. Clark tried to break away but Sean caught the collar of his shirt and dragged him back–the collar tore half loose in his hand and Sean hit him again. Clark slid down the wall until he was sitting against it and Sean stood panting over him.

'Get out,' said Clark. His teeth were stained pink by the blood in his mouth and a little of it spilled out on to his lips. His collar stood up at a jaunty angle under one ear.

There was no sound in the room except Sean's breathing.

'Get out,' said Clark again and the anger drained out of Sean leaving him trembling with reaction. He walked to the door.

'You too,' Clark pointed at Garrick. 'Get out and don't come back!'

'Come on, Garry,' said Sean.

Garrick stood up from his desk and limped across to Sean and together they went out into the school yard.

'What are we going to do now?' There was a big red lump on Garrick's forehead.

'I suppose we'd better go home.'

'What about our things?' asked Garrick.

'We can't carry all that–we'll have to send for them later. Come on.'

They walked out through the town and along the road to the farm. They had almost reached the bridge on the Baboon Stroom before either of them spoke again.

'What do you reckon Pa will do?' asked Garrick. He was only putting into words the problem that had occupied them both since they left the school.

'Well, whatever he does, it was worth it.' Sean grinned. 'Did you see me clobber him, hey? Smackeroo—right in the chops.'

'You shouldn't have done it, Sean. Pa's going to kill us. Me too and I didn't do anything.'

'You sniffed,' Sean reminded him.

They reached the bridge and leaned over the parapet side by side to watch the water.

'How's your leg?' asked Sean.

'It's sore—I think we should rest a bit.'

'All right, if you say so,' Sean agreed.

There was a long silence, then, 'I wish you hadn't done it, Sean.'

'Well, wishing isn't going to help. Old Nose-Holes is as punched up as he'll ever be and all we can do is think of something to tell Pa.'

'He hit me,' said Garrick. 'He might have killed me.'

'Yes,' agreed Sean righteously, 'and he hit me too.'

They thought about it for a while.

'Perhaps we should just go away,' suggested Garrick.

'You mean without telling Pa?' The idea had attraction.

'Yeah, we could go to sea or something,' Garrick brightened.

'You'd get seasick, you even get sick in a train.'

Once more they applied their minds to the problem. Then Sean looked at Garrick, Garrick looked at Sean and as though by agreement they straightened up and started off once more for Theunis Kraal.

Ada was in front of the house. She had on a wide-brimmed straw hat that kept her face in shadow and over one arm she carried a basket of flowers. Busy with her garden, she didn't notice them until they were halfway across the lawn and when she did she stood motionless. She was steeling herself, trying to get her emotions under control; from experience she had learned to expect the worst from her stepsons and be thankful when it wasn't as bad as that.

As they came towards her they lost momentum and finally halted like a pair of clockwork toys running down.

'Hello,' said Ada.

'Hello,' they answered her together.

Garrick fumbled in his pocket, drew out a handkerchief and blew his nose. Sean stared up at the deep Dutch-gabled roof of Theunis Kraal as though he had never seen it before.

'Yes?' Ada kept her voice calm.

'Mr Clark said we were to go home,' announced Garrick.

'Why? Ada's calm was starting to crack.

'Well—' Garrick glanced at Sean for support. Sean's attention was still riveted on the roof.

'Well . . . You see Sean sort of punched him in the head until he fell down. I didn't do anything.'

Ada moaned softly, 'Oh, no!' She took a deep breath. 'All right. Start at the beginning and give me the whole story.'

They told it in relays, a garbled rush of words, interrupting each other and arguing over the details. When they had finished Ada said, 'You better go to

your room. Your father is working in the home section today and he'll be back
for his lunch soon. I'll try and prepare him a little.'

The room had the cheery atmosphere of a condemned cell.

'How much do you reckon he'll give us?' asked Garrick.

'I reckon until he gets tired, then he'll rest and give us some more,' Sean
answered.

They heard Waite's horse come into the yard. He said something to the
stable boy and they heard him laugh; the kitchen door slammed and there was
half a minute of suspense before they heard Waite roar. Garrick jumped
nervously.

For another ten minutes they could hear Waite and Ada talking in the
kitchen, the alternate rumble and soothing murmur. Then the tap of Ada's feet
along the passage and she came into the room.

'Your father wants to see you—he's in the study.'

Waite stood in front of the fireplace. His beard was powdered with dust and
his forehead as corrugated as a ploughed land with the force of his scowl.

'Come in,' he bellowed when Sean knocked and they filed in and stood in
front of him. Waite slapped his riding-whip against his leg and the dust puffed
out of his breeches.

'Come here,' he said to Garrick and took a handful of his hair. He twisted
Garrick's face up and looked at the bruise on his forehead.

'Hmm,' he said. He let go of Garrick's hair and it stood up in a tuft. He
threw the riding-whip on the stinkwood desk.

'Come here,' he said to Sean. 'Hold out your hands—no palms down.'

The skin on both hands was broken and one knuckle was swollen and puffy
looking.

'Hmm,' he said again. He turned to the shelf beside the fireplace, took a pipe
out of the rack and filled it from the stone jar of tobacco.

'You're a pair of bloody fools,' he said, 'but I'll take a chance and start you
on five shillings a week all found. Go and get your lunch . . . we've got work to
do this afternoon.'

They stared at him a moment in disbelief and then back towards the door.

'Sean.' Sean stopped, he knew it was too good to be true. 'Where did you hit
him?'

'All over, Pa, anywhere I could reach.'

'That's no good,' Waite said. 'You must go for the side of his head—here,' he
tapped the point of his jaw with his pipe, 'and keep your fists closed tight or
you'll break every finger in your hands before you're much older.'

'Yes, Pa.'

The door closed softly behind him and Waite allowed himself to grin.

'They've had enough book learning anyway,' he said aloud and struck a
match to his pipe; when it was drawing evenly he blew out smoke.

'Christ, I wish I could have watched it. That little pen-pusher will know
better than to tangle with my boy again.'

Now Sean had a course along which to race. He was born to run and Waite Courtney led him out of the stall in which he had fretted and gave him his lead. Sean ran, unsure of the prize, unsure of the distance; yet he ran with joy, he ran with all his strength.

Before dawn, standing with his father and Garrick in the kitchen, drinking coffee with hands cupped around the mug, Sean felt excitement for each coming day.

'Sean, take Zama and N'duti with you and make sure there are no strays in the thick stuff along the river.'

'I'll only take one herdboy, Pa, you'll need N'duti at the dipping tank.'

'All right, then. Try and meet us back at the tank before midday, we've got to push through a thousand head today.'

Sean gulped the remains of his coffee and buttoned his jacket. 'I'll get going then.'

A groom held his horse at the kitchen door. Sean slid his rifle into the scabbard and went up into the saddle without putting his foot into the steel; he lifted a hand and grinned at Waite, then he swung the horse and rode across the yard. The morning was still dark and cold. Waite watched him from the doorway.

'So goddamned sure of himself,' thought Waite. Yet he had the son he had hoped for and he was proud.

'What you want me to do, Pa?' Garrick asked beside him.

'Well, there are those heifers in the sick paddock–'

Waite stopped. 'No. You'd better come with me, Garry.'

Sean worked in the early morning when the sunlight was tinted as a stage effect, all golden and gay, and the shadows were long and black. He worked in the midday sun and sweated in the heat; in the rain; in the mist that swirled down grey and dump from the plateau; in the short African twilight, and came home in the dark. He loved every minute of it.

He learned to know cattle. Not by name, for only the trek oxen were named, but by their size and colour and markings, so that by running his eye over one of the herds he knew which animals were missing.

'Zama, the old cow with the crooked horn. Where is she?'

'Nkosi,' no longer the diminutive Nkosizana–little lord.

'Nkosi, yesterday I took her to the sick paddock, she has the worm in her eye.'

He learned to recognize disease almost before it started. The way a beast moved and held its head. He learned the treatment for them. Screw worm–kerosene poured into the wound until the maggots fell out like a shower of rice. Opthalmia–rinse the eye with permanganate. Anthrax and quarter-evil–a bullet and a bonfire for the carcass.

He delivered his first calf among the acacia trees on the bank of the Tugela; he did it alone with his sleeves rolled up above the elbows and the soapy feel of the slime on his hands. Afterwards, while the mother licked it and it staggered at each stroke of the tongue, Sean felt a choking sensation in his throat.

All this was not enough to burn up his energy. He played while he worked.

Practising his horsemanship: swinging from the saddle and running beside his horse, up again and over the other side, standing on the saddle at full gallop and then opening his legs and smacking down on his backside—his feet finding the stirrups without groping.

Practising with his rifle until he could hit a running jackal at a hundred and fifty paces, cutting the fox-terrier-sized body in half with the heavy bullet.

Then there was much of Garrick's work to do also.

'I don't feel very well, Sean.'

'What's wrong?'

'My leg's sore, you know how it chafes if I ride too much.'

'Why don't you go home, then?'

'Pa says I've got to fix the fence round the Number Three dip tank.' Garrick leaned forward on his horse to rub his leg, giving a brave little smile.

'You fixed it last week,' Sean protested.

'Yes—but the wires sort of came loose again.' There was always a strange impermanency about any repairs that Garrick effected.

'Have you got the wire cutters?' and Garrick produced them with alacrity from his saddle bag.

'I'll do it,' said Sean.

'Hell, man, thanks a lot,' and then a second's hesitation. 'You won't tell Pa, will you?'

'No—you can't help it if your leg's sore,' and Garrick rode home, sneaked through to his bedroom and escaped with Jim Hawkins into the pages of *Treasure Island*.

From this work came a new emotion for Sean. When the rain brought the grass out in green and filled the shallow pans on the plateau with water it was no longer simply a sign that the bird-nesting season had begun and that the fishing in the Baboon Stroom would improve—now it meant that they could take cattle up from the valley, it meant that there would be fat on the herds they drove into the sale pens at Ladyburg, it meant that another winter had ended and again the land was rich with life and the promise of life. This new emotion extended to the cattle also. It was a strong, almost savage feeling of possession.

It was in the late afternoon. Sean was sitting on his horse among trees, looking out across open vleiland at the small herd that was strung out before him. They were feeding, heads down, tails flicking lazily. Between Sean and the main body of cattle was a calf—it was three days old, still pale-beige in colour and unsure of its legs. It was trying them out, running clumsy circles in the short grass. From the herd a cow lowed and the calf stopped dead and stood with its legs splayed awkwardly under it and its ears up. Sean grinned and picked up the reins from his horse's neck; it was time to start back for the homestead.

At that moment he saw the lammergeyer: it had already begun its stoop at the calf, dropping big and dark brown from the sky, wings cocked back and its talons reaching for the strike. The wind rustled against it with the speed of its dive.

Sean sat paralysed and watched. The eagle hit the calf and Sean heard bone break, sharp as the snap of a dry stick, and then the calf was down in the grass struggling feebly with the eagle crouched on top of it.

For a second longer Sean sat, dazed with the speed at which it had happened. Then hatred came on him. It came with a violence and twisted his stomach. He hit his horse with his heels and it jumped forward. He drove it at the eagle and as he rode he screamed at it, a high-pitched formless sound, an animal expression of hate.

The eagle turned its head, looking at him sideways with one eye. It opened its great yellow beak and answered his scream, then it loosed its claws from the calf and launched itself into the air. Its wings flogged heavily and it moved low along the ground, gaining speed, lifting, drawing away from Sean.

Sean pulled his rifle from the scabbard and hauled his horse back on to its haunches. He threw himself out of the saddle and levered open the breech of the rifle.

The eagle was fifty yards ahead of him rising fast now. Sean slipped a cartridge into the breech, closed it and brought the rifle up in one continuous movement.

It was a difficult shot. Moving away from him and rising, the beat of its wings jerking its body. Sean fired. The rifle jumped back into his shoulder and the gunsmoke whipped away on the wind, so he could watch the bullet connect.

The eagle collapsed in the air. It burst like a pillow in a puff of feathers and fell with its six-feet-long wings fluttering limply. Before it hit the ground Sean was running.

It was dead when he reached it, but he reversed his rifle: holding it by the muzzle, he swung the butt down from above his head on to its body. At the third blow the butt of his rifle broke off, but he kept on hitting. He was sobbing with fury.

When he stopped and stood panting the sweat was running down his face and his body was trembling. The eagle was a squashy mess of broken flesh and feathers.

The calf was still alive. The rifle was jammed. Sean knelt beside it with tears of anger burning his eyes and killed it with his hunting-knife.

13

So strong was this new feeling that Sean could hate even Garrick. He did not hate for long, though. Sean's anger and his hatred were quick things, with flames like those of a fire in dry grass: hot and high but soon burnt out and afterwards the ashes dead and no smouldering.

Waite was away when it happened. For three consecutive years Waite Courtney had been nominated for the chairmanship of the Beef Growers' Association and each time he had stood down. He was human enough to want the prestige the office carried with it, but he was also sensible to the fact that his farm would suffer from his frequent absences. Sean and Garrick had been working for two years when the annual election of office bearers came around again.

The night before Waite left for the meeting in Pietermaritzburg he spoke to Ada. 'I had a letter from Bernard last week, my dear,' he was standing before the mirror in their bedroom trimming his beard. 'They insist that I stand for the chair this year.'

'Very wise of them,' said Ada. 'They'd have the best man if you did.'

Waite frowned with concentration as he snipped at his whiskers. She believed so unquestioningly in him that he seldom doubted himself. Now

looking at his face in the mirror he wondered how much of his success was
owed to Ada's backing.

'You can do it, Waite.' Not a challenge, not a question, but a calm statement
of fact. When she said it he believed it.

He laid the scissors down on the chest of drawers and turned to her. She sat
cross-legged on the bed in a white nightgown, her hair was down in a dark
mass around her shoulders. 'I think Sean can look after things here,' she said,
and then quickly, 'and of course Garry.'

'Sean's learning fast,' Waite agreed.

'Are you going to take the job?'

Waite hesitated. 'Yes,' he nodded and Ada smiled.

'Come here,' she held out her hands to him.

Sean drove Waite and Ada to the station at Ladyburg: at the last minute Waite
had insisted that she go with him, for he wanted her to be there to share it with
him.

Sean put their luggage into the coach and waited while they talked with the
small group of cattlemen who were going up to the meeting. The whistle blew
and the travellers scattered to their compartments. Ada kissed Sean and
climbed up. Waite stayed a second longer on the platform.

'Sean, if you need any help go across to Mr Erasmus at Lion Kop. I'll be
back on Thursday.'

'I won't need any help, Pa.'

Waite's mouth hardened. 'Then you must be God, he's the only one who
never needs help,' Waite said harshly. 'Don't be a bloody fool—if you run into
trouble ask Erasmus.'

He climbed up after Ada. The train jerked, gathered speed and ran out
towards the escarpment. Sean watched it dwindle, then he walked back to the
buggy. He was master of Theunis Kraal and he liked the feeling. The small
crowd on the platform was dispersing and out of it came Anna.

'Hello, Sean.' She had on a green cotton dress that was faded with washing,
her feet were bare. She smiled with her small white teeth and watched his
face.

'Hello, Anna.'

'Aren't you going up to Pietermaritzburg?'

'No, I've got to look after the farm.'

'Oh!'

They waited in silence, uncomfortable before so many people. Sean
coughed and scratched the side of his nose.

'Anna, come on. We've got to get home.' One of her brothers called from in
front of the ticket office and Anna leaned towards Sean.

'Will I see you on Sunday?' she whispered.

'I'll come if I can. But I don't know—I've got to look after the farm.'

'Please try, Sean.' Her face was earnest. 'I'll be waiting for you, I'll take
some lunch and wait all day. Please come, even if it's only for a little while.'

'All right, I'll come.'

'Promise?'

'Promise.'

She smiled with relief. 'I'll wait for you on the path above the waterfall.'

She turned and ran to join her family and Sean drove back to Theunis Kraal.
Garrick was lying on his bed reading.

'I thought Pa told you to get on with the branding of those new cattle we bought on Wednesday.'

Garrick laid down his book and sat up. 'I told Zama to keep them in the kraal until you got back.'

'Pa told you to get on with it. You can't keep them there all day without feed or water.'

'I hate branding,' muttered Garrick. 'I hate it when they moo like that as you burn them, and I hate the stink of burning hair and skin—it gives me a headache.'

'Well someone's got to do it. I can't, I've got to go down and mix new dip into the tanks for tomorrow.' Sean was losing his temper. 'Hell, Garry, why are you always so damn helpless?'

'I can't help it, I can't help it if I've only got one leg.' Garrick was close to tears again. The reference to his leg had the desired effect—Sean's temper steadied instantly.

'I'm sorry,' Sean smiled his irresistible smile. 'I tell you what. I'll do the branding—you fix the tanks. Get the drums of dip loaded on to the Scotch cart, take a couple of the stable boys with you to help. Here are the keys of the storeroom.' He tossed the bunch on to the bed beside Garrick. 'You should be finished before dark.'

At the door he turned.

'Garry, don't forget to do all six tanks—not just the ones near the house.'

So Garrick loaded six drums of dip on to the Scotch cart and went off down the hill. He was home well before dark. The front of his breeches were stained with the dark, tarry chemical and some of it had soaked into the leather of his single riding-boot. As he came out of the kitchen into the passage Sean shouted from the study. 'Hey, Garry, did you finish them?'

Garrick was startled. Waite's study was a sacred place, the inner sanctum of Theunis Kraal. Even Ada knocked before going into it and the twins went there only to receive punishment. Garrick limped along the passage and pushed open the door.

Sean sat with his boots on top of the desk and his ankles neatly crossed. He leaned back in the swivel chair.

'Pa will kill you,' Garrick's voice was shaky.

'Pa's in Pietermaritzburg,' said Sean.

Garrick stood in the doorway and looked around the room. It was the first time he had really seen it. On every previous visit he had been too preoccupied with the violence to come and the only item in the room he had studied closely was the seat of the big leather easy chair as he bent over the arm of it and exposed his backside to the sjambok.

Now he looked at the room. The walls were panelled to the ceiling, the wood was dark yellow and polished. The ceiling was fancy plaster, in a pattern of oak leaves. A single lamp hung from the centre of it on a brass chain. You could walk into the fireplace of brown chipped stone and there were logs laid ready for the match.

Pipes and tobacco jar on the ledge beside the fireplace, guns in a rack along one wall, a bookcase of green and maroon leather bound volumes: encyclopaedias, dictionaries, books on travel and farming, but no fiction. There was an oil painting of Ada on the wall opposite the desk, the artist had captured a little of her serenity: she wore a white dress and carried her hat in her hand. A magnificent set of Cape buffalo horns above the fireplace dominated the room with their great crenellated bosses and wide sweep to the tips.

It was a man's room, with loose dog-hairs on the leopard-skin rugs, and the presence of the man strongly there—it even smelled of Waite. It was as distinctively his as the tweed coat and Terai hat that hung behind the door.

Next to where Sean sat the cabinet was open and bottle of brandy stood on top of it. Sean had a goblet in his hand.

'You're drinking Pa's brandy,' Garrick accused.

'It's not bad.' Sean lifted the glass and inspected the liquid; he took a careful sip and held it in his mouth, preparing himself to swallow. Garrick watched him with awe and Sean tried not to blink as it went down his throat.

'Would you like some?'

Garrick shook his head and the fumes came up Sean's nose and his eyes ran.

'Pa will kill you!' said Garrick again.

'Sit down,' ordered Sean, his voice husky from the brandy. 'I want to work out a plan for the time Pa's away.'

Garrick advanced on the armchair, but before he reached it he changed his mind—the associations were too painful. He went to the sofa instead and sat on the edge.

'Tomorrow,' Sean held up one finger, 'we'll dip all the cattle in the home section. I've told Zama to start bringing them early—you did do the tanks, didn't you?'

Garrick nodded and Sean went on.

'On Saturday,' Sean held up his second finger, 'we'll burn fire breaks along the top of the escarpment. The grass is dry as hell up there. You take one gang and start near the falls, I'll ride down to the other end, near Fredericks Kloof. On Sunday . . .' Sean said and then paused. On Sunday Anna.

'I want to go to church on Sunday,' said Garrick quickly.

'That's fine,' agreed Sean. 'You go to church.'

'Are you going to come?'

'No,' said Sean.

Garrick looked down at the leopard-skin rugs that covered the floor—he didn't try to persuade Sean for Anna would be at the service. Perhaps afterwards, if Sean wasn't there to distract her, he could drive her home in the buggy. He started a day dream and wasn't listening as Sean went on talking.

In the morning it was full daylight by the time Sean reached the dip tank. He pushed a small herd of stragglers before him and they came out through the trees and stirrup high grass into the wide area of trampled earth around the tank. Garrick had started running cattle through the dip and there were about ten head already in the draining kraal at the far end, standing wet and miserable, their bodies dark with drip.

Sean drove his herd through the gates of the entrance kraal into the solid pack of brown bodies that were already there. N'duti slid the bars of the gate back into place to hold them.

'I see you, Nkosi.'

'I see you, N'duti. Plenty of work today!'

'Plenty,' agreed N'duti, 'always plenty of work.'

Sean rode around the kraal and tied his horse beneath one of the trees, then walked across to the tank. Garrick was standing by the parapet and leaning against one of the columns that supported the roof.

'Hello, Garry, how's it going?'

'Fine.'

Sean leaned over the parapet next to Garry. The tank was twenty feet long and eight wide, the surface of the liquid was below ground level. Around the tank was a low wall and over it a roof of thatch to prevent rain diluting the contents.

The herdboys drove the cattle up to the edge and each beast hesitated on the brink.

'E'yapi, E'yapi,' screamed the herdboys and the push of bodies behind it forced it to jump. If one was stubborn, Zama leaned over the railing of the kraal, grabbed its tail and bit it.

Each beast jumped with its nose held high and its forefeet gathered up under its chest; it disappeared completely under the oil black surface and came up again swimming frantically along the tank until its hooves touched the sloping bottom at the far end and it could lumber up into the draining kraal.

'Keep them moving, Zama,' shouted Sean.

Zama grinned at him and bit with big white teeth into a reluctant tail.

The ox was a heavy animal and it splashed a drop up on to Sean's cheek as he leaned over the wall. Sean did not bother to wipe it off, he went on watching.

'Well, if we don't get top prices for this lot at the next sale then the buyers don't know good cattle,' he said to Garry.

'They're all right,' agreed Garry.

'All right? They're the fattest oxen in the district.' Sean was about to enlarge on the theme, but suddenly he was aware of discomfort—the drop of dip was burning his cheek. He wiped it off with his finger and held it to his nose; the smell of it stung his nostrils. For a second he stared at it stupidly and the spot on his cheek burned like fire.

He looked up quickly. The cattle in the draining kraal were milling restlessly and as he looked one of them staggered sideways and bumped against the railing.

'Zama!' shouted Sean, and the Zulu looked up. 'Stop them. For God's sake don't let any more through.'

There was another ox poised on the edge. Sean snatched off his hat and jumped up on to the wall, he beat the ox in the face with his hat trying to drive it back, but it sprang out into the tank. Sean caught hold of the railing and stepped into the space it had left on the edge of the tank.

'Stop them' he shouted. 'Get the bars in, don't let any more through.'

He spread his arms across the entrance, holding on to the railing on each side, kicking at the faces of the cattle in front of him.

'Hurry, damn you, get the bars in,' he shouted. The oxen pressed towards him, a wall of horned heads. Pushed forward by those behind and held back by Sean they started to panic; one of them tried to jump over the railing. As it swung its head its horn raked Sean's chest, up across the ribs, ripping his shirt.

Behind him Sean felt the wooden bars being dropped into place, blocking the entrance to the tank, and then Zama's hands on his arm pulling him up out of the confusion of horns and hooves. Two of the herdboys helped him over the railing and Sean shrugged their hands off as soon as he was on the ground.

'Come on,' he ordered and ran to his horse.

'Nkosi, you are bleeding.'

Blood had splotched in front of Sean's shirt but he felt no pain. The cattle that had been through the dip were now in terrible distress. They charged about the kraal, bellowing pitifully; one of them fell and when it got to its feet again its legs were shaking so that it could barely stand.

'The river,' shouted Sean, 'get them down to the river. Try and wash it off. Zama, open the gate.'

The Baboon Stroom was a mile away. One of the oxen died before they could get them out of the kraal, another ten before they reached the river. They died in convulsions, with their bodies shuddering and their eyes turned back into their heads.

Sean drove those that remained down the bank into the river. The water was clear and as each beast went into it, the dip washed off in a dark brown cloud.

'Stand here, Zama. Don't let them come out.'

Sean swam his horse to the far bank and turned back the oxen that were trying to climb it.

'Nkosi—one is drowning,' called N'duti and Sean looked across the river. A young ox was in convulsions in the shallows: its head was under the water and its feet thrashed the surface.

Sean slid off his horse and waded out to it. The water was up to his armpits. He tried to hold its head out and drag it to the bank.

'Help me, N'duti,' he shouted, and the Zulu came into the river. It was a hopeless task: each time the ox lunged it pulled them both under with it. By the time they got the ox to the bank it was dead.

Sean sat in the mud beside the body of the ox: he was exhausted and his lungs ached with the water he had breathed.

'Bring them out, Zama,' he gasped. The survivors were standing in the shallows or swimming in aimless circles. 'How many?' asked Sean. 'How many are dead?'

'Two more while you were in the water. Altogether thirteen, Nkosi.'

'Where's my horse?'

'It ran, and I let it go. It will be back at the house.'

Sean nodded.

'Bring them up to the sick paddock. We must watch them for a few days.'

Sean stood up and started walking back towards the dip tank. Garrick was gone, and the main herd was still in the kraal. Sean opened the gate and turned them loose. He felt better by then, and as his strength returned with it came his anger and his hatred. He started along the track towards the homestead. His boots squelched as he walked and he hated Garrick more strongly with each step. Garrick had mixed the dip. Garrick had killed his cattle and Sean hated him.

As Sean came up the slope below the house he saw Garrick standing in the yard. Garrick saw him also; he disappeared into the kitchen and Sean started to run. He went in through the kitchen door and nearly knocked down one of the servants.

'Garrick,' shouted Sean. 'Damn it—where are you?'

He searched the house; once quickly and then again thoroughly. Garrick was gone, but the window of the bedroom was open and there was a dusty boot print on the sill. Garrick had gone over it.

'You bloody coward,' howled Sean and scrambled out after him. He stood a second, with his head swinging from side to side and his fists opening and closing.

'I'll find out,' he howled again. 'I'll find you wherever you're hiding.'

He started across the yard towards the stables and halfway there he saw the door of the dairy was closed. When he tried it he found it was locked from inside. Sean backed away from it and then charged it with his shoulder—the lock burst and the door flew open. Sean skidded across the room and came up against the far wall. Garrick was trying to climb out of the window, but it was small and high up. Sean caught him by the seat of his pants and pulled him down.

'Watcha do to the dip, hey? Watcha do to it?' He shouted in Garrick's face.

'I didn't mean to. I didn't know it'd kill them.'

'Tell me what you did.' Sean had hold of the front of his shirt and was dragging him towards the door.

'I didn't do anything. Honest I didn't know.'

'I'm going to hammer you anyway, so you might as well tell me.'

'Please, Sean, I didn't know.'

Sean jammed Garrick against the doorway and held him there with his left hand—his right hand he drew back with the fist bunched.

'No, Sean. Please, no.'

And suddenly the anger was gone from Sean, his hands sank back to his sides.

'All right—just tell me what you did,' he said coldly. His anger was gone but not his hatred.

'I was tired and it was getting late and my leg was hurting,' whispered Garrick, 'and there were still four more tanks to do, and I knew you'd check that all the drums were empty, and it was so late . . . and . . .'

'And?'

'And so I emptied all the dip into the one tank . . . but I didn't know it would kill them, truly I didn't.'

Sean turned away from him and started walking slowly back towards the house. Garrick stumbled after him.

'I'm sorry, Sean, honest I'm sorry. I didn't know that . . .'

Sean walked ahead of him into the kitchen and slammed the door in his face. He went through into Waite's study. From the bookshelf he lifted down the heavy leather-covered stock register and carried it to the desk. He opened the book, picked up a pen and dipped it. For a moment he stared at the page and then in the 'deaths' column he wrote the number *13* and after it the words 'dip poisoning'. He pressed down so hard with the pen that the nib cut the paper.

It took Sean and the herdboys all the rest of that day and the next to bale out the tank, refill it with clean water and mix in fresh dip. He saw Garrick only at meals and they didn't speak.

The next day was Sunday. Garrick went into town early, for the church service started at eight o'clock. When he had gone Sean began his preparations. He shaved—leaning close to the mirror and handling the cut-throat gingerly, shaping his side-burns and clearing the hair from the rest of his face until his skin was smooth and fresh-looking. Then he went through to the master-bedroom and helped himself to a generous portion of his father's brilliantine, taking care to screw the lid back on the bottle and replace it exactly as he found it. He rubbed the brilliantine into his hair and sniffed its perfume appreciatively. He combed his hair over his forehead, parted it down the centre and polished it into a gloss with Waite's silver-backed brushes. Then a clean white shirt, breeches worn only once before, boots as shiny as his hair—and Sean was ready.

The clock on the mantelpiece in the lounge assured him that he was well ahead of time. To be exact, he was two hours early. Eight o'clock now: church didn't end until nine and it would be another hour before Anna could escape from under the eyes of her family and reach the rendezvous above the falls. He settled down to wait. He read the latest copy of the *Natal Farmer*. He had read it three times before for it was a month old, and now even the excellent article on 'Stomach parasites in Cattle and Sheep' had lost much of its punch. Sean's attention wandered—he thought about the day ahead and felt the familiar movement within his breeches. This necessitated a rearrangement for the breeches were tight fitting. Then fantasy palled: Sean was a doer not a thinker, and he went through to the kitchen to solicit a cup of coffee from Joseph. When he had finished it, there was still half an hour to go.

'The hell with it,' said Sean and shouted for his horse. He climbed the escarpment, letting his horse move diagonally up the slope and at the top he dismounted and let it blow. Today he could see the course of the Tugela river out across the plain—it was a belt of dark green. He could count the roofs of the houses in Ladyburg and the church spire, copper clad, shone in the sunlight like a beacon fire.

He mounted again and rode along the edge of the plateau until he reached the Baboon Stroom above the falls. He followed it back and forded it at a shallow place, lifting his feet up on the saddle in front of him to keep his boots dry. He off-saddled next to the pools and knee-haltered his horse, then he followed the path until it dropped over the edge of the plateau into the thick forest that surrounded the falls. It was cool and damp in the forest with moss growing on the trees, for the roof of leaves and creepers shut out the sun. There was a bottle-bird in the undergrowth.

'Glug, glug, glug,' it said, like water poured from a bottle, and its call was almost drowned in the ceaseless thunder of the falls.

Sean spread his handkerchief on a rock beside the path, sat down on it and waited. Within five minutes he was fidgeting impatiently—within half an hour he was grumbling aloud.

'I'll count to five hundred. . . . If she hasn't come by then I'm not going to wait.'

He counted and when he reached the promised figure he stopped and peered anxiously down the path. There was no sign of Anna.

'I'm not going to sit here all day,' he announced and made no effort to stand up. A fat yellow caterpillar caught his eye; it was on the trunk of a tree farther down the slope. He picked up a pebble and threw it. It bounced off the tree an inch above the caterpillar.

'Close,' Sean encouraged himself and stopped for another stone. After a while he had exhausted the supply of pebbles around his feet and the caterpillar was still moving leisurely up the trunk. Sean was forced to go out on a foraging expedition for more pebbles. He came back with both hands full and once more took up his position on the rock. He piled the pebbles between his feet and reopened the bombardment. He aimed each throw with the utmost concentration and with his third pebble he hit squarely and the caterpillar popped in a spurt of green juice. Sean felt cheated. He looked around for a new target and instead found Anna standing beside him.

'Hello, Sean.' She had on a pink dress. She carried her shoes in one hand and a small basket in the other. 'I brought some lunch for us.'

'What took you so long?' Sean stood up and wiped his hands on his breeches. 'I thought you weren't coming.'

'I'm sorry—everything went wrong.'

There was an awkward pause and Anna flushed slightly as Sean looked at her. Then she turned and started up the path. 'Come on–I'll race you to the top.'

She ran fast on bare feet, holding her skirts up to her knees and she was out in the sunshine before Sean caught her. He put his arms around her from behind and they fell together into the grass beside the path. They lay holding each other, laughing and panting at the same time.

'The service went on and on–I thought it would never finish,' said Anna, 'and afterwards–'

Before she could finish Sean covered her mouth with his and immediately her arms came up around his neck. They kissed with the tension building up steadily between them until Anna was moaning softly and moving her body against his. Sean released her mouth and moved his lips down across her cheek to her neck.

'Oh, Sean, it's been so long. It's been a whole week.'

'I know.'

'I've missed you so–I thought about you every day.'

Sean had his face pressed into her neck, he didn't answer.

'Did you miss me, Sean?'

'Hmm,' Sean murmured and lifted his mouth to take the lobe of her ear between his teeth.

'Did you think about me while you were working?'

'Hmm.'

'Tell me properly, Sean, say it properly.'

'I missed you, Anna, I thought about you all the time,' lied Sean and kissed her on the mouth. She clung to him and Sean's hand went down, right down to her knee and then up again under her clothes. Anna caught his wrist and held his hand away. 'No, Sean, just kiss me.'

Sean waited until her grip relaxed and then tried again, but this time she twisted away from him and sat up. 'Sometimes I think that's all you want to do.'

Sean felt his temper coming up, but he had the good sense to check it.

'That's not true, Anna. It's just that I haven't seen you for so long and I've missed you so much.'

She softened immediately and reached out to touch his cheek. 'Oh, Sean, I'm sorry. I don't mind really, it's just that–oh, I don't know.' She scrambled to her feet and picked up the basket. 'Come on, let's go on to the pools.'

They had a special place. It was walled in by the reeds and shaded by a big tree that grew on the bank above; the sand was washed clean and white. Sean spread his saddle blanket for them to sit on. They could hear the river, close by but hidden and the reeds rustled and nodded their fluffy heads with each breath of the wind.

'–and I couldn't get rid of him,' Anna chattered as she knelt on the blanket and unpacked the basket. 'He just sat there and every time I said something he blushed and wriggled on his seat. In the end I just told him, "I'm sorry, Garry, I have to go!"'

Sean scowled. The mention of Garrick had reminded him of the dip; he hadn't forgiven him yet.

'And then when I got into the house I found that Pa and Frikkie were fighting. Ma was in tears and the other kids were locked in the bedroom.'

'Who won?' asked Sean with interest.

'They weren't really fighting–they were just shouting at each other. They were both drunk.'

Sean was always slightly shocked at Anna's casual reference to her family's drinking habits. Everybody knew about Mr Van Essen and his two eldest boys but Anna didn't have to talk about it. Once Sean had tried to correct her. 'You shouldn't say things like that about your Pa. You should respect him.'

And Anna had looked at him calmly and asked, 'Why?' which was a difficult question. But now she changed the subject.

'Do you want to eat yet?'

'No,' said Sean and reached for her. She fought back, shrieking demurely until Sean held her down and kissed her. Then she lay quietly, answering his kisses.

'If you stop me now I'm going to get mad,' whispered Sean and deliberately unfastened the top button of her dress. She watched his face with solemn eyes and her hands stayed on his shoulders until he had undone her blouse down to the waist and then with her fingers she traced the bold black curves of his eyebrows.

'No, Sean, I won't stop you. I want to as well, I want to as much as you do.'

There was so much to discover and each thing was strange and wonderful and they were the first to find it. The way the muscles stood out down the side of his chest beneath his arms and yet left a place where she could see the outline of his ribs. The texture of her skin, smooth and white with the faint blue suggestion of veins beneath. The deep hollow down the centre of his back–pressing her fingers into it she could feel his spine. The down on her cheeks, so pale and fine he could see it only in the sunlight. The way their lips felt against each other and the tiny flutter of tongues between. The smell of their bodies, one milky warm and the other musky and vigorous. The hair that covered his chest and grew thicker under his arms, and hers: startlingly dark against white skin, and small silky nest of it. Each time there was something new to find and greet with soft sounds of delight.

Now, kneeling before her as she lay with her head thrown back and her arms half-raised to receive him, Sean suddenly bowed his head and touched her with his mouth. The taste of her was clean as the taste of the sea.

Her eyes flew open. 'Sean, no, you mustn't–oh no, you mustn't.' There were lips within lips and a bud as softly resilient as a tiny green grape. Sean found it with the tip of his tongue.

'Oh, Sean, you can't do that. Please, please, please.' And her hands were in the thick hair at the back of his head holding him there.

'I can't stand it any more, come over me . . . quickly, quickly, Sean.'

Filling like a sail in a hurricane, swollen and hard and tight, stretched beyond its limit until it burst and was blown to shreds in the wind and was gone. Everything gone. The wind and the sail, the tension and the wanting, all gone. There was left only the great nothingness which is peace. Perhaps a kind of death; perhaps death is like that. But, like death, not an ending–for even death contains the seeds of resurrection. So they came back from peace to a new beginning, slowly at first and then faster until they were two people again. Two people on a blanket among reeds with the sunlight white on the sand about them.

'Each time it's better and better–isn't it, Sean?'

'Ah!' Sean stretched, arching his back and spreading his arms.

'Sean, you do love me, don't you?'

'Sure. Sure I love you.'

'I think you must love me to have done'—she hesitated—'to do what you did.'

'I just said so, didn't I?' Sean's attention wandered to the basket. He selected an apple and polished it on the basket.

'Tell me properly. Hold me tight and tell me.'

'Hell, Anna, how many times have I got to say it?' Sean bit into the apple. 'Did you bring any of your Ma's shortbread?'

It was coming on night when Sean got back to Theunis Kraal. He turned his horse over to one of the grooms and went into the house. His body tingled from the sun, and he felt the emptiness and sadness of after-love, but it was a good sadness, like the sadness of old memories.

Garrick was in the dining-room, eating alone. Sean walked into the room and Garrick looked up nervously.

'Hello, Garry.' Sean smiled at him and Garrick was momentarily dazzled by it. Sean sat down in the chair beside him and punched him lightly on the arm.

'Have you left any for me?' His hatred was gone.

'There's plenty,' Garrick nodded eagerly. 'Try some of the potatoes, they're jolly good.'

14

'They say the Governor sent for your Pa while he was in Pietermaritzburg. Had him alone for nearly two hours.' Stephen Erasmus took the pipe out of his mouth and spat down on to the railway lines. In his brown homespun and *veldschoen* he did not look like a rich cattleman. 'Well, we don't need a prophet to tell us what it was about, do we?'

'No, sir,' Sean agreed vaguely. The train was late and Sean wasn't listening. He had an entry in the stock register to explain to his father and he was mentally rehearsing his speech.

'*Ja,* we know what it's about all right.' Old Erasmus put the pipe back between his teeth and spoke around it. 'It's been two weeks now since the British Agent was recalled from Cetewayo's kraal at Gingindhlovu. *Liewe Here!* in the old days we'd have called out the Commando long ago.' He packed his pipe, pushing down on to the glowing tobacco with a calloused forefinger. Sean noticed that the finger was twisted and scarred by the trigger-guards of a hundred heavy rifles.

'You've never been on commando have you, *Jong?*'

'No, sir.'

'About time you did then,' said Erasmus, 'about bledy time.'

Up on the escarpment the train whistled and Sean started guiltily.

'There she is.' Erasmus stood up from the bench on which they were sitting and the station master came out from his office with a rolled red flag in his hand. Sean felt his stomach sink slowly until it stopped somewhere just above his knees.

The train ran in past them, whooshing steam and brake-whining. The single passenger coach stopped precisely opposite the wooden platform. Erasmus came forward and took Waite's hand.

'*Goeie More,* Steff.'

'*More*, Waite. They tell me you're the new chairman now. Well done, man.'

'Thanks. Did you get my telegram?' Waite spoke in Afrikaans.

'*Ja*. I got it. I told the others, we'll all be out at Theunis Kraal tomorrow.'

'Good,' Waite nodded. 'You'll stay for lunch, of course. We've got a lot to talk about.'

'Is it what I think it is?' Erasmus grinned wickedly. The tobacco had stained his beard yellow around his mouth and his face was brown and wrinkled.

'I tell you all about it tomorrow, Steff,' Waite winked at him, 'but in the meantime you'd better get that old muzzle-loader of yours out of moth-balls.'

They laughed, one deep down and the other a rusty old laugh.

'Grab the bags, Sean. Let's get home.' Waite took Ada's arm and they walked with Erasmus to the buggy. Ada had on a new dress, blue with leg o'mutton sleeves and a picture hat; she looked lovely but a little worried as she listened to them talking. It's strange how women can never face the prospect of war with the same boyish enthusiasm as their men.

'Sean!' Waite Courtney's roar carried clearly from his study along the corridor and through the closed door of the sitting-room. Ada dropped her knitting into her lap and her features set into an expression of unnatural calm. Sean stood up from his chair.

'You should have told him earlier,' Garrick said in a small voice. 'You should have told him during lunch.'

'I didn't get a chance.'

'Sean!' Another blast from the study.

'What's happened now?' asked Ada quietly.

'It's nothing, Ma. Don't worry about it.'

Sean crossed to the door.

'Sean,' Garrick's stricken voice, 'Sean, you won't–I mean you don't have to tell–' He stopped and sat hunched in his chair, his eyes full of desperate appeal.

'It's all right, Garry, I'll fix it.'

Waite Courtney stood over the desk. Between his clenched fists the stock register lay open. He looked up as Sean came in and closed the door.

'What's this?' He prodded the page with a huge square-tipped finger. Sean opened his mouth and then closed it again.

'Come on. I'm listening.'

'Well, Pa–'.

'Well, Pa–be buggered. Just tell me how you've managed to massacre half the cattle on this farm in a little over a week?'

'It's not half the cattle–it's only thirteen.' Sean was stung by the exaggeration.

'Only thirteen,' bellowed Waite, '*only* thirteen. God Almighty, shall I tell you how much that is in cash? Shall I tell you how much that is in hard work and time and worry?'

'I know, Pa.'

'You know,' Waite was panting. 'Yes, you know everything. There's nothing anyone can tell you, is there? Not even how to kill thirteen head of prime oxen.'

'Pa–'

'Don't Pa me, by Jesus.' Waite slammed the heavy book closed. 'Just explain to me how you managed it. What's "dip poisoning"? What the bloody hell is "dip poisoning"? Did you give it to them to drink? Did you stick it up their arses?'

'The dip was too strong,' said Sean.

'And why was the dip too strong? How much did you put in?'

Sean took a deep breath, 'I put in four drums.'

There was silence and then Waite asked softly, *'How much?'*

'Four drums.'

'Are you mad? Are you raving bloody mad?'

'I didn't think it would harm them.' His carefully rehearsed speech forgotten, Sean unconsciously repeated the words he had heard from Garrick. 'It was getting late and my leg was—' Sean bit the sentence off and Waite stared at him, then the confusion cleared from his face.

'Garry!' he said.

'No,' shouted Sean. 'It wasn't him, I did it.'

'You're lying to me.' Waite came round from behind the desk. There was a note of disbelief in his voice. To his knowledge it was the first time it had ever happened. He stared at Sean and then his anger was back more violently than before. He had forgotten the oxen—it was the lie that concerned him now. 'By Christ, I'll teach you to tell the truth.' He snatched up his sjambok from the desk.

'Don't hit me, Pa,' Sean warned him, backing away. Waite threw up the sjambok and swung it down overarm. It hissed softly and Sean twisted away from it, but the tip of the lash caught his shoulder. Sean gasped at the pain and lifted his hand to it.

'You lying little bastard!' shouted Waite and swung the whip sideways as though he was scything wheat, and this time it curled around Sean's chest under his uplifted arm. It split his shirt like a razor cut and the cloth fell away to expose the red ridged welt across his ribs and around his back.

'Here's some more!' Waite lifted the sjambok again and as he stood with his arm thrown back and his body turned off balance he knew he had made a mistake. Sean was no longer clutching the whip marks; his hands were held low and his fists were bunched. At the corners his eyebrows were lifted, giving an expression of satanical fury to his face. He was pale and his lips were drawn back tight, showing his teeth. His eyes, no longer blue but burning black, were on a level with Waite's.

'He's coming for me.' Waite's surprise slowed his reflexes, he couldn't bring his whip-arm down before Sean was on him. Sean hit him, standing solidly on both feet, bringing the full weight of his body into the punch, hurling it into the middle of Waite's exposed chest.

Heart punched, strength oozing out of him, Waite staggered back against the desk. The sjambok fell out of his hand and Sean went after him. Waite had the sensation of being a beetle in a saucer of treacle: he could see and think but he could barely move. He saw Sean take three quick paces forward, saw his right hand cocked like a loaded rifle, saw it aimed at his defenceless face.

In that instant, while his body moved in slow motion but his mind raced, the scales of paternal blindness dropped from Waite Courtney's eyes and he realized that he was fighting a man who matched him in strength and height, and who was his superior in speed. His only advantage lay in the experience he had gathered in forty years of brawling.

Sean threw his punch: it had all the power of the first one and Waite knew that he could not survive that in his face—and yet he could not move to avoid it.

He dropped his chin on to his chest and took Sean's fist on the top of his head. The force of it flung him backwards over the desk, but as it hit he heard the brittle crackle of Sean's fingers breaking.

Waite dragged himself to his knees, using the corner of the desk as a support, and looking at his son. Sean was doubled up with pain, holding his broken hand against his stomach. Waite pulled himself to his feet and sucked in big breaths of air, he felt his strength coming back.

'All right,' he said, 'if you want to fight—then we fight.' He came round the desk, moving slowly, his hands ready, no longer underestimating his man.

'I am going to knock the daylights out of you,' announced Waite. Sean straightened up and looked at him. There was agony in his face now, but the anger was there also. Something surged up inside Waite when he saw it.

He can fight and he's game. Now we'll see if he can take a beating. Rejoicing silently Waite moved in on him, watching Sean's left hand, disregarding the broken right for he knew what pain was in it. He knew that no man could use a hand in that condition.

He shot out his own left hand, measuring with it, trying to draw Sean. Sean side-stepped, moving in past it. Waite was wide open for Sean's right, his broken right, the hand he could not possibly use—and Sean used it with all his strength into Waite's face.

Waite's brain burst into bright colours and darkness, he spun sideways, falling, hitting the leopard-skin rug with his shoulder and sliding with it across the floor into the fireplace. Then in the darkness he felt Sean's hands on him and heard Sean's voice.

'Pa, oh, my God, Pa. Are you all right?'

The darkness cleared a little and he saw Sean's face, the anger gone from it and in its place worry that was almost panic.

'Pa, oh, my God! Please, Pa.'

Waite tried to sit up, but he could not make it. Sean had to help him. He knelt next to Waite holding him, fumbling helplessly with his face, trying to brush the hair back off his forehead, stroking the rumpled beard into place. 'I'm sorry, Pa, truly I'm sorry. Let me help you to the chair.'

Waite sat in the chair and massaged the side of his jaw. Sean hovered over him, his own hand forgotten.

'What you want to do—kill me?' asked Waite ruefully.

'I didn't mean it. I just lost my temper.'

'I noticed,' said Waite, 'I just happened to notice that.'

'Pa—about Garry. You don't have to say anything to him, do you?'

Waite dropped his hand from his face and looked at Sean steadily.

'I'll make a bargain with you,' he said, 'I'll leave Garry out of it if you'll promise me two things. One: You never lie to me again.'

Sean nodded quickly.

'Two: If anybody ever takes a whip to you again you swear to me you'll give him the same as you just gave me.'

Sean started to smile and Waite went on gruffly. 'Now let's have a look at your hand.'

Sean held it out and Waite examined it, moving each finger in turn. Sean winced.

'Sore?' asked Waite. *He hit me with that. Sweet Jesus, I've bred me a wild one.*

'A little.' Sean was white-faced again.

'It's a mess,' said Waite. 'You'd better get into town right away and let

Doctor Van have a go at it.'

Sean moved towards the door.

'Hold on.' Sean stopped and Waite pulled himself out of his chair. 'I'll come with you.'

'I'll be all right, Pa, you stay and rest.'

Waite ignored this and walked towards him.

'Really, Pa, I'll be all right on my own.'

'I'm coming with you,' Waite said harshly; and then softly, almost inaudibly, 'I want to, dammit.'

He lifted his arm as though to put it around Sean's shoulders, but before it touched him he let it drop back to his side and together they went out into the corridor.

15

With two fingers in splints Sean handled his knife awkwardly at lunch the next day, but his appetite was unimpaired. As was only right and fitting he took no part in the conversation except on the rare occasions that a remark was addressed directly to him. But he listened, his jaws chewing steadily and his eyes moving from speaker to speaker. He and Garry sat side by side in a backwater of the luncheon board while the guests were grouped in order of seniority around Waite.

Stephen Erasmus by age and wealth was in the right-hand seat; opposite him Tim Hope-Brown, just as wealthy but ten years younger; below him Gunther Niewenhuizen, Sam Tingle and Simon Rousseau. If you added it all together you could say that Waite Courtney had about a hundred thousand acres of land and half a million sterling sitting around his table. They were brown men—brown clothing, brown boots and big brown, calloused, hands. Their faces were brown and battered-looking and now that the meal was in its closing stages their usual reserve was gone and there was a tendency among them to talk all at the same time and to perspire profusely. This was not entirely a consequence of the dozen bottles of good Cape Mossel that Waite had provided nor of the piles of food they had eaten—it was more than that. There was a sense of expectancy among them, an eagerness they were finding it difficult to suppress.

'Can I tell the servants to clear away, Waite?' Ada asked from the end of the table.

'Yes, thank you, my dear. We'll have coffee in here, please.'

He stood up and fetched a box of cigars from the sideboard and carried it to each of his guests in turn. When the ends were cut and the tips were glowing, every man leaning back in his chair with a recharged glass and a cup of coffee in front of him, Ada slipped out of the room and Waite cleared his throat for silence.

'Gentlemen.' They were all watching him. 'Last Tuesday I spent two hours with the Governor. We discussed the recent developments across the Tugela.'

Waite lifted his glass and sipped at it, then held it by the stem and rolled it between his fingers as he went on.

'Two weeks ago the British Agent at the Zulu king's kraal was recalled. Recalled is perhaps the wrong word—the king offered to smear him with honey and tie him over an ant-hill, an offer that Her Britannic Majesty's Agent declined with thanks. Shortly thereafter he packed his bags and made for the border.'

There was a small ruffle of laughter.

'Since then Cetewayo has collected all his herds which were grazing near the Tugela and driven them into the north; he has commanded a buffalo hunt for which he has decided he will need *all* his impis–twenty thousand spears. This hunt is to be held along the banks of the Tugela, where the last buffalo was seen ten years ago.' Waite sipped at his glass, watching their faces. 'And he has ordered that all wounded game is to be followed across the border.'

There was a sigh then, a murmur from them. They all knew that this was the traditional Zulu declaration of war.

'So, man, what are we going to do about it? Must we sit here and wait for them to come and burn us out?'

Erasmus leaned forward watching Waite.

'Sir Bartle Frere met Cetewayo's Indunas a week ago. He has given them an ultimatum. They have until January the eleventh to disband the impis and take the Queen's Agent back into Zululand. In the event that Cetewayo disregards the ultimatum, Lord Chelmsford is to command a punitive column of regulars and militia. The force is being assembled now and will leave Pietermaritzburg within the next ten days. He is to cross the Tugela at Rorkes Drift and engage the impis before they break out. It is intended to end this constant threat to our border and break the Zulu nation for ever as a military power.'

'It's about bledy time,' said Erasmus.

'His Excellency has gazetted me full colonel and ordered me to raise a commando from the Ladyburg district. I have promised him at least forty men fully armed, mounted and provisioned who will be ready to join Chelmsford at the Tugela. Unless any of you object I am appointing you gentlemen as my captains and I know I can rely upon you to help me make good my promise to His Excellency.'

Suddenly Waite dropped his stilted manner and grinned at them. 'You will collect your own pay. It will be in cattle, as usual.'

'How far north has Cetewayo driven his herds?' asked Tim Hope-Brown.

'Not far enough, I'll warrant,' cackled Stephen Erasmus.

'A toast,' said Simon Rousseau jumping to his feet and holding up his glass. 'I give you a toast: the Queen, Lord Chelmsford and the Royal Herds of Zululand.'

They all stood and drank it, and then suddenly embarrassed by their display they sat down again, coughing awkwardly and shuffling their feet.

'All right,' said Waite, 'let's get down to details. Steff, you'll be coming and your two eldest boys?'

'*Ja*, three of us and my brother and his son. Put down five, Erasmus.'

'Good. What about you, Gunther?'

They began the planning. Men, horses and wagons were marshalled on paper; each of the captains was allotted a series of tasks. There was question, answer and argument that filled the hours before the guests left Theunis Kraal. They rode in a bunch, trippling their horses, sitting slack and long-legged in the saddles, moving up the far slope along the road to Ladyburg. Waite and his sons stood on the front step and watched them go.

'Pa–' Garry tried tentatively for Waite's attention.

'Yes, boy?' Waite kept his eyes on the group. Steff Erasmus turned in the saddle and waved his hat above his head, Waite waved back.

'Why do we have to fight them, Pa? If the Governor just sent somebody to talk to them, then we wouldn't have to fight.'

Waite glanced at him, frowning slightly.

'Anything worth having is worth fighting for, Garry. Cetewayo has raised twenty thousand spears to take this from us—' Waite swept his arm in a circle that took in the whole of Theunis Kraal. 'I think it's worth fighting for—don't you, Sean?'

'You bet,' Sean nodded eagerly.

'But couldn't we just make a treaty with them?' Garry persisted.

'Another cross on a piece of paper.' Waite spoke with fierce disdain. 'They found one like that on Piet Retrief's body—hell of a lot of good it did him.'

Waite walked back into the house with his sons following him.

He lowered himself into his armchair, stretched his legs out in front of him and smiled at Ada. 'Damn good lunch, my dear.' He clasped his hands over his stomach, belched involuntarily and was immediately contrite. 'I beg your pardon—it just slipped out.'

Ada bent her head over her sewing to hide her smile.

'We've got a lot to do in the next few days.' He turned his attention back to his sons. 'We'll take one mule wagon and a pair of horses each. Now about ammunition. . . .'

'But, Pa, couldn't we just—?' Garry started again.

'Shut up,' said Waite, and Garry subsided miserably into one of the other chairs.

'I've been thinking,' announced Sean.

'Not you as well,' growled Waite. 'Damn it to hell, here's your chance to win your own cattle and. . . .'

'That's just what I've been thinking,' Sean cut in. 'Everybody will have more cattle than they know what to do with. The prices will drop way down.'

'They will at first,' admitted Waite, 'but in a year or two they'll climb back again.'

'Shouldn't we sell now? Sell everything except the bulls and breeding cows, then after the war we'll be able to buy back at half the price.'

For a moment Waite sat stunned and then slowly his expression changed.

'My God, I never thought of that.'

'And Pa,' Sean was twisting his hands together in his enthusiasm, 'we'll need more land. When we bring the herds back across the Tugela there won't be enough grazing to go round. Mr Pye has called the mortgages on Mount Sinai and Mahoba's Kloof. He's not using the land. Couldn't we lease them from him now before everybody starts looking for grazing?'

'We had a lot to do before you started thinking,' said Waite softly, 'but now we've really got to work.'

He searched his pockets, found his pipe and while he filled it with tobacco he looked at Sean. He tried to keep his face neutral but the pride kept showing.

'You keep thinking like that and you'll be a rich man one day.' Waite could not know how true his prophecy would prove—the time was still remote when Sean could drop the purchase price of Theunis Kraal across a gaming table, and laugh at the loss.

16

The Commando was moving out on New Year's Day. New Year's Eve was set down for a double celebration: 'Welcome 1879', and 'God speed the Ladyburg Mounted Rifles'. The whole district was coming into town for the *braaivleis* and dancing that was being held in the square. Feast the warriors–laugh, dance and sing, then form them up and march them out to war.

Sean and Garry rode in early. Ada and Waite were to follow later in the afternoon. It was one of those bright days of a Natal summer: no wind and no clouds, the kind of day when the dust from a wagon hangs heavy in the air. They crossed the Baboon Stroom and from the farther ridge looked down across the town and saw the wagon dust on every road leading into Ladyburg.

'Look at them come,' said Sean; he screwed up his eyes against the glare and stared at the north road. 'That will be the Erasmus wagon. Karl will be with them.'

The wagons looked like beads on a string.

'That's the Petersens',' said Garry, 'or the Niewehuisens'.'

'Come on,' shouted Sean, and slapped the free end of his reins across his horse's neck. They galloped down the road. The horses they rode were big glossy animals, with their manes cropped like English hunters.

They passed a wagon. There were two girls sitting beside mama on the box seat, the Petersen sisters. Dennis Petersen and his father were riding ahead of the wagon.

Sean whooped as he raced past the wagon and the girls laughed and shouted something that was lost in the wind.

'Come on, Dennis,' howled Sean as he swept past the two sedately trotting outriders. Dennis's horse reared and then settled in to run, chasing Sean. Garry trailed them both.

They reached the cross roads, lying flat along their horses' necks, pumping the reins like jockeys. The Erasmus wagon was trundling down to meet them.

'Karl,' Sean called as he held his horse a little to stand in the stirrups. 'Karl. Come on, man, catch a wayo, Cetewayo!'

They rode into Ladyburg in a bunch. They were all flush-faced and laughing, excited and happy at the prospect of dancing and killing.

The town was crowded, its streets congested with wagons and horses and men and women and girls and dogs and servants.

'I've got to stop at Pye's store,' said Karl, 'come with me–it won't take long.'

They hitched their horses and went into the store; Sean, Dennis and Karl walked noisily and talked aloud. They were men, big sun-burned raw-boned men, muscled from hard work, but uncertain of the fact that they were men. Therefore, walk with a swagger and laugh too loud, swear when Pa isn't listening and no one will know you have your doubts.

'What are you going to buy, Karl?'

'Boots.'

'That'll take all day–you'll have to try them on. We'll miss half the fun.'

'There'll be nothing doing for another couple hours,' protested Karl. 'Wait for me, you chaps.'

Karl sitting on the counter, trying boots on his large feet, was not a spectacle that could hold Sean's interest for long. He drifted away among the piles of merchandise that cluttered Pye's store. There were stacks of pick handles, piles of blankets, bins of sugar and salt and flour, shelves of groceries and clothing, overcoats and women's dresses and hurricane-lamps and saddles hanging from the roof, and all of it was permeated by the peculiar smell of a general dealer's store: a mixture of paraffin, soap and new cloth.

Pigeon to its coop, iron to magnet. . . . Sean's feet led him to the rack of rifles against the far wall of the room. He lifted down one of the Lee Metford carbines and worked the action; he stroked the wood with his fingertips, then he weighed it in his hands to feel the balance and finally brought it up to his shoulder.

'Hello, Sean.' His ritual interrupted, Sean looked up at the shy voice.

'It's Strawberry Pie,' he said smiling. 'How's school?'

'I've left school now. I left last term.'

Audrey Pye had the family colouring but with a subtle difference—instead of carrot her hair was smoked copper with glints in it. She was not a pretty girl, her face was too broad and flat, but she had that rare skin that too seldom goes with red hair: creamy unfreckled purity.

'Do you want to buy anything, Sean?'

Sean placed the carbine back in the rack.

'Just looking,' he said. 'Are you working in the store now?'

'Yes.' She dropped her eyes from Sean's scrutiny. It was a year since he'd last seen her. A lot can change in a year; she now had that within her blouse which proved she was no longer a child. Sean eyed it appreciatively and she glanced up and saw the direction of his eyes; the cream of her skin clouded red. She turned quickly towards the trays of fruit.

'Would you like a peach?'

'Thanks,' said Sean and took one.

'How's Anna?' asked Audrey.

'Why ask me?' Sean frowned.

'You're her beau, aren't you?'

'Who told you that?' Sean's frown became a scowl.

'Everybody knows that.'

'Well, everybody's wrong.' Sean was irritated by the suggestion that he was one of Anna's possessions. 'I'm nobody's beau.'

'Oh!' Audrey was silent a moment, then, 'I suppose Anna will be at the dance tonight?'

'Most probably.' Sean bit into the furry golden peach and studied Audrey. 'Are you going, Strawberry Pie?'

'No,' Audrey answered wistfully. 'Pa won't let me.'

How old was she? Sean made a quick calculation . . . three years younger than he was. That made her sixteen. Suddenly Sean was sorry she wouldn't be at the dance.

'That's a pity,' he said. 'We could have had some fun.' Linking them together, with the plural 'we', Sean threw her into confusion again. She said the first words she could think of, 'Do you like the peach?'

'Hmm.'

'It's from our orchard.'

'I thought I recognized the flavour.' Sean grinned and Audrey laughed. Her mouth was wide and friendly when she laughed. 'I knew you used to pinch them. Pa knew it was you. He used to say he'd set a mantrap in that hole in the hedge.'

'I didn't know he'd found that hole—we used to cover it up each time.'

'Oh, yes,' Audrey assured him, 'we knew about it all the time. It's still there. Some nights when I can't sleep I climb out of my bedroom window and go down through the orchard, through the hedge into the wattle plantation. It's so dark and quiet in the plantation at night—scary, but I like it.'

'You know something,' Sean spoke thoughtfully. 'If you couldn't sleep tonight and came down to the hedge at ten o'clock, you might catch me pinching peaches again.'

It took a few seconds for Audrey to realize what he had said. Then the colour flew up her face again and she tried to speak but no words came. She turned with a swirl of skirt and darted away among the shelves. Sean bit the last of the flesh off the peach pip and dropped it on the floor. He was smiling as he walked across to join the others.

'Hell's teeth, Karl, how much longer are you going to be?'

17

There were fifty or more wagons outspanned around the perimeter of the square but the centre was left open, and here the braaivleis pits were burning, the flames already sinking to form glowing beds. Trestle-tables stood in two lines near the fires and the women worked at them cutting meat and boerwors, buttering bread, arranging platoons of pickle bottles, piling the food on trays and sweetening the evening with their voices and laughter.

In a level place a huge buck-sail was spread for dancing and at each corner a lantern hung on a pole. The band was tuning with squeaks from the fiddles and preliminary asthma from the single concertina.

The men gathered in knots among the wagons or squatted beside the braaivleis pits, and here and there a jug pointed its base briefly at the sky.

'I don't like to be difficult, Waite,' Petersen came across to where Waite was standing with his captains, 'but I see you've put Dennis in Gunther's troop.'

'That's right.' Waite offered him the jug and Petersen took it and wiped the neck with his sleeve.

'It's not you, Gunther,' Petersen smiled at Gunther Niewehuisen, 'but I would be much happier if I could have Dennis in the same troop as myself. Keep an eye on him, you know.'

They all looked at Waite to hear what he would say. 'None of the boys are riding with their fathers. We've purposely arranged it that way. Sorry, Dave.'

'Why?'

Waite Courtney looked away, over the wagons at the furious red sunset that hung above the escarpment. 'This isn't going to be a bushbuck shoot, Dave. You may find that you'll be called upon to make decisions that will be easier for you if you're not making them about your own son.'

There was a murmur of agreement and Steff Erasmus took his pipe out of his mouth and spat into the fire. 'There are some things it is not pretty for a man to see. They are too hard for him to forget. He should not see his son kill his first man, also he should not see his son die.'

They were silent then, knowing this truth. They had not spoken of it before because too much talk softens a man's stomach, but they knew death and understood what Steff had said. One by one their heads turned until they were all staring across the square at the gathering of youngsters beyond the fires. Dennis Petersen said something but they could not catch the words and his companions laughed.

'In order to live a man must occasionally kill,' said Waite, 'but when he kills too young, he loses something . . . a respect for life: he makes it cheap. It is the same with a woman, a man should never have his first woman until he understands about it. Otherwise that too becomes cheap.'

'I had my first when I was fifteen,' said Tim Hope-Brown. 'I can't say it made them any cheaper; in fact I've known them to be bloody expensive.'

Waite's big boom led the laughter.

'I know your old man pays you a pound a week but what about us, Sean?' protested Dennis, 'we aren't all millionaires.'

'All right, then,' Sean agreed, 'five shillings in the pool. Winner takes the lot.'

'Five bob is reasonable,' Karl opined, 'but let's get the rules clear so there's no argument afterwards.'

'Kills only, woundings don't count,' said Sean.

'And they have to be witnessed,' insisted Frikkie Van Essen. He was older than the others; his eyes were already a little bloodshot for he had made a start on the evening's drinking.

'All right, dead Zulus only and a witness to each kill. The highest score takes the pool.' Sean looked around the circle of faces for their assent. Garry was hanging back on the fringe. 'Garry will be banker. Come on, Garry, hold out your hat.'

They paid the money into Garrick's hat and he counted it.

'Two pounds—from eight of us. That's correct.'

'Hell, the winner will be able to buy his own farm.'

They laughed.

'I've got a couple of bottles of smoke hidden in my saddle bags,' Frikkie said 'Let's go and try them.'

The hands of the clock on the church tower showed quarter before ten. There were silver-edged clouds around the moon, and the night had cooled. Rich meaty smelling steam from the cooking pits drifted across the dancers, fiddles sawed and the concertina bawled the beat, dancers danced and the watchers clapped in time and called encouragement to them. Someone whooped like a Highlander in the feverish pattern of movement, in the fever of fun. Damn the dribble of minutes with laughter, hold the hour, lay siege against the dawn!

'Where are you going, Sean?'

'I'll be back just now.'

'But where are you going?'

'Do you want me to tell you, Anna, do you really want to know?'

'Oh, I see. Don't be long. I'll wait for you by the band.'

'Dance with Karl.'

'No, I'll wait for you, Sean. Please don't be long. We've got such a little time left.'

Sean slipped through the circle of wagons, he kept in the tree shadow along the sidewalk, round the side of Pye's store and down the lane, running now, jumped the ditch and through the barbed wire fence. It was dark in the plantation and quiet as she had said; dead leaves rustled and a twig popped under his feet. Something ran in the darkness, scurry of small feet. Sean's stomach flopped over: nerves, only a rabbit. He came to the hedge and searched for the hole, missed it and turned back, found it and through into the orchard. He stood with his back against the wall of vegetation and waited. The trees were moon grey and black below. He could see the roof of the house beyond them. He knew she'd come, of course. He had told her to.

The church clock chimed the hour and then later the single stroke of the quarter hour. Angry now, damn her! He went up through the orchard, cautiously staying in shadow. There was a light in one of the side windows, he could see it spilling out into a yellow square on the lawn. He circled the house softly.

She was at the window with the lamp behind her. Her face was dark but lamplight lit the edges of her hair into a coppery halo. There was something of yearning in her attitude, leaning forward over the sill. He could see the outline of her shoulders through the white cloth of her gown.

Sean whistled, pitching it low to reach her only, and she started at the sound. A second longer she stared out from light into the dark and then she shook her head, slowly and regretfully from side to side. She closed the curtains and through them Sean saw her shadow move away. The lamp went out.

Sean went back through the orchard and the plantation. He was trembling with anger. From the lane he heard the music in the square and he quickened his pace. He turned the corner and saw the lights and movement.

'Silly little fool,' he said out loud, anger still there but something else as well. Affection? Respect?

'Where have you been? I've waited nearly an hour.' Possessive Anna.

'There and back to see how far it is.'

'Funny! Sean Courtney, where have you been?'

'Do you want to dance?'

'No.'

'All right, don't then.'

Karl and some of the others were standing by the cooking pits. Sean started for them.

'Sean, Sean, I'm sorry.' Penitent Anna. 'I'd love to dance, please.'

They danced, jostled by other dancers, but neither of them spoke until the band stopped to wipe their brows and wet dry throats.

'I've got something for you, Sean.'

'What is it?'

'Come, I'll show you.'

She led him from the light among the wagons and stopped by a pile of saddles and blankets. She knelt and opened one of the blankets and stood up again with the coat in her hands.

'I made it for you. I hope you like it.'

Sean took it from her. It was a sheepskin, tanned and polished, stitched with love, the inside wool bleached snowy white.

'It's beautiful,' Sean said. He recognized the labour that had gone into it. It made him feel guilty: gifts always made him feel guilty.

'Thank you very much.'

'Try it on, Sean.'

Warm, snug at the waist, room to move in the shoulders; it enhanced his considerable bulk. Anna stood close to him, arranging the collar.

'You look nice in it,' she said. Smug pleasure of the giver.

He kissed her and the mood changed. She held him tight around the neck.

'Oh, Sean, I wish you weren't going.'

'Let's say goodbye properly.'

'Where?'

'My wagon.'

'What about your parents?'

'They've gone back to the farm. Pa's coming in tomorrow morning. Garry and I are sleeping here.'

'No, Sean, there are too many people. We can't.'

'You don't want to,' Sean whispered. 'It's a pity because it might be the last time ever.'

'What do you mean?' She was suddenly still and small in his arms.

'I'm going away tomorrow. You know what might happen?'

'No. Don't talk like that. Don't even think it.'

'It's true.'

'No, Sean, don't. Please don't.'

Sean smiled in the darkness. So easy, so very easy.

'Let's go to my wagon.' He took her hand.

18

Breakfast in the dark, cooking fires around the square, voices quiet, men standing with their wives, holding the small children in farewell. The horses saddled, rifles in the scabbards and blanket rolls behind, four wagons drawn up in the centre of the square with the mules in the traces.

'Pa should be here any minute. It's nearly five o'clock,' said Garry.

'They're all waiting for him,' agreed Sean. He shrugged at the weight of the bandolier strapped over his shoulder.

'Mr Niewehuisen has made me one of the wagon drivers.'

'I know,' said Sean. 'Can you handle it?'

'I think so.'

Jane Petersen came towards them.

'Hello, Jane. Is your brother ready yet?'

'Nearly. He's just saddling up.'

She stopped in front of Sean and shyly held out a scrap of green-and-yellow silk.

'I've made you a cockade for your hat, Sean.'

'Thanks, Jane. Won't you put it on for me?' She pinned up the brim of Sean's hat; he took it back from her and set it at a jaunty angle on his head.

'I look like a general now,' he said and she laughed at him. 'How about a goodbye kiss, Jane?'

'You're terrible,' said little Jane and went away quickly, blushing. Not so little, Sean noticed. There were so many of them you hardly knew where to start.

'Here's Pa,' announced Garry as Waite Courtney rode into the square.

'Come on,' said Sean and untied his horse. From all around the square men were leading out their horses.

'See you later,' said Garry and limped off towards one of the waiting mule wagons.

Waite rode at the head of the column. Four troops of fifteen men in double file, four wagons behind them, and then the loose horses driven by black servants.

They moved out across the square, through the litter of the night's festivities, and into the main street. The women watched them in silence, standing motionless with the children gathered around them. These women had seen men ride out before against the tribes; they did not cheer for they were wise in the ways of death, they had learned that there is no room for glory in the grave.

Anna waved to Sean. He did not see her for his horse was skittish and he was past her before he had it under control. She let her hand drop back to her side and watched him go. He wore the sheepskin coat.

Sean did see the coppery flash and the swiftly-blown kiss from the upstairs window of Pye's store. He saw it because he was looking for it. He forgot his injured pride sufficiently to grin and wave his hat.

Then they were out of the town, and at last even the small boys and dogs that ran beside them fell back and the column trotted out along the road to Zululand.

The sun came up and dried the dew. The dust rose from under the hooves and drifted out at an angle from the road. The column lost its rigidity as men spurred ahead or dropped back to ride with their friends. They rode in groups and straggles, relaxed and cheerfully chatting, as informal as a party out for a day's shooting. Each man had taken to the field in the clothing he considered most suitable. Steff Erasmus wore his church suit, but he was the most formally attired of the group. They had only one standard item of uniform among them: this was the green-and-yellow cockade. However, even here there was scope for individual taste: some wore them on their hats, some on their sleeves and others on their chests. They were farmers, not fighting men, but their rifle scabbards were battered with use, their bandoliers worn with easy familiarity and the wood of their gun butts was polished from the caress of their hands.

It was middle afternoon before they reached the Tugela.

'My God, look at that!' whistled Sean. 'I've never seen so many people in one place in my life before.'

'They say there are four thousand,' said Karl.

'I know there are four thousand.' Sean ran his eyes over the camp. 'But I didn't know four thousand was that many.'

The column was riding down the last slope to Rorkes Drift. The river was muddy brown and wide, rippling over the shallows of the crossing place. The banks were open and grassy with a cluster of stone-walled buildings on the near side. In a quarter-mile radius around the buildings Lord Chelmsford's army was encamped. The tents were laid out in meticulous lines, row upon row with the horses picketed between them. The wagons were marshalled by the drift, five hundred at least, and the whole area swarmed with men.

The Ladyburg Mounted Rifles, in a solid bunch that overflowed the road behind their Colonel, came down to the perimeter of the camp and found their passage blocked by a sergeant in a dress coat and with a fixed bayonet.

'And who be you, may I ask?'

'Colonel Courtney—and a detachment of the Ladyburg Mounted Rifles.'

'What's that? Didn't catch it.'

Waite Courtney stood in his stirrups and turned to face his men.

'Hold on there, gentlemen. We can't all talk at once.'

The hubbub of conversation and comment behind him faded and this time the sergeant heard him.

'Ho! Beg your pardon, sir. I'll call the orderly officer.'

The orderly officer was an aristocrat and a gentleman. He came and looked at them. 'Colonel Courtney?' There was a note of disbelief in his voice.

'Hello,' said Waite with a friendly smile. 'I hope we are not too late for the fun.'

'No, I don't believe you are.' The officer's eyes fastened on Steff Erasmus. Steff lifted his top hat politely. *'More, Meneer.'* The bandoliers of ammunition looked a little out of place slung across his black frockcoat.

The officer tore his eyes away from him. 'You have your own tents, Colonel?'

'Yes, we've got everything we need.'

'I'll get the sergeant here to show you where to make camp.'

'Thank you,' said Waite.

The officer turned to the sergeant. So carried away was he that he took the man by the arm. 'Put them far away. Put them on the other side of the Engineers–' he whispered frantically. 'If the General sees this lot. . . .' He shuddered, but in a genteel fashion.

19

Garrick first became conscious of the smell. Thinking about it served as a rallying point for his attention and he could start to creep out of the hiding-place in his mind. For Garrick these returns to reality were always accompanied by a feeling of light-headedness and a heightening of the senses. Colours were vivid, skin sensitive to the touch, tastes and smells sharp and clear.

He lay on a straw mattress. The sun was bright, but he was in shade. He lay on the veranda of the stone-walled hospital above Rorkes Drift. He thought about the smell that had brought him back. It was a blending of corruption and sweat and dung, the smell of ripped bowels and congealing blood.

He recognized it as the smell of death. Then his vision came into focus and he saw the dead. They were piled along the wall of the yard where the cross-fire from the store and the hospital had caught them; they were scattered between the buildings, and the burial squads were busy loading them on to the wagons. They were lying down the slope to the Drift, they were in the water and on the far bank. Dead Zulus, with their weapons and shields strewn about them. Hundreds of them, Garrick thought with astonishment: no, thousands of them.

Then he was aware that there were two smells; but both of them were the smells of death. There was the stink of the black, balloon-bellied corpses swelling in the sun and there was the smell from his own body and the bodies of the men about him, the same smell of pain and putrefaction but mixed with the heaviness of disinfectant. Death wearing antiseptic–the way an unclean girl tries to cover her menstrual odour.

Garrick looked at the men around him. They lay in a long row down the veranda, each on his own mattress. Some were dying and many were not but on all of them the bandages were stained with blood and iodine. Garrick looked at his own body. His left arm was strapped across his bare chest and he felt the ache start beating within him, slow and steady as a funeral drum. There were bandages around his head. I'm wounded—again he was astonished. How? But how?

'You've come back to us, Cocky,' cheerful Cockney from beside him. 'We thought you'd gone clean bonkers.'

Garrick turned his head and looked at the speaker; he was a small monkey-faced man in a pair of flannel underpants and a mummy suit of bandages.

'Doc said it was shock. He said you'd come out of it soon enough.' The little man raised his voice, 'Hey, Doc, the hero is completely mentos again.' The doctor came quickly, tired-looking, dark under the eyes, old with overwork.

'You'll do,' he said, having groped and prodded. 'Get some rest. They're sending you back home tomorrow.' He moved away for there were many wounded, but then he stopped and looked back. He smiled briefly at Garrick, 'I doubt it will ease the pain at all but you've been recommended for the Victoria Cross. The General endorsed your citation yesterday. I think you'll get it.' Garrick stared at the doctor as memory came back patchily.

'There was fighting,' Garrick said.

'You're bloody well tooting there was!' the little man beside him guffawed.

'Sean!' said Garrick. 'My brother! What happened to my brother?' There was silence then and Garrick saw the quick shadow of regret in the doctor's eyes. Garrick struggled into a sitting position.

'And my Pa. What happened to my father?'

'I'm sorry,' said the doctor with simplicity, 'I'm afraid they were both killed.'

Garrick lay on his mattress and looked down at the Drift. They were clearing the corpses out of the shallows now, splashing as they dragged them to the bank. He remembered the splashing as Chelmsford's army had crossed. Sean and his father had been among the scouts who had led the column, three troops of the Ladyburg Mounted Rifles and sixty men of the Natal Police. Chelmsford had used these men who knew the country over which the initial advance was to be made.

Garrick had watched them go with relief. He could hardly believe the good fortune that had granted him a squirting dysentery the day before the ultimatum expired and the army crossed the Tugela.

'The lucky bastards,' protested one of the other sick as they watched them go. Garrick was without envy: he did not want to go to war, he was content to wait here with thirty other sick men and a garrison of sixty more to hold the Drift while Chelmsford took his army into Zululand.

Garrick had watched the scouts fan out from the Drift and disappear into the rolling grassland, and the main body of men and wagons follow them until they too had crawled like a python into the distance and left a well-worn road behind them through the grass.

He remembered the slow slide of days while they waited at the Drift. He remembered grumbling with the others when they were made to fortify the store and the hospital with bags and biscuit tins filled with sand. He remembered the boredom.

Then, his stomach tightened, he remembered the messenger.

'Horseman coming.' Garrick had seen him first. Recovered from his dysentery he was doing sentry duty above the Drift.

'The General's left his toothbrush behind, sent someone back for it,' said his companion. Neither of them stood up. They watched the speck coming across the plain towards the river.

'Coming fast,' said Garrick. 'You'd better go and call the Captain.'

'I suppose so,' agreed the other sentry. He trotted up the slope to the store and Garrick stood up and walked down to the edge of the river. His peg sank deep into the mud.

'Captain says to send him up to the store when he gets here.' Garrick's companion came back and stood beside him.

'Something funny about the way he's riding,' said Garrick, 'he looks tired.'

'He must be drunk. He's falling about in the saddle like it's Saturday night.'

Garrick gasped suddenly. 'He's bleeding, he's wounded.'

The horse plunged into the Drift and the rider fell forward on to its neck; the side of his shirt was shiny black with blood, his face was pale with pain and dust. They caught his horse as it came out of the water and the rider tried to shout but his voice was a croak. 'In the name of God prepare yourselves. The Column's been surrounded and wiped out. They're coming—the whole black howling pack of them. They'll be here before nightfall.'

'My brother,' said Garrick. 'What happened to my brother?'

'Dead,' said the man. 'Dead, they're all dead.' He slid sideways off his horse.

They came, the impis of Zulu in the formation of the bull, the great black bull whose head and loins filled the plain and whose horns circled left and right across the river to surround them. The bull stamped with twenty thousand feet and sang with ten thousand throats until its voice was the sound of the sea on a stormy day. The sunlight reflected brightly from the spear blades as it came singing to the Tugela.

'Look! Those in front are wearing the helmets of the Hussars,' one of the watchers in the hospital exclaimed. 'They've been looting Chelmsford's dead. There's one wearing a dress coat and some are carrying carbines.'

It was hot in the hospital for the roof was corrugated-iron and the windows were blocked with sandbags. The rifle slits let in little air. The men stood at the slits, some in pyjamas, some stripped to the waist and sweating in the heat.

'It's true then, the Column has been massacred.'

'That's enough talking. Stand to your posts and keep your mouths shut.'

The impis of Zulu crossed the Tugela on a front five hundred yards wide. They churned the surface to white with their crossing.

'My God! Oh, my God!' whispered Garrick as he watched them come. 'We haven't got a chance, there are so many of them.'

'Shut up. Damn you,' snapped the sergeant at the Gatling machine-gun beside him and Garry covered his mouth with his hand.

> '—Grabbed O'Riley by the neck
> Shoved his head in a pail of water
> Rammed that pistol up his—'

sang one of the malaria cases in delirium and somebody else laughed, shrill hysteria in the sound.

'Here they come!'

'Load!'

The metallic clashing of rifle mechanism. 'Hold your fire, men. Fire on command only.'

The voice of the bull changed from a deep sonorous chant to the shrill ululation of the charge—high-pitched frenzy of the blood squeal.

'Steady, men. Steady. Hold it. Hold your fire.'

'Oh, my God!' whispered Garrick softly, watching them come black up the slope. 'Oh, my God!—please don't let me die.'

'Ready!'

The van had reached the wall of the hospital yard. Their plumed head-dresses were the frothy crest of a black wave as they came over the wall.

'Aim!'

Sixty rifles lifted and held, aimed into the press of bodies.

'Fire!'

Thunder, then the strike of bullets into flesh, a sound as though a handful of gravel had been flung into a puddle of mud. The ranks reeled from the blow. The clustered barrels of the Gatling machine-gun jump—jump—jumped as they swung, cutting them down so they fell upon each other, thick along the wall. The stench of burnt black powder was painful to breathe.

'Load!'

The bullet-ravaged ranks were re-forming as those from behind came forward into the gaps.

'Aim!'

They were coming again, solid black and screaming halfway across the yard.

'Fire!'

Garrick sobbed in the shade of the veranda and pressed the fingers of his right hand into his eye sockets to squeeze out the memory.

'What's the trouble, Cocky?' The Cockney rolled painfully on to his side and looked at Garrick.

'Nothing!' said Garrick quickly. 'Nothing!'

'Coming back to you, is it?'

'What happened? I can only remember pieces of it.'

'What happened!' The man echoed his question, 'What didn't happen!'

'The doctor said—' Garrick looked up quickly, 'He said the General had endorsed my citation. That means Chelmsford's alive. My brother and my father—they must be alive as well!'

'No such luck, Cocky. The Doc's taken a fancy to you—you with one leg doing what you did—so he made inquiries about your folk. It's no use.'

'Why?' asked Garrick desperately. 'Surely if Chelmsford's alive they must be too?'

The little man shook his head. 'Chelmsford's made a base camp at a place called Isandhlwana. He left a garrison there with all the wagons and supplies. He took a flying column out to raid, but the Zulus circled around him and attacked the base camp, then they came on here to the Drift. As you know, we held them for two days until Chelmsford's flying column came to help us.'

'My folk—what happened to them?'

'Your father was at the Isandhlwana camp. He didn't escape. Your brother was with Chelmsford's column but he was cut off and killed in one of the skirmishes before the main battle.'

'Sean dead?' Garrick shook his head. 'No, it's not possible. They couldn't have killed him.'

'You'd be surprised how easily they did it,' said the Cockney. 'A few inches of blade in the right place is enough for the best of them.'

'But not Sean—you didn't know him. You couldn't understand.'

'He's dead, Cocky. Him and your Pa and seven hundred others. The wonder is we aren't too.' The man wriggled into a more comfortable position on his mattress. 'The General made a speech about our defence here. Finest feat of arms in the annals of British courage—or something like that.'

He winked at Garrick. 'Fifteen citations for the old V.C.—you's one of them. I ask you, Cocky, isn't that something? What's your girl friend going to do when you come home with a mucking great gong clanking around on your chest, hey?'

He stared at Garrick and saw the tears oozing in oily lines down his cheeks.

'Come on, Cocky. You're a bloody hero.' He looked away from Garrick's grief. 'Do you remember that part—do you remember what you did?'

'No,' Garrick's voice was husky. *Sean. You can't leave me alone. What am I going to do, now that you're gone?*

'I was next to you. I saw it all. I'll tell you about it,' said the Cockney.

As he talked so the events came back and fitted into sequence in Garrick's mind.

'It was on the second day, we'd held off twenty-three charges.'

Twenty-three, was it as many as that? Garrick had lost count; it might have been but a single surging horror. Even now he could taste the fear in the back of his throat and smell it rancid in his own sweat.

'Then they piled wood against the hospital wall and set fire to it.' Zulus coming across the yard carrying bundles of faggots, falling to the rifles, others picking up the bundles and bringing them closer until they too died and yet others came to take their place. Then flames pale yellow in the sunlight, a dead Zulu lying on the bonfire, his face charring, and the smell of him mingled with the smoke.

'We knocked a hole in the back wall and started to move the sick and wounded out through it and across to the store.'

The boy with the assegai through his spine had shrieked like a girl as they lifted him.

'Them bloody savages came again as soon as they saw we were pulling out. They came from that side,' he pointed with his bandaged arm, 'where the chaps in the store couldn't reach them, and there was only you and I and a couple of others at the loopholes—everyone else was carrying the wounded.'

There had been a Zulu with the blue heron feathers of an Induna in his head dress. He had led the charge. His shield was dried oxhide dappled black and white, and at his wrists and ankles were bunches of war rattles. Garrick had fired at the instant the Zulu half-turned to beckon to his warriors—the bullet sliced across the tensed muscles of his belly and unzipped it like a purse. The Zulu went down on his hands and knees with his entrails bulging out in a pink and purple mass.

'They reached the door of the hospital and we couldn't fire on them from the angle of the windows.'

The wounded Zulu started to crawl towards Garrick, his mouth moving and his eyes fastened on Garrick's face. He still had his assegai in his hand. The other Zulus were beating at the door and one of them ran his spear blade through a crack in the woodwork and lifted the bar. The door was open.

Garrick watched the Zulu crawling towards him through the dust with his pink wet bowels swinging like a pendulum under him. The sweat was running down Garrick's cheeks and dripping off the end of his chin, his lips were trembling. He lifted his rifle and aimed into the Zulu's face. He could not fire.

'That's when you moved, Cocky. I saw the bar lifted out of its brackets and I knew that in the next second there'd be a mob of them in through the door and we'd stand no chance against their spears at close range.'

Garrick let go his rifle and it rattled on the concrete floor. He turned away from the window. He could not watch that crippled, crawling thing. He wanted to run, to hide. That was it—to hide. He felt the fluttering start behind his eyes, and his sight began to grey.

'You were nearest to the door. You did the only thing that could have saved us. Though I know I wouldn't have had the guts to do it.'

The floor was covered with cartridge cases—brass cylinders shiny and treacherous under foot. Garrick stumbled; as he fell he put out his arm.

'Christ,' the little Cockney shuddered, 'to put your arm into the brackets like that—I wouldn't have done it.'

Garrick felt his arm snap as the mob of Zulus threw themselves against the door. He hung there staring at his twisted arm, watching the door tremble and shake as they beat against it. There was no pain and after a while everything was grey and warm and safe.

'We fired through the door until we had cleared them away from the other side. Then we were able to get your arm free, but you were out cold. Been that way ever since.'

Garrick stared out across the river. He wondered if they had buried Sean or left him in the grass for the birds.

Lying on his side Garrick drew his legs up against his chest, his body was curled. Once as a brutal small boy he had cracked the shell of a hermit crab. Its soft fat abdomen was so vulnerable that its vitals showed through the transparent skin. It curled its body into the same defensive attitude.

'I'll reckon you'll get your gong,' said the Cockney.

'Yes,' said Garrick. He didn't want it. He wanted Sean back.

20

Doctor van Rooyen gave Ada Courtney his arm as she stepped down from the buggy. In fifty years he had not obtained immunity from other people's sorrow. He had learned only to conceal it: no trace of it in his eyes, or his mouth, or his lined and whiskered face.

'He's well, Ada. They did a good job on his arm: that is, for military surgeons. It will set straight.'

'When did they arrive?' asked Ada.

'About four hours ago. They sent all the Ladyburg wounded back in two wagons.'

Ada nodded, and he looked at her with the professional shield of indifference, hiding the shock he felt at the change in her appearance. Her skin was as dry and lifeless as the petals of a pressed flower, her mouth had set determinedly against her grief and her widow's weeds had doubled her age.

'He's waiting for you inside.' They walked up the steps of the church and the small crowd opened to let them pass. There were subdued greetings for Ada and the usual funereal platitudes. There were other women there wearing black, with swollen eyes.

Ada and the doctor went into the cool gloom of the church. The pews had been pushed against the wall to make room for the mattresses. Women were moving about between them and men lay on them.

'I'm keeping the bad ones here, where I can watch them,' the doctor told her. 'There's Garry.'

Garrick stood up from the bench on which he was sitting. His arm was slung awkwardly across his chest. He limped forward to meet them, his peg tapped loudly on the stone floor.

'Ma, I'm–' he stopped. 'Sean and Pa–'

'I've come to take you home, Garry.' Ada spoke quickly, flinching at the sound of those two names.

'They can't just let them lie out there, they should–'

'Please, Garry. Let's go home,' said Ada. 'We can talk about it later.'

'We are all very proud of Garry,' said the doctor.

'Yes,' said Ada. 'Please, let's go home, Garry.' She could feel it there just below the surface and she held it in: so much sorrow confined in so small a place. She turned back towards the door, she mustn't let them see it. She mustn't cry here in front of them, she must get back to Theunis Kraal.

Willing hands carried Garrick's bags out to the buggy and Ada took the reins. Neither of them spoke again until they crossed the ridge and looked down at the homestead.

'You're the master of Theunis Kraal now, Garry,' said Ada softly and Garrick stirred uneasily on the seat beside her. He didn't want it, he didn't want the medal. He wanted Sean.

21

'I hope you don't mind me coming,' said Anna, 'but I had to talk to you.'

'No. I'm glad you did. Truly I'm glad,' Garrick assured her earnestly. 'It's so good to see you again, Anna. It feels like forever since we left.'

'I know, and so much–so much has happened. My Pa and yours. And–and Sean.' She stopped. 'Oh, Garry, I just can't believe it yet. They've told me and told me but I can't believe it. He was so–so alive.'

'Yes,' said Garrick, 'he was so alive.'

'He talked about dying the night before he left. I hadn't even thought about it until then,' Anna shook her head in disbelief, 'and I never dreamed it could happen to him. Oh Garry, what am I going to do?'

Garrick turned and looked at Anna. The Anna he loved, Sean's Anna. But Sean was dead. He felt an idea move within him, not yet formed in words, but real enough to cause a sick spasm of conscience. He shied away from it.

'Oh, Garry. What can I do?'

She was asking for help, the appeal was apparent in her voice. Her father killed at Isandhlwana, her elder brothers still with Chelmsford at Tugela, her mother and the three small children to feed. How blind of him not to see it!

'Anna, can I help you? Just tell me.'

'No, Garry. I don't think anyone can.'

'If it's money–' He hesitated discreetly. 'I'm a rich man now. Pa left the whole of Theunis Kraal to Sean and I, and Sean isn't–' She looked at him without answering.

'I can lend you some to tide you over–' blushed Garrick, 'as much as you need.'

She went on staring at him while her mind adjusted itself. Garrick master of Theunis Kraal, he was rich, twice as rich as Sean would have been. And Sean was dead.

'Please, Anna. Let me help you. I want to, really I do.'

He loved her, it was pathetically obvious–and Sean was dead.

'You will let me, Anna?'

She thought of hunger and bare feet, dresses washed until you could see through them when you held them to the light, petticoats patched and cobbled. And always the fear, the uncertainty you must live with when you are poor. Garry was rich and alive, Sean was dead.

'Please tell me you will.' Garrick leaned forward and took her arm, he gripped it fiercely in his agitation and she looked into his face. You could see the resemblance, she thought, but Sean had strength where here there was softness and uncertainty. The colour was wrong also, pale sand and paler blue instead of brutal black and indigo. It was as though an artist had taken a portrait and with a few subtle strokes had altered its meaning completely so as to make it into an entirely different picture. She did not want to think about his leg.

'It's sweet of you, Garry,' she said, 'but we've got a little in the bank and the plot is free of debt. We've got the horses; we can sell them if we have to.'

'What is it then? Please tell me.'

She knew then what she was going to do. She could not lie to him–it was too late for that. She would have to tell him, but she knew that the truth would not make any difference to him. Well, perhaps a little–but not enough to prevent her getting what she wanted. She wanted to be rich, and she wanted a father for the child she carried within her.

'Garry, I'm going to have a baby.'

Garrick's chin jerked up and his breathing jammed and then started again.

'A baby?'

'Yes, Garrick. I'm pregnant.'

'Whose? Sean's?'

'Yes, Garry. I'm going to have Sean's baby.'

'How do you know, are you sure?'

'I'm sure.'

Garrick pulled himself out of his chair and limped across the veranda. He stopped against the railing and gripped it with his good hand; the other was still in the sling. His back was turned to Anna and he stared out across the lawns of Theunis Kraal to the lightly-forested slope beyond.

Sean's baby. The idea bewildered him. He knew that Sean and Anna did that together. Sean had told him and Garrick had not resented it. He was jealous, but only a little, for Sean had let him share in it by telling him and so some of it had belonged to him also. But a baby. Sean's baby.

Slowly the full implication came to him. Sean's baby would be a living part of his brother, the part that had not been cut down by the Zulu blades. He had not completely lost Sean. Anna–she must have a father for her child, it was unthinkable that she could go another month without marrying. He could have both of them, everything he loved in one package. Sean and Anna. She must marry him, she had no other choice. Triumph surged up within him and he turned to her.

'What will you do, Anna?' He felt sure of her now. 'Sean's dead. What will you do?'

'I don't know.'

'You can't have the baby. It would be a bastard.' He saw her wince at the word. He felt very certain of her.

'I'll have to go away–to Port Natal.' She spoke without expression in her voice. Looking calmly at him, knowing what he would say, 'I'll leave soon,' she said, 'I'll be all right. I'll find some way out.'

Garrick watched her face as she spoke. Her head was small on shoulders wide for a girl, her chin was pointed, her teeth were slightly crooked but white–she was very pretty despite the catlike set of her eyes.

'I love you, Anna,' he said. 'You know that, don't you?'

She nodded slowly and her hair moved darkly on her shoulders. The cat eyes softened contentedly. 'Yes, I know, Garry.'

'Will you marry me?' He said it breathlessly.

'You don't mind? You don't mind about Sean's baby?' she said, knowing he did not.

'I love you, Anna.' He came towards her clumsily and she looked up at his face. She did not want to think about the leg.

'I love you, nothing else matters.' He reached for her and she let him hold her.

'Will you marry me, Anna?' He was trembling.

'Yes.' Her hands were quiescent on his shoulders. He sobbed softly and her expression changed to one of distaste, she made the beginnings of a movement to push him away but stopped herself.

'My darling, you won't regret it. I swear you won't,' he whispered.

'We must do it quickly, Garry.'

'Yes. I'll go into town this afternoon and speak to Padre–'

'No! Not here in Ladyburg,' Anna cut in sharply. 'People will have too much to say. I couldn't stand it.'

'We'll go up to Pietermaritzburg,' Garrick acquiesced.

'When, Garry?'

'As soon as you like.'

'Tomorrow,' she said. 'We'll go tomorrow.'

22

The Cathedral in Pietermaritzburg stands on Church Street. Grey stone with a bell-tower and iron railings between the street and the lawns. Pigeons strut puff-chested on the grass.

Anna and Garrick went up the paved path and into the semi-dark of the Cathedral. The stained glass window had the sun behind it, making the interior glow weirdly with colour. Because they were both nervous they held hands as they stood in the aisle.

'There's no one here,' whispered Garrick.

'There must be,' Anna whispered back. 'Try through that door there.'

'What shall I say?'

'Just tell him we want to get married.'

Garrick hesitated.

'Go on.' Anna still whispered, pushing him gently towards the door of the vestry.

'You come with me,' said Garrick. 'I don't know what to say.'

The priest was a thin man with steel-rimmed spectacles. He looked over the top of them at the nervous pair in the doorway and shut the book on the desk in front of him.

'We want to get married,' Garrick said and blushed crimson.

'Well,' said the priest drily, 'you have the right address. Come in.'

He was surprised at their haste and they argued a little, then he sent Garrick down to the Magistrates' Court for a special licence. He married them, but the ceremony was hollow and unreal. The drone of the priest's voice was almost lost in the immense cavern of the Cathedral as they stood small and awed before him. Two old ladies who came in to pray stayed on gleefully to witness for them, and afterwards they both kissed Anna and the priest shook Garrick's hand. Then they went out again into the sunlight. The pigeons still strutted on the lawn and a mule wagon rattled down Church Street with the coloured driver singing and cracking his whip. It was as though nothing had happened.

'We're married,' said Garrick doubtfully.

'Yes,' agreed Anna, but she sounded as though she didn't believe it either.

They walked back to the hotel side by side. They didn't talk or touch each other. Their luggage had been taken up to their room and the horses had been stabled. Garrick signed the register and the clerk grinned at him.

'I've put you in Number Twelve, sir, it's our honeymoon suite.' One of the eyelids drooped slightly and Garrick stammered in confusion.

After dinner, an excellent dinner, Anna went up to the room and Garrick sat on in the lounge drinking coffee. It was almost an hour later that he mustered the courage to follow her. He crossed the drawing-room of their suite, hesitated at the bedroom door then went in. Anna was in bed. She had pulled the bedclothes up to her chin and she looked at him with her inscrutable cat's eyes.

'I've put your nightshirt in the bathroom, on the table,' she said.

'Thank you,' said Garrick. He stumbled against a chair as he crossed the room. He closed the door behind him, undressed quickly and leaning naked over the basin splashed water on to his face; then he dried and pulled the nightshirt over his head. He went back into the bedroom: Anna lay with her face turned away from him. Her hair was loose on the pillow, shining in the lamp-light.

Garrick sat on the edge of the chair. He lifted the hem of his nightshirt above his knee and unfastened the straps of his leg, laid the peg carefully beside the chair and massaged the stump with both hands. It felt stiff. He heard the bed creak softly and he looked up. Anna was watching him, staring at his leg. Hurriedly Garrick pulled down his nightshirt to cover the protruding slightly enlarged end with its folded line of scar-tissue. He stood up, balancing, and then hopped one-legged across to the bed. He was blushing again.

He lifted the edge of the blankets and slipped into the bed and Anna jerked violently away from him.

'Don't touch me,' she said hoarsely.

'Anna. Please don't be scared.'

'I'm pregnant, you mustn't touch me.'

'I won't. I swear I won't.'

She was breathing hard, making no attempt to hide her revulsion.

'Do you want me to sleep in the drawing-room, Anna? I will if you say so.'

'Yes,' she said, 'I want you to.'

He gathered his dressing-gown from the chair and stooping picked up his leg. He hopped to the door and turned back to face her. She was watching him still.

'I'm sorry, Anna, I didn't mean to frighten you.' She did not answer him and he went on.

'I love you. I swear I love you more than anything in the world. I wouldn't hurt you, you know that, don't you? You know I wouldn't hurt you?'

Still she did not answer and he made a small gesture of appeal, the wooden leg clutched in his hand and the tears starting to fill his eyes. 'Anna, I'd kill myself rather than frighten you!'

He went quickly through the door and closed it behind him, Anna scrambled out of the bed and with her nightdress flurrying around her legs she ran across the room to the door and turned the key in the lock.

23

In the morning Garrick was bewildered to find Anna in a mood of girlish gaiety. She had a green ribbon in her hair and her green frock was faded but pretty. She chattered happily through breakfast and while they were having their coffee she leaned across the table and touched Garrick's hand. 'What shall we do today, Garry?'

Garrick looked surprised, he hadn't thought that far ahead. 'I suppose we'd better catch the afternoon train back to Ladyburg,' he said.

'Oh, Garry,' Anna pouted effectively. 'Don't you love me enough to give me a honeymoon?'

'I suppose—' Garrick hesitated and then 'of course, I didn't think of it.' He grinned excitedly. 'Where can we go?'

'We could take the mail boat down the coast to Capetown,' Anna suggested.

'Yes!' Garrick adopted the idea immediately. 'It'll be fun.'

'But, Garry—' Anna's eagerness faded. 'I only have two old dresses with me.' She touched her clothes. Garrick sobered also while he grappled with this new problem. Then he found the solution.

'We'll buy you some more!'

'Oh, Garry, could we? Could we really?'

'We'll buy you all you can use, more than you can use. Come on, finish your coffee and we'll go into town and see what they have.'

'I'm finished.' Anna stood up from the table ready to go.

24

They had a stateroom on the *Dunottar Castle* from Port Natal to Capetown. There were other young people aboard. Anna, in her elegant new clothing and sparkling with excitement, formed the centrepiece of a gay little group that played deck games, dined, danced and flirted as the mailboat drove south through the sunny golden days of early autumn.

At first Garrick was content to stay unobtrusively close to Anna. He was there to hold her coat, fetch a book or carry a rug. He watched her fondly, revelling in her success, hardly jealous when she almost disappeared behind a palisade of attentive young men, not resenting the sofa which formed his uncomfortable bed in the drawing-room of their suite.

Then gradually there came a realization among their travelling companions that Garrick was paying for most of the refreshments and other little expenses that came up each day. They became aware of him and of the fact that he appeared to be the richest of the group. From there it needed only a small adjustment to their thinking to admit Garrick to the circle. The men addressed remarks directly at him and some of the other girls flirted with him openly and sent him on small errands. Garrick was at once overjoyed and appalled by these attentions, for he could not cope with the lightning exchange of banter that flickered around him and left him stammering and blushing. Then Garrick found how easy it really was.

'Have a dram, old chap?'

'No, really. I don't, you know.'

'Nonsense, everybody does. Steward, bring my friend here a whisky.'

'Really, no really I won't.'

And of course Garrick did. It tasted foul and he spilt a little on Anna's evening dress; while he wiped it up with his handkerchief she whispered a barbed reprimand and then laughed gaily at a joke from the moustached gentleman on her right. Garrick shrank miserably back in his chair and forced down the rest of the whisky. Then slowly and exquisitely the glow came upon him, starting deep down inside him and spreading out warmly to the very tips of his fingers.

'Have another one, Mr Courtney?'

'Yes, thanks. I'll have the same again, but I think it's my round.' He had the next drink. They were sitting in deck-chairs on the upper deck in the shelter of the superstructure, there was a moon and the night was warm. Someone was talking about Chelmsford's Zulu campaign.

'You're wrong on that point,' Garrick said clearly. There was a small silence.

'I beg your pardon!' the speaker glanced at him with surprise. Garrick leaned forward easily in his chair and began talking. There was a stiffness at first but he made a witticism and two of the women laughed. Garrick's voice strengthened. He gave a quick and deep-sighted résumé of the causes and effects of the war. One of the man asked a question. It was a sharp one but Garrick saw the essence of it and answered neatly. It was all very clear and he found the words without effort.

'You must have been there,' one of the girls hazarded.

'My husband was at Rorkes Drift,' said Anna quietly, looking at him as though he were a stranger. 'Lord Chelmsford has cited him for the award of the Victoria Cross. We are waiting to hear from London.'

The party was silent again, but with new respect.

'I think it's my round, Mr Courtney. Yours is whisky, isn't it?'

'Thank you.'

The dry musty taste of the whisky was less offensive this time; he sipped it thoughtfully and found there was a faint sweetness in the dry.

As they went down to their staterooms later that night Garrick put his arm around Anna's waist.

'What fun you were tonight!' she said.

'Only a reflection of your charm, my darling, I am your mirror.' He kissed her cheek and she pulled away, but not violently.

'You're a tease, Garry Courtney.'

Garrick slept on his back on the sofa with a smile on his face and no dreams, but in the morning his skin felt tight and dry and there was a small ache behind his eyes. He went through to the bathroom and cleaned his teeth; it helped a little but the ache behind his eyes was still there. He went back to the drawing-room and rang for the cabin steward.

'Good morning, sir.'

'Can you bring me a whisky and soda?' Garry asked hesitantly.

'Certainly, sir.'

Garry did not put the soda into it but drank it neat, like medicine. Then afterwards miraculously the glow was there again, warming him. He had hardly dared to hope for it.

He went through to Anna's cabin. She was rosy with sleep, her hair a joyous tangle on the pillow.

'Good morning, my darling.' Garrick stooped over her and kissed her, and his hand moved to cover one of her breasts through the silk of her gown.

'Garry, you naughty boy.' She slapped his wrist, but jokingly.

There was another honeymoon couple aboard returning to their farm near Capetown—seventy-five acres of the finest vines on the whole of the Cape Peninsula, the man's own words. Anna and Garrick were forced by sheer persistence to accept their invitation to stay with them.

Peter and Jane Hugo were a delightful pair. Very much in love, rich enough, popular and in demand with Capetown society. With them Anna and Garrick spent an enchanted six weeks.

They went racing at Milnerton.

They swam at Muizenberg in the warm Indian Ocean. They picknicked at Clifton and ate cruyfish, fresh caught and grilled over open coals. They rode to hounds with the Cape Hunt and caught two jackals after a wild day's riding over the Hottentots' Holland. They dined at the Fort and Anna danced with the Governor.

They went shopping in the bazaars that were filled with treasures and curiosities from India and the Orient. Whatever Anna wanted she was given. Garry bought himself something as well—a silver flask, beautifully worked and set with cornelians. It fitted into the inside pocket of his coat without showing a bulge. With its help Garrick was able to keep pace with the rest of the company.

Then the time came for them to leave. The last night there were only the four of them for dinner and it was sad with the regret of present parting, but happy with the memory of shared laughter.

Jane Hugo cried a little when she kissed Anna goodnight. Garry and Peter lingered on downstairs until the bottle was finished and then they walked upstairs together and shook hands outside Garry's bedroom. Peter spoke gruffly. 'Sorry to see you two go. We've got used to having you round. I'll wake you early and we can go out for a last early morning ride before the boat leaves.'

Garry changed quietly in the bathroom and went through to the bedroom.

His peg made no sound on the heavily carpeted floor. He crossed to his own bed and sat down to unstrap his peg.

'Garry,' Anna whispered.

'Hullo, I thought you were asleep.'

There was a stirring and Anna's hand came out from under the bedclothes, held towards him in invitation.

'I was waiting to say goodnight to you.'

Garry crossed to her bed, suddenly awkward again.

'Sit down for a minute,' said Anna and he perched on the edge of her bed. 'Garry, you don't know how much I've enjoyed these last weeks. They've been the happiest days of my whole life. Thank you so much, my husband.'

She reached up and touched his cheek. She looked small and warm curled up in the bed.

'Kiss me goodnight, Garry.'

He leaned forward to touch her forehead with his lips but she moved quickly and took it full on her mouth.

'You can come in, if you like,' she whispered, her mouth still against his. She opened the bedclothes with one hand.

So Garry came to her when the bed was warm, and the wine still sang a little in her head and she was ready in the peculiar passion of early pregnancy. It should have been so wonderfully good.

Impatient now, ready to lead him, she reached down to touch and then stilled into surprised disbelief. Where there should have been hardness, male and arrogant, there was slackness and uncertainty.

Anna started to laugh. Not even the shotgun blast had hurt as deeply as that laugh.

'Get out,' she said through the cruel laughter. 'Go to your own bed.'

25

Anna and Garrick had been married two full months when they came back to Theunis Kraal. Garrick's arm was out of plaster, Peter Hugo's doctor had fixed that for him.

They took the road that by-passed the village and crossed the Baboon Stroom bridge. At the top of the rise Garry pulled the horses to a halt and they looked out across the farm.

'I can't understand why Ma moved into town,' said Garrick. 'She didn't have to do that. There's plenty of room for everybody at Theunis Kraal.'

Anna sat silently and contentedly beside him. She had been relieved when Ada had written to them at Port Natal after they had telegraphed her the news of their marriage. Young as she was Anna was woman enough to recognize the fact that Ada had never liked her. Oh, she was sweet enough when they met, but Anna found those big dark eyes of hers disconcerting. They looked too deep and she knew they found the things she was trying to hide.

'We'll have to go and see her as soon as we can. She must come back to the farm—after all Theunis Kraal is her home too,' Garrick went on. Anna moved slightly in her seat, *let her stay in the house in Ladyburg, let her rot there,* but her voice was mild as she answered, 'Theunis Kraal belongs to you now, Garry, and I'm your wife. Perhaps your stepmother knows what's best.' Anna touched his arm and smiled at him, 'Anyway we'll talk about it some other time. Let's get home now, it's been a long drive and I'm very tired.'

Immediately concerned, Garrick turned to her. 'I'm terribly sorry, my dear. How thoughtless of me.' He touched the horses with the whip and they went down the slope towards the homestead.

The lawns of Theunis Kraal were green and there were cannas in bloom, red and pink and yellow.

It's beautiful, thought Anna, *and it's mine. I'm not poor any more*. She looked at the gabled roof and the heavy yellow wood shutters on the windows as the carriage rolled up the drive.

There was a man standing in the shade of the veranda. Anna and Garrick saw him at the same time. He was tall with shoulders as wide and square as the crosstree of a gallows, he stepped out of the shadow and came down the front steps into the sunlight. He was smiling with white teeth in a brown burnt face; it was the old irresistible smile.

'Sean,' whispered Anna.

26

Sean really noticed him for the first time when they stopped to water the horses. They had left Chelmsford's Column the previous noon to scout towards the north-east. It was a tiny patrol—four mounted white men and half-a-dozen Nongaai, the loyal Native troops from Natal.

He took the reins from Sean's hands. 'I will hold your horse while you drink.' His voice had a resonance to it and Sean's interest quickened. He looked at the man's face and liked it immediately. The whites of the eyes had no yellow in them and the nose was more Arabic than negroid. His colour was dark amber and his skin shone with oil.

Sean nodded. There is no word in the Zulu language for 'thank you', just as there are no words for 'I am sorry'.

Sean knelt beside the stream and drank. The water tasted sweet for he was thirsty; when he stood again there were damp patches on his knees and water dripping from his chin.

He looked at the man who was holding his horse. He wore only a small kilt of civet-cat tails: no rattles nor cloak, no head-dress. His shield was black rawhide and he carried two short stabbing spears.

'How are you called?' Sean asked, noticing the breadth of the man's chest and the way his belly muscles stood out like the static ripples on a windswept beach.

'Mbejane.' Rhinoceros.

'For your horn?' The man chuckled with delight, his masculine vanity tickled.

'How are you called, Nkosi?'

'Sean Courtney.'

Mbejane's lips formed the name silently and then he shook his head.

'It is a difficult name.' He never said Sean's name—not once in all the years that were to follow.

'Mount up,' called Steff Erasmus. 'Let's get moving.'

They swung up on to the horses, gathered the reins and loosened the rifles in the scabbards. The Nongaai who had been stretched out resting on the bank stood up.

'Come on,' said Steff. He splashed through the stream. His horse gathered itself and bounded up the far bank and they followed him. They moved in line abreast across the grassland, sitting loose and relaxed in their saddles, the horses trippling smoothly.

At Sean's right stirrup ran the big Zulu, his long extended stride easily pacing Sean's horse. Once in a while Sean dropped his eyes from the horizon and looked down at Mbejane; it was a strangely comforting feeling to have him there.

They camped that night in a shallow valley of grass. There were no cooking fires; they ate biltong for supper, the black strips of dried salt meat, and washed it down with cold water.

'We're wasting our time. There hasn't been a sign of Zulu in two days' riding,' grumbled Bester Klein, one of the troopers.

'I say we should turn back and rejoin the Column. We're getting farther and farther away from the centre of things—we're going to miss the fun when it starts.'

Steff Erasmus wrapped his blanket more closely about his shoulders: the night's first chill was on them.

'Fun, is it?' He spat expertly into the darkness. 'Let them have the fun, if we find the cattle.'

'Don't you mind missing the fighting?'

'Look, you, I've hunted bushmen in the Karroo and the Kalahari, I've fought Xhosas and Fingoes along the Fish river, I went into the mountains after Moshesh and his Basutos. Matabele, Zulu, Bechuana—I've had fun with all of them. Now four or five hundred head of prime cattle will be payment enough for any fun we miss.' Steff lay back and adjusted his saddle behind his head. 'Anyway what makes you think there won't be guards on the herds when we find them? You'll get your fun—I promise you.'

'How do you know they've got the cattle up here?' insisted Sean.

'They're here,' said Steff, 'and we'll find them.' He turned his head towards Sean. 'You've got the first watch, keep your eyes open.' He tilted his top hat forward over his face, groped with his right hand to make sure his rifle lay beside him and then spoke from under the hat, 'Goodnight.' The others settled down into their blankets: fully-dressed, boots on, guns at hand. Sean moved out into the darkness to check the Nongaai pickets.

There was no moon, but the stars were fat and close to earth; they lit the land so that the four grazing horses were dark blobs against the pale grass. Sean circled the camp and found two of his sentries awake and attentive. He had posted Mbejane on the north side and now he went there. Fifty yards in front of him he picked up the shape of the small bush beside which he had left Mbejane. Suddenly Sean smiled and sank down on to his hands and knees, he cradled his rifle across the crooks of his elbows and began his stalk. Moving flat along the ground silently, slowly he closed in on the bush. Ten paces from it he stopped and lifted his head, careful to keep the movement inchingly slow. He stared, trying to find the shape of the Zulu among the scraggy branches and bunches of leaves. The point of a stabbing spear pricked him below the ear in the soft of his neck behind the jaw bone. Sean froze but his eyes rolled sideways and in the starlight he saw Mbejane kneeling over him holding the spear.

'Does the Nkosi seek me?' asked Mbejane solemnly, but there was laughter deep down in his voice. Sean sat up and rubbed the place where the spear had stung him.

'Only a night ape sees in the dark,' Sean protested.

'And only a fresh caught catfish flops on its belly,' chuckled Mbejane.

'You are Zulu,' Sean stated, recognizing the arrogance, although he had known immediately from the man's face and body that he was not one of the bastard Natal tribes who spoke the Zulu language but were no more Zulu than a tabby-cat is a leopard.

'Of Chaka's blood,' agreed Mbejane, reverence in his voice as he said the old king's name.

'And now you carry the spear against Cetewayo, your king?'

'My king?' The laughter was gone from Mbejane's voice. 'My king?' he repeated scornfully.

There was silence and Sean waited. Out in the darkness a jackal barked twice and one of the horses whickered softly.

'There was another who should have been king, but he died with a sharpened stick thrust up into the secret opening of his body, until it pierced his gut and touched his heart. That man was my father,' said Mbejane. He stood up and went back into the shelter of the bush and Sean followed him. They squatted side by side, silent but watchful. The jackal cried again up above the camp and Mbejane's head turned towards the sound.

'Some jackals have two legs,' he whispered thoughtfully. Sean felt the tingle along his forearms.

'Zulus?' he asked. Mbejane shrugged, a small movement in the darkness.

'Even if it is, they will not come for us in the night. In the dawn, yes, but never in the night.' Mbejane shifted the spear in his lap. 'The old one with the tall hat and grey beard understands this. Years have made him wise, that's why he sleeps so sweetly now but mounts up and moves in the darkness before each dawn.'

Sean relaxed slightly. He glanced sideways at Mbejane.

'The old one thinks that some of the herds are hidden near here.'

'Years have made him wise,' repeated Mbejane. 'Tomorrow we will find the land more broken, there are hills and thick thorn bush. The cattle will be hidden among them.'

'Do you think we'll find them?'

'Cattle are difficult to hide from a man who knows where to look.'

'Will there be many guards with the herds?'

'I hope so,' answered Mbejane, his voice a purr. His hand crept to the shaft of his assegai and caressed it. 'I hope there will be very many.'

'You would kill your own people, your brothers, your cousins?' asked Sean.

'I would kill them as they killed my father.' Mbejane's voice was savage now. 'They are not my people. I have no people. I have no brothers—I have nothing.'

Silence settled between them again, but slowly the ugliness of Mbejane's mood evaporated and in its place came a sense of companionship. Each of them felt comforted by the other's presence. They sat on into the night.

Mbejane reminded Sean of Tinker working a bird, he had the same half-crouched gait and the same air of complete absorption. The white men sat their horses in silence watching him. The sun was well up already and Sean unbuttoned his sheepskin coat and pulled it off. He strapped it on to the blanket roll behind him.

Mbejane had moved out about fifty yards from them and now he was working slowly back towards them. He stopped and minutely inspected a wet pat of cow dung.

'*Hierdie Kaffir verstaan wat hy doen,*' opined Steff Erasmus approvingly, but no one else spoke. Bester Klein fidgeted with the hammer of his carbine; his red face was already sweating in the rising heat.

Mbejane had proved right, they were in hilly country. Not the smoothly rounded hills of Natal but hills with rocky crests, deeply gullied and ravined between. There was thorn forest and euphorbia covering the sides of the hills with a lattice work of reptile grey trunks, and the grass was coarse and tall.

'I could use a drink,' said Frikkie Van Essen and wiped his knuckles across his lips.

'Chee peep, chee peep,' a barbet called stridently in the branches of the kaffir boom tree under which they waited. Sean looked up; the bird was brown and red among the scarlet flowers which covered the tree.

'How many?' asked Steff and Mbejane came to stand at his horse's head.

'Fifty—no more,' he answered.

'When?'

'Yesterday, after the heat of the day they moved slowly down the valley. They were grazing. They cannot be more than half an hour's ride ahead of us.'

Steff nodded. Fifty head only, but there would be more.

'How many men with them?'

Mbejane clucked his tongue disgustedly. 'Two *umfaans.*' He pointed with his spear at a dusty place where the print of a half-grown boy's bare foot showed clearly. 'There are no men.'

'Good,' said Steff. 'Follow them.'

'They told us that if we found anything we must go back and report,' protested Bester Klein quickly. 'They said we shouldn't start anything on our own.'

Steff turned in his saddle. 'Are you frightened of two *umfaans*?' he asked coldly.

'I'm not frightened of anything, it's just what they told us.' Klein flushed redder in his already red face.

'I know what they told us, thank you,' said Steff. 'I'm not going to start anything, we're just going to have a look.'

'I know you,' burst out Klein. 'If you see cattle you'll go mad for them. All of you, you're greedy for cattle like some men are for drink. Once you see them you won't stop.' Klein was a railway ganger.

Steff turned away from him. 'Come on, let's go.'

They rode out of the shade of the kaffir boom tree into the sunlight, Klein muttering softly to himself and Mbejane leading them down the valley.

The floor of the valley sloped gradually and on each side of them the ground rose steep and rocky. They travelled quickly with Mbejane and the other Nongaai thrown out as a screen and the horsemen cantering in a line with their stirrups almost touching.

Sean levered open the breech of his rifle and drew out the cartridge. He changed it for another from the bandolier across his chest.

'Fifty head is only ten apiece,' complained Frikkie.

'That's a hundred quid—as much as you earn in six months.' Sean laughed with excitement and Frikkie laughed with him.

'You two keep your mouths shut and your eyes open.' Steff's voice was phlegmatic, but he couldn't stop the excitement from sparkling in his eyes.

'I knew you were going to raid,' sulked Klein. 'I knew it, sure as fate.'

'You shut up also,' said Steff and grinned at Sean.

They rode for ten minutes; then Steff called softly to the Nongaai and the patrol halted. No one spoke and every man stood with his head alert and his ears straining.

'Nothing,' said Steff at last. 'How close are we?'

'Very close,' Mbejane answered. 'We should have heard them from here.'

Mbejane's exquisitely muscled body was shiny with sweat and the pride of his stance set him apart from the other Nongaai. There was a restrained eagerness about him, for the excitement was infectious.

'All right, follow them,' said Steff. Mbejane settled the rawhide shield securely on his shoulder and started forward again.

Twice more they stopped to listen and each time Sean and Frikkie were more restless and impatient.

'Sit still,' snapped Steff. 'How can we hear anything with you moving about?'

Sean opened his mouth, but before he could answer they all heard an ox low mournfully ahead of them among the trees.

'That's it!'

'We've got them!'

'Come on!'

'No, wait!' Steff ordered. 'Sean, take my farlookers and climb up that tree. Tell me what you can see.'

'We're wasting time,' argued Sean. 'We should—'

'We should learn to do as we're damn well told,' said Steff. 'Get up that tree.'

With the binoculars slung around his neck, Sean clambered upwards until he sat high in a crotch of two branches. He reached out and broke off a twig which obscured his vision, then exclaimed immediately, 'There they are, right ahead of us!'

'How many?' Steff called up to him.

'A small herd—two herdboys with them.'

'Are they among the trees?'

'No,' said Sean, 'they're in the open. Looks like a patch of swamp.'

'Make sure there aren't any other Zulus with them.'

'No—' Sean started to answer but Steff cut him short.

'Use the glasses, dammit. They'll be hiding if they're there.'

Sean brought up the glasses and focused them. The cattle were fat and sleek skinned, big horned and bodies dappled black on white. A cloud of white tick-birds hovered over them. The two herdboys were completely naked, youngsters with the thin legs and the disproportionately large genitals of the Africans. Sean turned the glasses slowly back and forth searching the patch of swamp and the surrounding bush. At last he lowered them.

'Only the two herdboys,' he said.

'Come down then,' Steff told him.

The herdboys fled as soon as the patrol rode out into the open. They disappeared among the fever trees on the far side of the swamp.

'Let them go,' laughed Steff. 'The poor little buggers are going to be in enough trouble as it is.'

He spurred his horse forward into the vivid green patch of swamp grass. It was lush: thick and tall enough to reach his saddle.

The others followed him in with the mud squelching and sucking at the hooves of the horses. They could see the backs of the cattle showing above the grass a hundred yards ahead of them. The tick-birds circled squawking.

'Sean, you and Frikkie cut around to the left—' Steff spoke over his shoulder and before he could finish the grass around them was full of Zulus, at least a hundred of them in full war dress.

'Ambush!' yelled Steff. 'Don't try and fight, too many of them. Get out!' and they dragged him off his horse.

Horses panicked in the mud, whinnying as they reared. The bang of Klein's rifle was almost drowned in the triumphant roar of the warriors. Mbejane jumped to catch the bridle of Sean's horse; he dragged its head around.

'Ride, Nkosi, quickly. Do not wait.'

Klein was dead, an assegai in his throat and the blood bursting brightly from the corners of his mouth as he fell backwards.

'Hold on to my stirrup leather.' Sean felt surprisingly calm. A Zulu came at him from the side; Sean held his rifle across his lap and fired with the muzzle almost in the man's face. It cut the top off his head. Sean ejected the cartridge case and reloaded.

'Ride, Nkosi!' Mbejane shouted again. He had made no effort to obey Sean: his shield held high he barged into two of the attackers and knocked them down into the mud. His assegai rose and fell, rose and fell.

'*Ngi Dhla*,' howled Mbejane. 'I have eaten.' Fighting madness on him, he jumped over the bodies and charged. A man stood to meet him and Mbejane hooked the edge of his shield under his and jerked it aside, exposing the man's left flank to his blade.

'*Ngi Dhla*,' Mbejane howled again.

He had torn an opening in the ring of attackers and Sean rode for it, his horse churning heavily through the mud. A Zulu caught at his reins and Sean fired with his muzzle touching the man's chest. The Zulu screamed.

'Mbejane,' shouted Sean. 'Take my stirrup!'

Frikkie Van Essen was finished; his horse was down and Zulus swarmed over him with red spears.

Leaning out of the saddle Sean circled Mbejane's waist with his arm and plucked him out of the mud. He struggled wildly but Sean held him. The ground firmed under his horse's hooves, they were moving faster. Another Zulu stood in their way with his assegai ready. With Mbejane kicking indignantly under one arm and his empty rifle in his other hand Sean was helpless to defend himself. He shouted an obscenity at the Zulu as he rode down on him. The Zulu dodged to one side and darted in again. Sean felt the sting of the blade across his shin and then the shock as it went on into his horse's chest. They were through, out of the swamp and into the trees.

Sean's horse carried him another mile before it fell. The assegai had gone in deep. It fell heavily but Sean was able to kick his feet out of the irons and jump clear. He and Mbejane stood looking down at the carcass—both of them were panting.

'Can you run in those boots?' asked Mbejane urgently.

'Yes.' They were light *veldschoen*.

'Those breeches will hold your legs.' Mbejane knelt swiftly and with his assegai cut away the cloth until Sean's legs were bare from the thighs down. He stood up again and listened for the first sounds of pursuit. Nothing.

Leave your rifle, it is too heavy. Leave your hat and your bandolier.'

'I must take my rifle,' protested Sean.

'Take it then,' Mbejane flashed impatiently. 'Take it and die. If you carry that they'll catch you before noon.'

Sean hesitated a second longer and then he changed his grip, holding the rifle by the barrel like an axe. He swung it against the trunk of the nearest tree. The butt shattered and he threw it from him.

'Now we must go,' said Mbejane.

Sean glanced quickly across at his dead horse, the leather thongs held his sheepskin coat on to the saddle. All Anna's hard work wasted, he thought wryly. Then following Mbejane he started to run.

The first hour was bad; Sean had difficulty matching his step to that of Mbejane. He ran with his body tensed and soon had a stabbing stitch in his side. Mbejane saw his pain and they stopped for a few minutes while Mbejane showed him how to relax it away. Then they went on with Sean running smoothly. Another hour went by and Sean had found his second wind.

'How long will it take us to get back to the main army?' grunted Sean.

'Two days perhaps . . . don't talk,' answered Mbejane.

The land changed slowly about them as they ran. The hills not so steep and jagged, the forest thinned and again they were into the rolling grassland.

'It seems we are not being followed.' It was half an hour since Sean had last spoken.

'Perhaps,' Mbejane was non-committal. 'It is too soon yet to tell.'

They ran on side by side, in step so their feet slapped in unison on the hard-baked earth.

'Christ, I'm thirsty,' said Sean.

'No water,' said Mbejane, 'but we'll stop to rest a while at the top of the next rise.'

They looked back from the crest. Sean's shirt was soaked with sweat and he was breathing deeply but easily.

'No one following us,' Sean's voice was relieved 'We can slow down a bit now.'

Mbejane did not answer. He also was sweating heavily but the way he moved and held his head showed he was not yet beginning to tire. He carried his shield on his shoulder and the blade of the assegai in his other hand was caked with black, dry blood. He stared out along the way they had come for fully five minutes before he growled angrily and pointed with his assegai.

'There! Close to that clump of trees. Can you see them?'

'Oh, hell!' Sean saw them: about four miles behind, on the edge of the forest where it thinned out, a black pencil line drawn on the brown parchment of grassland. But the line was moving.

'How many of them?' asked Sean.

'Fifty,' hazarded Mbejane. 'Too many.'

'I wish I had brought my rifle,' muttered Sean.

'If you had they would be much closer now—and one gun against fifty—' Mbejane left it unfinished.

'All right, let's get going again,' said Sean.

'We must rest a little longer. This is the last time we can stop before nightfall.'

Their breathing had slowed. Sean took stock of himself: he was aching a little in the legs, but it would be hours yet before he was really tired. He hawked a glob of the thick gummy saliva out of his throat and spat it into the grass. He wanted a drink but knew that would be fatal folly.

'Ah!' exclaimed Mbejane. 'They have seen us.'

'How do you know?' asked Sean.

'Look, they are sending out their chasers.' From the head of the line a trio of specks had detached themselves and were drawing ahead.

'What do you mean?' Sean scratched the side of his nose uneasily. For the first time he was feeling the fear of the hunted—vulnerable, unarmed, with the pack closing in.

'They are sending their best runners ahead to force us beyond our strength. They know that if they push us hard enough—even though they break their own wind while they do it—we will fall easily to the others that follow.'

'Good God,' Sean was now truly alarmed. 'What are we going to do about it?'

'For every trick, there is a trick,' said Mbejane. 'But now we have rested enough, let us go.'

Sean took off down the hill like a startled duiker, but Mbejane pulled him up sharply.

'That is what they want. Run as before.' And once again they fell into the steady lope, swinging long-legged and relaxed.

'They're closer,' said Sean when they reached the top of the next hill. Three specks were now well ahead of the others.

'Yes.' Mbejane's voice was expressionless. They went over the crest and down the other side, the slap-slap-slap of their feet together and their breathing an unaltering rhythm: suck blow, suck blow.

There was a tiny stream in the bottom of the valley, clean water rippling over white sand. Sean jumped it with only a single longing glance and they started up the far slope. They were just short of the crest when behind them they heard a thin distant shout. He and Mbejane looked round. On the top of the hill they had just left, only a half mile away, were the three Zulu runners, and as Sean watched they plunged down the slope towards him with their tall feather head-dresses bobbing and their leopard-tail kilts swirling about their legs. They had thrown aside their shields, but each man carried an assegai.

'Look at their legs,' exulted Mbejane. Sean saw that they ran with the slack, blundering steps of exhaustion.

'They are finished, they have run too hard.' Mbejane laughed. 'Now we must show them how afraid we are: we must run like the wind, run as though a hundred Tokoloshe* breathe on our necks.'

It was only twenty paces to the crest of the slope and they pelted panic-

*A chimera of Zulu mythology

stricken up and over the top. But the instant they were out of sight Mbejane caught Sean's arm and held him.

'Get down,' he whispered. They sank into the grass and then crawled back on their stomachs until they lay just below the crest.

Mbejane held his assegai pointed forward, his legs were gathered up under him and his lips were drawn back in a half grin.

Sean searched in the grass and found a rock the size of an orange. It fitted neatly into his right hand.

They heard the Zulus coming, their horny bare feet pounding up the hill and then their breathing, hoarse hissing gasps, closer and closer until suddenly they came up over the crest. Their momentum carried them down to where Sean and Mbejane stood up out of the grass to meet them. Their fatigue-grey faces crumbled into expressions of complete disbelief; they had expected to find their quarry half a mile ahead of them. Mbejane killed one with his assegai, the man did not even lift his arms to parry the thrust; the point came out between his shoulders.

Sean hurled the rock into the face of another. It made a sound like a ripe pumpkin dropped on a stone floor; he fell backwards with the assegai spinning from his hand.

The third man turned to run and Mbejane landed heavily on his back, bore him down and then astride his chest, pushed his chin back and cut his throat.

Sean looked down at the man he had hit; he had lost his head-dress and his face had changed shape. His jaw hung lopsided, he was still moving feebly.

I have killed three men today, thought Sean, *and it was so easy.*

Without emotion he watched Mbejane come across to his victim. Mbejane stooped over him and the man made a small gasping sound then lay still. Mbejane straightened up and looked at Sean.

'Now they cannot catch us before dark.'

'And only a night ape can see in the dark,' said Sean. Remembering the joke, Mbejane smiled; the smile made his face younger. He picked up a bunch of dry grass and wiped his hands on it.

The night came only just in time to save them. Sean had run all day and at last his body was stiffening in protest; his breathing wheezed painfully and he had no moisture left to sweat with.

'A little longer, just a little longer.' Mbejane whispered encouragement beside him.

The pack was spread out, the stronger runners pressing a scant mile behind them and the others dwindling back into the distance.

'The sun is going; soon you can rest.' Mbejane reached out and touched his shoulder; strangely, Sean drew strength from that brief physical contact. His legs steadied slightly and he stumbled less frequently as they went down the next slope. Swollen and red, the sun lowered itself below the land and the valleys were full of shadow.

'Soon now, very soon.' Mbejane's voice was almost crooning. He looked back: the figures of the nearest Zulu were indistinct. Sean's ankle twisted under him and he fell heavily; he felt the earth graze the skin from his cheek and he lay on his chest with his head down.

'Get up,' Mbejane's voice was desperate. Sean vomited painfully, a cupful of bitter bile.

'Get up,' Mbejane's hands were on him, dragging him to his knees.

'Stand up or die here,' threatened Mbejane. He took a handful of Sean's hair and twisted it mercilessly. Tears of pain ran into Sean's eyes, and he swore and lashed out at Mbejane.

'Get up,' goaded Mbejane and Sean heaved to his feet.

'Run,' said Mbejane, half-pushing him and Sean's legs began to move mechanically under him. Mbejane looked back once more. The nearest Zulu was very close but almost merged into the fading twilight. They ran on, Mbejane steadying Sean when he staggered, Sean grunting in his throat with each step, his mouth hanging open, sucking air across a swollen tongue.

Then quickly, in the sudden African transition from day to night, all colour was gone from the land and the darkness shut down in a close circle about them. Mbejane's eyes flicked restlessly back and forth, picking up shapes in the gloom, judging the intensity of the light. Sean reeled unseeing beside him.

'We will try now,' decided Mbejane aloud. He checked Sean's run and turned him right at an acute angle on their original track, now they were heading back towards the hunters at a tangent that would take them close past them but out of sight in the darkness.

They slowed to a walk, Mbejane holding Sean's arm across his shoulders to steady him, carrying his assegai ready in his other hand. Sean walked dully, his head hanging.

They heard the leading pursuers passing fifty paces away in the darkness and a voice called in Zulu, 'Can you see them?'

'*Aibo!*' Negative answered another.

'Spread out, they may try to turn in the dark.'

'*Yeh-bo!*' Affirmative.

Then the voices were passed and silence and night closed about them once more. Mbejane made Sean keep walking. A little bit of moon came up and gave them light and they kept going with Mbejane gradually working back on to a course towards the south-east. They came to a stream at last with trees along its bank. Sean drank with difficulty, for his throat was swollen and sore. Afterwards they curled together for warmth on the carpet of leaves beneath the trees and they slept.

28

They found Chelmsford's last camp on the following afternoon: the neat lines of black camp fires and the flattened areas where the tents had stood, the stakes which had held the horse pickets and the piles of empty bully-beef tins and five-pound biscuit tins.

'They left two days ago,' said Mbejane.

Sean nodded, not doubting the correctness of this. 'Which way did they go?'

'Back towards the main camp at Isandhlwana.'

Sean looked puzzled.

'I wonder why they did that.'

Mbejane shrugged. 'They went in haste—the horsemen galloped ahead of the infantry.'

'We'll follow them,' said Sean.

The spoor was a wide road for a thousand men had passed along it and the wagons and gun carriages had left deep ruts.

They slept hungry and cold beside the spoor and the next morning there was frost in the low places when they started out.

A little before noon they saw the granite dome of Isandhlwana standing out against the sky and unconsciously they quickened their pace. Isandhlwana, the Hill of the Little Hand. Sean was limping for his boot had rubbed the skin from one heel. His hair was thick and matted with sweat and his face was plastered with dust.

'Even army bully beef is going to taste good,' said Sean in English, and Mbejane did not answer for he did not understand, but he was looking ahead with a vaguely worried frown on his face.

'Nkosi, we have seen no one for two days' march. It comes to me that we should have met patrols from the camp before now.'

'We might have missed them,' said Sean without much interest, but Mbejane shook his head. In silence they went on. The hill was closer now so they could make out the detail of ledge and fissure that covered the dome in a lace-work pattern.

'No smoke from the camp,' said Mbejane. He lifted his eyes and started visibly.

'What is it?' Sean felt the first tingle of alarm.

'*N'yoni*,' said Mbejane softly and Sean saw them. A dark pall, turning like a wheel slowly, high above the hill of Isandhlwana, still so far off that they could not distinguish the individual birds: only a shadow, a thin dark shadow in the sky. Watching it Sean was suddenly cold in the hot noonday sun. He started to run.

There was movement below them on the plain. The torn canvas of an overturned wagon flapped like a wounded bird, the scurry and scuffle of the jackals and higher up the slope of the kopje the hunch-shouldered trot of a hyena.

'Oh, my God!' whispered Sean. Mbejane leaned on his spear; his face was calm and withdrawn but his eyes moved slowly over the field.

'Are they dead? Are they all dead?' The question required no answer. He could see the dead men in the grass, thick about the wagons and then scattered more thinly back up the slope. They looked very small and inconsequential. Mbejane stood quietly waiting. A big black kolbes vulture planed across their front, the feathers in its wing-tips flated like the fingers of a spread hand. Its legs dropped, touched and it hopped heavily to rest among the dead, a swift transformation from beautiful flight to obscene crouching repose. It bobbed its head, ruffled its feathers and waddled to dip its beak over a corpse that wore the green Hunting Tartan of the Gordons.

'Where is Chelmsford? Was he caught here also?'

Mbejane shook his head. 'He came too late.'

Mbejane pointed with his spear at the wide spoor that skirted the battlefield and crossed the shoulder of Isandhlwana towards the Tugela. 'He has gone back to the river. He has not stopped even to bury his dead.'

Sean and Mbejane walked down towards the field. On the outskirts they picked their way through the debris of Zulu weapons and shields; there was rust forming on the blades of the assegais. The grass was flattened and stained where the dead had lain, but the Zulu dead were gone—sure sign of victory.

They came to the English lines. Sean gagged when he saw what had been done to them. They lay piled upon each other, faces already black, and each one of them had been disembowelled. The flies crawled in their empty stomach cavities.

'Why do they do that?' he asked. 'Why do they have to hack them up like that?'

He walked on heavily past the wagons. Cases of food and drink had been smashed open and scattered in the grass, clothing and paper and cartridge cases lay strewn around the dead, but the rifles were gone. The smell of putrefaction was so thick that it coated his throat and tongue like castor oil.

'I must find Pa,' Sean spoke quietly in almost a conversational tone. Mbejane walked a dozen paces behind him. They came to the lines where the Volunteers had camped. The tents had been slashed to tatters and trampled into the dust. The horses had been stabbed while still tethered to their picket lines; they were massively bloated. Sean recognized Gypsy, his father's mare. He crossed to her.

'Hello, girl,' he said. The birds had taken her eyes out; she lay on her side, her stomach so swollen that it was as high as Sean's waist. He walked around her. The first of the Ladyburg men lay just beyond. He recognized all fifteen of them although the birds had been at them also. They lay in a rough circle, facing outwards. Then he found a sparse trail of corpses leading up towards the shoulder of the mountain. He followed the attempt that the Volunteers had made to fight their way back towards the Tugela and it was like following a paper chase. Along the trail, thick on each side of it, were the marks where the Zulus had fallen.

'At least twenty of them for every one of us,' whispered Sean, with a tiny flicker of pride. He climbed on up and at the top of the shoulder, close under the sheer rock cliff of Isandhlwana, he found his father.

There were four of them, the last four: Waite Courtney, Tim Hope-Brown, Hans and Nile Erasmus. They lay close together. Waite was on his back with his arms spread open, the birds had taken his face away down to the bone, but they had left his beard and it stirred gently on his chest as the wind touched it. The flies, big metallic green flies, crawled thick as swarming bees in the open pit of his belly.

Sean sat down beside his father. He picked up a discarded felt hat that lay beside him and covered his terribly mutilated face. There was a green-and-yellow silk cockade on the hat, strangely gay in the presence of so much death. The flies buzzed sullenly and some came to settle on Sean's face and lips. He brushed them away.

'You know this man?' asked Mbejane.

'My father,' said Sean, without looking up.

'You too.' Compassion and understanding in his voice, Mbejane turned away and left them alone.

'I have nothing,' Mbejane had said. Now Sean also had nothing. There was hollowness: no anger, no sorrow, no ache, no reality even. Staring down at this broken thing, Sean could not make himself believe that this was a man. Meat only; the man had gone.

Later Mbejane came back. He had cut a sheet of canvas from one of the unburned wagons and they wrapped Waite in it. They dug his grave. It was hard work for the soil was thick with rock and shale. They laid Waite in the grave, with his arms still wide-spread in *rigor mortis* beneath the canvas for Sean could not bring himself to break them. They covered him gently and piled rocks upon the place. They stood together at the head of the grave.

'Well, Pa—' Sean's voice sounded unnatural. He could not make himself believe he was talking to his father.

'Well, Pa–' he started again, mumbling self-consciously. 'I'd like to say thanks for everything you've done for me.' He stopped and cleared his throat. 'I reckon you know I'll look after Ma and the farm as best I can–and Garry also.' His voice trailed away once more and he turned to Mbejane.

'There is nothing to say.' Sean's voice was surprised, hurt almost.

'No,' agreed Mbejane. 'There is nothing to say.'

For a few minutes longer Sean stood struggling to grapple with the enormity of death, trying to grasp the utter finality of it, then he turned away and started walking towards the Tugela. Mbejane walked a little to one side and a pace behind him. *It will be dark before we reach the river,* thought Sean. He was very tired and he limped from his blistered heel.

29

'Not much farther,' said Dennis Petersen.

'No,' Sean grunted. He was irritated at statement of the obvious; when you come out of Mahoba's Kloof and have the Baboon Stroom next to the road on your left hand, then it is five miles to Ladyburg. As Dennis had said: not much farther.

Dennis coughed in the dust. 'That first beer is going to turn to steam in my throat.'

'I think we can ride ahead now.' Sean wiped at his face, smearing the dust. 'Mbejane and the other servants can bring them in the rest of the way.'

'I was going to suggest it.' Dennis was obviously relieved. They had almost a thousand head of cattle crowding the road ahead of them and raising dust for them to breathe. It had been two days' drive from Rorkes Drift where the Commando had disbanded.

'We'll hold them in the sale pens tonight and send them out tomorrow morning–I'll tell Mbejane.'

Sean clapped his heels into his horse and swung across to where the big Zulu trotted at the heel of the herd. A few minutes' talk and then Sean signalled to Dennis. They circled out on each side of the herd and met again on the road ahead of it.

'They've lost a bit of condition,' grumbled Dennis looking back.

'Bound to,' said Sean. 'We've pushed them hard for two days.'

A thousand head of cattle, five men's share of Cetewayo's herds–Dennis and his father, Waite, Sean and Garrick–for even dead men drew a full share.

'How far ahead of the others do you reckon we are?' asked Dennis.

'Dunno,' said Sean. It wasn't important and any answer would be only a guess: pointless question is just as irritating as obvious statement. It suddenly occurred to Sean that but a few months previously a question like that would have started a discussion and argument that might have lasted half an hour. What did that mean? It meant that he had changed. Having answered his own question, Sean grinned sardonically.

'What'er you laughing at?' asked Dennis.

'I was just thinking that a lot has changed in the last few months.'

'*Ja,*' said Dennis and then silence except for the broken beat of their hooves. 'It's going to seem funny without Pa,' Dennis said wistfully. Mr Petersen had been at Isandhlwana. 'It's going to seem funny being just Ma, the girls and me on the farm.'

They didn't speak again for a while. They were thinking back across the brief months and the events that had changed their lives.

Neither of them yet twenty years of age, but already head of his family, a holder of land and cattle, initiated into grief and a killer of men. Sean was older now with new lines in his face, and the beard he wore was square and spade-shaped. They had ridden with the Commandos who had burned and plundered to avenge Isandhlwana. At Ulundi they had sat their horses behind the ranks of Chelmsford's infantry in the hot sun, quietly waiting as Cetewayo massed his impis and sent them across open ground to overwhelm the frail square of men. They had waited through the din of the regular, unhurried volleys and watched the great black bull of Zulu tearing itself to shreds against the square. Then at the end the ranks of infantry had opened and they had ridden out, two thousand horsemen strong, to smash for ever the power of the Zulu empire. They had chased and hunted until the darkness had stopped them and they had not kept score of the kill.

'There's the church steeple,' said Dennis.

Sean came back slowly out of the past. They were at Ladyburg.

'Is your stepmother out at Theunis Kraal?' asked Dennis.

'No, she's moved into town—the cottage on Protea Street.'

'I suppose she doesn't want to be in the way now that Anna and Garry are married,' said Dennis.

Sean frowned quickly.

'How do you like old Garry getting Anna?' Dennis chuckled and shook his head. 'I reckon you could have got twenty-to-one odds he didn't have a chance.'

Sean's frown became a scowl. Garry had made him look such a damn fool—Sean hadn't finished with Anna.

'Have you heard from them yet? When are they coming home?'

'The last time we heard was from Pietermaritzburg; they sent a wire to Ma just to say they were married. She got it a couple of days before I arrived home from Isandhlwana. That was two months ago; as far as I know we haven't heard since.'

'I suppose Garry's so firmly settled on the nest they'll have to prise him off with a crowbar.' Dennis chuckled again, lewdly. Sean had a sudden and shockingly vivid mental picture of Garry on top of Anna; her knees were up high, her head was thrown back and her eyes were closed; she was making that little mewing sound.

'Shut up, you dirty bastard,' snarled Sean.

Dennis blinked. 'Sorry, I was only joking.'

'Don't joke about my family, he's my brother.'

'And she was your girl, hey?' murmured Dennis.

'Do you want a punch?'

'Cool down, man, I was joking.'

'I don't like that kind of joke, see?'

'All right. All right. Cool down.'

'It's dirty, that's dirty talk.' Sean was trying desperately to shut out the picture of Anna; she was in wild orgasm, her hands pleading at the small of Garrick's back.

'Jesus, since when have you become a saint?' asked Dennis and, urging his horse into a gallop, drew ahead of Sean; he kept going along the main street towards the hotel. Sean considered calling him back, but finally let him go.

Sean turned right into a shady side street. The cottage was the third house down, Waite had purchased it three years before as an investment. It was a charming little place, set among trees in a small green garden with flowers: thatched, whitewashed and surrounded by a wooden picket fence. Sean hitched his horse at the gate and went up the path.

There were two women in the sitting-room when he pushed the door open. They both stood up, surprise instantly becoming delight as they recognized him. It warmed him inside to see it—it's good to be welcome.

'Oh Sean, we weren't expecting you.' Ada came quickly to him. He kissed her and saw that sorrow had left its marks on her. He felt vaguely guilty that Waite's death had not wrought so obvious a change in him. He held her away at arm's length.

'You're beautiful,' he said. She was thin. Her eyes were too big for her face and the grief was in them like shadows in the forest, but she smiled and laughed at him.

'We thought you'd be back on Friday. I'm so glad you've come earlier.'

Sean looked past Ada.

'Hello, Strawberry Pie.' She was hovering impatiently for his attention.

'Hello, Sean.' She flushed a little with his eyes on her, but she did not drop hers.

'You look older,' she said, hardly noticing the dust that caked his skin, powdered his hair and eyelashes, and reddened his eyes.

'You've just forgotten what I look like,' he said, turning back to Ada.

'No, I'd never do that,' whispered Audrey so softly that neither of them heard her. She felt swollen up inside her chest.

'Sit down, Sean.' Ada led him to the big armchair across from the fireplace. There was a daguerreotype of Waite on the mantel.

'I'll get you a cup of tea.'

'How about a beer, Ma?' Sean sank into the chair.

'Of course—I'll get it.'

'No.' Audrey flew across the room towards the kitchen. 'I'll get it.'

'They're in the pantry, Audrey,' Ada called after her, and then to Sean, 'She's such a sweet child.'

'Look again,' Sean smiled. 'She's no child.'

'I wish Garry—' Ada cut herself short.

'What do you wish?' Sean prompted her. She was quiet for a moment, wishing that Garrick could have found a girl like Audrey instead of—

'Nothing,' she said to Sean and came to sit near him.

'Have you heard from Garry again?' asked Sean.

'No. Not yet, but Mr Pye says he had a cheque come through the bank—cashed in Capetown.'

'Capetown?' Sean raised a dusty eyebrow. 'Our boy's living life to the hilt.'

'Yes,' said Ada, remembering the size of that cheque. 'He is.'

Audrey came back into the room: she had a large bottle and a glass on a tray. She crossed to Sean's chair. Sean touched the bottle; it was cold.

'Quickly, wench,' Sean encouraged her. 'I'm dying of thirst.'

The first glass emptied in three swallows, Audrey poured again and, with the replenished glass in his fist, Sean settled back comfortably in the chair.

'Now,' said Ada, 'tell us all about it.'

In the warmth of their welcome—his muscles aching pleasantly, the glass in his hand—it was good to talk. He had not realized that there was so much to tell. At the first hint of slackening in his flow of speech either Ada or Audrey was ready with a question to keep him going.

'Oh, my goodness,' gasped Audrey at last. 'It's nearly dark outside, I must go.'

'Sean,' Ada stood up. 'Will you see that she gets home safely?'

They walked side by side in the half darkness, under the flamboyants. They walked in silence until Audrey spoke.

'Sean, were you in love with Anna?' She blurted out the question and Sean experienced his standard reaction: quick anger. He opened his mouth to blast her, then checked. It was a nice question. Had he been in love with Anna? He thought about it now for the first time, phrasing the question with care that he might answer it with truth. He felt a sudden rush of relief and he was smiling when he told her.

'No, Strawberry Pie, no, I was never in love with Anna.' The tone of his voice was right, he wasn't lying. She walked on happily beside him.

'Don't bother to come up to the house.' She noticed for the first time his stained and dirty clothing that might embarrass him in front of her parents. She wanted it to be right from the start.

'I'll watch you till you get to the door,' said Sean.

'I suppose you'll be going out to Theunis Kraal tomorrow?' she asked.

'First thing in the morning,' Sean assured her. 'There's a hell of a lot of work to do.'

'But you'll be coming to the store?'

'Yes,' said Sean and the way he looked at her made her blush and hate her redhead's skin which betrayed her so easily. She went quickly up the path and then stopped and looked back.

'Sean, please don't call me Strawberry Pie any more.'

Sean chuckled. 'All right, Audrey, I'll try to remember.'

30

Six weeks had gone since his return from the Zulu Campaign, Sean reflected, six weeks that had passed in a blur of speed. He sipped coffee from a mug the size of a German beer *stein*, sitting in the centre of his bed with his nightshirt hitched up to his waist and his legs crossed in comfortable Buddha fashion. The coffee was hot; he sipped noisily and then exhaled steam from his mouth.

The last six weeks had been full—too full for brooding grief or regret, although in the evenings, when he sat in the study with Waite's memory all about him, the ache was still there.

The days seemed to pass before they had fairly begun. There were three farms now: Theunis Kraal and the other two rented from old man Pye. He had stocked them with the looted cattle and the purchases he had made since his return. The price of prime beef had dropped to a new low, with nearly a hundred thousand cattle brought back from Zululand, and Sean could afford to be selective in his buying. He could also afford to wait while the price climbed up again.

Sean swung his legs off the bed and walked across the room to the washstand. He poured water from the jug into the basin and tested it tentatively with one finger. It was so cold it stung. He stood hesitating in his ridiculously feminine nightshirt, with dark chest hairs curling out above the elaborately embroidered front. Then he mustered his courage and plunged his face into the basin; he scooped water with both hands and poured it over the back of his neck, massaged it into his hair with hooked fingers and emerged at last blowing heavily with water dripping down on to his nightshirt. He towelled, stripped off the damp garment and stood naked peering out of the window. It had lightened enough for him to make out the smoky swirl of drizzle and mist beyond the pane.

'A hell of a day,' he grumbled aloud, but his tone was deceptive. He felt excitement for this day; he was fresh and sharp-edged, hungry for breakfast, ready to go for there was work to do.

He dressed, hopping on one leg as he got into his breeches, stuffing in the tails of his shirt and then sitting on the bed to pull on his boots. Now he was thinking about Audrey—he must try and get into town tomorrow to see her.

Sean had decided on matrimony. He had three good reasons. He had found that it was easier to get into the Bank of England's vaults than to get under Audrey's petticoats without marrying her. When Sean wants something no price was too high to pay.

Living at Theunis Kraal with Garry and Anna, Sean had decided that it would be pleasant to have his own woman to cook for him, mend his clothes and listen to his stories, for Sean was feeling a little left out.

The third consideration, by no means the least significant, was Audrey's connections with the local bank. She was one of the very few weaknesses in old man Pye's armour. He might even weigh in with Mahoba's Kloof Farm as a wedding present, though even the optimist in Sean realized that this hope was extravagant. Pye and his money were not easily parted.

Yes, Sean decided, he would have to find time to get into town and tell Audrey—in Sean's mind it wasn't a question of asking her. Sean brushed his hair, combed his beard, winked at himself in the mirror and went out into the passage. He could smell breakfast cooking and his mouth started to water.

Anna was in the kitchen. Her face was flushed from the heat of the stove.

'What's for breakfast, little sister?'

She turned to him, quickly brushing the hair off her forehead with the back of her hand.

'I'm not your sister,' she said, 'I wish you wouldn't call me that.'

'Where's Garry?' Sean asked as though he had not heard her protest.

'He's not up yet.'

'The poor boy's exhausted, no doubt.' Sean grinned at her and she turned away in confusion. Sean looked at her bottom without desire. Strange that Anna being Garry's wife should kill his appetite for her. Even the memory of what they had done before was vaguely obscene, incestuous.

'You're getting fat,' he said noticing the new heaviness of her body. She ducked her head but did not answer and Sean went on, 'I'll have four eggs, please, and tell Joseph not to dry them out completely.'

Sean went through into the dining-room and Garry came in through the side door at the same moment. His face was still vacant from sleep. Sean got a whiff of his breath; it smelled of stale liquor.

'Good morning, Romeo,' said Sean and Garry grinned sheepishly. His eyes were bloodshot and he hadn't shaved.

'Hello, Sean. How did you sleep?'

'Beautifully, thank you. I take it that you did also.' Sean sat down and spooned porridge from the tureen.

'Have some?' he asked Garry.

'Thanks.' Sean passed him the plate. He noticed how Garry's hand shook. *I'll have to talk to him about letting up on the bottle a trifle.*

'Hell, I'm hungry.' They talked the jerky, disconnected conversation of the breakfast table. Anna came through and joined them. Joseph brought the coffee.

'Have you told Sean yet, Garry?' Anna spoke suddenly, clearly and with decision.

'No.' Garry was taken by surprise, he spluttered his coffee.

'Told me what?' Sean asked. They were silent and Garrick fluttered his hand nervously. This was the moment he had been dreading–what if Sean guessed, what if he knew it was his baby and took them away, Anna and the baby, took them away and left Garry with nothing. Haunted by wild unreasonable fears, Garrick stared fixedly across the table at his brother.

'Tell him, Garry,' commanded Anna.

'Anna's going to have a baby,' he said. He watched Sean's face, saw the surprise change slowly to delight, felt Sean's arm close round his shoulders in a painful hug, almost crushing him.

'That's great,' Sean exulted, 'that's wonderful. We'll have the house full of kids in no time if you keep that up, Garry. I'm proud of you.'

Grinning stupidly with relief Garrick watched Sean hug Anna more gently and kiss her forehead.

'Well done, Anna, make sure it's a boy. We need cheap labour around here.'

He hasn't guessed, thought Garrick, *he doesn't know and it will be mine. No one can take it away from me now.*

That day they worked in the south section. They stayed together, Garry laughing in happy confusion at Sean's banter. It was delightful to have Sean give him so much attention. They finished early; for once Sean was in no mood for work.

'My reproductive brother, every barrel loaded with buck-shot.' Sean leaned across and punched Garry's shoulder. 'Let's knock it off and go into town. We can have a few quick ones to celebrate at the hotel and then go and tell Ada.'

Sean stood up in the stirrup and yelled above the moo and mill of the herd.

'Mbejane, bring those ten sick ones up to the house and don't forget that tomorrow we are going to fetch cattle from the sale pens.'

Mbejane waved in acknowledgement and Sean turned back to Garrick.

'Come on, let's get the hell out of here.'

They rode side by side, globules of moisture covering their oilskins and shining on Sean's beard. It was still cold and the escarpment was hidden in the wet mist.

'It's real brandy-drinking weather,' said Sean and Garrick did not answer. He was frightened again. He didn't want to tell Ada. She would guess. She guessed everything, she would know it was Sean's child. You couldn't lie to her.

The horses' hooves plopped wetly in the mud. They reached the spot where the road forked and climbed over the ridge to Ladyburg.

'Ada's going to love being a grandma,' chuckled Sean, and at that moment his horse stumbled slightly, broke its gait and started favouring its near fore.

Sean dismounted, lifted the hoof and saw the splinter driven deep into the frog.

'Damn it to hell,' he swore. He bent his head, gripped the hilt of the splinter with his teeth and drew it out.

'Well, we can't go into Ladyburg now, that leg will be sore for days.' Garry was relieved; it put off the time when he must tell Ada.

'Your horse isn't lame. Off you go, man, give her my love.' Sean looked up at him.

'We can tell her some other time. Let's get back home,' Garry demurred.

'Go on, Garry, it's your baby. Go and tell her.'

Garrick argued until he saw Sean's temper rising, then with a sigh of resignation he went and Sean led his own horse back to Theunis Kraal. Now that he was walking the oilskin was uncomfortably hot and heavy, Sean took it off and slung it over the saddle.

Anna was standing on the *stoep* as he came up to the homestead.

'Where's Garry?' she called.

'Don't worry. He's gone into town to see Ada. He'll be back by suppertime.'

One of the stable boys came to take Sean's horse. They talked together and then Sean stooped to lift the injured hoof. His breeches tightened across his buttocks and enhanced the long moulded taper of his legs. Anna looked at him. He straightened up and his shoulders were wide beneath the damp white linen of his shirt. He smiled at her as he came up the steps of the *stoep*. The rain had made his beard curl and he looked like a mischievous pirate.

'You must take better care of yourself now.' He put his hand on her upper arm to lead her inside. 'You can't stand around in the cold any more.' They went in through the glass doors. Anna looked up at him, the top of her head on a level with his shoulder.

'You're a damn fine woman, Anna, and I'm sure you're going to make a fine baby.' It was a mistake, for as he said it his eyes softened and his face turned down towards her. He let his arm drop around her shoulders.

'Sean!' She said his name as though it were an exclamation of pain. She moved quickly, fiercely within the circle of his arm, her body flattened itself against his and her hands went up to catch in the thick hair at the back of his head. She pulled his face down and her mouth opened warm and wet across his lips, her back arched and thrust her thighs against his legs. She moaned softly as she kissed him. For startled seconds Sean stood imprisoned in her embrace, then he tore his face away.

'Are you mad?' He tried to push her from him, but she fought her way back through his fending hands. She locked her arms around him and pressed her face against his chest.

'I love you. Please, please. I love you. Just let me hold you, that's all. I just want to hold you.' Her voice was muffled by the damp cloth of his shirt. She was shivering.

'Get away from me.' Roughly Sean broke her hold and almost threw her backwards on to the couch beside the fireplace.

'You're Garry's wife now, and you'll soon be the mother of his child. Keep your hot little body for him.' Sean stood back from her with his anger starting to mount.

'But I love you, Sean. Oh, my God, if I could only make you understand how I've suffered, living here with you and not being able to touch you even.'

Sean strode across to where she sat. 'Listen to me.' His voice was harsh. 'I don't want you. I never loved you, but now I could no more touch you than I could go with my own mother.' She could see the revulsion in his face. 'You're Garry's wife; if ever again you look at another man I'll kill you.'

He lifted his hands holding them with the fingers crooked ready. 'I'll kill you with my bare hands.'

His face was close to hers. She could not bear the expression in his eyes: she lashed out at him. He pulled back in time to save his eyes, but her nails gouged bloody lines across his cheek and down the side of his nose. He caught her wrists and held her while a thin trickle of blood dribbled down into his beard. She twisted in his hands, jerking her body from side to side, and she screamed at him.

'You swine, you dirty, dirty swine. Garry's wife, you say. Garry's baby, you say.' She threw her head back and laughed wildly through her screaming. 'Now I'll tell you the truth. What I have within me you gave me. It's yours! Not Garry's!' Sean let go her wrists and backed away from her.

'It can't be,' he whispered, 'you must be lying.' She followed him.

'Don't you remember how you said goodbye to me before you went to war? Don't you remember that night in the wagon? Don't you remember—don't you? Don't you?' She was talking quietly now, using her words to wound him.

'That was months ago. It can't be true,' Sean stammered, still moving away from her.

'Three and a half months,' she told him. 'Your brother's baby will be a little early, don't you think? But lots of people have premature babies—' Her voice droned on steadily, she was shivering uncontrollably now and her face was ghostly pale. Sean could stand it no longer.

'Leave me, leave me alone. I've got to think. I didn't know.' He brushed past her and went out into the passage. She heard the door of Waite's study slam shut and she stood still in the centre of the floor. Gradually her panting came under control and the storm surf of her anger abated to expose the black reefs of hatred beneath. She crossed the floor, went down the passage and into her own bedroom. She stood in front of the mirror and looked at herself.

'I hate him,' her lips formed the words in the mirror. Her face was still pale. 'There's one thing I can take from him. Garry's mine now, not his.'

She pulled the pins from her hair and let them drop on to the floor; her hair fell down her back. She shook it on to her shoulders then lifted her hands and tangled it into confusion. Her teeth closed on her own lips, she bit until she tasted blood.

'Oh, God, I hate him, I hate him,' she whispered through the pain. Her hands came down on to the front of her dress. She tore it open, then in the mirror looked without interest at the round bosses of her nipples that were already darkening with the promise of fruition. She kicked off her shoes.

'I hate him.' She stooped and her hands went up under her skirts into the petticoats. She loosened her pantaloons and stepped out of them; she held them across her chest to tear them, then threw them next to the bed. She swept her arm across the top of her dressing-table: one of the bowls hit the floor and burst with a splash of face-powder and there was the sudden pungent reek of spilled perfume. She crossed to the bed and dropped on to it. She lifted her knees and her petticoats fell back like petals of a flower: her white legs and lower body were the stamen.

Just before nightfall there was a shy knock on her door.

'What is it?' she asked.

'The Nkosikazi has not told me what I should cook for dinner.' Old Joseph's voice was raised respectfully.

'There will be no dinner tonight. You and all the servants may go.'

'Very well, Nkosikazi.'

Garrick came home in the dark. He had been drinking; she heard him stagger as he crossed the *stoep*, and his voice slur as he called.

'Hallo. Where's everybody? Anna! Anna! I'm back.' Silence for a while as he lit one of the lamps and then the hurried thump, thump of his peg along the passage and his voice again edged with alarm.

'Anna, Anna, where are you?'

He pushed the door open and stood with the lamp in his hand. Anna rolled away from the light, pressing her face into the pillow and hunching her shoulders. She heard him set the lamp down on the dressing-table, felt his hands pulling down her skirts to cover her nakedness, then gently turn her to face him. She looked into his face and saw the uncomprehending horror in it.

'My darling, oh Anna, my darling, what's happened?' He stared at her broken lips and her breasts. Bewildered he turned his head and looked at the bottles on the floor, at her torn pantaloons. His face hardened and came back to her.

'Are you hurt?' She shook her head.

'Who? Tell me who did it.' She turned away from him again, hiding her face.

'My darling, my poor darling. Who was it—one of the servants?'

'No,' her voice stifled with shame.

'Please tell me, Anna. What happened?'

She sat up quickly and threw her arms about him, holding him hard so her lips were near his ear. 'You know, Garry. You know who did it.'

'No, I swear I don't, please tell me.'

Anna drew her breath in deep, held it a second then breathed it out. 'Sean!'

Garrick's body convulsed in her arms, she heard him grunt as though he had been hit. Then he spoke. 'This too. Now this too.'

He loosened her hands from his neck and pushed her gently down on to the pillows. He crossed to the cupboard, opened one of the drawers and took out Waite's service pistol.

He's going to kill Sean, she thought. Garrick went out of the room without looking at her again. She waited with her hands clenched at her sides and her whole body stretched tightly. When the shot came at last it was surprisingly muted and unwarlike. Her body relaxed, her hands opened and she began to cry softly.

31

Garry limped down the passage. The pistol was heavy and the chequered grip rough in his hand. There was light showing under the study door at the end of the passage. It was unlocked. Garrick went in.

Sean sat with his elbows on the desk and his face in his hands but he looked up as Garrick came in through the door. The scratches had already dried black across his cheek, but the flesh around them was red and inflamed. He looked at the pistol in Garrick's hand.

'She has told you.' There was no question or expression in his voice.

'Yes.'

'I hoped that she wouldn't,' said Sean. 'I wanted her to spare you that at least.'

'Spare me?' Garrick asked. 'What about her? Did you think of her?'

Sean did not answer, instead he shrugged and laid back tiredly in his chair.

'I never realized before what a merciless swine you are,' choked Garrick. 'I have come to kill you.'

'Yes.' Sean watched the pistol come up. Garrick was holding it with both hands, his sandy hair hung forward on to his forehead.

'My poor Garry,' Sean said softly and immediately the pistol started to shake. It sank until Garrick held it, still with both hands between his knees. He crouched over it, blubbering–chewing at his lips to stop himself. Sean started out of his chair to go to him, but Garrick recoiled against the door-jamb.

'Keep away from me,' he yelled, 'don't touch me.' He threw the pistol, the sharp edge of the hammer cut across Sean's forehead, jerking his head back. The pistol glanced off and hit the wall behind him. It fired and the bullet splintered the panelled wood-work.

'We're finished,' Garrick screamed. 'We're finished for ever.' He groped wildly for the door and stumbled out into the passage, through the kitchens into the rain. He fell many times as the grass caught his peg, but each time he scrambled up and kept running. He sobbed with each step in the utter darkness of the night.

At last the growl of the rain-engorged Baboon Stroom blocked his way. He stood on the bank with the drizzle blowing into his face.

'Why me, why always me?' He screamed his agony into the darkness. Then with a rush of relief as strong as the torrent in the river-bed below him he felt the moth flutter its wings behind his eyes. The warmth and the greyness closed about him and he sank down on to his knees in the mud.

32

Sean took very little with him: his bed roll, a rifle and a spare horse. Twice in the darkness he lost the path to Mbejane's kraal but each time his horse found it again. Mbejane had built his big grass beehive hut well away from the quarters of the other servants, for he was Zulu of royal blood. When at last Sean came to it there were a few minutes of sleepy stirring and muttering within before Mbejane, with a blanket draped around his shoulders and an old paraffin lamp in his hand, came out to Sean's shouts.

'What is it, Nkosi?'

'I am going, Mbejane.'

'Where to?'

'Wherever the road leads. Will you follow?'

'I will get my spears,' said Mbejane.

Old man Pye was still in his office behind the bank when they reached Ladyburg. He was counting the sovereigns and stacking them in neat golden piles and his hands were as gentle on them as a man's hands on the body of the woman he loves, but he reached quickly for the open drawer at his side as Sean shouldered the door open.

'You don't need that,' said Sean and Pye lifted his hand guiltily off the pistol.

'Good gracious! I didn't recognize you, my boy.'

'How much have I got credited to my account?' Sean cut through the pleasantries.

'This isn't banking hours, you know.'

'Look here, Mr Pye, I'm in a hurry. How much have I got?'

Pye climbed out of his chair and crossed to the big iron safe. Shielding it with his body he tumbled the combination and swung open the door. He brought the ledger across to the desk.

'Carter–Cloete–Courtney,' he muttered as he turned the pages. 'Ah–Ada–Garrick–Sean. Here we are. Twelve hundred and ninety-six pounds eight and eight pence; of course, there are last month's accounts at the store still unpaid.'

'Call it twelve hundred then,' said Sean. 'I want it now and while you are counting it you can give me pen and paper.'

'Help yourself, there on the desk.'

Sean sat at the desk, pushed the piles of gold out of his way, dipped the pen and wrote. When he had finished he looked up at old Pye.

'Witness that, please.'

Pye took the paper and read it through. His face went limp with surprise.

'You're giving your half share of Theunis Kraal and all the cattle to your brother's first born!' he exploded.

'That's right, please witness it.'

'You must be mad,' protested Pye. 'That's a fortune you're giving away. Think what you're doing–think of your future. I had hoped that you and Audrey–' He stopped himself and went on. 'Don't be a fool, man.'

'Please witness it, Mr Pye,' said Sean and, muttering under his breath, Pye signed quickly.

'Thank you.' Sean folded the document, slipped it into an envelope and sealed it. He put it away inside his coat.

'Where's the money?' he asked.

Pye pushed a canvas bag across to him. His expression was one of disgust; he wanted no truck with fools.

'Count it,' he said.

'I'll take your word for it,' said Sean and signed the receipt.

Sean rode out past the sale pens and up the escarpment along the road to Pietermaritzburg. Mbejane trotted at his stirrup leading the spare horse. They stopped at the top of the escarpment. The wind had blown the clouds open and the starlight came through. They could see the town below them with here and there a lighted window.

I should have said goodbye to Ada, Sean thought. He looked down the valley towards Theunis Kraal. He could see no light. He touched the letter in the inside pocket of his coat.

'I'll post it to Garry from Pietermaritzburg,' he spoke aloud.

'Nkosi?' asked Mbejane.

'I said, "It's a long road, let us begin."'

'Yes,' agreed Mbejane. 'Let us begin.'

2. WITWATERSRAND

I

They turned north from Pietermaritzburg and climbed steadily up across bleak grassland towards the mountains. On the third day they saw the Drakensberg, jagged and black as the teeth of an ancient shark along the skyline.

It was cold; wrapped in his kaross Mbejane trailed far behind Sean. They had exchanged perhaps two dozen words since they left Pietermaritzburg for Sean had his thoughts and they were evil company. Mbejane was keeping discreetly out of his way. Mbejane felt no resentment, for a man who had just left his home and his cattle was entitled to brood. Mbejane was with sadness himself—he had left a fat woman in his bed to follow Sean.

Mbejane unplugged his small gourd snuff-box, picked a pinch and sniffed it delicately. He looked up at the mountains. The snows upon them were turning pink in the sunset and in a little while now they would make camp, and then again perhaps they would not. It made no difference.

Sean rode on after dark. The road crossed another fold in the veld and they saw the lights in the valley below.

'Dundee', Sean thought without interest. He made no effort to hasten his horse but let it amble down towards the town. Now he could smell the smoke from the coal mine, tarry and thick in the back of his throat. They entered the main street. The town seemed deserted in the cold. Sean did not intend stopping—he would camp on the far side; but when he reached the hotel he hesitated. There was warmth in there and laughter and the sound of men's voices and he was suddenly aware that his fingers were stiff with cold.

'Mbejane, take my horse. Find a place to camp beyond the town and make a fire so I won't miss you in the dark.'

Sean climbed down and walked into the bar. The room was full, miners most of them—he could see the grey coal dust etched into their skins. They looked at him incuriously as he crossed to the counter and ordered a brandy. He drank it slowly, making no attempt to join the loud talk around him.

The drunk was a short man built like Table Mountain, low, square and solid. He had to stand on tiptoe to put his arm around Sean's neck.

'Have a drink with me, *Boetie*.' His breath smelt sour and old.

'No thanks.' Sean was in no mood for drunks.

'Come on, come on,' the drunk insisted; he staggered and Sean's drink slopped on to the counter.

'Leave me alone.' Sean shrugged the arm away.

'You've got something against me?'

'No. I just feel like drinking alone.'

'You don't like my face, maybe?' The drunk held it close to Sean's. Sean didn't like it.

'Push off, there's a good fellow.'

The drunk slapped the counter.

'Charlie, give this big ape a drink. Make it a double. If he don't drink it, I ram it down his throat.'

Sean ignored the proffered glass. He swallowed what remained in his own and turned for the door. The drunk threw the brandy in his face. The spirit burned his eyes and he hit the man in the stomach. As his head came down Sean hit him again—in the face. The drunk spun sideways, fell and lay bleeding from his nose.

'What you hit him for?' Another miner was helping the drunk into a sitting position.

'It wouldn't cost you nothing to have a drink with him.' Sean felt the hostility in the room; he was the outsider.

'This boy is looking for trouble.'

'He's a tough monkey. We know how to handle tough monkeys.'

'Come on, let's sort this bastard out.'

Sean had hit the man as a reflex action. He was sorry now, but his guilt evaporated as he saw them gathering against him. Gone too was his mood of depression and in its place was a sense of relief. This was what he needed.

There were six of them moving in on him in a pack. Six was a fairly well-rounded number. One of them had a bottle in his hand and Sean started to smile. They were talking loudly, spreading courage and waiting for one of their fellows to start it.

Sean saw movement out of the side of his eye and jumped back to cover it with his hands ready.

'Steady on there,' a very English voice soothed him. 'I have come to offer my services. It seems to me you have adversaries and to spare.' The speaker had stood up from one of the tables behind Sean. He was tall, with a gauntly ravaged face and an immaculate grey suit.

'I want them all,' said Sean.

'Damned unsporting.' The newcomer shook his head. 'I'll buy the three gentlemen on the left if your price is reasonable.'

'Take two as a gift and consider yourself lucky.' Sean grinned at him and the man grinned back. They had almost forgotten the impending action in the pleasure of meeting.

'Very decent of you. May I introduce myself—Dufford Charleywood.' He shifted the light cane into his left hand and extended his right to Sean.

'Sean Courtney.' Sean accepted the hand.

'Are you bastards going to fight or what?' protested one of the miners impatiently.

'We are, dear boy, we are,' said Duff and moved lightly as a dancer towards him, swinging his cane. Thin as it was it made a noise like a well-hit baseball along the man's head.

'Then there were five,' said Duff. He flicked the cane and, weighted with lead, it made a most satisfactory swish. Like a swordsman he lunged into the throat of the second miner. The man lay on the floor and made a strangling noise.

'The rest are yours, Mr Courtney,' said Duff regretfully.

Sean dived in low, spreading his arms to scoop up all four pairs of legs at once. He sat up in the pile of bodies and started punching and kicking.

'Messy, very messy,' murmured Duff disapprovingly. The yelps and thuds gradually petered into silence and Sean stood up. His lip was bleeding and the lapel was torn off his jacket.

'Drink?' asked Duff.

'Brandy, please.' Sean smiled at the elegant figure against the bar. 'I won't refuse another drink this evening.'

They took the glasses to Duff's table, stepping over the bodies as they went.

'Mud in your eye!'

'Down the old red lane!'

Then they studied each other with frank interest, ignoring the clearing up operations being conducted around them.

'You are travelling?' asked Duff.

'Yes, are you?'

'No such luck. I am in the permanent employ of Dundee Collieries Ltd.'

'You work here?' Sean looked incredulous for Duff was a peacock among pigeons.

'Assistant Engineer,' nodded Duff. 'But not for long; the taste of coal-dust sticks in my craw.'

'May I suggest something to wash it out?'

'A splendid idea,' agreed Duff.

Sean brought the drinks to the table.

'Where are you headed?' asked Duff.

'I was facing north when I started,' shrugged Sean, 'I just kept going that way.'

'Where did you start from?'

'South.' Sean answered abruptly.

'Sorry, I didn't mean to pry.' Duff smiled. 'Yours is brandy, isn't it?'

The barman came round from behind the counter and crossed to their table.

'Hello, Charlie,' Duff greeted him. 'I take it you require compensation for the damage to your fittings and furniture?'

'Don't worry about it, Mr Charleywood. Not often we have a good barney like that. We don't mind the odd table and chair as long as it's worth watching. Have it on the house.'

'That's extremely good of you.'

'That's not what I came across for, Mr Charleywood. I've got something I'd like you to take a look at, you being a mining chap and all. Could you spare a minute, sir?'

'Come on, Sean. Let's see what Charlie's got for us. My guess is it's a beautiful woman.'

'It's not actually, sir,' said Charlie seriously and led the way through into the back room. Charlie reached up and took a lump of rock down from one of the shelves. He held it out to Duff. 'What do you make of that?'

Duff took it and weighed it in his hand, then peered closely at it. It was glassy grey, blotched with white and dark-red and divided by a broad black stripe.

'Some sort of conglomerate.' Duff spoke without enthusiasm. 'What's the mystery?'

'Friend of mine brought it down from Kruger's Republic on the other side of the mountains. He says it's gold bearing. They've made a big strike at a place called Witwatersrand just outside Pretoria. Of course, I don't put much store by these rumours 'cos you hear them all the time: diamonds and gold, gold and diamonds.'

Charlie laughed and wiped his hands on his apron.

'Anyway my friend says the Boers are selling mining licences to them as want to dig for the stuff. Thought I'd just get you to have a look.'

'I'll take this with me, Charlie, and pan it in the morning. Right now my friend and I are drinking.'

2

Sean opened his eyes the next morning to find the sun burning in through the window above his bed. He closed them again hurriedly and tried to remember where he was. There was a pain in his head that distracted him and a noise. The noise was a regular croaking rattle; it sounded as though someone was dying. Sean opened his eyes and turned his head slowly. Someone was in the bed across the room. Sean groped for a boot and threw it; there was a snort and Duff's head came up. For a second he regarded Sean through eyes as red as a winter sunset and then he subsided gently back into the blankets.

'Keep it down to a bellow,' whispered Sean. 'You are in the presence of grave illness.'

A long time later a servant brought coffee.

'Send word to my office that I am sick,' commanded Duff.

'I have done so.' The servant clearly understood his master. He went on, 'There is one outside who seeks the other Nkosi.' He glanced at Sean. 'He is greatly worried.'

'Mbejane. Tell him to wait,' said Sean.

They drank coffee in silence, sitting on the edge of their beds.

'How did I get here?' asked Sean.

'Laddie, if you don't know, then nobody does.' Duff stood up and crossed the room to find fresh clothing. He was naked and Sean saw that although he was slim as a boy his body was finely muscled.

'My God, what does Charlie put in his liquor?' complained Duff as he picked up his jacket.

He found the lump of rock in the pocket, brought it out and tossed it on to the packing-case that served as a table. He regarded it sourly as he finished dressing, then he went to the great pile of bachelor debris that filled one corner of the room. He scratched around and came out with a steel pestle-and-mortar and a battered black gold pan.

'I feel very old this morning,' he said as he started to crush the rock to powder in the mortar. He poured the powder into the pan, carried it out to the corrugated-iron water tank beside the front door and filled the pan from the tap.

Sean followed him and they sat together on the front step. Duff worked the pan, using a practised dip and swing that set the contents spinning like a whirlpool and slopped a little over the front lip with each turn. He filled it again with clean water.

Suddenly Sean felt Duff stiffen beside him. He glanced at his face and saw that his hangover had gone; his lips were shut in a thin line and his blood-shot eyes were fastened over the pan.

Sean looked down and saw the gleam through the water, like the flash of a trout's belly as it turns to take the fly. He felt the excitement prickle up his arms and lift the hair on his neck.

Quickly Duff splashed fresh water into the pan; three more turns and he flicked it out again. They sat still, not speaking, staring at the golden tail curved round the bottom of the pan.

'How much money have you got?' Duff asked without looking up.

'Little over a thousand.'

'As much as that. Excellent! I can raise about five hundred but I'll throw in my mining experience. Equal partners—do you agree?'

'Yes.'

'Then why are we sitting here? I'm going down to the bank. Meet me on the edge of town in half an hour.'

'What about your job?' Sean asked.

'I hate the smell of coal—the hell with my job.'

'What about Charlie?'

'Charlie is a poisoner—the hell with Charlie.'

3

They camped the night in the mouth of the pass with the mountains standing up before them. They had pushed the pace all that afternoon and the horses were tired—they turned their tails to the wind and cropped at the dry winter grass.

Mbejane built a fire in the shelter of a red stone outcrop and they huddled beside it brewing coffee, trying to keep out of the snow-cold wind, but it came down off the mountains and blew a plume of sparks from the fire. They ate; then Mbejane curled up beside the fire, pulled his kaross over his head and did not move again until morning.

'How far is it to this place?' Sean asked.

'I don't know,' Duff admitted. 'We'll go up through the pass tomorrow—fifty or sixty miles through the mountains—and then we'll be out into the high veld. Perhaps another week's riding after that.'

'Are we chasing rainbows?' Sean poured more coffee into the mugs.

'I'll tell you when we get there.' Duff picked up his mug and cupped his hands around it. 'One thing's certain—that sample was stinking with gold. If there's much of that stuff somebody's going to get rich.'

'Us, perhaps?'

'I've been on gold stampedes before. The first ones in make the killings. We might find the ground for fifty miles around as thick with claim pegs as quills on a porcupine's back.' Duff sipped noisily at his coffee. 'But we've got money—that's our ace in the hole. If we peg a proposition we've got capital to work it. If we're too late we can buy claims from the brokers. If we can't, well, there're other ways of getting gold than grubbing for it—a store, a saloon, a transport business, take your pick.'

Duff flicked the coffee grounds out of his mug. 'With money in your pocket you're somebody; without it anyone can kick you in the teeth.' He took a long black cheroot out of his top pocket and offered it to Sean. Sean shook his head and Duff bit the tip from the cheroot and spat it into the fire. He picked up a burning twig and lit it, sucking with content.

'Where did you learn mining, Duff?'

'Canada.' The wind whipped the smoke away from his mouth as Duff exhaled.

'You've been around?'

'I have, laddie. It's too damn cold to sleep; we'll talk instead. For a guinea I'll tell you the story of my life.'

'Tell me first, I'll see if it's worth it!' Sean pulled the blanket up around his shoulders and waited.

'Your credit is good,' agreed Duff. He paused dramatically. 'I was born thirty-six years ago, fourth and youngest son to the sixteenth Baron Roxby—that is, not counting the others who never made it to puberty.'

'Blue blood,' said Sean.

'Of course, just look at my nose. But please don't interrupt. Very early in the game my father, the sixteenth Baron, dispelled with a horsewhip any natural affection we may have owed him. Like Henry the Eighth he preferred children in the abstract. We kept out of his way and that suited everybody admirably. A sort of armed truce.

'Dear father had two great passions in life: horses and women. During his sixty-two glorious years he acquired a fine collection of both. My fifteen-year-old cousin, a comely wench as I recall, was his last and unattained ambition. He took her riding every day and fingered her most outrageously as he helped her in and out of the saddle. She told me about it with giggles.

'However father's horse, a commendably moral creature, cut short the pursuit by kicking father on the head, presumably in the middle of one of these touching scenes. Poor father was never the same again. In fact so much was he altered by this experience that two days later, to the doleful clangour of bells and a collective sigh of relief from his sons and his neighbours who owned daughters, they buried him.'

Dufford leaned forward and prodded the fire.

'It was all very sad. I or any of my brothers could have told father that not only was my cousin comely but she had the family sporting instincts developed to a remarkable degree. After all who should know better than we? We were her cousins and you know how cousins will be cousins. Anyway father never found out and to this day I feel guilty—I should have told him. He would have died happier . . . Do I bore you?'

'No, go on. I've had half a guinea's worth already,' Sean laughed.

'Father's untimely decease made no miraculous change in my life. The seventeenth Baron, brother Tom, once he had the title was every bit as tight-fisted and unpleasant as father had been. There I was at nineteen on an allowance too small to enable me to pursue the family hobbies, gathering mould in a grim old castle forty miles from London, with the development of my sensitive soul being inhibited by the undiluted company of my barbaric brothers.

'I left with three months' advance allowance clutched in my sweaty palm and the farewells of my brothers ringing in my ears. The most sentimental of these was "don't bother to write".

'Everybody was going to Canada; it seemed like a good idea so I went too. I made money and spent it. I made women and spent them also, but the cold got to me in the end.'

Duff's cheroot had died; he re-lit it and looked at Sean.

'It was so cold you couldn't urinate without getting frostbite on your equipment, so I began to think of lands tropical, of white beaches and sun, of exotic fruits and even more exotic maidens. The peculiar circumstances that finally decided me to leave are painful to recall and we will not dwell upon them. I left, to say the least, under a cloud. So here you see me freezing slowly to death, with a bearded ruffian for company and not an exotic maiden within a day's ride.'

'A stirring tale—well told,' applauded Sean.

'One story deserves another—let's hear your tale of woe.'

Sean's smile slid off his face. 'Born and bred here in Natal. Left home a week or so ago also in painful circumstances.'

'A woman?' asked Duff with deep compassion.

'A woman,' agreed Sean.

'The sweet bitches,' sighed Duff. 'How I love them.'

4

The pass ran like a twisted gut through the Drakensberg. The mountains stood up sheer and black on each side of them, so they rode in shadow and saw the sun only for a few hours in the middle of the day. Then the mountains dropped away and they were out into the open.

Open was the word for the high veld. It stretched away flat and empty, grass and brown grass dwindling to a distant meeting with the pale empty sky. But the loneliness could not blunt the edge of their excitement: each mile covered, each successive camp along the ribbon road ground it sharper until at last they saw the name in writing for the first time. Forlorn as a scarecrow in a ploughed land the signpost pointed right and said, 'Pretoria', pointed left and said, 'Witwatersrand'.

'The Ridge of White Waters,' whispered Sean. It had a ring to it that name—a ring like a hundred millions in gold.

'We're not the first,' muttered Duff. The left-hand fork of the road was deeply scored by the passage of many wagons.

'No time to worry about that.' Sean had the gold sickness on him now. 'There's a little speed left in these mokes—let's use it.'

It came up on the horizon as a low line above the emptiness, a ridge of hills like a hundred others they had crossed. They went up it and from the top looked down. Two ridges ran side by side, north and south, four miles or so apart. In the shallow valley between they could see the flash of the sun off the swamp pools that gave the hills their name.

'Look at them,' groaned Sean.

The tents and wagons were scattered along the length of the valley and in between them the prospect trenches were raw wounds through the grass. The trenches were concentrated along a line down the centre of the valley.

'That's the strike of the reef,' said Duff, 'and we're too late—it's all pegged!'

'How do you know?' protested Sean.

'Use your eyes, laddie. It's all gone.'

'There might be some they've overlooked.'

'These boys overlook nothing. Let's go down and I'll show you.' Duff prodded his horse and they started down. He spoke over his shoulder to Sean. 'Look up there near that stream—they aren't wasting time. They've got a mill going already. It's a four-stamp rig by the looks of it.'

They rode into one of the larger encampments of tents and wagons; there were women at work around the fires and the smell of food brought saliva jetting from under Sean's tongue. There were men also, sitting among the wagons waiting for their suppers.

'I'm going to ask some of these characters what's going on here,' said Sean. He climbed down off his horse and tossed the reins to Mbejane. Duff watched him with a wry grin as he tried in succession to engage three different men in conversation. Each time Sean's victim avoided his eyes, mumbled vaguely and withdrew. Sean finally gave up and came back to the horses.

'What's wrong with me,' he asked plaintively. 'Have I got a contagious clap?'

Duff chuckled. 'They've got gold sickness,' he said. 'You're a potential rival. You could die of thirst and not one of them would spit on you, lest it gave you strength to crawl out and peg something they hadn't noticed.'

He sobered. 'We're wasting time. There's an hour left before dark, let's go and have a look for ourselves.'

They trotted out towards the area of mauled earth. Men were working pick and shovel in the trenches, some of them lean and tough-looking with a dozen natives working beside them; others far from an office stool, sweating and gritting teeth against the pain of blistered palms, their faces and arms burnt angry red by the sun. All of them greeted Sean and Duff with the same suspicious hostility.

They rode slowly towards the north and every hundred yards with sickening regularity they came across a claim peg with a cairn of stones around its foot and the scrap of canvas nailed to it. Printed in crude capitals on the canvas was the owner's name and his licence number.

Many of the claims were as yet untouched and on these Duff dismounted and searched in the grass, picking up pieces of rock and peering at them before discarding them again. Then once more they moved on with sinking spirits and increasing exhaustion. They camped after dark in the open windy ridge and while the coffee brewed they talked.

'We're too late.' Sean scowled into the fire.

'We've got money, laddie, just remember that. Most of these gentlemen are broke—they are living on hope, not beef and potatoes. Look at their faces and you'll see despair starting to show. It takes capital to work reef gold: you need machinery and money for wages, you have to pipe in water and pile rock, you need wagons and time.'

'Money's no good without a claim to work,' brooded Sean.

'Stay with me, laddie. Have you noticed how many of these claims haven't been touched yet? They belong to speculators and my guess is that they are for sale. In the next few weeks you'll see the men sorted out from the boys—'

'I feel like packing up. This isn't what I expected.'

'You're tired. Sleep well tonight and tomorrow we'll see how far this reef runs—then we'll start some scheming.'

Duff lit one of his cheroots and sucked on it: in the firelight his face was as gaunt as a Red Indian's. They sat on in silence for a while, then Sean spoke.

'What's that noise?' It was a dull tom-tom beat in the darkness.

'You'll get used to that if you stay around here much longer,' said Duff. 'It's the stamps on that mill we saw from the high ground. It's a mile or so farther up the valley; we'll pass it in the morning.'

They were on the move again before the sun was up and they came to the mill in the morning's uncertain light. The mill crouched black and ugly on the smooth curve of the ridge, defiant as a quixotic monster. Its jaws thumped sullenly as it chewed the rock; it snorted steam and screeched metallically.

'I didn't realize it was so big,' said Sean.

'It's big all right,' agreed Duff, 'and they cost money, they don't give them away. Not many men around here can afford a set-up like that.'

There were men moving around the mill, tending its needs, feeding it rock and fussing about the copper tables over which its gold-laden fæces poured. One of the men came forward to offer them the usual hospitality. 'This is private ground. We don't want sightseers around here—keep going.'

He was a dapper little man with a round brown face and a derby hat pulled down to his ears. His moustache bristled like the whiskers of a fox terrier.

'Listen, François, you miserable bloody earthworm, if you talk to me like that I'll push your face around the back of your head,' Duff told him, and the dapper one blinked uncertainly and came closer, peering up at them.

'Who are you? Do I know you?'

Duff pushed his hat back so the man could see his face.

'Duff!' crowed the little man delightedly. 'It's old Duff.' He bounced forward to take Duff's hand as he dismounted. Sean watched the orgy of reunion with amusement. It lasted until Duff managed to bring it under control and lead the little Afrikander across to make the introduction.

'Sean, this is François du Toit. He's an old friend of mine from the Kimberley diamond fields.'

François greeted Sean and then relapsed once more into the excited chorus of '*Gott*, it's good to see you, old Duff.' He pounded Duff's back despite the nimble footwork that Duff was using to spoil his aim. Another few minutes of this passed before François composed himself to make his first coherent statement.

'Listen, old Duff, I'm just in the middle of cleaning the amalgam tables. You and your friend go down to my tent. I'll be with you in half an hour, tell my servant to make you some breakfast. I won't be long, man. *Gott*, man, it's good to see you.'

'An old lover of yours?' asked Sean when they were alone.

Duff laughed. 'We were on the diamond fields together. I did him a favour once—pulled him out of a caving drive when the rock fall had broken his legs. He's a good little guy and meeting him here is the proverbial answer to a prayer. What he can't tell us about the goldfield no one else can.'

François came bustling into the tent well under the promised half hour and during breakfast Sean was an outsider in a conversation where every exchange began, 'Do you remember—?' or 'What happened to old so and so?'

Then, when the plates were empty and the coffee mugs filled, Duff asked, 'So, what are you doing here, Franz? Is this your own outfit?'

'No, I'm still with the Company.'

'Not that whoreson Hradsky?' Duff registered mock alarm. 'That—that that's ta—ta—terrible,' he imitated a stutter.

'Cut it out, Duff.' François looked nervous. 'Don't do that, you want me to lose my job?'

Duff turned to Sean with an explanation. 'Norman Hradsky and God are equals, but in this part of the world God takes his orders from Hradsky.'

'Cut it out, Duff.' François was deeply shocked but Duff went on imperturbably.

'The organization through which Hradsky exercises his divine powers is referred to with reverently bated breath as "The Company". In actual fact its full and resounding title is The South African Mining and Lands Company. Do you get the picture?'

Sean nodded smiling and Duff added as an afterthought, 'Hradsky is a bastard and he stutters.'

It was too much for François He leaned across and caught Duff's arm. 'Please, man. My servant understands English, cut it out, Duff.'

'So the Company has started on these fields, hey? Well, well, it must be pretty big,' mused Duff and François followed with relief on to safer ground.

'It is! You just wait and see, it's going to make the diamond fields look like a church bazaar!'

'Tell me about it,' said Duff.

'They call it the Rotten Reef or the Banket or the Heidelberg Reef–but in fact there are three reefs, not one. They run side by side like layers in a sandwich cake.'

'All three have pay gold?' Duff shot the question and François shook his head. There was a light in his eyes; he was happy talking gold and mining.

'No–you can forget about the outer reef, just traces there. Then there's the Main Reef. That's a bit better, it's as much as six feet thick in places and giving good values, but it's patchy.'

François leaned eagerly across the table; in his excitement his thick Afrikaans accent was very noticeable.

'The bottom reef is the winner, we call it the Leader Reef. It's only a few inches thick and some places it fades out altogether, but it's rich. There's gold in it like plums in a pudding. It's rich, Duff, I'm telling you that you won't believe it until you see it!'

'I'll believe you,' said Duff. 'Now tell me where I can get some of this Leader Reef for myself.'

François sobered instantly, a shutter dropped over his eyes and hid the light that had shone there a moment before.

'It's gone. It's all gone,' he said defensively. 'It's all been pegged, you've come too late.'

'Well, that's that,' said Duff and a big silence settled on the gathering. François fidgeted on his stool, chewing at the ends of his moustache and scowling into his mug. Duff and Sean waited quietly; it was obvious that François was wrestling with himself, two loyalties tearing him down the middle. Once he opened his mouth and then closed it again; he blew on his coffee to cool it and the heat came off it in steam.

'Have you got any money?' He fired the question with startling violence.

'Yes,' said Duff.

'Mr Hradsky has gone down to Capetown to raise money. He has a list of a hundred and forty claims that he will buy when he gets back.' François paused guiltily. 'I'm only telling you this because of what I owe you.'

'Yes, I know.' Duff spoke softly. François took an audible breath and went on.

'On the top of Mr Hradsky's list is a block of claims that belongs to a woman. She is willing to sell and they are the most likely-looking propositions on the whole field.'

'Yes?' Duff encouraged him.

'This woman has started an eating-house about two miles from here on the banks of the Natal Spruit. Her name is Mrs Rautenbach, she serves good food. You could go and have a meal there.'

'Thanks, François.'

'I owed it to you,' François said gruffly, then his mood changed quickly and he chuckled. 'You'll like her, Duff, she's a lot of woman.'

Sean and Duff went to eat lunch at Mrs Rautenbach's. It was an unpainted corrugated-iron building on a wooden frame and the sign above the veranda said in letters of red and gold 'Candy's Hotel. High-class cuisine. Free toilet facilities. No drunks or horses admitted. Proprietor. Mrs Candella Rautenbach.'

They washed off the dust in the enamel basin which stood on the veranda, dried themselves on the free towel and combed in the free mirror on the wall.

'How do I look?' asked Duff.

'Ravishing,' said Sean, 'but you don't smell so good. When did you last bath?'

They went into the dining-room and found it almost full, but there was an empty table against the far wall. The room was hot and thick with pipe smoke and the smell of cabbage. Dusty bearded men laughed and shouted or ate silently and hungrily. They crossed the room to the table and a coloured waitress came to them.

'Yes?' she asked. Her dress was damp at the armpits.

'May we have the menu?'

The girl looked at Duff with faint amusement. 'Today we got steak and mashed potatoes with pudding afterwards.'

'We'll have it,' Duff agreed.

'You sure as hell won't get nothing else,' the girl assured him and trotted back to the kitchen.

'The service is good,' Duff enthused. 'We can only hope that the food and the proprietress are of the same high standard.'

The meat was tough but well flavoured and the coffee was strong and sweet. They ate with appreciation until Sean who was facing the kitchen stopped his fork on its way to his mouth. A hush was on the room.

'Here she is,' he said.

Candy Rautenbach was a tall and bright, shiny blonde and her skin was Nordic flawlessness as yet unspoiled by the sun. She filled the front of her blouse and the back of her skirt with a pleasant abundance. She was well aware of and yet not disconcerted by the fact that every eye in the room was on one of those areas. She carried a ladle which she twitched threateningly at the first hand that reached out to pinch her rump, the hand withdrew and Candy smiled sweetly and moved on among the tables. She stopped occasionally to chat with her customers and it was clear that many of these lonely men came here not only to eat. They watched her avidly, grinning with pleasure when she spoke to them. She reached their table and Sean and Duff stood up. Candy blinked with surprise.

'Sit down, please.' The small courtesy had touched her. 'You are new here?'

'We got in yesterday,' Duff smiled at her. 'And the way you cook a steak makes me feel as though I were home again.'

'Where are you from?' Candy looked at the two of them with perhaps just a shade more than professional interest.

'We've come up from Natal to have a look around. This is Mr Courtney—he is interested in new investments and he thought that these goldfields might provide an outlet for some of his capital.'

Sean just managed to stop his jaw dropping open and then quickly assumed the slightly superior air of a big financier as Duff went on.

'My name is Charleywood. I am Mr Courtney's mining adviser.'

'Pleased to meet you. I am Candy Rautenbach.' She was impressed.

'Won't you join us for a few minutes, Mrs Rautenbach?' Duff drew back a chair for her and Candy hesitated.

'I have to check up in the kitchen—perhaps later.'

'Do you always lie so smoothly?' Sean spoke with admiration when Candy had gone.

'I spoke no untruths,' Duff defended himself.

'No, but the way you tell the truth! How the hell am I going to play up to the role you have created for me?'

'You'll learn to live with it, don't worry. Just look wise and keep your mouth shut,' Duff advised. 'What do you think of her anyway?'

'Toothsome,' said Sean.

'Decidedly palatable,' agreed Duff.

When Candy came back Duff kept the conversation light and general for a while, but when Candy started asking some sharp questions it was immediately apparent that her knowledge of geology and mining was well above average and Duff remarked on it.

'Yes, my husband was in the game. I picked it up from him.' She reached into one of the pockets of her blue and white checked skirt and brought out a small handful of rock samples. She put them down in front of Duff. 'Can you name those?' she asked. It was the direct test, she was asking him to prove himself.

'Kimberlite. Serpentine. Feldspar.' Duff reeled them off and Candy relaxed visibly.

'As it happens I have a number of claims pegged along the Heidelberg Reef. Perhaps Mr Courtney would care to have a look at them. Actually, I am negotiating at the moment with The South African Mining and Lands Company who are very interested.'

Sean made his solitary but valuable contribution to the conversation. 'Ah yes,' he nodded sagely. 'Good old Norman.'

Candy was shaken—not many men used Hradsky's Christian name. 'Will tomorrow morning be convenient?' she asked.

5

That afternoon they bought a tent from a disillusioned hopeful who had thrown up his job on the Natal Railways to make the pilgrimage to Witwatersrand and now needed money to get home. They pitched it near the Hotel and went down to the Natal Spruit to take a long overdue bath. That night they held a mild celebration on the half bottle of brandy that Duff produced from his saddlebag and the next morning Candy took them out to the claims. She had twenty of them pegged right along the Banket. She led them to a spot where the reef outcropped.

'I'll leave you two to look around. If you're interested we can talk about it when you come to the Hotel. I've got to get back now, there'll be hungry mouths to feed.'

Duff escorted Candy to her horse, giving her his arm across the rough ground and helping her into the saddle in a manner he must have learned from his father. He watched her ride away then came back to Sean. He was elated.

'Tread lightly, Mr Courtney, walk with reverence for beneath your feet lies our fortune.'

They went over the ground, Sean like a friendly bloodhound and Duff cruising with the restless circling of a tiger shark. They inspected the claim notices, paced out the boundaries and filled their pockets with chips of rock, then they rode back to their tent and Duff brought out his pestle, mortar and pan. They took them down to the bank of the Natal Spruit and all afternoon crushed the rock and worked the pan. When they had tested the last sample Duff gave his judgement.

'Well, there's gold—and I'd say it's payable gold. It's not nearly as rich as the one we panned at Dundee but that must have been a selected piece of the Leader Reef!' He paused and looked seriously at Sean. 'I think it's worth a try. If the Leader Reef is there we'll find it and in the meantime we won't lose money by working the main reef.'

Sean picked up a pebble and tossed it into the stream in front of him. He was learning for the first time the alternate thrill and depression of gold sickness when one minute you rode the lightning and the next you dropped abruptly into the depths. The yellow tails in the pan had looked pathetically thin and undernourished to him.

'Supposing you're right and supposing we talk Candy into selling her claims, how do we go about it? That four-stamp mill looked a devilishly complicated and expensive bit of machinery to me, not the kind of thing you can buy over the counter in every general dealer's store.'

Duff punched his shoulder and smiled lopsidedly at him. 'You've got your Uncle Duff looking after you. Candy will sell her claims—she trembles when I touch her, a day or two more and she'll be eating out of my hand. As for the mill . . . When I came out to this country I fell in with a rich Cape farmer whose lifelong ambition had been to have his own gold mine. He selected a ridge which in his undisputed wisdom as a grower of grapes he considered to be an ideal place for his mine. He hired me to run it for him, purchased a mill of the latest and most expensive vintage and prepared himself to flood the market with gold. After six months when we had processed vast quantities of assorted quartz, schist and earth and recovered sufficient gold to fit into a mouse's ear without touching the sides my patron's enthusiasm was somewhat dampened and he dispensed with my invaluable services and closed the circus down. I left for the diamond fields and as far as I know the machinery is still lying there waiting for the first buyer with a couple of hundred pounds to come and pick it up.' Duff stood up and they walked back towards the tent. 'However, first things first. Do you agree that I should continue the negotiations with Mrs Rautenbach?'

'I suppose so.' Sean was feeling more cheerful again. 'But are you sure your interest in Mrs Rautenbach is strictly line of duty?'

Duff was shocked. 'Don't you think for a minute that my intentions are anything but to further the interests of our partnersnip. You can't believe that my animal appetite plays any part in what I intend doing?'

'No, of course not,' Sean assured him. 'I hope you can force yourself to go through with it.'

Duff laughed. 'While we are on the subject I think this is as good a time as any for you to develop a stomach ailment and retire to your lonely bed. From now on until we've got the agreement signed your boyish charm will be of no great value in the proceedings. I'll tell Candy that you've given me authority to act on your behalf.'

Duff combed his curls, put on the clothes that Mbejane had washed for him and disappeared in the direction of Candy's Hotel. Time passed slowly for Sean; he sat and chatted with Mbejane, drank a little coffee and when the sun went down returned to his tent. He read one of Duff's books by the light of the hurricane lamp but could not concentrate on it; his mind kept straying to thoughts of blonde hair. When someone scratched on the canvas door he leapt up with a confused hope that Candy had decided to come and deal with him direct. It was the coloured girl from the Hotel, her crinkly black hair at odds with what he had been thinking.

'Madame says she's sorry to hear about your sickness and to tell you to have two spoons of this,' she told him and offered Sean the bottle of castor oil.

'Tell your mistress, thank you very much.'

Sean accepted the medicine and started to close the tent flap again.

'Madame told me to stay and make sure that you took two full spoons—I have to take the bottle back and show her how much you've had.'

Sean's stomach cringed. He looked at the coloured girl standing resolute in the doorway, determined to carry out her instructions. He thought of poor Duff doing his duty like a man—he could do no less. He swallowed down the thick clinging oil with his eyes closed then went back to his book. He slept uneasily starting up occasionally to look at the empty bed across the tent. The medicine drove him out into the cold at half past two in the morning. Mbejane was curled up next to the fire and Sean scowled at him. His regular contented snoring seemed a calculated mockery. A jackal yelped miserably up on the ridge, expressing Sean's feelings exactly, and the night wind fanned his bare buttocks.

Duff came home in the dawning. Sean was wide awake.

'Well, what happened?' he demanded.

Duff yawned. 'At one stage I began to doubt whether I was man enough. However, it worked out to the satisfaction of all concerned. What a woman!' He pulled off his shirt and Sean saw the scratches across his back.

'Did she give you any castor oil?' Sean asked bitterly.

'I'm sorry about that.' Duff smiled at him sympathetically. 'I tried to dissuade her—truly I did. She's a very motherly person. Most concerned about your stomach.'

'You still haven't answered my question. Did you make any progress with the claims?'

'Oh that—' Duff pulled the blankets up under his chin. 'We disposed of that early on in the proceedings. She'll take a down payment of ten pounds each on them and give us an option to buy the lot at any time during the next two years for ten thousand. We arranged that over dinner. The rest of the time was devoted, in a manner of speaking, to shaking hands over the deal. Tomorrow afternoon—or rather this afternoon—you and I'll ride across to Pretoria and get a lawyer to write up an agreement for her to sign. But right now I need some sleep. Wake me at lunch time. Good-night, laddie.'

Duff and Sean brought the agreement back from Pretoria the following evening. It was an impressive four-page document full of 'in so much as' and 'party of the first part'. Candy led them to her bedroom and they sat around anxiously while she read it through twice.

She looked up at last and said, 'That seems all right–but there is just one other thing.' Sean's heart sank and even Duff's smile was strained. It had all been too easy so far.

Candy hesitated and Sean saw with faint surprise that she was blushing. It was a pleasant thing to see the peach of her cheeks turning to ripe apple and they watched it with interest, their tension lessening perceptibly. 'I want the mine named after me.'

They nearly shouted with relief.

'An excellent idea! How about the Rautenbach Reef Mine?'

Candy shook her head. 'I'd rather not be reminded of him–we'll leave him out of it.'

'Very well–let's call it the Candy Deep. A little premature, I suppose, as we are still at ground level, but pessimism never pays,' suggested Duff.

'Yes, that's lovely,' Candy enthused, flushing again but this time with pleasure. She scrawled her name across the bottom of the document while Sean fired out the cork of the champagne which Duff had bought in Pretoria. They clinked glasses and Duff gave the toast 'To Candy and the Candy Deep–may one grow sweeter and the other deeper with each passing day.'

6

'We'll need labour, about ten natives to start with. That'll be your problem,' Duff told Sean. It was the following morning and they were eating breakfast in front of the tent. Sean nodded but didn't try to answer until he had swallowed his mouthful of bacon.

'I'll get Mbejane on to that right away. He'll be able to get us Zulus, even if he has to drive them here with a spear at their backs.'

'Good–in the meantime you and I'll ride back to Pretoria again to buy the basic equipment. Picks, shovels, dynamite and the like.' Duff wiped his mouth and filled his coffee cup. 'I'll show you how to start moving the overburden and stacking the ore in a dump. We'll pick a site for the mill and then I'll leave you to get on with it while I head south for the Cape to see my farmer friend. God and the weather permitting ours will be the second mill working on these fields.'

They brought their purchases back from Pretoria in a small ox wagon. Mbejane had done his work well. There were a dozen Zulus lined up for Sean's approval next to the tent with Mbejane standing guard over them like a cheerful sheepdog. Sean walked down the line stopping to ask each man his name and joke with him in his own language. He came to the last in the line. 'How are you called?'

'My name is Hlubi, Nkosi.'

Sean pointed at the man's well-rounded paunch bulging out above his loincloth.

'If you come to work for me, we'll soon have you delivered of your child.'

They burst out in delightful laughter and Sean smiled at them affectionately: proud simple people, tall and big-muscled, completely defenceless against a well-timed jest. Through his mind flashed the picture of a hill in Zululand, a battlefield below it and the flies crawling in the pit of an empty stomach. He shut the picture out quickly and shouted above their laughter.

'So be it then—sixpence a day and all the food you can eat. Will you sign on to work for me?'

They chorused their assent and climbed up on to the back of the wagon. Sean and Duff took them out to the Candy Deep and they laughed and chattered like children going on a picnic.

It took another week for Duff to instruct Sean in the use of dynamite, to explain how he wanted the first trenches dug and to mark out the site for the mill and the dump. The moved the tent up to the mine and worked twelve hours every day. At night they rode down to Candy's Hotel to eat a full meal and then Sean rode home alone. He was so tired by evening that he hardly envied Duff the comfort of Candy's bedroom; instead he found himself admiring Duff's stamina. Each morning he looked for signs of fatigue in his partner but, although his face was lean and gaunt as ever, his eyes were just as clear and his lopsided smile just as cheerful.

'How you do it beats me,' Sean told him the day they finished marking out the mill site.

Duff winked at him. 'Years of practice, laddie, but between you and me the ride down to the Cape will be a welcome rest.'

'When are you going?' Sean asked.

'Quite frankly I think that every day I stay on here increases the risk of someone else getting in before us. Mining machinery is going to be a premium from now on. You have got things well in hand now . . . What do you say?'

'I was starting to think along the same lines,' Sean agreed. They walked back to the tent and sat down in the camp chairs, from where they could look down the length of the valley. The week before about two dozen wagons had been outspanned around Candy's Hotel, but now there were at least two hundred and from where they sat they could count another eight or nine encampments, some even larger than the one around Candy's place. Wood and iron buildings were beginning to replace the canvas tents and the whole veld was criss-crossed with rough roads along which mounted men and wagons moved without apparent purpose.

The restless movement, the dust clouds raised by the passage of men and beasts, the occasional deep crump, crump of dynamite firing in the workings along the Banket—all heightened the air of excitement, of almost breathless expectancy that hung over the whole goldfield.

'I'll leave at first light tomorrow,' Duff decided. 'Ten days' riding to the railhead at Colesberg and another four days by train will get me there. With luck I'll be back in under two months.' He wriggled round in his chair and looked directly at Sean. 'After Paying Candy her two hundred pounds and with what I spent in Pretoria I've only got about a hundred and fifty left. Once I get to Paarl I'll have to pay out three or four hundred for the mill, then I'll need to hire twenty or thirty wagons to bring it up here—say eight hundred pounds altogether to be on the safe side.'

Sean looked at him. He had known this man a few short weeks. Eight hundred was the average man's earnings for three years. Africa was a big land, a man could disappear easily. Sean loosened his belt and dropped it on to the table; he unbuttoned the money pouch.

'Give me a hand to count it out,' he told Duff.

'Thanks,' said Duff and he was not talking about the money. With trust asked for so simply and given so spontaneously the last reservations in their friendship shrivelled and died.

7

When Duff had gone Sean drove himself and his men without mercy. They stripped the overburden of the Reef and exposed it across the whole length of the Candy claims, then they broke it up and started stacking it next to the mill site. The dump grew bigger with every twelve-hour day worked. There was still no trace of the Leader Reef but Sean found little time to worry about that. At night he climbed into bed and slept away his fatigue until another morning called him back to the workings. On Sundays he rode across to François's tent and they talked mining and medicines. François had an enormous chest of patent medicines and a book entitled *The Home Physician*. His health was his hobby and he was treating himself for three major ailments simultaneously. Although he was occasionally unfaithful, his true love was sugar diabetes. The page in *The Home Physician* which covered this subject was limp and grubby from the touch of his fingers. He could recite the symptoms from memory and he had all of them. His other favourite was tuberculosis of the bone; this moved around his body with alarming rapidity taking only a week to leave his hip and reach his wrist. Despite his failing health, however, he was an expert on mining and Sean picked his brain shamelessly. François's sugar diabetes did not prevent him from sharing a bottle of brandy with Sean on Sunday evenings. Sean kept away from Candy's Hotel—that shiny blonde hair and peach skin would have been too much temptation. He couldn't trust himself not to wreck his new friendship with Duff by another importunate affair, so instead he sweated away his energy in the trenches of the Candy Deep.

Every morning he set his Zulus a task for the day, always just a little more than the day before. They sang as they worked and it was very seldom that the task was not complete by nightfall. The days blurred into each other and turned to weeks which quadrupled like breeding amœbæ and became months. Sean began to imagine Duff giving the Capetown girls a whirl with his eight hundred pounds. One evening he rode south for miles along the Cape road, stopping to question every traveller he met and when he finally gave up and returned to the goldfields he went straight to one of the canteens to look for a fight. He found a big, yellow-haired German miner to oblige him. They went outside and for an hour they battered each other beneath a crisp Transvaal sky surrounded by a ring of delighted spectators. Then he and the German went back into the canteen, shook each other's bleeding hands, drank a vow of friendship together and Sean returned to the Candy Deep with his devil exorcized for the time being.

The next afternoon Sean was working near the north boundary of the claims; at this point they had burrowed down about fifteen feet to keep contact with the reef. Sean had just finished marking the shot holes for the next blast and the Zulus were standing around him taking snuff and spitting on their hands before attacking the rock once more.

'Mush, you shag-eared villains. What's going on here, a trade union meeting?' The familiar voice came from above their heads, Duff was looking down at them. Sean scrambled straight up the side of the trench and seized him in a bear hug. Duff was thinner, his jowls covered with a pale stubble and his curly hair white with dust. When the fury of greeting had subsided a little Sean demanded, 'Well, where's the present you went to fetch me?'

Duff laughed, 'Not far behind, all twenty-five wagons full of it.'

'You got it then?' Sean roared.

'You're damn right I did! Come with me and I'll show you.'

Duff's convoy was strung out four miles across the veld, most of the wagons double-teamed against the enormous weight of the machinery. Duff pointed to a rust-streaked cylinder that completely filled one of the leading wagons.

'That is my particular cross, seven tons of the most spiteful stubborn and evil boiler in the world. If it's broken the wagon axle once it's broken it a dozen times since we left Colesberg, not to mention the two occasions on which it capsized itself—once right in the middle of a river.'

They rode along the line of wagons.

'Good God! I didn't realize there'd be so much.' Sean shook his head dubiously. 'Are you sure you know how it all fits together?'

'Leave it to your Uncle Duff. Of course, it's going to need a bit of work done on it, after all it's been lying out in the open for a couple of years. Some of it was rusted up solid, but the judicious use of grease, new paint and the Charleywood brain will see the Candy Deep plant breaking rock and spitting out gold within a month.' Duff broke off and waved to a horseman coming towards them. 'This is the transport contractor. Frikke Malan—Mr Courtney, my partner.'

The contractor pulled up next to them and acknowledged the introduction. He wiped the dust off his face with the sleeve of his shirt.

'*Gott,* man, Mr Charleywood, I don't mind telling you that this is the hardest money I've ever worked for. Nothing personal—but I'll be *vragtig* glad to see the last of this load.'

8

Duff was wrong; it took much longer than a month. The rust had eaten deep into parts of the machinery and each bolt they twisted open was red with the scaly cancer. They worked the usual twelve-hour day chipping and scraping, filing and greasing, knuckles knocked raw against steel and palms wet and red where the blisters had burst. Then one day suddenly and miraculously they were finished. Along the ridge of the Candy Deep, neat and sweet smelling in its new paint, thick with yellow grease and waiting only to be fitted together, lay the dismembered mill.

'How long has it taken us so far?' Duff asked.

'It seems like a hundred years.'

'Is that all?' Duff feigned surprise. 'Then I declare a holiday—two days of meditation.'

'You meditate, brother—I'm going to do some carousing.'

'That's an excellent alternative—let's go!'

They started at Candy's place but she threw them out after the third fight so they moved on. There were a dozen places to drink at and they tried them all. Others were celebrating, because the day before old Kruger, the President of the Republic, had given official recognition to the goldfields. This had the sole effect of diverting the payments for mining licences from the pockets of the farmers who owned the land into the Government coffers. No one worried about that, except possibly the farmers. Rather it was an excuse for a party. The canteens were packed with swearing, sweating men. Duff and Sean drank with them.

The Crown and Anchor boards were doing a steady business in every bar and the men who crowded around them were the new population of the goldfields. Diggers bare to the waist and caked with dirt, salesmen with loud clothes and louder voices selling everything from dynamite to dysentery cure, an evangelist peddling salvation, gamblers mining pockets, gentlemen trying to keep the tobacco juice off their boots, boys new-flown from home and wishing themselves back, Boers bearded and drab-suited, drinking little but watching with inscrutable eyes the invaders of their land. Then there were the others, the clerks and farmers, the rogues and contractors listening greedily to the talk of gold.

The coloured girl, Martha, came to find Sean and Duff on the afternoon of the second day. They were in a mud-brick and thatch hut called The Tavern of the Bright Angels. Duff was doing a solo exhibition of the Dashing White Sergeant partnered by a chair; Sean and the fifty or so other customers were beating the rhythm on the bar counter with glasses and empty bottles.

Martha skittered across to Sean, slapping at the hands that tried to dive up her skirts and squealing sharply every time her bottom was pinched. She arrived at Sean's side flushed and breathless.

'Madame says you must come quickly—there's big trouble,' she gasped and started to run the gauntlet back to the door. Someone flipped up her dress behind and a concerted masculine roar approved the fact that she wore nothing under the petticoats.

Duff was so engrossed in his dancing that Sean had to carry him bodily out of the bar and dip his head in the horse trough outside before he could gain his attention.

'What the hell did you do that for?' spluttered Duff and swung a round-arm punch at Sean's head. Sean ducked under it and caught him about the body to save him falling on his back.

'Candy wants us—she says there's big trouble.'

Duff thought about that for a few seconds, frowning with concentration, then he threw back his head and sang to the tune of 'London's Burning',

> 'Candy wants us—Candy wants us
> We don't want Candy, we want brandy.'

He broke out of Sean's grip and headed back for the bar. Sean caught him again and pointed him in the direction of the Hotel. Candy was in her bedroom. She looked at the two of them as they swayed arm-in-arm in the doorway.

'Did you enjoy your debauch?' she asked sweetly. Duff mumbled and tried to straighten his coat. Sean tried to steady him as his feet danced an involuntary sideways jig.

'What happened to your eye?' she asked Sean and he fingered it tenderly; it was puffed and blue. Candy didn't wait for an answer but went on, still sweetly:

'Well, if you two beauties want to own a mine by tomorrow you'd better sober up.'

They stared at her and Sean spoke deliberately but nevertheless indistinctly.

'Why, what's the matter?'

'They're going to jump the claims, that's the matter. This new proclamation of a State goldfield has given the drifters the excuse they've been waiting for. About a hundred of them have formed a syndicate. They claim that the old titles aren't legal any more; they are going to pull out the pegs and put in their own.'

Duff walked without a stagger across to the washbasin beside Candy's bed; he splashed his face, towelled it vigorously then stooped and kissed her. 'Thanks, my sweet.'

'Duff, please be careful,' Candy called after them.

'Let's see if we can't hire a few mercenaries,' Sean suggested.

'Good idea, we'll try and find a few sober characters—there should be some in Candy's dining-room.'

They made a short detour on their way back to the mine and stopped at François's tent; it was dark by then and François came out in a freshly ironed nightshirt. He raised an eyebrow when he saw the five heavily armed men with Sean and Duff.

'You going hunting?' he asked.

Duff told him quickly and François was hopping with agitation before he had finished.

'Steal my claims, the thunders, the stinking thunders!' He rushed into his tent and came out again with a double-barrelled shotgun.

'We'll see, man, we'll see how they look full of buckshot.'

'François, listen to me,' Sean shouted him down. 'We don't know which claims they'll go to first. Get your men ready and if you hear shooting our way come and give us a hand—we'll do the same for you.'

'*Ja, ja,* we'll come all right—the dirty thunders.' His nightshirt flapping around his legs François trotted off to call his men.

Mbejane and the other Zulus were cooking dinner, squatting round the three-legged pot. Sean rode up to them.

'Get your spears,' he told them. They ran for their huts and almost immediately came crowding back.

'Nkosi, where's the fight?' they pleaded, food forgotten.

'Come on, I'll show you.'

They placed the hired gunmen amongst the mill machinery from where they could cover the track which led up to the mine. The Zulus they hid in one of the prospect trenches. If it developed into a hand-to-hand fight the syndicate was in for a surprise. Duff and Sean walked a little way down the slope to make sure their defenders were all concealed.

'How much dynamite have we got?' Sean asked thoughtfully. Duff stared at him for a second, then he grinned.

'Sufficient, I'd say. You're full of bright ideas this evening.' He led the way back to the shed which they used as a storeroom.

In the middle of the track a few hundred yards down the slope they buried a full case of explosive and placed an old tin can on top of it to mark the spot. They went back to the shed and spent an hour making grenades out of bundles of dynamite sticks, each with a detonator and a very short fuse. Then they settled down huddled into their sheepskin coats, rifles in their laps and waited.

They could see the lights of the encampments straggled down the valley and hear an occasional faint burst of singing from the canteens, but the moonlit road up to the mine remained deserted. Sean and Duff sat side by side with their backs against the newly painted boiler.

'How did Candy find out about this, I wonder?' Sean asked.

'She knows everything. That hotel of hers is the centre of this goldfield and she keeps her ears open.'

They relapsed into silence again while Sean formed his next question.

'She's quite a girl—our Candy.'

'Yes,' agreed Duff.

'Are you going to marry her, Duff?'

'Good God!' Duff straightened up as though someone had stuck a knife into him. 'You going mad, laddie, or else that was a joke in the worst possible taste.'

'She dotes on you and from what I've seen you're fairly well disposed towards her.' Sean was relieved at Duff's quick rejection of the idea. He was jealous, but not of the woman.

'Yes, we've got a common interest, that I won't deny—but marriage!' Duff shivered slightly, not altogether from the cold. 'Only a fool makes the same mistake twice.'

Sean turned to him with surprise. 'You've been married before?' he asked.

'With a vengeance. She was half Spanish and the rest Norwegian, a smoking bubbly mixture of cold fire and hot ice.' Duff's voice went dreamy. 'The memory has cooled sufficiently for me to think of it with a tinge of regret.'

'What happened?'

'I left her.'

'Why?'

'We only did two things well together and one of them was fight. If I close my eyes I can still see the way she used to pout with these lovely lips and bring them close to my ear before she hissed out a particularly foul word, then—hey ho! back to bed for the reconciliation.'

'Perhaps you made the wrong choice. You look around, you'll see millions of happily married people.'

'Name me one,' challenged Duff and the silence lengthened as Sean thought.

Then Duff went on, 'There's only one good reason for marriage, and that's children.'

'And companionship—that's another good reason.'

'Companionship from a woman?' Duff cut in incredulously. 'Like perfume from garlic. They're incapable of it. I suppose it's the training they get from their mothers, who are after all women themselves, but how can you be friends with someone who suspicions every little move you make, who takes your every action and weighs it on the balance of he loves me, he loves me not?' Duff shook his head unhappily. 'How long can a friendship last when it needs an hourly declaration of love to nourish it? The catechism of matrimony, "Do you love me, darling?" "Yes, darling, of course I do, my sweet." It's got to sound convincing every time otherwise tears.'

Sean chuckled.

'All right, it's funny—it's hilarious until you have to live with it,' Duff mourned. 'Have you ever tried to talk to a woman about anything other than love? The same things that interest you leave them cold. It comes as a shock the first time you try talking sense to them and suddenly you realize that their attention is not with you–they get a slightly fixed look in their eyes and you know they are thinking about that new dress or whether to invite Mrs Van der Hum to the party, so you stop talking and that's another mistake. That's a sign; marriage is full of signs that only a wife can read.'

'I hold no brief for matrimony, Duff, but aren't you being a little unfair, judging everything by your own unfortunate experience?'

'Select any woman, slap a ring on her third finger and she becomes a wife. First she takes you into her warm, soft body, which is pleasant, and then she tries to take you into her warm, soft mind, which is not so pleasant. She does not share, she possesses–she clings and she smothers. The relation of man to woman is uninteresting in that it conforms to an inescapable pattern, nature has made it so for the very good reason that it requires us to reproduce; but in order to obtain that result every love, Romeo and Juliet, Bonaparte and Josephine not excepted, must lead up to the co-performance of a simple biological function. It's such a small thing–such a short-lived, trivial little experience. Apart from that man and woman think differently, feel differently and are interested in different things. Would you call that companionship?'

'No, but is that a true picture? Is that all there is between them?' Sean asked.

'You'll find out one day. Nature in her preoccupation with reproduction has planted in the mind of man a barricade; it has scaled him off from the advice and experience of his fellow men, inoculated him against it. When your time comes you'll go to the gallows with a song on your lips.'

'You frighten me.'

'It's the sameness of it all that depresses me–the goddamn monotony of it.' Duff shifted his seat restlessly then settled back against the boiler. 'The interesting relationships are those in which sex the leveller takes no hand–brothers, enemies, master and servant, father and son, man and man.'

'Homosexuals?'

'No, that's merely sex out of step and you're back to the original trouble. When a man takes a friend he does it not from an uncontrollable compulsion but in his own free choice. Every friendship is different, ends differently or goes on for ever. No chains bind it, no ritual or written contract. There is no question of forsaking all others, no obligation to talk about it–mouth it up and gloat on it the whole time.' Duff stood up stiffly. 'It's one of the good things in life. How late is it?'

Sean pulled out his watch and tilted its face to catch the moonlight. 'After midnight–it doesn't look as if they're coming.'

'They'll come–there's gold here, another uncontrollable compulsion. They'll come. The question is when.'

The lights along the valley faded out one by one, the deep sing-song voices of the Zulus in the prospect trench stilled and a small cold wind came up and moved the grass along the ridge of the Candy Deep. Sitting together, sometimes drowsing, sometimes talking quietly, they waited the night away. The sky paled, them pinked prettily. A dog barked over near Hospital Hill and another joined it. Sean stood up and stretched, he glanced down the valley towards Ferrieras Camp and saw them. A black moving blot of horsemen, overflowing the road, lifting no dust from the dew-damp earth, spreading out to cross the Natal Spruit then bunching together on the near bank before coming on.

'Mr Charleywood, we have company.'

Duff jumped up.

'They might miss us and go on to the Jack and Whistle first.'

'We'll see which road they take when they come to the fork. In the meantime let's get ready. Mbejane,' shouted Sean and the black head popped out of the trench.

'Nkosi?'

'Are you awake? They are coming.'

The blackness parted in a white smile. 'We are awake.'

'Then get down and stay down until I give the word.'

The five mercenaries were lying belly down in the grass, each with a newly-opened packet of cartridges at his elbow. Sean hurried back to Duff and they crouched behind the boiler.

'The tin can shows up clearly from here. Do you think you can hit it?'

'With my eyes closed,' said Sean.

The horsemen reached the fork and turned without hesitation towards the Candy Deep, quickening their pace as they came up the ridge. Sean rested his rifle across the top of the boiler and picked up the speck of silver in his sights.

'What's the legal position, Duff?' he asked out of the corner of his mouth.

'They've just crossed our boundary—they are now officially trespassers,' Duff pronounced solemnly.

One of the leading horses kicked over the tin can and Sean fired at the spot on which it had stood. The shot was indecently loud in the quiet morning and every head in the syndicate lifted with alarm towards the ridge, then the ground beneath them jumped up in a brown cloud to meet the sky. When the dust cleared there was a struggling tangle of downed horses and men. The screams carried clearly up to the crest of the ridge.

'My God,' breathed Sean, appalled at the destruction.

'Shall we let them have it, boss?' called one of the hired men.

'No,' Duff answered him quickly. 'They've had enough.'

The flight started, riderless horses, mounted men and others on foot were scattering back down the valley. Sean was relieved to see that they left only a half a dozen men and a few horses lying in the road.

'Well, that's the easiest fiver you've ever earned,' Duff told one of the mercenaries. 'I think you can go home now and have some breakfast.'

'Wait, Duff.' Sean pointed. The survivors of the explosion had reached the road junction again and there they were being stopped by two men on horseback.

'Those two are trying to rally them.'

'Let's change their minds, they're still within rifle range.'

'They are not on our property any more,' disagreed Sean. 'Do you want to wear a rope?'

They watched while those of the syndicate who had had enough fighting for one day disappeared down the road to the camps and the rest coagulated into a solid mass at the cross road.

'We should have shot them up properly while we had the chance,' grumbled one of the mercenaries uneasily. 'Now they'll come back—look at that bastard talking to them like a Dutch uncle.'

They left their horses and spread out, then they started moving cautiously back up the slope. They hesitated just below the line of boundary pegs then ran forward, tearing up the pegs as they came.

'All together, gentlemen, if you please,' called Duff politely and the seven rifles fired. The range was long and the thirty or so attackers ran doubled up and dodging. The bullets had little effect at first, but as the distance shortened the men started falling. There was a shallow donga running diagonally down the slope and as each of the attackers reached it he jumped down into it and from its safety started a heated reply to the fire of Sean's men. Bullets spanged off the machinery, leaving bright scars where they struck.

Mbejane's Zulus were adding their voices to the confusion.

'Let us go down to them now, Nkosi.'

'They are close—let us go.'

'Quiet down, you madmen, you'd not go a hundred paces against those rifles,' Sean snarled impatiently.

'Sean, cover me,' whispered Duff. 'I'm going to sneak round the back of the ridge, rush them from the side and lob a few sticks of dynamite into that donga.'

Sean caught his arm, his fingers dug into it so that Duff winced.

'You take one step and I'll break a rifle butt over your head—you're as bad as those Blacks. Now keep shooting and let me think.' Sean peered over the top of the boiler but ducked again as a bullet rang loudly against it, inches from his ear. He stared at the new paint in front of his nose, put his shoulder against it; the boiler rocked slightly. He looked up and Duff was watching him.

'We'll walk down together and lob that dynamite,' Sean told him. 'Mbejane and his boodthirsty heathens will roll the boiler in front of us. These other gentlemen will cover us, we'll do this thing in style.'

Sean called the Zulus out of the trench and explained to them. They chorused their approval of the scheme and jostled each other to find a place to push against the boiler. Sean and Duff filled the front of their shirts with the dynamite grenades and lit a short length of tarred rope each.

Sean nodded to Mbejane.

'Where are the children of Zulu?' sang Mbejane, shrilling his voice in the ancient rhetorical question.

'Here,' answered his warriors braced ready against the boiler.

'Where are the spears of Zulu?'

'Here,'

'How bright are the spears of Zulu?'

'Brighter than the Sun.'

'How hungry are the spears of Zulu?'

'Hungrier than the locust.'

'Then let us take them to the feeding.'

'*Yeh-bo.*' Explosive assent and the boiler revolved slowly to the thrust of the black shoulders.

'*Yeh-bo.*' Another reluctant revolution.

'*Yeh-bo.*' It moved more readily.

'*Yeh-bo.*' Gravity caught it. Ponderously it bumped down the slope and they ran behind it. The fire of the donga doubled its volume, rattling like hail against the huge metal cylinder. The singing of the Zulus changed its tone also; the deep-voiced chanting quickened, climbed excitedly and became the blood trill. That insane, horrible squealing made Sean's skin crawl, tickled his spine with the ghost fingers of memory, but it inflamed him also. His mouth opened and he squealed with them. He touched the first grenade with the burning rope then flung it in a high spluttering sparking arc. It burst in the air above the donga. He threw again. Crump, crump. Duff was using his explosive as well. The boiler crashed over the lip of the donga and came to rest in a cloud of dust; the Zulus followed it in, spreading out, still shrieking, and now their assegais were busy. The white men broke, clawed frantically out of the ravine and fled, the Zulus hacking at them as they ran.

When François arrived with fifty armed diggers following him the fight was over.

'Take your boys down to the camps. Comb them out carefully. We want every one of those that got away,' Duff told him. 'It's about time we had a little law and order on this field.'

'How will we pick out the ones that were in on it?' asked François.

'By their white faces and the sweat on their shirts you will know them,' Duff answered.

François and his men went, leaving Sean and Duff to clean up the battlefield. It was a messy job—the stabbing spears had made it so. They destroyed those horses that the blast had left still half alive and they gleaned more than a dozen corpses from the donga and the slope below it. Two of them were Zulus. The wounded, and there were many, they packed into a wagon and took them down to Candy's Hotel.

It was early afternoon by the time they arrived. They threaded the wagon through the crowd and stopped it in front of the Hotel. It seemed the entire population of the goldfield was there, packed around the small open space in which François was holding his prisoners.

François was almost hysterical with excitement. He was sweeping the shotgun around in dangerous circles as he harangued the crowd. Then he darted back to prod one of the prisoners with the twin muzzles.

'You thunders,' he screamed. 'Steal our claims—hey—steal our claims.'

At that moment he caught sight of Duff and Sean bringing the wagon through the press.

'Duff, Duff. We got them. We got the whole lot of them,' The crowd backed respectfully away from the menace of that circling shotgun and Sean flinched as it pointed directly at him for a second.

'So I see, François,' Duff assured him. 'In fact, I have seldom seen anyone more completely had.'

François's prisoners were swathed in ropes; they could move only their heads and as additional security a digger with a loaded rifle stood over each of them. Duff climbed down off the wagon.

'Don't you think you should slacken those ropes a little?' Duff asked dubiously.

'And have them escape?' François was indignant.

'Do you think they'd get very far?'

'No, I don't suppose so.'

'Well, another half an hour and they'll all have gangrene—look at that one's hand already, a beautiful shade of blue.'

Reluctantly François conceded and told his men to untie them.

Duff pushed his way through the crowd and climbed the steps of the Hotel. From there he held up his hands for silence.

'There have been a lot of men killed today—we don't want it to happen again. One way we can prevent it is to make sure that this lot get what they deserve.' Cheers were led by François.

'But we must do it properly. I suggest we elect a committee to deal with this affair and with any other problems that crop up on these fields. Say ten members and a chairman.'

More cheers.

'Call it the Diggers' Committee,' shouted someone and the crowd took up the name enthusiastically.

'All right, the Diggers' Committee it is. Now we want a chairman, any suggestions?'

'Mr Charleywood,' shouted François.

'Yes, Duff—he'll do.'

'Yes, Duff Charleywood.'

'Any other suggestions?'

'No,' roared the crowd.

'Thank you gentlemen.' Duff smiled at them. 'I am sensible of the honour. Now, ten members.'

'Jock and Trevor Heyns.'

'Karl Lochtkamper.'

'François du Toit.'

'Sean Courtney.'

There were fifty nominations. Duff baulked at counting votes so the committee was elected by applause. He called the names one at a time and judged the strength of the response to each. Sean and François were among those elected. Chairs and a table were brought out to the veranda and Duff took his seat. With a water-jug he hammered for silence, declared the first session of the Diggers' Committee open and then immediately fined three members of the crowd ten pounds each for discharging firearms during a meeting—gross contempt of Committee. The fines were paid and a proper air of solemnity achieved.

'I'll ask Mr Courtney to open the case for the prosecution.'

Sean stood up and gave a brief description of the morning's battle, ending, 'You were there, Your Honour, so you know all about it anyway.'

'So I was,' agreed Duff. 'Thank you, Mr Courtney. I think that was a very fair picture you presented. Now,' he looked at the prisoners, 'who speaks for you?'

There was a minute of shuffling and whispering, then one of them was pushed forward. He pulled off his hat and blushed purple.

'Your Worship,' he began, then stopped, wriggling with embarrassment.

'Your Worship.'

'You've said that already.'

'I don't rightly know where to begin, Mr Charleywood—I mean Your Honour, sir.'

Duff looked at the prisoners again.

'Perhaps you'd like to reconsider your choice.'

The first champion was withdrawn in disgrace and a fresh one sent forward to face the Committee. He had more fire.

'You bastards got no right to do this to us,' he started and Duff promptly fined him ten pounds. His next attempt was more polite.

'Your Honour, you can't do this to us. We had our rights, you know, the new proclamation and all, I mean, them old titles wasn't legal no more now, was they? We just came along as peaceful as you please, the old titles not being legal, we got a right to do what we done. Then you bastards, I mean Your Honour, dynamited us and like we had a right to protect ourselves,

I mean after all, didn't we, sir?'

'A brilliant defence most ably conducted. Your fellows should be grateful to you,' Duff complimented him, then turned to his Committee. 'Well now, how say you merry gentlemen. Guilty or not guilty?'

'Guilty.' They spoke together and François added for emphasis, 'the dirty thunders.'

'We will now consider sentence.'

'String them up,' shouted someone and instantly the mood changed. The mob growled: an ugly sound.

'I'm a carpenter, I'll whip you up a handsome set of gallows in no time at all.'

'Don't waste good wood on them. Use a tree.'

'Get the ropes.'

'String them up.'

The crowd surged in, lynch mad. Sean snatched François's shotgun and jumped up on to the table.

'So help me God, I'll shoot the first one of you that touches them before this court says so.' They checked and Sean pressed his advantage. 'At this range I can't miss. Come on, try me—there's two loads of buckshot in here. Someone will get cut in half.' They fell back still muttering.

'Perhaps you've forgotten, but there's a police force in this country and there's a law against killing. Hang them today and it'll be your turn tomorrow.'

'You're right, Mr Courtney, it'll be cruel heartless murder. That it will,' wailed the spokesman.

'Shut up, you bloody fool,' Duff snarled at him and someone in the crowd laughed. The laughter caught on and Duff sighed silently with relief. That had been very close.

'Give them the old tar and feathers.'

Duff grinned. 'Now you're talking sense. Who's got a few barrels of tar for sale?' He looked round. 'What, no offers? Then we'll have to think of something else.'

'I've got ten drums of red paint—thirty shillings each, good imported brand.' Duff recognized the speaker as a trader who had opened a general dealer's store down at Ferrieras Camp.

'Mr Tarry suggests paint. What about it?'

'No, it comes off too easily—that's no good.'

'I'll let you have it cheap—twenty-five shillings a drum.'

'No—stick your ruddy paint,' the crowd booed him.

'Give them a twist on Satan's Roulette Wheel,' shouted another voice, and the crowd clamoured agreement.

'That's it—give them the wheel.'

'Round and round and round she goes—where she stops nobody knows,' roared a black-bearded digger from the roof of the shanty across the road. The crowd howled.

Sean watched Duff's expression—the smile had gone. He was weighing it up. If he stopped them again they might lose all patience and risk the shotgun. He couldn't chance it.

'All right. If that's what you want.' He faced the terrified cluster of prisoners. 'The sentence of this court is that you play roulette with the devil for one hour and that you then leave this goldfield—if we catch you back here again you'll get another hour of it. The wounded are excused the first half of the sentence. I think they've had enough. Mr du Toit will supervise the punishment.'

'We'd prefer the paint, Mr Charleywood,' pleaded the spokesman again.

'I bet you would,' said Duff softly, but the crowd was carrying them away already, out towards the open veld beyond the Hotel. Most of them had staked claims of their own and they didn't like claim jumpers. Sean climbed down off the table.

'Let's go and have a drink,' Duff said to him.

'Aren't you going to watch?' asked Sean.

'I've seen it done once before down in the Cape. That was enough.'

'What do they do?'

'Go and have a look, I'll be waiting for you at the Bright Angels. I'll be surprised if you stay the full hour.'

By the time Sean joined the crowd most of the wagons had been gathered from the camps and drawn up in a line. Men swarmed round them fitting jacks under the axles to lift the big back wheels clear of the ground. Then the prisoners were hustled forward—one to each wheel. Eager hands lifted them and held them while their wrists and ankles were lashed to the rim of the wheel with the hub in the middle of their backs and their arms and legs spreadeagled like stranded starfish. François hurried along the line checking the ropes and placing four diggers at each wheel, two to start it and another two to take over when those were tired. He reached the end, came back to the centre again, pulled his watch from his pocket, checked the time, then shouted.

'All right—turn them, *kerels*.'

The wheels started moving, slowly at first then faster as they built up momentum. The bodies strapped to them blurred with the speed.

'Round and round and round she goes—round and round and round she goes,' chanted the crowd gleefully.

Within minutes there was a burst of laughter from the end of the line of wagons. Someone had started vomiting, it sprayed from him like yellow sparks from a catherine wheel. Then another and another joined in, Sean could hear them retching and gasping as the centrifugal force flung the vomit up against the back of their throats and out of their noses. He waited a few more minutes but when their bowels started to empty he turned away gagging and headed for the Bright Angel.

'Did you enjoy it?' asked Duff.

'Give me a brandy,' answered Sean.

9

With the Diggers' Committee dispensing rough justice a semblance of order came to the camps. President Kruger wanted no part in policing the nest of ruffians and cut-throats which was growing up just outside his Capital and he contented himself with placing his spies among them and leaving them to work out their own salvation. After all, the field was far from proved and the chances were that in another year the veld would again be as deserted as it had been nine months before. He could afford to wait; in the meantime the Diggers' Committee had his tacit sanction.

While the ants worked, cutting down into the reef with pick and with dynamite, the grasshoppers waited in the bars and shanties. So far only the Jack and Whistle mill was turning out gold, and only Hradsky and François du Toit knew how much gold was coming out of it. Hradsky was still in Capetown crusading for capital and François spoke to no one, not even to Duff, about the mill's productivity.

The rumours flew like sand in a whirlwind. One day it seemed that the reef had pinched out fifty feet below the surface, and the next the canteens buzzed with the news that the Heyns brothers had gone down a hundred feet and were pulling out nuggets the size of musket balls. Nobody knew but everybody was prepared to guess.

Up at the Candy Deep, Duff and Sean worked on relentlessly. The mill took shape on its concrete platform, its jaws open for the first bite at the rock. The boiler was swung up on to its cradle by twenty sweating, singing Zulus. The copper tables were fitted up ready to be smeared with quicksilver. There was no time to worry about the reef nor the dwindling store of money in Sean's cash belt. They worked and they slept—there was nothing else. Duff took to sharing Sean's tent up on the ridge and Candy had her featherbed to herself again.

On the twentieth of November they fired the boiler for the first time. Tired and horny-handed, their bodies lean and tempered hard with toil, they stood together and watched the needle creep up round the pressure gauge until it touched the red line at the top.

Duff grunted. 'Well, at least we've got power now.' Then he punched Sean's shoulder. 'What the hell are you standing here for—do you think this is a Sunday School picnic? There's work to do, laddie.'

On the second of December they fed the mill its first meal and watched the powdered rock flow across the amalgam tables. Sean threw his arm round Duff's neck in an affectionate half-Nelson, Duff hit him in the stomach and pulled his hat down over his eyes, they drank a glass of brandy each at supper and laughed a little but that was all. They were too tired to celebrate. From now on one of them must be in constant attendance of that iron monster. Duff took the first night shift and when Sean went up to the mill next morning he found him weaving on his feet, his eyes sunk deep in dark sockets. 'By my reckoning we've run ten tons of rock through her. Time to clean the tables and see just how much gold we've picked up.'

'You go and get some sleep,' said Sean and Duff ignored him.

'Mbejane, bring a couple of your savages here, we're going to change the tables.'

'Listen, Duff, it can wait an hour or two. Go and get your head down.'

'Please stop drivelling—you're as bad as a wife.'

Sean shrugged. 'Have it your own way, show me how you do it then.'

They switched the flow of powdered rock on to the second table that was standing ready; then with a broad bladed spatula Duff scraped the mercury off the copper top of the first table, collecting it in a ball the size of a coconut.

'The mercury picks up the tiny particles of gold,' he explained to Sean as he worked, 'and lets the grains of rock wash across the table and fall off into the dump. Of course it doesn't collect it all, some of it goes to waste.'

'How do you get the gold out again?'

'You put the whole lot in a retort and boil off the mercury—the gold stays behind.'

'Hell of a waste of mercury, isn't it?'

'No, you catch it as it condenses and use it again. Come on, I'll show you.'

Duff carried the ball of amalgam down to the shed, placed it in the retort and lit the blow-lamp. With the heat on it the ball dissolved and started to bubble. Silently they stared at it. The level in the retort fell.

'Where's the gold?' Sean asked at last.

'Oh, shut up,' Duff snapped impatiently, and then, repentant, 'Sorry, laddie, I feel a bit jaded this morning.'

The last of the mercury steamed off and there it was, glowing bright, molten yellow. A drop of gold the size of a pea. Duff shut off the blow-lamp and neither of them spoke for a while. Then Sean asked, 'Is that all?'

'That, my friend, is all,' agreed Duff wearily. 'What do you want to do with it—fill a tooth?'

He turned towards the door with a droop to his whole body.

'Keep the mill running, we might as well go down with our colours flying.'

10

It was a miserable Christmas dinner. They ate it at Candy's Hotel. They had credit there. She gave Duff a gold signet ring and Sean a box of cigars. Sean had never smoked before now the sting of it in his lungs gave him a certain masochistic pleasure. The dining-room roared with men's voices and cutlery clatter, the air was thick with the smell of food and tobacco smoke while in one corner—marooned on a little island of gloom—sat Sean, Duff and Candy.

Once Sean lifted his glass at Duff and spoke like an undertaker's clerk 'Happy Christmas.'

Duff's lips twitched back in a dead man's grin. 'And the same to you.'

They drank. Then Duff roused himself to speak. 'Tell me again—how much have we got left? I like to hear you say it; you have a beautiful voice, you should have played Shakespeare.'

'Three pounds and sixteen shillings.'

'Yes, yes, you got it just right that time—three pounds and sixteen shillings—now to really make me feel Christmasy, tell me how much we owe.'

'Have another drink,' Sean changed the subject.

'Yes, I think I will, thank you.'

'Oh please, you two, let's just forget about it for today,' pleaded Candy. 'I planned for it to be such a nice party—look, there's François! Hey, François—over here!'

The dapper du Toit bustled across to their table.

'Happy Christmas, kerels, let me buy you a drink.'

'It's nice to see you.' Candy gave him a kiss. 'How are you? You're looking fine.'

François sobered instantly. 'It's funny you should say that, Candy. As a matter of fact I'm a bit worried.' He tapped his chest and sank down into an empty chair. 'My heart, you know, I've been waiting for it to happen, and then yesterday I was up at the mill, just standing there, you understand, when suddenly it was as though a vice was squeezing my chest. I couldn't breathe—well, not very well anyway. Naturally I hurried back to my tent and looked it up. Page eighty-three. Under "Diseases of the Heart".' He shook his head sadly. 'It's very worrying. You know I wasn't a well man before, but now this.'

'Oh, no,' wailed Candy. 'I can't stand it—not you too.'

'I'm sorry, have I said something wrong?'

'Just in keeping with the festive spirit at this table.' She pointed at Duff and Sean. 'Look at their happy faces—if you'll excuse me I'm going to check up in the kitchen.' She went.

'What's wrong, old Duff?'

Duff flashed his death's head grin across the table at Sean.

'The man wants to know what's wrong—tell him.'

'Three pounds sixteen shillings,' said Sean and François looked puzzled.

'I don't understand.'

'He means we're broke—flat broke.'

'*Gott*, I'm sorry to hear that, Duff, I thought you were going good. I've heard the mill running all this month. I thought you'd be rich by now.'

'The mill's been running all right and we've recovered enough gold to block a flea's backside.'

'But why, man? You are working the Leader Reef aren't you?'

'I'm beginning to think this Leader Reef of yours is a bedtime story.'

François peered into his glass thoughtfully.

'How deep are you?'

'We've got one incline shaft down about fifty feet.'

'No sign of the Leader?' Duff shook his head and François went on.

'You know when I first spoke to you a lot of what I said was just guessing.'

Duff nodded.

'Well, I know a bit more about it now. What I am going to tell you is for you alone—I'll lose my job if it gets out, you understand?'

Duff nodded again.

'So far the Leader Reef has only been found at two places. We've got it on the Jack and Whistle and I know the Heyns brothers have struck it on the Cousin Jock Mine. Let me draw it for you.' He picked up a knife and drew in the gravy on the bottom of Sean's plate. 'This is the Main Reef running fairly straight. Here I am, here is the Cousin Jock and here you are in between us. Both of us have found the Leader and you haven't. My guess is it's there all right—you just don't know where to look.

'At the far end of the Jack and Whistle claims the Main Reef and the Leader are running side by side two feet apart but by the time they reach the boundary nearest to the Candy Deep they've opened up to seventy feet apart. Now on the boundary of the Cousin Jock they're back to fifty feet apart. To me it seems that the two reefs form the shape of a long bow, like this.' He drew it in. 'The Main Reef is the string and the Leader Reef is the wood. I'm telling you, Duff, if you cut a trench at right-angles to the Main Reef you'll find it—and when you do you can buy me a drink.'

They listened gravely and when François finished Duff leaned back in his chair. 'If we'd known this a month ago! Now how are we going to raise the money to cut this new trench and still keep the mill running?'

'We could sell some of our equipment,' suggested Sean.

'We need it, every scrap of it, and besides if we sold one spade the creditors would be on us like a pack of wolves, howling for their money.'

'I'd make you a loan if I had it—but with what Mr Hradsky pays me—' François shrugged. 'You'll need about two hundred pounds. I haven't got it.'

Candy came back to the table in time to hear François's last remark.

'What's this all about?'

'Can I tell her, François?'

'If you think it will do any good.'

Candy listened, then thought for a moment. 'Well, I've just bought ten plots of ground in Johannesburg, this new Government village down the valley, so I'm short myself. But I could let you have fifty pounds if that would help.'

'I've never borrowed money from a lady before—it'll be a new experience. Candy, I love you.'

'I wish you meant that,' said Candy, but luckily for Duff his hearing failed him completely just as Candy spoke. He went on hurriedly.

'We'll need another hundred and fifty or so—let's hear your suggestions, gentlemen.'

There was a long silence, then Duff started to smile and he was looking at Sean.

'Don't tell me, let me guess,' Sean forestalled him. 'You're going to put me out to stud?'

'Close—but not quite right. How are you feeling, laddie?'

'Thank you, I'm all right.'

'Strong?'

'Yes.'

'Brave?'

'Come on, Duff, let's have it. I don't like that look in your eye.'

Duff pulled a notebook out of his pocket and wrote in it with a stump of pencil. Then he tore out the page and handed it to Sean. 'We'll have posters like this put up in every canteen on the goldfields.'

Sean read it:

ON NEW YEAR'S DAY MR SEAN COURTNEY HEAVYWEIGHT CHAMPION OF
THE TRANSVAAL REPUBLIC WILL STAND TO MEET ALL COMERS IN FRONT
OF CANDY'S HOTEL FOR A PURSE OF FIFTY POUNDS A SIDE.

Spectators' Fee, 2s. All Welcome.

Candy was reading it over his shoulder. She squeaked.

'That's wonderful. I'll have to hire extra waiters to serve drinks and I'll run a buffet luncheon. I suppose I could charge two shillings a head?'

'I'll fix the posters,' François was not to be outdone, 'and I'll send a couple of my chaps down to put up a ring.'

'We'll close the mill down until New Year—Sean will have to get a lot of rest. We'll put him on light training only. No drinking, of course, and plenty of sleep,' said Duff.

'It's all arranged then, is it?' asked Sean. 'All I've got to do is go in there and get beaten to a pulp?'

'We're doing this for you, laddie, so that you can be rich and famous.'

'Thank you, thank you very much.'

'You like to fight, don't you?'

'When I'm in the mood.'

'Don't worry, I'll think up some dirty names to call you—get you worked up in no time.'

'How are you feeling?' Duff asked for the sixth time that morning.

'No change since five minutes ago,' Sean reassured him.

Duff pulled out his watch, stared at it, held it to his ear and looked surprised that it was still ticking.

'We've got the challengers lined up on the veranda. I've told Candy to serve them free drinks—as much as they want. Every minute we can wait here gives them a little longer to take on a load of alcohol. François is collecting the gate money in my valise; as you win each bout the stakes will go into it as well. I've got Mbejane stationed at the mouth of the alley beside the Hotel. If there's a riot one of us will throw the bag to him and he'll head for the long grass.'

Sean was stretched out on Candy's bed with his hands behind his head. He laughed. 'I can find no fault with your planning. Now for pity's sake calm down, man. You're making me nervous.'

The door burst open and Duff leapt out of his chair at the crash. It was François, he stood in the doorway holding his chest.

'My heart,' he panted. 'This is doing my heart no good.'

'What's happening outside?' Duff demanded.

'We've collected over fifty pounds gate money already. There's a mob up on the roof that haven't paid, but every time I go near them they throw bottles at me.'

François cocked his head on one side. 'Listen to them.' The noise of the crowd was barely softened by the flimsy walls of the Hotel. 'They won't wait much longer—you'd better come out before they start looking for you.'

Sean stood up. 'I'm ready.'

François hesitated.

'Duff, you remember Fernandes, that Portuguese from Kimberley?'

'Oh no!' Duff anticipated him. 'Don't tell me he's here.'

François nodded. 'I didn't want to alarm you but some of the local boys clubbed in and telegraphed south for him. He arrived on the express coach half an hour ago. I had hoped he wasn't going to make it in time, but–' He shrugged.

Duff looked at Sean sadly.

'Bad luck, laddie.'

François tried to soften the blow. 'I told him it was first come first served. He's sixth in the line so Sean will be able to make a couple of hundred quid anyway—then we can always say he's had enough and close the contest.'

Sean was listening with interest. 'This Fernandes is dangerous?'

'They were thinking of him when they invented that word,' Duff told him.

'Let's go and have a look at him.'

Sean led the way out of Candy's room and down the passage.

'Did you get hold of a scale to weigh them with?' Duff asked François as they hurried after Sean.

'No, there's not one on the fields that goes over a hundred and fifty pounds—but I have Gideon Barnard outside.'

'How does that help us?'

'He's a cattle dealer—all his life he's been judging animals on the hoof. He'll give us the weights to within a few pounds.'

Duff chuckled. 'That'll have to do then. Besides I doubt we'll be claiming any world titles.'

Then they were out on the veranda blinking in the brightness of the sun and the thunder of the crowd.

'Which is the Portuguese?' whispered Sean—he needn't have asked. The man stood out like a gorilla in a cage of monkeys. A shaggy coating of hair began on his shoulders and continued down his back and chest, completely hiding his nipples and exaggerating the bulge of his enormous belly.

The crowd opened a path for Sean and Duff and they walked along it to the ring. Hands slapped Sean's back but the well-wishes were drowned in the churning sea of sound. Jock Heyns was the referee—he helped Sean through the ropes and ran his hands over his pockets.

'Just checking,' he apologized. 'We don't want any scrap iron in the ring.' Then he beckoned to a tall, brown-faced fellow who was leaning on the ropes chewing tobacco.

'This is Mr Bernard—our weighing steward. Well, what do you say, Gideon?'

The steward hosed a little juice from the side of his mouth.

'Two hundred and ten.'

'Thank you.' Jock held up his hands and after a few minutes was rewarded with a comparative silence.

'Ladies and Gentlemen.'

'Who you talking to, Guvnor?'

'We are privileged to have with us today—Mr Sean Courtney.'

'Wake up, *Boet*, he's been with us for months.'

'The heavyweight champion of the Republic.'

'Why not make it the world, cock, he's got just as much right to that title.'

'Who will fight six bouts—'

'If it lasts that long.'

'—for his title and a purse of fifty pounds each.'

Sustained cheering.

'The first challenger—at two hundred and ten pounds—Mr Anthony—'

'Hold on,' Sean shouted, 'who says he's first?'

Jock Heyns had taken a deep breath to bellow the name, he let it escape with a hiss. 'It was arranged by Mr du Toit.'

'If I fight them, then I pick them—I want the Port . . .'

Duff's hand whipped over Sean's mouth and his whisper was desperate. 'Don't be a bloody fool—take the easy ones first. Use your head—we aren't doing this for fun, we're trying to finance a mine, remember?'

Sean clawed Duff's hand off his mouth. 'I want the Portuguese,' he shouted.

'He's joking,' Duff assured the crowd, then turned on Sean fiercely. 'Are you mad? That dago's a man-eater, we're fifty pounds poorer before you start.'

'I want the Portuguese,' repeated Sean with all the logic of a small boy picking the most expensive toy in the shop.

'Let him have the dago,' shouted the gentlemen on the hotel roof and Jock Heyns eyed them nervously; it was clear that they were about to add a few more bottles to the argument.

'All right,' he agreed hastily. 'The first challenger, at—' he glanced at Barnard and repeated after him, 'two hundred and fifty-five pounds—Mr Felezardo da Silva Fernandes.'

In a storm of hoots and applause the Portuguese waddled down off the veranda and into the ring. Sean had seen Candy at the dining-room window and he waved to her. She blew him a two-handed kiss and at that instant Trevor Heyns, the timekeeper, hit the bucket which served as a gong and Sean heard Duff's warning shout. Instinctively he started to duck. There was a flash of lightning inside his skull and he found himself sitting in among the legs of the first line of spectators.

'The bastard King hit me,' Sean complained loudly. He shook his head and was surprised to find it still attached to his body. Someone poured a glass of beer over him and it steadied him. He felt his anger flaming up through his body.

'Six,' counted Jock Heyns.

The Portuguese was standing at the ropes. 'Come back, Leetle Sheet, I haf some more for you, not half.'

Sean's anger jumped in his throat.

'Seven, eight.'

Sean gathered his legs under him.

'I kiss your mother.' Fernandes puckered his lips and smacked them. 'I love your sister, like this.' He demonstrated graphically.

Sean charged. With the full weight of his run behind it, his fist thudded into the Portuguese's mouth, then the ropes caught Sean and catapulted him back into the crowd once more.

'You weren't even in the ring, how could you hit him?' protested one of the spectators who had broken Sean's fall. He had money on Fernandes.

'Like this!' Sean demonstrated. The man sat down heavily and had nothing further to say. Sean hurdled the ropes. Jock Heynes was halfway through his second count when Sean interrupted him by lifting the reclining Portuguese to his feet, using the tangled bush of his hair as a handle. He balanced the man on his unsteady legs and hit him again.

'One, two, three . . .' resignedly Jock Heyns began his third count, this time he managed to reach ten.

There was a howl of protest from the crowd and Jock Heyns struggled to make himself heard above it.

'Does anyone want to lodge a formal objection?'

It seemed that there were those who did.

'Very well, please step into the ring. I can't accept shouted comments.' Jock's attitude was understandable—he stood to lose a considerable sum if his decision were reversed. But Sean was patrolling the ropes as hungrily as a lion at feeding time. Jock waited a decent interval, then held up Sean's right arm.

'The winner—ten minutes for refreshments before the next bout. Will the keepers please come and fetch their property.' He gestured towards the Portuguese.

'Nice going, laddie, unorthodox perhaps but beautiful to watch.' Duff took Sean's arm and led him to a chair on the veranda.

'Three more to go, then we can call it a day.' He handed Sean a glass.

'What's this?'

'Orange juice.'

'I'd prefer something a little stronger.'

'Later, laddie.'

Duff collected the Portuguese purse and dropped it into the valise while that gentlemen was being carried from the ring by his straining sponsors and laid to rest at the far end of the veranda.

Mr Anthony Blair was next. His heart was not in the encounter. He moved prettily enough on his feet but always in the direction best calculated to keep him out of reach of Sean's fists.

'The boy's a natural long-distance champ.'

'Watch it, Courtney, he'll run you to death.'

'Last lap, Blair, once more round the ring and you've done five miles.'

The chase ended when Sean, now sweating gently, herded him in a corner and there dispatched him.

The third challenger had by this time developed a pain in his chest.

'It hurts like you wouldn't believe it,' he announced through gritted teeth.

'Does it sort of gurgle in your lungs as you breathe?' asked François.

'Yes, that's it—gurgles like you wouldn't believe it.'

'Pleurisy,' diagnosed du Toit with more than a trace of envy in his voice.

'Is that bad?' the man asked anxiously.

'Yes it is. Page one hundred and sixteen. The treatment is—'

'Then I won't be able to fight. Hell, that's bad luck,' the invalid complained cheerfully.

'It's exceptionally bad luck,' agreed Duff. 'it means you'll have to forfeit your purse money.'

'You wouldn't take advantage of a sick man?'

'Try me,' Duff suggested pleasantly.

The fourth contestant was a German. Big, blond and happy-faced. He stumbled three or four times on his way to the ring. tripped over the ropes and crawled to his corner on hands and knees; once there he was able to regain his feet with a little help from the ring post. Jock went close to him to smell his breath and before he could dodge, the German caught him in a bear hug and led him into the opening steps of a waltz. The crowd loved it and there were no objections when at the end of the dance Jock declared Sean the winner on a technical knockout. More correctly the decison should have gone to Candy who had provided the free drinks.

'We can close down the circus now if you want to, laddie,' Duff told Sean. 'You've made enough to keep the Candy Deep afloat for another couple of months.'

'I haven't had a single good fight out of the lot of them. But I like the looks of this last one. The others were for business; this one I'll have just for the hell of it.'

'You've been magnificent—now you deserve a little fun,' agreed Duff.

'Mr Martin Curtis. Heavyweight champion of Georgia, U.S.A.' Jock introduced him.

Gideon Barnard put his weight at two hundred and ten pounds, the same as Sean's. Sean shook his hand and from the touch of it knew he was not going to be disappointed.

'Glad to know you.' The American's voice was as soft as his grip was hard.

'Your servant, sir,' said Sean and hit the air where the man's head had been an instant before. He grunted as a fist slogged into his chest under his raised right arm and backed away warily. A soft sigh blew through the crowd and they settled down contentedly. This was what they had come to see.

The red wine was served early; it flew in tiny drops every time a punch was thrown or received. The fight flowed smoothly around the square of trampled grass. The sound of bone on flesh was followed immediately by the growl of the crowd and the seconds between were filled with the hoarse breathing of the two men and the slither, slither of their feet.

'Yaaaa!' Through the tense half silence ripped a roar like that of a mortally wounded foghorn. Sean and the American jumped apart startled, and turned with everyone else to face Candy's Hotel. Fernandes was with them again; his mountain-wide hairiness seemed to fill the whole veranda. He picked up one of Candy's best tables and holding it across his chest tore off two of its legs as though they were the wings of a roasted chicken.

'François, the bag!' shouted Sean. François snatched it up and threw it high over the heads of the crowd. Sean held his breath as he followed its slow trajectory, then he blew out again with relief as he saw Mbejane field the pass and vanish around the corner of the Hotel.

'Yaaaa!' Fernandes gave tongue again. With a table leg in each hand he charged the crowd that stood between him and Sean; it scattered before him.

'Do you mind if we finish this some other time?' Sean asked the American.

'Of course not. Any time at all. I was just about to leave myself.'

Duff reached through the ropes and caught Sean's arm.

'There's someone looking for you—or had you noticed?'

'It might just be his way of showing friendliness.'

'I wouldn't bet on it—are you coming?'

Fernandes rumbled to a halt, braced himself and threw. The table leg whirred like a rising pheasant an inch over Sean's head, ruffling his hair with the wind of its passage.

'Lead on, Duff.' Sean was uncomfortably conscious of the fact that Fernandes was again in motion towards him, still armed with a long oak, and that three very thin ropes were all that stood between them. The speed that Sean and Duff turned on then made Mr Blair's earlier exhibition seem like that of a man with both legs in plaster. Fernandes, carrying top weight as he was, never looked like catching them.

François came up to the Candy Deep just after midday with the news that the Portuguese, after beating three of his sponsors into insensibility, had left on the noon coach back to Kimberley.

Duff uncocked his rifle. 'Thanks, Franz, we were waiting lunch for him. I thought he might call on us.'

'Have you counted the takings?'

'Yes, your commission is in that paper bag on the table.'

'Thanks, man, let's go down and celebrate.'

'You go and have one for us.'

'Hey, Duff, you promised—' Sean started.

'I said later—in three or four weeks' time. Now we've got a little work to do, like digging a trench fifty feet deep and three hundred yards long.'

'We could start first thing tomorrow.'

'You want to be rich, don't you?' asked Duff.

'Sure, but—'

'You want nice things, like English suits, French champagne and—'

'Yes, but—'

'Well, stop arguing, get off your fat arse and come with me.'

12

The Chinese use firecrackers to keep the demons away. Duff and Sean applied the same principle. They kept the mill running; as long as its clunking carried across the valley to the ears of their creditors all was well. Everyone accepted the fact that they were working a payable reef and left them alone, but the money they fed into the front of the mill had halved its value by the time it came out of the other side in those pathetic little yellow pellets.

In the meantime they cut their trench, tearing into the earth in a race against Settlement Day. They fired dynamite and as the last stones dropped back out of the sky they were in again, coughing with the fumes, to clear the loosened rock and start drilling the next set of holes. It was summer, the days were long and while it was light they worked. Some evenings they lit the last fuses by lantern light.

Sand fell through the hour-glass faster than they had bargained for, the money dribbled away and on the fifteenth of February Duff shaved himself, changed his shirt and went to see Candy about another loan. Sean watched him walk away down the slope. They had sold the horses a week before, and he said a small prayer–the first for many years.

Duff came back in the late morning. He stood on the edge of the trench and watched Sean tamping in the charges for the next cut. Sean's back was shiny with sweat; each individual muscle standing out in relief, swelling and subsiding as he moved.

'That's the stuff, laddie, keep at it.'

Sean looked up with dust-reddened eyes. 'How much?' he asked.

'Another fifty, and this is the last–or so she threatens.'

Sean's eyes fastened on the package Duff held under his arm.

'What's that?'

He could see the stains seeping through the brown paper and the saliva flooded out from under his tongue.

'Prime beef chops–no mealie meal porridge for lunch today.' Duff grinned at him.

'Meat.' Sean caressed the word. 'Underdone–bleeding a little as you bite it, a trace of garlic, just enough salt.'

'And you beside me, singing in the wilderness,' agreed Duff. 'Cut out the poetry, light those fuses and let's go and eat.'

An hour later they walked side by side along the bottom of their trench, Mbejane and his Zulus crowding behind them. Sean belched. 'Ah, pleasant memory, I'll never be able to look another plate of mealie meal in the face again.'

They reached the end, where the freshly broken earth and rock lay piled. Sean felt the thrill start in his hands, tingle up his arms and squeeze his lungs. Then Duff's fingers were biting into his shoulder; he could feel them trembling.

It looked like a snake, a fat grey python crawling down one wall of the trench, disappearing under the heap of new rubble and out the other side.

Duff moved first, he knelt and picked up a piece of the reef, a big grey mottled lump of it and kissed it.

'It must be it, hey, Duff? It must be the Leader?'

'It's the end of the rainbow.'

'No more mealie meal,' Sean said softly and Duff laughed. Then Sean laughed. Wildly, crazily, together they howled their triumph.

13

'Let me hold it again,' said Sean.

Duff passed it across to him.

'Hell, it's heavy.'

'There's nothing heavier,' agreed Duff.

'Must be all of fifty pounds.'

Sean held the bar in two hands, it was the size of a cigar box. 'More!'

'We've retrieved all our losses in two days' working.'

'And some to spare, I'd say.'

Sean placed the gold bar on the table between them. It shone with little yellow smiles in the lantern light and Duff leaned forward and stroked it; its surface felt knobbly from the rough casting.

'I can't keep my hands off it,' he confessed sheepishly.

'I can't either!' Sean reached out to touch it. 'We'll be able to pay Candy out for the claims in another week or two.'

Duff started. 'What did you say?'

'I said we'd be able to pay Candy out.'

'I thought I wasn't hearing things.' Duff patted his arm indulgently. 'Listen to me, laddie, I'll try and put it simply. How long have we got the option on these claims for?'

'Three years.'

'Correct—now the next question. How many people on these fields have any money?'

Sean looked mystified. 'Well, we have now and—and . . .'

'No one else, that is until Hradsky gets back,' Duff finished for him.

'What about the Heyns brothers? They've cut open the Leader Reef.'

'Certainly, but it won't do them any good, not until their machinery arrives from England.'

'Go on!' Sean wasn't quite sure where Duff was leading.

'Instead of paying Candy out now we are going to use this'—he patted the gold bar—'and all its little brothers to buy every likely claim we can lay our hands on. For a start there are Doc Sutherland's claims between us and the Jack and Whistle. Then we are going to order a couple of big ten-stamp mills and when those are spilling out gold we'll use it to buy land, finance brick works, engineering shops, transport companies and the rest. I've told you before there are more ways of making gold than digging for it.'

Sean was staring at him silently.

'Have you got a head for heights?' asked Duff.

Sean nodded.

'You're going to need it, because we are going up where the eagles fly—you are about to be a party to the biggest financial killing this country has ever seen.'

Sean lit one of Candy's cigars; his hand was a little unsteady.

'Don't you think it would be best to—well—not try and go too quickly. Hell, Duff, we've only been working the Leader for two days—'

'And we've made a thousand pounds,' Duff interrupted him. 'Listen to me, Sean, all my life I've been waiting for an opportunity like this. We're the first in on this field, it's as wide open as the legs of a whore. We're going to go in and take it.'

The next morning Duff had the good fortune to find Doc Sutherland early enough to talk business with him, before he began the day's drinking. Another hour would have been too late. As it was Doc knocked over his glass and fell out of his chair before he finally signed away twenty-five claims to Sean and Duff. The ink was hardly dry on the agreement before Duff was riding down to Ferrieras Camp to look for Ted Reynecke who held the claims on the other side of the Cousin Jack. Up on the Candy Deep Sean nursed the mill and bit his nails. Within seven days Duff had bought over one hundred claims and committed them to forty thousand pounds in debts.

'Duff, you're going mad.' Sean pleaded with him. 'We'll lose everything again.'

'How much have we pulled out of the Candy Deep so far?'

'Four thousand.'

'Ten per cent of what we owe in ten days—and with a miserable little four-stamp mill at that. Hold on to your hat, laddie, tomorrow I'm going to sign up for the forty claims on the other side of the Jack and Whistle. I would have had them today but that damned Greek is holding out for a thousand pounds apiece. I'll have to give it to him, I suppose.'

Sean clutched his temples.

'Duff—please, man, we're in over our necks already.'

'Stand back, laddie, and watch the wizard work.'

'I'm going to bed—I suppose I'll have to take your shift again in the morning if you're determined to spend tomorrow ruining us.'

'That's not necessary, I've hired that Yankee—Curtis. You know, your sparring partner. It turns out he's a miner and he's willing to work for thirty a month. So you can come to town with me and watch me make you rich. I'm meeting the Greek at Candy's Hotel at nine o'clock.'

14

At nine o'clock Duff was talking and Sean sat silently on the edge of his chair; at ten the Greek had still not put in an appearance, Duff was moody and Sean was garrulous with relief. At eleven Sean wanted to go back to the mine.

'It's an omen, Duff, God looked down and he saw us sitting here all ready to make a terrible mistake. "No," he said, "I can't let them do it—I'll have the Greek break a leg—I can't let it happen to such nice boys."'

'Why don't you go and join a Trappist monastery?' Duff checked his watch. 'Come on, let's go!'

'Yes, sir!' Sean stood up with alacrity. 'We'll get back in plenty of time to clean the tables before lunch.'

'We're not going home, we're going to look for the Greek.'

'Now listen, Duff.'

'I'll listen later—come on.'

They rode across to the Bright Angels, left the horses outside and walked in together. It was dark in the canteen after the sunshine outside, but even in the gloom a group at one of the tables caught their attention immediately. The Greek sat with his back to them; the line of his parting seemed to be drawn with white chalk and a ruler through the oily black waves of his hair. Sean's eyes switched from him to the two men that sat across the table from him. Jews, there was no mistaking it, but there any similarity ended. The younger one was thin with smooth olive skin drawn tight across the bold bones of his cheeks; his lips were very red and his eyes, fringed with girl's lashes, were coffee-brown and melting. In the chair beside him was a man with a body that had been shaped in wax then held near a hot flame. Shoulders rounded to the verge of deformity drooped down over a pear-shaped body; with difficulty they supported the great Taj Mahal domed head. His hair was styled in the fashion of Friar Tuck, thick only around the ears. But the eyes—flickering yellow eyes—there was nothing comical about them.

'Hradsky,' hissed Duff, then his expression changed. He smiled as he walked across to the table.

'Hello, Nikky, I thought we had an appointment.'

The Greek twisted quickly in his chair.

'Mr Charleywood, I'm sorry, I was held up.'

'So I see, the woods are full of highwaymen.'

Sean saw the flush start to come out of Hradsky's collar then sink back again.

'Have you sold?' Duff asked.

The Greek nodded nervously.

'I'm sorry, Mr Charleywood, but Mr Hradsky paid my price and no haggling—cash money, too!'

Duff let his eyes wander across the table.

'Hello, Norman. How's your daughter?'

This time the flush escaped from Hradsky's shirt and flooded over his face. He opened his mouth, his tongue clucked twice, then he closed it again.

Duff smiled, he looked at the younger Jew. 'Say it for him, Max.'

The toffee eyes dropped to the table top. 'Mr Hradsky's daughter is very well.'

'I believe she married soon after my involuntary departure from Kimberley.'

'That is correct.'

'Wise move, Norman, much wiser than having your bully boys run me out of town. That wasn't very nice of you.'

No one spoke.

'We must get together some time and have a chat about old times. Until then, fa–fa–fare ye we–we–well.'

On the way back to the mine Sean asked, 'He's got a daughter? If she looks like him you were lucky to escape.'

'She didn't—she was like a bunch of ripe grapes with the bloom on them.'

'I can hardly credit it.'

'Neither could I. The only conclusion I could reach was that Max did that job for him as well.'

'What's the story about Max?'

'He's the Court Jester. Rumour has it that after Hradsky has finished hanging it out, Max shakes it for him.'

Sean laughed and Duff went on, 'But don't underestimate Hradsky. His stutter is his only weakness and with Max to talk for him he's overcome that. Beneath that monumental skull is a brain as quick and merciless as a guillotine. Now that he's arrived on this goldfield there's going to be some action; we'll have to gallop to keep up with him.'

Sean thought for a few seconds, then, 'Talking about action, Duff, now that we've lost the Greek's claims and won't have to use all our ready money satisfying him, let's give some thought to ordering new machinery to work the claims we have got.'

Duff grinned at him.

'I sent a telegram to London last week. There'll be a pair of brand new ten-stamp mills on the water to us before the end of the month.'

'Good God, why didn't you tell me?'

'You were worried enough as it was—I didn't want to break your heart.'

Sean opened his mouth to blast Duff out of the saddle, Duff winked at him before he could talk and Sean's lips trembled. He felt the laughter in his throat, he tried to stop it but it swamped him.

'How much is it going to cost us?' he howled through his mirth.

'If you ask that question once more, I'll strangle you.' Duff laughed back at him. 'Rest content in the knowledge that if we're going to have enough to honour the bills of lading when those mills arrive at Port Natal, we'll have to run a mountain of Leader Reef through our little rig during the next few weeks.'

'What about the payments on the new claims?'

'That's my department—I'll worry about that.'

And so their partnership crystallized; their relationship was established over the weeks that followed. Duff with his magic tongue and his charming, lopsided grin was the one who negotiated, who poured the oil on the storm waters churned up by impatient creditors. He was the storehouse of mining knowledge which Sean tapped daily, he was the conceiver of schemes, some wild, others brilliant. But his fleeting nervous energy was not designed to bring them to fruition. He lost interest quickly and it was Sean who finally rejected the least likely Charleywood brain children and adopted the others that were more deserving; once he had made himself stepfather to them, he reared as though they were his own. Duff was the theorist, Sean the practician. Sean could see why Duff had never found success before, but at the same time he recognized that without him he would be helpless. He watched with profound admiration the way that Duff used the barely sufficient flow of gold from the Candy Deep to keep the mill running, pay the tradesmen, meet the claim monies as they fell due and still save enough for the new machinery. He was a man juggling with live coals: hold one too long and it burns, let one fall and all fall. And Duff, deep-down-uncertain Duff, had a wall to put his back against. His speech never showed it but his eyes did when he looked at Sean. Sometimes he felt small next to Sean's big body and bigger determination, but it was a good feeling: like being on a friendly mountain.

They put up the new buildings around the mill: storerooms, a smelting house and cabins for Sean and Curtis. Duff was sleeping at the Hotel again. The location for the Natives sprawled haphazard down the back slope of the ridge, retreating a little each week as the white mountain of the mine dump grew and pushed it back. The whole valley was changing. Hradsky's new mills arrived and stood up along the ridge, tall and proud until their own dumps dwarfed them. Johannesburg, at first a mere pattern of surveyors' pegs, sucked the scattered encampments on to her grassy chequer-board and arranged them in a semblance of order along her streets.

The Diggers' Committee, its members tired of having to scrape their boots every time they went indoors, decreed public latrines be erected. Then, flushed with their own audacity, they built a bridge across the Natal Spruit, purchased a water cart to lay the dust on the streets of Johannesburg and passed a law prohibiting burials within half a mile of the city centre. Sean and Duff as members of the Committee felt it their duty to demonstrate their faith in the goldfield, so they bought twenty-five plots of ground in Johannesburg, five pounds each to be paid within six months. Candy recruited all her customers and in one weekend of frantic effort they razed her Hotel to the ground, packed every plank and sheet of iron on to their wagons, carried it a mile down the valley and re-erected it on her own land in the centre of the township. During the party she gave them on that Sunday night they nearly succeeded in dismantling it for the second time. Each day the roads from Natal and the Cape fed more wagons, more men into the Witwatersrand goldfield. Duff's suggestion that the Diggers' Committee levy a guinea a head from all newcomers to help finance the public works was reluctantly rejected, the general feeling being that if it led to civil rebellion there were more newcomers than Committee members and no one fancied being on the losing side.

One morning, when he came out to the mine, Duff brought a telegram with him. He handed it to Sean without comment. Sean read it. The machinery had arrived.

'Good God, it's three weeks early.'

'They must have had a downhill sea, or a following wind or whatever it is that makes ships go faster,' muttered Duff.

'Have we got enough to pay the bill?' asked Sean.

'No.'

'What are we going to do?'

'I'll go and see the little man at the bank.'

'He'll throw you out in the street.'

'I'll get him to give us a loan on the claims.'

'How the hell are you going to do that—we haven't paid for them yet.'

'That's what you call financial genius. I'll simply point out to him that they're worth five times what we bought them for.' Duff grinned. 'Can you and Curtis carry on here without me for today while I go and arrange it?'

'You arrange it and I'll happily give you a month's holiday.'

When Duff came back that afternoon he carried a paper with him. It had a red wax seal in the bottom corner, across the top it said 'Letter of Credit' and in the middle, standing out boldly from the mass of small print, was a figure that ended in an impressive string of noughts.

'You're a bloody marvel,' said Sean.

'Yes, I am rather, aren't I?' agreed Duff.

15

The Heyns brothers' machinery was on the same ship. Jock and Duff rode down to Port Natal together, hired a hundred wagons and brought it all back in one load.

'I'll tell you what I'll do with you, Jock, I'll wager you that we get our mills producing before you do. Loser pays for the transport on the whole shipment,' Duff challenged him when they reached Johannesburg where, in Candy's new bar-room, they were washing the dust out of their throats.

'You're on!'

'I'll go further, I'll put up a side bet of five hundred.'

Sean prodded Duff in the ribs.

'Gently, Duff—we can't afford it.' But Jock had already snapped up the bet.

'What do you mean we can't afford it?' whispered Duff. 'We've got nearly fifteen hundred pounds left on the letter of credit.'

Sean shook his head. 'No, we haven't.'

Duff pulled the paper from his inside pocket and tapped Sean's nose with it. 'There—read for yourself.'

Sean took it out of Duff's hand.

'Thanks, old chap. I'll go and pay the man now.'

'What man?'

'The man with the wagons.'

'What wagons?'

'The wagons that you and Jock hired in Port Natal. I've bought them.'

'The hell you say!'

'It was your idea to start a transport business. Just as soon as they've off loaded they'll be on their way again to pick up a shipment of coal from Dundee.'

Duff grinned at him. 'Don't you ever forget an idea? All right, laddie, off you go—we'll just have to win the bet, that's all.'

One of the mills they placed on the Candy Deep, the other on the new claims beyond the Cousin Jock Mine. They hired two gangs from among the unemployed in Johannesburg. Curtis supervised one of them and Sean the other, while Duff darted back and forth keeping an eye on both. Each time he passed the Cousin Jock he spent a few minutes checking Trevor and Jock's progress.

'They've got the edge on us, Sean; their boilers are up and holding pressure already,' he reported fretfully, but the next day he was smiling again.

'They didn't mix enough cement in the platform—it started to crumble as soon as they put the crusher on it. They'll have to cast it again. That set them back three or four days.'

The betting down in the canteens fluctuated sharply with each change of fortune. François came up to the Candy Deep one Saturday afternoon. He watched them work, made a suggestion or two, then remarked, 'They're giving three-to-one against you at the Bright Angels; they reckon the Heynses will be finished by next weekend.'

'Go down and put another five hundred pounds on for me,' Duff told him, and Sean shook his head despairingly.

'Don't worry, laddie, we can't lose—that amateur mining engineer, Jock Heyns, has assembled his crusher jaws all arse-about-face. I only noticed it this morning—he's in for a surprise when he tries to start up. He'll have to strip the whole damn rig.'

Duff was right—they brought both their mills into production a comfortable fifteen hours before the Heyns brothers. Jock rode over to see them with his jaw on his chest. 'Congratulations.'

'Thanks, Jock, did you bring your cheque book?'

'That's what I came to talk about. Can you give me a little time?'

'Your credit's good,' Sean assured him, 'come and have a drink and let me sell you some coal.'

'Ah, yes, I heard your wagons arrived back this morning. What price are you charging?'

'Fifteen pounds a hundredweight.'

'Good God. You bloody bandit, I bet it cost you less than five shillings a hundredweight.'

'A man's entitled to a reasonable profit,' protested Sean.

It had been a long hard pull up to the top of the hill but Sean and Duff had arrived at last and from there it was downhill all the way. The money poured in.

The geological freak that had bowed the Leader Reef away from the Main across the Candy Deep claims had, at the same time, enriched it—injected it full of the metal. François was there one evening when they put the ball of amalgam into the retort. His eyes bulged as the mercury boiled away; he stared at the gold the way a man watches a naked woman.

'*Gott!* I'm going to have to call you two thunders "Mister" from now on.'

'Have you ever seen richer reef, François?' Duff gloated.

François shook his head slowly. 'You know my theory about the reef being the bed of an old lake—well this bears it out. The kink in your reef must have been a deep trench along the bottom of the lake. It would have acted as a natural gold trap. Hell, man, what luck. With your eyes closed you have picked the plum out of the pudding. The Jock and Whistle is half as rich as this.'

Their overdraft at the bank dropped like a barometer in a hurricane; the tradesmen started greeting them with a smile; they gave Doc Sutherland a cheque which would have kept even him in whisky for a hundred years. Candy kissed them both when they paid her out in full, plus interest at seven per cent. Then she built herself a new Hotel, double storied, with a crystal chandelier in the dining-room and a magnificent bedroom suite on the second floor done out in maroon and gold. Duff and Sean rented it immediately but with the express understanding that if ever the Queen visited Johannesburg they would allow her to use it. In anticipation Candy called it the Victoria Rooms.

François, with a little persuasion, agreed to take over the running of the Candy Deep. He moved his possessions, one chest of clothes and four chests of patent medicines, across from the Jack and Whistle. Martin Curtis was the manager of the mill on the new claims; they named it the Little Sister Mine. Although not nearly as rich as the Candy Deep it was producing a sweet fortune each month, for Curtis worked as well as he fought.

By the end of August Sean and Duff had no more creditors: the claims were theirs, the mills were theirs and they had money to invest.

'We need an office of our own here in town. We can't run this show from our bedrooms,' complained Sean.

'You're right,' agreed Duff, 'we'll build on that corner plot nearest the market square.' The plan was for a modest little four-room building, but it finally expanded to two stories, stinkwood floors, oak panelling and twenty rooms. What they couldn't use they rented.

'The price of land has trebled in three months,' said Sean, 'and it's still moving.'

'You're right—now's the time to buy,' Duff agreed. 'You're starting to think along the right lines.'

'It was your idea.'

'Was it?' Duff looked surprised.

'Don't you remember your "up where the eagles fly" speech?'

'Don't you forget anything?' asked Duff.

They bought land: one thousand acres at Orange Grove and another thousand around Hospital Hill. Their transport wagons, now almost four hundred strong, plied in daily from Port Natal and Lourenço Marques. Their brickfields worked twenty-four hours a day, seven days a week, to try to meet the demand for building materials.

It took Sean almost a week to dissuade Duff from building an Opera House but he succeeded and instead they joined most of the other members of the Diggers' Committee in financing a different type of pleasure palace. At Duff's suggestion they called it the Opera House. They recruited performers not from the great companies of Europe but from the dock areas of Capetown and Port Natal and chose as the conductor a Frenchwoman of vast experience named Blue Bessie after the colour of her hair. The Opera House provided entertainment on two levels. For the members of the Committee and the other emergent rich there was a discreet side entrance, a lavishly furnished lounge where one could buy the finest champagne and discuss the prices on the Kimberley Stock Exchange, and beyond the lounge were a series of tastefully decorated retiring-rooms. For the workers there was a bare corridor to queue in, no choice for your money and a five-minute time limit. In one month the Opera House produced more gold than the Jack and Whistle mine.

By December there were millionaires in Johannesburg: Hradsky, the Heyns brothers, Karl Lochtkamper, Duff Charleywood, Sean Courtney and a dozen others. They owned the mines, the land, the buildings and the city: the aristocracy of the Witwatersrand, knighted with money and crowned with gold.

A week before Christmas, Hradsky, their unacknowledged but undoubted king, called them all to a meeting in one of the private lounges of Candy's Hotel.

'Who the hell does he think he is,' complained Jock Heyns, 'ordering us round like a bunch of kaffirs.'

'*Verdammt Juden!*' agreed Lochtkamper.

But they went, every last man of them, for whatever Hradsky did had the smell of money about it and they could no more resist it than a dog can resist the smell of a bitch in season.

Duff and Sean were the last to arrive and the room was already hazed with cigar smoke and tense with expectation. Hradsky sagged in one of the polished leather armchairs with Max sitting quietly beside him; his eyes flickered when Duff walked in but his expression never changed. When Duff and Sean had found chairs Max stood up. 'Gentlemen, Mr Hradsky has invited you here to consider a proposition.'

They leaned forward slightly in their chairs and there was a glitter in their eyes like hounds close upon the fox.

'From time to time it is necessary for men in your position to find capital to finance further ventures and to consolidate past gains; on the other hand those of us who have money lying idle will be seeking avenues for investment.' Max cleared his throat and looked at them with his sad brown eyes.

'Up to the present there has been no meeting-place for these mutual needs such as exists in the other centres of the financial world. Our nearest approach to it is the Stock Exchange at Kimberley which, I'm sure you will agree, is too far removed to be of practical use to us here at Johannesburg. Mr Hradsky has invited you here to consider the possibility of forming our own Exchange and, if you accept the idea, to elect a chairman and governing body.'

Max sat down and in the silence that followed they took up the idea, each one fitting it into his scheme of thinking, testing it with the question 'How will I benefit?'

'*Ja*, it's dom fine idea.' Lochtkamper spoke first.

'Yes, it's what we need.'

'Count me in.'

While they schemed and bargained, setting the fees, the place and the rules, Sean watched their faces. The faces of bitter men, happy men, quiet ones and big bull-roarers but all with one common feature—that greedy glitter in the eyes. It was midnight before they finished.

Max stood up again.

'Gentlemen, Mr Hradsky would like you to join him in a glass of champagne to celebrate the formation of our new enterprise.'

'This I can't believe; the last time he paid for drinks was back in 'sixty,' declared Duff. 'Quickly somebody—find a waiter before he changes his mind.'

Hradsky hooded his eyes to hide the hatred in them.

16

With its own Stock Exchange and bordel Johannesburg became a city. Even Kruger recognized it; he deposed the Diggers' Committee and sent in his own police force, sold monopolies for essential mining supplies to members of his family and Government, and set about revising his tax laws with special attention to mining profits. Despite Kruger's efforts to behead the gold-laying goose, the city grew, overflowed the original Government plots and spread bawling and blustering out into the surrounding veld.

Sean and Duff grew with it. Their way of life changed swiftly; their visits to the mines fell to a weekly inspection and they left it to their hired men. A steady river of gold poured down from the ridge to their offices on Eloff Street, for the men they hired were the best that money could find.

Their horizons closed in to encompass only the two panelled offices, the Victoria Rooms and the Exchange. Yet within that world Sean found a thrill that he had never dreamed existed. He had been oblivious to it during the first feverish months; he had been so absorbed in laying the foundations that he could spare no energy for enjoying or even noticing it.

Then one day he felt the first voluptuous tickle of it. He had sent to the bank for a land title document he needed, expecting it to be delivered by a junior clerk—but instead the sub-manager and a senior clerk filed it respectfully into his office. It was an exquisite physical shock and it gave him a new awareness. He noticed the way men looked at him as he passed them on the street. He realized suddenly that over fifteen hundred human beings depended on him for their livelihood.

There was satisfaction in the way a path cleared for him and Duff as they crossed the floor of the Exchange each morning to take their places in the reserved leather armchairs of the members' lounge. When Duff and he leaned together and talked quietly before the trading began, even the other big fish watched them. Hradsky with his fierce eyes hooded by sleepy lids, Jock and Trevor Heyns, Karl Lochtkamper—any of them would have given a day's production from their mines to overhear those conversations.

'Buy!' said Sean.

'Buy! Buy! Buy!' clamoured the pack and the prices jumped as they hit them, then slumped back as they sucked their money away and put it to work elsewhere.

Then one March morning in 1886 the thrill became so acute it was almost an orgasm. Max left the chair at Norman Hradsky's side and crossed the lounge towards them. He stopped in front of them, lifted his sad eyes off the patterned carpet and almost apologetically proffered a loose sheaf of papers.

'Good morning, Mr Courtney. Good morning, Mr Charleywood. Mr Hradsky has asked me to bring this new share issue to your attention. Perhaps you would be interested in these reports, which are, of course, confidential, but he feels they are worthy of your support.'

You have power when you can force a man who hates you to ask for your favours. After the first advance by Hradsky they worked together often. Hradsky never acknowledged their existence by word or look. Each morning Duff called a cheerful greeting across the full width of the lounge, 'Hello, chatterbox,' or 'Sing for us, Norman.'

Hradsky's eyes would flicker and he would sag a little lower into his chair, but before the bell started the day's trading Max would stand up and come across to them, leaving his master staring into the empty fireplace. A few soft sentences exchanged and Max would walk back to Hradsky's side.

Their combined fortunes were irresistible: in one wild morning's trading alone they added another fifty thousand to their store of pounds.

An untaught boy handles his first rifle like a toy. Sean was twenty-two. The power he held was a more deadly weapon than any rifle, and much sweeter, more satisfying to use. It was a game at first with the Witwatersrand as a chessboard, men and gold for pieces. A word or a signature on a slip of paper would set the gold jingling and the men scampering. The consequences were remote and all that mattered was the score, the score chalked up in black figures on a bank statement. Then in that same March he was made to realize that a man wiped off the board could not be laid back in the box with as much compassion as a carved wooden knight.

Karl Lochtkamper, the German with a big laugh and a happy face, laid himself open. He needed money to develop a new property on the east end of the Rand; he borrowed and signed short-term notes on his loans, certain that he could extend them if necessary. He borrowed secretly from the men he thought he could trust. He was vulnerable and the sharks smelt him out.

'Where is Lochtkamper getting his money?' asked Max.

'Do you know?' asked Sean.

'No, but I can guess.'

Then the next day Max came back to them again.

'He has eight notes out. Here is the list,' he whispered sadly. 'Mr Hradsky will buy the ones that have a cross against them. Can you handle the rest?'

'Yes,' said Sean.

They closed on Karl on the last day of the quarter; they called the loans and gave him twenty-four hours to meet them. Karl went to each of the three banks in turn.

'I'm sorry, Mr Lochtkamper, we have loaned over our budget for this quarter.'

'Mr Hradsky is holding your notes—I'm sorry.'

'I'm sorry, Mr Lochtkamper, Mr Charleywood is one of our directors.'

Karl Lochtkamper rode back to the Exchange. He walked across the floor and into the lounge for the last time. He stood in the centre of the big room, his face grey, his voice bitter and broken.

'Let Jesus have this much mercy on you when your time comes. Friends! My friends! Sean, how many times have we drunk together? And you, Duff, was it yesterday you shook my hand?'

Then he went back across the floor, out through the doors. His suite in the Great North Hotel wasn't fifty yards from the Exchange. In the members' lounge they heard the pistol shot quite clearly.

That night Duff and Sean got drunk together in the Victoria Rooms.

'Why did he have to do it? Why did he have to kill himself?'

'He didn't,' answered Duff. 'He was a quitter.'

'If I'd known he was going to do that—my God, if only I'd known.'

'Damn it, man, he took a chance and lost—it's not our fault. He would have done the same to us.'

'I don't like this—it's dirty. Let's get out, Duff.'

'Someone gets knocked down in the rush and you want to cry "enough!"'

'It's different now somehow, it wasn't like this at the start.'

'Yes, and it'll be different in the morning. Come on, laddie, I know what you need.'

'Where are we going?'

'To the Opera House.'

'What will Candy say?'

'Candy doesn't have to know.'

Duff was right; it was different in the morning. There was the usual hurly-burly of work at the office and some tense action at the Exchange. He thought about Karl only once during the day and somehow it didn't seem to matter so much. They sent him a nice wreath.

He had faced the reality of the game he was playing. He had considered the alternative which was to get out with the fortune he had already made; but to do that would mean giving up the power he held. The addiction was already seated too deeply, he could not deny it. So his subconscious opened, sucked in his conscience and swallowed it deep down into its gut. He could feel it struggling there sometimes, but the longer it stayed swallowed the more feeble those struggles became. Duff comforted him: Duff's words were like a gastric juice that helped to digest that lump in the gut and he had not yet learned that what Duff said and what Duff did were not necessarily what Duff believed.

Play the game without mercy, play to win.

17

Duff stood with his back to the fireplace in Sean's office smoking a cheroot while they waited for the carriage to take them up to the Exchange. The fire behind him silhouetted his slimly tapered legs with the calves encased in polished black leather. He still wore his top coat, for the winter morning was cold. It fell open at his throat to show a diamond that sparkled and glowed in his cravat.

'. . . you get used to a woman somehow,' he was saying. 'I've known Candy four years now and yet it seems I've been with her all my life.'

'She's a fine girl,' Sean agreed absently as he dipped his pen and scribbled his signature on the document in front of him.

'I'm thirty-five now,' Duff went on. 'If I'm ever to have a son of my own . . .'

Sean laid down the pen deliberately and looked up at him; he was starting to grin.

'The man said to me once "They take you into their soft little minds" and again he said "They don't share, they possess". Is this a new tune I hear?'

Duff shifted uneasily from one foot to the other.

'Things change,' he defended himself. 'I'm thirty five . . .'

'You're repeating yourself,' Sean accused and Duff smiled weakly.

'Well, the truth is . . .'

He never finished the sentence; hooves beat urgently in the street outside and both their faces swung in the direction of the window.

'Big hurry!' said Sean coming quickly to his feet. 'Big trouble!' He crossed to the window. 'It's Curtis, and by his face it's not good news he brings.'

There were voices outside the door raised in agitation and the quick rush of feet, then Martin Curtis burst into the room without knocking. He wore a miner's overall and splattered gumboots. 'We've hit a mud rush on the ninth level.'

'How bad?' Duff snapped.

'Bad enough—it's flooded right back to number eight.'

'Jesus, that will take two months at least to clear,' Sean exclaimed. 'Does anyone else in town know—have you told anyone?'

'I came straight here—Cronje and five men were up at the face when it blew.'

'Get back there immediately,' ordered Sean, 'but ride quietly, we don't want the whole world to know there's trouble. Don't let a soul off the property. We must have time to sell out.'

'Yes, Mr Courtney.' Curtis hesitated. 'Cronje and five others were hit by the rush. Shall I send word to their wives?'

'Can't you understand English? I don't want a whisper of this to get out before ten o'clock. We're got to have time.'

'But, Mr Courtney—' Curtis was appalled. He stood staring at Sean and Sean felt the sick little stirring of guilt. Six men drowned in treacle-thick mud . . . He made an irresolute gesture with his hands.

'We can't—' He stopped and Duff cut in.

'They're dead now, and they'll be just as dead when we tell their wives at ten o'clock. Get going, Curtis.'

They sold their shares in the Little Sister within an hour of the start of trading and a week later they bought them back at half the price. Two months later the Little Sister was back on full production again.

18

They split their land at Orange Grove into plots and sold them, all but a hundred acres and on that they started building a house. Into the designing of it they poured their combined energy and imagination. With money Duff seduced the horticulturist of the Cape Town Botanical Gardens and brought him up by express coach. They showed him the land.

'Make me a garden,' said Duff.

'The whole hundred acres?'

'Yes.'

'It'll cost a pretty penny.'

'That is no problem.'

The carpets came from Persia, the wood from the Knysna forests and the marble from Italy. On the gates at the entrance to the main drive they engraved the words 'At Xanadu did Kublai Khan a stately pleasure dome decree'. As the gardener had predicted, it all cost a pretty penny. Each afternoon when the Exchange closed they would drive up together and watch the builders at work. One day Candy came with them and they showed it off to her like two small boys.

'This will be the ballroom.' Sean bowed to her. 'May I have the pleasure of this dance?'

'Thank you, sir.' She curtsied, then swept away on his arm across the unsanded boards.

'This will be the staircase,' Duff told her, 'marble—black and white marble—and there on the main landing in a glass case will be Hradsky's head, beautifully mounted with an apple in his mouth.'

They climbed laughing up the rough concrete ramp.

'This is Sean's room—the bed is being made of oak, thick oak to withstand punishment.' They trooped with linked arms down the passage.

'And this is my room—I was thinking of a solid gold bath but the builders says it's too heavy and Sean says it's too vulgar. Look at that view; from here you can see out across the whole valley. I could lie in bed in the mornings and read the prices in the Exchange floor with a telescope.'

'It's lovely,' Candy said dreamily.

'You like it?'

'Oh yes.'

'It could be your room too.'

Candy started to blush and then her face tightened with annoyance. 'He was right—you are vulgar.'

She started for the door and Sean fumbled for his cigars to cover his embarrassment. With two quick steps Duff caught her and turned her to face him. 'You sweet idiot, that was a proposal.'

'Let me go.' Near to tears she twisted in his hands. 'I don't think you're funny.'

'Candy—I'm serious. Will you marry me?'

The cigar dropped out of Sean's mouth but he caught it before it hit the ground. Candy was standing very still, her eyes fastened on Duff's face.

'Yes or no—will you marry me?'

She nodded once slowly and then twice very fast.

Duff looked at Sean over his shoulder. 'Leave us, laddie.'

On the way back to town Candy had regained her voice. She chattered happily and Duff answered her with his lopsided grin. Sean hunched morosely in one corner of the carriage. His cigar was burning unevenly and he threw it out of the window.

'You'll let me keep the Victoria Rooms, I hope, Candy.'

There was a silence.

'What do you mean?' asked Duff.

'Two's company,' Sean answered.

'Oh, no,' Candy cxclaimed.

'It's your house as well.' Duff spoke sharply.

'I give it to you—a wedding present.'

'Oh shut up,' Duff grinned, 'it's big enough for all of us.'

Candy crossed quickly to Sean's seat and put her hand on his shoulder.

'Please—we've been together a long time. We'd be lonely without you.'

Sean grunted.

'Please!'

'He'll come,' said Duff.

'Please.'

'Oh, well—' Sean frowned ungraciously.

19

They went racing at Milnerton. Candy with a hat full of ostrich feathers, Sean and Duff with pearl grey toppers and gold beads on their canes.

'You can pay for your wedding gown by putting fifty guineas on Trade Wind! She can't lose—' Duff told Candy.

'What about Mr Hradsky's new filly? I've heard she's a good bet,' Candy asked and Duff frowned.

'You want to go over to the enemy?'

'I thought you and Hradsky were almost partners.' Candy twirled her parasol. 'From the rumours I've heard you work with him all the time.'

Mbejane slowed the carriage as they ran into the crush of pedestrians and coaches outside the Turf Club gates.

'Well you've heard wrong both times. His Sun Dancer will never hold Trade Wind over the distance, she's bred too light in the legs. Frenchified with Huguenot blood; she'll fade within the mile. And as far as Hradsky being our partner, we throw him an occasional bone. Isn't that right, Sean?'

Sean was watching Mbejane's back. The Zulu, in loin cloths only and his spears laid carefully on the boards at his feet, was handling the horses with an easy familiarity. They cocked their ears back to catch his voice, deep and soft, as he talked to them.

'Isn't that right, Sean?' Duff repeated.

'Of course,' agreed Sean vaguely. 'You know—I think I'll get Mbejane a livery. He looks out of place in those skins.'

'Well, some of the other horses from the same stud were stayers. Sun Honey won the Cape Derby twice and Eclipse showed up the English stock in the Metropolitan Handicap last year,' Candy argued.

'Huh,' Duff smiled his superiority, 'well, you can take my word for it that Trade Wind will walk the main race today and he'll be back in his stable before Sun Dancer sees the finishing post.'

'Maroon and gold—the same as our racing colours,' Sean muttered thoughtfully. 'That would go very well with his black skin, perhaps a turban with an ostrich feather in it.'

'What the hell are you talking about?' complained Duff.

'Mbejane's livery.'

They left the carriage in the reserved area and went through to the members' grandstand, Candy sailing prettily between her escorts.

'Well, Duff, we've got the nicest looking woman here today.'

'Thank you.' Candy smiled up at Sean.

'Is that why you keep trying to look down the front of her dress?' challenged Duff.

'You filthy-minded beast.' Sean was shocked.

'Don't deny it,' Candy teased, 'but I find it very flattering—you're welcome.'

They moved through the throng of butterfly-coloured dresses and stiffly-suited men. A ripple of greetings moved with them.

'Morning, Mr Courtney.' The accent was on the 'Mister'. 'How's your Trade Wind for the big race?'

'Put your pants on him.'

'Hello, Duff, congratulations on your engagement.'

'Thanks, Jock, it's time you took the plunge as well.'

They were rich, they were young, they were handsome and all the world admired them. Sean felt good, with a pretty girl on his arm and a friend walking beside him.

'There's Hradsky—let's go across and engage in a little hog-baiting,' Duff suggested.

'Why do you hate him so much?' Candy asked softly.

'Look at him and answer your own question. Have you ever seen anything more pompous, joyless and unlovable?'

'Oh, leave him alone, Duff, don't spoil the day. Let's go down to the paddock.'

'Come on!' Duff steered them across to where Hradsky and Max were standing alone by the rail of the track.

'Salome, Norman, and peace to you also, Maximilian.'

Hradsky nodded and Max murmured sadly; his lashes touched his cheeks as he blinked.

'I noticed you two chatting away and thought I would come across and listen to your stimulating repartee.'

He received no answer and went on. 'I saw your new filly exercising on the practice track yesterday evening and I said to myself, Norman's got a girl friend—that's what it is—he's bought a hack for his lady. But now they tell me you are going to race her. Oh, Norman, I wish you'd consult me before you do these silly things. You're an impetuous little devil at times.'

'Mr Hradsky is confident that Sun Dancer will make a reasonable showing today,' Max murmured.

'I was about to offer you a side bet, but being a naturally kind-hearted person, I feel it would be taking an unfair advantage.'

A small crowd had gathered round them listening with anticipation. Candy tugged gently at Duff's elbow trying to lead him away.

'I thought five hundred guineas would be acceptable to Norman.' Duff shrugged. 'But let's forget it.'

Hradsky made a fierce little sign with his hands and Max interpreted smoothly. 'Mr Hradsky suggests a thousand.'

'Rash, Norman, extremely rash.' Duff sighed. 'But I suppose I must accommodate you.'

They walked down to the refreshment pavilion. Candy was quiet awhile, then she said, 'An enemy like Mr Hradsky is a luxury that even you two gods can't afford. Why don't you leave him alone?'

'It's a hobby of Duff's,' explained Sean as they found seats at one of the tables. 'Waiter—bring us a bottle of Pol Roger.'

Before the big race they went down to the paddock. A steward opened the wicket gate for them and they passed into the ring of circling horses. A gnome in silk of maroon and gold came to meet them and touched his cap then stood awkwardly fingering his whip.

'He looks good this morning sir.' The little man nodded at Trade Wind. There was a dark patch of sweat on the horse's shoulder and he mouthed the snaffle, lifting his feet delicately. Once he snorted and rolled his eyes in mock terror.

'He's got an edge on him, sir, eager kind of—if you follow me.'

'I want you to win, Harry,' said Duff.

'So do I, sir, I'll do my best.'

'There's a thousand guineas for you if you do.'

'A thousand—' the jockey repeated on an outgoing breath.

Duff looked across to where Hradsky and Max were standing talking to their trainer. He caught Hradsky's eye, glanced significantly at Hradsky's honey-coloured filly and shook his head sympathetically.

'Win for me, Harry,' he said softly.

'That I will, sir!'

The groom led the big stallion across to them and Sean flicked the jockey up into the saddle.

'Good luck.'

Harry settled his cap and gathered up the reins; he winked at Sean, his hobgoblin face wrinkling in a grin.

'There's no better luck than a thousand guineas, sir, if you follow me.'

'Come on.' Duff caught Candy's arm. 'Let's get a place at the rail.'

They hustled her out of the paddock and across the members' enclosure. The rail was crowded but a place opened for them respectfully and no one jostled them.

'I can't understand you two,' Candy laughed breathlessly. 'You make an extravagant bet, then you fix it so you can get nothing even if you win.'

'Money's not the problem,' Duff assured her.

'He won that much from me at Klabejas last night,' Sean commented. 'If Trade Wind beats the filly his prize will be the look on Hradsky's face—the loss of a thousand guineas will hurt him like a kick between the legs.'

The horses came parading past, stepping high next to the grooms who held them, then they turned free and cantered back, dancing sideways, throwing their heads, shining in the sunlight like the bright silk upon their backs. They moved away round the curve of the track.

The crowd rustled with excitement, a bookmaker's voice carried over the buzz.

'Twenty-to-one bar two. Sun Dancer at fives. Trade Wind even money.'
Duff showed his teeth as he smiled. 'That's right, you tell the people.'
Candy twisted her gloves nervously and looked up at Sean.
'You there in the grandstand–can you see what they're doing?'
'They're in line now, moving up together–it looks as though they'll get away
first time,' Sean told her without taking his binoculars from his eyes. 'Yes,
there they go–they're away!'
'Tell me, tell me,' commanded Candy, pounding Sean's shoulder.
'Harry's showing in front already–can you see the filly, Duff?'
'I saw a flash of green in the pack–yes, there she is lying sixth or seventh.'
'What horse is that next to Trade Wind?'
'That's Hamilton's gelding, don't worry about him, he won't last to the
turn.'
The frieze of horses, their heads going like hammers and the dust lifting pale
and thin behind them, were framed by the guide rail and the white mine
dumps beyond them. Like a string of dark beads they moved up the back
stretch and then bunched in the straight.
'Trade Wind's still there–I think he's making ground–the gelding's
finished and no sign of the filly yet.'
'Yes! There she is, Duff, wide on the outside. She's moving up.'
'Come on, my darling–' Duff half whispered. 'Let's see you foot it now.'
'She's clear of the pack–she's coming up, Duff, she's coming up fast,' Sean
warned.
'Come on, Trade Wind, hold her off,' Duff pleaded. 'Keep her there, boy.'
The pounding of the hooves reached them now, a sound like distant surf,
but rising sharply. The colours showed, emerald green above a honey skin and
maroon and gold leading on the bay.
'Trade Wind–come on Trade Wind,' shrieked Candy. Her hat flopped over
her eyes as she hopped; she ripped it off impatiently and her hair tumbled to
her shoulders.
'She's catching him, Duff!'
'Give him the whip, Harry, for Christ's sake–the whip, man.'
The hoof beats crescendoed, thundered up to them, then passed. The filly's
nose was at Harry's boot, creeping steadily forward, now level with Trade
Wind's heaving shoulder.
'The whip, God damn you,' screamed Duff, 'give him the whip.'
Harry's right arm moved, fast as a mamba–crack, crack; they heard the whip
above the howling crowd, above the drumming of hooves and the bay jumped
at its sting. Like a pair in harness the two horses swept over the finishing line.
'Who won?' Candy asked as though she were in pain.
'I couldn't see, damn it,' Duff answered.
'Nor could I–' Sean took out his handkerchief and wiped his forehead. 'That
didn't do my heart any good–as François would say. Have a cigar, Duff.'
'Thanks–I need one.'
Everyone in the crowd turned to face the board above the judges' box and an
uneasy silence held them.
'Why do they take such a long time to make up their minds?' complained
Candy. 'I'm so upset that I can only last a minute before I visit the Ladies'
Room.'
'The numbers are going up,' shouted Sean.
'Who is it?' Candy jumped to try and see over the heads of the crowd then

stopped hurriedly with an expression of alarm on her face.

'Number Sixteen,' bellowed Duff and Sean together, 'it's Trade Wind!'

Sean punched Duff in the chest and Duff leaned over and snapped Sean's cigar in half. Then they caught Candy between them and hugged her. She let out a careful shriek and fought her way out of their arms. 'Excuse me,' she said and fled.

'Let me buy you a drink.' Sean lit the mutilated stump of his cigar.

'No, it's my honour, I insist.' Duff took his arm and they walked with big satisfied grins towards the pavilion. Hradsky was sitting at one of the tables with Max. Duff walked up behind him, lifted his top hat off his head with one hand and with the other ruffled Hradsky's few remaining hairs.

'Never mind, Norman, you can't win all the time.'

Hradsky turned slowly. He retrieved his hat and smoothed back his hair, his eyes glittered yellow.

'He's going to talk,' whispered Duff excitedly.

'I agree with you, Mr Charleywood, you can't win all the time,' said Norman Hradsky. It came out quite clearly with only a small catch on the 'c's'–they were always difficult letters for him. He stood up, put his hat back on his head and walked away.

'I will have a cheque delivered to your office early on Monday morning,' Max told them quietly without taking his eyes off the table. Then he stood up and followed Hradsky.

20

Sean came through from the bathroom, his beard in wild disorder and a bath-towel around his wait.

> 'The famous Duke of York
> He had ten thousand men
> He marched them up to the top of the hill
> And he marched them down again.'

He sang as he poured bay rum from a cut-glass bottle into his cupped hands and rubbed it into his hair. Duff sat in one of the gilt chairs watching him. Sean combed his hair carefully then smiled at himself in the mirror.

'You magnificent creature,' Sean told his reflection.

'You're getting fat,' Duff grunted.

Sean looked hurt. 'It's muscle.'

'You've got a backside on you like a hippopotamus.'

Sean removed his towel and turned his back to the mirror; he surveyed it over his shoulder.

'I need a heavy hammer to drive a long nail,' he protested.

'Oh, no,' groaned Duff. 'Your wit at this time of the morning is like pork for breakfast, heavy on the stomach.'

Sean took a silk shirt out of his drawer, held it like a toreador's cape, made two passes and swirled it on to his back with a half veronica.

'*Olé!*' applauded Duff wryly. Sean pulled on his trousers and sat to fit his boots.

'You're in a nice mood this morning,' he told Duff.

'I've just come through an emotional hurricane!'

'What's the trouble?'

'Candy wants a church wedding.'

'Is that bad?'

'Well, it's not good.'

'Why?'

'Is your memory so short?'

'Oh, you mean your other wife.'

'That's right, my other wife.'

'Have you told Candy about her?'

'Good God, no.' Duff looked horrified.

'Yes, I see your problem—what about Candy's husband? Doesn't that even the score between you?'

'No, he has gone to his reward.'

'Well, that's convenient. Does anyone else know you're married already?' Duff shook his head.

'What about François?'

'No, I never told him.'

'Well, what's your problem—take her down to the church and marry her.' Duff looked uncomfortable.

'I don't mind marrying a second time in a magistrate's court, it would only be a couple of old Dutchmen I'd be cheating, but to go into a church—' Duff shook his head.

'I'd be the only one who'd know,' said Sean.

'You and the headman.'

'Duff,' Sean beamed at him. 'Duff, my boy, you have scruples—this is amazing!'

Duff squirmed a little in his chair.

'Let me think.' Sean held his forehead dramatically. 'Yes, yes, it's coming to me—that's it.'

'Come on, tell me.' Duff sat on the edge of his chair.

'Go to Candy and tell her it's all fixed, not only are you prepared to marry her in a church but you're even going to build your own church.'

'That's wonderful,' Duff murmured sarcastically, 'that's the way out of my difficulties all right.'

'Let me finish.' Sean started filling his silver cigar case. 'You also tell her that you want a civil ceremony as well—I believe that's what royalty do. Tell her that, it should win her over.'

'I still don't follow you.'

'Then you build your own chapel at Xanadu—we can find a distinguished-looking character, dress him up in a dog collar and teach him the right words. That keeps Candy happy. Immediately after the service the priest takes the coach for Capetown. You take Candy down to the magistrate's office and that keeps you happy.'

Duff looked stunned then slowly his face broke into a great happy smile. 'Genius—pure inspired genius.'

Sean buttoned his waistcoat. 'Think nothing of it. And now if you'll excuse me I'll go and do some work—one of us has to make sufficient to allow you to indulge these strange fancies of yours.'

Sean shrugged on his coat, picked up his cane and swung it. The gold head gave it a balance like a hand-made shotgun. The silk next to his skin and the halo of bay rum round his head made him feel good.

He went down the stairs. Mbejane had the carriage waiting for him in the hotel yard. The body tilted slightly at Sean's weight and the leather upholstery welcomed him with a yielding softness. He lit his first cigar of the day and Mbejane smiled at him.

'I see you, Nkosi.'

'I see you also, Mbejane, what is that lump on the side of your head?'

'Nkosi, I was a little drunk, otherwise that ape of Basuto would never have touched me with his fighting stick.'

Mbejane rolled the carriage smoothly out of the yard and into the street.

'What were you fighting about?'

Mbejane shrugged. 'Must a man have a reason to fight?'

'It is usual.'

'It is in my memory that there was a woman,' said Mbejane.

'That is also usual–who won this fight?'

'The man bled a little, his friends took him away. The woman, when I left, was smiling in her sleep.'

Sean laughed, then ran his eyes over the undulating plain of Mbejane's bare back. It was definitely not in keeping. He hoped his secretary had remembered to speak to the tailor. They pulled up in front of his offices. One of his clerks hurried down off the veranda and opened the door of the carriage.

'Good morning, Mr Courtney.'

Sean went up the stairs with his clerk running ahead of him like a hunting dog.

'Good morning, Mr Courtney,' another polite chorus from the row of desks in the main office. Sean waved his cane at them and went through into his own office. His portrait leered at him from above the fireplace and he winked at it.

'What have we this morning, Johnson?'

'These requisitions, sir, and the pay cheques, sir, and development reports from the engineers, sir, and . . .'

Johnson was a greasy-haired little man in a greasy-looking ulpaca coat, with each 'sir' he made a greasy little bow. He was efficient so Sean hired him, but that didn't mean he liked him.

'You got a stomach ache, Johnson?'

'No, sir.'

'Well, for God's sake, stand up straight, man.'

Johnson shot to attention.

'Now let's have them one at a time.'

Sean dropped into his chair. At this time of the day came the grind. He hated the paper work and so he tackled it with grim concentration, making random checks on the long rows of figures, trying to associate names with faces and querying requisitions that appeared exorbitant until finally he wrote his signature between the last of Johnson's carefully pencilled crosses and threw his pen on to the desk.

'What else is there?'

'Meeting with Mr Maxwell from the Bank at twelve-thirty, sir.'

'And then?'

'The agent for Brooke Bros. at one, and immediately after that Mr MacDougal, sir, then you're expected up at the Candy Deep mine.'

'Thank you, Johnson, I'll be at the Exchange as usual this morning if anything out of the ordinary comes up.'

'Very good, Mr Courtney. Just one other thing.' Johnson pointed at the brown paper parcel on the couch across the room. 'From your tailor.'

'Ah!' Sean smiled. 'Send my servant in here.' He walked across and opened the parcel. Within a few minutes Mbejane filled the doorway.

'Nkosi?'

'Mbejane—your new uniform.' Sean pointed at the clothes laid out on the couch. Mbejane's eyes switched to the gold and maroon finery, his expression suddenly dead.

'Put it on—come on, let's see how you look.'

Mbejane crossed to the couch and picked up the jacket. 'These are for me?'

'Yes, come on, put it on.' Sean laughed.

Mbejane hesitated, then slowly he loosened his loin cloth and let it drop. Sean watched him impatiently as he buttoned on the jacket and pantaloons, then he walked in a critical circle around the Zulu.

'Not bad,' he muttered and then in Zulu, 'Is it not beautiful?'

Mbejane wriggled his shoulders against the unfamiliar feel of the cloth and said nothing.

'Well, Mbejane, do you like it?'

'When I was a child I went with my father to trade cattle at Port Natal. There was a man who went about the town with a monkey on a chair, the monkey danced and the people laughed and threw money to it. That monkey had such a suit as this. Nkosi, I do not think he was a very happy monkey.'

The smile slipped off Sean's face. 'You would rather wear your skins?'

'What I wear is the dress of a warrior of Zululand.'

There was still no expression on Mbejane's face. Sean opened his mouth to argue with him but before he could speak he lost his temper.

'You'll wear that uniform,' he shouted. 'You'll wear what I tell you to wear and you'll do it with a smile, do you hear me?'

'Nkosi, I hear you.' Mbejane picked up his loin cloth of leopard tails and left the office. When Sean went out to the carriage Mbejane was sitting on the driver's seat in his new livery. All the way to the Exchange his back was stiff with protest and neither of them spoke. Sean glared at the doorman of the Exchange, drank four brandies during the morning, rode back to his office again at noon scowling at Mbejane's still protesting back, shouted at Johnson, snapped at the bank manager, routed the representative from Brooke Bros. and drove out to the Candy Deep in a high old rage. But Mbejane's silence was impenetrable and Sean couldn't re-open the argument without sacrifice of pride. He burst into the new administrative building of the Candy Deep and threw the staff into confusion.

'Where's Mr du Toit?' he roared.

'He's down the Number Three shaft, Mr Courtney.'

'What the hell is he doing down there? He's supposed to be waiting for me here.'

'He didn't expect you for another hour, sir.'

'Well, get me some overalls and a mining helmet, don't just stand there.'

He clapped the tin hat on his head and stamped his heavy gumboots across to the Number Three shaft. The skip dropped him smoothly five hundred feet into the earth and he climbed out at the tenth level.

'Where's Mr du Toit?' he demanded of the shift boss at the lift station.

'He's up at the face, sir.'

The floor of the drive was rough and muddy; his gumboots squelched as he set off down the tunnel. His carbide lamp lit the uneven rock walls with a flat white light and he felt himself starting to sweat. Two natives pushing a cocopan back along the railway lines forced him to flatten himself against one wall to allow them to pass and while he waited he felt inside his overalls for his cigar case. As he pulled it out it slipped from his hand and plunked into the mud. The cocopan was gone by that time so he stooped to pick up the case. His ear came within an inch of the wall and a puzzled expression replaced his frown of annoyance. The rock was squeaking. He laid his ear against it. It sounded like someone grinding his teeth. He listened to it for a while trying to guess the cause; it wasn't the echo of shovels or drills, it wasn't water. He walked another thirty yards or so down the drive and listened again. Not so loud here but now the grinding noise was punctuated with an occasional metallic snap like the breaking of a knife blade. Strange, very strange; he had never heard anything like it before. He walked on down the drive, his bad mood lost in his preoccupation with this new problem. Before he reached the face he met François.

'Hello, Mr Courtney.' Sean had long since given up trying to stop François calling him that. '*Gott*, I'm sorry I wasn't there to meet you. I thought you were coming at three.'

'That's all right, François, how are you?'

'My rheumatism's been giving me blazes, Mr Courtney, but otherwise I'm all right. How's Mr Charleywood?'

'He's fine.' Sean couldn't restrain his curiosity any longer. 'Tell me something, Franz, just now I put my ear against the wall of the drive and I heard an odd noise, I couldn't make out what it was.'

'What kind of noise?'

'A sort of grinding, like—like . . .' Sean searched for words to describe it, 'like two pieces of glass being rubbed together.'

François's eyes flew wide open and then began to bulge, the colour of his face changed to grey and he caught Sean's arm.

'Where?'

'Back along the drive.'

The breath jammed in François's throat and he struggled to speak through it, shaking Sean's arm desperately.

'Cave-in!' he croaked. 'Cave-in, man!'

He started to run but Sean grabbed him. François struggled wildly.

'François, how many men up at the face?'

'Cave-in.' François's voice was now hysterically shrill. 'Cave-in.' He broke Sean's grip and raced away towards the lift station, the mud flying from his gumboots. His terror infected Sean and he ran a dozen paces after François before he stopped himself. For precious seconds he wavered with fear slithering round like a reptile in his stomach; go back to call the others and perhaps die with them or follow François and live. Then the fear in his belly found a mate, a thing just as slimy and cold; its name was shame, and shame it was that drove him back towards the face. There were five blacks and a white man there, bare-chested and shiny with sweat in the heat. Sean shouted those two words at them and they reacted the way bathers do when someone on the beach shouts 'shark'. The same moment of paralysed horror, then the panic. They came stampeding back along the tunnel. Sean ran with them, the mud sucked at his heavy boots and his legs were weak with easy living and riding in carriages. One by one the others passed him.

'Wait for me,' he wanted to scream. 'Wait for me.' He slipped on the greasy footing, scraping his shoulder on the rough wall as he fell, and dragged himself up again, mud plastered in his beard, the blood humming in his ears. Alone now he blundered on down the tunnel. With a crack like a rifle shot one of the thick shoring timbers broke under the pressure of the moving rock and dust smoked from the roof of the tunnel in front of him. He staggered on and all around him the earth was talking, groaning, protesting with little muffled shrieks. The timbers joined in again, crackling and snapping, and as slowly as a theatre curtain the rock sagged down from above him. The tunnel was thick with dust that smothered the beam of his lamp and rasped his throat. He knew then that he wasn't going to make it but he ran on with the loose rock starting to fall about him. A lump hit his mining helmet and jarred him so that he nearly fell. Blinded by the swirling dust fog he crashed at full run into the abandoned cocopan that blocked the tunnel, he sprawled over the metal body of the trolley with his thigh bruised from the collision.

'Now I'm finished,' he thought, but instinctively he pulled himself up and started to grope his way around the cocopan to continue his flight. With a roar the tunnel in front of him collapsed. He dropped on his knees and crawled between the wheels of the cocopan, wriggling under the sturdy steel body just an instant before the roof above him collapsed also. The noise of the fall around him seemed to last for ever, but then it was over and the rustling and grating of the rock as it settled down was almost silence in comparison. His lamp was lost and the darkness pressed as heavily on him as the earth squeezed down on his tiny shelter. The air was solid with dust and he coughed; he coughed until his chest ached and he tasted salty blood in his mouth. There was hardly room to move, the steel body of the trolley was six inches above him, but he struggled until he managed to open the front of his overalls and tear a piece off the tail of his shirt. He held the silk like a surgical mask across his mouth and nose. It strained the dust out of the air so he could breathe. The dust settled; his coughing slowed and finally stopped. He felt surprised that he was still alive and cautiously be started exploring. He tried to straighten out his legs but his feet touched rock. He felt with his hands, six inches of head room and perhaps twelve inches on either side, warm mud underneath him and rock and steel all round. He took off his helmet and used it as a pillow. He was in a steel coffin buried five hundred feet deep. He felt the first flutter of panic. 'Keep your mind busy, think of something, think of anything but the rock around you, count your assets,' he told himself. He started to search his pockets, moving with difficulty in the cramped space.

'One silver cigar case with two Havanas.' He laid it down next to him.

'One box of matches, wet.' He placed it on top of the case.

'One pocket watch.'

'One handkerchief, Irish linen, monogrammed.'

'One comb, tortoiseshell—a man is judged by his appearance.' He started to comb his beard but found immediately that though this occupied his hands it left his mind free. He put the comb down next to his matches.

'Twenty-five pounds in gold sovereigns—' He counted them carefully, 'yes, twenty-five. I shall order a bottle of good champagne.' The dust was chalky in his mouth so he went on hurriedly, 'and a Malay girl from the Opera. No, why be mean—ten Malay girls. I'll have them dance for me, that'll pass the time. I'll promise them a sovereign each to bolster their enthusiasm.'

He continued the search, but there was nothing else. 'Gumboots, socks, well-cut trousers, shirt torn I'm afraid, overalls, a tin hat and that's all.'

With his possessions laid out carefully beside him and his cell explored he had to start thinking. First he thought about his thirst. The mud in which he lay was too thick to yield water. He tried straining it through his shirt without success, and then he thought about air. It seemed quite fresh and he decided that sufficient was filtering in from the loosely packed rock around him to keep him alive.

To keep him alive—alive until the thirst killed. Until he died curled up like a foetus in the warm womb of the earth. He laughed, a worm in a dark warm womb. He laughed again and recognized it as the beginnings of panic, he thrust his fist into his mouth to stop himself, biting down hard on his knuckles. It was very quiet, the rock had stopped moving.

'How long will it take? Tell me, Doctor. How long have I got?'

'Well, you are sweating. You'll lose moisture quite rapidly. I'd say about four days,' he answered himself.

'What about hunger, Doctor?'

'Oh, no, don't worry about that, you'll be hungry, of course, but the thirst will kill you.'

'And typhoid, or is it typhus, I can never remember. What about that, Doctor?'

'If there were dead men trapped in here with you there'd be a good chance, but you're alone, you know.'

'Do you think I'll go mad, Doctor, not immediately, of course, but in a few days?'

'Yes, you'll go mad.'

'I've never been mad before, not that I know of anyway, but I think it will help to go mad now, don't you?'

'If you mean, will it make it easier, well, I don't know.'

'Ah! now you're being obscure—but I follow you. You mean in that sleep of madness what dreams will come? You mean, will madness be more real than reality? You mean, will dying mad be worse than dying thirsty? But then I may beat the madness. This cocopan might buckle under the strain, after all there must be thousands of tons of rock bearing down on it. That's quite clever, you know, Doctor; as a medical man you should appreciate it. Mother Earth was saved but, alas, the child was stillborn, she bore down too hard.' Sean had spoken aloud, and now he felt foolish. He picked up a piece of stone and tapped the cocopan with it.

'It sounds firm enough. A most pleasing noise, really.' He beat harder on the metal body—one, two, three, one two, three—then dropped the stone. Soft as an echo, distant as the moon, he heard his taps repeated. His whole body stiffened at the sound, and he started to shiver with excitement. He snatched up the stone: three times he rapped, and three times the answer came back to him.

'They heard me, sweet merciful Christ, they heard me.' He laughed breathlessly. 'Dear Mother Earth, don't bear down, please don't bear down. Just be patient. Wait a few days and by Caesarian they'll take this child out of your womb.'

Mbejane waited until Sean disappeared down the Number Three shaft before he took off his new jacket. He folded it carefully on the driver's seat next to him. He sat and enjoyed the feel of the sun on his skin for a while, then he climbed off the carriage and went to the horses. He took them one at a time to the trough for water then returned them to their harnesses, buckling them in loosely. He picked up his spears from the footboard and moved across to a patch of short grass next to the administrative building. He sat down and went to work on the blade, humming softly to himself as he honed. At last he ran an expert thumb along each edge, grunted, shaved a few hairs off his forearm, smiled contentedly and laid his spears beside him in the grass. He lay back and the sun warmed him to sleep.

The shouting woke him. He sat up and automatically checked the height of the sun. He had slept an hour or more. Duff was shouting and François, mud-splattered and frightened-looking, was answering him. They were standing together in front of the administrative building. Duff's horse was sweating. Mbejane stood up and went across to them; he listened closely, trying to understand their staccato voices. They went too fast for him, but something was wrong, that much he knew.

'It's caved in almost to the Number Ten lift station,' François said.

'You left him in there,' accused Duff.

'I thought he was following me, but he turned back.'

'What for—why did he turn back?'

'To call the others—'

'Have you started clearing the drive?'

'No, I was waiting for you.'

'You stupid bloody idiot, he might be alive in there . . . every minute is vital.'

'But he hasn't a chance, Mr Charleywood, he must be dead.'

'Shut up, damn you.'

Duff swung away from him and started running towards the shaft. There was a crowd gathered beneath the high steel structure of the head gear, and suddenly Mbejane knew it was Sean. He caught up with Duff before he reached the shaft.

'Is it the Nkosi?'

'Yes.'

'What has happened?'

'The rock has fallen on him.'

Mbejane pushed his way into the skip next to Duff and neither of them spoke again until they reached the tenth level. They went down the drive, only a short way before they reached the end. There were men there with crowbars and shovels standing undecided, waiting for orders, and Mbejane shouldered a path through them. He and Duff stood together in front of the new wall of broken rock that sealed the tunnel, and the silence went on and on. Then Duff turned on the white shift-boss.

'Were you at the face?'

'Yes.'

'He went back to call you, didn't he?'

'Yes.'

'And you left him there?'

The man couldn't look at Duff.

'I thought he was following us,' he muttered.

'You thought only for your own miserable skin,' Duff told him, 'you filthy little coward, you slimy yellow bastard, you . . .'

Mbejane caught Duff's arm and Duff stopped his tirade. They all heard it then—clink, clink, clink.

'It's him—it must be him,' whispered Duff, 'he's alive!' He snatched a crowbar from one of the natives and knocked against the side of the tunnel. They waited, their breathing the only sound, until the answer came back to them louder and sharper than before. Mbejane took the crowbar out of Duff's hands. He thrust it into a crack in the rock jam and his back muscles bunched as he heaved. The bar bent like a liquorice stick, he threw it away and went at the stone with his bare hands.

'You!' Duff snapped at the shift-boss. 'We'll need timber to shore up as we clear the fall—get it.' He turned to the natives. 'Four of you working on the face at one time—the rest of you carry the stone away as we loosen it.'

'Do you want any dynamite?' asked the shift-boss.

'And bring the rock down a second time? Use your brains, man. Go and get that timber and call Mr du Toit while you're at the surface.'

In four hours they cleared fifteen feet of tunnel, breaking the larger slabs of stone with sledge hammers and prising the pieces out of the jam. Duff's body ached and his hands were raw. He had to rest. He walked slowly back to the lift station and there he found blankets and a huge dish of soup.

'Where did this come from?'

'Candy's Hotel, sir. Half Johannesburg is waiting at the head of the shaft.'

Duff huddled into a blanket and drank a little of the soup. 'Where's du Toit?'

'I couldn't find him, sir.'

Up at the face Mbejane worked on. The first four natives came back to rest and fresh men took their place. Mbejane led them, grunting an order occasionally but otherwise reserving his strength for the assault on the rock. For an hour Duff rested and when he returned to the head of the tunnel Mbejane was still there. Duff watched him curl his arms round a piece of stone the size of a beer keg, brace his legs and tear the stone out of the jam. Earth and loose rock followed it burying Mbejane's legs to the knees and Duff jumped forward to help him.

Another two hours and Duff had to rest again. This time he led Mbejane back with him, gave him a blanket and made him drink a little soup. They sat next to each other with their backs against the wall of the tunnel and blankets over their shoulders. The shift-boss came to Duff.

'Mrs Rautenbach sent this down for you, sir.'

It was a half-bottle of brandy.

'Tell her, thank you.' Duff pulled the cork with his teeth and swallowed twice. It brought the tears into his eyes—he offered the bottle to Mbejane.

'It is not fitting,' Mbejane demurred.

'Drink.'

Mbejane drank, wiped the mouth of the bottle carefully on his blanket and handed it back. Duff took another swallow and offered it again but Mbejane shook his head.

'A little of that is strength, too much is weakness. There is work to do now.' Duff corked the bottle.

'How long before we reach him?' asked Mbejane.

'Another day, maybe two.'

'A man can die in two days,' mused the Zulu.

'Not one with a body like a bull and a temper like a devil,' Duff assured him. Mbejane smiled and Duff went on groping for his words in Zulu.

'You love him, Mbejane?'

'Love is a woman's word.'

Mbejane inspected one of his thumbs; the nail was torn loose, standing up like a tombstone; he took it between his teeth, pulled it off and spat it on to the floor of the drive. Duff shuddered as he watched.

'Those baboons will not work unless they are driven.' Mbejane stood up. 'Are you rested?'

'Yes,' lied Duff, and they went back to the face.

Sean lay in the mud with his head on the hard pillow of the helmet. The darkness was as solid as the rock around him. He tried to imagine where the one ended and the other began—by doing that he could stop himself feeling his thirst so strongly. He could hear the ring of hammer on stone and the rattle of rock falling free but it never seemed to come any closer. The whole side of his body was stiff and sore but he could not turn over, his knees caught on the cocopan every time he tried and the air in his little cave was starting to taste stale—his head ached. He moved again, restlessly, and his hand brushed the small pile of sovereigns. He struck at them, scattering them into the mud. They were the bait that had led him into this trap. Now he would give them, and all the millions of others, for just the feel of the wind in his beard and the sun in his face. The darkness clung to him, thick and cloying as black treacle; it seemed to fill his nose, his throat and eyes, smothering him. He groped and found the matchbox. For a few seconds of light he would burn up most of the precious oxygen in his cave and call it fair exchange—but the box was sodden. He struck match after match but the wet heads crumbled without a spark and he threw them away and clenched his eyelids to keep the darkness out. Bright colours formed in front of his closed eyes, moving and rearranging themselves until suddenly and very clearly they formed a picture of Garrick's face. He hadn't thought about his family for months, he had been too busy reaping the golden harvest, but now memories crowded back. There were so many things he had forgotten. Everything else had become unimportant when compared with power and gold—even lives, men's lives, had meant nothing. But now it was his own life, teetering on the edge of the black cliff.

The sound of the sledge-hammers broke into his thoughts again. There were men on the other side of the blocked tunnel trying to save him, working their way into the treacherous rock pile which might collapse again at any minute. People were more valuable than the poisonous metal, the little gold discs that lay smugly beside him in the mud while men struggled to save him.

He thought of Garry, crippled by his careless shotgun, father to the bastard he had sired, of Ada whom he had left without a word of good-bye, of Karl Lochtkamper with the pistol in his hand and half his head splattered across the floor of his bedroom, or other nameless men dead or broken because of him.

Sean ran his tongue across his lips and listened to the hammers; he was certain they were nearer now.

'If I get out of here, it'll be different. I swear it.'

Mbejane rested for four hours in the next thirty-six. Duff watched the flesh melt off him in sweat. He was killing himself. Duff was worn out; he could no longer work with his hands but he was directing the teams who were shoring up the reclaimed tunnel. By the second evening they had cleared a hundred feet of the drive. Duff paced it out and when he reached the face he spoke to Mbejane.

'How long since you last signalled to him?'

Mbejane stepped back with a sledge-hammer in his tattered hands; its shaft was sticky and brown with blood.

'An hour ago and even then it sounded as though there were but the length of a spear between us.'

Duff took a crowbar from one of the other natives and tapped the rock. The answer came immediately.

'He's hitting something made of iron,' Duff said. 'It sounds as though he's only a few feet away. Mbejane, let these other men take over. If you wish you can stay and watch but you must rest again now.'

For answer Mbejane lifted the hammer and swung it against the face. The rock he hit cracked and two of the natives stepped up and levered it loose with their crowbars. At the back of the hole it left in the wall they could see the corner of the cocopan. Everyone stared at it, then Duff shouted.

'Sean, Sean, can you hear me?'

'Stop talking and get me out of here.' Sean's voice was hoarse with thirst and dust, and muffled by the rock.

'He's under the cocopan.'

'It's him.'

'Nkosi, are you all right?'

'We've found him.'

The shouts were picked up by the men behind them in the drive and passed back to those waiting at the lift station.

'They've found him—he's all right—they've found him.'

Duff and Mbejane jumped forward together, their exhaustion completely forgotten. They cleared the last few lumps of rock and with their shoulders touching knelt and peered under the cocopan.

'Nkosi, I see you.'

'I see you also, Mbejane, what took you so long?'

'Nkosi, there were a few small stones in the way.'

Mbejane reached under the cocopan and with his hands under Sean's armpits pulled him out

'What a hell of a place you choose to go to ground in, laddie. How are you feeling?'

'Give me some water and I'll be all right.'

'Water—bring water,' shouted Duff.

Sean gulped it, trying to drink the whole mug in one mouthful. He coughed and it shot out of his nose.

'Easy, laddie, easy.' Duff thumped his back. Sean drank the next mugful more slowly and finished panting from the effort.

'That was good.'

'Come on, we've got a doctor waiting up on top.' Duff draped a blanket over his shoulders. Mbejane picked Sean up across his chest.

'Put me down, damn you, I haven't forgotten how to walk.'

Mbejane set him down gently, but his legs buckled like those of a man just out of bed from a long illness and he clutched at Mbejane's arm. Mbejane picked him up again and carried him down to the lift station. They rode up in the skip into the open.

'The moon's shining. And the stars—my God, they're beautiful.' There was wonder in Sean's voice; he sucked the night air into his lungs but it was too rich for him and he started coughing again. There were people waiting at the head of the shaft and they crowded round them as they stepped out of the skip.

'How is he?'

'Are you all right, Sean?'

'Doc Symmonds is waiting in the office.'

'Quickly, Mbejane,' said Duff, 'get him out of the cold.'

One on either side of him they hurried Sean across to the administrative building and laid him on the couch in François's office. Symmonds checked him over, looked down his throat and felt his pulse.

'Have you got a closed carriage here?'

'Yes,' Duff answered.

'Well, wrap him up warmly and get him home to bed. With the dust and bad air he's been breathing there's serious danger of pneumonia. I'll come down with you and give him a sedative.'

'I won't need one, Doc,' Sean grinned at him.

'I think I know what's best for you, Mr Courtney.' Doctor Symmonds was a young man. He was the fashionable doctor among the rich of Johannesburg and he took it very seriously.

'Now if you please, we'll get you to your hotel.' He started to pack his instruments back into his valise.

'You're the doctor,' Sean agreed, 'but before we go will you have a look at my servant's hands, they're in a hell of a mess. There's hardly any meat left on them.'

Doctor Symmonds did not look up from what he was doing. 'I have no Kaffir practice, Mr Courtney, I'm sure you'll find some other doctor to attend to him when we get back to town.'

Sean sat up slowly, he let the blankets slip off his shoulders. He walked across to Doctor Symmonds and held him by the throat against the wall. The doctor had a fine pair of waxed moustaches and Sean took one of them between the thumb and forefinger of his free hand: he plucked it out like feathers from the carcass of a dead fowl and Doctor Symmonds squealed.

'Starting now, Doctor, you have a Kaffir practice,' Sean told him. He pulled the handkerchief out of Symmonds' top pocket and dabbed at the little drops of blood on the doctor's bare upper lip.

'Be a good fellow—see to my servant.'

21

When Sean woke the next morning the hands of the grandfather clock across the bedroom pointed at the top of their dial. Candy was in the room opening the curtains and with her were two waiters, each with a loaded tray.

'Good morning, how is our hero this morning?' the waiters put down their trays and went out as she came across to Sean's bed.

Sean blinked the sleep out of his eyes. 'My throat feels as though I've just finished a meal of broken glass.'

'That's the dust,' Candy told him and laid her hands on his forehead. Sean's hand sneaked round behind her and she squeaked as he pinched her. Standing well away from the bed she rubbed her bottom and made a face at him.

'There's nothing wrong with you!'

'Good, then I'll get up.' Sean started to pull back the bedclothes.

'Not until the doctor's had a look at you, you won't.'

'Candy, if that bastard puts one foot in this room I'll punch him so hard in the mouth his teeth will march out of his backside like soldiers.'

Candy turned to the breakfast trays to cover her smile. 'That's no way to talk in front of a lady. But don't worry, it isn't Symmonds.'

'Where's Duff?' Sean asked.

'He's having a bath, then he's coming to eat breakfast with you.'

'I'll wait for him, but give me a cup of coffee in the meantime, there's a sweetheart.'

She brought the coffee to him. 'Your savage has been camping on my trail all morning, he wants to see you. I've just about had to put an armed guard on this room to keep him out.'

Sean laughed. 'Will you send him in, Candy?'

She went to the door and stopped with a hand on the latch.

'It's nice to have you back, Sean, don't do anything silly like that again, will you?'

'That's a promise,' Sean assured her.

Mbejane came quickly and stood in the doorway. 'Nkosi, is it well with you?'

Sean looked at the iodine-stained bandages on his hands and the maroon and gold livery without answering. Then he rolled on his back and stared at the ceiling. 'I sent for my servant and instead there comes a monkey on a chain.'

Mbejane stood still, his face expressionless but for the hurt in his eyes.

'Go—find my servant. You will know him by his dress which is that of a warrior of Zululand.'

It took a few seconds for the laughter to start rolling around in Mbejane's belly; it shook his shoulders and creased the corners of his mouth. He closed the door very softly behind him and when he came back in his loin cloth Sean grinned at him.

'Ah! I see you, Mbejane.'

'And I see you also.'

He stood by the bed and they talked. They spoke little of the cave-in and not at all of Mbejane's part in the rescue. Between them it was understood, words could only damage it. Perhaps they would talk of it later, but not now,

'Tomorrow, will you need the carriage?' Mbejane asked at last.

'Yes—go now. Eat and sleep.' Sean reached out and touched Mbejane's arm. Just that small physical contact—that almost guilty touching—and Mbejane left him.

Then Duff came in in a silk dressing-gown and they ate eggs and steak from the trays and Duff sent down for a bottle of wine just to rinse the dust out of their throats once more.

'They tell me François is still down at the Bright Angels—he's been on the drink ever since he got out of that shaft. When he sobers up he can come to the office and collect his pay packet.'

Sean sat up. 'You're going to fire him?'

'I'm going to fire him so high he'll only touch the ground when he reaches Capetown.'

'What the hell for?' demanded Sean.

'What for?' Duff echoed. 'What for? For running—that's what for.'

'Duff, he was in a cave-in at Kimberley, wasn't he?'

'Yes.'

'Broke his legs, didn't you say?'

'Yes.'

'Shall I tell you something? If it were to happen to me a second time I'd run as well.'

Duff filled his wine glass without answering.

'Send down to the Bright Angels, tell him alcohol is bad for the liver—that should sober him—tell him unless he's back at work by tomorrow morning we'll dock it off his pay,' Sean said. Duff looked at him with a puzzled expression. 'What is this?'

'I had some time to think while I was down in that hole. I decided that to get to the top you don't have to stamp on everyone you meet.'

'Ah, I understand.' Duff gave his lopsided grin. 'A good resolution—New Year in August. Well, that's all right, you had me worried there, I thought a rock had fallen on your head. I also make good resolutions.'

'Duff, I don't want François fired.'

'All right, all right—he stays on. If you like we can open a soup kitchen at the office and turn Xanadu into a home for the aged.'

'Oh, go and burst. I just don't think it's necessary to fire François, that's all.'

'Who's arguing? I agreed with you, didn't I? I have deep respect for good resolutions. I make them all the time.'

Duff pulled his chair up to the bed. 'Quite by chance I happen to have a pack of cards with me.' He took them out of his dressing-gown pocket. 'Would you care for a game of Klabejas?'

Sean lost fifty pounds before he was saved by the arrival of the new doctor. The doctor tapped his chest and tut-tutted, looked down his throat and tut-tutted, wrote out a prescription and confined him to bed for the rest of the day. He was just leaving when Jock and Trevor Heyns arrived. Jock had a bunch of flowers which he presented to Sean in an embarrassed fashion.

Then the room began to fill in earnest: the rest of the crowd from the Exchange arrived, someone had brought a case of champagne, a poker game started in one corner and a political meeting in another.

'Who does this Kruger think he is, anyway—God or something? You know what he said last time we went to see him about getting the vote, he said "Protest, protest—I have the guns and you have not!"'

'Three Kings wins—you *are* holding cards!'

'—you wait and see. Consolidated Wits. will hit thirty shillings by the end of the month.'

'—and the taxes—they're putting another twenty per cent on dynamite.'

'—a new piece at the Opera, Jock's got a season ticket on her—no one else has had a look in yet.'

'All right, you two—stop that. If you want to fight go outside—this is a sick room.'

'This bottle's empty—break open a new one, Duff.'

Sean lost another hundred to Duff and then a little after five Candy came in. She was horrified. 'Out, all of you, out!'

The room emptied as quickly as it had filled and Candy wandered around picking up cigar butts and empty glasses.

'The vandals! Someone's burnt a hole in the carpet and look at this—champagne spilt all over the table.'

Duff coughed and started pouring himself another drink.

'Don't you think you've had enough of that, Dufford?'

Duff put down his glass. 'And it's time you went and changed for dinner.' Duff winked sheepishly at Sean, but he went.

Duff and Candy came back to his room after supper and had a liqueur with him.

'Now to sleep,' Candy commanded and went across to draw the curtains.

'It's still early,' protested Duff with no effect. Candy blew the lamp out.

Sean was not tired, he had lain in bed all day and now his brain was overactive. He lit a cigar and smoked, listening to the street noises below his window and it was past midnight before he finally drifted off. When he awoke, he woke screaming, for the darkness was on him again and the blankets pressed down on him suffocating him. He fought them off and stumbled blindly across the room. He had to have air and light. He ran into the thick velvet curtains and they closed around his face; he tore himself free and hit the french windows with his shoulder; they burst open and he was out on the balcony, out in the cold air with the moon fat and yellow in the sky above him. His gasping slowed until he was breathing normally again. He went back inside and lit the lamp, then he went through to Duff's empty bedroom. There was a copy of *Twelfth Night* on the bedside table and he took it back to his own room. He sat with the lamp at his elbow and forced his eyes to follow the printed words even though they made no sense. He read until the dawn showed grey through the open windows, then he put down the book. He shaved, dressed and went down the back stairs into the hotel yard. He found Mbejane in the stables.

'Put a saddle on the grey.'

'Where are you going, Nkosi?'

'To kill a devil.'

'Then I will come with you.'

'No, I will be back before midday.'

He rode up to the Candy Deep and tied his horse outside the administration buildings. There was a sleepy clerk in the front offices.

'Good morning, Mr Courtney. Can I help you?'

'Yes. Get me overalls and a helmet.'

Sean went to the Number Three Shaft. There was a frost on the ground that crunched as he walked on it and the sun had just cleared the eastern ridge of the Witwatersrand. Sean stopped at the hoist shed and spoke to the driver.

'Has the new shift gone on yet?'

'Half an hour ago, sir.' The man was obviously surprised to see him. 'The night shift finished blasting at five o'clock.'

'Good drop me down to the fourteenth level.'

'The fourteenth is abandoned now, Mr Courtney, there's no one working there.'

'Yes, I know.'

Sean walked across to the head of the shaft. He lit his carbide lamp and while he waited for the skip he looked out across the valley. The air was clear and the sun threw long shadows. Everything stood out in sharp relief. He had not been up this early in the morning for many months and he had almost forgotten how fresh and delicately coloured a new day was. The skip stopped in front of him. He took a deep breath and stepped into it. When he reached the fourteenth level he got out and pushed the recall signal for the skip and he was alone in the earth again. He walked up the tunnel and the echo of his footsteps went with him. He was sweating and a muscle in his cheek started to jerk; he reached the face and set the carbide lamp down on a ledge of rock. He checked to make sure his matches were in his pocket, then he blew out the lamp. The darkness came squeezing down on him. The first half hour was the worst. Twice he had the matches in his hand ready to strike but he stopped himself. The sweat formed cold wet patches under his arms and the darkness filled his open mouth and choked him. He had to fight for each lungful of air, suck in, hold it, breathe out. First he regulated his breathing and then slowly, slowly his mind came under control and he knew he had won. He waited another ten minutes breathing easily and sitting relaxed with his back against the side of the tunnel, then he lit the lamp. He was smiling as he went back to the lift station and signalled for the skip. When he reached the surface he stepped out and lit a cigar; he flicked the match into the square black opening of the shaft.

'So much for you, little hole.'

He walked back towards the administration building. What he could not know was that the Number Three shaft of the Candy Deep was to take something from him just as valuable as his courage and that, next time, what it took it would not give back. But that was many years ahead.

22

By October Xanadu was nearly finished. The three of them drove out to it as usual one Saturday afternoon.

'The builder is only six months behind schedule—now he says he'll be finished by Christmas and I haven't found the courage yet to ask him which Christmas,' Sean remarked.

'It's all the alterations Candy has thought up,' Duff said. 'She's got the poor man so confused he doesn't know whether he's a boy or a girl.'

'Well, if you'd consulted me in the first place it would have saved a lot of trouble,' Candy told them.

The carriage turned in through the marble gates and they looked around them. Already the lawns were smooth and green and the jacaranda trees lining the drive were shoulder high.

'I think it's going to live up to its name—that gardener's doing a good job,' Sean spoke with satisfaction.

'Don't you call him a gardener to his face or we'll have a strike on our hands. He's a horticulturist,' Duff smiled across at him.

'Talking about names,' Candy interrupted, 'don't you think Xanadu is—well, a bit outlandish?'

'No, I do not,' Sean said. 'I picked it myself. I think it's a damn good name.'

'It's not dignified—why don't we call it Fair Oaks?'

'Firstly, because there isn't an oak tree within fifty miles and secondly because it's already called Xanadu.'

'Don't get cross, it was just a suggestion.'

The builder met them at the top of the drive and they began the tour of the house. That took an hour, then they left the builder and went out into the garden. They found the gardener with a gang of natives near the north boundary.

'How's it going, Joubert?' Duff greeted him.

'Not bad, Mr Charleywood, but it takes time you know.'

'You've done a damn fine job so far.'

'It's kind of you to say so, sir.'

'When are you going to start laying out my maze?'

The gardener looked surprised; he glanced at Candy, opened his mouth, closed it again and looked once more at Candy.

'Oh, I told Joubert not to worry about the maze.'

'Why did you do that? I wanted a maze—ever since I visited Hampton Court as a child I've wanted my own maze.'

'They're silly things,' Candy told him. 'They just take up a lot of space and they're not even nice to look at.'

Sean thought Duff was going to argue, but he didn't. They talked to the gardener a little longer, then they walked back across the lawns in front of the house towards the chapel.

'Dufford, I've left my parasol in the carriage, would you mind getting it for me?' Candy asked.

When Duff was gone Candy took Sean's arm.

'It's going to be a lovely home. We're going to be very happy here.'

'Have you two decided on a date yet?' Sean asked.

'We want the house finished first so we can move straight in. I think we'll make it some time in February next year.'

They reached the chapel and stopped in front of it.

'It's a sweet little church.' Candy spoke dreamily. 'And such a nice idea of Dufford's—a special church of our own.'

Sean shuffled uncomfortably. 'Yes,' he agreed, 'it's a very romantic idea.' He glanced over his shoulder and saw Duff coming back with the parasol.

'Candy—it's none of my business. I don't know anything about marriage, but I know about training horses—you break them to the halter before you put the saddle on their backs.'

'I don't follow you.' Candy looked puzzled. 'What are you trying to say?'

'Nothing—just forget it. Here comes Duff.'

When they got back to the hotel there was a note at the reception desk for Sean. They went through into the main lounge and Candy went off to check the menu for dinner. Sean opened the envelope and read the note.

I should like to meet you and Mr Charleywood to discuss a matter of some importance. I will be at my hotel after dinner this evening and hope that it will be convenient for you to call on me then. N Hradsky.

Sean passed the note across to Duff.

'What do you suppose he wants?'

'He has heard of your deadly skill as a Klabejas player. He wants to take lessons,' Duff answered.

'Shall we go?'

'Of course. You know I can't resist Norman's exhilarating company.'

It was a superb dinner. The crayfish, packed in ice, had come up from Capetown by express coach.

'Candy—Sean and I are going across to see Hradsky. We might be back a little late,' Duff told her when they were finished.

'As long as it's Hradsky,' Candy smiled at him. 'Don't get lost—I have my spies at the Opera House you know.'

'Shall we take the carriage?' Duff asked Sean, and Sean noticed that he hadn't laughed at Candy's joke.

'It's only two blocks, we might as well walk.'

They walked in silence. Sean felt his dinner settling down comfortably inside him, he belched softly and took another puff from his cigar. When they had almost reached the Grand National Hotel Duff spoke.

'Sean . . .' He stopped.

'Yes?' Sean prompted him.

'About Candy . . .' He stopped again.

'She's a fine girl,' Sean prompted again.

'Yes, she's a fine girl.'

'Is that all you wanted to say?'

'Well—oh! never mind. Let's go and see what Saul and David want.'

Max met them at the door of Hradsky's suite.

'Good evening, gentlemen, I am so pleased you could come.'

'Hello, Max.' Duff went past him to where Hradsky was standing in front of the fireplace.

'Norman, my dear fellow, how are you?'

Hradsky nodded in acknowledgement and Duff took hold of the lapels of Hradsky's coat and adjusted them carefully; then he picked an imaginary piece of fluff off his shoulder.

'You have a way with clothes, Norman. Don't you agree that Norman has a way with clothes, Sean? I know of no one else who can put on a twenty-guinea suit and make it look like a half-filled bag of oranges.' He patted Hradsky's arm affectionately. 'Yes, thank you—I will have a drink.' He went across to the liquor cabinet and poured one for himself. 'Now, what can you gentlemen do for me?'

Max glanced at Hradsky and Hradsky nodded.

'I will come to the point immediately,' said Max. 'Our two groups of companies are the largest on the Witwatersrand.'

Duff put his glass back on top of the cabinet and dropped his grin. Sean sat down in one of the armchairs, his expression also serious; both of them could guess what was coming.

'In the past,' continued Max, 'we have worked together on numerous occasions and we have both benefited from it. The next logical step, of course, is to combine our strength, pool our resources and go on together to new greatness.'

'I take it that you are proposing a merger?'

'Precisely, Mr Courtney, a merger of these two vast financial ventures.'

Sean leaned back in his chair and started to whistle softly. Duff picked up his glass again and took a sip.

'Well, gentlemen, what are your feelings on the subject?' asked Max.

'Have you got a proposal worked out, Max, something definite for us to think about?'

'Yes, Mr Courtney, I have.' Max went to the stinkwood desk which filled one corner of the room and picked up a sheaf of papers. He carried it across to Sean. Sean scanned through it.

'You've done quite a bit of work here, Max. It's going to take us a day or two to work out exactly what you are offering.'

'I appreciate that, Mr Courtney. Take as long as you wish. We have worked for a month to draw up that scheme and I hope our labours have not been in vain. I think you will find our offer very generous.'

Sean stood up.

'We'll contact you again in the next few days, Max. Shall we go, Duff?'

Duff finished his drink.

'Goodnight, Max, look after Norman. He's very precious to us, you know.'

They went to their building on Eloff Street. Sean let them in through one of the side doors, lit the lamps in his office and Duff pulled up an extra chair to the desk. By two o'clock the following morning they understood the essentials of Hradsky's offer. Sean stood up and went to open one of the windows, for the room was thick with cigar smoke. He came back and flopped on to the couch, arranged a cushion behind his head and looked at Duff.

'Let's hear what you've got to say.'

Duff tapped his teeth with a pencil while he arranged his words.

'Let's decide first if we want to join with him.'

'If he makes it worth our while, we do,' Sean answered.

'I agree with you—but only if he makes it worth our while.' Duff laid back in his chair. 'Now the next point. Tell me, laddie, what is the first thing that strikes you about this scheme of Norman's?'

'We get nice-sounding titles and fat cash payments and Hradsky gets control,' Sean answered.

'You have laid your finger on the heart of it—Norman wants control. More than money, Norman wants control, so that he can sit at the top of the pile, look down on everyone else and say, "All right, you bastards, what if I do stutter?"'

Duff stood up, he walked round the desk and stopped in front of Sean's couch.

'Now for my next question. Do we give him control?'

'If he pays our price, then we give him control,' Sean answered. Duff turned away and went across to the open window.

'You know I rather like the feeling of being top man myself,' he said thoughtfully.

'Listen, Duff, we came here to make money. If we go in with Hradsky we'll make more,' Sean said.

'Laddie, we've got so much now that we could fill this room waist deep in sovereigns. We've got more than we'll ever be able to spend and I like being top man.'

'Hradsky's more powerful than we are—let's face up to that. He's got his diamond interests as well, so you're not top man even now. If we join him you still won't be top man and you'll be a damn sight richer.'

'Unassailable logic,' Duff nodded. 'I agree with you then. Hradsky gets control but he pays for it; we'll put him through the wringer until he's dry.'

Sean swung his legs off the couch. 'Agreed—now let's take this scheme of his by the throat, tear it to pieces and build it up again to suit ourselves.'

Duff looked at his watch. 'It's after two o'clock. We'll leave it now and start on it when we're fresh in the morning.'

They had their lunch brought down to the office the next day and ate it at the desk. Johnson, who had been sent up to the Stock Exchange with instructions to keep an eye on prices and call them immediately anything out of the ordinary happened, reported back after high change.

'It's been as quiet as a graveyard all day, sir, there's all sorts of rumours flying about. Seems someone saw the lights burning in this office at two o'clock this morning. Then when you didn't come to the Exchange but sent me instead—well, I can tell you, sir, there were a lot of questions asked.' Johnson hesitated, then his curiosity got the better of him.

'Can I help you at all, sir?' He started sidling across towards the desk.

'I think we can manage on our own, Johnson. Shut the door as you go out, please.'

At half-past seven they decided it was enough for one day and they went back to the hotel. As they walked into the lobby Sean saw Trevor Heyns disappear into the lounge and heard his voice.

'Here they are!'

Almost immediately Trevor appeared again with his brother.

'Hello, boys,' Jock appeared surprised to see them. 'What are you doing here?'

'We live here,' said Duff.

'Oh, yes, of course. Well, come and have a drink with us.' Jock smiled expansively.

'And then you can pump us and find out what we've been doing all day,' Duff suggested.

Jock looked embarrassed. 'I don't know what you mean, I just thought we'd have a drink together, that's all.'

'Thanks all the same, Jock, we've had a hard day. I think we'll just go on up to bed,' Duff said. They were halfway across the lobby before Duff turned back to where the two brothers were standing.

'I'll tell you boys something,' he said in a stage whisper. 'This is really big–it's so big it takes a while for the mind to grasp it. When you two realize that it's been right there under your noses all the time, you're going to kick yourselves.'

They left the Heyns brothers in the lobby staring after them and went up the stairs.

'That wasn't very kind,' Sean laughed. 'They won't sleep for a week.'

23

When neither Sean nor Duff put in an appearance at the Exchange the next morning, the rumours surged round the members' lounge and the prices started running amok. Reliable information that Sean and Duff had struck a rich new goldfield across the vaal sent the prices up like rocketing snipe; then twenty minutes later the denial came in and clipped fifteen shillings a share off the Courtney–Charleywood stock. Johnson ran backwards and forwards between the office and the Exchange all morning. By eleven he was so tired he could hardly talk.

'Don't worry any more, Johnson,' Sean told him. 'Here's a sovereign–go down to the Grand National and buy yourself a drink, you've had a hard morning.'

One of Jock Heyns's men, who had been detailed off to watch the Courtney–Charleywood office, followed Johnson down to the Grand National and heard him place his order with the barman. He raced back to the Exchange and reported to Jock.

'Their head clerk has just gone and ordered himself a bottle of French champagne,' he panted.

'Good God!' Jock nearly jumped out of his chair and beside him Trevor signalled frantically for his clerk.

'Buy,' he whispered in the man's ear. 'Buy every scrap of their script you can lay your hands on.'

Across the lounge Hradsky settled down a little further in his chair; he clasped his hands contentedly over the front of his stomach and he very nearly smiled.

By midnight Sean and Duff had completed their counter-proposal to Hradsky's offer.

'How do you think Norman will react to it?' asked Sean.

'I hope his heart is strong enough to stand the shock,' Duff grinned. 'The only reason that his jaw won't hit the floor is that his great gut will be in the way.'

'Shall we go down to his hotel now and show him?' suggested Sean.

'Laddie, laddie.' Duff shook his head sorrowfully. 'After all the time I've spent on your education, and you still haven't learned.'

'What do we do then?'

'We send for him, laddie, we make him come to us. We play him on the home ground.'

'How does that help?' Sean asked.

'It gives us an advantage immediately—it makes him remember that he's the one doing the asking.'

Hradsky came down to their office at ten o'clock the next morning; he came in state driven behind a four-in-hand and attended by Max and two secretaries. Johnson met them at the front door and ushered them into Sean's office.

'Norman, dear old Norman, I'm delighted to see you,' Duff greeted him and, fully aware of the fact that Hradsky never smoked, Duff thrust a cheroot between his lips. When everyone was seated Sean opened the meeting.

'Gentlemen, we have spent some time examining your proposition and in the main we find it just, fair and equitable.'

'Hear, hear,' Duff agreed politely.

'At the outset I want to make it quite clear,' Sean went on, 'that Mr Charleywood and myself feel strongly that the union of our two ventures is desirable—nay! essential. If you will forgive the quotation, "*ex unitate vires*".'

'Hear, hear—hear, hear.' Duff lit his cigar.

'As I was saying, we have examined your proposition and we accept it readily and happily, with the exception of a few minor details which we have listed.' Sean picked up the thick pile of paper. 'Perhaps you would care to glance through it and then we can proceed to the drawing-up of a formal agreement.'

Max accepted the sheaf gingerly. 'If you want privacy, Mr Charleywood's office which adjoins this room is at your disposal.'

Hradsky took his band next door and an hour later when he led them back again they looked like a party of pallbearers. Max was on the verge of tears, he cleared the lump from his throat.

'I think we should examine each item separately,' he said sadly, and three days later they shook hands on the deal.

Duff poured the drinks and gave each man a glass. 'To the new company, Central Rand Consolidated. It has been a long confinement, gentlemen, but I think we have given birth to a child of which we can be proud.'

Hradsky had control, but it had cost him dearly.

Central Rand Consolidated had its christening party on the main floor of the Johannesburg Stock Exchange; ten per cent of the shares were put out for sale to the public. Before the day's dealing began the crowd had overflowed the

Stock Exchange building and jammed in the street for a block in each direction. The President of the Exchange read the prospectus of Central Rand Consolidated; in the cathedral hush his every word carried clearly to the members' lounge. The bell rang and still the hush persisted. Hradsky's authorized clerk broke the silence timidly. 'I sell C.R.C.'s.'

It was nearly a massacre; two hundred men were trying to buy shares from him simultaneously. First his jacket and then his shirt disintegrated beneath the clutching hands; he lost his spectacles, crushed to powdered glass beneath the trampling feet. Ten minutes later he managed to fight his way out of the crowd and reported to his masters, 'I was able to sell them, gentlemen.'

Sean and Duff laughed. They had reason to laugh, for in those ten minutes their thirty per cent holding in C.R.C. had appreciated in value by half a million pounds.

24

That year Christmas dinner at Candy's Hotel was considerably better than it had been five years previously. Seventy-five people sat down to it at one table and by three o'clock, when it ended, only half of them were able to stand up. Sean used the banisters to get up the stairs and at the top he told Candy and Duff solemnly, 'I love you—I love you both desperately—but now I must sleep.' He left them and set off down the corridor bouncing against the walls like a trick billiard shot until he ricocheted through the door into his suite.

'You'd better make sure he's all right, Dufford.'

'A case of the blind drunk leading the blind drunk,' said Duff indistinctly, and also employing the wall to wall route followed Sean down the corridor. Sean was sitting on the edge of his bed wrestling with one of his boots.

'What you trying to do, laddie, break your ankle?'

Sean looked up and smiled beatifically. 'Come in, come in—all four of you. Have a drink.'

'Thanks, I brought my own.'

Duff closed the door behind him like a conspirator and produced a bottle from under his coat. 'She didn't see me—she didn't know her little Dufford had a big beautiful bottle in his inside pocket.'

'Would you mind helping me with this damn boot?' Sean asked.

'That's a very good question,' said Duff seriously as he set a course across the room for one of the armchairs. 'I'm glad you asked it.' He reached the chair and dropped into it. 'The answer, of course, is, Yes! I would mind.'

Sean let his foot drop and lay back on the bed.

'Laddie, I want to talk to you,' Duff said.

'Talk's free—help yourself.'

'Sean, what do you think of Candy?'

'Lovely pair of titties,' Sean opined.

'Sure, but a man cannot live by titties alone.'

'No, but I suppose she's also got the other basic equipment,' Sean said drowsily.

'Laddie, I'm being serious now—I want your help. Do you think I am doing the right thing—this marriage business, I mean.'

'Don't know much about marriage.' Sean rolled over on his face.

'She's calling me Dufford already—did you notice that, laddie? That's an omen, that's an omen of the most frightful portent. Did you notice, hey?' Duff waited a second for an answer which he didn't receive. 'That's what the other one used to call me. "Dufford," she'd say—I can hear it now—"Dufford, you're a pig".'

Duff looked hard at the bed. 'Are you still with me?'

No answer.

'Sean, laddie, I need your help.'

Sean snored softly.

'Oh, you drunken oaf,' said Duff miserably.

25

Xanadu was finished by the end of the January and the wedding was set for the twentieth of February. Duff sent the Commandant and the entire police force of Johannesburg an invitation: in return they put a twenty-four hour a day guard on the ballroom of Xanadu where the wedding gifts were laid out on long trestle tables. Sean drove up with Duff and Candy on the afternoon of the tenth, as Duff put it, to make the latest count of the booty. Sean gave the constable on duty a cigar and then they went through into the ballroom.

'Look, oh look,' squealed Candy. 'There's a whole lot of new presents!'

'This one's from Jock and Trevor,' Sean read the card.

'Open quickly, please, Dufford, let's see what they've given us.'

Duff prised the lid off the case and Sean whistled softly.

'A solid gold dinner service,' gasped Candy. She picked up one of the plates and hugged it to her chest. 'Oh, I just don't know what to say.'

Sean examined the other boxes. 'Hey, Duff, this one will make you specially happy—"Best wishes, N. Hradsky".'

'This I must see,' said Duff with the first enthusiasm he had shown in a month. He unwrapped the parcel.

'A dozen of them!' Duff hooted gleefully. 'Norman, you priceless little Israelite, a whole dozen dish towels.'

'It's the thought that counts,' laughed Sean.

'Dear old Norman, how it must have hurt him to shell out for them! I'll have him autograph them and I'll frame them and hang them in the front hall.'

They left Candy to arrange the presents and they went out into the garden.

'Have you got this mock priest organized?' asked Duff.

'Yes, he's at a hotel in Pretoria. He's in training now—he'll be able to rattle through the service like an old hand when the time comes.'

'You don't think that faking it is just as bad as doing it properly?' asked Duff dubiously.

'It's a hell of a time to think of that now,' said Sean.

'Yes, I suppose it is.'

'Where are you going for the honeymoon?' Sean asked.

'We'll coach down to Capetown and take the mail boat to London, then a month or so on the Continent. Be back here about June.'

'You should have a good time.'

'Why don't you get married as well?'

'What for?' Sean looked surprised.

'Well, don't you feel as though you're letting the old firm down a bit—me going into this alone?'

'No,' said Sean. 'Anyway, who is there to marry?'

'What about that lass you brought to the races last Saturday; she's a lovely piece of work.'

Sean raised an eyebrow. 'Did you hear her giggle?'

'Yes, I did,' admitted Duff. 'You couldn't very well miss it.'

'Can you imagine that giggle coming at you across the breakfast table?' Sean asked.

Duff shuddered. 'Yes, I see your point. But as soon as we get back I'll have Candy start picking you out a suitable female.'

'I've got a better idea, you let Candy run your life and I'll run my own.'

'That, laddie, is what I'm very much afraid is going to happen.'

Hradsky reluctantly agreed that the activities of the group—the mines, the workshops, the transport companies, all of them—should be suspended on the twentieth to allow their employees to attend Duff's nuptials. This meant that half the business on the Witwatersrand would shut down for the day. Consequently, most of the independent companies decided to close as well. On the eighteenth the wagons carrying the food and liquor started caravanning up the hill to Xanadu. Sean in a burst of benevolence that night invited the entire company from the Opera House to the wedding. He remembered it vaguely the next morning and went down to cancel the invitation but Blue Bessie told him that most of the girls had already gone into town to buy new dresses.

'The hell with it then—let them come. I just hope Candy doesn't guess who they are, that's all.'

On the night of the nineteenth Candy gave them the use of the dining-room and all the downstairs lounges of the Hotel for Duff's bachelor party. François arrived with a masterpiece made up in the mine workshops—an enormous ball and chain. This was formally locked on to Duff's leg and the party began.

Afterwards there was a school of thought that maintained that the building contractor commissioned to repair the damage to the Hotel was a bandit and that the bill for just under a thousand pounds that he presented was nothing short of robbery. However, none of them could deny that the Bok-Bok game in the dining-room, played by a hundred men, had done a certain amount of damage to the furniture and fittings; nor that the chandelier had not been able to support Mr Courtney's weight and on the third swing had come adrift from the ceiling and knocked a moderately large hole through the floor. Neither did anyone dispute the fact that after Jock Heyns had tried unsuccessfully for half an hour to shoot a glass off the top of his brother's head with champagne corks, the resulting ankle-deep lake of wine in the one lounge made it necessary for the floor to be relaid. Nevertheless they felt that a thousand was a little bit steep. On one point, however, everyone agreed—it was a memorable party.

At the beginning Sean was worried that Duff's heart wasn't in it for Duff stood by the bar with the metal ball under one arm listening to the lewd comment, with a lopsided grin fixed on his face. After seven or eight drinks Sean stopped worrying about him and went off to have his way with the chandelier. At midnight Duff talked François into releasing him from his chains and he slipped out of the room. No one—least of all Sean—noticed him go.

Sean could never remember how he got to bed that night but next morning he was tactfully awakened by a waiter with a coffee tray and a note.

'What time is it?' asked Sean as he unfolded the note.

'Eight o'clock, baas.'

'No need to shout,' muttered Sean. His eyes focused with difficulty for the pain in his head was pushing them out of their sockets.

Dear Best Man,
  This serves as a reminder that you and Duff have an appointment at eleven o'clock. I am relying on you to get him there, whole or in pieces. Love Candy.

The brandy fumes in the back of his throat tasted like chloroform, he washed them out with coffee and lit a cigar which started him coughing, and every cough nearly took the top off his head. He stubbed out the cigar and went to the bathroom. Half an hour later he felt strong enough to wake Duff. He went across the sitting-room and pushed open Duff's door; the curtains in the room were still drawn. He pulled them open and was nearly blinded by the sunlight that poured in through them. He turned to the bed and frowned with surprise. He walked slowly across and sat on the edge of it.

'He must have slept in Candy's room,' Sean muttered as he looked at the unused pillows and neatly tucked blankets. It took a few seconds for him to find the fault in his reasoning.

'Then why did she write that note?' He stood up, feeling the first twinge of alarm. A picture of Duff, drunk and helpless lying out in the yard or knocked over the head by one of the busy Johannesburg footpads, came very clear to mind. He ran across the bedroom and into the sitting-room. Halfway to the door he saw the envelope propped up on the mantelpiece and he took it down.

'What is this, a meeting of the authors' guild?' he muttered. 'The place is thick with letters.'

The paper crackled as he opened it and he recognized Duff's back sloping hand.

The first the worst, the second the same. I'm not going through with it. You're the best man so make my excuses to all the nice people. I'll be back when the dust has settled a little. D.

Sean sat down in one of the armchairs, he read through it twice more. Then he exploded.

'Damn you, Charleywood—"make my excuses". You craven bastard. Walk out and leave me to sweep up the mess.'

He rushed across the room with his dressing-gown flapping furiously round his legs. 'You'll make your own damned excuses—even if I have to drag you back on the end of a rope.'

Sean ran down the back stairs. Mbejane was in the stable yard talking to three of the grooms.

'Where is Nkosi Duff?' Sean roared.

They stared at him blankly.

'Where is he?' Sean's beard bristled.

'The baas took a horse and went for a ride,' answered one of the grooms nervously.

'When?' bellowed Sean.

'In the night—perhaps seven, eight hours ago. He should be back soon.'

Sean stared at the groom, breathing heavily. 'Which way did he go?'

'Baas, he did not say.'

Eight hours ago—he could be fifty miles away by now. Sean turned and went back to his room. He threw himself on the bed and poured another cup of coffee.

'This is going to break her up badly—' He imagined the tears and the chaos of undisciplined grief.

'Oh, hell—damn you to hell, Charleywood.' He sipped the coffee and thought about going as well—taking a horse and getting as far away as possible. 'It's no mess of my making—I want no part of it.' He finished the coffee and started dressing. He looked in the mirror to comb his hair and saw Candy standing alone in the chapel, waiting while the silence turned to murmuring and then to laughter.

'Charleywood, you pig,' Sean scowled. 'I can't let her go up there—it'll be bad enough without that. I'll have to tell her.'

He picked up his watch from the dressing-table, it was past nine.

'Damn you, Charleywood.'

He went down the passage and stopped outside Candy's door. He could hear women's voices inside and he knocked before he went in. There were two of Candy's friends and the coloured girl Martha. They stared at him.

'Where's Candy?'

'In the bedroom—but you mustn't go in. It's bad luck.'

'It's the worst bloody luck in the world,' agreed Sean. He knocked on the bedroom door.

'Who is it?'

'Sean.'

'You can't come in—what do you want?'

'Are you decent?'

'Yes, but you mustn't come in.'

He opened the door and looked in on a confusion of squealing females.

'Get out of here'—he said harshly—'I have to speak to Candy alone.'

They fled and Sean closed the door behind them. Candy was in a dressing-gown. Her face was quick with anticipation; her hair was pulled back and hung shiny and soft. She was beautiful, Sean realized. He looked at the frothy pile of her wedding-dress on the bed.

'Candy, bad news—I'm afraid. Can you take it?' He spoke almost roughly—hating it, hating every second of it.

He saw the bloom on her face wither until her expression was dead—blank and dead as a statue.

'He's gone,' said Sean. 'He's run out on you.'

Candy picked up a brush from her dressing-table and started stroking it listlessly through her hair. It was very quiet in the room.

'I'm sorry, Candy.'

She nodded without looking at him; instead she was looking down the lonely corridor of the future. It was worse than tears would have been, that silent acceptance. Sean scratched the side of his nose—hating it.

'I'm sorry—I wish I could do something about it.' He turned to the door.

'Sean, thank you for coming and telling me.' There was no emotion in her voice; like her face it was dead.

'That's all right,' Sean said gruffly.

He rode up to Xanadu. There were people clustered about the marquees on the lawn; by the quality of their laughter he could tell they were drinking already. The sun was bright and as yet not too hot, the band was playing from the wide veranda of the mansion, the women's dresses were gay against the green of the lawns. 'Gala day' fluttered the flags above the tents. 'Gala day' shouted the laughter.

Sean rode up the drive, lifting his hand in brief acknowledgement of the greetings that were shouted to him. From the vantage point of his horse's back he spotted François and Martin Curtis, glasses in hand, standing near the house talking to two of the Opera girls. He gave his horse to one of the native grooms and strode across towards them.

'Hello, boss,' called Curtis. 'Why so glum—you're not the one getting married.' They all laughed.

'François, Martin, come with me please.'

'What's the trouble, Mr Courtney?' François asked as he led them aside.

'The party's over,' Sean said grimly. 'There'll be no wedding.'

They gaped at him.

'Go around and tell everybody. Tell them they'll get their presents back.' He turned to leave them.

'What's happened, boss?' Curtis asked.

'Just tell them that Candy and Duff changed their minds.'

'Do you want us to send them home?'

Sean hesitated. 'Oh, the hell with it—let them stay—let them all get sick drunk. Just tell them there'll be no wedding.'

He went up to the house. He found the pseudo-priest waiting nervously in the downstairs study. The man's adam's apple had been rubbed raw by the starch-stiff dog collar.

'We won't need you,' Sean told him.

He took out his cheque book, sat down at the desk and filled in a cheque form.

'That's for your trouble. Now get out of town.'

'Thank you, Mr Courtney, thank you very much.' The man looked mightily relieved; he started for the door.

'My friend,' Sean stopped him. 'If you ever breathe a word about what we planned to do today, I'll kill you. Do I make myself clear?'

Sean went through to the ballroom, he slipped a small stack of sovereigns into the constable's hand.

'Get all these people out of here.' He gestured with his head at the crowds that were wandering among the tables looking at the gifts. 'Then lock the doors.'

He found the chef in the kitchen. 'Take all this food outside—give it to them now. Then lock up the kitchens.'

He went round the house closing the doors and drawing the curtains. When he walked into the study there was a couple on the big leather couch and the man's hand was under the girl's skirts; she was giggling.

'This isn't a whore house,' Sean shouted at them and they left hurriedly. He sank into one of the chairs. He could hear the voices and the laughter from outside on the lawn, the band was playing a Strauss waltz. It irritated him and he scowled at the marble fireplace. His head was aching again and the skin of his face felt dry and tight from the night's debauch.

'What a mess—what a bloody mess,' he said aloud. After an hour he went out and found his horse. He rode out along the Pretoria Road until he had passed the last houses, then he turned off into the veld. He cantered into the sea of grass with his hat pushed back on his head so the sun and the wind could find his face. He sat relaxed and loose in the saddle and let his horse pick its own way. In the late afternoon he came back to Johannesburg and left his horse with Mbejane in the stable yard. He felt better; the exercise and the fresh air had cleared his head and helped him to see things in truer perspective. He ran himself a deep hot bath, climbed into it and while he soaked the last of his anger at Duff smoothed out. He had control of himself again. He got out of the bath and towelled, then he slipped on his gown and went through to the bedroom. Candy was sitting on his bed.

'Hello, Sean.' She smiled at him, a brittle smile. Her hair was a little tangled now, her face was pale and unrouged. She had not changed from the dressing-gown he had seen her in that morning.

'Hello, Candy.' He picked up the cut-glass bottle of bay rum and rubbed some into his hair and beard.

'You don't mind me coming to see you, do you?'

'No, of course not.' He started combing his hair. 'I was about to come and see you myself.'

She drew her legs up under her in the double-jointed manner of women that is impossible for a man to copy.

'Can I have a drink, please?'

'I'm sorry—I thought you never touched the stuff.'

'Oh, today is special.' She laughed too gaily. 'It's my wedding day, you know.'

He poured the brandy without looking at her. He hated this suffering and he felt his anger at Duff coming back strongly. Candy took the drink and sipped it. She pulled a face. 'It tastes awful.'

'It'll do you good.'

'To the bride,' she said and drank it down quickly.

'Another one?' asked Sean.

'No thanks.' She stood up and went across to the window. 'It's getting dark now—I hate the darkness. Darkness distorts things so; what is bad in the daylight is unbearable at night.'

'I'm sorry, Candy, I wish I could help you.'

She whirled and came to him, her arms circled tight round his neck and her face pale and frightened pressed to his chest.

'Oh, Sean, please hold me—I'm so afraid.'

He held her awkwardly.

'I don't want to think about it. Not now, not now in the darkness,' she whispered. 'Please help me. Please help me not to think about it.'

'I'll stay with you. Don't get yourself upset. Come and sit down. I'll get you another drink.'

'No, no,' she clung to him desperately. 'I don't want to be alone. I don't want to think. Please help me.'

'I can't help you—I'll stay with you but that's all I can do.' Anger and pity mixed together in Sean like charcoal and saltpetre; his fingers tightened hard on her shoulders, digging into the flesh until they met bone.

'Yes, hurt me. That way I'll forget for a while. Take me to the bed and hurt me, Sean, hurt me deep.'

Sean caught his breath. 'You don't know what you're saying, that's crazy talk.'

'It's what I want—to forget for a little. Please, Sean, please.'

'I can't do that, Candy, Duff's my friend.'

'He's finished with me and I with him. I'm your friend too. Oh, God, I'm so alone. Don't you leave me too. Help me, Sean, please help me.'

Sean felt his anger slide down from his chest and flare up, cobra-headed, from his thighs. She felt it also.

'Yes, oh please, yes.'

He picked her up and carried her to the bed. He stood over her while he tore off his gown. She moved on the bed shedding her clothing and spreading herself to meet him, to take him in and let him fill the emptiness. He covered her quickly bayoneting through the soft veil and into the warmth of her body. There was no desire in it, it was cruel and hard drawn out to the frontiers of endurance. For him an expression of anger and pity; for her an act of renunciation. Once was not enough. Again and yet again he took her, until there were brown smudges on the bedclothes from his bleeding back, until her body ached and they lay entwined, wet and tired from the fury of it. In the quiescence of after-passion Sean spoke softly. 'It didn't help, did it?'

'Yes, it did.' Physical exhaustion had weakened the barriers that held back her grief. Still holding on to him, she started to cry.

A street lamp outside the room threw a silver square of light on the ceiling. Sean laid on his back and watched it, listening to Candy's sobs. He recognized the moment they reached their climax and followed their decline into silence. They slept then and later before the day woke together as if by arrangement.

'You are the only one who can help him now,' Candy said.

'Help him do what?' asked Sean.

'Find what he is looking for. Peace, himself—whatever you want to call it. He's lost, you know, Sean. He's lost and lonely, almost as lonely as I am. I could have helped him, I'm sure I could.'

'Duff lost?' Sean asked cynically. 'You must be mad!'

'Don't be so blind, Sean, don't be misled by the big talk and the grand manner. Look at the other things.'

'Like what?' asked Sean.

She didn't answer for a while. 'He hated his father, you know.'

'I guessed as much from the little he told me.'

'The way he revolts at any discipline. His attitude to Hradsky, to women, to life. Think about it, Sean, and then tell me if he acts like a happy man.'

'Hradsky did him a disservice once—he just doesn't like him,' Sean defended Duff.

'Oh, no—it's much deeper than that. In a way Hradsky is an image of his father. He's so broken up inside, Sean, that's why he clings to you. You can help him.'

Sean laughed outright. 'Candy, my dear, we like each other, that's all, there are no deep and dark motives in our friendship. Don't you start getting jealous of me now.'

Candy sat up and the blankets slipped down to her waist. She leaned towards Sean and her breasts swung forward, heavy, round and silver-white in the half light.

'There's a strength in you, Sean, a kind of solid sureness in you that you haven't discovered yet. Duff has recognized it and so will other unhappy people. He needs you, he needs you very badly. Look after him for me, help him to find what he seeks.'

'Nonsense, Candy,' Sean muttered with embarrassment.

'Promise me you'll help him.'

'It's time you went back to your room,' Sean told her. 'People will start talking.'

'Promise me, Sean.'

'All right, I promise.'

Candy slipped out of the bed. She dressed quickly. 'Thank you, Sean, goodnight.'

26

For Sean Johannesburg was poorer without Duff: the streets were not so busy, the Rand Club was drearier and the thrills at the Stock Exchange not so intense. However, there was work to do; his share and Duff's as well.

It was late every evening when the conferences with Hradsky and Max ended and he went back to the Hotel. In the reaction from the day's tension, when his brain was numb and his eyes burned, there was little energy to spare for regret. Yet he was lonely. He went to the Opera House and drank champagne with the crowd there. One of the girls did the Can-Can on the big table in the centre of the room and when she stopped in front of Sean and Trevor Heyns, with her forehead touching her knees and her petticoats hanging over her shoulders, Sean let Trevor whip her pants down—a week before he would have punched Trevor in the nose rather than concede the honour. It wasn't so much fun any more. He went home early.

The following Saturday noon Curtis and François came into the office for the weekly progress meeting. When they had finished and Hradsky had left, Sean suggested, 'Come along with me, we'll go and have a pot or twelve at the Grand National Bar, baptize the weekend so to speak.'

Curtis and François fidgeted in their chairs.

'We had arranged to meet some of the other boys down at the Bright Angels, boss.'

'That's fine, I'll come along with you,' said Sean eagerly, the prospect of being with ordinary men again was suddenly very attractive to him. He felt sickened of the company of those who shook his hand and smiled at him while they waited for a chance to wipe him off the board. It would be good to go along with these two and talk mining and not stocks and shares, to laugh with men who didn't give a damn if C.R.C.'s hit sixty shillings on Monday. He'd get a little drunk with François and Martin; later on perhaps he'd have a fight—an honest, snorting, stand-up fight. God, yes, it would be good to be with men who were clean inside—even if there was dirt under their nails and the armpits of their shirts were stained with sweat.

Curtis glanced quickly at François. 'There'll be just a crowd of roughnecks down there, boss, all the diggers come in on a Saturday.'

'That's fine,' said Sean. 'Let's go.'

He stood up and buttoned his dove-grey coat; the lapels were edged in black watered silk and matched the black pearl pin in his tie. He picked up his cane from the desk.

'Come on—let's get moving.'

They ran into the noise from the Bright Angels a block before they reached the building. Sean grinned and quickened his step like an old gun dog with the scent of the bird in its nostrils again. François and Curtis hurried along on either side of him. There was a big digger standing on the bar counter. Sean recognized him as one of his men from the Little Sister Mine; the man's body was tilted back to balance the weight of the demi-john he held to his lips and his throat jerked regularly as he swallowed. The crowd around his feet were chanting:

'Drink it, down, down, down, down, down.'

The digger finished, he threw the bottle against the far wall and belched like an air-locked geyser. He bowed to acknowledge the applause and then he caught sight of Sean standing in the doorway. He wiped his mouth guiltily with the back of his hand and jumped down off the counter. The other men in the crowd turned and saw Sean and the noise tapered off. They spread out along the bar in silence. Sean led François and Curtis into the room. He placed a pile of sovereigns on the counter.

'Set them up, barman, take the orders. Today is Saturday and it's time to tie the dog loose.'

'Cheers, Mr Courtney.'

'Good luck, sir.'

'*Gezondheid*, Mr Courtney.'

Their voices were subdued with respect.

'Drink up, man, there's plenty more where that came from.'

Sean stood with François and Martin at the bar. They laughed at his jokes. His voice was loud with good fellowship and his face flushed with happiness. He bought more drinks. After a while his bladder started making its presence felt and he went through the back door into the washrooms. There were men talking in there; he stopped before he rounded the edge of the screen into the room. '. . . what's he want to come here for, hey? This isn't the mucking Rand Club.'

'Shh! He'll hear you, man, do you want to lose your job?'

'I don't give a damn. Who does he think he is—"Drink up, boys, there's plenty more where that came from—I'm the boss, boys, do as you're told, boys, kiss my arse, boys."' Sean stood paralysed.

'Pipe down, Frank, he'll go just now.'

'The sooner the better, say I, the big dandy bastard with his ten-guinea boots and gold cane. Let him go back where he belongs.'

'You're drunk, man, don't talk so loud.'

'Sure I'm drunk, drunk enough to go in there and tell him to his face . . .'

Sean backed out through the door and walked slowly across the bar to François and Curtis.

'I hope you'll excuse me; I've just remembered there's something I've got to do this afternoon.'

'That's too bad, boss.' Curtis looked relieved. 'Perhaps some other time, hey?'

They were pleased to see him when he went up to the Rand Club. Three men nearly fought one another to buy him a drink.

27

He had dinner with Candy that night and over the liqueurs he told her about it. She listened without interruption until he finished.

'They didn't want me there. I don't see what I've done to them that they should dislike me that way.'

'And it worries you?' she asked.

'Yes, it worries me. I've never had people feel like that towards me before.'

'I'm glad it worries you.' She smiled gently at him. 'One day you're going to grow into quite a nice person.'

'But why do they hate me?' Sean followed his original line of thought.

'They're jealous of you—you say this man said, "ten-guinea boots and gold cane"—that is what's behind it. You're different from them now, you're rich. You can't expect them to accept that.'

'But I've never done anything to them,' he protested.

'You don't have to. One thing I've found in this life—for everything you get you have to pay a price. This is part of the payment you have to make for success.'

'Hell, I wish Duff was here,' said Sean.

'Then Duff would explain to you that it doesn't matter, wouldn't he?' said Candy. '"Who gives a damn for them, laddie, the unwashed herd? We can do without them,"' she mimicked. Sean scratched the side of his nose and looked down at the table.

'Please, Sean, don't ever let Duff teach you that people don't matter. He doesn't believe it himself—but he's so convincing. People are important. They are more important than gold or places or—or anything.'

Sean looked up at her. 'I realized that once; when I was trapped in the Candy Deep. I saw it very clear then in the darkness and the mud. I made a resolution.' He grinned sheepishly. 'I told myself I'd never hurt anyone again if I could help it. I really meant it, Candy. I felt it so strongly at the time—but, but . . .'

'Yes, I think I understand. That's a big resolution to make and a much bigger one to keep. I don't think any single experience is enough to change a person's way of thinking. It's like building a wall brick by brick. You add to it a little at a time until at last it's finished. I've told you before, Sean, that you have a strength in you. I think one day you'll finish building your wall—and when you do, it will have no weak spots.'

28

The next Tuesday Sean rode up to Xanadu for the first time since Duff had left. Johnson and four of the clerks from the office were at work in the ballroom, packing and labelling the presents.

'Nearly finished, Johnson?'

'Just about, Mr Courtney, I'll send a couple of wagons up tomorrow morning to fetch this lot.'

'Yes, do that. I don't want them lying around here any longer.'

He went up the marble staircase and stood on the top landing. The house had a dead feeling to it: new and sterile, it was waiting for people to come into it and bring it to life. He went down the corridor, stopping to look at the paintings that Candy had chosen. They were oils in soft pastels, woman's colours.

'We can do without these—I'll get some fire in them, scarlets and blacks and bright blues.'

He pushed open the door to his own bedroom. This was better: vivid Persian rugs on the floor, walls panelled in dark satiny wood and a bed like a polo field. He lay on the bed and looked up at the scrolled ornate plaster ceiling.

'I wish Duff were back—we can do some real living in this house.' He went downstairs again.

Johnson was waiting at the foot of the stairs. 'All finished, sir.'

'Good man! Off you go, then.'

He went through into the study and walked across to the gun rack. He took down a Purdey shotgun, carried it to the french windows and looked at it in the light. His nostrils flared a little at the nostalgic smell of gun oil. He brought the gun up to his shoulder, felt the true exciting balance of it and enjoyed it. He swung the barrels in an arc across the room, following the flight of an imaginary bird, and suddenly Duff's face was in his sights. Sean was taken so by surprise that he stood with the gun trained at Duff's head.

'Don't shoot, I'll come quietly,' said Duff solemnly.

Sean lowered the shotgun and carried it back to the rack.

'Hello.'

'Hello,' Duff answered, still standing in the doorway. Sean made a pretence of fitting the gun into the rack with his back to Duff.

'How are you, laddie?'

'Fine! Fine!'

'How's everybody else?'

'To whom do you refer, in particular?' Sean asked.

'Candy, for one.'

Sean considered the question. 'Well, you could have damaged her more by feeding her into a stamp mill.'

'Bad, hey?'

'Bad,' agreed Sean.

They stood in silence for a while.

'I take it that you are not very well disposed towards me either,' Duff said at last.

Sean shrugged his shoulders and moved across to the fireplace.

'Dufford, you're a pig,' he said conversationally.

Duff winced. 'Well, it was nice knowing you, laddie. I suppose from here on our paths diverge?'

'Don't drivel, Duff, you're wasting time. Pour the drinks and then you can tell me what it feels like being a pig. Also I want to discuss with you those paintings Candy has plastered along the upstairs corridor. I don't know whether to give them away or burn them.'

Duff straightened up from leaning against the door jamb; he tried to stop the relief showing on his face but Sean went on quickly, 'Before we close the lid on the subject and bury it, I want to tell you this. I don't like what you did. I can

see why you did it, but I don't like it. That's my piece said. Have you got
anything to add to it?'

'No,' said Duff.

'All right then. I think you'll find a bottle of Courvoisier right at the back of
the cabinet behind the whisky decanter.'

Sean went down to Candy's Hotel that evening and found Candy in her office.

'He's back, Candy.'

'Oh!' Candy caught her breath. 'How is he, Sean?'

'A little chastened, but not much.'

'I didn't mean that—I meant is he well?'

'The same as ever. He had the grace to ask how you were,' said Sean.

'What did you tell him?' asked Candy.

Sean shrugged and sat down in the chair next to her desk. He looked at the
tall stacks of sovereigns that Candy was counting.

'Is that last night's bar takings?' he asked, avoiding her question.

'Yes,' she answered absently.

'You're rich—will you marry me?' he smiled.

Candy stood up and walked across to the window.

'I suppose you two will be moving up to Xanadu now,' she said. Sean
grunted and she went on quickly. 'The Heyns brothers will take over the
Victoria Rooms—they've spoken to me about it already, so don't worry about
that. You'll have fun up there, it will be marvellous for you. I bet you'll have
parties every night and crowds of people. I don't mind, I've gotten used to the
idea now.'

Sean stood up and went to her, he took her gently by the elbow and turned
her to face him. He gave her the silk handkerchief out of his top pocket to blow
her nose.

'Do you want to see him again, Candy?'

She shook her head, not trusting her voice.

'I'll look after him like I promised.' He gave her a hug and turned to go.

'Sean,' she called after him. He looked back. 'You'll come to see me
sometimes. We could have dinner and talk a little. You'll still be my friend,
won't you?'

'Of course, Candy, of course, my dear.'

She smiled damply. 'If you pack your things and Duff's I'll have them sent
up to Xanadu for you.'

29

Sean looked across the boardroom table at Duff, seeking his support. Duff
blew a thick ring of cigar smoke. It spun and expanded like a ripple in a pond
before it hit the table top and disintegrated. Duff wasn't going to back him up,
Sean realized bitterly. They had argued half the previous night. He had hoped
that Duff might still change his mind. Now he knew he wouldn't. He made one
last appeal.

'They have asked for a ten per cent wage increase. I believe they need
it—prices have soared in this town, but wages have remained the same. These
men have wives and children, gentlemen, can't we take that into account?'

Duff blew another smoke ring and Hradsky pulled his watch from his pocket and looked at it pointedly. Max coughed and interrupted. 'I think we've been over that before, Mr Courtney. Could we put it to the vote now?'

Sean watched Hradsky's hand go up against him. He didn't want to look at Duff. He didn't want to see him vote with Hradsky, but he forced himself to turn his head. Duff's hands were on the table in front of him. He blew another smoke ring and watched it hit the table top.

'Those in favour of the motion?' asked Max, and Duff and Sean raised their right hands together. Sean realized then how much it would have meant if Duff had voted against him. Duff winked at him and he couldn't help grinning.

'That is thirty votes for, and sixty against,' declared Max. 'Therefore Mr Courtney's motion falls to the ground. I will inform the Mineworkers' Union of the decision. Now is there any other business before we close the meeting?'

Sean walked with Duff back to his own office.

'The only reason I supported you was because I knew Hradsky would win anyway,' said Duff pleasantly. Sean snorted.

'He's right, of course,' Duff went on unperturbed as he held open the door to Sean's office. 'A ten per cent wage increase would jump the group working costs up ten thousand a month.'

Sean kicked the door closed behind them and didn't answer.

'For God's sake, Sean, don't carry this goodwill-towards-men attitude to absurdity. Hradsky's right—Kruger is likely to slap another one of his taxes on us at any moment and we've got to finance all that new development on the East Rand. We can't let production costs creep up now.'

'All right,' gruffed Sean. 'It's all settled. I just hope we don't have a strike on our hands.'

'There are ways of dealing with strikes. Hradsky has got the police on our side and we can have a couple of hundred men up from Kimberley in no time at all,' Duff told him.

'Damn it, Duff, it's wrong. You know it's wrong. That grotesque Buddha with the little eyes knows it's wrong. But what can I do? Damn it, what can I do?' Sean exploded. 'I feel so bloody helpless.'

'Well, you're the one who wanted to give him control.' Duff laughed at him. 'Stop trying to change the world and let's go home.'

Max was waiting for them in the outer office. He looked nervous. 'Excuse me, gentlemen, could I have a word with you?'

'Who's talking,' Sean asked abruptly, 'you or Hradsky?'

'It's a private matter, Mr Courtney.' Max dropped his voice.

'Can't it wait until tomorrow?' Sean pushed past him and kept going for the door.

'Please, Mr Courtney, it's of the utmost importance.'

Max plucked desperately at Sean's arm.

'What is it, Max?' Duff asked.

'I have to speak to you alone.' Max dropped his voice again and glanced unhappily at the street door.

'Well, speak then,' Duff encouraged him. 'We're alone now.'

'Not here. Can you meet me later?'

Duff raised an eyebrow. 'What is this, Maximilian, don't tell me you are selling dirty pictures.'

'Mr Hradsky is waiting for me at the hotel. I told him I was coming to find some papers, he'll get suspicious if I don't go back immediately.' Max was nearly in tears; his Adam's apple played hide-and-seek behind his high collar, bobbing out and disappearing again. Duff was suddenly very interested in what Max had to say.

'You don't want Norman to know about this?' he asked.

'My goodness, no.' Max came closer to tears.

'When do you want to meet us?'

'Tonight, after ten o'clock when Mr Hradsky has retired.'

'Where?' asked Duff.

'There's a side road round the east end of the Little Sister Mine dump. It's not used any more.'

'I know it,' said Duff. 'We'll ride along there about half past ten.'

'Thank you, Mr Charleywood, you won't regret it.' Max scampered for the door and disappeared.

Duff adjusted his beaver at the correct angle, then he prodded Sean in the belly with the point of his cane.

'Smell it—suck it in.' Duff sniffed appreciatively and Sean did the same.

'I don't smell a thing,' Sean declared.

'The air is thick with it,' Duff told him. 'The sweet smell of treachery.'

They left Xanadu just after half past nine. Duff insisted on wearing a black opera cloak.

'Atmosphere is vital, laddie, you can't go to a rendezvous like this dressed in dirty khaki pants and *veldschoen*. It would ruin the whole thing.'

'Well, I'm damned if I'm going to get into fancy dress. This is a very good suit. It will have to do.'

'Can't I persuade you to wear a pistol in your belt?' asked Duff wistfully.

'No,' laughed Sean.

'No?' Duff shook his head. 'You're a barbarian, laddie. No taste, that's your trouble.'

They avoided the main streets on their way through Johannesburg and met the Cape road half a mile beyond the town. There was only a minute slice of moon left in the dark bowl of the sky. The stars, however, were big and by their light the white mine dumps, each the size of a large hill, stood out like pustules on the earth's face.

Despite himself, Sean felt a little breathless with excitement—Duff's zest was always infectious. They cantered with their stirrups almost touching. Duff's cloak billowing out behind him and the breeze of their passage fanning the tip of Sean's cigar to a fierce red spark.

'Slow down, Duff, the turning's just about here somewhere. It's overgrown, we'll miss it.'

They reined to a walk.

'What's the time?' asked Duff.

Sean drew on his cigar and held his watch close to the glow. 'A quarter after ten. We're early.'

'My bet is Maximilian will be there before us—here's the road.' Duff turned his horse on to it and Sean followed him. The Little Sister Mine dump rose up next to them, steep and white in the starlight. They skirted it but its bulk threw a shadow over them. Duff's horse snorted and shied and Sean gripped with his knees as his own horse danced sideways. Max had stepped out from a scraggy cluster of bushes next to the road.

'Well met by moonlight, Maximilian,' Duff greeted him.

'Please bring your horses off the road, gentlemen.' Max was still showing

signs of the afternoon's agitation. They tied their horses next to Max's among
the bushes and walked across to join him.

'Well, Max, what's new? How are the folks?' Duff asked.

'Before we go any further in this matter, I want you gentlemen to give me
your word of honour that, whether anything comes of it or not, you will never
say a word to anybody of what I tell you tonight.' Max was very pale, Sean
thought, or perhaps it was just the starlight.

'I agree to that,' said Sean.

'Cross my heart,' said Duff.

Max opened the front of his coat and brought out a long envelope. 'I think if
I show you these first it will make it easier to explain my proposition.'

Sean took the envelope from him. 'What are they, Max?'

'The latest statements from all four banks at which Mr Hradsky deals.'

'Matches, Sean, give us a light, laddie,' said Duff eagerly.

'I have a lantern with me,' Max said and he squatted down to light it. Sean
and Duff squatted with him and spread the bank statements in the circle of
yellow light. They examined them in silence until at last Sean rocked back on
his heels and lit another cigar.

'Well, I am glad I don't owe that much money,' Sean announced. Sean
folded up the sheets and put them back in the envelope. He slapped the
envelope into the palm of his free hand and started chuckling. Max reached
across, took it from him and placed it carefully back inside his coat.

'All right, Max, spell it out for us,' said Sean. Max leaned forward and blew
out the lantern. What he had to say was easier said in darkness.

'The large cash payment that Mr Hradsky had to make to you gentlemen
and the limitation of output from his diamond mines in terms of the new cartel
agreements in the diamond industry have forced him to borrow heavily on all
his banks.' Max stopped and cleared his throat. 'The extent of this borrowing
you have seen. Of course, the banks demanded security for the loans and Mr
Hradsky has given them his entire holding of C.R.C. shares. The banks have
set a limit on the shares of thirty-five shillings each. As you know C.R.C.'s are
currently quoted at ninety shillings, which leaves a wide margin of safety.
However, if the shares were to suffer a set-back and fall in price to thirty-five
shillings the banks would sell. They would dump every single share that Mr
Hradsky owns in C.R.C.'s on to the market.'

'Go on, Max,' said Duff. 'I'm beginning to like the sound of your voice.'

'It occurred to me that if Mr Hradsky was temporarily absent from
Johannesburg—say if he went on a trip to England to buy new machinery or
something of that nature—it would be possible for you gentlemen to force the
price of C.R.C.'s down to thirty-five shillings. Done correctly it would only
take three or four days to accomplish. You could sell short and start rumours
that the Leader Reef had pinched out at depth. Mr Hradsky would not be here
to defend his interests and as soon as C.R.C.'s hit thirty-five shillings the
banks would off-load his shares. The price would crash and you, with ready
cash available, would be in a position to buy up C.R.C. shares at a fraction of
their actual value. There is no reason why you shouldn't gain control of the
group and make a couple of million to boot.'

There was another silence. It lasted a long time before Sean asked, 'What do
you get out of it, Max?'

'Your cheque for one hundred thousand pounds, Mr Courtney.'

'Wages are going up,' remarked Sean. 'I thought the standard pay for this type of work was thirty pieces of silver. The rate, I believe, was set by a countryman of yours.'

'Shut up,' snapped Duff, then more pleasantly to Max, 'Mr Courtney likes his little jokes. Tell me, Max, is that all you want—just the money? I'll be frank with you—it doesn't ring true. You must be a moderately rich man as it is.'

Max stood up quickly and started towards the horses. He hadn't reached them before he swung around. His face was in darkness but his voice was naked as he screamed at them.

'Do you think I don't know what they call me—"The Court Jester", "Hradsky's tongue", "Lick-arse". Do you think I like it? Do you think I enjoy crawling to him every minute of every day? I want to be free again. I want to be a man again.' His voice choked off and his hands came up and covered his face. He was sobbing. Sean couldn't watch him and even Duff looked down at the ground in embarrassment. When Max spoke again it was in his usual soft and sad voice.

'Mr Courtney, if you wear your yellow waistcoat to the office tomorrow, I will take it as a sign that you intend to follow my suggestion and that my terms are acceptable to you. I will then make the necessary arrangements to ensure Mr Hradsky's absence from the country.' He untied his horse, mounted and rode away down the track towards the Cape Road. Neither Sean nor Duff moved to stand up. They listened to the hoof-beats of Max's horse fade into the darkness, before Duff spoke. 'Those bank statements were genuine—I had a good look at the seals.'

'And even more genuine was Max's emotion.' Sean flicked his cigar away into the bushes. 'No one could act that well. It made me feel quite sick listening to him. Hell, how can a man so cold-bloodedly betray his trust?'

'Laddie, let's not turn this into a discussion of Max's morals. Let's concern ourselves with the facts. Norman has been delivered into our hands, neatly trussed, spiced with garlic and with a sprig of parsley behind each ear. I say let's cook him and eat him.'

Sean smiled at him. 'Give me a few good reasons. I want you to convince me. The way I feel towards him after that meeting this afternoon, I shouldn't be surprised if I convince easily.'

'One,' Duff held up a finger. 'Norman deserves it.'

Sean nodded.

'Two,' another of Duff's fingers came up. 'If we gain control we can run things the way we want. You can indulge your good resolution and give everybody a pay rise and I'll be top man again.'

'Yes!' Sean tugged at his moustache thoughtfully.

'Three. We came here to make money, we'll never get another opportunity like this. And my last reason, but the most potent—you look so beautiful in that yellow waistcoat, laddie, I wouldn't miss seeing you in it tomorrow morning, not for a thousand C.R.C. shares.'

'It is rather natty,' admitted Sean. 'But listen, Duff, I don't want another Lochtkamper business. Messy, you know.'

Duff stood up.

'Norman's a big boy, he wouldn't do that. Anyway, he'll still be rich—he's got his diamond mines. We'll only be relieving him of his responsibilities on the Witwatersrand.'

They walked across to the horses. Sean had his foot in the stirrup when he stiffened and exclaimed, 'My God, I can't do it. It's all off.'

'Why?' Duff was alarmed.

'I spilt gravy on that waistcoat—I can't possibly wear it tomorrow. My tailor would murder me.'

30

There was no problem in arranging Hradsky's absence—someone had to go to London. There was machinery to buy for the new areas on the East Rand and they had to select two engineers from the hundred or so applicants waiting in England. Not ungraciously, Hradsky allowed himself to be elected for the job.

'We'll give him a farewell party,' Duff suggested to Sean during dinner that night. 'Well, not really a farewell party—but a wake.'

Sean started whistling the 'Dead March' and Duff tapped it out on the table with the handle of his knife.

'We'll have it at Candy's Hot—' Duff cut himself short. 'We'll have it here. We'll really lay it on for poor old Norman so afterwards he'll be able to say, "the bastards may have cleaned me out, but they certainly gave me a grand party".'

'He doesn't like parties,' said Sean.

'That's an excellent reason why we should give him one,' agreed Duff.

A week later when Hradsky and Max left on the morning coach for Port Natal there were fifty members of the Johannesburg Stock Exchange still in full evening dress from the night's party to wave him goodbye. Duff made a touching, if somewhat slurred, little speech and presented Hradsky with a bouquet of roses. Nervous of the crowd that milled about them, the horses bolted when the driver cracked his whip and Max and Hradsky were thrown together in an undignified heap on the rear seat of the coach. The crowd cheered them out of sight. With an arm around his shoulder Sean led Duff across the street to the office and deposited him in one of the deep leather armchairs.

'Are you sober enough to talk sense?' Sean asked dubiously.

'Sure. Always at your service as the lady said to the customer.'

'I managed to have a word with Max last night,' Sean told him. 'He will send us a telegram from Port Natal when he and Hradsky are safely on the mailboat. We won't start anything until we receive it.'

'Very wise—you're the wisest chap I know,' Duff grinned happily.

'You'd better go to bed,' Sean told him.

'Too far,' said Duff. 'I'll sleep here.'

It was another ten days before Max's telegram arrived. Sean and Duff were eating lunch in the Rand Club when it was delivered to their table. Sean slit open the envelope and read the message to Duff.

'Sailing four o'clock this afternoon. Good luck. Max.'

'I'll drink to that,' Duff lifted his wine glass.

'Tomorrow,' said Sean, 'I'll go up to the Candy Deep and tell François to pull all the men out of the bottom levels of the mine. No one's to be allowed in.'

'Put a guard at the fourteenth level,' suggested Duff. 'That'll make it more impressive.'

'Good idea,' agreed Sean. He looked up as someone passed their table and suddenly he started to smile. 'Duff, do you know who that is?'

'Who are you talking about?' Duff looked bewildered.

'That chap who's just gone out into the lounge–there he is, going into the lavatories.'

'Isn't that Elliott, the newspaper fellow?'

'Editor of the *Rand Mail*,' nodded Sean. 'Come with me, Duff.'

'Where are we going?'

'To get a bit of cheap publicity.'

Duff followed Sean out of the dining-room, across the lounge and into the men's lavatories. The door of one of the closets was closed and as they walked in someone farted softly behind it. Sean winked at Duff and went across to the urinal. As he addressed himself to it he said, 'Well, all we can hope for now, Duff, is that Norman will be able to work a miracle in England. Otherwise–' He shrugged his shoulder. Duff picked up his cue.

'We're taking a hell of a chance relying on that. I still say we should sell out now. C.R.C.'s were at ninety-one shillings this morning so it's obvious that the story hasn't leaked out yet. But when it does you won't be able to give the bloody shares away. I say we should get out while the going's good.'

'No,' Sean disagreed. 'Let's wait until we hear from Norman. It's taking a bit of a chance, I know, but we have a responsibility to the men working for us.' Sean took Duff's arm and led him out of the lavatory again; at the door he added the cherry to the top of the pie. 'If and when C.R.C. collapses there are going to be thousands of men out of work–do you realize that?'

Sean closed the door behind them and they grinned delightedly at each other.

'You're a genius, laddie,' whispered Duff.

'I'm happy to say I agree with you,' Sean whispered back.

The next morning Sean woke with the knowledge that something exciting was going to happen that day. He lay and savoured the feeling before he sent his mind out to hunt for the reason. Then he sat up suddenly and reached for the newspaper that lay folded on the coffee tray beside his bed. He shook it open and found what he was looking for on the front page, big headlines: *Is all well with the Central Rand Consolidated? Norman Hradsky's mystery journey.* The story itself was a masterpiece of journalistic evasion. Seldom had Sean seen anyone write so fluently or convincingly on a subject about which he knew nothing. 'It is suggested', 'Usually reliable sources report' and 'There is reason to believe'–all the old phrases of no significance. Sean groped for his slippers and padded down the corridor to Duff's room.

Duff had all the blankets and most of the bed; the girl was curled up like a pink anchovy on the outskirts. Duff was snoring and the girl whimpered a little in her sleep. Sean tickled Duff's lips with the tassel of his dressing-gown cord. Duff's nose twitched and his snores gurgled into silence. The girl sat up and looked at Sean with eyes wide but vacant from sleep.

'Quickly, run,' Sean shouted at her, 'the rebels are coming.'

She leapt straight into the air and landed three feet from the bed quivering with panic. Sean ran a critical eye of her. A pretty filly, he decided, and made a mental note to take her for a trot just as soon as Duff put her out to grass.

'All right,' he reassured her, 'they've gone away now.'

She became aware of her nakedness and Sean's frank appraisal of it. She tried to cover it with hands too small for the task. Sean picked up Duff's gown from the foot of the bed and handed it to her.

'Go and have a bath or something, sweetheart, I want to talk to Mr Charleywood.'

With the gown on she recovered her composure and told him severely, 'I didn't have any clothes on, Mr Courtney.'

'I would never have guessed,' said Sean politely.

'It's not nice.'

'You are too modest—I thought it was better than average. Off you go now, there's a good girl.' With a saucy flick of her head she disappeared into the bathroom and Sean transferred his attention to Duff. Duff had held grimly on to the threads of sleep throughout the exchange but he let go when Sean whacked him across the backside with the folded newspaper. Like a tortoise coming out of its shell his head emerged from the blankets. Sean handed him the paper and sat down on the edge of the bed. He watched Duff's face crease into laughter lines before he spoke.

'You better get down to the Editor's office and shout at him a little—just to confirm his suspicions. I'll go up to the Candy Deep and close all the bottom levels. I'll meet you back at the Exchange at opening time and don't forget to clean that grin off your face before you show it round town. Try to look haggard, it shouldn't be difficult for you.'

When Sean arrived at the Stock Exchange building the crowd had filled the street outside. Mbejane eased the landau into it and it opened to give them a passage. Sean scowled straight ahead and ignored the questions which were shouted at him from all around. Mbejane stopped the carriage outside the main entrance and four police constables held back the mob while Sean hurried across the pavement and through the double doors. Duff was there ahead of him, the centre of a turbulent circle of members and brokers. He saw Sean and waved frantically over the heads of his inquisitors. That was sufficient to switch their attention from Duff to Sean and they flocked to him, ringing him in with anxious angry faces. Sean's hat was knocked forward over his eyes and a button popped off his coat as one of them caught hold of his lapels.

'Is it true?' the man shouted, spittle flying from his lips into Sean's face. 'We've got a right to know if it's true.'

Sean swung his cane in a full overarm stroke on to the man's head and sent him tottering backwards into the arms of those behind him.

'Back, you bastards,' he roared at them using both the point and the edge of his cane to beat them away, scattering them across the floor until he stood alone, glowering at them with the cane still twitching restlessly in his hand.

'I'll make a statement later on. Until then, behave yourselves.' He adjusted his hat, picked the loose thread where the button had been from his coat and stalked across to join Duff. He could see Duff's grin starting to lift the corner of his mouth and he cautioned him silently with his eyes. Grim-faced they walked through into the members' lounge.

'How's it going your end?' Duff kept his voice low.

'Couldn't be better.' Sean contrived a worried expression. 'I've got an armed guard on the fourteenth level. When this bunch hear about that, they'll really start frothing at the mouth.'

'When you make your statement, let it ring with obvious false confidence,' Duff instructed. 'If it goes on like this we'll have the shares down to thirty-five shillings within an hour of opening.'

Five minutes before opening time Sean stood in the President's box and made his address to his fellow members, Duff listened to him with mounting admiration. Sean's hearty reassurances and verbal side-stepping were enough to strike despair into the souls of the most hardened optimists. Sean finished his speech and climbed down from the box amid a gloomy lack of applause. The bell rang and the brokers stood singly or in small disconsolate groups about the floor. The first tentative offer was made. 'I sell C.R.C.'

But there was no rush to buy. Ten minutes later there was a sale recorded at eighty-five shillings, six shillings lower than the previous day's closing price. Duff leaned across to Sean. 'We'll have to start selling some of our own shares to get things moving, otherwise everybody's going to keep sitting on the fence.'

'That's all right,' Sean nodded, 'we'll buy them back later at a quarter of the price. But wait until the news about the Candy Deep gets out.'

It was just before ten o'clock when that happened. The reaction was sharp. In one quick burst of selling C.R.C.'s dropped to sixty shillings. But there they hung, fluctuating nervously in the chaos of hope and doubt.

'We'll have to sell now,' whispered Duff, 'they are short of script. We'll have to give it to them otherwise the price will stick here.'

Sean felt his hands trembling and he clenched them in his pockets. Duff was showing signs of the strain as well, there was,a nerve jumping in his cheek and his eyes had receded into their sockets a little. This was a game with high stakes.

'Don't overdo it—sell thirty thousand.'

The price of C.R.C.'s sagged under the weight but levelled out at forty-five shillings. There was still another hour until high change and Sean's whole body was screwed up tight with tension. He felt the cold patches of sweat under his arms.

'Sell another thirty thousand,' he ordered his clerk and even to himself his voice sounded wheezy. He stubbed out his cigar in the copper ashtray next to his chair; it was already half full of butts. It was no longer necessary for either of them to act worried. This time the price stuck at forty shillings and the sale of sixty thousand more of their shares failed to move it down more than a few shillings.

'Someone's buying up,' muttered Sean uneasily.

'It looks like it,' agreed Duff. 'I'll lay odds it's that bloody Greek Efthyvoulos. It looks as if we'll have to sell enough to glut him before they'll drop any further.'

By high change Duff and Sean had sold three-quarters of their holdings in C.R.C.'s and the price still stood stubbornly at thirty-seven and sixpence. So tantalizingly close to the magic figure that would release a flood of Hradsky's shares on to the unprepared market, but now they were nearing the stage when they would no longer have any shares with which to force the price down that last two and sixpence.

The market closed and left Duff and Sean sitting limply in their armchairs, shaken and tired as prizefighters at the end of the fifteenth round. Slowly the lounge emptied but still they sat on. Sean leaned across and put his hand on Duff's shoulder. 'It's going to be all right,' he said. 'Tomorrow it will be all right.'

They looked at each other and they exchanged strength, each of them drawing it from the other until they were both smiling. Sean stood up. 'Come on, let's go home.'

Sean went to bed early and alone. Although he felt drained of energy, sleep was a long time coming to him and when it did it was full of confused dreams and punctuated with sharp jerks back into wakefulness. It was almost a relief to see the dawn define the windows as grey squares and to be released from his unrewarding rest. At breakfast he drank a cup of coffee and found that his stomach was unable to accept the plateful of steak and eggs that was offered it for it was already screwing up tight in anticipation of the day ahead. Duff was edgy and tired-looking as well; they spoke only a little during the meal and not at all in the carriage when Mbejane drove them down to the Exchange.

The crowd was outside the Stock Exchange again. They forced their way through it and into the building; they took their seats in the lounge and Sean looked round at the faces of his fellow members. In each of them were the marks of worry, the same darkness round the eyes and the jerkiness in movement. He watched Jock Heyns yawn extravagantly and had to do the same; he lifted his hand to cover his mouth and found it was trembling again. He laid the hand on the arm of his chair and kept it still. Across the lounge Bonzo Barnes caught Sean's eye and looked away quickly, then he also gaped into a cavernous yawn. It was the tension. In the years ahead Sean would see men yawn like that while they waited for the dawn to send them against the Boer guns. Duff leaned across to him and broke his line of thought.

'As soon as the trading starts, we'll sell. Try and panic them. Do you agree?'

'Sudden death,' Sean nodded. He couldn't face another morning of that mental agony. 'Couldn't we offer shares at thirty-two shillings and sixpence and get it over with?' he asked.

Duff grinned at him. 'We can't do that, it's too obvious—we'll just have to go on suffering to sell at best and let the price fall on its own.'

'I suppose you're right—but we'll play our high cards now and dump the rest of our shares as soon as the market opens. I don't see how the price can possibly hold after that.'

Duff nodded. He beckoned to their authorized clerk who was waiting patiently at the door of the lounge and when the man came up to them he told them, 'Sell one hundred thousand C.R.C.'s at best.'

The clerk blinked but he jotted the order down on his pad and went out on to the main floor where the other brokers were gathering. It was a few minutes from the bell.

'What if it doesn't work?' Sean asked. The tightness in his belly was nauseating him.

'It must work—it's got to work,' Duff whispered as much to himself as to Sean. He was twisting his fingers round the head of his cane and chewing against clenched teeth. They sat and waited for the bell and when it rang Sean jumped then reached sheepishly for his cigar case. He heard their clerk's voice, raised sharply, 'I sell C.R.C.'s,' and then the confused mumble of voices as the trading started. Through the lounge door he saw the recorder chalk up the first sale. 'Thirty-seven shillings.'

He drew hard on his cigar and lay back in his chair forcing himself to relax, ignoring the restless tapping of Duff's fingers on the arm of the chair next to him. The recorder wiped out the figures and wrote again. 'Thirty-six shillings.'

Sean blew out cigar smoke in a long jet. 'It's moving,' he whispered and Duff's hand clenched on the arm of the chair, his knuckles paling from the pressure of his grip.

'Thirty-five.' The elusive number at last. Sean heard Duff sigh next to him and his voice, 'Now! watch it go, laddie, now the banks will come on. Get ready, laddie, get ready now.'

'Thirty-four and six,' wrote the recorder.

'They must come in now,' said Duff again. 'Get ready to get rich, laddie.'

Their clerk was coming back across the floor and into the lounge. He stopped in front of their chairs. 'I managed to sell them, sir.'

Sean straightened up quickly. 'So soon?' he asked.

'Yes, sir, three big sales and I got rid of them all. I'm afraid the last was only at thirty-four and sixpence.'

Sean stared back at the board. The figure was still at thirty-four and sixpence.

'Duff, something's going on here. Why haven't the banks come in yet?'

'We'll force them to off-load.' Duff's voice was unnaturally hoarse. 'We'll force the bastards.' He pulled himself half out of his chair and snarled at the clerk.

'Sell another one hundred thousand at thirty shillings.' The man's face went slack with surprise. 'Hurry, man, do you hear me? What are you waiting for?' The clerk backed away from Duff, then he turned and scurried out of the lounge.

'Duff, for God's sake.' Sean grabbed his arm. 'Have you gone mad?'

'We'll force them,' muttered Duff. 'They'll have to sell.'

'We haven't got another hundred thousand shares.' Sean jumped up. 'I'm going to stop him.' He ran across the lounge but before he reached the door he saw the sale being chalked up on the board at thirty shillings. He pushed his way across the crowded floor until he reached his clerk. 'Don't sell any more,' he whispered.

The man looked surprised. 'I've sold them already, sir.'

'The whole hundred thousand?' There was horrified disbelief in Sean's voice.

'Yes, sir, someone took the lot in one batch.'

Sean walked back across the floor in a daze. He sank into the chair beside Duff.

'They're sold already.' He spoke as though he didn't believe himself.

'We'll force them, we'll force them to sell,' muttered Duff again and Sean turned to him with alarm. Duff was sweating in little dewdrops across his forehead and his eyes were very bright.

'Duff, for God's sake,' Sean whispered to him, 'steady man.' Sean knew that they were watched by everybody in the lounge. The watching faces seemed as large as those seen through a telescope and the buzz of their voices echoed strangely in his ears. Sean felt confused: everything seemed to be in slow motion like a bad dream. He looked through into the trading floor and saw the crude number thirty still chalked accusingly against C.R.C. Where are the banks? Why weren't they selling?

'We'll force them, we'll force the bastards,' Duff said again. Sean tried to answer him but the words wouldn't come. He looked back across the trading floor and now he knew it was a bad dream for Hradsky and Max were there, walking across the floor towards the members' lounge. Men were crowding around them and Hradsky was smiling and holding up his hands as if to fend off their questions. They came through into the lounge and Hradsky went to his chair by the fireplace. He lowered himself into it with his shoulder sagging forward and his waistcoat wrinkled tightly around the full bag of his belly. He was still smiling and Sean thought that his smile was one of the most unnerving things he had ever seen. He watched it with flesh-crawling fascination and beside him Duff was just as still and stricken. Max spoke quietly to Hradsky and then he stood up and walked across to Sean and Duff. He stopped in front of them.

'The clerk informs us that you have contracted to sell to Mr Hradsky five hundred thousand shares in C.R.C.'s at an average price of thirty-six shillings.' Max's lashes drooped sadly on to his cheeks. 'The total issue of C.R.C.'s, as you know, is one million shares. During the last two days Mr Hradsky was able to purchase another seventy-five thousand shares apart from the ones you sold to him. This makes his total holdings of C.R.C.'s almost six hundred thousand shares. It seems therefore that you have sold shares that don't exist. Mr Hradsky foresees that you will have some difficulty fulfilling your contract.'

Sean and Duff went on staring at him. He turned to leave them and Duff blurted out, 'But the banks—why didn't the banks sell?'

Max smiled a mournful little smile. 'The day he reached Port Natal Mr Hradsky transferred sufficient funds from his accounts there to liquidate his overdrafts in Johannesburg. He sent you that telegram and returned here immediately. We only arrived an hour ago.'

'But—but, you lied to us. You tricked us!'

Max inclined his head. 'Mr Charleywood, I will not discuss honesty with a man who does not understand the meaning of the word.' He went back to Hradsky's side. Everyone in the lounge had heard him and while Duff and Sean went on sitting among the ruins of their fortune the struggle to buy C.R.C. shares started on the main floor. In five minutes the price was over ninety shillings and still climbing. When it reached one hundred shillings, Sean touched Duff's arm.

'Let's go.' They stood up together and started for the door of the members' lounge. As they passed Hradsky's chair he spoke.

'Yes, Mr Charleywood, you can't win all the time.' It came out quite clearly with only a slight catch on the 'c's'—they were always difficult letters for Norman Hradsky.

Duff stopped, he turned to face Hradsky, his mouth opened as he struggled to find a reply. His lips moved, groping, groping for words—but there were none. His shoulders drooped, he shook his head and turned away. He stumbled once at the edge of the floor. Sean held his arm and guided him through the excited jabber of brokers. No one took any notice of the two of them. They were bumped and jostled before they were through the crush and out on to the pavement. Sean signalled Mbejane to bring the carriage. They climbed into it and Mbejane drove them to Xanadu.

They went through into the drawing-room.

'Get me a drink, please, Sean.' Duff's face was grey and crumpled-looking. Sean poured two tumblers half full of brandy and carried one across to Duff. Duff drank and then sat staring into the empty glass.

'I'm sorry—I lost my head. I thought we'd be able to buy those shares for dirt, when the banks started selling.'

'It doesn't matter,' Sean's voice was tired. 'We were smashed before that happened. Christ! What a well-laid trap it was!'

'We couldn't have known. It was so damn cunning, we couldn't have guessed, could we, Sean?' Duff was trying to excuse himself.

Sean kicked off his boots and loosened his collar. 'That night up at the mine dump–I would have staked my life Max wasn't lying.' He lay back in the chair and stirred his brandy with a circular movement of his hand. 'Christ, how they must have laughed to see us stampede into the pitfall!'

'But we aren't finished, Sean, we aren't completely finished, are we?' Duff was pleading with him, begging for a peg to hang his hope on. 'We'll come out of this all right, you know we will, don't you? We'll save enough out of the wreckage to start again. We'll build it all up again, won't we, Sean?'

'Sure,' Sean laughed brutally. 'You can get a job down at the Bright Angels cleaning out the spittoons and I'll get one at the Opera House playing the piano.'

'But–but–there'll be something left. A couple of thousand even. We could sell this house.'

'Don't dream, Duff, this house belongs to Hradsky. Everything belongs to him.' Sean flicked the brandy that was left in his glass into his mouth and swallowed it. He stood up quickly and went across to the liquor cabinet. 'I'll explain it to you. We owe Hradsky a hundred thousand shares that don't exist. The only way we can deliver them is to buy them from him first and he can set his own price on them. We're finished, Duff, do you know what that means? Smashed! Broken!' Sean poured brandy into his glass, slopping a little on the sideboard. 'Have another drink on Hradsky, it's his brandy now.' Sean swept his arm round the room, pointing at the rich furniture and heavy curtains. 'Take a last look at this lot. Tomorrow the Sheriff will be here to attach it; then through the due processes of the law it will be handed to its rightful owner–Mr Norman Hradsky.' Sean started back towards his chair and then he stopped. 'The due processes of the law,' he repeated softly. 'I wonder–it might just work.'

Duff sat up eagerly in his chair. 'You've got an idea?'

Sean nodded. 'Well, half an idea anyway. Listen, Duff, if I can save a couple of thousand out of this do you agree that we get out of here?'

'Where to–where will we go?'

'We were facing north when we started. It's as good a direction as any. They say there's gold and ivory beyond the Limpopo for those who want it.'

'But, why can't we stay here? We could play the stock market.' Duff looked uncertain, almost afraid.

'Damn it, Duff, we're finished here. It's a different story playing the market when you are paying the fiddler and calling the tune, but with a mere thousand or so we'd be among the dogs fighting for the scraps under Hradsky's table. Let's get out and start again. We'll go north, hunt ivory and prospect for a new reef. We'll take a couple of wagons and find another fortune. I bet you've forgotten how it feels to sit on a horse and handle a rifle, to have the wind in your face and not a whore or a stockbroker within five hundred miles.'

'But it means leaving everything we've worked for,' Duff groaned.

'Sweet merciful heavens, man, are you blind or just plain stupid?' Sean stormed at him. 'You don't own anything, so how the hell can you leave something you haven't got? I'm going down to see Hradsky and try to make a deal with him. Are you coming?'

Duff looked at him without seeing him, his lips were trembling and he was shaking his head. At last he was realizing the position they were in and the impact of it had dazed him. The higher you ride the further there is to fall.

'All right,' said Sean. 'Wait for me here.'

Hradsky's suite was full of talking, laughing men. Sean recognized most of them as the courtiers who used to cluster round the throne on which he and Duff had sat. The King is dead, long live the King! They saw him standing in the doorway and the laughter and loud voices fizzled out. He saw Max take two quick steps to the stinkwood desk in the corner, pull open the top drawer and drop his hand into it. He stood like that watching Sean. One by one the courtiers picked up their hats and canes and hurried out of the room. Some of them mumbled embarrassed greetings as they brushed past Sean. Then there were only the three of them left: Sean standing quietly in the doorway, Max behind the desk with his hand on the pistol and Hradsky in the chair by the fireplace watching through the yellow, half-hooded eyes.

'Aren't you going to invite me in, Max?' Sean asked and Max glanced quickly at Hradsky, saw his barely perceptible nod and looked back at Sean. 'Come in, please, Mr Courtney.'

Sean pushed the door shut behind him. 'You won't need the gun, Max, the game is over.'

'And the score is in our favour, is it not, Mr Courtney?'

Sean nodded. 'Yes, you've won. We are prepared to make over to you all the C.R.C. shares we hold.'

Max shook his head unhappily. 'I'm afraid it's not quite so easy as that. You have undertaken to sell us a certain number of shares and we must insist upon delivery in full.'

'Just where do you suggest we get them?' Sean asked.

'You could buy them on the Stock Exchange.'

'From you?'

Max shrugged but made no reply.

'So you are going to twist the knife, are you?'

'You put it very poetically, Mr Courtney,' agreed Max.

'Have you considered the consequences of forcing us into bankruptcy?'

'I will admit freely that the consequences to you do not concern us.'

Sean smiled. 'That was not very nice, Max, but I was talking about it from your point of view. Sequestration orders, creditors' meetings—you can rest assured that the liquidator appointed will be a member of the *Volksraad* or a relative of one. There will be court actions and counter actions, enforced sale of the shares in the estate and costs to pay. A liquidator with any sense at all could string it out for three or four years, all the time drawing a handsome commission. Have you thought about that, Max?'

The narrowing of Max's eyes showed that he hadn't. He looked at Hradsky with a trace of helplessness in his face, and Sean took a little comfort from that look.

'Now what I suggest is this—you let us draw ten thousand, take our horses and personal belongings. We in exchange will give you the rest. Shares, bank accounts, property, everything. You cannot possibly get more out of it if you force us into bankruptcy.'

Hradsky gave Max a message in their private facial code and Max interpreted it to Sean.

'Would you mind waiting outside, please, while we discuss this offer of yours.'

'I'll go down and have a drink at the bar,' said Sean. He pulled his watch from his waistcoat pocket and checked the time. 'Will twenty minutes be enough?'

'Ample, thank you, Mr Courtney.'

Sean had his drink by himself although the bar was nowhere near empty. This was not an arrangement of his own choosing, but he was flying the fever flag of failure and so he had to take an isolation berth at one end of the bar while all the other ships steered wide of him. No one looked in his direction and the conversation that went on round him was carefully arranged so as to exclude him. While he waited out the twenty minutes he amused himself by imagining the reactions of these his friends if he were to ask them for a loan. This helped to take the sting out of their snubs but still he felt it rankling. He looked at his watch again. The twenty minutes were up. Sean walked along the counter towards the door. Jock and Trevor Heyns saw him coming, they turned away abruptly and immediately became absorbed in staring at the bottle-lined shelves behind the bar counter. Sean stopped level with Jock and cleared his throat deferentially. 'Jock, could you spare a minute?'

Jock turned slowly. 'Ah, Sean. Yes, what is it?'

'Duff and I are leaving the Rand. I have something for you, just something to remember us by. I know Duff would want you to have it too.'

Jock reddened with embarrassment. 'That's not necessary,' he said and started to turn back to his drink.

'Please, Jock.'

'Oh, all right,' Jock's voice was irritable. 'What is it?'

'This,' Sean said and stepped forward, moving his weight behind the fist. Jock's large and whisky-flushed nose was a target to dream about. It was not one of Sean's best punches, he was out of training, but it was good enough to send Jock in a spectacular back-somersault over the counter. Dreamily Sean picked up Jock's glass and emptied it over Trevor's head.

'Next time you meet me smile and say "Hello",' he told Trevor. 'Until then—stay out of mischief.'

He went up the stairs to Hradsky's suite in much better spirits. They were waiting for him.

'Give me the word, Max,' Sean could even grin at him.

'Mr Hradsky has very generously–'

'How much?' Sean cut him short.

'Mr Hradsky will allow you to take fifteen hundred and your personal effects. As part of the agreement you will give an undertaking not to embark on any business venture on the Witwatersrand for a period of three years.'

'That will be too soon,' said Sean. 'Make it two thousand and you've got a deal.'

'The offer is not open to discussion.'

Sean could see they meant it. They didn't have to bargain; it was a statement.

'All right, I accept.'

'Mr Hradsky has sent for his lawyer to draw up the agreement. Would you mind waiting, Mr Courtney?'

'Not at all, Max, you forget I am a gentleman of leisure now.'

31

Sean found Duff still sitting in the chair where he had left him in the drawing-room of Xanadu. The bottle clutched in his hand was empty and he was unconscious. He had spilt brandy down the front of his waistcoat and three of the buttons were undone. Huddled in the big chair, his body seemed to have shrunk and the curly hair hanging on to his forehead softened the gaunt lines of his face. Sean loosened his fingers from the neck of the bottle and Duff moved restlessly, muttering and twisting his head.

'Bedtime for small boys,' said Sean. He lifted him out of the chair and hung him over one shoulder.

Duff sicked up copiously.

'That's the way, show Hradsky what you think of his bloody carpet,' Sean encouraged him. 'Give him another one for luck, but not on my boots.'

Duff did as he was bid and, chuckling, Sean carried him up the stairs. At the top he stopped and with Duff still bundled over one shoulder tried to analyse his own feelings. Damn it, he felt happy. It was ridiculous to feel so happy in the midst of disaster. He went on down the passage still wondering at himself and into Duff's room. He dropped Duff on the bed and stripped his clothes off, then he rolled him under the blankets. He brought the enamel wash basin from the bathroom and placed it next to the bed.

'You may need this—sleep well. There's a long ride ahead of us tomorrow.'

He stopped again at the top of the stairs and looked down their marble slope into the splendour of the lobby. He was leaving all of it and that was nothing to feel happy about. He laughed aloud. Perhaps it was because he had faced complete annihilation and at the last instant had changed it into something less; by avoiding the worst he had made defeat into a victory. A pathetic little victory to be sure, but at least they were no worse off now than they had been when they had arrived on the Rand. Was that the reason? Sean thought about it and found that it wasn't the whole truth. There was also a feeling of release. That was another part of it. To go on his way: north to a new land. He felt the tingle of anticipation.

'Not a whore or a stockbroker within five hundred miles,' he said aloud and grinned. He gave up trying to find words for his feeling. Emotion was so damned elusive: as soon as you cornered it, it changed its shape and the net of words which you had ready to throw over it was no longer suitable. He let it go free to range through his body, accepting and enjoying it. He ran down the stairs, out through the kitchens and into the stable yard.

'Mbejane!' he shouted, 'where the hell are you?'

The clatter of a stool overturning in the servants' quarters and the door of one of the rooms burst open.

'Nkosi—what is it?' The urgency of Sean's voice had alarmed Mbejane.

'Which are the best six horses we have?'

Mbejane named them, making no attempt to hide his curiosity.

'Are they all salted against the Nagana?'*

'All of them, Nkosi.'

*Sleeping sickness. Salting involved deliberate exposure to the sting of the tsetse fly. Animals that recovered were then immune.

'Good—have them ready before tomorrow's light.. Two with saddles, the others to carry the packs.'

Mbejane turned on his smile. 'Could it be we are going hunting, Nkosi?'

'It could easily be,' Sean agreed.

'How long will we be gone, Nkosi?'

'How long is for ever? Take leave of all your women, bring your kaross and your spears and we will see where the road leads.'

Sean went back to his bedroom. It took him half an hour to pack. The pile of discarded clothing in the centre of the room grew steadily and what he kept made only half a horseload. He crammed it into two leather valises. He found his sheepskin coat in the back of one of the closets and threw it over a chair with his leather breeches and slouch hat, ready to wear in the morning. He went down to the study and made his selection from the gun rack, ignoring the fancy doubles and obscure calibres. He took down a pair of shotguns and four Mannlichers.

Then he went to tell Candy goodbye. She was in her suite but she opened quickly to his knock.

'Have you heard?' he asked her.

'Yes, the whole town knows. Oh! Sean, I'm so sorry—please come in.' She held the door open for him. 'How is Duff?'

'He'll be all right—right now he's both drunk and asleep.'

'I'll go to him,' she said quickly. 'He'll need me now.'

For answer Sean raised an eyebrow and looked at her until she dropped her eyes.

'No, you're right. I suppose. Perhaps later, when he's got over the first shock.' She looked up at Sean and smiled. 'I suppose you need a drink. It must have been hell for you as well.' She went across to the cabinet. She had on a blue gown and it clung to the womanish thrust of her hips and did not go high enough to cover the cleft of her breasts. Sean watched her pour his drink and bring it to him. She was lovely, he thought.

'Till we meet again, Candy,' Sean lifted his glass.

Her eyes wide and very blue. 'I don't understand. Why do you say that?'

'We're going, Candy, first thing tomorrow.'

'No, Sean—you're joking.' But she knew he wasn't. There wasn't much to say after that. He finished his drink and they talked for a while, then he kissed her.

'Be happy, please,' he ordered her.

'I'll try. Come back one day soon.'

'Only if you promise to marry me,' he smiled at her and she caught hold of his beard and tugged his head from side to side.

'Get away with you—before I hold you to that.' He left her then because he knew she was going to weep and he didn't want to watch it.

The next morning Duff packed his gear under Sean's direction. He followed each instruction with a dazed obedience, answering when Sean spoke but otherwise withdrawn in a protective shell of silence. When he had finished Sean made him pick up his bags and marched him down to where the horses waited in the chill gloom of not-yet day. With the horses were men, four shapes in the darkness. Sean hesitated before going out into the yard.

'Mbejane,' he called. 'Who are these with you?'

They came forward into the light that poured through the doorway and Sean chuckled.

'Hlubi, of the noble belly! Nonga! and is it you, Kandhla?' Men who had worked beside him in the trenches of the Candy Deep, had plied the spades that had uncovered his fortune, had plied the spears that protected it from the first predators. Happy at his recognition of them, for it had been many years, they crowded forward smiling as widely and whitely as only a Zulu can.

'What brings you three rogues together so early in the day?' Sean asked, and Hlubi answered for them.

'Nkosi, we heard talk of a trek and our feet burned, we heard talk of hunting and we could not sleep.'

'There is no money for wages,' Sean spoke gruffly to cover the sudden rush of affection he felt for them.

'We made no talk of wages,' Hlubi answered with dignity. Sean nodded, it was the reply he had expected. He cleared his throat and went on.

'You would come with me when you know that I have the Tagathi on me?' He used the Zulu word for witchcraft. 'You would follow me knowing that behind me I leave a spoor of dead men and sorrow?'

'Nkosi,' Hlubi was grave as he answered. 'Something always dies when the lion feeds—and yet there is meat for those that follow him.'

'I hear the chatter of old women at a beer drink,' Mbejane observed drily. 'There is no more to say and the horses grow restless.'

They rode down the driveway of Xanadu between the jacaranda trees and the smooth wide lawns. Behind them the mansion was grey and unlighted in the half darkness. They took the Pretoria road, climbed to the ridge and checked their horses at the crest. Sean and Duff looked back across the valley. The valley was filled with early morning mist, and the mine headgears probed up out of it. They watched the mists turn to gold as the low sun touched them and a mine hooter howled dismally.

'Couldn't we stay for just a week longer—perhaps we could work something out?' Duff asked softly.

Sean sat silently staring at the golden mist. It was beautiful. It hid the scarred earth and it hid the mills—it was a most appropriate cloak for that evil, greedy city. Sean turned his horse away towards Pretoria and slapped the loose end of his reins across its neck.

3. THE WILDERNESS

I

They stayed five days in Pretoria, just long enough to buy the wagons and commission them, and when they left on the morning of the sixth day they went north on the Hunters Road. The wagons moved in column urged on by the Zulus and a dozen new servants that Sean had hired. They were followed by a mixed bag of black and white urchins and stray dogs; men called good luck after them and women waved from the verandas of the houses which lined the road. Then the town was behind them and they were out into the veld with only a dozen of the more adventurous mongrels still following them.

They made fifteen miles the first day and when they camped that night beside the ford of a small stream, Sean's back and legs ached from his first full day in the saddle in over five years. They drank a little brandy and ate steaks grilled over wood embers, then they let the fire die and sat and looked at the night. The sky was a curtain at which a barrel of grape-shot had been fired, riddling it with the holes through which the stars shone. The voices of the servants made a hive murmur as a background to the wailing of a jackal in the darkness beyond the firelight. They went to their living wagon early and for Sean the feel of rough blankets instead of silk sheets and the hardness of a straw mattress were not sufficient to keep him long from sleep.

From an early start the following morning they put another twenty miles behind them before outspan that night and twenty more the next day. The push and urgent drive were habits Sean had acquired on the Rand when every minute was vital and the loss of a day was a disaster. They were habits that stuck, and he pushed the caravan northward as impatiently as he would have chivvied the men on the Candy Deep who were cutting a drive to intersect the Reef. Then one morning, when they were inspanning the oxen at the usual hour of dawn, Mbejane asked him, 'Do we go to meet someone, Nkosi?'

'No. Why do you ask?'

'When a man moves fast there is usually a reason. I was seeking the reason for our haste.'

'The reason is—' Sean stopped. He looked around him quickly as if to find it, then he cleared his throat and scratched the side of his nose, '—outspan an hour before high sun,' he finished abruptly and went to his horse. He and Duff rode out a mile or two ahead of the wagons that day, then instead of keeping to the track or hurrying back to chase up the caravan Sean suggested, 'Let's ride across to the kopje over there. We'll leave the horses at the bottom and climb up to the top.'

'What for?' asked Duff.

'For the hell of it—come on.'

They hobbled the horses and set off up the steep side of the kopje, picking their way over the tumbled boulders and through the tangle of tree trunks. They were sweating and blowing hard when they came out on the summit and found a place with a shade and a flat rock ledge on which to sit. Sean gave Duff a cheroot and they smoked and looked out across the land that was spread like a map below them.

Here the grasslands of the high veld were starting to blend into the forests and hilly country of the bushveld. There were vleis open as wheatfields, ending suddenly against a hill or bounded by haphazard plantations of tall trees. From the height at which they sat they could trace the courses of underground rivers by the dark green and superior height of the trees that grew above them. Everything else was the colour of Africa—brown, a thousand different shades of brown. Pale brown grass on red brown soil, with twisted, chocolate-brown tree trunks reaching up to the moving masses of brown leaves at their tips. Flickering indefinite brown were the herds of springbok that fed among the trees and on the slopes of the bare bulging brown hills, and the brown land reached away vast and unhurried into immeasurable distance, unmarred by the scratchings of man: tranquil and dignified in its immensity.

'It makes me feel small, but sort of safe—as though no one will notice me here,' said Duff, then laughed self-consciously.

'I know what you mean,' Sean answered him. He saw that for the first time since they had left the Rand the strain was gone from Duff's face. They smiled at each other and leaned back against the rock face behind them. They watched their wagons, far below them, coil into the tight circle of the laager and the cattle turned free move out to graze. The sun sank and the shadows stretched out longer and longer across the land. At last they went down the hill and found their horses. That night they stayed later than usual next to the fire and though they talked little there was the old feeling between them again. They had discovered a new reef that was rich with the precious elements of space and time. Out here there was more of those two treasures than a man could use in a dozen life-times. Space to move, to ride or to fire a rifle; space spread with sunlight and wind, grass and trees, but not filled with them. There was also time. This was where time began: it was a quiet river, moving but not changed by movement; draw on it as much as you would and still it was always full. It was measured by the seasons but not restricted by them, for the summer that was now standing back to let autumn pass was the same summer that had flamed a thousand years before and would flame again a thousand years hence. In the presence of so much space and time all striving was futile.

From then on their lives took their tempo from the leisurely turning of wagon wheels. Sean's eyes which had been pointing straight ahead along the line of travel now turned aside to look about him. Each morning he and Duff would leave the wagons and wander out into the bush. Sometimes they would spend the day panning for gold in the sands of a stream, another day they would search for the first signs of elephant, but mostly they just rode and talked or lay hidden and watched the herds of game that daily became more numerous. They killed just enough to feed themselves, their servants and the pack of dogs that had followed them when they left Pretoria. They passed the little Boer settlement at Pietersburg and then the Zoutspansberg climbed up over the horizon, its sheer sides dark with rain forest and high rock cliffs. Here under the mountains they spent a week at Louis Trichardt, the most northerly permanent habitation of white men.

In the town they spoke with men who had hunted to the north of the mountains, across the Limpopo. These were taciturn brown-faced Boers with tobacco-stained beards—big men with the peace of the bush in their eyes. In

their courteous, unhurried speech Sean sensed a fierce possessive love of the
animals that they hunted and the land through which they moved so freely.
They were a different breed from the Natal Afrikanders and those he had met
on the Witwatersrand, and he conceived the respect for them that would grow
stronger in the years ahead when he would have to fight them.

There was no way through the mountains, they told him, but wagons could
pass around them. The western passage skirted the edge of the Kalahari desert
and this was bad country where the wagon wheels sank into the sandy soil and
the marches between water became successively longer. To the east there was
good rich forest land, well watered and stocked with game; low country, hotter
the nearer one went to the coast, but the true bushveld where a man could find
elephant.

So Sean and Duff turned east and, holding the mountains always in sight at
their left hand, they went down into the wilderness.

2

Within a week's trek they saw elephant sign: trees broken and stripped of their
bark. Although it was months old–the trees already dried out–nevertheless
Sean felt the thrill of it and that night spent an hour cleaning and oiling his
rifles. The forest thickened until the wagons had to weave continually between
the trunks of the trees. But there were clearings in the forest–open vleis filled
with grass where buffalo grazed like herds of domestic cattle and white tick
birds squawked about them. This country was well watered with streams as
clear and merry as a Scottish trout stream, but the water was blood-warm and
the banks thick with bush. Along the rivers, in the forest and in the open were
the herds of game: impala twisting and leaping away at the first approach with
their crumpled horns laid back, kudu with big ears and soft eyes, black sable
antelope with white bellies and horns curved like a naval cutlass, zebra trotting
with the dignity of fat ponies, while about them frolicked their companions,
the gnu, waterbuck, nyala, roan antelope and–at last–elephant.

Sean and Mbejane were ranging a mile ahead of the wagons when they
found the spoor. It was fresh, so fresh that sap still oozed from the mahoba-
hoba tree where the bark had been prised loose with the tip of a tusk and then
stripped off. The wood beneath was naked and white.

'Three bulls,' said Mbejane. 'One very big.'

'Wait here,' Sean spun his horse and galloped back to the column. Duff lay
on the driver's seat of the first wagon rocking gently to its motion, his hat
covering his face and his hands behind his head.

'Elephant! Duff,' Sean yelled. 'Not an hour ahead of us. Get saddled up,
man!'

Duff was ready in five minutes. Mbejane was waiting for them; he had
already worked the spoor a short distance and picked up the run of it and now
he went away on it. They followed him, riding slowly side by side.

'You've hunted elephant before, laddie?' asked Duff.

'Never,' said Sean.

'Good grief!' Duff looked alarmed. 'I thought you were an expert. I think
I'll go back and finish my sleep, you can call me when you've had a little more
experience.'

'Don't worry,' Sean laughed with excitement. 'I know all about it; I was raised on elephant stories.'

'That sets my heart at ease,' Duff murmured sarcastically and Mbejane glanced over his shoulder at them, not trying to conceal his irritation.

'Nkosi, it is not wise to talk now for we will soon come up with them.'

So they went on in silence: passing a knee-high pile of yellow dung that looked like the contents of a coir mattress, following the oval pad marks in the dust and the trail of torn branches.

It was a good hunt, this first one. The small breeze held steadily into their faces and the spoor ran straight and hot. They closed in, each minute strengthening the certainty of the kill. Sean sat stiff and eager in the saddle with his rifle across his lap, his eyes restlessly moving over the frieze of bush ahead of him. Mbejane stopped suddenly and came back to Sean's stirrup.

'Here they halted for the first time. The sun is hot and they will rest but this place was not to their liking and they have moved on. We will find them soon now.'

'The bush becomes too thick,' Sean grunted; he eyed the untidy tangle of catbush into which the spoor had led them. 'We will leave the horses here with Hlubi and go in on foot.'

'Laddie,' Duff demurred. 'I can run much faster on horseback.'

'Off!' said Sean and nodded to Mbejane to lead. They moved forward again. Sean was sweating and the drops clung heavily to his eyebrows and trickled down his cheeks; he brushed them away. The excitement was an indigestible ball in his stomach and a dryness in his throat.

Duff sauntered casually next to Sean with that small half-smile on his face, but there was a quickness in his breathing. Mbejane cautioned them with a gesture of his hand and they stopped. Minutes passed slowly and then Mbejane's hand moved again, pink-palmed eloquence.

'It was nothing,' said the hand. 'Follow me.'

They went on again. There were Mopani flies swarming at the corners of Sean's eyes, drinking the moisture, and he blinked them away. Their buzzing was so loud in his ears that he thought it must carry to their quarry. His every sense was tuned to its limit: hearing magnified, vision sharp and even his sense of smell so clear that he could pick up the taint of dust, the scent of a wild flower and Mbejane's faintly musky body-smell.

Suddenly in front of him Mbejane was still; his hand moved again gently, unmistakable.

'They are here,' said the hand.

Sean and Duff crouched behind him, searching with eyes that could see only brown bush and grey shadows. The tension coarsened their breathing and Duff was no longer smiling. Mbejane's hand came up slowly and pointed at the wall of vegetation in front of them. The seconds strung together like beads on the string of time and still they searched.

An ear flapped lazily and instantly the picture jumped into focus. Bull elephant, big and very close, grey among grey shadow. Sean touched Mbejane's arm. 'I had seen it,' said that touch.

Slowly Mbejane's hand swivelled and pointed again. Another wait, another searching and then a belly rumbled, a great grey belly filled with half-digested leaves. It was a sound so ridiculous in the silence that Sean wanted to laugh—a gurgling sloshy sound—and Sean saw the other bull. It was standing in shadow also, with long yellow ivory and small eyes tight-closed. Sean put his lips to Duff's ear.

'This one is yours,' he whispered. 'Wait until I get into position for the other,' and he began moving out to the side, each step exposing a little more of the second bull's flank until the shoulder was open to him and he could see the point of the elbow beneath the baggy, wrinkled skin. The angle was right; from here he could reach the heart. He nodded at Duff, brought his rifle up—leaning forward against the recoil, aiming close behind the massive shoulder—and he fired.

The gunfire was shockingly loud in the confined thorn bush; dust flew in a spurt from the bull's shoulder and it staggered from the strike of the bullet. Beyond it the third elephant burst from sleep into flight and Sean's hands moved neatly on his weapon, ejecting and reloading, swinging up and firing again. He saw the bullet hit and he knew it was a mortal wound. The two bulls ran together and the bush opened to them and swallowed them: they were gone, crashing away wounded, trumpeting in pain. Sean ran after them, dodging through the catbush, oblivious to the sting of the thorns that snatched at him as he passed.

'This way, Nkosi,' Mbejane shouted beside him. 'Quickly or we will lose them.' They sprinted after the sounds of flight—a hundred yards, two hundred, panting now and sweating in the heat. Suddenly the catbush ended and in front of them was a wide river-bed with steep banks. The river sand was blindingly white and in the middle was a sluggish trickle of water. One of the bulls was dead, lying in the stream with the blood washing off him in a pale brown stain. The other bull was trying to climb the far bank; it was too steep for him and he slid back wearily. The blood dripped from the tip of his trunk, and he swung his head to look at Sean and Mbejane. His ears cocked back defiantly and he began his charge, blundering towards them through the soft river sand.

Sean watched him come and there was sadness in him as he brought up his rifle, but it was the proud regret that a man feels when he watches hopeless courage. Sean killed with a brain shot, quickly.

They climbed down the bank into the river-bed and went to the elephant; it knelt with its legs folded under it and its tusks driven deep into the sand with the force of its fall. The flies were already clustering at the little red mouths of the bullet wounds. Mbejane touched one of the tusks and then he looked up at Sean.

'It is a good elephant,' He said no more, for this was not the time to talk. Sean leaned his rifle against the bull's shoulder; he felt in his top pocket for a cheroot and stood with it unlit between his teeth. He would kill more elephant, he knew, but always this would be the one he would remember. He stroked his hand over the rough skin and the bristles were stiff and sharp.

'Where is Nkosi Duff?' Sean remembered him suddenly. 'Did he also kill?'

'He did not shoot,' answered Mbejane.

'What!' Sean turned quickly to Mbejane. 'Why not?'

Mbejane sniffed a pinch of snuff and sneezed, then he shrugged his shoulders.

'It is a good elephant,' he said again, looking down at it.

'We must go back and find him.' Sean snatched up his rifle and Mbejane followed him. They found Duff sitting alone in the catbush with his rifle propped beside him and a water-bottle to his lips. He lowered the bottle as Sean came up and saluted him with it.

'Hail! the conquering hero comes.' There was something in his eyes that Sean could not read.

'Did you miss yours?' Sean asked.

'Yes,' said Duff, 'I missed mine.' He lifted the bottle and drank again. Suddenly and sickenly Sean was ashamed for him. He dropped his eyes, not wanting to acknowledge Duff's cowardice.

'Let's get back to the wagons,' he said. 'Mbejane can come with packhorses for the tusks.'

They did not ride together on the way home.

3

It was almost dark when they arrived back at the laager. They gave their horses to one of the servants and washed in the basin that Kandhla had ready for them, then they went to sit by the fire. Sean poured the drinks, fussing over the glasses to avoid looking at Duff. He felt awkward. They'd have to talk about it and he searched his brain for a way to bring it into the open. Duff had shown craven and Sean started to find excuses for him—he may have had a misfire or he may have been unsighted by Sean's shot. At all events Sean determined not to let it stay like this, sour and brooding between them. They'd talk it out then forget it. He carried Duff's glass to him and smiled at him.

'That's right, try to cover it with a grin,' Duff lifted his glass. 'To our big brave hunter. Dammit, laddie, how could you do it?'

Sean stared at Duff. 'What do you mean?'

'You know what I mean, you're so damned guilty you can't even look me in the face. How could you kill those bloody great animals—but even worse how could you *enjoy* doing it?'

Sean subsided weakly into his chair. He couldn't tell which of his emotions were uppermost—relief or surprise. Duff went on quickly.

'I know what you're going to say, I've heard the arguments before—from my dear father. He explained it to me one evening after we'd ridden down a fox. When I say "we", I mean twenty horsemen and forty hounds.'

Sean had not yet rallied from the shock of finding himself in the dock after preparing himself to play the role of prosecutor.

'Don't you like hunting?' he asked incredulously. The way he might have asked, 'don't you like eating?'

'I'd forgotten what it was like. I was carried away by your excitement, but when you started to kill them it all came back to me.' Duff sipped his brandy and stared into the fire. 'They never had a chance. One minute they were sleeping and the next you were ripping them with bullets the way the hounds ripped that fox. They didn't have a chance.'

'But, Duff, it wasn't meant to be a contest.'

'Yes, I know, my father explained that to me. It's a ritual—a sacred rite to Diana. He should have explained it to the fox as well.'

Sean was getting angry now. 'We came out here to hunt ivory—and that's what I'm doing.'

'Tell me that you killed those elephant only for their teeth, laddie, and I'll call you a liar. You loved it. Christ! You should have seen your face and the face of your damned heathen.'

'All right! I like hunting and the only other man I ever met who didn't was a coward,' Sean shouted at him.

Duff's face paled and he looked up at Sean. 'What are you trying to say?' he whispered. They stared at each other and in the silence Sean had to choose between letting his temper run or keeping Duff's friendship, for the words that would spoil it for ever were crowding into his mouth. He made his hands relax their grip on the arms of his chair.

'I didn't mean that,' he said.

'I hoped you didn't,' Duff's grin came precariously back on to his face. 'Tell me why you like hunting, laddie. I'll try and understand but don't expect me to hunt with you again.'

It was like explaining colour to a blind man, describing the lust of the hunter to someone who was born without it. Duff listened in agonized silence as Sean tried to find the words for the excitement that makes a man's blood sing through his body, that heightens his senses and allows him to lose himself in an emotion as old as the urge to mate. Sean tried to show him how the nobler and more beautiful was the quarry, the stronger was the compulsion to hunt and kill it, that it had no conscious cruelty in it but was rather an expression of love: a fierce possessive love. A devouring love that needed the complete and irrevocable act of death for its consummation. By destroying something, a man could have it always as his own: selfish perhaps, but then instinct knows no ethics. It was all very clear to Sean, so much a part of him that he had never tried to voice it before and now he stumbled over the words, gesticulating in helpless inarticulateness, repeating himself, coming at last to the end and knowing by the look on Duff's face that he had failed to show it to him.

'And you were the gentleman who fought Hradsky for the rights of man,' Duff said softly, 'the one who always talked about not hurting people.'

Sean opened his mouth to protest but Duff went on. 'You get ivory for us and I'll look for gold—each of us to what he is best suited. I'll forgive you your elephants as you forgave me my Candy—still equal partners. Agreed?'

Sean nodded and Duff held up his glass.

'It's empty,' he said. 'Do me a favour, laddie.'

4

There was never any aftertaste to their disputes, no rankling of unspoken words or lingering of doubt. What they had in common they enjoyed, where there were differences they accepted them. So when after each hunt the packhorses brought the tusks into the camp there was no trace of censure in Duff's face or voice; there was only the genuine pleasure of having Sean back from the bush. Sometimes it was a good day and Sean would cut the spoor, follow, kill and be back in the laager the same night. But more often, when the herd was moving fast or the ground was hard or he could not kill at the first approach, he would be gone for a week or more. Each time he returned they celebrated, drinking and laughing far into the night, lying late in bed the next morning, playing Klabejas on the floor of the wagon between their cots or reading aloud out of the books that Duff had brought with him from Pretoria.

Then a day or two later Sean would be gone again, with his dogs and his gunboys trotting behind him.

This was a different Sean from the one who had whored it up at the Opera House and presided over the panelled offices in Eloff Street. His beard, no longer groomed and shaped by a barber, curled on to his chest. The doughy colour of his face and arms had been turned by the sun to the rich brown of a newly-baked loaf. The seat of his pants that had been stretched to danger point across his rump now hung loosely; his arms were thicker and the soft swell of fat had given way to the flatness and bulge of hard muscle. He walked straighter, moved quicker and laughed more easily.

In Duff the change was less noticeable. He was lean and gaunt-faced as ever, but now there was less of the restlessness in his eyes. His speech and movements were slower and the golden beard he was growing had the strange effect of making him appear younger. Each morning he left the wagons, taking one of the servants with him, and spent the days wandering in the bush, tapping with his prospecting hammer at the occasional outcrops of rock or squatting beside a stream and spinning the gravel in his pan. Every evening he came back to camp and analysed the bag of rock samples he had collected during the day; then he threw them away, bathed and set out a bottle and two glasses on the table beside the fire. While he ate his supper he listened and waited for the dogs to bark, for the sound of horses in the darkness and Sean's voice. If the night remained silent he put the bottle away and climbed up into his wagon. He was lonely then, not with a deep loneliness but just enough to add relish to Sean's return.

Always they moved east, until gradually the silhouette of the Zoutpansberg softened as the mountains became less steep and began to fade into the tail of the range. Scouting along their edge Sean found a pass and they took the wagons up and over and down into the Limpopo valley beyond. Here the country changed character again; it became flat, the monotony of thorn scrub relieved only by the baobab trees with their great, swollen trunks crowned in a little halo of branches. Water was scarce and Sean rode ahead from each camp to find the next waterhole before they moved. However, the hunting was good for the game was concentrated on the isolated drinking places, and before they were halfway from the mountains to the Limpopo Sean had filled another wagon with ivory.

'We'll be coming back this way, I suppose?' Duff asked.

'I suppose so,' agreed Sean.

'Well then, I don't see any point in carrying a ton of ivory with us. Let's bury it and we can pick up on our way back.'

Sean looked at him thoughtfully. 'About once in every year you come up with a good idea—we'll do exactly that.'

The next camp was a good one. There was water—an acre of muddy liquid not as heavily salted with elephant urine as some of the previous ones had been; there was a shade provided by a grove of wild fig trees and the grazing was of a quality that promised to restore the condition that the oxen had lost since crossing the mountains. They decided to make it a rest camp: bury the ivory, do some repairs and maintenance on the wagons and let the servants and animals fatten up a little. The first task was to dig a hole large enough to contain all the hundred-odd tusks they had accumulated and it was evening on the third day before they finished.

5

Sean and Duff sat together inside the laager and watched the sun go down, bleeding below the land, and after it had gone the clouds were oyster and lilac-coloured in the brief twilight. Kandhla threw wood on the fire and it burnt up fiercely. They ate grilled kudu liver, and thick steaks with a rind of yellow fat on them, and they drank brandy with their coffee. The conversation lagged into contented silence for they were both tired. They sat staring into the fire, too lazy to make the effort required for bed. Sean watched the fire pictures form in the coals, the faces and the phantoms flickering and fading. He saw a tiny temple have its columns pulled out from under it by a fiery Samson and collapse in a shower of sparks–a burning horse changed magically into a dragon of blue flame. He looked away to rest his eyes and when he turned back there was a small black scorpion scuttling out from under the loose bark on one of the logs. It lifted its tail like the arm of a flamenco dancer and the flames that ringed it shone on its glossy body armour. Duff was also watching it, leaning forward with his elbows on his knees.

'Will he sting himself to death before the flames reach him?' he asked softly. 'I have heard that they do.'

'No,' said Sean.

'Why not?'

'Only man has the intelligence to end the inevitable; in all other creatures the instinct of survival is too strong,' Sean answered him, and the scorpion crabbed sideways from the nearest flames and stopped again with its raised sting jerking slightly. 'Besides he's immune to his own poison so he has no choice.'

'He could jump down into the fire and get it over with,' murmured Duff, subdued by the little tragedy.

The scorpion started its last desperate circuit of the closing ring. Its tail drooped and the grip of its claws was unsteady on the rough bark; it was shrivelling with the heat, its legs curling up and its tail subsiding. The flames caressed it with swift yellow hands and smeared its shiny body with the dullness of death. The log tipped sideways and the speck was gone.

'Would you?' asked Sean. 'Would you have jumped?'

Duff sighed softly. 'I don't know,' he said and stood up. 'I'm going to pump out my bilges and crawl into bed.' He walked away and went to stand at the edge of the circle of firelight.

Since they had left Pretoria the small voices of the jackals had yapped discreetly around each outspan–they were so much a part of the African night that they went unnoticed–but now suddenly there was a difference. Only one jackal spoke, and with a voice that stammered shrilly–a sound of pain, a crazy hysterical shrieking that made Sean's skin prickle. He scrambled to his feet and stood staring undecided into the darkness. The jackal was coming towards the camp, coming fast–and suddenly Sean knew what was happening.

'Duff!' he called. 'Come back here! Run, man, run!'

Duff looked back at Sean helplessly, his hands held low in front of him and his water arcing down, curving silver in the firelight from his body to the ground.

'Duff!' Sean's voice was a shout. 'It's a rabid jackal. Run, damn you, run!' The jackal was close now, very close, but at last Duff started to move. He was halfway back to the fire before he tripped. He fell and rolled over and brought his feet up and under his body to rise. His head turned to face the darkness from which it would come. Then Sean saw it. It flitted out of the shadows like a grey moth in the bad light and went straight for where Duff knelt. Sean saw him try to cover his face with his hands as the jackal sprang at him. One of the dogs twisted out of Mbejane's hand and brushed past Sean's legs. Sean snatched up a piece of firewood and sprinted after it, but already Duff was on his back, his arms flailing frantically as he tried to push away the terrier-sized animal that was slashing at his face and hands. The dog caught it and dragged it off, worrying it, growling through locked jaws. Sean hit the jackal with the club—breaking its back. He swung again and again, beating its body into shapelessness before he turned to Duff. Duff was on his feet now. He had unwound the scarf from his neck and was mopping with it at his face but the blood dribbled down his chin and blotched the front of his shirt. His hands were trembling. Sean led him close to the fire, pulled Duff's hands down and examined the bites. His nose was torn and the flesh of one cheek hung open in a flap.

'Sit down!'

Duff obeyed, holding the scarf to his face again. Sean went quickly to the fire: with a stick he raked embers into a pile, then he drew his hunting-knife and thrust the blade into the coals.

'Mbejane,' he called, without taking his eyes off the knife. 'Throw the jackal on to the fire. Put on plenty of wood. Do not touch its body with your hands. When you have done that tie up that dog and keep the others away from it.' Sean turned the knife in the fire. 'Duff, drink as much of that brandy as you can.'

'What are you going to do?'

'You know what I've got to do.'

'He bit my wrist as well.' Duff held up his hand for Sean to see the punctures, black holes from which the blood oozed watery and slow

'Drink.' Sean pointed at the brandy bottle. For a second they looked at each other and Sean saw the horror moving in Duff's eyes: horror of the hot knife and horror of the germs which had been injected into him. The germs that must burn out before they escaped into his blood, to breed and ferment there until they ate into his brain and rode him to a screaming, gibbering death.

'Drink,' said Sean again. Duff took up the bottle and lifted it to his mouth. Sean stooped and pulled the knife out of the fire. He held the blade an inch from the back of his hand. It was not hot enough. He thrust it back into the coals.

'Mbejane, Hlubi, stand on each side of the Nkosi's chair. Be ready to hold him.' Sean loosened his belt, doubled the thick leather and handed it to Duff. 'Bite on this.'

He turned back to the fire and this time when he drew the knife its blade was pale pink. 'Are you ready?'

'The work you are about to do will break the hearts of a million maids.' A last hoarse attempt at humour from Duff.

'Hold him,' said Sean.

Duff gasped at the touch of the knife—a great shuddering gasp—and his back arched, but the two Zulus held him down remorselessly. The edges of the wound blackened and hissed as Sean ran the blade in deeper. The stink of burning brought the vomit into his throat. He clenched his teeth. When he stepped back Duff hung slackly in the Zulu's hands, sweat had soaked his shirt and wet his hair. Sean heated the knife again and cleaned the bites in Duff's wrist while Duff moaned and writhed weakly in the chair. He smeared axle grease over the burns and bandaged the wrist loosely with strips torn from a clean shirt. They lifted Duff into the wagon and laid him on the cot. Sean went out to where Mbejane had tied the dog. He found scratches beneath the hair on its shoulder. They put a sack over its head to stop it biting and Sean cauterized its wounds also.

'Tie it to the far wagon, do not let the other dogs near it, see it has food and water,' he told Mbejane.

Then he went back to Duff. Delirious with pain and brandy Duff did not sleep at all that night and Sean stayed by his cot until the morning.

6

About fifty yards from the laager under one of the wild fig trees the servants built Duff a hut. The framework was of poles and over it they stretched a tarpaulin. They made a bed for him and brought his mattress and blankets from the wagon. Sean joined four trek-chains together, forging new links and hammering them closed. He passed one end of the chain round the base of the fig tree and riveted it back up on itself. Duff sat in the shade of a wagon and watched them work. His hurt hand was in a sling and his face was swollen, the wound crusty-looking and edged in angry red. When he was finished with the chain, Sean walked across to him.

'I'm sorry, Duff, we have to do it.'

'They abolished the slave trade some time ago—just in case you didn't know.' Duff tried to grin with his distorted face. He stood up and followed Sean to the hut. Sean looped the loose end of the chain round Duff's waist. He locked it with a bolt through two of the kinks then flattened the end of the bolt with a dozen strokes of the hammer.

'That should hold you.'

'An excellent fit,' Duff commended him. 'Now let us inspect my new quarters.'

Sean followed him into the hut. Duff lay down on the bed. He looked very tired and sick.

'How long will it take before we know?' he asked quietly.

Sean shook his head. 'I'm not sure. I think you should stay here at least a month—after that we'll allow you back into society.'

'A month—it's going to be fun. Lying here expecting any minute to start barking like a dog and lifting my leg against the nearest tree.'

Sean didn't laugh. 'I did a thorough job with the knife. It's a thousand to one you'll be all right. This is just a precaution.'

'The odds are attractive—I'll put a fiver on it.' Duff crossed his ankles and stared up at the roof. Sean sat down on the edge of the bed. It was a long time before Duff ended the silence.

'What will it be like, Sean, have you ever seen someone with rabies?'

'No.'

'But you've heard about it, haven't you? Tell me what you've heard about it,' Duff persisted.

'For Chrisake, Duff, you're not going to get it.'

'Tell me, Sean, tell me what you know about it.' Duff sat up and caught hold of Sean's arm.

Sean looked steadily at him for a moment before he answered. 'You saw that jackal, didn't you?'

Duff sank back on to his pillows. 'Oh, my God!' he whispered.

Together they started the long wait. They used another tarpaulin to make an open shelter next to the hut and under it they spent the days that followed.

In the beginning it was very bad. Sean tried to pull Duff out of the black despair into which he had slumped, but Duff sat for hours at a time gazing out into the bush, fingering the scabs on his face and only occasionally smiling at the banquet of choice stories that Sean spread for him. But at last Sean's efforts were rewarded—Duff began to talk. He spoke of things he had never mentioned before and listening to him Sean learned more about him than he had in the previous five years. Sometimes Duff paced up and down in front of Sean's chair with the chain hanging down behind him like a tail; at other times he sat quietly, his voice filled with longing for the mother he had never known.

'—there was a portrait of her in the upper gallery, I used to spend whole afternoons in front of it. It was the kindest face I had ever seen—'

Then it hardened again as he remembered his father, 'that old bastard'.

He talked of his daughter. '—she had a fat chuckle that would break your heart. The snow on her grave made it look like a big sugar-iced cake, she would have liked that—'

At other times his voice was puzzled as he examined some past action of his, angry as he remembered a mistake or a missed opportunity. Then he would break off and grin self-consciously. 'I say, I am talking a lot of drivel.'

The scabs on his face began to dry up and come away, and more often now his old gaiety bubbled to the surface.

On one of the poles that supported the tarpaulin roof he started a calendar, cutting a notch for each day. It became a daily ceremony. He cut each notch with the concentration of a sculptor carving marble and when he had finished he would stand back and count them aloud as if by doing so he could force them to add up to thirty, the number that would allow him to shed his chain.

There were eighteen notches on the pole when the dog went mad. It was in the afternoon. They were playing klabejas. Sean had just dealt the cards when the dog started screaming from among the wagons. Sean knocked over his chair as he jumped up. He snatched his rifle from where it leant against the wall and ran down to the laager. He disappeared behind the wagon to which the dog was tied and almost immediately Duff heard the shot. In the abrupt and complete stillness that followed, Duff slowly lowered his face into his hands.

It was nearly an hour before Sean came back. He picked up his chair, set it to the table and sat down.

'It's you to call—are you going to take on?' he asked as he picked up his cards. They played with grim intensity, fixing their attention on the cards, but both of them knew that there was a third person at the table now.

'Promise you'll never do that to me,' Duff blurted out at last.

Sean looked up at him. 'That I'll never do what to you?'

'What you did to that dog.'

The dog! The bloody dog. He should never have taken a chance with it, he should have destroyed it that first night.

'Just because the dog got it doesn't mean that you–'

'Swear to me,' Duff interrupted fiercely, 'swear you won't bring the rifle to me.'

'Duff, you don't know what you're asking. Once you've got it–' Sean stopped; anything he said would make it worse.

'Promise me,' Duff repeated.

'All right, I swear it then.'

7

It was worse now than it had been in the beginning. Duff abandoned his calendar and with it the hope that had been slowly growing stronger. If the days were bad then the nights were hell, for Duff had a dream. It came to him every night–sometimes two or three times. He tried to keep awake after Sean had left, reading by the light of a lantern; or he lay and listened to the night noises, the splash and snort of buffalo drinking down at the waterhole, the liquid half-warble of night birds or the deep drumming of a lion. But in the end he would have to sleep and then he dreamed.

He was on horseback riding across a flat brown plain: no hills, no trees, nothing but lawnlike grass stretching away on all sides to the horizon. His horse threw no shadow–he always looked for a shadow and it worried him that there never was one. Then he would find the pool–clear water, blue and strangely shiny. The pool frightened him but he would not stop himself going to it. He would kneel beside it and look into the water; the reflection of his own face looked up at him–animal-snouted, shaggy-brown with wolf teeth, white and long. He would wake then and the horror of that face would last until morning.

Nearly desperate with his own utter helplessness, Sean tried to help him. Because of the accord they had established over the years and because they were so close to each other, Sean had to suffer with him. He tried to shut himself off from it; sometimes he succeeded for an hour or even half a morning, but then it came back with a stomach-swooping shock. Duff was going to die–Duff was going to die an unspeakable death. Was it a mistake to let someone get too deep inside you, so that you must share his agony in every excruciating detail? Didn't a man have enough of his own that he must share the full measure of another's suffering?

By then the October winds had started, the heralds of the rain: hot winds full of dust, winds that dried the sweat on a man's body before it had time to cool him, thirsty winds, that during daylight brought the game to the waterhole in full view of the camp.

Sean had half a case of wine hoarded under his cot. That last evening he cooled four bottles, wrapping them in wet sacking. He took them up to Duff's shelter just before supper and set them on the table. Duff watched him. The scars on his face were almost completely healed now, glass red marks on his pale skin.

'Château Olivier,' said Sean and Duff nodded.

'It's a good wine–most probably travel-sick.'

'Well, if you don't want it, I'll take it away again,' said Sean.

'I'm sorry, laddie,' Duff spoke quickly. 'I didn't mean to be ungrateful. This wine suits my mood tonight. Did you know that wine is a sad drink?'

'Nonsense!' Sean disagreed as he twisted the corkscrew into the first cork. 'Wine is gay.' He poured a little into Duff's glass and Duff picked it up and held it towards the fire so the light shone through it.

'You see only the surface, Sean. A good wine has the elements of tragedy within it. The better the wine the more sad it is.'

Sean snorted. 'Explain yourself,' he invited.

Duff put his glass down on the table again and stared at it. 'How long do you suppose this wine has taken to reach its present perfection?'

'Ten or fifteen years, I suppose,' Sean answered.

Duff nodded. 'And now all that remains is to drink it—the work of years destroyed in an instant. Don't you think that is sad?' Duff asked softly.

'My God, Duff, don't be so damned morbid.'

But Duff wasn't listening to him. 'Wine and mankind have this in common. They can find perfection only in age, in a lifetime of seeking. Yet in the finding they find also their own destruction.'

'So you think that if a man lives long enough he will reach perfection?' Sean challenged him, and Duff answered him still staring at the glass.

'Some grapes grew in the wrong soil, some were diseased before they went to the press and some were spoiled by a careless vintner—not all grapes make good wine.' Duff picked up his glass and tasted from it, then he went on. 'A man takes longer and he must find it not within the quiet confines of the cask but in the cauldron of life; therefore his is the greater tragedy.'

'Yes, but no one can live for ever,' Sean protested.

'So you think that makes it less sad?' Duff shook his head. 'You're wrong, of course. It does not detract from it, it enhances it. If only there were some escape, some way of ensuring that what is good could endure instead of this complete hopelessness.'

Duff lay back in his chair, his face pale and gaunt-looking. 'Even that I could accept, if only they had given me more time.'

'I've had enough of this talk. Let's discuss something else. I don't know what you're worrying about. You're not fit to drink yet, you've got another twenty or thirty years to go,' Sean said gruffly and Duff looked up at him for the first time.

'Have I, Sean?'

Sean couldn't meet his eyes. He knew Duff was going to die. Duff grinned his lopsided grin and looked down again at his glass. Slowly the grin disappeared and he spoke again.

'If only I had more time, I could have done it. I could have found the weak places and fortified them. I could have seen the answers.' His voice rose higher. 'I could have! I know I could have! Oh God, I'm not ready yet. I need more time.' His voice was shrill and his eyes wild and haunted. 'It's too soon—it's too soon!'

Sean couldn't stand it, he jumped up and caught Duff's shoulders and shook him.

'Shut up, God damn you, shut up,' he shouted at him. Duff was panting, his lips were parted and quivering. He touched them with the tips of his fingers as though to stop them.

'I'm sorry, laddie, I didn't mean to let go like that.' Sean dropped his hands from Duff's shoulders.

'Both of us are too damned edgy,' he said. 'It's going to be all right, you wait and see.'

'Yes—it will be all right.' Duff ran his fingers through his hair, combing it back from his eyes. 'Open another bottle, laddie.'

8

That night after Sean had gone to bed, Duff had his dream again. The wine he had drunk slowed him down and prevented him from waking. He was trapped in his fancy, struggling to escape into wakefulness but only reaching the surface before he sank back to dream that dream again.

Sean went up to Duff's shelter the next morning early. Although the night's coolness still lingered under the spreading branches of the wild figs the rising day promised to blow dry and burn hot. The animals could sense it. The trek oxen were clustered among the trees and a small herd of eland was moving from the waterhole. The bull, with his short thick horns and the dark tuft on his forehead, was leading his cows away to find shade. Sean stood in the doorway of the hut and waited while his eyes adjusted themselves to its gloom. Duff was awake.

'Get out of bed or you'll have bed sores to add to your happiness.'

Duff swung his feet off the litter and groaned.

'What did you put in that wine last night?' He massaged his temples gently. 'I've got a hundred hobgoblins doing a Cossack dance around the roof of my skull.'

Sean felt the first twinge of alarm. He put his hand on Duff's shoulder feeling for the heat of fever, but Duff was quite cool. He relaxed.

'Breakfast's ready,' said Sean. Duff played with his porridge and barely tasted the grilled eland liver. He kept screwing his eyes up against the glare of the sun and when they had finished their coffee he pushed back his chair.

'I'm going to take my tender head to bed.'

'All right.' Sean stood up as well. 'We're a bit short of meat. I'll go and see if I can get a buck.'

'No, stay and talk to me,' Duff said quickly. 'We can have a few hands of cards.'

They hadn't played in days and Sean agreed readily. He sat on the end of Duff's bed and within half an hour he had won thirty-two pounds from him.

'You must let me teach you this game sometime,' he gloated.

Petulantly, Duff threw his hand in. 'I don't feel like playing any more.' He pressed his fingers to his closed eyelids. 'I can't concentrate with this headache.'

'Do you want to sleep?' Sean gathered up the cards and put them in their box.

'No. Why don't you read to me?'

Duff picked up a leather-bound copy of *Bleak House* from the table beside the bed and tossed it into Sean's lap.

'Where shall I start?' Sean asked.

'It doesn't matter, I know it almost by heart.' Duff lay back and closed his eyes. 'Start anywhere.'

Sean read aloud. He stumbled on for half an hour with his tongue never quite catching the rhythm of the words. Once or twice he glanced up at Duff, but Duff lay still with a faint sheen of sweat on his face and the scars very noticeable. He was breathing easily. Dickens is a powerful sleeping-draught for a hot morning and Sean's eyelids sagged down and his voice slowed and finally stopped. The book slid off his lap.

The small tinkle of Duff's chain disturbed him; he awoke and looked at the bed. Duff crouched apelike. The madness was a fire in his eyes and his cheeks twitched. A yellowish froth coated his teeth and formed a thin line of scum along his lips.

'Duff—' Sean said, and Duff lunged at him with fingers hooked and a noise in his throat that was not human nor yet animal. It was a sound that jellied Sean's stomach and took the strength from his legs.

'Don't!' screamed Sean, and the chain caught on one of the posts of the bed, jerking Duff back sprawling on to the bed before he could sink his teeth into Sean's paralysed body.

Sean ran. He ran out of the hut and into the bush. He ran with terror trembling in his legs and choking his breath. He ran with his heart taking its beat from his racing feet and his lungs pumping in disordered panic. A branch ripped across his cheek and the sting of it served to steady him. His feet slowed—he stopped and stood gasping, staring back towards the camp. He waited while his body settled and he forced his terror down until it was only a sickening sensation in his stomach. Then he circled through the thorn bush and approached the laager from the side farthest away from Duff's shelter. The camp was empty, the servants had fled in the same terror that had driven Sean. He remembered that his rifle was still in the hut beside Duff's bed. He slipped into his wagon and quickly opened the case of unused rifles. His hands were unsteady again as he fumbled with the locks, for the chain might have parted and at every second he expected to hear that inhuman sound behind him. He found his bandolier hanging on the end of his cot and he took cartridges from it. He loaded the rifle and cocked it. The weight of steel and wood in his hands gave him comfort. It made him a man again.

He jumped down out of the wagon and with the rifle held ready he went cautiously out of the circle of wagons. The chain had held. Duff stood in the shade of the wild fig plucking at it. He was making a sound like a new-born puppy. His back was turned to Sean and he was naked, his torn clothing scattered about him. Sean walked slowly towards him. He stopped outside the reach of the chain.

'Duff!' Sean called uncertainly. Duff spun and crouched, the froth was thick in his golden beard; he looked at Sean and his teeth bared. Then he charged screaming until the chain caught him and threw him on to his back once more. He scrambled to his feet and fought the chain, his eyes fastened hungrily on Sean. Sean backed away. He brought up the rifle and aimed between Duff's eyes.

Swear to me. Swear to me you won't bring the rifle to me.

Sean's aim wavered. He kept moving backwards. Duff was bleeding now. The steel links had smeared the skin off his hips, but still he pulled against them fighting to get at Sean—and Sean was shackled just as effectively by his promise. He could not end it. He lowered the rifle and watched in impotent pity.

Mbejane came to him at last.

'Come away, Nkosi. If you will not end it, come away. He no longer has need of you. The sight of you inflames him.'

Duff still struggled and screamed against his chain. From his torn waist the blood trickled down and clung in the hair of his legs with the stickiness of molten chocolate. With each jerk of his head the froth sprayed from his mouth and splattered his chest and arms.

Mbejane led Sean back into the laager. The other servants were there and Sean roused himself to give orders.

'I want everyone away from here. Take blankets and food—go camp on the far side of the water. I will send for you when it is over.' He waited until they had gathered their belongings and as they were leaving he called Mbejane back. 'What must I do?' he asked.

'If a horse breaks a leg?' Mbejane answered him with a question.

'I gave him my word,' Sean shook his head desperately, still facing towards the sound of Duff's raving.

'Only a rogue and a brave man can break an oath,' Mbejane answered simply. 'We will wait for you.' He turned and followed the others. When they were gone Sean hid in one of the wagons and through a tear in the canvas he watched Duff. He saw the idiotic shaking of his head, the curious shambling gait as he moved around the circle of the chain. He watched when the pain made him roll on the ground and claw at his head, tearing out tufts of hair and leaving long scratches down his face. He listened to the sounds of insanity: the bewildered bellows of pain, the senseless giggling and that growl, that terrible growl.

A dozen times he sighted along the rifle barrel, holding his aim until the sweat ran into his eyes and blurred them and he had to take the butt from his shoulder and turn away.

Out there on the end of the chain, its exposed flesh reddening in the sun, a piece of Sean was dying. Some of his youth, some of his laughter, some of his carefree love of life—so he had to creep back to the hole in the canvas and watch.

The sun reached its peak and started down again and the thing on the chain grew weaker. It fell and was a long time crawling on its hands and knees before it regained its feet again.

An hour before sunset Duff had his first convulsion. He was standing facing Sean's wagon, swinging his head from side to side, his mouth working silently. The convulsion took him and he stiffened; his lips pulled up grinning, showing his teeth, his eyes rolled back and disappeared leaving only the whites, and his body started to bend backwards. That beautiful body, still slim as a boy's with the long moulded legs, bending tighter and tighter until with a brittle crack the spine snapped and he fell. He lay wriggling, moaning softly and his trunk was twisted at an impossible angle from the broken spine.

Sean jumped from the wagon and ran to him: standing over him he shot Duff in the head and turned away. He flung his rifle from him and heard it clatter on the hard earth. He walked back to his wagon and took a blanket off Duff's cot. He came back and wrapped Duff in it, averting his eyes from the mutilated head. He carried him to the shelter and laid him on the bed. The blood soaked through the blanket, spreading on the cloth, like ink spilled on blotting-paper. Sean sank down on the chair beside the bed.

Outside the darkness gathered and became complete. Once in the night a hyena came and snuffled at the blood outside on the earth, then it moved away. There was a pride of lions hunting in the bush beyond the waterhole; they killed two hours before dawn and Sean sat in the darkness and listened to their jubilant roaring.

In the morning, Sean stood up stiffly from his chair and went down to the wagons. Mbejane was waiting beside the fire in the laager.

'Where are the others?' Sean asked.

Mbejane stood up. 'They wait where you sent them. I came alone—knowing you would need me.'

'Yes,' said Sean. 'Get two axes from the wagon.'

They gathered wood, a mountain of dry wood, and packed it around Duff's bed—then Sean put fire to it. Mbejane saddled a horse for Sean and he mounted up and looked down at the Zulu.

'Bring the wagons on to the next waterhole. I will meet you there.'

Sean rode out of the laager. He looked back only once and saw that the breeze had spread the smoke from the pyre in a mile-long smudge across the tops of the thorn trees.

9

Like a bag of pus at the root of an infected tooth the guilt and grief rotted in Sean's mind. His guilt was double-edged. He had betrayed Duff's trust, and he had lacked the courage to make the betrayal worthwhile. He had waited too long. He should have done it at the beginning, cleanly and quickly, or he should not have done it at all. He longed with every fibre of his body to be given the chance to do it again, but this time the right way. He would gladly have lived once more through all that horror to clear his conscience and clean the stain from the memory of their friendship.

His grief was a thing of emptiness, an aching void—so immense that he was lost in it. Where before there had been Duff's laughter, his twisted grin and infectious zest there was now only a grey nothingness. No glimmer of sun penetrated it and there were no solid shapes in it.

The next waterhole was shallow soup in the centre of a flat expanse of dry mud the size of a polo field. The mud was cracked in an irregular chequered pattern forming small brickettes, each the size of a hand. A man could have jumped across the water without wetting his feet. Scattered thickly round its circumference were the droppings of animals that had drunk there. Back and forth across its surface, changing direction as the wind veered, a few loose feathers sailed. The water was brackish and dirty. It was a bad camp. On the third day Mbejane went to Sean's wagon. Sean lay in his cot. He had not changed his clothes since leaving Duff. His beard was beginning to mat, sticky with sweat for it was hot as an oven under the wagon canvas.

'Nkosi, will you come and look at the water. I do not think we should stay here.'

'What is wrong with it?' Sean asked without interest.

'It is dirty, I think we should go on towards the big river.'

'Do whatever you think is right.' Sean rolled away from him, his face towards the side of the wagon.

So Mbejane took the wagon train down towards the Limpopo. It was two days later that they found the ribbon of dark green trees that lined the banks. Sean stayed in his cot throughout the trek, jolting over the rough ground, sweating in the heat but oblivious to all discomfort. Mbejane put the wagons into laager on the bank above the river-bed, then he and all the other servants waited for Sean to come to life again. Their talk round the fire at nights was baited with worry and they looked often towards Sean's living wagon, where it stood unlit by lantern, dark as the mood of the man that lay within.

Like a bear coming out of its cave at the end of winter, Sean came out of the wagon at last. His clothes were filthy. The dogs hurried to meet him, crowding round his knees, begging for attention and he did not notice them. Vaguely he answered the greeting of his servants. He wandered down the bank into the river-bed.

The summer had shrunk the Limpopo into a sparse line of pools strung out down the centre of the watercourse. The pools were dark olive green. The sand around them was white, glaring snowfield white, and the boulders that choked the barely moving river were black and polished smooth. The banks were steep, half a mile apart and walled in with trees. Sean walked through the sand, sinking to his ankles with each step. He reached the water and sat down at the edge, he dabbled his hand in it and found it warm as blood. In the sand next to him was the long slither mark of a crocodile, and a troop of monkeys were shaking the branches of a tree on the far bank and chattering at him. A pair of Sean's dogs splashed across the narrow neck between two pools and went off to chase the monkeys. They went half-heartedly with their tongues flapping at the corners of their mouths for it was very hot in the whiteness of the river-bed. Sean stared into the green water. It was lonely without Duff; he had only his guilt and his sorrow for company. One of the dogs that had stayed with him touched his cheek with its cold nose. Sean put his arm round its neck and the dog leaned against him. He heard footsteps in the sand behind him, he turned and looked up. It was Mbejane.

'Nkosi, Hlubi has found elephant not an hour's march up stream. He has counted twenty who show good ivory.'

Sean looked back at the water. 'Go away,' he said.

Mbejane squatted down beside him with his elbows on his knees. 'For whom do you mourn?' he asked.

'Go away, Mbejane, leave me alone.'

'Nkosi Duff does not need your sorrow—therefore I think that you mourn for yourself.' Mbejane picked up a pebble and tossed it into the pool.

'When a traveller gets a thorn in his foot,' Mbejane went on softly, 'and he is wise he plucks it out—and he is a fool who leaves it and says "I will keep this thorn to prick me so that I will always remember the road upon which I have travelled." Nkosi, it is better to remember with pleasure than with pain.' Mbejane lobbed another pebble into the pool, then he stood up and walked back to the camp. When Sean followed him ten minutes later he found a saddle on his horse, his rifle in the scabbard and Mbejane and Hlubi waiting with their spears. Kandhla handed him his hat, he held it by the brim, turning it in his hands. Then he clapped it on to his head and swung up on to the horse.

'Lead,' he ordered.

During the next weeks Sean hunted with a single-mindedness that left no time for brooding. His returns to the wagons were short and intermittent; his only reasons for returning at all were to bring in the ivory and change his horse. At the end of one of these brief visits to camp and as Sean was about to mount up for another hunt, even Mbejane complained. 'Nkosi, there are better ways to die than working too hard.'

'You look well enough,' Sean assured him, although Mbejane was now as lean as a greyhound and his skin shone like washed anthracite.

'Perhaps all men look healthy to a man on horseback,' Mbejane suggested and Sean stopped with one foot in the stirrup. He looked at Mbejane thoughtfully, then he lowered his leg again. 'We hunt on foot now, Mbejane, and the first to ask for mercy earns the right to be called "woman" by the other.'

Mbejane grinned; the challenge was to his liking. They crossed the river and found spoor before midday—a small herd of young bulls. They followed it until nightfall and slept huddled together under one blanket, then they went on again next morning. On the third day they lost the spoor in rocky ground and they cast back towards the river. They picked up another herd within ten miles of the wagons, went after them and killed that evening—three fine bulls, not a tusk between them under fifty pounds weight. A night march back to the wagons, four hours' sleep and they were away again. Sean was limping a little now and on the second day out, during one of their infrequent halts, he pulled off his boot. The blister on his heel had burst and his sock was stiff with dried blood. Mbejane looked at him expressionlessly. 'How far are we from the wagons?' asked Sean.

'We can be back before dark, Nkosi.' Mbejane carried Sean's rifle for him on the return. Not once did his mask of solemnity slip. Back in camp Kandhla brought a basin of hot water and set it in front of Sean's chair. While Sean soaked his feet in it his entire following squatted in a circle about him. Every face wore an expression of studied concern and the silence was broken only by the clucking sounds of Bantu sympathy. They were loving every minute of it and Mbejane with the timing of a natural actor was building up the effect, playing to his audience. Sean puffed at a cheroot, scowling to stop himself laughing. Mbejane cleared his throat and spat into the fire. Every eye was on him; they waited breathlessly.

'Nkosi,' said Mbejane, 'I would set fifty head of oxen as your marriage price—if you were my daughter.'

One instant more of silence, then a shout of laughter. Sean laughed with them at first, but after a while when Hlubi had nearly staggered into the fire and Nonga was sobbing loudly on Mbejane's shoulder with tears of mirth streaming down his cheeks, Sean's own laughter stopped. It wasn't *that* funny.

He looked at them sourly—at their wide open pink mouths and their white teeth, at their shaking shoulders and heaving chests and suddenly it came to him very clearly that they were no longer laughing at him. They were laughing for the joy of it. They were laughing because they were alive. A chuckle rattled up Sean's throat and escaped before he could stop it, another one bounced around inside his chest and he lay back in his chair, opened his mouth and let it come. The hell with it, he was alive, too.

In the morning when he climbed out of his wagon and limped across to see what Kandhla was cooking for breakfast, there was a faint excitement in him again, the excitement of a new day. He felt good. Duff's memory was still with him, it always would be, but now it was not a sickening ache. He had plucked out the thorn.

10

They moved camp three times in November, keeping to the south bank of the river, following it back towards the west. Slowly the wagons which they had emptied of ivory beside the waterhole began to fill again, for the game was concentrated along the river. The rest of the land was dry but now each day there was promise of relief.

The clouds that had been scattered across the sky began to crowd together, gathering into rounded dark-edged masses or rearing proudly into thunderheads. All of nature seemed impressed by their growing importance. In the evenings the sun dressed them in royal purple and during the day the whirlwinds did dervish dances for their entertainment. The rains were coming. Sean had to make a decision, cross the Limpopo and cut himself off from the south when the river flooded, or stay where he was and leave the land beyond undisturbed. It wasn't a difficult decision. They found a place where the banks flattened out a little on both sides of the river. They unloaded the first wagon and double-teamed it; then with everybody shouting encouragement the oxen galloped down the steep slope into the river-bed. The wagon bounced behind them until it hit the sand where it came to a halt, tilted at an abandoned angle, with its wheels sunk axle-deep into the sand.

'On to the spokes,' shouted Sean. They flung themselves on the wheels and strained to keep them turning, but half the oxen were down on their knees, powerless in the loose footing.

'Damn it to hell.' Sean glared at the wagon. 'Outspan the oxen and take them back. Get out the axes.'

It took them three days to lay a bridge of corduroyed branches across the river and another two to get all the wagons and ivory to the far bank. Sean declared a holiday when the last wagon was manhandled into the laager and the whole camp slept late the next morning. The sun was high by the time Sean descended from his wagon. He was still muzzy and a little liverish from lying abed. He yawned wide and stretched like a crucifix. He ran his tongue round his mouth and grimaced at the taste, then he scratched his chest and the hair rasped under his fingers.

'Kandhla, where's the coffee? Don't you care that I am near dead from thirst?'

'Nkosi, the water will boil very soon.'

Sean grunted and walked across to where Mbejane squatted with the other servants by the fire watching Kandhla.

'This is a good camp, Mbejane.' Sean looked up at the roof of leaves above them. It was a place of green shade, cool in the late morning heat. Christmas beetles were squealing in the wide stretched branches.

'There is good grazing for the cattle,' Mbejane agreed; he stretched out his hand towards Sean.

'I found this in the grass—someone else has camped here.' Sean took it from him and examined it, a piece of broken china with a blue fig-leaf pattern. It was a shock to Sean, that little fragment of civilization in the wilderness; he turned it in his fingers and Mbejane went on. 'There are the ashes of an old fire there against the shuma tree and I found the ruts where wagons climbed the bank at the same place as ours.'

'How long ago?'

Mbejane shrugged. 'A year perhaps. Grass has grown in the wagon tracks.'

Sean sat down in his chair, he felt disturbed. He thought about it and grinned as he realized he was jealous; there were strangers here in the land he was coming to regard as his own, those year-old tracks gave him a feeling of being in a crowd. Also there was the opposite feeling, that of longing for the company of his own kind. The sneaking desire to see a white face again. It was strange that he could resent something and yet wish for it simultaneously.

'Kandhla, am I to have coffee now or at supper tonight?'

'Nkosi, it is done.' Kandhla poured a little brown sugar into the mug, stirred it with a stick and handed it to him. Sean held the mug in both hands, blowing to cool it, then sipping and sighing with each mouthful. The talk of his Zulus passed back and forth about the circle and the snuff-boxes followed it, each remark of worth being greeted with a solemn chorus of 'It is true, it is true,' and the taking of snuff. Small arguments jumped up and fell back again into the leisurely stream of conversation. Sean listened to them, occasionally joining in or contributing a story until his stomach told him it was time to eat. Kandhla started to cook, under the critical supervision and with the helpful suggestions of those whom idleness had made garrulous. He had almost succeeded in grilling the carcass of a guinea-fowl to the satisfaction of the entire company, although Mbejane felt that he should have added a pinch more salt, when Nonga sitting across the fire from him jumped to his feet and pointed towards the north. Sean shaded his eyes and looked.

'For Chrissake,' said Sean.

'Ah! ah! ah!' said his servants.

A white man rode towards them from the trees; he cantered with long stirrups, slouched comfortably, close enough already for Sean to make out the great ginger beard that masked the bottom half of his face. He was a big man; the sleeves of his shirt rolled high around thick arms.

'Hello,' shouted Sean and went eagerly to meet him. The rider reined in at the edge of the laager. He climbed stiffly out of the saddle and grabbed Sean's outstretched hand. Sean felt his fingerbones creak in the grip.

'Hello, man! How goes it?' He spoke in Afrikaans. His voice matched the size of his body and his eyes were on a level with Sean's. They pumped each other's arms mercilessly, laughing, putting sincerity into the usual inanities of greeting.

'Kandhla—get out the brandy bottle,' Sean called over his shoulder, then to the Boer, 'Come in, you're just in time for lunch. We'll have a dram to celebrate. Hell, it's good to see a white man again!'

'You're on your own, then?'

'Yes—come in, man, sit down.'

Sean poured drinks and the Boer took one up.

'What's your name?' he asked.

'Courtney—Sean Courtney.'

'I'm Jan Paulus Leroux—glad to meet you, meneer.'

'Good health, meneer,' Sean answered him and they drank. Jan Paulus wiped his whiskers on the palm of his hand and breathed out heavily, blowing the taste of the brandy back into his mouth.

'That was good,' he said and held out his mug. They talked excitedly, tongues loose from loneliness, trying to say everything and ask all the questions at once—meetings in the bush are always like this. Meanwhile the tide was going out in the bottle and the level dropped quickly.

'Tell me, where are your wagons?' Sean asked.

'An hour or two behind. I came ahead to find the river.'

'How many in your party?' Sean watched his face, talking just for the sound of it.

'Ma and Pa, my little sister and my wife—which reminds me—you had better move your wagons.'

'What?' Sean looked puzzled.

'This is my outspan place,' the Boer explained to him. 'See, there are the marks of my fire—this is my camp.'

The smile went out of Sean's voice. 'Look around you, Boer, there is the whole of Africa. Take your pick—anywhere except where I am sitting.'

'But this is my place.' Jan Paulus flushed a little. 'I always camp at the same place when I return along a spoor.'

The whole temper of their meeting had changed in a few seconds. Jan Paulus stood abruptly and went to his horse. He stooped and tightened the girth, hauling so savagely on the strap that the animal staggered off balance. He flung himself on to its back and looked down at Sean.

'Move your wagons,' he said, 'I camp here tonight.'

'Would you like to bet on that?' Sean asked grimly.

'We'll see!' Jan Paulus flashed back.

'We certainly shall,' agreed Sean.

The Boer wheeled his horse and rode away. Sean watched his back disappear among the trees and only then did he let his anger slip. He rampaged through the laager working himself into a fury, pacing out frustrated circles, stopping now and then to glare out in the direction from which the Boer's wagons would come—but under all the external signs of indignation was his unholy anticipation of a fight. Kandhla brought him food, hurrying along behind him with the plate. Sean waved him away impatiently and continued his pugnacious patrol. At last a trek whip popped in the distance and an ox lowed faintly, to be answered immediately by Sean's cattle. The dogs started barking and Sean crossed to one of the wagons on the north side of the laager and leaned against it with assumed nonchalance. The long line of wagons wound out of the trees towards him. There were bright blobs of colour on the high box seat of the lead wagon. Women's dresses! Ordinarily they would have made Sean's nostrils flare like those of a stud stallion, but now his whole attention was concentrated on the larger of the two outriders. Jan Paulus cantered ahead of his father, and Sean, with his fists clenched into bony hammers at his sides, watched him come. Jan Paulus sat straight in the saddle; he stopped his horse a dozen paces from Sean and shoved his hat on to the back of his head with a thumb as thick and as brown as a fried sausage; he tickled his horse a little with his spurs to make it dance and he asked with mock surprise, 'What, *Rooi Nek*, still here?'

Sean's dogs had rushed forward to meet the other pack and now they milled about in a restrained frenzy of mutual bottom-smelling, stiff-limbed with tension, backs abristle and legs cocking in the formal act of urination.

'Why don't you go and climb a tree? You'll feel more at home there,' Sean suggested mildly.

'Ah! so?' Jan Paulus reared in his stirrups. He kicked loose his right foot, swung it back over his horse's rump to dismount and Sean jumped at him. The horse skittered nervously, throwing the Boer off balance and he clutched at the saddle. Sean reached up, took a double handful of his ginger beard and leaned back on it with all his weight. Jan Paulus came over backward with his arms windmilling, his foot caught in the stirrup and he hung suspended like a hammock, held at one end to the plunging horse and at the other by his chin to Sean's hands. Sean dug his heels in, revelling in the Boer's bellows.

Galvanized into action by Sean's example, the dogs cut short the ceremony and went at each other in a snarling, snapping shambles; the fur flew like sand in a Kalahari dust-storm.

The stirrup-leather snapped; Sean fell backwards and rolled to his feet just in time to meet Jan Paulus's charge. He smothered the punch that the Boer bowled overarm at him, but the power behind it shocked him; then they were chest to chest and Sean felt his own strength matched. They strained silently with their beards touching and their eyes inches apart. Sean shifted his weight quickly and tried for a fall, but smoothly as a dancer Jan Paulus met and held him. Then it was his turn; he twisted in Sean's arms and Sean sobbed with the effort required to stop him. Oupa Leroux joined in by driving his horse at them, scattering the dogs, his hippo-hide sjambok hissing as he swung it. 'Let it stand! you thunders, give over—hey! Enough, let it stand!'

Sean shouted with pain as the lash cut across his back and at the next stroke Jan Paulus howled as loudly. They let go of each other and massaging their whip-weals retreated before the skinny old white-beard on the horse.

The first of the wagons had come up now and two hundred pounds of woman, all in one package, called out from the box seat, 'Why did you stop them, Oupa?'

'No sense in letting them kill each other.'

'Shame on you—so you must spoil the boys' fun. Don't you remember how you loved to fight? Or are you now so old you forget the pleasures of your youth? Leave them alone!'

Oupa hesitated, swinging the sjambok and looking from Sean to Jan Paulus.

'Come away from there, you old busybody,' his wife ordered him. She was solid as a granite kopje, her blouse packed full of bosom and her bare arms brown and thick as a man's. The wide brim of her bonnet shaded her face but Sean could see it was pink and pudding-shaped, the kind of face that smiles more easily than it frowns. There were two girls on the seat beside her but there was no time to look at them. Oupa had pulled his horse out of the way and Jan Paulus was moving down on him. Sean went up on his toes, crouching a little, preoccupied with the taste he had just had of the other's strength, watching Jan Paulus close in for the main course and not too certain he was going to be able to chew this mouthful.

Jan Paulus tested Sean with a long right-hander but Sean rolled his head with it and the thick pad of his beard cushioned the blow; he hooked Jan Paulus in the ribs under his raised arm and Jan Paulus grunted and circled away.

Forgetting his scruples, Oupa Leroux watched them with rising delight. It was going to be a good fight. They were well matched—both big men, under thirty, quick and smooth on their feet. Both had fought before and that often; you could tell it by the way they felt each other out, turning just out of reach, moving in to offer an opening that a less experienced man might have attempted and regretted, then dropping back.

The fluid, almost leisurely pattern of movement exploded. Jan Paulus jumped in, moving left, changed direction like the recoil of a whip lash and used his right hand again; Sean ducked under it and laid himself open to Jan Paulus's left. He staggered back from its kick, bleeding where it had split the flesh across his cheek-bone, and Jan Paulus followed him eagerly, his hands held ready, searching for the opening. Sean kept clear, instinct moving his feet until the blackness faded inside his head and he felt the strength in his arms again. He saw Jan Paulus following him and he let his legs stay rubbery; he dropped his hands and waited for Jan Paulus to commit himself. Too late Jan Paulus caught the cunning in Sean's eyes and tried to break from the trap, but clenched bone raked his face. He staggered away and now he was bleeding also.

They fought through the wagons with the advantage changing hands a dozen times. They came together and used their heads and their knees, they broke and used their fists again. Then locked chest to chest once more they rolled down the steep bank into the river-bed of the Limpopo. They fought in the soft sand and it held their legs, it filled their mouths when they fell and clung like white icing-sugar to their hair and beards. They splashed into one of the pools and they fought in the water, coughing with the agony of it in their lungs, floundering like a pair of bull hippos, their movements slowing down until they knelt facing each other, no longer able to rise, the water running from them and the only sound their gasping for air.

Not sure whether the darkness was actuality or a fantasy of fatigue, for the sun had set by the time they were finished, Sean watched Jan Paulus starting to puke, retching with a tearing noise to bring up a small splash of yellow bile. Sean crawled to the edge of the pool and lay with his face in the sand. There were voices echoing in his ears and the light of a lantern—the light was red—filtered through the blood that had trickled into his eyes. His servants lifted him and he hardly felt them. The light and the voices faded into blackness as he slipped over the edge of consciousness.

The sting of iodine woke him and he struggled to sit up but hands pushed him down.

'Gently, gently, the fight is over.' Sean focused his one eye to find the voice. The pinkness of Ouma Leroux hung over him. Her hands touched his face and the antiseptic stung him again. He exclaimed through puffed lips.

'So! Just like a man,' Ouma chuckled. 'Your head nearly knocked off without a murmur but one touch of medicine and you cry like a baby.'

Sean rang his tongue round inside his mouth; one tooth loose but all the others miraculously present. He started to lift his hand to touch his closed eye but Ouma slapped it down impatiently and went on working over him.

'Glory, what a fight!' She shook her head happily. 'You were good, *kerel*, you were very good.'

Sean looked beyond her and saw the girl. She was standing in shadow, a silhouette against the pale canvas. She was holding a basin. Ouma turned and dipped the cloth in it, washing out the blood before she came back to his face. The wagon rocked under her weight and the lantern that hung from the roof swung, lighting the girl's face from the side. Sean's legs straightened on his cot and he moved his head slightly to see her better.

'Be still, *jong*,' Ouma commanded. Sean looked past her at the girl—at the full serene line of her lips and the curve of her cheek. He saw the pile of her hair fluff up in happy disarray and then, suddenly penitent, slide down behind her neck, curl over her shoulder and hang to her waist in a plait as thick as his wrist.

'Katrina, do you expect me to reach right across to the basin each time? Stand closer, girl.'

She stepped into the light and looked at Sean. Green, laughing, almost bubbling green was the colour of her eyes. Then she dropped them to the basin. Sean stared at her, not wanting to miss the moment when she would look up again.

'My big bear,' Ouma spoke with grudging approval. 'Steal our camp site, fight my son and ogle my daughter. If you go on like this I might have to knock the thunder out of you myself. Glory, but you are a dangerous one! Katrina, you had better go back to our wagons and help Henrietta see to your brother. Leave the basin on the chest there.'

She looked at Sean once more before she left. There were secret shadows in the green—she didn't have to smile with her mouth.

I I

Sean woke to the realization that something was wrong. He started to sit up but the pain checked him: the stiffness of bruised muscle and the catch of half-dried scab. He groaned and the movement hurt his lips. Slowly he swung his legs off the cot and roused himself to take stock of the damage. Dark through the hair of his chest showed a heel imprint of Jan Paulus's boot. Sean prodded round it gently, feeling for the give of a broken rib; then, satisfied with that area, he went on to inspect the raw graze that wrapped round on to his back, holding his left arm high and peering closely at the broken skin. He picked a bit of blanket fluff from the scab. He stood up, only to freeze as a torn muscle in his shoulder knifed him. He started to swear then softly monotonously, and he kept it up all through the painful business of climbing down out of the wagon.

His entire following watched his descent—even the dogs looked worried. Sean reached the ground and started to shout.

'What the hell—' He stopped hurriedly as he felt his lip crack open again and start to bleed.

'What the hell'—he said again, keeping his lips still—'are you doing standing round like a bunch of women at a beer drink—is there no work here? Hlubi, I thought I sent you out to look for elephant.' Hlubi went. 'Kandhla, where's breakfast? Mbejane, get me a basin of water and my shaving-mirror.' Sean sat in his chair and morosely inspected his face in the mirror.

'If a herd of buffalo had stampeded across it they would have done less damage.'

'Nkosi, it is nothing compared to his face,' Mbejane assured him.

'Is he bad?' Sean looked up.

'I have spoken to one of his servants. He has not left his bed yet and he lies there, growling like a wounded lion in a thicket; but his eyes are as tightly closed as those of a new cub.'

'Tell me more, Mbejane. Say truly, was it a good fight?'

Mbejane squatted down next to Sean's chair. He was silent a moment as he gathered his words.

'When the sky sends its cloud impis against the peaks of the Drakensberg, with thunder and the spears of lightning, it is a thing to thrill a man. When two bull elephants fight unto death there is no braver show in all the veld. Is this not so?'

Sean nodded, his eyes twinkling.

'Nkosi, hear me when I tell you these things were as the play of little children beside this fight.'

Sean listened to the praises. Mbejane was well versed in the oldest art of Zululand and when he had finished he looked at Sean's face. It was happy. Mbejane smiled and took a fold of paper out of his loin cloth. 'A servant from the other camp brought this while you slept.'

Sean read the note. It was written in a big round schoolgirl hand and worded in High Dutch. He liked that writing. It was an invitation to dinner.

'Kandhla, get out my suit and my number one boots.' He picked up the mirror again. There wasn't very much he could do about his face—trim the beard, perhaps, but that was all. He laid the mirror down and looked upstream to where the Leroux wagons were half hidden among the trees.

Mbejane carried a lantern in front of Sean. They walked slowly to enable Sean to limp with dignity. When they reached the other laager, Jan Paulus climbed stiffly out of his chair and nodded an equally stiff greeting. Mbejane had lied—except for a missing tooth there was little to choose between their faces. Oupa slapped Sean's back and pressed a tumbler of brandy into his hand. He was a tall man, but twenty thousand suns had burnt away his flesh and left only stringy muscle, had faded his eyes to a pale green and toughened his skin to the texture of a turkey's neck. His beard was yellowish-white with still a touch of ginger round the mouth. He asked Sean three questions without giving him time to answer the first, then he led him to a chair.

Oupa talked, Sean listened and Jan Paulus sulked. Oupa talked of cattle and hunting and the land to the north. After a few minutes Sean realized that he was not expected to take part in the conversation: his few tentative efforts were crushed under Oupa's verbal avalanche. So Sean listened half to him and half to the whisper of women's voices from the cooking fires behind the laager. Once he heard her laugh. He knew it was her for it was the rich sound of the thing that he had seen in her eyes. At last the women's business with food and pots was finished and Ouma led the girls to where the men sat. Sean stood up and saw that Katrina was tall, with shoulders like a boy. As she walked towards him the movement pressed her skirt against her legs—they were long but her feet was small. Her hair was red-black and tied behind her head in an enormous bun.

'Ah, my battling bear,' Ouma took Sean's arm, 'let me present my daughter-in-law, Henrietta—here is the man that nearly killed your husband.' Jan Paulus snorted from his chair and Ouma laughed, her bosom wobbling merrily. Henrietta was a small dark-eyed girl. *She doesn't like me*, Sean guessed instantly. He bowed slightly and took her hand. She pulled it away.

'This is my youngest daughter, Katrina. You met her last night.'

She does like me. Her fingers were long and square-tipped in his. Sean risked his lips with a smile.

'Without her ministrations I might have bled to death,' he said. She smiled straight back at him but not with her mouth.

'You wear your wounds well, meneer, the blue eye has an air of distinction.'

'That will be enough from you, girl,' Oupa spoke sharply. 'Go and sit by your mother.' He turned to Sean. 'I was telling you about this horse—well, I said to the fellow, "He's not worth five pounds let alone fifteen, look at those hocks, thin as sticks." So he says to me, trying to get me away, you follow, he says, "Come and look at the saddle." But I can see he's worried–'

The thin cotton of the girl's blouse could hardly contain the impatient push of her breasts, Sean thought that he had never seen anything so wonderful.

There was a trestle-table next to the cooking fire: they went to it at last. Oupa said grace. Sean watched him through his lashes. Oupa's beard waggled as he spoke and at one point he thumped the table to emphasize the point he was making to the Almighty. His 'amen' had such an impressive resonance that Sean had to make an effort to stop himself applauding and Oupa fell back spent.

'Amen,' said Ouma and ladled stew from a pot the size of a bucket. Henrietta added pumpkin fritters and Katrina stacked slices of fresh mealie bread on each plate. A silence fell on the table, spoiled only by the clank of metal on china and the sound of Oupa breathing through his nose.

'Mevrouw Leroux, I have waited a long time to taste food like this again.' Sean mopped up the last bit of gravy with a piece of mealie bread. Ouma beamed.

'There's plenty more, meneer. I love to see a man eat. Oupa used to be a great trencherman. My father made him take me away for he could not afford to feed him every time he came courting.' She took Sean's plate and filled it. 'You look to me like a man who can eat.'

'I think I'll hold my own in most company,' Sean agreed.

'So?' Jan Paulus spoke for the first time. He passed his plate to Ouma. 'Fill it up, please, Mother, tonight I am hungry.'

Sean's eyes narrowed, he waited until Jan Paulus had his plate back in front of him, then he took up his fork deliberately. Jan Paulus did the same.

'Glory,' said Ouma happily. 'Here we go again. Oupa, you may have to go out and shoot a couple of buffalo before dinner is finished tonight.'

'I will bet one sovereign on Jan Paulus,' Oupa challenged his wife. 'He is like an army of termites. I swear that if there was nothing else he'd eat the canvas off the wagons.'

'All right,' agreed Ouma. 'I've never seen the Bear eat before, but it seems to me he has plenty of room to put it.'

'Your woollen shawl against my green bonnet that Jan Paulus gives up first,' Katrina whispered to her sister-in-law.

'When Jannie has finished the stew he'll eat the Englishman,' Henrietta giggled. 'But it's a pretty bonnet–I'll take the wager.'

Plateful for plateful, Ouma measuring out each ladle with scrupulous fairness, they ate against each other. The talk round the table dwindled and halted.

'More?' asked Ouma each time the plates were clean, and each time they looked at each other and nodded. At last the ladle scraped the bottom of the pot.

'That's the end of it, my children, we will have to call it another draw.'

The silence went on after she had spoken. Sean and Jan Paulus sat very still looking at their respective plates. Jan Paulus hiccupped, his expression changed. He stood up and went into the darkness.

'Ah! listen! listen!' crowed Ouma. They waited and then she exploded into laughter. 'The ungrateful wretch, is that what he thinks of my food? Where's your sovereign, Oupa?'

'Wait, you greedy old woman, the game's not finished yet.' He turned and stared at Sean. 'To me it looks as though your horse is nearly blown.'

Sean closed his eyes. The sounds of Jan Paulus's distress came to him very clearly.

'Thank you for a–' He didn't have time to finish. He wanted to get far away so the girl couldn't hear him.

12

The following morning during breakfast Sean thought about his next move. He would write an invitation to dinner and then he would deliver it himself. They would have to ask him to stay for coffee and then, if he waited, there would be a chance. Even Oupa would have to stop talking sometime and Ouma might relax her vigilance. He was sure there'd be a chance to talk to the girl. He didn't know what he would say to her but he'd worry about that when the time came. He climbed into the wagon and found pencil and paper in his chest. He went back to the table and spread the paper in front of him. He chewed the end of the pencil and stared out into the bush. Something moved against the trees. Sean put the pencil down and stood up. The dogs barked then stopped as they recognized Hlubi. He was coming at a trot–he was coming with news. Sean waited for him.

'A big herd, Hkosi, with many showing ivory. I saw them drink at the river and then go back into the bush, feeding quietly.'

'When?' asked Sean to gain time. He was searching for a plausible excuse to stay in camp–it would have to be good to satisfy Mbejane who was already saddling one of the horses.

'Before the sun this morning,' answered Hlubi and Sean was trying to remember which was his sore shoulder–he couldn't hunt with a sore shoulder. Mbejane led the horse into the laager. Sean scratched the side of his nose and coughed.

'The tracker from the other camp follows close behind me, Nkosi, he too has seen the herd and brings the news to his master. But I, being as swift as a springbok when I run, have outdistanced him,' Hlubi ended modestly.

'Is that so?' For Sean it changed the whole problem, he couldn't leave the herd to that red-bearded Dutchman. He ran across to the wagon and snatched his bandolier from the foot of the cot. His rifle was already in the scabbard.

'Are you tired, Hlubi?' Sean buckled the heavy ammunition belt across his chest. The sweat had run in oily streaks down the Zulu's body; his breathing was deep and quick.

'No, Nkosi.'

'Well, then, lead us to these elephants of yours, my fleet-footed springbok.' Sean swung up on to his horse. He looked over his shoulder at the other camp. She would still be there when he came back.

Sean was limited to the speed of Hlubi's feet while the two Leroux had only to gallop along the easy spoor left by Sean's party and they caught up with him before he had gone two miles.

'Good morning to you,' Oupa greeted him as he drew level and pulled his horse in to a trot. 'Out for a morning's ride, I see.'

Sean made the best of it with a grin. 'If we are all to hunt then we must hunt together. Do you agree?'

'Of course, meneer.'

'And we must share the bag equally, one third to each man.'

'That is always the way.' Oupa nodded.

'Do you agree?' Sean turned in his saddle towards Jan Paulus. Jan Paulus grunted. He showed little inclination to open his mouth since he had lost his tooth.

They found the spoor within an hour. The herd had wrecked a road through the thick bush along the river. They had stripped the bark from the saplings and left them naked and bleeding. They had knocked down bigger trees to reach the tender top leaves and they had dropped their great piles of dung in the grass.

'We need no trackers to follow this.' Jan Paulus had the first excitement on him. Sean looked at him and wondered how many elephant had died in front of his rifle. A thousand perhaps, and yet the excitement was on him again now.

'Tell your servants to follow us. We'll go ahead. We'll catch them within an hour.' He smiled at Sean, gap-toothed, and Sean felt the excitement lift the hair on his own forearms. He smiled back.

They cantered in rough line abreast, slack-reined to let the horses pick their own way among the fallen trees. The river bush thinned out as they moved north and soon they were into parkland. The grass brushed their stirrups and the ground beneath it was firm and smooth.

They rode without talking, leaning forward in their saddles, looking ahead. The rhythmic beat of hooves was a war drum. Sean ran his fingers along the row of bullets strapped across his chest, then he drew his rifle, checked the load and thrust it back into its scabbard.

'There!' said Oupa and Sean saw the herd. It was massed among a grove of fever trees a quarter of a mile ahead.

'Name of a name,' Paulus whistled. 'There must be two hundred at least.'

Sean heard the first pig-squeal of alarm, saw ears fan out and trunks lift. Then the herd bunched together and ran with their backs humped, a thin screen of dust trailing behind them.

'Paulus take the right flank. You, meneer, in the middle and I'll ride left,' shouted Oupa.

Sean jammed his hat down over his ears and his horse jumped under him as he hit it with his heels. Like a thrown trident the three horsemen hurled themselves at the herd. Sean rode into the dust. He picked an old cow elephant from the moving mountain range in front of him and pressed his horse so close upon her that he could see the bristles in her tail tuft and the erosion of her skin, wrinkled as an old man's scrotum. He touched his hand to his horse's neck and it plunged—from full gallop to standstill in half a dozen strides. Sean threw his feet free of the stirrups and hit the ground, loose-kneed to ride the shock. The cow's spine was a line of lumps beneath the grey skin—Sean broke it with his first bullet and she dropped, sliding on her hindquarters like a dog with worms. His horse started to run again before he was properly in the saddle and everything became movement and noise, dust and the smell of burnt powder. Chase them, coughing in the dust. Close with them. Off the horse and shoot. Wet blood on grey skin. Slam, slam of the rifle—its barrel hot, recoiling savagely. Sweat in the eyes, stinging. Ride. Shoot again. Two more down, screaming, anchored by paralysed legs. Blood-red as a flag. Load, cramming cartridges into the rifle. Ride. Chase them, shoot again and again. The bullets striking on flesh with a hollow sound, then up and ride again. Ride—until the horse could no longer keep up with them and he had to let them go. He stood holding his horse's head, the dust and the thirst closed his throat. He could not swallow. His hands trembled in reaction. His shoulder was aching again. He untied his silk scarf, wiped his face with it and blew the mud out of his nose, then he drank from his water-bottle. The water tasted sweet.

The hunt had led from parkland into mopani bush. It was very thick, shiny green leaves hanging to the ground and pressing close around him. The air was still and warm to breathe. He turned back along the line of the chase. He found them by their squealing. When they saw him they tried to charge, dragging themselves towards him—using the front legs only and groping with their trunks. They sagged into stillness after the head shot. This was the bad part. Sean worked quickly. He could hear the other rifles in the mopani forest around him and when he came to one of the long clearings among the trees he saw Jan Paulus walking towards him, leading his horse.

'How many?' called Sean.

'*Gott*, man, I didn't count. What a killing, hey? Have you got a drink for me? I dropped my water-bottle somewhere.'

Jan Paulus's rifle was in its saddle scabbard. The reins were slung over his shoulder and his horse followed him with its head drooping from exhaustion. The clearing was walled in with the dense mopani trees and a wounded elephant broke into the open. It was lung shot—the side of its chest painted with froth—and when it squealed the blood sprayed in a pink spout from the end of its trunk. It went for Jan Paulus, streaming the black battle ensigns of its ears. His horse reared, the reins snapped, it turned free and galloped away, leaving him full in the path of the charge. Sean went up on to his horse's back without touching stirrups. His horse threw its head, dancing in a tight circle, but he dragged it around and drove it to intercept the charge.

'Don't run, for God's sake, don't run!' he shouted as he cleared his rifle from the scabbard. Jan Paulus heard him. He stood with his hands at his sides, his feet apart and his body braced. The elephant heard Sean shout also and it swung its head and Sean saw the first hesitation in its run. He fired, not trying to pick his shot, hoping only to hurt it, to bring it away from Jan Paulus. The bullet slapped into it with the sound of a wet towel flicked against a wall. The elephant turned, clumsy with the weakness of its shattered lungs. Sean gathered his horse beneath him and wheeled it away and the elephant followed him.

Sean fumbled as he reloaded, his hands were slippery with sweat. One of the brass shells slipped through his fingers, tapped against his knee and dropped into the grass under his horse's hooves. The elephant gained on him. He loosened his bed-roll from the saddle and let it fall—they would sometimes stop to savage even a fallen hat, but not this one. He turned in the saddle and fired into it. It squealed again so close upon him that the brown blood splattered into his face. His horse was almost finished; he could feel its legs flopping with every stride and they were nearly at the end of the clearing racing towards the solid wall of green mopani. He pushed another round into the breech of his rifle and swung his body across the saddle. He slid down until his feet touched the ground and he was running next to his horse. He let go and was flung forward, but he fought to keep his balance, his body jarring with the force of his run. Then, still on his feet, he turned for his first steady shot. The elephant was coming in fast, almost on top of him, hanging over him like a cliff. Its trunk coiled on its chest and the curves of its ivory were lifted high.

It's too close, much too close. I can't hit the brain from here.

He aimed at the hollow in its forehead just above the level of its eyes. He fired and the elephant's legs folded up; its brain burst like an overripe tomato within the bone castle of its skull.

Sean tried to jump aside as the massive body came skidding down upon him, but one of its legs hit him and threw him face down into the grass. He lay there. He felt sick, for his stomach was still full of warm oily fear.

After a while he sat up and looked at the elephant. One of its tusks had snapped off flush with the lip. Jan Paulus came, panting from his run. He stopped next to the elephant and touched the wound in its forehead, then he wiped his fingers on his shirt.

'Are you all right, man?'

He took Sean's arm and helped him to his feet; then he picked up Sean's hat and dusted it carefully before handing it to him.

13

In the three-sided shelter formed by the belly and out-thrust legs of one of the dead elephants they made their camp that night. They drank coffee together and Sean sat between the two Leroux with his back against the rough skin of the elephant's belly. The silhouettes of the tree against the night sky were deformed by the shapes of the vultures that clustered in them and the darkness was ugly with the giggling of hyena. They had set a feast for the scavengers. They spoke little for they were tired, but Sean could feel the gratitude of the men who sat beside him and before they rolled into their blankets Jan Paulus said gruffly, 'Thank you, *kerel.*'

'You might be able to do the same for me one day.'

'I hope so, *ja*! I hope so.'

In the morning Oupa said, 'It's going to take us three or four days to cut out all this ivory.' He looked up at the sky. 'I don't like these clouds. One of us had better ride back to camp to fetch more men and wagons to carry the ivory.'

'I'll go.' Sean stood up quickly.

'I was thinking of going myself.' But Sean was already calling to Mbejane to saddle his horse and Oupa couldn't really argue with him, not after yesterday.

'Tell Ouma to take the wagons across the river,' he acquiesced. 'We don't want to be caught on this side when the river floods. Perhaps you wouldn't mind helping her.'

'No,' Sean assured him. 'I don't mind at all.'

His horse was still tired from the previous day's hunt and it was three hours before he reached the river.

He tied his horse on the bank and went down to one of the pools. He stripped off his clothes and lowered himself into the water. He scrubbed himself with handfuls of the coarse sand and when he waded out of the pool and dried on his shirt his skin was tingling. He rode along the bank and the temptation to gallop his horse was almost unbearable. He laughed to himself a little.

'The field's almost clear, though I wouldn't put it past that suspicious old Dutchman to follow me.'

He laughed again and thought about the colour of her eyes, green as *crème-de-menthe* in a crystal glass, and the shape of her bosom. The muscles in his legs tightened and the horse lengthened its stride in response to the pressure of his knees. 'All right, run then,' Sean encouraged it, 'I don't insist on it, but I would be grateful.'

He went to his own wagons first and changed his sweaty shirt for a fresh one, his leather breeches for clean calico and his scuffed boots for soft polished leather. He scrubbed his teeth with salt and dragged a comb through his hair and beard. He saw in the mirror that the battle damage to his face was fading and he winked at his image. 'How can she resist you?' He gave his moustache one more twirl, climbed out of the wagon and was immediately aware of a most uncomfortable feeling in his stomach. He walked towards the Leroux' laager thinking about it, and he recognized it as the same feeling he used to have when Waite Courtney called him to the study to do penance for his boyhood sins.

'That's odd,' he muttered. 'Why should I feel like that?' His confidence faded and he stopped. 'I wonder if my breath smells—I think I'd better go back and get some cloves.' He turned with relief, knew it as cowardice and stopped again. 'Get a grip on yourself. She's only a girl, an uneducated little Dutch girl. You've had fifty finer women.'

'Name me two,' he shot back at himself.

'Well, there was—Oh! for Chrissake, come on.' Resolutely he set off for the Leroux' laager again.

She was sitting in the sun within the circle of wagons. She was leaning forward on the stool and her newly-washed hair fell thickly over her face almost to the ground. With each stroke of the brush it leapt like a live thing and the sun sparkled the red lights in it. Sean wanted to touch it—he wanted to twist fistfuls of it round his hands and he wanted to smell it, it would smell warm and slightly milky like a puppy's fur. He stepped softly towards her but before he reached her she took the shiny mass with both hands and threw it back over her shoulders—a startled flash of green eyes, one despairing wail, 'Oh, no! not with my hair like this.' A swirl of skirts that sent the stool flying and she was gone into her wagon. Sean scratched the side of his nose and stood awkwardly.

'Why are you back so soon, meneer?' she called through the canvas. 'Where are the others? Is everything all right?'

'Yes, they're both fine. I left them and came to fetch wagons to carry the ivory.'

'Oh, that's good.' Sean tried to interpret the inflexion of her voice: was it good that they were fine, or good that he had left them? So far the indications were favourable; her confusion at seeing him boded well.

'What's wrong?' Ouma bellowed from one of the other wagons. 'It's not Oupa, don't tell me something has happened to him?' The wagon rocked wildly and her pink face, puckered with sleep, popped out of the opening. Sean's reassurances were smothered by her voice.

'Oh, I knew this would happen. I had a feeling. I shouldn't have let him go.' 'Paulus, oh, Jan Paulus—I must go to him. Where is he?'

Henrietta came running from the cooking fire behind the wagons and then the dogs started barking and the servants added their chatter to the confusion. Sean tried to shout them all down and watch Katrina emerging from her wagon at the same time. She had disciplined her hair now—it had a green ribbon in it and hung down her back. She was laughing and she helped him to quieten Ouma and Henrietta.

They brought him coffee, then they sat round him and listened to the story of the hunt. Sean went into detail on the rescue of Jan Paulus and was rewarded by a softening of the dislike in Henrietta's eyes. By the time Sean had finished talking it was too late to start moving the wagons across the river. So he talked some more, it was most agreeable to have three women as an attentive audience, and then they ate supper.

With ostentatious tact Ouma and Henrietta retired early to their respective living wagons and left Sean and Katrina sitting by the fire. At carefully-spaced intervals there was a stage cough from Ouma's wagon, a reminder that they were not entirely alone. Sean lit a cheroot and frowned into the fire searching desperately for something intelligent to say, but all his brain could dredge up was, 'Thank God, Oupa isn't here.' He sneaked a glance at Katrina: she was staring into the fire as well and she was blushing. Instantly Sean felt his own cheeks starting to heat up. He opened his mouth to talk and made a squawking noise. He shut it again.

'We can speak in English if you like, meneer.'

'You speak English?' Sean's surprise brought his voice back.

'I practise every night—I read aloud out of my books.'

Sean grinned at her delightedly—it was suddenly very important that she could speak his language. The dam, holding back all the questions that there were to ask and all the things there were to say, burst and the words came pouring out over each other. Katrina fluttered her hands when she couldn't find the word she wanted and then lapsed back into Afrikaans. They killed the short taut silences with a simultaneous rush of words, then laughed together in confusion. They sat on the edges of their chairs and watched each other's faces as they talked. The moon came up, a red rain moon, and the fire faded into a puddle of ashes.

'Katrina, it's long past the time decent people were asleep. I'm sure Meneer Courtney is tired.'

They dropped their voices to a whisper, drawing out the last minutes.

'In just one minute, girl, I'm coming out to fetch you to bed.'

They walked to her wagon and with each step her skirts brushed against his leg. She stopped with one hand on the wagon step. She wasn't as tall as he'd imagined, the top of her head came to his chin. The seconds slid by as he hesitated, reluctant to touch, strangely frightened to test the delicate thread they had spun together lest he destroy it before it became strong. Slowly he swayed towards her and something surged up inside him as he saw her chin lift slightly and the lashes fall over her eyes.

'Goodnight, Meneer Courtney.' Ouma's voice again, loud and with an edge to it. Sean started guiltily.

'Goodnight, mevrouw.'

Katrina touched his arm just above the elbow, her fingers were warm.

'Goodnight, meneer, I shall see you in the morning.'

She rustled up the steps and slipped through the opening of the canvas. Sean scowled at Ouma's wagon.

'Thanks very much—and if there is ever anything I can do for you, please don't hesitate to ask.'

14

They started moving the wagons early next morning. There was no time to talk to Katrina in the bustle of inspanning and working the wagons across the corduroy bridge. Sean spent most of the morning in the river-bed and the white sand bounced the heat up at him. He threw off his shirt and sweated like a wrestler. He trotted beside Katrina's wagon when they ran it through the river-bed. She looked once at his naked chest and arms; her cheeks darkened in the shadow of her bonnet and she dropped her eyes and didn't look at him again. With only the two wagons that were going back to fetch the ivory still on the north bank and the rest safely across, Sean could relax. He washed in one of the pools, put on his shirt and went across to the south bank looking forward to a long afternoon of Katrina's company.

Ouma met him. 'Thank you, my bear, the girls have made you a parcel of cold meat and a bottle of coffee to eat on your way.' Sean's face went slack. He had forgotten all about that stinking ivory; as far as he was concerned Oupa and Paulus could keep the lot of it.

'Don't worry about us any more now, meneer. I know how it is with a man who is a man. When there's work to do everything else comes after.'

Katrina put the food in his hands. Sean looked for a sign from her. One sign and he'd defy even Ouma.

'Don't be too long,' she whispered. The thought that he might shirk work had obviously not even occurred to her. Sean was glad he hadn't suggested it.

It was a long ride back to the elephant.

'You've taken your time, haven't you?' Oupa greeted him with sour suspicion. 'You'd better get to work if you don't want to lose some of your share.'

Taking out the tusks was a delicate task: a slip of the axe would scar the ivory and halve its value. They worked in the heat with a blue haze of flies around their faces, settling on their lips and crawling into their nostrils and eyes. The carcasses had started to rot and the gases ballooned their bellies and escaped in posthumous belches. They sweated as they worked and the blood caked their arms to the elbows, but each hour the wagons filled higher until on the third day they loaded the last tusk. Sean reckoned his share at twelve hundred pounds, the equivalent of a satisfactory day on the Stock Exchange.

He was in a good mood on the morning that they started back to the camp, but it deteriorated as the day wore on and they struggled with the heavily-loaded wagons. The rain seemed to have made up its mind at last and now the sky's belly hung down as heavily as that of a pregnant sow. The clouds trapped the heat beneath them and the men panted and the oxen complained mournfully. At mid-afternoon they heard the first far thunder.

'It will be on us before we pass the river,' fretted Oupa. 'See if you can't get some pace out of those oxen.'

They reached Sean's camp an hour after dark and threw his share of the ivory out of the wagons almost without stopping; then they went down to the river and across the bridge to the south bank.

'My mother will have food ready,' Jan Paulus called back to Sean. 'When you have washed come across and eat with us.'

Sean had supper with the Leroux, but his attempts to get Katrina by herself were neatly countered by Oupa whose suspicions were now confirmed. The old man played his trump card immediately after supper and ordered Katrina to bed. Sean could only shrug helplessly in reply to Katrina's appealing little glance. When she had gone Sean went back to his own camp. He was dizzy with fatigue and he fell on to his cot without bothering to undress.

The rains opened their annual offensive with a midnight broadside of thunder. It startled Sean to his feet before he was awake. He pulled open the front of the wagon and heard the wind coming.

'Mbejane, get the cattle into the laager. Make sure all the canvas is secure.'

'It is done already, Nkosi, I have lashed the wagons together so the oxen cannot stampede and I have—' Then the wind whipped his voice away.

It came out of the east and it frightened the trees so they thrashed their branches in panic; it drummed on the wagon canvas and filled the air with dust and dry leaves. The oxen turned restlessly within the laager. Then came the rain: stinging like hail, drowning the wind and turning the air to water. It swamped the sloping ground that could not drain it fast enough, it blinded and it deafened. Sean went back to his cot and listened to its fury. It made him feel drowsy. He pulled the blankets up to his chin and slept.

In the morning he found his oilskins in the chest at the foot of his cot. They crackled as he pulled them on. He climbed out of the wagon. The cattle had churned the inside of the laager to calf-deep mud and there was no chance of a fire for breakfast. Although the rain was still falling the noise was out of proportion to its strength. Sean paused in his inspection of the camp; he thought about it and suddenly he knew that it was the flood voice of the Limpopo that he heard. Sliding in the mud, he ran out of the laager and stood on the bank of the river. He stared at the mad water. It was so thick with mud it looked solid and it raced so fast it appeared to be standing still. It humped up over piles of submerged rock, gullied through the deeps and hissed in static waves through the shallows. The branches and tree trunks in it whisked past so swiftly that they did little to dispel the illusion that the river was frozen in this brown convulsion.

Reluctantly Sean lifted his eyes to the far bank. The Leroux' wagons were gone.

'Katrina,' he said with the sadness of the might-have-been, then again, 'Katrina,' with the sense of his loss melting in the flame of his anger; and he knew that his wanting was not just the itch that is easily scratched and forgotten, but that it was the true ache, the one that gets into your hands and your head and your heart as well as your loins. He couldn't let her go. He ran back to his wagon and threw his clothes on to the cot.

'I'll marry her,' he said and the words startled him. He stood naked, with an awed expression on his face.

'I'll marry her,' he said again; it was an original thought and it frightened him a little. He took a pair of shorts out of his chest and put his legs into them; he pulled them up and buttoned the fly.

'I'll marry her!' He grinned at his own daring. 'I'm damned if I won't!' He buckled his belt on and tied a pair of *veldschoen* to it by their laces. He jumped down into the mud. The rain was cold on his bare back and he shivered briefly. Then he saw Mbejane coming out of one of the other wagons and he ran.

'Nkosi, Nkosi, what are you doing?' Sean put his head down and ran faster with Mbejane chasing him out on to the bank of the river.

'It's madness . . . let us talk about it first,' Mbejane shouted. 'Please, Nkosi, please.' Sean slipped in the mud and slithered down the bank. Mbejane jumped down after and caught him at the edge of the water, but the mud had coated Sean's body like grease and Mbejane couldn't hold him. Sean twisted out of his hands and sprang far out. He hit the water flat and swam on his back trying to avoid the undertow. The river swept him away. A wave slapped into his mouth and he doubled up to cough; immediately the river caught him by the heels and pulled him under the surface. It let him go again, just long enough to snatch air then it stirred him in a whirlpool and sucked him under once more. He came up beating at the water with his arms, then it tumbled him over a cascade and he knew by the pain in his chest that he was drowning. He swooped down a shute of swift water between rocks and it didn't matter any more. He was too tired. Something scraped against his chest and he put out his hand to protect himself; his fingers closed round a branch and his head lifted out of the water. He drank air and then he was clinging to the branch, still alive and wanting to live. He started kicking, edging across the current, riding the river with his arms around the log.

One of the eddies beneath the south bank swung the log in, under the branches of a tree. He reached up, caught them and dragged himself out. He knelt in the mud and water came gushing up out of him, half through his mouth and half through his nose. He had lost his *veldschoen*. He belched painfully and looked at the river. How fast was it moving, how long had he been in the water? He must be fifteen miles below the wagons. He wiped his face with his hand. It was still raining. He stood shakily and faced upstream.

It took him three hours to reach the spot opposite his wagons. Mbejane and the others waved in wild relief when they saw him, but their shouts could not carry across the river. Sean was cold now and his feet were sore. The tracks of the Leroux' wagons were dissolving in the rain. He followed them and at last the pain in his feet healed as he saw the flash of canvas in the rain mist ahead of him.

'Name of a name,' shouted Jan Paulus. 'How did you cross the river?'

'I flew, how else?' said Sean. 'Where's Katrina?'

Paulus started to laugh, leaning back in the saddle. 'So that's it then, you haven't come all this way to say goodbye to me.'

Sean flushed. 'All right, laughing boy. That's enough merriment for today . . . Where is she?'

Oupa came galloping back towards them. He asked his first question when he was fifty yards away and his fifth as he arrived. From experience Sean knew there was no point in trying to answer them. He looked beyond the two Leroux and saw her coming. She was running back from the lead wagon, her bonnet hanging from its ribbon around her throat and her hair bouncing loosely with each step. She held her skirts out of the mud, her cheeks flushed darker than the brown of her face and her eyes were very green. Sean ducked under the neck of Oupa's horse and went wet, muddy and eager to meet her.

Then the shyness stopped them and they stood paces apart. 'Katrina, will you marry me?'

She went pale. She stared at him then turned away, she was crying and Sean felt the bottom drop out of his stomach.

'No,' shouted Oupa furiously. 'She won't marry you. Leave her alone, you big baboon. You've made her cry. Get out of here. She's only a baby. Get out of here.' He forced his horse between them.

'You hold your mouth, you old busybody.' Ouma came panting back to join the discussion. 'What do you know about it anyway? Just because she's crying doesn't mean she doesn't want him.'

'I thought he was going to let me go,' sobbed Katrina, 'I thought he didn't care.'

Sean whooped and tried to dodge around Oupa's horse.

'You leave her alone,' shouted Oupa desperately, manœuvring his horse to cut Sean off. 'You made her cry. I tell you she's crying.'

Katrina was undoubtedly crying. She was also trying to get around Oupa's horse.

'*Vat haar,*' shouted Jan Paulus. 'Get her, man, go and get her!'

Ouma caught the horse by the reins and dragged it away; she was a powerful woman. Sean and Katrina collided and held tight.

'Hey, that's it, man,' Jan Paulus jumped off his horse and pounded Sean's back from behind. Unable to protect himself Sean was driven forward a pace with each blow.

Much later Oupa muttered sulkily. 'She can have two wagons for her dowry.'

'Three!' said Katrina.

'Four!' said Ouma.

'Very well, four. Take your hands off him, girl. Haven't you any shame?' Hastily Katrina dropped her arm from Sean's waist. Sean had borrowed a suit of clothing from Paulus and they were all standing round the fire. It had stopped raining but the low clouds were prematurely bringing on the night.

'And four of the horses,' Ouma prompted her husband.

'Do you want to beggar me, woman?'

'Four horses,' repeated Ouma.

'All right, all right . . . four horses.' Oupa looked at Katrina, his eyes were stricken. 'She's only a baby, man, she's only fifteen years.'

'Sixteen,' said Ouma.

'Nearly seventeen,' said Katrina, 'and anyway you've promised, Pa, you can't go back on your word now.'

Oupa sighed; then he looked at Sean and his face hardened.

'Paulus, get the Bible out of my wagon. This big baboon is going to swear an oath.'

Jan Paulus put the Bible on the tailboard of the wagon. It was thick and the cover was of black leather, dull with use.

'Come here,' Oupa said to Sean. 'Put your hand on the book . . . don't look at me. Look up, man, look up. Now say after me, "I do most solemnly swear to look after this woman"–don't gobble, speak slower–"until I can find a priest to say the proper words. Should I fail in this then I ask you, God, to blast me with lightning, sting me with serpents, burn me in eternal fire–"' Oupa completed the list of atrocities, then he grunted with satisfaction and tucked the Bible under his arm. 'He won't have a chance to do all that to you . . . I'll get you first.'

Sean shared Jan Paulus's wagon that night; he wasn't in a mood for sleep and anyway Jan Paulus snored. It was raining again in the morning, depressing weather for farewells. Jan Paulus laughed, Henrietta cried and Ouma did both. Oupa kissed his daughter.

'Be a woman like your mother,' he said, then he scowled at Sean.

'Remember, just you remember!'

Sean and Katrina stood together and watched the trees and the curtain of rain hide the wagon train. Sean held Katrina's hand. He could feel the sadness on her; he put his arm round her and her dress was damp and cold. The last wagon disappeared and they were alone in a land as vast as solitude. Katrina shivered and looked up at the man beside her. He was so big and overpoweringly male; he was a stranger. Suddenly she was frightened. She wanted to hear her mother's laugh and see her brother and father riding ahead of her wagon, the way it had always been.

'Oh, please, I want . . .' she pulled out from his arm. She never finished that sentence, for she looked at his mouth and his lips were full and burnt dark by the sun—they were smiling. Then she looked at his eyes and her panic smoothed away. With those eyes watching over her she was never to feel frightened again, not until the very end and that was a long time away. Going into his love was like going into a castle, a thick-walled place. A safe place where no one else could enter. The first feeling of it was so strong that she could only stand quietly and let the warmth wrap her.

15

That evening they outspanned Katrina's wagons back at the south bank of the river. It was still raining. Sean's servants waved and signalled to them, but the brown water bellowed down between them cutting off all sound and hope of passage. Katrina looked at the water. 'Did you really swim that, meneer?'

'So fast that I hardly got wet.'

'Thank you,' she said.

Despite the rain and smoky fire Katrina served up a meal as good as one of Ouma's. They ate it in the shelter of the tarpaulin beside her wagon. The wind guttered the hurricane lamp, flogged the canvas and blew a fine haze of rain in on them. It was so uncomfortable that when Sean suggested that they go into the wagon Katrina barely hesitated before agreeing. She sat on the edge of her cot and Sean sat on the chest opposite her. From an awkward start their conversation was soon running as fast as the river outside the wagon.

'My hair is still wet,' Katrina exclaimed at last. 'Do you mind if I dry it while we talk?'

'Of course not.'

'Then let me get my towel out of the chest.'

They stood up at the same time. There was very little space in the wagon. They touched. They were on the cot. The movement of his mouth on hers, the warm taste of it, the strong pleading of his fingers at the nape of her neck and along her spine—all these things were strangely confusing. She responded slowly at first, then faster with bewildered movements of her own body and little graspings at his arms and shoulders. She did not understand and she did not care. The confusion spread through her whole body and she could not stop it, she did not want to. She reached up and her fingers went into his hair. She pulled his face down on hers. His teeth crushed her lips—sweet, exciting pain. His hand came round from her back and enclosed a fat round breast. Through the thin cotton he found the erectness of her nipple and rolled it gently between his fingers. She reacted like a filly feeling the whip for the first time. One instant she lay under the shock of his touch and then her convulsive heave caught him by surprise. He went backwards off the cot and his head cracked against the wooden chest. He sat on the floor and stared up at her, too surprised even to rub the lump on his head. Her face was flushed and she pushed the hair back from her forehead with both hands. She was shaking her head wildly in her effort to speak through her gasping. 'You must go now, meneer—the servants have made a bed for you in one of the other wagons.'

Sean scrambled to his feet. 'But, I thought . . . surely we are . . . well, I mean.'

'Keep away from me,' she warned anxiously. 'If you touch me again tonight, I'll . . . I'll bite you.'

'But, Katrina, please, I can't sleep in the other wagon.' The thought appalled him.

'I'll cook your food, mend your clothes . . . everything! But until you find a priest . . .' She didn't go on, but Sean got the idea. He started to argue. It was his introduction to Boer immovability and at last he went to find his own bed. One of Katrina's dogs was there before him—a three-quarters-grown brindle hound. Sean's attempts to persuade it to leave were as ill-fated as had been his previous arguments with its mistress. They shared the bed. During the night a difference of opinion arose between them as to what constituted a half-share of the blankets. From it the dog earned its name—Thief.

16

Sean determined to show Katrina just how strongly he resented her attitude. He would be polite but distant. Five minutes after they had sat down to breakfast the next morning this demonstration of disapproval had deteriorated to the stage where he was unable to take his eyes off her face and he was talking so much that breakfast lasted an hour.

The rain held steadily for three more days and then it stopped. The sun came back, as welcome as an old friend, but it was another ten days before the river regained its sanity. Time, rain or river meant very little to the two of them. They wandered out into the bush together to pick mushrooms; they sat in camp and when Katrina was working Sean followed her around. Then, of course, they talked. She listened to him. She laughed at the right places and gasped with wonder when she was meant to. She was a good listener. As for Sean, if she had repeated the same word over and over the sound of her voice alone would have held him entranced. The evenings were difficult. Sean would start getting restless and make excuses to touch her. She wanted him to, but she was frightened of the confusion that had so nearly trapped her the first night. So she drew up a set of rules and put them to him. 'Do you promise not to do anything more than kiss me?'

'Not unless you say I can,' Sean agreed readily.

'No.' She saw the catch in that.

'You mean, I must never do anything but kiss you even if you say I can?'

She started to blush. 'If I say so in the daytime, that's different . . . but anything I say at night doesn't count, and if you break your promise I'll never let you touch me again.'

Katrina's rules stood unchanged by the time the river had dropped enough for the wagons to be taken across to the north bank. The rains were resting, gathering their strength, but soon they would set in once more. The river was full but no longer murderous. Now was the time to cross. Sean took the oxen across first, swimming them in a herd. Holding on to one of their tails he had a Nantucket sleigh-ride across the river and when he reached the north bank there was a joyous welcome awaiting him.

They took six thick coils of unused rope from the stores wagon and joined them together. With the end of the rope round his waist Sean made one of his horses tow him back across the river, Mbejane paying out the line to him as he went. Then Sean supervised Katrina's servants as they emptied all the water barrels and lashed them to the sides of the first wagon to serve as floats. They ran the wagon into the water, tied on the rope and adjusted the barrels so that the wagon floated level. Sean signalled to Mbejane and waited until he had made the other end of the rope fast to a tree on the north bank. Then they pushed the wagon into the current and watched anxiously as it swung across the river like a pendulum, the current driving it but the tree anchoring it. It hit the north bank a distance the exact width of the river downstream of the tree, and Sean's party cheered as Mbejane and the other servants ran down the bank to retrieve it. Mbejane had a team of oxen standing ready and they dragged it out. Sean's horse towed him across the river again to fetch the rope.

Sean, Katrina and all her servants rode across on the last wagon. Sean stood behind Katrina with his arms round her waist, ostensibly to steady her, and the servants shouted and chattered like children on a picnic.

The water piled up brown against the side of the wagon, tilting it and making it roll, and with an exhilarating swoop they shot across the river and crashed into the far bank. The impact tumbled them overboard, throwing them into the knee-deep water beside the bank. They scrambled ashore. The water streamed out of Katrina's dress, her hair melted wetly over her face; she had mud on one cheek and she was gasping with laughter. Her sodden petticoats clung to her legs, tripping her, and Sean picked her up and carried her to his own laager. His servants shouted loud encouragement after him and Katrina shrieked genteelly to be put down, but held tight round his neck with both arms.

17

Now that the rains had changed every irregularity in the land into a waterhole and sowed new green grass where before had been dust and dry earth, the game scattered away from the river. Every few days Sean's trackers came into camp to report that there were no elephant. Sean condoled with them and sent them out again. He was well satisfied; there was a new quarry now, more elusive and therefore more satisfying than an old bull elephant with a hundred and fifty pounds of ivory on each side of his face. Yet to call Katrina his quarry was a lie. She was much more than that.

She was a new world—a place of endless mysteries and unexpected delights, an enchanting mixture of woman and child. She supervised the domestic routine with deceptive lack of fuss. With her there, suddenly his clothes were clean and had their full complement of buttons; the stew of boots and books and unwashed socks in his wagon vanished. There were fresh bread and fruit preserves on the table; Kandhla's eternal grilled steaks gave way to a variety of dishes. Each day she showed a new accomplishment. She could ride astride, though Sean had to turn his back when she mounted and dismounted. She cut Sean's hair and made as good a job of it as his barber in Johannesburg. She had a medicine chest in her wagon from which she produced remedies for every ailing man or beast in the company. She handled a rifle like a man and could strip and clean Sean's Mannlicher. She helped him load cartridges, measuring the charges with a practised eye. She could discuss birth and procreation with a clinical objectivity and a minute later blush all over when he looked at her that way. She was as stubborn as a mule, haughty when it suited her, serene and inscrutable at times and at others a little girl. She would push a handful of grass down the back of his shirt and run for him to chase her, giggle for minutes at a secret thought, play long imaginative games in which the dogs were her children and she talked to them and answered for them. Sometimes she was so naïve that Sean thought she was joking until he remembered how young she was. She could drive him from happiness to spitting anger and back again within the space of an hour. But, once he had won her confidence and she knew that he would play to the rules, she responded to his caresses with a violence that startled them both. Sean was completely absorbed in her. She was the most wonderful thing he had ever found and, best of all, he could talk to her. He told her about Duff. She saw the extra cot in his wagon and found clothing that was obviously too small for him. She asked about it and he told her all of it and she understood.

The days became weeks. The cattle grew fat, their skins sleek and tight. Katrina planted a small vegetable garden and reaped a crop from it. Christmas came and Katrina baked a cake. Sean gave her a kaross of monkey skins that Mbejane had worked on in secret. Katrina gave Sean hand-sewn shirts, each with his initials embroidered on the top pocket, and she relaxed the rules a fraction.

Then when the new year had begun and Sean hadn't killed an elephant in six weeks, Mbejane headed a deputation from the gunboys. The question he had to ask, though tactfully disguised, was simply, 'Did we come here to hunt, or what?'

They broke camp and moved north again and the strain was showing on Sean at last. He tried to sweat it out by long days of hunting but this didn't help for conditions were so bad that they added to his irritability. The grass in most places was higher than a mounted man's head, its sharp edges cut as he passed through it. But the grass seeds were the worst. half an inch long and barbed like an arrow they worked their way quickly through clothing and into the skin. In the humid heat the small wounds they made festered within hours. Then there were the flies. Hippo-flies, green-headed flies, sand-flies and with one thing in common—they stung. The soft skin behind the ears was their favourite place. They'd creep upon him, settle so lightly he wouldn't feel it—then, ping with the red-hot needle. Always wet, sometimes with sweat, other times with rain, Sean would close with a herd of elephant. He would hear them moving in the long grass around him and see the white canopy of egrets fluttering over them, but it was seldom he could get a shot at them. If he did he had to stand in the centre of a storm of blundering bodies. Often they would be following a herd, almost upon them, when Sean would lose interest and they'd all go back to camp. He couldn't keep away.

He was miserable, his servants were miserable, and Katrina was happy as a bird at daybreak. She had a man, she was mistress of a household which she ran with confidence and, because her senses were not yet as seasoned as Sean's, she was physically content. Even with Sean's strict adherence to the rules, their evenings in her wagon would end for her with a sigh and a shudder and she would go dreamy-eyed to bed and leave Sean with a burning devil inside of him. The only person Sean could complain to was Thief. He would lie with his snout buried in Sean's armpit, with at least his share of the blankets over him, and listen quietly.

The Zulus could see what the trouble was but they didn't understand it. They didn't discuss it, of course, but if one of them spread his hands expressively or coughed in a certain way the others knew what he meant. Mbejane came closest to actually putting it into words. Sean had just thrown a tantrum. It was a matter of a lost axe and who was responsible. Sean lined them up and expressed doubts as to their ancestry, present worth and future prospects, then he stormed off to his wagon. There was a long silence and Hlubi offered his snuff-box to Mbejane.

Mbejane took a pinch and said, 'It's a stupid stallion that doesn't know how to kick down a fence.'

'It is true, it is true,' they agreed, and there the matter rested.

18

A week later they reached the Sabi river. The mountains on the far side were blue-grey with distance and the river was full—brown and full.

The next morning was fresh and cool from the night's rain. The camp smelt of wood-smoke, cattle and wild mimosa. From one of the ostrich eggs that Mbejane had found the day before, Katrina made an omelette the size of a soup-plate. It was flavoured with nutmeg and chunks of mushroom, yellow and rich. Afterwards there were scones and wild honey, coffee and a cheroot for Sean.

'Are you going out today?' Katrina asked.

'Uh huh.'

'Oh!'

'Don't you want me to?'

'You haven't stayed in camp for a week.'

'Don't you want me to go?'

She stood up quickly and started clearing the table. 'Anyway you won't find any elephant . . . you haven't found anything for ages.'

'Do you want me to stay?'

'It's such a lovely day.' She signed to Kandhla to take the plates away.

'If you want me to stay, ask me properly.'

'We could look for mushrooms.'

'Say it,' said Sean.

'All right then, please!'

'Mbejane! Take the saddle off that horse, I won't be using him.'

Katrina laughed. She ran to her wagon, skirts swirling around her legs, calling to the dogs. She came back with her bonnet on and a basket in her hand. The dogs crowded round them, jumping up and barking.

'Go on . . . seek up then,' Sean told them and they raced ahead, circling back barking, chasing one another. Sean and Katrina walked holding hands. The brim of Katrina's bonnet kept her face in shadow, but even then her eyes when she looked at him were bright green. They picked the new mushrooms, round and hard, brown and slightly sticky on top, fluted underneath delicately as a lady's fan. In an hour they had filled the basket and they stopped under a marula tree. Sean lay on his back. Katrina broke off a blade of grass and tickled his face with it until he caught her wrist and pulled her down on to his chest. The dogs watched them, sitting around them in a circle, their tongues hanging out pink and wet.

'There's a place in the Cape, just outside Paarl. The mountains stand over it and there's a river . . . the water's very clear, you can see the fish lying on the bottom,' said Katrina. Her ear was against his chest and she was listening to his heart. 'Will you buy me a farm there one day?'

'Yes,' said Sean.

'We'll build a house with a wide veranda and on Sundays we'll drive to church with the girls and the little ones in the back and the bigger boys riding next to the buggy.'

'How many will there be?' asked Sean. He lifted the side of her bonnet and looked at her ear. It was a very pretty ear, in the sunlight he could see the fine fur on the lobe.

'Oh lots . . . boys mostly, but a few girls.'

'Ten?' suggested Sean.

'More than that.'

'Fifteen?'

'Yes, fifteen.'

They lay and thought about it. To Sean it seemed a fairly well-rounded number.

'And I'll keep chickens, I want lots of chickens.'

'All right,' said Sean.

'You don't mind?'

'Should I?'

'Some people mind chickens, some people don't like them at all,' said Katrina. 'I'm glad you don't mind them. I've always wanted them.'

Stealthily Sean advanced his mouth towards her ear but she felt him move and sat up.

'What are you doing?'

'This,' said Sean and his arm shot out.

'No, Sean, they're watching us.' She waved her hand at the dogs.

'They'll understand,' said Sean and then they were both quiet for a long time.

The dogs burst out together in full hunting chorus. Katrina sat up and Sean turned his head and saw the leopard. It stood fifty yards away on the edge of the thick bush along the river bank watching them, poised elegantly in tights of black and gold, long and small-bellied. It moved then, blurring with speed, touching the ground as lightly as a swallow touches the water when it drinks in flight. The dogs went after it in a pack, Thief leading them, his voice cracking with excitement.

'Back, come back,' shouted Sean. 'Leave it, damn you, come back.'

'Stop them, Sean, go after them. We'll lose them all.'

'Wait here,' Sean told her.

He ran after the sound of the pack. Not shouting, saving his wind. He knew what would happen and he listened for it. He heard the tone of the hunt change–sharper now. Sean stopped and stood panting, peering ahead. The dogs were not moving. The sound of their barking was steady in volume.

'The swine has stopped; he's going to take them.'

He started running again and almost immediately heard the first dog scream. He kept running. He found the dog lying where the leopard had flung it–the old bitch with white ears, her stomach was stripped out. Sean went on. The tan ridgeback next, disembowelled, still alive and crawling to meet him. He ran on; always the hunt was out of sight ahead of him but he kept after it. He no longer stopped to help the dogs that had been mauled. Most of them were dead before he reached them. The saliva thickened in his mouth, his heart jumped against his ribs and he reeled as he ran.

Suddenly he was in the open and the hunt was spread out before him. There were three dogs left. One of them was Thief. They were circling the leopard, belling him, darting in at his back legs, snapping, then jumping back as the leopard spun snarling. The grass was short and green in the clearing. The sun was directly overhead: it threw no shadow, it lit everything with a flat, even light. Sean tried to shout but his throat wouldn't let the sound out. The leopard dropped on to its back and lay with the sprawled grace of a sleeping cat, its legs open and its belly exposed. The dogs hung back, hesitating. Sean shouted again but his voice still would not carry. That creamy yellow belly, soft and fluffy, was too much temptation. One of the dogs went for it, dipping its head, its mouth open. The leopard closed on it like a spring trap. It caught and held the dog with its front paws and its back legs worked quickly. The dog yammered at the swift surgeon strokes and then it was thrown aside, its bowels hanging out. The leopard relaxed again to show the yellow bait of its belly. Sean was close now and this time the two dogs heard his shout. The leopard heard it also. It flashed to its feet and tried to break, but the instant it turned Thief was at it, slashing at its back legs forcing it to swing and crouch.

'Here, boy, leave him! Here, Thief, come here!'

Thief took Sean's shout as encouragement. He danced just out of reach of the flicking paws, shrilly taunting the leopard. The hunt was finely balanced now. Sean knew if he could get the dogs to slacken their attack the leopard would run. He went forward a pace, stooped to pick up a stone to throw at Thief and his movement tipped the balance. When he straightened up the leopard was watching him and he felt the eel of fear move in his stomach. It was going to come for him. He knew it by the way its ears flattened against its head and its shoulders bunched like loaded springs. Sean dropped the stone and reached for the knife on his belt.

The leopard's lips peeled back. Its teeth were yellow, its head with the ears flattened was like a snake's. It came fast and low against the ground, brushing the dogs aside. Its run was long-reaching, smoothly beautiful. It snaked towards him, fast over the short grass. It came into the air, lifting high, very fast and very smoothly. Sean felt the shock and the pain together. The shock threw him backwards and the pain sucked the breath from his lungs. Its claws hooked into his chest, he felt them scrape his ribs. He held its mouth from his face, his forearm against its throat and he smelt the overripe grave smell of its breath. They rolled together in the grass, its front claws still holding in the flesh of his chest, and he felt its back legs coming up to rake his stomach. He twisted desperately to keep clear of them, using his knife at the same time, slipping the blade into its back. The leopard screamed, its back legs came up again; he felt the claws go into his hip and tear down his thigh. The pain was deep and strong and he knew he was badly hurt. The legs came up again. This time they would kill him.

Thief locked his teeth in the leopard's leg before the claws could catch in Sean's flesh, he dragged back, digging in with his front feet, holding the leopard stretched out across Sean's body. Sean's vision was dissolving into blackness and bright lights. He pushed the knife into the leopard's back, close to the spine and pulled it down between the ribs the way a butcher cuts a chop. The leopard screamed again with its body shuddering and its claws curling in Sean's flesh. Sean cut again, deep and long–and again, then again. Tearing at it, mad with the pain, its blood gushed out and mixed with his and he rolled away from it. The dogs were worrying it, growling. It was dead. Sean let the knife slip out of his hand and touched the tears in his leg. The blood was dark red, pouring with the thickness of treacle, much blood. He was looking down a funnel of darkness. The leg was far away, not his–not his leg.

'Garry,' he whispered, 'Garry, oh God! I'm sorry. I slipped, I didn't mean it, I slipped.' The funnel closed and there was no leg–only darkness. Time was a liquid thing, all the world was liquid, moving in darkness. The sun was dark and only the pain was steady, steady as a rock in the dark moving sea. He saw Katrina's face indistinct in the darkness. He tried to tell her how sorry he was. He tried to tell her it was an accident, but the pain stopped him. She was crying. He knew she would understand so he went back into the dark sea. Then the surface of the sea boiled and he choked in the heat, but always the pain was there like a rock to hold on to. The steam from the sea coiled up around him and it hardened into the shape of a woman and he thought it was Katrina, then he saw its head was a leopard's head and its breath stank like the rotting of a gangrenous leg.

'I don't want you–I know who you are,' he shouted at it. 'I don't want you. It's not my child,' and the thing broke into steam, twisting grey steam, and came back gibbering at him on a chain that tinkled, frothing yellow from the grey misty mouth, and terror came with it. He twisted and covered his face, holding on to the pain for the pain was real and steady.

Then after a thousand years the sea froze and he walked on it and the white ice stretched away wherever he looked. It was cold and lonely on the ice. There was a small wind, a cold small wind, the wind whispered across the ice and its whispering was a sad sound, and Sean held his pain, hugging it close to him for he was lonely and only the pain was real. Then there were other figures moving around him on the ice, dark figures all hurrying one way, crowding him, pushing him along with them and he lost his pain, lost it in the desperate hurrying press. And though they had no faces, some of the figures wept and others laughed and they hurried forward until they came to the place where the crevasse split across the ice in front of them. The crevasse was wide and deep and its sides were white, then pale-green shading to blue and at last to infinite blackness, and some of the figures threw themselves joyfully into it singing as they fell. Others clung to edges, their formless faces full of fear, and still others stepped off into the void, tiredly, like travellers at the end of a long journey. When Sean saw the crevasse he began to fight, throwing himself back against the crowd that bore him forward, carrying him to the edge of the pit, and his feet slid over the edge. He clawed with his fingers at the slippery edge of the ice. He fought and he shouted as he fought for the dark drop sucked at his legs. Then he lay quietly and the crevasse had closed and he was alone. He was tired–wasted and terribly tired. He closed his eyes and the pain came back to him, throbbing softly in his leg.

He opened his eyes and he saw Katrina's face. She was pale and her eyes were big and heavily underscored in blue. He tried to lift his hand to touch her face but he couldn't move.

'Katrina,' he said. He saw her eyes go green with surprise and happiness.

'You've come back. Oh, thank God. You've come back.'

Sean rolled his head and looked at the canvas of the wagon tent.

'How long?' he asked. His voice was a whisper.

'Five days . . . Don't talk—please, don't talk.'

Sean closed his eyes. He was very tired so he slept.

19

Katrina washed him when he woke. Mbejane helped her lift and turn him, his big pink-palmed hands very gentle as he handled the leg. They washed the smell of fever off him and changed the dressings. Sean watched Katrina as she worked and every time she looked up they smiled at each other. Once he used a little of his strength to ask Mbejane, 'Where were you when I needed you?'

'I slept in the sun, Nkosi, like an old woman,' Mbejane half-laughed, half-apologized. Katrina brought him food and when he smelt it he was hungry. He ate it all and then he slept again.

Mbejane built a shelter with open sides and a roof of thatch. He sited it in the shade on the bank of the Sabi. Then he made a bed of poles and laced leather thongs. They carried Sean from the wagon, Katrina fussing around them until they had laid him in the shelter. Katrina went back to the wagon for pillows and when she returned she found Thief and Sean settling down comfortably.

'Sean, get that monster out of there—those blankets have just been washed.'

Thief flattened his body and hid his head in Sean's armpit.

'It's all right, he's quite clean,' Sean protected him.

'He smells.'

'He does not.' Sean sniffed at Thief. 'Well, not much anyway.'

'You two!' She put the pillows under Sean's head and went round to his leg. 'How does it feel?'

'It's fine,' said Sean. Thief inched himself up the bed until he reached the pillows.

In the slow slide of days Sean's body healed and the well of his strength filled. The moving air under the shelter dried the scabs off his chest and leg, but there would be scars. In the mornings, after breakfast, Sean held court from his couch. Katrina sat on the end of the bed and his servants squatted around him. First they talked over domestic matters—the health of the oxen, mentioning them by name, discussing their eyes, hooves and stomachs. There was a tear in the canvas of one wagon. The single remaining bitch was in season—was Thief man enough for the job yet? There was meat to kill—perhaps the Nkosikaze would take the rifle later today. Hlubi had caught four barbel of medium size in his fish trap, and here the talk turned to the bush around them. A lion had killed a buffalo below the first bend in the river—there you could see the vultures. During the night a herd of cow elephant had drunk a mile upstream. Each item was considered by the meeting. Everyone felt free to comment or argue against any view which conflicted with his own. When everything had been said Sean gave them their tasks for the day and sent them away. Then he and Katrina could be alone.

From the shelter they could see the full sweep of the river, with the crocodiles lying on the white sandbars and the kingfishers plopping into the shallows. They sat close to each other and they talked of the farm they would have. Sean would grow grapes and breed horses and Katrina would keep chickens. By the next rainy season they would have filled all the wagons; one more trip after that and they would have enough to buy the farm.

Katrina kept him in bed long after he was strong enough to leave it. She mothered him and he loved it. Shamelessly, in the fashion of the male, he accepted her attentions and even exaggerated his injuries a little. Finally but reluctantly Katrina let him up. He stayed in camp a week more, until his legs stopped wobbling, then one evening he took his rifle and went with Mbejane to shoot fresh meat. They went slowly, Sean favouring his leg, and he shot a young eland not far from the laager. Sean sat against a msasa tree and smoked a cheroot while Mbejane went back to fetch servants to carry the meat. Sean watched them butcher the carcass; there were slabs of white fat on the meat. They slung it on poles and carried it between them, two men to a pole, and when they got back to camp Sean found Katrina in one of her inscrutable moods. When he talked to her at supper she answered him from far away and afterwards by the fire she sat detached from him. She was very lovely and Sean was puzzled and a little resentful. At last he stood up.

'It's time for bed--I'll see you to your wagon.'

'You go. I'll sit a little longer.'

Sean hesitated. 'Is there something wrong? Have I done something wrong?'

'No,' she said quickly. 'No. I'm all right. You go to bed.'

He kissed her cheek. 'If you need me I'll be close. Goodnight, sleep sweet.' He straightened up. 'Come on, Thief,' he said. 'Time for bed.'

'Leave Thief with me, please.' Katrina caught the skin at the back of the dog's neck and restrained him.

'Why?'

'I just feel like company.'

'Then I'll stay as well,' Sean moved to sit down again.

'No, you go to bed.' She sounded desperate and Sean looked hard at her.

'Are you sure you're all right?'

'Yes, please go.'

He went to his wagon and looked back at her. She was sitting very straight, holding the dog. He climbed into the wagon. The lamp was lit and he stopped in surprise when he saw his cot. There were sheets on it, not just the rough blankets. He ran his hand over the smooth fabric; it was crisp from new ironing. He sat on the cot and pulled off his boots. He undid his shirt and threw it on to the chest, then he lay back and looked up at the lamp.

'There's something bloody funny going on here,' he said.

'Sean'--her voice just outside the wagon. Sean jumped up and opened the flap. 'Can I come in?'

'Yes, of course.' He gave her his hand and lifted her into the wagon. He looked at her face. She was frightened.

'There *is* something wrong,' he said.

'No, don't touch me. There's something I've got to tell you. Sit down on the cot.'

Sean watched her face. He was worried.

'I thought I loved you when I came away with you. I thought we had for ever to be together.' She swallowed painfully. 'Then I found you there in the grass—torn and dead. Before our life together had begun you were dead.'

Sean saw the pain come back into her eyes; she was living it again. He put out his hand to her but she held his wrist.

'No, wait ... please let me finish. I have to explain to you. It's very important.'

Sean dropped his hand and she went on speaking quickly.

'You were dead and I, too, was dying inside. I felt empty. There was nothing left. Nothing ... just the hollowness inside and the dry dead feeling on the outside. I touched your face and you looked at me. I prayed then, Sean, and I prayed through the days when you fought the rotting of your body.'

She knelt in front of him and held him around the waist.

'Now we are alive and together again, but I know that it cannot be for ever. A day more, a year, if we are lucky, twenty. But not for ever. I see how small I have been to us. I want to be your wife.'

He bent to her quickly but she pulled away and stood up. She slipped the buttons and her clothing fell away. She loosed her hair and let it drop shiny bright down the whiteness of her body.

'Look at me, Sean, I want you to look at me. This and my love I can give you ... is it enough?'

There was smoothness, hollow and swell, hair like black fire and soft light on soft skin. He saw the flush from her cheeks spread on to her breasts until they glowed, pink and shy but proud in their perfection. He looked no further. He took her to him and covered her nakedness with his big body. She was trembling and he put her between the sheets and gentled her with his voice until the trembling stopped and she lay with her face pressed up under his beard into his neck.

'Show me how ... I want to give everything to you. Please show me how,' she whispered.

So they married each other and their marriage was a commingling of many things. There was the softness of the wind in it and wanting, the way the baked earth wants the rain. There was pain sharp and swift, movement like running horses, sound low as voices in the night but glad as a greeting, joy climbing on eagles' wings, the triumphant surge and burst of wild water on a rock shore and then there was stillness and warmth within and the snuggling of drowsy puppies, and sleep. Yet it did not end in the sleep, it went on to another seeking and finding, another union and a stranger mystery in the secret depths of her body.

20

In the morning she brought her Bible to him.

'Hey, hey,' protested Sean, 'I've already sworn one oath.' Katrina laughed at him, the memory of the night still warm and happy inside her. She opened the book at its fly leaf.

'You've got to write your name in it ... here, next to mine.'

She watched him, standing next to his chair with her hip touching his shoulder.

'And your date of birth,' she said.

Sean wrote: 'Ninth Jan. 1862.' Then he said: 'What's this "date of death" . . . do you want me to fill that in as well?'

'Don't talk like that,' she said quickly and touched the wooden table.

Sean was sorry he'd said it. He tried to cover up. 'There's only space for six children.'

'We can write the others in the margin. That's what Ma did . . . hers even go over on to the first page of Genesis. Do you think we'll get that far, Sean?'

Sean smiled at her. 'The way I feel now we should reach the New Testament without much trouble.'

They had made a good start. By June the rains were over and Katrina walked with her shoulders back to balance her load. There was a good feeling in the camp. Katrina was more woman than child now. She was big and radiant, pleased with the awe her condition inspired in Sean. She sang to herself often and sometimes in the night she would let him share in it. She would let him pull the nightdress back from the mound of her stomach and lay his ear against the tight-stretched, blue-veined skin. He listened to the suck and gurgle and felt the movement against his cheek. When he sat up his eyes would be full of the wonder of it and she would smile proudly at him and take his head on her shoulder and they would lie together quietly. In the daytime things were right as well. Sean laughed with the servants and hunted without the intensity of before.

They moved north along the Sabi river. Sometimes they camped for a month at one place. The game came back to the rivers as the veld dried out and once more the ivory started piling up in the wagons.

One afternoon in September Sean and Katrina left the camp and walked along the bank. The land was brown again and smelt of dry grass. The river was pools and white sand.

'Hell, it's hot.' Sean took off his hat and wiped the sweat off his forehead. 'You must be cooking under all those clothes.'

'No, I'm all right.' Katrina was holding his arm.

'Let's have a swim.'

'You mean with no clothes on?' Katrina looked shocked.

'Yes, why not?'

'It's rude.'

'Come on.' He took her down the bank protesting every step and at a place where boulders screened the water he prised her out of her dress. She was laughing and gasping and blushing all at the same time. He carried her into the pool and she sat down thankfully with the water up to her chin.

'How's that feel?' Sean asked.

She let her hair down and it floated out round her, she wriggled her toes in the sand and her stomach showed through the water like the back of a white whale.

'It's nice,' she admitted. 'It feels like silk underwear against my skin.'

Sean stood over her with only his hat on. She looked at him.

'Sit down,' she said uncomfortably and looked away from him.

'Why?' he asked.

'You know why . . . you're rude, that's why.'

Sean sat down beside her.

'You should be used to me by now.'

'Well, I'm not.'

Sean put his arm around her under the water.

'You're lovely,' he said. 'You're my fancy.'

She let him kiss her ear.

'What's it going to be?' He touched the ripe swelling. 'Boy or girl?' This was currently the favourite topic of conversation.

'Boy.' She was very definite.

'What shall we call him?'

'Well, if you don't find a *predikant* soon we'll have to call him the name you're always giving to the servants.'

Sean stared at her. 'What do you mean?'

'You know what you call them when you're cross.'

'Bastard,' said Sean, then really concerned, 'Hell, I hadn't thought of that! We'll have to find a priest. No child of mine will be a bastard. We'll have to go back to Louis Trichardt.'

'You've got about a month,' Katrina warned him.

'My God, we'll never make it. We've left it too late.' Sean's face was ghastly. 'Wait, I've got it. There are Portuguese settlements across the mountains on the coast.'

'Oh, Sean, but they're Roman Catholics.'

'They all work for the same boss.'

'How long will it take to cross the mountains?' Katrina asked doubtfully.

'I don't know. Perhaps two weeks to reach the coast on horseback.'

'On horseback?' Katrina looked still more doubtfully.

'Oh hell . . . you can't ride.' Sean scratched the side of his nose. 'I'll have to go and fetch one. Will you stay on your own? I'll leave Mbejane to look after you.'

'Yes, I'll be all right.'

'I won't go if you don't want me to. It's not that important.'

'It is important, you know it is. I'll be all right, truly I will.'

Before he left the next morning Sean took Mbejane aside. 'You know why you're not coming with me, don't you?'

Mbejane nodded, but Sean answered his own question. 'Because there is more important work for you to do here.'

'At night,' said Mbejane, 'I will sleep beneath the Nkosikazi's wagon.'

'You'll sleep?' asked Sean threateningly.

'Only once in a while and then very lightly,' Mbejane grinned.

'That's better,' said Sean.

21

Sean said goodbye to Katrina. There were no tears, she understood necessity and helped him to a quiet acceptance of it. They stood a long while beside their wagon, holding each other, their lips almost touching as they whispered together and then Sean called for his horse. Hlubi followed him leading the packhorse when he crossed the Sabi and when Sean reached the far bank he turned and looked back. Katrina was still standing by their wagon and behind her hovered Mbejane. In her bonnet and green dress she looked very young. Sean waved his hat over his head and then set off towards the mountains.

The forest dwindled into grassland as they climbed and each night was colder than the last. Then, in its turn the grassland conceded to the sheer bluffs and misty gorges of the mountain back. Sean and Hlubi struggled upwards, following the game trails, losing them, turning back from impassable cliffs, scouting for a pass, leading the horses over the steep pitches and at night sitting close to the fire and listening to the baboons barking in the kranses around them. Then suddenly, in the middle of a morning that was bright as a cut diamond, they were at the top. To the west the land lay spread out like a map and the distance they had travelled in a week was pathetically small. By straining his eyes and his imagination Sean could make out the dark-green belt of the Sabi watercourse. To the east the land merged with a blueness that was not the sky and for a while he failed to recognize it. Then–'the sea,' he shouted and Hlubi laughed with him for it was a godlike feeling to stand above the world. They found an easier route down the eastern slopes and followed it on to the coastal plain. At the bottom of the mountains they came to a native village. To see cultivated lands and human dwellings again was a small shock to Sean. He had come to accept the fact he and his retinue were the only people left on earth.

The entire population of the village fled when they saw him. Mothers snatched up a child in each hand and ran as fast as their menfolk–memories of the slave-traders still persisted in this part of Africa. Within two minutes of his arrival Sean again had the feeling that he was the only person left on earth. With the contempt of the Zulu for every other tribe in Africa, Hlubi shook his head sadly.

'Monkeys,' he said.

They dismounted and tied their horses under the big tree that was the centre of the village. They sat in the shade and waited. The huts were grass beehives, their roofs blackened with smoke, and a few chickens picked and scratched at the bare earth between them. Half an hour later Sean saw a black face watching him from the edge of the bush and he ignored it. Slowly the face emerged, followed closely by a reluctant body. With a twig, Sean went on drawing patterns in the dust between his feet. Out of the corner of his eye he watched the hesitant approach. It was an old man with stork thin legs and one eye glazed into a white jelly by tropical ophthalmia. Sean concluded that his fellows had picked him to act as ambassador on the grounds that all their number he would be the least loss.

Sean looked up and gave him a radiant smile. The old man froze and then his lips twitched into a sickly grin of relief. Sean stood up, dusted his hands on the sides of his breeches and went to shake the old man's hand. Immediately the bush around them swarmed with people, they poured back into the village jabbering and laughing: they crowded round Sean and felt his clothing, peered into his face and exclaimed delightedly. It was obvious that most of them had never seen a white man before. Sean was trying to shake off One-Eye, who still had a possessive hold on Sean's right hand, and Hlubi leaned disdainfully against the tree, taking no part in the welcome. One-Eye ended the confusion by screeching at them in a voice rusty with age. The courage he had displayed earlier now earned its reward. At his command a dozen of the younger women scampered off and came back with a carved wooden stool and six earthenware pots of native beer. By the hand, on which he had not for an instant relaxed his grip, One-Eye led Sean to the stool and made him sit; the rest of the villagers squatted in a circle round him and one of the girls brought the biggest beer-pot to Sean. The beer was yellow and it bubbled sullenly. Sean's stomach shied at the sight of it. He glanced at One-Eye who was watching him anxiously, he lifted the pot and sipped. Then he smiled with surprise; it was creamy and pleasantly tart.

'Good,' he said.

'Goot,' chorused the villagers.

'Your health,' said Sean.

''ealt,' said the village as one man, and Sean drank deep. One of the girls took another beer-pot to Hlubi. She knelt in front of him and shyly offered it. She had a plaited-grass string around her waist from which a small kilt hung down in front, but her stern was completely exposed and her bosoms were the size and shape of ripe melons. Hlubi looked at them until the girl hung her head, then he lifted the beer-pot.

Sean wanted a guide to the nearest Portuguese settlement. He looked at One-Eye and said, 'Town? Portagee?'

One-Eye was almost overcome by Sean's attention. He grabbed Sean's hand again before he could pull it away and shook it vigorously.

'Stop that, you bloody fool,' said Sean irritably and One-Eye grinned and nodded, then without releasing Sean's hand he began an impassioned speech to the other villagers. Sean meanwhile was searching his memory for the name of one of the Portuguese ports on this coast.

'Nova Sofala,' he shouted as he got it.

One-Eye broke off his speech abruptly and stared at Sean.

'Nova Sofala,' said Sean again pointing vaguely towards the east and One-Eye showed his gums in his biggest grin yet.

'Nova Sofala,' he agreed pointing with authority and then it was only a matter of minutes before it was understood between them that he would act as guide. Hlubi saddled the horses, One-Eye fetched a grass sleeping mat and a battle-axe from one of the huts. Sean mounted and looked at Hlubi to do the same but Hlubi was acting strangely.

'Yes?' Sean asked with resignation. 'What is it?'

'Nkosi.' Hlubi was looking at the branches of the tree above them. 'The Old One could lead the packhorse.'

'You can take it in turns,' said Sean.

Hlubi coughed and transferred his eyes to the fingernails of his left hand.

'Nkosi, is it possible that you will return to this village on the way back from the sea?'

'Yes, of course,' said Sean, 'we'll have to leave the Old One here. Why do you ask?'

'I have a thorn in my foot, Nkosi, it gives me pain. If you do not require me I will wait here for you. Perhaps the torn wound will have healed by then.' Hlubi looked up at the tree again and shuffled his feet with embarrassment. Sean had not noticed him limping and he was puzzled as to why Hlubi should start malingering now. Then Hlubi could not stop himself from glancing at where the girl stood in the circle of villagers. Her kilt was very small and from the sides gave her no cover at all. Understanding came to Sean and he chuckled.

'The thorn you have is painful, but it's not in your foot.' Hlubi shuffled his feet again. 'You said they were monkeys . . . have you changed your mind?' Sean asked.

'Nkosi, they are indeed monkeys,' Hlubi sighed. 'But very friendly monkeys.'

'Stay then . . . but do not weaken yourself too much. We have mountains to cross on the way home.'

One-Eye led the packhorse—this made him very proud. Through tall grass, mangrove swamp and thick hot jungle, then through white coral sand and the curving stems of palm trees, they came at last to the sea. Nova Sofala was a fort with brass cannon and thick walls. The sea beyond it was muddy brown from the estuary that flowed into it.

The sentry at the gates said, *'Madre de Dio'* when he saw Sean, and took him to the Commandant. The Commandant was a small man with fever-yellowed face and a tired, sweat-darkened tunic. The Commandant said, *'Madre de Dio,'* and shot his chair back from his desk. It took some time for him to realize that contrary to appearance this dirty, bearded giant was not dangerous. The Commandant could speak English and Sean laid his problem before him.

For a certainty he could be of assistance. There were three Jesuit missionaries in the fort, freshly arrived from Portugal and eager for employment. Sean could take his pick but first he must bath, eat dinner with the Commandant and help him sample the wines that had arrived on the same boat as the missionaries. Sean thought that was a good idea.

At dinner he met the missionaries. They were young men, pinkfaced still, for Africa had not yet had a chance to mark them. All three of them were willing to go with him and Sean selected the youngest—not for his appearance but rather for his name. 'Father Alphonso' had a heroic ring to it. The Jesuits went early to bed and left the Commandant, the four junior officers and Sean to the port. They drank toasts to Queen Victoria and her family and to the King of Portugal and his family. This made them thirsty so they drank to absent friends, then to each other. The Commandant and Sean swore a mutual oath of friendship and loyalty and this made the Commandant very sad, he cried and Sean patted his shoulder and offered to dance the Dashing White Sergeant for him. The Commandant said that he would esteem it as a very great honour and furthermore he would be delighted. He himself did not know this dance but perhaps Sean would instruct him. They danced on the table. The Commandant was doing very well until in his enthusiasm he misjudged the size of the table. Sean helped the junior officers put him to bed and in the morning Sean, Father Alphonso and One-Eye started back towards the mountains.

Sean was impatient of any delay now; he wanted to get back to Katrina. Father Alphonso's English was on a par with Sean's Portuguese. This made conversation difficult, so Alphonso solved the problem by doing all the talking. At first Sean listened but when he decided that the good father was trying to convert him he no longer bothered. Alphonso did not seem put out—he just went on talking and clinging to the horse with both hands while his cassock flapped about his legs and his face sweated in the shade of his wide-brimmed hat. One-Eye followed them like an ancient stork.

It took them two days back to One-Eye's village and their entry was a triumphal procession. Father Alphonso's face lit up when he saw so many prospective converts. Sean could see him mentally rubbing his hands together, and he decided to keep going before Alphonso forgot the main object of the expedition. He gave One-Eye a hunting-knife in payment for his services. One-Eye sat down under the big tree in the centre of the village, his own thin legs no longer able to support his weight and the knife clutched to his chest.

'Hlubi, you've had enough of that ... come on now!' Sean had not dismounted and was restlessly waiting for Hlubi to say his farewells to three of the village girls. Hlubi had displayed traditional Zulu taste—all three of them were big-breasted, big-bottomed and young. They were also crying.

'Come on, Hlubi ... what's the trouble?'

'Nkosi, they believe that I have taken them for my wives.'

'What made them think that?'

'Nkosi, I do not know.' Hlubi broke the armhold that the plumpest and youngest had around his neck, he snatched up his spears and fled. Sean and Alphonso galloped after him. The villagers shouted farewells and Sean looked back and saw One-Eye still sitting at the base of the big tree.

The pace which Sean set was at last telling on Alphonso. His verbal spring-tides slackened and he showed a measure of reluctance to let his backside touch the saddle; he rode crouched forward on his horse's neck with his buttocks in the air. They crossed the mountains and went down the other side; the ground levelled out into the Sabi Valley and they rode into the forest. On the ninth day out from Nova Sofala they reached the Sabi river. It was late afternoon. Flocks of guinea-fowl were drinking in the river-bed, they went up in a blue haze of whirling wings as Sean led his party down the bank. While the horses watered Sean spoke with Hlubi.

'Do you recognize this part of the river?'

'Yes, Nkosi, we are two hours' march upstream from the wagons ... we held too far to the north coming through the forest.'

Sean looked at the sun, it was on the tree-tops.

'Half an hour's light left ... and there's no moon tonight.'

'We could wait until morning,' Hlubi suggested hopefully. Sean ignored him and motioned to Alphonso to mount up. Alphonso was prepared to debate the advisability of moving on. Sean took a handful of his cassock and helped him into the saddle.

23

In the darkness the lantern burning in Katrina's wagon glowed through the canvas and guided them the last half mile into camp. Thief bayed them welcome and Mbejane ran out at the head of the other servants to take Sean's horse. His voice was loud with worry and relief.

'Nkosi, there is little time ... it has begun.'

Sean jumped off his horse and ran to the wagon. He tore open the canvas flap.

'Sean.' She sat up. Her eyes were very green in the lantern light, but they were dark-ringed. 'Thank God, you've come.'

Sean knelt beside her cot and held her. He said certain things to her and she clung to him and moved her lips across his face. The world receded and left one wagon standing in darkness, lit by a single lamp and the love of two people.

Suddenly she stiffened in his arms and gasped. Sean held her, his face suddenly helpless and his big hands timid and uncertain on her shoulders.

'What can I do, my fancy? How can I help you?'

Her body relaxed slowly and she whispered, 'Did you find a priest?'

'The priest!' Sean had forgotten about him. Still holding on to her he turned his head and bellowed, 'Alphonso . . . Alphonso. Hurry, man.'

Father Alphonso's face in the opening of the wagon was pale with fatigue and grimy with dust.

'Marry us,' said Sean. 'Quickly, man, che-cha, chop-chop . . . you savvy?'

Alphonso climbed into the wagon. The skirts of his cassock were torn and his knees were white and bony through the holes. He stood over them and opened his book. 'Ring?' he asked in Portuguese.

'I do,' said Sean.

'No! No! Ring?' Alphonso held up a finger and made an encircling gesture. 'Ring?'

'I think he wants a wedding ring,' whispered Katrina.

'Oh, my God,' said Sean. 'I'd forgotten about that.' He looked round desperately. 'What can we use? Haven't you got one in your chest or something?'

Katrina shook her head, opened her lips to answer but closed them again as another pain took her. Sean held her while it lasted and when she relaxed he looked up angrily at Alphonso.

'Marry us . . . damn you. Don't you see there's not time for all the trimmings?'

'Ring?' said Alphonso again. He looked very unhappy.

'All right, I'll get you a ring.' Sean leapt out of the wagon and shouted at Mbejane.

'Bring my rifle, quickly.'

If Sean wanted to shoot the Portuguese that was his business and Mbejane's duty was to help him. He brought Sean the rifle. Sean found a gold sovereign in the pouch of his belt, he threw it on the ground and held the muzzle of the rifle on it. The bullet punched a ragged hole through it. He tossed the rifle back to Mbejane, picked up the small gold circle and scrambled back into the wagon.

Three times during the service the pains made Katrina gasp and each time Sean held her tight and Alphonso increased the speed of his delivery. Sean put the punctured sovereign on Katrina's finger and kissed her. Alphonso gabbled out the last line of Latin and Katrina said, 'Oh, Sean, it's coming.'

'Get out,' Sean told Alphonso and made an expressive gesture towards the door—thankfully Alphonso went.

It did not take long then, but to Sean it was an eternity—like that time when they had taken Garrick's leg. Then in a slippery rush it was finished. Katrina lay very quiet and pale, while on the cot below her, still linked to her, purple-blotched and bloody lay the child that they had made.

'It's dead,' croaked Sean. He was sweating and he had backed away against the far wall of the wagon.

'No,' Katrina struggled up fiercely. 'No, it's not . . . Sean, you must help me.'

She told him what to do and at last the child cried.

'It's a boy,' said Katrina softly. 'Oh, Sean . . . it's a boy.' She was more beautiful than he had ever seen her before; pale and tired and beautiful.

24

Sean's protests were in vain—Katrina left her bed the next morning and squeezed into one of her old dresses. Sean hovered between her and the child on the cot.

'I'm still so *fat*,' she lamented.

'Fancy, please stay in bed another day or two.'

She pulled a face at him and went on struggling with the lacing of her bodice.

'Who's going to look after the baby?'

'I will!' said Sean earnestly. 'You can tell me what to do.'

Arguing with Katrina was like trying to pick up quicksilver with your fingers, not worth the effort. She finished dressing and took up the child.

'You can help me down the steps.' She smiled at him. Sean and Alphonso set a chair for her in the shade of one of the big shuma trees and the servants came to see the child. Katrina held him in her lap and Sean stood over them in uncertain possession. For Sean it seemed unreal yet . . . too much for his mind to digest in so short a time. He grinned dazedly at the steady stream of comment from his servants and his arm was limp when Alphonso shook his hand for the twentieth time that morning.

'Hold your child . . . Nkosi. Let us see you with him on your arm,' called Mbejane and the other Zulus took up the cry. Sean's expression changed slowly to one of apprehension.

'Pick him up, Nkosi.'

Katrina proffered the bundle and a hunted look came into Sean's eyes.

'Have no fear, Nkosi, he has no teeth, he cannot harm you,' Hlubi encouraged him. Sean held his first-born awkwardly and assumed the hunchbacked posture of the new father. The Zulus cheered him and slowly Sean's face relaxed and his smile was a glow of pride.

'Mbejane, is he not beautiful?'

'As beautiful as his father,' Mbejane agreed.

'Your words are a blade with two edges,' laughed Sean. He looked at the child closely. It wore a cap of dark hair, its nose was flat as a bulldog's, its eyes were milky-grey and its legs were long, skinny and red.

'How will you name him?' asked Hlubi. Sean looked at Katrina.

'Tell them,' he said.

'He shall be called Dirk,' she said in Zulu.

'What is the meaning?' asked Hlubi, and Sean answered him.

'It means a dagger . . . a sharp knife.'

There was immediate nodded approval from all the servants. Hlubi produced his snuff-box and passed it among them and Mbejane took a pinch.

'That,' he said, 'is a good name.'

25

Paternity, the subtle alchemist, transformed Sean's attitude to life within twelve hours. Never before had anything been so utterly dependent upon him, so completely vulnerable. That first evening in their wagon he watched Katrina sitting cross-legged on her cot, stooping forward over the child to give it her breast. Her hair hung in a soft wing across one cheek, her face was fuller, more matronly and the child in her lap fed with a red face and small wheezings. She looked up at him and smiled and the child tugged her breast with its tiny fists and hunting mouth.

Sean crossed to the cot, sat beside them and put his arm around them. Katrina rubbed her cheek against his chest and her hair smelt warm and clean. The boy went on feeding noisily. Sean felt vaguely excited as though he were on the threshold of a new adventure.

A week later, when the first rain clouds built up in the sky, Sean took the wagon across the Sabi and on to the slopes of the mountains to escape the heat of the plains. There was a valley he had noticed when he and Hlubi had made their journey to the coast. The valley bottom was covered with short sweet grass and cedar trees grew along a stream of clear water. Sean took them to this place.

Here they would wait out the rainy season and when it was finished and the baby was strong enough to travel they could take the ivory south and sell it in Pretoria. It was a happy camp. The oxen spread out along the valley, filling it with movement and the contented sound of their lowing; there was laughter among the wagons and at night when the mist slumped down off the mountains the camp fire was bright and friendly. Father Alphonso stayed with them for nearly two weeks. He was a pleasant young man and although he and Sean never understood what the other was saying yet they managed well enough with sign language. He left at last with Hlubi and one of the other servants to escort him back over the mountains, but before he did he managed to embarrass Sean by kissing him goodbye. Sean and Katrina were sorry to see him go. They had grown to like him and Katrina had almost forgiven him his religion.

The rains came with the usual flourish and fury. Weeks drifted into months. Happy months, with life centring around Dirk's cot. Mbejane had made the cot for him out of cedarwood and one of Katrina's chests produced the sheets and blankets for it. The child grew quickly: each day he seemed to occupy more of his cot, his legs filled out, his skin lost its blotchy-purple look and his eyes were no longer a vague milky-blue. There was green in them now—they would be the same colour as his mother's.

To fill the long lazy days Sean started to build a cabin beside the stream. The servants joined in and from a modest first plan it grew into a thing of sturdy plastered walls and neatly thatched roof with a stone fireplace at one end. When it was finished Sean and Katrina moved into it. After their wagon with its thin canvas walls, the cabin gave a feeling of permanence to their love. One night, when the rain hissed down in darkness outside and the wind whined at the door like a dog wanting to be let in, they spread a mattress in front of the fireplace and there in the moving firelight they started another baby.

Christmas came, and after it the New Year. The rains stuttered and stopped and still they stayed on in their valley. Then at last they had to go, for their supplies of basic stores—powder, salt, medicines, cloth—were nearly finished. They loaded the wagons, inspanned and left in the early morning. As the line of wagons wound down the valley towards the plains Katrina sat on the box seat of the lead wagon holding Dirk on her lap and Sean rode beside her. She looked back—the roof of their cabin showed brown through the branches of the cedar trees. It seemed forlorn and lonely.

'We must come back one day, we've been so happy here,' she said softly. Sean leaned out of the saddle towards her and touched her arm.

'Happiness isn't a place, my fancy, we aren't leaving it here, we're taking it with us.'

She smiled at him. The second baby was starting to show already.

26

They reached the Limpopo river at the end of July and found a place to cross. It took three days to unload the wagons, work them through the soft sand and then carry the ivory and stores across. They finished in the late afternoon of the third day and by then everyone was exhausted. They ate an early supper and an hour after sunset the Zulus were rolled in their blankets, and Sean and Katrina were sleeping arms-around and head-on-chest in the wagon. In the morning Katrina was quiet and a little pale. Sean didn't notice it until she told him that she felt tired and was going to lie down—immediately he was all attentive. He helped her into the wagon and settled the pillows under her head.

'Are you sure you're all right?' he kept asking.

'Yes . . . it's nothing, I'm just a bit tired. I'll be all right,' she assured him. She appreciated his concern but was relieved when finally he went to see to the business of reloading the wagons, for Sean's ministrations were always a little clumsy. She wanted to be left alone, she felt tired and cold.

By midday the wagons were loaded to Sean's satisfaction. He went to Katrina's wagon, lifted the canvas and peeped in. He expected her to be asleep. She was lying on the cot with her eyes open and two of the thick grey blankets wrapped around her. Her face was as pale as a two-day corpse. Sean felt the first leap of alarm, he scrambled into the wagon.

'My dear, you look ghastly. Are you sick?' He put his hand on her shoulder and she was shivering. She didn't answer him, instead her eyes moved from his face to the floor near the foot of the bed and Sean's eyes followed hers. Katrina's luxury was her chamber-pot; it was a massive china thing with red roses hand-painted on it. She loved it dearly and Sean used to tease her when she was perched on top of it. Now the pot stood near the foot of the bed and when Sean saw what was in it his breathing stopped. It was half full of a liquid the colour of milk stout. 'Oh, my God,' he whispered. He went on staring at it, standing very still while a gruesome snatch of doggerel he remembered hearing sung in the canteens of the Witwatersrand began trotting through his brain like an undertaker's hack.

> Black as the Angel,
> Black as disgrace
> When the fever waters flow
> They're as black as the ace.

Roll him in a blanket
Feed him on quinine
But all of us we know
It's the end of the line.

Black as the Angel
Black as disgrace
Soon we'll lay him down below
And chuck dirt in his face.

He raised his head and looked steadily at her, searching for the signs of fear. But just as steadily she looked back at him.

'Sean, it's blackwater.'

'Yes . . . I know,' Sean said, for there was nothing to be gained by denial, no room for extravagant hope. It was blackwater fever: malaria in its most malignant form, attacking the kidneys and turning them to fragile sacks of black blood that the slightest movement could rupture. Sean knelt by her cot. 'You must lie very still.' He touched her forehead lightly with the tips of his fingers and felt the heat of her skin.

'Yes,' she answered him, but already the expression in her eyes was blurring and she made the first restless movement of delirium. Sean put his arm across her chest to hold her from struggling.

By nightfall Katrina was deep in the nightmare of malaria. She laughed, she screamed in senseless terror, she shook her head and fought him when he tried to make her drink. But she had to drink, it was her one chance, to flush out her kidneys that she might live. Sean held her head and forced her.

Dirk started crying, hungry and frightened by the sight of his mother.

'Mbejane!' shouted Sean, his voice pitched high with desperation. Mbejane had waited all afternoon at the entrance of the wagon.

'Nkosi, what can I do?'

'The child . . . can you care for him?'

Mbejane picked up the cot with Dirk still in it. 'Do not worry about him again. I will take him to the other wagon.'

Sean turned his whole attention back to Katrina. The fever built up steadily within her. Her body was a furnace, her skin was dry and with every hour she was wilder and her movements more difficult to control.

An hour after dark Kandhla came to the wagon with a pot of steaming liquid and a cup. Sean's nose wrinkled as he caught the smell of it.

'What the hell is that?'

'I have stewed the bark from a maiden's breast tree . . . the Nkosikazi must drink it.'

It had the same musty smell as boiling hops and Sean hesitated. He knew the tree. It grew on high ground, it had a diseased-looking lumpy bark and each lump was the size and shape of a breast surmounted by a thorn.

'Where did you get it? I have seen none of these trees near the river.' Sean was marking time while he decided whether to make Katrina drink the brew. He knew these Zulu remedies, what they didn't kill they sometimes cured.

'Hlubi went back to the hills where we camped four days ago . . . he brought the bark into the camp an hour ago.'

A thirty-mile round journey in something under six hours—even in his distress Sean could smile.

'Tell Hlubi the Nkosikazi will drink his medicine.'

Kandhla held her head and Sean forced the evil-smelling liquid between her lips—he made her finish the whole potful. The juice of the bark seemed to relieve the congestion of her kidneys; four times before morning she passed frothy black water. Each time Sean held her gently, cushioning her body from any movement that might have killed her. Gradually her delirium became coma; she lay huddled and still in the cot, shaken only by the brief fits of shivering. When the morning sun hit the wagon canvas and lit the interior, Sean saw her face, and he knew that she was dying. Her skin was an opaque yellowish white, her hair had lost its glow and was lifeless as dry grass. Kandhla brought another pot of the medicine and they fed it to her. When the pot was empty Kandhla said, 'Nkosi, let me lay a mattress on the floor beside the Nkosikazi's bed. You must sleep and I will stay here with you and wake you if the Nkosikazi stirs.'

Sean looked at him with haunted eyes. 'There will be time to sleep later, my friend.' He looked down at Katrina and went on softly. 'Perhaps, very soon there will be time.'

Suddenly Katrina's body stiffened and Sean dropped on his knees beside her cot. Kandhla hovered anxiously behind him. It took Sean a while to understand what was happening and then he looked up at Kandhla.

'Go! go quickly!' he said and the suffering in his voice sent Kandhla stumbling blindly from the wagon. Sean's second son was born that morning and while Kandhla watched over Katrina Sean wrapped the child in a blanket, took him into the veld and buried him. Then he went back to Katrina and stayed with her while days and nights blended together into a hopeless muddle of grief. As near as Katrina was to death, that near was Sean to insanity. He never moved out of the wagon, he squatted on the mattress next to her cot, wiping the perspiration from her face, holding a cup to her lips or just sitting and watching her. He had lost his child and before his eyes Katrina was turning into a wasted yellow skeleton. Dirk saved him. Mbejane brought the boy to him and he romped on the mattress, crawling into Sean's lap and pulling his beard. It was the one small glimmer of light in the darkness.

27

Katrina survived. She came back slowly from the motionless coma that precedes death and with her hesitant return Sean's despair changed to hope and then to a wonderful relief. Her water was no longer black but dark pink and thick with sediment. She was aware of him now and, although she was so weak that she could not lift her head off the pillow, her eyes followed him as he moved about the wagon. It was another week before she learned about the baby. She asked him, her voice a tired whisper, and Sean told her with all the gentleness of which he was capable. She did not have the strength for any great show of emotion; she laid quietly staring up at the canvas above her head and her tears slid down across her yellow cheeks.

The damage that the fever had done to her body was hardly credible. Her limbs were so thin that Sean could completely encircle her thigh with one hand. Her skin hung in loose yellow folds from her face and body and pink blood still stained her water. This was not all: the fever had sucked all the strength from her mind. She had nothing left to resist the sorrow of her baby's death, and the sorrow encased her in a shell through which neither Sean nor

Dirk could reach her. Sean struggled to bring her back to life, to repair the terrible damage to her mind and body. Every minute of his time he employed in her service.

He and the servants scoured the veld for thirty miles around the laager to find delicacies to tempt her appetite, wild fruits, honey, giraffe marrows, the flesh of a dozen animals: kabobs of elephant heart and duiker liver, roasted iguana lizard as white and tender as a plump pullet, golden fillets of the yellow-mouthed bream from the river. Katrina picked at them listlessly then turned away and lay staring at the canvas wall of the cot.

Sean sat beside her and talked about the farm they would buy, trying vainly to draw her into a discussion of the house they would build. He read to her from Duff's books and the only reaction he received was a small quivering of her lips when he read the words 'death' or 'child'. He talked about the days on the Witwatersrand, searching his mind for stories that might amuse her. He brought Dirk to her and let him play about the wagon. Dirk was walking now, his dark hair had started to curl and his eyes were green. Dirk, however, could not be too long confined in the wagon. There was too much to do, too much to explore. Before long he would stagger to the entrance and issue the imperial summons: 'Bejaan! Bejaan!'

Almost immediately Mbejane's head would appear in the opening and he would glance at Sean for permission.

'All right, take him out then . . . but tell Kandhla not to stuff him full of food.'

Quickly, before Sean changed his mind, Mbejane would lift Dirk down and lead him away. Dirk had nearly two dozen Zulus to spoil him. They competed hotly for his affections, no effort was too much—dignified Mbejane down on his hands and knees being ridden mercilessly in and out among the wagons, Hlubi scratching himself under the arms and gibbering insanely in his celebrated imitation of a baboon while Dirk squealed with delight, fat Kandhla raiding Katrina's store of fruit preserves to make sure Dirk was properly fed and the others keeping in the background, anxious to join the worship but fearful of incurring the jealously of Mbejane and Hlubi. Sean knew what was happening but he was powerless to prevent it. His time was completely devoted to Katrina.

For the first time in his life Sean was giving more than just a superficial part of himself to another human being. It was an isolated sacrifice: it went on throughout the months it took for Katrina to regain sufficient of her strength to enable her to sit up in bed without assistance; it continued through the months that she needed before Sean judged it safe to resume the trek towards the south. They built a litter for her—Sean would not risk the jarring of the wagon—and the first day's trek lasted two hours. Four of the servants carried the litter and Katrina lay in it, protected from the sun by a strip of canvas spread above her head. Despite the gentleness with which the Zulus handled her, at the end of the two hours Katrina was exhausted. Her back ached and she was sweating in small beads from her yellow skin. The next week they travelled two hours daily and then gradually increased the time until they were making a full day's journey.

They were halfway to the Magaliesberg, camped at a muddy waterhole in the thorn flats, when Mbejane came to Sean.

'There is still one wagon empty of ivory, Nkosi.'

'The others are full,' Sean pointed out.

'Four hours' march from this place there is enough ivory buried to fill those wagons.'

Sean's mouth twisted with pain. He looked away towards the south-east and he spoke softly. 'Mbejane, I am still a young man and yet already I have stored up enough ugly memories to make my old age sad. Would you have me steal from a friend not only his life but his share of ivory also?'

Mbejane shook his head. 'I asked, that is all.'

'And I have answered, Mbejane. It is his . . . let it lie.'

28

They crossed the Magaliesberg and turned west along the mountain range. Then, two months after they had left the Limpopo river, they reached the Boer settlement at Louis Trichardt. Sean left Mbejane to outspan the wagons on the open square in front of the church and he went to search for a doctor. There was only one in the district, Sean found him in his surgery above the general dealer's store and took him to the wagons. Sean carried his bag for him and the doctor, a greybeard and unused to such hardships, trotted to keep up with Sean. He was panting and pouring sweat by the time they arrived. Sean waited outside while the doctor completed his examination and when he finally made his descent from the wagon Sean fell on him impatiently. 'What do you think, man?'

'I think, meneer, that you should give hourly thanks to your Maker.' The doctor shook his head in amazement. 'It seems hardly possible that your wife could have survived both the fever and the loss of the child.'

'She is safe then, there's no chance of a relapse?' Sean asked.

'She is safe now . . . but she is still a very sick woman. It may take a year before her body is fully mended. There is no medicine I can give you. She must be kept quiet, feed her well and wait for time to cure her.' The doctor hesitated. 'There is other damage—' he tapped his forehead with his forefinger. 'Grief is a terrible destroyer. She will need love and gentleness and after another six months she will need a baby to fill the emptiness left by the one she lost. Give her those three things, meneer, but most of all give her love.' The doctor hauled his watch from his waistcoat and looked at it. 'Time! there is so little time. I must go, there are others who need me.' He held out his hand to Sean. 'Go with God, meneer.'

Sean shook his hand. 'How much do I owe you?'

The doctor smiled, he had a brown face and his eyes were pale blue; when he smiled he looked like a boy. 'I make no charge for words. I wish I could have done more.' He hurried away across the square and when he walked you could see that his smile lied, he was an old man.

'Mbejane,' said Sean. 'Get a big tusk out of the wagon and take it to the doctor's room above the store.'

Katrina and Sean went to the morning service in the church next day. Katrina could not stand through the hymns. She sat quietly in her pew, watching the altar, her lips forming the words of the hymn and her eyes full of her sorrow.

They stayed on for three more days in Louis Trichardt and they were made welcome. Men came to drink coffee with them and see the ivory and the women brought them eggs and fresh vegetables, but Sean was anxious to move south. So on the third day they started the last stage of their trek.

Katrina regained her strength rapidly now. She took over the management of Dirk from the servants, to their ill-concealed disappointment, and soon she left her litter and rode on the box seat of the lead wagon again. Her body filled out and there was colour showing once more through the yellow skin of her cheeks. Despite the improvement to her body the depression of her mind still persisted and there was nothing that Sean could do to lift it.

A month before the Christmas of 1895 Sean's wagon train climbed the low range of hills above the city and they looked down into Pretoria. The jacaranda trees that filled every garden were in bloom—masses of purple—and the busy streets spoke well of the prosperity of the Transvaal Republic. Sean outspanned on the outskirts of the city, simply pulling the wagons off the road and camping beside it, and once the camp was established and Sean had made certain that Katrina no longer needed his help he put on his one good suit and called for his horse. His suit had been cut to the fashion of four years previously and had been made to encompass the belly he had acquired on the Witwatersrand. Now it hung loosely down his body but bunched tightly around his thickened arms. His face was burnt black by the sun and his beard bushed down on to his chest and concealed the fact that the stiff collar of his shirt could no longer close around his neck. His boots were scuffed almost through the uppers, there was not a suspicion of polish on them and they had completely lost their shape. Sweat had soaked through his hat around the level of the band and left dark greasy marks; the brim drooped down over his eyes so he had to wear it pushed on to the back of his head. There was, therefore, some excuse for the curious glances that followed him that afternoon as he rode down Church Street with a great muscular savage trotting at his one stirrup and an overgrown brindle hound at the other. They pushed their way between the wagons that cluttered the wide street; they passed the Raadsaal of the Republican Parliament, passed the houses standing back from the road in their spacious purple and green gardens and came at last to the business area of the city that crowded round the railway station. Sean and Duff had bought their supplies at a certain general dealer's stores and now Sean went back to it. It was hardly changed—the signboard in front had faded a little but still declared that I. Goldberg, Importer & Exporter, Dealer in Mining Machinery, Merchant & Wholesaler, was prepared to consider the purchase of gold, precious stone, hides and skins, ivory and other natural produce. Sean swung down from the saddle and tossed his reins to Mbejane. 'Unsaddle, Mbejane. This may take time.'

Sean stepped up on to the sidewalk, lifted his hat to two passing ladies and went through into the building where Mr Goldberg conducted his diverse activities. One of the assistants hurried to meet him, but Sean shook his head and the man went back behind the counter. He had seen Mr Goldberg with two customers at the far end of the store. He was content to wait. He browsed around among the loaded shelves of merchandise, feeling the quality of a shirt, sniffing at a box of cigars, examining an axe, lifting a rifle down off the rack and sighting at a spot on the wall, until Mr Goldberg bowed his customers through the door and turned to Sean. Mr Goldberg was short and fat. His hair was cropped short and his neck bulged over the top of his collar. He looked at Sean and his eyes were expressionless while he rifled through the index cards of his memory for the name. Then he beamed like a brilliant burst of sunlight. 'Mr Courtney, isn't it?'

Sean grinned. 'That's right. How are you, Izzy?' They shook hands. 'How's business?'

Mr Goldberg's face fell. 'Terrible, terrible, Mr Courtney. I'm a worried. man.'

'You look well enough on it,' Sean prodded his stomach. 'You've put on weight.'

'You can joke, Mr Courtney, but I'm telling you it's terrible. Taxes and worry, taxes and worry,' Mr Goldberg sighed, 'and now there's talk of war.'

'What's this?' Sean frowned.

'War, Mr Courtney, war between Britain and the Republic.'

Sean's frown dissolved and he laughed. 'Nonsense, man, not even Kruger could be such a bloody fool! Get me a cup of coffee and a cigar and we'll go through to your office and talk business.'

Mr Goldberg's face went blank and his eyelids drooped almost sleepily.

'Business, Mr Courtney?'

'That's right, Izzy, this time I'm selling and you're buying.'

'What are you selling, Mr Courtney?'

'Ivory!'

'Ivory?'

'Twelve wagon loads of it.'

Mr Goldberg sighed sadly. 'Ivory's no good now, the bottom's fallen out of it. You can hardly give it away.' It was very well done; if Sean had not been told the ruling prices two days before he might have been convinced.

'I'm sorry to hear that,' he said. 'If you're not interested, I'll see if I can find someone else.'

'Come along to my office anyway,' said Mr Goldberg. 'We can talk about it. Talk costs nothing.'

Two days later they were still talking about it. Sean had fetched his wagons and had off-loaded the ivory in the back yard of the store. Mr Goldberg had personally weighed each tusk and written the weights down on a sheet of paper. He and Sean had added the columns of figures and agreed on the total. Now they were in the last stages of agreeing the price.

'Come on, Izzy, we've wasted two days already. That's a fair price and you know it . . . let's get it over with,' Sean growled.

'I'll lose money on this,' protested Mr Goldberg. 'I've got to make a living, every man's got to live.'

'Come on,' Sean held out his right hand. 'Let's call it a deal.'

Mr Goldberg hesitated a second longer, then he put his pudgy hand in Sean's fist and they grinned at each other, both well satisfied. One of Mr Goldberg's assistants counted out the sovereigns, stacking them in piles of fifty along the counter, then Sean and Mr Goldberg checked them and agreed once more. Sean filled two canvas bags with the gold, slapped Mr Goldberg's back, helped himself to another cigar and headed heavily laden for the bank.

'When are you going into the veld again?' Mr Goldberg called after him.

'Soon!' said Sean.

'Don't forget to get your supplies here.'

'I'll be back,' Sean assured him.

Mbejane carried one of the bags and Sean the other. Sean was smiling and streamers of cigar smoke swirled back from his head as he strode along the sidewalk. There's something in the weight of a sack of gold that makes the man who holds it stand eight feet tall.

That night as they lay together in the darkness of the wagon Katrina asked him.

'Have we enough money to buy the farm yet, Sean?'

'Yes,' said Sean. 'We've got enough for the finest farm in the whole Cape peninsula . . . and, after one more trip, we'll have enough to build the house and the barns, buy the cattle, lay out the vineyard and still have some left over.'

Katrina was silent for a moment then, 'So we are going back into the bushveld again?'

'One more trip,' said Sean. 'Another two years and then we'll go down to the Cape.' He gave her a hug. 'You don't mind, do you?'

'No,' she said. 'I think I'd like that. When will we leave?'

'Not just yet awhile,' Sean laughed. 'First we're going to have some fun.' He hugged her again, her body was still painfully thin; he could feel the bones of her hips pressed against him.

'Some pretty clothes for you, my fancy, and a suit for me that doesn't look like a fancy dress. Then we'll go out and see what this burg has to offer in the way of entertainment–' He stopped as the idea swelled up in his mind. 'Damn it! I know what we'll do. We'll hire a carriage and go across to Jo'burg. We'll take a suite at the Grand National Hotel and do some living. Bath in a china bath, sleep in a real bed; you can have your hair prettied-up and I'll have my beard trimmed by a barber. We'll eat crayfish and penguin eggs . . . I can't remember when I last tasted pork or mutton . . . we'll wash it down with the old bubbling wine and waltz to a good band–' Sean raced on and when he stopped for breath Katrina asked softly, 'Isn't the waltz a very sinful dance, Sean?'

Sean smiled in the darkness. 'It certainly is!'

'I'd like to be sinful just once . . . not too much, just a little with you to see what it's like.'

'We will be'–said Sean–'as wicked as hell.'

29

The next day Sean took Katrina to the most exclusive ladies' shop in Pretoria. He chose the material of half a dozen dresses. One of them was to be a ball gown in canary-yellow silk. It was extravagance and he knew it, but he didn't care once he saw the flash of guilty delight in Katrina's cheeks and the old green sparkle in her eyes. For the first time since the fever she was living again. He spilled out his sovereigns with thankful abandon. The sales girls were delighted with him, they crowded round him with trays of feminine accessories.

'A dozen of those,' said Sean and, 'yes, those will do.' Then a flash of green on the racks across the room caught his eye–it was Katrina's green.

'What's that?' He pointed and two sales girls nearly knocked each other down in the rush to get it for him. The winner carried the shawl back to him and Sean took it and placed it around Katrina's shoulders. It was a beautiful thing.

'We'll take it,' said Sean and Katrina's lips quivered–then suddenly she was crying, sobbing brokenly. The excitement had been too much. There was immediate consternation among the shop assistants, they flapped around Sean like hens at feeding time while he picked Katrina up and carried her out to the hired carriage. At the door he paused and spoke over his shoulder.

'I want those dresses finished by tomorrow evening. Can you do it?'

'They'll be ready, Mr Courtney, even if my girls have to work all night on them.'

He took Katrina back to the wagons and laid her on her cot.

'Please forgive me, Sean, I've never done that in my life before.'

'It's all right, my fancy, I understand. Now you just go to sleep.'

The following day Katrina stayed at the camp resting, while Sean went to see Mr Goldberg again and buy from him the stores they would need for the next expedition. It took another day to load the wagons and by then Katrina seemed well enough to make the trip to Johannesburg.

They left in the early afternoon. Mbejane driving, Sean and Katrina sitting close together on the back seat holding hands under the travelling rug and Dirk bouncing round the interior of the carriage, pausing now and then to flatten his face against a window and keeping up a flow of comment in the peculiar mixture of English, Dutch and Zulu that Sean called Dirkese. They reached Johannesburg long before Sean expected to. In four years the town had doubled its size and had spread out into the veld to meet them. They followed the main road through the new areas and came to the centre. There were changes here as well but it was, in the main, the way he remembered it. They threaded their way through the babble of Eloff Street, and around them, mingling with the crowds on the sidewalks, were the ghosts of the past. He heard Duff laugh and twisted quickly in his seat to place the sound; a dandy in a boater hat with gold fillings in his teeth laughed again from a passing carriage and Sean heard that it was not Duff's laugh. Very close, but not the same. All of it was like that—similar but subtly changed, nostalgic but sad with the knowledge of loss. The past was lost—and he knew then that you can never go back. Nothing is the same, for reality can exist at one time only and in one place only. Then it dies and you have lost it and you must go on to find it at another time and in another place.

They took a suite at the Grand National, with a sitting-room and two bedrooms, a private bathroom and a balcony that looked out over the street—over the rooftops to where the headgears and white dumps stood along the ridge. Katrina was exhausted. They had supper sent up to the room early and when they had eaten Katrina went to bed and Sean went down alone to drink a nightcap at the bar. The bar-room was crowded. Sean found a seat in the corner and sat silently in the jabber of conversation. In it, but no longer a part of it.

They had changed the picture above the bar—it used to be a hunting print; but now it was a red-coated general, impressively splattered with blood, taking leave of his staff in the middle of a battlefield. The staff looked bored. Sean let his eyes wander on along the dark panelled walls. He remembered—there was so much to remember! Suddenly he blinked. Near the side door was a star-shaped crack in the wooden panelling. Sean started to grin and put down his glass and massaged the knuckles of his right hand. If Oakie Henderson hadn't ducked under that punch it would have taken his head off.

Sean signalled to the barman. 'Another brandy, please.' While the man was pouring, Sean asked, 'What happened to that panel near the door?'

The man glanced up and then back at the bottle. 'Some fellow put his fist through it in the old days. Boss left it like that, sort of souvenir, you know.'

'He must have been quite a fellow . . . that wood's an inch thick. Who was he?' Sean asked expectantly.

The man shrugged. 'One of the drifters. They come and they go. Make a few pounds, piss it against the wall and then go back where they came from.' He looked at Sean with bored eyes. 'That'll be half a dollar, mate.' Sean drank the brandy slowly, turning the glass in his hands between sips and watching the liquor cling to its sides like thin oil. By a cracked panel in a bar-room they shall remember you.

And now I shall go to bed, he decided, this is no longer my world. My world is upstairs sleeping—I hope! He smiled a little to himself and finished the brandy in his glass.

'Sean'—a voice at his ear and a hand on his shoulder as he turned to leave. 'My God, Sean, is it really you?'

Sean stared at the man beside him. He did not recognize the neatly clipped beard and the big sun-burned nose with the skin peeling off the tip, but suddenly he knew the eyes.

'Denis, you old rogue. Denis Petersen from Ladyburg. That's right, isn't it?'

'You didn't recognize me!' laughed Denis. 'So much for our friendship—you disappear without a word and ten years later you don't even know me!'

Now they were both laughing.

'I thought they would have hanged you long ago—' Sean defended himself. 'What on earth are you doing in Johannesburg?'

'Selling beef—I'm on the committee of the Beef Growers' Association.' There was pride in Denis's voice. 'I have been up here negotiating the renewal of our contracts.'

'When are you going back?'

'My train leaves in an hour.'

'Well, there's time for a drink before you go—what will it be?'

'I'll have a small brandy, thanks.'

Sean ordered the drinks and they took them up and stood, suddenly awkward in the awareness that ten years were between their once complete accord.

'So, what have you been doing with yourself?' Denis ended the pause.

'This and that, you know—a bit of mining, just come back from the bushveld. Nothing very exciting.'

'Well, it's good to see you again anyway. Your health.'

'And yours,' said Sean, and then suddenly he realized that here was news of his family—news he had been without for many years.

'How's everyone at Ladyburg—your sisters?'

'Both married—so am I, with four sons,' and the pride was in Denis's voice again.

'Anyone I know?' asked Sean.

'Audrey—you know old Pye's daughter.'

'No!' Sean ripped out the word, and then quickly, 'That's wonderful, Denis. I'm pleased for you—she was a lovely girl.'

'The best,' agreed Denis complacently. He had the sleek well-fed, well-cared for look of a married man, fatter in the face and his stomach starting to show. I wonder if I have it yet, Sean thought. 'Of course, old man Pye's dead now—that's one creditor he couldn't buy off. Ronnie's taken over the bank and the store.'

'The bat-eared bush rat,' said Sean and knew immediately that he had said the wrong thing. Denis frowned slightly. 'He's family now, Sean. A very decent chap really—and a clever business man.'

'I'm sorry, I was joking. How's my mother?' Sean changed the subject by asking the question that had been in the forefront of his mind and he had picked the right topic. Denis's expression softened immediately—you could see the warmth in his eyes.

'The same as ever. She's got a dress shop now, next door to Ronnie's store. It's a gold mine—no one would think of buying anywhere else but at Aunt Ada's. She's godmother to my two eldest. I guess she's godmother to half the kids in the district,' and then his expression hardened again. 'The least you could have done was write to her sometime, Sean. You can't imagine the pain you have caused her.'

'There were circumstances.' Sean dropped his eyes to his glass.

'That's no excuse—you have a duty which you neglected. There is no excuse for it.'

You little man, Sean lifted his head and looked at him without trying to disguise his annoyance. You pompous, preaching little man peering out at the world one-eyed through the keyhole of your own self-importance. Denis had not noticed Sean's reaction and he continued. 'That's a lesson a man must learn before he grows up—we all have our responsibilities and our duties. A man grows up when he faces those duties, when he accepts the burdens that society places on him. Take my own case: despite the vast amount of work I have on the farms—I now own Mahoba's Kloof as well—and despite the demands made on me by my family, yet I have time to represent the district on the committee of the Beef Growers' Association, I am a member of the Church Council and the village management board, and I have every reason to believe that next month I will be asked to accept the office of mayor.' Then he looked steadily at Sean. 'What have *you* done with your life so far?'

'I've lived it,' Sean answered, and Denis looked a little perplexed—then he gathered himself.

'Are you married yet?'

'I was—but I sold her to the Arab slavers up north.'

'You did what?'

'Well,' grinned Sean, 'she was an old wife and the price was good.'

'That's a joke, hey? Ha, ha!' You couldn't fool good old Denis—Sean laughed out loud. This unbelievable little man!

'Have a drink, Denis,' he suggested.

'Two is my limit, thanks Sean.' Denis pulled the gold hunter from his waistcoat pocket and inspected it. 'Time to go—I'm afraid. Nice seeing you again.'

'Wait,' Sean stopped him. 'My brother—how's Garry?'

'Poor old Garry.' Denis shook his head solemnly.

'What's wrong with him?' Sean's voice was sharp with his sense of dread.

'Nothing—' Denis reassured him quickly. 'Well, I mean nothing more than ever was.'

'Why did you say "poor old Garry" then?'

'I don't really know—except that everybody says it. It's habit, I suppose—he's just one of those people you say *poor old* in front of.'

Sean suppressed his irritation, he wanted to know. He had to know.

'You haven't answered me—how is he?'

Denis made a significant gesture with his right hand. 'Looking into the bottle quite a bit these days—not that I blame him with that woman he married. You were well out of it there if I may say so, Sean.'

'You may,' Sean acquiesced, 'but is he well? How are things at Theunis Kraal?'

'We all took a bit of a beating with the rindepest* but Garry—well, he lost over half of his herds. Poor old Garry, everything happens to him.'

'My God—fifty per cent!'

'Yes—but, of course, Ronnie helped him out. Gave him a mortgage on the farm to tide him over.'

'Theunis Kraal bonded again,' groaned Sean. 'Oh Garry, Garry.'

'Yes—well,' Denis coughed uneasily. 'Well, I think I'd better be going. *Totsiens*, Sean.' He held out his hand. 'Shall I tell them I saw you?'

'No,' said Sean quickly. 'Just leave it stand.'

'Very well then.' Denis hesitated. 'Are you all right, Sean? I mean'—he coughed again—'are you all right for money?'

Sean felt his unhappiness dissolve a little; this pompous little man was going to offer him a loan. 'That's very good of you, Denis. But I've got a couple of pounds saved up—enough to eat on for a few days,' he spoke seriously.

'All right then.' Denis looked mightily relieved. 'All right then—*totsiens*, Sean,' and he turned and walked quickly out of the bar. As he left the room so he went out of Sean's mind, and Sean was thinking of his brother again.

Then suddenly Sean decided. I will go back to Ladyburg when this next trip is over. The dream farm outside Paarl would not lose anything in being transplanted to Natal—and he suddenly longed to sit in the panelled study at Theunis Kraal again, and to feel the mist come cold down the escarpment in the mornings, and see the spray blowing off the white falls in the wind. He wanted to hear Ada's voice again and to explain to her, knowing she would understand and forgive.

But more, much more it was Garry—poor old Garry. I must go back to him—ten years is a long time and he will have lost the bitterness. I must go back to him—for his sake and for Theunis Kraal. With the decision made, Sean finished his drink and went up the stairs to his suite.

Katrina was breathing softly in her sleep, the dark mass of her hair spread out on the pillow. While he undressed he watched her and slowly the melancholy dissolved. Gently he pulled back the blankets on his side of the bed and just then Dirk whimpered from the next room. Sean went through to him. 'All right, what's the trouble?'

Dirk blinked owlishly and searched for an excuse, then the relief flooded into his face and he produced the one that creaked with age. 'I want a drink a water.'

The delay while Sean went through to the bathroom gave Dirk an opportunity to rally his forces and when Sean came back he opened the offensive in earnest.

'Tell me a story, Daddy.' He was sitting up now, bright-eyed.

'I'll tell you a story about Jack and a Nory—' said Sean.

'Not that one—' protested Dirk. The saga of Jack and his brother lasted five seconds and Dirk knew it. Sean sat down on the edge of the bed and held the glass for him.

'How about this one? There once a king who had everything in the world . . .

* An epidemic cattle disease.

but when he lost it he found out that he had never had anything and that he now had more than he ever had before.'

Dirk looked stunned.

'That's not a very good one,' he gave his opinion at last.

'No,' said Sean. 'It isn't . . . is it? But I think we should be charitable and admit that it's not too bad for this time of night.'

30

Sean woke feeling happy. Katrina was sitting up in bed filling cups from a pewter coffee pot and Dirk was hammering at the door to be let in. Katrina smiled at him. 'Good morning, meneer.'

Sean sat up and kissed her. 'How did you sleep, fancy?'

'Well, thank you,' but there were dark rings under her eyes. Sean went across to the bedroom door.

'Prepare to receive cavalry,' he said and swung it open, Dirk's charge carried him on to the bed and Sean dived after him. When two men are evenly matched, weight will usually decide and within seconds Dirk had straddled Sean's chest, pinning him helplessly and Sean was pleading for quarter.

After breakfast Mbejane brought the carriage round to the front of the hotel. When the three of them were settled in it, Sean opened the small window behind the driver's seat and told Mbejane, 'To the office first. Then we have to be at the Exchange by ten o'clock.'

Mbejane grinned at him. 'Yes, Nkosi, then lunch at the Big House.' Mbejane had never been able to master the word Xanadu.

They went to all the old places. Sean and Mbejane laughing and reminiscing at each other through the window. There was a panic at the Exchange, crowds on the pavement outside. The offices on Eloff Street had been refaced and a brass plate beside the front door carried the roll of the subsidiaries of Central Rand Consolidated. Mbejane stopped the carriage outside and Sean boasted to Katrina. She sat silently and listened to him, suddenly feeling inadequate for a man who had done so much. She misinterpreted Sean's enthusiasm and thought he regretted the past and wished he were back.

'Mbejane, take us up to the Candy Deep,' Sean called at last. 'Let's see what's happening there.'

The last five hundred yards of the road was overgrown and pitted with disuse. The administration block had been demolished and grass grew thick over the foundations. There were new buildings and headgears half a mile farther along the bridge, but here the reef had been worked out and abandoned. Mbejane pulled up the horses in the circular drive in front of where the offices had stood. He jumped down and held their heads while Sean helped Katrina out of the carriage. Sean lifted Dirk and sat him on his shoulder and they picked their way through the waist-high grass and piles of bricks and rubbish towards the Candy Deep Number Three Shaft.

The bare white concrete blocks that had held the machinery formed a neat geometrical pattern in the grass. Beyond them reared the white mine dump; some mineral in the powdered rock had leaked out in long yellow stains down its sides. Duff had once had the mineral identified. It was of little commercial value, used occasionally in the ceramics industry. Sean had forgotten the name of it; it sounded like the name of a star—Uranus perhaps.

They came to the shaft. The edges of it had crumbled and the grass hung into it, the way an unkempt moustache hangs into an old man's mouth. The headgear was gone and only a rusty barbed-wire fence ringed the shaft. Sean bent his knees: keeping his back straight for Dirk still sat on his shoulder, he picked up a lump of rock the size of a man's fist and tossed it over the fence. They stood quietly and listened to it clatter against the sides as it fell. It fell for a long time and when at last it hit the bottom the echo rang faintly up from a thousand feet below.

'Throw more!' commanded Dirk, but Katrina stopped him.

'No, Sean, let's go. It's an evil place.' She shuddered slightly. 'It looks like a grave.'

'It very nearly was,' said Sean softly, remembering the darkness and the rock pressing down upon him.

'Let's go,' she said again, and they went back to where Mbejane waited with the carriage.

Sean was gay at lunch, he drank a small bottle of wine, but Katrina was tired and more miserable than she had been since they left Louis Trichardt. She had begun to realize the type of life he had led before she met him and she was frightened that now he wanted to return to it. She had only known the bush and the life of the Trek-Boer, she knew she could never learn to live like this. She watched as he laughed and joked during the meal, she watched the easy assurance with which he commanded the white head waiter, the way he picked his way through the maze of cutlery that was spread out on the table before them and at last she could hold it in no longer.

'Let's go away, let's go back into the bush.'

Sean stopped with a loaded fork halfway to his mouth. 'What?'

'Please, Sean, the sooner we go the sooner we'll be able to buy the farm.'

Sean chuckled. 'A day or two more won't make any difference. We're starting to have fun. Tonight I'll take you dancing—we were going to be sinful, remember?'

'Who will look after Dirk?' she asked weakly.

'Mbejane will—' Sean looked at her closely. 'You have a good sleep this afternoon and tonight we'll go out and tie the dog loose.' He grinned at the memories that expression invoked.

When Katrina woke from her rest that evening she found the other part of the reason for her depression. For the first time since the baby her periodic bleeding had started again, the tides of her body and mind were at their lowest ebb. She said nothing to Sean, but bathed and put on the yellow gown. She brushed her hair furiously, dragging the brush through it until her scalp tingled, but still it hung dull and lifeless—as dull as the eyes that looked back at her out of the yellow face in the mirror.

Sean came up behind her and leaned over her to kiss her cheek. 'You look,' said he, 'like a stack of gold bars five-and-a-half feet high.' But he realized that the yellow gown had been a mistake: it matched too closely the fever colour of her skin. Mbejane was waiting in the sitting-room when they went through.

'It may be late before we return,' Sean told him.

'That is of no account, Nkosi,' Mbejane's face was as impassive as ever, but Sean caught a sparkle of anticipation in his eyes and realized that Mbejane could hardly wait to get Dirk to himself.

'You are not to go into his room,' Sean warned.

'What if he cries, Nkosi?'

'He won't . . . but if he does see what he wants, give it to him then leave him to sleep.'

Mbejane's face registered his protest.

'I'm warning you, Mbejane, if I come home at midnight and find him riding you round the room I'll have both your hides for a kaross.'

'His sleep shall be unspoiled, Nkosi,' lied Mbejane.

In the hotel lobby Sean spoke to the receptionist. 'Where can we find the best food in this town?' he asked.

'Two blocks down, sir, the Golden Guinea. You can't miss it.'

'It sounds like a gin palace,' Sean was dubious.

'I assure you, sir, that you'll have no complaint when you get there. Everyone goes there. Mr Rhodes dines there when he's in town, Mr Barnato, Mr Hradsky–'

'Dick Turpin, Cesare Borgia, Benedict Arnold,' Sean continued for him. 'All right, you have convinced me. I'll take a chance on having my throat cut.'

Sean went out through the front entrance with Katrina on his arm. The splendour of the Golden Guinea subdued even Sean a little. A waiter with a uniform like a major-general's led them down a marble staircase, across the wide meadow of carpet between the group of elegant men and women to a table that even in the soft light dazzled with its bright silver and snowy linen. Chandeliers of crystal hung from the vaulted ceiling, the band was good, and the air was rich with the fragrance of perfume and expensive cigars.

Katrina stared helplessly at the menu until Sean came to her rescue and ordered the meal in a French accent that impressed her but not the waiter. The wine came and with it Sean's high spirits returned. Katrina sat quietly opposite him and listened. She tried to think of something witty to answer him with; in their wagon or alone in the veld they could talk for hours at a time but here she was dumb.

'Shall we dance?' Sean leaned across the table and squeezed her hand. She shook her head.

'Sean, I couldn't. Not with all these people watching. I'd only make a fool of myself.'

'Come on, I'll show you how . . . it's easy.'

'No, I couldn't, truly I couldn't.'

And to himself Sean had to admit that the dance floor of the Golden Guinea on a Saturday night was not the best place for a waltz lesson. The waiter brought the food, great steaming dishes of it. Sean addressed himself to it and the one-sided conversation wilted. Katrina watched him, picking at the too rich food herself, acutely conscious of the laughter and voices around them, feeling out of place and desperately miserable.

'Come on, Katrina,' Sean smiled at her. 'You've hardly touched your glass. Be a devil and get a little of that in you to warm you up.'

Obediently she sipped the champagne. She didn't like the taste. Sean finished the last of his crayfish thermidor and leaning back in his chair glowing with wine and good food said, 'Man . . . I only pray the chef can keep the rest of the meal up to that standard.' He belched softly behind his fingers and ran his eyes contentedly round the room. 'Duff used to say that a well-cooked crayfish was proof that–'

Sean stopped abruptly. He was staring at the head of the marble staircase–a party of three had appeared there. Two men in evening dress hovering attentively on each side of a woman. The woman was Candy Rautenbach. Candy with her blonde hair piled on top of her head. Candy with diamonds in her ears and at her throat, her bosom overflowing her gown as white as the frothy head on a beer tankard. Candy with bright blue eyes above a red mouth, Candy poised and lovely. Laughing, she glanced towards him and her eyes met his across the room. She stared in open disbelief, the laughter frozen on her lips, then suddenly her pose was gone and she was running down the stairs towards him, holding her skirts up to her knees, her escorts cantering after her in alarm, waiters scattering out of her path and every head in the room turning to watch her. Sean pushed back his chair, stood up to meet her and Candy reached him and jumped up to throw her arms around his neck. There was a long incoherent exchange of greetings and at last Sean prised her loose from his neck and turned her to face Katrina. Candy was flushed and panting with excitement; with every breath her bosom threatened to spring out of her bodice, and she was still holding on to Sean's arm.

'Candy, I want you to meet my wife, Katrina. My dear, this is Candy Rautenbach.'

'How do you do.' Katrina smiled uncertainly and Candy said the wrong thing.

'Sean, you're joking! You married?'

Katrina's smile faded. Candy noticed the change and went on quickly, 'But I must applaud your choice. I am so pleased to meet you, Katrina. We must get together sometime and I'll tell you all about Sean's terrible past.'

Candy was still holding Sean's arm and Katrina was watching her hand–the long tapered fingers against the dark cloth of Sean's suit. Sean saw the direction of Katrina's eyes and tried tactfully to disengage himself but Candy held on. 'Sean, these are my two current beaux.' They were standing to heel behind her like well-trained gundogs. 'They are both so nice I can't make up my mind about them. Harry Lategaan and Derek Goodman. Boys, this is Sean Courtney. You've heard lots about him.'

They shook hands all round.

'Do you mind if we join you?' asked Derek Goodman.

'I'd be upset if you didn't!' said Sean. The men spread out to find chairs while Candy and Katrina studied each other. 'Is this your first visit to Johannesburg, Mrs Courteney?' Candy smiled sweetly. *I wonder where Sean found her, she's thin as a stick and that complexion!–that accent! he could have done better for himself–he could have had his pick.*

'Yes, we won't be here very long though.' *She's a harlot. She must be–her breasts half-naked and the paint on her face and the way she touches Sean. She must have been his mistress. If she touches him again I'll–I'll kill her.*

Sean came back to the table carrying a chair and set it down for Candy. 'Candy's one of my old friends, my dear, I'm sure you two will like each other.'

'I'm sure we will,' said Candy but Katrina didn't answer and Candy turned back to him. 'Sean, how wonderful it is to see you again. You look so well . . . as sunburnt and handsome as the first time I met you. Do you remember that day you and Duff came to eat at the Hotel?

A shadow fell across Sean's face at the mention of Duff's name. 'Yes, I remember.' He looked round and snapped his fingers for the waiter. 'Let's have some more champagne.'

'I'll get it,' Candy's escorts cut in simultaneously and then started wrangling good-naturedly as to whose turn it was.

'Is Duff with you tonight, Sean?' Candy asked.

'Candy, didn't Derek get the drinks last time? It's my turn now.' Harry sought her support. Candy ignored them and looked at Sean for a reply but he turned and went round the table to the seat beside Katrina.

'I say, old girl, can I have the first dance?' asked Derek.

'I'll spin you for it, Derek, winner pays but gets first dance,' Harry suggested.

'You're on.'

'Sean, I said is Duff here tonight?' Candy looked at him across the table.

'No, he's not. Listen, you two, how about letting me in on this.' Sean avoided her eyes and joined in the haggle with Harry and Derek. Candy bit her lip—she wanted to press Sean further. She wanted to know about Duff—then suddenly she turned on her smile again. She wasn't going to plead with him.

'What is this?' She tapped Harry's shoulder with her fan. 'Am I going to be the prize in a game of chance? Derek will pay for the wine and Sean gets first dance.'

'I say, old girl, that's a bit rough, you know.' But Candy was already standing up.

'Come on, Sean, let's see if you can still tread a stately measure.'

Sean glanced at Katrina. 'You don't mind, do you . . . just one dance?'

Katrina shook her head.

I hate her. She's a harlot. Katrina had never in her life spoken the word out loud, she had seen it only in her Bible, but now it gave her a fierce pleasure to think it. She watched Sean and Candy walk arm-in-arm to the dance floor.

'Would you care to dance, Mrs Courtney?' said Derek. Katrina shook her head again without looking at him. She was staring at Sean and Candy. She saw Sean take her in his arms and a cold lump settled in her stomach. Candy was looking up into Sean's face, laughing at him, her arm on his shoulder, her hand in his.

She's a harlot. Katrina felt her tears very near the surface and thinking that word held them back. Sean swirled Candy into a turn—Katrina stiffened in her chair, her hands clenching in her lap—their legs were touching, she saw Candy arch her back slightly and press her thighs against Sean. Katrina felt as though she were suffocating, jealousy had spread up cold and tight through her chest.

I could go and pull him away, she thought. *I could stop him doing that. He has no right. It's as though the two of them are doing—doing it together. I know they have before, I know it now—Oh God, make them stop it. Please make them stop.*

At last Sean and Candy came back to the table. They were laughing together and when he reached her chair Sean dropped his hand on Katrina's shoulder. She moved away from it but Sean seemed not to notice. Everybody was having a good time. Everybody except Katrina. Harry and Derek were jostling for position. Sean's big laugh kept booming out and Candy was sparkling like the diamonds she wore. Every few minutes Sean turned to Katrina and tried to draw her into the conversation but Katrina stubbornly refused to be drawn. She sat there hating them all. Hating even Sean—for the first time she was unsure of him, jealous and frightened for him. She stared down at her hands on the tablecloth in front of her and saw how bony they were, chapped and reddened by the sun and wind, ugly compared to Candy's. She pulled them quickly into her lap and leaned across towards Sean. 'Please, I want to go back to the hotel. I don't feel well.'

Sean stopped in the middle of a story and looked at her with a mixture of concern and dismay. He didn't want to leave and yet he knew she was still sick. He hesitated one second and then he said, 'Of course, my fancy, I'm sorry. I didn't realize–' He turned to the others. 'We'll have to be going . . . my wife's not too strong . . . she's just had one hell of a go of blackwater.'

'Oh, Sean, must you?' Candy couldn't hide her disappointment. 'There's still so much to talk about.'

'I'm afraid so. We'll get together another night.'

'Yes,' agreed Katrina quickly, 'next time we come to Johannesburg we'll see you.'

'Oh, I don't know . . . perhaps before we go,' Sean demurred. 'Some night next week. How about Monday?'

Before Candy could answer Katrina interrupted. 'Please, Sean, can we go now. I'm very tired.' She started towards the stairs but looked back to see Candy jump up and take Sean's arm, hold her lips close to his ear and whisper a question. Sean answered her tersely and Candy turned back to the table and sat down. When they were out on the street Katrina asked, 'What did she say to you?'

'She just said goodbye,' muttered Sean and Katrina knew he was lying. They didn't talk again on the way back to the hotel. Katrina was preoccupied with her jealousy and Sean was thinking about what Candy had asked and what he had answered.

'Sean, where's Duff? You must tell me.'

'He's dead, Candy.'

The second before she turned back to the table Sean had seen her eyes.

31

Sean woke with a headache and Dirk's jumping on his chest did not help to ease it at all. Sean had to bribe him off with the promise of sweets. Dirk, sensing his advantage, raised his price to a packet of bull's eyes and two lollipops, the kind with red stripes, before he allowed Katrina to lead him away to the bathroom. Sean sighed and settled back under the blankets. The pain moved up and crouched just behind his eyes. He could taste stale champagne on his own breath and his skin smelt of cigar smoke. He drowsed back in half sleep and the ache faded a little.

'Sean, it's Sunday you know. Are you coming to church with us?' Katrina asked coldly from the bedroom door. Sean squeezed his eyelids tighter closed.

'Sean!' No answer.

'Sean!' He opened one eye.

'Are you going to get up?'

'I don't feel very well,' he croaked. 'I think I have a touch of malaria.'

'Are you coming?' Katrina demanded remorselessly. Her feelings towards him had not softened during the night.

'I don't feel up to it this morning, truly I don't. I'm sure the Good Lord will understand.'

'Thou shalt not take the Lord's name in vain,' Katrina warned him with ice in her voice.

'I'm sorry.' Sean pulled the blankets up to his chin defensively. 'But truly, fancy, I can't get up for another couple of hours. My head would burst.'

Katrina turned back into the sitting-room and Sean heard her speak to Dirk in a voice purposely pitched to reach him.

'Your father's not coming with us. We will have to go down to breakfast by ourselves. Then we will have to go to church on our own.'

'But,' Dirk pointed out, 'he's going to buy me a packet of bull's eyes and *two* lollipops with red stripes.' In Dirk's opinion that levelled the score. Sean heard the door of the suite close and Dirk's voice receded down the passage. Sean relaxed slowly and waited for the ache behind his eyes to diminish. After a while he became aware of the coffee tray on the table beside the bed and he weighed the additional pain that the effort of sitting up would involve against the beneficial effect of a large cup of coffee. It was a difficult decision but in the end he carefully raised his body to a sitting position and poured a cupful. There was a small jug of fresh cream on the tray, he took it in his right hand and was just about to add a little to the cup when there was a knock on the sitting-room door.

'Come in!' called Sean. He supposed it was the waiter coming to collect the tray. Sean searched his mind for a really scathing remark to send him on his way. He heard the sitting-room door open.

'Who is it?' he asked. There were quick footsteps and then Sean started so violently that the cream slopped out of the jug on to his sheets and his new nightshirt.

'Good God, Candy, you shouldn't have come here.' Sean was in a frenzy of agitation. He put the jug back on the tray with nervous haste and wiped ineffectually at the mess on his nightshirt with his hands. 'If my wife . . . Did anyone see you? You mustn't stay. If Katrina knows you've been here she'll . . . well I mean, she won't understand.'

Candy's eyes were puffy and rimmed with red. She looked as though she hadn't slept. 'It's all right, Sean, I waited across the street until I saw your wife leave. One of my servants followed her, she went to the Dutch church on Commissioner Street and there the service lasts about fifty years.' She came into the room and sat down on the edge of his bed.

'I had to talk to you alone. I couldn't let you go without knowing about Duff. I want you to tell me about it . . . everything about it. I promise not to cry, I know how you hate it.'

'Candy, let's not torture ourselves with it. He's dead. Let's remember him alive.' Sean had forgotten his headache for its place had been taken by pity for her and worry at the position in which she had placed him.

'Tell me, please. I must know. I'd never rest again if I didn't,' she said quietly.

'Candy, don't you see that it doesn't matter? The way in which he went is not important. All that you need to know is he's gone.' Sean's voice faded but went on softly, almost to himself, 'He's gone, that is the only thing that matters, he's gone and left us richer for knowing him and a little poorer for having lost him.'

'Tell me,' she said again and they looked at each other, their emotions locked behind expressionless faces. Then Sean told her, his words limping at first, then faster and stronger as the horror of it came back to him. When he had finished she said nothing. She sat on the edge of the bed staring down at the patterned carpet. Sean moved closer to her and put his arm around her.

'There is nothing we can do. That's the thing about death, there is nothing you can do to make it change its mind.'

She leaned against him, against the comfort of his big body and they sat silently until suddenly Candy pulled away from him and smiled her gay brittle smile.

'And now tell me about you. Are you happy? Was that your son with Katrina? He's a lovely child.'

With relief Sean followed her away from the memory of Duff. They talked about each other, filling in the blanks from the time they had last met until suddenly Sean returned to reality.

'Good God, Candy, we've been talking for ages. Katrina will be back at any moment. You had better run.'

At the door she turned, buried her fingers in his beard and tugged his head from side to side. 'If she ever throws you out, you magnificent brute, here's somebody who'll have a place for you.'

She stood up on her toes and kissed him. 'Be happy,' she commanded and the door closed softly behind her.

Sean rubbed his chin, then he pulled off his nightshirt, screwed it into a ball, tossed it through the open door of the bedroom and went to the bathroom. He was towelling himself and whistling the waltz that the band had played the night before, sweating a little in the steamy warmth of the bathroom when he heard the front door open. 'Is that you, Fancy?'

'Daddy! Daddy! Mummy got sweets for me.' Dirk hammered on the bathroom door, and Sean wrapped the towel round his waist before opening it.

'Look! Look at all my sweets,' gloated Dirk. 'Do you want one, Pa?'

'Thank you, Dirk,' Sean put one of the huge striped humbugs in his mouth, moved it to one side and spoke around it.

'Where's your Mummy?'

'There.' Dirk pointed at the bedroom. He closed the sweet packet carefully. 'I'll keep some for Bejaan,' he announced.

'He'll like that,' Sean said and went across to the bedroom. Katrina lay on the bed; as soon as he saw her he knew something was desperately wrong. She lay staring up at the ceiling, her eyes unseeing, her face as yellow and set as that of a corpse. Two quick strides carried him to her. He touched her cheek with his fingers and the sense of dread settled on him again, heavily, darkly.

'Katrina?' There was no response. She lay still without a flicker of life in her eyes. Sean swung round and ran out of the suite, down the corridor to the head of the stairs. There were people in the lobby below him and he yelled over their heads to the clerk behind the desk.

'Get a doctor, man, as fast as you can . . . my wife's dying.'

The man stared up at him blankly. He had a neck too thin for his high stiff collar and his black hair was parted down the centre and polished with grease.

'Hurry, you stupid bastard, get moving,' roared Sean. Everybody in the lobby was looking at him. He still wore only a small towel around his waist and, heavy with water, his hair hung down over his forehead.

'Move, man! Move!' Sean was dancing with impatience. There was a heavy stone vase on the banister at Sean's side, he picked it up threateningly and the clerk jerked out of his trance and scuttled for the front door. Sean ran back to the suite.

Dirk was standing by Katrina's bed, his face distorted by the humbug it contained and his eyes large with curiosity. Sean snatched him up, carried him through to the other bedroom and locked the door on his outraged howls. Dirk was unused to being handled in that manner. Sean went back to Katrina and knelt beside her bed. He was still kneeling there when the doctor arrived. Tersely Sean explained about the blackwater, and the doctor listened then sent him to wait in the sitting-room. It was a long wait before the doctor came through to him and Sean sensed that behind his professional poker face the man was puzzled.

'Is it a relapse?' Sean demanded.

'No, I don't think so. I've given her a sedative.'

'What's wrong with her? What is it?' Sean pursued him and the doctor hedged.

'Has your wife had some sort of shock . . . some bad news, something that could have alarmed her? Has she been under nervous strain?'

'No . . . she's just come back from church. Why? What's wrong?' Sean caught the doctor's lapels and shook him in his agitation.

'It appears to be some sort of paralytic hysteria. I've given her laudanum. She'll sleep now and I'll come back to see her this evening.'

The doctor was trying to loosen Sean's hands from his jacket. Sean let him go and pushed past him to the bedroom.

The doctor called again just before dark, Sean had undressed Katrina and put her into the bed, but apart from that she had not moved. Her breathing was shallow and fast despite the drug she had been given. The doctor was baffled.

'I can't understand it, Mr Courtney. There is nothing I can find wrong with her apart from her general run-down condition. I think we'll just have to wait and see, I don't want to give her any more drugs.'

Sean knew the man could be of no more help to him and he hardly noticed when he left with a promise to come again in the morning. Mbejane gave Dirk his bath, fed him and put him to bed and then he slipped quietly out of the suite and left Sean alone with Katrina. The afternoon of worry had tired Sean. He left the gas burning in the sitting-room and stretched out on his own bed. After a while he slept.

When the rhythm of his breathing changed Katrina looked across at him. Sean lay fully clothed on top of his blankets, one thickly-muscled arm thrown above his head and his tension betrayed by the twitching of his lips and the frown that puckered his face. Katrina stood up and moved across to stand over him, lonely as she had never been in the solitude of the bush, hurt beyond the limits of physical pain and with everything that she believed in destroyed in those few minutes that it had taken for her to discover the truth.

She looked down at Sean and with surprise realized that she still loved him, but now the security that she had found with him was gone. The walls of her castle had proved paper. She had felt the first cold draughts blowing in through them as she watched him reliving his past and regretting it. She had felt the walls tremble and the wind howl stronger outside when he danced with that woman–then, they had collapsed into ruin around her. Standing in the half-darkened room, watching the man she trusted so completely and who just as completely had betrayed her, she went carefully over the ground again to make sure there was no mistake.

That morning, she and Dirk had stopped at the sweet shop on the way back from church. It was almost opposite the hotel. It had taken Dirk a long time to select his tuppenny worth. The profusion of wares on display unmanned him and reduced him to a state of dithering indecision. Finally, with the assistance of the proprietor and a little prompting from Katrina his purchases were made and packed into a brown paper bag. They were just about to go when Katrina looked out through the large front window of the shop and saw Candy Rautenbach leaving the hotel. She came quickly down the front steps, glanced about her, crossed the street to a waiting carriage and her coachman whisked her away. Katrina had stopped the instant she caught sight of her. A pang of last night's jealousy returned, for Candy looked very lovely even in the morning sunlight. It was not until Candy's carriage disappeared that Katrina began to question her presence at their hotel at eleven o'clock on a Sunday morning. Her jealousy was a bayonet thrust up under her ribs: it made her catch her breath. Vividly she remembered Candy's whispered question as they left the Golden Guinea the previous night. She remembered the way Sean had answered and the way he had lied about it afterwards. Sean knew that Katrina would go to church that morning. How simple it all was! Sean had arranged to meet her, he had refused to accompany Katrina and while Katrina was out of the way that harlot had gone to him.

'Mummy, you're hurting me.' Unconsciously she had tightened her grip on Dirk's hand. She hurried out of the shop, dragging Dirk with her. She almost ran across the hotel lobby, up the stairs and along the passage. The door was closed. She opened it and the smell of Candy's perfume met her. Her nostrils flared at it. There was no mistaking it, she remembered it from the previous evening—the smell of fresh violets. She heard Sean call from the bathroom, Dirk ran across the room and hammered on the door.

'Daddy! Daddy! Mummy got sweets for me.'

She put her Bible down on top of the writing desk and moved across the thick carpet with the smell of violets all around her. She stood in the doorway of the bedroom. Sean's nightshirt lay on the floor, there were still damp stains on it. She felt her legs begin to tremble. She looked up and saw the stains on the bed, grey on the white sheets. She felt giddy, her cheeks burned; she only just managed to reach her own bed.

32

She knew there was no mistake. Sean had taken that woman in such a casually blatant manner—in their own bedroom, almost before her eyes, that his rejection of her could hardly have been more final if he had slapped her face and thrown her into the street. Weakened by fever, depressed by the loss of her child and the phase of her cycle, she had not the resilience to fight against it. She had loved him but she had proved insufficient for him. She could not stay with him: the stubborn pride of her race would not allow it. There was only one alternative.

Timidly she bent over him and as she kissed him she smelt the warm man-smell of his body and felt his beard brush her cheek. Her determination wavered; she wanted to throw herself across his chest, lock her arms around his neck and plead with him. She wanted to ask for another chance. If he could tell her how she had failed him she could try to change, if only he could show her what she had done wrong. Perhaps if they went back into the bush again. She dragged herself away from his bed. She pressed her knuckles hard against her lips. It was no use. He had decided and even if she begged him to take her back there would always be this thing between them. She had lived in a castle and she would not change it now for a mud hut. Driven by the trek whip of her pride she moved quickly across to the wardrobe. She put on a coat and buttoned it—it reached to her ankles and covered her nightdress; she spread the green shawl over her head, winding the loose end around her throat. Once more she looked across at Sean. He slept with his big body sprawled and the frown still on his face.

In the sitting-room she stopped beside the writing desk. Her Bible lay where she had left it. She opened the front cover, dipped the pen and wrote. She closed the book and went to the door. There she hesitated once more and looked back at Dirk's bedroom. She could not trust herself to see him again. She lifted an end of the shawl to cover her mouth, then she went out into the passage and closed the door softly behind her.

33

Sean was surprised to find himself fully dressed and lying on top of his bed when he woke next morning. It was still half dark outside the hotel windows and the room was cold. He propped himself up one elbow and rubbed at his eyes with the back of a clenched fist. Then he remembered and he swung his legs off the bed and looked at Katrina's bed. The blankets were thrown back and it was empty. Sean's first feeling was relief, she had recovered enough to get up on her own. He went through to the bathroom, stumbling a little from the stiffness of uneasy sleep. He tapped on the closed door.

'Katrina?' he questioned and then again louder. 'Katrina, are you in there?'

The handle turned when he tried it and the door swung open without resistance. He blinked at the empty room, white tiles reflecting the uncertain light, a towel thrown across a chair where he had left it. He felt the first twinge of alarm. Dirk's room—the door was still locked, the key on the outside. He flung it open. Dirk sat up in bed, his face flushed, his curls standing up like the leaves of a sisal bush. Sean ran out into the passage, along it and looked down into the lobby. There was a light burning behind the reception desk. The clerk slept with his head on his arms, sitting forward on his chair snoring. Sean went down the stairs three at a time. He shook the clerk.

'Has anybody been out through here during the night?' Sean demanded.

'I . . . I don't know.'

'Is that door locked?' Sean pointed at the front door.

'No, sir, there's a night latch on it. You can get out but not in.'

Sean ran out on to the pavement. Which way, which way to search for her? Which way had she gone? Back to Pretoria to the wagons? Sean thought not. She would need transport and she had no money to hire it. Why should she leave without waking him, leave Dirk, leave her clothing and disappear into the night. She must have been unbalanced by the drugs the doctor had given her. Perhaps there was something in his theory that she had suffered a shock, perhaps she was wandering in her nightdress through the streets with no memory, perhaps—Sean stood in the cold grey Transvaal morning, the city starting to murmur into wakefulness around him, the questions crowding into his head and finding there no answers with which to mate.

He turned and ran back through the hotel, out of the rear door into the stable yard.

'Mbejane,' he shouted, 'Mbejane, where the hell are you?'

Mbejane appeared quickly from the stall where he was currying one of the hired horses.

'Nkosi.'

'Have you seen the Nkosikazi?'

Mbejane's face creased into a puzzled frown. 'Yesterday–'

'No, man,' shouted Sean. 'Today, last night . . . have you seen her?'

Mbejane's expression was sufficient reply.

Sean brushed impatiently past him and ran into the stable. He snatched a saddle off the rack and threw it on to the back of the nearest horse. While he clinched the girth and forced a bit between its teeth he spoke to Mbejane.

'The Nkosikazi is sick. She has left during the night. It is possible that she walks as one who still sleeps. Go quickly among your friends and tell them to search for her, tell them that there's ten pounds in gold for the one who finds her. Then come back here and care for Dirk until I return.'

Sean led the horse from the stable and Mbejane hurried off to spread the word. Sean knew that within minutes half the Zulus in Johannesburg would be looking for Katrina–tribal loyalty and ten pounds in gold were strong incentives. He swung up on to the horse and galloped out of the yard. He tried the Pretoria road first. Three miles out of town a native herd boy grazing sheep beside the road convinced him that Katrina had not passed that way. He turned back. He paid a visit to the police station at Marshal Square. The Kommandant remembered him from the old days; Sean could rely on his co-operation. Sean left him and rode fast through the streets that were starting to fill with the bustle of a working day. He hitched his horse outside the hotel and took the front steps three at a time. The clerk had no news for him. He ran up the stairs and along the passage to his suite. Mbejane was feeding Dirk his breakfast. Dirk beamed at Sean through a faceful of egg and spread his arms to be picked up but Sean had no time for him.

'Has she come back?'

Mbejane shook his head. 'They will find her, Nkosi. Fifty men are searching for her now.'

'Stay with the child,' said Sean and went down to his horse. He stood beside it ready to mount but not knowing which way to go. 'Where the hell has she got to?' he demanded aloud. In her night clothes with no money, where the hell had she gone?

He mounted and rode with aimless urgency through the streets, searching the faces of the people along the sidewalks, turning down the sanitary lanes and peering into backyards and vacant plots. By midday he had tired his horse and worked himself into a ferment of worry and bad temper. He had searched every street in Johannesburg, made a nuisance of himself at the police station and sworn at the hotel clerk, but there was still no sign of Katrina. He was riding down Jeppe Street for the fifth time when the imposing double-storey of Candy's Hotel registered through his preoccupation.

'Candy,' he whispered. 'She can help.'

He found her in her office among Persian rugs and gilt furniture, walls covered with pink and blue patterned wallpaper, a mirrored ceiling hung with six crystal waterfalls of chandeliers and a desk with an Indian mosaic top. Sean pushed aside the little man in the black alpaca coat who tried to stop him entering and burst into the room. Candy looked up and her small frown of annoyance smoothed as she saw who it was.

'Sean . . . oh, how nice to see you.' She came round from behind the desk, the bell tent of her skirts covering the movement of her legs so she seemed to float. Her skin was smooth white and her eyes were happy blue. She held out her hand to him, but hesitated as she saw his face. 'What is it, Sean?'

He told her in a rush and she listened and when he had finished she rang the bell on her desk.

'There's brandy in the cabinet by the fireplace,' she said, 'I expect you are in need of one.'

The little man in the alpaca coat came quickly to the bell. Sean poured himself a large brandy and listened to Candy giving orders.

'Check the railway station. Telegraph the coach stages on each of the main roads. Send someone up to the hospital. Check the registers of every hotel and boarding-house in town.'

'Very well, madame.' The little man bobbed his head as he acknowledged each instruction and then he was gone.

Candy turned back to Sean.

'You can pour a drink for me also and then sit down and simmer down. You're behaving just the way she wanted you to.'

'What do you mean?' demanded Sean.

'You are being given a little bit of wifely discipline, my dear. Surely you have been married long enough to recognize that?'

Sean carried the glass across to her and Candy patted the sofa next to her.

'Sit down,' she said. 'We'll find your little Cinderella for you.'

'What do you mean . . . wifely discipline?' he demanded again.

'Punishment for bad behaviour. You may have eaten with your mouth open, answered back, taken more than your share of the blankets, not said good morning with the right inflection or committed one of the other mortal sins of matrimony, but–' Candy sipped her drink and gasped slightly, 'I see that time has not given you a lighter hand with the brandy bottle. One Courtney tot always did equal an imperial gallon . . . but, as I was saying, my guess is that little Katy is having an acute attack of jealousy. Probably her first, seeing that the two of you have spent your whole married life out in the deep sticks and she has never had an opportunity of watching the Courtney charm work on any other female before.'

'Nonsense,' said Sean. 'Who's she got to be jealous of?'

'Me,' said Candy. 'Every time she looked at me the other night I felt as though I'd been hit in the chest with an axe.' Candy touched her magnificent bosom with her fingertips, skilfully drawing Sean's attention to it. Sean looked at it. It was deeply cleft and smelt of fresh violets. He shifted restlessly and looked away.

'Nonsense,' he said again. 'We're just old friends, almost like–' he hesitated.

'I hope, my dear, that you weren't going to say "brother and sister" . . . I'll not be party to any incestuous relationship . . . or had you forgotten about that?'

Sean had not forgotten. Every detail of it was still clear. He blushed and stood up.

'I'd better be going,' he said. 'I'm going to keep looking for her. Thanks for your help, Candy, and for the drink.'

'Whatever I have is yours, m'sieur,' she murmured, lifting an eyebrow at him, enjoying the way he blushed. 'I'll let you know as soon as we hear anything.'

The assurance that Candy had given him wore thinner as the afternoon went by with no news of Katrina. By nightfall Sean was again wild with worry, it had completely swamped his bad temper and even anæsthetized his fatigue. One by one Mbejane's tribesmen came in to report a blank score, one by one the avenues Candy's men were exploring proved empty and long before midnight Sean was the only hunter left. He rode hunched in the saddle, a lantern in his hand, riding the ground that had already been covered a dozen times, visiting the mining camps along the ridge, stopping to question late travellers he met along the network of roads between the mines. But the answer was always the same. Some thought he was joking: they laughed until they saw that his face was haunted and dark-eyed in the lantern light, then they stopped laughing and moved hurriedly on. Others had heard about the missing woman; they started to question him, but as soon as Sean realized they could not help him, he pushed past them and went on searching. At dawn he was back at the hotel. Mbejane was waiting for him.

'Nkosi, I have had food ready for you since last night. Eat now and sleep a little. I will send the men out to search again today, they will find her.'

'Tell them, I will give one hundred pounds to the one who finds her.' Sean passed his hand wearily across his face. 'Tell them to hunt the open veld beyond the ridges, she may not have followed a road.'

'I will tell them . . . but now you must eat.'

Sean blinked his eyes, they were red-veined and each had a little lump of yellow mucus in the corner.

'Dirk?' he asked.

'He is well, Nkosi, I have stayed with him all the while.'

Mbejane took Sean firmly by the arm. 'There is food ready. You must eat.'

'Saddle me another horse,' said Sean. 'I will eat while you do it.'

Without sleep, unsteady in the saddle as the day wore on, Sean widened the circle of his search until he was out into the treeless veld and the mine headgears were small spidery triangles on the horizon.

A dozen times he met Zulus from the city, big black men in loin cloths, moving at their businesslike trot, hunting the ground like hounds. There was a concealed sympathy behind their greetings

'Mbejane has told us, Nkosi. We will find her.' And Sean left them and rode on alone, more alone that he had ever been in his life before. After dark he rode back into Johannesburg, the faint flutter of hope inside him stilled as he limped stiffly into the gas-lit lobby of the hotel and saw the pity in the reception clerk's face.

'No word, I'm afraid, Mr Courtney.'

Sean nodded. 'Thanks anyway. Is my son all right?'

'Your servant has taken good care of him, sir. I sent dinner up to him an hour ago.'

The stairs seemed endless as he climbed them. By God, he was tired—sick-tired and sick with worry. He pushed open the door of his suite and Candy stood up from a chair across the room. The hope flared up in him again.

'Have you—' he started eagerly.

'No,' she said quickly. 'No, Sean, I'm sorry.' He flopped into one of the chairs and Candy poured a drink for him from a decanter that was waiting on the writing desk. He smiled his thanks and took a big gulp at the glass. Candy lifted his legs one at a time and pulled off his boots, ignoring his faint protest. Then she took up her own glass and went to sit across the room from him.

'I'm sorry I joked yesterday,' she apologized softly. 'I don't think I realized how much you love her.' She lifted her glass to him. 'Here's a speedy end to the search.'

Sean drank again, half a glass at a swallow.

'You do love her, don't you?' Candy asked.

Sean answered her sharply. 'She's my wife.'

'But it's not only that,' Candy went on recklessly, knowing his anger was just below the surface of his fatigue.

'Yes, I love her. I'm just learning how much, I love her as I'll never be able to love again.' He drained his glass and stared at it, his face grey under the brown and his eyes dark with unhappiness. 'Love,' he said. 'Love,' mouthing the word, weighing it. 'They've dirtied that word . . . they sell love at the Opera House . . . they have used that word so much that now when I want to say "I love Katrina" it doesn't sound what I mean.' Sean hurled the glass against the far wall, it shattered with a crack and a tingle and Dirk stirred in the bedroom. Sean dropped his voice to a fierce whisper. 'I love her so it screws my gut, I love her so that to think of losing her now is like thinking of dying.'

He clenched his fists and leaned forward in his chair. 'I'll not lose her now, by Christ, I'll find her and when I do I'll tell her this. I'll tell her just like I'm telling you.' He stopped and frowned. 'I don't think I've ever said to her "I love you." I've never liked using that word. I've said "Marry me" and "You're my fancy," but I've never said it straight before.'

'Perhaps that's part of the reason she ran away, Sean, perhaps because you never said it she thought you never felt it.' Candy was watching him with a strange expression—pity and understanding and a little yearning.

'I'll find her,' said Sean, 'and this time I'll tell her . . . if it's not too late.'

'You'll find her and it won't be too late. The earth can't have swallowed her, and she'll be glad to hear you say it.' Candy stood up. 'You must rest now, you have a hard day ahead of you.'

Sean slept fully dressed in the chair in the sitting-room. He slept brokenly, his mind struggling and kicking him back to half wakefulness every few minutes. Candy had turned the gas low before she left and its light fell in a soft pool on to the writing desk beneath it. Katrina's Bible lay where she had left it and each time Sean started awake the fat, leather-covered book caught his eye. Some time before dawn he woke for the last time and knew he could not sleep again.

He stood up and his body still ached and his eyes felt gritty. He moved across to the gas lamp and turned it up high, he let his hand drop from the lamp on to the Bible. Its leather was cool and softly polished beneath his fingers. He opened the front cover and caught his breath with a hiss.

Beneath Katrina's name, in her carefully rounded writing, the ink still freshly blue, *she had filled in the date of death.*

The page magnified slowly in front of his eyes until it filled the whole field of his vision. There was a rushing sound in his ears, the sound of a river in flood, but above it he heard voices, different voices.

'Let's go, Sean, it looks like a grave.'

'But more than anything she needs love.'

'The earth can't have swallowed her.'

And his own voice, 'If it's not too late, if it's not too late.'

The morning light was gathering strength as he reached the ruins of the old Candy Deep office block. He left his horse and ran through the grass towards the mine dump. The wind was small and cold; it moved the tops of the grass and went on to where Katrina's green shawl was caught on the barbed wire fence that ringed the shaft. In the wind the shawl flapped its wings like a big green bird of prey.

Sean reached the fence and looked down into the mouth of the shaft. At one place the grass had been torn away from the edge as though someone had snatched at it as they fell.

Sean loosed the shawl from the spikes of the barbed wire, he balled the heavy material in his fists, then he held it out over the shaft and let it drop. It spread out as it floated down into the blackness, and it was the bright green of Katrina's eyes.

'Why?' whispered Sean. 'Why have you done this to us, my fancy?' He turned away and walked back to his horse, stumbling carelessly in the rough footing.

Mbejane was waiting for him in the hotel suite.

'Get the carriage,' Sean told him.

'The Nkosikazi—?'

'Get the carriage,' Sean repeated.

Sean carried Dirk downstairs. He paid his bill at the reception desk and went out to where Mbejane had the carriage ready. He climbed up into it and held Dirk on his lap.

'Drive back to Pretoria,' Sean said.

'Where's Mummy?' Dirk demanded.

'She's not coming with us.'

'Are we going alone?' Dirk insisted and Sean nodded wearily.

'Yes, Dirk, we are going alone.'

'Is Mummy coming just now?'

'No, Dirk. No, she's not.'

It was finished, Sean thought. It was all over—all the dreams and the laughter and the love. He was too numbed to feel the pain yet—it would come later.

'Why are you squeezing me so hard, Daddy?'

Sean slackened his grip and looked down at the child on his lap. It was not finished, he realized; it was only a new beginning.

But first I must have time for this to heal: time—and a quiet place to lie up with this wound. The wagons are waiting and I must go back into the wilderness.

Perhaps after another year I will have healed sufficiently to start again, to go back to Ladyburg with my son, back to Ladyburg, and to Ada and to Garry—he thought. Then suddenly and sickeningly he felt the pain again, and the deep raw ache of it frightened him.

Please God, prayed Sean who had never prayed before, *please God, give me the strength to endure it.*

'Are you going to cry, Daddy? You look like you're going to cry.' Dirk was watching Sean's face with solemn curiosity. Sean pulled the child's head gently against his shoulder and held it there.

If tears could pay both our debts, thought Sean, if with my tears I could buy for you an indulgence from all pain, if by weeping now I could do all your weeping for you—then I would cry until my eyes were washed away.

'No, Dirk,' he answered. 'I am not going to cry—crying never helps very much.'

And Mbejane took them to where the wagons waited at Pretoria.

The Sound of Thunder

This book is for my children –
SHAUN and LAWRENCE
and CHRISTIAN LAURIE

Chapter One

Four years of travel in the roadless wilderness had battered the wagons. Many of the wheel-spokes and *disselbooms* had been replaced with raw native timber; the canopies were patched until little of the original canvas was visible; the teams were reduced from eighteen to ten oxen each, for there had been predators and sickness to weed them out. But this exhausted little caravan carried the teeth of five hundred elephant; ten tons of ivory; the harvest of Sean Courtney's rifle; ivory that he would convert into nearly fifteen thousand gold sovereigns once he reached Pretoria.

Once more Sean was a rich man. His clothing was stained and baggy, crudely mended; his boots were worn almost through the uppers and clumsily resoled with raw buffalo hide; a great untrimmed beard covered half his chest and a mane of black hair curled down his neck to where it had been hacked away with blunt scissors above the collar of his coat. But despite his appearance he was rich in ivory, also in gold held for him in the vaults of the Volkskaas Bank in Pretoria.

On a rise of ground beside the road he sat his horse and watched the leisurely plodding approach of his wagons. It is time now for the farm, he thought with satisfaction. Thirty-seven years old, no longer a young man, and it was time to buy the farm. He knew the one he wanted and he knew exactly where he would build the homestead – site it close to the lip of the escarpment so that in the evenings he could sit on the wide stoep and look out across the plain to the Tugela River in the blue distance.

'Tomorrow early we will reach Pretoria.' The voice beside him interrupted his dreaming, and Sean moved in the saddle and looked down at the Zulu who squatted beside his horse.

'It has been a good hunt, Mbejane.'

'Nkosi, we have killed many elephant.' Mbejane nodded and Sean noticed for the first time the strands of silver in the woolly cap of his hair. No longer a young man either.

'And made many marches,' Sean went on and Mbejane inclined his head again in grave agreement.

'A man grows weary of the trek,' Sean mused aloud. 'There is a time when he longs to sleep two nights at the same place.'

'And to hear the singing of his wives as they work the fields.' Mbejane carried it further. 'And to watch his cattle come into the kraal at dusk with his sons driving them.'

'That time has come for both of us, my friend. We are going home to Ladyburg.'

The spears rattled against his raw-hide shield as Mbejane stood up, muscles moved beneath the black velvet of his skin and he lifted his head to Sean and smiled. It was a thing of white teeth and radiance, that smile. Sean had to return it and they grinned at each other like two small boys in a successful bit of mischief.

'If we push the oxen hard this last day we can reach Pretoria tonight, Nkosi.'

'Let us make the attempt.' Sean encouraged him and walked his horse down the slope to intercept the caravan.

As it toiled slowly towards them through the flat white glare of the African morning a commotion started at its rear and spread quickly along the line, the dogs clamoured and the servants shouted encouragement to the rider who raced past them towards the head of the caravan. He lay forward in the saddle, driving the pony with elbows and heels, hat hanging from the leather thong about his neck and black hair ruffled with the speed of his run.

'That cub roars louder than the lion that sired him,' grunted Mbejane, but there was a fondness in his expression as he watched the rider reach the leading wagon and drag the pony from full run down on to his haunches.

'Also he spoils the mouth of every horse he rides.' Sean's voice was as harsh as Mbejane's, but there was the same fond expression in his eyes as he watched his son cut loose the brown body of a springbok from the pommel of his saddle and let it drop into the road beside the wagon. Two of the wagon drivers hurried to retrieve it, and Dirk Courtney kicked his pony and galloped down to where Sean and Mbejane waited beside the road.

'Only one?' Sean asked as Dirk checked the pony and circled back to fall in beside him.

'Oh, no. I got three – three with three shots. The gunboys are bringing the others.' Offhanded, taking as natural that at nine years of age he should be providing meat for the whole company, Dirk slouched down comfortably in the saddle, holding the reins in one hand and the other resting negligently on his hip in faithful imitation of his father.

Scowling a little to cover the strength of his pride and his love, Sean examined him surreptitiously. The beauty of this boy's face was almost indecent, the innocence of the eyes and faultless skin should have belonged to a girl. The sun struck ruby sparks from the mass of dark curls, his eyes spaced wide apart were framed with long black lashes and overscored by the delicate lines of the brow. His eyes were emerald and his skin was gold and there were rubies in his hair – a face fashioned by a jewelsmith. Then Sean looked at the mouth and experienced a twinge of uneasiness. The mouth was too big, the lips too wide and soft. The shape of it was wrong – as though it were about to sulk or whine.

'We are making a full day's trek today, Dirk. No *outspan* until we reach Pretoria. Ride back and tell the drivers.'

'Send Mbejane. He's doing nothing.'

'I told *you* to go.'

'Hell, Dad! I've done enough today.'

'Go, damn you!' Sean roared with unnecessary violence.

'I've only just come back, it's not fair that—' Dirk started, but Sean did not let him finish.

'Every time I ask you to do something I get a mouthful of argument. Now do what I tell you.' They held each other's eyes; Sean glaring and Dirk resentful, sulky. Sean recognized that expression with dismay. This was going to be another of those tests of will that were becoming more frequent between them. Would this end as most of the others had? Must he admit defeat and use the *sjambok* again? When was the last time – two weeks ago – when Sean had reprimanded Dirk on some trivial point concerning the care of his pony. Dirk had stood sullenly until Sean was finished, and then he had walked away among the wagons. Dropping the subject from his mind, Sean was chatting with Mbejane when suddenly there was a squeal of pain from the laager and Sean ran towards it.

In the centre of the ring of wagons stood Dirk. His face still darkly flushed with temper, and at his feet the tiny body of one of the unweaned puppies flopped and whimpered with its ribs stoved in from Dirk's kick.

In anger Sean had beaten Dirk, but even in his anger he had used a length of rope and not the viciously tapered *sjambok* of hippo hide. Then he had ordered Dirk to his living-wagon.

At noon he had sent for him and demanded an apology – and Dirk, uncrying, with lips and jaw set grimly, had refused it.

Sean beat him again, with the rope, but this time coldly – not for the sake of retribution. Dirk did not break.

Finally, in desperation Sean took the *sjambok* to him. For ten hissing strokes, each of which ended with a wicked snap across his buttocks, Dirk lay silently under the whip. His body convulsed slightly at each lash but he would not speak, and Sean beat him with a sickness in his own stomach and the sweat of shame and guilt running into his eyes, swinging the *sjambok* mechanically with his fingers clawed around the butt of it, and his mouth full of the slimy saliva of self-hatred.

When at last Dirk screamed, Sean dropped the *sjambok*, reeled back against the side of the wagon and leaned there gasping – fighting down the nausea which flooded acid-tasting up his throat.

Dirk screamed again and again, and Sean caught him up and held him to his chest.

'I'm sorry, Pa! I'm sorry. I'll never do it again, I promise you. I love you, I love you best of all – and I'll never do it again,' screamed Dirk, and they clung to each other.

For days thereafter not one of the servants had smiled at Sean nor spoken to him other than to acknowledge an order. For there was not one of them, including Mbejane, who would not steal and cheat and lie to ensure that Dirk Courtney had whatever he desired at the exact moment he desired it. They could hate anyone, including Sean, who denied it to him.

That was two weeks ago. And now, thought Sean watching that ugly mouth, do we do it all again?

Then suddenly Dirk smiled. It was one of those changes of mood that left Sean slightly bewildered, for when Dirk smiled his mouth came right. It was irresistible.

'I'll go, Dad.' Cheerfully, as though he was volunteering, he prodded the pony and trotted back towards the wagons.

'Cheeky little bugger!' gruffed Sean for Mbejane's benefit, but silently he queried his share of the blame. He had raised the boy with a wagon as his home and the veld as his schoolroom, grown men his companions and authority over them as his undisputed right of birth.

Since his mother had died five years before he had not known the gentling influence of a woman. No wonder he was a wild one.

Sean shied away from the memory of Dirk's mother. There was guilt there also, guilt that had taken him many years to reconcile. She was dead now. There was no profit in torturing himself. He pushed away the gloom that was swamping the happiness of a few minutes before, slapped the loose end of the reins against the horse's neck and urged it out on to the road – south towards the low line of hills upon the horizon, south towards Pretoria.

He's a wild one. But once we reach Ladyburg he'll be all right, Sean assured himself. They'll knock the nonsense out of him at school, and I'll knock manners into him at home. No, he'll be all right.

That evening, the third of December, 1899, Sean led his wagons down the hills and laagered them beside the Apies River. After they had eaten, Sean sent Dirk to his cot in the living wagon. Then he climbed alone to the crest of the hills and looked back across the land to the north. It was silver-grey in the moonlight, stretching away silent and immeasurable. That was the old life and abruptly he turned his back upon it and walked down towards the lights of the city which beckoned to him from the valley below.

Chapter Two

There had been a little unpleasantness when he had ordered Dirk to stay with the wagons; in consequence Sean was in an evil mood as he crossed the bridge on the Apies and rode into the city the following morning. Beside him Mbejane ran to keep pace with his horse.

Deep in his own thoughts Sean turned into Church Street before he noticed the unusual activity about him. A column of horsemen forced him to rein his horse to the side of the road. As they passed Sean examined them with interest.

Burghers in a motley of homespun and store clothes, riding in a formation which might imaginatively have been called a column of fours. But what excited Sean's curiosity was their numbers – By God! there must be two thousand of them at least, from lads to greybeards each of them was festooned with bandoliers of ammunition and beside each left knee the butt of a bolt-action Mauser rifle stuck up from its scabbard. Blanket-rolls tied to the saddles, canteens and cooking-pots clattering, they filed past. There was no doubting it. This was a war commando.

From the sidewalk women and a few men called comment at them.

'*Geluk boor!* Shoot straight.'

'*Spoedige terugkoms*.'

And the commandos laughed and shouted back. Sean stooped to a pretty girl who stood beside his horse. She was waving a red scarf and suddenly Sean saw that though she smiled her eyelashes were loaded with tears like dew on a blade of grass.

'Where are they going?' Sean raised his voice above the uproar.

She lifted her head and the movement loosed a tear; it dropped down her cheek, slid from her chin and left a tiny damp spot on her blouse.

'To the train, of course.'

'The train? Which train?'

'Look, here come the guns.'

In consternation Sean looked up as the guns rumbled past, two of them. Uniformed gunners in blue, frogged with gold, sitting stiffly to attention on the carriages, the horses leaning forward against the immense weight of the guns. Tall wheels shod with steel, bronze glittering on the breeches in contrast to the sombre grey of the barrels.

'My God!' breathed Sean. Then turning back to the girl he grasped her shoulder and shook it in his agitation. 'Where are they going? Tell me quickly – where?'

'*Menheer!*' She bridled at his touch and wriggled away from it.

'Please. I'm sorry – you must tell me.' Sean called after her as she disappeared into the crowd.

A minute longer Sean sat stupefied, then his brain began to work again. It was war, then. But where and against whom?

Surely no tribal rising would call out this array of strength. Those guns were the most modern weapons Sean could conceive.

No, this was a white man's war.

Against the Orange Republic? Impossible, they were brothers.

Against the British, then? The idea appalled him. And yet – and yet five years ago there had been rumours. It had happened before. He remembered 1895, and the Jameson Raid. Anything could have happened during the years he had been cut off from civilization – and now he had stumbled innocently into the midst of it.

Quickly he considered his own position. He was British. Born in Natal under the Union Jack. He looked like a burgher, spoke like one, rode like one, he was born in Africa and had never left it – but technically he was just as much an Englishman as if he had been born within sound of Bow bells.

Just supposing it was war between the Republic and Britain, and just supposing the Boers caught him – what would they do with him?

Confiscate his wagons and his ivory certainly, throw him into prison perhaps, shoot him as a spy possibly!

'I've got to get to hell out of here,' he mumbled, and then to Mbejane, 'Come on. Back to the wagons, quickly.' Before they reached the bridge he changed his mind. He had to learn with certainty what was happening. There was one person he could go to, and he must take the risk.

'Mbejane, go back to the camp. Find Nkosizana Dirk and keep him there – even if you have to tie him. Speak to no man and, as you value your life, let Dirk speak with no man. It is understood?'

'It is understood, Nkosi.'

And Sean, to all appearances another burgher among thousands of burghers, worked his way slowly through the crowds and the press of wagons towards a general dealer's store at the top end of the town near the railway station.

Since Sean had last seen it the sign above the entrance had been freshly painted in red and gold. 'I. Goldberg. Importer & Exporter, Dealing in Mining Machinery, Merchant & Wholesaler, Purchasing Agent: gold, precious stones, hides and skins, ivory and natural produce.'

Despite this war, or because of it, Mr Goldberg's emporium was doing good business. It was crowded and Sean drifted unnoticed among the customers, searching quietly for the proprietor.

He found him selling a bag of coffee beans to a gentleman who was plainly sceptical of its quality. The discussion of the merits of Mr Goldberg's coffee beans as opposed to those of his competitor across the street was becoming involved and technical.

Sean leaned against a shelf full of merchandise, packed his pipe, lit it and while he waited he watched Mr Goldberg in action. The man should have been a barrister, his argument was strong enough to convince first Sean and finally the customer. The latter paid, slung the bag over his shoulder and grumbled his way out of the shop, leaving Mr Goldberg glowing pink and perspiring in the flush of achievement.

'You haven't lost any weight, Izzy,' Sean greeted him.

Goldberg peered at him uncertainly over his gold-framed spectacles, beginning to smile until suddenly he recognized Sean. He blinked with shock, jerked his head in a gesture of invitation so his jowls wobbled, and disappeared into the back office. Sean followed him.

'Are you mad, Mr Courtney?' Goldberg was waiting for him, quivering with agitation. 'If they catch you . . .'

'Listen, Izzy. I arrived last night. I haven't spoken to a white man in four years. What the hell is going on here?'

'You haven't heard?'

'No, damn it, I haven't.'

'It's war, Mr Courtney.'

'I can see that. But where? Against whom?'

'On all the borders – Natal, the Cape.'

'Against?'

'The British Empire.' Goldberg shook his head as though he did not believe his own statement. 'We've taken on the whole British Empire.'

'We?' Sean asked sharply.

'The Transvaal Republic and the Orange Free State. Already we have won great victories – Ladysmith is besieged, Kimberley, Mafeking—'

'You, personally?'

'I was born here in Pretoria. I am a burgher.'

'Are you going to turn me in?'

'No, of course not. You've been a good customer of mine for years.'

'Thanks, Izzy. Look, I've got to get out of here as fast as I can.'

'It would be wise.'

'What about my money at the Volkskaas – can I get it out?'

Izzy shook his head sadly. 'They've frozen all enemy accounts.'

'Damn it, God damn it!' Sean swore bitterly, and then, 'Izzy, I've got twenty wagons and ten tons of ivory parked out there on the edge of town – are you interested?'

'How much?'

'Ten thousand for the lot; oxen, wagons, ivory – the lot.'

'It would not be patriotic, Mr Courtney,' Goldberg decided reluctantly. 'Trading with the enemy – besides I have only your word that it's ten tons.'

'Hell, Izzy, I'm not the British Army – that lot is worth twenty thousand quid.'

'You want me to buy sight unseen – no questions asked? All right. I'll give you four thousand – gold.'

'Seven.'

'Four and a half,' countered Izzy.

'You bastard.'

'Four and a half.'

'No, damn you. Five!' growled Sean.

'Five?'

'Five!'

'All right, five.'

'Thanks, Izzy.'

'Pleasure, Mr Courtney.'

Sean described the location of his laager hurriedly.

'You can send someone out to pick it up. I am going to run for the Natal border as soon as it's dark.'

'Keep off the roads and well clear of the railway. Joubert has thirty thousand men in Northern Natal, massed around Ladysmith and along the Tugela heights.' Goldberg went to the safe and fetched five small canvas bags from it. 'Do you want to check?'

'I'll trust you as you trusted me. Good-bye, Izzy.' Sean dropped the heavy bags down the front of his shirt and settle them under his belt.

'Good luck, Mr Courtney.'

Chapter Three

There were two hours of daylight left when Sean finished paying his servants. He pushed the tiny pile of sovereigns across the tailboard of the wagon towards the last man and went with him through the complicated ritual of farewell, the hand-clapping and clasping, the repetition of the formal phrases – then he stood up from his chair and looked around the circle. They squatted patiently, watching him with wooden black faces – but reflected back from them he could sense his own sorrow at this parting. Men with whom he had lived and worked and shared a hundred hardships. It was not easy to leave them now.

'It is finished,' he said.

'*Yebho*, it is finished.' They agreed in chorus and no one moved.

'Go, damn you.'

Slowly one of them stood and gathered the bundle of his possessions, a *kaross* (or skin blanket), two spears, a cast-off shirt that Sean had given him. He balanced the bundle on his head and looked at Sean.

'Nkosi!' he said and lifted a clenched fist in salute.

'Nonga,' Sean replied. The man turned away and trudged out of the laager.

'Nkosi!'

'Hlubi.'

'Nkosi!'

'Zama.'

A roll call of loyalty – Sean spoke their names for the last time, and singly they left the laager. Sean stood and watched them walk away in the dusk. Not one of them looked back and no two men walked together. It was finished.

Wearily Sean turned back to the laager. The horses were ready. Three with saddles, two carrying packs.

'We will eat first, Mbejane.'

'It is ready, Nkosi. Hlubi cooked before he went.'

'Come on, Dirk. Dinner.'

Dirk was the only one who spoke during the meal. He chattered gaily, wrought up with excitement by this new adventure, while Sean and Mbejane shovelled fat Hlubi's stew and hardly tasted it.

Out in the gathering darkness a jackal yelped, a lonely sound on the evening wind, fitting the mood of a man who had lost friends and fortune.

'It is time.' Sean shrugged into his sheepskin jacket and buttoned it as he stood to kick out the fire, but suddenly he froze and stood with his head cocked as he listened. There was a new sound on the wind.

'Horses!' Mbejane confirmed it.

'Quickly, Mbejane, my rifle.' The Zulu leapt up, ran to the horses and slipped Sean's rifle from its scabbard.

'Get out of the light and keep your mouth shut,' Sean ordered as he hustled Dirk into the shadows between the wagons. He grabbed the rifle from Mbejane and levered a cartridge into the breech and the three of them crouched and waited.

The click and roll of pebbles under hooves, the soft sound of a branch brushed aside.

'One only,' whispered Mbejane. A pack-horse whickered softly and was answered immediately from the darkness. Then silence, a long silence broken at last by the jingle of a bridle as the rider dismounted.

Sean saw him then, a slim figure emerging slowly out of the night and he swung the rifle to cover his approach. There was something unusual in the way the stranger moved, gracefully but with a sway from the hips, long-legged like a colt and Sean knew that he was young, very young to judge by his height.

With relief Sean straightened up from his crouch and examined him as he stopped uncertainly beside the fire and peered into the shadows. The lad wore a peaked cloth cap pulled down over his ears and his jacket was an expensive, honey-coloured chamois. His riding breeches were beautifully tailored and hugged his buttocks snugly. Sean decided that his backside was too big and out of proportion to the small feet clad in polished English hunting boots. A regular dandy, and the scorn was in Sean's tone as he called out.

'Stay where you are, friend, and state your business!'

The effect of Sean's challenge was unexpected. The lad jumped, the soles of his glossy boots cleared the ground by at least six inches, and when he landed again he was facing Sean.

'Talk up. I haven't got all night.'

The lad opened his mouth, closed it again, licked his lips and spoke.

'I was told you were going to Natal.' The voice was low and husky.

'Who told you that?' demanded Sean.

'My uncle.'

'Who is your uncle?'

'Isaac Goldberg.'

Sean digested this intelligence and while he did so he examined the face before him. Cleanshaven, pale, big dark eyes and a laughing kind of mouth that was now pursed with fright.

'And if I am?' Sean demanded.

'I want to go with you.'

'Forget it. Get back on your horse and go home.'

'I'll pay you – I'll pay you well.'

Was it the voice or the posture of the lad, Sean pondered, there was something very odd about him. He stood with a flat leather pouch held in both hands across the front of his hips – in an attitude of defence, as though he were protecting – protecting what? And suddenly Sean knew what it was.

'Take off your cap,' he ordered.

'No.'

'Take it off.'

A second longer the lad hesitated, then in a gesture that was almost defiance he jerked off the cap and two thick black braids of hair, shiny in the firelight, dropped and hung down almost to his waist and transformed him instantly from gawky masculinity into stunning womanhood.

Although he had guessed it, Sean was unprepared for the shock of this revelation. It was not so much her beauty, but her attire that caused the shock. Never in his life had Sean seen a woman in breeches, and now he gasped. Breeches, by God, she might as well be naked from the waist down – even that would be less indecent.

'Two hundred pounds—' She was coming towards him now, offering the pouch. At each step the cloth of the breeches tightened across her thighs and Sean dragged his eyes guiltily back to her face.

'Keep your money, lady.' Her eyes were grey, smoky grey.

'Two hundred on account, and as much again when we reach Natal.'

'I'm not interested.' But he was, those soft lips started to quiver.

'How much then? Name your price.'

'Look, lady. I'm not heading a procession. There are three of us already – one a child. There is hard riding ahead, plenty of it, and an army of Boers in between. Our chances are slim enough as it is. Another member to the party, and a woman at that, will make them prohibitive. I don't want your money, all I want is to get my son to safety. Go home and sit this war out – it won't last long.'

'I'm going to Natal.'

'Good. You go then – but not with us.' Sean could not trust himself longer to resist the appeal of those grey eyes and he turned to Mbejane. 'Horses,' he snapped and walked away from her. She stood watching him quietly as they mounted up, making no protest. She semed very small and alone as Sean looked down at her from the saddle.

'I'm sorry,' he growled. 'Go home now like a good girl,' and quickly he wheeled away and trotted out into the night.

All night they rode, east through the open moonlit land. Once they passed a darkened homestead and a dog barked, but they sheered away and then turned east again and held the great crucifix of the Southern Cross at their right-hand. When Dirk fell asleep in the saddle and slipped sideways, Sean caught him before he hit the ground, pulled him across into his lap and held him there for the rest of the night.

Before dawn they found a clump of bush on the bank of a stream, hobbled the horses and made camp. Mbejane had the billy-can boiling over a small well-screened fire and Sean had rolled Dirk unconscious into his blankets when the girl rode into camp and jumped down from her horse.

'I nearly lost you twice.' She laughed and pulled off the cap. 'Gave me a horrible fright.' She shook down the shiny braids. 'Coffee! Oh good, I'm famished.'

Menacingly Sean climbed to his feet and with clenched fists he glared at her, but undismayed she hobbled her horse and turned it loose before acknowledging him again.

'Don't stand on ceremony, please be seated.' And she grinned at him with such devilment in her grey eyes, aping so faithfully his stance with hands on those indecent hips, that Sean suddenly found himself smiling. He tried to stop it for he knew it was an admission of surrender, but his effort was so unsuccessful that she burst into delighted laughter.

'How's your cooking?' he demanded.

'So, so.'

'You'd better brush up on it because from now on you're working your passage.'

Later, when he had sampled it for the first time, he admitted grudgingly:

'Not bad – in the circumstances,' and wiped the plate with a crust of bread.

'You are too kind, sir.' She thanked him and lugged her blanket-roll into the shade, spread it, pulled off her boots, wriggled her toes and lay back with a sigh.

Sean positioned his own bedroll with care so that, when he opened his eyes, without turning his head he could watch her from under the brim of the hat that covered his face.

He woke at midday and saw that she slept with one cheek in her open hand, the lashes of her eyes meshed together and a few loose strands of dark hair across a face that was damp and flushed in the drowsy heat. He watched her for a long time before silently rising and crossing to his saddle-bags. When he went down to the stream he took with him his flat canvas toilet-bag, the remaining pair of breeches that were neither patched nor too badly stained and a clean silk shirt.

Sitting on a rock beside the water, naked and freshly scrubbed, he regarded his face in the polished steel mirror.

'A big job.' He sighed and started snipping at the great bush of beard which had not felt the scissors in three years.

At dusk, self-conscious as a girl in her first party dress, Sean walked back into the camp. They were all awake. Dirk and the girl sat together on her blanket in such earnest conversation that neither of them noticed his arrival. Mbejane was busy at the fire; he rocked back on his heels and examined Sean without change of expression.

'We'd better eat and get going.'

Dirk and the girl looked up. Her eyes narrowed and then widened thoughtfully.

Dirk gaped at him, and then, 'Your beard's all funny—' he announced, and the girl tried desperately to quell her laughter.

'Get your blankets rolled up, boy.'

Sean tried to break Dirk's grip on the subject, but like a bulldog Dirk held on relentlessly.

'—and why are you wearing your best clothes, Dad?'

Chapter Four

They rode three abreast in the darkness, Dirk between them and Mbejane trailing behind with the pack-horses. The land rose and fell beneath them like the swells of an endless sea and the way in which the grass moved with the night wind heightened the illusion of waves. Islands in the sea were the dark bulks of the kopjes they passed, and the yelp of a jackal was the voice of a seabird.

'Aren't we holding too far east?' The girl broke the silence and her voice blended with the soft sound of the wind.

'Intentionally,' Sean answered. 'I want to cross the tail of the Drakensberg well clear of the Boer concentrations around Ladysmith and the line of rail,' and he looked over Dirk's head at her. She rode with her face lifted to the sky.

'You know the stars?' he asked.

'A little.'

'So do I. I know them all.' Dirk accepted the challenge and swivelled towards the south. 'That's the Cross with the pointers, and that's Orion with his sword on his belt, and that's the Milky Way.'

'Tell me some others,' the girl invited.

'The others are just ordinary ones – they don't count. They haven't even got names.'

'Oh, but they have and most of them have got a story.'

There was a pause. Dirk was now in an invidious position; either he had to admit ignorance, and Dirk's pride was too large to swallow with ease, or else he would forgo what promised to be a choice series of stories. Large as was his pride, his appetite for stories was even larger.

'Tell me some,' he conceded.

'You see that little clump there underneath the big bright one? They are called the Seven Sisters. Well, once upon a time—'

Within minutes Dirk was completely absorbed. These were even better than Mbejane's stories – probably because they were new, while Dirk could recite from memory Mbejane's entire repertoire. He fell upon any weakness in the plot like a prosecuting attorney.

'But why didn't they just shoot the old witch?'

'They didn't have guns in those days.'

'They coulda used a bow and arrow.'

'You can't kill a witch with a bow and arrow. The arrow just goes – psst straight through her without hurting her.'

'Hangs teeth!' That was really impressive, but before accepting it Dirk found it necessary to corroborate with expert opinion. He checked with Mbejane, translating the problem to the Zulu. When Mbejane supported the girl Dirk was convinced, for Mbejane was a celebrated authority on the supernatural.

That night Dirk did not fall asleep in the saddle and when they camped before dawn the girl's voice was hoarse with overwork, but her conquest of Dirk was complete and that of Sean was well advanced.

All night while he listened to her voice and the husky bursts of laughter that punctuated it Sean had felt the seed that was planted at their first meeting sinking its roots down into his lower belly and loins, spreading its tendrils up through his chest. He wanted this woman so violently that in her presence his wits failed him. Many times during the night he had attempted to join the discussions, but each time Dirk had brushed his efforts aside with contempt and turned avidly back to the girl. By morning he had made the disturbing discovery that he was jealous of his own son – jealous of the attention Dirk was getting, and for which he hungered so strongly.

While they drank coffee after the morning meal lying on their blankets beneath a grove of syringa trees, Sean remarked:

'You haven't told us your name yet.' And of course it was Dirk that answered.

'She told me. Your name's Ruth – isn't it?'

'That's right, Dirk.'

With an effort Sean clamped down on the senseless anger that boiled up through him, but when he spoke his voice carried traces of it.

'We've heard enough from you for one night, my boy. Now get your head down, close your eyes and your mouth and keep them that way.'

'I'm not sleepy, Dad.'

'Do what I tell you.' Sean jumped up and strode out of the camp. He climbed the small kopje above them. By now it was full daylight and he searched the veld to the horizon on all sides. There was no trace of habitation or human. He climbed down again and fussed with the hobbles of the horses before returning to the grove of syringas.

Despite his protestations Dirk was curled like a sleeping puppy and, near the fire from a large bundle of blankets issued the unmistakable snoring of Mbejane. Ruth lay a little apart from them, a blanket thrown over her legs, her eyes closed and the front of her shirt rising and falling in a manner that gave Sean two good reasons for not sleeping. He lay propped on one elbow and fed his eyes and his imagination on her.

These four years past he had not seen a white woman, four years without the sound of a woman's voice or the comfort of her body. In the beginning it had worried him – the restlessness, the undirected fits of depression, and sudden bursts of temper. But gradually in the long days of hunting and riding, in the endless struggle with drought and storm, with beasts and the elements, he had brought his body under control. Women had faded into unreality, vague phantoms that plagued him only in the night so he twisted and sweated and cried out in his sleep until nature gave him release and the phantoms dispersed for a while to gather strength for their next visitation.

But this was no phantom that lay beside him now. By stretching out a hand he could stroke the faint down on her cheek and feel the blood-warm silk of her skin.

She opened her eyes, they were milky grey with sleep, slowly focusing until they levelled with his and returned his scrutiny.

Because of what she read there, she lifted her left hand from the blanket and held it out towards him. Her riding gloves were off. For the first time he noticed the slender gold ring that encircled her third finger.

'I see,' he muttered dully, and then in protest: 'But you are too young – you're too young to be married.'

'I'm twenty-two years old,' she told him softly.

'Your husband – where is he?' Perhaps the bastard was dead, his one last hope.

'I am going to him now. When war seemed inevitable he went to Natal, to Durban, to find a job and a home for us there. I was to follow him – but the war came earlier than we expected. I was stranded.'

'I see.' I am taking you to another man, he thought with bitterness, and put it in different words. 'So he is sitting in Durban waiting for you to make your own way through the lines.'

'He is with the army of Natal. A week ago he got a message through to me. He wanted me to stay on in Johannesburg and wait until the British capture the city. He says that with so great a force they will be in Johannesburg within three months.'

'Why didn't you wait, then?'

She shrugged. 'Patience is not one of my virtues,' and then the devilment was in her eyes again. 'Besides, I thought it would be fun to run away – it was so terribly dull in Johannesburg.'

'Do you love him?' he demanded suddenly. The question startled her and the smile died on her lips.

'He's my husband.'

'That doesn't answer my question.'

'It was a question you had no right to ask.' She was angry now.

'You have to tell me.'

'Do you love your wife?' she snapped at him.

'I did. She's been dead five years.' And her anger flickered out as swiftly as it had blazed.

'Oh, I'm sorry. I didn't know.'

'Forget it. Forget I ever asked.'

'Yes, that's best. We are getting into an awful tangle.' Her hand with the ring upon it was still held out towards him, lying between them on the soft carpet of fallen leaves. He reached out and lifted it. It was a small hand.

'Mr Courtney – Sean, it's best if – we mustn't – I think we'd better sleep now.' And she withdrew the hand and rolled away from him.

The wind woke them in the middle of the afternoon, it roared in from the east, flattening the grass on the hills and thrashing the branches above their heads.

Sean looked up at the sky with the wind fluttering his shirt and ruffling his beard. He leaned forward against it, towering over Ruth so that suddenly she realized how big he was. He looked like a god of the storm, with long powerful legs braced apart and the muscles of his chest and arms standing out proudly beneath the white silk of his shirt.

'Clouds building up,' Sean shouted above the rush of the wind. 'No moon tonight.'

She stood up quickly and a sudden violent gust threw her off balance. She staggered against him and his arms closed about her. For a moment she was pressed to his chest, could feel the lean, rubbery resilience of his body and smell the man smell of it. It was a shock for both of them, this unexpectedly intimate contact and when she broke away her eyes were wide and grey with fear of the thing she had felt stir within her.

'I'm sorry,' she whispered. 'That was an accident.' And the wind caught her hair and streamed it across her face in a dancing, snapping black tangle.

'We'll upsaddle and ride with the daylight that is left,' Sean decided. 'We won't be able to move tonight.'

The clouds rolled in on the wind, spreading upon themselves, changing shape and dropping closer to the earth. Clouds the colour of smoke and bruises, heavy with the rain they carried.

The night came early, but still the wind roared and buffeted them in the gloom.

'It will drop in an hour or so, then we'll get the rain. We'll try and find shelter while there's still light enough to see.'

On the reverse slope of a kopje they found an overhang of rock and offloaded the packs beneath it. While Sean pegged the horses out on their head ropes to prevent them walking away before the storm, Mbejane cut grass and piled it into a mattress on the rock floor beneath the overhang. Huddled in their oilskins they ate biltong and cold mealie bread and afterwards Mbejane withdrew discreetly to the far end of the shelter and disappeared under his blankets. He had that animal knack of being able to sleep instantly and completely even under the most adverse conditions.

'All right, boy. Get into your blankets.'

'Can't I just . . .' Dirk began his nightly protest.

'No, you can't.'

'I'll sing for you,' Ruth offered.

'What for?' Dirk was puzzled.

'A sleepy-time song – haven't you ever had a lullaby?'

'No.' But Dirk was intrigued. 'What you going to sing?'

'Into your blankets first.'

Sitting beside Sean in the darkness, very conscious of his bulk and the touch of his shoulder against hers, the muted roar of the wind as her accompaniment – Ruth sang.

First the old Dutch folksongs, 'Nooi, Nooi' and 'Jannie met die Hoepel been', then other old favourites like 'Frère Jacques'. Her voice meant something to each of them.

Mbejane woke to the sound of it and made him remember the wind on the hills of Zululand and the singing of the young girls in the fields at harvest-time. It made him glad he was going home.

To Dirk it was the voice of the mother he had hardly known. A safe sound – and soon he slept.

'Don't stop,' whispered Sean.

So she sang for him alone. A love-song from two thousand years ago, filled with all the suffering of her people, but with joy in it also. The wind died away while she sang and her voice died away with it into the vast silence of the night.

The storm broke. The first thunder crashed and the lightning forked jagged-blue through the clouds. Dirk whimpered a little but slept on.

In the stark, blue light Sean saw that Ruth's cheeks were wet with tears and when the darkness closed around them again she started to tremble against him. He reached out for her and she clung to him, small and warm against his chest, and he could taste the salt of her tears on his lips.

'Sean, we mustn't.'

But he lifted her and held her across his chest as he walked out into the night. The lightning blazed again and lit the land with startling brilliance so he could see the horses huddling heads down, and the crisp outline of the kopje above them.

The first raindrops splashed against his shoulders and into his face. The rain was warm and he walked on carrying Ruth. Then the air was filled with rain, an encompassing pearly mist of it in the next flash of lightning, and the night was filled with the odour of rain on dry earth – a clean warm smell.

Chapter Five

In a still morning, washed so clean by the rain that they could see the mountains, blue and sharp on the southern horizon, they stood together on the crest of the kopje.

'That's the tail of the Drakensberg, we've cleared it by twenty miles. There's very little chance of a Boer patrol this far out. We can ride by day now. Soon we'll be able to work in again and meet the railway beyond the battle lines.'

Because of the beauty of the morning, of the land that dripped away into the great, grassy bowl that was Natal, and of the woman that stood beside him, Sean was gay.

Because of the promise of an end to the journey and the promise of a new one with this woman as his companion, he was content.

When he spoke she turned slowly to look up at him, her chin lifting in acknowledgement of his superior height. For the first time Sean realized that his own mood was not reflected in her eyes.

'You are very lovely,' he said, and still she remained silent, but now he could recognize the shadows in her eyes as sorrow or something even stronger.

'Ruth, you'll come with me?'

'No.' She shook her head slowly, regretfully. The fat black python of hair rolled across her shoulder and hung down against the honey chamois leather of her jacket.

'You must.'

'I cannot.'

'But, last night.'

'Last night was madness ... the storm.'

'It was right. You know that.'

'No. It was the storm.' She looked away from him towards the sky. 'And now the storm is ended.'

'It was more than that. You know it. It was from the first moment of our meeting.'

'It was a madness based upon deceit. Something that I will have to cover with lies – the way we had to cover it with darkness at the time.'

'Ruth. My God, don't talk about it like that.'

'Very well, I won't. I won't talk about it again, ever.'

'We can't leave it now. You know we can't.'

And in answer she held up her left hand so that the gold upon it caught the sun.

'We'll say good-bye here on a mountain in the sunlight. Though we'll ride together a little farther – it's here we'll say good-bye.'

'Ruth . . .' he started, but she placed the hand across his mouth and he felt the metal of the ring on his lips and it seemed to him that the ring was as cold as his dread of the loss she was about to inflict upon him.

'No,' she whispered. 'Kiss me once more and then let me go.'

Chapter Six

Mbejane saw it first and spoke quietly to Sean, perhaps two miles out on their flank, like a smudge of brown smoke rising beyond the fold of the nearest ridge, so faint that Sean had to search a moment before he found it. Then he swivelled away from it and hunted frantically for cover. The nearest was an outcrop of red stone half a mile away, much too far.

'What is it, Sean?' Ruth noticed his agitation.

'Dust,' he gold her. 'Horsemen. Coming this way.'

'Boers?'

'Probably.'

'What are we to do?'

'Nothing.'

'Nothing?'

'When they show on the ridge I'll ride to meet them. Try to bluff our way through.' He turned to Mbejane and spoke in Zulu. 'I will go to them. Watch me carefully, but keep moving away. If I lift my arm let the pack-horses go and ride. I will hold them as long as I can, but when I lift my arm then it is finished.' Quickly he unbuckled the saddle-bag which held the gold and handed it to the Zulu. 'With a good start you should be able to hold them off until nightfall. Take the Nkosikazi where she wishes to go and then with Dirk return to my mother at Ladyburg.'

He looked again at the ridge just in time to see two horsemen appear upon it. Sean lifted the binoculars from his chest; in the round field of the glasses the two riders stood broadside, their faces turned towards him so he could make out the shape of their helmets. He saw the burnished sparkle of their accoutrements, the size of their mounts and their distinctive saddlery and he yelled with relief.

'Soldiers!'

As if in confirmation a squadron of cavalry in two neat ranks broke over the skyline with the pennants fluttering gaily on the forest of their lances.

Dirk hooting with excitement, Ruth laughing beside him and Mbejane dragging the pack-horses after them, Sean galloped standing in the stirrups and waving his hat above his head to meet them.

Unaffected by the enthusiasm of the welcome the lancers sat stolidly and watched them come and the subaltern at their head greeted Sean suspiciously as he arrived.

'Who are you, sir?' But he seemed less interested in Sean's reply than in Ruth's breeches and what they contained. During the explanations that followed Sean conceived for the man a growing dislike. Although the smooth, sun-reddened skin and the fluffy, yellow moustache aggravated this feeling, the central cause was the pair of pale blue eyes. Perhaps they always popped out that way, but Sean doubted it. They focused steadily on Sean only during the short period when Sean reported that he had made no contact with the Boer, then they swivelled back to Ruth.

'We'll not detain you longer, Lieutenant,' Sean grunted and gathered his reins to turn away.

'You are still ten miles from the Tugela River, Mr Courtney. Theoretically this area is held by the Boers and although we are well out on the flank of their main army it would be much safer if you entered the British lines under our protection.'

'Thank you, no. I want to avoid both armies and reach Pietermaritzburg as soon as possible.' The subaltern shrugged. 'The choice is yours. But if it were my wife and child . . .' He did not finish, but turned in the saddle to signal the column forward.

'Come on, Ruth.' Sean caught her eye, but she did not move.

'I'm not going with you.' There was a flat quality in her voice and she looked away from him.

'Don't be silly.' It shocked him and gave his reply a harshness that lit sparks of anger in her eyes.

'May I travel with you?' she demanded of the subaltern.

'Well, ma'am.' he hesitated, glancing quickly at Sean before he went on. 'If your husband . . .'

'He's not my husband. I hardly know him.' She cut in and ignored the exclamation of protest from Sean. 'My husband is with your army. I want you to take me with you, please.'

'Well, now . . .! That's a horse of another colour,' the officer drawled, but the lazy arrogance of his tone barely concealed his pleasure at the prospect of Ruth's company. 'I'd be delighted to escort you, ma'am.'

With her knees Ruth backed her mount and fell in beside the subaltern. This small manoeuvre placed her directly facing Sean – as though she were on the far side of a barrier.

'Ruth, please. Let me talk to you about this. Just a few minutes.'

'No.' There was no expression in her voice, nor in her face.

'Just to say good-bye,' he pleaded.

'We've said good-bye.' She glanced from Sean to Dirk and then away.

The subaltern raised his clenched fist high and lifted his voice. 'Column! Column, Forward!' and as his big, glossy hunter started he grinned maliciously at Sean and touched the brim of his helmet in ironical salute.

'Ruth!'

But she was no longer looking at Sean. Her eyes were fixed ahead and as she swept away at the head of the column her chin was up, that smiling type of mouth was drawn into two straight lips and the thick braid of hair thumped against her back with each thrust of the horse beneath her.

'Rough luck, matey!' called a trooper from the rear rank and then they were past.

Hunched in the saddle Sean stared after them.

'Is she coming back, Pa?' Dirk inquired.

'No, she's not coming back.'

'Why not?'

Sean did not hear the question. He was watching, waiting for Ruth to look back at him. But he waited in vain, for suddenly she was gone over and beyond the next fold in the land and a few seconds later the column had followed her. Afterwards there was only the vast emptiness of the land and the sky above – as vast as the emptiness within him.

Chapter Seven

Sean rode ahead. Ten yards behind they followed, Mbejane restraining Dirk from a closer approach for he understood that Sean must now be left alone. Many times in the years they had been together Mbejane and Sean had travelled in this formation – Sean riding ahead with his sorrow or his shame and Mbejane trailing him patiently, waiting for Sean's shoulders to straighten and his chin to lift from where it dropped forward on his chest.

There was no coherence in Sean's thoughts, the only pattern was the rise and swoop of alternate anger and despair.

Anger at the woman, anger almost becoming hatred before the plunge of despair as he remembered she was gone. Then anger building up towards madness, this time directed at himself for letting her go. Again the sickening drop as he realized that there was no means by which he could have held her. What could he have offered her? Himself? Two hundred pounds of muscle and bones and scars supporting a face like a granite cliff? Poor value! His wordly goods? A small sack of sovereigns and another woman's child – By God, that was all he had. After thirty-seven years that was all he had to show! Once more his anger flared. A week ago he had been rich – and his anger found a new target. There was at least somewhere he could seek vengeance, there was a tangible enemy to strike, to kill. The Boer. The Boer had robbed him of his wagons and his gold, had sent him scurrying for safety; because of them the woman had come into his life and because of them she had been snatched away from him.

So be it, he thought angrily, this then is the promise of the future. War!

He straightened in his saddle, his shoulders seemed to fill out wide and square. He lifted his head and saw the shiny snake of a river in the valley below. They had reached the Tugela. Without pause Sean pushed his horse over the lip of the escarpment. On its haunches, loose rock rolling and slithering beneath its hooves, they began the descent.

Impatiently Sean followed the river downstream, searching for a drift.

But between the sheer banks it ran smooth and swift and deep, twenty yards wide and still discoloured with mud from the storm.

At the first place where the far bank flattened sufficiently to promise an easy exit from the water, Sean checked his horse and spoke brusquely.

'We'll swim.'

In reply Mbejane glanced significantly at Dirk.

'He's done this before,' Sean answered him as he dismounted and began to shed his clothing, then to the boy, 'Come on, Dirk. Get undressed.'

They drove the pack-horses in first, forcing them to jump from the steep bank and watched anxiously until their heads reappeared above the surface and they struck out for the far bank. Then all three of them naked, their clothing wrapped in oilskins and lashed to the saddles, they remounted.

'You first, Mbejane.'

A splash that rose above the bank.

'Off you go, Dirk. Remember to hang on to the saddle.'

Another high splash, and Sean flogged his mount as it baulked and danced sideways along the bank. A sudden lunge outwards and the long drop before the water closed over them.

Snorting water, they surfaced and with relief Sean saw Dirk's head bobbing beside that of his horse and heard his shouted excitement. Moments later they stood on the far bank, water streaming from their naked bodies, and laughed together at the fun of it.

Abruptly the laughter was strangled to death in Sean's throat. Lining the bank above them, grinning with the infection of merriment but with Mauser rifles held ready, stood a dozen men. Big men, bearded, festooned with bandoliers of ammunition, dressed in rough clothing and a selection of hats that included a brown derby and a tall beaver.

In imitation of Sean, both Mbejane and Dirk stopped laughing and stared up at the frieze of armed men along the bank. A complete silence fell on the gathering.

It was broken at last by the man in the brown derby as he pointed at Sean with the barrel of his Mauser.

'*Magtig!* But you'd need a sharp axe to cut through that branch.'

'Don't anger him,' warned the gentleman in the beaver. 'If he hits you over the head with it, it will crack your skull!' and they all laughed.

It was hard for Sean to decide which was the more discomforting; the intimate discussion of his nudity, or the fact that the discussion was conducted in the Taal (or Cape Dutch). In his impatience he had walked, or rather swum, into the arms of a Boer patrol. There was just a forlorn hope that he might be able to bluff his way through, and he opened his mouth to make the attempt. But Dirk forestalled him.

'Who are they, Pa, and why are they laughing?' he asked in clear piping English, and Sean's hope died as abruptly as did the Boer laughter when they heard that hated language.

'Oh! So!' growled the man in the beaver, and gestured eloquently with his Mauser. 'Hands up please, my friend.'

'Will you allow me to put my trousers on first?' Sean asked politely.

'Where are they taking us?' For once Dirk was subdued and there was a quiver in his voice that touched Beaver, who rode beside him. He answered for Sean.

'Now don't you worry, you're going to see a general. A real live general.' Beaver's English was intelligible and Dirk studied him with interest.

'Will he have medals and things?'

'*Nee*, man. We don't use such rubbish.' And Dirk lost interest. He turned back to Sean.

'Pa, I'm hungry.'

Again Beaver intervened. He pulled a long black stick of biltong, dried meat, from his pocket and offered it to Dirk.

'Sharpen your teeth on that, *Kerel*.'

With his mouth full Dirk was taken care of and Sean could concentrate on the other Boers. They were convinced they had caught a spy, and were discussing the impending execution. In a friendly manner Sean was admitted to the argument, and they listened with respectful attention to his defence. This was interrupted while they forded the Tugela and climbed the escarpment once more, but Sean continued it while they rode in a bunch along the crest. Finally, he convinced them of his innocence – which they accepted with relief, as none of them were really looking forward to shooting him.

Thereafter the talk turned to more pleasant topics. It was a glorious day, sunshine lit the valley in gold and green. Below them the river twisted and sparkled, working its devious way down from the smoky blue wall of the Drakensberg that stood along the far horizon. A few fat clouds dawdled across the sky, and a light breeze took the edge off the heat.

The youngsters in the party listened avidly as Sean spoke of elephant beyond the Limpopo, and of the wide land that waited for men to claim it.

'After the war . . .' they said, and laughed in the sun. Then a change in the wind and a freak lie of the hills brought a faint but ugly sound down to them and the laughter died.

'The guns,' said one of them.

'Ladysmith.'

Now it was Sean's turn to ask the questions. They told him how the commandos had raced down on the town of Ladysmith and rolled up the force that stood to oppose them. Bitterly they remembered how old Joubert had held his horsemen and watched while the broken English army streamed back into the town.

'Almighty! Had he loosed us on them then! We would sweep them into the sea.'

'If Oom Paul had commanded instead of old Joubert, the war would be finished already – but instead we sit and wait.'

Gradually Sean filled in the picture of the war in Natal. Ladysmith was invested. General George White's army was bottled and corked within the town. Half the Boer army had moved forward along the railway and taken up a defensive line straddling the Escarpment, overlooking the river and the tiny village of Colenso.

Below them on the great plain of the Tugela, General Buller was massing his army for the breakthrough to relieve Ladysmith.

'But let him try – Oom Paul is waiting for him.'

'Who is Oom Paul – Surely not Kruger?' Sean was puzzled. Oom Paul was the affectionate nickname of the President of the South African Republic.

'*Nee*, man! This is another Oom Paul. This one is Vecht-General Jan Paulus Leroux of the Wynberg commando.' And Sean caught his breath.

'Is he a big man with red hair and a temper to go with it?'

Laughter, and then. '*Ja!* that's the one. Do you know him?'

'Yes. I know him.'

So my brother-in-law is now a general, Sean grinned to himself, and then asked:

'Is this the general we are going to visit?'

'If we can find him.'

Young Dirk will meet his uncle at last – and Sean found himself anticipating the reunion with a tingle of pleasure.

Chapter Eight

The canvas of the tent did little to moderate the volume of the voice within. It carried clearly to where Sean waited with his escort.

'Must I drink coffee and shake hands with ever *rooinek* we catch? Have I not already enough work for ten men, but you must bring me more? Send him to one of the Field-Cornets! Send him to Pretoria and let them lock him up! Do whatever you like with him if he is a spy – but, in the name of a merciful providence, don't bring him to me.'

Sean smiled happily. Jan Paulus certainly hadn't lost his voice. There was an interval of comparative quiet while Beaver's voice mumbled within the tent. Then again the muted bellow.

'No! I will not! Take him away.'

Sean filled his lungs, cupped his hands about his mouth and shouted at the tent.

'Hey, you bloody Dutchman! Are you afraid to meet me again? You think I'll knock your teeth out like I did last time.'

A few moments of appalling stillness, then the clattering of an overturned stool and the flap of the tent was thrown open. Into the sunlight, blinking in the glare, but scowling, the red hair that fringed his bald plate burning like a bush-fire, and his shoulders hunched aggressively, came Jan Paulus. His face turned from side to side as he searched for the source of the insult.

'Here,' called Sean, and Jan Paulus stopped dead. Uncertainly he peered at Sean.

'You!' He took a pace forward and then, 'It is you, isn't it. Sean!' And he began to laugh. His right hand that had been clenched into a huge fist unfolded and was thrust forward.

'Sean! Hell, man! Sean!'

They gripped hands and grinned at each other.

'Come into the tent. Come on in, man.'

Once they were inside, Jan Paulus's first question was:

'Where's Katrina? Where is my little sister?' and immediately the smile was gone from Sean's face. He sat down heavily on the *reimpje* stool and took off his hat before he answered.

'She's dead, Paulus. She's been dead these last four years.'

Slowly the expression on Jan Paulus's face changed until it was bleak and hard.

'How?' he asked.

And what can I answer him, thought Sean. Can I tell him she killed herself for some reason that no one will ever know.

'Fever,' he said. 'Blackwater fever.'

'You did not send word to us.'

'I did not know where to find you. Your parents—'

'They too are dead,' Jan Paulus interrupted brusquely and turned away from Sean to stare at the white canvas wall of the tent. There was silence between them then as they remembered the dead in sorrow, made more poignant by its utter helplessness. At last Sean stood up and went to the entrance of the tent.

'Dirk. Come here.'

Mbejane pushed him forward and he crossed to Sean and took his hand. Sean led him into the tent.

'Katrina's son,' he said and Jan Paulus looked down at him.

'Come here, boy.' Hesitantly Dirk went to him. Suddenly Jan Paulus dropped into a squat so that his eyes were on a level with those of the child. He took Dirk's face between the palms of his hands and studied it carefully.

'Yes,' he said. 'This is the type of son she would breed. The eyes—' His voice stumbled and stopped. A second longer he looked into Dirk's eyes. Then he spoke again.

'Be proud,' he said and stood up. Sean motioned at the flap of the tent, and thankfully Dirk scampered out to where Mbejane waited.

'And now?' Jan Paulus asked.

'I want passage through the lines.'

'You are going over to the English?'

'I am English,' said Sean. Frowning a little, Jan Paulus considered this before he asked:

'You will give me your word not to take up arms with them?'

'No,' answered Sean and Jan Paulus nodded, it was the answer he had expected.

'There is a debt between us,' he decided. 'I have not forgotten the time of the elephant. This is full payment of that debt.' He crossed to the portable desk and dipped a pen. Still standing he wrote rapidly, fanned the paper dry and proffered it to Sean.

'Go,' he said. 'And I hope we do not meet again, for next time I will kill you.'

'Or I you,' Sean answered him.

Chapter Nine

That afternoon Sean led his party across the steel railway bridge over the Tugela, on through the deserted village of Colenso and out again across the plain. Far ahead, sown on the grass plain like a field of white daisies, were the tents of the great British encampment at Chievely Siding. But long before he reached it Sean came to a guard post manned by a sergeant and four men of an illustrious Yorkshire regiment.

"Ullo, Piet. And where the hell do you think you're off to?"

'I am a British subject,' Sean informed them. The sergeant ran an eye over Sean's beard and patched coat. He glanced at the shaggy pony he rode, and then considered the direction from which Sean had approached.

'Say that again,' he invited.

'I am a British subject,' Sean repeated obligingly in an accent that fell heavily on the Yorkshireman's ear.

'And I'm a ruddy Japanee,' agreed the sergeant cheerfully. 'Let's have your rifle, mate.'

Two days Sean languished in the barbed-wire prison compound while the Intelligence Department cabled the Registrar of Births at Ladyburg and waited for his reply. Two long days during which Sean brooded incessantly, not on the indignities which had been inflicted on him, but on the woman he had found and loved and lost again so quickly. These two days of enforced inactivity came at precisely the worst moment. By repeating over and over in his imagination each word that had passed between them, by feeling again each contact of their hands and bodies, by forming her face in his mind's eye and gloating over every detail of it – Sean burned her memory so deeply into himself that it was there for all time. Although he did not even know her surname, he would never forget her.

By the time he was released with apologies and given back his horses, rifle, moneybag and packs – Sean had driven himself into a mood of such overpowering depression that it could only be alleviated by liquor or physical violence.

The village of Frere, which was the first station south on the line to the coast, promised both of these.

'Take Dirk with you,' instructed Sean, 'beyond the town find a camp beside the road and make a big fire, so I can find you in the dark.'

'What will you do, Nkosi?'

Sean started towards the dingy little canteen that catered for the thirsty of Frere.

'I'm going there,' he answered.

'Come, Nkosizana.' As he and Dirk continued on down the street Mbejane was deciding how long he should give Sean before coming to fetch him. It was many years since the Nkosi had headed for a bar in such a determined fashion, but then there had been much to distress him these last few days. He will need until midnight, Mbejane decided, then he will be in a condition conducive to sleep.

From the door Sean surveyed the interior of the canteen. A single large room with a trestle bar counter along the back wall, and the room was comfortably full of warmth and men and the smell of liquor and cigars. Still standing in the entrance, Sean slipped his hand into the pocket of his trousers and surreptitiously counted his money – ten sovereigns he had allowed himself, more than sufficient for the purchase of the liquor he intended to consume.

As he worked his way through the crowd towards the bar, he looked at the men about him. Soldiers mostly, from a dozen different regiments. Colonials and Imperial troops, other ranks predominating, although a party of junior officers sat at a table against the far wall. Then there were a few civilians whom he judged to be transport drivers, contractors and business men, two women with the officers whose profession was never in doubt, and a dozen black waiters.

'What will it be, ducks?' the large woman behind the counter asked as he reached it and Sean regarded her moustache and her term of address with disfavour.

'Brandy.' He was in no mood for the niceties.

'You want the bottle, ducks?' She had recognized his need.

'That will do for a start,' he agreed.

He drank three large brandies, and with a faint dismay knew that they were having no effect – apart from sharpening his imagination to the point where he could clearly see Ruth's face before his eyes, complete in every detail down to the little black beauty spot high on her cheek and the way the corners of her eyes slanted upwards as she smiled. He would have to make a more active approach to forgetfulness.

Leaning back with both elbows on the counter and the glass clutched in his right hand, he studied the men about him once more. Evaluating each of them as a source of distraction and then discarding and moving his attention on, he was finally left with the small group around the gaming-table.

Seven players, the game draw poker, and from what he could see the stakes were modest. He picked up his bottle, crossed the room to join the circle of spectators and took up his position behind a sergeant of yeomanry who was receiving a battering from the cards. A few hands later the sergeant drew one to fill his flush, missed and pushed the bluff – raising twice until he was called by two pairs across the table. He threw his hand in and blew through his lips in disgust.

'That cleans me out.' He gathered the few coins left on the table in front of him and stoop up.

'Rough luck, Jack. Anyone care to take his place?' The winner looked around the circle of spectators. 'Nice friendly little game, table stakes.'

'Deal me in.' Sean sat down, placed his glass and bottle strategically at his right hand and stacked five gold sovereigns in front of him.

'The man's got gold! Welcome.'

Sean ducked the first hand, lost two pounds to three queens on the next, and won five pounds on the third. The pattern of his luck was set, he played with cold single-mindedness – and when he wanted cards it seemed he had only to wish for them.

What was the old adage? – 'Unlucky in love, and the cards turn hot.' Sean grinned without amusement and filled a small straight with the five of hearts, beat down the three sevens that came against him and drew the pot towards him to swell the pile of his winnings. Up about thirty or forty pounds. He was enjoying himself now.

'A small school, gentlemen.' Three players had dropped out in the last hour leaving four of them at the table. 'How about giving the losers a chance to recoup?'

'You want to raise the stakes?' Sean asked the speaker. He was the only other winner, a big man with a red face and the smell of horses about him. Transport rider, probably.

'Yes, if everyone agrees. Make the minimum bet five pounds.'

'Suits me,' grunted Sean, and there was a murmur of agreement round the table. With heavy money out an air of caution prevailed at first, but slowly the game opened up. Sean's luck cooled a little, but an hour later he had built up his kitty on a series of small wins to a total of seventy-five pounds. Then Sean dealt a strange hand.

The first caller on Sean's left raised before the draw, and was raised in turn by the gentleman with the horsy smell, number three called and Sean fanned his cards open.

With a gentle elation he found the seven, eight, nine and ten of Clubs – with a Diamond six. A pretty little straight dealt pat.

'Call your twenty, and raise it twenty,' he offered, and there was a small stir of excitement among the onlookers.

'Call.' Number one was short of cash.

'Call,' echoed Horse Odour and his gold clinked into the pot.

'I'm dropping.' Number three closed his cards and pushed them away. Sean turned back to number one.

'How many cards?'

'I'll play with these.' Sean felt the first premonition of disaster.

'And you?' he asked Horse Odour.

'I'm also happy with what I have.'

Two pat hands against his small straight; and from the suit distribution, Sean's four Clubs, one of them would certainly be a flush. With a queasy feeling in his stomach Sean knew he was in trouble, knew his hand to be a loser.

Break the straight and go for the other Club, still not a certain winner, but the only thing worth trying.

'I'll draw one.' He tossed the six of Diamonds into the welter of discards, and dealt to himself from the top of the pack.

'My bet.' Number one's face was glowing with confidence. 'I'll raise the maximum – another forty. Cost you eighty pounds to look at me, boys. Let's see the colour of your money.'

'I'd like to push you – but that's the limit. I'll call.' Horse Odour's expression was completely neutral but he was sweating in a light sheen across his forehead.

'Let me go to the books.' Sean picked up his cards and, from behind the other four, pressed out the corner of the card he had drawn. It was black, he opened it a little more – a black six. Slowly he felt the pressure build up within him like a freshly fired boiler. He drew a long breath and opened the card fully.

'I'll call also.' He spoke on a gusty outgoing breath.

'Full house,' shouted number one. 'Queen's full – beat that, you bastards!'

Horse Odour slapped his cards down viciously, his red face crumbling in disappointment. 'Goddam it – of all the filthy luck. I had an ace-high flush.' Number one giggled with excitement and reached for the money.

'Wait for it, friend,' Sean advised him, and spread his cards face up upon the table.

'It's a flush. My full house beats you,' protested number one.

'Count the pips—' Sean touched each card as he named them, 'six, seven, eight, nine and the ten – all Clubs. Straight flush! You come second by a day's march.' He lifted number one's hands off the money, pulled it towards him and began stacking it in columns of twenty.

'Pretty hot run of luck you're having,' Horse Odour gave his opinion, his face still twisted with disappointment.

'Yes,' agreed Sean. Two hundred and sixty-eight pounds. Very pretty.

'Funny how it comes to you on the big hands,' Horse Odour went on. 'And especially when you're dealing. What did you say your profession was?'

Without looking up Sean began transferring the stacks of sovereigns to his pockets. He was smiling a little. The end to a perfect evening, he decided.

Satisfied that the money was secure Sean looked up at Horse Odour and turned that smile full upon him.

'Come along then, laddie,' he said.

'It will be a pleasure.' Horse Odour shoved his chair back and stood up.

'It will indeed,' agreed Sean.

Horse Odour led down the back-stairs into the yard, followed by Sean and the entire clientèle of the canteen. At the bottom he paused, judging Sean's footstep on the wooden stairs behind him – then he spun and hit, swinging his body into the punch.

Sean rolled his head, but it caught him on the temple and he went over backwards into the crowd behind him. As he fell he saw Horse Odour jerk back the tail of his jacket and bring out the knife. It shone dull silver in the light from the canteen windows – skinning knife, curved, eight inches of blade.

The crowd scattered leaving Sean lying on the stairs, and Horse Odour came in to kill him, making an ugly sound, bringing the knife arching down from overhead, a clumsy, unprofessional blow.

Only slightly stunned, Sean followed the silver sweep of the knife with ease and the man's wrist slapped loudly into Sean's open left hand.

For a long moment the man lay on top of Sean, his knife-arm helpless in Sean's grip, while Sean assessed his strength – and with regret realized it was no match. Horse Odour was big enough, but the belly pressed against

Sean's was flabby and large, and the wrist in Sean's hands was bony without the hard rubbery give of sinew and muscle.

Horse Odour started to struggle, trying to wrestle his knife-arm free, the sweat dewed on his face and then began to drip – it had an oily, unpleasant smell like rancid butter that blended poorly with the odour of horses.

Sean tightened his grip on the man's wrist, at first using only the strength of his forearm.

'Aah!' Horse Odour stopped struggling. Sean brought in the power of his whole arm, so he could feel his shoulder muscles bunching and writhing.

'Jesus Christ!' Shrieking, as bone cracked in his wrist, Horse Odour's fingers sprang open and the knife thumped on to the wooden stairs.

Still holding him, Sean sat up, then came slowly to his feet.

'Leave us, friend.' Sean flung him backwards into the dust of the yard. He was breathing easily, still feeling cold and detached as he looked down and watched Horse Odour scrabbling to his knees, nursing his broken wrist.

Perhaps it was the man's first movement towards flight that triggered Sean – or perhaps it was the liquor he had drunk that twisted his emotions, aggravated his sense of loss and frustration and channelled it into this insane outburst of hatred.

Suddenly it seemed to Sean that here before him on the ground was the source of all his ills – this was the man who had taken Ruth from him.

'You bastard!' he growled. The man sensed the change in Sean and scrambled to his feet, his face turning desperately from side to side as he sought an avenue of escape.

'You filthy bastard!' Sean's voice rose, shrill with the strength of this new emotion. For the first time in his life Sean craved to kill. He advanced upon the man slowly, his fists opening and closing, his face contorted and the words that spilled from his mouth no longer making sense.

A great stillness had fallen upon the yard. In the shadows the watchers stood, chilled with the dreadful fascination of it. The man was frozen also, only his head moved and no sound came from his open lips – and Sean closed in with the weaving motion of a cobra in erection.

At the last moment the man tried to run, but his legs were slack and heavy with fear – and Sean hit him in the chest with a sound like an axe swung against a tree-trunk.

As he fell Sean went in after him, straddling his chest, roaring incoherently with only a single word recognizable – the name of the woman he loved. In his madness he felt the man's face breaking up under his fists, felt the warm splatter of blood thrown into his own face and on to his arms, and heard the shouts of the crowd.

'He'll kill him!'

'Get him off!'

'For Chrissake give me a hand – he's as strong as a bloody ox.'

Their hands upon him, an arm locked around his throat from behind, the shock as someone hit him with a bottle, the press of their bodies as they swarmed over him.

With men clinging to him, two of them riding his back and a dozen others on his arms and legs, Sean came to his feet.

'Pull his legs out from under him.'

'Get him down, man. Get him down.'

With a convulsive heave Sean swung the men on his arms into violent collision with each other. They released him.

He kicked his right leg free, and those on his other leg let go and scattered. Reaching over his shoulders he plucked the men off his back and stood alone, his chest swelling and subsiding as he breathed, the blood from the bottle gash in his scalp trickling down his face and soaking into his beard.

'Get a gun!' someone shouted.

'There's a shotgun under the bar.' But no one left the circle that ringed him in, and Sean glared around at them his eyes staring wildly from the plain of glistening blood that was his face.

'You've killed him!' a voice accused him. And the words reached Sean through the madness, his body relaxed slightly and he tried to wipe away the blood with the open palm of his hand. They saw the change in him.

'Cool down, mate. Fun's fun but the hell with murder.'

'Easy, now. Let's have a look what you've done to him.'

Sean looked down on the body, and he was confused and then suddenly afraid. The man was dead – he was certain of it.

'Oh, my God!' he whispered, backing away, wiping at his eyes ineffectually and smearing blood.

'He pulled a knife. Don't worry, mate, you've got witnesses.' The temper of the crowd had changed.

'No,' Sean mumbled; they didn't understand. For the first time in his life he had abused his strength, had used it to kill without purpose. To kill for the pleasure of it, to kill in the manner in which a leopard kills.

Then the man moved slightly, he rolled his head and one of his legs flexed and straightened. Sean felt hope leap within him.

'He's alive!'

'Get a doctor.'

Fearfully Sean approached and knelt beside the man, he unknotted the scarf from around his own throat and cleaned the bloody mouth and nostrils.

'He'll be all right – leave him to the Doc.'

The doctor came, a lean and laconic man chewing tobacco. In the yellow light of a hurricane lamp he examined and prodded while they crowded close about him craning to see over his shoulders. At last the doctor stood up.

'All right. He can be moved. Carry him up to my surgery.' Then he looked at Sean. 'Did you do it?'

Sean nodded.

'Remind me not to annoy you.'

'I didn't mean to – it just sort of happened.'

'Is that so?' The doctor shot a stream of yellow tobacco juice into the dust of the yard. 'Let's have a look at your head.' He pulled Sean's head down to his own level and parted the sodden black hair.

'Nicked a vein. Doesn't need a stitch. Wash it and a little iodine.'

'How much, Doc, for the other fellow?' Sean asked.

'You paying?' The doctor looked at him quizzically.

'Yes.'

'Broken jaw, broken collar-bone, about two dozen stitches and a few days in bed for concussion,' he mused, adding it up. 'Say two guineas.'

Sean gave him five. 'Look after him, Doc.'

'That's my job.' And he followed the men who were carrying Horse Odour out of the yard.

'Guess you need a drink, mister. I'll buy you one,' someone offered. The whole world loves a winner.

'Yes,' agreed Sean. 'I need a drink.'

Sean had more than one drink. When Mbejane came to fetch him at midnight he had a deal of difficulty getting Sean up on to the back of the horse. Half-way to the camp Sean slid off and subsided into the road, so Mbejane loaded him sideways – head and arms hanging over to port and legs dangling starboard.

'It is possible that tomorrow you will regret this,' Mbejane told him primly as he unloaded him beside the fire and rolled him still booted and bloody into his blanket.

He was correct.

Chapter Ten

In the dawn as Sean cleaned his face with a cloth dipped in a mug of hot water, regarding its reflection in the small metal mirror, the only fact that gave him the faintest satisfaction was the two hundred-odd sovereigns he had salvaged from the night's debauch.

'Are you sick, Pa?' Dirk's ghoulish interest in Sean's condition added substantially to his evil temper.

'Eat your breakfast.' Sean's tone was calculated by its sheer malevolence to dry up further questioning.

'There is no food.' Mbejane fell into the familiar role of protector.

'Why not?' Sean focused his bloodshot eyes upon him.

'There is one among us who considers the purchase of strong drink, and other things, more important than food for his son.'

From the pocket of his jacket Sean drew a handful of sovereigns. 'Go!' he ordered. 'Buy food and fresh horses. Go quickly so that in my grave illness I may not be afflicted with the wisdom of your counsel. Take Dirk with you.'

Mbejane examined the money, and grinned.

'The night was not wasted.'

When they had gone back to Frere, Dirk trotting beside the huge half-naked Zulu and his voice only fading at a distance of a hundred yards, Sean poured himself another mug of coffee and cupping it in his hands he sat staring into the ash and pink coals of the fire. He could trust Mbejane to use the money with care, he had the bargaining patience peculiar to his race that could if necessary devote two days to the purchase of a single ox. These things did not concern Sean now. Instead he went over the events of the previous night. Still sickened by his display of murderous rage, he tried to justify it. Taking into account the loss of nearly all he owned, the accumulation of years of hard work that had been stripped from him in a single day; the hardship and uncertainty that had followed. And finally he had reached the flash point when liquor and poker-tensed nerves had snapped the last reserve in him and translated it all into that violent outburst.

But that was not all, he knew he had avoided the main issue. *Ruth*. As he came back to her a wave of hopeless longing overwhelmed him, a tender despair such as he had never experienced before. He groaned aloud, and lifted his eyes to the morning star which was fading on the pink horizon as the sun came up behind.

For a while longer he wallowed in the softness of his love, remembering the way she walked, the dark serenity of her eyes and her mouth when she smiled and her voice when she sang – until it threatened to smother him in its softness.

Then he sprang to his feet and paced restlessly in the grass beside the fire. We must leave this place, ride away from it – go quickly. I must find something to do, some way to keep from thinking of it, something to fill my hands which ache now from the need to hold her.

Along the road, going north to Colenso, a long column of infantry filed past him in the dawn. He stopped his pacing and watched them. Each man leaned forward against his pack and the rifles stood up behind their shoulders.

Yes, he thought, I will go with them. Perhaps at the place to which they march I can find what I could not find last night. We will go home to Ladyburg, riding hard on fresh horses. I will leave Dirk with my mother, then come back to this war.

He began to pace again impatiently. Where the hell was Mbejane?

From the heights above, Sean looked down on Ladyburg. The village spread in a neat circle around the spire of the church. He remembered the spire as beacon-bright in its cladding of new copper, but nineteen years of weather had dulled it to a mellow brown.

Nineteen years. It did not seem that long. There were goods yards around the station now, a new concrete bridge over the Baboon Stroom, the blue gums in the plantation beyond the school were taller, and the flamboyants that had lined the main street were gone.

With a strange reluctance Sean turned his head and looked out to the right, across the Baboon Stroom, close in against the escarpment, to where he had left the sprawling Dutch gabled homestead of Theuniskraal with its roof of combed yellow thatch and the shutters of yellow-wood across the windows.

It was there, but not as he remembered it. Even at this distance he could see the walls were flaking and mottled with patches of dampness; the thatch was shaggy as the coat of an airedale; one of the shutters tilted slightly from a broken hinge; the lawns were brown and ragged where the bare earth showed through. The dairy behind the house had crumbled, its roof gone and the remains of its walls jutted forlornly upwards to the height of a man's shoulder.

'Damn the little bastard!' Sean's anger flared abruptly as he saw the neglect with which his twin brother had treated the lovely old house. 'He's so lazy he wouldn't get out of a bed he'd peed in.'

To Sean it was not just a house. It was the place his father had built, which had sheltered Sean on the day of his birth and through the years of his childhood. When his father died under the Zulu spears at Isandlawana, half the farm and the house had belonged to Sean; he had sat in the study at nights with the logs burning in the stone fireplace and the mounted buffalo head above it throwing distorted, moving shadows up on to the plaster ceiling. Although he had given his share away – yet it was still his home. Garry, his brother, had no right to let it decay and fall apart this way.

'Damn him!' Sean voiced his thoughts out loud – then almost immediately his conscience rebuked him. Garry was a cripple, his lower leg shot away by the blast of a careless shotgun. And Sean had fired that shotgun. Will I never be free of that guilt, how long must my penance continue? He protested at the goad of his conscience.

That is not your only trespass against your brother, his conscience reminded him. Who sired the child he calls his son? Whose loins sowed the seed that became man-child in the belly of Anna, your brother's wife?

'It has been a long time, Nkosi.' Mbejane had seen the expression on his face as Sean looked towards Theuniskraal and remembered those things from the past that were better forgotten.

'Yes.' Sean roused himself, and straightened in the saddle. 'A long road and many years. But now we are home again.'

He looked back towards the village, searching the quarter beyond the main street and the hotel for the roof of that little cottage on Protea Street. As he found it, showing through the tall, fluffy blue gum trees, there was a lift in his mood, a new excitement. Did she live there still? How would she look – a little grey surely; had her fifty years marked her deeply, or had they treated her with the same consideration which she showed all those with whom *she* came in contact? Had she forgiven him for leaving without a farewell? Had she forgiven his long years of silence since then? Did she understand the reasons why he had never written – no word or message, except that anonymous gift of ten thousand pounds he had transferred to her bank account. Ten thousand miserable little pounds, which he had hardly noticed among all the millions he had won and lost in those days long ago when he was one of the lords of the Witwatersrand goldfields.

Again the sense of guilt closed in upon him. As he knew with utter certainty that she *had* understood, that she *had* forgiven. For that was Ada, the woman who was his stepmother – and whom he loved beyond the natural love one owes their own full-blooded mother.

'Let's go down,' he said and kicked his horse to a canter.

'Is this home, Pa?' Dirk shouted as he rode beside him.

'Yes, my boy. This is home.'

'Will Gran'ma be here?'

'I hope so,' Sean answered, and then softly, 'Beyond all other things, I hope that she will.'

Over the bridge above the Baboon Stroom, past the cattle-pens alongside the line of rail, past the old wood and iron station buildings with the sign, white and black faded to grey, 'Ladyburg. Altitude 2,256 ft. above sea level', swinging left into the dusty main street which was wide enough to turn a full span of oxen, and down to Protea Street rode Sean and Dirk, with Mbejane and the pack-mule trailing far behind.

At the corner Sean checked his mount to a walk, drawing out the last few minutes of anticipation until they stopped outside the wicket fence of white that encompassed the cottage. The garden was neat and green, gay with beds of Barberton daisies and blue rhododendrons. The cottage had been enlarged, a new room built on the far side, and it was crisp-looking in a coat of new whitewash. A sign at the gate said in gold letters on a green ground.

'Maison Ada.
High-class Costumier'

Sean grinned. 'The old girl's gone all French, by God.' Then to Dirk, 'Stay here!'

He swung down from his horse, handed the reins to Dirk and went through the gate. At the door he paused self-consciously and adjusted his cravat. He glanced down at the severe dark broadcloth suit and new boots which he had purchased in Pietermaritzburg, slapped the dust from his breeches, stroked his newly trimmed beard into place, gave his moustache a twirl and knocked on the door.

It was opened at last by a young lady. Sean did not recognize her. But the girl reacted immediately, flushing slightly, attempting to pat her hair into place without drawing attention to its disarray, trying to dispose of the sewing in her hands, and exhibiting all the signs of confusion peculiar to the unmarried female who finds herself suddenly and unexpectedly in the presence of a large, well-dressed and attractive male. But Sean felt a twinge of pity as he looked at her scarred face, ugly with the purple cicatrice of acne.

Sean lifted his hat. 'Is Mrs Courtney here?'

'She's in the workroom, sir. Who shall I tell her is calling?'

'Don't tell her anything – it's a surprise,' Sean smiled at her, and she lifted her hands self-consciously in an attempt to mask the ruin of her face.

'Won't you come in, sir?' She turned her head aside, shyly – as though to hide it.

'Who is it, Mary?' Sean started at the voice from the depths of the cottage, it hadn't changed at all – and the years dropped away.

'It's a gentleman, Aunt Ada. He wants to see you.'

'I'm coming. Ask him to sit down, and please bring us coffee, Mary.'

Mary escaped thankfully and left Sean standing alone in the small sitting-room, twisting his hat in big brown hands, staring up at the daguerreotype print of Waite Courtney above the mantel. Although he did not recognize the fact, the face of his father in the picture was almost his own – the same eyes under heavy black brows, the same arrogance about the mouth, even the identical thrust of stubbornness in the jaw beneath the thick spade-shaped beard – and the big, hooked Courtney nose.

The door from the work-room opened and Sean swung quickly to face it. Ada Courtney came through it smiling, until she saw him, then she stopped and the smile died on her lips and she paled. Uncertainly her hand lifted to her throat and she made a small choking sound.

'Dear God,' she whispered.

'Ma.' Sean fidgeted his feet awkwardly. 'Hello, Ma. It's good to see you.'

'Sean.' The colour flooded back into her cheeks. 'For a moment I thought – you're grown so much like your father. Oh, Sean!' And she ran to him. He tossed his hat on to the sofa and caught her around the waist as she came.

'I've waited for you. I knew you'd come.'

Sean scooped her up and kissed her into a confusion of joy and laughter, swinging her while he did it, laughing himself.

'Put me down,' Ada gasped at last, and when he did she clung to him.

'I knew you'd come back. At first there were bits in the newspaper about you, and people told me things – but these last years there has been nothing, nothing at all.'

'I'm sorry.' Sean sobered.

'You're a bad boy.' She was sparkling with excitement, her hair had escaped from its bun and a wisp of it hung down her cheek. 'But it's so good to have you back—' and suddenly she was crying.

'Don't, Ma. Please don't.' He had never seen her cry before.

'It's just that . . . It's the surprise.' She brushed impatiently at her tears. 'It's nothing.'

Desperately Sean sought something to distract her. 'Hey!' he exclaimed with relief, 'I've another surprise for you.'

'Later,' she protested. 'One at a time.'

'This won't wait.' He led her to the door and out on to the front stoep with his arm around her shoulders.

'Dirk,' he shouted. 'Come here.'

He felt her standing very still as they watched Dirk coming up the garden walk.

'This is your Gran'ma.' He introduced them.

'Why is she crying?' Dirk eyed her with frank curiosity.

Later they sat at the table in the kitchen while Ada and Mary plied them with food. Ada Courtney believed that the first thing to do with a man was feed him.

Mary was almost as excited as Ada, she had taken full advantage of the few minutes she had been alone, and now her hair was freshly brushed and she wore a gay new apron, but the powder with which she had tried to cover the terrible disfiguration of the skin served only to call attention to it. In sympathy Sean refrained from looking at her, and Mary noticed. Shyly she devoted herself to winning Dirk's attention. She fussed over him quietly – and Dirk accepted this as the natural order of things.

While they ate Sean filled in the missing years for Ada with a brief outline of his activities, glossing over the death of Dirk's mother, and other things of which he had no reason to be proud. He came to the end of it.

'And so here we are.

> "Home is the sailor, home from the sea,
> And the hunter home from the hill."

Dirk, don't put so much in your mouth and keep it closed when you chew.'

'How long will you stay? Mary, see if there are any cream-puffs in the jar – Dirk is still hungry,' said Ada.

'You'll make him sick. I don't know; not long though – there's a war on.'

'You're going to join?'

'Yes.'

'Oh, Sean. Must you?' Knowing that he must. While he selected a cheroot from his case Sean studied her closely for the first time. There was grey now as he had known there would be, almost as much grey as black; long streaks of it across her temples and the texture of her skin had altered, losing the moisture of youth, drying out so that it creased around the eyes and stretched tight across her hands to show the knuckles more prominently and the blueness of veins beneath it. She was plumper also, her bosom was full and round, each breast having lost its separate identity in the whole.

Yes the other qualities whose memories he had treasured so long ago still persisted, seemed indeed to have grown stronger; the composure which showed in the stillness of her hands and body, yet was given the lie by the humour that hovered around her lips; the eyes whose depths held compassion and a sure understanding of those things they looked upon. But mostly it was the indefinable aura of goodness about her – looking at her, he sensed again that behind those eyes no destructive thought could live for long.

Sean lit the cheroot and spoke while the smoke masked his face.

'Yes, Ma. I must go.'

And Ada, whose husband had ridden to war also, and not ridden home, could not prevent the sadness showing for an instant in her eyes.

'Yes. I suppose you must. Garry has gone already and Michael has been agitating to follow him.'

'Michael?' Sean fired the question.

'Garry's son – he was born a short while after – after you left Ladyburg. He will be eighteen this winter.'

'What's he like?' Sean's voice was too eager. Michael – so that is what my son is named. My first-born. By God, my first-born, and I didn't even know his name until he was almost fully grown. Ada was looking at him with her own question unasked in her eyes.

'Mary, take Dirk through to the bathroom please. Try and get a little of that food from around his mouth.' When they had gone she answered Sean's question.

'He's a tall boy, tall and lean. Dark like his mother, but a serious lad. He doesn't laugh much. Always top of his class. I like him very much. He comes here often.' She was silent for a moment, then, 'Sean . . .'

Quickly Sean cut in. 'And how is Garry?' He sensed what she was going to ask.

'Garry has not changed very much. He has had a run of bad luck . . .

Poor Garry, things have been bad on the farm. The rinder-pest ravaged his herds, he had to borrow money from the bank.' She hesitated an instant. 'And he is drinking a lot these days. I can't be sure of it – he never visits the hotel and I have never seen him take a drink. But it must be that.'

'I'll find out where he is when I go up to Colenso.'

'You'll have no difficulty finding him. Garry is a lieutenant-colonel on the General's staff. He was given promotion from major last week, and he has been awarded the Distinguished Service Order to go with his Victoria Cross. He is in charge of liaison between the Imperial and the Colonial troops.'

'Good God!' Sean was stunned. 'Garry a colonel!'

'General Buller thinks very highly of him. The General is also a holder of the Victoria Cross.'

'But,' Sean protested. 'You know how Garry got that decoration. It was a mistake. If Garry is on the General's staff – then Lord have mercy on the British Army!'

'Sean, you mustn't talk about your brother that way.'

'Colonel Garrick Courtney.' Sean laughed out loud.

'I don't know what there is between you and Garry. But it's something very nasty – and I don't want any of it in this house.' Ada's tone was fierce and Sean stopped laughing.

'I'm sorry.'

'Before we close the subject, I want to warn you. Please be very careful how you handle Garry. Whatever happened between you two – and I don't want to know what it is – Garry still hates you. Once or twice he started talking about you but I stopped him. Yet I know it from Michael – the boy has picked it up from his father. It's almost an obsession with him. Be careful of Garry.'

Ada stood up. 'And now about Dirk. What a lovely child he is, Sean. But I'm afraid you've spoiled him a little.'

'He's a tiger,' Sean admitted.

'What schooling has he been given?'

'Well, he can read a little—'

'You'll leave him here with me. I'll enrol him when the school term begins.'

'I was going to ask. I'll leave money with you.'

'Ten years ago there was a very large and mysterious deposit to my bank account. It wasn't mine – so I placed it out at interest.' She smiled at him and Sean looked guilty. 'We can use that.'

'No,' he said.

'Yes,' she contradicted. 'And now tell me when you are leaving.'

'Soon.'

'How soon?'

'Tomorrow.'

Chapter Eleven

Since climbing the World's View road out of Pietermaritzburg, Sean and Mbejane had travelled in sunshine and in companionship. The feelings between them were solid, compacted by time and the pressure of trouble and shared laughter into a shield of affection – so that now they were happy as only men can be together. The jokes were old jokes, and the responses almost automatic – but the excitement between them was new, in the same way that each day's sun is new. For they were riding to war, to another meeting with death, so that everything else lost significance. Sean felt free, the thoughts and relationships with other people which had weighed him down over the past months slipped away. Like a ship clear for action he hurried with a new lightness to meet his chance.

At the same time he could stand aside from himself and grin tolerantly at his own immaturity. By God, we're like a couple of kids sneaking out of school. Then, following the thought further – he was suddenly thankful. Thankful that this was so; thankful that there was still this capacity to forget everything else and approach the moment in childlike anticipation. For a while this new habit of self-appraisal asserted itself; I am no longer young and I have learned much, gathered it brick by brick along the way and trimmed each brick and cemented it into the wall. The fortress of my manhood is not yet completed, but what I have built so far is strong. Yet the purpose of a fortress is to protect and hold safely those things that are precious; if, during the building, a man loses and expends those things which he wishes to protect, then the finished fortress is a mockery. I have not lost it all, a little I have used in barter. I have traded a little faith for the knowledge of evil; exchanged a little laughter for the understanding of death; a measure of freedom for two sons (and this was a good trade) – but I know there is still something left.

At his side Mbejane noticed the change of Sean's mood, and he moved in front of it to turn it once more into the sunshine.

'Nkosi, we must hurry if you wish to reach your drinking-place at Frere.'

With an effort Sean thrust his thoughts aside, and laughed. They rode on into the north, and on the third day they reached Chievely.

Sean remembered his innocent amazement when, as a youth, he had joined Lord Chelmsford's column at Rorke's Drift at the beginning of the Zulu War. He had believed then no greater accumulation of men was possible. now he looked across the encampment of the British Army before Colenso and smiled; Chelmsford's little force would have been lost in the artillery and ordnance park, yet beyond that the tents stretched away for two miles. Row upon row of white canvas cones with the horse lines in between – and to the rear the orderly acres of transport vehicles, thousands of them, with the draught animals scattered grazing across the veld almost to the range of the eye.

It was an impressive sight not only in its immensity but also in its neat and businesslike layout; so was the military precision of the blocks of men at drill, the massed glitter of their bayonets as they turned and marched and countermarched.

When Sean wandered into the camp and read the names of the regiments at the head of each row of tents he recognized them as the sound of glory. But the new khaki uniforms and pith helmets had reduced them all to a homogeneous mass. Only the cavalry retained a little of the magic in the pennants that fluttered gaily at their lance-tips. A squadron trotted past him and Sean eyed their mounts with envy. Great shiny beasts, as arrogant as the men upon their backs. Horse and rider given an air of inhuman cruelty by the slender bright-tipped lance they carried.

A dozen times Sean asked his question, 'Where can I find the Guides,' and though the answer was given in the dialects of Manchester and Lancashire, in the barely intelligible accents of Scotland and Ireland, each had a common factor – they were all singularly unhelpful.

Once he stopped to watch a group training with one of the new Maxim machine-guns. Clumsy, he decided, no match against a rifle. Later he would remember this judgement and feel a little foolish.

All morning he trudged through the camp, with Mbejane trailing him, and at noon he was tired and dusty and bad-tempered. The Natal Corps of Guides appeared to be a mythical unit. He stood on the edge of the camp and looked out across the open veld, pondering his next move in the search.

Half a mile out on the grassy plain a thin drift of blue smoke caught his eye. It issued from a line of bush that obviously marked the course of a stream. Whoever had picked that spot to camp certainly knew how to make himself comfortable in the veld. Compared to the bleak surroundings of the main encampment it would be paradise; protected from the wind, close to firewood and water, well away from the attention of senior officers. That was his answer, Sean grinned and set out across the plain.

His guess was proved correct by the swarm of black servants among the trees. These could only be Colonial troops, each with a personal retainer. Also, the wagons were drawn up in the circular formation of the laager. With a feeling of homecoming Sean approached the first white man he saw.

In an enamel hipbath beneath the shade of a mimosa tree this gentleman sat, waist deep, while a servant added hot water from a large black kettle.

'Hello,' Sean greeted him. The man looked up from his book, removed the cheroot from his mouth and returned Sean's greeting.

'I'm looking for the Guides.'

'Your search is ended, my friend. Sit down.' Then to the servant, 'Bring the Nkosi a cup of coffee.'

Thankful, Sean sank into the *reimpje* chair near the bath and stretched his legs out before him. His host laid aside the book and began to lather his hairy chest and armpits while he studied Sean with frank appraisal.

'Who's in charge here?' Sean asked.

'You want to see him?'

'Yes.'

The bather opened his mouth and yelled.

'Hey! Tim!'

'What you want?' The reply came from the nearest wagon.

'Fellow here to see you.'

'What's *he* want?'

'Says he wants to talk to you about his daughter.'

There was a long silence while the man in the wagon digested this, then: 'What's he look like?'

'Big bloke, with a shotgun.'

'You're joking!'

'The hell I am! Says if you don't come out he's coming in to get you.'

The canvas of the wagon canopy was lifted cautiously and an eye showed behind the slit. The ferocious bellow that followed startled Sean to his feet. The canvas was thrown aside and out of the wagon vaulted the Commanding Officer of the Guides. He moved in on Sean with his arms held like a wrestler. For a moment Sean stared at him, then he answered the bellow and dropped into a defensive crouch.

'Yaah!' The man charged and Sean met him chest to chest, locking his arms around him as they closed.

'Tim Curtis, you miserable bastard,' he roared in laughter and in pain as Tim tried to pull his beard out by the roots.

'Sean Courtney, you evil son of a bitch,' breathless as the air was forced from his lungs by Sean's hug.

'Let's have a drink.' Sean punched him.

'Let's have a bottle.' Tim caught his ears and twisted.

At last they broke apart and stood laughing incoherently in the pleasure of meeting again.

The servant returned with Sean's coffee and Tim waved him away disgustedly. 'None of that slop! Get a bottle of brandy out of my chest.'

'You two know each other, I presume.' The man in the bath interrupted them.

'Know each other! Jesus, I worked five years for him!' snorted Tim. 'Digging his dirty gold out of the ground. Worst boss I ever had.'

'Well, now's your chance,' Sean grinned, 'because I've come to work for you.'

'You hear that Saul? The idiot wants to join.'

'*Mazeltov.*' The bather dunked the tip of his cheroot in his bath water, flicked it away and stood up. He offered Sean a soapy hand.

'Welcome to the legion of the lost. My name's Saul Friedman. I gather yours is Sean Courtney. Now where's that bottle and we'll celebrate your arrival.'

The commotion had summoned the others from their wagons and Sean was introduced to each of them. It seemed the uniform of the Guides was a khaki tunic without insignia or badges of rank, slouch hats and riding breeches. There were ten of them. A tough-looking bunch and Sean found their company to his liking.

Naked except for a towel draped round his waist, Saul did duty as barman, then they all settled down in the shade to a bout of drinking. Tim Curtis entertained them for the first twenty minutes with a biographical and biological account of Sean's career, to which Saul contributed comments that were met with roars of laughter. It was obvious that Saul was the Company wit, a function which he performed with distinction. He was the youngest of them all, perhaps twenty-five years old, and physically the smallest. His body was thin and hairy, and in a pleasant sort of way he was extremely ugly. Sean liked him.

An hour later when the brandy had taken them to the stage of seriousness which precedes wild and undirected hilarity, Sean asked,

'Captain Curtis . . .'

'Lieutenant, and don't forget it,' Tim corrected him.

'Lieutenant, then. What is our job, and when do we do it?'

Tim scowled at his empty glass, then looked across at Saul. 'Tell him,' he instructed.

'As mentioned earlier, we are the legion of the lost. People look on us with pity and a mild embarrassment. They pass us by on the far side of the street, making the sign of the Cross and murmuring a spell to avert the evil eye. We live here in our own little leper colony.'

'Why?'

'Well, first of all, we belong to the most miserable little runt in the entire army of Natal. An officer, who, despite a formidable array of medals, would not inspire confidence in a young ladies' choir. He is chief liaison officer for the Colonial troops on the general staff. Lieutenant-Colonel Garrick Court- ney, V.C., D.S.O.' Saul paused and his expression changed. 'No relation of yours, I trust?'

'No,' lied Sean without hesitation.

'Thank God,' Saul continued. 'Anyway, this is why people pity us. The embarrassment arises from the fact that nobody recognizes our official existence. Even the drawing of rations must be preceded by a comic opera dialogue between Tim and the Quartermaster. But because we are called "Guides" everybody expects us to get out there and start doing a bit of guiding. So in some weird fashion the failure of General Buller to advance even one hundred yards in three months is laid at our door.' Saul filled his glass. 'Anyway, we haven't run out of brandy yet.'

'You mean we don't do anything?' Sean asked incredulously.

'We eat, we sleep and we drink.'

'Occasionally we go visiting,' Tim added. 'Now is as good a time as any.'

'Who do we visit?'

'There is a most enterprising woman in the area, not five miles distant. She owns a travelling circus – forty wagons and forty girls. They follow along behind the main army to comfort and encourage it. Let's go and get some comfort and encouragement. If we start now we'll get to the head of the line – first come, first served.'

'I'll leave you to it,' Saul stood up and drifted away.

'He's a good kid,' Tim observed as he watched him leave.

'Is it against his religion?'

'No. But he's married and takes it seriously. How about you?'

'I'm not married.'

'Let's go then.'

Much later they rode home together in the moonlight, both pleasantly melancholy with love and liquor. The girl who had taken Sean to her wagon was a friendly lass with a pair of fat maternal bosoms.

'I like you, mister,' she had told him afterwards.

'I like you also,' he replied truthfully.

Although Sean experienced no more shame or guilt than after satisfying any of his other bodily needs, yet he knew that half an hour with a stranger in a wagon bed was a very poor substitute.

He began to hum the tune that Ruth had sung on the night of the storm.

Chapter Twelve

Lieutenant-Colonel Garrick Courtney removed his uniform jacket and hung it carefully on the dumb-valet beside his desk. The way a houseproud wife straightens a picture on her wall, he touched the purple watered silk on which was suspended the heavy, bronze cross, until it hung to his satisfaction. His lips moving, he read the inscription again. 'For Valour', and smiled.

The champagne he had drunk during lunch made his brain feel like a great brilliant diamond set in his skull, sharp and hard and clear.

He sat down, swivelled the chair sideways to the desk and stretched his legs out in front of him.

'Send him in, Orderly!' he shouted, and dropped his eyes to his boots. You couldn't tell the difference, he decided. No one could tell by looking at them which one was flesh and bone beneath the polished leather – or which leg was carved wood with a cunningly articulated ankle.

'Sir.' The voice startled him and he pulled his legs in guiltily, hiding them beneath his chair.

'Curtis!' He looked up at the man who stood before his desk. Tim stood rigidly to attention, staring stolidly over Garry's head, and Garry let him stand. He felt satisfaction that this hulking bastard must use those two powerful legs to pay respect to Garrick Courtney. Let him stand. He waited, watching him, and at last Tim fidgeted slightly and cleared his throat.

'At ease!' There was no doubt now as to who held the power. Garry picked up the paper-knife from his desk and turned it in his hands as he spoke.

'You're wondering why I sent for you.' He smiled expansively. 'Well, the reason is that I have a job for you at last. I lunched with General Buller today.' He paused to let that absorb. 'We discussed the Offensive. He wanted my views on certain plans he has in mind.' Garry caught himself. 'Anyway, that is beside the point. I want you and your men to reconnoitre the river on both sides of Colenso. See here.' Garry spread a map on the desk in front of him. 'There are fords marked here and here.' He jabbed at the map with the paper-knife. 'Find them and mark them well. Check the bridges – both the railway and the road bridge, make certain they are intact. Do it tonight. I want your full report in the morning. You can go.'

'Yes, sir.'

'Oh, Curtis—' Garry stopped him as he stooped in the entrance of the tent. 'Don't fail. Find those fords.' The canvas flap dropped closed behind the American, and Garry opened the drawer of his desk and took out a silver flask set with carnelians. He unscrewed it and sniffed the contents before he drank.

With the dawn, in bedraggled pairs the Guides dribbled into camp. Sean and Saul were the last to return. They dismounted, turned their horses over to the servants and joined the group around the fire.

'Yes?' Tim looked up from where he squatted with a mug of coffee cupped in his hands. His clothing was soaked and steam lifted off it as it dried in the heat from the flames. 'They've blown the rail bridge – but the road bridge is still intact.'

'You're sure?'

'We walked across.'

'That's something anyway,' grunted Tim, and Sean raised a sceptical eyebrow.

'You think so. Hasn't it occurred to you that they've left the bridge because that is where they *want* us to cross?'

No one replied and Sean went on wearily:

'When we checked the bridges, Saul and I did a bit of exploring on the far side. Just beyond the railway bridge there is a series of little kopjes. We crawled around the bottom of them.'

'And?'

'There are more Boers sitting on those kopjes than there are quills on a porcupine's back. Whoever tries to cross those bridges in daylight is going to get the Bejesus shot out of him.'

'Lovely thought!' growled Tim.

'Charming, isn't it? Further contemplation of it will make me puke. What did you find?'

'We found plenty of water.' Tim glanced down at his sodden clothing. 'Deep water.'

'No ford,' Sean anticipated gloomily.

'None. But we found a ferryboat on the bank with the bottom knocked out of it. That could be the excuse for marking a ford on the map.'

'So now you can go and tell our beloved Colonel the glad tidings.' Saul grinned. 'But one gets you five that it has no effect. My guess is that Buller will attack Colenso within the next two days. He might just be able to get a couple of thousand men across that bridge, then we'd have a chance.'

Tim regarded him balefully. 'And the Guides will be the first across. All very well for you. The Rabbi has reduced your target area considerably – but what about us?'

'But it's marked on the map,' protested Lieutenant-Colonel Garrick

Courtney. His head was bowed so that Tim could see the pink scalp through the furrows the comb had left in his sandy-brown hair.

'I've seen dragons and sea monsters marked on maps, sir,' Tim answered, and Garry looked up at him coldly with pale blue eyes.

'You're not paid to be a comedian, Curtis.'

'I beg your pardon, sir,' and Garry frowned. Curtis could make the 'sir' sound like an insult.

'Who did you send?' he demanded.

'I went myself, sir.'

'You could have missed it in the dark.'

'If there is a ford there, it would have a road or at least a path leading down to it. I wouldn't have missed that, sir.'

'But in the darkness you could have been mistaken,' insisted Garry. 'You might have missed something that would be obvious in daylight.'

'Well, sir . . .'

'Good.' Briskly Garry went on. 'Now, the bridges. You say these are still intact.'

'Only the road bridge, but . . .'

'But what?'

'The men I sent report that the hills beyond the river are heavily defended. Almost as though the bridge has been preserved to bait a trap.'

'Curtis.' Deliberately Garry laid his paper-knife upon the map before him. His nose was too large for the space between his eyes and when he pursed his lips this way he looked, Tim thought, like a bird – a sparrow, a little brown sparrow.

'Curtis,' Garry repeated softly. 'It seems to me you have very little enthusiasm for this business. I send you out to do a job and you come back with a long list of excuses. I don't think you realize how important this is.'

Chirp, chirp – little sparrow. Tim smiled secretly and Garry flushed.

'For instance. Who did you sent to reconnoitre these bridges – reliable men, I hope?'

'They are, sir.'

'Who?'

'Friedman.'

'Oh! The little Jewish lawyer. A wise choice, Curtis, a commendably wise choice.' Garry sniffed and picked up the paper-knife.

My God! Curtis marvelled. *He's a Jew-baiter as well, this little sparrow has all the virtues.*

'Who else did you send?'

'A new recruit.'

'A new recruit? A new recruit!' Garry dropped the knife and lifted his hands in appeal.

'I happen to have worked for him before the war. I know him well, sir. He's a first-class man. I'd trust him before anyone else you could name. In fact, I was going to ask you to approve his promotion to sergeant.'

'And what is the name of this paragon?'

'Funnily enough it's the same as yours, sir. Although he tells me you're not related. His name is Courtney. Sean Courtney.'

Slowly, very slowly, the expression of Garry's face altered. It became

smooth, neutral. Pale also, the lifeless, translucent paleness of a corpse's face.
All life died in his eyes as well – they were looking inwards, back into the
secret places of long ago. The dark places. They saw a small boy climbing
a hill.

*He was climbing up through thick bush, young legs strong beneath him.
Climbing in deep shade, with the smell of leaf-mould and the soft murmur
of insects, sweating in the heat of a Natal summer's morning, eyes straining
ahead through the dense green foliage for a glimpse of the bush buck they
were hunting, the dog leaning eagerly against the leash and the same
eagerness pumping in his own chest.*

*The dog barked once, and immediately the brush and stir of a big body
moving ahead of them, the click of a hoof against rock, then the rush of its
run.*

*The shot, a blunt burst of sound, and the buck bleating wounded as it
thrashed through the grass, and Sean's voice high and unbroken: 'I got him.
I got him first shot! Garry. Garry! I got him, I got him!'*

*Into the sunlight, the dog dragging him. Sean wild with excitement,
running down the slope towards him with the shotgun. Sean falling, the gun
flung from his hands, the roar of the second shot and the blow that knocked
Garry's leg out from under him.*

*Sitting now in the grass and staring at the leg. The little white splinters
of bone in the pulped flesh and the blood pumping dark and strong and thick
as custard.*

*'I didn't mean it . . . Oh God, Garry, I didn't mean it. I slipped. Honest,
I slipped.'*

Garry shuddered, a violent almost sensual spasm of his whole body, and
the leg beneath the desk twitched in sympathy.

'Are you all right, sir?' There was an edge of concern on Tim's voice.

'I am perfectly well, thank you, Curtis.' Garry smoothed back the hair
from his temples. There were deep bays of baldness there and his hairline
was frayed and irregular. 'Please continue.'

'Well, I was saying – it looks like a trap. They've left those bridges
because . . .'

'It is your duty to collect information, Curtis. It is the duty of the general
staff to evaluate it. I think that completes your report? Good, then you may
leave.'

He must have a drink now, already his hand was on the handle of the
drawer.

'Oh, Curtis.' His voice croaked with the terrible dryness in his throat, but
he spoke on through it. 'That promotion you spoke of is approved. Make
the man a sergeant.'

'Very well, sir.'

'Of course, in the event of a frontal assault on the bridges he will act as
guide for the first attack.'

'Sir?'

'You see the need for it, don't you?' Tim had never heard this wheedling
tone from him before. It was almost as though he wanted Tim's approval.
As though he were trying to justify his decision. 'I mean, he knows the
bridges. He's been over them. He's the one who knows them, isn't he?'

'Yes, sir.'

'And after all, he's a sergeant. I mean, we should send someone with rank – we can't just send anybody.'

'I could go, sir.'

'No. No. We'll need you at the ford.'

'As you wish.'

'You won't forget, will you? You *will* send him, won't you?' Almost pleading now.

'I'll send him,' agreed Tim and stooped out of the tent. Garry jerked open the drawer and his fingernails scrabbled on the rough wood in their haste to find the flask.

Chapter Thirteen

To General Sir Redvers Buller, V.C.,
Officer Commanding,
British Expeditionary Army of Natal

At Chievely

December 19th 1899

Sir,

I have the honour to report that in accordance with orders received a reconnaissance was carried out by officers and men of the Natal Corps of Guides on the night of December 18th. The results of which are set out below:

Ford marked 'A' on attached Map: Although the ford promises passage for a large body of men, it is difficult to locate in darkness and a night crossing is not recommended.

Bridge marked 'B' on attached Map: This is a road bridge of metal construction. At present it is undamaged, probably due to its sturdy construction resisting demolition by the enemy.

Bridge marked 'C' on attached Map: This is a railway bridge also constructed of metal, but has been demolished by the enemy.

General: Limited penetration of the area beyond the Tugela River by elements of the N.C.G. revealed the presence of the enemy on the hills marked 'D' and 'E'. However, no evidence of artillery or excessive force was noted.

Courtney G., Lieutenant-Colonel
Officer Commanding N.C.G.,
In the Field.

EXTRACT FROM THE BATTLE ORDERS OF GENERAL SIR REDVERS BULLER V.C.
MADE AND SIGNED ON THE NIGHT OF DECEMBER 19TH 1899.

.. The force commanded by Brigadier Lyttelton will advance on and
capture the village of Colenso. Thereafter it will seize and cross the metal
bridge, and drive the enemy from the kopjes on the far bank. (See attached
Map.)'

Chapter Fourteen

They lay in the grass, side by side, and the dew had soaked through the
backs of their tunics. The night was still and silent. No clouds above and the
fat stars were very bright. Ahead of them the silver smear of the Milky Way
threw the silhouette of the Tugela heights into bold relief, gave it an aspect
of brooding menace.

Saul yawned loudly, and immediately Sean was forced to do the same.
Though they had not slept that night, it was not the weariness – but the
symptom of nerves wound tight at the prospect of going in against the Boer
guns . . .

'Another hour and a half until dawn,' Saul whispered, and Sean grunted.
There was no profit in counting the hours. At forty-seven minutes past six
the sun would rise, and from behind them the British Army would move
forward across the brown grass plain.

Once more Sean rose to his knees and swept the ground before them with
his eyes, letting them move slowly along the bank of the Tugela, picking up
the loom of the steel road bridge a hundred paces ahead of them, accounting
for each bush on this bank, that they had not multiplied or moved. Then
satisfied, he sank down again.

'My God, it's cold!' He could feel Saul shivering beside him.

'It will warm up quite soon.' Sean grinned in the darkness as he answered.
The clear night sky had allowed yesterday's warmth to escape, the grass and
their clothing were wet, even the steel of the rifles was painfully cold to
touch – but Sean had long ago learned to ignore physical discomfort. He
could, when necessary, lie completely motionless while tsetse flies settled on
his neck and sank their red-hot needles into the soft skin behind his ears.
Nevertheless, it was a relief when the false dawn showed and it was time
to move.

'I'll go in now,' he whispered.

'Good luck – I'll have breakfast ready when you come back.'

This was a job for one man. A job than Sean did not relish. They had made certain that there were no enemy on this side of the river, now at the last minute when it was too late for the Boers to alter their dispositions – someone had to cross and find out in what strength they were holding the bridge. A couple of Boer Maxims sited to command the bridge at short range, or even demolition charges set ready to blow, would mean that the chances of success instead of being slim would be non-existent.

Sean slung his rifle across his back and began crawling forward through the grass. Twice he stopped to listen briefly, but there was little time – true dawn in an hour. He reached the bridge and lay in its heavy shadow, staring across at the far bank. Nothing moved. In the starlight the kopjes loomed like the backs of dark whales in the grassy sea. He waited five minutes – long enough for a restless sentry to fidget – still nothing.

'Here we go,' he whispered aloud, and suddenly he was afraid. For an instant he did not recognize the sensation, for he had experienced it only three or four times in his life, but never with so little cause. He crouched beside the steel girders of the bridge, with the weakness in his legs and his belly full of the oiliness. It was only when he caught the taste of it at the back of his throat, a taste a little like that of fish oil mixed with the effluence of something long dead, that he knew what it was.

I'm afraid. His first reaction was of surprise, which changed quickly to alarm.

This was how it happened. He knew it happened to other men. He had heard them talk of it around the camp fires, remembered the words and the pity underlying them.

'Ja, his gunboy led him back to camp. He was shaking like a man with fever, and he was crying. I thought he was hurt. "Daniel," I said, "Daniel, what is wrong?"

' "It broke," he said with the tears running into his beard. "It broke there in my head, I heard it break. I threw the gun away and I ran."

' "Did he charge, Daniel?" I asked.

' "No, man. I didn't even see him, just heard him feeding close by in the catbush. Then it broke in my head and I was running."

'He was no coward. I had hunted with him many times, seen him kill an elephant from a charge so that it fell close enough to touch with the gunbarrel. He was good, but he had lived too close to it. Then suddenly it broke in his head. He hasn't hunted again.'

I have accumulated fear the way an old ship collects barnacles and weed below the water-line, now it is ready to break in me also – Sean knew. Knew also that if he ran now, as the old hunter had run, he would never hunt again.

Crouching in the darkness, sweating in the cold of dawn with the iciness of his fear, Sean wanted to vomit. He was physically sick, breathing heavily through his open mouth, the warm oiliness in his belly coming close to venting itself, so weak with it that his legs began to tremble and he caught at one of the iron girders of the bridge for support.

A minute that seemed like all eternity, he stood like that. Then he began to fight it, bearing down on it, stiffening his legs and forcing them to move forward. Consciously he checked the relaxation of his sphincter muscle – that close he had come to the ultimate degradation.

He knew then that the old joke about cowards was true. And that it applied to him also.

He went up on to the bridge; picking up each foot deliberately, swinging it forward, laying it down and moving the weight of his body over it. His breathing was deliberate, each breadth taken and expelled at the command of his brain. He couldn't trust his body now to perform even the simplest task – not after it had betrayed him so monstrously.

Had they been waiting at the bridge, the Boers would have killed him that morning. Without caution he paced slowly down the centre of it, big and heavily moving in the starlight and his footsteps rang on the metal.

Under his feet the metal gave way to gravel. He was across. He kept walking, down the middle of the road, following the gentle curve towards the dark hills.

He walked on with his terror and the sound of it roared in his head like the sound of the sea. The sling of his rifle slipped from his shoulder and the weapon clattered into the road. He stood for a full minute before he could gather himself to stoop and pick it up. Then he turned and went back. Pacing slowly, counting his footsteps, measuring them out – one each second – timing them carefully to prevent himself from running. Because if he ran he knew it was finished. He too would never hunt again.

'You all right?' Saul was waiting.

'Yes.' Sean sank down beside him.

'See anything?'

'No.'

Saul was staring at him. 'Are you sure you're all right?'

Sean sighed. Once before he had been afraid. Fear had come to him in a caved-in mineshaft, later he had gone back and left his fear in the same mineshaft, and had walked away from it alone. In the same way he had hoped to leave it now beyond the river, but this time it had followed him back. With a certainty he knew that it would never leave him from now onwards. It would always be near.

I will have to tame it, he thought. I will have to break it to the halter and the curb.

'Yes, I'm all right,' he answered Saul. 'What's the time?'

'Half-past five.'

'I'll send Mbejane back now.'

Sean stood up and went to where Mbejane waited with their horses. He handed Mbejane the small square of green cloth which was the prearranged signal that neither the bridge nor the town was defended in force. The red square he replaced in his breast-pocket.

'I will come back,' Mbejane told him.

'No.' Sean shook his head. 'There is nothing for you here.'

Mbejane untied the horses. 'Stay in peace.'

'Go in peace.' Sean was thankful that Mbejane would not be there as witness, should he break under his new-found fear.

But I must not break, he decided grimly. Today will be the test. If I can last out this day, then perhaps I will have tamed it.

He went back to where Saul waited in the darkness, and together they lay and watched the dawn come on.

Chapter Fifteen

The darkness drew back, each minute enlarging the circle of their vision. Now the upper words of the bridge stood out, a neat geometrical pattern against the dark bulk of the heights. Then he could see the patterns of dark bush against pale grass and rock.

The new light distorted distance, made the high ground seem remote and no longer hostile. A flight of egrets flew in long formation above the course of the river, high enough to catch the sun so that they were birds of bright, glowing gold in a world of shadow. And the dawn brought with it a small cold wind whose voice in the grass blended with the murmur of the river.

Then the sun hit the heights as though to bless the army of the Republic. The mist in the gullies writhed in agony at its warmth, lifted into the wind and smeared away.

The rim of the sun pushed up over the edge of the land, and the day came bright and clean with dew.

Through his glasses Sean studied the crest of the high ground. At a hundred paces there were traces of smoke as the Boer Army brewed coffee.

'You think they'll spot us?' asked Saul.

Sean shook his head without lowering his glasses. Two small bushes and the thin screen of grass they had constructed during the night hid them effectively.

'Are you sure you are all right?' Saul asked once more. From the set of his face Sean seemed to be in pain.

'Stomach gripes,' Sean grunted. Let it start soon, please let it start. The waiting is the worst.

Then the ground trembled under his chest, the faintest vibration, and Sean felt relief flood through him. 'Here come the guns,' he said, and using the cover of one of the bushes, he stood up and looked behind him.

In a single column, following each other at strictly spaced intervals, the guns were moving into action. They were coming in fast, still tiny with distance but growing as the gunners astride the lead horses of each team urged them on. Closer now so that Sean could see the whip arms rising and falling, he heard the rumble and rattle of the carriage and faintly the shouts of the outriders.

Sixteen guns, one hundred and fifty horses to drag them, and a hundred men to serve them. But in the vastness of the great plain before Colenso the column seemed small and insignificant. Sean looked beyond them and saw the foot soldiers following them, line upon line, like the poles of a fence,

thousands of them creeping forward across the plain. Sean felt the old wild
elation begin. He knew the army was centred upon the line of markers
which he and Saul had laid early the previous night, and that the two of
them would be the first across the bridge – the first of all those thousands.

But it was elation of a different quality to anything he had experienced
before. It was sharper and more poignant, seasoned by the red pepper of his
fear. So that for the first time in his life Sean learned that fear can be a
pleasurable sensation.

He watched the patterns of men and guns evolve upon the brown gaming-
table – counters thrown down at chance, to be won or irretrievably lost at
the fall of the dice of war. Knowing also that he was one of the counters,
afraid and strangely jubilant in this knowledge.

The guns were close now. He could make sense of the shooting, see the
features of the men and even recognize his own feelings in their faces.

Close, perhaps too close. Uneasily Sean glanced back at the forbidding
heights beyond the river and gauged the range. Two thousand yards perhaps,
long rifle shot. And still the guns came on.

'Jesus Christ! Are they mad?' Sean asked aloud.

'They must engage now.' Saul also saw the danger. 'They can't come
closer.'

And still the guns came on. The sound of their charge was low thunder;
dust from the dew-damp earth rose reluctantly behind them; horses with
wide mouths throwing froth as they drove against the traces.

'They're in range now. They must stop, they must!' groaned Sean.

Then at last the column splayed open, alternate guns wheeling left and
right still at full gallop. Swinging broadside to the waiting Boer rifles.

'My God! My God!' Sean mouthed the blasphemy in agony as he watched.
'They'll be massacred.'

Gunners rising in the stirrups, leaning back to check the carriages. The
Gun-Captains jumping from their mounts, letting them gallop free as they
ran to begin the unhitching and the pointing.

In this helpless moment while men swarmed over the guns, man-handling
them to train upon the heights; while the horses still reared and whinnied
in hysterical excitement; before the shells could be unloaded and stacked
beside their pieces – in that moment the Boer rifles opened together. It was
a sound that lacked violence, strangely unwarlike, muted by distance to the
popping of a hundred strings of fireworks, and at first there was no effect.
The grass was thick enough to hide the strike of the bullets, the dust too lazy
with dew to jump and mark their fall.

Then a horse was hit and fell kicking, dragging its mate on to its knees
also. Two men ran to cut it loose, but one of them never reached it. He sat
down suddenly in the grass with his head bowed. Two more horses dropped,
another reared and pawed wildly at the air with one front leg flapping
loosely where a bullet had broken the bone above the knee.

'Get out!' roared Sean. 'Pull back while there's still time,' but his voice
did not carry to the gun crews, could not carry above the shouting and the
screaming of wounded horses.

There was a new sound now which Sean could not identify, a sound like
hair on a tin roof, isolated at first then more frequent until it was a hundred

hammers clanging together in broken rhythm – and he knew it was the sound of bullets striking the metal of the guns.

He saw:

A gunner fall foward and jam the breech of the piece until he was dragged clear;

A loader drop the shell he was carrying and stumble on with his legs folding until he subsided and lay still;

One of the horses break loose and gallop away across the plain dragging a tangle of torn traces behind it;

A covey of wild pheasant rise together out of the grass near the batteries and curve away along the river before dropping on stiff wings back into cover;

And behind the guns the infantry in neat lines advancing placidly towards the huddle of deserted cottages that was Colenso.

Then, with a crash that made the earth jump, and with sixteen long spurts of blue smoke, the guns came into action.

Sean focused his glasses on the ridge in time to see the first shells burst along the crest. The evil blossoms of greenish-yellow lyddite fumes bloomed quickly in the sunlight, then drifted oily-thick on the wind.

Again the guns crashed, and again – each salvo more ragged than the last until it became a continuous stuttering, hammering roar. Until the stark outline of the ridge was blurred and indefinite in the dust and lyddite fumes. There was smoke also, a fine greyish mist of it banked along the heights – the smoke of thousands of rifles.

Quickly Sean set the rear sight of his Lee-Metford at a thousand yards, wriggled forward on his elbows, hunched down over his rifle and began shooting blindly into the smoke on the heights. Beside him Saul was firing also.

Twice Sean emptied his magazine before looking back at the guns. The tempo of their fire had slackened. Most of the horses were down in the grass. Dead men were draped across the gun carriages, others badly wounded crouched for cover behind the mountings, and where six men had served each piece before, now four or only three carried shell and loaded and fired.

'The fools, the bloody fools,' Sean whispered, and began to shoot again, concentrating his whole attention on the routine of jerking the bolt back, sliding it forward in the same motion, sighting up into the mist of gun smoke, and firing. He did not count the shots and each time the weapon clicked empty he groped for another clip from his bandolier and re-loaded. He was starting to sweat now, could feel it trickling down his armpits, his ears buzzed from the concussion of the rifle and his shoulder was beginning to throb.

Gradually a sense of unreality induced by the clamour of the guns and the smell of burnt powder came over him. It seemed that all he would ever do was lie and shoot at nothing, shoot at smoke. Then reality faded further so that all of existence was the vee and dot of a rifle sight, standing solid in mist. And the mist had no shape. In his ears was the vast buzzing silence that drowned all the other sounds of battle. He was alone and tranquil, heavy and dulled by the hypnotic drift of smoke and the repetitive act of loading and firing.

Abruptly the mood was broken. Over them passed a rustle like giant wings, then a crack as though Satan had slammed the door of hell. Startled he looked up and saw a ball of shimmering white smoke standing in the air above the guns, spinning and spreading, growing in the sky like a flower.

'What the . . .'

'Shrapnel,' grunted Saul. 'Now they're finished.'

Then crack and crack again as the Boer Nordenfeldts planted their cotton flowers of smoke above the plain, flailing the guns and the men who still worked them with a buzzing, hissing storm of steel.

Then there were voices. Confused and dazed by the gunfire, it took Sean a minute to place them. He had forgotten the infantry.

'Close up there.'

'Close up on the right. Keep the line!'

'Don't run. Steady, men. Don't run.'

Long lines of men, lines that bulged and lagged and straightened again at the urging of their officers. Evenly spaced, plodding quietly with their rifles held across their chests, they passed the guns. Behind them they left khaki bundles lying on the plain, some of the bundles lay still but others writhed and screamed. As the gaps appeared in the lines they were quickly filled at the chant of 'Close up. Close up there on the flank.'

'They are heading for the railway bridge.' Sean felt the first premonition of disaster. 'Don't they know that it's been destroyed?'

'We'll have to stop them.' Saul scrambled to his feet beside Sean.

'Why didn't the fools follow our markers?' Angrily Sean shouted the question that had no answer. He did it to gain time, to postpone the moment when he must leave the flimsy cover of the grass shelter and go out into the open where the shrapnel and the Mausers swept the ground. Sean's fear came back on him strongly. He didn't want to go out there.

'Come on, Sean. We must stop them.' And Saul started to run. He looked like a skinny little monkey, capering out towards the advancing waves of foot soldiers. Sean sucked in his breath and held it a moment before he followed.

Twenty yards ahead of the leading rank of infantry, carrying a naked sword in one hand and stepping out briskly on long legs, came an officer.

'Hey, you!' Sean shouted at him, waving his hat to catch his attention. He succeeded. The officer fixed him with bright blue eyes like a pair of bayonets and the waxed points of his grey moustache twitched. He strode on towards Sean and Paul.

'You're heading for the wrong bridge,' Sean yelled at him, his voice high-pitched with agitation. 'They've blown the rail bridge, you'll never get across there.'

The officer reached them and checked his stride.

'And who the hell are you, if it's not a rude question?'

'We're the ground scouts . . .' Sean started, then leapt in the air as a Mauser bullet flicked into the ground between his legs. 'And put that bloody sword away – you'll have every Boer on the Tugela competing for you.'

The officer, a colonel by the crowns on his shoulders, frowned at Sean.

'The correct form of address, Sergeant . . .'

'The hell with that!' Sean roared at him. 'Swing your advance on to the road bridge.' He pointed with agitation at the metal superstructure of the bridge that showed on the left through the thorn trees. 'If you continue as you're going they'll cut you to pieces.'

A moment longer the Colonel fixed Sean with his bayonet eyes, then he lifted a silver whistle to his lips and blew a piercing blast.

'Take cover,' he shouted. 'Take cover!'

And immediately the first rank dropped into the grass. Behind them the other ranks lost their rigidity, as men hesitated.

'Get into the town,' a voice shouted. 'Take cover in the buildings.' And they broke and ran, a thousand men, jostling each other, racing for the security of the cottages of Colenso. Pouring into the single street, diving into doorways and windows. Within thirty seconds they had all gone to ground.

'Now, what's this all about?' demanded the Colonel, turning back to Sean. Impatiently Sean repeated himself, standing out in the open and uncomfortably aware that for absence of other targets the Boers were beginning to take a very active interest in them.

'Are you sure?'

'Dammit! Of course, I'm sure. The bridge is destroyed and they have torn up all the barbed wire fences and thrown them into the river. You'll never get across there.'

'Come along.' The Colonel set off towards the nearest cottage and Sean walked beside him. Afterwards he was never certain how he had managed to cover that hundred yards without running.

'For God's sake, put that sword away,' he growled at the Colonel as they walked with the flit, spang, flit, spang of bullets around them.

'Nervous, Sergeant?' And for the first time the Colonel grinned.

'You're damn right, I am.'

'So am I. But it would never do to let the men see that, would it?' He steadied the scabbard on his hips and ran the sword back into it. 'What's your name, Sergeant?'

'Sean Courtney, Natal Corps of Guides. What's yours?' Sean ducked instinctively as a bullet cracked past his head, and the Colonel smiled again at the familiarity.

'Acheson. John Acheson. 2nd Battalion, Scots Fusiliers.'

And they reached the cottage. No longer able to restrain himself, Sean dived thankfully through the kitchen door and found Saul already there. He handed Sean a cheroot and held a match for him.

'These crazy Souties!' he observed. 'And you're as bad as he is – strolling around in the middle of a battle.'

'Right, Courtney.' Acheson followed him into the kitchen. 'Let's go over the situation.'

He listened quietly while Sean explained in detail. He had to shout to lift his voice above the whistle and rack of the Boer artillery and the roar of a thousand Lee-Metford rifles as they replied from the windows and doorways of the village. Around them the kitchen was being used as a dressing-station and the moan and whimper of wounded men added to the hubbub of battle.

When Sean had finished Acheson turned away and strode to the window. He looked out across the railway tracks, to where the guns stood. They were drawn up in precise parade-ground formation. But now they were silent.

Dribbling back towards the shelter of a deep donga – or gully – in the rear, the surviving gunners dragged their wounded with them.

'The poor bastards,' Sean whispered, as he saw one of the retreating gunners killed, shot in the head so that his helmet was thrown spinning upwards in a brief pink cloud of blood.

The sight seemed to rouse Acheson also.

'All right,' he said. 'We'll advance on the road bridge. Come on, Courtney.'

Behind him someone cried out, and Sean heard him fall. But he did not look round. He watched the bridge ahead of him. Although his legs moved mechanically under him it seemed to come no nearer. The thorn trees were thicker here beside the river and they gave a little cover from the merciless marksmen on the far bank. Yet men were falling steadily, and the shrapnel raged and cracked above them.

'Let's get across. Get the best seats on the other side,' Saul shouted beside him.

'Come on, then,' agreed Sean and they ran together. They were first on to the bridge, with Acheson just behind them. Bullets left bright scars on the grey painted metal, and then suddenly, miraculously, they were across. They had crossed the Tugela.

A drainage ditch beside the road and they dived into it, both of them panting. Sean looked back. Over the bridge poured a mass of khaki, all semblance of order gone as they crowded into the bottleneck and the fire from the Boers churned into them.

Once across, the leaders fanned out along the river, crouching below the dip of the bank, while behind them the slaughter on the bridge continued. A struggling mass of cursing, running, angry, frightened and dying men.

'It's a bloody abattoir.' Sean was appalled as he watched it. Dead and wounded men were falling over the low guard rail, splashing into the brown waters of the Tugela to sink or strike out clumsily for the banks. But a steady stream of men was coming across and going to ground in the two-deep drainage ditches, and beneath the angle of the river bank.

It was clear to Sean that the attack was losing its impetus. As the men jumped down into the ditches he saw in their faces and in the way they flattened themselves into shelter that they had lost all stomach for the attack. The ordeal of the bridge had destroyed the discipline that had held their steady advance into those neatly controlled ranks; Officers and men were inextricably mixed into a tired and badly frightened rabble. There was no contact between the different groups in the drainage trenches and those lying in the lee of the river banks – and already there was little cover for the men who were still coming across. The fire from the Boer positions never faltered, and now the bridge was blocked with the bodies of the fallen, so that each new wave had to climb over them, stepping on dead and wounded alike, while the storm of Boer rifle-fire lashed them like wind-driven rain.

Rivulets of fresh bright blood dribbled down the supports of the bridge in ghastly contrast to the grey paint, and the surface of the river was stained by a chocolate-brown cloud of it spreading slowly downstream. Here and there a desperate rallying voice was lifted in the hubbub of incoherent shouts and groans.

'Here the 21st. Form on me the 21st.'

'Independent fire. On the heights. Ten rounds rapid.'

'Stretcher-bearer!'

'Bill. Where are you, Bill?'

'Jesus Christ! Jesus sobbing Christ!'

'Up, you men! Get up!'

'Come on the 21st. Fix bayonets.'

Some of them were head and shoulders out of the ditch returning the Boer fire, a few were drinking from their water-bottles already. A sergeant struggled with a jammed rifle and swore softly without looking up, while beside him a man sat with his back against the wall of the ditch, his legs sprawled open, and watched while the blood pumped from the wound in his belly.

Sean stood and felt the wind of a bullet slap against his cheek, while low in his stomach the slimy reptile of fear coiled itself tighter. Then he scrambled up the side of the ditch.

'Come on!' he roared and started running towards the hills. It was open here, like a meadow, and ahead of him an old barbed-wire fence sagged on rotten poles. He reached it, lifted his foot and kicked with his heel. The fence pole snapped level with the ground, the wire collapsed. He jumped over it.

'They're not coming,' Saul shouted beside him, and Sean stopped. The two of them were alone in the middle of the field – and the Boer rifles were seeking them eagerly.

'Run, Saul!' Sean shouted and snatched off his hat. 'Come on, you bastards.' He waved at the men behind him.

A bullet missed him so narrowly that he staggered in the wind of its passage.

'This way! Follow us! Come on!' Saul had not left him. He was dancing with excitement, and flapping his arms.

'Come back.' Acheson's voice floated across to them. He stood in the drainage ditch, showing clear from the waist up. 'Come back, Courtney!'

The attack was finished. Sean knew it in that instant, and saw the wisdom of Acheson's decision. Further advance over the open meadowland below the heights was suicide. The resolve that had carried him this far collapsed, and his terror snapped the leash he had held upon it. He ran back blindly, sobbing, leaning forward, his elbows pumping in time to his fear-driven feet.

Then suddenly Saul was hit beside him. It took him in the head, threw him forward, his rifle spinning from his hands, squawking hoarsely with pain and surprise as he went down skidding on his belly. And Sean ran on.

'Sean!' Saul's voice left behind him.

'Sean!' A cry of dreadful need, and Sean closed his mind against it and ran on towards the safety of the ditch.

'Sean. Please!' and he checked and stood uncertain with the Mausers barking above and the bullets clipping the grass around him.

Leave him, shrieked Sean's terror. *Leave him. Run! Run!*

Saul crawled towards him, blood on his face and his eyes fastened on Sean's face.

'Sean!'

Leave him. Leave him.

But there was hope in that pitiful blood-smeared face, and the fingers of Saul's hands clawed among the coarse grass roots as he dragged himself forward.

It was beyond all reason. But Sean went back to him.

Beneath the spurs of his terror Sean found the strength to lift him and run with him.

Hating him as he had never hated before, Sean blundered towards the drainage ditch carrying Saul. The acceleration of his brain slowed down the passage of time so that he seemed to run for ever.

'Damn you!' he mouthed at Sean, hating him.

'Damn you to hell!' The words came easily from his mouth, an inarticulate expression of his terror.

Then the ground gave way beneath his feet and he fell. Together they dropped into the drainage ditch and Sean rolled away from him. He lay on his stomach and pressed his face into the earth and shook as a man shakes in high fever.

Slowly he came back from that far place where fear had driven him, and he lifted his head.

Saul sat against the bank of the ditch. His face was streaked with a mixture of blood and dirt.

'How are we doing?' Sean croaked and Saul looked at him dully. It was bright and very hot here in the sun. Sean unscrewed the stopper of his water-bottle and held it to Saul's lips. Saul swallowed painfully and water spilled from the corner of his mouth down his chin and on to his tunic.

Then Sean drank and finished panting with pleasure.

'Let's have a look at your head.'

He lifted Saul's hat from his head, and the blood that had accumulated around the sweat band poured in a fresh flood down Saul's neck. Parting the sodden black hair Sean found the groove in the flesh of his scalp.

'Grazed you,' he grunted and groped for the field dressing in the pocket of Saul's tunic. While he bound an untidy turban round Saul's head he noticed that a strange stillness had fallen on the field, a stillness accentuated rather than broken by the murmur of voices from the men around him and the occasional report of a rifle from the heights above.

The battle was over. At least we got across the river, he thought bitterly. The only problem that now remains is getting back again.

'How's that feel?' He had wet his handkerchief and wiped some of the blood and dust from Saul's face.

'Thank you, Sean.' Suddenly Sean realized that Saul's eyes were full of tears and it embarrassed him. He looked away from them.

'Thank you for . . . for coming back to get me.'

'Forget it.'

'I'll never forget it. Never as long as I live.'

'You'd have done the same.'

'No, I don't think so. I wouldn't have been able to. I was so scared, so afraid, Sean. You'd never know. You'll never know what it's like to be that afraid.'

'Forget it, Saul. Leave it alone.'

'I've got to tell you. I owe it to you – from now on I owe you . . . If you hadn't come back I'd be . . . I'd still be out there. I owe you.'

'Shut up, damn you!' He saw that Saul's eyes were different, the pupils had shrunk to tiny black specks and he was shaking his head in a meaningless idiotic fashion. The bullet had concussed him. But this could not prevent Sean's anger. 'Shut up,' he snarled. 'You think I don't know about fear. I was so scared out there – I hated you. Do you hear that? I hated you!'

And then Sean's voice softened. He had to explain to Saul and himself. He had to tell him about it, to justify it and place it securely in the scheme of things.

Suddenly he felt very old and wise. In his hands he held the key to the whole mystery of life. It was all so clear, for the first time he understood and he could explain it.

They sat close together in the sun, isolated from the men around them, and Sean's voice sank to an urgent whisper as he tried to make Saul understand, tried to pass on to him this knowledge that embraced all truth.

Beside them lay a corporal of the Fusiliers. He lay on his back, dead, and the flies swarmed over his eyes and laid their eggs. They looked like tiny grains of rice clustered in the lashes around his dead open eyes.

Saul leaned heavily against Sean's shoulder, now and then he shook his head in confusion as he listened to Sean. Listened to Sean's voice tripping and stumbling then starting to hurry as his ideas broke up and crumpled, heard the desperation in it as Sean strove to retain just a few grains of all that knowledge which had been his a few moments before. Heard it peter out into silence and sorrow as he found that it was gone.

'I don't know,' Sean admitted at last.

Then Saul spoke, his voice was dull and his eyes would not focus properly as he peered at Sean from beneath the blood-soiled turban of bandages.

'Ruth,' he said, 'You speak like Ruth does. Sometimes in the night when she cannot sleep she tries to tell me. Almost I understand, almost she finds it and then she stops "I don't know," she says at last. "I just don't know." '

Sean jerked away from him, and stared into his face. 'Ruth?' he asked quietly.

'Ruth – my wife. You'd like her, Sean – she'd like you. So brave   she came to me through the Boer lines All the way from Pretoria – riding alone. She came to me. I couldn't believe it. All that way. She just walked into camp one day and said, "Hello, Saul. I'm here!" just like that! You'll like her when you meet her, Sean. She's so beautiful, so serene . . .'

In October when the big winds blow they come for the first time on a still day. It has been hot and dry for perhaps a month, then you hear them from far away, roaring softly. The roar mounts quickly, the dust races brown on the wind and the trees lean away from it, threshing and churning their branches. You see it coming but all your preparations are nothing when it hits. The vast roaring and the dust envelope you and you are numbed and blinded by the violence of it.

In the same way Sean saw it coming, he recognized it as the murderous rage which before had nearly killed a man, but still he could not prepare himself. And then it was upon him and the roaring filled his head and narrowed his vision so that all he could see was the face of Saul Friedman. The face was in profile for Saul was staring back across the plain of Colenso towards the English lines.

Sean lifted the dead corporal's rifle and laid it across his lap. With his thumb he slipped off the safety-catch, but Saul did not notice the movement.

'She's in Pietermaritzburg, I had a letter from her last week,' he murmured, and Sean shifted the rifle in his lap so that the muzzle aimed into the side of Saul's chest below the armpit.

'I sent her down to Pietermaritzburg. She's staying with her uncle there.' Saul lifted his hand and touched his head. Sean curled his finger on the trigger. 'I wish you could meet her, Sean. She'd like you.' Now he looked into Sean's face, and there was such pathetic trust in his eyes. 'When I write I am going to tell her about today – about what you did.'

Sean took up the slack in the trigger until he could feel the final resistance.

'We both owe you—' Saul stopped and smiled shyly. 'I just want you to know that I'll never forget it.'

Kill him, roared Sean's head. Kill him now – kill him quickly. Don't let him talk.

It was the first conscious command his instinct had issued.

Now! Do it now! But his trigger-finger relaxed.

This is all that stands between you and Ruth. Do it, do it now. The roaring in his head abated. The big wind had passed by and he could hear it receding. He lifted the rifle and slowly pushed the safety-catch across.

In the stillness after the wind he knew suddenly that from now on Saul Friedman was his special charge. Because he had come so close to taking it from him, Saul's life had become a debt of honour.

He laid the rifle aside and closed his eyes wearily.

'We'd better think about getting out of here,' he said quietly. 'Otherwise I might never get around to meeting this beauty of yours.'

Chapter Sixteen

'Hart has got himself into a mess out there!' General Sir Redvers Buller's voice matched the pompous jut of his belly and he leaned back against the weight of the telescope he held to his eye. 'What do you think, Courtney?'

'Well, he certainly hasn't reached the drift, sir. It looks to me as though he's been pinned down in the loop of the river,' Garry agreed.

'Damn the man! My orders were clear,' growled Buller. 'What can you make of the guns – can you see anything there?'

Every telescope in the party of officers swivelled back to the centre, to where the corrugated iron roofs of Colenso showed above the thorn trees, dimly through the dust and the smoke.

'I can't . . . Garry started, then jumped uncontrollably as the naval 4·7 bellowed from its emplacement beside them. Every time that morning it had fired, Garry had jumped. If only I knew when it was going to, he thought and jumped again as it bellowed.

'They are not being served,' one of the other staff officers interposed and Garry envied him his composure and his calmness of voice. His own hands were trembling so that he must grip hard with both hands to keep his binoculars focused on the town. Each time the naval gun fired the dust of its recoil drifted over them, also the sun was fierce and he was thirsty. He thought of the flask in his saddle-bags and the next bellow of the gun caught him completely off guard. This time both his feet left the ground.

'. . . Do you agree, Courtney?' Buller's voice, he had not heard the beginning of the question.

'I do indeed, sir.'

'Good.' The General turned to his A.D.C. 'Send a rider to Hart. Tell him to pull out of there before he gets badly mauled. Quick as you can, Clery.'

At that moment Garry made a remarkable discovery. Behind the inscrutable mask of his face with its magnificent silver moustache, behind the bulging expressionless eyes – General Sir Redvers Buller was every bit as agitated and uncertain as was Garry Courtney. His continual appeals to Garry for support confirmed this. Of course, Garry did not consider that another reason why Buller addressed his appeals to him, rather than the regular officers of his staff, was because this was the one quarter from which Buller could rely on unquestioning support.

'That takes care of the left flank.' Buller was clearly relieved at his decision as he searched out towards the right, fixing the low round bulk of Hlangwane Kopje in the field of his telescope. 'Dundonald seems to be keeping his end up.' Earlier, there had been desultory rifle and pompom fire from the right flank. Now it was silent.

'But the centre . . .' As though he had been delaying the moment, Buller at last turned his attention on the holocaust of dust and flame and shrapnel that enveloped Colenso.

'Come along.' He snapped his telescope closed. 'We'd better have a closer look at what they've accomplished there.' And he led his staff back to the horses. Careful that no one should usurp his place at the General's right hand, Garry limped along beside him.

At the headquarters of Lyttelton's Brigade, established in a deep donga half a mile before the first scattered buildings of the town, it took Buller half a minute to find out what had been accomplished. It appalled him.

'We hold the town, sir. And three companies have advanced to the road bridge and seized it. But we cannot hope to hold it. I have sent a runner ordering them to withdraw on the town.'

'But why aren't the guns firing? What's happened to Colonel Long?'

'The guns have been silenced. Long is badly wounded.'

While Buller sat his horse, slowly absorbing this, a sergeant of the Transvaal Staats Artillerie jerked the lanyard of his quick-firing Nordenfeldt and fired the shell which changed a British reverse into a resounding defeat that would echo around the world.

From out of the broken and rocky complex of hills on the north bank the shell arched upwards; over the river with its surface churned to brown by shrapnel and short shell and blood; high over the deserted guns manned only by corpses; shrieking over the heads of the surviving gunners as they crouched in the rear with their wounded, forcing them to duck as they had ducked a thousand times before; plunging in its descent over the town of Colenso where weary men waited; down across thorn tree and mimosa and brown grass veld littered with dead men; falling at last in a tall jump of dust and smoke in the midst of General Buller's staff.

Beneath him Garry's horse dropped, killed instantly, pinning his leg so that had it been flesh and bone, not carved oak, it would have been crushed. He felt the blood soaking through his tunic and splattered in his face and mouth.

'I've been hit. Help me, God help me, I'm wounded.' And he writhed and struggled in the grass, wiping the blood on his face.

Rough hands freed his leg and dragged him clear of his horse.

'Not your blood. You're all right. Not your blood, it's his.'

On his hands and knees Garry stared in horror at the Surgeon-Major who had stood beside him and who had shielded him from the blast. Shrapnel had cut his head away, and the blood still spouted from his neck as though it were a severed hose.

Around him men fought their panic-stricken horses as they reared and whinnied. Buller was doubled up in the saddle, clutching the side of his chest.

'Sir, sir, Are you all right?' An A.D.C. had the reins and was bringing Buller's horse under control. Two officers ran to Buller and helped him down. He stood between them, his face contorted with pain, and and his voice when he spoke was shaky, but hoarse.

'Disengage, Lyttelton! Disengage on your whole front!'

'Sir,' protested the Brigadier. 'We hold the town. Let me cover the guns until nightfall when we can retrieve them at our . . .'

'Damn you, Lyttelton. You heard me. Pull your brigade back immediately. The attack has failed.' Buller's breathing wheezed in his throat and he still clutched the side of his chest with both hands.

'To withdraw now will mean accepting heavier losses than we have suffered already. The enemy artillery is accurately ranged . . .'

'Pull them out, do you hear me!' Buller's voice rose to a shout.

'The guns . . .' Lyttelton tried again, but Buller had already turned to his A.D.C.

'Send riders to Lord Dundonald's Brigade. He must retire immediately. I give him no latitude of discretion, he is to disengage his force at once and withdraw. Tell him . . . tell him the attack has failed on left and centre, tell him the guns are lost and he is in danger of being surrounded. Go. Ride fast.'

There was a murmur among them, horrified as they listened to these orders. Miserably every eye turned to Lyttelton, silently they pleaded with him, for he was the senior officer present.

'General Buller.' He spoke softly, but with an urgency that caught even Buller's shell-shocked attention. 'At least, let me try to recover the guns. We cannot abandon them. Let me call for volunteers. . . .'

'I'll go, sir. Please let me try.' A young subaltern elbowed Garry aside in his eagerness. Garry knew who he was, all of them did, for apart from being one of the most promising and popular youngsters in Buller's command – he was also the only son of the legendary Lord Roberts.

Assisted by his A.D.C., Buller moved to the shade of a mimosa tree and sank down heavily with his back against the rough bark of the trunk. He looked up at young Roberts, dully, without apparent interest.

'All right, Bobbie, Lyttelton will give you men. Off you go then.' He pronounced the sentence of death upon him, and Roberts laughed excitedly, gaily, and ran to his horse.

'I think we are all in need of refreshment. Will you join me in a sandwich and a glass of champagne, gentlemen?' Buller nodded to his A.D.C., who hurried to bring food and drink from his saddle-bags. A stray shell burst twenty yards away, scattering clods of earth over them. Stolidly Buller brushed a piece of dry grass from his whiskers and selected a smoked salmon sandwich.

Chapter Seventeen

Sean crawled down the drainage ditch towards the bank of the river. A shell burst on the edge of the ditch and scattered clods of earth over his back. He paused to brush a tangle of grass roots out of his whiskers and then crawled on to where Colonel Acheson squatted on his haunched in earnest conversation with a captain of the Fusiliers.

'Hey, Colonel Acheson. I doubt you'll need me again, will you?' The Captain looked shocked at Sean's term of address, but Acheson grinned briefly.'

'A runner just got through. We have been ordered to withdraw.'

'What a pity!' Sean grunted sarcastically. 'Just when we were knocking the daylights out of old brother Boer,' and all three of them ducked as a machine-gun hammered lumps of dirt out of the bank above their heads. Then Sean took up from where he had been interrupted. 'Well, in that case – I'll be leaving you.'

'Where are you going?' the Captain demanded suspiciously.

'Not across that bridge.' Sean removed the stub of his cheroot from his mouth and pointed with it at the grey structure with its gruesome streaks of new paint. 'I've got a wounded man with me. He'll never make it. Have you got a match?'

Automatically the Captain produced a box of wax matches from his breast-pocket. 'Thanks. I'm going to swim him downstream and find a better place to cross.' Sean re-lit his cheroot, blew a cloud of smoke and returned the Captain's matches.

'A pleasure meeting you, Colonel Acheson.'

'You have permission to fall out, Courtney.' A second longer they looked into each other's eyes, and Sean experienced a powerful desire to shake this man's hand but instead he started crawling back along the ditch.

'Courtney!' Sean paused and glanced over his shoulder. 'What's the name of the other Guide?'

'Friedman. Saul Friedman.'

Acheson scribbled briefly in his notebook, then returned it to his pocket.

'You'll hear more about today – good luck.'

'And to you, sir.'

From a tree that hung out over the brown water of the Tugela, Sean hacked a bushy green branch with his bayonet.

'Come on,' and Saul slid down the greasy clay of the bank, waist-deep into the river beside Sean.

'Leave your rifle.' Obediently Saul dropped it into the river.

'What's the bush for?'

'To cover our heads.'

'Why are we waiting?'

'For Acheson to create a diversion when he tries to get back across the bridge.'

At that moment a whistle shrilled on the bank above them. Immediately a fierce covering fire blared out and a party of khaki-clad figures stampeded out on to the bridge.

'Now,' grunted Sean. They sank together into the blood-warm water with only their heads, wreathed in leaves, above the surface. Sean pushed out gently and the current caught them. Neither of them looked back at the shrieking carnage on the bridge as they drifted away.

Twenty minutes later and a half-mile downstream, Sean edged across the current towards the remains of the railway bridge that hung like a broken drawbridge into the river. It offered a perfect access to the south and the embankment of the railway would cover them in their retreat across the plain.

Sean's feet touched mud bottom, then they were under the sagging bridge like chickens under the wing of a hen. He let the branch float away and dragged Saul to the bank between the metal girders.

'Five minutes' rest,' he told him and squatted beside him to rewind the bandage that had come down over Saul's ears. Muddy water streamed from sodden uniforms, and Sean mourned the cheroots in his tunic pocket.

There was another drainage ditch running beside the high gravel embankment of the railway. Along it, walking in a crouch, Sean prodded Saul ahead of him, yelling at him every time he attempted to straighten up and relieve his aching back. Once a sniper on the kopjes behind them thumped a bullet into the gravel near Sean's head, and Sean swore wearily and almost touched his knees with his nose. But Saul did not notice it. With his legs sloppy under him he staggered along in front of Sean, until finally he fell and lay in a sprawling, untidy heap in the bottom of the ditch.

Sean kicked him.

'Get up, damn you!'

'No, Ruth. Don't wake me up yet, It's Sunday. I don't have to work today.' Speaking quite clearly in a reasonable persuasive tone Saul looked up at Sean, but his eyes were matt and the pupils shrunken to black points.

'Get up. Get up!' The use of Ruth's name inflamed Sean. He caught Saul's shoulder and shook him. Saul's head jerked crazily and fresh blood seeped through his bandage. Instantly contrite, Sean laid him back gently.

'Saul, please. You must try. Just a little farther.'

'Glossless,' whispered Saul. 'There is no gloss on it. I don't want it.' And he closed his eyes, his lips bulged open and his breath snored through them in tiny bubbles of spittle.

A suffocating despair dropped down over Sean as he studied Saul's face. The eyes had receded into dark plum-coloured cavities, leaving the skin stretched tight across his cheeks and across the gaunt bony nose.

Not because I nearly killed him, not because I owe it to him. But because – but because? How can you define your feelings for another man. All you can say is – because he is my friend. Then, because he is my friend I cannot leave him here.

Sinking down beside him, Sean lifted his slack body into a sitting position, draped one of Saul's arms around his shoulder and stood up. Saul hung beside him, his head lolled forward on his chest, and Sean looked ahead. He could see the survivors from the bridge struggling back through the village, dragging their wounded with them.

Across the whole breadth of the plain, singly and in twos and threes, harried by shrapnel, beaten, broken, Buller's mighty army was in retreat. And there, not a hundred yards from where Sean crouched in the railway ditch, drawn up neatly in the grass, deserted, forlorn, stood the field guns.

Quickly Sean averted his eyes from them and began plodding away from the river. Over his shoulder he held Saul's wrist, his free arm was wrapped around Saul's waist.

Then slowly he was aware that the Boer fire was crescendoing once more Shell that had fallen haphazard among the retreating men began to concentrate on an area directly ahead of Sean. Behind him the rifle fire that had popped spasmodically on the heights now swelled into a fierce, sustained crackle like a bushfire in green forest.

Leaning against the side of the ditch Sean peered ahead through the mimosa trees and the storm of dust and bursting shell. He saw horses, two teams in harness, men with them racing in through the thorn trees, lifting pale dust in a cloud to mingle with the dust of the shells. Far ahead of them, brandishing his cane, leading them in towards the abandoned guns, galloped a figure on a big shiny bay.

'He's laughing.' In wonder, Sean watched the leading rider disappear behind a column of dust and high explosive, only to emerge again as he swerved his mount like a polo player. His mouth was open and Sean saw the glint of white teeth. 'The fool is laughing his head off!'

And suddenly Sean was cheering wildly.

'Ride, man, Ride!' he shouted and his voice was lost in the shriek and crash of the bombardment.

'They've come to fetch the guns,' howled Sean. 'Saul, they've come for the guns.' Without knowing how he had done it, mad with the excitement of it, Sean found himself out of the ditch, running with new strength, running with Saul's unconscious weight slung over his shoulder, running through the grass towards the guns.

By the time he reached the battery the first team was already there. The men were down struggling to back the horses up to the trail of the Number One gun. Sean slid the inert body from his shoulder and dropped it in the grass. Two of them were trying to lift the trail of the field gun, but this task required four men.

'Get out of the way!' Sean shouted at them and straddled the long wedge-shaped trail of steel. He locked his hands into the grips and heaved upwards, lifting it clear and high.

'Get the carriage.' Quickly they rolled the detachable axle and wheels in under the trail and locked them into position. Sean stepped back panting.

'Well done!' The younger officer leaned forward in his saddle as he shouted at Sean. 'Get up on the carriage.'

But Sean turned and ran to Saul, he picked him up and stumbled with him to the carriage.

'Grab him!' he grunted at the two soldiers who were already aboard. Between them they dragged Saul up on to the carriage seat.

'No room for you, cock. Why don't you take Taffy's place on the right-hand wheeler?' one of them shouted down, and Sean saw he was correct. The drivers were mounting up, but one saddle was empty.

'Look after him,' he told the man who held Saul.

'Don't worry, I've got him,' the gunner assured him, and then urgently, 'You'd best grab a seat – we're pulling out.'

'Look after him,' Sean repeated and started forward.

In that moment the luck which had protected him all that morning ran out. A shell burst beside him. He felt no pain but his right leg gave under him and he went down on his knees.

He tries to stand but his body would not obey.

'Forward!' shouted the subaltern, and the gun carriage trundled away, gathering speed, beginning to jolt and bounce as the drivers lashed the horses. Sean saw the gunner who held Saul staring back at him from the carriage, his face was contorted with helplessness.

'Look after him!' Sean shouted. 'Promise me you'll look after him.'

The gunner opened his mouth to reply, but another shell burst between them, throwing up a curtain of dust that hid the carriage. This time Sean felt the shrapnel tear into his flesh. It stung like the cut of a razor and he sagged sideways. As he went down he saw that the subaltern had been hit as well. Saw him throw up his arms and fall backwards over the rump of his horse, rolling from the saddle, hitting the ground with his shoulder, one foot caught in the stirrup so that he dragged over the rough ground until the stirrup leather snapped and left him lying. His horse galloped away in pursuit of the careering gun carriage.

Sean dragged himself after it. 'Look after him,' he shouted. 'For God's sake, look after Saul.' But nobody heard that shout for they were gone away amongst the trees, gone away in the dust with the shellfire escorting them like a troop of brown demons.

Still Sean crawled after them, using one hand to reach ahead and claw into the earth and inch his whole body belly down through the grass. His other arm dragged at his side, and he could feel his right leg slithering after him, until it caught and tethered him. He struggled against it, but his toe had hooked in a tuft of coarse grass and he could not free it. He wriggled on to his side and doubled up with his broken arm beneath him to look back at his leg.

There was much blood, a wet, slippery drag-mark of it across the flattened grass, and still it welled up out of his body. But there was no pain, only a dizziness and a weariness in his head.

His leg twisted at a ridiculous angle from his trunk, and the spur on his boot stood up jauntily. He wanted to laugh at the leg, but somehow the effort was too great and he closed his eyes against the glare of the sun.

Near him he heard somebody groaning and for a while he thought it must be Saul. Then he remembered that Saul was safe, and it was the young subaltern. With his eyes closed Sean lay and listened to him die. It was an ugly sound.

Chapter Eighteen

Battle-General Jan Paulus Leroux stood upon the heights above the Tugela and removed his Terai hat. His head was bald with a fringe of ginger hair above the ears and thick around the back. The skin of his pate was smooth and creamy white where the hat had protected it from the sun, but his face had been weathered and sculptured by the elements until it looked like a cliff of red-stone.

'Bring my pony, Hennie.' He spoke to the lad who stood beside him.

'*Ja*, Oom Paul.' And he hurried away down the reverse slope to the pony laager.

From the firing trench at Jan Paulus's feet one of his burghers looked up at him.

'God has heard our prayers, Oom Paul. He has given us a great victory.'

Jan Paulus nodded heavily, and his voice as he replied was low and humble, without any trace of jubilation.

'*Ja*, Fredevik. In God's name, a great victory.'

But not as great as I had planned it, he thought.

Out of cannon shot, almost out of range of the naked eye, the last tattered remnants of the British were dwindling into the brown distance.

If only they could have waited, he thought with bitterness. So clearly I explained it to them, and they did not heed me.

His whole strategy had revolved upon the bridge. If only his burghers on the kopje below the heights had held their fire and let them cross. Then God would have delivered the enemy to them in thousands instead of hundreds. Caught in the amphitheatre of the heights with the river at their backs none of them would have escaped when his artillery destroyed the bridge behind them. Sadly he looked down upon the trap he had laid with such infinite care. From above he could see the trenches, each of them, masked and cunningly overlapped so that an unbearable fire could sweep the grassy bowl into which he had hoped to lure the British centre. The trap that would never be sprung, for he knew they would not come again.

Hennie climbed back to him, leading his pony, and Jan Paulus mounted quickly.

'Come, let us go down.'

At forty-two years of age, Jan Paulus Leroux was very young for the command he held. There had been opposition in Pretoria to his appointment when old Joubert retired, but President Kruger had ridden rough-shod over it and forced the Volkraad to accept. Ten minutes before, Jan Paulus had sent him a telegraphed message which had justified this confidence.

With long stirrup leathers, his massive body loose and relaxed in the saddle, his *sjambok* trailing from his wrist and the wide-brimmed hat shading his face, Jan Paulus went down to gather the harvest of war.

As he reached the kopjes and rode in among them, his burghers rose from their trenches on the slopes and cheered him. Their voices blended in a savage roar that echoed from the heights like the jubilation of lions on a new kill. Impassively Jan Paulus examined their faces as he passed. They were coated with red dust and burned powder, and sweat had run in dark lines through the grime. One man used his rifle as a crutch to balance himself against his wound, and there were harsh lines of pain around his mouth as he cheered. Jan Paulus checked his pony. 'Lie down, don't be a fool, man!' The man grinned painfully and shook his head.

'*Nee*, Oom Paul. I'm going with you to fetch the guns.'

Brusquely Jan Paulus motioned to the men who stood beside the wounded burgher. 'Take him away. Take him to the doctors.' And he trotted on to where Commandant Van Wyk waited for him.

'I told you to hold your men until they crossed,' he greeted him, and Van Wyk's grin faded.

'*Ja*, Oom Paul. I know. But I could not hold them. The young ones started it. When they saw the guns right there under their noses – I could not hold them.' Van Wyk turned and pointed across the river. 'Look how near they were.'

Jan Paulus looked across the river. The guns were standing in the open, so close and so lightly screened by the intervening thorn scrub that he could count the spokes of the wheels and see the sparkle of the brass breech fittings.

'It was too much temptation,' Van Wyk ended lamely.

'So! It is done, and we cannot undo it with words.' Grimly Jan Paulus determined that this man would never command again. 'Come, we will fetch them.'

At the road bridge Jan Paulus halted the long column of horsemen behind him. Although none of it showed on his face, yet his stomach heaved with horror at what he saw.

'Move them,' he ordered, and as the thirty burghers dismounted and went forward to clear the bridge he called out after them. 'Handle them gently, lift them – do not drag them away like mealie sacks. These were men. Brave men.' Beside him the boy, Hennie, was crying openly. The tears falling on to his patched tweed jacket.

'Be still, Jong,' Jan Paulus murmured gently. 'Tears are for women.' And he urged his pony into the narrow passage between the dead. It was the dust and the sun and the lyddite fumes which had irritated his own eyes, he told himself angrily.

Quietly, lacking the triumphant bearing of victors, they came to the guns and spread out among them. Then a single rifle-shot cracked out and a burgher staggered and clutched the wheel of a gun carriage for support.

Whirling his pony, and flattening himself along its neck, Jan Paulus charged the donga beyond the guns from which the shot had come. Another shot hissed past his head, but by then Jan Paulus had reached the donga. Pulling his mount down from full gallop on to its haunches, he jumped from the saddle and kicked the rifle out of the British private's hands before dragging him to his feet.

'We have killed too much already, you fool.' Stumbling over the English words, his tongue clumsy with rage, he roared into the soldier's face. 'It is finished. Give up.' And then turning on the surviving gunners who huddled along the donga. 'Give up, give up, all of you!' None of them moved for a long minute, then slowly one at a time they stood up and shuffled out of the donga.

While a party of Boers led the prisoners away, and the others went about the business of hitching up the guns and the ammunition wagon, the British stretcher-bearers began filtering forward through the mimosa trees. Soon khaki figures were mingled everywhere with the burghers as they searched like bird-dogs for the wounded.

Two of them, dark-skinned Indians of the Medical Corps, had found a man lying out on the left flank. They were having difficulty with him, and Jan Paulus handed the reins of his pony to Hennie and walked across to them.

In semi-delirium the wounded man was cursing horribly and resisting all attempts by the two Indians to fix splints on his leg.

'Leave me alone, you bastards,' and a flying fist knocked one of them sprawling. Jan Paulus, recognizing the voice and the punch, started to run.

'You behave yourself, or I'll klop you one,' he growled as he reached them. Groggily Sean rolled his head and tried to focus on him.

'What's that? Who are you? Get the hell away from me.'

Jan Paulus did not answer. He was looking at the wounds and they made him want to vomit.

'Give to me.' He took the splints from the shaken bearers and squatted down beside Sean.

'Get away!' Sean screamed at him. 'I know what you're going to do. You're going to cut it off!'

'Sean!' Jan Paulus caught his wrist and held it while Sean writhed and swore.

'I'll kill you, you filthy bastard. I'll kill you if you touch it.'

'Sean! It's me. Look at me!'

And slowly Sean relaxed, his eyes steadied.

'It's you? It's really you?' he whispered. 'Don't let them ... don't let them take my leg. Not like they did to Garry.'

'Be still, or I'll break your stupid head,' growled Jan Paulus. Like his face, his hands were beefy and red, big hands with fingers like calloused sausages, but now they worked as gently as those of a mother on her child. At last, holding the ankle, he looked at Sean.

'Hold fast, now. I must straighten it.'

Sean tried to grin, but his face was grey beneath the coating of battle filth, and sweat squeezed from his skin like a rash of tiny blisters.

'Don't talk so much, you bloody Dutchman. Do it!'

Bone grated on broken bone deep in the torn flesh and Sean gasped. Every muscle in his body convulsed and then relaxed again as he fainted.

'*Ja*', grunted Jan Paulus. 'That's better,' and for the first time the set of his features betrayed his compassion. He finished with the bandages, and for a few seconds continued to squat beside Sean's unconscious body. Then he whispered so low that the two bearers could not catch the words.

'Sleep well, my brother. May God spare you your leg.'

And he stood, all trace of pity and sorrow locked away behind the red-stone of his face.

'Take him away,' he ordered, and waited while they lifted the stretcher and staggered away with it.

He went to his pony, and his feet dragged a little through the grass. From the saddle he looked once more towards the south but the two bearers had disappeared with their burden among the mimosa trees. He touched spurs to his pony's flanks and followed the long procession of wagons, prisoners and guns back towards the Tugela. The only sound was the jingle of harness and the melancholy rumble of wheels.

Chapter Nineteen

Garrick Courtney watched the champagne spilling into the crystal bowl of his glass. The bubbles swirled in golden patterns, catching the lantern light. The mess corporal lifted the bottle, dexterously caught a drop of wine on his napkin and moved behind Garry to fill the glass of Brigadier Lyttelton, who sat beside him.

'No.' Lyttelton placed a hand over his empty glass to prevent him doing so.

'Come, come, Lyttelton.' Sir Redvers Buller leaned forward and looked down the table. 'That's an excellent wine.'

'Thank you, sir, but champagne is for victory – perhaps we should have a case sent across the river.'

Buller flushed slowly and looked down at his own glass. Once more an ugly silence descended on the mess. In an effort to break it Garry spoke up.

'I do think the withdrawal today was made in extremely good order.'

'Oh. I agree most heartily.' From across the table Lord Dundonald's icy sarcasm added to the gaiety. 'But in all fairness, Colonel, we were travelling very light on our return.'

This oblique reference to the guns sent every eye to Buller's face – Dundonald was showing a reckless disregard of that notorious temper. But as a peer of the realm he could take the chance. With a courteous insolence he met Buller's glare, and held it until the pale bulging eyes faded and dropped.

'Gentlemen.' Buller spoke heavily. 'We have had a most trying day, and for all of us there is still work to do.' He glanced at his A.D.C. 'Clery, will you be kind enough to propose the Queen?'

Alone, Garry limped from the huge marquee mess tent. The smaller tents, lit internally, were a vast field of luminous cones, and above them the night was black satin sown with silver stars. The wine that Garry had drunk during dinner hummed in his head so that he did not notice the dejected silence that smothered the encampment as he picked his way through it.

As Garry entered his headquarters a man stood up from the camp chair beside his desk. In the light of the lantern his features were gaunt, and weariness showed in every line of his body.

'Ah! Curtis.'

'Good evening, sir.'

'You've come to make your report?'

'I have, sir. For what it's worth.'

'Tell me, Curtis – how many casualties?' There was an eagerness behind the question which Tim found ghoulish. Speculatively he examined Garry's face before replying.

'We suffered heavily, out of a strength of twenty we had four killed, two missing and five wounded – three of them seriously.'

'Have you made out a list?'

'Not yet.'

'Well, tell me. Who were they?'

'Killed were Booth, Amery . . .'

No longer could Garry hold his impatience, he blurted out suddenly:

'What about that sergeant?'

'You mean Courtney?'

'Yes. *Yes*.' And now with his impatience was mingled a dread that made his stomach feel hollow.

'Wounded, sir.'

And Garry felt a lift of relief so intense that he must close his eyes and suck in his breath to ride it up.

Sean was still alive! Thank God. Thank God for that.

'Where is he now?'

'They've got him down at the railhead hospital. He's being sent out with the first batch of badly wounded.'

'Badly?' Garry's relief changed quickly to concern, and he demanded harshly, 'How badly? *How badly?*'

'That's all they told me. I went down to the hospital but they wouldn't allow me to see him.'

Garry sank into his chair and instinctively reached for the drawer before he checked himself.

'Very well, Curtis. You may go.'

'The rest of my report, sir?'

'Tomorrow. Leave it till tomorrow.'

With the liquor glowing hotly in his belly, Garry set off through the night towards the hospital. It did not matter now that he had planned and hoped that Sean would die. He no longer reasoned, but hurried through the sprawling camp, driven by his desperate need. Unrecognized but strong within him was the hope that he might again draw comfort and strength from that fountain as he had done so long ago. He started to run, stiffly, so the toe of his boot scuffed in the dust with each pace.

Desperately he searched through the hospital. He hurried along the rows of stretchers examining the faces of the wounded; he saw pain and mutilation and slow creeping death soaking like spilt red ink through the white bandages. He heard the moan and murmur and delirious laughter, he smelt the taint of agony-induced sweat blended with the heavy sweetness of corruption and disinfectant – and he hardly noticed them. One face, one face only, he wanted. And he did not find it.

'Courtney.' The medical orderly examined his list, tilting it to catch the lamplight. 'Ah! Yes. Here it is – let's see. Yes! He's gone already – left on the first train an hour ago . . . I can't say, sir, probably to Pietermaritzburg. They've established a big new hospital there. I can't tell you that either, I'm afraid, but they've got him listed here as *dangerous* . . . that's better than *critical* anyway.'

Wearing his loneliness like a cloak, Garry stumbled back to his quarters.

'Good evening, sir.' His servant was waiting for him. Garry always made them wait up. A new man this, they changed so fast. Never could keep a batman more than a month.

Garrick pushed past him, and half fell against the camp bed.

'Steady on, sir. Let's get you on to the bed, sir.' The man's voice was insidiously servile, the voice men used towards drunks. The touch of his hands infuriated Garry.

'Leave me.' He lashed out with a clenched fist across the man's face, throwing him back. 'Leave me. Get out and leave me!'

The servant rubbed his bruised cheek uncertainly, backing away.

'Get out!' Garry hissed at him.

'But, sir—'

'Get out, damn you. Get out!'

The man went out and closed the tent flap softly behind him. Garry stumbled across to it and laced it closed. Then he stood back. Alone. They can't see me now. They can't laugh now. They can't. Oh God, Sean!

He turned from the flap. The dummy leg caught on the rough floor and he fell. One of the straps parted and the leg twisted under him. On his hands and knees he crawled towards the commode across the tent, and the leg jerked and twisted grotesquely behind him.

Kneeling beside the commode he lifted the china basin from its recess and reached into the space below it and he found the bottle. His fingers were too clumsy for the cork, he pulled it with his teeth and spat it on to the floor. Then he held the bottle to his lips and his throat jerked rhythmically as he swallowed. A little of the brandy spilled on to his tunic and stained the ribbon of the Victoria Cross.

He lowered the bottle and rested, panting from the sting of the liquor. Then he drank again more slowly. The trembling of his hands stilled. His breathing smoothed out. He reached up and took the tumbler from the top of the commode, filled it, then placed the bottle beside him on the floor and wriggled into a more comfortable position against the commode.

In front of him his artificial leg twisted on its broken straps at an unnatural angle below the knee. He contemplated it, sipping the brandy slowly and feeling it numb the taste-buds of his tongue.

The leg was the centre of his existence. Insensate, unmoving, still as the eye of a great storm upon which the whole turmoil of his life revolved. The leg – always the leg. Always and only the leg.

Now under the lulling spell of the liquor he had drunk, from the stillness at the centre where the leg lay, he looked outward at the gigantic shadows of the past, and found them preserved and perfect, not distorted or blurred by time, whole and complete in each detail.

While they paraded through his mind, the night telescoped in upon itself so that time had no significance. The hours endured for a few minutes and were gone while the level in the bottle fell and he sat against the commode sipping at the tumbler and watching while the night wasted away. In the dawn the final act was played out before him.

Himself on a horse in the darkness riding in cold soft rain towards Theuniskraal. One window showing a yellow oblong of lantern light, the rest dark in the greater dark mass of the homestead.

The unaccountable premonition of coming horror closing cold and soft as the rain around him, the silence spoiled only by the crunch of his horse's hooves in the gravel of the drive. The thump of his pegleg as he climbed the front steps and the chill of the brass doorknob in his hand as he turned it and pushed it in upon the silence.

His own voice slurred with drink and dread. 'Hello. Where's everybody? Anna! Anna! I'm back!'

The blue flare of his match and the smell of burnt sulphur and paraffin as he lit the lamp, then the urgent echoing thump of his pegleg along the passage.

'Anna, Anna, where are you?'

Anna, his bride, lay upon the bed in the darkened room, half-naked, turning quickly away from the light, but he had seen the dead-white face with swollen and bruised lips.

The lamp from the table threw bloated shadows on the wall as he stooped over and gently drew down the petticoats to cover the whiteness of her lower body, then turned her to face him. 'My darling, oh Anna, my darling. What's happened?' Through the torn blouse her breasts were engorged and darkly nippled with pregnancy. 'Are you hurt? Who? Tell me who did it?' But she covered her face and broken lips with her hands.

'My darling, my poor darling. Who was it – one of the servants?'

'No.'

'Please tell me, Anna. What happened?'

Suddenly her arms were about his neck and her lips close against his ear. 'You know, Garry! You know who did it.'

'No, I swear I don't. Please tell me.'

Her voice tight and hoarse with hatred, uttering that word, that one unbelievable horrible word. 'Sean!'

'Sean!' he said aloud in his desolation. 'Sean. Oh God! and then savagely, 'I hate him. I hate him! Let him die – please God, let him die.'

He closed his eyes, losing his grip upon reality, and felt the first dizzy swing of vertigo as the liquor took firm hold upon him.

Too late now to open his eyes and focus them upon the bed across the tent, the giddiness had begun – now he would not be able to hold it down. The warm, acid-sweet taste of brandy welled up into his throat and mouth and nose.

Chapter Twenty

When his servant found him it was the middle of the morning. Garry lay fully dressed but asleep upon the bed with his sparse hair ruffled, his uniform stained and grubby, and the leg lying derelict in the centre of the floor.

The servant closed the door softly and studied his master, his nostrils flaring at the sour smell of stale brandy and vomit.

'Had yourself one hell of a bust-out. Hey – Hop, Skip and Jump?' he murmured without sympathy. Then he picked up the bottle and examined the inch of liquor remaining in it. 'Your bloody good health, cock,' he saluted Garry and drained the bottle, patted his lips delicately and spoke again. 'Right! Let's get your sty cleaned up.'

'Leave me alone,' Garry groaned.

'It's eleven o'clock, sir.'

'Leave me. Get out and leave me.'

'Drink this coffee, sir.'

'I don't want it. Leave me.'

'I've got your bath filled, sir, and a clean uniform laid out for you.'

'What time is it?' Garry sat up unsteadily.

'Eleven o'clock,' the man repeated patiently.

'My leg?' Garry felt naked without it.

'One of the harness makers is stiching the straps, sir. It'll be ready by the time you've bathed.'

Even in a position of rest Garry's hands, laid upon the desk in front of him trembled slightly, and the rims of his eyelids prickled. The skin of his face was stretched like that of a drum over the slow pain that throbbed within his skull.

At last he sighed and picked Lieutenant Curtis's report from the top of the slim sheaf of papers that waited for his attention. Garry skimmed through it dully, few of the names upon it meant anything to him. He saw Sean's name headed the list of wounded, and below him was the little Jewish lawyer. At last satisfied that the report contained nothing to the discredit of Colonel Garrick Courtney, he initialled it and laid it aside.

He picked up the next document. A letter addressed to him as Officer Commanding the Natal Corps of Guides, from a Colonel John Acheson of the Scots Fusiliers. Two pages of neat, pointed handwriting. He was about to discard it and leave it to his Orderly's attention when the name in the body of the text caught his eye. He leaned forward attentively and read quickly from the beginning.

'. . . pleasure in bringing to your attention . . . conduct beyond the call of . . . under intense enemy fire . . . once more, initiated an advance . . . although wounded . . . disregard of personal danger . . . two members of your Guides.

    Sergeant Sean Courtney.

    Pte. Saul Friedman.

. . . earnestly recommend . . . Distinguished Conduct Medal . . . great gallantry and powers of leadership.'

Garry dropped the letter and leaned back in his chair, staring at it as though it were his own death warrant. For a long while he did not move, while the pain kept beating in his head. Then he picked it up once more. Now his hands trembled so violently that the paper fluttered like the wing of a wounded bird.

'Everything of mine, everything I've ever owned – he's taken it from me,' and he looked down at the ribbons on his breast 'I've never had Now this, the one thing.'

A drop of moisture fell on to the letter, blurring the ink.

'I hate him,' he whispered and tore the letter across. 'I hope he dies,' and he tore again and again, ripping it to shreds and at last screwing them into a ball in his clenched fist.

'No. You'll not get that from me. It's mine – it's the one thing you'll never have!' He hurled the crumpled ball against the canvas of the tent, and lowered his head on to his arms upon the desk. His shoulders shook as he sobbed:

'Don't die. Please, Sean, don't die.'

Chapter Twenty-one

Simply by putting his shoulder against her and shoving her aside, Dirk Courtney cleared a small girl from the doorway and was first down the steps and out into the sun. Without looking back at the schoolhouse he headed for the hole in the back hedge, the others would be following.

They caught up with him while he was selecting a *klei-lat* from the hedge.

'Hurry up,' Dirk ordered. 'We got to get to the river first else they'll get the best place.'

They spread out along the hedge, small boys chattering like a troop of excited monkeys.

'Lend me your knife, Dirkie.'

'Hey, look at my lat.' Nick Peterson brandished the short rod of Port Jackson Willow he had cut and peeled. It whipped with a satisfying swish.

'It's not a lat,' Dirk informed him. 'It's a Lee-Metford.' He looked round at the rest of his team. 'You remember now – I'm Lord Kitchener, and you got to call me "My Lord".'

'And I'm General French,' announced Nick. This was fair enough, after all, he was Dirk's chief lieutenant. It had taken Dirk a mere two weeks and five bloody fist-fights to reach his position as unchallenged leader.

'And I'm General Methuen!' one of the lesser members yelped.

'And I'm General Buller!'

'And I'm General Gatacre!'

'You can't all be generals.' Dirk glared around. 'Only Nick and I are generals. You are all just privates and things.'

'Gee, man, Dirkie! Why you always got to spoil things?'

'You shut your mouth, Brian.' Dirk sensed mutiny, and quickly he diverted their attention. 'Come on, let's go and get ammo.'

Dirk took the long route down the sanitary lane. This way he was unlikely to meet adults and have any of his force seconded to serve elsewhere at wood chopping or gardening under parental control.

'Peaches are nearly ripe,' Nick commented as they passed the Pye orchard.

'Another week,' Dirk agreed, and crawled through the hedge into the Van Essen plantation that spread down to the Baboon Stroom.

'There they are!' someone shouted as they emerged from the trees.

'Boers, General!'

Out on the right, busy along the bank of the river was another bunch of small figures – sons of the Dutch families in the district.

'I'll go and talk to them,' Dirk said. 'You go for ammo.' They trotted off towards the river and Dirk called after them: 'Hey, Nick, get me a good dollop of clay.'

'All right, My Lord.'

With all the dignity of a general, officer and a peer of the realm, Dirk approached the enemy and stopped a short distance from them.

'Hey, Piet, are you ready yet?' he asked haughtily. Piet Van Essen was his second cousin twice removed. A chunky lad but not as tall as Dirk.

'*Ja.*'

'The same rules?' Dirk asked.

'*Ja*, the same rules.'

'No clothes,' Dirk warned him.

'And no throwing with stones,' Piet shot back.

'How many you got?' Dirk began counting the enemy suspiciously.

'Fifteen – same as you.'

'All right then,' Dirk nodded.

'All right then!'

Nick was waiting for him below the bank. Dirk jumped down beside him and accepted the large ball of blue clay that Nick handed him.

'It's just right, Dirkie, not too wet.'

'Good – let's get ready.'

Quickly Dirk stripped off his clothing, pulled the belt from the loops of his pants and buckled it around his waist to hold his spare lats.

'Hide the clothes, Brian,' Dirk ordered and surveyed his naked warriors. Nearly all of them still retained the almost womanly shape of youth; undeveloped chests, protruding stomachs and fat white buttocks.

'They'll come down the river like they do every time,' Dirk said. 'This time we're going to ambush them.' As he spoke he kneaded a handful of clay into a ball and spiked it on to the end of the lat. 'Me and Nick'll wait here – the rest of you on top of the bank in those bushes back there.'

He was looking for a target to practise on, and found it in a water tortoise which was laboriously climbing the far bank.

'Watch that old skilpad.' He interrupted himself; stepped forward with his right hand holding the lat thrown back, then whipped it through in an overhead swing. The ball of clay flew from the end of the rod with a vicious hum and smacked on to the shiny black carapace with a force that left a white starshaped crack upon the shell. The tortoise jerked in its head and limbs and toppled backwards into the stream.

'Good shot!'

'There he is, let me have a shot.'

'That's enough! You'll get plenty shots just now.' Dirk stopped them. 'Now listen to me! When they come me and Nick will hold them here for a bit, then we'll run back along the river and they'll chase us. Wait until they are right underneath you – then give it to them.'

Dirk and Nick crouched side by side, close in against the bank with the water up to their noses. A tuft of reeds hid those parts of their heads still above the surface and within easy reach their loaded clay-lats lay on dry land.

Below water Dirk felt Nick's elbow nudge his ribs, and he nodded carefully. He also had heard the whisper of voices around the bend of the river, and the roll and plop of loose earth dislodged by a careless foot. He turned his head and answered Nick's grin with one just as bloodthirsty, then he peered around the reeds.

Twenty paces in front of him a head appeared cautiously around the angle of the bank and the expression of its face was set and nervous – and Dirk moved his own head back behind the bunch of reeds.

A long silence broken suddenly. 'They're not here.' The voice was squeaky with adolescence and tension. Boetie was a delicate child, small for his age, who insisted on joining the rest of them in games beyond his strength.

Another long silence and then the sound of a wholesale but stealthy approach. Dirk reached out and gripped Nick's arm – the enemy were committed, out in the open – he lifted his mouth above the surface.

'Now!' he whispered and they reached for their lats. The surprise was complete and devastating. As Dirk and Nick rose dripping, with throwing arms cocked, the attackers were bunched in such a way that they could neither run nor return the fire unhampered.

The clay pellets flew into them, slapping loudly on bare flesh, producing howls of anguish and milling, colliding confusion.

'Give it to them,' shouted Dirk, and threw again without picking his man, blindly into the mass of legs and arms and pink backsides. Beside him Nick worked in a silent frenzy of load and throw.

The confusion lasted perhaps fifteen seconds, before the howls of pain became shouts of anger.

'It's only Dirk and Nick.'

'Get them – it's only two of them.'

The first pellet flipped Dirk's ear, the second hit him full in the chest. 'Run! he gasped through the pain, and floundered to the bank. Bent forward to climb from the stream he was frighteningly vulnerable, and a pellet thrown at point-blank range took him in that portion of his anatomy which he was offering to the enemy. The sting of it propelled him from the water and clouded his vision with tears.

'Chase them!'

'Hit them!'

The pack bayed after them, pellets hissed about them and slapped at them as they pelted back along the stream. Before they reached the next bend their backs and bottoms were dappled with the angry red spots which tomorrow would be bruises.

Without discretion, hot with the chase, shouting and laughing, the attackers poured into the trap and as they rounded the bend it closed upon them.

Dirk and Nick stood poised to meet them, and suddenly the bank above their heads was lined with squealing, dancing, naked savages, who hurled a steady stream of missiles into them.

For a minute they stood it, then completely broken they scrambled out of the river-bed with pellets flailing them and raced panic-stricken for the shelter of the plantation.

One of them remained below the bank, kneeling in the mud, sobbing softly. But according to the unspoken laws that governed them this one was exempt from further punishment.

'It's only Boetie,' Nickie shouted. 'Leave him. Come on! Chase the others!' And he scrambled up the bank and led them after the flight. Yelling and shrilling with excitement they streamed away through the brown grass to where Piet Van Essen was desperately trying to stay the route on the edge of the plantation, and gather his men to meet the charge.

But another of them remained below the bank – Dirk Courtney.

There were just two of them now. Screened by the bank, completely alone. Boetie looked up and through his tears saw Dirk coming slowly towards him. He saw the lat in Dirk's hand and the expression on his face. He knew he was alone with Dirk.

'Please, Dirk,' he whispered. 'I give up. Please. I give up.'

Dirk grinned. Deliberately he moulded the clay pellet on to his lat.

'I'll give you all my lunch tomorrow,' pleaded Boetie. 'Not just the sweets, I'll give you all of it.'

Dirk hurled the clay. Boetie's shriek thrilled his whole body. He began to tremble with the pleasure of it.

'I'll give you my new pocket-knife.' Boetie's voice was muffled by sobs and his arms which he had crossed over his face.

Dirk loaded the lat, slowly so he could savour this feeling of power.

'Please, Dirkie. Please, man, I'll give you anything you—' and Boetie shrieked again.

'Take your hands off your face, Boetie.' Dirk's voice was strangled, thick with pleasure.

'No, Dirkie. Please no!'

'Take your hands away, and I'll stop.'

'You promise, Dirkie. You promise you'll stop.'

'I promise,' whispered Dirk.

Slowly Boetie lowered his arms, they were thin and very white, for he always wore long sleeves against the sun.

'You promised, didn't you. I did what you—' and the clay hit him across the bridge of his nose, spreading as it struck, jerking his head back. Immediately there was blood from both nostrils.

Boetie clawed at his face, smearing blood on to his cheeks.

'You promised,' he whimpered. 'You *promised*!' But Dirk was already moulding the next pellet.

Dirkie walked home alone. He walked slowly, smiling a little, with soft hair falling forward on to his forehead and a smear of blue clay on one cheek.

Mary was waiting for him in the kitchen of the cottage of Protea Street. She watched from the window while he slipped through the hedge and crossed the yard. As he came towards the door she noticed the smile on his face. There was hardly sufficient room in her chest for what she felt as she looked at the innocent beauty of his face. She opened the door for him.

'Hello, darling.'

'Hello, Mary,' Dirk greeted her, and his little smile became a thing of such radiance that Mary had to reach for him.

'My goodness, you're covered in mud. Let's get you bathed before your gran'ma gets home.'

Dirk extricated himself from her embrace and moved in on the biscuit-tin.

'I'm hungry.'

'Just one,' Mary agreed, and Dirk took a handful. 'Then I've got a surprise for you.'

'What is it?' Dirk was more interested in the biscuits. Mary had a surprise for him every evening and usually it was something silly like a new pair of socks she had knitted.

'I'll tell you when you're in the bath.'

'Oh, all right.' Still munching Dirk set off for the bathroom. He began to disrobe along the passage dropping first his shirt and then his pants for Mary to retrieve as she followed.

'What is the surprise?'

'Oh Dirk, you've been playing that horrible game again.' Mary knelt beside the tub and gently passed the soapy flannel down his bruised back and buttocks. 'Please promise me you'll never play it again.'

'All right.' It was a very simple matter to extract a promise from Dirk, he had made this particular one before. 'Now, what's your surprise?'

'Guess.' Mary was smiling now, a secret knowing smile which immediately caught Dirk's attention. He studied her scarred face, her ugly loving face.

'Sweets?' he hazarded, and she shook her head and caressed his naked body with the flannel.

'Not socks!'

'No.' She dropped the flannel into the soap-scummed water and clasped him to her chest. 'No, not socks,' she whispered.

He knew then.

'Is it . . .? Is it . . .'

'Yes, Dirkie, it's about your father.'

Instantly he began to struggle.

'Where is he, Mary? Where is he?'

'Into your nightshirt first.'

'Is he here? Has he come home?'

'No, Dirk. He isn't here yet. He's in Pietermaritzburg. But you're going to see him soon. Very soon. Gran'ma has gone now to make reservations on the train. You're going to see him tomorrow.'

His hot, wet body began to tremble in her arms, quivering with excitement.

Chapter Twenty-two

'In some respects, Mrs Courtney, it was possibly all to the good that we were unable to contact you before.' The Surgeon-Major tamped tabacco into his pipe, and began methodically searching all his pockets.

'Your matches are on the desk.' Ada came to his assistance.

'Oh! Thank you.' He got the pipe drawing, and continued, 'You see, your son was attached to an irregular unit – there was no record of next-of-kin, and when he came to us from Colenso six weeks ago he was, shall we say, in no condition to inform us of your address.'

'Can we see Pa now?' Dirk could no longer contain himself, for the past five minutes he had wriggled and fidgeted on the the couch beside Ada.

'You'll see your father in a few minutes, young man.' And the surgeon turned back to Ada. 'As it so happens, Mrs Courtney, you have been spared a great deal of anxiety. At first there were grave doubts that we would be able to save your son's life, let alone his right leg. Four weeks it hung in the balance, so to speak. But now' – and he beamed at Ada with justifiable pride – 'well, you'll see for yourself.'

'He's well?' Quickly, anxiously she asked.

'What a formidable constitution your son has, all muscle and determination.' He nodded, still smiling. 'Yes, he's well on the road to recovery. There may be a slight limp in the right leg – but when you weigh that against what might have been . . .' He spread his hands eloquently. 'Now the sister will take you through to him.'

'When can he come home?' Ada asked from the doorway.

'Soon – another month, perhaps.'

A deep veranda, cool with shade and the breeze that came in across the hospital lawns. A hundred high metal beds along the wall, a hundred men in grey flannel nightshirts propped against white pillows. Some of them slept, a few were reading, others talked quietly or played chess and cards on boards set between the beds. But one lay withdrawn, staring at, but not seeing, the pair of fiscal shrikes which squabbled raucously over a frog on the lawn.

The beard was gone, removed while he was too weak to protest on the orders of the ward sister who considered it unhygienic, and the result was a definite improvement that even Sean secretly admitted. Shielded for so long, the skin on the lower half of his face was smooth and white like that of a boy; fifteen years had been shaved away with that coarse black matt. Now emphasis was placed on the heavy brows which, in turn, directed attention to his eyes, dark blue, like cloud shadow on mountain lakes. Darker blue at this moment as he considered the contents of the letter he held in his right hand.

The letter was three weeks old, and already the cheap paper was splitting along the creases from constant refolding. It was a long letter, much of it devoted to detailed description of the clumsy sparring along the Tugela River in which Buller's army was now engaged. There was one reference to the headaches from which the writer periodically suffered as a result of his wound which was now externally healed, and many more to the deep gratitude that Saul felt for him. These embarrassed Sean to such an extent that when re-reading the letter he scowled and skipped each one as he came to it.

But there was one paragraph to which Sean returned each time, and read slowly, whispering it to himself so that he could savour each word:

I remember telling you about Ruth, my wife. As you know, she escaped from Pretoria and is in Pietermaritzburg staying with relatives of hers. Yesterday I had a letter from her that contained the most wonderful tidings. We have been married four years this coming June, and now at last as a result of our brief meeting when she arrived in Natal – I am to become a father! Ruth tells me she has determined on a daughter (though I am certain it will be a son!) and she has selected a name. It is a most unusual name, to be charitable – I can see that it will require a great deal of diplomacy on my part to make her change her mind. (Among her many virtues is an obstinacy reminiscent of the rock of ages.) She want to name the poor waif '*Storm*' – Storm Friedman – and the prospect appals me!

Although our faiths differ, I have written to Ruth asking her to agree to your election as 'Sandek' – which is the equivalent of godfather. I can foresee no objection from Ruth (especially in view of the debt which we both owe you) and it needs now only your consent. Will you give it?

At the same time I have explained to Ruth your present situation and address (c/o Greys Hospital!) and asked her to visit you there so that she can thank you personally. I warn you in advance that she knows as much about you as I do – I am not one to hide my enthusiasms!

Lying with the letter clutched in his hand, Sean stared out across the lawns into the sunlight. Beneath the bedclothes, swelling up like a pregnant belly, was the wicker basket that cradled his leg. '*Storm!*' he whispered, remembering the lightning playing blue and blinding white upon her body.

'Why doesn't she come?' Three weeks he had waited for her. 'She knows that I am here, why doesn't she come to me?'

'Visitors for you.' The sister paused beside him and straightened the bedclothes.

'Who?' He struggled up on to his good elbow, with the other arm still in its sling across his chest.

'A lady.' And he felt it surge through him. 'And a small boy.' The cold backwash of disappointment, as he realized it was not her. Then immediately guilt – Ada and Dirk, how could he hope it was someone else?

Without the beard Dirk did not recognize him until he was ten paces away. Then he charged, his cap flew from his head and his dark hair, despite the bonds of brilliantine, sprang up into curls as he ran. He was squeaking incoherently as he reached the bed, clambered up on to Sean's chest to lock both arms around his neck.

It was some time before Sean could prise him loose and look at him.

'Well, boy,' he said, and then again, 'well, my boy.' Unable to trust himself not to lay his love for the child bare for all to see – there were a hundred men watching and grinning – Sean sought diversion by turning to Ada.

She waited quietly, as she had spent half her life waiting, but when he looked at her the tenderness showed in her smile.

'Sean.' She stooped to kiss him. 'What happened to your beard? You look so young.'

They stayed for an hour, most of which was taken up by a monologue from Dirk. In the intervals while he regained his breath Ada and Sean were able to exchange all their accumulated news. Finally, Ada stood up from the chair beside Sean's bed.

'The train leaves in half an hour, and Dirk has school tomorrow. We'll come up from Ladyburg each week-end until you are ready to return home.'

Getting Dirk out of the hospital was like evicting an unruly drunk from a bar. Alone Ada could not manage it and she enlisted a male hospital orderly to the cause. Kicking and struggling in tantrum, Dirk was carried down the veranda with his screams ringing back to Sean long after he had disappeared from view.

'I want my Dad. I want to stay with my Dad.'

Chapter Twenty-three

Benjamin Goldberg was the executor of his brother's estate. This estate consisted of a forty-per-cent shareholding in Goldberg Bros. Ltd., a company which listed among its assets a brewery, four small hotels and a very large one situated on the Marine Parade at Durban, sixteen butcher shops, and a factory devoted to the manufacture of polony, pork sausages, bacon and smoked ham. The last products caused Benjamin some embarrassment, but their manufacture was too profitable to be discontinued. Benjamin was also the Chairman of the Board of Goldberg Bros., and a sixty-per-cent share-holder. The presence of an army of twenty-five thousand hungry and thirsty men in Natal had increased the consumption of beer and bacon in a manner that caused Benjamin further embarrassment, for he was a peaceable man.

The huge profits forced upon him by the hostilities both troubled and delighted him.

These same two emotions were evoked by the presence in his household of his niece. Benjamin had four sons and not a single daughter, his brother Aaron had left one daughter for whom Benjamin would gladly have traded all four of his own sons. Not that the boys weren't doing very well, all of them settled into the business very nicely. One of them running the Port Natal Hotel, the eldest managing the brewery and the two others in the meat section. But – and here Benjamin sighed – but Ruth! There was a girl for a man's old age. He looked at her across the polished stinkwood breakfast table with its encrustation of silver and exquisite bone china, and he sighed again.

'Now, Uncle Ben, don't start again. Please.' Ruth buttered her toast firmly.

'So all I'm saying is that we need him here. Is that so bad?'

'Saul is a lawyer.'

'*Nu?* Is that so bad. He's a lawyer, but we need a lawyer with us. The fees I pay out to those other *schmoks*!'

'He doesn't want to come into the Company.'

'All right. We know he doesn't want charity. We know he doesn't want your money working for him. We know all about his pride – but now he's got responsibilities. Already he should be thinking about you – and the baby – not so much about what he wants.'

At the mention of the baby, Ruth frowned slightly. Benjamin noticed it, there were few things he did not notice. Young people! If only you could tell them. He sighed again.

'All right. We'll leave it until Saul comes back on leave,' he agreed heavily.

Ruth, who had never mentioned her uncle's offers of employment to Saul, had a momentary vision of living in Pietermaritzburg – close enough to be drowned in the tidal waves of affection that emanated from her Uncle Benjamin, caught like a tiny insect in the suffocating web of family ties and duties. She flashed at him in horror.

'You even mention it to Saul and I'll never speak to you again.'

Her cheeks flushed wondrously and fire burned in her eyes. Even the heavy braid of dark hair seemed to come alive like the tail of an angry lioness, flicking as she moved her head.

Oi Yoi Yoi! Benjamin hid his delight behind hooded lids. *What a temper! What a woman! She could keep a man young for ever.*

Ruth jumped up from the table. For the first time he noticed that she wore riding habit.

'Where are you going? Ruth, you're not riding again today.'

'Yes I am.'

'The baby!'

'Uncle Ben, why did you never learn to mind your own business?' And she marched out of the room. Her waist was not yet thickened with pregnancy and she moved with a grace that played a wild discord on the old man's heart strings.

'You should not let her treat you that way, Benjamin.' Mildly, the way she did everything, his wife spoke from across the table.

'There's something troubling that girl.' Carefully Benjamin wiped egg from his moustache, laid the napkin on the table, consulted the gold fob watch he drew from his waistcoat, and stood up. 'Something big. You mark my words.'

It was Friday, strange how Friday had become the pivot on which the whole week turned. Ruth urged the chestnut stallion, and he lengthened his stride under her, surging forward with such power that she had to check him a little and bring him down into an easy canter.

She was early and waited ten impatient minutes in the oak-lined lane behind Greys Hospital before, like a conspirator, the little nurse slipped out through the hedge.

'Have you got it?' Ruth demanded. The girl nodded, glanced around quickly and took an envelope out of her grey nursing cloak. Ruth exchanged it for a gold sovereign. Clutching the coin the nurse started back for the hedge.

'Wait.' Ruth stopped her. This was her only physical contact and she was reluctant to break it so soon. 'How is he?'

'It's all there, m'am.'

'I know – but tell me how he looks. What he does and says,' Ruth insisted.

'Oh, he's looking fine now. He's been up and about on his sticks all week, with that big black savage helping him. The first day he fell and you should have heard him swear. Lordy!' They both laughed together.

'He's a real card, that one. He and sister had another tiff yesterday when she wanted to wash him. He called her a shameless strumpet. She gave him what for all right. But you could see she was ever so pleased and she went around telling everybody about it.'

She burbled on and Ruth listened enchanted, until:

'Then yesterday, you know what he did when I was changing his dressing?' She blushed coyly. 'He gave me a pinch behind!'

Ruth felt a hot flood of anger wash over her. Suddenly she realized that the girl was pretty in an insipid fashion.

'And he said . . .'

'Thank you!' Ruth had to restrain the hand that held her riding-crop. 'I have to go now.' Usually the long skirts of her habit hampered her in mounting, but this time she found herself in the saddle without effort.

'Next week, m'am?'

'Yes,' and she hit the stallion across his shoulder. He lunged forward so violently that she had to clutch at the pommel of the saddle. She rode him as she had never ridden a horse befor, driving him with whip and spur until dark patches of sweat showed on his flanks and froth spattered back along his shoulders, so that by the time she reached a secluded spot on the bank of the Umgeni River far out of town her jealousy had abated and she felt ashamed of herself. She loosened the stallion's girth and petted him a little before leaving him tethered to one of the weeping willows, and picking her way down the bank to her favourite log on the water's edge.

There she settled herself and opened the envelope. If only Sean could have known that his temperature chart, progress report, house-doctor's recommendations, and the sucrose content of his urine were being so avidly studied, he would probably have added a ruptured spleen to his other ills.

At last Ruth folded the pages into their envelope and tucked it away in her jacket of her habit. He must look so different without his beard. She stared into the pool below her and it seemed as though his face formed in the green water and looked back at her. She touched the surface with the toe of her riding-boot so that the ripples spread and shattered the image.

She was left with only the feeling of loneliness.

'I must not go to him,' she whispered, steeling the resolve which had kept her from him these past weeks since she had known he was there. So close – so terribly near.

Determinedly she looked down again into the pool and tried to conjure up the face of her husband. All she saw was a yellowfish, gliding quietly across the sandy bottom with the pattern of its scales showing like the teeth of a file along its sides. She dropped a pebble into the water and the fish darted away.

Saul. Merry little Saul with his monkey face, who made her laugh the way a mother laughs at her child. *I love him*, she thought. And it was true, she loved him. But love has many shapes, and some are the shapes of mountains – tall and jagged and big. While others are the shape of clouds – which have no shape, no sharp outline, soft they blow against the mountain and change and stream away but the mountain stands untouched by them. The mountain stands for ever.

'My mountain,' she murmured, and she saw him again so vividly, standing tall above her in the storm.

'Storm,' she whispered and clasped her open hands across her belly that was still flat and hard.

'Storm,' she whispered and felt the warmth within her. It spread outwards from her womb, the heat rising with it until it was a burning madness she could no longer control. With her skirts flying about her legs she ran to the stallion, her hands trembled on the straps of the girth.

'Just once,' she promised herself. 'Just this once more.' Desperately she clawed up into the saddle.

'Just this once, I swear it!' and then brokenly, 'I can't help myself. I've tried – oh God, how I've tried!'

An appreciative stirring and hum of comment from the beds along the wall followed her as she swept down the hospital veranda. There was urgent grace in the way she held her skirts gathered in one hand, in the crisp staccato tap of her pointed boots along the cement floor and the veiled swing of her hips above. There was unrestrained eagerness in the sparkle in her eyes and the forward thrust of her breasts beneath the wine-coloured jacket. The wild ride which brought her here had flushed her cheeks and tumbled her hair glossy black down her temple and on to her forehead.

Those sick and lonely men reached as though a goddess had passed them by, thrilled by her beauty, yet saddened because she was unattainable. She did not notice them, she did not feel their hungry eyes upon her nor hear the aching whisper of their voices – for she had seen Sean.

He came slowly across the lawns towards the veranda, using the stick awkwardly to balance the drag of his leg. His eyes were downcast and he frowned in thought. Her breath caught in her throat as she saw how wasted was his body. She had not remembered him so tall with shoulders gaunt and wide like the cross-tree of a gallows. Never before had she seen the bony thrust of his jawline, nor the pale smoothness of his skin faintly blue with newshaved beard. But she remembered the eyes heavily overscored with black browns, and his great beaky nose above the wide sensuality of his mouth.

On the edge of the lawn he stopped with feet apart, set the point of the cane between them with both hands clasped over the head of it, and he lifted his eyes and looked at her.

For many seconds neither of them moved. He stood balancing on the cane with his shoulders hunched and his chin raised as he stared at her. She in the shadow of the veranda, her skirts still held in one hand – but the other at her throat, fingers trying to still the emotions that fluttered there.

Gradually his shoulders straightened until he stood tall. He hurled the cane aside and reached both hands open towards her.

Suddenly she was running over the smooth, green lawn. Into his arms, trembling in silent intensity, while he held her.

With both arms around his waist and her face pressed against his chest she could smell the man smell of him and feel the hard muscle of his arms as he enfolded her – and she knew she was safe. As long as she stayed like this – nothing, nobody could touch her.

Chapter Twenty-four

On the slope of the table-topped mountain that crouches over the town of Pietermaritzburg there is a glade among the wattle trees. It is a secret place where even the timid little blue buck come out to graze in daylight. On a still day you can hear very faintly the pop of the wagon whips on the road below, or farther off the steam whistle of a train. But that is all that intrudes in this wild place.

A butterfly crossed the glade in uncertain wobbling flight, it came out of the sunlight into the dappled, moving shade along the edge, and settled.

'That's good luck,' Sean murmured lazily and Ruth lifted her head from the plaid rug on which they lay. As the butterfly moved its wings, fanning them gently, the iridescent green and yellow markings sparkled in the speck of sunlight that pierced the roof of leaves above them and fell upon it like a spotlight.

'It tickles,' she said, and the insect moved like a living jewel across the smooth white field of her belly. It reached her navel and paused. Then the tiny tendril of its tongue uncurled and dabbed at the fine sheen of moisture that their loving had left upon her skin.

'He's come to bless the baby.'

The butterfly skirted the deep, delicately chisseled pit and moved on downwards.

'Don't you think he's being just a little forward – he doesn't have to bless that as well?' Ruth asked.

'He certainly seems to know his way around,' Sean admitted dubiously.

The butterfly found its road southwards blocked by a forest of dark curls, so laboriously it turned and retraced its steps towards the north. Once more it detoured round her navel and then headed uneeringly for the pass between her breasts.

'Keep right on, friend,' Sean cautioned, but it turned suddenly and climbed the steep slope until at last it sat triumphant on the peak.

Sean watched it throbbing its wings, blazing in oriental splendour upon her nipple, and he felt himself stirred once more.

'Ruth.' His voice was husky again. She rolled her head to look into his eyes.

'Go away, little butterfly,' and she brushed it from her breast.

Later, after they had slept a little, Ruth woke him and they sat facing each other on the rug with the open hamper between them.

While Sean uncorked the wine she worked over the hamper with the dedication of a priestess preparing a sacrifice. He watched her split the bread rolls and fill them with salty, yellow butter, then open the screw-topped jars of soused beans and pickled onions and beetroot. A heart of young lettuce rustled crisply as she plucked its leaves into a wooden bowl, and poured dressing over them.

Her hair, released from its braid, broke like a black wave over the marble of her shoulders, then rippled and swung with the small movements of her body. With the back of her hand she brushed it from her forehead, then looked up at him and smiled.

'Don't stare. It's bad manners.' She took the glass he offered her and sipped the cool yellow wine, set it aside and went on to dismember the fat-breasted chicken. Pretending to ignore his eyes upon her body, she began to sing, sofly, the love-song she had sung on the night of the storm and shyly her breasts peeped at him through the black curtain of her hair.

She wiped her fingers carefully on a linen napkin, took up the wineglass again and with elbows on her knees leaned forward slightly and returned his scrutiny with equal frankness.

'Eat,' she said.

'And you?'

'In a little while. I want to watch you.'

Then he was hungry.

'You eat the way you make love – as though tomorrow you die.'

'I'm taking no chances.'

'You're covered with scars, like an old tom-cat who fights too much,' and she leaned forward and touched his chest with one finger. 'What happened there?'

'Leopard.'

'And there?' She touched his arm.

'Knife.'

'And there?' his wrist.

'Burst shotgun.'

She dropped her hand and caressed the fresh purple cicatrice that twined around his leg like some grotesque parasitic vine.

'This one I know,' she whispered and her eyes were sad as she touched it.

Quickly, to change her mood, he spoke.

'Now it's my turn to ask the questions.' He reached across and laid his open hand upon her stomach where the first faint bulge pressed warmly into his palm.

'What happened there?' he demanded, and she giggled before she replied. 'Burst shotgun – or was it a cannon?'

When she had repacked the hamper she knelt beside him. He lay flat on his back with a long black cheroot between his teeth.

'Have you had sufficient?' she asked.

'My God, yes,' and he sighed happily.

'Well, I haven't.' She leaned over him, took the cheroot from his mouth and flicked it into the brambles.

With the first faint flush of evening in the sky a small breeze came down from the mountain and rustled the leaves above them. The fine hairs upon her forearms came erect, each on its tiny pimple of gooseflesh, and her nipples stood out dark and hard.

'You must not be late back to the hospital on the very first day they've let you out.' She rolled away from him and reached for her clothing. 'Matron will have me hung, drawn and quartered.' Sean agreed. They dressed quickly, and she was remote from him. All the laughter gone from her voice and her face cold and expressionless.

He stood behind her to lace the whalebone corset. He hated to cage that lovely body and was about to say so.

'Saul is coming tomorrow. A month's leave.' Her voice was harsh. His hands stilled and they stood without moving. It was the first time either of them had referred to Saul since that morning a month ago when she had come to him at the hospital.

'Why didn't you tell me sooner?' His voice also was harsh.

'I didn't want to spoil today.' She had not turned towards him, but stood staring out across the glade to the far hills beyond the town.

'We must decide what we are going to tell him.'

'There is nothing to tell him,' she answered flatly.

'But what are we going to do?' Now his voice was ugly with mingled dread and guilt.

'Do, Sean?' She turned slowly and her face was still cold and expressionless. 'We are going to do nothing – nothing at all.'

'But you belong to me?' he cried in protest.

'No,' she answered.

'The child – it's mine!'

At his words her eyes narrowed and the sweet line of her lips hardened in anger.

'No, damn you, it isn't! Not yours – although you sired it.' She flamed at him. It was the first time she had unleashed her temper at him. It startled Sean. 'The child belongs to Saul – and I belong to Saul. We owe you nothing.'

He stared at her. 'You don't mean that,' and the flames of her anger faded. Quickly he tried to press his advantage.

'We'll go away together.'

'*Run away* – you mean. *Sneak away* like a pair of thieves. What would we take with us, Sean? The happiness of a man who loves and trusts us both – that, and your own guilt. You'd never forgive me, nor I you. Even now when we talk of it you cannot meet my eyes. Already you are beginning to hate me a little'

'No! No!'

'And I would hate you,' she whispered. 'Call for my horse, please.'

'You don't love him.' The agonized accusal was wrung from him, but it was as though he had not spoken. She went on dressing.

'He'll want to see you. Half of every letter he writes is about you. I've told him that I've visited you at the hospital.'

'I'm going to tell him,' Sean shouted. 'I'll tell him everything.'

'No, you won't.' She answered him calmly. 'You did not save him at Colenso to destroy him now. You would destroy him – and us. Please call for my horse.'

Sean whistled and they stood together, not touching, not talking, not even looking at each other. Until Mbejane emerged from the bush below the glade leading the horses.

Sean lifted her into the saddle.

'When?' he asked quietly.

'Perhaps never,' she answered and swung the horse away. She did not look back so Sean never saw the tears that streamed down her face. The muffled drum of hooves drowned her sobs and she held her back and her shoulders stiff so that he would not know.

Chapter Twenty-five

The War Council ended long after dark and when his commandants had upsaddled and ridden away to their laagers among the hills, Jan Paulus sat alone beside the fire.

He was tired, as though his brain was the cold, flabby body of an octopus and its tentacles spread out to every extremity of his body. He was lonely.

Now at the head of five thousand men he was alone as he had never been in the vast solitude of the open veld.

Because of the loneliness and because of the companionship she had given him these past twenty years his thoughts turned to Henrietta, and he smiled in the darkness and felt the longing blunt the edge of his determination.

I would like to go back to the farm, for a week only. Just to see that they are all well. I would like to read to them from the Book and watch the faces of the children in the lamplight. I would like to sit with my sons on the stoep and hear the voices of Henrietta and the girls as they work in the kitchen. I would like . . .

Abruptly he stood up from beside the fire. *Ja*, you would like this and you would like that! Go, then! Give yourself leave of absence as you have refused it to so many others. He clenched his jaw, biting into the stem of his pipe. Or else, sit here and dream like an old woman while twenty-five thousand Englishmen pour across the river.

He strode out of the laager, and the earth tilted upwards beneath his feet as he headed for the ridge. Tomorrow, he thought. Tomorrow.

God has been merciful that they did not rush the ridge two days ago when I had three hundred men to hold it. But now I have five thousand to their twenty-five – so let them come!

Suddenly, as he reached the crest, the valley of the Tugela lay below him. Soft with moonlight so that the river was a black gash in the land. He scowled as he saw the field of bivouac fires that straddled the drift at Trichardts farm.

They have crossed. May God forgive me that I had to let them cross, but I could not meet and hold them with three hundred. Two days I have waited in agony for my columns to cover the twenty miles from Colenso. Two days while the cannon bogged down in the mud. Two days while I watched their cavalry and their foot soldiers and their wagons crossing the drift and I could not stop them.

Now they are ready. Tomorrow they will come up to us. This is where they will come, to try at any other place is madness, a stupidity far beyond any they have shown before.

They cannot try the right, for to reach it they must march across our front. With little cover and the river fencing them in they would expose their flank to us at two thousand yards. No, they cannot try the right – not even Buller will try the right.

Slowly he turned his head and looked out to the left where the tall peaks rose sheer out of the heights. The formation of the ground resembled the back of a gigantic fish. Jan Paulus stood upon its head, on the relatively smooth slope of Tabanyama – but on his left rose the dorsal fin of the fish. This was a series of peaks – Vaalkrans, Brakfontein, Twin Peaks, Conical Hill and, the highest and the most imposing of all, Spion Kop.

Once again, he experienced the nagging prickle of doubt. Surely no man, not even Buller, would throw any army against that line of natural fortresses. It would be senseless as the sea hurling its surf at a line of granit cliffs. Yet the doubt remained.

Perhaps Buller, that pedestrian and completely predictable man; Buller who seemed eternally committed to the theory of frontal assault, perhaps this time he would know that the slopes of Tabanyama were *too* logically the only point at which he could break through. Perhaps he would know that the whole of the Boer Army waited for him there with all their guns. Perhaps he would guess that only twenty burghers guarded each of the peaks on the left flank – that Jan Paulus had not dared to spread his line so thin, and had risked everything on Tabanyama.

Jan Paulus sighed. Now it was past the time for doubt. He had made the choice and tomorrow they would know. Tomorrow, *van more.*

Heavily he turned away and started down towards the laager. The moon was setting behind the black massif of Spion Kop, and its shadow hid the path. Loose rock rolled under his feet. Jan Paulus stumbled and almost fell.

'*Wies Daar?*' The challenge from an outcrop of granite beside the path.

'A friend.' Jan Paulus saw the man now, he leaned against the rock with a Mauser held low across his hips.

'Tell me – what commando are you with?'

'The Wynbergers under Leroux.'

'So! Do you know Leroux?' the sentry asked.

'Yes.'

'What colour is his beard?'

'Red – red as the flames of hell.'

The sentry laughed.

'Tell Oom Paul from me I'll tie a knot in it next time I see him.'

'Best you shave before you try – he might do the same for you,' Jan Paulus warned him.

'Are you his friend?'

'And his kinsman too.'

'The hell with you then also.' The sentry laughed again. 'Will you drink coffee with us?'

It was an ideal opportunity for Jan Paulus to mingle with his men and gauge their temper for tomorrow. '*Dankie.*' He accepted the invitation.

'Good.' The sentry straightened up and Jan Paulus saw he was a big man, made taller by the homburg hat he wore. 'Karl, is there any coffee left in the pot?' He yelled into the darkness beyond the rocks and was answered immediately.

'In the name of God, must you bellow? This is a battlefield, not a political meeting.'

'The English are as loud. I've heard them all night.'

'The English are fools. Must you be the same?'

'For you, only for you.' The sentry dropped his voice to a sepulchral whisper, and then roared again suddenly: 'But what about that damned coffee?'

This one is not short of stomach, Jan Paulus grinned to himself, as the man, still chuckling happily, placed an arm about his shoulder and led him to the screened fire among the rocks. Three burghers squatted about it with blankets draped over their shoulders. They were talking among themselves as the sentry and Jan Paulus approached.

'The moon will be down in half an hour,' one of them said. '*Ja.* I will not be happy to see it gone. If the English plan a night attack, then they will come in the dark of the moon.'

'Who is with you?' Karl asked as they came towards the fire.

'A friend,' the sentry replied.

'From what commando?'

'The Wynbergers,' Jan Paulus answered for himself, and Karl nodded and lifted the battered enamel coffee-pot from the fire.

'So, you are with Oom Paul. And what does he think of our chances for tomorrow?'

'That of a man with one bullet left in thick catbush with a lungshot buffalo coming down in full charge.'

'And does it worry him?'

'Only a madman knows no fear. Oom Paul is afraid. But he tries not to show it, for fear spreads among men like the white sore throat diphtheria,' Jan Paulus replied as he accepted the mug of coffee and settled down against a rock out of the firelight so they would not recognize his face nor the colour of his beard.

'Show it or not,' grunted the sentry as he filled his mug. 'But I reckon he'd give one of his eyeballs to be back on his farm at Wynberg with his wife beside him in the double bed.'

Jan Paulus felt the glow of anger in his belly and his voice as he replied was harsh.

'You think him a coward?'

'I think I would rather stand on a hill a mile behind the fighting and send other men in to die,' the sentry chuckled again, but there was a sardonic note in it.

'I've heard him swear that tomorrow he will be in front wherever the fight is fiercest,' growled Jan Paulus.

'Oh, he said so? So that we fight more cheerfully? But when the Lee-Metfords rip your belly open – how will you know where Oom Paul is?'

'I have told you he is my kin. When you insult him you insult me.' Anger had closed Jan Paulus's throat so that his voice was hoarse.

'Good!' The sentry stood up quickly 'Let us settle it now.'

'Be still, you fools.' Karl spoke irritably. 'Save your anger for the English,' and then more softly, 'all of us are restless, knowing what tomorrow will bring. Let your quarrel stand.'

'He is right,' Jan Paulus agreed, still choked with anger. 'But when I meet you again . . .!'

'How will you know me?' the sentry demanded.

'Here!' Jan Paulus jerked the wide-brimmed Terai hat from his head and flung it at the man's feet. 'Wear that and give me yours in exchange.'

'Why?' The sentry stood puzzled.

'Then if ever a man comes up to me and says, "You're wearing my hat", he will be saying, "Jan Paulus Leroux is a coward!" '

The man grinned so that his teeth glittered in the firelight, then he dropped his own black homburg into Jan Paulus's lap and stooped to pick up the Terai. In that instant, faintly on the wind, soft as the crackle of dried twigs, they heard the rifle-fire.

'Mausers!' shouted Karl and he leapt to his feet sending the coffee-pot flying.

'On the left,' moaned Jan Paulus in anguish. 'Oh, God help us! They've tried the left.'

The chorus of rifle-fire rose, swelling urgently; and now blending with the crisp crackle of the Mausers was the deep belling of the Le-Metfords.

'Spion Kop! They're on Spion Kop,' and Jan Paulus ran, hurling himself down the path towards the laager with the black homburg jammed down over his ears.

Chapter Twenty-six

The mist lay heavily on the peak of Spion Kop that morning, so that the dawn was a thing of liquid, pearly light. A soft uncertain thing that swirled about them and condensed in tiny drops upon the metal of their rifles.

Colonel John Acheson was breakfasting on ham sandwiches spread thickly with Gentleman's Relish. He sat on a boulder with his uniform cloak draped over his shoulders and chewed morosely.

'No sign of the jolly old Boer yet,' the captain beside him announced cheerfully.

'That trench is not deep enough.' Acheson glowered at the shallow ditch which had been scraped in the stony soil and which was now filled to capacity with men in all the various attitudes of relaxation.

'I know, sir. But there's not much we can do about it. We're down to bedrock and it would need a wagon-load of dynamite to sink another foot.' The captain selected a sandwich and upended the Relish bottle over it. 'Anyway, all the enemy fire will be from below and the parapets will cover that.' Along the front edge of the trench clods of earth and loose rock had been piled to a height of two feet. Pathetic cover for two thousand men.

'Have you ever been on this mountain before?' Acheson asked politely.

'No, sir, Of course not.'

'Well, what makes you so bloody certain how the land lies. You can't see a thing in this mist.'

'Well, sir, we *are* on the crest, and it *is* the highest . . .' But Acheson interrupted him irritably. 'Where are those damned scouts? Haven't they come in yet?' He jumped up and with his cloak swirling about him strode along the trench. 'You men. Can't you get that parapet higher there'.

At his feet a few of them stirred and began half-heartedly piling stone. They were exhausted by the long night climb and the skirmish which had driven the Boer garrison from the mountain, and Acheson heard them muttering sullenly behind him as he walked on.

'Acheson!' Out of the mist ahead of him loomed the figure of General Woodgate followed closely by his staff.

'Sir!' Acheson hurried to meet him.

'Are your men entrenched?'

'As best they can.'

'Good. What of the enemy? Have your scouts reported back yet?'

'No. They're still out there in the mist.' And Acheson pointed into the smoky billows that limited the range of their vision to fifty feet.

'Well, we should be able to hold until we are reinforced. Let me know the moment ...' A small commotion in the mist behind them, and Woodgate paused. 'What is it?'

'My scouts, sir.'

Saul Friedman began delivering his report from a range of twenty feet. His face was working with excitement as he scurried out of the mist.

'False crest! We're on the false crest. The true summit is two hundred yards ahead and there's a rise of ground out on our right flank, like a little knoll all covered with aloes, that enfilades our whole position. There are Boers everywhere. The whole bloody mountain is crawling with them.'

'Good God, man! Are you certain?'

'Colonel Acheson,' snapped Woodgate, 'turn your right flank to face the knoll,' and as Acheson strode away he added under his breath, 'if you have time!' and he felt the agitated swirl of the mist as it was swept away before the wind.

Chapter Twenty-seven

Jan Paulus stood beside his pony. The mist had dewed in his beard and set it a-sparkle in red-gold. Across both shoulders heavy bandoliers of ammunition drooped, and the Mauser rifle seemed like a child's toy in his huge hairy hands. His jaw was thrust forward in thought as he reviewed his dispositions. All night he had flogged his pony from laager to laager, all night he had roared and bullied and driven men up the slopes of Spion Kop. And now around him the mountain rustled and murmured with five thousand waiting burghers, and in an arc of 120 degrees behind it stood his guns. From Green Hill in the north-west to the reverse slopes of the Twin Peaks in the east, his gunners crouched beside their creusots and their Nordenfeldts, ready to range in upon the crest of Spion Kop.

All things are ready and now I must earn the right to wear this hat. He grinned and settled the homburg more firmly over his ears.

'Hennie, take my horse back to the laager.'

The boy led it away and he started up the last slope towards the summit. The light strengthened as he climbed and the burghers among the rocks recognized the flaming beacon of his beard.

'*Goeie Jag*, Oom Paul,' and, '*Kom saam om die Rooi Nekke te skiet*,' they called. Then two burghers ran down to meet him.

'Oom Paul. We've just been forward to Aloe Knoll. There are no English on it!'

'Are you sure?' It seemed too generous a gift of fortune.

'*Ja*, man. They are all on the back of the mountain. We heard them digging and talking there.'

'What commando are you?' Jan Paulus demanded of the men massed around him in the mist.

'The Carolina commando,' voices answered.

'Come,' ordered Jan Paulus. 'Come, all of you. We are going to Aloe Knoll.'

They followed. Skirting the summit, with the brush, brush, brush of hundreds of feet through the grass, hurrying so that their breathing steamed in the moist air. Until abruptly ahead of them humped the dark mound of Aloe Knoll and they swarmed over it and disappeared among the rocks and crevices like a column of ants returning to their nest.

Lying on his belly Jan Paulus lit his pipe and tamped down on the glowing tobacco with a fire-calloused thumb, sucked the smoke into his mouth and peered into the solid white curtain of mist. In the eerie silence that had fallen upon the mountain his stomach rumbled loudly and he remembered that he had not eaten since the previous noon. There was a stick of biltong in his coat pocket.

A lion hunts best on an empty stomach, he thought and drew again on his pipe.

'Here comes the wind,' a voice whispered near him, and he heard the rising sibilance of it through the aloes above his head. The aloes stood tall as a man, multi-headed, green candelabra tipped in crimson and gold, nodding slightly in the morning wind.

'*Ja*.' Jan Paulus felt it stirring deep in his chest, that blend of fear and exhilaration that drowned his fatigue. 'Here it comes.' He knocked out his pipe, stuffed it still hot into his pocket and lifted his rifle from the rock in front of him.

Dramatically, as though unveiling a monument, the wind stripped the mists away. Beneath a sky of cobalt blue, soft golden brown in the early sunshine, lay the rounded peak of Spion Kop. A long uneven scar of red earth five hundred yards long was slashed across it.

'*Almagtig!*' Jan Paulus gasped. 'Now we have them.'

Above the crude parapet of the trench, like birds on a fence rail, so close that he could see the chinstraps and the button on each crown, the light khaki helmets contrasted clearly with the darker earth and grass. While beyond the trench, completely exposed from boots to helmets, standing in the open or moving leisurely forward with ammunition and water canteens, were hundreds of English soldiers.

For long seconds the silence persisted, as though the burghers who stared over their rifles at this unbelievable target could not bring themselves to press the triggers on which their fingers rested. The English were too close, too vulnerable. A universal reluctance held the Mausers silent.

'Shoot!' roared Jan Paulus. '*Skiet, Kerels, Skiet*,' and his voice carried to the English behind the trenches. He saw all movement among them suddenly paralysed, white faces turn to stare in his direction – and he sighted carefully into the chest of one of them. The rifle jumped against his shoulder, and the man went down into the grass.

That single shot broke the spell. Gunfire crackled in hysterical unison and the frieze of khaki figures along the trench exploded into violent movement as the bullets thudded amongst them. At that range most of Jan Paulus's burghers could be trusted to knock down four running springbok with five shots. In the few seconds that it took the English to dive into the trench, at least fifty of them went down, dead or wounded, and lay sprawled against the red earth.

Now there were only the helmets and heads above the parapet to shoot at and these were never still. They ducked and weaved and bobbed as Woodgate's men fired and reloaded, and seventeen hundred Lee-Metford rifles added their voices to the pandemonium.

Then the first shell, lobbed from a field gun on the reverse slope of Conical Hill, shrieked over the heads of the burghers and burst in a leap of smoke and red dust fifty feet in front of the English trench. A lull while Jan Paulus's heliograph team below the crest signalled the range correction to the battery, then the next shell burst beyond the trench; another lull and the third fell full upon the trench. A human body was thrown high, legs and arms spinning like the spokes of a wagon wheel. When the dust cleared there was a gap in the parapet and half a dozen men frantically trying to plug it with loose rock.

Together all the Boer guns opened. The constant shriek of big shells was punctuated by the vicious whine of the quick-firing pompoms. And once again a mist covered the peak, this time a thin sluggish mist of dust and lyddite fume which diluted the sunlight and clogged the nostrils and eyes and mouths of men for whom a long, long day had begun.

Chapter Twenty-eight

Lieutenant-Colonel Garrick Courtney was damnably uncomfortable. It was hot in the sun. Sweat trickled down under his tunic and moistened his stump so that already it was chafed. His field-glasses magnified the glare as he looked out across the Tugela River to the great hump of the mountain four miles away. The glare aggravated the ache behind his eyes, which was a memorial to last night's drinking.

'Woodgate seems to be holding very well. His reinforcements should be up to him soon enough.'

Sir Redvers Buller appeared to be satisfied, and none of his staff had any comment to add. Stolidly they stood and stared through their glasses at the peak which was now faintly blurred with the dust and smoke of battle.

Garrick was puzzling once more the devious lines of authority which

Buller had established for the attack on Spion Kop. Commanding the actual assault was General Woodgate, who was now 'holding very well' on the peak, yet Woodgate was responsible not to Buller but to General Charles Warren, who had his headquarters beyond Trichardts Drift where the column had crossed. Warren was in turn responsible to Buller, who was well back behind the river, standing on a pleasant little hill called Mount Alice.

Everyone on the staff was aware that Buller hated Warren. Garrick was certain that Warren had been given command of an operation which Buller considered very risky, so that in the event it failed Warren would be discredited and goaded into resigning. Of course, if he succeeded, Sir Redvers Buller was still supreme Commander and the credit would therefore accrue to him.

It was a line of reasoning Garrick found easy to follow, in fact, had he been in Buller's position he would have done exactly the same thing. This secret knowledge gave Garry a deal of satisfaction, and standing beside Buller on the slope of Mount Alice he felt very much in tune with him. He found himself hoping that Spion Kop would soon be a bloody slaughter-house, and that Warren would retreat across the river in disgrace. He remembered the occasion in the mess when Sir Charles had referred to him as an 'irregular, and a damned *colonial* irregular – at that!' Garry's fingers tightened on his field-glasses and he glared out at the mountain. He was so deep in his resentment that he hardly noticed the signaller who came running from the mule wagon that housed the field telegraph which connected Buller's headquarters with those of Warren beyond the river.

'Sir! Sir! A message from General Warren.' The urgency of the man's tone caught all their attentions. As one man the entire general staff lowered their glasses and turned to him.

'Let's have it then, my man!' Buller snatched the sheet of notepaper and read it slowly. Then he looked up at Garry and there was something in those pale, bulging eyes, a pleasure, a conspiratory gleam that made Garry almost grin.

'What do you make of that, Courtney?' He handed the sheet across and waited while Garry read it.

'Message from Colonel Crofton on the Spion Kop. *Reinforce at once or all is lost. General Woodgate dead. What do you suggest. Warren.*'

'It seems to me, sir,' Garry spoke slowly, trying to mask the fierce jubilation he felt, 'that Sir Charles Warren is on the verge of panic.'

'Yes, that's the way it looks.' Buller was openly gloating now.

'I would suggest sending him a message that will stiffen him, sir.'

'Yes, I agree.' Buller turned to the signaller and began to dictate. 'The mountain must be held at all costs. No withdrawal. I repeat no withdrawal. Reinforce with Middlesex and Dorset regiments.' Then he hesitated and looked around his staff. 'What do you know of this fellow Crofton. Is he the right man to command on the peak?'

There were non-committal sounds of negation from them until A'Court, Buller's A.D.C., spoke up.

'Sir. There is one excellent man up there – Acheson – Colonel John Acheson. You remember his showing at Colenso?'

Buller nodded thoughtfully and turning back to the signaller he went on with his dictation. 'You must put some really good hard fighting man in command on the peak. Suggest you promote Acheson fo Major-General.'

Chapter Twenty-nine

In front of the trench the grass was flattened by the repeated counter-attacks that had swept across it, stained by the blood of those who had dragged themselves back from the Boer positions along the crest, and littered with the twisted corpses of those who had not. Every few seconds a shell exploded along the British line, so there was a continual moving forest of bursts, and the shrapnel hissed like the flails of threshing giants.

John Acheson forced himself to his feet and climbed on to the parapet and shouted, 'Come on, lads. This time they'll not stop us!' In the trench below him the dead and the wounded lay upon each other two and three deep, all of them coated with a layer of red dust. The same red dust coated the faces that looked up at him as he shouted again.

'Bugler, sound the charge. Come, lads, forward. Take the bayonet to them.'

The bugle started to sing, brassy and urgent. Acheson hopped like a gaunt, old stork from the parapet and flapped his sword. Behind him he heard laughter from a dozen throats, not the laughter of ordinary men, but the chilling discord of insanity.

'Follow me, the Lancs! Follow me!' His voice rose to a shriek and they scrambled from the trench behind him. Dusty spectres with bloodshot eyes, smeared with dust and their own sweat. Their laughter and their curses blended with the babbling of the wounded, outstripped it and climbed into a chorus of wild cheers. Without form, spreading like spilled oil, the charge flowed out towards the crest. Four hundred men staggering through the dust-storm of shell-fire and the tempest of the Mausers.

Acheson stumbled over a corpse and fell. His ankle twisted with a shock of pain that jolted his dulled senses. He recovered his sword, dragged himself up and limped grimly on towards the rampart of boulders that marked the crest. But this time they did not reach it to be thrown back as they had before. This time the charge withered before it had covered half the distance. In vain Acheson waved them forward, yelling until his voice was a hoarse croak. They slowed and wavered, then at last they broke and streamed back down the open bullet-swept slope to the trench. Tears of frustrated anger streaking his dusty cheeks, Acheson hobbled after them. He fell over the parapet and lay face down on the corpses that lined the trench.

A hand shaking his shoulder roused him and he sat up quickly and tried to control the breathing that shuddered up his throat. Dimly he recognized the man who crouched beside him.

'What is it, Friedman?' he gasped. But the reply was drowned in the arrival of another shell, and the delirious shrieks of a man wounded in the belly in the trench beside them.

'Speak up, man!'

'Heliograph message from Sir Charles Warren,' shouted Saul. 'You have been promoted General. You are in command of the peak.' And then with a dusty sweat-streaked grin he added: 'Well done, sir.'

Acheson stared at him aghast. 'What about General Woodgate?'

'He was shot through the head two hours ago.'

'I didn't know.' Since morning Acheson had known nothing that was happening outside his own small section of the line. His whole existence had closed down to a hundred yards of shrapnel-and-bullet-swept earth. Now he peered out at the halocaust around him and whispered, 'In command! No man commands here! The devil is directing this battle.'

'Sir Charles is sending up three more battalions to reinforce us,' Saul shouted into his ear.

'We can well use them,' Acheson grunted, and then, 'Friedman, I've sprained my ankle. I want you to lace up my boot as tight as you can – I'm going to need this foot again before the day is done.'

Saul knelt without argument and began working over his foot. One of the riflemen at the parapet beside him was thrown sideways. He fell across Acheson's lap, and from the wound in his temple the contents of his skull splattered them both. With an exclamation of surprise and disgust Saul pulled back and wiped his face, then he reached forward to drag the body from Acheson's legs.

'Leave him.' Acheson prevented him sharply. 'See to that boot.' While Saul obeyed, Acheson unwound the silk scarf from around his own neck and covered the mutilated head. It was a wound he had seen repeated a hundred times that day, all of them shot through the right side of the head.

'Aloe Knoll,' he whispered fiercely. 'If only we'd taken Aloe Knoll.' Then his tone dulled. 'My poor lads.' And gently he eased the shattered head from his lap.

Chapter Thirty

'They are ripe now, let us pluck them!' With five hundred of his burghers Jan Paulus had left the shelter of Aloe Knoll and worked his way forward, crawling belly down through the jumble of rocks, until now they were crouched in a line along a fold of dead ground below the false crest. Twenty yards ahead of them was the right-hand extremity of the English trench.

They could not see it, but clearly they heard the incoherent cries of the wounded; the shouts of 'Stretcher-bearer! Stretcher-bearer!' and 'Ammunition boys, here!' and above the splutter of musketry, the continuous metallic rattle of breech bolts reloading.

'You must signal to the guns, Oom Paul.' The burgher next to him reminded him.

'*Ja*,' Jan Paulus removed the homburg from his head and waved with it at the fat mound at Aloe Knoll behind them. He saw his signal briefly acknowledged and knew that the order to cease fire was being flashed by heliograph to the batteries.

They waited, tensed to charge, a long line of men. Jan Paulus glanced along them and saw that each man stared ahead fixedly. Most of their faces masked by beards of fifty different hues, but here and there a lad too young for this work, too young to hide his fear. Thank God my eldest is not yet twelve, or he would be here. He stopped that train of thought guiltily, and concentrated his whole attention on the volume of shell-fire that raged just ahead of them. Abruptly it ceased, and in the comparative silence the rifle-fire sounded strangely subdued. Jan Paulus let the slow seconds pass, counting silently to ten, before he filled his lungs and roared:

'*Vrystaat!* Come on the Free Staters!'

Echoing his cry, yelling wildly, his burghers surged forward over the crest on to the English flank. They came from so close in, seeming to appear as a solid wall from under the English parapet, that the momentum of their charge carried them instantly into the depleted line of shell-shocked, thirst-tormented and dazed Lancashires. Hardly a shot was fired, and though a few individual scuffles rippled the smooth onward flow of the charge – most of the English responded immediately to the shouts of 'Hands Op! Hand Op!' by throwing down their rifles and climbing wearily to their feet with hands held high. They were surrounded by jubilant burghers and hustled over the parapet and down the slope towards Aloe Knoll. A great milling throng of burghers and soldiers spread over fifty yards of the trench.

'Quickly!' Jan Paulus shouted above the hubbub. 'Catch them and take them away.' He was well aware that this was only a very localized victory, involving perhaps a tenth of the enemy. Already cries of 'The Lancs are giving in!', 'Where are the officers?', 'Back, you men', were spreading along the English line. He had planted the germ of defeat among them, now he must spread it through them before he could carry the entire position. Frantically he signalled for reinforcements from the Boer positions along the crest, hundreds of his burghers were already running forward from Aloe Knoll. Another five minutes and complete victory would emerge from the confusion.

'Damn you, sir! What do you think you're doing!' The voice behind him was impregnated with authority, unmistakably that of a high-ranking officer. Jan Paulus wheeled to face a tall and enraged old gentleman, whose pointed grey whiskers quivered with fury. The apoplectic crimson of his countenance clashed horribly with its coating of red dust.

'I am taking your men hands-up away.' Jan Paulus struggled gutturally with the foreign words.

'I'll be damned if you are, sir.' Leaning heavily on the shoulder of a skinny little dark-haired man who supported him, the officer reached forward and shook a finger in Jan Paulus's face. 'There will be no surrender on this hill, Kindly remove your rabble from my trench!'

'Rabble, is it!' roared Jan Paulus. Around them the Boers and the British had ceased all activity and were watching with interest. Jan Paulus turned to the nearest burghers: '*Vat hulle weg!* Take them away!' His gesture that accompanied the order was unmistakable.

'We'll have none of that, sir!' Acheson glared at him before issuing his own order. 'You men, fall back and re-form on the Devonshires. Hurry it up, now. Come along. Come along.'

'Hey!' Jan Paulus held up his hand. 'These are my . . .' He groped for the word. 'My captures.'

'Sir.' Acheson released his grip on Saul's shoulder, drew himself up to his full height and glared up into Jan Paulus's face. 'I will give you five minutes to vacate this trench – otherwise you will become my prisoner. Good day to you.' And he hobbled away through the grass. Jan Paulus stared in disbelief when fifty paces away Acheson turned, folded his arms across his chest, and waited grimly for the expiry of the five minutes. About him he had gathered a handful of battle-stained soldiers and it was clearly his intention to implement his threat with this pitiful little band. Jan Paulus wanted to laugh with frustration – the skinny old goat. But he realized with dismay that most of his prisoners were filtering away and hurrying to join Acheson. He must do something, but what? The whole position was deteriorating into a farce.

'Stop them!' he shouted at his burghers. 'Hold those men – they went hands-up. They cannot change their minds now.'

Then abruptly the whole position altered. Over the skyline behind Acheson and his tiny party poured a solid phalanx of fresh khaki-clad figures. The three battalions of reinforcements sent up from the foot of the mountain by Sir Charles Warren had at last arrived. Acheson glanced over his shoulder and saw them swarming forward. The brown parchment of his face tore laterally in a wide and wicked grin.

'Fix bayonets!' he shrieked, and drew his sword. 'Buglers sound the charge. Charge, men! Charge!'

Hopping and stumbling like a stork with a broken leg, he led them. Behind him, the glittering crest of a wave, a line of bayonets raced down on the trench. Jan Paulus's burghers hated naked steel. There were five hundred of them against two thousand. They broke and blew away like smoke on a high wind. Their prisoners ran with them.

Jan Paulus reached the crest and dropped behind a boulder that already sheltered three men.

'Stop them! Here they come!' he panted.

While the British wave slowed and expended itself against the reef of hidden Mausers, while they fell back with the shrapnel scourging them once more – Jan Paulus knew that he would not stand in the British trench again that day.

He could sense the despondency among his burghers. He knew that already the faint-hearted were slipping away to where their ponies waited at the foot of the mountain. He knew with sickened acceptance that he had lost Spion Kop. Oh! The English had paid a heavy price all right, there must be fifteen hundred of their dead and wounded strewn upon the peak, but they had torn a gap in his line. He had lost Spion Kop and through this breach would pour twenty-five thousand men to relieve Ladysmith, and to drive his burghers out of Natal and into the Transvaal. They had lost. It was finished.

John Acheson tried desperately to ignore the agony of his bloated foot, he tried to shut out the shrill chorus of the wounded pleading for water. There was no water on the peak. He turned his gaze away from the trench where men, drugged with exhaustion, oblivious to the thunder of the bombardment that still raged about them, lay in sleep upon the bodies of their dead and dying comrades.

He looked instead at the sun, that great, bloody orb lightly screened with long streamers of cloud. In an hour it would be dark – and he knew he had lost. The message he held in his hands admitted it, the grotesque piles of dead men that clogged the trench proved it. He re-read the message with difficulty for his vision jerked and swam giddily.

'If you cannot hold until tomorrow, retire at your discretion. Buller.'

Tomorrow. What would tomorrow bring, if not a repetition of today's horror? They had lost. They were going down from this mountain. They had lost.

He closed his eyes and leaned back against the rough stone of the parapet. A nerve in his eyelid began to twitch insistently, he could not stop it.

Chapter Thirty-one

How many are there left? Half, perhaps. I do not know. Half my men gone, all night I heard their ponies galloping away, and the crack and rumble of their wagons, and I could not hold them.

Jan Paulus stared up at the mountain in the dawn.

'Spion Kop.' He mouthed the name with loathing, but its outline was blurred for his eyes could not focus. They were rimmed with angry red and in each corner was a lump of yellow mucus. His body seemed to have shrunk, dried out like that of an ancient mummy. He slumped wearily in the saddle, every muscle and nerve in his body screamed for rest. To sleep a while. Oh God, to sleep.

With a dozen of his loyal commandants he had tried all night to staunch the dribble of deserters that was bleeding his army to death. He had ridden from laager to laager, blustering, pleading, trying to shame them. With many he had succeeded, but with many he had not – and once he had himself been shamed. He remembered the old man with the long white beard straggling from his yellow, wizened face, his eyes glistening with tears in the firelight.

'Three sons I have given you today, Jan Paulus Leroux. My brothers have gone up your accursed mountain to beg for their bodies from the English. Three sons! Three fine sons! What more do you want from me?' From where he sat against the wheel of his wagon the old man struggled to his feet hugging the blanket around his shoulders, 'You call me coward, Leroux. You say I am afraid.' He stopped and struggled with his breathing, and when he went on his voice was a croak. 'I am seventy-eight years old and you are the first man to ever call me that – if God is merciful you'll be the last.' He stopped again. 'Seventy-eight years. Seventy-eight! and you call me that! Look, Leroux. Look well!' He let the blanket fall away and Jan Paulus stiffened in the saddle as he saw the bloody mess of bandages that swathed the old man's chest 'Tomorrow morning I will be with my sons. I wait for them now. Write on our grave, Leroux! Write "*Cowards*" on our grave!' And through the old lips burst a froth of pink bubbles.

Now with red eyes Jan Paulus stared up at the mountain. The lines of fatigue and shame and defeat were etched deep beside his nostrils and around his mouth. When the mists cleared they would see the English on the crest and with half his men he would go back. He touched the pony with his spurs and started him up the slope.

The sun gilded the mountain mist, it swirled golden and began to dissipate.

Faintly on the morning wind he heard the cheering and he frowned. *The English cheer too soon*, he thought. *Do they think we will not come again?* He urged his pony upward, but as it scrambled over loose rock and scree he reeled drunkenly in the saddle and was forced to cling to the pommel.

The volume of cheering mounted, and he peered uncomprehendingly at the crest above him. The skyline was dotted with figures who danced and waved their hats, and suddenly there were voices all around him.

'They've gone.'

'The mountain is ours.'

'We've won! Praise God, we've won. The English have gone.'

Men crowded about his pony, and dragged him from the saddle. He felt his legs buckle under him, but rough hands were there to support him, and half dragging, half carrying, they bore him up towards the peak.

Jan Paulus sat upon a boulder and watched them harvest the rich crop of battle. He could not sleep yet, not until this was done. He had allowed the English stretcher-bearers to come up his mountain and they were at work along the trench while his own burghers gleaned their dead from along the crest.

Four of them approached Jan Paulus, each holding the corner of a grey woollen blanket as though it were a hammock. They staggered under the load, until they reached the neat line of corpses already laid out on the grass.

'Who knows this man?' one of them called, but there was no reply from the group of silent men who waited with Jan Paulus.

They lifted the body out of the blanket and laid it with the others. One of the burghers who had carried him removed from his clutching, dead fingers a wide Terai hat and placed it over his face. Then he straightened and asked:

'Who claims him?' Unless a friend or a kinsman claimed the corpse it would be buried in a communal grave.

Jan Paulus stood up and walked across to stand over the body. He lifted the hat and replaced it with the homburg from his own head.

'*Ja*. I claim him,' he said heavily.

'Is he kin or friend, Oom Paul?'

'He is a friend.'

'What is his name?'

'I do not know his name. He is just a friend.'

Chapter Thirty-two

Saul Friedman fidgeted impatiently. In his eagerness he had arrived half an hour before visiting-time began and for this he was doing penance in the bleak little waiting-room of Greys Hospital. He sat forward on the straight-backed chair, twisted his helmet between his fingers and stared at the large sign on the opposite wall.

'Gentlemen are requested *Not* to smoke'.

He had asked Ruth to come with him, but she had pleaded a headache. In a sneaking fashion Saul was glad. He knew that her presence would inhibit his reunion with Sean Courtney. He didn't want polite conversation about the weather and how was he feeling now, and he must come round to dinner some evening. It would have been difficult not to be able to swear if they wanted – it would have been even more difficult in view of Ruth's attitude.

Yesterday, the first day of his leave, he had spoken of Sean with enthusiasm. How many times had she visited him? How was he? Did he limp badly? Didn't Ruth think he was a wonderful person? Twice she replied and, well, no not badly, yes he was very nice. Just about then Saul perceived the truth. Ruth did not like Sean. At first he could hardly believe it. He tried to continue the conversation. But each of her monosyllabic replies confirmed his first suspicion. Of course, she had not said so, but it was so obvious. For some reason she had taken a dislike to Sean which was close to loathing.

Now Saul sat and pondered the reason. He discounted the possibility that Sean had offended her. If that were the case Sean would have received as good as he gave and afterwards Ruth would have related the whole tale with glee and relish.

No, Saul decided, it was something else. Like a swimmer about to dive into icy water, Saul drew a metaphorical deep breath and plunged into the uncharted sea of feminine thought processes. Was Sean's masculinity so overpowering as to be offensive? Had his attention to her been below average (Ruth was accustomed to extravagant reactions to her beauty)? Could it be that . . .? Or, on the other hand, did Sean . . .? Saul was floundering heavily when suddenly, as a shipwrecked victim surfacing for the last time finds a tall ship close alongside with lifeboats being lowered from every derrick, the solution came to him.

Ruth was jealous!

Saul leaned back in the chair, astounded at the depth of his own perception. His lovely, hot-tempered wife was jealous of the friendship between Sean and himself!

Chuckling tenderly, Saul laid plans to appease Ruth. He'd have to be less fulsome in his praises of Sean. He must get them together and in Sean's presence pay special attention to Ruth. He must . . .

Then his thoughts richocheted off in another direction and he began to think about Ruth. As always when he thought too intensely about her, he experienced a feeling of bemusement similar to what a poor man feels on winning a large lottery.

He had met her at the Johannesburg Turf Club during the big Summer Meeting, and he had fallen in love at a range of fifty paces, so that when he was presented to her, his usually nimble tongue lay like a lump of heavy metal in his mouth and he squirmed and was silent. The friendly smile she bestowed upon him licked across his face like a blow torch, heating it until he felt the skin would blister.

That night, alone in his lodging, he planned his campaign. To its conduct he allocated the sum of five hundred guineas, which was exactly half his savings. The following morning he began his intelligence work, and a week later he had collected a massive volume of information.

She was eighteen years old and was on a visit to relations in Johannesburg, a visit scheduled to last a further six weeks. She came from a rich Natal family of brewers and hotel-keepers, but she was an orphan and a ward of her uncle. While in Johannesburg she rode every day, visited the theatre or danced every night with an assortment of escorts, except Fridays when she attended the Old Synagogue in Jeppe Street.

His opening manoeuvre was the hire of a horse and he waylaid her as she rode out with her cousin. She did not remember him and would have ridden on, but at last his tongue, which was sharpened by three years of practice at the Johannesburg Bar, came to life. Within two minutes she was laughing and an hour later she invited him back to tea with her relatives.

The following evening he called for her in a splendid carriage and they dined at Candy's Hotel and went on to the Ballet in company with a party of Saul's friends.

Two nights later she went with him to the Bar Association Ball and found that he was a superb dancer. Resplendent in brand-new evening dress, with an ugly yet mobile and expressive face, an inch taller than her five feet six, with wit and intelligence that had earned him a wide circle of friends – he was the perfect foil for her own beauty. When he returned her home Ruth had a thoughtful but dreamy look in her eye.

The following day she attended Court and listened to him successfully defend a gentleman accused of assault with intent to do grievous bodily harm. She was impressed by his display and decided that in time he would reach the heights of his profession.

A week later Saul again proved his command of the spoken word in an impassioned declaration of love. His suit was judged and found worthy, and after that it was merely a case of informing the families and sending out the invitations.

Now, at last, four years later they were to have their first child. Saul grinned happily as he thought about it. Tomorrow he would begin his attempt to discourage the adoption of the name 'Storm'. It would be a difficult case to win, one worthy of his talents. In the preceding four years Saul had learned that once Ruth set her small white teeth into something she had a bulldog grip. A great deal of finesse was needed to loosen that grip without invoking her wrath. Saul had an awesome respect for his wife's wrath.

'It's four o'clock.' The little blonde nurse poked her head around the waiting-room door and smiled at him. 'You may go in now. You'll find him out on the veranda.'

Saul's eagerness returned in full flood and he had to restrain himself from bouncing too boisterously down the veranda.

He recognized Sean's bulk, clad in uniform khaki, reclining elegantly in a cane-backed chair and chatting to the men in the row of beds in front of him. He came up behind the chair.

'Don't stand up, Sergeant. Just toss me a salute from where you are.'

'Saul!' Lugging himself out of the chair and pivoting easily on his game leg, Sean gripped both Saul's shoulders in the old show of affection. The pleasure that fired Sean's expression was genuine and that was enough for Saul.

'Good to see you, you old bastard.' He returned Sean's grip, grinning happily. He did not notice how swiftly Sean's pleasure faded, and was replaced by a shifty, nervous smile.

'Have a drink.' They were the first words that came into Sean's mind. He must have time to feel his way. Had Ruth said anything to Saul, had he guessed?

'Water?' Saul grimaced.

'Gin,' whispered Sean, guilt making him garrulous and he went on in a clumsy attempt at humour. 'Water carafe is full of gin. For God's sake don't tell Matron. I smuggle it in. Argue with the nurse whenever she tries to change it – she says "Water stale, must change!" I say, "Like stale water, raised on stale water, stale water strongly indicated in all cases of leg injury!" '

'Give me stale water too,' laughed Saul.

While he poured Sean introduced Saul to the gentleman in the next bed, a Scotsman who agreed with them that stale water was a sovereign therapeutic for shrapnel wound in the chest – a complaint from which he was currently suffering. The three of them settled down to a course of intensive treatment.

At Sean's prodding Saul embarked on a long account of the battle of Spion Kop. He made it seem very funny. Then he went on to describe the final break through at Hlangwane, Buller's eventual relief of Ladysmith, and his cautious pursuit of Leroux's army which was now in full retreat into the Transvaal.

They discussed Lord Roberts's offensive that had driven up from the

Cape, relieved Kimberley, swept on to take Bloemfontein and was now poised for the final thrust up through the belly of the Transvaal to Pretoria which was the heart.

'It will all be over in three months.' The Scotsman gave his opinion.

'You think so?' Sean sneered at him a little, and succeeded in provoking an argument whose flames were fed with gin.

As the level in the carafe fell the time for sober and serious discussion passed and they became sentimental. Tenderly Saul inquired after their injuries.

The Scotsman was being shipped home across the sea, and at the thought of parting they became sad.

Sean was returning the following day to Ladyburg for convalescent leave. At the end of which, if the doctors were satisfied that the pieces of shrapnel in his leg were satisfactorily encysted (two words which Sean had difficulty enunciating) he would be returned to duty.

The word '*duty*' aroused their patriotism and Sean and Saul with arms around each other's shoulders swore a mighty oath that together, comrades in arms, brothers in blood, they would see this war out. Never counting the cost in hardship and danger, together they would ride against the foe.

Suitable music was needed for their mood, and the Scotsman gave them 'The Wild Colonial Boy'. His eyes were moist and his voice quavered with emotion.

Deeply touching, but not entirely appropriate to the occasion, Sean and Saul did 'Hearts of Oak' as a duet, then all three launched into a lively rendition of 'Are you awake, Johnny Cope?'

The Matron arrived in the middle of the third chorus, by which time Johnny Cope and anybody else within a hundred yards could not possibly have been sleeping.

'Gentlemen, visiting hour ended at five o'clock.' She was a fearsome woman with a voice like a cavalry charge, but Saul who had pleaded before hanging judges rose undaunted to the defence.

'Madam.' He opened his address with a bow. 'These men – nay, let me speak with truth – these heroes have made great sacrifice in the name of freedom. Their blood has flowed like gin in defence of that glorious ideal – Freedom! All I ask is that a little of that precious stuff be granted unto them. Madam. In the name of honour, of fairness, and of gratitude I appeal to you.' He ended with one fist clenched above his heart and his head tragically bowed.

'Hoots, mon!'

'Oh good! Very good!'

The two heroes burst into spontaneous and heartwarming applause, but over the Matron's features descended a frosty veil of suspicion. She elevated her nose a little and sniffed.

'You're drunk!' she accused grimly.

'Oh, foul libel! Oh, monstrous untruth.' Saul backed hurriedly out of range.

'All right, Sergeant.' She turned grimly on Sean. 'Where is it?'

'What?' Sean was all helpless innocence.

'The bottle!' She lifted the bedclothes and began her search. Saul picked up his helmet, saluted them behind her back and tiptoed down the veranda.

Chapter Thirty-three

Sean's leave in Ladyburg passed quickly, much too quickly. Mbejane had disappeared on a mysterious errand into Zululand. Sean guessed that it related to the two wives and their offspring that Mbejane had cheerfully sent to the kraals of their parents when he and Sean had left Ladyburg so many years before.

Dirk was incarcerated each morning in the schoolhouse, and so Sean was free to roam alone upon the hills and over the veld that surrounded the town. Most of his time he spent covering the huge derelict ranch called Lion Kop which spread above the escarpment. After a month he knew the course of every stream and each fold and slope of the land. His leg strengthened with the exercise. It no longer pained him and the scar lost its purple shine and dulled down to a closer match with his skin colour.

But as his strength returned and flesh filled out his shoulders and padded the gaunt bones of his face, so restlessness came back to him. His daily pilgrimage to Lion Kop Ranch became an obsession. He wandered through the bare rooms of the old homestead and saw them as they could be with the thatched roof replaced to keep out the rain and the flaking plaster renewed and freshly painted. He stood before the empty, smoke-blackened fireplace and imagined the glow and the warmth it could give. Stamping across the dusty floors he judged the yellow-wood planking as sound as the massive beams that supported the roof. Then he wandered out across the land, stooping now and then to take up a handful of earth and feel its rich loamy texture.

In the May of 1900 he went to the Deeds Registry at the Magistrate's office and surreptitiously inspected the title. He found that the fifteen thousand acres of Lion Kop Ranch had been purchased from the estate of the late Stephanus Johannes Erasmus by the Ladyburg Banking & Trust Co. Ltd. Transfer had been signed by Ronald Pye, Esq., in his capacity as Chairman of the Bank. Sean grinned. Ronny Pye was his most cherished childhood enemy. This could be very amusing.

Sean settled himself in the deep, soft nest of polished leather formed by the arm-chair and glanced curiously around the panelled office.

'A few changes since you were last here. Hey, Sean?' Ronny Pye interpreted his thoughts accurately.

'A few.' The Ladyburg Banking & Trust Co. was doing very prettily, judging by the furnishings. Some of its prosperity showed on the figure of its Chairman. Plenty of flesh under the solid gold watch-chain, dark but expensive jacket to offset the extravagant waistcoat, fifteen-guinea hand-made boots. Very nice until you looked at the face; pale so that the freckles showed like irregular gold coins, greedy eyes, ears like the handles of a shaving-mug – that much hadn't changed. But although Ronny was just two years Sean's senior, there was plenty of grey in his ginger sideburns and little wrinkles of worry around his eyes.

'Been out to Theuniskraal to visit your sister-in-law yet?' There was a sly expression in Ronny's face as he asked.

'No.'

'No, of course you wouldn't,' Ronny nodded understandingly and managed to convey that the scandal, though old, was by no means dead. Sean felt a repugnance that made him shift in his chair. The little ginger moustache heightened Ronny's resemblance to a bush rat. Now Sean wanted to end the business and get out into the fresh air again.

'Listen, Ronny. I've searched title on Lion Kop. You own it,' he began abruptly.

'Lion Kop?' The previous morning the clerk from the Registry had hurried down to Mr Pye with news that earned him a sovereign. There had been many others calling with the news that Sean had visited the ranch every day for a month. But now Ronny had to search his memory to place the name. 'Lion Kop? Ah, yes! The old Erasmus place. Yes, I do believe we picked it up from the estate. Paid too much for it, I'm afraid.' Here he sighed with resignation. 'But we can hold on to it for another ten years or so and get our money back. No hurry to sell.'

'I want it.' Sean cut short the preliminaries and Ronny laughed easily.

'You're in good company. Half the farmers in Natal want it – but not enough to meet our price.'

'How much?'

The established price of grazing land in the Ladyburg area was one shilling and sixpence an acre. Ten minutes before Ronny had set himself to ask two shillings. But now he was looking into Sean's eyes and remembering a fist crushing his nose and the taste of his own blood. He heard again Sean's arrogant laughter rejecting his overtures of friendship. No, he thought with hatred. No, you big cocky bastard, now you pay for those.

'Three shillings,' he said.

Sean nodded thoughtfully. He understood. Then suddenly he grinned. 'My God, Ronny, I heard you were a pretty sharp business man. But I must have heard wrong. If you paid three shillings for Lion Kop they really caught you with your skirts up.' And Ronny flushed. Sean had probed deep into his pride.

'I paid ninepence,' he snapped. 'I'm selling for three shillings.'

'Make out the deed of sale for £2,250. I'll take it.'

Damn it! Damn it to hell! Ronny swore silently. *He would have paid five.*

'That's for the land only. An extra £1,000 for the improvements.'

'Anything else?' Sean inquired.

'No.'

Sean calculated quickly, with transfer tax he could meet the price with a few hundred spare.

'I'll still take it.'

Ronny stared at him while his brain wriggled like a snake. *I didn't realize he wanted it that badly – I could have had his soul!*

'Of course, my Board will have to approve the sale. It depends on them really.' Ronny's Board of Directors consisted of himself, his little sister Audrey, and her husband Dennis Petersen. Ronny held eighty per cent of the shares, and Sean knew this. He had examined the Company's Articles that were lodged with the Registrar.

'Listen to me, dear friend of my youth.' Sean leaned forward across the stinkwood desk and picked up a heavy silver cigar-box. 'You made an offer. I accepted it. I'll be here at four o'clock this afternoon with the money. Please have the documents ready.' Sean lifted the cigar-box in one fist and started to squeeze. The muscles in his forearm writhed like mating pythons and the box crumpled and burst open at the seams. Sean placed the distorted lump of metal on the blotter in front of Ronny.

'Don't misunderstand me, Sean.' Ronny grinned nervously and dragged his eyes away from the box. 'I'm certain I'll be able to convince my Board.'

Chapter Thirty-four

The following day was a Saturday. No school for Dirk and Sean took him along on the daily ride out to the ranch. Almost beside himself with joy at being alone with his god, Dirkie raced his pony ahead and then circled at full gallop to fall in beside Sean once more. Laughing with excitement, chattering ecstatically for a while, then he could no longer contain his high spirits and he galloped ahead. Before Sean reached the cross-roads below the escarpment he met a small caravan of travellers coming in the opposite direction.

Sean greeted the leader solemnly. 'I see you, Mbejane.' Mbejane had the jaded and slightly sheepish look of a tom-cat returning from a busy night out. 'I see you also, Nkosi.'

There was a long, embarrassed silence while Mbejane took a pinch of snuff and stared fixedly at the sky above Sean's head. Sean was studying Mbejane's travelling companions. There were two in their middle age, which is about thirty-five years old for a Zulu woman. Both of them wore the tall head-dress of clay which denotes matronhood. Though they retained the proud, erect carriage, their breasts were pendulous and empty and the skin of their bellies above the brief aprons was wrinkled with the marks of child-bearing. There were also two girls just beyond puberty, moon-faced, skins glowing with youth, straight and well-muscled, buttocks like ripe melons and firm, round breasts. They hung their heads and giggled shyly.

'Perhaps it will rain tonight,' Mbejane remarked.

'Perhaps.'

'It will be good for the grazing,' Mbejane ploughed on doggedly.

'Who the hell are these women?' Sean could contain his curiosity no longer and Mbejane frowned at this breach of etiquette. Observations on the weather and the grazing should have continued another five minutes.

'Nkosi, these two are my wives.' He gestured at the matrons.

'The other two your daughters?'

'No.' Mbejane paused, then went on gravely: 'It is not fitting that a man of my years should have but two women who are old for work and the bearing of children. I have purchased two younger wives.'

'I see,' said Sean, and kept the grin off his face. Mbejane had invested a large percentage of his capital. 'And what do you propose doing with all your wives, you know we must soon return again to fight?'

'When the time comes they will go to the kraals of their fathers and wait for me there.' Mbejane hesitated delicately. 'I bring them with me until I am certain that I have trodden on the moon of each of them.'

Treading on a woman's moon was the Zulu expression for interrupting her menstrual cycle. Mbejane was making sure his investment bore interest.

'There is a farm upon the hills up there.' Sean seemed to be changing the subject.

'Many times, Nkosi, you and I have spoken of it.' But Mbejane understood and there was an anticipatory gleam in his eyes.

'It is a good farm?' Sean held him a little longer in suspense.

'It is truly an excellent and beautiful farm. The water is sweeter then the juice of the sugar-cane, the earth is richer than the flesh of a young ox, the grass upon it as thick and as full of promise as the hair on a woman's pudendum.' Now Mbejane's eyes were shining with happiness. In his book a farm was a place where a man sat in the sun with a pot of millet beer beside him and listened to his wives singing in the fields. It meant cattle, the only true wealth, and many small sons to herd them. It meant the end of a long weary road.

'Take your wives with you and select the place where you wish to build your kraal.'

'Nkosi.' There is no Zulu equivalent of *thank you*. He could say *I praise you*, but that was not what Mbejane felt. At last he found the word. '*Bayete! Nkosi, Bayete!*' The salute to a King.

Dirk's pony was tethered to the hitching-post in front of the homestead. Using a charred stick Dirk was writing his name in big crude capitals on the wall of the front veranda.

Although the entire house would be replastered and painted Sean found himself quivering with anger. He jumped from his horse roaring and brandishing his *sjambok* and Dirk disappeared round the corner of the house. By the time Sean had regained self-control and was sitting on the veranda wall revelling in the pride of ownership, Mbejane arrived. They chatted a while and then Mbejane led his women away. Sean could trust him to build the beehive huts of his kraal on the richest earth of Lion Kop.

The last girl in the line was Mbejane's youngest and prettiest wife. Balancing the large bundle on her head, her back straight, her buttocks bare except for the strip of cloth that covered the cleft, she walked away with such unconsciously regal grace that Sean was instantly and forcibly reminded of Ruth.

His elation subsided. He stood up and walked away from the old building. Without Ruth in it, this house would not be a home.

He sat alone on the slope of the hills. Again he was reminded of Ruth. This place was so much like their secret glade. Except, of course, there were no wattle trees here.

Chapter Thirty-five

'Wattle!' exclaimed Ronny Pye and glared at his sister and his brother-in-law. 'He's planting wattle.'

'What for?' Dennis Petersen asked.

'For the bark, man. The bark! There's a fortune in it. Twenty pounds a ton!'

'What do they use it for?'

'The extract is used in tanning leather.'

'If it's so good why haven't other people—' Dennis began, but Ronny brushed him aside impatiently.

'I've gone into it thoroughly. Lion Kop is ideal wattle ground, high and misty. The only other really good ground in the district is Mahobo's Kloof Ranch and Theuniskraal. Thank God you own Mahobo's Kloof! Because that's where we're going to plant our own wattle.' He looked at Dennis but without seeing him as he went on. 'I've spoken to Jackson at Natal Wattle Company. He'll sell us the saplings on the same terms as he's supplying that bastard Courtney, and he'll buy our bark – every scrap of it at a guaranteed twenty pounds a ton. I've hired two men to supervise the planting. Labour will be our big problem, Sean has grabbed every native within twenty miles. He's got an army of them up there.' Suddenly Ronny stopped. He had seen the expression on Dennis's face 'What's wrong with you?'

'Mahobo's Kloof!' Dennis moaned. 'Oh God! Oh my God!'

'What do you mean?'

'He came to see me last week. Sean . . . He wanted an option to purchase. A five years' option.'

'You didn't give it to him!' Ronny screamed.

'He offered three shillings an acre – that's six times as much as I paid for it. How could I refuse.'

'You fool! You blithering bloody idiot! In five years that land will be worth . . .' Ronny gulped, 'It will be worth at least ten pounds!'

'But nobody told me!' Dennis wailed the age-old cry of the might-have-been, the lament of those that never quite succeed.

'Nobody told Sean either.' Audrey spoke softly for the first time and there was that in her voice that made Ronny turn savagely on his handsome sister.

'All right – we all know about you and Sean. But he didn't stay around long enough for you to get your hooks into him, did he?' Ronny stopped himself and glanced guiltily at Dennis. It was years before Audrey had abandoned all hope of Sean's return to Ladyburg and succumbed to Dennis's gentle but persistent courtship. Now Dennis coughed awkwardly and looked at his hands on the desk in front of him.

'Well, anyway,' he murmured, 'Sean's got it and there's nothing we can do about it.'

'Isn't there – hell!' Ronny pulled a notebook towards him and opened it. 'This is how I see it. He's borrowed that ten thousand from his mother – you know the money we tried to get her to invest in the Burley deal.' They all remembered the Burley deal and looked a little ashamed. Ronny hurried on. 'And he's borrowed another five thousand from Natal Wattle – Jackson let is slip out.' Ronny went on with his calculations. When he finished he was smiling again. 'Mr Sean Courtney is stretched about as thin as he can get without breaking. Just one slip, one little slip and – Pow!' He made a chopping motion with his open hand. 'We can wait!'

He selected a cigar from the leather box which had replaced the silver one and lit it before he spoke again. 'By the way – did you know he hasn't been discharged from the army yet? The way the war is going they certainly need good fighting men. That leg of his looks all right to me. Perhaps a word in the right ear – a little pressure somewhere.' Ronny was positively grinning now. His cigar tasted delicious.

Chapter Thirty-six

The doctors at Greys Hospital had given Sean his final examination a week before Christmas. They had judged his disability as roughly one per cent, a slight limp when he was physically tired. This disqualified him from a war wound pension and had made him available for immediate return to duty.

A week after New Year's Day of 1901 the first letter from the army arrived. He was to report immediately to the Officer Commanding the Natal Mounted Rifles – the regiment which had now swallowed up the old Natal Corps of Guides.

The war in South Africa had entered a new phase. Throughout the Transvaal and Orange Free State the Boers had begun a campaign of guerilla warfare alarming in its magnitude. The war was far from over and

Sean's presence was urgently required to swell the army of a quarter of a million British troops already in the field.

He had written begging for an extension of his leave, and had received in reply a threat to treat him as a deserter if he wasn't in Johannesburg by February 1st.

The last two weeks had been filled with frantic activity. He had managed to finish the planting of ten thousand acres of wattle begun the previous May. He had arranged a further large loan from Natal Wattle to pay for the tending of his trees. The repairs and renovation of the Homestead on Lion Kop were completed and Ada had moved from the cottage in Protea Street to act as caretaker and manager of the estate during his absence.

Now, as he rode alone over his land in a gesture of farewell, he had an opportunity to think of other things. The main one of these was his daughter. His first and only daughter. She was two months old now. Her name was Storm and he had never seen her. Saul Friedman had written a long, joyous letter from the front where Sean was soon to join him. Sean had sent hearty congratulations and then tried once again to contact Ruth. He had written her without result and, finally, had abandoned his work on Lion Kop and gone up to Pietermaritzburg. Four days he waited, calling morning and afternoon at the Goldberg mansion – and each time Ruth was either out or indisposed. He had left a bitter little note for her and gone home.

Deep in gloom he rode through his plantations. Great blocks of young trees, row upon endless row, covered the hills of Lion Kop. The older wattle planted ten months before had started to come away. Already it was waist high with fluffy green tops. It was an achievement of almost superhuman proportion, ten months of ceaseless gruelling labour by two thousand native labourers. Now it was done. He had retained a gang of fifty Zulus, who would work under Ada's supervision, clearing the undergrowth between the rows and guarding against fire. That was all there was to it; four years of waiting until the trees reached maturity and were ready for stripping.

But now he was so completely absorbed in thought that he passed over the boundary of Lion Kop without noticing, and rode on along the foot of the escarpment. He crossed the road and the railway line. From ahead the murmur of the White Falls blended with the wind whisper in the grass, and he glimpsed the flash of water cascading down from the high rock in the sunshine. The acacia trees were in bloom, covered with the golden mist of their flowers above, gloomy with shadows beneath.

He crossed the river below the pool of the falls. The escarpment rose steeply above him, striped with dark dense bush in the gulleys, a thousand feet high so it blocked out the sunlight. The pool was a place of fern and green moss, and the rocks were black and slippery with the spray. A cold place, out of the sun – and the water roared as it fell in a white, moving veil like smoke.

Sean shivered and rode on, ambling up the slope of the escarpment. Then he knew that instinct had directed him. In his distress he had come back to the first home he had ever known. This was Courtney land beneath his feet, and spreading down and out towards the Tugela. The nostalgia came upon him more strongly as he climbed, until at last he reached the rim and stood looking down upon the whole of Theuniskraal.

He picked out the landmarks below him; the homestead with the stables and the servants' quarters behind it; the paddocks with the horses grazing heads down and tails swinging; the dip-tanks among the trees – and each of them had some special memory attached to it.

Sean dismounted and sat down in the grass. He lit a cheroot, while his mind went back and picked over the scrap-heap of the past. An hour, and then another, passed before he came back to the present, pulled his watch from the front pocket of his waistcoat and checked the time.

'After one!' he exclaimed, and stood to dust the seat of his pants and settle his hat on to his head before beginning the descent of the escarpment. Instead of crossing the river at the pool, he stayed on Theuniskraal and keeping to higher ground aimed to intersect the road on this side of the bridge. Occasionally he found cattle feeding together in herds of less than a dozen; they were all in condition, fat on the new grass, for the land was not carrying nearly its full capacity. As he passed they lifted their heads and watched him with vacant, bovine expressions of unsurprise.

The forest thickened, then abruptly ended and before him lay one of the small swampy depressions that bellied out from the river. From his look-out on the escarpment this area had been screened by trees, so now for the first time Sean noticed the saddled horse tethered on the far edge of the swamp. Quickly Sean searched for its rider, and found him in the swamp – only his head visible above the bright poisonous green field of papyrus grass. The man's head disappeared again and there was a commotion in the grass; a wild thrashing and the sudden panic-ridden bellow of a beast.

Sean worked his way quickly round the edge of the swamp until he reached the horse. The head and shoulders of the man in the swamp reappeared and Sean could see that he was splattered with mud.

'What's the trouble?' Sean shouted, and the head turned towards him.

'There's a beast bogged down here.'

'Hold on, I'll give you a hand.' Sean stripped his jacket, waistcoat and shirt and hung them with his hat on a branch before going in. Ploughing knee-deep through ooze that bubbled and belched gas as he disturbed it, using both arms to part the coarse tangle of reeds and marsh grass, Sean finally reached them.

The beast was an old black cow; her hindquarters completely submerged in a mudhole and her front legs twisted helplessly under her chest.

'She's just about finished,' said the man. Sean looked at him and saw he was not a man but a youth. Tall for his age, but lightly built. Dark hair, cropped short and the big nose to show he was a Courtney.

With an unnatural tightness in his gut and a shortening of his breath, Sean knew that he was looking at his son.

'Don't just stand there,' snapped the boy. He was covered from the chest down in a glistening evil-smelling coat of mud, sweat pouring down his face and dissolving the spots of mud on his forehead and cheeks, breathing heavily through open mouth, crouching over the animal to hold its head above the surface.

'Have to roll her,' said Sean. 'Keep her head up.' He waded to the hindquarters and the mud bubbled greasily up around his waist. He thrust his arms down through it – groping for the trapped legs.

Sean's hands could only just encompass the thick bone and sinew of the hock. He settled his grip and leaned back against it, straining upwards, gradually bringing the full strength of his body into the pull until he knew that something in his belly was on the point of tearing. He held like that, his whole face contorted, mouth wide open so that his breathing rattled hoarsely up his throat, the great muscles of his chest and arms locked in an iron convulsion.

A minute, two minutes, he held the stance while the boy watched him with a mingled expression of alarm and wonder. Then suddenly there was a squelching popping escape of swamp gas around Sean's chest, and the beast began to move. Slowly at first, reluctantly up through the ooze showed the swell of its rump – then faster, as the mud lost its hold, until, with a final belch and sigh, it yielded and Sean came to his feet holding the legs above the surface – the cow lying exhausted on her side.

'Hell's teeth!' breathed the boy in open admiration. For a moment the beast lay quiescent, then realizing that its legs were free, it began to struggle, thrashing wildly to regain them.

'Hold the head,' shouted Sean, and blundered sideways until he could grab its tail and prevent it from attempting to stand. When the animal was quiet again he began to drag it, moving backwards, towards the firm ground. Like a bobsleigh the carcass slid easily over the carpet of mud and flattened reeds until it grounded. Then Sean jumped clear while she struggled up, stood a moment and then lumbered unsteadily away into the trees.

Sean and his son stood together, gasping, covered with filth, still ankle-deep in mud, watching the cow disappear.

'Thanks. I'd never have done it on my own, sir.' The form of address and the boy's tone touched something deep in Sean.

'It needed two of us,' he agreed. 'What's your name?'

'Courtney, sir. Michael Courtney.' He held out his hand towards Sean.

'Nice to meet you, Mike.' Sean took the hand.

'I know you, don't I, sir? I'm sure I've seen you before – it's been worrying me.'

'I don't think so.' With an effort Sean kept his feelings from showing in his voice and face.

'I'd . . . I'd count it an honour to know *your* name.' As Michael spoke a shyness came upon them both.

What can I tell him? thought Sean. For I must not lie – and yet I cannot tell him the truth.

'My God, what a bloody mess,' he laughed instead. 'We stink like we've been dead ten days.'

Michael seemed to notice their condition for the first time. 'Ma will have a hernia when she sees me,' he laughed also, then, 'Come up to the house. It's not far from here. Have lunch with us and you can clean up – the servants will wash your clothes for you.'

'No.' Sean shook his head. 'I must get back to Ladyburg.'

'Please. I'd like you to meet my mother. My father's not here – he's at the war. But, please come home with me.'

He really wants me to. As Sean looked into his son's eyes the warm feeling that he had been struggling to suppress flooded up from his chest and he felt his face flush with the pleasure of it.

'Mike,' he spoke slowly, groping for the right words. 'Things are a bit difficult right now. I can't take you up on the invitation. But I'd like to see you again and I'll be through this way one day. Shall we leave it until then?'

'Oh!' Michael made no attempt to hide his disappointment. 'Anyway, I'll ride with you as far as the bridge.'

'Good.' Sean picked up his shirt and wiped off the surplus mud, while Michael unhitched their horses.

They rode slowly, in silence at first with the shyness still on them. Then they started to talk, and quickly the barriers between them crumbled. With a feeling of pride that was ridiculous in the circumstances, Sean became aware of the quickness of Michael's brain, the ease of expression unusual in one so young, and the maturity of his views.

They spoke of Theuniskraal.

'It's a good farm.' There was pride in Michael's voice. 'My family has owned it since 1867.'

'You're not running much stock,' Sean grunted.

'Pa has had a run of bad luck. The rinderpest hit us but we'll build it up again – you wait and see.' He was silent a moment, then, 'Pa's not really a cattleman, instead of putting money into stock he spends it on horses – like Beauty here.' He patted the neck of his magnificent golden mare. 'I've tried to argue with him, but—' Then he realized that he was steering close to the leeshore of disloyalty, and he checked himself then went on hurriedly: 'Don't misunderstand me, my father is an unusual man. Right now he's on the army staff – a colonel, and one of General Buller's right-hand men. He is a holder of the Victoria Cross for bravery, and he has been awarded the D.S.O. for the job he is doing now.'

Yes, thought Sean, I have defended Garry also; many times, as often as you will by the time you reach my age. In understanding he changed the direction of the conversation.

They spoke of the future:

'So you want to be a farmer, then?'

'I love this place. I was born here. To me it is not just a piece of land and a house. It is part of a tradition to which I belong – built by men of whom I am proud. After Pa, I will be the only one left to continue it. I won't fail that trust. But . . .'

They had reached the rise above the road, and Michael stopped and looked at Sean as though trying to make up his mind how much he should tell this stranger.

'But?' Sean prompted him gently. For a moment longer Michael stared at him, trying to account for his certainty in this man – for the conviction he had that he could trust him beyond all other men on earth. He felt that he had known him all his life, and between them was something so strong – so good and strong as to be almost tangible.

'But,' he jerked himself back to their conversation, 'that is not all. I want something beyond just land and cattle. It's so difficult to explain. My grandfather was a big man; he worked with people as well as animals. He had . . . you do understand me, don't you?'

'I think so,' Sean nodded 'You feel you'd like to make a place for yourself in the scheme of things.'

'Yes, that's it. I'd like to make decisions other than when to cull and when to brand, or where to build a new dip-tank.'

'What are you going to do about it then?'

'Well, I'm at Cape Town University. This is my third year – I'll have my degree by Christmas.'

'Then what?'

'I don't know, but I'll find something.' Then Michael smiled. 'There's a lot to learn first. Sometimes when I realize how much it frightens me a little.'

They walked their horses down towards the road, so completely absorbed in each other that neither of them noticed the buggy coming towards them from the direction of Ladyburg until it was almost on them.

Then Michael glanced up. 'Hey! Here comes my mother. Now you can meet her.'

With a sense of dread numbing him, Sean realized he was trapped. There was no escape – the buggy was less than fifty yards away, and he could see Anna sitting up behind the coloured driver staring at them.

Michael shouted, 'Hello, Ma!'

'Michael! Whatever have you been doing? Look at you!' There was a shrewishness in her voice now. The years had treated Anna in the manner she deserved, had sharpened her features and exaggerated the catlike set of her eyes. She turned those eyes on Sean and she frowned. The frown cut deep grooves in her forehead and showed the heavy lines of flesh beneath her chin.

'Who's that with you?' she asked Michael.

'A friend. He helped me free a bogged animal. You should have seen him, Ma. He lifted it clean out of the mud.'

Sean saw that she was expensively dressed, ostentatiously so for a farmer's wife on a working day. Velvet and ostrich feathers – those pearls must have cost Garry a small fortune. The rig was new, polished black lacquer picked out with scarlet, and brass fittings – another few hundred pounds' worth. Sean ran his eyes over the horses, matched bays, blood stock – Jesus! he thought.

Anna was still frowning at him, recognition and doubt mixed in her expression. She was starting to flush, her lips trembling.

'Hello, Anna.'

'Sean!' She spat the word.

'It's been a long time. How are you?'

Her eyes slanted venomously. She hardly moved her lips as she snapped at Michael, 'Get away from that man!'

'But . . .' The bewildered look on Michael's face hurt Sean like a spear thrust.

'Do as your mother says, Michael,' Sean told him.

'Are you . . . are *you* my Uncle Sean?'

'Yes.'

'Get away from him,' shrilled Anna. 'Don't you ever speak to him again. Do you hear me, Michael? He's evil – evil! Don't ever let him near you.

He'll destroy you.' Anna was panting, shaking with rage and hatred, babbling like a madwoman. 'Get off our land, Sean Courtney. Get off Theuniskraal and don't come on again.'

'Very well, Anna. I'm going.'

'Michael. Get on your horse!' she screamed at him. 'Hurry. Come away from him.'

Michael swung up into the saddle.

'Drive on. Drive quickly,' she ordered the coloured coachman. At the touch of the whip the big bays jumped forward and Anna was thrown back against the padded seat. 'Come on, Michael. Come home immediately.'

Michael looked across at Sean. He was bewildered, uncertain. 'I don't . . . I don't believe that you . . .'

'We'll talk again some other time, Mike.'

And suddenly Michael's expression changed, the corners of his mouth drooped and his eyes were dark with regret at having found, and lost, so soon.

'No,' he said, lifted his hand in a gesture of farewell, and wheeled his horse. Crouched forward on its neck he drove in savage pursuit of the buggy.

'Michael,' Sean called after him, but he did not seem to hear.

Chapter Thirty-seven

And so Sean went back to war. The farewell was an ordeal. Ada was so brave about it that Sean wanted to shake her and shout, 'Cry, damn you! Get it over with!' Dirk threw one of his more spectacular fits. He clung to Sean and yelled until he almost suffocated himself. By the time the train pulled out Sean was in a towering rage that lasted until they reached Pietermaritzburg four hours later.

He took his anger into the saloon on the station and sedated it with half a dozen brandies. Then, with Mbejane carrying his luggage, he worked his way through the crowd on the platform, searching for an empty compartment on the northbound express. As all traffic was on military permit only, his fellow-travellers were exclusively clad in khaki. A vast, drab throng speckled with gay spots of colour, women who were sending men to war and not very happy about it. The sound of weeping blended with the roar of loud voices, men's laughter and the occasional squeal of a child. Suddenly, above it all Sean heard his name called. He peered about and saw an arm waving frantically above the heads of the crowd.

'Sean! Hey, Sean!' Saul's head bobbed into view and then disappeared as he hopped up and down. Sean fought his way through to him and they shook hands delightedly.

'What the hell are you doing here?' Saul demanded.

'Heading back to duty – and you?'

'A week's leave just ended. Came down to see the baby. My God, what luck I spotted you!'

'Is Ruth here?' Sean could not contain the question.

'She's waiting in the carriage outside.'

'I'd like to have a look at this infant.'

'Of course. Let's find a couple of seats first and dump our luggage, then we've got twenty minutes before the train leaves.'

Sean saw her as they came out on to the front steps of the station building. She sat in an open carriage while a coloured coachboy held a parasol over her. She was dressed in dove-grey with big leg-o'-mutton sleeves slashed with pink and a huge hat piled with pink roses. Her face was in profile as she leaned forward over the bundle of white lace on her lap. Sean felt the leap in his chest as he looked at the calm lines of her face. He stopped and whispered,

'My God, she's lovely,' and beside him Saul laughed with pleasure.

'Wait until you meet my daughter!'

She did not see them approach the carriage, she was too intent on her child.

'Ruth, I've a surprise for you,' bubbled Saul. She looked up and Sean was watching her. She went rigid with shock, staring at him while all colour drained away from her face.

'Hello, Ruth.'

She did not reply immediately. Sean saw her mask her face with a pale impassivity.

'Hello, Sean. You startled me.'

Saul had missed the interplay of their emotions. He was climbing up into the carriage beside her.

'Come, have a look.' Now he was opening the lace shawl, leaning over the infant, his face alight with pride.

Silently Sean climbed up into the carriage and sat opposite them.

'Let Sean hold her, Ruth.' Saul laughed. 'Let him get a good look at the loveliest girl in the world.' And he did not notice the way in which Ruth froze again and hugged the child to her protectively.

'Take her, Sean. I promise she'll not wet you too badly, though she might pick up a little,' Saul went on happily.

Sean held out his hands for the infant, watching Ruth's face. It was defiant, but afraid.

'Please,' he said. The colour of her eyes seemed to change a darker bluer grey. The hard lines around her mouth dissolved and her lips quivered pink and moist. She leaned forward and placed her daughter in his arms.

Chapter Thirty-eight

It was a long, slow journey up to Johannesburg – a journey broken by interminable halts. At every siding there was a delay, sometimes of half an hour but usually of three times that length. Occasionally, without apparent reason, they groaned to a stop in the middle of the veld.

'What the hell is the trouble now?'

'Somebody shoot the driver.'

'Not again!'

Protest and comment were shouted by the angry heads that protruded from the windows of every coach. And when the guard trotted up along the gravelled embankment towards the front of the train, he was followed by a chorus of catcalls and hooting.

'Please be patient, gentlemen. We have to check the culverts and bridges.'

'The war's over.'

'What are you worried about?'

'The jolly old Boer is running so hard he hasn't got time to worry about bridges.'

Men climbed down beside the tracks, and stood in small impatient groups until the whistle blew and they scrambled aboard as the train jolted and began crawling forward again.

Sean and Saul sat together in a corner of a crowded compartment and played Klabrias. Because the majority regarded the cold clean highveld air with the same horror as if it had been a deadly cyanide gas, the windows were tightly closed. The compartment was blue with pipe-smoke and fetid with the smell of a dozen unwashed bodies. The conversation was inevitable. Confine a number of men in a small space and they'll get round to it in under ten minutes.

This company had a vast experience in matters pornographic.

A sergeant had served three years in Bangkok, but it took him two hours to convince his companions that what rumour placed horizontally, nature, in fact, had maintained at the vertical. He carried his point only after an expedition down the corridor from which he returned with another old China hand. This expert produced photographic evidence which was studied minutely and deemed conclusive.

It served also to remind a corporal who had done a tour of duty in India of his visit to the Temple of Konarak. A subject which was good for another hour and paved the way for a smooth entry into a discussion of the famous Elephant House in Shanghai.

They kept it up from noon until nightfall.

In the meantime, Saul had lost interest in the cards and taken a book from his bag and started reading. Sean was bored. He cleaned his rifle. Then he picked his teeth with a match and stared out of the window at the small herds of springbok that grazed along the line of rail. He listened to a detailed account of the pleasures provided by the proprietress of the Elephant House, and decided to give it a wide berth if he ever visited Shanghai.

'What are you reading?' he demanded of Saul at last.

'Huh?' Saul looked up vaguely and Sean repeated the question. '*The Westminster System of Government*', Saul held the book so that Sean could see the title.

'Jesus!' grunted Sean. 'What do you read that stuff for?'

'I am interested in politics,' Saul explained defensively and returned to reading.

Sean watched him for a while then, 'Have you got any other books with you?'

Saul opened his bag again. 'Try this.'

'*The Wealth of Nations*'. Sean handled the book dubiously. 'What's it about?' But Saul was reading again.

Sean opened the heavy volume and glanced idly at the first page. He sighed with resignation for it was a long time since he had read anything but a letter or a bank statement – then his eyes started moving back and forth across the page like the shuttle of a loom. Without knowing it, they were weaving the first threads into a fabric that would cover a part of his soul which until now had been naked.

After an hour Saul looked across. 'What do you make of it?' he asked.

Sean grunted without looking up. He was completely absorbed. This was important. The language of Adam Smith had a certain majestic clarity. With some of his conclusions Sean did not agree but the reasoning evoked a train of thought in Sean's own brain, stimulating it to race ahead and anticipate – sometimes correctly, but often reaching a point wide of where the author was aimed.

He read quickly, knowing that he would go back and read it all again for this was only a scouting party into the unknown territory of economics. With his eyes still fixed on the pages, he groped in the pockets of his tunic, found a stub of pencil and underlined a passage to which he wanted to return. Then he left it and went on. Now he used the pencil frequently.

'No!' he wrote in the margin at one place.

'Good,' at another.

Saul looked up again and frowned as he realized Sean was defacing the book. Then he noticed Sean's expression, saw its scowling concentration and his own face relaxed. He watched Sean from under lowered eyelashes. His feeling for this man of muscle and moods and unexpectedly soft places had passed affection and now reached the borders of adulation. He did not know why Sean had placed protecting wings above him, nor did he care. But it was good to sit quietly, no longer reading, and watch the face of this big man who was more than just a friend.

Alone in the midst of a multitude they sat together. The train snaked northwards across the grassland, spreading a long trail of silver-grey smoke behind it and the sun sank exhausted to the earth and bled on to the clouds. After it was gone the darkness came quickly.

They ate canned meat spread on coarse bread with the blade of a bayonet. There was no lighting in the compartment, so after they had eaten they sat together wrapped in their blankets and talked in darkness. Around them all other conversation died and was replaced by the sounds of sleep. Sean opened one of the windows and the cold sweet air cleaned their minds and sharpened them so that they talked in quietly suppressed excitement.

They talked of men and land and the welding of the two into a nation; and how that nation should be governed. They spoke a little of war and much of the peace that would follow it; of the rebuilding of that which had been destroyed into something stronger.

They saw the bitterness ahead that would flourish like an evil weed nourished on blood and the corpses of the dead and they discussed the means by which it should be rooted out before it strangled the tender growth of a land that could be great.

They had never spoken like this before. Saul hugged his blankets about his shoulders and listened to Sean's voice in the darkness. Like most of his race his perception had been sensitized and sharpened so that he could pick up a new quality, a new sense of direction in this man.

I have had a hand in this, he thought, with a stirring of pride. He is a bull, a wild bull, charging anything that moves; charging without purpose, then breaking his run and swinging on to something new; using his strength to destroy because he had never learned to use it in any other way; confused and angry, roaring at the barbs in his shoulders; chasing everything and as a consequence catching nothing. Perhaps I can help him, show him a purpose and a way out of the arena.

And so they talked on into the night. The darkness added another dimension to their existence. Unseen, their physical forms no longer limited them and it seemed that their minds were freed to move out and meet in the darkness, to combine into a cushion of words that carried each idea forward. Until abruptly, the whole delicate pattern was shattered and lost in the concussion of dynamite and the shriek of escaping steam, the roar of breaking timber and glass, and the confusion of equipment and sleeping bodies thrown violently together as the train reared and twisted and plunged from the tracks. Almost immediately a further sound blended into it all – the crackling of musketry at close range and the steady hammering beat of a Maxim machine-gun.

Sean was pinned helplessly in the complete darkness unable to breathe under an immense weight. He struggled wildly, tearing at the men and baggage above him, his legs bound by loose blankets. The weight eased enough for him to drag air into his lungs, but a knee was driven into his face with such force that his lip burst open and the blood oozed saltily into his mouth. He lashed out and felt the stinging rake of broken glass along his arm.

In the darkness men screamed in terror and in pain, leading the hideous chorus of groans and oaths and gunfire.

Sean dragged his body free of the press, felt men thrashing under him as he stood.

Now he could hear the repeated splintering thud of bullets into woodwork much louder than the guns that fired them.

Someone reeled against him and Sean caught him.

'Saul?'

'Leave me, let me go.' A stranger, Sean released him.

'Saul. Saul. Where are you?'

'Sean.'

'Are you hurt?'

'No.'

'Let's get out of here.'

'My rifle.'

'Bugger your rifle.'

'Where's the window?'

'Blocked.'

At last Sean was able to get some idea of their situation. The coach was on its side with the windows against the earth and the whole welter of dead and broken men piled upon them. The door was high above them, probably jammed.

'We'll have to break out through the roof.' He groped blindly, then swore and jerked his hand back as a splinter of wood knifed up under a fingernail, but he felt a draught of cold air on his face.

'There's a hole.' He reached out again eagerly and felt the torn timber. 'One of the planks is sprung.'

Immediately there was a rush of bodies in the darkness, hands clawed at him as half a dozen men fought to find the opening.

'Get back, you bastards.' Sean struck out with both fists and felt them connect. He was panting and he could feel the sweat sliding down his back. The air was heavy with the body warmth and breath of terrified men.

'Get back. I'll work on it.' He forced his hands into the crack and tore the loose plank out. For an instant he struggled with the temptation to press his face to the narrow opening and suck in the clean air. Then he locked his hands on to the next plank, braced his legs against the roof and heaved back with all his strength. It wouldn't budge. He felt the panic mounting in him once more.

'Find me a rifle, somebody,' he shouted above the uproar.

'Here.' Saul's voice, and the rifle was thrust into his hands. He ran the barrel into the opening and using it as a lever flung his weight on to it. He felt wood tearing, moved the barrel and pulled again. It gave and he cleared the plank and started on the next.

'All right. One at a time. Saul, you first.' With his panic just below the surface, Sean shoved each man unceremoniously through the jagged opening. A fat one stuck and Sean put a boot behind him and pushed. The man squeaked and went out like a champagne cork.

'Is there anyone else?' he shouted in the darkness.

'Sean,' Saul's voice from outside. 'Get out of there.'

'You get under cover,' Sean roared back at him.

The Boer fire still flailed the wrecked train. Then he asked again, 'Is there anyone else?' and a man groaned at Sean's feet.

Quickly Sean found him. Hurt badly, his head twisted. Sean cleared the tangle of baggage from above his body and straightened him out. Can't move him, he decided, safer here until the medicos come. He left him and stumbled over another.

'Damn them,' he sobbed in his dreadful anxiety to get out. This one was dead. He could feel the reptilian clamminess of death on his skin, and he left him and scrabbled his way out into the open night.

After the utter blackness of the comparment, the stars lit the land with a pearly light and he saw the fog of steam hanging above the locomotive in a high, hissing bank, and the leading coaches telescoped into each other, and the others jack-knifed and twisted into a weird sculpture of destruction. At intervals along the chain a few rifles winked a feeble reply to the Boer fire that poured down upon them.

'Sean,' Saul called from where he was crouched beside the overturned coach. Sean ran to him and lifted his voice above the clamour.

'Stay here. I'm going back to look for Mbejane.'

'You'll never find him in this lot. He was with the horses – listen to them.'

From the horse-boxes at the rear of the train came such a sound that Sean hoped never to hear again. Two hundred trapped and frenzied animals – it was far worse than the sound of those men still in the wreckage.

'My God!' whispered Sean. Then his anger rose higher than his fear. 'The bastards,' he grated and looked up at the high ground above them.

The Boers had chosen a place where the line curved along the bank of a river. The watercourse cut off escape on that side, and on the other the ground rose steeply in a double fold that commanded the full length of the railway line.

Along the first fold lay their riflemen, two hundred of them at least, judging by the intensity of their fire, while from above them on the summit ridge the muzzle flashes of the Maxim gun faded and flared as it traversed relentlessly back and forth along the train. Sean watched it hungrily for a moment, then he lifted the rifle that he still carried and emptied the magazine, firing at the Maxim. Immediately the flashes grew brighter as it came questing back to find him, and around Sean's head the air was filled with the swishing crack of a hundred whips.

Sean ducked down while he reloaded, then stood up again to shoot.

'You bastards,' he shouted at them, and his voice must have carried for now the riflemen up there were helping the Maxim to search him out. They were getting very close.

Sean crouched down once more, and beside him Saul was firing also.

'Where did you get the rifle?'

'I went back for it.' Saul punctuated his reply with gunfire and Sean grinned as his fingers fumbled with the reload. 'You're going to get hurt one day,' he said.

'You taught me how to go about it,' Saul retorted.

Once more Sean emptied his magazine to no effect, except that the recoil of the rifle invoked the old high madness in him. It needed only Mbejane's voice beside him to trigger it completely.

'Nkosi.'

'Where the hell have you been?' Sean demanded.

'My spears were lost. I spent much time finding them in the darkness.'

Sean was silent for a moment while he peered up at the ridge. Out on the left there was a gap in the line of riflemen where a narrow donga ran through them and down towards the railway. A small party might be able to go up that gully and pass through the rear of the Boer firing-line. From there the solitary Maxim on the ridge would be very vulnerable.

'Bring your spears, Mbejane.'

'Where are you going?' Saul asked.

'I'm going to try for that machine-gun. Stay here and keep these gentlemen's mind on other things.'

Sean started off along the train towards the outlet of the donga. He covered fifty yards before he realized that not only Mbejane but Saul was with him.

'Where do you think you're going?'

'With you.'

'The hell you are!'

'Watch me.' There was that peculiar note of obstinacy in Saul's voice that Sean had come to recognize, and there was no time to argue. He ran on until he was opposite the donga where again he sought shelter in the lee of an overturned coach while he made his final assessment of the position.

The donga looked narrow but deep, and the scrub-bush that filled it would give them cover to the top where there was a definite gap in the Boer Line.

'It'll do,' he decided aloud, and then to the other two, 'I'll go first, then you follow me, Saul, and watch those big feet of yours.'

He was vaguely aware that some show of resistance was being organized among the survivors of the wreck. He could hear the officers rallying them and now a hundred rifles were returning the Boer fire.

'All right. I'm off.' Sean stood up. 'Follow me as soon as I get across.'

At that moment a new voice hailed them. 'What are you men up to?'

'What's it to you?' Sean flashed impatiently.

'I'm an officer,' and then Sean recognized the voice and the lanky figure with a bared sabre in one hand. 'Acheson!'

A second's hesitation before Acheson recognized him. 'Courtney. What are you doing?'

'I'm going up that donga to attack the Maxim.'

'Think you can reach it?'

'I can try.'

'Good fellow – off you go then. We'll be ready to support you if you make it.'

'See you at the top,' said Sean and ran out towards the mouth of the donga.

They moved quietly in single file upwards and the guns and the shouting cloaked the soft sounds of their advance. Sean could hear the voices of the burghers above them growing closer and louder as they approached – very close now – on the side of the donga just above their heads – then behind them, and they were through.

The donga was shallower here, starting to flatten out as it neared the crest. Sean lifted his head above the side and looked out. Below him he could just make out the lumpy shapes of the Boers in the grass but their rifles threw long orange spouts of flames when seen from above – while the British replies were mere pinpricks of light from around the dark tangle of coaches.

Then Sean's attention focused on the Maxim and he could see why the rifle-fire from below had made no effect on it. Sited just below the crest of the ridge on a forward bulge of the slope, it was protected by a scharnz of rock and earth that had been thrown up in front of it. The thick water-jacketed barrel protruded through a narrow opening and the three men that served it crouched low behind the wall.

'Come on,' whispered Sean, and wriggled up out of the donga on to his belly to begin the stalk.

One of the gunners saw him when he was a few yards from the gun. *'Magtig! Pasop, daars 'n –'* and Sean went in with the rifle clubbed in both hands and the man never finished his warning. Mbejane and Saul followed him in, and for a few seconds the emplacement was filled with a struggling mass of bodies. Then it was over and the three of them panted heavily in the stillness.

'Do you know how to work this thing, Saul?'

'No.'

'Nor do I.' Sean squatted behind the gun and settled his hands on to the twin grips, his thumbs automatically resting on the firing-button.

'Wat makeer julle daar bo? Skiet, man, skiet!' a Boer shouted from below, and Sean shouted back, *'Wag maar 'n oomblik – dan skiet ek bedonderd.'*

'Wie's daar? Who's that?' the Boer demanded and Sean depressed the gun.

It was too dark to use the sights, so he took a vague aim over the barrel and thrust his thumbs down on the button. Immediately his shoulders shook like those of a man using a jack hammer and he was deafened by the harsh beat of the gun, but he swung the barrel in a low, sweeping arc across the ridge below him.

A storm of shouts and cries of protest broke out along the Boer line, and Sean laughed with savage delight. The Boer fire upon the train withered miraculously as men jumped up and scattered beneath the spray of bullets. Most of them streamed back to where their horses waited behind the crest, keeping well out on the flanks of the Maxim, while a line of cheering British infantry followed them up from the train – giving the support that Acheson had promised.

Only a tiny but determined group of Boers came up the slope towards Sean, yelling angrily and shooting as they came. There was dead ground directly below the emplacement where Sean could not reach them with the Maxim.

'Get out of here. Run out to the sides,' Sean shouted back at Saul and Mbejane as he hoisted the heavy gun on to the rock wall in front of him to improve its field of fire. But the movement twisted the belt of ammunition and after the first burst the gun jammed hopelessly. Sean lifted it above his head, stood like that for an instant and then hurled it among the men below him. It knocked two of them down into the grass. Sean snatched up a pumpkin-sized rock from the top of the wall and sent it after the gun – and another, and another. Howling with the laughter of fear and excitement, he rained rocks upon them. And they broke. Most of them veered out to the sides and joined the general rush for the horses.

Only one man kept coming, a big man who climbed quickly and silently.

Sean missed him with three rocks, and suddenly he was too close – not ten feet away. There he paused and lifted his rifle. Even in the dark, at that range, the Boer could hardly miss and Sean sprang from the top of the wall. For an instant he dropped free, and then with a shock that knocked the wind from both of them, he drove into the burgher's chest. They rolled down the slope, kicking and grappling, bouncing over the rocky ground, until a small thorn bush held them.

'Now, you bloody Dutchman!' rasped Sean. He knew there was only one possible outcome to this encounter. With supreme confidence in his own strength Sean reached for the man's throat, and with a sense of disbelief felt his wrist held in a grip that made the bone creak.

'*Kom, ons slaat aan,*' the burgher's mouth was an inch from Sean's ear, and the voice was unmistakable.

'Jan Paulus!'

'Sean!' The shock of recognition eased his grip for an instant, and Sean broke his hand loose.

Only once in his life had Sean met a man whose strength matched his own – and now again they were pitted against each other. He drove the heel of his right hand up under Jan Paulus's chin, forcing his head back against the encircling left arm. It should have broken Jan Paulus's neck. Instead he locked his arms around Sean's chest below the level of his armpits – and squeezed. Within seconds Sean felt his face swelling and congesting with blood, his mouth opened and his tongue came out between his teeth.

Without breath, yet he maintained the pressure on Jan Paulus's neck, felt it give fractionally – and knew that another inch of movement would snap the vertebrae.

The earth seemed to tilt and turn beneath him, he knew he was going for his vision was blotched with moving patches of deeper darkness – the knowledge gave him a little more strength. He flung it all on to Jan Paulus's neck. It moved. Jan Paulus gave a wild muffled cry and his grip on Sean's chest eased a fraction.

Again, Sean told himself, again. And he gathered all of what was left for the final effort.

Before he could make it, Jan Paulus moved quickly under him, changing his grip, lifting Sean clear of his chest. Then his knees came up under Sean's pelvis and with a convulsive heave drove Sean's lower body forward and over – cartwheeling him so that he was forced to release Jan Paulus's neck and use his hands to break his own fall.

A rock caught him in the small of the back and agony flared in him like sheet lightning in a summer sky. Dimly through it he heard the shouts of the British infantry very near, saw Jan Paulus scramble up and glance down the slope at the starlight on the bayonets, and saw him take off up the slope.

Sean dragged himself to his feet and tried to follow him but the pain in his back was an effective hobble and Jan Paulus reached the crest ten paces ahead of him. But as he ran, another dark shape closed on his flank the way a good dog will quarter on a running rybuck. It was Mbejane and Sean could see the long steel in his hand as he lifted it above Jan Paulus's back.

'No!' shouted Sean. 'No, Mbejane! Leave him! Leave him!'

Mbejane hesitated, slowed his run, stopped and looked back at Sean.

Sean stood beside him, his hands clasped to his back and his breathing hissing in his throat. Below them from the dark rear slope of the ridge came the hoof-beats of a single running pony.

The sound of Jan Paulus's flight dwindled, and they were engulfed in the advance of the lines of the bayonet men from the train. Sean turned and limped back through them.

Chapter Thirty-nine

Two days later, on the relief train, they reached Johannesburg.

'I suppose we should report to somebody,' Saul suggested as the three of them stood together on the station platform beside the small pile of luggage they had been able to salvage from the train wreck.

'You go and report, if that's what you want,' Sean answered him. 'Me, I'm going to look around.'

'We've got no billets,' Saul protested.

'Follow your Uncle Sean.'

Johannesburg is an evil city, sired by Greed out of a dam named Gold. But it has about it an air of gaiety, of brittle excitement and bustle. When you are away from it you can hate it – but when you return you are immediately re-infected. As Sean was now.

He led them through the portals of the railway building into Eloff Street and grinned as he looked up that well-remembered thoroughfare. It was crowded. The carriages jostled for position with the horse-drawn trams. On the sidewalks beneath the tall three- and four-storeyed buildings the uniforms of a dozen different regiments set off the butterfly colours of the women's dresses.

Sean paused on the station steps and lit a cigar. At that moment the sounds of carriage wheels and human voices were drowned by the plaintive wail of a mine hooter and immediately others joined in signalling the noon. Automatically Sean reached for his pocket-watch to check the time, and noticed the same general movement in the crowded street. He grinned again.

Jo'burg hasn't changed much – still the old habits, the same feeling about it. The mine dumps higher than he remembered them, a few new buildings, a little older and a little smarter – but still the same heartless bitch beneath it all.

And there on the corner of Commissioner Street, ornate as a wedding-cake with its fancy ironwork and corniced roof, stood Candy's Hotel.

With rifle and pack slung over each shoulder, Sean pushed his way through the press on the sidewalk with Saul and Mbejane in his wake. He reached the hotel and went in through the revolving glass doors.

'Very grand.' He looked about the lobby as he dumped his pack on the thick pile of the carpet. Crystal chandeliers, velvet curtains roped with silver, palms and bronze urns, marble tables, fat plush chairs.

'What do you think, Saul. Shall we give this flophouse a try?' His voice carried across the lobby and stilled the murmuring of polite conversation.

'Don't talk so loudly,' Saul cautioned.

A general officer in one of the plush chairs hoisted himself and slowly turned his head to train a monocled stare upon them, while his aide-de-camp leaned across and whispered, '*Colonials*'.

Sean winked at him and moved across to the reception desk.

'Good afternoon, sir.' The clerk regarded them frostily.

'You have reservations for my chief of staff and myself.'

'What name, sir?'

'I'm sorry, I can't answer that question. We are travelling incognito,' Sean told him seriously, and a helpless expression appeared on the man's face. Sean dropped his voice to conspiratory level. 'Have you seen a man come in here carrying a bomb?'

'No.' The man's eyes glazed a little. 'No, sir. No, I haven't.'

'Good.' Sean appeared relieved. 'In that case we'll take the Victoria Suite. Have our luggage sent up.'

'General Caithness has the Victoria Suite, sir.' The clerk was becoming desperate.

'What?' Sean roared. 'How dare you!'

'I didn't . . . We had no . . .' Stuttering, the clerk backed away from him.

'Call the owner,' ordered Sean.

'Yes, sir.' And the clerk disappeared through a door marked 'Private'.

'Have you gone mad?' Saul was fidgeting with embarrassment. 'We can't afford to stay at this place. Let's get out of here.' Under the concentrated scrutiny of every guest in the lobby he was very conscious of their grubby travel-stained uniforms.

Before Sean could answer a woman came through the 'Private' doorway, a very lovely but very angry woman with eyes that blazed like the blue sapphires at her throat.

'I am Mrs Rautenbach – the owner. You asked to see me.'

Sean just smiled at her, and her anger withered slowly as she began to recognize him beneath the creased ill-fitting tunic and without the beard.

'Do you still love me, Candy?'

'Sean?' She was still uncertain.

'Who else?'

'Sean!' And she came to him on the run. Half an hour later General Caithness had been evicted and Sean and Saul were settling comfortably into the Victoria Suite.

Freshly bathed, with only a towel round his waist, Sean lay back in his chair while the barber scraped away his three-day growth of beard.

'Some more champagne?' Candy had not taken her eyes off him for the last ten minutes.

'Thanks.'

She filled his glass, replaced it at his right hand and then touched the thick muscles of his upper arm. 'Still hard,' she murmured. 'You've kept ahead of the years.' Her fingers moved on to his chest. 'Just a little grey here and there – but it suits you,' and then to the barber, 'Haven't you finished yet?'

'One moment more, madam.' He again scissored along the line of Sean's temple, stood back and studied his masterpiece – then, with modest pride, held the mirror for Sean's approval.

'Excellent. Thank you.'

'You may go now. See to the gentleman next door.' Candy had waited long enough. As the door closed behind the barber she turned the key. Sean stood up from the chair and they faced each other across the room.

'My God, but you're big.' Her voice was husky, unashamedly hungry.

'My God, but you're beautiful,' Sean answered her, and they moved slowly to meet in the centre of the floor.

Later they lay quietly while the darkness gathered in the room as evening fell. Then Candy moved her mouth across his shoulder and, the way a cat cleans its kittens, she began gently to lick the long red scratches upon his neck.

When the room was truly dark Candy lit one of the shaded gas-lights and sent down for biscuits and a bottle of champagne. They sat together upon the rumpled bed and talked.

At first there was a shyness between them because of what they had done together – but soon it passed – and they sat up far into the night.

Rare it is for a man to have a friend as well as a lover in one woman – but with Candy this was possible. And to her he released all those things that had been bottled and fomenting within him.

He told her of Michael, and the strange bond between them.

He told her of Dirk, and hinted at his misgivings for the boy.

He spoke of the war and of what he would do when it finished.

He told her of Lion Kop and his wattle.

But one thing he could not tell her. He could not speak of Ruth or the man who was her husband.

Chapter Forty

During the next few days Sean and Saul reported to the headquarters of the Regional Commander and were assigned neither billets nor duties. Now that they had arrived no one seemed very interested in them. They were told to report daily, and turned loose again. They returned to Candy's Hotel and spent most of the days playing billiards or cards and most of the evenings eating and drinking and talking.

A week of this and Sean was getting bored. He began to feel like a stud stallion. Even a solid diet of heavenly mana begins to pall after a while – so when Candy asked him to escort her to a reception and dinner with which

Lord Kitchener was celebrating his promotion to Supreme Command of the Army in South Africa, Sean accepted with relief.

'You look like some sort of god,' Candy told him as he entered her suite through the concealed doorway which connected it with his own bedroom in the Victoria rooms. When she had shown him this discreet little panel and demonstrated how at a touch it slid silently aside, Sean had thrust down the temptation of asking how many others had used it. It was senseless to resent the nameless host who had passed through the panel to teach Candy all those little tricks with which she now delighted him.

'You don't look too bad yourself.' She was dressed in blue silk, the colour of her eyes, and she wore diamonds at her throat.

'How gallant you are!' She came to him and stroked the silk lapels of his newly tailored evening jacket. 'I wish you'd wear your medals.'

'I haven't any medals.'

'Oh Sean! You must have! With all those bullet holes in you, you must have medals.'

'I'm sorry, Candy.' Sean grinned. At times she was so far from being the glittering sophisticated woman of the world. Although she was a year older than he was, time had not destroyed that fragile quality of skin and hair that most women lose so quickly. There was no thickening of her body, no coarsening of her features.

'Never mind – even without medals, you'll be the handsomest man there tonight.'

'And you the loveliest girl.'

As the carriage rolled down Commissioner Street towards the Grand National Hotel, Sean lay back against the yielding support of soft polished leather. His cigar was drawing evenly with an inch of firm grey ash, the single brandy he had drunk before leaving glowed beneath the starched front of his dress-shirt, a faint aura of bay rum clung and hovered around him – and Candy's hand lay lightly upon his leg.

All these things induced in him a mood of deep contentment. He laughed easily at Candy's chatter and let the smoke of his cigar trickle through his lips – tasting it with an almost childlike pleasure. When the carriage stopped before the entrance to the hotel and rocked gently on its superb springing, he climbed down and stood by the big rear-wheel to guard Candy's skirt as she descended.

Then, with her fingers on his forearm, he guided her up the front steps and through the glass doors into the lobby of the hotel. The splendour of the place did not equal Candy's own establishment. But it was impressive enough – and so was the reception line that awaited them. While they took their places among those waiting to meet the Commander-in-Chief, Sean spoke quietly to an aide-de-camp.

'My Lord, may I present Mr Courtney and Mrs Rautenbach.'

Lord Kitchener had a formidable presence. His hand was cold and hard and he stood as tall as Sean. The eyes that stared for an instant into Sean's held a disqueting rigidity of purpose. Then he turned to Candy and his expression softened momentarily as he bowed over her hand.

'Very kind of you to come, madam.'

Then they were past and into the gaudy of uniforms and velvet and silk.

The whole was dominated by dress scarlet of the Guards and Fusiliers, but there was also the gold-frogged blue of the Hussars, the green of the Foresters, kilts of half a dozen Highland reigments, so that Sean's black dress was conspicuously conservative. Among the glitter of orders and decorations shone the jewellery and white skins of the women.

Here assembled were the prize blooms of the huge tree that was the British Empire. A tree grown strong above the rest of the forest. Two centuries of victory in war had nurtured it, two hundred million persons were its roots that sucked in the treasures of half the world and sent them up along the shipping lanes to that grey city astride the Thames that was its heart. And there this rich sap was digested and transmuted into men. These were the men whose lazy speech and careful nonchalance reflected the smugness and arrogance which made them hated and feared by even the trunk of the great tree that gave them flower. While the lesser trees crowded closer and sent their own roots out to divert a little of its sustenance to themselves, the first disease had already eaten into the wood beneath the bark of the giant. America, India, Afghanistan, and South Africa, had started the dry rot that one day would bring it crashing down with a force that would shatter its bulk into so many pieces as to prove it not teak but soft pine.

Watching them now, Sean felt himself apart from them, closer in spirit and purpose to those shaggy men whose Mausers still shouted desperate defiance at them from the vast brown veld.

These thoughts threatened to spoil his mood and he thrust them down, exchanged his empty glass for another filled with bubbling yellow wine and attempted to join the banter of the young officers who surrounded Candy. He succeeded only in conceiving a burning desire to punch one of them between his downy moustaches. He was savouring the idea with increasing relish when a touch on his arm turned him.

'Hello, Courtney. Seem to find you everywhere there is either a fight or a free drink.' Startled, Sean turned to look into the austere face and incongruously twinkling eyes of Major-General John Acheson.

'Hello, General. I notice you frequent the same areas.' Sean grinned at him.

'Bloody awful champagne. Old K. must be economizing.' Then he ran his eyes over Sean's immaculate evening dress. 'A bit difficult to tell whether you have received the awards for which I recommended you.'

Sean shook his head. 'Still a sergeant. I didn't want to embarrass the General Staff by appearing in my chevrons.'

'Ah!' Acheson's eyes narrowed slightly. 'Must be some hold up. I'll look into it.'

'I assure you I'm quite happy this way.'

Acheson nodded and changed the subject. 'You haven't met my wife?' This was patronage on the grand scale. Sean was not to know that Acheson considered him his personal good luck charm. His own rapid promotion dated from their first meeting. Sean blinked in surprise before answering,

'I haven't yet had the honour.'

'Come along then.'

Sean excused himself from Candy, who dismissed him with a tap of her fan and Acheson steered him through the press towards a group at the end of the room. A dozen paces from it Sean stopped abruptly.

'Something wrong?' Acheson asked.

'No. Nothing.' Sean started forward again, but now his eyes were fastened with fascination on one of the men who was a part of the group towards which they were headed.

A slim figure in the dark blue dress uniform of the Natal Mounted Rifles. Sandy brown hair brushed straight back from his high forehead, nose too big for the mouth and the chin beneath it, slightly round-shouldered but with the highest reward for bravery showing purple and bronze beside the striped ribbon of the Distinguished Service Order on his chest, while on his shoulders the silver crowns and lace proclaimed him a colonel.

Slowly, with a new awakening of his guilt, Sean let his eyes move down to this man's legs. With incomprehension he saw them perfectly matched, booted in polished black leather. Only when the man moved slightly, shifting his weight, Sean saw the leadenness in one of them and understood.

'My dear – I would like to present Mr Courtney. I think you have heard me speak of him. He was with me at Colenso, and on the train a few weeks ago.'

'Indeed. Mr Courtney, this is a great pleasure.' She was plump and friendly but Sean was hardly able to murmur the correct response so conscious was he of the other eyes upon his face.

'And this is Major Peterson of my staff.'

Sean nodded.

'Colonel Courtney you will probably know – seeing that you bear the same name, and not to mention the fact that he is your Commanding Officer.'

For the first time in nineteen years Sean looked into the face of the man he had crippled.

'Hello, Garry,' he said and held out his hand. He stood with it out and waited.

Garry Courtney's lips moved. He hunched his shoulders and his head swung slightly from side to side.

Take it, Garry. Please take my hand. Sean tried silently to urge him. Realizing the forbidding set of his own countenance, Sean forced his lips into a smile. It was an uncertain thing that smile, it trembled a little at the corners of his mouth.

In response Garry's own lips relaxed and for a moment Sean saw the terrible longing in his brother's eyes.

'It's been a long time. Garry. Much too long.' Sean prodded forward with his open right hand. *Take it. Oh God, please make him take it.*

Then Garry straightened. As he did so the toe of his right boot scraped softly, awkwardly on the marble floor. The naked longing in his eyes was glazed over, the corners of his mouth lifted upwards in something close to a sneer.

'Sergeant,' his voice was too loud, too high. 'Sergeant, you are incorrectly dressed!' Then he turned, pivoting on the dead leg, and limped slowly away through the throng.

Sean stood with his hand still out and the smile frozen on his mouth.

*You shouldn't have done that to us. We both wanted – I know you wanted
it as much as I.*

Sean let his hand fall empty to his side and balled it into a fist.

'You know him?' Acheson asked softly.

'My brother.'

'I see,' Acheson murmured. He saw many things – and one of them was
the reason why Sean Courtney was still a sergeant.

Major Peterson coughed and lit a cigar. Mrs Acheson touched the
General's arm. 'My dear, Daphne Langford arrived yesterday. There she
is with John – we must have them to dinner.'

'Of course, my dear. I will ask them this evening.'

They turned their attention on each other, giving Sean the respite he
needed to recover from his snubbing.

'Your glass is empty and so is mine, Courtney. I suggest we go on to
something more substantial than K's cooking champagne.'

Brandy, fiery Cape brandy, very different from that soapy liquor they
make in France. A dangerous spirit to take in his present mood. And only
one mood was possible for Sean after what Garry had done to him – cold,
murderous rage.

His face was impassive, politely he responded to Mrs Acheson's charm,
once he smile at Candy across the room, but always he sent brandy after
brandy down to feed the rage that seethed in his belly; his eyes followed the
figure in dark blue as it limped from group to group.

The aide-de-camp who arranged the dinner seating could never have
known that Sean was a mere sergeant. As Mrs Rautenbach's guest he
believed him to be an influential civilian and placed him high at the long
table, between Candy and Mrs Acheson, with Major Peterson below him
and a brigadier and two colonels opposite. One of the colonels was Garrick
Courtney.

Beneath the almost uninterrupted stare which Sean fastened on him,
Garry became nervously garrulous. Never once meeting Sean's eyes, he
aimed his remarks higher up the table, and that bronze cross suspended on
the ribbon of shot purple silk that bumped against his chest each time he
leaned forward gave a weight to his opinions that was evident in the attention
they received from the officers of general rank.

The food was excellent. Rock lobster that had run the gauntlet of Boer
blockade from the Cape, plump young pheasant, venison, four assorted
sauces – even the quality of the champagne had improved. But Sean ate
little, instead he gave permanent employment to the wine steward who
hovered behind his chair.

'And so' said Garrick as he selected a cigar from the cedarwood box that
was offered him, 'I cannot see hostilities continuing another three months
at the outside.'

'I agree with you sir,' Major Peterson nodded. 'We'll be back in London
for the season.'

'Poppycock!' Sean made his first contribution to the discussion. It was a
word he had learned only recently – but he liked it. Besides, there were
ladies present.

Peterson's face chameleoned to a creditable match with the scarlet of his dress coat, Acheson started to smile then changed his mind, Candy wriggled in anticipation for she had reached the edge of boredom, and a chilly stillness fell over that area of the table.

'I beg your pardon?' Garry looked at him for the first time.

'Poppycock,' Sean repeated, and the wine steward stepped forward to cascade champagne into the crystal bowl of his glass, an operation which he had repeated at least a dozen times during the course of the evening – but this time it commanded the attention of the entire company.

'You don't agree with me?' Garry challenged.

'No.'

'Why not?'

'Because there are still eighteen thousand Boers in the field, because they are still an organized army, because not once have they had a decisive defeat inflicted on them – but mainly because of the character of these eighteen thousand that are left.'

'You don't—' Garry's voice was petulant, but Acheson interrupted smoothly. 'Excuse me, Colonel Courtney.' Then he turned to Sean. 'I believe you know these people—' he hesitated and then went on, 'you are even related through marriage.'

'My brother-in-law leads the Wynberg commando,' Sean affirmed. The old boy knew more of his past than he suspected – must have made a few inquiries. Sean was flattered and the harshness gone from his voice.

'What in your opinion, will be their course of action from now on?' Acheson pursued the subject and Sean tasted his champagne while he considered his reply.

'They will scatter – break up into their traditional fighting units, the commando.' Acheson nodded, from his position on the General Staff he knew this had already happened.

'In so doing they will avoid the necessity of dragging a supply column with them. Once the rainy season begins these small units will find grazing less of a problem for their horses.'

'Yes.' Sean saw they were all listening now. He thought quickly, cursing the wine that had dulled his brain 'They will avoid battle, run from it and swing round to jab at the flanks, then run again.'

'Supplies?' asked the Brigadier.

'The veld is their storeroom, each farm upon it a haven.'

'Ammunition, weapons, clothing?' persisted the Brigadier.

'Every British soldier they capture or kill will provide a brand-new Lee-Metford rifle and a hundred rounds of ammunition.'

'But how long can they live like that?' Garry spoke indulgently, as though to a child. 'How far can they run?' He glanced around at the others seeking their support, but everyone was watching Sean.

'How wide is the veld – that is how far they can run.' Sean turned on him, stung by the tone of his voice. 'My God, you know them. Hardship is a way of life with them. Pride, the watchword that will carry them on.'

'You paint a pretty picture.' Garry smiled easily. 'It is unusual to find such appreciation of grand strategy among the rank and file.' Then he looked higher up the table once more with an emphasis that excluded Sean from the conversation. 'As I was saying, General Acheson, I believe—'

'One moment please, Colonel.' Acheson in turn excluded him and put his question to Sean. 'If you had the running of it, what plan of action would you adopt?'

Across the table Garrick Courtney coughed in a manner intended to inform the company that his brother was about to make a fool of himself.

It was not lost on Sean. 'The problem revolves around one single fact. The mobility of the enemy,' he stated grimly.

'Your perception does you great credit,' murmured Garry.

'Our first problem is to contain him and then to wear him down,' Sean went on, trying to ignore the taunts of his brother.

'Contain him?' The Brigadier fired the question.

'Hold him into a limited area,' Sean explained.

'How?'

'Say by a series of set fortifications,' Sean suggested.

'Correct me if I'm wrong – but you propose to divide the whole of the highveld into paddocks and farm the enemy as one would dairy cattle?' Garry was still smiling.

'The new blockhouse lines along the line of rail are proving effective. It should be possible to extend them across the open veld – every time the enemy had to pass through them he would be subject to a mauling by the garrisons and his position would immediately be pin-pointed.

'The cost would be enormous,' Acheson pointed out.

'Not as great as supporting an army of a quarter of a million men in the field for another five years,' Sean brushed his objection aside, he was set on his run of ideas. 'Then, within the defined areas small well-mounted bodies of men, unimpeded by supply wagons and artillery, could be used to raid the commandos – hitting them in an unrelenting series of raids and ambushes. Driving them on to the blockhouse lines, wearing down their horses, giving them no chance to rest, employing exactly their tactics of skirmishing. Against the commandos use counter-commandos.'

Acheson nodded thoughtfully. 'Go on,' he said.

'Then, clear out the farms,' Sean went on recklessly. 'Bring in the women and old men whose crops keep the commandos fed. Force them to operate in a vacuum.'

In the years ahead Sean was to regret the impulse that made him say it. Perhaps Kitchener would have scorched the land without Sean's suggestion, perhaps he had no hand in the formation of the concentration camps that bred bitterness Sean would spend the rest of his life trying to sweeten. But he could never be certain. He was drunk and angry – but later this knowledge would not comfort him.

Now suddenly he felt empty as though in a premonition of the monstrous seed he had sown and he sank into brooding silence while the others passed his ideas back and forth, building on them, already beginning to plan.

When the dinner party broke up and they drifted through to drink coffee, Sean made one more attempt to tear down the barrier between his brother and himself. He went to him with his pride in his hands and offered it. 'I was in Ladyburg last month. All's well there. Ada writes to say—'

'I receive a weekly letter not only from my wife but from my stepmother

and my son. I am fully aware of the latest news from home. Thank you.'
Garry stared over Sean's shoulder as he replied.

'Garry . . .'

'Excuse me.' Garry nodded briefly and limped away to speak to a brother officer. He kept his back towards Sean.

'Let's go home, Candy.'

'But Sean . . .'

'Come on.'

Sean slept very little that night.

Chapter Forty-one

The Headquarters of the General Officer Commanding the eastern sector were tastefully situated in the offices of a brewery company in Plein Street. Major Peterson was waiting for Garry when he arrived.

'I sent for you two hours ago, sir.'

'I was indisposed,' Garry told him.

'Old Ach is not in a very good mood today – we'd better not keep him waiting any longer. Come along.'

Down the passage, where orderlies bustled, Peterson led him, and to a door at the far end. He knocked once and then opened it. Acheson looked up from his paperwork.

'Colonel Courtney is here, sir.'

'Thank you, Peterson. Come in, Courtney.'

Peterson closed the door and left Garry standing alone on the thick Persian rug in front of Acheson's desk.

'I sent for you two hours ago, Courtney.' Acheson used the same reprimand, and Garry shifted his leg uncomfortably.

'I wasn't too well this morning, sir. Had to get the doctor in.'

Acheson fingered his white moustache as he examined the dark circles beneath Garry's eyes, and the chalky colour of his face. 'Sit down,' he ordered.

Acheson was silent, watching him. But Garry avoided his eyes. He felt brittle from the previous night's drinking, his skin dry and sensitive, and he fidgeted in the chair, clasping and unclasping the hand that lay in his lap.

'I want one of your men,' Acheson spoke at last.

'Of course, sir,' Garry nodded.

'That sergeant – Courtney. I want to give him an independent command.'

Garry sat very still.

'You know who I mean?' Acheson persisted.

'Yes, sir.'

'You should,' Acheson murmured dryly. 'I have personally recommended him to you on two occasions for recognition.' He flicked through the sheaf of papers in front of him.

'Yes, sir.' Garry's right hand was opening and closing again.

'I notice you took no action on either of my recommendations.'

'No, sir.'

'May I ask why?'

'I didn't have . . . I didn't think the occasions merited further action.'

'You thought that my judgement was in error?' Acheson asked politely.

'No sir. Of course not, sir.' Garry answered quickly.

'Well, then?' Acheson's eyes were pale blue, but cold.

'I spoke to the man. Congratulated him. After Colenso I gave him leave.'

'Very decent of you – in view of the wounds he received there.'

'I didn't want to . . . You see – he's my brother. It was difficult – favouritism. I couldn't really do much.' Garry wriggled sideways in his chair, his hands came up pawing the air as though to pluck words from it.

'Your brother?' Acheson demanded.

'Yes. My brother. I know him, I know him – you don't. You can't have any idea.' Garry could feel the pattern of his thoughts disintegrating, his voice sounded shrill in his own ear. He had to explain, he had to tell Acheson. 'My leg,' he shrilled, 'my leg. You see it. Look at it! He did that. He took my leg. You don't know him. He's evil. He's evil, evil. I tell you he's evil.'

Achesons expression had not changed, but his eyes were colder, more watchful. Garry had to reach him and make him understand.

'Anna.' Garry's lips were wet and blubbery. 'My wife, Anna. He did that to her. Everything he touches – you can't know how he is. I know. He's evil. I tried, I hoped at Colenso – but you can't destroy him. He is the destroyer.'

'Colonel Courtney!' Acheson's voice cut into his tirade, and Garry jerked at the crack of it. He covered his lips with his fingers and slowly he subsided into the chair.

'I just want to explain. You don't understand.'

'I think I do,' Acheson clipped the words short and harsh. 'I am granting you indefinite leave on grounds of ill-health.'

'You can't do that – I won't resign my commission.'

'I have not asked you to,' Acheson snapped. 'I will send the papers to your hotel this afternoon. You can take tomorrow's train south.'

'But – but, sir—'

'That will be all, Courtney. Thank you.'

Acheson turned his attention once more to his papers.

Chapter Forty-two

That afternoon Sean spent two hours with Acheson, then he returned to Candy's Hotel and found Saul in the billiard room. Sean selected a cue. Saul laid both balls against the far cushion and straightened.

'Well?' he asked, as Sean chalked his stick.

'You'll never believe it.'

'Tell me, and let me be the judge.'

Grinning secretly Sean cannoned twice and then sank the red.

'From sergeant without portfolio, to a full-blown major and an independent command,' he announced.

'*You?*'

'Me.' Sean chuckled and missed a cannon.

'They must be crazy.'

'Crazy or not. From now on you will stand in my presence, adopt a respectful tone of speech – and miss that shot.'

Saul missed.

'If you're an officer and a gentleman why don't you behave like one and keep your mouth shut when I'm making a play.'

'You also have changed your status.'

'How?'

'You're now a lieutenant,' Sean informed him.

'No!'

'With a gong.'

'A gong?'

'A medal, you fool.'

'I'm overcome. I am speechless.' At last Saul broke down and began to laugh. It was a sound which Sean enjoyed. 'What kind of a gong – and what for?'

'Distinguished Conduct Medal – for the night of the train.'

'But Sean, you . . .'

Sean interrupted. 'Yes, they gave me one also. Old Acheson got quite carried away. He started hanging medals and promotions on everything that moved, with the same dedicated fervour as a bill-poster putting up advertisements for Bovril. He damned nearly pinned a medal on the orderly who brought in the coffee.'

'He gave you coffee?'

'And a cigar,' Sean answered. 'He counted not the cost. It was like two lovers on an assignation. Repeatedly he addressed me as *My dear fellow.*'

'And what is this command he gave you?'

Sean racked his cue and stopped laughing.

'You and I are to head one of the first counter-commandos. Small, lightly equipped units to ride in and ginger up the Boer. Harass him, wear him down, chase the guts out of his horses and keep him moving until he runs on to one of the big columns.'

The following morning they rode out with Major Peterson to inspect the band of volunteers he had assembled for them.

'A mixed bag I'm afraid, Courtney. We've scratched together three hundred and fifteen.' Peterson was gloating a little behind the apology. He had not forgotten that *poppycock*.

'It must have been difficult,' Sean agreed. 'You only had a quarter of a million to choose from. What abour officers?'

'Sorry. Only Friedman here. But I have got you an absolute gem. Sergeant-major. Snaffled him from the Dorsets. Fellow by the name of Eccles. First-class, absolutely first-class.'

'And Tim Curtis – the one I asked for?'

'Sorry again. They've reopened the gold mines. All engineers are being pulled out and sent back to work.'

'Damn it, I wanted him. What about machine-guns?'

'Four Maxims. Bloody lucky to get them.'

'Horses?'

'A bit of a struggle – but you can go down to remount and take your pick.'

Sean went on relentlessly with his demands and questions during the ride out towards Randfontein. His excitement for the challenge of this venture rose steadily as they argued and talked. At last he was taking it seriously. He asked the final and crucial question as they trotted past the sentries into the great army camp on the outskirts of Johannesburg.

'Has Acheson decided in which area I will be operating?'

'Yes.' Peterson dropped his voice. 'South-east Transvaal.'

'That's where Leroux is!'

'That's right. The gentleman who met your train the other day.'

Jan Paulus again!

'Here you are, Courtney.'

A little apart from the main camp stood three lines of white canvas tents. A field kitchen smoked at the far end and around it were clustered Sean's warriors.

'My God, Peterson. You said a mixed bag! You've robbed the army of cooks and batmen. And what are those – *sailors*, Bejusus!'

Peterson smiled thinly and shifted in the saddle.

'Press-ganged them,' he admitted. 'Gunnery detail from *Repulse*. Ah, here comes your sergeant-major.'

Eccles approached in column of fours; bull-built black moustache, a few inches over six feet and all of it held stiffly erect. Peterson introduced them and they appraised each other.

'A right scruffy lot we got here, sir.'

'We've got a bit of work to do, Eccles.'

'That we'ave, sir.'

'Let's get started then.' And they glowered at each other in mutual respect and liking.

A week later they were ready to go. Saul had named them 'Courtney's Fighting Scouts'. They were all well mounted, altough there were some interesting styles of horsemanship evident – especially among the delegates from the Royal Navy. By bullying the quartermaster Sean had arrived at a standard uniform similar to that of the Imperial Light Horse; slouch hats, khaki tunics and riding breeches, bandoliers, puttees and issue boots. They had forty fat and healthy pack-mules, four Maxim machine-guns and Eccles had trained teams to serve them.

Acheson had approved Sean's request to use Charlestown as a base. He had arranged rail transport south to this tiny village near the Natal border, promised support from the big flying columns in the area, and informed Sean that he was expecting *big things* from him. He made it sound like a threat.

Chapter Forty-three

'But, darling, you haven't even been given a real uniform. You look so drab.' Candy, who was watching him dress from the double bed, held very definite views on what constituted a real uniform. It had gold lace and frogging with, say a Star of the Garter on a rich scarlet ground. 'Lock at those buttons – they're not even shiny.'

'Boers like shiny things – makes good shooting in the sun.' Sean glanced over his shoulder at her. Her hair was fluffed into golden disorder and the blue gown was arranged to provoke rather than conceal. Hastily Sean returned his eyes to his own reflection in the full-length mirror and brushed the hair back along his temples. A touch of grey in it now. Quite dignified, he decided. Pity about the nose. He took it between his fingers and straightened it, a hell of a nose, but when he released his grip it returned immediately to a half-cock position.

'Well, I'll be leaving you now,' he said, and she stood up quickly and the laughter was gone from her lips, they trembled a little.

'I'll come down with you.' She rearranged the gown quickly.

'No.'

'Yes, I have a farewell present for you.'

In the hotel yard, hitched behind four fat mules, was a scotch-cart. She led him to it and lifted the tarpaulin cover.

'A few things I thought you might need.'

Against the cold she had provided a sheepskin coat, six fine woollen blankets and a silk eiderdown, two feather pillows and a mattress; a case of Courvoisier brandy and a case of Veuve Clicquot champagne. Against starvation there was potted salmon, strawberry jam, caviar in little glass jars, tinned delicacies all carefully packed in wooden boxes. For his health a medicine chest complete with a set of surgical instruments. Against the Boer there was a Toledo steel sabre in a leather scabbard worked with silver and a matched pair of Colt revolvers in a mahogany presentation case.

'Candy . . .' Sean stumbled. 'I don't know what to say.'

She smiled a little and took his arm, hugging it. 'There's something else also.' She nodded to one of the grooms who disappeared into the stables and led out a full-blooded Arab stallion with an English hunting saddle on its back.

'My God!' exclaimed Sean, and the stallion danced sideways so that the early sun glowed on the sheen of its coat. It flared the great pink pits of its nostrils and rolled its eyes before rearing high and dragging the groom off his feet.

'Candy, my dear,' Sean repeated.

'Good-bye, Sean.' She lifted her lips for his kiss and then broke away and almost ran back to the hotel.

While Saul shouted ribald encouragement, Mbejane and the groom held its head. Sean mounted the stallion, then they turned it loose and Sean fought to quieten it. At last he brought it under a semblance of control and, crabbing and pracing with arched neck and dainty high-stepping gait, persuaded it to head off in the general direction of Johannesburg railway station.

Eccles watched his approach impassively.

'What the hell are you laughing at, Sergeant-Major?'

'I wasn't laughing, sir.'

Sean dismounted and, with relief, gave the stallion into the care of two of his troopers.

'Nice bit of horseflesh, sir.'

'What do you think he'll fetch?'

'You're going to sell him, sir?' Eccles could not hide his relief.

'You're damn right, I am. But it's a gift, so no sale here in Johannesburg.'

'Well, Colonel Jordan at Charlestown is usually in the market for a good nag. I should be able to get you a price sir. We'll see what we can do.'

Colonel Jordan purchased not only the stallion but the pistols and the sabre as well. The secretary of the Charlestown garrison officers' mess frothed at the mouth with excitement when Eccles drew back the tarpaulin cover from the scotchcart.

When Sean's column rode out into the brown open winter grassland towards the jagged line of the Drakensberg, the little scotch-cart trotted behind with the Maxims and a dozen ammunition cases making a full load.

Chapter Forty-four

There was cold that first night, and the stars were brilliant, clear and very far away. In the morning the land lay white and brittle in the grip of frost; each blade of grass each twig and fallen leaf transformed into a white-jewelled wonder. A thin scum of ice covered the pool beside which the column had camped.

Mbejane and Sean squatted together. Mbejane with his monkey-skin kaross draped over his shoulders and Sean with the sheepskin coat buttoned to the throat.

'Tonight we will camp below that mountain.' Sean pointed away towards the west at the blue cone that stood out against the lighter blue of the dawn sky. 'You will find us there.'

'Nkosi,' Mbejane nodded over his snuffbox.

'These others.' Sean pointed with his chin at the group of four natives who waited quietly with the spears beside the pool. 'Are they men?'

Mbejane shrugged. 'I know little of them. The best of those I spoke with, perhaps. But they work for gold – and of their hearts I do not know.' Before going on, he regarded their clothing; tattered European cast-offs which were everywhere replacing the traditional tribal costume. 'They dress without dignity. But beneath the rags it is possible that they are men.'

'They are all we have so we must use them. Yet I wish we had those others who now grow fat in the company of their women.'

Mbejane smiled. A week before he had put the message into the grapevine and he knew that both Hlubi and Nonga were at that moment dissipating their accumulations of fat as they trotted north from their kraals along the Umfolozi River. They would be here soon.

'This is the way we will hunt,' Sean told him. 'Your men will spread out ahead of us and search for sign. The horses of those we seek will carry no steel on their hooves. If you find it fresh, then follow it until the run and direction of it is clear. Then return to me in haste.'

Mbejane nodded and sniffed a pinch from his snuffbox.

'While you search, stop at the kraals you find along the way. Speak with the people there, clearly, if the Mabune are here these people will know of it.'

'It will be as you say, Nkosi.'

'The sun comes.' Sean looked up at the glow of it upon the high places while the valleys were blue with shadow. 'Go in peace, Mbejane.'

Mbejane folded his kaross and tied it with a strip of leather. He picked up his stabbing spear and slung the great oval war shield on his shoulder. 'Go in peace, Nkosi.'

Sean watched while he talked with the other trackers, listening to the sonorous rise and fall of his voice. Then they scattered, trotting away into the veld, dwindled and were gone.

'Eccles.'

'Sir.'

'Finished breakfast?'

'Yes, sir.'

The men stood to their horses, blanket-rolls and carbines on the saddles, slouch hats pulled well down and the collars of their greatcoats turned up against the cold. Some were still eating with their bayonets from the cans of shredded beef.

'Let's go, then.'

The column closed up, riding four abreast, the pack-mules and the scotchcart in the centre, the outriders fanning out ahead to screen the advance. It was a tiny command, not a hundred and fifty paces long even with the pack animals, and Saul smiled as he remembered the massive fifteen-mile column that had marched from Colenso to Spion Kop.

Yet it was enough to tickle his pride. Courtney's Fighting Scouts. The task now was to justify the second word of their title.

Saul hooked one leg over the saddle, balanced his notebook upon it – and while they rode he and Sean planned a thorough re-organization of the column.

When they halted at midday the planning was put into effect. A patrol of ten men in charge of the mules, for this duty Sean picked those who were fat, old or ungainly in the saddle. These men would also act as horseholders when the unit went in to fight on foot.

From among his sailors, Sean selected the gunners to captain the four Maxim teams. The riflemen were divided into patrols of ten with the most likely men promoted Sergeant Patrol Leaders, and their warrants noted in Saul's little book.

It was well after nightfall when they offsaddled that night below the dark massif of the mountain. Mbejane was waiting with his men beside a small, well-screened fire.

'I see you, Mbejane.'

'I see you, Nkosi.'

In the firelight Mbejane's legs were coated with dust to the knees and his face was grey with fatigue.

'What news?'

'Old sign. Perhaps a week ago, many men camped over there below the river. Twenty fires not in lines as the soldiers make them. They left no little tin pots as the soldiers do when they have emptied them of meat. No tents, but beds of cut grass – many beds.'

'How many?' It was an idle question for Mbejane could not count as a white man counts. He shrugged.

'As many beds as there are men with us?' Sean sought a comparison.

'More.' Mbejane thought carefully before answering.

'As many again?' Sean persisted.

'Perhaps as many again – but no more than that.'

Probably five hundred men, Sean guessed. 'Which way were they moving?'

Mbejane pointed south-west.

Back towards Vryheid and the protection of the Drakensberg mountain. Yes, it was part of the Wynberg commando without doubt.

'What news from the kraals?'

'There is fear among them. They tell little, and that of no importance.' Mbejane made no attempt to hide his disgust, the contempt that the Zulu feels for every other tribe in Africa.

'You have done well, Mbejane. Rest now for we ride before the dawn.'

Four more days they moved south-west, Sean's trackers sweeping the ground ten miles on each side of their path and finding it empty.

The Drakensberg reared up like a serrated back of a prehistoric monster along the south horizon. There was snow on the peaks.

Sean exercised his men in the counters to a surprise attack. Riflemen wheeling out and dismounting in line to cover the Maxims as they galloped wildly for the nearest high ground. Holders gathering the loose horses and pelting away to the cover of the nearest donga or kopje. Again and again they repeated this manoeuvre.

Sean worked them until they leaned forward in their saddles to nurse aching backsides and cursed him as they rode. He worked them to the edge of exhaustion and then on to a new physical fitness. They sprouted beards, their faces reddened and peeled, then darkened with the sun, their uniforms darkened also, but with dirt. Now they no longer cursed him. There was a new feeling among them, they laughed more and sat solid in the saddle, slept soundly at night despite the cold and woke with eagerness.

Sean was moderately satisfied.

On the morning of the tenth day Sean was scouting ahead of the column with two of his troopers. They had just dismounted to rest among an outcrop of boulders when Sean picked up movement out on the plain ahead. With a savage lift of aniticipation he scrambled down from the boulder on which he was sitting and ran to his horse for his binoculars.

'Damn it!' he mouthed his disappointment as he saw the lance blades glitter in the round strangely fore-shortened field of the glasses. 'Cavalry'.

Half an hour later they met the small patrol of lancers from one of the big columns that were driving south from the line of blockhouses. The young subaltern in command gave Sean a cigar, and the latest news of the war.

De la Rey and Smuts were rampaging north of Johannesburg in the Magaliesberg with forty thousand men chasing their three thousand. South in the Free State another of the great De Wet hunts was in full swing. But this time they would catch him, the subaltern assured Sean. Fifty thousand foot and horse had driven his commando into the angle between the block-house line and the flooded Riet River. In the east it was quieter. The commandos there lacked leadership and were lying up in the mountains around Komatipoort.

'So far it's quiet here also, sir. But I don't like the looks of it. This man Leroux is a nasty piece of work, clever man too, So far he's limited his activities to a few raids. Ten days ago about five hundred of his men hit one of our supply columns near Charlestown. Wiped out the guard and collected enough ammunition to fight a full-scale battle, then made off towards the mountains.'

'Yes,' Sean nodded grimly. 'We found one of his camps.'

'No sign of him since then, sir. We've been scouring the ground for him but so far without luck.'

'What's his force?' Sean asked.

'He can muster three thousand, so they say. My guess is that he's getting himself poised for something really big.'

That night Mbejane came into camp well after midnight. He came to where Sean slept under the scotchcart and with him were two other men.

'Nkosi.'

Sean rolled on his side, instantly awake at the touch. 'Mbejane?' He crawled out from under the cart and stood up.

The moon was up, silver and round and bright. By its light he recognized the men with Mbejane and exclaimed with pleasure:

'By God! Hlubi! Nonga!' Then remembering his manners, 'I see you.'

He stepped forward grinning broadly to clasp their shoulder in turn. And each replied gravely as they returned his embrace. 'I see you, Nkosi.'

'Are you well?'

'I am well. Are you well?'

The catechism of Zulu greeting can be carried on for as long as there is time available. More than a year had passed since Sean had discharged them from his service outside Pretoria, and so Sean must ask each of them for news of his father, his brothers, his herds, and the journey they had made, before he could put his own question.

'You came through Ladyburg?'

'We came that way,' agreed Hlubi.

'You saw the Nkosana Dirk?'

Now for the first time they both smiled, white teeth in the moonlight.

'We sat in council with the Nkosizana,' Hlubi chuckled. 'He grows like a bull calf. Already he wears scars of battle, honourable blackening of one of his eyes.'

'He grows in wisdom also,' Nonga boasted. 'Saying aloud to us those things which are written in the book.'

Hlubi went on: 'He sends greetings to the Nkosi, his father, and asks that he be allowed now to leave his school and join with him once more. For now he is skilled in the matter of books and numbers.'

Sean laughed. 'And what of the Nkosikazi, my mother?' he asked.

'She is well, She sends you this book.' Hlubi produced a travel-stained envelope from his loin-cloth. Sean tucked it away inside his coat to be read at leisure.

'Now.' The formula of greeting completed, Sean could come to the present. 'What news of Mabunu? Have you found sign?'

Mbejane squatted on his haunches and laid his spear and shield beside him. The other followed his example. The meeting came to order.

'Speak,' Mbejane ordered Hlubi.

'We came through the mountains, this being the shorter way,' Hlubi explained. 'In the hills below the mountains we found the road made by many horses, and following it we came upon a level place surrounded by rock. The Mabunu are there with cattle and wagons.'

'How far is this place?' Sean asked eagerly.

'A day's long journey.' Thirty miles.

'How many Mabunu?' Sean asked and Mbejane explained, 'As many as camped at the place I told you of.'

It made sense, Sean decided. Jan Paulus would have split his force into smaller units, for reasons of supply and concealment, until such time as he needed them.

'We will go then,' he said and stood up.

Eccles woke quickly.

'Sergeant-Major. The guides have found a small Boer commando in laager below the mountains. Get the men mounted up.'

'Sir!' Eccles's moustache, rumpled with sleep, quivered like the whiskers of a hunting dog.

While around him the commotion of upsaddling began. Sean kicked life into the fire and in its yellow flickering light he tore a page from his notebook and licked the point of a pencil.

> *To all British troops in the field:*
>
> I am in contact with a Boer commando of 500. Will attempt to contain them pending your arrival. The bearer will act as a guide.
>
> S. Courtney (Major).
>
> 5th August, 1900. Time 00.46 hours.

'Hlubi,' he called.

'Nkosi!'

'Take this book,' he handed him the note. 'There are soldiers out there.' He swept his arm towards the north. 'Give it to them.'

Chapter Forty-five

Bunched into a compact column with the gallant little scotchcart bouncing and jolting in the rear, Courtney's Fighting Scouts cantered southwards with the brown winter grass brushing their stirrups.

With Saul beside him and the two Zulus ranging ahead like hunting dogs, Sean rode in the van. He slouched easily in the saddle and tried with both hands to steady Ada's letter as it fluttered in the wind of his passage. It was strange to read the gentle reassuring words as he hurried into battle.

All was well at Lion Kop. The wattle grew apace – free from fire, drought or pestilence. She had hired an assistant manager who worked afternoons only; his mornings required attendance at Ladyburg School. Dirk was earning his princely salary of two shillings and sixpence a week and seemed to be enjoying the work. The arrival of his school report for the period ended at Easter was the occasion for some concern. His average high marks for each subject was followed by the notation, 'Could do much better' or 'Lacks concentration'. The whole was summarized by the Headmaster, 'Dirk is a high-spirited and popular boy. But he must learn to control his temper and to apply himself with more diligence to those subjects he finds distasteful.'

Dirk had recently fought an epic bout of fisticuffs with the Petersen boy, who was two years his senior, and had emerged blooded and bruised, but victorious. Here Sean detected a note of pride in Ada's prim censure. There followed half a page of messages dictated by Dirk in which protestations of filial love and duty were liberally punctuated with requests for a pony, a rifle, and permission to terminate his scholastic career.

Ada went on tersely to say that Garry had recently returned to Ladyburg, but had not yet called upon her.

Finally, she instructed him to take pains with his health, invoked the Almight to his protection, anticipated his swift return to Lion Kop – and ended with love.

Sean folded the letter carefully and tucked it away. Then he let his mind drift, lolling in the saddle while the brown miles dropped steadily behind his horse. There were so many loose or ravel threads to follow – Dirk and Ada, Ruth and Saul, Garrick and Michael – and all of them made him sad.

Then suddenly he glanced sideways at Saul and straightened in the saddle. This was not the time to brood. They had entered the mouth of one of the valleys that sloped upwards towards the massive snow-plastered ramparts of the Drakensberg, and were following a stream whose banks dropped ten feet to the water that gurgled and tinkled over the polished round boulders in its bed.

'How much farther, Nonga?' he called.

'Close now, Nkosi.'

In another valley that ran parallel to the one Sean was following, separated from it by two ridges of broken rock, a young Boer asked the same question.

'How much farther, Oom Paul?'

But before answering, Vecht-Generaal Jan Paulus Leroux eased himself around in the saddle and looked back along the commando of one thousand burghers he was leading to a rendezvous at his laager in the mountains. They rode in a solid mass that clogged the floor of the valley, bearded men in a motley of dark homespun clothing, on ponies shaggy in their winter coats – yet Jan Paulus felt pride swell in his chest as he looked at them. These were the bitter-enders, veterans of half a hundred fights, men forged and tempered in the furnace of battle, razor-sharp and resilient as the finest steel. Then he looked at the boy beside him – a boy in years only for his eyes were old and wise.

'Close now, Hennie.'

'Eccles, we'll halt here. Water the horses. Loosen the girths but don't offsaddle. No fires but the men can rest and eat.'

'Very well, sir.'

'I am going forward to have a look at the laager. While I am away I want you to issue an extra hundred rounds of ammunition to each man. Check the Maxims. I should be back in two hours.'

'When will it be, sir?'

'We'll move forward at dusk, I want to be in position to attack as soon as the moon rises. You can tell the men now.'

As Sean and Nonga left the column and moved on foot up the valley, two men watched them from the ridge. They lay on their bellies among the rocks. Both of them were bearded. One of them wore a British officer's Sam Browne belt over his patched leather jacket, but the rifle that rested on the rock in front of him was a Mauser.

'They send spies to the laager,' he whispered, and his companion answered in the Taal.

'*Ja*, they have found it.'

'Go! Ride quickly to Oom Paul and say for him that we have three hundred khaki ripe and ready for the plucking.'

The other Boer grinned and wriggled backwards, working his way off the skyline. Once below it he ran to his pony and led it down into the grass which would muffle its hoof-beats, before he mounted.

An hour later Sean returned from his reconnaissance.

'We've got them, Eccles,' he grinned savagely at Saul and Eccles.

'They're about two miles ahead in a hidden basin of hills.' He squatted down and smoothed a patch of earth with the palm of his hand. 'Now here is the way we'll do it.' With a twig he drew quickly in the dirt. 'This is our valley. Here we are. This is the laager, hills here and here and here. This is the entrance to the basin. Now, we'll place two Maxims here, with a hundred men below and in front of them like this. I want you—'

Abruptly his earthen map exploded, throwing dirt into his eyes and open mouth. 'What the bloody—' he mouthed as he clawed at his face but the rest of it was lost in the blast of the Mausers.

Through streaming eyes Sean looked up at the ridge. 'Oh my God!' A fire haze of gunsmoke drifted across it like sea spray on a windy day, and he sprang to his feet.

'Into the river. Get the horses into the river,' he roared above the murderous crackle, the shrill fluting whine of ricochets and the continuous slapping of bullets into earth and flesh.

'Into the river. Get into the river!' He ran down the column shouting at the men who were struggling to clear their rifles from the scabbards of plunging, rearing horses. The Boer fire flogged into them, dropping men and horses screaming in the grass. Loose horses scattered along the valley, reins trailing and empty stirrups bouncing against their flanks.

'Leave them! Let them go! Get into the river!' Two of the mules were down, kicking, wounded in the traces of the scotchcart. Sean tore the tarpaulin loose and lifted out one of the Maxims. A bullet splintered the woodwork under his hands.

'You!' he shouted at one of his sailors. 'Grab this!' He passed the gun to

him and the man ran with it cradled in his arms and jumped over the river
bank. With a case of ammunition under each arm Sean followed him. It
seemed as though he ran waist-deep in water, each pace dragging with
painful deliberation and his fear came strongly upon him. A bullet flipped
his hat forward over his eyes, the ammunition cases weighted him down,
and he blundered panic-stricken towards the river. The earth was gone
abruptly from under his feet and he fell, dropping free until, with a shock
that jarred his spine, he struck and toppled forward face-down into the icy
water.

Immediately he scrambled up and, still clutching the Maxim ammunition,
floundered to the steep bank. Above him the Boer fire whipped and sang,
but the bed of the river was crowded with his men, and others still fell and
jumped from the bank to add to the congestion.

Panting and streaming water from his clothing Sean leaned against the
bank while he gathered himself. The stream of survivors into the river-bed
dwindled and stopped. The Boer fire also stuttered out and a comparative
quiet fell over the field, spoiled only by the groaning and cursing of the
wounded.

Sean's first coherent thought was for Saul. He found him holding two
pack-mules under the bank with Nonga and Mbejane beside him holding
another pair. He sent Saul to take command at the far end of the line.

'Sergeant-Major!' Sean shouted, and with relief heard Eccles's reply from
close at hand.

'Here, sir.'

'Spread them out along the bank. Get them to cut firing platforms.'

'Very good, sir,' and immediately he began. 'Here you lot, you heard the
Major! Up off your backsides!'

Within ten minutes there were two hundred rifles lining the bank and the
Maxim was sited and manned behind a scharnz of stone and earth. Those
men who had lost their weapons were tending the wounded. This pitiful
little group were gathered in the middle of the line, they were propped
against the bank, sitting waist-deep in slush and their blood stained the
water pinky-brown.

Sean climbed up on to one of the firing platforms beside Eccles and lifted
his head to peer cautiously over the bank. The area in front of him was a
sickening sight. Dead mules and horses with their packs burst open littering
the grass with blankets and provisions. Wounded animals flopping helpless
or standing quietly with their heads hanging.

'Is there anyone out there still alive?' Sean called, but the dead men gave
him no answer. A sniper on the ridge ploughed a bullet into the ground in
front of Sean's face and he ducked down quickly.

'Most of them managed to crawl in, sir. Those that didn't are better out
there than in the mud here.'

'How many did we lose, Eccles?'

'About a dozen dead, sir, and twice as many wounded. We got off very
lightly.'

'Yes,' Sean nodded 'Most of their initial fire went high. It's a mistake
even the best shots make when shooting downhill.'

'They fair caught us with our pants down,' mused Eccles and Sean did not miss the censure in his tone.

'I know. I should have placed look-outs on the ridge,' he agreed. You're no Napoleon, he told himself, and you've got casualties to prove it.

'How many of them lost their weapons?' he asked.

'We've got two hundred and ten rifles and one Maxim, sir, and I issued an extra hundred rounds to each man just before the attack.'

'Should be enough,' Sean decided. 'Now all that remains is to sweat it out until my native guide brings up reinforcements.'

For half an hour nothing happened beyond a little desultory sniping from the ridge. Sean moved along the line talking to the men.

'How's it going, sailor?'

'Me old ma would have a fit, sir. "George," she'd say, "sitting in the mud is not going to do your piles no good," she'd say, sir.' The man was shot through the stomach and Sean had to force his chuckle through his throat.

'I could use a smoke, though. That I could.'

Sean found a damp cigar in his pocket for him and moved on. A youngster, one of the Colonials, was crying silently as he held against his chest the blood-soaked bundle of bandages that was his hand.

'Giving you pain?' Sean asked gently. The boy looked up at him, the tears smearing his cheeks. 'Go away,' he whispered. 'Please go away.'

Sean walked on. I should have put look-outs on the ridge, he thought again. I should have—

'Flag of truce on the ridge, sir,' a man shouted excitedly and Sean clambered up beside him.

Immediately a hum of comment ran along the line.

'They're hanging out their washing.'

'The bastards want to surrender. They know we've got them licked.'

Sean climbed out of the river-bed and waved his hat at the speck of white that fluttered on the ridge, and a horseman trotted down towards him.

'*Middag, Menheer*,' Sean greeted him. He received only a nod in reply and took the note the man proffered:

Menheer,
   I expect the arrival of my Hotchkiss gun at any moment. Your position is not safe. I suggest you lay down your guns to prevent further killing.
                    J. P. Leroux, Vecht-Generaal,
                                        Wynberg commando.

It was written on an irregular scrap of brown wrapping paper in High Dutch.

'My greetings to the General, *Menheer*, but we will hold out here a little longer.'

'As you wish,' the Boer acquiesced, 'but first you must see if any of these' – he pointed at the khaki figures that were scattered among the dead mules and horses – 'you must see if any of them are still alive. And you must destroy the wounded animals.'

'It is kind of you, *Menheer*.'

'You will, of course, make no attempt to pick up weapons or ammunition.'

'Of course.'

The Boer stayed with them while Eccles and half a dozen men searched the field, destroying the maimed animals and examining the fallen troopers. They found one man still alive. The air hissed softly from his severed windpipe and a froth of blood bubbles writhed about the hole. On a blanket they carried him down to the river-bed.

'Eleven dead, sir,' Eccles reported to Sean.

'Eccles, as soon as the truce ends we are going to recover another Maxim and the two cases of ammunition.'

They stood beside the scotchcart and Sean inclined his head to indicate the bulky, blue-metalled weapon that showed from beneath the tarpaulin.

'Very good, sir.'

'I want four men ready below the lip of the bank. Make sure each man has a knife to cut the pack ropes.'

'Yes, sir.' Eccles grinned like a playful walrus and drifted back towards the river, and Sean strolled across to the mounted Boer.

'We have finished, *Menheer.*'

'Good. As soon as I cross the skyline up there – then we'll start again.'

'I agree.' Sean walked back to the river, picking his way through the dead. Already the flies were there, swarming green and metallic, rising like a migrating hive of bees as he passed, then settling again.

Sean reached the bank and below him Saul crouched at the head of a bunch of unarmed men. Behind them stood a very disgruntled Eccles, his moustache drooping in disappointment. Instantly Sean saw what had happened – Saul had used his superior rank to take over command of the volunteers. 'What the hell do you think you're doing?' Sean demanded, and Saul answered him with an obstinate stare.

'You'll stay where you are. That's an order!' He turned to Eccles. 'Take over, Sergeant-Major,' and Eccles grinned.

This was no time to argue. Already the Boer horseman was half way up the ridge. Sean raised his voice and shouted at the long line of men below the bank.

'Listen, all of you. No one is to fire until the enemy do. That way we may be able to spin it out a little longer.' Then less loudly as he spoke to Eccles. 'Don't run, just walk out casually.' Sean jumped down the bank and stood between Eccles and Saul. All three of them peered up at the ridge and saw the Boer reach the crest, wave his hat and disappear.

'Go!' Sean said, and all of them went. Eccles, the four volunteers – and Saul. Flabbergasted, Sean stared at the six of them as they strolled out towards the scotchcart. Then his anger flared. *The stupid little bastard*, and he went also.

He caught up with them as they reached the scotchcart, and in the strained silence of the suspended storm he growled at Saul:

'I'll fix you for this!' and Saul grinned triumphantly.

Still there was a puzzled silence from the ridge – but it could not last much longer.

Together Saul and Eccles slashed at the ropes that held the tarpaulin, and Sean pulled it back and reached for the gun.

'Take it.' He passed it to the man behind him. At that moment a warning shot cracked over their heads.

'Grab one each and run!'

From the ridge and the river came gunfire like a long roll of drums, and they ran doubled beneath their loads and dodging, back towards the river.

The man carrying the Maxim fell headlong. Sean threw the ammunition case he carried, it dropped short of the bank, but skidded forward and toppled over the edge. Hardly pausing in his run, he stooped and gathered the fallen Maxim and went on. Ahead of him first Eccles, then Saul jumped into safety and Sean followed them with the three surviving troopers.

It was over, Sean sat waist-deep in the icy water with the machine-gun clutched to his chest, and all he could think of was his anger at Saul. He glared at him, but Saul and Eccles knelt facing each other grinning and laughing.

Sean handed the gun to the nearest trooper and crossed to Saul. His hand fell heavily on his shoulder and he pulled him to his feet.

'You—' He could not find words cutting enough. If Saul had been killed out there, Ruth would never have believed Sean had not ordered it so. 'You fool,' he said and might have hit him, but he was distracted by the cries from the firing platform beside him.

'The poor bastard!'

'He's up.'

'Lie down, for God's sake, lie down.'

Sean released Saul, jumped up on to the platform and stared through the loophole in the scharnz.

Out in the open the trooper who had carried the Maxim was on his feet. He was moving parallel to the bank, shambling with a curious idiot gait, his hands hanging loosely by his sides. They were shooting at him from the ridge.

Held in the paralysis of horror, none of them went to him. He was hit and he lurched but tottered on with the Boer rifles hunting him, staggering in a circle away from the river. Then, suddenly they killed him and he dropped on to his face.

The gunfire stopped and in the silence the men in the river-bed began to move around, and talk of trivial things, avoiding each other's eyes, ashamed to have watched such a naked intimate thing as that man's dying.

Sean's anger was gone, replaced by guilty thankfulness that it had not been Saul out there in the open.

Chapter Forty-six

In the long period of stagnation that followed, Sean and Saul sat together against the bank. Though they talked little, the old sense of companionship was restored.

With a rush and rattle the first shell ripped the air above their heads, and with everyone else Sean ducked instinctively. The shell burst in a tall brownish-yellow spurt on the far slope. Consternation bushfired along the river.

'Lummy, they've got a gun!'

'Book me on the next train, mate!'

'Nothing to worry about, boys,' Sean shouted reassuringly. 'They can't reach us with that piece.'

And the next shell burst on the lip of the bank, showering them with earth and pebbles. One startled second they stood dazed and coughing in the fumes, and the next they fell on the bank like a band of competitive grave-diggers. Dust from their exertions rose in a pale brown mist over the river to puzzle the Boers on the ridge. Almost before the arrival of the next shell, each man had hacked out a small earthen cupboard into which he could squeeze himself.

The Boer gunners were alarmingly inconsistent. Two or three rounds would fly wildly overhead and burst in the open veld. The next would land squarely in the river spraying mud and water high in the air. When this happened the sound of sustained cheering drifted faintly down from the ridge, followed by a long pause – presumably while the gunners received the congratulations of their fellows. Then the bombardment would recommence with enthusiastic rapidity, which slowly wound down into another long pause while everybody rested.

During one of these intervals Sean peered through his loop-hole. From a dozen points along the ridge rose pale columns of smoke.

'Coffee break up there, Eccles.'

'The way they do things we can expect another white flag and a couple of their lads coming down with coffee for us as well.'

'I doubt it,' Sean grinned. 'But I think we can expect them to come down though.' Sean pulled out his watch. 'Half-past four now. Two hours to sundown. Leroux must try for a decision before dark.'

'If they come, they'll come from behind,' Saul announced cheerfully and pointed to the slope of ground that menaced their rear. 'To meet a charge from there, we would have to line the far bank and expose our backs to sniping from the ridge.'

Sean considered the problem for a minute. 'Smoke! That's it!'

'I beg yours, sir?'

'Eccles, get the men to build fireplaces of stone along the bed and set grass and branches ready to light,' Sean ordered. 'If they do come from behind we'll screen ourselves with smoke.'

Fifteen minutes of furious activity completed the work. At intervals of ten paces along the river-bed they built flat-topped cairns of stone that rose above the level of the water. On each was piled a large heap of grass and wild hemlock branches gathered from where they overhung the bank of the river.

A little before sunset, in that time of shadows and deceptive light, with a haze rising in the still, cold air to mask them, Leroux charged his horsemen at the river.

Sean heard a low drumming of hooves as though a train passed in the distance and started to his feet.

'Here they come!' somebody shouted. 'The bastards are coming from behind.'

With the low sun at their backs throwing big, distorted shadows ahead of them, they swept down in a long line from the west.

'Light the fires!' bellowed Sean. They were lying flat on their horses, five hundred of them coming in at full gallop and shooting as they came.

'Maxims!' Sean shouted. 'Get the Maxims across!' The teams dragged the heavy unwieldy weapons from their emplacements and floundered with them across the stream. From each of the fires blue smoke spread and lifted. Men coughed and swore and splashed to their new positions. From the ridge a furious covering fire raked the river and then the field-piece crashed shell after shell amongst them.

'Fire at will!' Sean shouted. 'Hit the bastards. Hit them. Hit them hard.'

The din was appalling – gunfire and bursting shells, the hammering beat of the Maxims, shouts of defiance and pain, the thunder of charging hooves, crackling of the flames. Over it all a dense fog of smoke and dust.

With elbows on the rough shale of the bank, Sean aimed and fired and a horse went down, throwing rider and rifle high and clear. Without taking the butt from his shoulder he worked the bolt and fired again. Got him! swaying and twisting in the saddle. Drop, you bastard! That's it – slide forward and fall. Shoot again, and agin. Empty the magazine. Hitting with every shot.

Beside him the matelot traversed the Maxim in a deliberate hammering arc. Fumbling, as he reloaded, Sean watched the Maxim scythe its slow circle of destruction, leaving a shambles of downed horses and struggling men, before its beat stopped abruptly and the matelot crouched over it to fit a fresh belt from the wooden case. A bullet from the ridge, fired blindly into the smoke, hit him in the back of the neck and he fell forward, jamming the gun, blood gushing from his open mouth over the jacketed barrel. His limbs twitched and jerked in the epilepsy of death.

Sean dropped his rifle and dragged the matelot off the gun, levered the first round of the belt into the breech and thrust his thumbs down on the buttons.

They were close now. Sean bore down on the firing handles to raise his fire, aiming at the chests of the horses. The sailor's blood fried and sizzled on the hot barrel, and the grass in front of the muzzle flattened and quivered in the continuous blast.

Above him a solid frieze of milling horses was outlined against the darkening sky, the men upon them pouring their bullets into the crowded river-bed. Wounded horses plunged down the bank, rolling and kicking into the mud.

'Dismount! Dismount! Go in after them!' an old burgher with a neat blond beard yelled.

Sean dragged the gun around to get him. The man saw him in the smoke but his right leg was out of the stirrup, his rifle held in the left hand, helpless in the act of dismounting. Sean saw his eyes were grey and without fear as he looked down into the muzzle of the Maxim. The burst hit him across the chest, his arm windmilled, his left foot caught in the stirrup as he went backwards and his pony dragged him away.

The attack broke. The Boer fire slackened, ponies wheeled away, and raced back for the shelter of the hills. The old burgher Sean had killed went with them, dragged upon his back with his head bouncing loosely over the broken ground. leaving a long slide mark of flattened grass.

Around him Sean's men cheered and laughed and chattered with jubilation. But in the mud there were many who did not cheer and with a guilty shock Sean realized he had been standing on the corpse of the sailor who had died over the gun.

'Our round, that one!' Eccles beamed. Callous among the dead as only an old soldier can be.

'Yes,' Sean agreed.

Out in the open a horse heaved itself up and stood shivering, one leg hanging broken under it. A wounded burgher started to cough in the grass, choking and gasping as he drowned in his own blood.

'Yes, our round, Eccles. Put up the flag. They must come down and collect the wounded.'

They used lanterns in the darkness to find the wounded and kill the horses.

'Nkosi, at a place where the river turns and the banks are low, they have placed men,' Mbejane reported, back from the reconnaissance on which Sean had sent him. 'We cannot escape that way.'

'I thought as much,' Sean nodded, and held out the open can of bully beef to Mbejane. 'Eat,' he said.

'What's he say, sir?' Eccles asked.

'The river is held in force downstream.' Sean lit one of the cheroots that he had recovered in the darkness from the saddle-bag of his dead horse.

'Ruddy cold sitting here in the mud,' Eccles hinted.

'Patience, Sergeant-Major,' Sean smiled. 'We'll give them until midnight. By then most of them will be down the other side of the ridge drinking coffee around the fires.'

'You are going to rush the ridge, sir?' Eccles obviously approved.

'Yes. Tell the men. Three hours' rest and then we'll take the ridge.'

'Very good, sir.'

Sean lay back and closed his eyes. He was very weary, his eyes felt gritty from the dust and smoke, his lower body was wet and cold his boots heavy with mud. Lyddite fumes had given him a blinding headache.

I should have put a look-out on the ridge, he thought again. My God! What a mess I've made of this. My first command and already I've lost all the horses and damn-nigh half of my men. I should have put a look-out on the ridge.

Chapter Forty-seven

They took the ridge a few minutes after midnight with hardly any opposition. The few Boer sentries made good time down the far slope and Sean looked down upon the Boer laagers. The camp fires glimmered in an irregular line along the valley. Men stood around them staring up at the ridge. Sean scattered them with a dozen lusty volleys, and then yelled. 'Cease firing. Eccles, get the men settled in. We are going to have visitors fairly soon.'

The Boers had built scharnzes along the crest which saved Sean's men much inconvenience and within ten minutes the Maxims were emplaced and Sean's two hundred unwounded men waited behind walls of rough rock for the Boer counter-attack. This took some time to develop for the situation necessitated a hurried War Council in the valley below. But at last they heard the first stealthy approach of the attackers.

'Here they come, Sergeant-Major. Hold your fire, please.'

The burghers worked their way up cautiously and when Sean could hear their voices whispering among the rocks he decided they were close enough and discouraged further intimacy with volleyed rifle-fire and the use of all his Maxims. The Boers replied with heat and at the height of the exchange the Hotchkiss gun joined in from the valley. Its first shell passed but a few feet over Sean's head, then burst in the valley behind him. The second and third shots dropped neatly among the attacking Boer riflemen and raised such a howl of protest that the gunners, their efforts not appreciated, maintained an aloof and offended silence for the rest of the night.

Sean had expected a determined night attack but it soon became clear that Leroux was fully aware of the danger of closely engaging an inferior force in the dark. He contented himself with keeping Sean awake all night, his burghers taking it in turn to come up and keep the short-range rifle duel going – and Sean began to have qualms about the wisdom of his offensive. Dawn would find him on a rocky ridge, facing a numerically superior force, with his line enchored at neither end, and short enough to be easily flanked and enfiladed. He remembered Spion Kop – and there was little comfort in the memory. But the alternative was to fall back on the river, and his hackles rose at the thought. Unless relief came soon, defeat was certain – better here on the high ground than in the mud. We'll stay, he decided.

In the dawn there was a lull but although the gunfire dwindled to an occasional crack and flash on the lower slope yet Sean could sense an increase of activity among the Boers. Ominous rustlings and the muted sounds of movement on his flanks confirmed his misgivings. But now it was too late to retreat on the river, for already the mountains were showing stark silhouettes against the dawn sky. They seemed very close, as close and unfriendly as the unseen multitude of the enemy waiting out there for the light to come.

Sean stood up. 'Take the gun,' he whispered to the man beside him as he relinquished the Maxim.

All night he had fought with that wicked clumsy weapon and now his hands were claws shaped to the firing grips, and his shoulders ached intolerably. He flexed them as he moved down the line, stopping to chat with the men who lay belly-down behind the scharnz, trying to make his words of encouragement sound convincing.

In their replies he sensed the respect they were forming for him as a fighting man. It was more than respect – closer to a tolerant affection. The same feeling old General Buller had evoked amongst his men. He made mistakes, a lot of men died when he led, but they liked him and followed cheerfully. Sean reached the end of the line.

'How's it going?' he asked Saul softly.

'Fair enough.'

'Any sign of the old Boer?'

'They're pretty close – we heard them talking a few minutes ago. My guess is they're as ready as we are.'

'How's your ammunition?'

'We've got enough to finish this business.'

To finish this business! That would be his decision. When the massacre began, how much must he make them endure before he called for quarter, and they stood up with arms raised in the most shameful of all attitudes?

'You'd better get under cover, Sean. Light's coming fast.'

'Who the hell is looking after whom,' Sean grinned at him. 'I want no more heroics from you,' he said, and walked quickly to his station on the other flank.

The night lifted quickly from the land, and morning came as abruptly as it does only in Africa. The Boer laagers were gone. The Hotchkiss gun was gone. Sean knew that the gun and the Boer horses had been moved back behind the new ridge which now faced their position. He knew also that the rocky ground below him was crawling with the enemy, that they were on his flanks and probably in his rear as well.

Slowly, the way a man looks at a place before he begins a long journey, Sean looked around him at the mountains and the sky and the valley. In the soft light it was very beautiful.

He looked down the gut of the valley towards the grass plains of the highveld. His head jerked with surprise. He felt excitement lift the hair on his forearms. The mouth of the valley was blocked by a dark mass. In the uncertain light it could have been a plantation of wattle trees – oblong and regular and black against the pale grass. But this plantation was moving, changing shape, elongating. Birnam Wood to Dunsinane.

The first rays of the sun slanted in across the crest of the ridge and lit the lance-heads into a thousand minute dazzles.

'Cavalry!' roared Sean. 'By Jesus, look at them.'

The cry was taken up and thrown along the line, yelling, cheering wildly they fired down upon the tiny brown figures that were scurrying away to meet the Boer pickets who galloped in across the floor of the valley, each of them dragging a bunch of a dozen horses after him.

Then above the cheering and the gunfire, high above the sounds of hooves and the cries of panic, a bugle began to sing: 'Bonnie Dundee' – sharp and clear and urgently it commanded the charge.

Sean's rifles fell silent. The cheering faltered and stopped. One by one his men stood up to watch as the lines of lancers moved forward. Walk. Trot. Canter. Gallop. The lance heads dropped Belly-high they flitted like fireflies in front of the solid dark ranks, and that terrible thing swept down upon the tangle of men and frenzied, struggling horses.

Some of the Boers were up now, wheeling away, breaking like game before the beaters.

'My God!' breathed Sean, tensing himself for the burst of sound as the charge struck home. But there was only the drum of hooves – no check, no distortion as the dark squadrons drove through the Boers. Precisely they wheeled, and came back. Broken lances thrown aside, sabres unsheathed, bright and long.

Sean watched a burgher dodging desperately as a lancer followed him. Saw him turning at the last moment and crouching with his arms covering his head. The lancer stood in his stirrups and swung he sabre backhanded. The burgher dropped. Like a polo player the trooper pivoted his horse and rode back over the Boer, leaning low out of the saddle to sabre him again as he knelt in the grass.

'Quarter!' growled Sean, then his voice rising shrilly in horror and disgust. 'Give them quarter. For the love of God, give them quarter!'

But cavalry gives no quarter. They butchered with dispassionate parade-ground precision. Hack and cut, turn and trample until the blades blurred redly – until the valley was strewn with the bodies of men wounded a dozen times.

Sean tore his eyes away and saw the remains of Leroux's commando scattered into the broken ground where the big cavalry mounts could not follow.

Sean sat down on a rock and bit the end off a cheroot. The rank smoke helped cleanse his mouth of the taste of victory.

Two days later Sean led his column into Charlestown. The garrison cheered them and Sean grinned as he watched his men react. Half an hour before they had bumped along, hunched unhappily on their borrowed mounts. Now they sat erect and jaunty, eating the applause and liking the taste.

Then the grin faded from Sean's face as he saw how his band was depleted, and he looked back at the fifteen crowded wagons that carried the wounded.

If only I'd put look-outs on the ridge.

Chapter Forty-eight

There was an urgent summons from Acheson waiting for Sean. He caught the northbound express twenty minutes after arriving in Charlestown, hating Saul for the hot bath in which he left him, and for the uniform which Mbejane had persuaded a plump Zulu maid to wash and iron, hating him still more venomously for the invitation to be guest of honour at the officers' mess that night – and knowing that Saul would drink deep on Veuve Clicquot and Courvoisier which had once belonged to Sean.

When Sean arrived in Johannesburg the following morning, with soot from the locomotive adding a subtle touch to the fragrance he had gathered from two unwashed weeks in the veld, there was an orderly to meet him and conduct him to Acheson's suite in the Grand National Hotel.

Major Peterson was patently taken aback by Sean's turn-out, he eyed the stains and tears and dried mud with genteel horror at the contrast they afforded to the breakfast table's crisp white linen and splendid silver. The ripeness of Sean's odour impaired Peterson's appetite and he dabbed at his nose with a silk handkerchief. But Acheson seemed not to notice, he was in festive mood.

'Damned fine show, Courtney. Oh, damned fine. Proved your point entirely. We'll not have much trouble from Leroux for some time, I warrant you. Have another egg? Peterson, pass him the bacon.'

Sean finished eating and filled his coffee cup before he made his request. 'I want to be relieved of this command, I made a bloody mess of it.'

Both Acheson and Peterson stared in horror. 'Good God, Courtney. You've achieved a notable success – the most spectacular in months.'

'Luck,' brusquely Sean interrupted. 'Another two hours and we would have been wiped out.'

'Lucky officers are more valuable to me than clever ones. Your request is refused, Colonel Courtney.' So it's Colonel now, a bribe to get me into the dentist's chair. Sean was mildly amused.

A knock at the door prevented Sean continuing his protestation, and an orderly came into the room and handed Acheson a message.

'Urgent dispatch from Charlestown,' he whispered. Acheson took the paper from him and used it like a conductor's baton as he went on talking.

'I have got three junior officers for you, men to replace your losses. You catch them for us and hold them for my cavalry. That's all I want from you. While you're doing your bit the columns are going to start a series of new drives. This time we are going to sweep every inch of the ground between the blockhouse lines. We are going to destroy the crops and the livestock; burn the farms; take every woman, man and child off the land and put them in detainment camps. By the time we're finished there will be nothing but bare veld out there. We will force them to operate in a vacuum, while we wear them down with a relentless series of drives and raids.' Acheson slapped the table so that the crockery jingled. 'Attrition, Courtney. From now on it's a war of attrition!'

Those words had an uncomfortable familiarity for Sean. And suddenly a picture of desolation formed in his mind. He saw the land – his land – blackened with fire, and the roofless homesteads standing in the wastes. The sound of the empty winds across the land was the wailing of orphans, and the protest of a lost people.

'General Acheson—' he began, but Acheson was reading the dispatch.

'Damn!' he snapped. 'Damn and blast! Leroux again. He doubled back and caught the transport column of those same lancers who cut him up. Wiped it out and disappeared into the mountains.' Acheson laid the message on the table in front of him and stared at it. 'Courtney,' he said, 'go back and, this time, catch him!'

Chapter Forty-nine

'Breakfast is ready, Nkosi.' Michael Courtney looked up from his book at the servant. 'Thank you, Joseph, I'm coming now.'

These two hours of study each morning passed so quickly. He checked the clock on the shelf above his bed – half-past six already – closed the book and stood up.

While he brushed his hair he watched his reflection in the mirror without attention. His mind was fully occupied with events that would fill this new day. There was work to do.

His reflection looked back at him with serious grey eyes from a face whose lean contours were marred by the big Courtney nose. His hair was black and springy beneath the brush.

He dropped the brush and while he shrugged into his leather jacket he flipped open the book to check a passage. He read it through carefully, then turned and went out into the corridor.

Anna and Garrick Courtney were seated at opposite ends of the long dining-table of Theuniskraal and they both looked up expectantly as he entered.

'Good morning, Mother.' She held up her face for his kiss.

'Good morning, Pa.'

'Hello, my boy.' Garry was wearing full dress, complete with crowns and decorations, and Michael felt a flare of irritation. It was so damned ostentatious. Also it reminded him that he was nineteen years old and there was a war going on while he sat at home on the farm.

'Are you going into town today, Pa?'

'No, I'm going to do some work on my memoirs.'

'Oh,' Michael glanced pointedly at the uniform and his father flushed slightly and applied himself to his meal.

'How are your studies, darling?' Anna broke the silence.

'Well enough, thank you, Mother.'

'I'm certain you'll have as little trouble with the final examinations as you had with the others.' Anna smiled at him possessively and stretched out to touch his hand. Michael withdrew it quickly and laid down his fork.

'Mother, I want to talk to you about enlisting.' Anna's smile froze. At the end of the table Garry straightened in his chair.

'No,' he snapped with unusual violence. 'We've been over this before. You're still a minor and you do as you're told.'

'The war is almost over, darling. Please think of your father and me.'

It began then. Another of those long wheedling, pleading arguments that sickened and frustrated Michael until he stood up abruptly and left the room. His horse was waiting saddled for him in the yard. He threw himself on to its back and swung its head at the gate, lifting it over, and scattering chickens as he landed. He galloped furiously away towards the main dip-tank.

From the dining-room they heard the hooves beat away until they had dwindled into silence. Garry stood up.

'Where are you going?' snapped Anna.

'To my study.'

'To the brandy bottle in your study,' she corrected him contemptuously.

'Don't, Anna.'

'*Don't, Anna*,' she mimicked him. '*Please don't, Anna.* Is that all you can say?' Her voice had lost the genteel inflexion she had cultivated so carefully. Now it contained all the accumulated bitterness of twenty years.

'Please, Anna. I'll stop him going. I promise you.'

'You'll stop him!' She laughed. 'How will you stop him? Will you rattle your medals at him? How will you stop him – you, who have never done one useful thing in all your life?' She laughed again, shrilly. 'Why don't you show him your leg and say, "Please don't leave your poor crippled Daddy".'

Garry drew himself up. His face had gone very pale. 'He'll listen to me. He's my son.'

'Your son!'

'Anna, please—'

'Your son! Oh, that's choice! He's not your son. He's Sean's son.'

'Anna.' He tried to stop her.

'How could you have a son?' She was laughing again, and he could not stand it. He started for the door but her voice followed him, cutting into the two most sensitive places in his soul; his deformity and his impotence.

He stumbled into his study, slammed the door and locked it. Then he crossed quickly to the solid cabinet that stood beside his desk.

He poured the tumbler half-full and drank it. Then he sank into his chair and closed his eyes and reached for the bottle behind him. He poured again carefully and screwed the cap back on to the bottle. This one he would sip slowly, making it last perhaps an hour. He had learned how to keep the glow.

He unbuttoned and removed his tunic, stood up and hung it over the back of the chair, seated himself once more, sipped at the tumbler, then drew towards him the pile of handwritten sheets, and read the one on top.

'Colenso: An account of the campaign in Natal under General Buller.' By Colonel Garrick Courtney, V.C., D.S.O.

He lifted it, laid it aside, and began to read what followed. Having read it so many times before, he had come to believe in it. It was good. He knew it was good. So too did Messrs William Heinemann in London, to whom he had sent a draft of the first two chapters. They were anxious to publish as soon as possible.

He worked on quietly and happily all morning. At midday old Joseph brought a meal to the study. Cold chicken and salads on Delft-ware china, with a bottle of white Cape wine wrapped in a snowy napkin. He worked as he ate.

That evening when he had altered the last paragraph on the final page and laid his pen on the inkstand, he was smiling.

'Now, I will go and see my darling.' He spoke aloud and put on his tunic.

The homestead of Theuniskraal sat on the crest of a rise below the escarpment. A big building of whitewashed walls, thatch and Dutch gables. In front of it the terraced lawns sprawled away, contoured by beds of azaleas and blue rhododendrons and bounded on the one side by the horse paddocks: two large paddocks for the brood mares and the yearlings, where Garry paused beside the low fence and watched the foals nuzzling upwards at the udders.

Then he limped on along the fence towards the smaller enclosure with its nine-foot fence of thick, canvas-padded gumpoles that contained his stud stallion.

Gypsy was waiting for him, nodding his almost snakelike head so that his mane flared golden in the late sunlight, flattening his ears, then pricking them forward, dancing a little with impatience.

'Hey, Boy. Hey there, Gypsy,' Garry called and the stallion thrust his head between the poles to nibble with soft lips at Garry's sleeve.

'Sugar, is that what you're after.' Garry chuckled and cupped his hands while the stallion fed delicately from them.

'Sugar, my darling,' Garry whispered in sensual delight at the touch of the soft muzzle on his skin and Gypsy cocked his ears to listen to his voice.

'That's all. All finished.' The stallion nuzzled his chest and Garry wiped his hands on its neck, caressing the warm and silky coat.

'That's all, my darling. Now run for me. Let me watch you run.' He stepped back and clapped his hands loudly. 'Run, my darling, run.'

The stallion pulled his head back between the poles and went up on his hind legs, whinnying as he reared, cutting at the air with his fore-hooves.

The veins stood out along the belly and upon the tight double-swollen bag of its scrotum.

Swift and virile and powerful, it pivoted upon its quarters.

'Run for me!' shouted Garrick. The stallion came down into full gallop along the track worn by its hooves, sweeping around the paddock with loose dirt flying and the light dancing on his coat as the great muscles bulged beneath.

'Run.' Leaning against the poles of the fence, Garrick watched him with an expression of terrible yearning.

When he stopped again with the first dark patches of sweat dulling his shoulders, Garrick straightened up and shouted across the stable yard.

'Zama, bring her now!'

On a long rein two grooms led the brood mare down towards the paddock. Gypsy's nostrils flared into dark pink caverns and he rolled his eyes until the whites showed.

'Wait, my darling,' whispered Garrick in a voice tight with his own excitement.

Chapter Fifty

Michael Courtney dismounted among the rocks on the highest point of the escarpment. For a week he had denied the impulse to return to this place. Somehow it seemed a treachery – a disloyalty to both his parents.

Far below and behind him in the forest was the tiny speck of Theuniskraal. Between them the railway angled down towards the sprawled irregular pattern of rooftops that was Ladyburg.

But Michael did not look that way. He stood behind his mare and gazed along the line of bare hills to the gigantic quilt of trees that covered them in the north.

The wattle was tall now, so that the roads between the blocks no longer showed. It was a dark smoky green that undulated like the swells of a frozen sea.

This was as close as he had ever been to Lion Kop. It was a forbidden land, like the enchanted forest of the fairy-tale. He took the binoculars from his saddle-bag and scanned it carefully, until he came to the roof of the homestead. The new thatch, golden and unweathered, stood out above the wattle.

Grandma is there. I could ride across to visit, there would be no harm in that. *He* is not there. *He* is away at the war.

Slowly he replaced the binoculars in the saddle-bag, and he knew he would not go to Lion Kop. He was shackled by the promise he had made to his mother. Like so many other promises he had made.

With dull resignation he remembered the argument at breakfast that morning, and new that they had won again. He could not leave them, knowing that without him they would wither. He could not follow *him* to war.

He smiled ironically as he remembered the fantasies he had imagined. Charging into battle with *him*, talking with *him* beside the camp fire in the evenings, throwing himself in front of a bayonet meant for *him*.

From the look-out on the escarpment Michael had spent hours each day of the last Christmas holiday waiting for a glimpse of Sean Courtney. Now with guilt he remembered the pleasure he had experienced whenever he picked up that tall figure in the field of his binoculars and followed it as it moved between the newly planted rows of wattle.

But he's gone now. There would be no disloyalty if I rode across to see Grandma. He mounted the superb golden mare and sat deep in thought. At last he sighed, swung her head back towards Theuniskraal – and rode away from Lion Kop.

I must never come up here again, he thought determinedly, especially after *he* comes home.

Chapter Fifty-one

They are tired, tired to the marrow of their bones. Jan Paulus Leroux watched the lethargy of his burghers as they off-saddled and hobbled their horses. They are tired with three years of running and fighting, sick-tired in the certain knowledge of defeat, exhausted with grief for the men they have buried, with grief also for the children and the women with them in the camps. They are wearied by the sight of burned homes scattered about with the bones of their flocks.

Perhaps it is finished, he thought and lifted the battered old Terai from his head. Perhaps we should admit that it is finished, and go in to them. He wiped his face with his scarf and the cloth came away discoloured with the grease of his sweat and the dust of the dry land. He folded the scarf into the pocket of his coat and looked at the fire-blackened ruins of the homestead on the bluff above the river. The fire had spread into the gum trees and the leaves were sere and yellow and dead.

'No,' he said aloud. 'It is not finished – not until we try for this last time,' and he moved towards the nearest group of his men.

'*Ja*, Hennie. How goes it?' he asked.

'Not too bad, Oom Paul.' The boy was very thin, but then all of them were thin. He had spread his saddle-blanket in the grass and lay upon it.

'Good.' Jan Paulus nodded and squatted beside him. He took out his pipe and sucked on it. There was still the taste of tobacco from the empty bowl.

'Will you take a fill, Oom Paul?' One of the others sat up and proffered a pouch of springbok skin.

'*Nee, dankie.*' He looked away from the pouch, shutting out the temptation. 'Keep it for a smoke when we cross the Vaal.'

'Or when we ride into Cape Town,' joked Hennie, and Jan Paulus smiled at him. Cape Town was a thousand miles south of them, but that was where they were going.

'*Ja*, keep it for Cape Town,' he agreed and the smile on his face turned bitter. Bullets and disease had left him with six hundred ragged men on horses half-dead with exhaustion to conquer a province the size of France. But it was the last try. He started to speak then.

'Already Jannie Smuts is into the Cape with a big commando. Pretorius also has crossed the Orange, De la Rey and De Wet will follow – and Zietsmann is waiting for us to join him on the Vaal River. This time the Cape burghers must rise with us. This time . . .'

He spoke slowly, leaning forward with his elbows on his knees, a gaunt giant of a man with his unkempt, ginger beard wiry with dust and streaked about the mouth with yellowish grey. The cuffs of his sleeves were stained with the discharge from the veld sores on his wrists. Men came across from the other groups and squatted in a circle about him to listen and take comfort.

'Hennie, bring my Bible from the saddle-bag. We will read a little from the Book.'

The sun was setting when he closed the Book and looked around at them. An hour had gone in prayer that might more profitably have been spent in rest, but when he looked at their faces he knew the time had not been wasted.

'Sleep now, *Kerels*. We will upsaddle early tomorrow.' If they do not come in the night, he qualified himself silently.

But he could not sleep. He sat propped against his saddle and for the hundredth time re-read the letter from Henrietta. It was dated four months earlier, had taken six weeks to reach him along the chain of spies and commandos which carried their mail. Henrietta was sick with dysentery and both the younger children, Stephanus and baby Paulus, were dead from the *witseerkeel*. The concentration camp was ravaged by this disease and she feared for the safety of the older children.

The light had failed so he could not read further. He sat with the letter in his hands. With such a price as we have paid, surely we could have won something.

Perhaps there is still a chance. Perhaps.

'Upsaddle! Upsaddle! Khaki is coming.' The warning was shouted from the ridge across the river where he had placed his pickets. It carried clearly in the still of the evening.

'Upsaddle! Khaki is coming.' The cry was taken up around the camp. Jan Paulus leaned over and shook the boy beside him, who was too deep in exhaustion to have heard.

'Wake up, Hennie. We must run again.'

Five minutes later he led his commando over the ridge and southward into the night.

Chapter Fifty-two

'Still holding southwards,' Sean observed. 'Three days' riding and they haven't altered course.'

'Looks like Leroux has got his teeth into something,' agreed Saul.

'We'll halt for half an hour to blow the horses.' Sean lifted his hand and behind him the column lost its shape as the men dismounted and led their horses aside. Although the entire unit had been remounted a week before, the horses were already losing condition from the long hours of riding to which they had been subjected. However, the men were in good shape, lean and hard-looking. Sean listened to their banter and watched the way they moved and laughed. He had built them into a tough fighting force that had proved itself a dozen times since that fiasco a year ago when Leroux had caught them in the mountains. Sean grinned. They had earned the name under which they rode. He handed his horse to Mbejane and moved stiffly towards the shade of a small mimosa tree.

'Have you got any ideas about what Leroux is up to?' he asked Saul as he offered him a cheroot.

'He could be making a try at the Cape railway.'

'He could be,' Sean agreed as he lowered himself gratefully on to a flat stone and stretched his legs out in front of him. 'My God, I'm sick of this business. Why the hell can't they admit it's finished – why must they go on and on?'

'Granite cannot bend.' Saul smiled dryly. 'But I think that now it is very near the point where it must break.'

'We thought that six months ago.' Sean answered him, then looked beyond him. 'Yes, Mbejane, what is it?'

Mbejane was going through the ritual which preceded serious speech. He had come and squatted half a dozen paces from where Sean sat, had laid his spears carefully beside him in the grass, and now he was taking snuff.

'Nkosi.'

'Yes?' Sean encouraged him and waited while Mbejane tapped a little of the dark powder on to his fingernail.

'Nkosi, this porridge has an unusual taste.' He sniffed and sneezed.

'Yes?'

'It seems to me that the spoor has changed.' Mbejane wiped the residual snuff from his nostrils with the pink palm of his hand.

'You speak in riddles.'

'These men we follow ride in a different manner from the way they did before.'

Sean thought about that for a few seconds before he saw it. Yes! He was right. Where previously Leroux's commando had spread and trampled the grass in a road fifty feet wide, since this morning they had ridden in two files as though they were regular cavalry.

'They ride as we do, Nkosi, so the hooves of the horses fall in the tracks of those that lead. In this way it is difficult to tell how many men we follow.'

'We know there are about six hundred. . . . Hold on! I think I see what you . . .'

'Nkosi, it comes to me that there are no longer six hundred men ahead of us.'

'My God! You could be right.' Sean jumped up and began to pace restlessly. 'He is splitting his commando again. We've crossed a dozen rocky places where he could have detached small groups of his men. By evening we'll be following less than fifty men – when that happens they'll break up into individuals, lose us in the dark and head separately for a pre-arranged rendezvous.' He punched his fist into the palm of his hand. 'That's it, by God!' He swung round to face Saul.

'You remember that stream we crossed a mile back – that would have been an ideal place.'

'You're taking a big risk,' Saul cautioned him. 'If we go back now and it turns out you're wrong – then you've lost him for good.'

'I'm right,' Sean snapped. 'I know I am. Get them mounted up – we're going back.'

Sean sat his horse on the bank of the stream and looked down into the clear water that sparkled over gravel and small round boulders.

'They will have gone downstream, otherwise the mud they stirred up would have washed down across the ford.' He turned to Saul. 'I'm going to take fifty men with me so as not to raise too much dust. Give me an hour's start and then follow with the rest of the column.'

'*Mazeltov.*' Saul grinned at him.

With a Zulu tracker on each bank Sean and Eccles and fifty men followed the stream towards the north-west. Behind them the mountains of the Drakensberg were an irregular pale blue suggestion against the sky and around them the brown winter-sere veld spread away in the folded complexity of ridges and the shallow valleys. In the rocky ground along the ridges grew the squat little aloe plants, holding up their multiple flowers like crimson candelabra while in the valleys the stunted thorn bushes huddled along the course of the stream. High, cold cloud obscured the sky. There was no warmth in the pale sunlight, and the wind had a knife-edge to it.

Two miles below the ford Sean was showing his anxiety by leaning forward in the saddle and checking the ground that Mbejane had already covered. Once he called, 'Mbejane, are you sure you haven't missed them?'

Mbejane straightened from his crouch and turned slowly to regard Sean with a look of frigid dignity. Then he shifted his war shield to the other shoulder and, not deigning to answer, he returned to his search.

Fifty yards farther on he straightened again and informed Sean.

'No, Nkosi. I have not missed them.' He pointed with his assegai at the deeply scarred bank up which horses had climbed, and the flattened grass which had wiped the mud from their legs.

'Got them!' Sean exulted in his relief; behind him he heard the stir of excitement run through his men.

'Well done, sir.' Eccles's moustache twitched ferociously as he grinned.

'How many, Mbejane?'

'Twenty, not more.'

'When?'

'The mud has dried.' Mbejane considered the question, stooping to touch the earth and determine its texture. 'They were here at half sun this morning.'

The middle of the morning; they had a lead of five hours.

'Is the spoor fat enough to run upon?'

'It is, Nkosi.'

'Then run, Mbejane.'

The spoor bellied towards the west then swung and steadied in the same persistently southward direction, and Sean's column closed up and cantered after Mbejane.

Southward, always southward. Sean pondered the problem – what could he hope to accomplish with a mere six hundred?

Unless! Sean's brain started to harry a vague idea. Unless he intended slipping through the columns of infantry and cavalry that lay before him and trying for a richer prize.

The railway, as Saul had suggested? No, he discounted that quickly. Jan Paulus would not risk his whole command for such low stakes.

What then? The Cape? By God, that was it – the Cape! That rich and lovely country of wheatlands and vineyards. That serene and secure land, lazing in the security of a hundred years of British rule – and yet peopled by men of the same blood as Leroux and De Wet and Jan Smuts.

Smuts had already taken his commando across the Orange River. If Leroux followed him, if De Wet followed him, if the Cape burghers broke their uneasy neutrality and flocked to join the commandos – Sean's mind baulked at the thought. He left the wider aspect of it and came back to the moment.

All right then, Jan Paulus was riding to the Cape with only six hundred men? No, he must have more. He must be riding to a rendezvous with one of the other commandos. Who? De la Rey? No, De la Rey was in the Magaliesberg. De Wet? No, De Wet was far south – twisting and turning away from the columns that harried him. Zietsmann? Ah, Zietsmann! Zietsmann with fifteen hundred men. That was it.

Where would they meet? On a river obviously, for they must have water for two thousand horses. The Orange was too dangerous – so it must be the Vaal, but whereabouts on the Vaal? It must be a place easily recognizable. One of the fords? No, cavalry used the fords. A confluence of one of the tributaries? Yes, that was it.

Eagerly Sean unbuckled his saddle-bag and pulled from it his map-case.

Holding the heavy cloth map folded against his thigh he twisted sideways in the saddle to study it.

'Here we are now,' he muttered and ran his finger south. 'The Padda River!'

'I beg your pardon, sir.'

'The Padda, Eccles, the Padda!'

'Very well, sir,' agreed Eccles with stolid features covering his bewilderment.

In the dark valley below them the single fire flared briefly, then died to a tiny glow.

'All ready, Eccles,' Sean whispered.

'Sir!' Without raising his voice Eccles placed affirmative emphasis on the monosyllable.

'I'll go down now.' Sean resisted the impulse to repeat his previous orders. He wanted to say again how important it was that no one escaped, but he had learned that once was enough with Eccles. Instead he whispered, 'Listen for my signal.'

The Boers had only one sentry. Secure in the knowledge that their stratagem had thrown off all pursuit, they slept around the poorly screened fire. Sean and Mbejane moved down quietly and squatted in the grass twenty paces from the high rock on which the sentry sat. The man was outlined darkly against the stars and Sean watched him intently for a full minute before he decided.

'He sleeps also.'

Mbejane grunted.

'Take him quietly,' Sean whispered. 'Make sure his rifle does not fall.' Mbejane moved and Sean laid a hand on his shoulder to restrain him. 'Do not kill – it is not necessary.' And Mbejane moved silently as a leopard towards the rock.

Sean waited straining his eyes into the darkness. The seconds dragged by – and suddenly the Boer was gone from the rock. A gasp, a soft sliding sound and stillness.

Sean waited, and then Mbejane was back as silently as he had left.

'It is done, Nkosi.'

Sean laid his rifle aside and cupped his hands over his lips, filled his cheeks and blew the long warbling whistle of a nightbird. At the fire one of the sleepers stirred and muttered. Farther off a horse stamped and blew softly through its nostrils. Then Sean heard a pebble click and the cautious swish of feet through grass, small sounds lost in the wind.

'Eccles?' Sean murmured.

'Sir.'

Sean stood up and they closed in on the camp.

'Wake up, gentlemen. Breakfast is ready.' Sean shouted in the Taal, and each burgher woke to find a man standing over him and the muzzle of a Lee-Metford pressing into his chest.

'Build up that fire,' Sean ordered. 'Take their rifles.' It had been too easy, he spoke roughly in the irritation of anti-climax.

'Mbejane, bring the one from the rock – I want to see how gently you dealt with him.'

Mbejane dragged him into the firelight and Sean's lips tightened as he saw the way the man's head lolled and his legs hung.

'He's dead,' Sean accused.

'He sleeps, Nkosi,' Mbejane denied.

Sean knelt beside him and twisted his face to catch the light. Not a man, a lad with a thin bitter face and the fluff of pale, immature beard on his cheeks. In the corner of his eye a stye had burst to matt the closed lashes with yellow pus. He was breathing.

Sean glanced up at the other prisoners. They were being herded away out of earshot.

'Water, Mbejane.' And the Zulu brought a canteen from the fire while Sean explored the hard swelling above the boy's temple.

'He'll do,' Sean grunted, and curled his lips in distaste at what he must do as soon as the lad recovered. He must do it while he was still groggy and bemused by the blow. From his cupped hand he splashed cold water into his face and the boy gasped and rolled his head.

'Wake up,' Sean urged quietly in the Taal. 'Wake up.'

'Oom Paul?' The Boer mumbled.

'Wake up.' The lad struggled to sit.

'Where . . . You're English!' As he saw the uniform.

'Yes,' Sean snapped. 'We're English. You've been caught.'

'Oom Paul?' The boy looked round wildly.

'Don't worry about him. He'll be with you on the boat to St Helena. Leroux and Zietsmann were both caught on the Vaal yesterday. We were waiting for them at the Padda and they walked right into the trap.'

'Oom Paul caught!' The boy's eyes were wide with shock, still dazed and out of focus. 'But how did you know? There must have been a traitor – someone must have told. How did you know about the meeting-place?' He stopped abruptly as his brain caught up with his tongue. 'But how . . . Oom Paul couldn't be on the Vaal yet, we left him only yesterday.' Then sickeningly he realized what he had done 'You tricked me,' he whispered. 'You tricked me.'

'I'm sorry,' Sean said simply. He stood up and walked across to where Eccles was securing his prisoners.

'When Captain Friedman arrives tell him to bring the column in to the garrison at Vereeniging and wait for me there. I am going ahead with my servant,' he said abruptly, then called across to Mbejane.

'Mbejane, bring my horse.' He would trust no one else to carry the news to Acheson.

The following afternoon Sean reached the railway line guarded by its blockhouses and flagged a northbound train. The next morning he de-trained with soot-inflamed eyes, tired and filthy, at Johannesburg station.

Chapter Fifty-three

Jan Paulus Leroux checked his horse and behind him the tiny fragment of his commando bunched up and all of them peered eagerly ahead.

The Vaal is a wide, brown river, with sandbanks through which it cuts its own channel. The banks are steep and along them are scattered a few of the ugly, indigenous thorn trees, which provide no cover for an army of three thousand men and horses. But Leroux had chosen the rendezvous with care. Here the tiny Padda River looped down through a complex of small kopjes to join the Vaal and among these kopjes an army might escape detection – but only if it exercised care. Which Zietsmann was not doing.

The smoke from a dozen fires hazed out in a long pale smear across the veld, horses were being watered on one of the sandbanks in the middle of the river, and a hundred men were bathing noisily from the bank, while laundry decked the thorn trees.

'The fool,' snarled Leroux and kicked his pony into a run. He stormed into the laager, flung himself off his horse and roared at Zietsmann.

'*Menheer*, I must protest.'

Zietsmann was nearly seventy years old. His beard was pure white and hung to the fifth button of his waistcoat. He was a clergyman, not a general, and his commando had survived this long because it was so ineffectual as to cause the British no serious inconvenience. Only great pressure from Delarey and Leroux had forced him to take part in this wild plan. For the last three days, as he waited for Leroux to join him, he had been harassed by doubts and misgivings. These doubts were shared by his wife – for he was the only Boer general who still had his woman with him in the field.

Now he stood up from his seat by the fire and glared at this red-bearded giant Leroux, whose face was mottled with fury.

'*Menheer*,' he growled. 'Please remember you are speaking not only to your Elder, but also to a Dominie of the Church.'

In this way was set the tone for the long discussions which were to fill the next four days. During this time Leroux saw his bold design bog down in a welter of trivialities. He did not resent the loss of the first day which was spent in prayer, indeed he realized that this was essential. Without God's blessing and active intervention the enterprise must fail, so the sermon he delivered that afternoon lasted a little over two hours and the text he selected was from Judges – 'Shall I yet again go out to battle against the children of Benjamin, my brother, or shall I cease?' and the Lord said, 'Go up; for tomorrow I will deliver them into thine hand.'

Zietsmann bettered his time by forty minutes. But then, as Leroux's men pointed out, Zietsmann was a professional while Oom Paul was only a lay-preacher.

The next and most critical question was the election of the Supreme Commander for the combined enterprise. Zietsmann was the older by thirty years, a factor heavily in his favour. Also, he had brought sixteen hundred men to the Vaal against Leroux's six hundred. Yet Leroux was the victor of Colenso and Spion Kop, and since then he had fought consistently and with not a little success, including the wrecking of eight trains and the annihilation of four British supply columns. Zietsmann had been second in command at Modder River, but since then he had done nothing but keep his commando intact.

For three days the debate continued with Zietsmann dourly refusing to bring the matter to the vote until he sensed that opinion had swung to his side. Leroux wanted command; not only for personal satisfaction, but also because he knew that under this cautious and stubborn old man they would be lucky to reach the Orange River, let alone force an effective entry into the Cape.

The card that won the hand belonged to Zietsmann, and it was ironic that he had it simply because of his inactivity over the last eighteen months.

When Lord Roberts had marched into Pretoria two years before, his entry had been offered only token resistance, for the Government of the South African Republic had withdrawn along the eastern railway line to Komatipoort. With them went the entire contents of the Pretoria Treasury, which totalled two million pounds in gold Kruger sovereigns. Later, when old President Kruger left for Europe, a part of this treasure went with him, but the balance had been shared out among the remainder of the commando leaders as their war chests to continue the fight.

Months before most of Leroux's share had been expended on the purchase of supplies from the native tribes, on ammunition from the Portuguese gun runners and on payment to his men. During a desperate night action with one of the raiding British columns he had lost the balance along with his Hotchkiss gun, twenty of his best men and a hundred irreplaceably precious horses.

Zietsmann, however, had come to the meeting with a pack-mule carrying thirty thousand sovereigns. The successful invasion of the Cape would depend largely upon this gold. On the evening of the fourth day he was duly elected Commander by a majority of two hundred, and within twelve hours he had demonstrated how well-equipped he was for the task.

'So we start in the morning, then,' one of the burghers beside Leroux grunted.

'About time,' another commented. They were breakfasting on biltong – sticks of hard dried meat – for Leroux had succeeded in convincing Zietsmann that cooking-fires were dangerous.

'No sign of Van der Bergh's men?' asked Leroux.

'Not yet, Oom Paul.'

'They are finished, or else they would have been here days ago.'

'Yes, they are finished,' agreed Leroux. 'They must have run into one of the columns.' Twenty good men, he sighed softly, and Hennie was with them. He was very fond of the boy, all of them were. He had become the mascot of the commando.

'At least they are out of it now – the lucky thunders.' The man had spoken without thinking, and Leroux turned on him.

'You can go too hands-up for the British, there is no one to stop you.' The softness of his voice did not cover the ferocity in his eyes.

'I didn't mean it that way, Oom Paul.'

'Well, don't say it then,' he growled, and would have continued, but a shout from the sentry on the kopje above them brought them all to their feet.

'One of the scouts coming!'

'Which way?' Leroux bellowed upwards.

'Along the river. He's riding to burst!'

And the sudden stilling of voices and movement was the only outward sign of the dread that settled upon all of them. In these days a galloping rider carried only evil tidings.

They watched him splash through the shallows and slide from the saddle to swim beside his horse across the deep channel. Then pony and rider, both streaming water, came lunging up the near bank and into the camp.

'Khaki,' shouted the man. 'Khaki coming!'

Leroux ran to catch the pony's head and demanded,

'How many?'

'A big column.'

'A thousand?'

'More than that. Many more – six, seven thousand.'

'*Magtig!*' swore Leroux. 'Cavalry?'

'Infantry and guns.'

'How close?'

'They will be here before midday.'

Leroux left him and ran down the slope to Zietsmann's wagon.

'You heard, *Menheer?*'

'*Ja*, I heard.' Zietsmann nodded slowly.

'We must mount up,' Leroux urged.

'Perhaps they will not find us. Perhaps they will pass us by.' Zietsmann spoke hesitantly, and Leroux stared at him.

'Are you mad?' he whispered, and Zietsmann shook his head – a confused old man.

'We must mount up and break away towards the south.' Leroux grabbed the lapels of Zietsmann's frock coat and shook them in his agitation.

'No, not the south – it is finished. We must go back,' the old man muttered, then suddenly his confusion cleared. 'We must pray. The Lord will deliver us from the Philistine.'

'*Menheer*, I demand . . .' Leroux started, but another urgent warning shouted from the kopje interrupted him.

'Riders! To the south! Cavalry!'

Running to one of the horses Leroux vaulted on to its bare back, with a handful of its mane he turned it towards the kopje and flogged it with his heels, driving it up the steep rocky side, scrambling and sliding in the loose rock until he reached the top and jumped down beside the sentry.

'There!' The burgher pointed.

Like a column of safari ants, tiny and insignificant in the immensity of brown grass and open sky, still four or five miles distant, the squadrons were strung out in extended order across the southern hills.

'Not that way. We cannot go that way. We must go back.' He swung round to the north. 'We must go that way.'

Then he saw the dust in the north also and he felt his stomach slide sickly downwards. The dust drifted low, so thin it might have been only heat haze or the passing of a dust devil – but he knew it was not.

'They are there also,' he whispered. Acheson had thrown his column in from four directions. There was no escape.

'Van der Bergh!' whispered Leroux bitterly. 'He has gone hands-up to the English and betrayed us.' A moment longer he stared at the dust, then quickly he adjusted to the problem of defence.

'The river is our one line,' he muttered. 'With the flanks anchored on this kopje and that one there.' He let his eyes run back up the little valley of the Padda River, carefully memorizing the slope and lay of the land, storing in his mind each of its salient features, already siting the captured Maxims, picking the shelter of the hills and river bank for the horses, deciding where the reserves should be held.

'Five hundred men can hold the north kopje, but we will need a thousand on the river.' He vaulted up on to the pony and called down to the sentry, 'Stay here. I will send men up to you. They must build scharnzes along the ridge – there, and there.'

Then he drove the pony down the slope, sliding on its haunches until it reached the level ground.

'Where is Zietsmann?' he demanded.

'In his wagon.'

He galloped across to it and jerked open the canvas at the entrance.

'*Menheer*,' he began and then stopped. Zietsmann sat on the wagon bed with his wife beside him. A Bible was open on his lap.

'*Menheer*, there is little time. The enemy closes from all sides. They will be upon us in two hours.'

Zietsmann looked up at him, and from the soapy glaze of his eyes Leroux knew he had not heard.

'Thou shalt not fear the arrow that flieth by day, nor the terror that walketh by night,' he murmured.

'I am taking command, *Menheer*,' Leroux grunted. Zietsmann turned back to the book and his wife placed an arm round his shoulders.

We can hold them for this day, and perhaps tomorrow, Leroux decided from where he lay on the highest kopje. They cannot charge their cavalry against these hills, so they must come for us with the bayonet.

It is the guns first that we must fear, and then the bayonet.

'Martinus Van der Bergh,' he said aloud. 'When next we meet I will kill you for this.' And he watched the batteries unlimbering out of rifle-shot across the river, forming their precise geometrical patterns on the brown grass plain.

'*Nou skiet hulle*,' muttered a burgher beside him.

'*Ja*,' agreed Leroux. 'Now they will shoot,' and the smoke gushed from the muzzle of one of the guns out on the plain. The shell burst thunderously on the lower slopes and for an instant the lyddite smoke danced like a yellow ghost, swirling and turning upon itself, before the wind drifted it up to them. They coughed in the bitter-tasting fumes.

The next shell burst on the crest, throwing smoke and earth and rock high into the air, and immediately the rest of the batteries opened together.

They lay behind their hastily constructed earthworks while the shellfire battered the ridge. The shrapnel buzzed and hummed and struck sparks from the rocks, the solid jarring concussions made the earth jump beneath their bellies and dulled their ears so they could hardly hear the screaming of the wounded, and slowly a great cloud of dust and fumes climbed into the sky above them. A cloud so tall that Sean Courtney could see it from where he waited fifteen miles north of the Vaal.

'It looks as though Acheson has caught them,' murmured Saul.

'Yes, he's caught them,' Sean agreed, and then softly, 'The poor bastards.'

'The least they could have done was to let us be in at the kill,' growled Sergeant-Major Eccles. The distant rumble of the guns had awakened his blood lust and his great moustache wriggled with frustration. 'Don't seem right to me, seeing as how we been following the old Boer for going on a year and a half – the least they could have done was to let us be there at the end.'

'We are the cover guns, Eccles. General Acheson is trying to drive them south on to his cavalry, but if any of the birds break back through his line of beaters then they're ours,' Sean explained.

'Well, it just don't seem right to me,' Eccles repeated, then suddenly remembering his manners, he added, 'Begging your pardon, sir.'

Chapter Fifty-four

Exultantly General Acheson traversed his binoculars across the group of hills. Vaguely through the dust and smoke he could pick out their crests.

'A fair cop, sir!' Peterson grinned.

'A fair cop indeed,' Acheson agreed. They had to shout above the thunder of the guns and beneath them their horses fidgeted and trembled. A dispatch-rider galloped up, saluted and handed Peterson a message.

'What is it?' Acheson asked without lowering his glasses.

'Both Nichols and Simpson are in position for the assault. They seem anxious to engage, sir.' Then Peterson looked up at the holocaust of dust and flame upon the hills. 'They'll be lucky if they find anyone left to fight up there.'

'They will,' Acheson assured him. He was not misled by the deceptive fury of the barrage. They had survived worse at Spion Kop.

'Are you going to let them go, sir?' Peterson insisted gently. For another minute Acheson watched the hills, then he lowered his glasses and pulled his watch from his breast pocket. Four o'clock – three hours more of daylight.

'Yes!' he said. 'Send them in.'

And Peterson scribbled the order and handed it to Acheson for his signature.

'*Hier Kom Hulle.*' Leroux heard the shout in the ceaseless roar of the shells, heard it taken up and passed along the line.

'Here they come.'

'*Pasop!* They are coming.'

He stood up and his stomach heaved at the movement. Poisoned by the lyddite fumes, he fought his nausea and when he had controlled it he looked out along the river. For a second the veil of dust opened so he could see the tiny lines of khaki moving in towards the hills. Yes, they were coming.

He ran down his own line towards the river, shouting as he went.

'Wait until they are certain! Don't shoot until they reach the markers!'

From this corner of the kopje he could look out over every quarter of the field.

'*Ja*, I thought so!' he muttered. 'They come from two sides to split us.' Advancing on the frontage of the river were those same lines of tiny figures. The lines bulged and straightened and bulged again, but always they crept slowly nearer. Already the leading rank was moving up on his thousand-yard markers, in another five minutes they would be in range.

'They stand out well,' Leroux muttered as he ran his eyes along the rows of markers. While most of his men were building the earthworks along the kopjes and the river, others had paced out the ranges in front of these defences. Every two hundred and fifty yards they had erected those small cairns of stones, and over each they had smeared whitish grey mud from the river. It was a trick the British never seemed to understand, and as they advanced the Boer rifles had their range almost to the yard.

'The river is safe,' he decided. 'They cannot break through there,' and he allowed himself time to grin. 'They never learn. Every time they come against the worst side.' Then he switched his attention to the assault on his left flank. This one was dangerous, this was where he must command in person, and he ran back to his original position while around him and overhead the storm of shrapnel and lyddite roared on unabated.

He dropped on his belly between two of his burghers, wriggled forward unbuckling the bandolier from around his chest and draped it over the boulder beside him.

'Good luck, Oom Paul,' a burgher called.

'And to you, Hendrik,' he answered as he set the rear sight of his Mauser at a thousand yards, then laid the rifle on the rock in front of him.

'Close now,' the burgher beside him muttered.

'Very close. Good luck and shoot straight!'

Suddenly the storm lifted and there was silence. A vast aching silence, more shocking than the buzzing, howling roar of the guns. The dust and the smoke drifted away from the crests and after its gloom the sunshine burned down brightly on the hills and the golden brown plain, it sparkled with dazzling brilliance on the sweeping waters of the Vaal, and it lit each tiny khaki figure with stark intensity, so their shadows lay dark on the earth beneath them. They reached the line of markers.

Leroux picked up his rifle. There was one man he had been watching, a man who walked a little ahead of his line. Twice Leroux had seen him pause as if to shout an order to those who followed him.

'You first, my friend,' and he took the officer in his sights, holding him carefully in the notch with the bead obscuring his trunk. Gently he took up the slack in the trigger and the recoil slammed back into his shoulder. With the vicious and characteristic crack of the Mauser stinging his eardrums, Leroux watched the man go down into the grass.

'*Ja!*' he said and reloaded.

Not in simultaneous volley, not with the continuous wild crackle which they had used at Colenso – but in a careful, steady stutter which showed that each shot was aimed – the Boer rifles started the hunt.

'They have learned,' Leroux muttered as he worked the bolt of his rifle, and the empty case pinged away among the rocks. 'They have learned well,' and he killed another man. At two places on the ridge the Maxim guns began their frenzied hammering bursts.

Before it reached the second row of markers, the first line of infantry no longer existed, it was scattered back in the grass, completely annihilated by the terrible accuracy of the Boer fire. The second line walked over them and came on steadily.

'Look at them come,' shouted a burgher farther down the line. Though they had seen it a dozen times before, all of these ragged farmers were awed by the passive, impersonal advance of British infantry.

'These men fight not to live but to die!' muttered the man who lay beside Leroux.

'Then let us help them to die,' Leroux shouted. And below him on the plain the slow inexorable ranks moved forward towards the third row of markers.

'Shoot, *Kerels*. Shoot straight,' Leroux roared, for now he could see the bayonets. He pressed a clip full of ammunition down into the magazine, and with the back of his hand brushed the clinging drops of sweat from his eyebrows, pushed the rifle forward and knocked down four men with his next six shots. Then he saw the change. At one place the line bulged as men began to hurry forward, while on the flanks it wavered and disintegrated as others hung back or crouched down behind pitifully inadequate cover.

'They are breaking!' Leroux howled excitedly. 'They won't reach the slopes.'

The forward movement faltered, no longer able to stand the mauling they were receiving, men turned back or went to ground while their officers hurried along the ranks goading them on. In so doing they proclaimed to the Boer riflemen that they were officers and at that range they did not survive long.

'They're finished!' shouted Leroux, and a thin burst of cheering ran along the ridge while the Boer fire increased in volume, flailing into the milling confusion of a broken infantry assault.

'Hit them, *Kerels*. Keep hitting them!' The following ranks overran the leaders, then in turn faltered and failed as the Maxim and Mauser fire churned into them.

Out on the plain a bugle began to lament, and as it mourned, the last spasmodic forward movement of the assault ceased, and back past the dead and the wounded streamed the retreat.

A single shell rushed overhead to burst in the valley beyond and immediately, as if in frustrated fury, the guns lashed the kopje once more. But in the jump and flash of the shells five hundred Boers cheered and laughed and waved their rifles at the retreating infantry.

'What happened on the river?' Leroux called in the tumult, and after a while the answer came back.

'They did not reach the river. They are broken there also.'

Leroux lifted his hat from his head and wiped the sweat and the dust from his face. Then he looked at the sunset.

'Almighty God, we give you thanks for this day. We ask your mercy and guidance in the days that are to come.'

The shellfire lashed the hills like the surf of a storm-driven sea until the night came. Then in the darkness they saw the fires of the British bivouacs spread like a garden of yellow flowers on the plains around them.

Chapter Fifty-five

'We must break out tonight.' Leroux looked across the fire at Zietsmann.

'No.' The old man spoke softly, not looking at him.

'Why?' demanded Leroux.

'We can hold these hills. They cannot drive us from them.'

'*Ja!* We can hold them tomorrow – two days, a week – but then it is finished. We lost fifty men today from the guns.'

'They lost many hundreds. The Lord smote them and they perished.' Zietsmann looked up at him now and his voice gathered strength. 'We will stay here and place our trust in the Lord.' There was a murmur of agreement from those who listened.

'*Menheer*.' Leroux covered his eyes for a moment, pressing fingers into them to still the terrible aching. He was sick from the lyddite, and tired – tired to the depths of his soul. It would be easier to stay. There would be no dishonour in it for they had fought like no men before them. Two more days and then it would be over without dishonour. He removed his hands from his face. '*Menheer*, if we do not break out tonight we never will. By tomorrow we will not have the strength.' He stopped for the words came slowly, slurred a little from a brain dulled by the lyddite and the hammering of big guns. He looked at his hands and saw the suppurating sores on his wrists. There would be no dishonour. They would fight this last time and then it would be finished.

'But it is not a matter of honour,' he mumbled. Then he stood up and they watched him in silence for he was going to speak. He spread his hands out in appeal, and the firelight lit his face from below leaving his eyes in shadow, dark holes like the sockets of a skull. He stood like that for a while and his rags hung loosely on the gaunt wasted body.

'Burghers . . .' he started. But the words were not there. There was nothing except the need to fight on. He dropped his hands to his sides.

'I am going,' he said with simplicity. 'When the moon goes down I ride,' and he walked away from the fire. One by one other men rose and followed him, and all of them were men of his own commando.

Six men squatted in a circle and watched the moon as it touched the hills. Behind them the horses were saddled and the rifles stuck up from their scabbards. By each of the six hundred horses a burgher lay fully clothed, wrapped in his blanket and trying to sleep. Though the horses stamped and moved restlessly there was no jingling of bits for all of them were carefully muffled.

'We will say it again, so that each of us knows his part.' Leroux looked around the circle. 'I will go first with a hundred men and follow the river towards the east. What is your route, Hendrik?'

'South, through the cavalry until the dawn, then round towards the mountains.'

Leroux nodded and asked the next man:

'And yours?'

'West along the river.'

'*Ja*, and yours?'

He asked each in turn and when all had answered – 'The place of meeting is the old laager by the Hill of Inhlozana. Is this agreed?'

And they waited, watching the moon and listening to the jackals squabbling over the British corpses on the plain. Then the moon went down below the hills and Leroux stood up stiffly.

'*Totsiens, Kerels*. Good luck to all of us.' He took the reins of his pony and led it down towards the Vaal, while in silence a hundred men led their horses after him. As they passed the single wagon beside the Padda, old Zietsmann was waiting and he came forward leading a pack-mule.

'You are going?' he asked.

'*Ja, Menheer*. We must.'

'God go with you.' Zietsmann thrust out his hand and they gripped briefly.

'The mule is loaded. Take the money with you. We will not need it here.'

'Thank you, *Menheer*.' Leroux motioned to one of his men to take the mule. 'Good luck.'

'Good luck, General.' For the first time Zietsmann used his title, and Leroux went down to the perimeter of their defences and out into the veld where the British waited.

With the first pale promise of dawn in the sky, they were through and clear. Though twice during the night heavy outbursts of firing in the darkness far behind them showed that not all of the escaping bands had been so fortunate.

Chapter Fifty-six

Sean and Saul stood beside the little scotchcart and Mbejane brought them coffee.

'My God, it's cold enough to freeze the hanger off a brass monkey.' Sean cupped his hands around the mug and sipped noisily.

'At least you've got a hood to keep your tip warm,' Saul retorted. 'We'd better get moving before we all freeze to the ground.'

'Dawn in an hour,' Sean agreed. 'Time to start walking our beat,' and he called across to Mbejane, 'Kill the fire and bring my horse.'

In double file with the scotchcart bumping along in the rear they started on the outward leg of their patrol. In the last four days they had covered the same ground as many times, tacking backwards and forwards across the beat that Acheson had assigned them. The grass was brittle with frost and crunched under the horses' hooves.

While ahead of them the Zulu trackers ranged like gundogs, and behind the troopers huddled miserably in their greatcoats, Sean and Saul picked up their endless discussion from the point at which they had left it the previous evening. Already they had reached so far into the future that they were talking of a federation under responsible government that would encompass all the territories south of the Zambesi.

'That's what Rhodes has proposed for the last ten years,' Saul pointed out.

'I don't want any part of that wily bastard.' Sean spoke emphatically. 'He'll keep us tied for ever to the apron strings of Whitehall the sooner we get rid of him and Milner the better, say I.'

'You want to get rid of Imperial rule?' Saul asked.

'Of course, let's end this war and send all of them back across the sea. We can run our own affairs.'

'Colonel, it seems to me you are fighting on the wrong side,' Saul remarked, and Sean chuckled.

'But seriously, Saul . . .' He never finished. Mbejane came out of the darkness, running with silent purpose so that Sean checked his horse and felt the skin along his arms prickle with nervous excitement.

'Mbejane?'

'Mabuna!'

'Where? How many?'

He listened to Mbejane's hurried explanation, then swung round to face Sergeant-Major Eccles, who was breathing heavily down his neck.

'Your birds, Eccles. A hundred or so of them, only a mile ahead and coming straight towards us.' Sean's voice was tight with the same excitement that made Eccles's moustache wriggle like an agitated caterpillar on the impassive oval of his face. 'Deploy in single line. They'll walk right on top of us in the dark.'

'Dismounted, sir?'

'No,' Sean answered. 'We'll gun charge them as soon as they show. But for God's sake keep it quiet.'

As Sean sat on his horse with Saul beside him, the two files of troopers opened on each side of them. There was no talking; only the clicking of iron-shod hooves on rock, the rustling of men struggling out of their heavy greatcoats, and the soft rattle and snick of breech-bolts opening and closing.

'Once more into the breach, dear friends,' whispered Saul, but Sean did not answer because he was wrestling with his fear. Even in the cold of dawn his hands were damp. He wiped them on the thighs of his breeches and slid his rifle from the scabbard.

'What about the Maxims?' Saul asked.

'No time to set them up.' Sean knew his voice was hoarse and he cleared his throat before he went on. 'We won't need them – it's six to one.'

He looked along the silent line of his men. A dark line against the grass that was paling in the dawn. He could see that each of his troopers leaned forward in the saddle with his rifle held across his lap. The tension was a tangible thing in the half-darkness; even the horses were infected, they moved beneath their riders, shifting their bodies, nodding with impatience. Please God, let none of them whicker now.

And he peered ahead into the darkness. Waiting with his own fear and the fear of his men so strong that the Boers must surely smell it.

A patch of greater darkness in the dawn, ahead and slightly to the left of centre. Sean watched it for a few seconds and saw it move, slowly, like the moonlit shadow of a tree on the open veld.

'Are you sure they're Boers?' Saul whispered, and the doubt startled Sean. While he hesitated the shadow spread towards them and now he could hear the hooves.

Are they Boers? Desperately he searched for some sign that would allow him to loose his charge. Are they Boers? But there was no sign – only the dark advance and the small sounds of it, the click and creak in the dawn.

They were close now, less than a hundred yards, although it was impossible to tell with certainty for the dark, moving mass seemed to float towards them.

'Sean . . .' Saul's whisper was cut off by the shrill nervous whinny of his horse. The sound was so unexpected that Sean heard the man beside him gasp. Almost immediately came the sign for which Sean waited.

'*Wie's daar?*' The challenge from ahead was in the guttural of the Taal.

'Charge!' yelled Sean and hit his horse with his heels. Instantly the whole of his line jumped forward to hurl itself upon the Boers.

Forward in the pounding hooves, forward in the shouting, in the continuous crackle of rifle-fire that sparkled along the line – with his fear left behind him, Sean spurred at them. Steadying the butt of his rifle under hi right armpit, firing blind, blending his voice with the yelling of six hundred others, leading slightly in the centre of the line; he took his commando down upon the Boers.

They broke before the charge. They had to break for they could not hope to stand against it. They swung and drove their exhausted horses back towards the south.

'Bunch up!' roared Sean. 'Bunch on me!' And his line shortened so they charged knee to knee in a solid wall of men and horses and gunfire before which the Boers fled in wild despair.

Directly in Sean's path lay a struggling, badly wounded horse with its rider pinned underneath it. Jammed into the charge he could not swerve.

'Up, Boy!' he shouted and lifted his horse with his knees and his hands, clearing the tangle and stumbling as they landed. Then forward again in the urgent, jostling clamour of the charge.

'We're gaining!' yelled Saul. 'This time we've got them.'

The horse beside him hit a hole and went down with its leg breaking like a pistol-shot. The trooper was thrown from it high and clear, turning in the air as he fell. The line closed to fill the gap, and pounded on over the grassland.

'There's a kopje ahead,' Sean shouted as he saw the ragged loom of it against the dawn sky. 'Don't let them reach it!' And he raked his spurs along his horse's ribs.

'We won't catch them,' warned Saul. 'They'll get into the rocks.'

'Damn it! God damn it!' groaned Sean. In the past few minutes the light had strengthened. Dawn in Africa comes quickly once it starts. Clearly he could see the leading Boers ride into the rocks, throw themselves from their ponies and duck into cover.

'Faster!' shouted Sean in agony. 'Faster!' as he saw the chance of quick success slip from his grasp. Already Mausers were talking back from the lower slopes of the kopje, and the last burghers were down and scurrying into the rocks. Loose ponies turned wildly into his line, empty stirrups flapping, eyes wide with terror – forcing his men to swerve into each other, dissipating the force of the charge. A loose pack-mule with a small leather pack upon its back climbed up through the rocks until a stray bullet killed it and it rolled into a deep crevice. But nobody saw it fall.

Sean felt the horse between his legs jerk and he was thrown with such violence that the stirrup leathers snapped like cotton and he went up and out, hung for a sickening moment and then swooped down to hit the ground with his chest and shoulder and the side of his face.

While he lay in the grass the charge spent itself like a wave on the kopje, then eddied and swirled into confusion. Dimly Sean was aware of the hooves that trampled about his head, of the sound of the Mausers and the shouts of the men who were swept by them.

'Dismount! Get down and follow them.' Saul's voice and the tone of it roused Sean. With his hands under his chest he pushed himself into a sitting position. The side of his face burned where the skin had been smeared away, his nose was bleeding and the blood turned the earth in his mouth to a gritty paste. His left arm was numb to the shoulder and he had lost his rifle.

Dully he tried to spit the filth from his mouth while he peered at the chaos about him, trying to make sense of it. He shook his head, to joggle the apathy from his brain, while all around him men were being cut down at point-blank range by the Mausers.

'Dismount! Dismount!' The urgency of Saul's voice brought Sean unsteadily to his feet.

'Get down, you bastards!' He took up the cry. 'Get down and chase them.' A horse brushed against him and he staggered but kept his balance. The trooper slid down from its back beside Sean.

'Are you all right, Colonel?' He reached out to steady Sean, but a bullet took him in the chest below his raised arm and killed him instantly. Sean stared down at the body and felt his brain click back into focus.

'The bastards,' he snarled and snatched up the man's rifle, then, 'Come on!' he roared. 'Follow me!' and he led them out of the shambles of struggling horses into the rocks.

In the next half-hour, grimly and irresistibly, they used their superior numbers to drive the Boers back up the kopje. Each outcrop of rocks was a strongpoint that had to be assaulted and carried, and paid for in blood. On a front of perhaps two hundred yards, the attack became a series of isolated skirmishes over which Sean could not maintain command. He gathered those men who were near him and boulder by boulder they fought their way towards the top, while the burghers in front of him held each position until the last moment and then fell back on the next.

The top of the kopje was flattened into a saucer with fifty feet of steep open ground falling away on all sides, and finally sixty burghers reached this natural fortress and held it with the determination of men who knew that they fought for the last time. Twice they threw the British from the lip of the saucer and sent them scrambling and sliding back into the shelter of the broken rock below. After the second repulse a heavy unnatural silence settled on the kopje.

Sean sat with his back to a rock and took the water-bottle that a corporal offered him. He rinsed the slime of blood and congealing saliva from his mouth and spat it pink on to the ground beside him. Then he tilted the bottle and swallowed twice with his eyes tightly closed in the intense pleasure of drinking.

'Thanks.' He passed the bottle back.

'More?' the corporal asked.

'No.' Sean shook his head and looked back down the slope. The sun was well up now, throwing long shadows behind the horses that were grazing far out across the veld below. But at the foot of the slope lay the dead animals, most of them on their sides with legs thrust stiffly out. Blanket-rolls had burst open to litter the grass with the pathetic possessions of the dead men around them.

The men in their khaki and brown were as inconspicuous as piles of dead leaves in the grass, mostly British but with here and there a burgher lying amongst them in the fellowship of death.

'Mbejane.' Sean spoke softly to the big Zulu who squatted beside him. 'Find Nkosi Saul and bring him to see me here.'

He watched the Zulu crawl away. Mbejane had been left behind at the start of that wild gallop, but before Sean was half-way up the kopje he had glanced back to find him kneeling two paces behind, ready with a bandolier of ammunition for the moment when Sean needed it. Neither of them had spoken until this moment. Between them words were seldom necessary.

Sean fingered the raw graze on his face and listened to the murmured conversation of the men around him. Twice he heard clearly the voices of Boers from the saucer above them and once he heard a burgher laugh. They were very close, and Sean moved uneasily against the rock.

Within minutes Mbejane was back with Saul crawling behind him. When he saw Sean, Saul's expression changed quickly.

'Your face! Are you all right?'

'Cut myself shaving.' Sean grinned at him. 'Have a seat. Make yourself comfortable.'

Saul crawled the last few yards and settled himself against Sean's rock. 'Now what?' he asked.

'Ten minutes' rest, then we're going up again,' Sean told him. 'But this time with a little more purpose. I want you to work around the back of the kopje with half the men. Take Eccles with you. We'll rush their whole perimeter at the same moment. When you're in position fire three shots in quick succession then count slowly to twenty. I'll back you from this side.'

'Good.' Saul nodded. 'It'll take me a little while to get round – don't be impatient.' And he was smiling as he rose to his knees and leaned forward to touch Sean's shoulder.

Sean would always remember him like that: big mouth creased at the corners, smiling with white teeth through three days' growth of beard, slouch hat pushed to the back of his head, so his hair fell forward on to his forehead, and sunburned skin flaking from the tip of his nose.

The rock behind them was cracked through. If Saul had not leaned forward to make that gesture of affection he would not have exposed himself.

The sniper on the ridge had seen the brim of his hat above the rock and he held his aim into the crack. At the moment that Saul's fingers touched Sean's shoulder his head moved across the gap and the Boer fired.

The bullet hit Saul in the right temple, slanted diagonally back through his head and came out behind his left ear.

Their faces were but eighteen inches apart and Sean was smiling into Saul's eyes as the bullet hit. Saul's whole head was distorted by the impact, swelling and bursting like a balloon. His lips stretched so that for an instant his smile was a hideous rubbery thing and then he was snatched away and thrown sideways down the slope. He slid to a stop with his head and shoulders mercifully covered by a tuft of the coarse grey grass that grew among the rocks, but his trunk shivered and his legs danced and kicked convulsively.

For a slow count of ten Sean did not move nor did his expression alter. It took him that long to believe what he had seen. Then his face seemed to crumple.

'Saul!' His voice was a croak.

'Saul!' It rose higher, sharp with the realization of his loss.

He came slowly to his knees. Now Saul's body was still, very still and relaxed.

Again Sean opened his mouth but this time the sound he uttered was without form. The way an old bull buffalo bellows at the heart shot, that way Sean gave expression to his grief. A low shuddering cry that carried to the men in the rocks around him and to the Boers in the saucer above.

He made no attempt to touch Saul. He stared at him.

'Nkosi.' Mbejane was appalled at what he saw on Sean's face. His tunic was stiff with his own dried blood. The graze across his cheek was swollen and inflamed and it wept pale lymph. But it was the eyes that alarmed Mbejane.

'Nkosi.' Mbejane tried to restrain him, but Sean did not hear. His eyes were glazing over with the madness that had taken the place of his grief. His head hunched down on his shoulders and he growled like an animal.

'Take them! Take the bastards!' And he went up and over the rock in a twisting leap with the bayoneted rifle held against his chest.

'Come on!' he roared and went up the slope so fast that only one bullet hit him. But it did not stop him and he was over the lip, roaring and clubbing and hacking with the bayonet.

From the rocks four hundred of his men swarmed up after him and boiled over the lip of the saucer. But before they reached Sean he was face to face with Jan Paulus Leroux.

This time it was no match. Jan Paulus was wasted and sick. A gaunt skeleton of the man he had been. His rifle was empty and he fumbled with the reload. He looked up and recognized Sean. Saw him tall and splattered with blood. Saw the bayonet in his hands and the madness in his eyes.

'Sean!' he said and lifted the empty rifle to meet the bayonet. But he could not hold it. With Sean's weight behind it the bayonet glanced off the stock and went on. Jan Paulus felt the tingling slide of the steel through his reluctant flesh and he went over backwards with the bayonet in him.

'Sean,' he cried from his back. Sean stood over him and plucked the bayonet out. He lifted it high with both hands, his whole body poised to drive it down again.

They stared at each other. The British charge swept past them and they were alone. One man wounded in the grass and the other wounded above him with the bayoneted rifle and the madness still on him.

The vanquished in the grass, who had fought and suffered and sacrificed the lives of those he loved.

The victor above him, who had fought and suffered and sacrificed the lives of those he loved.

The game was war. The prize was a land. The penalty for defeat was death.

'*Maak dit klaar!* Make it finished!' Leroux told him quietly. The madness went out in Sean like the flame of a candle. He lowered the bayoneted rifle and let it drop. The weakness of his wound caught up with him and he staggered. With surprise he looked down at his belly and clasped his hands over the wound, and then he sank down to sit beside Jan Paulus.

In the saucer the fight was over.

Chapter Fifty-seven

'We're ready to move, sir.' Eccles stood beside the scotchcart and looked down at Sean. A massive scowl concealed his concern. 'Are you comfortable?'

Sean ignored the question. 'Who is in charge of the burial details, Eccles?'

'Smith, sir.'

'You have told him about Saul – about Captain Friedman?'

'Yes, sir. They will bury him separately.'

Sean lifted himself painfully on to an elbow and for a minute stared at the two gangs working bare to the waist on the communal graves. Beyond them lay the rows of blanket-wrapped bundles. A fine day's work, he thought bitterly.

'Shall we start, sir?' Eccles asked.

'You've given Smith my orders? Burghers to be buried with their comrades – our men with theirs?'

'It's all taken care of, sir.'

Sean lay back on the bedding that covered the floor of the scotchcart.

'Please send my servant to me, Eccles.'

While he waited for Mbejane, Sean tried to avoid contact with the man who lay beside him in the scotchcart. He knew Jan Paulus was watching him.

'Sean – *Menheer*, who will say the words for my men?'

'We have no Chaplain.' Sean did not look at him.

'I could say them.'

'General Leroux, it will be another two hours before the work is completed. You are wounded, and it is my duty to get this column with the other wounded back to Vereeniging as soon as I can. We are leaving the burial detail and when they're finished they'll catch us up.' Sean spoke lying on his bank staring up at the sky.

'*Menheer*, I demand—' Jan Paulus began, but Sean turned angrily towards him.

'Listen, Leroux. I've told you what I'm going to do. The graves will be carefully marked, and later the War Graves Commission will send a Chaplain.'

There was very little room in the scotchcart and they were both big men. Now, as they glared at each other their faces were a foot apart. Sean would have said more, but as he opened his mouth the wound in his guts caught him and he gasped. The sweat broke out heavily across his forehead.

'Are you all right?' Jan Paulus's expression altered.

'I'll feel better once we get to Vereeniging.'

'*Ja*, you're right. We must go,' agreed Leroux.

Eccles came back with Mbejane.

'Nkosi, you sent for me?'

'Mbejane, I want you to stay here and mark the place where they bury Nkosi Saul. Remember it well, for later you must be able to bring me back to it,' Sean mumbled.

'Nkosi.' Mbejane went away.

'Very well, Eccles. You can start.'

It was a long column. Behind the van rode the prisoners, many of them mounted two up. Then followed the wounded, each in a horse litter of poles and blankets, behind them the scotchcart, and finally Eccles and two hundred troopers of the rearguard. Their progress was slow and dismal.

In the scotchcart neither of them spoke again. They lay in pain, bracing themselves against the jolt and lurch, with the sun beating down mercilessly upon them.

In that dreamlike state induced by pain and loss of blood, Sean was thinking of Saul. At times he would convince himself that it had not happened and he would experience a rush of relieve as though he had woken from a nightmare to find it was not reality. Saul was alive after all. Then his mind would focus with clarity and Saul was dead again. Saul was wrapped in a blanket with the earth above him, and all they had planned was down there with him. Then Sean would grapple once more with the unanswerable.

'Ruth!' he cried aloud, so that Jan Paulus beside him stirred uneasily.

'Are you all right, Sean?'

But Sean did not hear him. Now there was Ruth. Now there was Ruth alone. He felt joy then in his loss, joy quickly swamped with guilt. For an instant he had been glad that Saul was dead, and his treachery sickened him and ached like the bullet in his guts. But still there was Ruth, and Saul was dead. I must not think of it like that. I must not think! And he struggled up into a sitting position and clung to the side of the scotchcart.

'Lie down, Sean,' Jan Paulus told him gently. 'You'll bleed again.'

'You!' Sean shouted at him. 'You killed him.'

'*Ja.*' Leroux nodded his red beard into his chest. 'I killed them, but you also – all of us. *Ja*, we killed them.' And he reached up and took Sean's arm and drew him down into the blankets. 'Now, lie still or we'll bury you also.'

'But why, Paul. Why?' Sean asked softly.

'Does it matter why? They are dead.'

'And now what happens?' Sean covered his eyes from the sun.

'We go on living. That is all, we just go on.'

'But what was it about. Why did we fight?'

'I don't know. Once I knew clearly, but now I have lost the reason,' Leroux answered.

They were silent for a long time and then they began to talk again. Groping together for the things that must take the place of that which had filled these last three years.

Twice that afternoon the column halted briefly while they buried men who had died of their wounds. And each of these deaths – one a burgher and the other a trooper – gave poignancy and direction to the talk in the scotchcart.

In the evening they met a patrol that was scouting ahead of the big columns returning from the Padda River. A young lieutenant came to the scotchcart and saluted Sean.

'I have a message for you from General Acheson, sir.'

'Yes?'

'This fellow Leroux got away from us at the Padda. Zietsmann, the other Boer leader, was killed, but Leroux got away.'

'This is General Leroux,' Sean told him.

'Good God!' He stared at Leroux. 'You caught him. I say – well done, sir. Jolly well done.' In the past two years Jan Paulus had become a legend to the British, so that the lieutenant examined him now with frank curiosity.

'What is your message?' Sean snapped.

'Sorry, sir.' The youngster dragged his eyes away from Jan Paulus. 'All the Boer leaders are meeting at Vereeniging. We are to give them safe conduct into the garrison. General Acheson wanted you to try to contact Leroux with the offer – but, that won't be difficult now. Jolly good show, sir.'

'Thank you, Lieutenant. Please tell General Acheson that we'll be in Vereeniging tomorrow.'

They watched the patrol ride away and disappear over a fold in the land.

'So!' growled Leroux. 'It's surrender then.'

'No,' Sean contradicted him. 'It's peace!'

Chapter Fifty-eight

The primary school at Vereeniging had been converted into an officers' hospital. Sean lay on his field cot and regarded the picture of President Kruger on the wall opposite him. In this way he was putting off the moment when he must continue with the letter he was writing. So far he had written the address, the date and the salutation: 'My dear Ruth'.

It was ten days since the column had returned from the veld. It was also ten days since the surgeons had cut him open and tied together those parts of his alimentary canal that the bullet had disrupted. He wrote:

I am at this moment well on the way to recovering from a small wound received two weeks ago near the Vaal River – so please take no notice of my current address. [He started a new paragraph.]

God knows I wish the circumstances in which I write were less painful to both of us. You will by now have received an official notification of Saul's death, so there is nothing I can add but to say that he died in circumstances of great personal gallantry. While about to lead a bayonet charge he was shot and killed *instantly*.

I know you will want to be alone in your grief. It will be some weeks before the doctors allow me to travel. By the time I reach Pietermaritzburg I hope you will be sufficiently recovered to allow me to call on you in the hope that I may be able to give you some comfort.

I trust that small Storm continues to increase in weight and beauty. I look forward to seeing her again.

A long while he pondered the ending, and finally decided on 'Your true friend'. He signed it, folded it into its envelope and laid it on the locker beside his bed for posting.

Then he lay back on his pillows and surrendered himself to the ache of loss and the dull pain in his belly.

After a while his physical pain dominated, and he glanced surreptitiously around the ward to ensure there were no nurses about. Then he lifted the sheet, pulled up his nightshirt and began picking at the bandage until he had exposed the edge of the wound with the black horsehair stitches standing stiffly out of it like the knots in a strand of barbed wire. An expression of comical disgust curled his lips. Sean hated sickness – but especially he hated it in his own flesh. The disgust gave way slowly to a helpless anger and he glared at the wound.

'Leave it stand, old Sean. Looking won't make it better.' Sean had been so intent on the evil gash in his stomach that he had not heard the speaker approach. Despite the cane and the limp that dragged his right leg, Leroux moved silently for a big man. He stood now beside the bed and smiled shyly down at Sean.

'Paul!' Guiltily Sean covered himself.

'*Ja*, Sean. How goes it?'

'Not too bad, And you?'

Leroux shrugged. 'They tell me I will need this for a long time to come.' He tapped the ferrule of the cane on the floor. 'May I sit down?'

'Of course.' Sean moved to give him the edge of the bed and Leroux lowered himself with his bad leg stretched stiffly in front of him. His clothing was newly washed and the cuffs of his jacket darned; patches on the elbows, and a long tear in the knee of his breeches had been cobbled together with crude, masculine stitches.

His beard had been trimmed and squared. There were iodine-stained bandages covering the open sores on his wrists, but a red mane of hair hung to the collar of his jacket and the bones of his forehead and cheeks made harsh angles beneath skin that was desiccated and browned by the sun.

'So!' said Sean.

'So!' Leroux answered him and looked down at his hands . Both he and Sean were silent then, awkward and inarticulate, for neither of them dealt easily in words.

'Will you smoke, Paul?' Sean reached for the cheroots on his locker.

'Thank you.' They made a show of selecting and lighting, then silence overwhelmed them again and Leroux scowled at the tip of his cheroot.

'This is good tobacco,' he growled.

'Yes,' agreed Sean and regarded his own cheroot with equal ferocity. Leroux coughed and rolled his cane between the fingers of his other hand.

'*Toe maar*, I just thought I'd come and see you,' he said.

'I'm glad of it.'

'So, you're all right then, hey?'

'Yes. I'm all right,' Sean agreed.

'Good.' Leroux nodded sagely. 'Well, then!' He stood up slowly. 'I had better be going. We are meeting again in an hour. Jannie Smuts has come up from the Cape.'

'I heard so.' Even the hospital was penetrated by rumours of what was happening in the big marquee tent pitched on the parade-ground near the station. Under the chairmanship of old President Steyn the Boer leaders were talking out their future. De Wet was there, and Niemand and Leroux. Botha was there and Hertzog and Strauss and others whose names had echoed across the world these last two years. And now the last of them, Jannie Smuts, had arrived. He had left his commando besieging the little town of O'Kiep in the Northern Cape and travelling up the British-held railway. Now they were all assembled. If they had gained nothing else in these last desperate years, they had at least won recognition as the leaders of the Boer people. This tiny bank of tired and warsick men was treating with the representatives of the greatest military power on earth.

'*Ja*, I have heard so,' Sean repeated, and impulsively he thrust out his hand. 'Good luck, Paul.'

Leroux seized his hand and held it hard, his mouth moved with the pressure of his emotion.

'Sean, we must talk. We have to talk!' he blurted.

'Sit down,' Sean told him and Leroux freed his hand and sank on to the bed once again.

'What must I do, Sean?' he asked. 'It's you who must advise me. Not these . . . not these others from over the sea.'

'You have seen Kitchener and Milner.' It was not a question for Sean knew of the meeting. 'What do they ask of you?'

'They ask everything.' Leroux spoke bitterly. 'They ask for surrender without terms.'

'Will you agree to that?'

For a minute Leroux was silent, and then he lifted his head and looked full into Sean's face.

'So far we have fought to live,' he said and what Sean saw in those eyes he would never forget. 'But now we will fight to die.'

'And by this, what will you achieve?' Sean asked softly.

'Death is the lesser evil. We cannot live as slaves.' Leroux's voice rose sharply. 'This is my land,' he cried.

'No,' Sean told him harshly. 'It is also my land, and the land of my son,' and then his voice softened. 'And the blood of my son is your blood.'

'But these others – this Kitchener, this devil Milner.'

'They are a people apart,' Sean said.

'But you fought with them!' Leroux accused.

'I have done many foolish things,' agreed Sean. 'But, from them I have learned.'

'What are you saying?' demanded Leroux, and Sean could see the sparkle of hope in his eyes. I must say this carefully, thought Sean, I must be very careful. He drew a long breath before he spoke.

'As it stands this moment your people are scattered but alive. If you fight on, the British will stay until you have found the annihilation you seek. If you stop now, then soon they will leave.'

'Will you leave?' demanded Leroux savagely.

'No.'

'And you are British! The British will stay – you and those like you.'

Then Sean grinned at him. It was so sudden, so irresistible that grin, that it threw Leroux off balance.

'Do I look and talk like a *rooinek*, Paul?' he asked in the Taal. 'Which half of my son is burgher and which half British?'

Confused by this sneak attack Leroux stared at him for a long time before he dropped his eyes and fiddled with his cane.

'Come on, man,' Sean told him. 'Make an end to this foolishness. You and I have a lot of work to do.'

'You and I?' Leroux asked suspiciously.

'Yes.'

Leroux laughed, a sudden harsh bellow of laughter.

'You are a *slim Kerel*,' he roared.

'I'll have to think about what you have said.' He rose from the bed and seemed to stand taller now. The laughter filled out his gaunt features and wrinkled his nose.

'I'll have to think very carefully about it.' He reached out his hand again and Sean took it. 'I will come and talk with you again. He turned away abruptly and limped down the ward with his cane tapping loudly.

Jan Paulus kept his word. He visited Sean daily, an hour or so at a time, and they talked. Two days after the Boer surrender he brought another man with him.

Jan Paulus stood a good four inches over him, but though he was slimly built the visitor gave the impression of size.

'Sean, this is Jan Christian Niemand.'

'Perhaps I am lucky we did not meet before, Colonel Courtney.' Niemand's voice, high in timbre, was crisp and authoritative. He spoke the perfect English he had learned at Oxford University. 'What do you think, *Oubas?*' He addressed Jan Paulus by the title which was obviously a private joke between them, and Jan Paulus chuckled.

'Very lucky. Otherwise you also might be using a stick.'

Sean examined Niemand with interest. Hard years of war had muscled his shoulders and he walked like a soldier, yet above the pointed blond beard was the face of a scholar. The skin had a youthful clarity which was almost maidenly, but the eyes were a penetrating blue, the merciless blue of a Toledo steel blade.

His mind had the same resilience, and before many minutes Sean was using all his wits to meet and answer questions that Niemand asked him. It was clear that he was being subjected to some sort of test. At the end of an hour he decided he had passed.

'And now, what are your plans?'

'I must go home,' Sean answered, 'I have a farm and a son – soon, perhaps, a wife.'

'I wish you happiness.'

'It is not yet settled.' Sean admitted. 'I still have to ask her.'

Jannie Niemand smiled. 'Well, then, I wish you luck with your suit. And strength to build a new life.' Suddenly he was serious. 'We also must rebuild what has been destroyed.' He stood up from the bed and Jan Paulus stood with him.

'There will be need of good men in the years ahead.' Niemand held out his hand and Sean took it. 'We will meet again. Count on that.'

Chapter Fifty-nine

As the train ran in past the great, white mine dumps and Sean leaned from the window of the coach to look ahead at the familiar skyline of Johannesburg, he wondered how such an unlovely city still had the power to draw him back each time. It was as though he was connected to it by an elastic umbilical cord which allowed him a wide range. But when he reached its limit it pulled him back.

'Two days,' he promised himself. 'Two days I'll stay here. Just long enough to hand old Acheson my formal resignation and tell Candy Good-bye. Then I'll head south to Ladyburg – and leave this town to stew in its own evil juices.'

Near at hand a midday hooter howled from one of the mines, and immediately its cry was taken up and answered by the other mines. It sounded as though a pack of hungry wolves were hunting across the valley, the wolves of greed and gold. Those mines that had been forced to close during the hostilities were now back in production, and the black smoke from their stacks sullied the sky and drifted in a dirty mist across the crest of the ridge.

The train slowed, and the unexpected clatter and lurch of the points broke the rhythm of its run. Then it was sliding in along the concrete platform of Johannesburg Station. Sean lifted his luggage down from the rack above his head and passed it out of the open window to Mbejane. The exertion of lifting and carrying no longer caught in his guts; except for the irregular scar near his navel he was completely healed. When he strode down the platform towards the exit he held himself erect, no longer stooping to favour his stomach.

A horsedrawn cab deposited them on the pavement outside Acheson's headquarters, and Sean left Mbejane guarding the luggage while he pushed his way across the crowded lobby and climbed the staircase to the first floor.

'Good afternoon, Colonel.' The orderly sergeant recognized him immediately and jumped to attention with such alacrity that he overturned his stool.

'Afternoon, Thompson,' Sean told him. The honours of his rank still

embarrassed him. Thompson relaxed and inquired with more than just the
formal concern:

'How are you, sir? Sorry to 'ear about your belly, sir.'

'Thank you, Thompson, I am fine now. Is Major Peterson in?'

Peterson was delighted to see him. He made tender inquiries after the
movement of Sean's bowels, for irregularity was often one of the unpleasant
aftermaths of a stomach wound. Sean reassured him and Peterson went on:

'Have some tea. The old man is busy right now but he'll see you in ten
minutes,' and he shouted for Thompson to bring tea before he returned to
the subject of Sean's wound. 'Much of a scar, old chap?' he asked.

Sean loosened his Sam Browne belt, unbuttoned his tunic and pulled his
shirt out from his trousers. Peterson came round the desk and inspected
Sean's hairy stomach at close range.

'Very neat. Damn good job they did on you.' Peterson gave his expert
opinion. 'I got one at Omdurman – one of those fuzzy wuzzies pegged me
with his dirty great spear.' And he in turn partially disrobed and displayed
his pale hairless chest. From common courtesy Sean was forced to cluck and
shake his head at the small triangular cicatrice on Peterson's bosom, although
secretly he was not impressed. The attention went to Peterson's head.

'Got another one – damn painful it was too!' and he unbuckled his belt
and had his trousers half down when the interleading door opened.

'Hope I'm not interrupting anything, gentlemen?' General Acheson
inquired politely. There were a few moments of confusion while they both
attempted to dress and make the correct military salutations. Peterson had
the nicest decision to make, one not covered by the Articles of War. It was
one of the few occasions in history where a divisional commander was
received by a senior field officer standing at rigid attention with his trousers
round his ankles. Major Peterson affected a rather startling line in scarlet
flannel underwear. Once Acheson had understood the reason for this irregularity of dress among his officers, he was strongly tempted to join in the
exhibition, for he also had some fine scars, but he restrained himself
admirably. He led Sean through to the inner office and gave him a cigar.

'Well, Courtney. I hope you haven't come looking for a job.'

'On the contrary – I want to get the hell out of this business, sir.'

'I think we can arrange that. The Paymaster will be relieved.' Acheson
nodded. 'I'll get Peterson to draw up your papers.'
papers.'

'I want to leave tomorrow,' Sean insisted, and Acheson smiled.

'You're in a big hurry. All right. Peterson can post them to you for your
signature – your unit has already been disbanded so there is no point in
kicking your heels around here.'

'Good!' Sean had anticipated resistance, and he laughed with relief.

'There are just three other items,' Acheson went on, and Sean frowned
with quick suspicion.

'Oh?'

'Firstly, a parting gift from His Majesty. A Distinguished Service Order
for catching Leroux – there will be an investiture next week. Lord K. would
like you to attend personally.'

'Hell, no! If I've got to stay in Johannesburg – I don't want it.'

And Acheson chuckled. 'A surprising lack of gratitude! Peterson can post it to you also. Secondly, I've been able to bring a little influence to bear on the War Claims Adjustment Board. Although Parliament hasn't passed the Bill, they've gone ahead and sanctioned your claim.'

'Good God!' Sean was stunned. At Acheson's suggestion he had registered a claim for ten thousand pounds, his deposit in the Volkskaas Bank, which had been seized by the Boers at the outbreak of war. He had expected nothing from it, and had promptly forgotten about it. 'They haven't made a full award, have they?'

'Don't be naïve, Courtney.' Acheson chuckled. 'Only twenty per cent against a possible further adjustment once the Bill is through the House. Still, two thousand is better than a poke in the eye with a blunt stick. Here's their cheque. You'll have to sign for it.'

Sean examined the slip of paper with rising delight. It would go a little way towards paying off his loan from Natal Wattle. He looked up quickly. 'And the third item?' he asked.

Acheson slipped a small square of cardboard across the desk. 'My card – and a standing invitation to visit and stay as long as you like whenever you are in London.' He stood up and extended his hand. 'Good luck, Sean. And I'd like to think it isn't good-bye.'

In a rosy state of elation induced by freedom and the prospect of a loving farewell with Candy Rautenbach, Sean stopped the cab first at the railway station to reserve a seat on the following morning's southbound train, and to cable Ada of his homecoming. Then, on to Commissioner Street and the lobby of Candy's Hotel to ask for the proprietress.

'Mrs Rautenbach is resting, sir, and cannot be disturbed,' the clerk informed him.

'Good man!' Sean passed him half a guinea and ignored his squawks of protest as he climbed the marble staircase.

He let himself silently into Candy's suite and crossed to her bedroom. He wanted to surprise her; and there could be no doubt that he succeeded beyond his wildest expectations. Candy Rautenbach was not resting. In fact she was most strenuously employed in the entertainment of a gentleman whose tunic, hanging over the back of one of the gilt and red velvet chairs, showed him to be a subaltern in one of His Majesty's regiments.

Sean supported his subsequent actions on the hypothesis that Candy was his exclusive property. In the flood of righteous indignation that overwhelmed him, he took no account of the fact that his visit was a farewell gesture, that his relationship with Candy had been at best vague and intermittent, and that he was the following morning leaving to propose matrimony to someone else. All he saw was the cuckoo in the nest.

So that no discredit may reflect on the courage of the subaltern or the honour of his regiment, we must remember that his knowledge of Candy's domestic arrangements, if not those of her anatomy, was incomplete. She had been introduced to him as *Mrs Rautenbach* and now in this terrible moment as he returned to reality he assumed that the large and angry man who bore down on the bed roaring like a wounded bull, was the one and only Mr Rautenbach come home from the wars. He made preparation for departure, which began with a rapid descent from the high four-poster bed on the opposite side to that of Sean's approach. In a condition of stark mental clarity induced by a super-abundance of adrenalin in the blood stream, the subaltern became aware of his own nudity which prevented flight into the public gaze, of the fact that Mr Rautenbach's threatening advance made such flight imperative, and finally that Mr Rautenbach wore the uniform and insignia of a full colonel. This last consideration weighed most heavily with him, for despite his age he came from an old and respected family with an impressive record of military service and he understood the decencies and orders of society of which one of the strictest was that you did not unite with the wife of an officer who outranked you.

'Sir,' he said, and drew himself up with dignity. 'I think I can explain.'

'You little bugger!' Sean answered him in a tone that suggested his explanation would have little consequence. Taking the shortest route, which was over the bed, Sean went for him. Candy, who had in these first few seconds been too preoccupied with pulling the coverlets over herself to take any active part in the proceedings, now shrieked and lifted the silk eiderdown in such a way that it wrapped around Sean's boots as he leaped over her, and became tangled in his spurs. Sean fell with a crash that reverberated through the whole building and startled the guests in the lobby below, and he lay for the moment stunned with his feet on the bed and his head and shoulders on the floor.

'Get out!' Candy shouted at the subaltern, as Sean began to stir ominously. Then she gathered up an armful of bedclothes and spread them over Sean, winding him and smothering him.

'Hurry up. For God's sake, hurry!' she entreated as her friend hopped with one leg in his breeches. 'He'll tear you to pieces.' And she pounced on top of the struggling, cursing mount of sheets and blankets.

'Don't worry about the boots,' and the subaltern tucked them under one arm, slung his tunic over his shoulders and placed his helmet on the back of his head.

'Thank you, ma'am,' he said, and then with gallantry, 'I sincerely regret any inconvenience I have caused you. Please give my apologies to your husband.'

'Get out, you fool,' she pleaded clinging desperately to Sean as he heaved and swore. After he had left she stood up and waited for Sean to emerge.

'Where is he? I'll kill him. I'll murder the little bastard!' Sean threw off the bedclothes, scrambled to his feet and glared wildly around him. But the first thing he saw was Candy, and Candy was shaking with laughter. There was a lot of Candy to shake and most of it was white and round and smooth, and even if the laughter was a little hysterical it was still a very pleasing spectacle.

'Why did you stop me?' Sean demanded, but he was fast transferring his interest from the subaltern to Candy's bosom.

'He thought you were my husband,' she gasped.

'The little bastard,' growled Sean.

'He was sweet.' And abruptly she stopped laughing. 'And who the hell are you to come barging in here, anyway? Do you think you own the world and everything in it?'

'You belong to me.'

'Like hell, I do!' Candy exploded. 'Now get out of here, you big lumbering ox.'

'Put some clothes on.' Things were taking an unforeseen turn. Sean had expected her to be guilty and contrite.

'Get out of here,' she yelled, as her temper started to run. Sean had never seen her like this and he only just managed to field the large vase she hurled at his head. Frustrated in her desire to hear breaking china, Candy grabbed another missile, an ornamental mirror, which crashed with satisfying violence against the wall behind him. Her boudoir was furnished in splendid Victorian taste and provided an almost unlimited supply of ammunition. Despite Sean's nimble footwork, he could not remain unscathed for ever and finally he was hit by a gilt-framed picture of some nameless officer. Candy's taste leaned rather heavily towards martial men.

'You little bitch!' roared Sean in pain, and he launched a counter-attack. Candy fled, naked and squealing, but he caught her at the door, lifted her on to his shoulder and carried her kicking to the bed.

'Now, my girl,' he grunted as he arranged her, pink bottom up, across his lap. 'I'm going to teach you some manners.'

The first slap left a perfect red print of his hand upon her chubby cheeks, and stilled her struggles. The second slap had considerably less force behind it, and the third was an affectionate pat. But Candy was sobbing pitifully.

With his right hand raised, Sean realized with dismay that for the first time in his life *he was striking a woman!* 'Candy!' He spoke uncertainly, and was amazed that she twisted and sat up in his lap, clasped him about the neck and pressed a damp cheek against him.

Words welled up in his throat, words of apology, a plea for forgiveness – but his good sense prevented them from emerging and instead he demanded huskily, 'Are you sorry for your behaviour?'

Candy gulped and nodded shakily. 'Please forgive me, darling. I deserved that.' And her fingers fluttered at his throat and across his lips. 'Please forgive me, Sean. I'm so terribly sorry.'

They ate dinner in bed that evening. In the early morning, while Sean soaked lazily in the sunken bath and the hot water stung the scratches on his back, they talked.

'I'm catching the morning train home, Candy. I want to be home for Christmas.'

'Oh, Sean! Can't you stay – just a few days?'

'No.'

'When will you come back?'

'I don't know.'

There was a long silence before she spoke again.

'I take it then that I am not included in your plans for the future?'

'You are my friend, Candy,' he protested.

'Now, isn't that nice.' And she stood up. 'I'll order your breakfast.'

In the bedroom she paused and regarded herself slowly in the full-length mirror. The blue silk of her gown matched the blue of her eyes, but at this time of the day there were tiny creases in the skin of her throat.

I am rich, she thought, *I don't have to be lonely*. She walked on past the mirror.

Chapter Sixty

Sean walked slowly up the gravel drive towards the Goldberg mansion. He walked between an avenue of 'Pride of India' trees and around him the green lawns climbed in a series of terraces towards the rococo façade of the house. It was a morning of drowsy warmth and the doves in the Pride of Indias cooed sleepily.

Faintly from among the ornamental shrubbery he heard the tinkle of laughter. He stopped and listened to the sound of it. Suddenly he was shy, loth to meet her again – unable to know how she would receive him for she had not replied to his letter.

At last he left the drive and crossed the carpet of lawn until he reached the lip of an amphitheatre. In the bowl below him stood a miniature replica of the Parthenon temple. Clean, white, marble columns in the sunshine, with a circular fish-pond like a moat around it. He could see the shapes of carp gliding slowly through the green water below the lily pads. The lily blossoms were white and gold and purple.

Ruth sat upon the raised marble edge of the pond. She was dressed all in black from her throat to her toes, but her arms were bared and she held them out and cried:

'Walk, Storm. Walk here to me.'

Ten paces away, her solid bottom solidly planted on the lawn, Storm Friedman regarded her mother seriously from under a bang of dark hair.

'Come on, baby,' Ruth urged her, and very deliberately the child leaned forward. Slowly she elevated her plump posterior until it was pointed towards the sky, displaying a laced and be-ribboned pair of pantaloons beneath the short skirt. She remained like that for a few seconds and then, with an effort, came up on to her feet and stood balanced precariously on her fat, pink legs. Ruth clapped her hands in spontaneous delight, and Storm smiled in triumph, displaying four large white teeth.

'Come here to Mummy,' laughed Ruth and Storm completed a dozen unsteady paces before abandoning this form of locomotion as impractical. Dropping to her hands and knees she finished the course at a canter.

'You cheated!' Ruth accused, and jumped up to catch her under the arms and swing her high. Storm squealed ecstatically. 'More!' she commanded. 'More!'

Sean wanted to laugh with them. He wanted to run down to them and gather them both in his arms. For suddenly he knew that here was the whole meaning of life, his excuse for existing. A woman and a child. *His* woman, and *his* child.

Ruth looked up and saw him. She froze with the child held to her chest. Her face was without expression as she watched him come down the steps into the amphitheatre.

'Hello.' He stopped in front of her, twisting his hat awkwardly between his hands.

'Hello, Sean,' she whispered, then the corners of her mouth lifted in a shy, uncertain smile and she flushed. 'You took so long. I thought you weren't coming.'

A great grin split Sean's face and he stepped forward, but at that moment Storm, who had been staring at him with solemn curiosity, began a series of convulsive leaps accompanied by yells of:

'Man! Man!' Her feet were anchored against Ruth's stomach, which gave power to her thrusts. She leaned out towards Sean determined to reach him, and Ruth was taken by surprise. Sean had to drop his hat and catch Storm before she fell.

'More! More!' yelled Storm, continuing to bounce in Sean's arms. One of the few things Sean knew about babies was that they have a soft pulsing spot on the top of their heads which is very vulnerable, so he clung to his daughter in terror that he drop her and in equal terror that he crush her. Until Ruth stopped laughing, relieved him of his burden and said,

'Come up to the house. You're just in time for tea.'

They crossed the lawn slowly, each of them holding one of Storm's hands, so that the child need no longer concentrate on balancing and could devote her whole attention to the fascinating manner in which her feet kept alternately appearing and disappearing under her.

'Sean. There is one thing I have to know before anything else.' Ruth was looking down at her child, not at him. 'Did you . . .' She paused. 'Saul – Could you have prevented what happened to him. I mean, you didn't . . .' Her voice trailed off.

'No, I didn't,' he said harshly.

'Swear it to me, Sean. As you hope for salvation, swear it to me,' she pleaded.

'I swear it to you. I swear on . . .' He sought for an oath, not on his own life, for that was not strong enough. 'I swear on the life of our daughter.'

And she sighed with relief. 'That was why I did not write to you. I had to know first.'

He wanted to tell her than that he was taking her away with him, he wanted to tell her about Lion Kop and the huge empty house that waited for her to make it into a home. But he knew it was not the moment – not immediately after they had spoken of Saul. He would wait.

He waited while he was introduced to the Goldbergs and was left with them when Ruth took the child into the house to deliver her into the care of the nurse. She returned and he made small conversation during tea and tried not to let them see it in his eyes when he looked at Ruth.

He waited until they were alone together on the lawn and then he blurted it out:

'Ruth, you and Storm are coming home with me.'

She stopped over a rosebush and picked a butter-yellow blossom, then with a slight frown on her face she broke each of the tiny red thorns off the stem before she looked at him.

'Am I, Sean?' she asked innocently, but he should have been warned by the chips of diamond brightness in her eyes.

'Yes,' he said. 'We can be married within the next few days. It will take that long to arrange a special licence and for you to pack. Then I'll take you to Lion Kop – I haven't told you about . . .'

'Damn you,' she said softly. 'Damn your conceit. Damn your arrogance.' And he gawked at her.

'You stroll in with your whip in your hand, crack it once and expect me to bark and jump through the hoop.' She was working herself into a fury now. 'I don't know what dealings you've had with women before – but I for one am not a camp-follower, nor do I intend being treated like one. Did it ever occur to you for one single second that I might not be prepared to accept this favour you intend bestowing on me? How long did it take you to forget that I have been a widow for three short months? What supreme lack of perception made you believe I would run from one man's grave and throw myself into your condescending arms?'

'But, Ruth, I love you.' He tried to stop her outburst, but she shouted at him.

'Then prove it, damn you. Prove it by being gentle. Prove it by treating me like a woman and not a chattel – by *understanding*.'

Now his surprise gave way to an anger every bit as intense as hers, and in his turn he shouted at her.

'You weren't so bloody fussy on the night of the storm – or afterwards!'

As though he had struck her, she stepped back a pace and the mutilated rosebud dropped from her hand.

'You swine,' she whispered. 'Get out, and don't come back.'

'Your servant, ma'am.' He clapped his hat on to his head, swung round and strode away across the lawn. When he reached the gravel drive his steps slowed and he stopped and wrestled with his anger and his pride.

Then slowly he turned. The lawn was an empty sweep of smooth green. She was gone.

Ruth ran up the wide marble staircase, but by the time she reached her bedroom window he was half-way down the drive. From the height of the second floor his figure was foreshortened so he appeared massive, and his dark suit stood out clearly against the pale gravel of the drive. He reached the gates and stopped, she leaned forward eagerly across the sill of the window so he could see her more easily when he turned to look back. She saw him deliberately light a long black cheroot, flick away the match, adjust the hat on his head, square his shoulders – and walk away.

In disbelief she stared at the twin columns of the gate, and the dark green hawthorn hedge behind which he had disappeared. Then slowly she left the window and crossed to the bed and sat down.

'Why didn't he understand?' she asked softly.

She knew she would cry later, in the night when the real loneliness began.

Chapter Sixty-one

Sean returned to Ladyburg in the middle of a misty Natal winter's day. As the train huffed over the rim of the escarpment, he stood on the balcony of his coach and looked out at the vast green stain upon the hills of Lion Kop. The sight of it moved him, but his elation was toned with dark colours.

This is the middle of the way. This year I will be forty-one years old. Out of all that striving and folly something must have emerged. Let me total my assets.

In cash I have a little over two thousand pounds (compliments of the War Claims Adjustment Board). In land I have fifteen thousand acres, with an option to purchase as many more. I have ten thousand acres of standing wattle which, in another year, will be ready for cutting. My loans against this are heavy but not oppressive, so I am a wealthy man.

In things of the flesh I have a number of grey hairs, a fine collection of scars and a broken nose. But I can still lift and carry a two-hundred-pound sack of mealies under each arm, I can eat half a young sheep at a sitting; without field-glasses I can count the number of head in a herd of springbok at a distance of two miles, and Candy who knows about these things made no complaint about my stamina. I am not yet old.

Apart from these things I have a son who belongs to me (and a son and a daughter who do not). Although I have lost the best of them, I have friends – perhaps more friends than enemies.

But as important as any of these is the purpose and direction I have at least achieved. I know what I want. My course is plotted and the wind stands fair.

These are my assets. These are mine to use and enjoy.

What are my liabilities? Borrowed money, the hatred of a brother and a son, and Ruth.

Ruth is gone! Ruth is gone! Clattered the crossties under the coach, Ruth is gone! Ruth is gone! They mocked him.

Sean scowled and forcibly changed the words in his mind.

'The wind is fair! The wind is fair!'

Over the months that followed Sean used his whole energy in the development of Lion Kop. He planned the cutting of his standing bark and decided to reap one-third of it a year before maturity, and another third in each of the subsequent two years. To replace it he used his two thousand pounds not to pay off his loans, but to plant the rest of his land to wattle. When this was done he had to keep busy. He bought himself a theodolite and a book of instruction in elementary survey, and mapped his lands, laid out his block of trees, pegged new roads for access to his plantations when the cutting began.

Once again he had nothing to do, so he went to see Dennis Petersen and spent a long day arguing the purchase of Mahobo's Kloof Ranch on which he had bought an option. He had no cash, and Jackson at Natal Wattle baulked at the suggestion of further loans. When Dennis refused to consider extended terms of payment, Sean called on Ronny Pye at the Ladyburg Banking & Trust. It was a forlorn chance and Sean was genuinely surprised when Ronny gave him a cup of coffee and a cigar, then listened politely to his proposition.

'You're putting it all on one horse, Sean,' Ronny warned him.

'There's only one horse in this race. It can't lose.'

'Very well.' Ronny nodded. 'Here's what I will do with you. I will advance you the full purchase price of Mahobo's Kloof, plus a further ten thousand pounds to develop it. In return you will give me a first bond on Mahobo's Kloof, and a second bond on Lion Kop after Natal Wattle Company's loan.'

Sean took it. A week later Ronny Pye called on Jackson in Pietermaritzburg. After the preliminary sparring Ronny asked him:

'Are you quite happy about those Notes you have out to Courtney?'

'The security is good.' Jackson hesitated. 'But he seems to be going a little wild.'

'I might be willing to take them over for you,' Ronny hinted delicately, and Jackson rubbed his nose thoughtfully to mask his relief.

Happily Sean flung his army of Zulus at the virgin grasslands of Mahobo's Kloof. He delighted in the long ranks of sweating, singing blackmen as they opened the rich, red earth and placed the fragile little saplings.

Dirk was Sean's constant companion in these days. His attendance in the schoolhouse became more sporadic. Convinced that Dirk would never become a scholar, Sean tacitly condoned the gastric disturbances that prevented Dirk leaving for school in the mornings, but cleared miraculously a few minutes later and allowed him to follow Sean out into the plantations. Dirk aped Sean's stance, his seat in the saddle, and his long reaching walk. He listened carefully to Sean's words and repeated them later without omitting the oaths. In the late afternoons they hunted quail and pheasant and guinea-fowl along the slopes of the escarpment. On Sunday when Sean rode across to his neighbours for a bush buck shoot, or a poker session, or merely to drink brandy and talk, then Dirk went with him.

Despite Sean's protest, Ada returned with her girls to the cottage on Protea Street. So the homestead of Lion Kop was a vast empty shell. Sean and Dirk used only three of the fifteen rooms, and even these were sparsely furnished. No carpets on the floor, nor pictures on the walls. A few leather-thonged chairs, iron bedstead, plain deal tables, and a cupboard or two. Piled in odd corners were the books and fishing-rods; a pair of shotguns and a rifle on the rack beside the fireplace. The yellow-wood floor was unpolished with dust and bits of fluff beneath the chairs and beds, dark stains left by the litter of pointer puppies; and in Dirk's bedroom, which Sean never visited, there was a welter of old socks and soiled shirts, school exercise books and trophies of the hunt.

Sean had no interest in the house. It was a place to eat and sleep, it had a roof to keep the rain out, a fireplace for warmth, and lamplight so that he could indulge his new appetite for reading. With reading glasses purchased from a travelling salesman on his nose, Sean spent his evenings wading through books on politics and travel, economics and surveying, mathematics and medicine, while Dirk, ostensibly preparing his schoolwork, sat across the fireplace from him and watched him avidly. Some nights when Sean was engaged in correspondence, he would forget that Dirk was there and the boy would sit up until after midnight.

Sean was now corresponding with both Jannie Niemand and Jan Paulus Leroux. These two had become a political team in the Transvaal, and were already bringing gentle pressure to bear on Sean. They wanted him to organize the equivalent of their South Africa Party, and to lead it in Natal. Sean hedged. Not yet, perhaps later he told them.

Once a month he received and answered a long letter from John Acheson. Acheson had returned to England and the gratitude of the nation. He was now Lord Caisterbrook and from his seat in the House of Lords he kept Sean informed of the temper and mood of the English people and the affairs of State.

Sometimes, more often than was healthy, Sean thought about Ruth. Then he became angry and sad and desperately lonely. Slowly it would build up within him until he could not sleep, then he would go down at night to a friendly widow who lived alone in one of the gangers' cottages beside the new railways yards.

Yet he counted himself happy, until that day at the beginning of September 1903, when he received an embossed card. It said simply:

Miss Storm Friedman requests the pleasure of the company of Colonel Sean Courtney, D.S.O., D.C.M., at a party to celebrate her third birthday. 4 p.m., September 26th.

  R.S.V.P.
The Golds, Chase Valley,
  Pietermaritzburg.

In the bottom right-hand corner was an inky finger-print about the size of a threepenny-piece.

Chapter Sixty-two

On the 24th, Sean left by train for Pietermaritzburg. Dirk came back from the station with Ada to his old room in the cottage on Protea Street.

That night Mary lay awake and listened to him cry for his father. Only a thin wooden partition separated them. Ada's cottage had not been designed as a workshop and hostel for her girls. She had solved the problem by enclosing the wide, back veranda and dividing it into cubicles each large enough to hold a bed, a cupboard and a washstand. One of these was Mary's and tonight Dirk was in the cubicle next to hers.

For an hour she lay and listened to him weep, praying quietly that he would exhaust himself and fall asleep. Twice she thought he had done so, but each time after a silence of only a few minutes the tear-muffled sobs started again. Each of them drove needles of physical pain deep into her chest, so that she lay rigid in her bed with her fists clenched until they ached.

Dirk had become the central theme of her existence. He was the one bright tower in the desolation. She loved him with obsessive devotion, for he was so beautiful, so young and clean and straight. She loved the feel of his skin and the springy silk of his hair. When she looked at Dirk her own face did not matter. Her own scarred ruin of a face did not matter.

The months she had been separated from him had been an agony and a dark lonely time. But now he was back and once again he needed her comfort. She slipped from her bed and stood taut with her love, her whole attitude portraying her compassion. The moonlight that filtered in through the mosquito-screened window treated her with the same compassion. It toned down the mottled cicatrice that coarsened the planes of her face and it showed them as they might have been. Her twenty-year-old body beneath the thin nightgown was slender but full-breasted, innocent of the marks that marred her face. A young body, a soft body clad in moon-luminous white like that of an angel.

Dirk sobbed again and she went to him.

'Dirk,' she whispered as she knelt beside his bed. 'Dirk, please don't cry, please, my darling.'

Dirk gulped explosively and rolled away from her, folding his arms across his face.

'Shh! my darling. It's all right now.' She began to stroke his hair. Her touch evoked a fresh outburst of grief from him, liquid choking grief that spluttered and throbbed in the darkness.

'Oh Dirk, please. . . .' And she went into his bed. The sheets were warm and moist where he had lain. She gathered him, held his hot body to her bosom and began to rock him in her arms.

Her own loneliness at last overwhelmed her. Her voice took on a husky quality as she whispered to him. She strained to him – her need growing much greater than his.

One last convulsive sob and Dirk was silent. She felt the tension go out of his back and out of his hard round buttocks that were pressed into her stomach. Straining him even closer, her fingers moved down across his cheek to caress his throat.

Dirk turned towards her, turning within the circle of her arms. She felt his chest heave and subside as he sighed, and his voice stifled with misery.

'He doesn't love me. He went away and left me.'

'I love you, Dirk,' she whispered. 'I love you – we all love you, darling.' And she kissed his eyes and his cheeks and his mouth. The taste of his tears was hot salt.

Dirk sighed again and bowed his head until it was on her bosom. She felt his face nuzzling into the softness and her hands went to the back of his head and drew it closer.

'Dirkie. . . .' Her voice dried up in the strange new heat within her.

In the morning Dirk woke slowly, but with a feeling of wonder. He lay a while and thought about it, unable at first to place the formless shimmering sense of well-being that possessed him.

Then he heard Mary moving about behind the partition of her cubicle. The gurgle and splash of water poured from jug to basin, the rustle of cloth. Finally, the sound of her door softly opened and closed, and her steps moving away towards the kitchen.

The events of the previous evening came back to him, crisp and stark in every detail. Not fully understood, but looming large to overshadow all else in his mind.

He threw the sheets aside and lifted himself on both elbows, drew up his nightshirt and contemplated his body as though he had never seen it before.

He heard footsteps approaching. Quickly he covered himself, pulled the bedclothes over and feigned sleep.

Mary came in quietly and placed a cup of coffee, with a rusk in the saucer, on the bedside table.

Dirk opened his eyes and looked at her.

'You're awake,' she said.

'Yes.'

'Dirk . . .' she started, and then she blushed. It mottled the puckered skin of her cheeks. Her voice fell to a whisper, scratchy with her shame. 'You mustn't ever tell anybody. You must forget about . . . what happened.'

Dirk did not reply.

'Promise me, Dirkie, Please promise me.'

He nodded slowly. Not trusting himself to speak, his throat filled with a knowledge of domination over her.

'It was wrong, Dirkie. It was a terrible thing. We mustn't even think about it again.'

She walked to the door.

'Mary.'

'Yes.' She stopped without turning, her whole body poised like a bird on the point of flight.

'I won't tell anyone – if you come again tonight.'

'No,' she hissed violently.

'Then, I'll tell Granny.'

'No. Oh, Dirkie. You wouldn't.' She was beside the bed now, kneeling, reaching for his hand. 'You mustn't – you mustn't. You promised me.'

'Will you come?' he asked softly. She peered into his face, into the serene perfection of warm brown skin and green eyes with the black silk of his hair curling on to the forehead.

'I can't – it's a terrible, terrible thing that we did.'

'Then I'll tell,' he said.

She stood up and walked slowly out of the cubicle, her shoulders slumped forward in the attitude of surrender. He knew she would come.

Chapter Sixty-three

In a hired carriage Sean arrived punctually at the Goldberg residence. He arrived like a column of wise men from the east. The seats of the carriage were piled with fancy-wrapped packages. However, Sean's limited knowledge of a three-year-old female's tastes were reflected in his choice of gifts. Every single package contained a doll. There were large china dolls that closed their eyes when reclining, small rag dolls with blonde plaits, a doll that passed water, a doll that squawked when its stomach was squeezed, dolls in a dozen national costumes and dolls in swaddling clothes.

Mbejane followed the carriage leading the gift which Sean considered a master stroke of originality. It was a piebald Shetland pony, complete with a hand-fashioned English saddle and a tiny martingale and reins.

The gravel drive was crowded with carriages. Sean was forced to walk the last hundred yards, his arms filled with presents. Under these circumstances navigation was a little difficult. He took a fix on the hideously ornamented roof of the mansion, which he could just see over the top of his load, and set off blind across the lawns. He was aware of the continuous and piercing shrieking which grew louder as he proceeded, and finally of an insistent tugging on his right trouser leg. He stopped.

'Are those *my* presents?' a voice from somewhere above the level of his knee asked. He craned his head out to one side and looked down into the upturned face of a miniature Madonna. Large shining eyes in an oval of innocent purity framed with shiny dark curls. Sean's heart flipped over.

'That depends what your name is,' he hedged.

'My name is *Miss* Storm Friedman of the Golds, Chase Valley, Pietermaritzburg. *Now* are they my presents?'

Sean bent his knees until he squatted with his face almost on a level with that of the Madonna.

'Many happy returns of the day, Miss Friedman,' he said.

'Oh goody!' She fell on the packages, trembling with excitement while from the mass of fifty children who ringed them in the shrieking continued unabated.

Storm demolished the wrappings in very short order, using her teeth when her fingers were inadequate for the task. One of her small guests attempted to assist her, but she flew at him like a panther kitten with a cry of 'They're *my* presents!' He retired hastily.

At last she sat in a litter of wrappings and dolls and pointed at the single remaining package in Sean's hands.

'That one?' she asked.

Sean shook his head. 'No, that one is for your Mummy. But if you look behind you, you might find something else.'

Mbejane, grinning widely, was holding the Shetland. For seconds Storm was too overcome to speak and then with a sound like a steam-whistle she flew to her feet. Deserting her newly adopted children, she ran to the pony. Behind her a flock of small girls descended on the dolls, vultures when a lion leaves the kill.

'Lift me! Lift me!' Storm was hopping with delirious impatience. Sean took her up and the warm, wriggling little body in his hands made his heart flip again. Gently he set her on the saddle, handed her the reins and led the pony towards the house.

A queen riding in state, followed by an army of her attendants, Storm reached the upper terrace.

Ruth was standing beside the delicacy-laden trestle table with the parents of Storm's guests. Sean handed the lead rein to Mbejane. 'Look after her well,' and he crossed the terrace, very conscious of the many adult eyes upon him, thankful for the hour he had spent that morning at the barber's shop, and for the care he had taken with his attire – a brand-new suit of expensive English broadcloth, boots burnished to a gloss, solid gold watch chain across his belly and a white carnation in his buttonhole.

He stopped in front of Ruth and removed his hat. She held out her hand, palm downwards. Sean knew that he was *not* expected to shake that hand.

'Sean, how good of you to come.'

Sean took her hand. It was a measure of his feelings that he bowed to touch it with his lips – a gesture which he considered French, foppish and undignified.

'It was good of you to ask me, Ruth.'

He produced the box from under his arm and held it out to her. She opened it without a word and her cheeks flushed with pleasure when she saw the long-stemmed roses it contained.

'Oh, how sweet of you!' And Sean's heart did its trick again as she smiled full into his eyes, then slipped her hand into the crook of his arm.

'I'd like you to meet some friends of mine.'

That evening when the other guests had left and Storm, prostrated with nervous and physical exhaustion, had been put to bed, Sean stayed on to dinner with the Goldbergs. By now both Ma and Pa Goldberg were fully aware that Sean's interest in Ruth was not on account of his previous friendship with Saul. All afternoon Sean had followed Ruth around the lawns like a huge St Bernard behind a dainty poodle.

During dinner Sean, who was extremely pleased with himself, Ruth, the Goldbergs and life in general, was able to endear himself to Ma Goldberg and also dull Ben Goldberg's suspicions that he was a penniless adventurer. Over brandy and cigars Sean and Ben discussed the ventures on Lion Kop and Mahobo's Kloof. Sean was completely frank about the financial tightrope which he was walking, and Ben was impressed with the magnitude of the gamble and Sean's cold appraisal of the odds. It was just such a *coup* as this that had put Ben Goldberg where he was today. It made him feel nostalgic and vaguely sentimental of *the old days*, so that when they went through to join the ladies he patted Sean's arm and called him 'My boy'.

On the front steps, while he was preparing to leave, Sean asked, 'May I call on you again, Ruth?' and she answered,

'I'd like that very much.

Now began what was for Sean a novel form of courtship. To his surprise he found he rather enjoyed it. Every Friday night he would entrain for Pietermaritzburg and install himself in the White Horse Hotel. From this base he conducted his campaign. There were dinner parties, either at The Golds or with Ruth's friends or at one of the local hostelries where Sean played host. There were balls and dances, days at the races, picnics and rides over the surrounding hills with Storm on her Shetland bouncing along between them. During Sean's absences from Ladyburg, Dirk moved into the cottage on Protea Street and Sean was relieved that he seemed to accept it with better grace.

The time arrived when at last the first blocks of wattle were ready for the axe. Sean determined to use this as an excuse to inveigle Ruth away to Ladyburg. The Goldbergs froze up solid at the suggestion and only thawed when Sean produced a written invitation from Ada for Ruth to be her guest for the week. Sean went on to explain that it was to be a celebration of his first cutting of bark, which would begin at the end of the week, and that thereafter he could not leave Ladyburg for months.

Ma Goldberg, who was secretly delighted at having Storm all to herself for a whole week, exerted a subtle influence on Ben, and very grudgingly he gave his approval.

Sean decided that Ruth would be treated like visiting Royalty – the grand climax to his suit.

Chapter Sixty-four

As one of the biggest landowners in the district and because of his war honours, Sean ranked high in the complicated social structure of Ladyburg. Therefore, preparations for Ruth's visit produced an epidemic of excitement and curiosity that affected the entire Ladyburg district. The flood of invitations he released sent women to their wardrobes and sewing-baskets, while the outlying farmers begged accommodation from relatives and friends nearer town. Other leading members of the community, jealous of their social status, road out to Lion Kop with offers to provide entertainment on those three days of the week which Sean had left empty. Reluctantly Sean agreed – he had private plans for those three days.

Ada and her girls were inundated with orders for new clothing, but they still made one afternoon free and came up to the Lion Kop homestead armed with brooms and dusters and tins of polish. Sean and Dirk were driven from the house. They spent that afternoon riding over Sean's estate, looking for the best place to hold the big bush-buck shoot which would be the climax of the week.

With a gang of his Zulus, Mbejane hacked down the jungle of undergrowth around the homestead and dug the barbecue pits.

The Village Management Board met in secret conclave, infected by the general excitement and armed with strict instructions from their wives, they voted unanimously for a civic reception of Ruth Friedman at the station and a formal Ball that night. Dennis Petersen, who had Sean's consent to a barbecue on the night of Ruth's arrival, was placated with the promise that he would be allowed to make a short speech of welcome at the station.

Sean called upon Ronny Pye and was again surprised when Ronny agreed cheerfully to a further loan of one thousand pounds. Ronny signed the cheque with the satisfied air of a spider putting the final thread into his web, and Sean left immediately for Pietermaritzburg to visit a jeweller. He returned home five hundred pounds poorer, with a packet in his breast-pocket that contained a huge square-cut diamond set in a band of platinum. Dirk was at the station to meet him. Sean took one look at him and ordered him to the village barber.

The night before Ruth's arrival Sean and Mbejane fell upon Dirk in a surprise attack and dragged him protesting to the bathroom. Sean was astounded by the large quantities of foreign matter that he removed from Dirk's ears, and by the way in which Dirk's suntan dissolved so readily under an application of soap.

The following morning as her railway coach ground to a jerky halt in front of the station building, Ruth looked down on a mass of strangers surrounding the roped-off area in front of her. Only one family was not represented in the crowd, which included the young ladies and gentlemen of Ladyburg High School in their church clothes.

She stood uncertainly on the balcony of the coach and heard the hum of appreciative comment and speculation. Ruth had relieved the plain black mourning with a wide ribbon of pink around the crown of her hat, pink gloves and gauzy pink veil, which shrouded her face in a misty and mysterious fashion. It was very effective.

Convinced that there was some misunderstanding, Ruth was about to withdraw into the coach, when she noticed a deputation approaching along the roped-off passageway. It was headed by Sean and she recognized the thunderous scowl he wore as his expression of acute embarrassment. She felt an inexplicable urge to burst out laughing, but managed to keep it to a smile as Sean climbed up on to the balcony and took her hand.

'Ruth, I'm terribly sorry. I didn't plan all this – things got a little out of control,' he whispered hurriedly, then he muttered an introduction to Dennis Petersen, who had ponderously mounted the steps behind him. Now Dennis turned to face the crowd and spread his arms in the gesture that Moses might have employed on his return from the mountain.

'Ladies and gentlemen, citizens of Ladyburg, friends—' he began, and from the way he said it Sean knew he was good for another half-hour. He glanced sideways at Ruth and saw that she was smiling. It came as a surprise to him when he realized she was enjoying herself. Sean relaxed a little.

'It gives me great pleasure to welcome to our fair town this lovely lady, friend of one of our foremost . . .' Ruth's fingers found their way surreptitiously into Sean's hand, and Sean relaxed a little more. He saw the wide brim of Ada's hat standing out in the crowd and he smiled at her. She replied with a nod of approval towards Ruth.

By some curious twist of oratory, Dennis was now talking about the new water filtration plant and its benefit to the community.

'—But, my friends, this is only the first of a series of projects planned by your Board.' He paused significantly.

'Hear, hear,' Sean interjected loudly and clapped his hands. The applause was taken up by the crowd, and Sean stepped past Dennis to the rail of the balcony.

'On behalf of Mrs Friedman and myself, I thank you for your friendship and your hospitality.' Then, leaving Dennis on the balcony making helpless little movements with his hands, and silently opening and closing his mouth, Sean spirited Ruth away, ran her through a rapid fire series of introductions and handshakes, gathered Ada and Dirk and got them all into the carriage.

While Sean and Mbejane fussed with the luggage, Ruth and Ada settled their skirts and adjusted their hats before meeting each other's eyes again.

'Although Sean warned me, I didn't expect you to be quite so lovely,' Ada said. Flushing with pleasure and relief, Ruth leaned impulsively across to touch her arm.

'I've been longing to meet you, Mrs Courtney.'

'If you promise to call me Ada, then I'll call you Ruth.'

Sean scrambled into the carriage, flustered and perspiring. 'Let's get the hell out of here.'

That week was to be remembered for many years. The usual Christmas festivities paled into insignificance beside it.

Matrons competed fiercely to provide food, mountains of it, prepared from their closely guarded recipe books. In between cooking they conducted old feuds, began new ones and worried about their daughters.

The young bucks competed on the gymkhana and polo field, then again on the dance floor. Dirk Courtney won the junior tent-pegging event. Then against a visiting team from Pietermaritzburg College he captained the school rugby team to an inglorious 30-0 defeat.

The young ladies competed with equal ferocity, covering it with giggles and blushes. The success of their efforts was measured in the outbreak of betrothals and scandals during the week.

The older men smiled indulgently, until, fortified with bottled spirit, they discarded their dignity and capered and panted around the dance floor. There were three bouts of fisticuffs – but these were between old enemies and none of them were really worth watching.

Only one family held aloof from the festivities. There were many of the young ladies who missed Michael Courtney.

During one of the infrequent lulls of the week, Sean managed to separate Ruth from Ada, and take her out to the homestead at Lion Kop. She moved silently through the empty rooms, appraising each with narrowed thoughtful eyes while Sean hovered anxiously behind her, certain that her silence was disapproval. In fact, Ruth was in ecstasy; a shell, a magnificent shell of a house, with no trace of another woman in it, waiting for her to bring it to life. She could imagine exactly the curtains she wanted, her Persian carpets sent down by Uncle Isaac from Pretoria and now in storage, would look just right once she had the yellow-wood floors polished to a gloss. The kitchen, of course, would have to be completely rebuilt – with a new double Agar stove. The bedroom . . .

Unable to contain himself, Sean blurted out:

'Well, do you like it?'

She turned slowly to him, the mists of thought clearing from her eyes.

'Oh, Sean! It's the most beautiful house in all the world.'

In this emotional moment, Sean put forward the proposition he had planned for that evening.

'Ruth, will you marry me?'

And Ruth, who had planned to hesitate and ask for a little time to consider, replied instantly:

'Oh, yes please!'

She was truly impressed with the ring.

Chapter Sixty-five

The finale to the week was Sean Courtney's bush-buck shoot.

Sean and Dirk arrived at Protea Cottage with the dawn. They were dressed in rough hunting clothes and the leather gun-cases lay on the floor of the mule-wagon under Sean's feet. It took nearly fifteen minutes for Sean to transfer Ruth, Ada and her girls from the cottage to the carriage. In the same way a man might drive a flock of chickens towards the door of a henhouse. He would get them all moving slowly in front of him, down the path towards the carriage, clucking and fussing. Almost there when suddenly one of them would shriek softly and double back towards the cottage for a forgotten parasol or work-basket and the general movement would break down again.

The third time this happened Sean felt something snap inside his head. He bellowed. A vast hush fell over the ladies and two of them looked as though they might cry.

'Now don't get worked up, dear.' Ada tried to soothe him.

'I am not getting worked up.' Sean's voice quivered with the effort of restraint. 'But if everybody is not in the carriage by the count of ten – then I might easily get that way.'

They were all seated by the count of five and he drove out to the stockpens – a very ruffled rooster.

Carriages and mule-wagons carrying the entire population of the Ladyburg district were waiting in a disorderly tangle in the field beside the stockpen. Sean trotted past in a babble of greeting and comment. One at a time the waiting carriages wheeled into line behind him and the long convoy wound out towards Mahobo's Kloof Farm. The big shoot had begun.

In the middle of the line someone was playing a concertina and the singing started. It spread to each carriage in turn and blended with the sound of wheels and hooves and laughter.

Gradually Sean's irritation smoothed out. Ada's girls were singing *Boland Se Nooinentje* in the back seat. Dirk had jumped down from the carriage and with half a dozen of the youngsters from the village ran ahead of the horses. Ruth's hand touched Sean's leg uncertainly and as he turned and grinned at her he saw the relief in her answering smile.

'What a beautiful day, Sean.'

'Sorry I nearly spoiled it—' he answered.

'Oh, nonsense!' She moved closer to him and suddenly he was happy. All the preparation was worth it. Beside him Ruth laughed softly.

'What's the joke?' Sean reached out and took her hand.

'No joke. I just felt like laughing,' she answered. 'Look how green everything is.' She said it to distract him, to make him look away so that she could study his face. The subterfuge worked.

'The land seems so young now.' His eyes, as he looked at it, took on that gentleness she knew so well. By now she knew many of his moods and she was learning how to induce or redirect each of them. He was such a simple man, yet in that simplicity lay his strength. He is like a mountain, she thought. You know how it will be with the sun on it in the early morning. You know that when the wind is in the south there will be mist covering the crest, and in the evening the shadows will fall in certain patterns across the slopes and the gorges will look dark and blue. Yet also you know the shape of the mountain is unchanged, that it will never change.

'I love you, my mountain,' she whispered, and anticipated the startled expression before it flashed across his face.

'Hey?'

'I love you, my man,' she amended.

'Oh! I love you too.'

And now he is vaguely embarrassed. Oh, God, I could eat him! If I were to reach over and kiss him now in front of everybody . . .! Secretly she savoured the idea.

'What devilment are you planning?' he demanded gruffly. He wasn't supposed to read her so accurately. Taken off balance she stared at him. Suddenly the mountain had shown that it understood exactly the way she felt when she looked at it.

'Nothing,' she denied in confusion. 'I wasn't . . .' Before she realized fully what he was about, he had turned half-way in his seat towards her and lifted her bodily into his lap.

'Sean, no!' she gasped and then her protests were muffled. She heard the laughter of Ada's girls, the hoots of encouragement and applause from the other carriages, and she kicked and struggled, pushing with one hand against his chest and trying to keep her hat on with the other.

By the time he replaced her on the seat beside him, her hair had come down behind, her hat was off and her cheeks and ears were flaming red. She had been very thoroughly kissed.

'Nice shot, Sean!'

'Author! Author!'

'Arrest that man!' The cries and the laughter added to her confusion.

'You're terrible!' Ruth used her hat as a screen behind which she tried to control her blushes. 'In front of all those people, too!'

'That should keep you out of mischief for a while, me lass!'

And suddenly she wasn't so sure of the shape of her mountain.

The cavalcade turned off along the rough track from the main road, splashed through the drift, climbed the far bank and spread out among the trees. Servants, who had been waiting since the previous evening, ran to their masters' horses as they halted. Each vehicle disgorged a noisy blast of children and dogs, and then a more dignified trickle of adults. The women moved without hesitation towards the two huge marquees that had been erected among the trees, while the men unloaded the gun-cases and began assembling their weapons.

Still sitting on the front seat of the wagon, Sean opened the leather case at his feet and while his hands automatically fitted the barrels into the breech piece of his shotgun he allowed himself to review his preparations with a certain amount of satisfaction.

He had selected this site not only for the cool grove of syringa trees which provided shade above and a soft carpet of fallen leaves below, nor for the proximity of the tinkling stream where all the animals could be watered, but also because it was situated within fifteen minutes' walk of the first beat.

Days before a gang of Zulus working under Mbejane had cleared out all the undergrowth beneath the trees, had erected the marquee tents and the trestle tables, dug the cooking pits and even built two grass-walled pit latrines discreetly out of view of the main camp.

Huge log fires were burning in the cooking pits now, but by noon they would have burned down to glowing coal beds. The trestle tables about which the women had already begun working were laden with food. There was a great deal of activity going on in that direction at the moment – most of it talking.

From the other wagons men were starting to drift towards him, buckling on their cartridge belts, hefting shotguns, chatting together nonchalantly in an attempt to disguise their excitement. Under instruction from Sean, Dirk had assembled a rabble of those males who were too young to handle shotguns but too old to stay with the women. These were making no effort to hide *their* excitement. Armed with *sikelas* (the Zulu fighting sticks) they were showing every indication of getting out of hand. Already one small boy was weeping loudly and massaging the welt he had received from a playful *sikela*.

'All right – shut up, all of you,' Sean shouted 'Dirk will take you up to the beaters. But remember! Once the hunt starts, keep in the line and listen to what you're told. If I catch anybody running about or getting ahead of the line – I'll personally wallop the tar out of him. Do you understand?' It was a long speech to shout and Sean ended with his face flushed ferociously. This gave weight to his words and resulted in a respectful chorus of:

'Yes, Mr Courtney.'

'Off you go, then.'

Whooping, racing each other they poured away through the trees and a comparative peace descended on the camp.

'My God, let alone bush buck, that lot would drive elephant, buffalo and lion panic-stricken ahead of them,' observed Dennis Petersen dryly. 'How about our positions, Sean?'

Aware that he had their complete attention, Sean drew the moment out a little.

'We are going to drive the Elands' Kloof first,' he announced. 'Mbejane and two hundred Zulus are waiting at the head of the Kloof for the signal. The guns will take station at the tail of the Kloof.' Sean paused.

'How about our positions?'

'Patience. Patience.' Sean chided them. 'I know I shouldn't have to repeat the safety rules, but . . .' and he immediately went on to do so. 'No rifles – shotguns only. You'll shoot only in an arc of 45 degrees directly ahead of you – no passing shots to either side. Especially you, Reverend!' That gentleman, who was notoriously trigger-happy, looked suitably abashed.

'My whistle will mean the beaters are too close – all guns up and unloaded immediately.'

'It's getting late, Sean.'

'Let's get on with it.'

'Right,' Sean agreed. 'I'll take centre gun.' There was a murmur of agreement. That was fair enough, the plum to the man who provided the hunt, no one could grudge that. 'On my left flank in this order, Reverend Smiley – since the Almighty will obviously send most of the game his way, I might as well profit by it.' A burst of laughter as Smiley wavered between horror at the blasphemy and delight at his own good fortune. 'Then Ronny Pye, Dennis Petersen, Ian Vermaak, Gerald and Tony Erasmus (you two fight it out in a brotherly fashion), Nick . . .' Sean read from the list in his hand. This in strict order of seniority was the social register of Ladyburg, a proper and exact balancing of wealth and influence, ofpopularity and age. Apart from placing himself in the centre of the line, Sean had not taken much part in the preparation of the list – quite correctly Ada had not trusted his sense of social perception.

'That takes care of the left flank.' Sean looked up from the list. He had been so engrossed in reading that he had not sensed the air of tension and expectancy which had fallen over his audience. A single horseman had crossed the drift and walked his magnificent thoroughbred into the camp. He had dismounted quietly and servants had led his horse away. Now, carrying a shotgun, he was walking towards Sean's wagon.

Sean looked up and saw him. He stared in surprise, while slowly elation mounted within him until it reached his face in a wide grin.

'Garry, glad you could make it!' he called out spontaneously, but Garry's face remained without expression. He nodded a curt greeting. At least he's come, exulted Sean. This is the first overture. Now it's up to me.

'You can take the first position on my right, Garry.'

'Thank you.' Now Garry smiled, but it was a curiously cold grimace and he turned away to talk with the nearest man. A small shiver of disappointment moved the crowd. They had expected something spectacular to happen. All of them knew of the feud between the Courtney brothers and the mystery that surrounded it. But now, with a feeling of anti-climax they turned their attention back to Sean's reading. Sean finished and jumped down from the wagon, and immediately the crowd moved away. Sean sought Garrick and saw him far ahead near the head of the long file of men that was strung out along the footpath that led to Elands' Kloof.

The file moved fast as the hunters stepped out eagerly. Unless he ran, Sean knew he would not be able to pass the men ahead of him and catch up with Garry. I'll wait until we reach the beat, he decided. My God, what a wonderful ending to this week. I have Ruth, now if only I can get back my brother and with him Michael!

From the shoulder of the gorge Sean looked down across Elands' Kloof. A deep slot of a valley, two miles long and five hundred yards wide at this end, but it tapered slowly upwards until it lost its identity in the high ground. The full length of it was clogged solid with dark green bush, a seemingly impenetrable mass above which a few tall trees reared up in a desperate attempt to reach the sunlight. Like the tentacles of a giant squid, creepers and vines lifted from the dark bush to overpower them and drag them down. Here on the shoulder the air was dry and wholesome – down there it would stink of damp earth and rotting vegetable matter.

Lingering as though suddenly reluctant to go down into the humid discomfort of the Kloof, the hunters gathered on the shoulder. Shading eyes against the glare, they peered up towards the head of the gorge where the beaters were a line of dark specks against the green spring grass.

'There go the kids,' someone pointed. Dirk was leading his band along the high ground above the Kloof.

Sean moved across to his twin brother.

'Well, Garry, how are things out at Theuniskraal?'

'Not bad.'

'I read your book – I think it's excellent. It certainly deserved the reception it got in London. Lord Caisterbrook wrote to me to say that your concluding chapter is giving the War Office much food for thought. Well done, Garry.'

'Thank you.' But there was an evasive lack of warmth in Garry's reply. He made no attempt to continue the conversation.

'Michael didn't come out with you today?'

'No.'

'Why not, Garry?' And Garry smiled for the first time, a cool, spiteful smile.

'He didn't want to.'

'Oh!' The hurt showed in Sean's face for an instant, then he turned to the men around him. 'Right, gentlemen, let's get down there.'

In position now, a line of men standing quietly in the gloom and stagnant heat. Each man's neighbour visible only as an indefinite shape among the leaves and vines and fallen trees. Few things sharp – the outline of a hat-brim, the glint of a random beam of sun on gun-metal, a human hand framed in a hole of dark green leaves. The silence heavy as the heat – spoiled by the nervous rustle of a branch, a hastily smothered cough, the click of a shotgun breech.

Sean hooked his thumb across both hammers of his gun and pulled them back to full cock, lifted the twin muzzles to the roof of leaves above his head and fired in rapid succession. He heard the deep booming note of the gun bouncing against the sides of the valley, echoing and fragmenting as it was thrown back upon itself. Then swiftly the silence closed in again.

He stood motionless, tuning his hearing as finely as was possible, but his reward was the thin drone of an insect and the harsh startled cry of a bush lourie. He shrugged, two miles of distance and the mass of vegetation would blanket completely the cries of the beaters and the clatter of their sticks as they thrashed the bush. But they were coming now, of this he was certain, they would have heard his signal shots. He could imagine them moving down the line, two hundred black men interspersed with the small white boys, chanting the rhetorical question which was as old as the drive hunt itself.

'*E'yapi?*' Repeated over and over again, the accent on the first half of the word, shrilling it.

'*E'yapi?* Where are you going?'

And between him and the beaters, in that wedge of tangled bush, there would be the first uneasy stirring. Dainty bodies, dappled with grey, rising from the secret beds of fallen leaves. Hooves, pointed and sharp, splayed and driven deep into soft leaf-mould by the weight of tensed muscle. Ears pricked forward, eyes like wet black satin, shiny moist muzzles quivering and snuffling, corkscrew horns laid back. The whole poised on the edge of flight.

With the taint of gunsmoke in his notrils, Sean opened the action of his shotgun and the empty shells ejected crisply, pinging out to leave the eyes of the breech empty. He selected two fresh cartridges from his belt and slid them home, snapped the gun closed and thumbed the hammers on to half-cock.

Now they would be moving. The does first, ginger-brown and dappled like roe-deer, slipping away down the valley with their fawns long-legged beside them. Then the bucks, the Inkonka, black and big and silent as shadows; crouching as they moved, horns flat against their shoulders. Moving away from the faint cries and the commotion, moving their mates and their young away from danger – down towards the waiting guns.

'I heard something then!' The Reverend Smiley's voice sounded as though he were being strangled, probably by the dog collar which showed as a pale spot in the gloom.

'Shut up, you fool!' Sean gambled his chance of salvation on the rebuke, but he need not have worried for the endearment was drowned by the double blast of Smiley's shotgun – so indecently loud and totally unexpected that Sean's feet left the ground.

'Did you get him?' Sean asked, his voice a little shaky from the fright. No reply.

'Reverend, did you get one?' Sean demanded. He had seen nothing, and heard nothing that might by the most generous stretch of imagination lead anyone to suspect the presence of a bush buck.

'My goodness, I could have sworn . . .' Smiley's reply was in the kind of voice you would expect from beyond the grave. 'Oh dear, I think I must have been mistaken.'

Here we go again, thought Sean with resignation.

'If you run out of cartridges let me know,' he called softly and grinned at Smiley's injured silence. The shots would have turned the game back towards the beaters, they would be starting to mill now as they sought an avenue of escape. Perhaps moving out on the flanks. As if in confirmation of Sean's thoughts, a shotgun thudded out on the left, then another, then two more on the right.

The fun had started in earnest.

In the brief silence he heard the beaters now, their excited cries muffled but urgent.

A blur of movement ahead of him through the screen of branches, just a flick of dark grey and he swung the gun and fired, wallop of the butt on to his shoulder, and thud and scuffle and roll and kick in the undergrowth.

'Got him!' exulted Sean. Still kicking, the head and shoulders of a half-grown ram emerged from under a bramble bush. It was down, mouth open, bleeding, crabbing against the earth, leaving a drag mark through the dead leaves. Boom again, the mercy stroke, and it lay still. Head speckled with tiny buckshot woulds, eyelids quivering into death and the swift rush of blood from the nostrils.

The din of gunfire all about, cries of the beaters and the answering shouts of the gunners, the panic-stricken run and crackle in the bush ahead.

Inkonka, big one, black as a hellhound, three twists in the horn, eyes staring, lunging into the clearing to halt with head up and front legs braced wide, hunted, panting, wild with terror.

Lean forward against the gun, hold the pip on his heaving chest and fire. The bounce of the gun and the long blue gush of smoke. Knock him down with the solid charge of short range buckshot. Cleanly, quickly, without kicking.

'Got him!'

Another one, blundering straight into the gun line, blind with panic, bursting out of the undergrowth almost on top of Sean. Doe with fawn at her heels – let her go.

The doe saw him and wheeled left to take the gap between Sean and Garrick. As it dashed through, Sean looked beyond and saw his brother. Garrick had left his position and closed in on Sean. He was crouched slightly, the shotgun held in both hands, hammers fully cocked – and his eyes were fastened on Sean.

Garrick waited quietly during the initial stages of the beat. The tree-trunk on which he sat was soft and rotten, covered with moss and the orange and white tongues of fungus. From the inside pocket of his jacket he took the silver flask inlaid with carnelians. The first mouthful started his tears and numbed his tongue, but he swallowed it painfully and lowered the flask.

'He has taken from me everything I ever had of value:

My leg: Garry looked down at the way it stuck out stiffly ahead of him with the heel buried in the damp leaf-mould. He drank again quickly, closing his eyes against the sting of brandy.

My wife: In the dark redness behind his eyelids he saw her again, as Sean had left her, lying in torn clothing with bruised and swollen lips.

My manhood: Because of what he did to her that night, Anna has never let me touch her body. Until then there was hope. But now I am forty-two years old and I am virgin. It is too late.

My position: That swine Acheson would never have thrown me out – but for Sean.

And now he will take Michael from me.

He remembered again the premonition of disaster that he had experienced when Anna reported to him how she had found Michael and Sean together on Theuniskraal. It had started then, each little incident building up. The day Michael had stared at the faded but bold entries in the leather-bound stock register. 'Is that Uncle Sean's handwriting?'

That battered saddle Michael had found in the loft above the stables; he had polished it lovingly and restitched the seams, fitted new stirrup leathers, and used it for a year. Until Garry had noticed the crude initials cut into the leather of the flap. 'S.C.' That night Garry had taken the saddle and thrown it into the furnace of the hot-water boiler.

Eight months ago, on Michael's twenty-first birthday, Garry had called him into the panelled study of Theuniskraal, and reluctantly told him of Sean's legacy to him. Michael had held the dog-eared sheet and read it through with his lips moving silently. Then at last he looked up and his voice was shaky. 'Uncle Sean gave me a half-share in Theuniskraal even before I was born. Why, Dad? Why did he do that?' And Garry had no answer for him.

This last week had been the climax. It had taken all Anna's and Garrick's combined influence and entreaties to prevent Michael responding to the invitations Sean had sent. Then the Zulu herd-boy, whose duty was to follow Michael and come to Garrick immediately Michael crossed the boundary of Theuniskraal, reported that each evening Michael rode up to the high ground on the escarpment and sat there until after dark staring in the direction of Lion Kop ranch.

I am going to lose him, He is my son, even if Sean sired him. But he is my son, and unless I prevent it Sean is going to take that away from me also.

Unless I prevent it. He lifted the flask to his lips once more and found with surprise that it was empty. He screwed the stopper down and returned the flask to his pocket.

Around him the gunfire and the shouting began. From the log beside him he picked up the shotgun and loaded it. He stood up and cocked the hammers.

Sean saw him, coming slowly, limping a little, crouching, making no attempt to fend off the branches that dragged across his face.

'Don't bunch up, Garry. Stay in your position, you're leaving a gap in the line.'

Then he noticed Garry's expression. It seemed that the skin had been stretched tight across the cheek-bones and the nose, so the rims of his nostrils were white. His jaws were chewing nervously and there was a fine sheen of sweat across his forehead. He looked sick or deadly afraid.

'Garry, are you all right?' Alarmed, Sean started towards him – then stopped suddenly. Garry had lifted the shotgun.

'I'm sorry, Sean. But I can't let you have him,' he said. The blank double eyes of the muzzles were all Sean saw of the gun, and below them, Garry's knuckles white with pressure, as he gripped the stock. One finger was hooked forward around the triggers.

Sean was afraid then. He stood without moving for his legs were heavy and numb under him.

'I've got to.' Garry's voice was a croak. 'I have to do it – otherwise you'll take him. You'll destroy him also.'

With fear making his legs clumsy and slow, Sean turned deliberately away from him and walked back to his station. The muscles of his back were stiff with anticipation, knotted so tightly that they ached.

The beaters were close now, he could hear them shouting and thrashing the bush just ahead. He lifted the whistle to his lips and blew three shrill blasts. The shouting died away, and in the comparative silence Sean heard a sound behind him, a sound half-way between a sob and a cry of pain.

Slowly, inchingly, Sean turned his head to look back. Garry was gone.

Beneath him Sean's legs began to tremble, and a muscle in his thigh twitched spasmodically. He sank down and sat on the carpet of soft damp leaves. When he lit a cheroot he used both hands to steady the fluttering flame of the match.

'Dad! Dad!' Dirk came pelting out into the tiny clearing. 'Dad, how many did you get?'

'Two,' said Sean.

'Only two?' And Dirk's voice went flat with disappointment and shame. 'Even Reverend Smiley beat you hollow. He got four!'

Chapter Sixty-six

Ruth returned to Pietermaritzburg the afternoon following the hunt Sean insisted on accompanying her home. Ada, Dirk and a dozen of the friends Ruth had made during the week were at the station to see them leave. Sean was trying to detach Ruth from the earnest discussion into which all women seem to fall on the eve of a major parting. His repeated, 'You'd better get aboard, my dear,' and 'The flag's up, Ruth', were studiously ignored by all of them, until he found it necessary to take Ruth's arm and bundle her up into the coach. Her head reappeared instantly at the window to take up the discussion at the exact point where Sean had interrupted it. Sean was about to follow her when he saw Dirk. With a stab of guilt Sean realized how blatantly he had neglected Dirk during the week.

'Cheerio, Dirkie,' Sean called gruffly and the boy flew to him and wound his arms tightly around Sean's neck.

'Come on, Dirk. I'll be back tomorrow morning.'

'I want to go with you.'

'You have school tomorrow.' Sean tried to loosen Dirk's hold. The women were watching in silence now, and Sean felt himself flushing with embarrassment. *My God, he's not a baby any more – he's nearly fifteen.* He tried to keep his irritation from showing in his voice as he whispered:

'Stop that now. What will people think of you?'

'Take me with you, Dad. Please take me,' and Dirk quivered against him. The whistle blew and with voluble relief the women turned away and began talking all at once.

'Do you think I'm proud of you when you act like this?' Sean hissed at him. 'Now, behave yourself and shake hands properly.'

Dirk clutched his hand, with the tears filling his eyes.

'Stop it this instant!' Sean turned abruptly and swung himself up into the coach as the train jerked forward and started sliding out of the platform.

Dirk took a few indeterminate paces after it and then stopped with his shoulders shaking uncontrollably, his eyes still fastened on Sean's face as it protruded from the window.

'Your father will be back tomorrow, Dirkie.' Ada laid her hand consolingly on Dirk's shoulder.

'He doesn't love me,' whispered Dirk. 'He never even . . .'

'Of course he does,' Ada interrupted quickly. 'It was just that he was so . . .' But Dirk did not wait for her to finish. He shrugged her hand away, spun round and jumped blindly from the platform on to the tracks, ducked through the barbed-wire fence beyond and ran out across the fields to intercept the train as it made its first long turn on to the slope of the escarpment.

He ran with his face contorted, and the harsh grass brushing his legs, he ran with his arms pumping the rhythm of his racing feet – and ahead of him the train whistled mournfully and crawled out from behind the Van Essen plantation.

It was crossing his front, still fifty yards away, slowly gathering speed for its assault on the escarpment. He would not reach it – even though Sean's coach was the last before the guard's van – he would not reach it.

He stopped, panting, searching wildly for a glimpse of his father – but the window of Sean's compartment was blank.

'Pa!' he shrieked, and his voice was lost in the clatter of the crossties and the hoarse panting of steam.

'Pa!' He waved both arms wildly above his head. 'Pa! It's me. Me – Dirk.'

Sean's compartment moved slowly across his line of vision. For a few brief seconds he looked into the interior.

Sean stood sideways to the window, he was leaning forward with his shoulders hunched and Ruth was in his arms. Her head thrown back, the hat gone from her head and her dark hair in abundant disarray. She was laughing, white teeth and eyes asparkle. Sean leaned forward and covered her open mouth with his own. And then they were past.

Dirk stood like that with his arms raised. Then slowly they sank to his sides. The tension in his lips and around he eyes smoothed away. All expression faded from his eyes and he stood and watched the train puff and twist up the slope until with a last triumphant spurt of steam it disappeared over the skyline.

Dirk crossed the railway line and found the footpath that climbed the hills. Once he lifted his hands and with his thumbs wiped the tears from his cheeks. Then he stopped listlessly to watch a scarab beetle at his feet. The size of a man's thumb, glossy black and horned like a demon, it struggled with a ball of cow-dung three times its own size. Standing on its back legs, thrusting with its front, it rolled the perfect sphere of dung before it. Oblivious of everything but the need to spawn, to bury the ball in a secret place and deposit its eggs upon it, it laboured in silent dedication.

With the toe of his book Dirk flicked the ball away into the grass. The beetle stood motionless, deprived of the whole purpose of its existence. Then it began to search. Back and forth, clicking and scraping its shiny body armour across the hard, bare earth of the path.

Watching its frenzied search dispassionately, Dirk's face was calm and lovely. He lifted his foot and brought his heel down gently on the beetle.

He could feel it wriggling under his boot until with a crunch its carapace collapsed and it spurted brown as tobacco juice. Dirk stepped over it and walked on up the hill.

In the night Dirk sat alone. His arms were clasped around his legs and his forehead rested on his knees. The shafts of moonlight through the canopy of wattle branches had a cold white quality, similar to the emotion that held Dirk's body rigid. He lifted his head. Moonlight lit his face from above, accentuating the perfection of his features. The smooth, broad depth of his forehead, the flaring dark lines of his brows set off the large but delicately formed plane of his nose. But now his mouth was a line of pain, of cold white pain.

'I hate him.' His mouth did not lose the shape of pain as he whispered the words, 'and I hate her. He doesn't care about me any more – all he cares about is that woman.'

The vicious hiss of breath through his lips was the sound of despair.

'I always try to show him . . . No one else but him, but he doesn't care. Why doesn't he understand – Why? Why? Why?'

And he shivered feverishly,

'He doesn't want me. He doesn't care.'

The shivering ceased, and the shape of his mouth changed from pain to hatred.

'I'll show him. If he doesn't want me – then I'll show him.' And the next words he spat as though they were filth from his mouth, 'I hate him.' Around him the wattle branches rustled in the wind. He jumped to his feet and ran, following the moonlit road deeper into the plantations of Lion Kop.

A *meerkat* hunting alone along the road saw him and scampered into the trees like a small grey ferret. But Dirk ran on, faster now as his hatred drove him and his breathing sobbed in rhythm with his feet. He ran with the dry west wind into his face – he needed the wind. His revenge would ride on the wind.

'Now, we'll see,' he shouted suddenly as he ran. 'You don't want me – then have this instead!' And the wattle and wind answered him with a sound like many voices far away.

At the second access road he turned right and ran on into the heart of the plantations. He ran for twenty minutes and when he stopped he was panting wildly.

'Damn you – God damn you all.' His voice came catchy from his dried-out mouth.

'Damn you, then.' And he walked off the road and fought his way into the trees. They were two-year growth not yet thinned, and the branches interlaced to dispute his passage – hands trying to hold him, small desperate hands clutching at him, tugging at his clothing like the supplicating hands of a beggar. But he shrugged them away and beat them off until he was deep in amongst them.

'Here!' he said harshly and dropped to his knees in the soft crackling trash of small twigs and dry leaves that carpeted the earth. Hooking his fingers he raked a pyramid of the stuff, and he sobbed as he worked so that his muttering was broken and without coherence.

'Dry, it's dry. I'll show you then – you don't want— Everything I've done you've. ... I hate you ... Oh, Pa! Why? Why don't you – what have I done?'

And the matchbox rattled. Twice he struck and twice the match broke in his fingers. The third flared blue, spitting tiny sparks of sulphur, burning acrid, settling down to a small yellow flame that danced in the cup of his hands.

'Have this instead!' And he thrust the flame into the pile of kindling. It fluttered, almost died and then grew again as a wisp of grass caught it.

Consumed instantly, the grass was gone and the flame died, gone – almost, but then a leaf and it jumped brightly, orange points of flame in the twigs. The first tiny popping and it spread sideways, a burning leaf swirled upwards.

Dirk backed away as the flame leapt jubilantly into his face. He was no longer sobbing.

'Pa,' he whispered and the flame fastened on to the living leaves of a branch that hung over it. A gust of wind hit it and sprayed sparks and golden orange flame against its neighbour.

'Pa.' Dirk's voice was uncertain, he stood up and wiped his hands nervously against his shirt.

'No.' He shook his head in bewilderment, and the sapling bloomed with fire and the fire whispered softly.

'No.' Dirk's voice rose. 'I didn't really mean ...' but it was lost in the pistol-shots of flame and the whisper that was now a drumming roar.

'Stop it,' he shouted. 'Oh God, I didn't mean it. No! No!' And he jumped forward into the heat of it, into the bright orange glare, kicking wildly at the flaming kindling, scattering it so that it fell and caught again in fifty new points of fire.

'No, stop it. Please stop it!' And he clawed at the burning tree until the heat drove him back. He ran to another sapling and tore a leafy branch from it. He rushed at the fire, beating at it, sobbing again in the smoke and the flame.

Riding joyously on the west wind, roaring red and orange and black, the flames spread out among the trees and left him standing alone in the smoke and the swirling ash.

'Oh Pa! I'm sorry, I'm sorry – I didn't mean it.'

Chapter Sixty-seven

A shutter kept slamming softly in the wind, but this was not the only reason Michael Courtney could not sleep. He felt trapped, chained by loyalties he could not break; he was aware of the dark oppressive bulk of the Theuniskraal homestead around him. A prison, a place of bitterness and hatred.

He moved restlessly on his bed and the shutter banged and banged. He threw back the single sheet and the floorboards creaked as he stood up from the bed.

'Michael!' The voice from the next room was sharp, suspicious.

'Yes, Mother.'

'Where are you going, darling?'

'There's a loose shutter. I'm going to close it.'

'Put something on, darling. Don't catch cold.'

Stifling, beginning to sweat now in physical discomfort, Michael knew he must get out of this house into the cool freedom of the wind and the night. He dressed quickly but silently, then carrying his boots he crept down the long passage and out on the wide front stoep.

He found the shutter and secured it, then he sat upon the front steps and pulled on his boots before standing again and moving out across the lawns. He stood on the bottom terrace of Theuniskraal's gardens and around him the west wind soughed and shook the trees.

The restlessness of the wind increased his own, so he must get out of the valley – get up on to the high ground of the escarpment. He started to walk, hurrying past the paddocks towards the stables. In the stable yard he stopped abruptly, his tall lean body caught in mid-stride. There was a glow, a soft orange glow on the far hills of Lion Kop.

Then Michael ran, shouting as he passed the grooms' quarters. He threw open the half-door of one of the stalls and snatched the bridle from its peg as he ran to his horse. Hands clumsy with haste, he forced the bit between the animal's teeth and buckled the cheek strap. When he led it out into the yard two of the grooms were standing there, bewildered with sleep.

'Fire!' Michael pointed along the hills. 'Call everybody and bring them to help.' He went up on to the bare back of his horse and looked down at them. 'Bring every man from the location, come in the mule-wagon. Come as fast as you can.' Then he hit his heels into the mare's flanks and drove her out of the yard, laying forward across her back.

Twenty minutes later Michael checked her on the crest of the escarpment. She was blowing heavily between his knees. Still five miles ahead, bright even in the bright moonlight, a circle of fire lay on the dark plantations of

Lion Kop. Above it a black cloud, a cloud that climbed and spread on the wind to hide the stars.

'Oh God – Uncle Sean!' The exclamation wrung from Michael was a cry of physical pain, and he urged the mare forward again. Charging her recklessly through the ford of the Baboon Stroom so that the water flew like exploding glass, then lunging up the far bank and on along the hills.

The mare was staggering in her gallop as Michael kneed her through the gates into the yard of the Lion Kop homestead. There were wagons and many blackmen carrying axes. Michael hauled the mare back so violently that she nearly fell.

'Where is the Nkosi?' he shouted at a big Zulu he recognized as Sean's personal servant.

'He has gone to Pietermaritzburg.'

Michael slid down from his horse and turned her loose.

'Send a man to the village to ask for help.'

'It is done,' the Zulu replied.

'We must move all the livestock from the top paddocks, get the horses out of the stables – it may come this way,' Michael went on.

'I have sent all the wives to do these things.'

'You have done well, then. Now let us go.'

The Zulus were swarming up on to the wagons, clutching the long-handled axes. Michael and Mbejane ran to the lead wagon. Michael took the reins. At that moment two horsemen galloped into the yard. He could not see their faces in the night.

'Who's that? Michael shouted.

'Broster and Van Wyk!' The nearest neighbours.

'Thank God! Will you take the other wagons?'

They dismounted and ran past Michael.

Michael stood with his legs braced apart, he threw his shoulders open as he wielded the whip and then sent it snaking forward to crack an inch above the ears of the lead mules. They lunged forward into the traces and the wagon bounced and clattered out of the yard.

As they galloped in frantic convoy along the main acesss road towards the plantations they met the Zulu women with their children from the location streaming down towards the homestead, their soft voices calling greeting and speed to their men as they passed.

But Michael hardly heard them, he stood with his eyes fastened on the pillar of red flame and smoke that rose from the heart of Sean's trees.

'It is in the trees we planted two years ago.' Mbejane spoke beside him. 'But already it will be close upon the next block of older trees. We cannot hope to stop it there.'

'Where then?'

'This side there are more young trees and a wide road. We can try there.'

'What is your name?' Michael asked.

'Mbejane.'

'I am Michael. The Nkosi's nephew.'

'I know.' Mbejane nodded, then went on, 'Turn off where next the roads meet.'

They came to the cross-roads. In the sector ahead were the young trees

– ten feet high, thick as a man's arm, massed dark leaves and interlacing branches. Far out beyond them in the tall mature wattle was the line of flame. Above it a towering wall of sparks and dark smoke, coming down swiftly on the wind. It would be upon them in less than an hour at its present rate of advance.

A fire like this would jump a thirty-foot road without checking – they must cut back into the young wattle and increase the gap to sixty feet at the least.

Michael swung the wagon off the road and hauled the mules to a halt. He jumped down to meet the other wagons as they came up.

'Go on for two hundred yards – then start your boys in chopping out the wattle towards the fire – we've got to widen the road. I'll start my gang here,' he shouted at Van Wyk.

'Right.'

'Mr Broster – go on to the end of the block and start working back this way – cut the timber out another thirty feet.'

Without waiting to hear more, Broster drove on. These two men, twice Michael's age, conceded him the right of command without argument.

Snatching an axe from the nearest Zulu, Michael issued his orders as he ran to the young wattle. The men crowded after him and Michael selected a tree, took his stance and swung the axe in a low arc from the side. The tree quivered and rained loose leaves upon him at the blow. Smoothly he reversed his grip on the shaft of the axe and swung again from the opposite side. The blade sliced through the soft wood, the tree sagged wearily away from him and groaned as it subsided. He stepped past it to the next. Around him the Zulus spread out along the road and the night rang with the beat of their axes.

Four times during the next half-hour fresh wagons galloped in, wagons loaded with men and driven by Sean's neighbours, until almost three hundred men were using the ax on Sean's lovingly planted and tenderly nursed wattle.

Shoulder to shoulder, chopping in wordless frenzy, trampling the fallen sapling as they moved forward.

Once a man yelled in pain and Michael looked up to see two Zulus dragging another back to the road with his leg half severed by the slip of a careless axe. Dark blood in the moonlight.

One of the neighbours hurried to tend the injured man and Michael turned back to the destruction of the wattle.

Swing, change hands and swing again, the solid *thunk!* and the tree swaying. Shove it over and struggle through the fallen tangle of branches to the next. Swing again, and smell the sweet bleeding sap – feel the ache in the shoulders and the sting of sweat in the burst blisters of the palms.

Then suddenly the other smell, acrid on the wind. Smoke. Michael paused and looked up. The men on each side of him stopped work also and the firelight danced on their naked, sweat-greased bodies as they leaned on their axes and watched it come.

On a front four hundred yards wide, ponderously it rolled down towards them. Not with the explosive white heat of a burning pine forest, but in the awful grandeur of orange and dark red, billowing smoke and torrential sparks.

Gradually the sound of axes died along the line as men stopped and watched this appalling thing come down towards them. It lit their faces clearly, revealing the awe that was on all of them. They could feel the heat now, great gusts of it that shrivelled the tender growth ahead of the flames – and suddenly a freak of the wind sent a bank of black smoke billowing down over the motionless line of men and blotted them out from each other. It cleared as swiftly as it came, and left them coughing and gasping.

'Back! Get back to the road!' yelled Michael and the cry was taken up and thrown along the line. They waded back through the morass of waist-high vegetation and assembled in small subdued groups along the road, standing together helplessly with the axes idle in their hands, fearful in the face of that line of flame and smoke.

'Cut branches to beat with!' Michael whipped their apathy. 'String out along the edge.' He hurried along the road, pushing them back into line, bullying them, cursing in his own fear. 'Come on, the flames will drop when they reach the fallen trees. Cover your faces – use your shirts. Hey, you – don't just stand there.'

With renewed determination each man armed himself with a green branch, and they re-formed along the road.

Quietly they stood in the daylight glare of the flames – black faces impassive, white ones flushed with heat and working anxiously.

'Do you think we'll be able to . . .' Michael started as he reached Ken Broster, and then he stopped. The question he had been about to ask had no answer. Instead he said, 'We've lost three thousand acres already – but if it gets away from us here!'

Involuntarily both of them glanced back at the tall mature wattle behind them.

'We'll hold it here,' Broster stated with a certainty he did not feel.

'I hope you're right,' whispered Michael, then suddenly Broster shouted: 'Oh Christ look!'

For a moment Michael was blinded by the red glare and unsighted by the smoke. The fire burned unevenly. In places it had driven forward in great wedge-shaped salients of flame and left behind bays of standing wattle that were withering and browning in the heat.

From out of one of these bays, into the springy matt of fallen and trampled branches staggered a man.

'Who the hell . . .' started Michael. The man was unrecognizable. His short ripped to shreds by branches that had also scourged his face into a bloody mask. He floundered forward towards the road, two slack exhausted paces before he fell and disappeared under the leaves.

'The Nkosana.' Mbejane's voice boomed above the thunder of the flames.

'Dirk! It's Dirk Courtney!' Michael started forward.

The heat was painful in Michael's face. How much more intense must it be out there where Dirk was lying. As if they knew their prey was helpless the flames raced forward eagerly, triumphantly to consume him. Whoever went in to rob them would meet the full fury of their advance.

Michael plunged into the brush and ploughed his way towards where

Dirk thrashed feebly, almost encircled by the deadly embrace of the flames
– and the heat reached out ahead of the flames to welcome him. Mbejane
ran beside him.

'Go back,' shouted Mbejane. 'It needs only one of us.' But Michael did
not answer him and they crashed side by side through the brush, racing the
fire with Dirk as the prize.

Mbejane reached him first and lifting him, turned back for the road. He
took one step before he fell and rose again unsteadily from the mass of
branches. Even his vast strength was insufficient in this vacuum of heat. His
mouth was open, a pink cave in the glistening black oval of his face, wide
open and his chest heaved strenuously as he hunted air, but instead sucked
the scalding heat into his throat.

Michael threw himself forward against the heat to reach him. It was
almost a solid thing, a barrier of red shimmering glare. Michael could feel
it swelling and tightening the skin of his face and drying the moisture from
his eyeballs.

'I'll take his legs,' he grunted and reached for Dirk. A patch of brown
appeared miraculously on the sleeve of his shirt – singed by the flames as
though it had been carelessly ironed. Beneath it the heat sunk a barb of
agony into his flesh.

Half a dozen paces together with Dirk between them before Michael
tripped and fell, dragging Mbejane down with him. They were a long time
rising, all movements slowing down – but when they did they were
surrounded.

Two prongs of flame had reached the area of fallen saplings on either side
of them. This had slowed them and diminished their fury. But a chance gust
of the wind and fuel had forced them to curl inwards on each other, spreading
horns of fire ahead of Michael and Mbejane and leaving them enclosed by
a dancing, leaping palisade of flame.

'Go through!' croaked Michael, his throat scalded and swollen. 'We must
break through.'

And they churned their way towards the encircling wall. Through it,
vague and unreal, he could see men beating at the flames – distorted
phantoms trying desperately to open a path for them. Mbejane wore only
a loin cloth, no breeches, coat nor boots to protect him, as Michael had. He
was very near the limit of his strength.

Now looking at Michael across the body of the boy they carried, Mbejane
saw a curious thing. Michael's hair crinkled slowly and then began to smoke
– smouldering like an old sack.

Michael screamed at the agony of it, a hideous sound that shrilled above
the roar and crackle of the flames. But agony was the key that unlocked the
last storehouse of his strength. As though it were a rag doll he snatched
Dirk's body from Mbejane's grasp and lifting it with both hands on to his
shoulders he charged into the fire.

The flames reached to his waist, clawing greedily at him as he ran and
the smoke eddied and swirled about him – but he was through.

'Help Mbejane!' he shouted at the Zulu beaters and then he was out on
the road. He dropped Dirk and beat at his clothing with his bare hands. His

boots were charred and his clothing was alight in a dozen places. He fell and rolled wildly in the dusty road to smother it.

Two Zulus went in to help Mbejane. Two nameless blackmen, two labourers – men of no distinction. Neither of them wore boots. Both of them reached Mbejane as he tottered weakly towards them. One on each side they urged him back towards the road.

At this moment Michael rolled to his knees in the road and despite his own agony watched them with a sickened fascination.

Leading Mbejane between them as though he were a blind man, they stumbled barefooted into the flames and stirred up a great cloud of sparks around them. Then the smoke rolled down over them and they were gone.

'Mbejane!' croaked Michael, and pushed himself to his feet to go to him – then:

'Oh God – Oh, thank God.' Mbejane and one of the Zulus stumbled out of the smoke into the arms of the men who waited for them.

No one went back for the other Zulu. No one went back for him until two hours later when the dawn had broken and the fire had been stopped at the road and the mature wattle had been saved. Then Ken Broster led a small party gingerly into the wilderness of still smouldering ash, into the black desert. They found him on his face. Those parts of him that had lain against the earth were still recognizable as belonging to a human being.

Chapter Sixty-eight

'Ladyburg in twenty minutes, Mr Courtney.' The conductor put his head round the door of the compartment.

'Thanks, Jack.' Sean looked up from his book.

'I see from this morning's paper that you're engaged to be married?'

'That's right.'

'Well, then, break clean, no hitting low – let's have a good clean fight and good luck to both of you.' Sean grinned and the man went down the passage. Sean packed his book into the briefcase, stood up and followed him.

On the balcony of the coach he stopped and lit a cheroot, then he leaned on the railings and looked out across the veld for his first glimpse of Lion Kop. This had become a ritual whenever he returned to Ladyburg.

This morning he was as happily content as he had ever been in his life. Last night, after conferring with Ma and Pa Goldberg, Ruth had set the wedding date for March next year. By then Sean would have completed his first cutting of bark, and they would take a month to honeymoon in the Cape.

Now, at last, I have everything a man could reasonably ask for, he thought, and smiled and in that moment he saw the smoke. He straightened up and flicked the cheroot away.

The train snaked up towards the rim of the escarpment, slowing as the gradient changed beneath it. It reached the crest and the whole vista of the Ladyburg valley opened below it. Sean saw the great irregular blot upon his trees, with the thin grey streams of smoke drifting wearily away across the hills.

He opened the balcony gate and jumped down from the train. He hit and slid and rolled down the gravel embankment. The skin was scraped from his knees and the palms of his hands. Then he was on his feet, running.

Along the road where the fire had been stopped men waited. Sitting quietly or sprawled in exhausted sleep, all of them were coated with ash and soot. Their eyes were smoke-inflamed and their bodies ached with fatigue. But they waited while the black acres smouldered and smoked sullenly – for if the wind came up again it would fan the ashes to life.

Ken Broster lifted his head from his arm, then sat up quickly.

'Sean's here!' he said. The men around him stirred and then stood up slowly. They watched Sean approaching, he came with the sloppy, blundering legs of a man who has run five miles.

Sean stopped a little way off and his breathing wheezed and heaved in this throat.

'How? How did it happen?'

'We don't know, Sean.' In sympathy Ken Broster dropped his eyes from Sean's face. You do not stare at a man in anguish. Sean leaned against one of the wagons. He could not bring himself to look again at the vast expanse of smouldering desert with the skeletons of the tree-trunks standing out of it like the twisted and blackened fingers of an arthritic hand.

'One of your men was killed,' Ken told him softly. 'One of your Zulus.' He hesistated – then went on firmly. 'Others were hurt, badly burned.' Sean made no reply, he did not seem to understand the words.

'Your nephew and your boy – Dirkie.' Still Sean stared at him dully.

'Mbejane also.' This time Sean seemed to cringe away from him.

'I sent them down to the homestead – the doctor's there.'

Still no reply from Sean, but now he wiped the palm of his hand across his mouth and eyes.

'Mike and Dirk aren't too bad, skin burns – but Mbejane's feet are in a hell of a mess.' Ken Broster spoke quickly now. 'Young Dirk got trapped in front of the flames. Mike and Mbejane went to get him . . . surrounded . . . down . . . picked him up . . . tried to help . . . useless . . . badly burned . . . meat off his feet . . .

To Sean the words were disjointed, meaningless. He leaned against the wagon. There was looseness in him, a lack of will. *It was too much. Let it go. Let it all go.*

'Sean, are you all right?' Broster's hands on his shoulders. He straightened up and looked around him again.

'I must go to them. Lend me a horse.'

'You go ahead, Sean. We'll stay on here and watch it for you. Don't worry about it, we'll make bloody sure she doesn't start again.'

'Thank you, Ken.' Then he looked around the circle of anxious compassionate faces. 'Thank you,' he said again.

Sean rode slowly into the stable yard on Lion Kop. There were many carriages and servants, black women and children, but a hush came upon them when they recognized him. Surrounded by women, a crude litter lay near the far wall of the yard and Sean walked across to it.

'I see you, Mbejane.'

'Nkosi.' Mbejane's eyelashes were burned away giving his face a bland and slightly puzzled expression. His hands and his feet were bound loosely in bundles of crisp white bandages through which ointment had soaked in yellow patches. Sean squatted behind him. He could not speak. He reached out almost hesistantly and touched Mbejane's shoulder.

'Is it bad?' he asked then.

'No, Nkosi. It is not too bad. My wives have come for me. I will return when I am ready.'

They spoke together a little while, and Mbejane told him of Dirk and how Michael had come. Then he murmured, 'This woman is the wife of the one who died.'

Sean noticed her for the first time. She sat alone in the crowded yard, on a blanket against the wall. A child stood beside her; leaning forward, naked, holding one of her fat, black breasts with both hands as he fed from it. She sat impassively with her legs folded under her, a cloak of ochre-dyed leather draped loosely over her shoulders, but open at the front for the child. Sean moved across to her. The child watched him with large dark eyes, but without removing the nipple from his mouth and the corners of his mouth were wet with spilled milk.

'He was a man,' Sean greeted the woman.

She inclined her head gravely. 'He was a man!' she agreed.

'Where will you go?' Sean asked.

'To my father's kraal.' The high headdress of red clay enhanced the quiet dignity of her reply.

'Select twenty head of cattle from my herds to take with you.'

'*Ngi Yabonga* – I praise you, Nkosi.'

'Go in peace.'

'Stay in peace.' She stood, lifted the child on to her hip and walked slowly from the yard without looking back.

'I will go now, Nkosi.' Mbejane spoke from the litter. The colour of his skin was grey with pain. 'And when I return we will plant again. It was only a small fire.'

'It was only a small fire.' Sean nodded. 'Go in peace, my friend. Drink much beer and grow fat. I will visit you.'

Mbejane chuckled softly and signalled his wives to their places around the litter. They lifted him, young women strong from their work in the fields.

'Stay in peace, Nkosi.' Mbejane lay back painfully upon the soft mattress of fur, and they carried him out of the yard. They began to sing as they passed the gates, moving in double file on each side of the litter, stately and tall, their naked backs glistening with oil, rumps swaying together beneath the brief loin cloths, and their voices joined high and proud in the ancient song of welcome to the warrior returned from battle.

Gathered on the stoep of Lion Kop were many of his neighbours and their wives, come with sympathy and offers of assistance.

Ada was waiting for him as Sean climbed the steps.

'Dirk?' he asked.

'He is well, asleep now. Laudanum.'

'Michael?'

'He is waiting for you. He refused the drug. I've put him in your room.'

On his way down the passage Sean stopped at Dirk's room and looked in. Dirk lay on his back with bandaged hands folded across his chest. His face was swollen and laced with ugly red lines where the wattle branches had clawed him. On the chair beside his bed Mary sat in patient vigil. She looked at Sean and made to rise. Sean shook his head.

'No. I will come back when he is awake.' He went on down the passage to his own room.

Three of Ada's girls hovered and chirruped about Michael's bed like birds whose nests are endangered. They saw him and stopped their chatter. All Ada's girls held Sean in unexplained awe.

'Oh, Mr Courtney. His poor hands . . .' one little lass began, then blushed crimson, dropped a hurried curtsy and escaped from the room. The others followed quickly.

Sean moved across to the bed.

'Hello, Mike.' His voice was gruff, as he saw the blister that hung like a pale grape on Michael's cheek.

'Hello, Uncle Sean.' The raw places of his face and lips were smeared with yellow ointment. Sean sat down gingerly on the edge of the bed.

'Thank you, Michael,' he said.

Chapter Sixty-nine

Ronny Pye called early the following morning. With him came Dennis Petersen and both of them were wearing suits.

'Very fancy turn-out,' Sean greeted them. 'Business or social?'

'Well, you might say a little of each.' Ronny paused at the top of the veranda steps. 'May we come in?'

Sean led them to the end of the veranda, and they seated themselves before anyone spoke again.

'I heard about the fire, Sean. Terrible business. I heard there was a native killed and both Dirk and Michael were hurt. Terrible business.' Ronny shook his head in sympathy.

'Did you also hear that I lost four thousand acres of timber?' Sean inquired politely.

'Heard that also.' Ronny nodded solemnly. 'Terrible business.'

Ronny and Dennis glanced at each other furtively, and then looked down at their hands.

'Very nasty,' Ronny repeated and a silence fell upon them.

'Anything else worrying you?' Sean inquired politely.

'Well, now that you've brought it up—' Ronny reached inside his jacket and withdrew a long folded document tied with a red ribbon. 'Mind you, we don't have to discuss it today. Leave it until you feel better?'

'Talk!' Sean grunted.

'Clause eight.' Ronny spread the document between the coffee-cups on the table. 'In the event of the said security, namely, a certain block of wattle known as No. 2 block of Lion Kop Estates in extent approximately . . .' Ronny hesitated. 'Guess there's no sense in me reading it all. You know what it says. That wattle was part of the collateral for the loan.'

'How long will you give me to raise the money?' Sean asked.

'Well, Sean, you understand there is no period of grace allowed in the contract. Seems to me you'll have to put it up right away.'

'I want a month,' Sean told him.

'A month!' Ronny was shocked and hurt by the request. 'See here now, Sean. I don't honestly— I mean, surely you've got the money. I mean why do you need a month. Just let us have your cheque.'

'You know damned well I haven't got it.'

'Seems to me—' Ronny offered delicately. 'Seems to me if you haven't got it now, there's not much chance you'll have it in a month. No offence, Sean, but we have to look at this thing from a business angle. If you follow me.'

'I follow you.' Sean nodded. 'And I want a month.'

'Give it to him,' blurted Dennis Petersen, his first contribution, and Ronny turned on him instantly with his face twisting into a snarl. The struggle he had within himself to smooth out his features and to restore his voice to its level and reasonable tone lasted fully five seconds.

'Well now, Dennis,' he murmured. 'That's an unusual way to look at it. Seems to me—'

'I spoke to Audrey before we came up here. I promised her . . . Anyway, we both agreed.' Dennis was staring out across the valley, unable to meet his partner's eyes.

Suddenly Ronny Pye chuckled. Yes, by God! It would be even better that way – watching this big arrogant bastard crawling round begging, with his hat in his hands. Sean would go to Jackson first and Ronny had telegraphed Jackson the previous afternoon. He had also telegraphed Nichols at the Standard Bank. By now the message would be spreading swiftly along the network of South African banking channels. Sean Courtney would find it difficult to borrow the price of a meal.

'All right then, Sean. As a special concession you can have a month.' Then all the laughter was gone and he leaned forward in his chair. 'You've got exactly thirty days. Then, by Christ, I am going to sell out under you.'

After they were gone Sean sat alone on the wide veranda. The sunlight on the hills was bright and hot, but in the shade it was cool. He heard Ada's girls chattering somewhere in the house, then one of the giggled shrilly. The sound irritated Sean, his frown deepened and he drew a rumpled envelope from his jacket pocket and smoothed it out on the arm of his chair. Awhile he sat in thought nibbling the stub of a pencil.

Then he wrote: 'Jackson. Natal Wattle'. And again, 'Standard Bank'. Then 'Ben Goldberg'. He paused and considered this last name on his list. Then he grunted aloud and scratched it out with two hard strokes of the pencil. Not from the Godbergs. Leave them out of this.

He wrote again quickly, scrawling a single word – 'Candy' and below it 'Tim Curtis'.

That was all. John Acheson was in England. It would take two months to receive a reply from him.

That was all. He sighed softly and folded the envelope into his pocket. Then he lit a cheroot, sank down in the chair and placed his feet on the low veranda wall in front of him. I'll leave on tomorrow morning's train, he thought.

The windows behind him were open. Lying beyond them in the bedroom Michael Courtney had heard every word of their conversation. Now he stood up painfully from the bed and began to dress. He went out the back way and nobody saw him leave. His mare was in the stables, and on a borrowed saddle he rode back to Theuniskraal.

Anna saw him coming and ran out into the yard to meet him. 'Michael! Oh, Michael. Thank God you are safe. We heard . . .' Then she saw his face and the raw, swollen burns on it and she froze. Michael dismounted slowly and one of the grooms led his horse away.

'Michael, darling. Your poor face.' And she embraced him quickly.

'It's nothing, Mother.'

'Nothing!' She pulled away from him, lips drawn into a tight, hard line. 'You run away in the middle of the night to that . . . that . . . Then you come home days later with your face and your hands in a terrible mess – is that nothing!'

'I'm sorry, Mother. Gran'ma looked after me.'

'You knew I'd be half-dead with worry, sitting here imagining all sorts of things. You didn't send word to me you just let me . . .'

'You could have come to Lion Kop,' he said softly.

'To the home of that monster? Never!' And Michael looked away from her.

'Where's Father?'

'In his study, as usual. Oh, darling, you don't know how I've missed you. Tell me you love me, Michael.'

'I love you,' he repeated automatically and the sensation of suffocating was on him again. 'I must see Dad. It's very urgent.'

'You've just arrived. Let me fix something to eat – let me see to your poor face.'

'I have to see Dad now. I'm sorry.' And he went past her towards the house.

Garry was sitting at his desk when Michael walked into the study.

Michael hated this room. He hated the high smoke-stained ceiling, the oppressive darkness of the panelled walls, the massive hunting trophies, he hated even the carpets and the smell of old paper and dust. From this room had issued the decrees and the pronouncements which had restricted and predetermined his life. This room was the symbol of everything from which he wished to escape. Now he glared around it defiantly, as though it were a living thing – I've come back to extract from you what you owe me, he thought, you've had value from me, now pay me back!

'Michael!' Garrick's boot scraped on the wooden floor as he stood to greet him, and Michael winced at the sound.

'Hello, Dad.'

'Your mother and I, we have been so worried. Why didn't you send word to us?' The hurt was there in Garrick's voice. Michael opened his mouth to apologize in automatic guilt, but the words came out differently from the way he had intended.

'I was busy. I didn't have a chance.'

'Sit down, my boy.' Garrick gestured to one of the polished leather armchairs. He removed the metal-framed spectacles from his nose, but he did not look at Michael's injured face again. He would not think about Sean and Michael together.

'I'm glad you've come back. I was just working on the opening chapters of my new book. It's a history of our family from the time of your great-great-grandfather's arrival at the Cape. I'd very much like your opinion. I'd value it immensely. The considered opinion of a graduate from the South African College.'

The trap was closing. It was so obvious that Michael squirmed. He could almost feel the panelled walls moving in on him. He started to protest: 'Dad, I have to speak to you.' But already Garrick was adjusting his spectacles and shuffling through the papers on his desk, talking quickly.

'I think you'll like it. It should interest you.' Garrick glanced up and smiled at Michael with the eagerness of a child that brings a gift. 'Here we are. I'll start at the beginning. You must allow for it being the first rough draft. It's not polished yet.' And he began to read. At the end of each paragraph he searched for Michael's approval, smiling in anticipation of it. Until Michael could bear it no longer, until he shouted suddenly in the middle of a sentence.

'I want you to pay me out my share of Theuniskrraal.'

There was a momentary break in Garrick's reading, just a flutter in his voice to acknowledge Michael's request and then he went on steadily, but his voice had lost its timbre and was now a lifeless monotone. He finished the paragraph, laid the sheet aside, removed his spectacles and placed them in their case. The lid of the case snapped shut against the tension of its spring and Garry lifted his head slowly.

'Why?'

'I need the money.'

'What for?'

'I need it.'

Garry stood up and moved across to the window. He stood before it with his hand clasped behind him. The green lawns flowed down to the fence that bounded the gardens, and upon them the poinsettia bushes were vivid patches of scarlet. Beyond, the land lifted into the first long roll, golden grass and scattered forest with the cattle feeding beneath and the massive silver and blue clouds piled above.

'It will rain tonight,' Garrick murmured, but Michael did not answer. 'We need it. Three weeks of dry, and the pasture is withering.' Still no reply and Garry returned to his desk.

'I hear there was a fire on Lion Kop last night.'

'There was.'

'They say that your uncle is finished. They say the fire finished him.'

'No!' Michael denied it quickly. 'That's not true.'

'Is that why you want the money, Michael?'

'Yes.'

'You want to give it to Sean?'

'I want to buy a share in Lion Kop Wattle. I don't want to give anything – it will be a business offer.'

'And what about Theuniskraal – it's your home. You were born here.'

'Please, Dad. I've made up my mind.'

'Did Sean suggest this?'

'He did not. He knows nothing about it.'

'It's your idea then. You thought it up all on your own. You're going to sell out your own parents for him. My God, what sort of hold has he over you that you would do that for him.'

Flushing a dusty brick colour, Michael kicked back his chair and jumped to his feet.

'You make it sound like treachery.'

'That's exactly what it is!' shouted Garrick. 'It's Judas's work. Your mother and I – we raised you with everything. We scraped to send you to University, we built our whole lives around you. We worked for the day you would return here to Theuniskraal and . . .' He stopped, panting, and wiped from his chin the bubble of saliva that had burst through his lips. 'Instead you ran off to joint that . . . that swine. How do you think we liked that? Don't you think it nearly broke our hearts? Of all people you had to go to him! And now, now you want half of Theuniskraal to take him as a gift – to buy his . . .'

'Stop that!' Michael warned him sharply. 'And before you go on remember where I got my half of Theuniskraal. Remember who made the original gift.' He picked up his hat and riding-crop and strode towards the door.

'Michael.' The terrible appeal in Garry's voice checked him.

'What is it?'

'Your share – it isn't very much. I hadn't told you before, but there was a time – when you were very young. The rinderpest, I had to—' He couldn't go on.

'What are you trying to tell me?'

'Sit down, Michael. Sit down and I'll show you.' Reluctantly, afraid of what he was about to hear, Michael returned and stood beside his chair.

Garry selected a key from the bunch on his watch-chain and opened the top drawer of his desk. He selected a rolled document, slipped it from its retaining ribbon and handed it without speaking to his son.

Michael spread it and read the words upon the cover.

'Deed of Mortgage'.

With a sliding sensation in his stomach, he turned the page. He did not read it all. Words and groups of words stood out in bolder print, and they were sufficient:

'The Ladyburg Trust & Banking Co.' ... 'A certain piece of land in extent approx. 25,000 morgen situate in the district of Ladyburg, Magisterial Division of Pietermaritzburg, known as the farm Theuniskraal' ... 'All constructions, erections and improvements thereon ... Plus interest at eight and one half per cent.'

'I see.' Michael handed the document back to his father and stood up.

'Where are you going?'

'Back to Lion Kop.'

'No!' Garry whispered. 'No, Michael. Please, my son. No – O God – No!' Michael left the room and closed the door softly behind him.

When Anna came into the room Garry was sitting behind the desk, sitting quietly with his shoulders slumped forward.

'You let him go!' she hissed. Garry did not move, he did not seem to hear.

'He's gone. Gone to your brother – and you let him.' Her voice was very low, but now it rose harshly and she shrieked at him. 'You useless drunken animal. Sitting here playing with your little books. You were not man enough to breed him – your brother had to do that for you! And you are not man enough to keep him – again your brother! You let him go. You've taken my son from me.'

Garry sat unmoving. He saw nothing. He heard nothing. In his head was a soft, misty greyness, and the mist blotted out all sight and sound. It was warm in the mist – warm and safe. No one could reach him here for it wrapped and protected him. He was safe.

'This is all you are good for.' Anna snatched a handful of the manuscript sheets from the desk in front of him. 'Your little pieces of paper. Your dreams and stories of other men – real men.'

She ripped the pages through and through again, then flung them at him. The pieces fluttered and swirled, then settled like dead leaves on his shoulders and in his hair. He did not move. Panting in her grief and anger, she took up what remained of the manuscript and shredded that also, scattering the tiny white scraps about the room.

Chapter Seventy

The two of them stood together on the station platform. They did not speak. Most of the previous day and night had been spent talking and now there was nothing more to say. They stood together in quiet companionship – and a stranger looking at them would have known immediately they were father and son. Though Michael was not as tall, and he was lean beside Sean's bulk – yet the tone of the skin and the colour of the hair were the same. Both had the big Courtney nose and their mouths were wide and full-lipped.

'I'll telegraph as soon as I hit gold.' Sean had explained to Michael in detail the financial structure of Lion Kop. He had told him how he intended to find the money which would keep it from collapsing.

'I'll hold this end up.' Michael was to begin cutting the wattle which had survived the fire. They had ridden the previous afternoon through the plantations and marked the blocks which were ripe for the axe. 'Good luck, Uncle Sean.'

'Since we are working together now, Mike, I suggest you drop the "Uncle". It's too clumsy for everyday use.'

Michael grinned. 'Good luck, Sean.'

'Thanks, Mike.' They clasped hands, gripping hard, then Sean climbed up into the coach.

Jackson was friendly but firm and Nichols at the Standard Bank was very polite and full of sympathy. Sean caught the northbound train for Johannesburg to fire his last two bullets.

'Colonel Courtney. How good to see you.' The reception clerk at Candy's Hotel came round from behind his desk to greet Sean. 'We were only talking about you last week. Welcome back to Johannesburg.'

'Hello, Frank. Putting on a little weight there, aren't you?' Sean prodded his waistcoat and the man chuckled. 'Tell me, Frank, is Candy . . . is Mrs Rautenbach in?'

'Ah! There've been some changes since you left, sir.' The clerk grinned with just a trace of malice. 'It's not Mrs Rautenbach any longer. No, sir. Mrs Heyns – Mrs Jock Heyns now!'

'Good God! She married Jock!'

'That she did. Two weeks ago – biggest wedding in Jo'burg since the war. Two thousand guests.'

'Where is she now?'

'On the water. Off to England and the Continent for six months' honeymoon.'

'I hope she'll be happy,' Sean murmured softly, remembering the loneliness he had seen in her eyes when he left.

'With all Mr Heyns's money? How can she be otherwise?' the clerk asked in genuine surprise.

'Will you be staying, Colonel?'

'If you have a room.'

'We always have a room for our friends. How long, sir?'

'Two days, Frank.'

Tim Curtis was Chief Engineer on the City Deep. When Sean spoke to him about a loan he laughed.

'Christ! Sean, I only work there – I don't own the bloody mine.'

Sean had dinner with him and his bride of two years' standing. At their urging Sean examined their newborn infant and secretly decided that it looked like an unweaned bulldog.

Extending his stay in Johannesburg, Sean visited the banks. He had dealt with most of them long ago, but the personnel had changed, so he was puzzled that the manager of each institution seemed to have heard of him.

'Colonel Courtney. Now would you be Colonel Sean Courtney of Lion Kop Wattle Estates down in Natal?' And when he nodded he saw the shutters come down in their eyes, like windows barred by a prudent householder against burglars.

On the eighth night he ordered liquor to be sent to his suite – two full bottles of brandy. He drank steadily and desperately. The brandy would not quieten the violent struggles of his brain, but seemed to goad it, distorting his problems and deepening his melancholia.

He lay alone until the dawn paled out the yellow gaslight of the lamps. The brandy hummed giddily in his head and he longed for peace – the peace he had found only in the immense silence and space of the veld. Suddenly a picture formed in his mind of a lonely grave below a little hill. He heard the wind moan over it and saw the brown grass sway. That was peace.

He sat up unsteadily.

'Saul,' he said, and the sadness was heavy on him for the pilgrimage he had promised himself and had not made.

'It is finished here. I'll go now,' and he stood up. The giddiness caught him and he clutched at the head-rail of the bed to steady himself.

Chapter Seventy-one

He recognized the kopje from four miles off. Into his memory its shape was indelibly etched, the symmetrical slope of the sides cobbled with boulders that glinted dully in the sunshine like the scales of a reptile, the flattened summit ringed by a bolder stratum of rock, the high altar on which the sacrifice to greed and stupidity had been made.

Closer he could discern the aloe plants upon the slopes, fleshy leaves spiked like crowns and jewelled with scarlet blooms. On the plain below the kopje, in the short brown grass, stood a long line of white specks. Sean rode towards them and as he approached each speck evolved into a cairn of whitewashed stones and on each stood a metal cross.

Stiff from the long day in the saddle Sean dismounted slowly. He hobbled the horses, dropped saddle and pack from their backs and turned them loose to feed. He stood alone and lit a cheroot, suddenly reluctant to approach the line of graves.

The silence of the empty land settled gently upon him, a silence not broken but somehow heightened by the sound of the wind across the plain. The harsh tearing as his mount cropped at the dry brown grass seemed sacrilegious in this place, but it roused Sean from his thoughts. He walked towards the double line of graves and stood before one of them. Stamped crudely into the metal of the cross the words 'Here lies a brave burgher'.

He moved along the line of crosses and on each he read those same words. On some of them the printing was irregular, on one the 'r' in burgher had been replaced by a 'g'. Sean stopped and glared at it, hating the man who in his haste and unconcern thad made the epitaph an insult.

'I'm sorry.' He spoke aloud, apologizing to the man who lay beneath it. Then he was embarrassed, angry at himself for the weakness. Only a madman speaks aloud to the dead. He strode away towards the second row of crosses.

'Leading Seaman W. Carter, R.N.' The fat one.

'Corporal Henderson C.F.S.' Twice in his chest and another in the belly.

He walked along the line and read their names. Some were just names, others he saw instantly and vividly. He saw them laughing, or frightened, saw the way they rode, remembered the sound of their voices. This one still owed him a guinea, he remembered the bet.

'Keep it.' He spoke and immediately checked himself again.

Slowly he went on to the end of the line, his momentum running down as he approached the grave that stood separate from the others – the way he had ordered it.

He read the inscription. Then he squatted down comfortably on his haunches beside it and stayed there until the sun settled and the wind turned cold and plaintive. Only then he went to his saddle and loosened the blanket-roll. There was no firewood and he slept fitfully in the cold of the night and the icier cold of his throughts.

In the morning he went back to Saul's grave. For the first time he noticed that grass was growing up between the stones of the cairn and that the cross sagged a little to one side. He shrugged off his coat and went down on his knees, working like a gardener over the grave, weeding out the grass with his hunting knife, making certain the roots were removed. Then he went to the head and lifted the rocks away from around the cross. He tore the cross from the ground and re-dug the hole for it, setting it up again carefully, plugging the base with pebbles and earth and at last packing the whitewashed rocks firmly around it once more.

He stood back, brushed earth and flakes of whitewash from his hands and surveyed his handiwork. It still was not right, there was something missing. He thought about it, frowning heavily until he found the answer.

'Flowers,' he grunted and lifted his head towards the aloes on the kopje above him. He set off up the slope, picking his way through the little of boulders towards the summit. His knife slipped easily through the soft thick stems and the juice oozed heavily from the wounds. With an armful he started back down the slope. Out to one side a patch of colour caught his eye, a sprinkling of pink and white amoung the boulders. He detoured towards it. Hottentot Daisies, each one in perfect trumpet with a pink throat and a fragile yellow tongue. Delighted with his find, Sean laid aside his burden of aloe blooms and went in amongst them. Stooping like a reaper he worked through them towards the lip of a narrow ravine. gathering the flowers into posies and binding the stems together with grass. Finally he reached the ravine and straightened up to rest his aching back.

The ravine was narrow, he could have jumped across it with little effort – but it was deep. He peered down into it without much interest. The cleft was floored with rainwashed sand, and his interest quickened as he made out the half-buried bones of a large animal. But what made him climb down into the ravine was not the bones, but the bulky leather object entangled with them.

Sliding on his backside the last few feet of the descent he reached the bottom, and examined his find. A leather mule-pack, double pouches, and the buckles of the harness almost rusted away. He tugged the whole lot loose from the sand and was surprised at the weight of it.

The leather was dry and brittle, faded almost white with exposure and the locks of the pouches were rusted solid. With his knife he slit the flap of one pouch and out of it cascaded a stream of sovereigns. They fell into the sand, clinking upon each other in a heap that glittered with merry golden smiles.

Sean stared at them in disbelief. He dropped the pack and squatted on his haunches over the pile. Timidly he picked up one of the discs and examined the portrait of the old President, before lifting the coin to his mouth and biting down upon it. His teeth sank into the soft metal and he removed it from his mouth.

'Well, damn me sideways,' he invited, and he laughed out loud. Rocking back on his haunches and lifting his face to the sky he roared out his jubilation and his relief. It went on and on until his laughter dried suddenly, and he sobered.

Cupping a double handful of the gold he asked it:

'Now, where the hell did you come from?' And his answer was in the grim face embossed upon each coin. Boer Gold.

'And who do you belong to?'

The answer was the same, and he let the coins trickle through his fingers. Boer Gold.

'The hell it is!' he growled angrily. 'Starting this minute it's Courtney Gold.' And he began to count it.

As his fingers worked so did his brain. He prepared his case against his own conscience. They owed him the balance outstanding on a train of wagons filled with ivory, they owed him his deposits in the Volkskaas Bank, they owed him for a shrapnel wound in the leg and a bullet in the belly, they owed him for three years of hardship and danger, and they owed him for a friend. As he stacked the sovereigns into piles of twenty he considered his case, found it good and proven, justified it and gave judgement in his own favour.

'I find for the appellant,' he announced, and concentrated his whole attention on the counting. An hour and a half later he reached the total.

There was a huge pile of coins upon the flat rock he had used as a desk. He lit a cheroot and the smoke he drew into his lungs made him lightheaded. His conscience had surrendered unconditionally and in its place was a sense

of well-being. All the more intense for the period of depression through
which he had come.

'Sean Courtney accepts from the Government of the one-time Republic
of the Transvaal an amount of twenty-nine thousand, two hundred pounds,
in full discharge of all debts and claims.' He chuckled again and began
shovelling the gold back into the leather pouches.

With the heavy pack slung over his shoulders and with his arms full of
wild flowers, Sean went down the kopje. He saddled his horse and loaded
the pack on to his mule before he went to pile the flowers on Saul's grave.
They made a brave show of colour against the brown grass.

He lingered another hour, fussing over his floral arrangements and
resisting the temptation to thank Saul. For now he had decided the gold was
not a gift from the Republican Government – but from Saul Friedman. This
made it even easier to accept.

At last he mounted and rode away. As the man and his horses dwindled
into insignificance on the great brown plain, a dust devil came dancing up
from the south. A tall, spinning column of heated air and dust and fragments
of dry grass, it weaved and swayed towards the graveyard below the kopje.
For a time it seemed as though it would pass wide of it, but suddenly it
changed direction and dashed down upon the double row of crosses. It
snatched up the flowers on Saul's grave, lifted them ripped their petals and
scattered them widely across the plain.

Chapter Seventy-two

With Michael beside him lugging the carpet-bag which was the heaviest
item of luggage, Sean left the buggy and crossed the sidewalk into the offices
of the Ladyburg Banking & Trust Co.

'Oh! Colonel Courtney,' the young lady at the reception desk enthused.
'I'll tell Mr Pye you are here.'

'Please don't bother. I'll carry the glad news myself.'

Ronny Pye looked up in alarm as the door of his office flew open and the
two of them walked in.

'Good morning, Ronny,' Sean greeted him cheerfully. 'Have you bled any
good stones today, or is it still too early?'

Guardedly Ronny murmured a reply and stood up.

Sean selected a cigar from the leather box on the desk and sniffed it.

'Not a bad line in horse-dung you've got here,' he remarked and bit the
end off. 'Match please, Ronny, I'm a customer, where are your manners?'

Reluctantly, suspiciously, Ronny lit the cigar for him. Sean sat down and
placed his feet on the desk with ankles neatly crossed.

'How much do I owe you?' he asked. The question heightened Ronny's suspicion and his eyes settled on the carpet-bag in Michael's hands.

'You mean altogether? Capital *and* interest?'

'Capital *and* interest,' Sean affirmed.

'Well, I'd have to work that out.'

'Give it to me in round figures.'

'Well, very roughly, you understand, it would be around – oh, I don't know – say . . .' He paused. That carpet-bag looked confoundedly heavy. Its sides bulged and he could see the tension in Michael's arm muscles as he held it. 'Say, twenty-two thousand, eight hundred and sixteen pounds, fifteen shillings.' As he named the exact figure Ronny dropped his voice in veneration the way a primitive tribesman might invoke the name of his god.

Sean lowered his feet. Then he leant forward and swept the papers that covered the desk to one side.

'Very well. Pay the man, Michael.'

Solemnly Michael placed the bag in the cleared space. But when Sean winked at him his solemnity cracked and he grinned.

Making no attempt to hide his agitation, Ronny plunged both hands into the mouth of the bag and withdrew two pouches of unbleached vancas. He loosened the draw string of one and spilled gold on to his desk.

'Where did you get this?' he demanded angrily.

'At the end of the rainbow.'

'There's a fortune here,' Ronny protested, as he dipped into the carpet-bag again.

'A Goodly amount, I'll admit.'

'But, but . . .' Ronny was scratching in the pile of coins, hunting for the secret of their origin like a hen for a worm. However, Sean had spent a week in Johannesburg and another two days in Pietermaritzburg visiting every bank and exchanging small parcels of Kruger coin for Victorian and Portuguese, and the coin of half a dozen other States. For a minute Sean watched his efforts with a smile of happy contempt. Then he excused himself.

'We'll be getting on home now.' Sean placed an arm around Michael's shoulder and led him to the door.

'Deposit the balance to my account, there's a good fellow.'

Further protest stillborn on his lips, and despair mingled with frustration, Ronny Pye watched through the window as Lion Kop Wattle Estates climbed up into the buggy, settled its hat firmly, waved a whip in a courteous farewell and trotted sedately out of his clutches.

All that summer the hills of Lion Kop echoed to the thud of axes and the singing of hundreds of Zulus. As each tree toppled and fell in a froth of heaving branches, men with cane-knives moved forward to strip the rich bark and tie it in bundles. Every train that left for Pietermaritzburg towed truckloads of it to the extract plant.

Each long day together strengthened the bonds between Sean and Michael. The evolved a language of their own, notable only for its economy of words. Without lengthy discussion each took charge of a separate sphere of Lion Kop activity. Michael made himself responsible for the maintenance of equipment, the loading and dispatch, all the paperwork and the ordering of material. At first Sean surreptitiously checked his work, but when he found no fault in it he no longer bothered. They parted only at the end of each week; Sean to Pietermaritzburg for obvious reasons, and Michael to Theuniskrral in duty. Michael hated those returns home, he hated Anna's endless accusations of disloyalty and her occasional fits of weeping. But even worse was the silent reproach in Garry's face. Early each Monday morning, with the joy of a released convict he set off for Lion Kop and Sean's welcome:

'What about those bloody axe handles, Mike?'

Only in the evenings they talked freely sitting together on the stoep of the homestead. They spoke of money and war and politics and women and wattle – and they talked as equals, without reserve, as men who work together with a common purpose.

Dirk sat quietly in the shadows and listened to them. Fifteen years old, but Dirk had a capacity for hatred out of all proportion to his age, and he used it all on Michael. Sean's handling of Dirk was in no way different; his school attendance was still spasmodic, he trailed Sean about the plantations and received his full share of rough affection and even rougher discipline – yet he sensed in the relationship between Sean and Michael a terrible threat to his security. Merely by reason of age and experience he was excluded from the evening discussions on the stoep. His few contributions were received with indulgent attention, then the talk would be resumed as though he had not spoken. Dirk sat quietly planning in lurid detail his assassination of Michael. On Lion Kop that summer there were small thefts and unexplained acts of vandalism, all of which affected only Michael. His best riding-boots vanished, his single dress shirt was ripped down the back when he came to don it for the monthly dance at the schoolhouse, his pointer bitch whelped a litter of four puppies, which survived only a week before Michael found them dead in the straw of the barn.

Ada and her young ladies began preparing for the Christmas of 1904 in the middle of December. As their guests, Ruth and Storm came down from Pietermaritzburg on the twentieth and Sean's frequent absences from Lion Kop left a heavy burden of work on Michael. There was an air of mystery in the Protea Street cottage. Sean was strictly excluded from the long sessions in Ada's private rooms, where she and Ruth retired to plan the wedding dress, but this was not the only secret. There was something else, which was keeping all the young ladies in fits of suppressed giggles and excitement. With a little eavesdropping Sean gathered it was something to do with his Christmas present from Ruth. However, Sean had other worries, chief of which was maintaining his position in the fierce competition for Miss Storm Friedman's favours. This included a heavy expenditure on sweetmeats, which were delivered to Storm without Ruth's knowledge. The Shetland pony had been left in Pietermaritzburg and Sean was required to substitute at the cost of his dignity and grass stains on the knees of his breeches. As reward he was invited to take tea each afternoon with Storm and her dolls.

Favourite among all Storm's dolls was a female child with human hair and an insipid expression on its large china face. Storm wept with a broken heart when she found that china head shattered into many pieces. With Sean's help she buried it in the back yard and they stripped Ada's garden of flowers for the grave. Sullenly Dirk watched the funeral. Storm was now completely reconciled to her loss and so thoroughly enjoyed the ceremony that she insisted Sean exhume the body and start again. In all the doll was buried four times and Ada's garden looked as though a swarm of locusts had descended upon it.

Chapter Seventy-three

Christmas Day started early for Sean. He and Michael supervised the slaughter of ten large oxen for the Zulu labour force, then distributed pay and gifts. To each man a khaki shirt and short pants, and for each of their wives a double handful of coloured beads. There was much singing and laughter. Mbejane, risen from his sickbed for the occasion, made a speech of high dramatic content. Unable to prance on his freshly healed legs, yet he shook his spears, postured and roared his questions at them.

'Has he beaten you?'

'*Ai-bho!*' They hurled the negative back at him.

'Has he fed you?'

'*Yhe-bho!*' explosive accent.

'Is there gold in your pockets?'

'*Yhe-bho!*'

'Is he our father?'

'He is our father!'

All to be construed not too literally, Sean grinned. Then he stepped forward to accept the large earthen pot of millet beer that Mbejane's senior wife presented to him. It was a matter of honour that this be emptied without removing it from the lips, a feat which Sean and then Michael both accomplished. Then they climbed up into the waiting buggy. Mbejane took the reins and with Dirk on the seat beside him drove them down to Ladyburg.

After the first flurry of greeting and good wishes, Ruth led Sean into the back yard followed by everyone else. There stood a large object covered by a tarpaulin which was ceremoniously removed and Sean gaped at what Ruth had given him.

Its paintwork burnished to a high gloss, metal parts and polished leather upholstery sparkling in the sun – stood a motor vehicle.

Stamped in the huge metal wheel hubs, and below the mascot on the radiator were the words 'Rolls-Royce'.

Sean had seen these fiendishly beautiful machines in Johannesburg, and now he was overcome by the feeling of unease they had given him then.

'My dear Ruth, I haven't the words to thank you.' He kissed her heartily to delay the moment when he must approach the monster.

'Do you really like it?'

'Like it? It's the most magnificent thing I have ever seen.' Over her shoulder Sean noticed with relief that Michael had taken over. As the only engineer present, he was seated behind the wheel and speaking authoritatively to the crowd about him.

'Get in!' Ruth ordered.

'Let me look at it first.' With Ruth on his arm, Sean circled the Rolls, never approaching closer than half a dozen paces. The great headlights glared at him malevolently and Sean averted his eyes. His unease was slowly becoming genuine fear as he realized that he was expected not only to ride in the thing, but to direct its course and speed.

Unable to delay longer, he approach and patted the bonnet.

'Hey there!' he told it grimly. With an unbroken animal you must establish mastery from the first contact.

'Get in!' Michael was still in charge and Sean obeyed, placing Ruth in the middle of the front seat and himself nearest the door. On Ruth's lap Storm bounded and squealed with excitement. The delay while Michael consulted the handbook at length did nothing for Sean's confidence.

'Ruth, don't you think it wise to leave Storm behind – just this first time?'

'Oh, she isn't any trouble.' Ruth regarded him quizzically, then smiled. 'It's really quite safe, darling.' Despite her assurance, Sean stiffened in terror when the motor finally roared into life; and he held that pose, staring fixedly ahead, during the whole of their triumphal progress through the streets of Ladyburg. Citizens and servants boiled from the houses along their route and lined the road to cheer in wonder and delight.

At last they were back in Protea Street and when Michael stopped outside the cottage Sean escaped from the vehicle like a man waking from a nightmare. He firmly vetoed the suggestion that the family motor to church, on the grounds that it was irreverent and in bad taste. The Reverend Smiley was flattered that Sean remained awake throughout his sermon, and judged by Sean's worried expression that at last he was in fear for his soul.

After church Michael went out to Theuniskraal to eat Christmas dinner with his parents, but returned early in the afternoon to begin Sean's instruction. The entire population of Ladyburg turned out to watch Sean and Michael circling the block at a walking pace. By early evening Michael decided that Sean was ready for a solo circuit and accordingly he disembarked.

Alone at the wheel, sweating nervously, Sean looked at the sea of expectant faces around him and saw Mbejane grinning hugely in the background.

'Mbejane!' he bellowed.

'Nkosi!'

'Come with me,' and Mbejane's grin dissolved. He backed away a little. It was unnatural that a vehicle should move of its own accord – and Mbejane wanted no part of it.

'Nkosi, there is much pain still in my legs.'

Among the crowd were many of the Zulu labourers from Lion Kop, who had come down from the hills when news of the miracle reached them. Now one of these laughed in such a manner as to cast doubt on Mbejane's courage.

Mbejane drew himself to his full height and withered the man with his eyes, then he stalked proudly to the Rolls, sat on the seat beside Sean and folded his arms across his chest.

Sean drew a deep breath and gripped the steering-wheel with both hands, his eyes narrowed and he scowled ahead down the road.

'Clutch in!' he muttered to himself. 'In gear! Brake off! Throttle down! Clutch out!'

The Rolls leapt forward so violently that both he and Mbejane were nearly thrown over the back of the seat. Fifty yards farther on the machine expired from lack of fuel, a stroke of good fortune because it was unlikely that Sean would have been able to remember the procedure for stopping it.

Grey of face and unsteady of limb, Mbejane alighted from the Rolls for the last time. He never rode in it again – and secretly Sean envied him his freedom. He was greatly relieved to hear that it would be weeks before more fuel could be sent up from Cape Town.

Chapter Seventy-four

Three weeks before Sean's wedding Ada Courtney went into her orchard one morning early to pick fruit for breakfast. She found Mary there, dressed in her white nightgown, and hanging by her neck from the big avocado tree. Ada cut her down and sent one of the servants to call Doctor Fraser.

Between them they carried the dead girl to her cubicle and laid her on her bed. While Doc Fraser made a hasty examination Ada stood staring down at the face that death had made more pitiful.

'What depths of loneliness drove her to this,' she whispered, and Doc Fraser pulled the sheet over the corpse and looked across at Ada.

'That wasn't the reason – in fact, it might have been better if she were a little more lonely.' He pulled out his tobacco pouch and began to load his pipe. 'Who was her boy friend, Aunt Ada?'

'She had none.'

'She must have.'

'Why do you say that?'

'Aunt Ada, this girl was four months pregnant.'

It was a small funeral, just the Courtney family and Ada's girls. Mary was an orphan and she had no other friends.

Two weeks before the wedding, Sean and Michael finished the season's cut of bark and switched the Zulus to planting out the blocks destroyed by the fire. Together they drew up a draft Profit and Loss Account. Combining their rudimentary knowledge of accounting and arguing far into the night,

they finally agreed that from fifteen hundred acres of wattle they had cut
fourteen hundred and twenty tons of bark, to gross a little over twenty-eight
thousand pounds sterling.

But here all agreement ended. Michael insisted that the stocks of material
and expenditure on planting of new trees be carried forward, giving a net
profit for the year of nine thousand pounds. Sean wanted to write all
expenditure off against income and show a profit of one thousand, so they
deadlocked and finally sent all the books to a qualified accountant in
Pietermaritzburg. This gentleman sided with Michael.

They then considered the prospects for the coming season and were a
little awed when they realized that there would be four thousand acres of
wattle to reap and an expected gross of eighty thousand pounds sterling –
always providing there were no more fires. That evening, without Sean's
knowledge, Michael wrote two letters. One to a manufacturer of heavy
machinery in Birmingham, whose name and address Michael had furtively
copied from one of the huge boilers in the Natal Wattle Estate Company's
plant. The other to the firm of Foyle's booksellers in Charing Cross Road,
London, requesting the immediate dispatch of all and any literature on
processing of wattle bark. Michael Courtney had caught from Sean the habit
of dreaming extravagantly. He had also acquired the trick of setting out to
make those dreams become reality.

Three days before the wedding Ada and her young ladies set out for
Pietermaritzburg by train and Sean, Michael and Dirk followed in the
Rolls.

The three of them arrived dusty and bad-tempered outside the White
Horse Hotel. It had been a nerve-racking journey. Sean had enlivened it by
shouting incessant warnings, instruction and blasphemy at Michael, the
driver.

'Slow down, for God's sake, slow down! Do you want to kill us all!'

'Look out! What that cow!'

'Don't drive so close to the verge!'

Dirk had done his share by demanding halts for urination, hanging over
the sides, climbing tirelessly between the front and back seats, and urging
Michael to exceed the speed-limit set by Sean. Finally, in anger, Sean had
Michael stop the car and administered corporal punishment with the birch
of a melkbos tree cut from beside the road.

On arrival Dirk was met by Ada, and led away snivelling. Michael took
the Rolls and disappeared in the direction of the Natal Wattle Company's
plant, where he was to spend most of the following three days snooping and
asking questions, and Sean went to find Jan Paulus Leroux, who had come
down from Pretoria in response to Sean's wedding invitation. By the day of
the wedding Michael Courtney had complied a small volume of notes on
wattle processing, and Jan Paulus had given Sean a minute account of the
aims and objects of the South African Party. But in response to his urgings
Sean had promised only to 'think about it'.

The wedding ceremony had given everybody much cause for thought.
Although Sean had no qualms about marrying in a synagogue, yet he

steadfastly refused to undergo the painful little operation which would enable him to do so. His half-hearted suggestion that Ruth should convert to Christianity was met with a curt rejection. Finally, a compromise was agreed, and Ben Goldberg persuaded the local Magistrate to perform a civil ceremony in the dining-room of The Golds.

Ben Goldberg gave the bride away and Ma Goldberg wept a little. Ruth was mangificent in Ada's creation of green satin and seed pearls. Storm wore an exact miniature of Ruth's dress and sparked off a minor brawl with the other flower girls during the ceremony. Michael as Best Man conducted himself with aplomb. He quelled the riot among the flower girls, produced the wedding ring on cue and prompted the groom when he muffed his lines.

The reception on the lawns was attended by a huge crowd of the Goldbergs' friends and business associates and by half the population of Ladyburg, including Ronny Pye, Dennis Petersen and their families. Garrick and Anna Courtney were not there, nor had they acknowledged the invitation.

Brilliant sunshine blessed the day and the lawns were smooth and green as expensive carpets. There were long trestle tables laden with the fruits of Ma Goldberg's kitchen and the products of Ben Goldberg's brewery.

Storm Friedman went from group to group of guests, boosting up her skirts to display the pink ribbons in her pantaloons, until Ruth caught her at it.

Having found his first taste of champagne very much to his liking, Dirk went on to drink six glasses of it behind the rose bushes. He was then copiously ill. Fortunately Michael found him before Sean did, and spirited him away to one of the guest bedrooms and left him there to languish.

With Ruth on his arm, Sean inspected the display of wedding gifts and was impressed. He then circulated among the crowds on the lawn until he reached Jan Paulus and fell into an earnest political discussion. Ruth left them to it and went to change into her going-away clothes.

The prettiest and most blonde of Ada's young ladies caught the bouquet. Immediately thereafter she caught Michael's eye and blushed to match the crimson carnations in her hand.

Amid a hum of appreciative comment and a snowstorm of confetti Ruth returned and, a queen ascending the throne, took her seat in the Rolls. Beside her Sean, in dustcoat and goggles, steeled himself, muttered his usual incantations and gave the Rolls its head. Like a wild horse the machine seemed to rear on its hind wheels and then tear down the driveway scattering gravel and guests. Ruth cluthing desperately at a large hatful of ostrich feathers and Sean shouting at the Rolls to 'Whoa! There, girl,' – they headed out along the road that led through the Valley of a Thousand Hills to Durban and the sea, and disappeared in a tall column of dust.

Chapter Seventy-five

Three months later, having picked up Storm from Ma Goldberg *en passant*, they reappeared at Lion Kop homestead. Sean had put on weight and both of them had that smugly complacent look found only in the faces of couples returning from a successful honeymoon.

On the front stoep and in the outbuildings of Lion Kop were the crates and packing-cases which contained wedding gifts, Ruth's furniture and carpets, and the additional furniture and curtains they had purchased in Durban. Ruth, ably assisted by Ada, threw herself joyously into the task of unpacking and moving in. Meanwhile Sean began a tour of inspection of the estate to determine how much of it had suffered in his absence, and he felt vaguely cheated when he found that Michael had managed very well without him. The plantations were trim and cleared of undergrowth, the vast black scar through their centre was nearly obliterated with freshly planted rows of saplings, the labour force was half as productive again under the new incentive payment scheme which Michael, in consultation with the Accountant, had introduced. Sean gave Michael a lecture on 'not getting too bloody clever' and 'learning to walk before you run' which he ended with a few words of praise.

Thus encouraged, Michael approached Sean one night when he was alone in his study. Sean was in a state of deep contentment induced by a meal from an enormous roast sirloin which he was digesting, by the fact that Ruth had finally agreed to his adoption of Storm and the change of her name from Friedman to Courtney, and by the prospect of joining Ruth in their gartantuan double bed just as soon as he finished his brandy and his hand-rolled Havana cigar.

'Come in, Michael. Sit down. Have a brandy.' Sean greeted him genially, and almost defiantly Michael crossed the Persian carpet and laid a thick sheaf of papers on the desk in front of him.

'What's this all about?' Sean smiled at him.

'Read it and you'll see.' Michael retreated to a chair across the room. Still smiling Sean glanced at the heading on the top sheet.

'Preliminary estimates and ground plan for proposed Tannin Extraction Plant. Lion Kop Estates.'

The smile faded. Sean turned the page and as he read he began to frown and then to scowl. When at last he finished he relit his dead cigar and sat in silence for five minutes while he recovered from the shock.

'Who put you up to this?'

'Nobody.'

'Where would you sell your extract?'

'Page 5. The outlets are listed there – and the ruling prices over the last ten years.'

'This plant needs 20,000 tons of bark a year – if we planted every foot of Lion Kop and Mahobo's Kloof to wattle we could only supply half of that.'

'We'd buy the rest from the new estates along the valley – we could offer a better price than Jackson, because we'd save railage to Pietermaritzburg.'

'Who would run the plant?'

'I'm an engineer.'

'On paper you are,' Sean grunted. 'What about water?'

'We'd dam the Baboon Stroom above the falls.'

For an hour Sean poked and prodded at the scheme, seeking for a soft spot. His agitation mounted as Michael calmly met each of his queries.

'All right.' Sean growled. 'You've done your homework. Now answer me this one. How the hell do you propose finding seventy thousand pounds to finance this little lot?'

Michael closed his eyes as though he were praying, his jaw was a hard, thrusting line. And suddenly Sean wondered why he had never noticed the strength in that face, the stubborn almost fanatical determination. Michael opened his eyes again and spoke softly.

'A loan on Lion Kop and Mahobo's Kloof for twenty-five thousand, a notarial bond on the plant for as much again – and a public share issue on the balance.'

Sean jumped up from his desk and roared.

'No!'

'Why not?' still calmly and reasonably.

'Because I've spent half my life in debt up to here!' Sean grabbed his own throat. 'Because now at last I'm in the clear and I want to stay that way. Because I know what it feels like to have more money than I need, and I don't like the feeling. Because I'm happy just the way things are now – and I don't want to catch another lion by the tail and have him turn round and claw the hell out of me.' He stopped panting and then shouted: 'Because a certain amount of money belongs to you, but more than that you belong to it. Because I don't want to be that wealthy again!'

Lean and fast as an angry leopard, Michael came out of his chair and smashed a balled fist on to the top of the desk. He glared across at Sean, flushed angry red under his tan, quivering like an arrow.

'Well, I do! Your only objection to my plan is that it's sound,' he blazed. Sean blinked in surprise and then rallied.

'If you get it, you won't like it!' he bellowed, and Michael matched his volume.

'Let me be the judge of that!'

At that moment the door of the study opened and Ruth stood on the threshold and stared at them. They looked like a pair of game cocks with their hackles up.

'What on earth is going on?' she demanded. Both Michael and Sean looked up guiltily, then slowly they relaxed. Michael sat down and Sean coughed awkwardly.

'We are just having a discussion, my dear.'

'Well, you've woken Storm and just about torn the roof off.' Then she smiled and crossed to take Sean's arm. 'Why don't you leave it until tomorrow. Then you can continue your discussion at twenty paces with pistols.'

The pygmies of the Ituri Forests hunt elephant with tiny arrows. Once the barb is lodged they follow quietly and doggedly, camping night after night on the spoor until at last the poison works its way to the animal's heart and brings it down. Michael had placed his arrow-head deep in Sean's flesh.

Chapter Seventy-six

At Lion Kop Ruth found a happiness she had never expected, had not believed existed.

Up to this time her existence had been ordered and determined by an adoring but strict father, and then in the same manner by Ben Goldberg. The few short years with Saul Friedman has been happy, but now they were as unreal as memories of childhood. Always she had been wrapped in a cocoon of wealth, hemmed in by social taboos and the dignity of the family. Even Saul had treated her as a delicate child for whom all decisions must be made. Life had been placid and orderly, but deadly dull. Only twice she had rebelled, once to run away from Pretoria and again when she had gone to Sean in the hospital. Boredom had been her constant companion.

But now suddenly she was mistress of a complex community. The sensation had been a little overpowering at first and from habit she had appealed to Sean for him to make the fifty decisions that each day brought forward.

'I'll make a bargain with you,' he answered. 'You don't tell me how to grow wattle and I'll not tell you how to run the house – put the damn sideboard where it looks best.'

Hesitantly at first, then with growing confidence and at last with sureness and pride she made Lion Kop into a home of beauty and comfort. The coarse grass and scrub around the homestead fell back to make room for lawns and flower-beds, the outer walls of Lion Kop gleamed in a crisp new coat of whitewash. Inside, the yellow-wood floors shone like polished amber setting off the vivid Bokhara carpets and draped velvet curtains.

After a few disastrous experiments the kitchens began to yield a succession of meals that moved Michael to raptures, and even Sean pronounced them edible.

Yet, with a dozen servants, she had time for other things. To read, to play with Storm and to ride. Sean's wedding gift to her was a string of four golden palaminos. There was time also for long visits from and with Ada

Courtney. The two of them established an accord stronger than that of mother and daughter.

There was time for dancing and barbecues, there was time for laughter and for long quiet evenings when she and Sean sat alone on the wide front stoep or in his study and talked of many things.

There was time for love.

Her body, hard from riding and walking, was also healthy and hot. It was a sculpture sheathed in velvet and fashioned for love.

There was only one dark place in her happiness – Dirk Courtney.

When her overtures were met with sullenness and her small specially cooked gifts were rejected, she realized the cause of his antagonism. She sensed the bitter jealousy which was eating like a canker behind those lovely eyes and the passionately beautiful face. For days she prepared what she would say to him. Then she found the opportunity when he came into the kitchens while she was alone. He saw her and turned quickly to leave, but she stopped him.

'Oh, Dirk, please don't go. I want to discuss something with you.' He came back slowly and leaned against the table. She saw how tall he had grown in the last year, his shoulders were thickening into the shape of manhood and his legs were strong and tapered from the narrow hips that he thrust forward in a calculated insolence.

'Dirk . . .' she began and paused. Suddenly she was unsure of herself. This was not a child as she had imagined; there was a sensuality in that beautiful face she found disturbing – he carried his body with awareness, moving like a cat. Suddenly she was afraid, and she swallowed jerkily before she went on:

'I know how difficult it has been for you – since Storm and I came to live here. I know how much you love your father, how much he means to you. But . . .' She spoke slowly, her carefully prepared speech forgotten so that she had to grope for the words to explain. She tried to show him that they were not in competition for Sean's love; that all of them – Ruth, Michael, Storm and Dirk – formed a whole; that their interests did not overlap, but that each of them gave to Sean and received from him a different kind of love. When at last she faltered into silence she knew he had not listened nor tried to understand. 'Dirk, I like you and I want you to like me.'

With a thrust of his buttocks against the table, Dirk straightened up. He smiled then and let his eyes move down over her body, slowly.

'Can I go now?' he asked, and Ruth stiffened. Then she knew there was no compromise, that she would have to fight him.

'Yes, Dirk. You may go,' she answered. She knew with sudden clarity that he was evil, and if she lost this contest he would destroy her and her child. In that moment she was no longer afraid.

Catlike, Dirk seemed to sense the change in her. For a moment she thought she saw a flicker of doubt, of uncertainty in his eyes – then he turned away and sauntered out of the kitchen.

She guessed that it would come soon, but not as soon as it did.

Every afternoon Ruth would ride out into the plantations with Storm's pony on a lead rein beside her. They made a game of finding Sean and Michael, following the labyrinth of roads that criss-crossed through the blocks of trees, guided by the vague directions of the gangs of Zulus until finally they ran them down and delivered the canteens of coffee and the hamper of sandwiches. Then, all four of them would picnic on the soft carpet of dead leaves beneath the trees.

This afternoon, dressed in riding habit and carrying the hamper, Ruth came out into the kitchen yard. The young Zulu nursemaid was sitting in the shade of the kitchen wall flirting with one of the grooms. Storm was nowhere in sight, and Ruth asked sharply:

'Where is Miss Storm?'

'She went with Nkosana Dirk.' And Ruth felt the tingling premonition of danger.

'Where are they?' and the nursemaid pointed vaguely in the direction of the stables and outbuildings that sprawled away down the back slope of the hill.

'Come with me.' Ruth dropped the hamper and ran with her skirts gathered in one hand. She reached the first row of stables and hurried down them, glancing into each stall as she passed. Then into the feed rooms with the big concrete bins and the smell of oats and molasses and chopped lucerne mixing with the sharp tang of dung and dubbined leather, out again into the sunlight, running for the barns.

Storm screamed in terror, just once, but high and achingly clear, so the silence afterwards quivered with the memory of it.

The harness room. Ruth swirled in her run. *God, please No! Don't let it happen. Please! Please!*

She reached the open door of the harness room. It was gloomy and cool within the thick stone walls, and for a moment the scene made no sense to Ruth.

Her back wedged into the far corner, Storm stood with hands lifted to shield her face – small fingers rigid, splayed open, spread like the tip feathers of a bird's wing. Her body shook silently with her sobs.

In front of Storm, squatting on his heels, Dirk leaned forward with one hand outstretched as though he offered a gift. He was laughing.

Then Ruth saw the thing in Dirk's hand move and she froze with horror. It uncoiled from around his wrist, and slowly reached out towards Storm, its head cocked back in a half-loop of its body, tiny black tongue vibrating between the grinning pink lips.

Ruth screamed, and Dirk jumped to his feet and spun to face her with his right hand hidden behind his back.

From the corner Storm darted across the room and buried her face in Ruth's skirts, weeping piteously. Ruth picked her up and held her tight against her shoulder, but she never took her eyes off Dirk's face.

'It's only a *rooi-slang*.' Dirk laughed again, but nervously. 'They're harmless – I was only having a joke.' He brought the snake out from behind his back, dropped it on to the stone-flagged floor and crushed its head under the heel of his riding-boot. He kicked it away against the wall, then with an impatient gesture he brushed the black curls from his forehead and made to leave the room. Ruth stepped across to block his path.

'Nannie, take Miss Storm back to the house.' Gently Ruth handed the child to the Zulu nursemaid and closed the door after them and slid the bolt across.

Now it was darker in the room, two square shafts of sunlight filled with moving dust motes fell from the high windows, and the quiet was spoiled only by the sound of Ruth's laboured breathing.

'I was only having a joke,' Dirk repeated, and grinned defiance at her. 'I suppose you'll run and tell my father?'

The walls of the room were studded with wooden pegs from which were suspended the harness and saddlery. Beside the door hung Sean's raw-hide stockwhips, eight foot of braided leather tapering from the butt handle into nothingness. Ruth lifted one down from the rack and flicked the lash out to lie upon the floor between them.

'No, Dirk, I'm not going to tell your father. This thing is between you and me alone.'

'What are you going to do?'

'I'm going to settle it.'

'How?' Still grinning, he placed his hands on his hips. Beneath rolled sleeves his upper arms bulged smooth and brown as though they had been freshly oiled.

'Like this.' Ruth flicked her skirt aside and stepped forward, using the whip underhand she sent the lash snaking out to coil around Dirk's ankle and immediately she jerked back on it. Taken completely off balance, Dirk went over backwards. His head hit the wall as he fell and he lay stunned.

To give herself space in which to wield the whip, Ruth moved into the centre of the room. Her anger was cold as dry ice, it gave strength to arms already finely muscled from riding, and it seared away all mercy. Now she was a female animal fighting for the survival of herself and her child.

She had learned to use a stockwhip in the process of becoming an expert horsewoman, and her first blow split Dirk's shirt from the shoulder to the waist. He shouted with anger and rolled on to his knees. The next blow cut down from the base of his neck along his spine, paralysing him in the act of rising. The next, across the back of both knees, knocked his legs out from under him.

On his belly Dirk reached for the pitchfork against the wall, but braided leather exploded around his wrist. He shouted again and rolled on his side to nurse the hand against his chest.

Ruth hit him and he writhed across the floor towards her like a wounded leopard with its hindquarters shattered by buckshot. Step by step Ruth retreated before him, and the long lash hissed and cracked.

Without mercy she beat him until his shirt hung in tatters from his waist and shoulders, exposing the smooth white skin with the fat crimson welts superimposed upon it.

She beat him until his shouts turned to shrieks and finally to sobbing.

She beat him until he lay shivering, moaning, moving feebly with his blood sprinkled in dark blobs on the stone paving around him.

Then she folded the whip and turned to open the door. In the stable yard, standing in silent curiosity, were gathered all the grooms and the household servants.

Ruth selected four of them.

'Take the Nkosana to his room.'
Then to one of the grooms,
'Ride to the Nkosi. Tell him to come quickly.'

Sean came quickly, he came wild with anxiety and nearly tore the door off Dirk's bedroom in his haste. He stopped dead on the threshold and stared aghast at Dirk's back.

Stripped to the waist, Dirk lay face downwards on his bed and Ruth worked over him with a sponge. On the table beside her stood a steaming basin and the pungent reek of antiseptic filled the room.

'Good God! What happened to him?'

'I beat him with a stockwhip.' Ruth answered him calmly and Sean gaped at her, then dropped his gaze to Dirk.

'You did that?'

'Yes.'

The anger tightened Sean's mouth.

'Jesus God! You've cut him to pieces. You've half killed him.' And he glanced at Ruth. 'Why?'

'It was necessary.' The absolute assurance and lack of remorse in her reply, confused Sean. He was suddenly uncertain in his anger.

'What did he do?'

'I can't tell you that. It is something private between us. You must ask Dirk.'

Sean crossed quickly to the bed and knelt beside it.

'Dirk. Dirkie, my boy, what happened. What did you do?' And Dirk lifted his face from the pillow and looked at his father.

'It was a mistake. It doesn't matter.' Then he buried his face in the pillow once more, and his voice was muffled, so Sean had excuse for not believing that he had heard correctly.

'What did you say?' he demanded, and there was a short delay before Dirk replied quite distinctly,

'I said – it was my fault.'

'That's what I thought you said.' Sean stood up with a puzzled expression on his face. 'Well, I don't know why you sent for me, Ruth. You seem to have the situation fairly well in hand.' He moved to the door, looked back as though he were going to speak, then, changing his mind, he shook his head and went out.

That night in the quiet, exhausted minutes before sleep, Sean murmured against her cheek, 'I think you did today what I should have done years ago.' And then, with a sleepy chuckle, 'At least there's no doubt in anyone's mind as to who is the mistress of Lion Kop.'

Chapter Seventy-seven

There was a guileless simplicity in Sean's approach to life – in his mind any problem when met with direct action disintegrated.

If you became obsessed with a woman, you tumbled her. If that didn't produce the desired effect, then you married her.

If you wanted a piece of land or a horse or a house or a gold mine, then you paid your money and took it. If you didn't have the money, you went out and found it.

If you liked a man you drank with him, hunted with him, laughed together. If you disliked him, you either punched him in the head or subjected him to a ponderous sarcasm and mockery. Either way you left him in no doubt of your feelings.

When a son got out of hand you whaled the tripe out of him, then gave him an expensive present to demonstrate your affection. Now he admitted he had been tardy in the matter of Dirk; but Ruth had done a most effective job. It only remained for him to call Dirk into the study and shout at him a little. A week later he returned from a trip to Pietermaritzburg and with an embarrased scowl presented to Dirk his peace offerings. The first was a brassbound leather case, which contained a hand-made shotgun by Greener of London; tooled silver inlay, glossy walnut stock and butt, and interchangeable Damascus barrels. The other was a two-year-old filly from the Huguenot stud at Worcester in the Cape. By Sun Lord out of Harvest Dance, Sun Dancer was an animal of the most distinguished blood in Africa and of surpassing beauty and speed. Sean paid a thousand guineas for her and considered he had got the best of the bargain.

As far as he was concerned there was no longer any problem with Dirk, and Sean could devote all his energy to furthering the three major ventures in which he was engaged.

Firstly, there was the matter of putting Ruth with child. Here he had her wholehearted co-operation. But their efforts, apart from providing a deal of healthy exercise and pleasure, were singularly unproductive. Sean remembered the deadly skill he had shown in their first encounter and was puzzled. Ruth suggested they keep in training until the rainy season began; she had developed a superstitious belief in the power of thunder. On one of his trips to Pietermaritzburg Sean saw a carved wooden statue of Thor in a junk dealer's window. He bought it for her, and from then on the god stood on their bedside table clutching his hammer and overlooking their strivings with such a knowing expression that at last Ruth turned him face to the wall.

Then there was Michael's Tannin Extract Plant. He had resorted to a piece of underhand villainy that shocked Sean and, he professed, killed his

belief in the essential decency of mankind. Michael had visited each of the
new growers along the valley, men who had followed Sean's lead in the
planting of wattle, and after swearing them to secrecy had offered them
shares in the Company. They were enthusiastic and with Michael at the
head they visited Lion Kop in formal deputation. The meeting was conducted
with so much verbal thunder and lightning thrown about that the Great
God Thor might have been in the Chair. At the end Sean, who had teased
the idea all the months since Michael had approached him and who was
now as enthusiastic as any of them, allowed himself to be persuaded. He
spoke for seventy per cent of the shares and the balance was allotted to the
other growers. A Board of Directors, with Sean as Chairman, was elected
and the Accountant was instructed to proceed with the registration of The
Ladyburg Wattle Co-operative Ltd. For the first time Sean exercised his
majority vote to crush the misgivings of the other shareholders and appoint
Michael Courtney as Plant Engineer. Then, with an older director to act
as a steadying influence, Michael was put aboard the next Union Castle
mailship for England, a letter of authority in his pocket and Sean's warnings
and words of wisdom in his head. Remembering himself at the age of twenty-
three, Sean decided it necessary to point out to Michael that he was being
sent to London to buy machinery and increase his knowledge of it, not to
populate the British Isles nor to tour their hostelries and gaming
establishments.

There was swift reaction from Jackson at Natal Wattle, who regretted
that the contracts between the Tugela Valley growers and his company
would not be renewed – and that owing to heavy demands from elsewhere
he could no longer supply seed or saplings. But Sean's seedbeds were now
well enough established to meet the needs of the whole valley – and, with
luck, their plant would be in production by the beginning of the next cutting
season.

Before Michael and his chaperon returned flushed with the success of
their mission, Sean had another visitor. Jan Paulus Leroux, weary of the
three-year argument he and Sean had conducted with the aid of the postal
authority, arrived at Ladyburg and expressed his intention of staying until
Sean agreed to head the Natal branch of the South African Party and to
contest the Ladyburg seat at the next Legislative Assembly elections. Two
weeks later, after he and Sean had hunted and killed a number of guinea-
fowl, pheasant and bush buck; had consumed huge quantities of coffee and
more moderate quantities of brandy; had talked each other hoarse and had
closed the last gap between them, Jan Paulus left on the Johannesburg train
with the parting words:

'*Toe Maar!* It is settled then.'

The South African Party's platform was a Federation of the Cape, the
Transvaal, the Orange Free State and Natal, under government responsible
to Whitehall. It was opposed by extreme English and Dutch opinion – the
jingoes who shouted 'God Save the King', and the Republicans who wanted
the Almighty to treat the King differently.

After meeting with the men on the list Jan Paulus had given him, Sean
began the campaign. His first convert was Ruth Courtney, won over by the
prospect of the excitement associated with an election battle rather than by

Sean's oratory. Now a week or more of every month was spent in travelling about Natal to attend political gatherings. Ruth rehearsed Sean in his speech – he had only one – until he was word perfect. She kissed the babies and played hostess to the wives, tasks in which Sean showed no special aptitude. She sat beside him on the platform and restrained him from going down into the audience to engage in hand-to-hand combat with hecklers. The way she smiled and the way she walked certainly lost no votes for the South African Party. From London Lord Caisterbrook promised his support, and it looked as though Sean could count on twenty-two seats out of the Assembly's thirty.

On the level ground below the escarpment, hard by the Baboon Stroom, the plant of the Ladyburg Wattle Co-operative took shape. It covered ten acres of ground and beyond it the cottages of the employees were laid out in neat blocks.

Despite Michael's vehement protests, Sean bowed to the will of his fellow directors and a consulting engineer was employed until such time as the plant was in production. Without him they would have lost a year's harvest of bark, for although Michael was eager and tireless, yet he was a young man with no practical experience. Even with the older man to help him, the plant was still a long way from ready before the season's cutting began. When at last the tall silver smoke stack began spewing smoke and the furnaces lit the night with a satanic glow, there were thousands of tons of bark piled up in the open-sided warehouses around the factory.

It was a wonderful season. Good rains had filled the bark with rich sap and when the year ended the Co-operative had shown a profit of ten thousand pounds on its first year's operation – Lion Kop Estates a profit four times greater. Sean had been in and out of debt as swiftly as a small boy visits the bathroom when sent to wash his face.

Despite the good rains, there were only three spectacular storms that summer. On each occasion Sean was away from Lion Kop on business. While the lightning leapt across the hills and the hammer strokes of thunder broke over the valley, Ruth stood at the window of their bedroom and lamented another wasted opportunity. Mbejane did much better – all his seed brought forth fruit and he reaped four fat sons that season.

Chapter Seventy-eight

It was a busy year for Dirk Courtney also. After his resounding defeat at the thin end of the stockwhip, Dirk and Ruth fell into a state of wary neutrality – but he conceded control of Lion Kop to her

Storm Courtney he ignored, unless she was in Sean's lap or riding on his shoulder. Then he watched them covertly until he could find an excuse to interrupt their play or to get away from Lion Kop. His absences became more frequent; there were trips to Pietermaritzburg and the surrounding districts to play rugby and polo; there were mysterious night excursions to Ladyburg, and in the day he rode away at dawn each morning – Sean believed he rode to school until he received a note from the headmaster asking him to call.

After showing him the attendance register and a copy of Dirk's academic record, the headmaster leaned back in his chair and waited for Sean's comments.

'Not so good, hey?'

'I agree, Mr Courtney. Not so good.'

'Couldn't we send him to a boarding establishment somewhere, Mr Besant?'

'Yes, you could do that,' Besant agreed dubiously, 'but would it serve any real purpose – apart from providing him with expert coaching in rugby football?'

'How else will he get his University entrance?' Sean was impressed with what higher education had done for Michael. He looked upon it as a sovereign alchemy for all the ills of youth.

'Mr Courtney . . .' The headmaster hesitated delicately. He had heard of Sean's temper and did not want a personal demonstration of it. 'Some young men are not really suited for University training.'

'I want Dirk to go,' Sean interjected.

'I doubt that either Stellenbosch or Cape Town Universities share your ambitions.' The schoolroom manner re-asserted itself for a moment, and Besant spoke with dry sarcasm.

'You mean he's stupid?' Sean demanded.

'No, no.' Hurriedly Besant soothed him. 'It's just that he's not, shall we say, academically inclined.'

Sean pondered on that awhile. It seemed a very nice distinction, but he let it go and asked:

'Well, what do you suggest?'

Besant's suggestion was that Dirk Courtney get the hell out of his school – but he phrased it gently.

'Although Dirk is only sixteen – he is very mature for his age. Say you were to start him at the Wattle Company . . .?'

'You recommend I take him away from school, then?' Sean asked thoughtfully, and Besant suppressed a sigh of relief.

Dirk Courtney was apprenticed to the foreman boilermaker at the factory. His first action was to inform his journeyman that he'd be running this show one day and what was he going to do about it? That gentleman, forewarned by Dirk's reputation, regarded him dolefully, spat a long squirt of tobacco juice an inch from Dirk's gleaming toecap, and replied at some length. He then pointed to a kettle on the workshop forge and told Dirk to make him a cup of coffee, and while he was about it to remove his thumb from his posterior orifice. Within a week the two of them were cronies and the man, whose name was Archibald Frederick Longworthy, began to instruct Dirk in arts other than the fabrication of steelplate. Archy was thirty-six years old. He had come out to Africa after completing a five-year term in Leavenworth Prison for the intriguing offence of *Crimen Injuria* – and when he explained the meaning Dirk was delighted.

Archy introduced Dirk to one of his friends, Hazel, a plump and friendly girl who worked at the Ladyburg Hotel as a barmaid and dispensed her favours in the same cheerful manner that she did her liquor – but Dirk quickly became her favourite, and he learned some pretty little tricks from her.

Shrewdly, Archibald Longworthy examined the situation and decided that nothing but profit could come from friendship with Sean Courtney's heir. Besides which the boy was a lot of fun. He could tumble a tart and swig gin with the best of them – also he had a seemingly inexhaustible supply of sovereigns.

In exchange Dirk hero-worshipped Archy, diverting much of his feelings from his father to his first real friend. Ignoring the grey wrists and neck which bespoke Archy's disaffection for soap and water, the pale wispy hair through which pink scalp showed, ignoring also the black tooth in the front of his mouth – Dirk invested him with the glamour and excitement of an old-time pirate.

When Dirk found himself to be suffering from a painless but evil-smelling condition, it was Archy who assured him it was only '*whites*' and went with him to a doctor in Pietermaritzburg. On the train coming home they planned their revenge with much laughter, comradely banter – and rising anticipation.

Hazel was surprised to see them in the middle of a Sunday afternoon, she sat up quickly as they came into her room overlooking the backyard of the hotel.

'Dirkie, you shouldn't come here in the daytime – your Pa will find out.' It was warm in the shabby little room, and the smell of cheap scent and a half-filled chamber-pot blended harshly with the odour of female perspiration. Hazel's thin chemise clung damply to her body and outlined the heavy hang of her breasts and the deep lateral fold around the level of her navel. There were dark smudges below her eyes and a curl was sweat-plastered down her cheek where the pillow had left little creases in the skin. The two of them stood in the doorway and grinned at her, from many experiences Hazel recognized the wolfish eagerness those grins masked.

'What do you want?' Suddenly she was afraid and instinctively she covered the deep cleft of her bosom with one hand.

'Dirkie here wants to have a little chat with you.' Carefully Archy closed the door and turned the key in the lock, then he ambled towards the bed. Manual labour had sheathed his arms in hard, knotty muscle and the hands that hung at his sides were disproportionately large and coated with coarse, blond hair.

'You keep away from me, Archy Longworthy.' Hazel swung her legs off the bed, the chemise pulled up to expose fat white thighs. 'I don't want no trouble, you just leave me alone.'

'You give Dirkie here a clap. Now Dirkie here is my friend and he don't like what you give him.'

'I didn't! It couldn't have been me. I'm clean – I tell you.' She stood up, still holding the front of her chemise closed and back away before him. 'You keep away from me.' Then as Archy jumped forward, 'No – don't I'll . . .' And she opened her mouth to scream, but Archy's hand closed over it like a great hairy spider. She struggled desperately, clawing at the hand over her face.

'Come on, Dirk.' Archy chuckled, as he held her easily with one arm around her waist. Uncertainly Dirk hesitated at the door, no longer grinning.

'Come on, man. I'll hold her.' With a sudden swing of his arm Archy hurled the girl face down on the bed, then jumped across to keep her mouth smothered in the pillow. 'Come on, Dirk, use this!' With his free hand Archy unbuckled the wide belt he wore. The leather was studded with blunt metal spikes. 'Double it over!'

'Hell's teeth, Arch – you reckon we should?' Dirk still hesitated, the belt hanging limply from his hands.

'You scared, or something?' And Dirk's mouth hardened at the gibe. He stepped forward and swung the belt in a full overarm stroke across the wriggling body. Hazel froze at the sting of it and she gasped explosively into the pillow.

'That's the stuff – hold on a second.' Archy hooked his thumb into the thin fabric of her chemise and ripped it down from the shoulder-blades to the hem. Her fat woman's buttocks bulged through, dimpled and white. 'Now, give it hell!'

Again Dirk lifted the heavy doubled leather, he stood poised like that while a sensation of giddy power buoyed him upwards to the level of the gods, then he swung his body down into the next stroke.

Chapter Seventy-nine

'He's unopposed,' Ronny Pye murmured, and beside him Garrick Courtney stirred uneasily.

'Have you heard him speak?' Ronny persisted.

'No.'

'He wants to throw in Natal with that bunch of Dutchmen up in the Free State and Transvaal.'

'Yes, I know.'

'Do you agree with him?'

Garry was silent, he seemed to be engrossed with the antics of the small herd of foals in the paddock in front of them as they chased each other on legs that seemed to have too many joints, clumsy in their fluffy baby coats.

'I'm sending twenty yearlings up to the show sales in Pietermaritzburg

– should average about four, five hundred a head because they're all first-class animals. Be able to let you have a sizable payment on the bond.'

'Don't worry about that now, Garry. I didn't come out here looking for money.' Ronny offered his cigar-case, and when Garry refused he selected one himself and began preparing it carefully. 'Do you agree with this idea of a Union?'

'No.'

'Why not?' Ronny did not look up from his cigar, he did not want to show his eagerness prematurely.

'I fought them – Leroux, Niemand, Botha, Smuts. I fought them – and we won. Now they're sitting up there in Pretoria calmly plotting to take over the whole country – not just the Free State and Transvaal, but Natal and the Cape as well. Any Englishman who helps them is a traitor to his King and his country. He should be put against the wall and shot.'

'Quite a few people round here think that way – quite a few. And yet no one is opposing Sean Courteney – he's just going to walk into the Assembly.'

Garry turned and began limping slowly along the paddock fence towards the stables, and Ronny fell in beside him.

'Seems to me and the others we need a good man to put against him – someone with a lot of prestige. Good war record, man who has written a book and knows what's going on – knows how to use words. If we could find someone like that, then we'd be happy to put up the expense money.' He struck a match and waited for the sulphur to clear before he lit his cigar and spoke through the smoke. 'Only three months to election time – we got to get organized right away. He's holding a meeting at the schoolhouse next week.'

Sean's political campaign, which had been ambling along mildly without causing much interest, suddenly took on new dramatic quality.

His first meeting in Ladyburg was attended by most of the local population – all of them so starved for entertainment that they were prepared to listen to Sean reel off the little speech that they had already read reported verbatim in most of the Natal newspapers. With hardy optimism they hoped that question time might be more rewarding – and some of them had prepared queries on such momentous matters as the price of hunting licences, the public library system, and the control of foot and mouth disease. At the very least it was an opportunity to meet friends from the outlying areas.

But apart from Sean's employees, friends and neighbours, others arrived at the schoolhouse and filled the first two rows of desks. All of them were young men Sean had never seen before, and he eyed them with heavy disapproval while they laughed and joked loudly during the preliminaries.

'Where did this bunch come from?' he demanded of the Chairman.

'They came in on the afternoon train – all in one party.'

'Seems as though they're looking for trouble.' Grimly Sean sensed in them the slightly feverish excitement of men steeling themselves to violence. 'Most of them have been on the bottle.'

'Now, Sean.' Ruth leaned across and laid her hand on his knee. 'You must promise not to get worked up. Don't antagonize them.' Sean opened his mouth to reply, then left it like that as Garry Courtney came in through the crowd around the doorway and moved across to sit with Ronny Pye in the back row.

'Close your mouth, darling,' Ruth murmured and Sean obeyed, then smiled and waved a greeting to his brother. Garry replied with a nod, and immediately fell into deep discussion with Ronny Pye.

Amid coughing and feet shuffling the Chairman rose to introduce Sean to men who had been his schoolmates, who had drunk his brandy and hunted with him. He went on to tell them how Sean had won the Anglo-Boer war virtually single-handed, how he had brought prosperity to the district with his factory and his wattle. Then he ended with a few remarks that had Sean squirming in his seat and trying to get two fingers into his collar.

'So, ladies and gentlemen of our fair district – I give you a man of vision and foresight, a man with a heart as big as his fists – your candidate and mine, Colonel Sean Courtney!'

Sean stood up smiling, to be rocked by a blast of jeers and catcalls from the front rows. The smile faded and his fists curled into great bony hammers on the table in front of him. He scowled down on them, beginning to sweat with anger. A light tug on the tail of his coat steadied him and his fists opened a little. He began to speak, bellowing above the shouts of 'Sit down!', 'Speak up!', 'Give him a chance!', 'Stand down!', and the thunder of booted feet stamping in unison on the wooden floor.

Three times in the uproar he lost the run of his speech and had to turn to Ruth for prompting, scarlet in the face with anger and mortification, while waves of derisive laughter broke over him. He ended up reading out the last half from his notebook – it made little difference that he stumbled and lost his place repeatedly for no one more than three feet away could hear a word. He sat down and a sudden silence descended on the hall, an air of expectancy that made Sean realize that this must have been carefully planned – and that the main entertainment was still to follow.

'*Mr* Courtney.' At the back of the hall Garry Courtney was on his feet, and every head was craned around towards him. 'May I ask you a few questions?'

Sean nodded slowly. So that is it! Garry planned this reception.

'My first question, then. Can you tell us what the name is for a man who sells his country to the enemies of his King?'

'Traitor!' howled the hecklers.

'Boer!' They stood up in a mass and roared at him. The pandemonium lasted perhaps five minutes.

'I'm taking you out of here,' Sean whispered to Ruth and reached for her arm, but she pulled away.

'No, I'm staying.'

'Come on, do as I tell you. This is going to get rough.'

'You'll have to carry me out first,' she flared at him, angry and beautiful.

Sean was about to accept the challenge, when suddenly the uproar ceased abruptly. Again, all heads turned towards Garrick Courtney, where he stood ready with his next question. In the silence he grinned maliciously.

'One other thing, do you mind telling us the nationality and faith of your wife?'

Sean's head jerked back. He felt the sickening physical jolt of it in his stomach, and he started to struggle to his feet. But Ruth was already standing, and she laid a hand on his shoulder to prevent him rising.

'I think I will answer that one, Garry.' She spoke clearly with just that trace of huskiness in her voice.

'I am a Jewess.'

That silence persisted. Still with her hand on Sean's shoulder, standing straight and proud beside him, she held Garry's stare across the room. Garry broke first. Flushing up along his neck, he dropped his eyes and shifted clumsily on his bad leg. Among the men in the front rows the same guilty reaction followed her words. They glanced at each other and then away, moving awkwardly in shame. A man stood up, and started down the aisle towards the door. Half-way there he stopped and turned.

'Sorry, Missus. I didn't know there'd be any of that,' and he went on towards the door. As he passed Ronny Pye he tossed a sovereign into his lap. Another man stood up, grinned uneasily at Ruth and hurried out. Then in twos and threes the others followed him. The last of them trooped out in a bunch, and Sean noted with relish that not all of them returned Ronny's sovereigns.

At the end of the schoolroom Garry dithered, uncertain whether to leave or to stay and attempt to brazen his way out of a situation he had so seriously misjudged.

Sean stood up slowly and encircled Ruth's waist with one arm, he cleared his throat for it was choked with his pride of her.

'Not only that,' he called, 'but she's one of the best goddamned cooks in the district also.' In the laughter and cheers that followed Garry stumbled and pushed his way out of the room.

Chapter Eighty

The following day Garrick Courtney announced his intention of contesting the Ladyburg seat as an Independent, but not even the Loyalist newspapers gave him an outside chance of winning – until six weeks before polling-day.

On that evening, long after dark, Dirk hitched Sun Dancer at the rail outside the hotel. After he had loosened the girth and slipped the bit from her mouth, he left her to drink at the trough and went up on to the sidewalk. As he sauntered past the bar he peered in through the large window with its gold-and-red-lettered slogan, 'Got a thirst, drink a Goldberg Beer!'

Quickly he checked the clientele at the bar for informers. There were none of his father's foremen – they were always dangerous, nor were Messrs

Petersen or Pye or Erasmus present this evening. He recognized two of the
factory mechanics, a couple of railway gangers, a bank clerk, a counter-hand
from the Co-operative Society among the half-dozen strangers – and he
decided that it was safe. None of these ranked high enough in Ladyburg
society to carry news to Sean Courtney of his son's drinking habits.

Dirk walked to the end of the block, paused there for a few seconds, and
then strolled casually back. But his eyes were restlessly checking the shadows
for tale carriers. Tonight the main street was deserted, and as he came level
with the swing doors of the bar he stepped sideways through them and into
the warm yellow lamplight of the saloon. He loved this atmosphere – he
loved the smell of sawdust, liquor, tobacco smoke and men. It was a place
of men. A place of rough voices and laughter, of crude humour and
companionship.

A few of the men along the bar glanced up as he entered.

'Hey, Dirk!'

'We've missed you – where have you been all week?'

Dirk returned Archy's greeting self-consciously and when he walked to
take the stool beside him at the end of the bar counter he held himself erect
and swaggered a little – for this was a place of men.

'Good evening, Dirk. What will it be?' The barman hurried across to
him.

'Hello, Henry – is it all right tonight?' Dirk dropped his voice to a
whisper.

'Should be – we aren't expecting any snoopers.' Henry reassured him.
'But the door behind you isn't locked.'

Dirk's seat in the corner had been selected with care. From it he could
survey each newcomer to the room while being screened himself by the
drinkers along the counter. Behind him a door led through the washup into
the back yard – a necessary precaution when you're seventeen and both the
law and your father forbid you liquor.

'Very well, then – give me the usual.' Dirk nodded.

'You're out late tonight.' Henry remarked as he poured gin into a tumbler
and filled it with bottled gingerbeer. 'You been out hunting again?' Henry
was a small man in his early fifties, with a pale unsunned face and little
blue eyes, and now as he asked the question he winked one of them at Archy
Longworthy.

'Did you get it tonight?' Archy took over the catechism.

Dirk laid a finger along the side of his nose. 'What do you think?'
He grinned and they all laughed delightedly.

'Who was it? *Madame?*' Archy drew him out, playing for the other
listeners, who were leaning forward still chuckling.

'Oh, her!' Dirk shrugged contemptuously. *Madame* was the code name
of the wife of one of the railway drivers. Her husband ran the night train
to Pietermaritzburg every alternate day. She was not considered much of a
conquest.

'Who then?' Henry kidded softly.

'I'll let you know when I'm finished nesting there myself,' Dirk promised.

'A pretty one?' they insisted. 'Young, hey?'

'She's all right – not too bad.' Dirk tasted his gin.

'Man, you get so much you don't hardly 'preciate it any more,' Archy chided him, grinning at his audience, and Dirk bridled with pleasure. 'Come on, Dirk – tell us, man. Is she hot?'

For answer Dirk extended one finger cautiously and touched his glass, hissed sharply as though he had touched red hot steel and jerked his hand back with an exclamation of pain. They roared with appreciation and Dirk laughed with them, flushing, eager for their acceptance.

'Give us the story—' Henry insisted. 'You don't have to give us the name, just give us the details. Where did you take her?'

'Well—' Dirk hesitated.

'Come on, Dirk. Tell us about it.'

And of course he obliged. Telling it in detail so that the indulgent quality of their laughter changed and they leaned closer to him listening hungrily.

'Jesus! Did she say *that*?'

'Then what did you do?' they encouraged him.

And Dirk told them. He was a natural storyteller and he built up the suspense until there was a small island of attentive silence around him. But the rest of the bar-room was louder with laughter and voices than it had been when he entered. One group in particular were feeling their liquor.

'– So I took her hand,' Dirk went on, 'and I said, "Now I've got a little surprise for you." "What is it?" she asked, as though she didn't know. "Close your eyes and I'll show you." I told her . . .' And a voice rang loudly from across the room:

'– You take that big ugly bastard Courtney. What does he do except drive round in a big motor-car and make speeches.'

Dirk stopped in the middle of a sentence and looked up. Suddenly his face was pale. The man who had spoken was one of the group at the far end of the bar. He was dressed in a shabby overall of blue denim. A man no longer young, with the lines of hardship etched deep around his eyes and mouth.

'You know who gives him his money? I tell you – we give it to him. Without these he'd be finished – he wouldn't last a month.' The man held up his hands, they were calloused and the nails were split and ragged, encrusted with dark semi-circles of dirt. 'That's where he gets his money. Colonel Bloody Courtney.'

Dirk was staring across at the speaker; his hands lay clenched on the counter in front of him. Now suddenly the room was very quiet – so that the man's next words seemed even louder.

'You know what he pays – thirty-two pounds a month top journeyman's wages! Thirty-two pounds a month!'

'The minimum rate is twenty-five—' one of his companions observed dryly. 'I reckon you're free to move on to a better job – if you can find it. Me, I'll stay on here.'

'That's not the point. That big idle bastard's making a fortune out of us – I reckon he can afford to pay more. I reckon . . .'

'Do you reckon you're worth that much?' Dirk jumped up from his stool and shouted the question down the length of the counter. There was a stir of interest and every head turned towards him.

'Leave him, Dirk, he's drunk. Don't start anything,' Henry whispered in agitation, and then raising his voice and turning to the other, 'You've had

enough, Norman. Time you were on your way. Your old lady will be waiting
dinner for you.'

'Good God!' Norman was peering in Dirk's direction, his eyes focusing
blearily.

'Good God! It's Courtney's pup.'

And Dirk's face set into nervous rigidity. He began to walk slowly down
the room towards the man.

'Leave him, Dirk.' To restrain him Archy caught his arm as he passed.
But Dirk shrugged it off.

'You insulted my father. You called him a bastard!'

'That's right.' Norman nodded. 'Your daddy's a bastard all right. Your
daddy's a big lucky bastard who's never done a full day's work in his life
– a big, lucky, bloodsucking bastard. And he's whelped an equally useless
pup, who spends his time . . .'

Dirk hit him in the mouth, and he went over backwards off the stool,
flailing his arms as he fell. He hit the floor with his shoulders and rolled up
on to his knees spitting blood and a broken tooth from his mouth.

'You little bastard—' he mouthed through the blood. Dirk stepped forward
with his left foot and swung his boot with the whole weight of his body
behind it. The toe of his boot thudded into the man's chest and flung him
on to his back.

'Christ, stop him,' shouted Henry from behind the bar. But they sat
paralysed as Dirk stooped for the bar stool, lifted it above his head and then
brought it down, swinging his body with it as though he were chopping a
log. The heavy wooden seat hit the man in the centre of his forehead, it hit
solidly for the back of his head was against the floor and could not give with
the blow. It split his skull cleanly and twin spurts of blood shot from his
nostrils into the sawdust on the floor.

'You've killed him.' A single voice broke the long silence that followed.

'Yes.' Dirk agreed. *I've killed him. I've killed a man.* It sang within him
savagely. It came up and filled his chest so that he could hardly breathe.
And he stood over the corpse not wanting to miss a moment of it. He felt
his legs trembling under him, the muscles of his cheeks so tight with
excitement they felt they must tear.

'Yes, I killed him.' His voice was choked with the violence of the pleasure
that gripped him. His vision narrowed down so that the dead man's face
filled the whole field of it. The forehead was deeply dented and the eyes
bulged from their sockets.

Around him there was a sudden bustle of consternation.

'You'd better send for his father.'

'I'm getting out of here!'

'No, stay where you are. Nobody must leave.'

'My God, call Doc Fraser.'

'Doc's not wanted – get the police.'

'He was so quick – like a bloody leopard—'

'Christ, I'm getting out of here.'

Two of them stooped over the body.

'Leave him!' snapped Dirk. 'Don't touch him.' Jealous as a young lion of its kill. And instinctively they obeyed. They stood up and moved away. With them everyone else drew back, leaving Dirk standing alone.

'Get his father,' repeated Henry. 'Someone ride out and call Sean Courtney.'

An hour later Sean strode into the room. He wore an overcoat over his nightshirt and his boots had been pulled hurriedly over his bare feet. He stopped on the threshold and glared around the room, his hair in wild disorder from sleep – but when he entered, the atmosphere in the room changed. The tense silence relaxed and every face turned eagerly towards him.

'Mr Courtney – thank God you've come,' blurted the young police constable who was standing beside Dr Fraser.

'How bad is it, Doc?' Sean asked.

'He's dead, Sean.'

'Pa, he insulted . . .' Dirk started.

'Shut up!' Sean ordered him grimly. 'Who is he?' he fired at the constable.

'Norman Ven Eek – one of your fitters from the mill.'

'How many witnesses?'

'Fourteen of them, sir. They all saw it.'

'Right,' Sean ordered, 'get the body down to the police station. You'll be able to take statements from them tomorrow morning.'

'What about the accused . . . I mean what about your son, sir?' The constable corrected himself.

'I'll be responsible for him.'

'I'm not sure that I shouldn't . . .' He saw the expression on Sean's face. 'Well, that will be all right, I suppose,' he agreed reluctantly.

'Pa . . .' Dirk started again.

'I told you to keep your mouth shut – you've done enough damage for one night.' Sean spoke without looking at him, then to the barman,

'Fetch a blanket.' Then to the police constable, 'Get some of them to help you,' and he pointed towards the window which was lined four deep with curious faces.

'Very well, Mr Courtney.'

After they had shuffled out with the blanket-wrapped body, Sean glanced significantly at Dr Fraser.

'I'd better get down there – complete my examination.'

'You go ahead,' Sean agreed and the doctor packed his bag and went. Sean closed the door behind him and slammed the shutters across the window. Then he turned to the men who stood anxiously along the bar.

'What happened?' They stirred restlessly and looked everywhere but at him.

'You, George?' Sean selected one of his mechanics.

'Well, Mr Courtney, your Dirk went up to Norman and hit him off the stool. Then he kicked him as he was trying to get up, then he picked up the stool and hit him with it.' The mechanic stumbled hoarsely through his explanation.

'Did this man provoke him?' Sean demanded.

'Well, he called you a – begging your pardon, Mr Courtney – he called you a big, idle, bloodsucking bastard.'

Sean frowned quickly. 'Did he now! What else did he say?'

'He said you were a slave owner – that you starved your men. He said that he was going to get even with you sometime.' Archy Longworthy took over the telling of it with a note of interrogation in his voice as he glanced round at the others for support. After a few seconds there was a guilty nodding of heads and a few murmurs of agreement. Archy took courage from it. 'He sort of hinted that he was going to wait for you one night and get even.'

'Did he say that in so many words?' Sean's presence dominated the room with such an obvious air of authority that when Archy looked again for support he found it in their faces.

'He said: "One night I'm going to wait for that big bastard – then I'll show him a few things." ' Archy gave them the exact words. No one protested.

'Then what happened?'

'Well then he sort of picked on young Dirk. And "Here's Courtney's brat," he said. "Yellow as his old man, I reckon!" '

'What did Dirk do?' Sean asked.

'Well, Mr Courtney, he just laughed – like a gentleman, sort of, nice and friendly. 'Forget it, he said, – you've had too much to drink.'

A sudden thought occurred to Sean. 'What was Dirk going in here, anyway?'

'Well, it's like this, Mr Courtney – a few weeks ago he lent me a couple pounds. I asked him to call round here tonight so I could give it back to him – that's all it was.'

'He wasn't drinking then?' Sean asked suspiciously.

'Good Lord, no!' Archy was so obviously shocked at the suggestion that Sean nodded.

'All right, what happened then?' he pursued.

'Well, Norman went on ribbing him. Called him a coward and all that – I can't remember the exact words. But at last young Dirk lost his temper. He walked across and hit him off the stool. Well, I guess Norman deserved that – what do you think, boys?' Archy looked at them again.

'That's right – fair made my blood boil to hear him picking on Dirk like that.' The mechanic backed him up and the others murmured agreement.

'Well, then,' Archy took up the tale again, 'Norman's lying on the floor and pulls out his knife.' There was a rustle of astonishment from along the bar. One man opened his mouth and lifted his hand in protest, but suddenly embarrassed, he carried the gesture through and massaged his neck.

'Knife. What knife – where's it now?' Sean leaned forward eagerly. Standing beside him Dirk began to smile softly. When he smiled his face was beautiful.

'Here's the knife.' Henry, the barman, reached under the counter and brought out a large bone-handled clasp knife. Everybody in the room stared at it blankly.

'How did it get there?' Sean asked, and now for the first time he was aware of the sickly guilt-ugly faces in front of him. He knew then for certain it was a lie.

'I took it off Norman afterwards. We thought it best you should be the first to know the truth – you being his father, and all.' Archy wriggled his shoulders ingratiatingly and smiled around at his witnesses.

Slowly Sean turned to the man nearest to him, the bank clerk.

'Is this the knife with which Norman Van Eek threatened my son?'

'Yes, Mr Courtney.' The man's voice squeaked unnaturally.

Sean looked at the man beyond him and repeated the question exactly.

'Yes, that's the one, sir.'

'That's it.'

'Yes.'

'No doubt about it – that's it.'

He asked each man in turn and each answered the same.

'Dirk.' Sean came last to him. He asked it slowly and heavily. Looking into the clear innocent eyes of his son. 'As God is your witness – did Norman Van Eek draw thisknife on you?'

Please, my son, deny it now. Say it so they all can hear you. If you value my love – tell me the truth now. Please, Dirk, please. All this he tried to say, tried to convey it with the sheer force of his gaze.

'As God is my witness, Pa,' Dirk answered him and was silent again.

'You have not answered,' Sean insisted. *Please, my son.*

'He drew that knife from the hip pocket of his overalls – the blade was closed. He opened it with the thumbnail of his left hand, Pa,' Dirk explained softly. 'I tried to kick it out of his hand, but hit his chest instead. He fell on to his back and I saw him raise the knife as though he were going to throw it. I hit him with the stool. It was the only way I could stop him.'

All the passion went out of Sean's face. It was stony and hard.

'Very well,' he said. 'We'd better get home now.' Then he addressed the rest of the bar-room. 'Thank you, gentlemen.' And he walked out through the door to the Rolls. Dirk followed him meekly.

The next afternoon Dirk Courtney was released by the local magistrate into his father's custody on bail of fifty pounds, pending the visit of the Circuit Court two weeks later, when he was to stand trial on a charge of manslaughter.

His case was set down at the head of the Court list. The whole district attended the trial, packing the tiny Courthouse and clustering at each of its windows.

After a retirement of seven minutes the jury brought back its verdict and Dirk, walking out of the dock, was surrounded by the laughing, congratulating crowd and borne out into the sunlight.

In the almost deserted Courtroom Sean did not rise from his seat in the front row of chairs. Peter Aaronson, the defence lawyer Sean had imported from Pietermaritzburg, shuffled his papers into his briefcase, made a joke with the Registrar, then walked across to Sean.

'In and out again in seven minutes already – that's one for the record book.' When he smiled he looked like a koala bear. 'Have a cigar, Mr Courtney.' Sean shook his head and Peter thrust a disproportionately large cigar into his own mouth and lit it. 'I tell you truly, though, I was worried by the knife business. I expected trouble there. I didn't like that knife.'

'No more did I,' Sean agreed softly, and Peter held his head on one side examining Sean's face with bright, birdlike eyes.

'But I liked those witnesses – a troupe of performing seals. "Bark," you say to them – Woof! Woof! Just like magic. Someone trained them pretty well.'

'I don't think I understand you,' Sean said to him grimly, and Peter shrugged.

'I'll post my account – but I warn you I'm going to hit you with a big one. Say, five hundred guineas?'

Sean lay back in his seat and looked up at the little lawyer.

'Say, five hundred,' he agreed.

'Next time you need representation – I recommend a bright youngster name of Rolfe. Humphrey Rolfe,' Peter went on.

'You think I'll need a lawyer again?'

'With your boy – you'll need a lawyer,' Peter told him with certainty.

'And you don't want the job?' Sean leaned forward with sudden interest. 'At five hundred guineas a throw?'

'Money I can get anywhere.' Peter took the cigar from his mouth and inspected the fluffy grey ash at its tip. 'Remember the name, Mr Courtney – Humphrey Rolfe. He's a bright boy – and not too fussy.'

He walked away down the aisle lugging his heavy briefcase, and Sean stood up and followed him slowly. Pausing on the steps of the Courthouse he looked across the square. The centre of a small knot of men, Dirk stood laughing, with Archy Longworthy's arm around his shoulder. Archy's voice carried to where Sean stood.

'Don't let any of you get the idea you can tangle with Dirkie here – you'll end up with your teeth busted clean out the back of your head.' Archy grinned so that the blackened tooth showed. 'I say it so you can all hear me. Dirkie here is my friend – and I'm proud of him.'

You alone, thought Sean. He looked at his son and saw how tall he stood. Shaped like a man – broad in the shoulders with muscle in his arms, no fat on the belly and long legs dropping away clean from hips.

'But he is only sixteen. He's a child – perhaps there is still time to prevent him setting hard. Then with truth he knew he was deceiving himself, and he remembered what a friend had said to him long ago:

'*Some grapes grew in the wrong soil, some were diseased before they went to the press, and others were spoiled by a careless vintner – not all grapes make good wine.*'

And I am the careless vintner, he thought.

Sean walked across the square. 'You're coming home,' he told Dirk harshly, knowing as he looked at the lovely face that he no longer loved his son. The knowledge nauseated him.

'Congratulations, Colonel. I knew we'd win,' Archy Longworthy beamed, and Sean glanced up him.

'I'll be in my office ten o'clock tomorrow morning. I want to talk to you.'

'Yes, sir!' grinned Archy happily, but he was not grinning when he left Ladyburg on the following evening's train with a month's pay in lieu of notice to compensate him.

Chapter Eighty-one

With the storm of adverse editorial comment raised by Dirk's trial, Garry Courtney's chances in the coming election increased significantly. The jingo press spoke darkly of a 'surprise outcome, which thinking men will welcome as a true assessment of the worth of the two candidates of the Ladyburg constituency'. Only the Liberal papers reported the generous pension which the Ladyburg Wattle Co-operative Co. voted to Norman Van Eek's widow and orphan.

But everyone knew that Sean Courtney was still a long way ahead. He could be certain of the vote of the two hundred men employed at the factory and on his estates, the other wattle producers of the valley and their employees, as well as a good half of the townsfolk and ranchers – that was until the *Pietermaritzburg Farmer & Trader* devoted a full front page to the exclusive story of one Archibald Frederick Longworthy.

Mr Longworthy related how, by the threat of physical violence and loss of employment, he had been forced to perjure himself in court. How, after the case, he had been summarily dismissed from his work. The exact nature of his perjury was not revealed.

Sean cabled his lawyers in Pietermaritzburg to begin immediate proceedings against the *Farmer & Trader* for defamation of character, libel, contempt, treason, and anything else they could think of. Then, reckless of his own safety, he climbed into the Rolls and raced at thirty miles an hour in pursuit of his cable. He arrived in Pietermaritzburg to find that Mr Longworthy, after signing a sworn statement and graciously accepting a payment of fifty guineas, had departed without leaving a forwarding address. Legal advice was against Sean visiting the editor of the *Farmer & Trader* and laying himself open to a counter-suit of assault and battery. It would be two months before the defamation trial was heard in court, and the election was to be held in ten days' time.

All Sean could do was publish a full-page denial in each of the Liberal papers, then return to Ladyburg at a more sedate pace. There a telegram awaited him from Pretoria. Jan Paulus and Jan Niemand suggested that in the circumstances it might be better if Sean withdraw from nomination. Sean's reply went sizzling back over the wires.

Like a pair in harness, Garry and Sean Courtney swept up to the polling-day finishing line.

The actual voting took place in the Ladyburg Village Management offices under the beady eyes of two Government registration officers. Thereafter, the ballot boxes would be removed to Pietermaritzburg, where on the following day in the City Hall the votes would be counted and the official results announced.

On opposite sides of the square the opposing candidates set up the large marquee tents from which free refreshments would be served to the voters. Traditionally the candidate who fed the largest number would be the loser. Nobody wished to put *their* choice to additional expense, so they patronized the other man's stall. This day, however, both candidates served an almost equal amount of food.

It was a day that threatened the approach of the wet season, humid heat lay trapped beneath grey overcast clouds and the occasional bursts of sunlight stung like the blast of an open furnace door. Sean, suited and waistcoated, sweated with anxiety as he greeted each visitor to his stall with a booming, false *camaraderie*. Beside him Ruth looked like a rose petal, and smelled as sweet. Storm, demure for once, stood between them. Dirk was not there – Sean had found work for him on the far side of Lion Kop. Many sly eyes and snide sallies remarked his absence.

Ronny Pye had persuaded Garry not to wear his uniform. Anna was with him, pretty in mauve and artificial flowers. It was only at closer range that the ugly little lines around her mouth and eyes, and the grey hairs that were woven in the shiny black mass of her hair showed up. Neither she nor Garry let their eyes wander across the square.

Michael arrived and spoke first with his father, kissed his mother dutifully, then crossed to resume the argument Sean had broken off the night before. Michael wanted Sean to buy ten thousand acres of the coastal lowlands around Tongaat and plant it to sugar-cane. Within a few minutes he realized that this was not the best time to push his idea; Sean greeted each of his points with hearty laughter and offered him a cigar. Discouraged but not resigned, Michael went into the ballot office and, settling his problem of divided loyalty, deliberately spoiled his paper. Then he returned to his office at the wattle factory to whip his sugar estimates into shape for the next attack on Sean.

Ada Courtney never left the Protea Street cottage all that day. She had steadfastly denied appeals to join either camp, and refused to allow any of her girls to help in the preparations. She had prohibited any political discussion in her house – and ordered Sean to leave when he had disregarded this rule. Only after Ruth had interceded and Sean had made an abject apology, was he allowed to return. She disapproved of the whole business and considered it undignified and common that members of her family should not only be standing for public office but actually competing for it. Her deep distrust of and contempt for officialdom stemmed from the time the Village Board had wanted to place street lamps along Protea Street. She had attended their next meeting armed with an umbrella, and in vain they had tried to convince her that street lights did not attract mosquitoes.

However, Ada was the only person in the district who did not attend. From mid-morning until polling closed at five o'clock the square was jammed solid with humanity, and when the sealed ballot boxes were borne in state to the railway station, many of them climbed on the same train and went up to Pietermaritzburg for the official counting.

It had been a day of unremitting nervous tension, so a very short time after entering their suite in the White Horse Hotel, Ruth and Sean fell into exhausted sleep in each other's arms . When, in the early morning a brilliant electrical storm raged down upon the town, Ruth moved restlessly in her sleep, coming slowly back to consciousness – and to the realization that she and Sean were already engaged in the business that had been delayed so long. Sean woke at the same time and, for the few seconds that it took him to understand what was happening, was as bewildered as she – then both of them went to it with a will. By dawn Ruth knew that she would bear a son, though Sean felt it was a little soon to tell for certain.

After bathing, they ate breakfast in bed together with a renewed sense of intimacy. Ruth in a white silk gown, with her hair loosed into a shiny mass on her shoulders and her skin glowing as though she had been freshly scrubbed, was extreme provocation to Sean. Consequently they arrived late at the City Hall, much to the agitation of Sean's supporters.

The counting was well advanced. In a roped-off section of the hall ballot officers sat in silent industry at the tables piled with the small pink slips of paper. On a placard above each table was printed the name of the district and the candidates, and between the tables scrutineers paced watchfully.

The body of the hall was filled with a milling, humming swarm of men and women. Before it engulfed them Sean caught a glimpse of Garry and Anna moving through the press, then for the next ten minutes he was subjected to an orgy of hand-shaking, back-slapping and well wishes – interrupted by a bell and a complete silence.

'The result for the legislative assembly seat of Newcastle . . .' a high thin voice announced in the hush '. . . Mr Robert Sampson 986 votes. Mr Edward Sutton 423 votes . . .' And the rest was lost in a burst of cheers and groans. Sampson was the South African Party candidate, and Sean fought his way through the pack that surrounded him.

'Well done, you old son of a gun,' shouted Sean and beat him between the shoulder-blades.

'Thanks, Sean. It looks as though we are home and dry I never expected a majority that size!' and they wrung each other's hands deliriously.

The morning went on with intervals of excited, buzzing tension exploding into applause as each result was announced. Sean's confidence rose as his party captured each seat that had expected, and one that they were resigned to lose – but then the bell rang again and in the same impersonal tone the Chief Registration Officer at last announced:

'The result for the legislative assembly seat of Ladyburg and the lower Tugela—' he felt the cold emptiness of apprehension in his stomach, and his breath burning up the back of his throat. Standing beside him he could sense the rigidity of Ruth's body and he groped for her hand.

'Colonel *Garrick* Courtney 638 votes. Colonel *Sean* Courtney 631 votes.'

Ruth's hand squeezed hard, but Sean did not reply to the pressure. The two of them stood very still, a tiny island of quiet in the surge and roar – in the triumphant cheers and despairing groans – until Sean said softly: 'I think we'll go back to the hotel, my dear.'

'Yes,' she answered as softly, and the sound of her voice was helpless pity. Together they started across the floor and a way opened to them. A passage lined by faces that bore expressions of regret, happiness, curiosity, indifference and triumphant malice.

Out into the sunlight and across the street to the rank of hirecabs they walked together, while behind them the uproar was muted – sounding at this distance like the voices of wild animals.

Sean handed Ruth up into the coach and was about to join her before he remembered what there was still to be done. He spoke to the driver and gave him money before coming back to Ruth.

'Please wait for me at the hotel, my dear.'

'Where are you going?'

'I must offer Garry our congratulations.'

Through the screen of bodies that surrounded him Garry saw Sean approaching and he felt his body tensing involuntarily – racked by that conflict of hatred and love he bore for this man.

Sean stopped in front of him and smiled. 'Well done, Garry!' he said and offered his right hand. 'You beat me in a hard straight fight – and I'd like to shake your hand.'

Garry took the words up with temerity, examined them with growing realization of their meaning and found that they were true. He had fought Sean and beaten him. This was something that could not be destroyed – something that Sean could never take away from him. *I've beaten him.* For the first time – the very first time in all my life!

It was an emotional orgasm so intense that for a long moment Garry could not move or make any reply.

'Sean . . .' His voice choked up. He caught Sean's outstretched hand in both of his and held it with desperate strength.

'Sean, perhaps now . . .' he whispered, 'I'd like to . . . I mean, when we get back to Ladyburg . . .' Then he stopped and blushed scarlet with embarrassment. Quickly he released Sean's hand and stepped back. 'I thought you might like to come out to Theuniskraal,' he mumbled, 'some day when you're not busy. Look around the old place.' Then more eagerly, 'It's been a long time. I've still got Pa's old . . .'

'Never!' Anna Courtney hissed the word. Neither of them had noticed her cross the hall, but now she appeared suddenly at Garry's side. Her eyes were bright gems of hatred set in their patterns of wrinkles, and her face was white as she glared at Sean. 'Never.' She hissed again, and took Garry's arm. 'Come with me,' she commanded, and Garry followed her meekly. But he glanced back at where Sean still stood, and there was a desperate plea in his eyes. A plea for understanding, for forgiveness of this weakness.

Chapter Eighty-two

Like one who lives in a hurricane belt, and recognizes the shape of clouds and the breathless hush that precedes high wind – Ruth knew she would have to deal with the brooding undirected rage which would be Sean's reaction to this failure of his plans. His moods came at widely spaced intervals and did not last long – but she feared those moods of his, and like the prudent householder forewarned of the hurricane's approach, she took precautions to minimize its wrath.

When she reached the hotel she sent an urgent summons to the Manager.

'In half an hour I want lunch served in the suite – not your ordinary bill of fare. Something really good.' The Manager thought a moment. 'Oyster! We have a barrel just arrived from Umhlanga Rocks.'

'Excellent.' Ruth liked the man's response to the emergency.

'Then I could do a smoked ham, cold venison, cold rock lobster, salads?'

'Excellent again. What about cheese?'

'Gruyère. Danish Blue. Camembert.'

'Wine?'

'Champagne?'

'Yes,' Ruth agreed instantly. She would shamelessly exploit Sean's weakness for it. 'A bottle of Veuve Clicquot – no, on second thoughts, three bottles.'

'I'll send the wine up first?'

'Immediately – with your best glass and a silver bucket,' Ruth told him.

Then she fled to her toilet. Thank the Lord for French perfume and this morning dress of grey silk she had been saving for just such an occasion. She worked quickly, but with skill, upon her face and hair, and when she was finished she sat quietly before the mirror and composed her features into an expression of peace. The effect was very satisfactory, she decided after critical contemplation. Since it was the way he had first seen it, Sean could never resist her hair in braids. It made her look like a little girl.

'Shall I open the wine, Madam?'

'Yes, please.' She called into the sitting-room, then went through to await the onslaught of the hurricane.

Ten minutes later it came wafting in like a gentle zephyr, with a cigar clamped between its teeth, its hands thrust deep into trouser pockets and a bemused expression on its face.

'Hey, now!' Sean stopped when he saw her, and removed the cigar. 'That's nice!'

The fact that he had noticed her appearance was proof that her weather forecast was hopelessly incorrect and she burst out laughing.

'What's so funny?' Sean asked mildly.

'Nothing and everything. You and me. Have a glass of champagne.'

'Mad woman,' Sean said and kissed her. 'I like your hair like this.'

'Aren't you disappointed?'

'About the result, you mean? Yes, I suppose I am.' He went to the central table and poured wine into the crystal glasses, handed one to her and took up the other.

'I give you a toast – the short, exciting political career of Sean Courtney.'

'You wanted to win so badly – but now . . .?'

Sean nodded. 'Yes, I always want to win. But now that the game is lost . . .' He shrugged. 'Shall I tell you something? I was getting a big sick of all the speechifying and hand-shaking. I feel that even in my sleep I have a vacant grin on my face.' He crossed to one of the leather arm-chairs and sank down into it gratefully. 'There is something else also. Come here and let me tell you about it.'

She went to him, sat in his lap and slid her hand into the front of his shirt so that she could feel the soft springy hair of his chest, and the hard rubbery flesh beneath.

'Tell me,' she said, and he told her about Garry. He spoke slowly, telling her everything – about the leg, how it was when they were children, and finally, about Michael. She was quiet for a while, and he could see the hurt in her eyes that Sean had been another woman's lover. At last she asked:

'Does Garry know that Michael is your son?'

'Yes. Anna told him one night. She told him the night I left Ladyburg – he wanted to kill me.'

'Why did you leave?'

'I couldn't stay on. Garry hated me for siring his son – and Anna hated me because I would not go to her.'

'She still wanted you, then?'

'Yes. That night – the night I left, Anna came to me and asked me to . . .' Sean paused. 'You know what I mean.'

'Yes.' Ruth nodded, hurt still and jealous, but making the effort to understand.

'I refused her – and she went to Garry and, in spite, she told him about the child. My God, what a poisonous bitch she is!'

'But if she wanted you, why did she marry Garry?'

'She was with child. She thought I had been killed in the Zulu war – she married him to provide a father for her child.'

'I see,' Ruth murmured. 'But why do you tell me this?'

'I wanted you to understand how I feel about Garry. After what he did to you at that meeting I can't expect you to have much sympathy for him – but he wasn't trying to hurt you, he was aiming at me. I owe him so much, I never seem able to pay him. That's why . . .'

'That's why you are glad he won today?' Ruth finished for him.

'Yes,' Sean answered eagerly. 'You see, don't you, how important this must have been to him. For the first time he was able to . . . able to . . .' Sean fluttered his hands in frustration as he sought the words.

'He was able to compete with you on equal terms,' Ruth supplied them for him.

'Exactly!' Sean struck the arm of his chair with clenched fist. 'When I went to congratulate him, he was ready to meet me. He invited me out to Theuniskraal – just then that evil, bloody woman interfered and took him away. But somehow I know it's going to be all right now.'

A knock on the outer door interrupted him, and Ruth jumped up from his lap.

'That will be the waiter with the lunch,' but before she was half-way across the room, the knock was repeated with such insistence that it threatened to loosen the plaster.

'I'm coming.' Irritated, Ruth raised her voice and swung the door open.

Led by Bob Sampson a flood of men rushed into the room; jabbering and gesticulating they bore down on Sean.

'What the hell's going on?' he demanded.

'You've won!' shouted Bob. 'A recount, you won on a recount – by ten votes!'

'My God!' breathed Sean, and then so softly that only Ruth heard him, 'Garry. Poor Garry!'

'Open that champagne – send for another case. We're in solidly – all of us!' exulted Bob Sampson. 'So let's drink to the Union of South Africa!'

Chapter Eighty-three

'Not even this once. Out of so many times, so many things – not even this once.' Already Garry Courtney was drunk. He lay deep in his chair with a tumbler held in both hands, stirring the brown liquid with a circular movement so a few drops slopped over the rims and stained the cloth of his trousers.

'No,' agreed Anna. 'Not even this once.' She stood with her back to him, staring out of the window of their suite into the gaslit street below, for she did not want him to see her face. But she could not control the harsh, gloating quality of her voice. 'Now you can go back to writing your little books. You've made your point – you've proved to yourself and the rest of the world how effective you are.'

Moving her hands slowly, she began to massage her own upper arms with sensual pleasure. A tiny shudder thrilled her so she moved restlessly and her skirts rustled like leaves in the wind. God, how close it had been – and she had been afraid.

'You're a loser, Garry Courtney. You *have* always been – and you *will* always be.'

Again she shuddered with the memory of her fear. He had so nearly escaped. She had seen it begin from the moment the first result was announced, every minute it had grown stronger. Even his voice had changed, deeper with the first hint of confidence in it. He had looked at her strangely, without submission, with the beginning of his contempt. Then the flare of rebellion when he had spoken to Sean Courtney. She had been truly afraid then.

'You are a loser,' she repeated, and heard the sound he made – half-gulp, half-sigh. She waited and when she heard the soft gurgle of brandy poured from bottle to glass she hugged herself tighter and now she smiled as she remembered the announcement of the recount. The way he had shrunk, the way he had crumpled and turned to her with all of it gone – the confidence and contempt wiped away. Gone! Gone for ever. Sean Courtney would never have him. She had made that oath – and now it would be kept.

As so many times before, she played over in her mind the details of that night. The night she had made the oath.

It was raining. She was standing on the wide stoeh of Theuniskraal, and Sean was leading his horse up across the lawns of Theuniskraal. The damp linen of his shirt clung to his shoulders and chest, the rain had made his beard break out in tiny curls so he looked like a mischievous pirate.

'Where's Garry?' Her own voice, and his voice answering.

'Don't worry. He's gone into town to see Ada. He'll be back by supper-time.'

Then he was coming up the steps towards her, standing tall above her, and his hand on her arm was cold from the rain.

'You must take better care of yourself now. You can't stand in the cold any more.' And he led her through the french doors. The top of her head was on a level with his shoulders, and his eyes as he looked down at her were gentle with masculine awe of pregnancy.

'You're a damn fine woman, Anna. And I'm sure you're going to make a fine baby.'

'Sean!' She remembered how his name had come up her throat like an involuntary exclamation of pain. The fierce forward surge that had flattened her body against his, back arching to send her hips forward searching for his manhood. The coarse electric feeling of his hair in her hands as she pulled his face down and the taste of his mouth opened warm and moist.

'Are you mad!' As he tried to break away from her, her arms locked around his body and her face pressed to his chest.

'I love you. Please, Sean, please. Just let me hold you, that's all. I just want to hold you.'

'Get away from me!' And she felt herself thrown roughly on to the couch beside the fireplace.

'You're Garry's wife and you'll soon be the mother of his child. Keep your hot little body for him.' And his face thrust forward, close to hers. 'I don't want you. I could no more touch you than I could go with my own mother. You're Garry's wife. If ever again you look at another man I'll kill you. I'll kill you with my bare hands.'

Love congealing instantly, transformed to hatred by his words. Her fingernails raking across his cheek so the blood slid down into his beard, and he caught her wrists. Holding her while she struggled and screamed at him.

'You swine, you dirty, dirty swine. Garry's wife you say. Garry's baby you

say! Now hear the truth. What I have within me you put there. It's yours
– not Garry's!'

Then he was backing away from her. 'You're lying. It can't be.'

Following him now, speaking those cruel words softly. 'You remember how
we said good-bye when you went to war? You remember that night in the
wagon?'

'Leave me, leave me alone. I've got to think. I didn't know.' And he was
gone. She heard the door of his study slam, and she stood in the centre of the
floor while the storm surf of her anger abated and exposed the black reefs of
hatred beneath.

Then she was alone in her bedroom, standing before the mirror – making
her oath.

'I hate him. There's one thing I can take from him. Garry belongs to me
now. Mine, not his. I will take that away from him.'

The pins pulled from her hair, so it tumbled to her shoulders. Her fingers
tangling it into confusion. Teeth closing on her own lips so she could taste
the blood.

'Oh God, I hate him' she whispered through the pain. Tearing open the
blouse of her dress, watching in the mirror the great pink bosses of her
nipples already darkening with the promise of fruition.

'I hate him.' Pantaloons torn and discarded, bowls of face powder and
cosmetics swept from the dressing-table to burst and fill the room with the
pungent reek of perfume.

Then lying alone in the darkening room. Waiting for Garry to come.

Now she turned away from the window and looked down at Garry,
triumphantly, knowing he could never escape again.

I have kept my oath, she thought, and crossed to the chair.

'Poor Garry.' She forced her voice to croon gently, and she stroked the
hair back from his forehead. He looked up at her, surprised, but eager for
affection. 'Poor Garry. Tomorrow we'll go home to Theuniskraal.'

She moved the bottle on the side table closer to his hand. Then she kissed
his cheek lightly, and went on into the bedroom of the suite – smiling again,
secure and safe in his weakness.

Chapter Eighty-four

Four months passed quickly. Sean, distracted by the responsibilities of his
office, the mountains of correspondence, the meetings and sessions, the
petitioners and the schemers – offered only a token resistance to Michael's
sugar plans. Michael went off to the coast, purchased the land, and became
deeply involved with the seller's eldest daughter. This young lady had the
dubious distinction of being one of the few divorcees in Natal. When the

scandal reached his ears, Sean, secretly pleased that Michael's chastity was at last shed, boarded the Rolls and went off on a flying mission of rescue. He returned to Ladyburg with a penitent Michael in tow. Two weeks later the young lady married a travelling salesman and moved from Tongaat to Durban, whereupon Michael was allowed to return to Tongaat and begin the development of the sugar estate.

Ruth no longer accompanied Sean on all of his absences from Ladyburg. Her swiftly increasing girth and a mild malady which assailed her in the mornings kept her at Lion Kop, where she and Ada spent much time in the design and fabrication of babywear. In this Storm rendered assistance. The matinée jacket, which took three months to knit, was certain to fit the infant perfectly – provided it was a hunchback with its one arm twice as long as the other.

Kept busy from early morning to nightfall in the capacity of overseer on Mahobo's Kloof, Dirk found little time for distraction. Ladyburg was now well covered by Sean's espionage system, and Dirk's few visits were reported in detail.

But on the far side of Ladyburg, derelict and shabby from want of love, brooded the great homestead of Theuniskraal. In the night a single window showed a pale yellow square of light as Garry Courtney sat alone at his desk. In front of him lay a pathetically thin sheaf of papers. Hour after hour he stared at it – but no longer seeing it. He was dry inside, deprived of the juice of life and seeking its substitute in the bottle, which was always near him.

The days drifted into weeks, and they in turn became months – and he drifted with them.

Each afternoon he would go down to the paddocks, then, leaning against the heavy wooden paling, he would watch his bloodstock. Hour after hour he stood unmoving and it seemed that, in time, he left his own body and lived within those richly gleaming skins, as though his own hooves drove deep into the turf as he ran, as though his own voice squealed and his muscles bunched and moved in the savage mating of heaving bodies.

Ronny Pye found him there one afternoon; without Garry being aware of his presence, he came up silently and stood beside him, studying the pale intense face with the chisel-marks of pain and doubt and terrible yearning sculptured deep around the mouth and below the pale blue eyes.

'Hello, Garry.' He spoke softly, but recognizing the pity in his own voice he thrust it aside. There was no room for softness now, and ruthlessly he hardened his resolve.

'Ronny.' Vaguely, Garry turned to him, and when he smiled it was shyly. 'Business or social?'

'Business, Garry.'

'The bond?'

'Yes.'

'What do you want me to do?'

'How about coming into town – we can go over things in my office.'

'Now?'

'Yes, please.'

'Very well.' Garry straightened up slowly. 'I'll come with you.'

They rode together over the crest of ground and down towards the concrete bridge over the Baboon Stroom. Both of them silent – Garry because there was nothing in him, nothing to give voice to; Ronny Pye because of his sense of shame for the thing he was about to do. He was going to take a man's home from him and turn him loose upon a world in which he would have no chance of survival.

At the bridge they stopped automatically to rest their horses, and they sat without speaking, an incongruous pair. One man sitting quietly, slim and wasted, his clothing slightly rumpled, his face austere with suffering; the other plump, red-faced below bright ginger hair, dressed in expensive cloth, fidgeting in the saddle.

There was little sign of life across the river. A long, tired smear of smoke from the wattle factory stack rising straight into the still hot air, a black boy moving cattle down to drink at the river, the huff and clatter and clang of a locomotive shunting in the goods-yards – but otherwise the town of Ladyburg lay slumbering in the heat of a summer afternoon.

Then on the open grassy plain below the escarpment, urgent movement caught Ronny's eye, and he focused his attention upon it with relief.

A horseman riding fast, and even at this distance Ronny recognized him.

'Young Dirk,' he grunted, and Garry roused himself and peered out across the river. Horse and rider blended into one unit, seeming to touch the earth so lightly they were bound to it only by a pale feather of dust that drifted low behind them.

'My God, that little bastard can ride.' In reluctant admiration Ronny shook his head solemnly and a drop of perspiration broke from his hairline and slid down his cheek. The horse reached the road and pivoted neatly, flattening into the increased speed of its run. Movement of such rhythmic grace and power that the watchers were stirred.

'Look at him go!' whistled Ronny. 'Don't reckon there's anything to catch that horse in the whole of Natal.'

'You think so?' Garry's voice was suddenly alive, and his lips were pursed in anger.

'I'm damned certain of it.'

'Mine. My colt – Grey Weather. Over a point-to-point course, I'd match him against any of Sean Courtney's stud.'

And those words gave Ronny Pye the idea. He turned it over in his mind while with slightly narrowed eyes he watched Dirk Courtney race Sun Dancer down towards the wattle factory. When horse and rider had disappeared through the tall gates, Ronny spoke softly:

'Would you back your colt with money?'

'I'd back him with my life.' There was savagery in Garry's voice.

Yes, thought Ronny, this way at least I will give him a chance. This way the fates will make the decision – there will be no blame to my account.

'Would you back him with Theuniskraal?' he asked, and the silence drew out.

'How do you mean?' whispered Garry.

'If you win, the bond on Theuniskraal is set aside.'

'And if I lose?'

'You lose the farm.'

'No,' snapped Garry. 'Christ, no! That's too much.'

Ronny shrugged indifferently. 'It was just an idea – you're probably wise. You wouldn't have much of a chance against Sean.'

Garry gasped sharply, that challenge had wounded deep as a lance. Made it a direct competition between Sean and himself; to ignore it would be to admit he could never win.

'I'll take the bet.'

'The whole bet? You'll cover my money with what you have left of Theuniskraal?'

'Yes, damn you. Yes. I'll show you how much chance I have against him.'

'We'd better get it down in writing,' Ronny suggested gently. 'Then I'll see if I can arrange it with Sean.' He touched his mount with his spurs and they moved forward across the bridge. 'By the way, I think it best we tell nobody about our little bet. We'll pretend it's just an honour match.'

Garry nodded his agreement. But that night when he wrote to Michael he told him about it, then went on to plead with Michael to ride Grey Weather in the race.

Two days before the competition Michael confided in his grandmother. Ada went out to Theuniskraal to try and dissuade Garry from this reckless gamble, without success. Garry was almost fanatical in his determination. The stake meant nothing to him – it was the prospect of winning.

And now he had Grey Weather and Michael to run for him. This time he would win. This time!

Chapter Eighty-five

In the dark Sean walked with Dirk down the lane to the stables. The clouds banked along the escarpment were fired red by the hidden sun and the wind fretted through the plantations, so that the wattle moaned and shook.

'North wind,' grunted Sean. 'It'll rain before nightfall.'

'Sun Dancer loves the rain,' Dirk answered him tensely, and Sean glanced at him.

'Dirk – if you lose today . . .' he started, but Dirk cut him short.

'I won't lose,' and again as though it were a vow, 'I won't lose!'

'If you'd only show as much determination in other things – the more important . . .'

'Important! Pa, this is important. This is the most important thing I've ever done.' Dirk stopped and turned to his father. He caught Sean's sleeve, clinging to him. 'Pa, I'm doing this for you – for you, Pa!'

Sean looked down and what he saw in his son's face, in that beautiful face, silenced the retort that he was about to make. Where did I go wrong with you, he asked himself with love stained by loathing. Where did you get this blood, why are you this way, demanded his pride and his contempt.

'Thank,' he said dryly, freed his arm and walked on towards the stables.

Sightless in his deep preoccupation with Dirk, Sean was into the stable yard before he noticed Mbejane.

'Nkosi. I see you.' Mbejane rose solemnly from the hand-carved stool on which he sat.

'I see you also,' Sean cried with pleasure, and then controlled himself. A display of emotion in front of lesser persons would embarrass Mbejane. 'You are well?' he asked gravely, and restrained the desire to prod the swelling dignity of Mbejane's stomach, reminding himself that Mbejane's abundant flesh and fat had been carefully cultivated as a sign to the rest of the world of his prosperity.

'I am well,' Mbejane assured him.

'That you have come gives me pleasure.'

'Nkosi, on a day of importance it is right that we should be together – as it was before.' And Mbejane allowed himself to smile for the first time, a smile that within seconds became a mischievous grin that Sean gave back to him. He should have guessed that Mbejane would never miss a fight, or a hunt, or a contest.

Then Mbejane turned to Dirk.

'Do us honour today,' he commanded, as though he spoke to one of his own sons. 'Your father and I will be watching you.' He placed a huge black hand upon Dirk's shoulder as though in benediction, then he turned to gesture with his fly-whisk at the stable-boys waiting behind him.

'Bring the horse!'

Two of them led her out, her hooves ringing on the paving of the yard as she danced a little. Head up, moving greyhound-bellied, pricking her ears forward and back, she saw Dirk and wrinkled the soft velvet of her nostrils as she whickered.

'Hey, girl!' Dirk walked towards her. At his approach she rolled her eyes until the whites showed and her small dainty ears flattened wickedly against her neck.

'Stop that nonsense,' Dirk admonished, and she bared yellow teeth menacingly and reached with her slender snakelike neck. He put out his hand to her and she took his fingers between those terrible teeth and nibbled them tenderly. Then, finished with pretence, she snorted, pricked her ears and nuzzled his chest and neck.

'Where is her blanket? Has she eaten? Put the saddle and bridle in the car.' Dirk snapped a chain of questions and instructions at the stable-boys as he caressed Sun Dancer's face with the gentle hands of a lover.

So many contradictions in one person. Sean watched his son with sadness heavy upon him, oppressive as this red dawn. Where did I go wrong?

'Nkosi, I will walk down with the horse.' Mbejane sensed his mood and sought to end it.

'Better that a man of your station should ride with me in the motor-car,' Sean demurred, and took a fiendish pleasure in the shifty glance that Mbejane cast at the great gleaming Rolls parked at the far end of the yard. It has eyes like a monster, thought Mbejane and looked quickly away.

'I will walk with the horse and see that it comes to no harm,' he announced.

'As you wish,' Sean agreed. The small procession set off towards Ladyburg. The two grooms leading Sun Dancer in her red tartan blanket, and Mbejane following sedately with his small black sons carrying his carved stool and his spears behind him.

Two hours later Sean drove the Rolls into the field behind the stockyards. Staring straight ahead, both hands gripping the wheel so that the knuckles of his hands gleamed white – Sean did not hear the shouted greetings nor see the gala crowds and the bunting until the Rolls bumped to a halt in the grass and his hands unfroze slowly from the wheel. Then he exhaled gently and the rigid muscles of his face softened into a grin of uncertain triumph.

'Well, we made it!' He spoke as if he were not quite certain.

'You did very well, my dear.' Ruth's voice was also a little scratchy and she relaxed her protective hold on Storm.

'You should let me drive, Pa.' Dirk was lounging against the saddlery on the back seat. Sean turned furiously upon him, but Dirk was too quick. He flung open the door and was absorbed into the crowd that had gathered around the Rolls before Sean could assemble his words. Sean glowered after him.

'Hello, Sean. Nice to see you.' Dennis Petersen had opened the door at his elbow and Sean hastily rearranged his features into a smile.

'Hello, Dennis. Nice turn-out.'

'Everybody in the district,' Dennis assured him, as they shook hands, and then looked with satisfaction around the field. There were at least fifty carriages parked haphazard along the stockyard fence, an open wagon had been arranged as a refreshment stall with silver urns of coffee and piles of cakes laid out upon it. A dog fight was in progress near the gate, while small boys in already wilted church clothes shrieked and whooped and chased each other through the crowd.

'Who's responsible for the decorations?' Sean asked, surveying the flags and bunting that fluttered from the poles that marked the finishing line and from the wide roped-off lane that led up to them.

'The Board – we voted it last week.'

'Very nice.' Sean was looking now at the stockpen where the horses were. A solid barricade of humanity lined the railings, but he saw Dirk climb over and jump down beside Sun Dancer amid a splatter of applause from the onlookers.

'Good-looking lad.' Dennis was watching Dirk also, but there was something in his tone that added, *but I'm glad he's not mine.*

'Thanks.' The defiance in Sean's voice was not lost on Dennis and he smiled ironically.

'We'd better go across and talk to the other judges, Garrick is waiting.' Dennis jerked his head towards the carriage at the end of the line, and although he had been painfully aware of it, Sean looked at it for the first time.

Together with Pye, Erasmus and his father, Michael was standing beside it watching them. Tall and lean in tight black riding-boots, and an open shirt of white silk accentuating the breadth of his shoulders, he leaned against the wheel. Above him Ada and Anna sat together on the rear seat and suddenly Sean felt a twist of anger in his stomach that Ada should be there with *them*.

'Mother.' He greeted her without smiling.

'Hello, Sean.' And he could not fathom the tone of her voice nor her expression. Was it regret, or perhaps a reluctant rejection? For a long minute they held each other's eyes – until at last Sean had to break, because now, instead of anger, he felt guilty. But he did not understand the source of his guilt – it was only the sorrowful accusation in Ada's eyes that had given it to him.

'Anna.' He greeted her and received in exchange a stiff nod.

'Garry.' Sean tried to smile. He made a movement to lift his right hand, but as he did so he knew it would be rejected, for the same accusation that he had seen in Ada's eyes was also in Garry's. He turned with relief to Michael.

'Hello, Mike. You know you're going to get the pants thrashed off you?'

'I'm going to make you eat those words without salt!' And they laughed together easily, laughed with such obvious joy in each other that Anna moved restlessly in her seat and spoke sharply.

'Can't we get this over with, Ronny?'

'Yes,' Ronny Pye agreed hastily. 'Well, then. Where is young Dirk? We'd better go and find him.'

In a group they left the women and moved through the crowd towards the stockpen where Dirk stood laughing with two girls that Sean recognized as daughters of one of the factory foremen. They were both looking up at Dirk and reacting with such unashamed adoration that Sean felt a lift of indulgent pride. Casually Dirk dismissed the girls and came across to meet them.

'All set, Pa.'

'So I see,' Sean gruffed, and waited for Dirk to show courtesy to the men with him, but Dirk ignored them and spoke only to Ronny Pye.

'Let's hear it.'

'Well, then. A contest between Garry Courtney's colt Grey Weather and Sean Courtney's filly Sun Dancer. An honour match with no stake put up by the owners. Agreed?'

'Right,' said Sean.

Garry opened his mouth and then closed it firmly and nodded. He was sweating a little. He unfolded the handkerchief in his hand and wiped his forehead.

'The distance approximately five miles around four points. The points being firstly the posts that have been erected on this field, secondly the north-eastern boundary marker of the farm Theuniskraal.' Ronny pointed at the crest of the escarpment that stood above them, its slope golden with grass in the morning sun and smeared with streaks of dark green bush. 'Thirdly, the No. 3 diptank of Mahobo's Kloof farm, which you can't see from here as it is behind those trees.' Ronny's arm described a long arc along the crest of the escarpment and stopped pointing at the spires of a clump of saligna gums. 'But both of you know it?' 'Sure,' agreed Dirk, and Michael nodded.

'The fourth and finishing-point is the same as the starting-point – here.' He jerked his thumb at the two posts that fluttered gay with flags.

'Stewards have been posted at the Theuniskraal boundary and the dip-tank – make sure you pass on the far side of them. The judges are Messrs Petersen, Erasmus and myself. All and any dispute regarding the running or interpretation of the rules will be decided by us. . . .' Ronny went on talking and Sean felt his excitement mounting from his stomach and beginning to tingle along his forearms. It was taking a hold on all of them now, even Ronny's voice had an edge to it. Though Sean did not understand that the foxlike eagerness of his face came from the knowledge that this was a contest in which he stood to gain more than any of them. But Garrick understood fully, and his eyes watched Ronny's lips hypnotically.

'That's it, then,' Ronny finished and then to the riders, 'Get saddled up, and bring your horses to the start.'

The judges walked away and left the four Courtneys standing together.

'Sean . . .' Garry spoke first, his eyes were stricken. 'I think you should know . . .' but he did not finish.

'What?' Sean asked abruptly, and at the tone of his voice Garrick straightened up. The thing in his eyes changed shape, and became what Sean had never expected to see there – pride.

'It doesn't matter.' Garry turned and walked purposefully towards his horse, and there was a spring in his stride and a set to his shoulders.

'Good luck, Mike.' Sean punched his arm.

'And the same to you.' Michael started after Garrick, then stopped and turned back to Sean. 'Whatever anyone else says, Sean, I know you didn't plan this.' Then he was striding away.

'What the hell did he mean by that?' puzzled Sean, but Dirk cut into his thoughts.

'Why did you have to do that, Pa?' he demanded.

'What?' Sean looked at him uncomprehendingly.

'Give him luck. Why did you have to give him luck? I'm riding for you – not him. I'm your son – not him!'

The two riders moved together towards the start, and buzzing with excitement the crowd went with them.

Sean walked beside Sun Dancer, with Dirk leaning attentively from the saddle to listen to him.

'Take it gently to the swamp, don't push her for she'll need all her steam in the mud. Michael will gain there, that colt is strong in the leg, but heavy. Follow him and let him break a path for you. Out of the swamp you can catch up and pass him on the slope, push hard there. You must lead him to the top and hold your lead along the crest to the dip-tank.'

'All right, Pa.'

'Now, when you start down again keep well out beyond the Van Essen plantation on to hard ground – that way you can cut the edge of the swamp. My guess is that Mike will come straight down and plough through the middle – but you must take the longer route – and use Sun Dancer's speed against Grey Weather's strength.'

They had reached the starting-posts and the crowd scattered and spread away to line the ropes. An open funnel of humanity faced the two horsemen, then the swamp with its deceptively lush papyrus grass concealing the glutinous mudholes. Beyond it the great soar of the escarpment. A long course. A hard course.

'Are both of you ready?' called Ronny Pye from the sidelines. 'Clear the field, please, Sean.'

Sean put his hand on Dirk's knee.

'Let's see what you can do, boy.' Then he ducked under the ropes into the crowd.

Sun Dancer was skittering nervously, coming up on her back legs and throwing her head so that the mane flew red-gold in the sunlight. She was sweating in dark patches on her shoulders. Michael was circling Grey Weather, keeping him moving gently, leaning forward and patting his neck, talking to him so that he switched his ears, cocking them half back to listen.

'Quiet, please, everybody!' Dennis was using a megaphone, and the buzz of voices descended into an expectant rustling.

'You're under starter's orders now,' he shouted at the riders, 'Turn wide, and walk up together.'

They swung away from the posts, and came together. Dirk touched Sun Dancer with the spur and she jumped back thrusting her quarters into Michael's leg.

'Keep your bloody animal under control,' he snarled at Michael. 'Don't crowd me!'

'Are you nervous, Dirkie?' Obediently Michael wheeled his mount aside.

'Damn you! – I'll show you who's nervous,' and Sun Dancer threw her head in protest, as Dirk sawed her with the curb.

'Come round, swing them round.' Dennis's voice through the megaphone boomed distortedly.

They turned in line and started walking up, twenty yards from the start, two horses with the sunlight glowing on their polished skins. Pale gold and dark red. The crowd sighed softly like wind in the grass.

Ten paces and Sun Dancer was pushing forward, lengthening her stride, crabbing a little.

'Hold your line! Keep together,' Dennis cautioned them, and Dirk yanked her back roughly. The rims of his nostrils were flared and white with tension.

Michael moved up beside him, holding his hands low. The big red colt stepping high in the exaggerated action of an animal under restraint.

Quickening together over the last five paces, their riders hunching lower in the saddles, they came to the posts.

'Go!' bellowed Dennis, and 'Go!' roared a hundred voices. Still in line, matching each other's stride, they changed from a walk into an easy, free, swinging canter. Both Dirk and Michael rising slightly in their stirrups to hold them from headlong flight. Half a mile ahead lay the swamp and beyond it five miles of mountain and rough, rocky ground, of donga and thornbush. They cantered down between the yelling lines and out of the funnel into the open.

The crowd broke and scattered to various points of vantage and Sean ran with them, unslinging his binocular-case, chuckling with excitement in the general confusion of shouts and laughter.

Ruth was waiting for him beside the Rolls and he caught her around the waist and lifted her on to the bonnet.

'Sean, you'll scratch the paintwork,' she protested, as she clutched at her hat and teetered dangerously on the high, round bonnet.

'The hell with the paintwork,' he laughed as he climbed up beside her and she clung to him for support. 'There they are!'

Far out across the field the two horses ran down towards the bright green of the swamp. Sean lifted and focused his binoculars, and suddenly they were so close he expected to hear the drumming of the hooves. Grey Weather was pulling ahead, forcing powerfully with his great shoulders lunging into each stride – and Sun Dancer trailed him with her neck arched against the pressure of the bit. On her back Dirk sat upright with his elbows pressed into his flanks as he held her.

'The little bugger is listening to advice,' Sean growled. 'I quite expected him to be using the whip already.'

Across the distance that separated them Sean could feel as a tangible thing Dirk's determination to win, he could see it in the way he held his shoulders, he could see it in the rigid lines of his arms. But what he did not see were the harsh lines of hatred in Dirk's face as he stared at Michael's back ahead of him.

The beat of hooves changed its tone, no longer ringing on hard ground, but dulling as they reached the swamp. Now lumps of damp clay flew from Grey Weather's hooves and a piece hit Dirk's chest and sprayed dirt on the white silk of his shirt. Sun Dancer's gait altered as she felt the soft ground.

'Easy, girl. Hey there, girl,' Dirk whispered and held her firmly with his knees to give her confidence. The grass brushed his stirrups and ahead of him Grey Weather splashed into the first mudhole, plunged through it and into the swamp proper. The tall papyrus engulfed him.

'The old man was right,' Dirk smiled for the first time. Michael was forcing a path through the reeds, flattening them for Dirk to follow with half the effort. Twice Grey Weather sunk to his belly in potholes of black glue, rearing and struggling to free himself while Dirk skirted them.

Both horses were shiny with mud, and their riders were soaked to the waist and splattered above. The swamp stank like an animal cage and marsh gas erupted sullenly as they disturbed it. Clouds of insects rose about them, a sakabula bird fled shrieking as they ploughed through the papyrus. One of the razor leaves lashed Michael's cheek and a thread of blood ran down his jaw washing the blobs of mud with it and dripped on to his shirt.

Then suddenly the ground firmed under them, the solid papyrus broke into clumps, thinned and was left behind and Grey Weather led them out on to the first slope of the escarpment. He was running heavily now, and grunting with each stride, while Sun Dancer moved up beside him.

'You're finished!' Dirk shouted at Michael as they drew level. 'I'll see you at the finish-line,' and he leaned forward in the saddle and gave Sun Dancer the spurs and the whip together.

Without pressing his horse Michael angled him off towards the right, letting him move under slack rein to pick his own way and he began the first leg of a series of zigzags that would take him to the top.

On the steep ground below the crest Dirk used the whip incessantly, and Sun Dancer went up in a series of scrambling leaps with the loose rock rolling under her hooves. The sweat had washed away the mud from her shoulders and she landed with less control at each jump. 'Pull, you bitch. Pull!' Dirk shouted at her, and looked back in agony at Michael's sedate ascent. He was two hundred yards below and coming steadily. Dirk's movement caught Sun Dancer off balance and she landed awkwardly at the next jump, her hooves scrabbled and she started to fall. Dirk kicked his feet from the stirrups and jumped with the reins still in his hands. The instant he landed he leaned back on the reins to hold her, but she was down on her knees now, sliding back and she pulled Dirk down with her on to the level place below.

They struggled together and when at last he got her on her feet she was trembling with terror, dust and pieces of dry grass coated her muddy legs.

'Damn you! Damn you, you clumsy bitch,' whispered Dirk as he ran his hands over her hocks to check for damage. He glanced back at Michael and found him much closer now.

'Oh, God!' he blurted, snatched up Sun Dancer's reins and ran at the slope dragging her after him. Dirk came out on the crest with sweat pouring down his face and soaking through his shirt. Saliva had dried to a thick gummy froth in his mouth and he was panting harshly – but he had held on to his lead and Sun Dancer was over her trembling fit. She had recovered sufficiently to cavort a little as he mounted.

'This way, Dirkie!' The two stewards standing on the pile of stones that marked the Theuniskraal boundary were waving and shouting wild encouragement. Dirk clouted the spurs into her and was off again, galloping along the ridge, sweeping past them and on towards the clump of gums three miles ahead.

'Catch him, Mike. Ride, man, ride!' Faint shouts behind him – and Dirk knew without looking back that Mike had reached the top and was chasing him. He rode on, grimly mourning the time lost on the ascent and hating both Sun Dancer and Michael for it. At this point he should have led by four hundred yards – not fifty.

Directly ahead now was the gorge through which the Baboon Stroom dropped down the escarpment, its side choked with dark green river bush. Dirk found the path and turned away from the skyline aiming upstream at the ford. Without grass to muffle them Sun Dancer's hooves hammered in staccato rhythm on the hard-packed earth of the path, but also he could hear behind him like an echo the beat of other hooves – Michael was on to the path behind him. Dirk looked back under his own arm. Michael was so close that he could see the laughter lines creasing the corners of his mouth, and the mockery inflamed him.

'I'll show him—!' And Dirk started with the whip again, cracking it across Sun Dancer's flanks and shoulders so that she jumped forward with

a new urgency. Down the steep bank of the river and out on to the white
sandbank, he plunged with Grey Weather's nose drawing level with his
boot. Into the dark green water they rode abreast, throwing up a veil of
spray that sparkled in the sunlight, slipping from their saddles to swim
beside the horses through the deep, while the current moved them down
towards the falls. Up into the saddles again the instant the horses found the
bottom and splashed towards the far bank. Out on to the sand, with water
streaming from sodden clothing, shouting with excitement as they raced for
the narrow path that climbed the far bank. First man on to it would hold
the advantage.

'Give way! I'm leading – give me way,' screamed Dirk furiously.

'Make your own way!' Michael laughed back at him.

'You bastard!' Dirk used his knees and reins to thrust Sun Dancer's
shoulder into Michael, trying to force him clear.

'None of that!' Michael warned him.

'You bastard – I'll show you.'

They rode knee to knee now. Dirk sat up quickly and twisted his foot,
placing his booted toe under Michael's instep. With a sudden vicious lift of
his leg he slipped Michael's foot from the stirrup and threw him sideways.
As he felt himself going over Michael clutched desperately at the pommel,
pulling the saddle with him so it slid on to Grey Weather's flank and the
shift of weight forced the horse to disengage and slew away from the path.
Michael went down on his shoulder into the sand and rolled with his knees
drawn up against his stomach.

'That's for you!' Dirk yelled in defiance as he went up the bank and out
into the open veld again. Behind him in the river-bed Michael staggered to
his feet, his wet clothing coated white with sand, and ran after Grey Weather
who was trotting back towards the water with the saddle hanging under his
chest.

'The dirty little swine. My God, if only Sean knew!' Michael caught the
horse before it started to drink, wrestled the saddle on to his back again and
clinched the girth.

'Now, I can't let him win!' He jumped up on to Grey Weather and booted
him towards the bank. 'I can't let him win.'

Two hundred yards ahead Dirk's shirt was a white blob against the
brown grass. As he rounded the dip-tank and pointed Sun Dancer's head
at the ridge for the last leg, one of the stewards shouted:

'What happened to Michael?'

'He fell in the river,' Dirk called back. 'He's finished!' And his voice rang
with triumph.

'He's leading – Dirk's leading!' Sean stood on the Rolls with his glasses
trained on the clump of gum-trees, and now he was the first to spot the tiny
figure of the horseman as it showed on the crest of the escarpment.

'Where's Michael?' Ruth asked.

'He can't be far behind,' Sean muttered and waited anxiously for him to
appear. He had fretted while he watched Dirk's reckless ascent of the slope,
and cursed him loudly for his brutal treatment of Sun Dancer. Then he had

entreated him to *get a bloody move on* during the run along the ridge with Michael gaining steadily on him. When the two horsemen had veered away from the skyline to cross the Baboon Stroom they had disappeared from view and this was the first glimpse the spectators had received of either competitor since that moment.

'The little idiot's riding too wide. I told him to cut the edge of the swamp – not ride round it altogether.'

'Where's Michael?' Ruth repeated. Sean swung the glasses back and scanned the crest with the first twinges of concern.

'Not showing yet – he must have run into trouble.'

'Do you think he's all right? Has he been hurt?'

'How should I know?' Sean's anxiety made him irritable, but immediately he was penitent and encircled Ruth's waist with his arm. 'He can look after himself, that one. No sense fussing about him.'

Dirk was well down the slope now, leaving a thin trail of dust, for Sun Dancer skidded on her haunches most of the way.

'Still no sign of Michael?' Ruth moved restlessly against him.

'No. Not yet,' Sean grunted. 'Dirk can afford to miss the swamp – he's leading by a quarter of a mile.'

Suddenly a sigh of relief moved the crowd like a gust of wind through a field of wheat.

'There he is!'

'He's coming straight down the slope.'

'He can't make it unless he flies!'

Sean swung his glasses from Dirk to Michael and back, estimating their speeds and positions, allowing for Michael's delay in the swamp, but setting against that the additional distance that Dirk had to cover.

'It's going to be close—' he decided aloud. 'Dirk's got the edge, but it's going to be very close.'

Ada did not see it that way. Dirk was leading and Dirk was going to win. She looked across at Garrick. He stood beside the finishing-post a hundred yards away, but even at that distance there was no mistaking the droop of his shoulders and the air of misery that surrounded him like an aura of defeat. Sun Dancer's hooves were slashing his life to threads.

Unable to bear it a moment longer, Ada jumped down from the carriage and ran through the crowd to where Sean stood like a triumphant colossus on the bonnet of the Rolls.

'Sean.' She reached up and touched his leg, but he was so engrossed he did not feel or hear her.

'Sean,' she shouted and tugged at his trouser-leg.

'Mother?' He turned vaguely to look down at her.

'I must talk to you,' Ada shouted above the sound of the crowd that was rising with excitement.

'Not now. They're coming in to the finish – climb up here where you can see it.'

'Now. I must speak to you now. Come down this instant!' Her tone shocked him, for a second he wavered and peered furtively back at the race. Then he shrugged with resignation and jumped down beside her.

'What is it? Please be quick – I don't want to miss—'

'I'll be quick.' Sean had never seen such a cold fury on her before. 'I wanted to say that I never thought I'd see that day when I had nothing left for you but contempt. Thoughtless you've been often – but never downright merciless.'

'Mother, I . . .' He was bewildered.

'Listen to me. You set out to destroy your brother and you've done it. Well, I hope you have the pleasure of it. You've got Theuniskraal now. Enjoy it, Sean. Sleep well at night.'

'Theuniskraal! What do you mean?' He shouted at her now in his confusion. 'I didn't wager for the farm!'

'Ah, no,' Ada scoffed at him. 'Of course you didn't – you let Ronny Pye do that for you.'

'Pye? What's he got to do with it?'

'Everything! He helped you plan it. He helped you provoke Garry into this stupidity. He holds the mortgage on Theuniskraal.'

'But . . .' Slowly the enormity of it all began to shape up in Sean's mind.

'You took his leg – now take Theuniskraal, but pay for it with my love.' She looked steadily into his eyes, but the pain was there clouding her own. 'Good-bye, Sean. we won't speak to each other again.' And she walked slowly away. She walked like an old woman at last, a tired and worn old woman.

Sean understood and began to run towards the finishing-line. He drove through the crowd like a shark through a shoal of sardines. Over their heads he saw the two horsemen galloping in across the field.

Dirk was leading, standing in the stirrups to thrash Sun Dancer with the whip. His black hair fluttered in the wind, and his shirt filthy with thrown mud. Under him the filly danced on flying hooves and the beat of them drummed above the rising roar of the crowd. Her body was black and shiny with sweat, and froth flew from her gaping pink mouth to form white lace on her chest and flanks.

Fifty hopeless yards behind her plunged the colt with Michael flogging his heels into him with despair. Michael's face was twisted in an agony of frustration. Grey Weather was finished, his legs loose with exhaustion and his breath sawing hoarsely with each stride.

Sean tore his way through the press of bodies that lined the guide ropes. He reached the front rank and shouldered two women from his path. Then he stooped and ducked under the rope into the open.

Sun Dancer was almost up to him, hammering down in a crescendo of hooves, her head nodding with each stride.

'Dirk! Stop her!' roared Sean.

'Pa! Pa! Get out of the way . . .' Dirk screamed back at him, but Sean sprang to intercept him.

'Pa!'

Sean was in front of him, crouching with arms extended. Too close to swing Sun Dancer's head away from him, too late to stop her charge.

'Jump, girl, jump,' shouted Dirk and gathered the horse with his knees, feeling her respond with a bunching of her quarters; feeling her lift her forelegs against her chest and drive upwards in a high parabola. But sensing also the sluggishness of her exhausted body and knowing she had not gone high enough to clear Sean's head.

An aching moment as Sun Dancer lifted clear of the ground, the horrified groan of the crowd as her forelegs smashed into Sean and she twisted in the air, falling. Dirk thrown, his stirrup leathers parting like whip cracks. Then all of them down together in the grass. Shrill screams of women in the crowd.

Sun Dancer struggling up again with a foreleg swinging loosely from the knee, whinnying in the pain of broken bone.

Sean on his back, his head twisted to the side and blood from his torn cheek dribbling into his nose and mouth so that his breathing snored hoarsely.

Dirk with the skin smeared from elbows and one cheek, crawling towards Sean, kneeling beside him, raising both hands clenched, hammering down with them so that his fists splattered the blood, beating them into the chest and slack, unconscious face of his father.

'Why did you? Oh, God, I hate you.' Shock and fury and despair. 'For you! You stopped me, you stopped me.'

Michael dragging Grey Weather down on his haunches, flinging from the saddle, running to them, holding Dirk's arms, dragging him off, fighting him.

'Leave him, you little bastard.'

'He didn't want me to. He stopped me, I hate him. I'll kill him.'

The crowd surging forward, flattening the guide ropes, two men helping Michael hold Dirk, the rest of them ringing Sean's body.

The cries and questions:

'Where's Doc Fraser?'

'Jesus, he's badly hurt!'

'Catch that horse. Get a gun.'

'What about the bets?'

'Don't touch him. Wait . . .'

'Got to straighten his arm.'

'Get a gun. For Christ sake, get a gun.'

Then a new silence on them, their ranks opening quietly and Ruth coming through to him running – Mbejane behind her.

'Sean.' She knelt beside him, clumsy in her pregnancy. 'Sean,' she began again, and the men about her could not look at her face.

'Mbejane, bring him to the car,' she whispered.

He slipped the monkey-skin cloak from his shoulder and let it drop, stooped over Sean and lifted him. The great black muscles of his chest and arms swelled, and he stood with his legs braced wide against the weight.

'His arm, Nkosikazi.'

She arranged the hanging arm comfortably across his chest.

'Bring him,' she repeated and together they walked through the crowd. Sean's head lolled against Mbejane's shoulder like that of a sleeping child. Mbejane laid Sean gently on the back seat with his head in Ruth's lap.

'My daddy,' she kept repeating, her face screwed up with horror at the blood and her tiny body trembling like that of a frightened rabbit.

'Will you drive us please, Michael?' Ruth looked up at him as he stood beside the Rolls. 'Take us to Protea Street.'

With Mbejane loping alongside, the big car bumped across the field

through the throng of anxious watchers, then swung on to the main road
and moved away towards Ladyburg.

Chapter Eighty-six

While about him the crowds scattered slowly and drifted to their carriages,
Dirk Courtney stood alone and watched the Rolls disappear in its own
blown dust.

Waves of reaction shivered up his legs and turned to heavy nausea in his
gut. The open gravel rash on his face burned like acid spilled upon the skin.

'You'd better go in and have Doc Fraser put something on your face.'
Coming from his carriage with a heavy service revolver, Dennis Petersen
paused beside him.

'Yes,' Dirk answered dully, and Dennis walked on to where two native
grooms held Sun Dancer. Unsteadily on three legs, but quiet now, she stood
between them with her head hanging dejectedly.

Dennis touched the muzzle of the revolver to her forehead, and at the shot
she recoiled violently and dropped, shuddering. Her legs stiffened in one last
convulsion, then she lay still.

Watching, Dirk shuddered in sympathy and then leaned forward to vent
his nausea in the grass. It came up sour and scalding hot. He wiped it from
his mouth with the palm of his hand, then he began to walk. Without
direction, blindly, from the field towards the escarpment.

Over in his mind, keeping pace with his legs like the refrain of a marching
song:

He doesn't want me. He doesn't want me.

And then savagely:

I hope he dies. Please let him die.

'Please let him die.' Anna Courtney said it softly, so that Garry standing
below her seat in the buggy did not hear her. He stood with his shoulders
hunched, and his head thrust forward in thought, hands hanging at his sides
slowly folding and unfolding, then he raised one of them and squeezed the
fingers into his closed eyelids.

'I'm going to him,' he said. 'God help me, but I'm going to him.'

'No! I forbid it. Leave him – let him suffer as I suffered.'

Slowly, bewildered, Garry shook his head.

'I must. It's too long, too much. I must. Pray God it's not too late.'

'Let him die.' Then suddenly it snapped in her head, broke under the
weight of the hatred so long sustained.

She rose screaming in her seat. 'Die! Damn you. Die!' And Garry uncovered his eyes, and looked at her in alarm.

'Compose yourself, my dear.'

'Die! Die!' Her face was blotched with flaming spots of red, and her voice squawked as though she were being strangled. Garry scrambled up beside her and flung his arms around her protectively.

'Get away from me. Don't touch me.' She screamed at him: fighting from his embrace. 'Because of you I lost him. He was so big, so strong. He was mine – and because . . .'

'Anna, Anna, Please don't.' He tried to soothe her raving. 'Please stop it, my dear.'

'You, you crawling, crippled thing. Because of you.' And suddenly it had to come out, like pus from a canker. 'But I paid you back. I took him from you also – and now he's dead. You'll never have him.' She laughed, gloating, demented.

'Anna. Stop it.'

'That night – do you remember that night? Will you or he ever forget it? I wanted him, I wanted him big like a bull on top of me, I wanted him rutting deep like it was before – I begged him. I pleaded – but because of you. Because of his crippled little weakling brother. Christ, I hated him!' She laughed again, a shriek of pain and hatred. 'I tore my clothing and bit into my own lips, as I had wanted him to do. When you came – I wanted you to . . . but you, I had forgotten you were only half a man! I wanted you to kill him – *kill him!*'

Pale, so that the sweat on his face shone like water on white marble, Garry pulled away from her with loathing.

'All this time I thought he – I believed you.' And he half fell from the buggy, leaning against it for a moment to steady himself. '. . . All this time wasted.' Then he launched himself and began to run, his bad leg jerking and catching under him.

'You want a lift, Garry?' Dennis Petersen drew level with him and called down from the carriage.

'Yes. Oh, yes.' Garry caught the handrail and dragged himself up beside Dennis. 'Take me to him, please, as fast as you can.'

Chapter Eighty-seven

Silent, deserted, the great house crouched over her. Dark with the shutters closed against the sun, brooding and immense, smelling musty as though old passions had died within its walls.

Anna stood alone in the huge central room and screamed its name.

'Theuniskraal!'

And the thick stone walls smothered the sound of her madness.

'He is dead! Do you hear me? I took him away from all of you.'

And she shrieked in triumphant laughter, with the tears greasing her cheeks. 'I won! Do you hear me? I won!' And her grief distorted the laughter.

She picked up the heavy glass lamp and hurled it across the room; it burst and the paraffin sprayed wide, glistening on the walls and soaking into the carpet.

'Theuniskraal! Hear me! I hate you also. I hate him. I hate you all – all of you.'

She raged through the room, tearing down the gilt-framed pictures and smashing them so that the glass sparkled like tiny jewels in the gloom; she used a chair to smash in the front of the display cabinet and wreck the old china and glassware in it; she swept the books from the shelves into fluttering heaps, and threw their torn pages in the air.

'I hate!' she screamed. 'I hate!' And the great house waited silent. Exhausted with worn-out emotions – old and sad and wise.

'I hate you – all of you.' And she ran out into the passage, through the kitchens to the pantries. On the lowest shelf stood a four-gallon drum of methylated spirit and she panted as she struggled with the stopper. The stopper came out, the clear liquid welled and ran down the metal sides, and she picked the drum up across her chest and stumbled back into the kitchen. It spilled down her skirts, soaking in, drenching the heavy cloth, forming a spreading pool on the stone flags.

'I hate!' She laughed and stumbled, staggering off balance, still clutching the drum she fell against the kitchen range. Hot metal scorched her clothing and burned through to the flesh of her hip, but she did not feel it. Her sodden skirts brushed over the fire-box, a tiny point of flame caught and grew. So when she ran on into the house a fiery train swept behind her.

Back in the central room, she poured from the drum over the books and the carpet, laughing as she splashed the long-draped velvet curtains.

Oblivious of the flames that followed, until her petticoats caught and burned against her legs. Then she screamed again at the agony of her tortured flesh and brain. She dropped the metal drum and it exploded, showering her with liquid blue flame, turning her hair and her face and her whole body into a living torch, a torch that fell and writhed and died before the flames reached the thatch of the roof of Theuniskraal.

Chapter Eighty-eight

They faced each other across the waist of the dhow, and the bright sunlight threw their shadows along the filthy planking of the deck. Two tall young men, both dark-haired and burned rich brown by the sun, both with the big

Courtney nose – both angry. From the poop three of the Arab crew watched with mild curiosity.

'So, you won't come home, then?' Michael asked. 'You're going through with this childishness?'

'Why do you want me to?'

'Me? Good God, if I never see you again it would be too soon. Ladyburg will be a cleaner town without you.'

'Then why did you come?'

'Your father asked me.'

'Why didn't he come himself?' Dirk's bitterness echoed in his voice.

'He's still a sick man – his head. Hurt badly.'

'If he wanted me, he would have come.'

'He sent for you, didn't he?'

'But why did he want you to win – why did he stop me?'

'Listen to me, Dirk. You're young yet. There are many things you don't understand.'

'Don't I!' And Dirk threw back his head and laughed scornfully. 'Oh, I understand all right. You'd better get off this boat, we're just about to sail.'

'Listen, Dirk . . .'

'Get off. Run back to him – you can have my share.'

'Dirk, listen to me. He said if you refused to come – then I was to give you this.' From inside his coat Michael drew an envelope and offered it.

'What is it?'

'I don't know – but I expect that it's money.'

Dirk came slowly across the deck and took the envelope from him.

'Have you a message for him?' Michael asked, and when Dirk shook his head he turned and jumped down on to the wooden jetty. Immediately a bustle began behind him as the Arab crew cast off the lines.

Standing on the edge of the jetty, Michael watched the stubby little craft drift out on the waters of Durban Bay. He could smell the stench of her bilges, her sides were streaked with human filth, and the single sail that rose slowly as the crew hoisted the long teak boom was stained and patched like a quilt.

The wind took her and the pregnant belly of the sail bulged out, she heeled and thrust forward through the chop of dirty green water – headed towards the bar, where a low surf broke in languid lines of white.

The two half-brothers stared at each other across the widening gap. Neither of them lifted an arm or smiled. The dhow bore away. Dirk's face was a tiny brown fleck above the white of his tropical suit, then suddenly his voice.

'Tell him . . .' Small in the distance. 'Tell him . . .' and the rest of it was lost on the wind, in the soft lap and sigh of the wavelets beneath the jetty.

Chapter Eighty-nine

Below where they sat on the lip of the escarpment, the walls of Theuniskraal stood up like smoke-browned tombstones marking the burial ground of hatred.

'About time you started rebuilding,' Sean grunted, 'you can't stay on at Protea Street for ever.'

'No.' Garry paused before going on: 'I've picked out the new site for the homestead – there, beyond the number two dip.'

Both of them looked away from the roofless ruins, and they were silent again until shyly Garry asked, 'I'd like you to have a look at the plans. It won't be as big as the old house now that there is just Michael and I. Could you . . .?'

'Good,' Sean cut in quickly. 'Why don't you bring them across to Lion Kop tomorrow evening? Ruth will want you to stay for dinner.'

'I'd like that.'

'Come early,' said Sean, and started to stand up from the rock on which he sat. He moved heavily, awkwardly – and Garry jumped up to help him. Hating the weakness of his slowly mending body, Sean would have brushed Garry's eager hands away. But he saw the expression on his brother's face and instead he submitted meekly.

'Give me an arm over the rough ground, please.' He spoke gruffly.

Side by side, with Sean's arm across Garry's shoulder, they moved to where the buggy waited.

Ponderously Sean climbed up and settled himself into the padded leather seat.

'Thanks.' He gathered up the reins and smiled down at Garry, and Garry flushed with pleasure and looked away to the infinite lines of young wattle trees that covered the hills of Theuniskraal.

'Looks good, doesn't it?' he asked.

'You and Michael have done wonders up here,' Sean agreed, still smiling.

'Courtney Brothers and Son.' Softly Garry spoke the name of the new company which had merged the lands of Theuniskraal and Lion Kop into one vast estate. 'Now at last it is the way it should have been long ago.'

'Until tomorrow, Garry.' Sean flipped the reins and the buggy rolled forward, rocking gently over the uneven surface of the new road.

'Until tomorrow, Sean,' Garry called after him, and watched until the buggy was lost to sight among the blocks of dark mature wattle. Then he walked to his horse and mounted. He sat a while watching the distant ranks of Zulu labourers singing as they worked. He saw Michael moving on horseback amongst them, stopping occasionally to lean from the saddle and urge them on.

And Garry began to smile. The smile smoothed away the lines from around his eyes. He touched the horse with his spurs and cantered down to join Michael.

A Sparrow Falls

For Danielle

A sky the colour of old bruises hung low over the battlefields of France, and rolled with ponderous dignity towards the German lines.

Brigadier-General Sean Courtney had spent four winters in France and now, with the eye of a cattleman and a farmer, he could judge this weather almost as accurately as that of his native Africa.

'It will snow tonight,' he grunted, and Lieutenant Nick van der Heever, his orderly officer, glanced back at him over his shoulder.

'I shouldn't wonder, sir.'

Van der Heever was heavily laden. In addition to his service rifle and webbing, he carried a canvas kitbag across his shoulder, for General Courtney was on his way to dine as a mess guest of the 2nd Battalion. At this moment the Colonel and officers of the 2nd Battalion were completely unaware of the impending honour, and Sean grinned in wicked anticipation at the panic that his unannounced arrival would create. The contents of the kitbag would be some small compensation for the shock, for it included half a dozen bottles of pinch bottle Haig and a fat goose.

Nevertheless, Sean was aware that his officers found his informal behaviour and his habit of arriving suddenly in the front lines, unannounced and un-attended by his staff, more than a little disconcerting. Only a week before, he had overheard a field telephone conversation on a crossed line between a major and a captain.

'The old bastard thinks he's still fighting the Boer War. Can't you keep him in a cage back there at HQ?'

'How do you cage a bull elephant?'

'Well, at least warn us when he's on his way –'

Sean grinned again and trudged on after his orderly officer, the folds of his great-coat flapping about his putteed legs and, for warmth, a silk scarf wrapped around his head beneath the soup-plate shape of his helmet. The boards bounced under his feet and the gluey mud sucked and gurgled beneath them at the passing weight of the two men.

This part of the line was unfamiliar, the brigade had moved in less than a week previously, but the stench was well remembered. The musty smell of earth and mud, overladen with the odour of rotting flesh and sewage, the stale lingering whiff of burned cordite and high explosive.

Sean sniffed it and spat with distaste. Within an hour he knew he would be so accustomed as not to notice it, but now it seemed to coat the back of his throat like cold grease. Once again he looked up at the sky, and now he frowned. Either the wind had shifted into the east a point or two, or they had taken a wrong turning within the maze of trenches, for the low cloud was no longer rolling in the direction that fitted with the map that Sean carried in his head.

'Nick!'

'Sir?'

'Are you still right?'

And he saw at once the uncertainty in the young subaltern's eyes as he looked back.

'Well, sir –'

The trenches had been deserted for the last quarter of a mile, not a single soul had they passed in the labyrinth of high earthen walls.

'We'd better take a look, Nick.'

'I'll do it, sir.' Van der Heever glanced ahead along the trench, and found what he was looking for. At the next intersection a wooden ladder was fastened into the wall. It reached to the top of the sand-bagged parapet. He started towards it.

'Careful, Nick,' Sean called after him.

'Sir,' the young man acknowledged, and propped his rifle before swarming upwards.

Sean calculated they were still three or four hundred yards from the front line yet, and the light was going fast. There was a purple velvet look to the air beneath the clouds, not shooting light at all, and he knew that, despite his age, van der Heever was an old soldier. The glance he took over the top would be swift as a meerkat looking out of its hole.

Sean watched him crouch at the top of the ladder, lift his head for a single quick sweep and then duck down again.

'The hill is too much on our left,' he called down.

The hill was a low, rounded mound that rose a mere hundred and fifty feet above the almost featureless plain. Once it had been thickly forested, but now only the shattered stumps stood waist-high and the slopes were dimpled with shell craters.

'How far is the farm house?' Sean asked, still peering upwards. The farm house was a roofless rectangle of battered walls that stood foursquare facing the centre of the Battalion's sector. It was used as a central reference point for artillery, infantry and aircorps alike.

'I'll have another look,' and van der Heever lifted his head again.

The Mauser has a distinctive cracking report, a high and vicious sound that Sean had heard so often as to be able to judge with accuracy its range and direction.

This was a single shot, at about five hundred yards, almost dead ahead.

Van der Heever's head snapped backwards as though he had taken a heavy punch, and the steel of his helmet rang like a gong. The chin-strap snapped as the round helmet spun high in the air and then dropped to the floorboards in the bottom of the trench and rolled on its rim into a pool of grey mud.

Van der Heever's hands remained locked closed on the top rung of the ladder for a moment, then the nerveless fingers opened, and he tumbled backwards, falling heavily into the bottom of the trench with the skirts of his greatcoat ballooning around him.

Sean stood frozen and disbelieving, his mind not yet accepting the fact that Nick was hit, but, as a soldier and a hunter, judging that single shot with awe.

What kind of shooting was that? Five hundred yards in this murky light; one fleeting glimpse of a helmeted head above the parapet; three seconds to set the range and line up, then another instant of time to sight and fire as the head bobbed up again. The Hun that fired that shot was either a superb marksman with reflexes like a leopard – or the flukiest sniper on the western front.

The thought was fleeting and Sean started forward heavily and knelt beside his officer. He turned him with a hand upon the shoulder and felt the sickening slide in his guts and the cold grip on his chest.

The bullet had entered at the temple and exited behind the opposite ear.

Sean lifted the shattered head into his lap, removed his own helmet and began to unwind the silk scarf from around his head. He felt a desolation of loss.

Slowly he wrapped the boy's head into the scarf, and immediately the blood soaked through the thin material. It was a futile gesture – but it served to keep his hands occupied and detract from his sense of helplessness.

He sat on the muddy floorboards, holding the boy's body, his heavy shoulders bowed forward. The size of Sean's bared head was accentuated by the thick curls of dark wiry hair shot through with splashes and strands of grey that sparkled frostily in the fading light. The short thick beard was laced with grey as well, and the big beaked nose was twisted and battered-looking.

Only the black curved eyebrows were sleek and unmarked, and the eyes were clear and dark cobalt blue, the eyes of a much younger man, steady and alert.

Sean Courtney sat for a long time holding the boy, and then he sighed once, deeply, and laid the broken head aside. He stood up, hefted the kitbag on to his own shoulder, and set off along the communications trench once again.

At five minutes before midnight, the Colonel commanding the 2nd Battalion stooped through the blackout curtains that screened the entrance to the mess, and beat the snow from his shoulders with a gloved hand as he straightened.

The mess had been a German dugout six months before, and was the envy of the brigade. Thirty feet below ground level, it was impregnable, even to the heaviest artillery barrage. The floor was of heavy timber boarding and even the walls were panelled against the damp and the cold. A pot-bellied stove stood against the far wall, glowing cheerfully.

Gathered about it in a half circle of looted armchairs sat the off-duty officers.

However, the Colonel had eyes only for the burly figure of his General, seated in the largest and most comfortable chair closest to the stove, and he shed his great-coat as he hurried across the dugout.

'General, my apologies. If I'd known you were coming I was making my rounds.'

Sean Courtney chuckled and rose ponderously from the chair to shake his hand. 'It's what I would expect of you, Charles, but your officers have made me very welcome – and we have kept a little of the goose for you.'

The Colonel glanced quickly about the circle and frowned as he saw the hectic cheeks and sparkling eyes of some of his younger subalterns. He must warn them of the folly of trying to drink level with the General. The old man was steady as a rock, of course, and those eyes were like bayonets under the dark brows, but the Colonel knew him well enough to guess that he had a full quart of Dimple Haig in his belly, and that something was troubling him deeply. Then it came to him. Of course –

'I'm terribly sorry to hear about young van der Heever, sir. Sergeant-Major told me what happened.'

Sean made a gesture of dismissal, but for a moment the shadows darkened about his eyes.

'If I'd only known you were coming up into the line this evening, I would have warned you, sir. We have had the devil of trouble with that sniper ever since we moved up. It's the same fellow, of course – absolutely deadly. I've never heard of anything like it. Dreadful nuisance when everything else is so quiet. Only casualties we've had all week.'

'What are you doing about him?' Sean asked harshly. They all saw the flush of anger darken his face, and the Adjutant intervened swiftly.

'I've been on to Colonel Caithness at 3rd Battalion, and we did a deal, sir. He has agreed to send us Anders and MacDonald –'

'You got them!' The Colonel looked delighted. 'Oh, I say, that's excellent. I didn't think Caithness would part with his prize pair.'

'They came in this morning – and the two of them have been studying the ground all day. I gave them a free hand, but I understand they are setting up the shoot for tomorrow.'

The young Captain who commanded 'A' Company pulled out-his watch and studied it a moment. 'They are going out from my section, sir. As a matter of fact, I was going to go down and give them a send-off, they will be moving into position at half past twelve. If you'll excuse me, sir.'

'Yes, of course, off with you, Dicky – wish them good luck from me.' Everybody in the brigade had heard of Anders and MacDonald.

'I'd like to meet that pair.' Sean Courtney spoke suddenly, and dutifully the Colonel agreed.

'Of course, I'll come out with you, sir.'

'No, no, Charles – you've been out in the cold all night as it is. I'll just go along with Dicky here.'

The snow came down thickly out of the utter darkness of the midnight sky. It damped down the night sounds in its thick muffling cloak, muting the regular bursts of a Vickers firing at a hole in the wire on the battalion's left.

Mark Anders sat wrapped in his borrowed blankets and he bowed his head to the book in his lap, adjusting his eyes to the yellow wavering light of the candle-stump.

The rise in temperature that accompanied the first fall of snow and the changed quality of sound entering the small dugout awakened the man who slept beside him. He coughed, and rolled over to open a chink in the canvas curtain beside his head.

'Damn,' he said, and coughed again, the harsh hammering sound of a heavy smoker. 'Damn it to hell. It's snowing.' Then he rolled back to Mark. 'You still reading?' he demanded roughly. 'Always with your nose in a bloody book. You'll ruin your shooting eyes.'

Mark lifted his head. 'It's been snowing for an hour already.'

'What you want all that learning for?' Fergus MacDonald was not so easily distracted. 'It won't do you no good.'

'I don't like the snow,' said Mark. 'We didn't reckon on the snow.'

The snow complicated the task ahead of them. It would cover the ground out there with a sensitive mantle of white. Anybody moving out from the trench into no-man's-land would leave tracks that the dawn light would instantly betray to an observant enemy.

A match flared and Fergus lit two Woodbines and passed one to Mark. They sat shoulder to shoulder, huddled in their blankets.

'You can call off the shoot, Mark. Tell 'em to shove it. You're a volunteer lad.'

They smoked in silence for a full minute before Mark replied.

'That Hun is a bad one.'

'If it's snowing, he probably won't be out tomorrow. Snow will keep him in bed also.'

Mark shook his head slowly. 'If he's that good, he'll be out.'

'Yes.' Fergus nodded. 'He's that good. That shot he made last evening – after lying up all day in the cold, then five hundred yards if it was an inch, and in that light –' Fergus cut himself off, and then went on quickly, 'But you're good also, lad. You're the best, boy.'

Mark said nothing, but carefully pinched out the glowing tip of the Woodbine.

'You're going?' Fergus asked.

'Yes.'

'Get some sleep then, lad. It's going to be a long day.'

Mark blew out the candle flame as he lay back and pulled the blankets over his head.

'You get a good sleep,' Fergus said again. 'I'll wake you in plenty of time,' and he resisted the paternal urge to pat the thin bony shoulder under the blanket.

The young Captain spoke quietly with one of the sentries on the forward firing step, and the man whispered a reply and pointed with his chin along the darkened trench.

'This way, sir.' He went on down the boards, swaddled in clothing so that he had the shape of a bear, and Sean towered head and shoulders above him as he followed.

Around the next revert, through the soft curtains of falling snow, there was the subdued red glow of a brazier from the shallow dugout in the side of the trench. Dark figures squatted close about it, like witches at a sabbat.

'Sergeant MacDonald?' One of the figures rose and stepped forward.

'That's me.' There was a cocky, self-assured tone to the reply.

'Is Anders with you?'

'Present and correct,' said MacDonald, and one of the other figures rose from the circle about the brazier and came forward. He was taller, but moved with grace, like an athlete or a dancer.

'You are ready, Anders?' the Captain went on, speaking in the soft half-whisper of the trenches, and MacDonald replied for him

'The lad is fighting fit, sir.' He spoke with the proprietary tone of the manager of a prize-fighter. It was clear that the boy was his property, and that ownership gave him a distinction he would never have achieved on his own.

At that moment another flare burst high overhead, a brilliant white and silent explosion of light, softened by the snow.

Sean could judge a man like he could a horse. He could pick the rotten ones, or the big-hearted, from the herd. It was a trick of experience and some deeper inexplicable insight.

In the light of the flare his eyes flickered across the face of the older Sergeant. MacDonald had the bony under-nourished features of the slum-dweller, the eyes too close set, the lips narrow and twisted downwards at the corners. There was nothing to interest Sean there and he looked at the other man.

The eyes were a pale golden brown, set wide, with the serene gaze of a poet or a man who had lived in the open country of long distant horizons. The lids were held wide open, so that they did not overlap the iris, leaving a clear glimpse of the clean white about the cornea so that it floated free like a full moon. Sean had seen it only a few times before, and the effect was almost hypnotic, of such direct and searching candour that it seemed to reach deep into Sean's own soul.

After the first impact of those eyes, other impressions crowded in. The first was of the man's extreme youth. He was nearer seventeen than twenty, Sean judged – and then saw immediately how finely drawn the boy was. Despite the serenity of his gaze, he was stretched out tight and hard, racked up with strain close to the snapping point. Sean had seen it so often in the past four years. They had found this child's special talent and exploited it ruthlessly, all of them – Caithness at 3rd Battalion, the ferrety MacDonald, Charles, Dicky and, by association, himself. They had worked him mercilessly, sending him out time and again.

The boy held a steaming tin mug of coffee in one hand, and the wrist that protruded from the sleeve of his coat was skeletal, and speckled with angry red bites of body lice. The neck was too long and thin for the head it supported, and the cheeks were hollow, the eye-sockets sunken.

'This is General Courtney,' said the Captain; and as the light of the flare died, Sean saw the eyes shine suddenly with a new light, and heard the boy's breath catch with awe.

'Hello, Anders, I've heard a lot about you.'

'And I've heard about you, sir.' The transparent tones of hero-worship irritated Sean. The boy would have heard all the stories, of course. The regiment boasted of him, and every new recruit heard the tales. There was nothing he could do to prevent them circulating.

'It's a great honour to meet you, sir.' The boy tripped on the words, stuttering a little – another sign of the terrible strain he was under – yet the words were completely sincere.

The legendary Sean Courtney, the man who had made five million pounds on the goldfields of the Witwatersrand and lost every penny of it in a morning at a single coup of fortune. Sean Courtney, who had chased the Boer General Leroux across half of Southern Africa and caught him at last after a terrible hand-to-hand fight. The soldier who had held Bombata's ravaging Zulu impis at the gorge and then driven them on to the waiting Maxims, who had planned with his erstwhile enemy Leroux and helped build the Charter of Union which united the four independent states of Southern Africa into a single mighty whole, who had built another vast personal fortune in land and cattle and timber, who had given up his position in Louis Botha's Cabinet and at the head of the Natal Legislative Council to bring the regiment out to France – it was natural the boy's eyes should shine that way and his tongue trip, but still it annoyed Sean. At fifty-nine I'm too old to play the hero now, he thought wryly – and the flare went down, plunging them back into the darkness.

'If there's another mug of that coffee,' said Sean. 'It's bloody cold tonight.'

Sean accepted the chipped enamel mug and hunkered down close to the brazier, cupped the mug between his hands, blowing on the steaming liquid and sipping noisily, and after a moment the others followed his example hesitantly. It was strange to be squatting like old mates with a General and the silence was profound.

'You're from Zululand?' Sean asked the boy suddenly, his ear had picked up the accent, and without waiting for a reply went on in the Zulu tongue, '*Velapi wena?* Where are you from?'

The Zulu language came naturally and easily to Mark's lips though he had not spoken it for two years. 'From the north beyond Eshowe, on the Umfolosi River.'

'Yes. I know it well. I have hunted there.' Sean changed back to English. 'Anders? I knew another Anders. He rode transport from Delagoa Bay back in '89. John? Yes, that's it. Old Johnny Anders. Any relation? Your father?'

'My grandfather. My father's dead. My grandfather has land on the Umfolosi. That's where I live.' The boy was relaxing now. In the brazier glow, Sean thought he saw the lines of strain around his mouth ironing out.

'I didn't think you'd know poor folk, like us – sir.' Fergus MacDonald spoke with cutting edge in his voice, leaning forward towards the brazier with his head turned towards him so that Sean could see the bitter line of his mouth.

Sean nodded slowly. MacDonald was one of them then. One of those who were intent on the new order – trade unions and Karl Marx, Bolsheviks who threw bombs and called themselves comrades. Irrelevantly he noticed for the first time that MacDonald had ginger hair, and big golden freckles on the backs of his hands. He turned back to Mark Anders.

'He taught you to shoot?'

'Yes, sir.' The lad grinned for the first time, warmed by the memory. 'He gave me my first rifle, a Martini Hendry that blew a cloud of gunsmoke like a bush fire but would throw dead true at a hundred and fifty yards.'

'I've hunted elephant with it. A great rifle,' Sean agreed, and suddenly across an age difference of forty years they were friends.

Perhaps, for Sean, the recent death of that other bright young man, Nick van der Heever, had left an aching gap in his life, for now he felt a flood of paternal protection for the youngster. Fergus MacDonald seemed to sense it also, for he cut in like a jealous woman.

'You'd best be getting ready now, lad.' The smile was gone from Mark's lips, the eyes were too calm, and he nodded his thin neck stiffly.

Fergus MacDonald fussed over the lad, and once again Sean was reminded of a trainer preparing his fighter in the dressing-room. He stripped off the heavy, voluminous great-coat and the battle-dress jacket. Over the long woollen full-length underwear went a woollen shirt and two kitted jerseys. A woollen scarf around the throat.

Then a mechanic's boiler-suit which covered the layers of clothing in a single neat skin that would not snag, or flutter in a breeze to draw an enemy eye. A woollen balaclava over the head, and a leather airman's helmet, and Sean saw the reason. The British steel helmet had a distinctive brim, and anyway was no protection from a Mauser bullet.

'Keep your nut down, Mark, me boy.'

Knitted mittens with fingers cut out, and then thick loose gloves over them. 'Keep the old fingers working, lad. Don't let them stiffen up on you.'

A small leather shoulder bag that slung comfortably under the left armpit.

'Ham sandwiches with plenty of mustard, chocolate and barley sugar – just the way you like it. Don't forget to eat, keep you warm.'

Four full clips of .303 cartridges, three slipped into the thigh pockets of the boiler-suit – and one into the special pocket sewn into the forearm of the left sleeve.

'I waxed each round myself,' Fergus announced mainly for the benefit of the listening General. 'They'll slide in like –' and the simile was crude and obscene, meant to show Fergus's scorn of rank and class. But Sean let it pass easily, he was too interested in the preparations for the hunt.

'I won't show Cuthbert until the sun is right.'

'Cuthbert?' Sean asked, and Fergus chuckled and indicated a third figure that lay quietly at the back of the dugout. It was the first time Sean had noticed him and Fergus chuckled again at his puzzled expression and reached out to the reclining figure.

Only then Sean realized it was a dummy, but in the light of the brazier the features were realistic and the helmeted head rode at a natural angle on the shoulders. The model ended abruptly at the hips and below it there was only a broom handle.

'I'd like to know how you are going to do it?' Sean addressed the question to young Mark Anders, but Fergus replied importantly.

'Yesterday the Hun was shooting from low on the northern slope of the hill. Mark and me worked out the angles of the two shots he made and we've got him pegged to within fifty yards.'

'He may change position,' Sean pointed out.

'He'll not leave the north slope. It's in shadow all day, even if the sun comes out. He will want to shoot from shade into light.' Sean nodded at the logic of it.

'Yes,' he agreed, 'but he may shoot from a stand in the German line.'

And Mark answered quietly, 'I don't think so, sir. The lines are too far apart here' – the German line ran across the crest of the hill – 'he'd want a shorter range. No, sir, he's shooting from close in. He makes a stand in no-man's-land, probably changes it every day – but each time he comes close as he can get to our lines while still staying in the shadow.' The boy had not tripped on a single word now that his mind had locked on to the problem. His voice was low and intense.

'I picked out a good stand for the lad, just beyond the farm house. He can cover the whole of the northern slope at less than two hundred yards. He'll move out now and settle in while it's still dark. I'm sending him out early. I want him to make his move before the Hun. I don't want the lad walking on top of the bastard in the dark.' Fergus MacDonald took over from Mark with an air of authority. 'Then we both wait until the light is good and clean, then I start working with Cuthbert here,' he patted the dummy and chuckled again. 'It's damned difficult to give him a nice natural look, like some stupid rooky sticking his head up to take a first look at France. If you let the Hun get too long a look at him, then he'll tumble to the trick, but if you make it too quick, he won't get a chance for a shot. No, it's not easy.'

'Yes, I should imagine,' Sean murmured wryly, 'that it's the most dangerous and difficult part of the whole thing.' And he saw the deadly expression flit across Fergus MacDonald's face before he turned to Mark Anders.

'Another mug of coffee, lad – and then it's time to be getting on. I want you in place before the snow stops.'

Sean reached into the breast of his great-coat and brought out the silver flask that Ruth had given him on the day the regiment sailed.

'Put some fangs in the coffee.' He offered the flask to Mark.

The boy shook his head shyly. 'No thank you, sir. Makes me see squiff.'

'Don't mind if I do, sir.' Fergus MacDonald reached swiftly across the brazier. The clear brown liquid glugged freely into his own mug.

The Sergeant-Major had sent out a patrol before midnight to cut a lane through the wire in front of 'A' Company.

Mark stood at the foot of the trench ladder and changed his rifle from the right hand; another flare burst overhead and in its light Sean saw how intent the boy was on his task. He pulled back the bolt of the rifle, and Sean noted that he was not using the standard No. 1 short Lee-Enfield, which was the work-horse of the British army, but that he favoured the American P.14 which also fired the .303 calibre but had the longer barrel and finer balance.

Mark stripped two clips of ammunition into the magazine and closed the bolt, levering a round of carefully selected and waxed ammunition into the breach.

In the last light of the flare he looked across at Sean, and nodded slightly. The flare died and in the darkness that followed Sean heard the quick light steps on the wooden ladder. He wanted to call 'good luck' after the boy, but suppressed the whim and instead patted his pockets for his cheroot case.

'Shall we get on back, sir?' the Captain asked quietly.

'Off with you,' growled Sean, his voice gruff with the premonition of coming tragedy. 'I'll stay on a while.' Though he could give no help, somehow it seemed like deserting the boy to leave now.

Mark moved quickly along the line that the patrol had laid to guide him through the wire. He stooped to keep contact with the line in his left hand, and he carried the P.14 in his right. He lifted his feet carefully, and stepped lightly, trying not to scuff the snow, trying to spread his weight evenly on each foot so as not to break the crust.

Yet every time a flare went up, he had to fall face forward and lie still and huddled, a dark blot in the electric glare of light against the sheet of white, screened only by the persistently falling veils of snow. When he scrambled up in the darkness and moved on, he knew he left a disturbed area of snow. Ordinarily it would not have mattered, for in the barren, shell-churned wilderness of no-man's-land, such light scrabble marks passed unnoticed. But Mark knew that in the first cold light of dawn an unusual pair of eyes would be scrutinizing every inch of the ground, hunting for just this kind of sign.

Suddenly, colder than the icy snow-laden air against his cheeks, was the deep chill of loneliness. The sense of vulnerability, of being pitted against a skilled and implacable enemy, an invisible, terrifying, efficient adversary who would deliver instant death at the slightest error.

The latest flare sank and died, and he scrambled to his feet and blundered to the dark, jagged wall of the ruined farm house. He crouched against it, and tried to control his breathing for this newly conceived terror threatened to smother him. It was the first time it had come upon him. Fear he had known — had lived with it as his constant companion these last two years, but never this terrible paralyzing terror.

When he touched his fingers of his right hand to his ice-cold cheek, he felt the tremble in them, and in sympathy his teeth chattered in a short staccato rhythm.

'I can't shoot like this,' he thought wildly, clenching his jaw until it ached and locking his hands together and holding them hard against his groin, 'and I can't stay here.' The ruin was too obvious a stand to make. It would be the first point the German sniper would study. He had to get out of there, and quickly. Back to the trenches. Suddenly his terror was panic, and he lifted himself to begin the crazed flight back, leaving his rifle propped against the ruined wall.

'*Bist du da?*' a voice whispered softly near him in the darkness. Mark froze instantly.

'*Ja!*' The reply was further along the wall and Mark found the rifle with his left hand settling naturally on to the stock and his right curling about the pistol grip, forefinger hooking over the trigger.

'*Komm, wir gehen zurück.*' Close beside Mark, sensed rather than seen in the darkness, passed a heavily laden figure. Mark swung the rifle to follow him, his thumb on the safety-catch ready to slip it. The German stumbled heavily in the treacherous snowy footing, and the wiring tools he carried clanked together. The man cursed.

'*Scheisse!*'

'*Halt den Mond,*' snapped the other, and they moved on back towards the German line above them on the crest of the hill.

Mark had not expected a wiring detail to be out in this weather. His first thought had been for the German sniper, but now his mind leaped forward at this sudden good fortune.

The patrol would lead him through the German wire, and their heavy blundering tracks would hide his own from the sniper.

It was only when he had decided this that he realized with surprise that his panic had passed, his hands were rock steady and his breathing was deep and slow. He grinned without humour at his own frailty and moved forward lightly after the German patrol.

They were a hundred paces beyond the farm house when it stopped snowing. Mark felt the slide of dismay in his chest. He had relied heavily on the snow holding, at least until dawn, but he kept on after the patrol. They were moving faster and more confidently as they neared their own lines.

Two hundred yards below the crest Mark left them to go on alone, and began working his way sideways around the slope, groping his way painstakingly through the heavily staked wire, until at last he recognized and reached the stand that he and Fergus had picked out through binoculars the previous afternoon.

The main trunk of one of the oaks that had covered the hill had fallen directly down the slope, pulling up a great matted tangle of roots from the soft high-explosive-ploughed earth.

Mark crawled among the tangle of roots; selecting the side which would be in deepest shadow from the winter-angled sun, he wriggled in on his belly until he was half covered by them, but with head and shoulders able to turn to cover the full curve of the northern slope ahead of him.

Now his first concern was to check the P.14 carefully, paying particular attention to the vulnerable, high-mounted Bisley-type rear sight to make sure that it had not been knocked or misaligned during the journey across no-man's-land. He ate two of the ham sandwiches, drank a few rationed mouthfuls of sweet coffee and adjusted the woollen scarf over his mouth and nose, for warmth and to prevent the steaming of his breath. Then he laid his forehead carefully against the wooden butt of his rifle. He had developed the knack of instant sleep, and while he slept it snowed again.

When Mark woke in the sickly grey light of dawn, he was blanketed by the fine white flakes. Careful not to disturb them, he lifted his head slowly, and blinked his eyes rapidly to clear them. His fingers were stiff and cold; he worked them steadily in the gloves, forcing warm blood to flow.

He had been lucky again – twice in one night was too much. First the patrol to lead him through the wire and now this thin white coat of natural camouflage to blend his shape with the tangled roots of the oak. Too much luck, the pendulum must swing.

Slowly the darkness drew back, widening his circle of vision, and as it expanded so the whole of Mark's existence came to centre in those two wide golden brown eyes. They moved quickly in the pattern of search, touching in turn each irregularity and fold, each feature, each object, each contrasting colour or texture of snow and mud and earth, each stump of shattered timber or fallen branch, the irregular rim of every shell hole, looking for shadows where they should not have been, seeking the evidence of disturbance beneath the new thin coat of snow, seeking, searching – for life, literally for life.

The snow stopped again a little before nine, and by noon the sky had lightened and there were holes in the cloud-cover, a single watery ray of sun fell and moved like a searchlight across the southern slope of the hill.

'Right, Cuthbert, let's draw some Hun fire.'

Fergus had marked each of the German sniper's kills on the trench map the Sergeant-Major had loaned him. There were two black spots close to each other in the same section of trench. At those places the parapet was too low for the commanding bulk of the hill that commanded the front line. After five men had been killed at those two spots the parapet had been raised with sand-bags and crudely lettered notices warned the unwary.

'KEEP YOUR HEAD DOWN. SNIPER AT WORK.'

The two black spots were only fifty paces apart, and Fergus guessed that the sniper had achieved his successes here by waiting for a victim to pass down the trench. He would get a glimpse of a head in the first gap, and would be aiming into the second gap with his finger on the hair-trigger as the man passed it. He explained this to Sean Courtney as he made his preparations, for by this time Sean was so intrigued by the hunt that only a major German offensive would have lured him back to his headquarters. During the morning he had spoken to his aide-de-camp over the field telephone, and told them where they could find him in an emergency.

'But make sure it's an emergency,' he had growled ferociously into the head-set.

'I'll draw him from south to north,' Fergus explained, 'that will force the bloody Hun to turn away from Mark's stand, it will give the lad an extra second while he swings back towards the ridge.'

Fergus MacDonald was good with the dummy, Sean had to concede it. He carried it two feet higher than natural man height, to compensate for the raised parapet, and he gave it a realistic roll of the shoulders, like a hurrying man as he passed it through the first gap.

Sean, the young Captain and the beefy red-faced Sergeant-Major were waiting with a half dozen other ranks beyond the second gap, watching Fergus come down the boards towards them steadily.

Instinctively they all drew breath and held it as he came up to the second gap, all of them tensed with suspense.

Up the slope of the hill, the Mauser cracked, like a bull-whip on the icy air, and the dummy kicked sharply in Fergus MacDonald's hands.

Fergus jerked it down out of sight, and fell to his knees to examine the neat round hole punched through the papier-mâché head.

'Oh shit!' he whispered bitterly. 'Oh, shit all over it!'

'What is it, MacDonald?'

'The bloody Hun – oh, the sodding bastard –'

'MacDonald!'

'He's picked the same stand as my boy.'

Sean did not understand for a moment. 'He's in among the oak trunks, he's sitting right on top of Mark. They picked the same stand.'

The vicious stinging discharge of the Mauser was so close, so high and sharp, that for a few seconds afterwards, Mark's ear-drums buzzed with the mosquito hum of auditory memory.

For seconds he was stunned, frozen with the shock of it. The German sniper was somewhere within twenty feet of where he lay. By some freak of coincidence, he had chosen the same point on the slope as Mark. No, it was no freak of coincidence. With the hunter's eye for ground, both men had selected the ideal position for their common purpose – to deliver swift death from hiding. The pendulum of Mark's fortune had swung to the other end of its arc.

Mark had not moved in the seconds since the Mauser shot, but every sense was heightened by the adrenalin that sang through his veins and his heart beat with a force that seemed to reverberate against the cage of his ribs.

The German was on his left, higher up the slope, slightly behind his shoulder. The left was his unprotected side, away from the tangled oak roots.

He trained his eyes around, without moving his head, and in the periphery of his vision saw another of the fallen oak trunks close by. He did not move for another full minute, watching for the flicker of movement in the corner of his eye. There was nothing, and the silence was awesome and oppressive – until a Spandau fired a short burst, a mile or more away down the line.

Mark began to turn his head towards the left, as slowly as a chameleon stalking a fly. Gradually the distortion of periphery vision cleared, and he could sweep the whole of the slope above him.

The nearest oak trunk had been savaged with shrapnel, all the bark was torn away and raw chunks of timber ripped from it. It had fallen across a hollow in the earth, forming a bridge; and although the snow had piled up against it, there was a narrow gap between earth and oak. The gap was perhaps three inches wide at the centre, and Mark could see reflected light from the snow beyond.

At that moment, a minute blur of movement snapped his eyes in his skull. It was a fleeting movement of a mere sixteenth of an inch, but it riveted Mark's attention. He stared for fully five seconds, before he realized what he was seeing.

Beyond the screening end of the oak trunk, the very tip of a Mauser barrel protruded. It had been bound with burlap to break the stark outline and to prevent reflection of light off metal – but the cruel little mouth of the muzzle was uncovered.

The German was lying behind the oak log, like Mark his right flank protected, facing half-way from Mark – and less than twenty feet separated them.

Mark watched the tip of the Mauser barrel for ten minutes more, and it did not move again. The German had stillness and patience. Once he had reloaded, he had frozen again into that rigour of watchfulness.

'He's so good that there is no way I can clear the shot,' Mark thought. 'If I move an inch, he'll hear me, and he'll be fast. Very fast.'

To get a clear shot, Mark would have to move back twenty feet or more, and then he would be looking directly into the muzzle of the Mauser; a head-on shot, with the German alerted by his movements. Mark knew he could not afford to give away that much advantage, not against an adversary of this calibre.

The long still minutes crawled by without any break in tension. Mark had the illusion that every nerve and sinew of his body was quivering visibly, but in reality the only movement was in the glove of his right hand. The fingers moved steadily in a kneading motion, keeping supple and warm, and the eyes moved in Mark's skull, swivelling slowly back and forth across the battered trunk of the oak, blinking regularly to clear the tears that tension and the icy air induced.

'What the hell is happening up there?' Fergus MacDonald fretted nervously, peering into the lens of the periscope that allowed the observer to keep well down below the sand-bagged parapet.

'The boy is pinned down.' General Sean Courtney did not remove his own eyes from the other periscope, but swung it slightly, sweeping back and forth across the slope. 'Try the Hun with Cuthbert again.'

'I don't think he'll fall for it again,' Fergus began to protest immediately, looking up with those close-set eyes, rimmed with pink now by the cold and the strain of waiting.

'That's an order, Sergeant.' Sean Courtney's broad forehead wrinkled and the dark brows drew sharply together, his voice growled like an old lion and the dark-blue eyes snapped. The power and presence of the man in this mood awed even Fergus MacDonald.

'Very well, sir,' he muttered sulkily, and went to where the dummy was propped against the firing step.

The lash of the Mauser cracked again, and at the shock Mark Anders's eyelids blinked twice very quickly and then flared wide open. The golden brown eyes stared fixedly up the slope, intent as those of the hunting peregrine.

The instant after the shot, he heard the rattle of the Mauser bolt being drawn back and then thrust forward to reload, and again the tip of the hessian wrapped muzzle stirred slightly – but then Mark's eyes flicked sideways.

There had been another movement, so fine that it might have gone unnoticed by eyes less keen. The movement had been a mere breath, and it had been in the narrow three-inch gap between the oak trunk and the snow-coated earth. Just that one brief stir and then stillness once more.

Mark stared into the gap for long seconds, and saw nothing. Merely shadow and undefined shape, trickily reflected light from the snow beyond. Then suddenly, he was seeing something else.

It was the texture of cloth, a thin sliver of it in the narrow gap, then his eyes picked up the stitched seam in the grey cloth, bulging slightly over the living flesh beneath.

There was some small portion of the German's body showing through the gap. He was lying close up on the far side of the log, and his head was pointed in the direction from which the muzzle of the Mauser projected.

Carefully Mark proportioned the man's body in his imagination. Using the rifle muzzle as his only reference point, he placed the man's head and shoulders, his trunk and his hips –

'Yes, his hips,' Mark thought. 'That is his hip or upper thigh –' and then there was a change in the light. The sun found a weak spot in the cloud cover overhead and the light brightened briefly.

In the better light, Mark made out a small portion of a German service belt, with the empty loop which should have held a bayonet. It confirmed his guess. Now he knew that the slight bulge in the field grey material was caused by the head of the femur where it fitted into the cup of the pelvic girdle.

'Through both hips,' Mark thought coldly. 'It's a pinning shot, and then there is the femoral artery –' Carefully he began to work the glove off his right hand.

He must roll on his side, and swing the long barrel of the P.14 through an arc of over ninety degrees, without making the least sound.

'Please, God,' Mark asked silently, and began to make the move. Achingly slowly, the barrel of his rifle swung and, at the same time, he began to transfer his weight on to his other elbow.

It seemed to be a complete round of eternity before the P.14 pointed into the narrow gap below the oak trunk, and Mark was doubled up, straining to keep the barrel bearing from this unnatural position. He could not slip the safety-catch from the rifle before firing; even that tiny metallic snick would alert the German.

He curled his finger on the trigger, and took up the pull, feeling the dead lock of the safety mechanism. He aimed carefully, his head twisted awkwardly, and he began to push the safety-catch across with his thumb, while holding pressure on the hair trigger. It had to be done smoothly, so as not to pull his aim off the sliver of grey uniform cloth.

The thunder of the shot seemed to bounce against the low grey sky, and the bullet crashed through the tiny gap. Mark saw the impact of it, the rubbery shock of metal into flesh.

He heard the German cry out, a wild sound without form or meaning, and Mark swept back the bolt of the P.14, and reloaded with instinctive dexterity. The next shot blended with the echo of the first, coming so close together that they seemed as one. The jacketed bullet crashed through the gap, and this time Mark saw blood spurt, a bright scarlet spray of it that splattered the snow, turning swiftly to pale pink as it was diluted by the melt of its own heat.

Then there was nothing in the gap, the German had been thrown back by the impact – or had rolled aside. Only the smear of pink stained snow.

Mark waited, a fresh cartridge in the breach of the P.14, turned now to face the oak trunk, tensed for the next shot. If it had not been a decisive wound, the German would be coming after him, and he was ready for the snap shot.

He felt coldly unemotional, but vitally aware, his every fibre and nerve pitched to its utmost, his vision sharp and bright and his hearing enhanced.

The silence drew out for a while longer – and then there was a sound. For a moment Mark did not recognize it, then it came again. The sound of a man sobbing.

It came stronger now, more hysterical, gut-racking.

'*Ach, mein Gott – mein lieber Gott –*' the man's voice, pitiful, broken. '*Das Blut – ach Gott – das Blut.*'

Suddenly the sound was tearing at Mark's soul, cutting deeply into his being. His hand began to shake, and he felt the tremor of his lips once again. He tried to clench his jaw, but now his teeth were chattering wildly.

'Stop it, oh God, stop it,' he whispered, and the rifle fell from his hands. He pressed his mittened hands to his ears, trying to shut out the terrible sounds of the dying German.

'Please, please,' Mark pleaded aloud. 'Stop it, please.'

And the German seemed to hear him.

'*Hilf mir, lieber Gott – das Blut!*' His voice was broken by the wet helpless sounds of his despair.

Suddenly Mark was crawling forward, through the snow, blindly up the slope.

'I'm coming. It's all right,' he muttered. 'Only stop it.' He felt his senses swaying.

'*Ach mein lieber Gott, ach, meine Mutti . . .*'

'Oh Jesus – stop it. Stop it.'

Mark dragged himself around the end of the oak log.

The German was half propped against the log. With both hands he was trying vainly to stem the fountain of bright pulsing arterial blood that flowed through his fumbling fingers. The two bullets had shattered both his hips, and the snow was a sodden mushy porridge of blood.

He turned his face to Mark, and already it was drained of all colour, a shiny greyish white, slick with a fine sheen of perspiration. The German was young, as young as Mark, but swiftly approaching death had smoothed out his features so he seemed younger still. It was the face of a marble angel, smooth and white, and strangely beautiful, with blue eyes in pale blue sockets, a burst of pale golden curls escaping from under the helmet on to the smooth pale forehead.

He opened his mouth and said something that Mark did not understand, and the teeth were white and even, beyond the full pale lips.

Then, slowly, the German sagged back against the log still staring at Mark. His hands fell away from his groin and the regular pulsing spurt of blood from the shattered flesh slowed and shrivelled away. The pale blue eyes lost their feverish lustre, and dulled, no longer focused.

Mark felt a thread pull in the fabric of his mind, like silk beginning to tear. It was almost a physical thing – he could hear it beginning to give way inside him.

His vision wavered, the dead German's features seemed to run like melting wax, and then slowly reform again. Mark felt the tear widening, the silken veil of his reason ripping through; beyond it was a dark and echoing chasm.

The dead German's features went on reforming, until they hardened and Mark was looking into his own face as through a wavering distorted mirror. His own haunted face, the eyes golden brown and terrified, the mouth that was his mouth opened – and a cry came from it that was the despair and the agony of all the world.

The last shreds of Mark's reason whipped away on the tempest of horror, and he heard himself screaming – and felt his feet running under him, but there was only blackness in his head, and his body was light and without weight, like the body of a bird in flight.

The German machine-gunner cocked the Maxim with a single savage wrench on the crank handle, and traversed sharply left, at the same time depressing the thick water-jacketed barrel of the weapon until it pointed directly down the slope below the sand-bagged emplacement towards the British lines.

The single wildly running figure was angling away towards the left, and the gunner pulled the wooden butt of the Maxim into his shoulder and fired a single short traversing burst, aiming a fraction low to counteract the natural tendency to shoot high at a downhill target.

Mark Anders hardly felt the mighty hammer strokes of the two bullets that smashed into his back.

Fergus MacDonald was crying. That surprised Sean, he had not expected it. The tears slid slowly from pink-rimmed eyes, and he struck them away with a single angry movement.

'Permission to take out a patrol, sir?' he asked, and the young Captain glanced uncertainly at Sean over the Sergeant's shoulder.

Sean nodded slightly, a mere inclination of the head.

'Do you think you can find volunteers?' the Captain asked uncertainly, and the red-faced Sergeant answered gruffly.

'There'll be volunteers, sir, the lads have a feeling for what that youngster did.'

'Very well, then – as soon as it's dark.'

They found Mark a little after eight o'clock. He hung in the rusting barbed wire at the bottom of the slope, like a broken doll. Fergus MacDonald had to use a pair of wire-cutters to cut him down, and it took them nearly another hour to get him back to the British lines, dragging the stretcher between them through the mud and slushy snow.

'He's dead,' said General Courtney, looking down at the white drained face on the stretcher in the lantern light.

'No, he's not,' Fergus MacDonald denied it fiercely. 'They don't kill my boy that easy.'

The locomotive whistled shrilly as it clattered over the steel-work of the bridge. Silver steam flew high in a bright plume, and then smeared back on the wind.

Mark Anders leaned far out over the balcony of the single passenger carriage and the same wind ruffled the soft brown wing of his hair and a spattering of ash particles from the furnace stung his cheek, but he screwed up his eyes and looked down into the bed of the river as they roared across.

The water flowed down under the dipping reeds, and then met the pylons of the bridge and swirled sullenly, flowing green and strong and full down to the sea.

'Water's high for this time of year,' Mark muttered aloud. 'Grandpapa will be happy,' and he felt his lips tugging up into the unaccustomed smile. He had smiled only infrequently during the past months.

The locomotive hurtled across the steel bridge, and threw itself at the far slope. Immediately, the beat of its engine changed and its speed bled away.

Mark stooped and hefted his old military pack, opened the gate of the balcony and clambered down on to the steel steps, hanging with one arm over the racing gravel embankment.

The train slowed rapidly as the incline steepened and he swung the pack off his shoulder and leaned far out to let it drop as gently as possible on to the gravel. It bounced once and went bounding away down the embankment, crashing into the shrubbery like a living animal in flight.

Then he swung down towards the racing earth himself and, judging his moment finely as the train crested the ridge, he let go to hit the embankment on flying feet, throwing his weight forward to ride the impact and feel the gravel sliding under him.

He stayed upright, and came to a halt as the rest of the train clattered past him, and the guard looked out sternly from the last van and called a reprimand.

'Hey, that's against the law.'

'Send the sheriff,' Mark shouted back, and gave him an ironic salute as the locomotive picked up speed on the reverse slope with explosive grunts of power, the rhythm of the tracks rising sharply. The guard clenched a fist and Mark turned away.

The jolt had hurt his back again and he slipped a hand into his shirt and ran it around under his armpit as he started back along the tracks. He fingered the twin depressions below the shoulder blade and marvelled again at how close one of them was to the bony projections of the spine. The scar tissue had a silky, almost sensuous feel, but they had taken long months to close. Mark shuddered involuntarily as he remembered the rattle of the trolley that carried the dressings, and the impassive almost masculine face of the matron as she stuffed the long cotton plugs into the open mouths of the bullet wounds; he remembered also the slow tearing agony as the bloody dressing was pulled out again with the glittering steel forceps, and his own breathing sobbing in his ears and the matron's voice, harsh and impersonal.

'Oh, don't be a baby!'

Every day – day after day, week after week – until the hot feverish delirium of the pneumonia that had attacked his bullet-damaged lung had seemed a blessed relief. How long had it been – from the VAD Station in a French field with the muddy snow deeply rutted by the ambulances and the burial details digging graves beyond the tented hospital – to the general hospital near Brighton and the dark mists of pneumonia, the hospital ship home down the length of the Atlantic, baking in the airless tropics, the convalescent hospital with its pleasant lawns and gardens – how long? Fourteen months in all, months during which the war which men were already misnaming 'Great' had ended. Pain and delirium had clouded the passage of time, yet it seemed a whole lifetime.

He had lived one life in the killing and the carnage, in the pain and the suffering, and now he was reborn. The pain in his back abated swiftly. It was almost mended now, he thought happily, and he pushed away the dark and terrible memories and scrambled down the embankment to retrieve his pack.

Andersland was almost forty miles downstream, and the train had been behind schedule, it was noon already. Mark knew that he would not make it before the following evening – and strangely, now that he was almost home, the sense of urgency was gone.

He moved easily, falling into that long, familiar stride of the hunter, easing the pack on his back slightly as soon as the newly healed wounds stiffened, feeling the good sweat springing cool on his face and through the thin cotton of his shirt.

Absence of so many years had sharpened his appreciation of the world through which he moved, so that which before had warranted only passing attention become now a new and unfamiliar delight.

Along the banks the dense riverine bush was alive with myriad life. The bejewelled dragonflies that skimmed the surface on transparent wings or coupled in flight, male upon female, his long glittering abdomen arched to join with hers; the hippopotamus that burst through the surface in an explosive exhalation of breath, and stared at Mark upon the bank with pink watery eyes, flicking the tiny ears, and wallowing like a gargantuan black balloon in the green swirling current.

It was like moving through an ancient Eden, before the coming of man, and suddenly Mark knew that this solitude was what his body and mind needed to complete the healing process.

He camped that night on a grassy bluff above the river, above the mosquitoes and the unpleasant darkness of the thick bush.

A leopard woke him after midnight, sawing hoarsely down in the river bottom, and he lay and listened to it moving slowly upstream until he lost it among the crags of high ground. He did not sleep again immediately, but lay and examined, with the pleasure of anticipation, the day ahead of him.

For every day of the past four years, even the very bad days of darkness and ghosts, he had thought of the old man. Some days it had been only a fleeting thought, on other days he had dwelt upon him as a homesick schoolboy tortures himself with thoughts of home. The old man was home, of course, both the mother and father Mark had never known. Always there from his first vaguest memory to the present, unchanging in his strength and quiet understanding.

Mark felt a deep physical pang of longing, as he recalled clearly a picture of the old man sitting on the hard carved rocker on the wide boarded stoep, the crumpled old khaki shirt, crudely patched and in need of laundering, open at the neck to expose a fuzz of silver-white chest hair; the neck and jowls wrinkled like those of a turkey cock, but burned dark brown and pelted with five days' growth of silver stubble that sparkled like glass chips; the huge moustaches of glistening white, the ends curled with beeswax into fearsome spikes, the wide terai hat pulled low over the bright toffee-coloured humorous eyes. The hat was always in place, sweat-soaked and greasy around the band, but never removed, not even at meal-times – nor, Mark suspected, in the big brass bed at night.

Mark remembered him pausing from working with the whittling knife, rolling the quid from one cheek to the other, then letting fly at the old five-gallon Tate and Lyle golden syrup can that was his spittoon. Hitting solidly at ten feet, spilling not a single drop of the dark brown juice, and then continuing the story as though there had been no interruption. And what stories! Stories to start a small boy's eyes popping from their sockets and wake him in the night to peer fearfully under the bed.

Mark remembered the old man in small things, stooping to take up a handful of his rich soil and let it run through his fingers, then wiping them on the seat of his pants with the proud fierce expression on his withered old features. 'Good land – Andersland,' he would say, and nod like a sage. Mark remembered him in the big things, standing tall and skinny beside Mark in thick thorn bush with the big old Martini Hendry rifle bellowing and smoking, the recoil shaking his frail old body as, like a black mountain, the buffalo bull came down upon them, blood mad and crazed with its wounds.

Four years since last he had seen him, since last he had heard news of him. At first he had written, long homesick letters, but the old man could not read nor write. Mark had hoped that he might take them to a friend, the postmistress perhaps, and that they might read them to him and write back to Mark.

It had been a vain hope. The old man's pride would never allow him to admit to a stranger that he could not read. Nevertheless, Mark had continued to write, once every month for all those long years; but only tomorrow he would have his first news of the old man in all that time.

Mark slept again for another few hours, then built up the fire again in the darkness before dawn and brewed coffee. He was moving again as soon as it was light enough to see his feet on the path.

From the escarpment he watched the sun come up out of the sea. There were mountains of cumulus thunder clouds standing tall over the distant sea, and the sun came up behind them so that they glowed with red and roses, wine and deep purples, each cloud etched in outline by brilliant red-gold and shot through with shafts of light.

At Mark's feet the land dropped away into the coastal lowlands, that rich littoral of densely forested valleys and smooth golden grassy hills that stretched to the endless white beaches of the Indian Ocean.

Below where Mark stood, the river tumbled over the edge of the escarpment, leaping in sheets of white and silver from wet black rock to deep dark pools which turned upon themselves in foam like huge wheels, as though they rested before the next wild plunge downwards.

Mark began to hurry for the first time, following the steep path downwards with the same urgency as the river, but it was mid morning before he came out on to the warm and drowsing sweep of land below the escarpment.

The river widened, and became shallower, changing its mood completely as it meandered between the exposed sandbanks. There were new birds here, different beasts in the forest and upon the hills, but now Mark had no time for them. Hardly glancing at the flocks of long, heavy-beaked storks and scimitar-billed ibis on the sandbanks, even when the hadedah ibis rose with their wild insanely ringing shrieks of laughter, he hurried on.

There was a place, unmarked except for a small tumbled cairn at the foot of a huge wild fig tree, that had a special significance to Mark, for it marked the western boundary of Andersland.

Mark stopped to rebuild the cairn among the grey scaly roots that crawled across the earth like ancient reptiles, and while he worked, a flock of fat green pigeons exploded on noisy wings from the branches above him where they had been feeding on the bitter yellow fruit.

When Mark went on beyond the fig tree, he walked with a new lightness and resilience to his step, a new set to his shoulders and a new brightness in his eyes – for he walked once again on Andersland. Eight thousand acres of rich chocolate loamy ground, four miles of river frontage, water that never failed, softly rounded hills covered with thick sweet grass, Andersland, the name the old man had given it thirty years before.

Half a mile further on, Mark was about to leave the river and take a short cut across the next ridge to the homestead, when there was a distant but earth-trembling thud, and immediately afterwards the faint sound of human voices on the still warm air.

Puzzled, Mark paused to listen, and again the thudding sound – but this time preceded by the crackling and snapping of branches and undergrowth. The unmistakable sound of timber being felled.

Abandoning his original intention, Mark kept on down the river, until he emerged suddenly from forest into open country that reminded him at first of those terrible devastated fields of France, torn and ravaged by shell and high explosive until the raw earth lay exposed and churned.

There were gangs of dark men in white linen dhotis and turbans felling the heavy timber and clearing out the undergrowth along the river. For a moment Mark did not understand who these strange men were, and then he remembered reading a newspaper report that Hindu labourers were being brought out in their thousands from India to work for the new sugar cane estates. These were the wiry, very dark-skinned men that worked now like a colony of ants along the river. There were hundreds of them – no, Mark realized that they were in their thousands – and there were oxen teams as well. Big spans of heavy, strong-looking beasts plodding slowly as they dragged the fallen timber into rows for burning.

Not truly understanding what he was seeing, Mark left the river and climbed the slope beside it. From the crest he had a new uninterrupted view across Andersland – and beyond, eastwards towards the sea.

The devastation stretched as far as he could see, and now there was something else to ponder. The land was going to the plough, all of it. The forest and grazing land had been torn out, and the trek oxen moved slowly over the open ground, one team following the next, the rich chocolate earth turning up under the plough shares in thick shiny welts. The cries of the ploughmen and the muted popping of the long trek whips carried to where Mark stood, bewildered, upon the slope of the hill.

He sat down on a boulder and for almost an hour watched the men and the oxen at work, and he was afraid. Afraid for what this all meant. The old man would never let this happen to his land. He had a hatred of the plough and the axe; he loved too deeply the stately trees which now groaned and crackled as they toppled. The old man hoarded his grazing like a miser, as though it were as precious as its golden colour suggested. He would never allow it to be turned under – not if he were alive.

That was why Mark was afraid. If he were alive. For, God knows, he would never sell Andersland.

Mark did not truly want to know the answer. He had to force himself to rise and go down the hill.

The dark turbaned labourers did not understand his questions, but they directed him with expressive gestures to a fat babu in a cotton jacket who strutted importantly from work gang to work gang, snapping at a naked black back with a light cane or pausing to write a laborious note in the huge black book he carried.

He looked up, startled, and then immediately became obsequious in the presence of a white man.

'Good day, master –' He would have gone on, but the shiny acquisitive eyes darted over Mark and they saw how young he was, unshaven, his cheap army issue suit was stained with travel and rumpled from having been slept in. It was obvious he carried his entire worldly possessions in his back-pack.

'To tell the truth, we are not needing more men here.' His manner changed instantly, becoming lordly. 'I am being in charge here –'

'Good.' Mark nodded. 'Then you can tell me what these men are doing on Andersland.'

The man irritated him, he had known so many like him in the army – bully those below and lick the backsides of those above.

'Beyond doubt we are making ground clear for sugar.'

'This ground belongs to my family,' said Mark, and instantly the man's manner changed again.

'Ah, good young master, you are from the company at Ladyburg?'

'No, no – we live here. In the house,' Mark pointed at the ridge of the hill, beyond which lay the homestead, 'this is our ground.'

The babu chuckled like a fat dark baby, and shook his head.

'Nobody living here now. Alas! The company owns everything.' And he made a wide gesture that took in the whole landscape from escarpment to the sea. 'Soon everything is sugar, you will see, man. Sugar, sugar.' And he laughed again.

From the ridge the old homestead looked the same, just a green-painted roof of corrugated iron showing above the dark green of the orchard, but as Mark came up the overgrown path past the hen coops, he saw that all the window panes had been removed, leaving blank dark squares, and there was no furniture on the wide stoep. The rocker was gone, and there was a sag to the roof timbers at one end of the veranda; a drainpipe had come loose and hung away from the wall.

The garden had the wild untended look of neglect, the plants beginning to encroach on the house itself. The old man had always kept it trimmed and neat with the leaves swept up daily from under the trees and the white-painted beehives set up in orderly rows in the shade. Somebody had robbed the hives with brutal carelessness, smashing them open with an axe.

The rooms were bare, stripped of anything of possible value, even the old black wood-burning stove in the kitchen, everything except the Tate and Lyle spittoon on the stoep which lay on its side; its spilled contents had left a dark stain on the woodwork.

Mark wandered slowly from room to empty room, feeling a terrible sense of loss and desolation as the wind-blown leaves rustled under his feet, and the big black and yellow spiders watched him with myriad glittering eyes from the webs they had spun in the corners and across the jambs of the door-ways.

Mark left the house and went down to the small family graveyard, feeling a quick lift of relief when he realized there were no new graves there. Grand-mother Alice, her eldest daughter, and her cousin who had died before Mark was born. Still three graves – the old man was not there.

Mark drew a bucket from the well and drank a little of the cold sweet water, then he wandered into the orchard and picked a hatful of guavas and a ripe yellow pineapple. In the backyard strutted a young cockerel who had escaped the plunderers. Mark had to hunt him for half an hour before a stone brought him down off the roof in a squawking flutter of feathers.

Plucked and cleaned, he went into the canteen over the fire that Mark made in the backyard – and while he boiled, Mark had a sudden thought.

He went back into the old man's bedroom and in the far corner, where the big brass bed had once stood, he knelt and felt for the loose board. He prised the single nail that held it down with his clasp knife and then lifted the plank.

He reached down into the opening below and brought out first a thick bundle of envelopes tied with a strip of raw-hide. Mark riffled the edge of the pack and saw that not a single envelope had been opened. They were all addressed in his own spiky hand. They had been carefully stored in this hiding place. Yet not all Mark's letters were there. The sequence ended abruptly and Mark, checking the last letter, found it post-marked eleven months previously. Mark felt a choking sensation in the base of his throat, and the sharp sting of tears.

He placed the bundle of letters aside and reached again into the opening to bring out the Mazzawatee tea caddy, with the picture of the grandmother in steel-rimmed spectacles on the lid. It was the old man's treasure-chest.

He carried the can and the bundle of letters out into the backyard for the late afternoon light was going fast in the unlit rooms. He sat on the kitchen step, and opened the tea caddy.

There were forty gold sovereigns in a leather purse, some of them had the bearded head of Kruger the old president of the South African Republic, the others of Edward and George. Mark slipped the purse into the inner pocket of his jacket and in the fading light examined the rest of the old man's treasure. Photographs of grandmother Alice as a young woman, yellowed and dog-eared with age, a wedding certificate, old newspaper clippings from the Boer War, cheap articles of women's jewellery, the same as those that Alice wore in the photographs, a medal in a presentation case, a Queen's South Africa medal with six bars including those for Tugela, Ladysmith and the Transvaal campaigns, Mark's own school reports from the Ladyburg School and then the diploma from the University College at Port Natal – these the old man valued especially, with the illiterate's awe of learning and the written word. He had sold some of his prize livestock to pay for Mark's education, he rated it that highly. Nothing in the tea caddy, apart from the sovereigns, was of any value, but it had all been precious beyond price to the old man. Carefully Mark repacked the tin and placed it in his back-pack.

In the last light of day Mark ate the stringy cockerel and the fruit, and when he rolled into his blanket on the wooden kitchen floor he was still thinking.

He knew now that the old man, wherever he had gone, had intended returning to Andersland. He would never have left that precious hoard behind unless that had been his intention.

A boot in the ribs brought Mark awake, and he rolled over and sat up, gasping with the pain of it.

'On your feet! Get your arse moving – and keep it going.'

It was not yet fully light, but Mark could make out the man's features. He was clean-shaven with a heavy smooth jaw, and his teeth seemed to have been ground down to a flat even line – very white against the dark suntan. His head was round, like a cannon ball, and gave the impression of vast weightiness, for he carried it low on a thick neck like a heavyweight boxer shaping up.

'Up!' he repeated, and drew back the scuffed brown riding-boot again. Mark came up on his feet and squared to defend himself. He found the man was shorter than he was, but he was stocky and solid, with broad thick shoulders and the same weightiness in his frame. 'This is private property, we don't want tramps hanging about.'

'I'm not a tramp,' Mark started, but the man cut him short with a snort of brusque laughter.

'You with the fancy clothes, and the Rolls parked at the door – you had me fooled for a moment there.'

'My name is Mark Anders,' he said. 'This land belongs to my grandfather – John Anders –'

He thought he saw something move in the man's eyes, a change in the set of his mouth, doubt or worry perhaps. He licked his lips, a quick nervous gesture, but when he spoke his voice was still flat and quiet.

'I don't know nothing about that – all I know is this land belongs to the

Ladyburg Estates now, and I am the foreman for the company, and neither me nor the company wants you hanging around here,' he paused and settled on his feet, dropping his shoulders and pushing out his heavy jaw, 'and one other thing I know is I like to break a head now and then, and I haven't broken one for God knows a long time.'

They stared at each other, and Mark felt a sudden hot rush of anger. He wanted to take up the man's challenge, even though he realized how powerful and dangerous he was. He had the look of a killer, and the weight and the strength, but Mark felt himself coming into balance, his own shoulders dropping.

His tormentor saw it also and his relish was obvious. He smiled thinly, clenching his jaw around the smile so that the cords stood out in his throat, swaying slightly up on to the balls of his feet. Then suddenly Mark felt revolted and sickened by the presence of violence. There had been too much of it in his life already – and there was no reason to fight now. He turned away and picked up his boots.

The man watched him dress, disappointed perhaps, but ready for further confrontation. When he swung his pack up on to his shoulder, Mark asked, 'What's your name?'

The man answered him lightly, still keyed up for violence. 'My friends call me Hobday,' he said.

'Hobday who?'

'Just Hobday.'

'I won't forget it,' said Mark. 'You've been a real brick, Hobday.' He went down the steps into the yard, and fifteen minutes later when Mark looked back from the ridge where the Ladyburg road crossed on its way northwards, Hobday was still standing in the kitchen yard of Andersland, watching him intently.

Fred Black watched Mark come up the hill. He leaned against the rail of the dipping tank and chewed steadily on his quid of tobacco, stringy and sun-blackened and dry as a stick of chewing tobacco himself.

Although he was one of John Anders's cronies, and had known Mark since he was a crawler, it was clear he did not recognize him now. Mark stopped fifteen paces off and lifted his hat.

'Hello, Uncle Fred,' Mark greeted him, and still it was a moment before the older man let out a whoop and leapt to embrace Mark. 'God, boy, they told me you'd got yourself killed in France.'

They sat together on the rail of the cattle pen, while the Zulu herd boys drove the cattle below them through the narrow race, until they reached the ledge from which they made the wild scrambling leap into the deep stinking chemical bath, to come up again, snorting fearfully, and swim, nose up, for the slope ramp beyond.

'He's been dead almost a year – no, longer, over a year now – lad, I'm sorry. I never thought to let you know. Like I said, we thought you were dead in France.'

'That's all right, Uncle Fred.' Mark was surprised that he felt no shock. He had known it, accepted it already, but there was still the grief that lay heavy on his soul. They were both silent for a longer time, the old man beside him respecting his grief.

'How did he –' Mark hesitated over the word, 'how did he go?'

'Well, now.' Fred Black lifted his hat and rubbed the bald pink pate lovingly. 'It was all a bit sudden like. He went off to poach a little biltong with Piet Greyling and his son up at Chaka's Gate.' Vivid memories crowded back for Mark. Chaka's Gate was the vast wilderness area to the north where the old man had taught him the craft of the hunter. Years before, back in 1869 it had been declared a hunting reserve but no warden had been appointed, and the men of northern Natal and Zululand looked upon it as their private hunting reserve.

'On the fifth day, the old man did not come back into camp. They searched for him another four days before they found him.' He paused again and glanced at Mark. 'You feeling all right, boy?'

'Yes, I'm all right.' Mark wondered how many men he had seen die, how many he had killed himself – and yet the death of one more old man could move him so. 'Go on, please, Uncle Fred.'

'Piet said it looked like he had slipped while he was climbing a steep place, and he had fallen on his rifle and it had gone off. It hit him in the stomach.' They watched the last ox plunge into the dip, and Fred Black climbed stiffly down from the pole fence. He held the small of his back for a moment. 'Getting old,' he grunted, and Mark fell in beside him as they started up towards the house.

'Piet and his boy buried him there. He wasn't fit to bring back, he'd been in the sun four days. They marked the place and made a sworn statement to the magistrate when they got back to Ladyburg.'

Fred Black was interrupted by a cry and the sight of a female figure racing down the avenue of blue gum trees towards them – slim and young, with honey brown hair in a thick braid bouncing on her back, long brown legs and grubby bare feet beneath the skirts of the faded cheap cotton skirt.

'Mark!' she cried again. 'Oh Mark!' But she was close before he recognized her. She had changed in four years.

'Mary.' The sadness was still on Mark, but he could not talk further now. There would be time later. Even in the sadness, he could not miss the fact that Mary Black was a big girl now, no longer the mischievous imp who once had been below his lordly notice when he had been a senior at Ladyburg High School.

She still had the freckled laughing face and the prominent, slightly crooked front teeth, but she had grown into a big, wide-hipped, earthy farm girl, with a resounding jolly laugh. She was as tall as Mark's shoulder and her shape under the thin, threadbare cotton was rounded and full; she had hips and buttocks that swung as she walked beside him, a waist like the flared neck of a vase and fat heavy breasts that bounced loosely at each stride. As they walked, she asked questions, endless questions in a demanding manner, and she kept touching Mark, her hand on his elbow, then grabbing his hand to shake out the answers to her questions, looking up at him with mischievous eyes, laughing her big ringing laugh. Mark felt strangely restless.

Fred Black's wife recognized him from across the yard and let out a sound like a milch cow too long deprived of her calf. She had nine daughters, and she had always pined for a son.

'Hello, Aunt Hilda,' Mark began, and then was folded into her vast pneumatic embrace.

'You're starved,' she cried, 'and those clothes, they stink. You stink too, Marky – your hair, you'll be sitting on it next.'

The four unmarried girls, supervised by Mary, set the galvanized bath in the centre of the kitchen floor and filled it with buckets of steaming water from the stove. Mark sat on a stool on the back veranda with a sheet around his shoulders, while Aunt Hilda sheared him of his long curling locks with a huge pair of blunt scissors.

Then she drove her daughters protesting from the kitchen. Mark fought desperately for his modesty, but she brushed his defence aside.

'An old woman like me, you haven't got anything I haven't seen bigger and better.' She stripped him determinedly, hurling the soiled and rumpled clothing through the open doorway to where Mary hovered expectantly.

'Wash them, child – and you get yourself away from that door.'

Mark blushed furiously and dropped quickly into the water.

In the dusk, Fred Black and Mark sat together on the coping of the well in the yard, with a bottle of brandy between them. The liquor was the fierce 'Cape Smoke' with a bite like a zebra stallion, and after the first sip Mark did not touch his glass again.

'Yes, I've thought about that often,' Fred agreed, already slightly owl-eyed with the brandy. 'Old Johnny loved that land of his.'

'Did he ever speak of selling it to you?'

'No, never did. I always thought he'd be there for ever. Often talked of being buried next to Alice. He wanted that.'

'When did you last see Grandpapa, Uncle Fred?'

'Well, now,' he rubbed his bald head thoughtfully, 'it would be about two weeks before he left for Chaka's Gate with the Greylings. Yes, that's right. He'd been into Ladyburg to buy cartridges and provisions. Pitched up here one night in the old scotch-cart, and we had a good old chat.'

'He didn't say anything then – about selling?'

'No, not a word.'

The kitchen door flew open, spilling yellow lantern light into the yard, and Aunt Hilda bellowed at them.

'Food's up. Come along now, Fred, don't you keep that boy out there, teaching him your evil ways – and don't you bring that bottle into this house. You hear me!'

Fred grimaced, poured the last three inches of dark brown liquor into his tumbler and shook his head at the empty bottle.

'Farewell, old friend.' He sent it sailing over the hedge, and drained the tumbler like medicine.

Mark was crowded into the bench against the kitchen wall with Mary on one side of him and another of the big buxom daughters on the other. Aunt Hilda sat directly opposite him, shovelling food on to his plate, and loudly berating him if his rate of ingestion faltered.

'Fred needs somebody here to help him now. He's getting old, though the old fool doesn't know it.'

Mark nodded, his mouth so full he was unable to reply, and Mary reached across him for another hunk of home-baked bread that was still warm from the oven. Her big loose breast pressed against Mark and he almost choked.

'The girls don't get much chance to meet nice boys – stuck out here on the farm.'

Mary shifted in her seat, and her upper thigh came firmly against Mark's.

'Leave the lad alone, Hilda, you scheming old woman,' Fred slurred amiably from the head of the table.

'Mary, give Mark some more gravy on those potatoes.' The girl poured the gravy, steadying herself as she leaned over towards Mark by placing her free hand on Mark's leg above the knee.

'Eat up! Mary's done you a special milk tart for afters.'

Mary's hand still rested on his leg, and now it moved slowly but purposefully upwards. Instantly Mark's entire attention focused on the hand and the food turned to hot ashes in his mouth.

'Some more pumpkin, Marky?' Aunt Hilda asked with concern, and Mark shook his head weakly. He could not believe what was happening below the level of the table – and directly in front of Mary's mother.

He felt a rising sense of panic.

As casually as he could in the circumstances, he dropped one hand into his lap, and without looking at the girl, gripped her wrist firmly.

'Have you had enough, Mark?'

'Yes, oh yes, indeed,' Mark agreed fervently, and tried to drag Mary's hand away, but she was a big powerful lass and not easily distracted.

'Clear Mark's plate, Mary love, and give him some of your lovely tart.'

Mary seemed not to hear. Her head was bowed demurely over her plate, her cheeks were flushed bright glowing pink, and her lips trembled slightly. Beside her, Mark writhed and squirmed in his seat.

'Mary, what's wrong with you, girl?' Her mother frowned with irritation. 'Do you hear me, child?'

'Yes, Mother, I hear you.' At last she sighed and roused herself. She stood up slowly and reached for Mark's plate with both hands, while he sagged slightly on the bench, weak with relief.

Mark was exhausted from the long day's march and the subsequent excitement, but though he fell asleep almost instantly, it was a sleep troubled by dreams.

Through a ghostly, brooding landscape of swirling mist and weird unnatural light, he pursued a dark wraith – but his legs were slowed, as though he moved through a bath of treacle, and each pace was an enormous effort.

He knew the wraith that flitted through the mist ahead of him was the old man, and he tried to cry out, but though he strained with open mouth no sound came. Suddenly a small red hole appeared in the wraith's dark back and from it flowed a bright pulsing stream of blood, and the wraith turned to face him.

For a moment he looked into the old man's face, the intelligent yellow eyes smiled at him over the huge spiked moustache, and then the face melted like hot wax and the pale features of a beautiful marble statue came up like a face through water. The face of the young German – at last Mark cried out and fell to cover his face. In the darkness he sobbed softly, until another sensation came through to his tortured imagination.

He felt a slow cunning caress. The sobbing shrivelled in his throat, and gradually he abandoned himself to the wicked delight of his senses. He knew what was coming, it had happened so often in the lonely nights and he welcomed it now, drifting up slowly out of the depths of sleep.

At the edge of his awareness there was a voice now, whispering, crooning gently.

'There now, don't fuss, there now – it's all right now, it's going to be all right. Don't make that terrible noise.'

He came awake gradually, for long moments not realizing that the warm firm flesh was reality. Above him were heavy white breasts, hanging big and heavy to sweep across his chest, white bare skin shining in the moonlight that spilled through the window above his narrow steel bed.

'Mary will make it better,' the voice whispered with husky intensity.

'Mary?' he choked out the name, and tried to sit up, but she pushed him back gently with her full weight on his chest. 'You're mad.'

He began to struggle, but her mouth came down over his, wet and warm and all engulfing, and his struggles abated at the shock of this new sensation. He felt his sense whirl giddily.

Against the rising turmoil within him was balanced the terrible things that he knew about women. Those strange and awful things that the regimental chaplain had explained to him, the knowledge that had sustained him against all the blandishments of the bold little *poules* of France and the ladies who had beckoned to him from the dark doorways of London's back streets.

The chaplain had told them how two equally evil terrible consequences came from unlawful union with a woman. Either there was a disease that was without cure, which ate away the flesh, left a rotting hole in a man's groin and finally drove him insane, or there was a child without a father – a bastard to darken a man's honour.

The threat was too much, and Mark tore his mouth free from the girl's sucking hungry lips and the thrusting, driving tongue.

'Oh God!' he whispered. 'You'll have a baby.'

'That's all right, silly,' she whispered in a cheerful husky voice. 'We can get married.'

She shifted suddenly as he lay stunned by this intelligence, and she swung one knee over his supine body, pinning him under the heavy soft cushion of her flesh, smothering him with the fall of bright clinging hair.

'No.' He tried to wriggle out from under her. 'No, this is mad. I don't want to marry –'

'Yes, there – oh yes.'

For another instant he was paralyzed by the feeling of it, and then with a violent wrench he toppled her over. She fell sideways, her hands clutched wildly at his shoulders for an instant before she went over the side of the bed.

The washstand crashed over, and the thud of the girl's big body upon the floorboards echoed through the silent sleeping house.

For a moment afterwards the echoes died, the silence returned and then was split by a chorus of screams from the bedroom of the younger girls across the passage.

'What is it?' bellowed Fred Black, from the big bedroom.

'There's somebody in the house.'

'Get him, Fred, don't just lie there.'

'Where's my shotgun?'

'Help, papa! Help!'

With a single bound, Mary leapt up from the bedroom floor, snatched her nightgown off the chair and swept it over her head.

'Mary!' Mark sat up, he wanted to explain, to try and tell her about the chaplain. He leaned towards her and even in the faint moonlight he could see the fury that contorted her features.

'Mary –' He did not have time to avoid the blow, it came full-armed and flat-handed, smashing into the side of his head with a force that rattled his teeth and starred his vision. She was a big strong girl. When his head cleared, she was gone, but his ear still sang with the sound of a thousand wild bees.

A dusty Daimler lorry pulled up beside Mark as he trudged along the side of the deeply rutted road with thick grass growing along the central hump.

There was a middle-aged man and his wife in the front seat, and he called to Mark.

'Where are you going, son?'

'Ladyburg, sir.'

'Jump in the back, then.'

Mark rode the last twenty miles sitting high on bagged maize, with a coop of cackling hens beside him and the wind ruffling his stiff newly cropped hair.

They rattled over the bridge across the Baboon Stroom, and Mark marvelled at how it had all changed. Ladyburg was no longer a village, but a town. It had spread out as far as the stream itself, and there was a huge new goods yard below the escarpment in which half a dozen locomotives busily shunted trucks heavily laden with freshly sawn timber from the mills, or with bagged sugar from the new factory.

The factor itself was a monument to the town's progress, a towering structure of steel girders and huge boilers. Smoke and steam boiled from a half dozen stacks to form a grey mist that smeared away on the gentle breeze.

Mark wrinkled his nose at the faint stink of it on the wind, and then looked with awe down Main Street. There were at least a dozen new buildings, their ornate façades decorated with scrolls of ironwork, and beautifully intricate gables, stained glass in the main doors and the owner's name and date of construction in raised plaster lettering across the front; but these were all over-shadowed by a giant structure four stories tall, crusted with ornamentation like a wedding cake of a wealthy bride. Proudly it bore the legend 'Ladyburg Farmers Bank'. The driver of the truck dropped Mark on the sidewalk in front of it, and left him with a cheery wave.

There were at least a dozen motor vehicles parked among the scotch-carts and horse-drawn carriages, and the people on the streets were well dressed and cheerful-looking, the citizens of a prosperous and thriving community.

Mark knew one or two of them from the old days, and as he trudged down Main Street with his pack slung over one shoulder, he paused to greet them. There was always a momentary confusion until they recognized him, and then, 'But, Marky, we heard – we thought you'd been killed in France. It was in the *Gazette*.'

The Land Deeds Registrar's Office was in the sprawled labyrinth of Government offices behind the Magistrate's Court and Police Station. There had been plenty of time to think on the long journey up from Andersland, and Mark knew exactly what he was going to do, and in what order.

There was a cramped space in the front of the office with an uninviting wooden bench, and a plain deal counter. There was an elderly clerk with nearsighted eyes behind steel-rimmed spectacles, and a peaked green eyeshade on his forehead. He looked like an ancient crow in his black alpaca jacket with paper guards over his cuffs, and a bony beak of a nose, as he crouched over his desk making a Herculean task of stamping a pile of documents.

He worked on for a few minutes. Mark patiently read the Government notices that plastered the walls, until the clerk looked up at last with the exasperated air of a man interrupted in a labour that might alter the destiny of mankind.

'I'd like to look at a land deed, please sir.'

A certain piece of extinguished quit-rent land situate in the division of Ladyburg being Erf. No. 42 of Division A of One. The farm known as ANDERSLAND ...

*Deed of Transfer passed in favour of Ladyburg Estates Ltd registered at Ladyburg
on 1st day of June, 1919.*
*Know all men whom it may concern that DENNIS PETERSEN appeared before
me, Registrar of Deeds, he, the said appearer, being duly authorized by a power
of attorney executed at Ladyburg on the 12th day of May, 1919, by JOHN
ARCHIBALD ANDERS which power was witnessed in accordance with law … and
that the said appearer declared that his principal had truly and legally sold …*

Mark turned to the next document.

Agreement of Sale of Immovable property
*That JOHN ARCHIBALD ANDERS, hereinafter known as the Seller, and
LADYBURG ESTATES LTD hereinafter known as the purchaser – the Farm
known as ANDERSLAND – together with all improvements and buildings, standing
crops, implements and livestock – for the consideration of Three Thousand Pounds
Sterling –*
 In witness whereof the parties set their hand.
 JOHN ARCHIBALD ANDERS (his mark) X
 *For and on behalf of LADYBURG ESTATES LTD – DIRK COURTNEY
 (DIRECTOR)*
 As witnesses of the above:–
  PIETER ANDRIES GREYLING
  CORNELIUS JOHANNES GREYLING

Mark frowned at the two names. Piet Greyling and his son had accompanied
the old man up to Chaka's Gate almost immediately after witnessing the Deed
of Sale, and they had found him dead a few days later and buried him out
there in the wilderness.

General Power of Attorney
in favour of DENNIS PETERSEN.
I, the undersigned, JOHN ARCHIBALD ANDERS
do hereby empower the above-mentioned DENNIS …
signed JOHN ARCHIBALD ANDERS X (his mark)
as witness PIETER ANDRIES GREYLING.
  CORNELIUS JOHANNES GREYLING.

Mark pored over the bundle of stiff legal parchment with its fancy printing
and red wax seals with dangling ribbons of watered silk. Carefully he copied
out the names of the parties involved in the transaction into his notebook
and when he had finished, the clerk who had been jealously watching his
precious papers reclaimed them and reluctantly handed over an official receipt
for the five-shilling search fee.
 The office of the registrar of companies was directly across the narrow lane,
and here Mark was received in a different mood. The keeper of this gloomy
cavern was a young lady dressed in severe dove-grey jacket and long sweeping
skirt which was at odds with her lively eyes and pert air.
 The pretty little face, with freckled snub nose, lit with a quick appreciative
smile as Mark came in through the door and within minutes she was helping
him in a comradely and conspiratorial manner as he perused the memoranda
and articles of association of Ladyburg Estates Ltd.
 'Do you live here?' asked the girl. 'I haven't seen you before.'
 'No, I don't,' Mark answered warily without looking up at her. He was

finding it difficult to concentrate on the documents, and he remembered vividly his last encounter with a young girl.

'You're lucky.' The girl sighed dramatically. 'It's so dull here, nothing to do after work in the evenings.' She waited hopefully, but the silence drew out.

The Directors of Ladyburg Estates were Messrs Dirk Courtney and Ronald Beresford Pye, but they held only a single share each, just sufficient to qualify them to act as officers of the company.

The other nine hundred and ninety-nine thousand, nine hundred and ninety-eight ordinary fully paid up five-shilling shares were held by the Ladyburg Farmers Bank.

'Thank you very much,' said Mark, returning the file to the girl while avoiding her frank gaze. 'Could I see the file for Ladyburg Farmers Bank please?'

She brought it promptly.

The one million one-pound shares of the Ladyburg Farmers Bank were owned by three men, all of them Directors of the Company.

Dirk Courtney:	600,000 fully paid-up shares.
Ronald Beresford Pye:	200,000 fully paid-up shares.
Dennis Petersen:	200,000 fully paid-up shares.

Mark frowned, the web was tangled and intricately woven, the same names again and again. He wrote the names into his notebook.

'My name is Marion, what's yours?'

'Mark – Mark Anders.'

'Mark, that's a strong romantic name. Have you read *Julius Caesar*? Mark Antony was such a strong romantic character.'

'Yes,' agreed Mark. 'He was. How much do I owe you for the search fee?'

'Oh, I'll just forget about that.'

'No, look don't do that – I want to pay.'

'All right then – if you want to.'

At the door he paused.

'Thanks,' he said shyly. 'You were very kind.'

'Oh it's a pleasure. If there's anything else – well, you know my name and where to find me.' Then suddenly and unaccountably, she blushed scarlet. To hide it, she turned away with the files. When she looked again, he was gone, and she sighed, holding the files to her plump little bosom.

Mark found the accounts of the old man's estate filed with the Master of the Court almost contemptuously under the heading 'Intestate Estates less than £100'.

On the credit side were listed two rifles and a shotgun, four trek oxen and scotch-cart – sold at public auction to realize eighty-four pounds sixteen shillings. On the debit side were legal and commission fees accruing to one Dennis Petersen – and costs of winding up the estate. The total was one hundred and twenty-seven pounds; the account had been in deficit – a distribution had been made and the estate closed. John Archibald Anders had gone, and left hardly a ripple behind him, not even the three thousand pounds he had been paid for Andersland.

Mark hefted his pack again and went out into the brilliant sunlight of afternoon. A water cart was moving slowly down Main Street drawn by two oxen, its sprinklers pouring fine jets of water into the roadway to lay the thick dust.

Mark paused and inhaled the smell of water on dry earth, and looked across the street at the towering building of the Ladyburg Farmers Bank.

For a brief moment, he touched the idea of crossing and entering, demanding of the men in there what had made the old man change his firm resolve to die and be buried on Andersland, how the money had been paid to him – and what he had done with it.

But the idea passed swiftly. The men who worked in that building were creatures of a different breed from the penniless grandson of an illiterate hard-scrabble farmer. There were orders in society, unseen barriers which a man could not cross, even if he had a university diploma, a military medal for gallantry and an honourable discharge from the army.

That building was the shrine of wealth and power and influence, where dwelt men like giants, like gods. The likes of Mark Anders did not barge in there demanding answers to unimportant questions about an old man of no account.

'Intestate estate less than £100,' Mark whispered aloud, and set off across town, towards the clanking, huffing sounds of the railway goods yard.

'Yes,' agreed the station master, 'Piet Greyling was a main-line loco driver, and his son fired for him – but they threw in their time months ago, back in 1919, both of them.' He rubbed his chin thoughtfully. 'No, I don't know where they were headed, just too damned happy to see them go, I guess. Oh, yes, now I come to think on it, the son did say something about they were going to Rhodesia. Going to buy a farm, or something,' and the man chuckled. 'Buy a farm! With what, I wonder – wishes and dreams – not on the salary of a loco driver or fireman.'

The board room of the Ladyburg Farmers Bank occupied half of the top floor of the building; one set of floor-to-ceiling windows faced eastwards to catch the cool sea breeze on hot summer days, the other windows faced the tall escarpment. This made a fine backdrop to the town, and gave an interesting aspect to the huge room with its high ornately plastered ceiling where dancing white cherubs bearing bunches of grapes were suspended upside-down, frozen in their endless jollification.

The walls were panelled in dark mahogany that set off the green velvet curtaining with golden corded edges.

The carpet was green also, and thick enough to muffle the hoofs of a cavalry charge. The board room table was of marble with golden ormolu work, vine leaves and nude female figures clambering up the legs, playing harps or dancing demurely.

At one end of the table, a man stood respectfully, a man with the short neck and heavy shoulders of a wrestler. The seat of his khaki breeches was shiny from the saddle, and his boots were dusty from hard riding. He twisted the rim of a slouch hat nervously between his fingers.

Opposite where he stood at the far end of the marble table, another man slouched elegantly in the leather-padded chair. Even seated, it was clear that he was a big man, the shoulders under the expensive British broadcloth were wide and powerful.

However, his head was nicely balanced on these shoulders, a glorious head of lustrous but skilfully barbered hair, dark curls that extended low down on to his cheeks into magnificent sideboards. The strong smoothly shaven chin had the jut and set of a man accustomed to command, a wide determined mouth and perfect white teeth with which he now nibbled thoughtfully at his lower lip. A small frown formed a bird's foot at the bridge of his nose, between the dark intelligent eyes, and one carefully manicured fist supported his chin as he listened quietly.

'Anyway, I thought you might like to know, Mr Courtney,' the speaker ended lamely, and shuffled his dusty boots on the thick carpet. For a long moment there was silence. The man glanced uneasily at the other two gentlemen who flanked Dirk Courtney, but then flicked back to the central figure.

Dirk Courtney dropped his hand into his lap, and the frown cleared. 'I suspect you did the right thing, Hobday.' He smiled slightly, a smile that enhanced his powerful good looks. 'You can rest in the antechamber. The clerk there will find refreshment for you, but I will want to talk to you again later. Wait.'

'Yes, sir, Mr Courtney, sir.' The man crossed to the door with alacrity, and as it closed behind him the two men flanking Dirk Courtney burst out together.

'I told you at the time something like this would happen –'
'But you told us he had been killed –'
'I never liked the idea –'
'Oh, I thought it was going too far this time –'

They spoke across each other, quick breathless outbursts while Dirk Courtney sat with an enigmatic half-smile hovering on his lips, examining with attention the diamond on the little finger of his right hand, turning the big white stone to catch the light from the windows so that it flicked spots of brilliant light across the ceiling high above where he sat.

After a few minutes, the two of them faltered into silence, and Dirk Courtney looked up politely.

'Have you both finished? I found that most helpful, constructive, imaginative.' He looked from one to the other expectantly, and then when they were silent he went on, 'Unfortunately, you are not in possession of all the facts. Here is some more news for you. He arrived in town this morning, and he went straight to the Land Deeds, from there to the Register of Companies, the Master's Office –' There was a fresh outburst of lamentation from his listeners, while Dirk Courtney selected a cigar from the humidor and prepared it carefully, cutting the end with a gold-plated pocket-knife and moistening it between his lips, then he held it poised between thumb and forefinger while he waited for silence again.

'Thank you, gentlemen – but as I was saying, the gentleman in question then went down to the goods yard – and began making inquiries about Greyling and son.'

This time they were silent, exchanging appalled and disbelieving glances, and the silence drew out while Dirk Courtney struck a Swan Vesta and waited for the sulphur to burn off before he lit the cigar.

'It was all your idea,' said Ronald Pye. He was at least thirty years senior to Dirk Courtney. Once prosperously bulging flesh had sagged beneath his expensive waistcoat, his jowls drooped also, like the wattles of a rooster, and his cheeks were mottled with faded freckles and old man's blemishes, little darker liver spots. His hair also had faded and thinned, stained only by residual traces of the fiery ginger it had once been. But his prominent ears stood out from his head, giving him an alert listening look, like a desert fox, and his eyes had a fox's cunning glitter as they watched Dirk Courtney's face.

'Yes,' Dirk Courtney agreed. 'Most ideas around here are mine indeed. That's why the net reserves of the Farmers Bank have increased from one and a half to fifteen million pounds in the ten years since I started contributing my ideas –'

Ronny Pye went on staring at him, regretting bitterly for the ten thousandth time in those ten years that he had ever been tempted to sell control of the bank to this young adventurer, this elegant buccaneer.

God knows, there had been occasion for doubt, for caution, and he had hesitated long enough before accepting the fantastic offer that Dirk Courtney had made. He had known too much of the lad's history, how he had left his home here in Ladyburg in unsavoury circumstances, estranged from his father and family.

Then, years later, he had sauntered into Ronald Pye's office, unannounced and unheralded, and made his offer.

He had seen at a glance that the boy had grown into a hard man, but the offer had been too good to dismiss, and then immediately after, he had begun to hear the dark rumours that followed the man as vultures follow the lion. He should have been warned, the fact that Dirk Courtney could offer six hundred thousand pounds in cash for sixty per cent of the Bank's shares and support the offer with a Bank guarantee from Lloyds Bank of London was, in itself, enough to give substance to the dark rumours. How often does an honest man make that kind of money in a few short years, he asked himself.

In the end the money had tempted Ronny Pye, that and the chance to score over an old enemy, General Sean Courtney. He had delighted in the prospect of setting up the estranged son, setting him up in almost baronial circumstances in the very centre of Courtney country. The delight in doing so had swung the balance, spite and six hundred thousand pounds cash money.

It had been a bad bargain. 'I was against this from the beginning,' he said now.

'My dear Pye, you are against every new idea – on principle. Yet only a week ago you were swooning like a virgin bride over the balance sheet of Ladyburg Estates, and Zululand sugar.'

Dirk stood up from the chair. His full height was imposing, he smoothed his hair lightly with both hands while his cigar was gripped between strong white teeth, then he arranged the folds of his cravat, touching the pearl pin before swinging away and striding to the far wall of the board room.

He drew down the rolled map of Zululand and north Natal that covered half the wall, and stood back from it. The boundary of every farm was marked in large-scale topography. The farms belonging to Ladyburg Estates had been carefully shaded in green chalk. They made an impressive sweep of colour from sea to mountains, a great phalanx of land and natural wealth.

'There it is now, gentlemen – the scheme that you opposed so violently.' He smiled again. 'It was too rich for your watery blood.' The smile faded, and he scowled. When he scowled, the line of the wide mouth became bitter and the set of the lustrous eyes altered, with a mean pinched expression. 'The key to the whole thing was here on the Umfolosi – the water, we had to have it or none of it made sense. One stupid, stubborn, uneducated old bastard –' he cut it off abruptly, and in a moment his smile was back, the voice tight with excitement. 'It is all ours now, the full south bank of the river, and it's not going to end there!' His spread hands clammed down on the map, hooked like claws. 'Here,' he said, 'and here, and here –' his hands marched northwards greedily.

He swung away from the map, laughing, and cocked his big handsome head at them. 'Look at you,' he laughed. 'It's running down your legs, you're so terrified – and all because I'm making you rich.'

Dennis Petersen spoke now. He was the same age as Ronny Pye, married to his sister, and, but for that connection, he would never have been seated at the ormolu marble table, for he was the least significant of the three men. His features were indefinite and slightly blurred, his body in expensive clothing was pudgy and shapeless, while the colour of his eyes was difficult to fathom.

'What are we going to do?' he asked, and though his hands were clasped in his lap, it seemed that he was actually wringing them plaintively.

'We?' Dirk asked kindly, and crossed to his chair. 'We, my dear Dennis?' he patted the man's shoulder like a father, despite the age difference. '*We* aren't going to do a thing. You just go back to your own office now – and I will tell you about it once it's over.'

'Listen, Dirk.' Dennis lifted his chin firmly. 'No more of that – that rough stuff, do you hear?' Then he saw Dirk's eyes and dropped his chin. 'Please,' he mumbled.

Dirk chuckled. 'Off you go and do your sums, both of you, add up the money. Don't worry about a thing.' He helped them from their seats, a hand on each shoulder, and shepherded them towards the door. 'We have a board meeting tomorrow at nine o'clock, Dennis, I will be discussing the new extraction plant at Stanger. I will want the figures, make sure I have them.'

Alone for a moment, Dirk Courtney's face changed and the eyes narrowed. He pressed out the stub of the cigar in the onyx ashtray as he crossed to the door that led to the antechamber.

'Hobday,' he called softly. 'Come in here a moment, please.'

There are occasions in a hunter's experience when a spoor begins hot and true and then fades. Mark remembered a hunt like that which he and the old man had made up near Chaka's Gate.

'Dead spoor, gone away,' he muttered aloud now, and stood uncertainly in the main street of Ladyburg. There seemed no way that he might find the old man's grave. No way that he could bring the body back and rebury it beside Alice on Andersland.

Less important was the money that the old man had been paid for Andersland. Three thousand pounds. It was a vast fortune in Mark's eyes and it would be good to know what had happened to it. With that amount, he could afford land of his own somewhere.

Then Mark faced the issue he had avoided up until now and admitted that there was just one more faint chance, but he felt his stomach tighten at what he had to do. With a physical effort he steeled himself and set off steadily down the street towards the towering building of the Ladyburg Farmers Bank. He had not reached it before the church clock on the spire at the end of the street sounded the hour, five clear chimes that echoed across the valley, and a dozen bank employees came out in a group through the front door, smiling and chatting gaily in the relief of the day's work ended – while a uniformed guard began closing and locking the solid mahogany doors.

Mark felt a sneaking sense of relief, and he turned away. 'I'll come back tomorrow,' he told himself firmly.

The boarding house behind the church offered dinner and a bed for seven shillings and sixpence, and Mark thought about it for only a moment. The sovereigns that he had from the old man's hoard might have to carry him long and far.

He went on out to the bridge over the Baboon Stroom and climbed down on to the bank, moving upstream to find a place to camp.

There was a fine site, with trees and firewood a quarter of a mile above the bridge, but when Mark went down the bank to the water, he could smell the stink of it before he touched the surface with the canteen; he paused, squatting on his haunches.

There was a thick soapy scum thrown up along the edge, and it had coated the stems of the reeds. For the first time Mark realized that the reeds were dead and brown, and that the water bubbled with sullen beads of gas. He scooped a handful and sniffed at it, then flicked it away with disgust and stood up, wiping his hand on the seat of his pants.

There was a big yellow fish, at least four pounds in weight, its swollen belly upwards and rotting opaque eyes bulging from its head as it floated in the sluggish current, turning gently in the eddy at the edge of the reeds. Mark watched it with a feeling of disquiet, of foreboding, as though that poisoned and rotting carcass had some special significance in his life. He shuddered softly and turned away, climbed the bank again and shouldered his pack.

He made his way upstream, pausing now and then to peer down into the river-bed, until he was opposite the steel structure of the new sugar mill; here the waters of the stream boiled and steamed with wisps of pale gas that hung like mist in the stiff brown reeds. Around the next bend, he came upon the effluent pipe, a six-inch black iron pipe that stuck out over the far side of the bank from which the hot, steaming discharge poured in a continuous stream.

A change in the breeze carried the acrid chemical stench of it to where Mark stood, and he coughed and turned away.

A hundred yards further upstream, the clear water chuckled through clean stands of green reeds that bowed and swung gracefully on the breeze, and Mark saw the deep waving shape of an eel in the pool beyond, and watched the small black and pink crabs scurrying across the sugar-white sand below the surface.

He found another camp site on the first slope of the escarpment, beside a waterfall and its slowly swirling pool. In the trees above him, the ferns hung like soft green veils, and when he stripped his clothing and went into the pool, the water was a cool and refreshing delight.

He shaved with the old cut-throat, sitting naked on a mossy rock beside the pool. He dried himself on his shirt and then rinsed it out and hung it beside the small bright fire to dry, and while he waited for the canteen to boil he wandered, bare to the waist, on to the open slope and looked down into the valley.

The sun was already touching the rim of the escarpment, and its low rays were ruddy and warm rose. They burnished the iron roofs of the town, and tinted the column of smoke that rose from the chimney stack of the sugar mill to a beautiful golden bronze. The smoke rose tall into the evening sky, for the breeze had dropped in that peculiar stillness and hush of the African evening.

Movement caught his eye, and he blinked to clear his vision.

There was a hunting party in the open land beyond the town. Even at this distance, Mark could tell they were hunters. Four horsemen moving slowly in a group, one with a rifle or shotgun held against his hip, its barrel pointing to the sky as he leaned forward intently in the saddle. The other three were armed also; he could see the guns in the scabbards at their knees, and they also had that intent air of suppressed excitement, the air of the hunter. Ahead of the group was a single figure, a Zulu in ragged cast-off western clothing but he led the horsemen in the characteristic attitude of the tracker, trotting in that deceptively fast gait of the Zulu, head down, eyes on the ground, carrying a stripped reed in one hand, the tracker's wand to part the grass, or touch the spoor.

Idly Mark wondered what they were hunting, so close to town, and on the bank of that dying and poisoned river, for they were coming along the same trail that Mark had followed to the escarpment.

The light was going swiftly now, the shining beacons of the iron roofs winked out swiftly as the sun went below the crest, but in the last of the light, Mark saw the leader of the group of horsemen rein in his mount and straighten in the saddle. He was a stocky figure, sitting square on his mount. The man looked up towards the escarpment where Mark stood, then the light was gone and the group became a dark blob against the darkening land.

Vaguely disturbed, and troubled by the day just past, by the cold memories of the old man, by the sadness of that dying river, and at last by that distant figure, Mark crouched over his fire, munching his stew of tinned bully and then sipping his coffee.

When at last he pulled on his coat and rolled into his blanket close beside the fire, he could not sleep. The sense of disquiet seemed to grow rather than abate, and he found himself wondering again what four horsemen could find to hunt on the edge of a busy town. Then he thought again about the way that they had followed his own path along the river, and the disquiet deepened, sleep receded.

Suddenly he remembered how the old man would never sleep beside his cooking fire.

'I learned that when we was a chasing the Boer. A light in the night brings things other than moths – lions, hyenas and men.' He could almost hear the old man's voice saying it, and he rose immediately, with the blanket still around his shoulders, and moved away up the slope fifty yards until he found a hollow filled with dead leaves.

Sleep came at last and the soft skirt of it was falling lightly across his eyes when a Scops owl called in the forest near him; instantly he was fully awake. It was a familiar night sound, but this one had jarred some deep chord in him. The imitation had been clever, but it did not deceive an ear so closely tuned to the sounds of the wild.

Tense and listening, Mark lifted his head slowly and peered down the slope. His fire was a puddle of pink embers and above him the shapes of the trees were dark and fluffy against a crisp sky of white stars.

The owl called again down near the pool, and, at the same moment, Mark heard something move stealthily near him in the darkness, something big and heavy, the brush brush of footfalls in the dead leaves. Then there was silence again.

Mark strained his eyes and ears into the darkness, but it was impenetrable under the trees.

Far below in the valley, a locomotive whistled three times, the sounds carrying clearly in the stillness, and then there was the huff and puff of the train pulling out from the goods yard and settling into a steady rhythmic beat of boiler and tracks.

Mark tried to put that sound beyond his hearing, trying to filter it out so that he could discern the closer softer sounds in the night around him.

Something moved down the slope, he heard the silky soft whisper of it and then he saw movement, outlined against the glowing ashes of his fire, a man's booted legs stepped out of the darkness and halted beside the fire, standing completely still.

Nearer Mark, there was another movement, a stir of impatient feet in dead leaves – and then, unmistakably, the metallic snick of gun-metal as a safety-catch was slipped to the 'fire' position. The sound struck like electricity along Mark's nerve ends, and his breath caught in his throat. It was very close, six feet away, and now he thought he could make out the loom of the man against the stars. He was standing almost on top of Mark's bed in the hollow, staring down at the fire beside the camp.

The man at the fire spoke now, softly, but his voice carried clearly. 'The bastard has gone – he's not here.' He stooped to the pile of dry firewood that Mark had cut and stacked. He threw a piece on to the embers, and sparks flew upwards in the fiery spiral and the branch flamed, throwing out a circle of yellow light.

Then he exclaimed sharply, 'His pack is still here,' and he hefted the shotgun expectantly, glaring into the night.

'Remember, there's a hundred pounds on it.'

The words and the way the man was handling the shotgun made his intention clear beyond doubt. Mark felt the warm flood of adrenalin rush through his body, and he was poised and quivering with suppressed energy, ready to burst into explosive movement in an instant.

The man near him moved again, and Mark heard the muted tap of metal on metal, the sound of the man's breathing also, hoarse with tension – and then suddenly and with devastating shock, bright white light split the darkness. A lantern beam swivelled and then fastened on Mark's blanket-wrapped crouching form.

In the instant before he moved, Mark saw the shape of the man beyond the dazzle of the light. He carried the lantern in his right hand holding it high, at the level of his head, and the rifle was in his left hand, hanging at the trail.

He was completely unprepared to find Mark lying almost at his feet, and his shout was wild.

'He's here. My God.' He tried to bring up the rifle, but his right hand held the lantern.

'Shoot! Shoot, damn it!' another voice shouted, a voice somehow familiar, and beside Mark the man dropped the lantern and began to swing up the rifle. Mark launched himself straight at him.

He used the man's own momentum, taking the upswing of the rifle; seizing the muzzle of the barrel in one hand and the stock in the other, he smashed the weapon into the man's face with the full weight and force of his body behind it. He heard gristle and bone crunch, while the solid impact of the steel breach striking into the man's face was transmitted through the rifle into his arms, jarring him to the shoulders.

The man went over backwards, with a cry that bubbled with the quick burst of blood into his nose and mouth. Mark bounded over him and ran at the slope.

Behind him there was a chorus of shouts and cries, and then the blam, blam of a shotgun and the double glow of the muzzle flashes. Mark heard the heavy charges of shot slash into the leaves beside him, and something burned his upper arm like the sting of a wild bee.

'The light. Get the light!'

'There he is, don't let him get away.'

A rifle fired three times in quick succession, it sounded like a .303 Lee-Enfield. The bullet hit a rock and howled away into the sky, another thumped into a tree trunk close beside him as he ran.

Mark fell heavily in the dark and felt his ankle go, the pain of it exploded up his leg into his groin and lower belly. He rolled on to his knees, and the beam of the lantern swept over, and then fastened hungrily on him.

'We've got him.'

A fusillade of shots, and a triumphant chorus of shouts. The shot and bullets shattered the air around him, one so close that the whip of it deafened one ear and he threw himself forward at the slope.

The pain in his foot made Mark cry out. It was white-hot shooting agony that burst from his ankle and broke like brilliant phosphorescent surf against the roof of his skull, but he drove himself on, soaked with sweat, swerving as he ran, sobbing and hobbling on the damaged leg.

They were spread out in the bush behind him, and it seemed that the slope was tiring them quickly, men accustomed to riding horseback, for the cries were becoming strained and breathless, edged with worry and the first fear that their quarry might escape them.

Mark was trying to think between the bursts of agony with which each step racked him. He thought to drop into thick cover and lie until they passed him, but they were too close for that, and they had a tracker with them, a tracker who had brought them unerringly to his camp, even in darkness. To lie down now would be surrender – and suicide, but he could not go on much longer. Already the pain was threatening to swamp him, there was a sound in his head like great wings and his vision was starting to break up and star.

He fell to his knees and vomited, gagging and choking on the acid gall of it, and within seconds the voice of the pursuit was closer and more urgent. He dragged himself up, and the lantern beam caught him squarely, a rifle bullet disrupted the air about his head so that he staggered as he blundered onwards, using the screen of bush to avoid the beam of light. Quite suddenly he felt the ground tilt upwards under his feet sharply.

He lost his footing again, but in the same movement rolled to his feet and stumbled over a lip on to level ground where there was the sudden sugary crunch of gravel under his feet. Three stumbling paces and he came down heavily, his feet knocked out from under him and as he went down, steel smeared the skin from his outflung forearm.

He lay panting and blinded for long seconds and heard the hunters bay like hounds down the slope. The sound goaded him and he groped with outstretched hands for purchase to push himself on to his feet once more.

He found the cold smooth steel that had tripped him; it trembled like a living thing under his hands. It came to him then that he had climbed the embankment of the railway line and fallen across the rails of the permanent way.

He pushed himself to his knees, and now he heard the deep panting rush in the night; suddenly the whole slope of the escarpment was lit by reflected light that swung dramatically and brightened like daylight as the locomotive he had heard leaving the goods yard in the valley came roaring out of the deep cutting that skirted the steepest part of the escarpment, before crossing the deep gorge of the river.

The long white beam of the lamp struck him like a solid thing and he flung up his arm to shield his eyes and rolled off the rails, crouching down on the gravel on the opposite side to that of his pursuers.

In the light of the locomotive lamp, Mark saw a stocky agile figure come up the embankment at a run. He ducked across the tracks, directly under the roaring throbbing loco. The dazzle of light prevented Mark seeing his face, yet there was something familiar in the way the man moved and held his shoulders.

The engine came thundering down on Mark, and as it drew level a spurt of steam from the driving pistons scalded him with its hot breath. Then it was past and there was just the dark blurred rush of the boxcars above him.

Mark dragged himself upright, balancing on his good foot and struck the streams of sweat from his eyes, peering upwards to judge his moment.

When it came, he almost missed it; his hands were slippery with sweat and the railing was almost jerked from his grip even though the train had lost much of its speed and power on the slope.

The strain in his shoulder shot an arrow of pain along his arm, and he was torn off his feet, swinging against the side of the boxcar while he grappled wildly for a grip with his other hand.

He found purchase and clung on to the side of the boxcar, his feet still free but scrabbling for the footplates – and at that moment hands like steel claws seized his injured ankle, the full weight of a heavy body bore him down, racking him out against the side of the car.

Mark screamed with the unbearable white-hot pain of the grip on his ankle, and it took all his strength and courage to maintain his double grip on the rail.

His body was penduluming, as the man who held him was himself swung off the ground and then came back to skid and run in the loose gravel of the embankment, as though he were driving a dog-sledge.

Mark twisted his head back and judged the white blob of the man's face and aimed the kick with his free foot, but it was an impossible target. At that instant the sound of the locomotive altered, as it hit the steel of the bridge where it crossed the deep gorge of the river.

The uprights of the bridge sprang out of the rushing corridor of blackness; Mark heard the deadly hiss of the riveted steel girders flit past his head, and at the same moment the grip on his leg was released. He clung with his remaining strength and resolve to the railing of that goods truck, while the train racketed over the bridge and ploughed on steadily up the slope, until it burst at last over the crest on to the level ground of the plateau. It picked up speed sharply, and Mark dragged himself inch by agonized inch up the railing, until at last he tumbled over the side of the open boxcar on to the load of sugar sacks and lay face downwards, sobbing for each breath, while he rode the high storm surf of pain from his leg.

The cold roused him at last. His sweat-sodden coat was turned icy by the rush of night air and he crawled painfully forward towards the shelter of the high steel side of the car. He checked quietly and found with relief that his purse and notebook were still in his pocket.

Suddenly he was aware that he was not alone and fresh panic gripped him. 'Who's that?' he croaked, recoiling quickly into a defensive attitude.

A voice answered quickly in deep Zulu. 'I mean no harm, Nkosi,' and Mark felt a quick rush of relief. A man crouched against the side of the car, out of the wind, and it was clear that he was as alarmed by Mark's presence as Mark had been by his.

'I mean no harm, lord. I am a poor man without the money to pay to ride the steamer. My father is sick and dying in Tekweni, Durban town.'

'Peace,' grunted Mark in the same language. 'I am a poor man also.' He dragged himself into shelter beside the Zulu, and the movement twisted his ankle and he gasped at the fresh pain.

'Hau!' the black man's eyes caught the starlight as he peered at Mark. 'You are hurt.'

'My leg,' Mark grunted, trying to ease it into a more comfortable position

– and the Zulu leaned forward and Mark felt his gentle hands on the ankle.

'You are without shoes?' The man was surprised at Mark's torn and bloodied feet.

'I was chased by bad men.'

'Ha,' the Zulu nodded, and Mark saw in the starlight that he was a young man. 'The leg is bad. I do not think the bone is broken, but it is bad.'

He untied the small pack beside him and took out some article of clothing. Deliberately he began to tear the material into strips.

'No,' Mark protested sharply. 'Do not destroy your clothes for me.' He knew how each article of western clothing, however ragged and threadbare, was treasured.

'It is an old shirt,' said the Zulu simply and began to bind up the swollen ankle skilfully. When he had finished, it felt easier.

'*Ngi ya bone* – I praise you,' Mark told him, and then he shivered violently as the delayed but icy fist of shock clamped down on him; he felt nausea rise in his throat and he shivered again.

The Zulu took the blanket from around his own shoulders and placed it carefully over Mark.

'No. I cannot take your blanket.' The blanket smelled of smoke from a dung fire, and of the Zulu himself – the earthy African tang. 'I cannot take it.'

'You need it,' said the Zulu firmly. 'You are sick.'

'Very well,' Mark muttered, as another shivering fit caught him. 'But it is a large blanket, big enough for two –'

'It is not fitting.'

'Come,' said Mark roughly, and the Zulu hesitated a moment longer before drawing closer and taking up a fold of the woollen blanket.

Shoulder to shoulder, they sat on into the night, and Mark found himself dropping into a haze of exhaustion and pain, for the swollen ankle still beat like a drum. The Zulu beside him was silent, and Mark thought he slept, but as the train slowed after two hours' hard run across the plateau, he whispered quietly,

'This is Sakabula halt. It stops here for to let the other train pass.'

Mark remembered the desolate siding with its double loop of line. No buildings and only a signboard to identify it. He would have lapsed once more into half sleep, but something warned him, a strange sense of danger which he had developed so acutely in France.

He shrugged aside the blanket, and dragged himself up on his knees to peer ahead. The track came into the siding on a gentle curve, and the silver rails glittered in the lamp of the locomotive.

Far ahead was the sign-post of the halt, stark white in the beam from the locomotive, but there was something else. Parked on the track beside the halt was a dark vehicle, a heavy lorry, and its headlights still burned. In the puddle of yellow light Mark made out the dark shapes of waiting men. Alarm jarred his bowels and clutched at his chest with a cold cramping fist.

A motor lorry from Ladyburg could not have reached here ahead of them, but a telegraph message could have alerted –

'I must go,' Mark blurted, and with stiff fingers he hooked a sovereign out of his money belt and pressed it quickly into the Zulu's hand.

'There is no call for –' the man began, but Mark cut him off brusquely.

'Stay in peace.' He dragged himself to the side of the car furthest from the waiting men, and lowered himself down the steel ladder until he hung just above the tracks.

He waited for the locomotive to slow down, groaning and creaking and sighing steam, and then he braced himself and dropped – trying to take most of his weight on his good leg.

He collapsed forwards as he struck the ground; ducking his head, he rolled on to his shoulders and, drawing up his knees, went down the embankment like a rubber ball.

In the dry pale grass beside the line, he did not rise but dragged himself on elbows and belly to a low dark thorn bush, fifty yards from the rails. Slowly he worked himself under its low spiny branches and lay face down, gritting his teeth against the dull beat of his ankle.

The train had halted with its van level with Mark's hiding place; the guard climbed down, flashing his lantern, while from the head of the train a group of men, each one carrying a lantern, hurried back towards him, searching the open trucks as they came.

Mark could see they were all armed, and their voices carried loudly as they called explanations to the driver and fireman who leaned from the cab of the locomotive.

'What's the trouble?'

'You've got a fugitive from justice aboard.'

'Who are you?'

'We're special constables.'

'Who's the fellow?'

'He robbed a bank –'

'He killed four men in Ladyburg –'

'He jumped your train on the escarpment –'

'Don't take any chances, you fellows, the bastard is a killer –'

They came swiftly down the train, talking loudly and calling to each other to bolster their courage, and at the last moment Mark remembered the Zulu. He should have warned the man, but he had been too concerned with his own danger. He wanted to shout now, warn him to run, but he could not bring himself to do it. The Zulu would be all right, they would not shoot when they saw he was a black, they might slap him around a little and throw him off –

The Zulu darted out from between two of the boxcars from where he had climbed down on to the coupling. He was a dark flitting shape, and somebody yelled a warning. Immediately there was a shot.

Mark saw the dust from the bullet fly in the lamplight, and the Zulu swerved and ran directly out into the open grassland. Half a dozen shots ripped the night, the muzzle flashes were angry red blooms in the night, but the Zulu ran on.

One of the men on the track dropped to his knee, and Mark saw his face white and eager in the light of the torches. He aimed deliberately, and his rifle kicked up sharply.

The Zulu collapsed in the grass without a cry, and they raced forward in an excited pack to gather around his body.

'Oh, Jesus, it's only a black.' There was confused angry discussion and argument for five minutes, and then four of them took an arm and leg each and carried the Zulu between them to the parked lorry.

The black man's head lolled back, almost sweeping the earth, his mouth gaped open and the blood that dripped from it was black as tar in the lamplight and his head swung loosely to the uneven stride of the men who carried him. They lifted him into the back of the lorry.

The north-bound train came thundering through the siding, its whistle shrilling on a high piercing shriek, and then it was gone on its way to Ladyburg.

The men climbed into the lorry and the engine fired, and it moved away with its headlights sweeping sky and earth as it pitched over the bumpy track.

The stationary train whistled mournfully and it began to roll forward, rumbling slowly over the tracks. Mark crawled out from his hiding-place beneath the bush, and hopped and stumbled after it, catching it just before its speed built up.

He crawled over the sugar bags into the lee of the steel side, and found the Zulu had left his blanket. As he wrapped it around his icy body, he felt the guilt flood over him, guilt for the man's death, the man who had been a friend – then the guilt turned to anger.

Bitter corrosive anger that sustained him through the night as the train rushed southwards.

Fordsburg is a squalid suburb of Johannesburg, three hundred miles from the golden grassy hills of Zululand and the beautiful forested valley of Lady-burg. It is an area of mean cottages, tiny workers' houses of galvanized iron on timber frames, each with a bleak little garden. In some of the gardens there were brave and defiant shows of bright blooms, barbeton daisies, cannas and flaming red poinsettia, but in most of them the bare untended earth, patched with blackjack and khaki-bush, told of the tenants' indifference.

Over the narrow streets and crowded cottages, the mine dumps held majestic sway, towering table-topped mountains of poisonous yellow earth from which the gold had been extracted. The cyanide process of extraction ensured that the earth of the dumps was barren and sterile. No plants grew upon them, and on windy days the yellow dust and grit whipped over the grovelling cottages beneath them.

The dumps dominated the landscape, monument to the antlike endeavours of man, symbols of his eternal greed for gold. The mine headgears were spidery steel structures against the pale cloudless blue of the highveld winter sky. The huge steel wheels on their heights spun endlessly, back and forth, lowering the cages filled with men deep into the earth, and rising again with the ore bins loaded with the gold-rich rock.

Mark made his way slowly down one of the narrow, dusty streets. He still limped slightly, and a cheap cardboard suitcase carried the few possessions he had bought to replace those he had lost on the escarpment.

The clothes he wore were an improvement on the shapeless demobilization suit that the army had given him. His flannels were neatly creased and the blue blazer fitted his good shoulders and narrow flanks, the open-necked white shirt was snowy clean and set off the smooth brown skin of his neck and face.

He reached the cottage numbered fifty-five on the gate, and it was a mirror image of those on each side and opposite. He opened the gate and went up the short flagged path, aware that somebody was watching him from behind the lace curtain in the front room.

However, when he knocked on the front door it was only opened after a delay of many minutes, and Mark blinked at the woman who stood there.

Her dark short hair was freshly combed, and the clothes she wore had clearly been hastily put on in place of dowdier everyday dress. She was still fastening the belt at her slim waist. It was a dress of pale blue with a design of yellow daisies, and it made her appear young and gay, although Mark saw at once that she was at least ten years older than he was.

'Yes?' she asked, tempering the abrupt demand with a smile.

'Does Fergus MacDonald live here?' He saw now that she was good-looking, not pretty, but fine-looking with good bones in her cheeks and dark intelligent eyes.

'Yes, this is Mr MacDonald's house.' There was a foreign inflection in her voice that was intriguing. 'I am Mrs MacDonald.'

'Oh,' he said, taken by surprise. He had known Fergus was married. He had spoken about it often, but Mark had never really thought about his wife before – not as a real flesh and blood woman, and certainly not one like this. 'I am an old friend of Fergus's from the army.'

'Oh, I see –' she hesitated.

'My name's Mark, Mark Anders.' Instantly her attitude changed, the half smile bloomed and lit her whole face. She gave a small gasp of pleasure.

'Mark, of course, Mark.' She took his arm impetuously and drew him over the threshold. 'He has spoken of you so often – I feel I know you so well. Like a member of the family, like a brother,' she still had his arm, standing close to him, laughing up at him. 'Come in, Mark, come in. I am Helena.'

Fergus MacDonald sat at the head of the deal table in the dingy kitchen. The table was covered with sheets of newsprint instead of a cloth and Fergus hunched over his plate, and scowled angrily as he listened to Mark's account of his flight from Ladyburg.

'The bastards, they are the enemy, Mark. The new enemy.'

His mouth was filled with potato and heavily spiced boerewors, thick farmer's sausage, and he spoke through it.

'We are in another war, lad – and this time they are worse than the bloody Hun.'

'More beer, Mark.' Helena leaned across to fill his tumbler from the black quart bottle.

'Thank you.' Mark watched the foaming head rise in his glass, and he pondered Fergus's statement.

'I don't understand, Fergus. I don't know who these men are, I don't know why they tried to kill me.'

'They are the bosses, lad. That's who we are fighting now. The rich, the mine-owners, the bankers, all those who oppress the working man.'

Mark took a long swallow of his beer, and Helena smiled at him from across the table.

'Fergus is right, Mark. We have to destroy them.' And she began to talk. It was strange confusing talk from a woman, and there was a fanatical light in her dark eyes. The words had a compelling power in her clear articulate voice with its lilting accent, and Mark watched the way she used her hands to emphasize each point. They were neat strong hands with gracefully tapered fingers and short nails. The nails were clean and trimmed but the first two fingers of her right hand were stained pale yellow. Mark wondered at that, until suddenly Helena reached across and took a cigarette from the packet at Fergus's elbow.

Still talking, she lit the cigarette from a match in her cupped hands, and drew deeply before exhaling forcibly through pursed lips. Mark had never seen a woman smoke before, and he stared at her. She shook her head vehemently.

'The history of the people's revolt is written in blood. Look at France, see how the revolution sweeps forward in Russia.'

The short dark shining curls danced around her smooth pale cheeks, and she pursed her lips again to drag at the cigarette, and in some strange fashion Mark found the mannish act shocking – and exciting.

He felt his groin clenching, the tight swollen hardening of his flesh, beyond his reason – far beyond his control. His breathing caught with shock and embarrassment, and he leaned back and slipped one hand into his trouser pocket, certain that both of them must be aware of his shameful reaction, but instead Helena reached across the table and seized his other wrist in a surprisingly powerful grip.

'We know our enemy, we know what must be done and how we must do it, Mark.'

Her fingers seemed to burn like heated iron into his flesh, he felt dizzy with the force of it. His voice was hoarse as he forced himself to reply.

'They are strong, Helena, powerful –'

'No, no, Mark, the workers are strong, the enemy are weak, and smug. They suspect nothing, they wallow like hogs in the false security of their golden sovereigns, but in reality they are few and unprepared. They do not know their own weakness – and as yet the workers do not realize their great strength. We will teach them.'

'You're right, lass.' Fergus wiped the gravy from the plate with a crust of bread and stuffed it into his mouth. 'Listen to her, Mark, we are building a new world, a brave and beautiful new world.'

He belched loudly and pushed his plate away, leaving both elbows on the table. 'But first we have to tear down and destroy this rotten, unjust and corrupt society. There will be hard fighting, and we will need good hard fighting men.' He laughed harshly and slapped Mark's shoulder. 'They'll call for MacDonald and Anders again, lad, you hear me.'

'There is nothing for us to lose, Mark.' Helena's cheeks were flushed. 'Nothing but our chains – and there is a whole world to win. Karl Marx said that, and it's one of the great truths of history.'

'Helena, are you,' he hesitated to use the word, 'are you and Fergus – well I mean, you aren't Bolsheviks are you?'

'That's what the bosses, and their minions, the police, call us.' She laughed contemptuously. 'They try to make us criminals, already they fear us. With reason, Mark, we will give them reason.'

'No, lad, don't call us Bolsheviks. We are members of the communist party, dedicated to universal communism. I'm the local party secretary and shop steward of the mineworkers' union for the boilermakers' shop.'

'Have you read Karl Marx?' Helena demanded.

'No.' Mark shook his head, dazed and shocked, but still sexually excited by her to the edge of pain. Fergus a Bolshevik? A bomb-throwing monster? But he knew he was not. He was an old and trusted comrade.

'I will lend you my copy.'

'Come on, lass,' Fergus chuckled, and shook his head. 'We are going too fast for the lad. He's got a right barmy look right now.' He leaned over and placed an affectionate arm around Mark's shoulders, drawing him close. 'Have you a place to stay, lad? A job? A place to go?'

'No.' Mark flushed. 'I haven't, Fergus.'

'Oh, yes you have,' Helena cut in quickly. 'I have fixed the bed in the other room – you'll stay there, Mark.'

'Oh, but I couldn't –'

'It's done,' she said simply.

'You'll stay, lad.' Fergus squeezed him hard. 'And we'll see about a job for you tomorrow – you're book-learned. You can read and write and figure, it will be easy to fix you. I know they need a clerk up at the pay office, and the paymaster is a comrade, a member of the party.'

'I'll pay you for lodging.'

'Of course you will,' Fergus chuckled again, and filled his glass to the brim with beer. 'It's good to see you again, son,' and he raised his own glass. 'Send down the line for MacDonald and Anders – and warn the bastards we are coming!' He took a long swallow, the pointed Adam's apple bobbing in his throat, then wiped the froth from his upper lip with the back of his hand.

The regimental chaplain had called it the 'sin of Onan', while the rankers had many more ribald terms for it, 'toss the caber' or 'visit Mrs Hand and her five daughters'. The chaplain had warned of the dire consequences that it would bring – failing sight, and falling hair, a palsied shaking hand and at last idiocy and the insane asylum. Mark lay in the narrow iron bed and stared with unseeing eyes at the faded pink rose-pattern wallpaper of the tiny room. It had the musty smell of being long closed, and there was a wash-basin in an iron frame with an enamel basin against the far wall. A single unshaded bulb hung on a length of flex from the ceiling, and the white plaster around it was fly-speckled; even at the moment three drowsy flies sat on the flex in a stupor. Mark swivelled his attention to them, trying to put aside the waves of temptation that flowed up through his body.

Light steps in the passage stopped opposite his bedroom door, and now there was a tap on the woodwork.

'Mark?'

He sat up quickly, letting the single thin blanket fall to his waist.

'May I come in?'

'Yes,' he husked, and the door swung open. Helena crossed to his bed. She wore a gown of light pink shiny material that buttoned down the front; the skirt opened at each step and there was a glimpse of smooth white flesh above her knees.

She carried a slim book in one hand. 'I said I would lend it to you,' she explained. 'Read it, Mark.' She held out the volume.

The Communist Manifesto was the title, and Mark took it from her, opening it at random. He bowed his head over the open pages to cover the confusion into which her near presence plunged him.

'Thank you, Helena.' He used her name for the first time, wanting her to leave and yet hoping she would stay. She leaned over him a little, looking at the open book, and the bodice of her gown fell apart an inch. Mark looked up, and saw the incredibly silky sheen where the beginning of one white breast pressed against the lace that edged the neck of the gown. Swiftly he dropped his eyes again, and they were both silent until Mark could stand it no longer, and he looked up at her.

'Helena,' he began, and then stopped. There was a smile, a secret womanly smile on her lips, lips that were slightly parted and moist in the harsh electric light. The dark eyes were half hooded but glowed again with that fierce fanatical light, and her bosom beneath the pink satin rose and fell with quick soundless breathing.

He flushed a sultry red under the dark tan of his cheeks and he rolled abruptly on to his side, drawing up his knees.

Helena straightened up slowly, still smiling. 'Goodnight, Mark.' She touched his shoulder, fire sprang afresh from her finger-tips and then she turned and went slowly towards the door. The slippery material of the gown slid softly across the tight double rounds of her buttocks.

'I'll leave the light on.' She looked back at him, and now the smile was knowing. 'You'll want to read.'

The Pay Office of Crown Deep Mines Ltd was a long austere room where five other clerks worked at high desks set in a line down one wall. They were mostly men in advanced middle age, two of them sufferers from phthisis, that dreaded disease of the miners in which the rock dust from the drills settled in the lungs, building up slowly until the lung turned to stone and gradually crippled the man. Employment in the mine offices was a form of pension. The other three were grey and drab men, stooped from poring over their ledgers. The atmosphere in the office was quiet and joyless, as in some monastic cloister.

Mark was given charge of the files and personnel R to Z, and the work was dull and repetitive, soon becoming automatic as he calculated overtime and leave pay, made deductions for rent and union fees and struck his totals. It was drudgery, not nearly enough to engage a bright and active young brain, and the narrow confines of the office were a cage for a spirit that was at home in the wide open sweep of sky and veld and had known the cataclysmic universe of the battlefields of France.

On the weekends, he escaped from his cage and rode on an old bicycle for miles into the open veld, following dusty paths along the base of the rocky kopjes on which grew the regal candelabra of giant aloes, their blooms burning in bright scarlet against the clear pale blue of the highveld sky. He sought seclusion, wilderness, secret places far from other men, but it seemed that always there were the barriers of barbed wire to limit his range; the grasslands had gone to the plough, the pale dust devils swirled and danced over red earth from which the harvest had been stripped, leaving the dried sparse stubble of maize stalks.

The great herds of game that once had covered the open grassland to the full range of the eye were long gone, and now small scrub cattle, multi-coloured and scrawny, grazed in mindless bovine herds tended by almost naked black piccaninnies who paused to watch Mark pedalling by, and greeted him with solemnity which turned to wide-eyed pleasure when he returned the greeting in their own language.

Once in a while Mark would start a small grey duiker from its lay and send it bounding and bouncing away through the dry grass with small sharp horns and ears erect, or else catch a glimpse of a springbuck drifting elusive as smoke across the plain, lonely survivors of the long rifles. Then the delight of their wild presence stayed long with him, warming him on the dark cold ride home.

He needed these times of quiet and solitude to complete the healing process, not only of the Maxim bullet wounds in his back but of the deeper wounds, soul damage caused by too early an exposure to war in all its horror.

He needed this quietness also to evaluate the swift rush of events that filled his evenings and nights in direct contrast to the grey drudgery of his working days.

Mark was carried along by the fanatical energy of Fergus MacDonald and Helena. Fergus was the comrade who had shared with him experience that most men never knew, the stark and terrible involvement of combat. He was also much older than Mark, a paternal figure, filling a deep need in his life. It was easy to suspend the critical faculties and believe; not to think, but to follow blindly wherever Fergus's bitter restless energy led them.

There was excitement and a sense of commitment in those meetings with men like him, men with an ideal and a sense of destiny. The secret meetings in locked rooms with armed guards at the doors, the atmosphere quivering with the promise of forbidden things. The cigarette-smoke spiralling upwards until it filled the room with a thick blue haze, like incense burning at some mystic rite; the faces shining with sweat and quiet frenzy of the fanatic, as they listened to the speakers.

Harry Fisher, the Chairman of the Party, was a tall fierce man with a heavy gut, the brawny shoulders and hairy muscular arms of a boilermaker, an unkempt shock of coarse wiry black hair laced with strands of silver and dark burning eyes.

'We are the Party, the praetorian guard of the proletariat, and we are not bound by law or the ethical considerations of the bourgeois age. The Party in itself is the new law, the natural law of existence.'

Afterwards he shook hands with Mark, while Fergus stood by with paternal pride. Fisher's grip was as fierce as his stare.

'You're a soldier,' he nodded. 'We will need you again, comrade. There is bloody work ahead.'

The disquieting presence of the man stayed to haunt Mark long afterwards, even when they rode home in the crowded tramcar, the three of them squeezed into a double seat so that Helena's thigh was pressed hard against his. When she spoke to him, she leaned sideways, her lips almost touching his cheek, and her breath smelling of liquorice and cigarettes, a smell that mingled with the cheap flowery perfume she wore, and the underlying musky warmth of her woman's body.

There were other meetings on the Friday evenings, great raucous shouting gatherings where hundreds of white miners crowded into the huge Fordsburg Trades Union Hall, most of them boozy with cheap brandy, loud and inarticulate and spoiling for trouble. They roared like the crowd at a bull fight as the speakers harangued them; occasionally one of the audience climbed on to his chair to sway there, shouting meaningless confused slogans until his laughing comrades dragged him down.

One of the most popular speakers at these public meetings was Fergus MacDonald, he had a dozen tricks to excite his audience, he probed their secret fears and twisted the probe until they howled half in pain and half in adulation.

'You know what they are planning, the bosses, you know what they are going to do? First they will fragment the trades –'

A thunderous ugly roar, that shook the windows in their frames, and Fergus paused on the stage, sweeping his sparse sandy hair back off his forehead and grinning down at them with his thin bitter mouth until the sound subsided.

'– the trade that took you five years to learn, they will split it up and now there will be three unskilled men to do your job, with only a year's training to learn that fragment, and they will pay them a tenth of the wage you draw.'

A storming roar of 'No!' and Fergus flung it back at them.

'Yes!' he shouted. 'Yes! Yes! And yes again. That is what the bosses are going to do. But that's not all, they are going to use blacks in your jobs, black men are going to take those jobs away from you – black men who will work for a wage that you cannot live on.'

They screamed now, frantic with anger, a terrible anger which had no object on which to focus.

'What about your kids, are you going to feed them on mealies, are your wives going to wear limbo? That's what will happen, when the blacks take your jobs!'

'No!' they roared. 'No!'

'Workers of the world,' Fergus shouted at them, 'workers of the world unite – and keep our country white!'

The bellow of applause, the rhythmic stamp of feet on the wooden floor lasted for ten minutes, while Fergus strutted back and forth across the stage, clasping his hands above his head like a prize-fighter. When at last the cheering faltered, he flung back his head and bellowed the opening line of 'The Red Flag'.

The entire hall came crashing to its feet, and stood at attention to sing the revolutionary song:

> *Then raise the scarlet standard high,*
> *Within its shade we'll live or die.*
> *Tho' cowards flinch and traitors sneer,*
> *We'll keep the red flag flying here.*

Mark walked home with the MacDonalds in the frosty night, their breathing smoking like ostrich plumes in the lights of the street lamps. Helena walked between the men, a small dainty figure in her black overcoat with rabbit-fur collar and a knitted cap pulled down over her head.

She had slipped a hand into the crook of the elbows of each of them, a seemingly natural impartial gesture, but there was a disturbing pressure of fingers on the hard muscle of Mark's upper arm, and her hip touched his as she skipped occasionally to catch the longer stride of the men.

'Listen, Fergus, what you were saying there in the hall doesn't make sense, you know,' Mark broke the silence, as they turned into the home street. 'You can't have it both ways, workers unite and keep it white.'

Fergus chuckled appreciatively. 'You're a bright lad, comrade Mark.'

'But, I'm serious, Fergus – it's not the way Harry Fisher –'

'Of course not, lad. Tonight I was shovelling up swill for the hogs. We need them fighting mad, we have things to tear down, bloody work to do.' He stopped and turned to face Mark over the woman's head. 'We need cannon fodder, lad, and plenty of it.'

'So it won't be like that?' Mark asked.

'No, lad. It will be a beautiful brave new world. All men equal, all men happy, no bosses – a workers' state.'

Mark tried to control his pricking nagging doubts.

'You keep talking of fighting, Fergus. Do you mean that, literally? I mean, will it be a shooting war?'

'A shooting war, comrade, a bloody shooting war. Just like the revolution in Russia, where comrade Lenin has shown us the way. We have to burn away the dross, we have to soak this earth with the blood of the rulers and the bosses, we have to flood it with the blood of their minions – the petit bourgeois officer's class of the police and military.'

'What will –' Mark almost said 'we' but it would not come to his lips. He could not make that commitment. 'What will you fight with?'

Fergus chuckled again, and winked slyly. 'Mum's the word, lad, but it's time you knew a little more.' He nodded. 'Yes, tomorrow night,' he decided.

On Saturday there was a bazaar being held in the Trades Hall, a Women's Union fund-raising drive for building the new church. Where the crazed mob had screamed murder and bloody revolution the previous night, now there were long trestle tables set out and the women hovered over their displays of baked and fancily iced cakes, trays of tarts, preserved fruit in jars and jams.

Mark bought a packet of tarts for a penny and he and Fergus munched them as they wandered idly down the hall, stopping at the piles of second-hand clothing while Fergus tried a maroon cardigan and, after careful deliberation, purchased it for half a crown. They reached the top of the hall, and stood beneath the raised stage.

Fergus surveyed the room casually and then took Mark's arm and led him up the steps. They crossed the stage quietly, and went in through a door in the wings, into a maze of small union offices and storerooms, all deserted now on a Saturday afternoon.

Fergus used a key from his watch-chain to unlock a low iron door, and they stooped through it. Fergus relocked behind him, and they went down a narrow flight of steps that descended steeply. There was a smell of damp and earth, and Mark realized that they were descending to the cellars.

Fergus tapped on the door at the bottom of the stairs, and after a moment a single eye regarded them balefully through a peep hole.

'All right, comrade. Fergus MacDonald – a committee member.'

There was the rattle of chains and the door opened. A disgruntled, roughly dressed man stood aside for them. He was unshaven and sullen, and against the wall of the tiny room was a table and chair, still spread with the remains of a meal and the crumpled daily newspaper.

The man grunted, and Fergus led Mark across the room and through another door into the cellars.

The floor was earthen and the arched columns were in raw unplastered brick. There was the stench of dust and rats, stale dank air in confined space. A single bulb lit the centre starkly, but left the alcoves behind the arches in shadow.

'Here, lad, this is what we are going to use.'

There were wooden cases stacked neatly to the height of a man's head in the alcoves, and the stacks were draped with heavy tarpaulin, obviously stolen from the railway yards for they were stencilled SAR & H.

Fergus lifted the edge of one tarpaulin, and grinned that thin humourless smile.

'Still in the grease, lad.' The wooden cases were branded with the distinctive arrow-head and WD of the British War Department, and below that the inscription: '6 pieces. Lee-Enfield Mark IV (CNVD)'.

Mark was stunned. 'Good God, Fergus, there are hundreds of them.'

'That's it, lad – and this is only one arsenal. There are others all along the Rand.'

He lifted another tarpaulin, walking on down the length of the cellar. The ammunition cases, with the quick-release catches on the detachable lids that were painted: '1000 rounds .303.'

'We have enough to do the job.' Fergus squeezed Mark's arm, and led him on.

There were racks of rifles now, ready for instant use, blued steel glistening with gun oil in the electric light. Fergus picked out a single rifle and handed it to Mark.

'This one has got your name on it.'

Mark took the weapon, and the feel of it in his hands was terribly familiar.

'It's the only one we've got, but the moment I saw it, I thought of you. When the time comes, you'll be using it.'

The P.14 sniper's rifle had that special balance that felt just right in his hands but made Mark sick in the stomach. He handed it back to Fergus without a word, but the older man winked at him before racking it again carefully.

Like a showman, Fergus had kept the best for last. With a flourish he whipped the canvas off the heavy weapon, with its thick corrugated water-jacketed barrel, that squatted on its steel tripod. The Maxim machine gun, in its various forms, had the dubious distinction of having killed more human beings than any other single weapon that man's destructive genius had been able to devise.

This was one of that deadly family, the Vickers–Maxim .303 Mark IV.B, and there were boxes stacked beside it. Each containing a belt of 250 rounds. The gun could throw those at 2440 feet per second and at a cyclic rate of 750 rounds a minute.

'How about that, comrade? You asked what we are going to fight with – how will that do for a beginning?'

In the silence Mark could hear faintly, but distinctly, the sound of children's laughter from the hall above them.

Mark sat alone upon the highest crest of the low kopjes that stretched into the west, black ironstone ridges breaking out of the flat dry earth like the crested back of a crocodile surfacing from still lake water.

The memory of the hidden arsenal had stayed with him through the night, keeping him from sleep, so that now his eyes felt gritty and his skin stretched tight and dry across the bones of his cheeks.

Lack of sleep had left him with that remote feeling, a lightness of thought, detached from reality, so now he sat in the bright sunlight blinking like a day-flying owl, and looking like a stranger into his own mind.

He felt a rising sense of dismay as he realized how idly he had drifted along the path that had brought him here to the very brink of the abyss. It had taken the feel of the P.14 in his hands, and the laughter of children to bring him up at the end of a rope.

All his training, all his deepest beliefs were centred on the sanctity of law, on the order and responsibilities of society. He had fought for that, had spent all of his adult life fighting for that belief. Now suddenly he had drifted, out of apathy, to the camp of the enemy; already he was numbered with the legions of the lawless, already they were arming him to begin the work of destruction. There was no question now that it was merely empty rhetoric shouted at gatherings of drunken labourers – he had seen the guns. It would be cruel and without mercy. He knew Harry Fisher, had recognized the forces that drove him. He knew Fergus MacDonald, the man had killed before and often; he would not flick an eyelid when he killed again.

Mark groaned aloud, aghast at what he had let happen to himself. He who knew what war really was, he who had worn the king's uniform, and won his medal for courage.

He felt the oily warmth of shame in this throat, a gagging sensation, and, to arm himself against future weakness of this same kind, he tried to find the reasons why he had been drawn in.

He realized now that he had been lost and alone, without family or home, and Fergus MacDonald had been the only shelter in the cold. Fergus the older comrade of shared dangers, whom he had trusted without question. Fergus the father figure – and he had followed again, grateful for the guidance, not questioning the destination.

There had, of course, been Helena as well and the hold she had over him, the tightest grip any human could have over another. He had been, and still was, totally obsessed with her. She had awakened his long suppressed and tightly controlled sexuality. Now it was but a breath away from bursting the wall he had built to dam it; when it burst, it might be a force he could not control, and that thought terrified him almost as much as the other.

He tried now to separate the woman from her womanhood, tried to see the person beyond this devastating web she wove around his senses, and he succeeded in as much that he realized that she was not a person he could admire, not the mother he would choose for his children. Also, she was the wife of an old comrade who trusted him completely.

Now he felt he was ready to make the decision to leave, and to carry that resolve through firmly.

He would leave Fordsburg immediately, leave Fergus MacDonald and his dark, cataclysmic schemes. He felt his spirits lighten instantly at the prospect. He would not miss him, nor that drab monastic pay office with its daily penance of boredom and drudgery. He felt the bright young spirit of anticipation flame again.

He would leave Fordsburg on the next train – and Helena. Immediately the flame flickered and his spirit plunged. There was a physical pain in his groin at the prospect, and he felt the cracks open in the dam wall of his passions.

It was dark when he left his bicycle in the garden shed, and he heard voices raised jovially in the house and bursts of laughter. Lights blazed beyond the curtained kitchen windows and when he stepped into the room there were four men at the table. Helena crossed quickly and hugged him impulsively, laughing, with high spots of colour in her cheeks, before taking his hand and leading him to the table.

'Welcome, comrade.' Harry Fisher looked up at Mark with those disturbing eyes and the shock of dark wiry hair hanging on to his forehead. 'You are in time to join the celebration.'

'Grab the lad a glass, Helena,' laughed Fergus, and she dropped his hand and hurried to the cupboard to fetch a glass and fill it with black stout from the bottle.

Harry Fisher raised his own glass to Fergus. 'Comrades, I give you the new member of the Central Committee – Fergus MacDonald.'

'Isn't it wonderful, Mark?' Helena squeezed Mark's hand.

'He's a good man,' growled Harry Fisher. 'The appointment isn't too soon. We need men with Comrade MacDonald's guts.' The others nodded agreement over their stout glasses, the two of them were both members of the local committee of the party; Mark knew them well from the meetings.

'Come, lad.' Fergus made room for him at the table and he squeezed in beside him, drawing all their attention.

'And you, young Mark,' Harry Fisher laid a powerful hairy hand on his shoulder, 'we are going to issue your party card –'

'How about that, lad!' Fergus winked and nudged Mark in the ribs. 'Usually it takes two years or more, we don't let the rabble into the party, but you've got friends on the Central Committee now.'

Mark was about to speak, to refuse the honour he was being accorded. Nobody had asked him, they had taken it that as he was Fergus's protégé, he was for them. Mark was about to deny it, to tell them the decision he had made that day – when that sense of danger warned him. He had seen the guns, if he was not a friend then he was an enemy with a fatal secret. A secret that they could not risk. He had no doubts at all about these men, now. If he was an enemy, then they would see that he never passed that secret on to another man. But the moment for refusal had passed.

'Comrade MacDonald, I have a mission for you. It is urgent – and vital. Can you leave your work for two weeks?'

'I've got a sick mother,' Fergus chuckled. 'When do you want me to go, and what do you want me to do?'

'I want you to leave, say Wednesday, that will give me time to give you your orders and for you to make your arrangements.' Harry Fisher took a swallow of stout and the froth stayed on his upper lip. 'I'm sending you to visit all the local committees – Capetown, Bloemfontein, Port Elizabeth – so that each of them can be coordinated.'

Mark felt a guilty lift of relief at the words, there would be no confrontation with Fergus now. He could merely slip away while he was gone on his mission. Then he glanced up and was startled by the gaze that Helena had fastened upon him. She stared at him with the fixed hungry expression of a leopard watching its prey from cover in the last instant before its spring.

Now when their eyes met, she smiled again that secret knowing smile, and the tip of her pink tongue dabbed at her slightly parted lips.

Mark's heart pounded to the point of physical pain and he dropped his eyes hurriedly to his glass. He was to be alone with Helena, and the prospect filled him with dread and a surging passionate heat.

Mark carried Fergus's cheap and badly battered suitcase down to the station, and as they took the short cut across open veld, the thick frost crunched like sugar under their feet, and sparkled in myriad diamond points of light in the first rays of the sun.

At the station they waited with four other members of the party for the southbound mail, and when at last it came, puffing hoarsely, shooting steam high into the frosty air, it was thirty-five minutes late.

'Thirty-five minutes late is almost early for the railways,' Fergus laughed, and shook hands with each of them in turn, slapping their shoulders before scrambling up the steel ladder into the coach. Mark passed his suitcase up through the open window.

'Look after Helena, lad, and yourself.'

Mark stood and watched the train run out southwards, shrinking dramatically in size until the sound of it was a mere whisper fading to nothingness. Then he turned and started up the hill towards the mine just as the hooters began their mournful wailing howl that echoed off the yellow mesas of the dumps, summoning the disorderly columns of men to their appointed labours. Mark walked with them, one in a thousand, distinguished from the others neither in appearance nor achievement. Once again he felt a sense of seething discontent, a vague but growing knowledge that this was not all that was life, not all that he was capable of doing with his youth and energy; and he looked curiously at the men who hurried with him towards the iron gates at the mine hooter's imperious summons.

All of them wore that closed withdrawn look, behind which Mark was convinced lurked the same misgivings as now assaulted him. Surely they also felt the futility of the dull daily repetition – the young ones at least must feel it. The older and greyer must regret it; deep down they must mourn for the long sunny days, now past, spent toiling in endless drudgery for another man's coin. They must mourn the fact that when they went, they would leave no footprints, no ripple on the surface, no monument, except perhaps a few sons to repeat the meaningless cycle, all of them interchangeable, all of them dispensable.

He paused at the gates, standing aside while the stream of humanity flowed past him, and slowly the sense of excitement built up in him, the certainty that there was something, some special and worthwhile task for him to perform. Some special place that waited for him, and he knew he must go on and find it.

He hurried forward, suddenly grateful to Fergus MacDonald for placing this pressure on him, for forcing him to face himself, for breaking the easy drifting course he had taken since his flight from Ladyburg.

'You are late, Anders.' The supervisor looked up from his ledgers severely, and each of his juniors repeated the gesture, a long row of them with the same narrow disapproving expressions.

'What have you got to say?'

'I merely called in to clean out my desk,' said Mark smiling, the excitement still on him. 'And to throw in my time.'

The disapproving expressions changed slowly to shock.

It was dusk when Mark opened the back gate of the cottage and went up the short walk to the kitchen. He had walked all day at random, driven on restlessly by a new torrent of energy and exciting thoughts; he had not realized how hungry he was until he saw the lights in the window and smelled the faint aroma of cooking.

The kitchen was deserted, but Helena called through from the front.

'Mark, is that you?' Before he could answer, she appeared in the kitchen door, and leaned one hip against the jamb. 'I thought you weren't coming home tonight.'

She wore the blue dress, and Mark knew now that it was her best, reserved for special occasions, and she wore cosmetics – something that Mark had never seen her do before. There were spots of rouge on her cheeks and her lips were painted, giving new lustre to her usually sallow skin. The short dark hair was newly washed, shiny in the lamplight, and brushed back, caught over one ear with a tortoise-shell clasp.

Mark stared at her. Her legs were smooth and sleek in silken stockings, the feet neatly clad in small pumps.

'Why are you staring, Mark?'

'You are –' Mark's voice turned husky, and caught. He cleared his throat. 'You are very pretty tonight.'

'Thank you, sir.' She laughed, a low throaty chuckle, and she did a slow pirouette, flaring the blue filmy skirt above the silken legs. 'I'm glad you like it.' Then she stopped beside him and took his arm. Her touch was a delicious shock, like diving into a mountain pool.

'Sit down, Mark.' She led him to the chair at the head of the table. 'Let

me get you a nice beer.' She went to the ice box, and while she pulled the
cap on the bottle and poured, she ran on gaily. 'I found a goose at the butcher's
– do you like roast goose?'

Saliva poured from under Mark's tongue. 'I love it.'

'With roast potato and pumpkin pie.'

'For that I would sell my soul.'

Helena laughed delightedly, it wasn't one of Mark's usual shy and reserved
replies. There was a sense of excitement surrounding him like an aura this evening,
echoing her own excitement.

She brought the two glasses, and propped one hip on the table.

'What shall we drink to?'

'To freedom,' he said without hesitation, 'and a good tomorrow.'

'I like that,' she said, and clinked his glass, leaning over him so that the
bodice of her dress was at the level of his eyes. 'But why only tomorrow –
why can't the good times start right now this minute?'

Mark laughed. 'All right, here's to a good tonight and a good tomorrow.'

'Mark!' Helena pursed her lips in mock disapproval, and immediately he
blushed and laughed in confusion.

'Oh no, I didn't mean – that sounded dreadful. I didn't –'

'I bet you say that to all the girls.' Helena stood up quickly. She did not
want to embarrass him and break the mood, so she crossed to the stove.

'It's ready,' she announced, 'if you want to eat now.'

She sat opposite him, anticipating his appetite, buttering the thick slices
of bread with yellow farm butter and keeping his glass fully charged.

'Aren't you eating?'

'I'm not hungry.'

'It's good – you don't know what you are missing.'

'Better than your other girls cooked for you?' she demanded playfully, and
Mark dropped his eyes to his plate and busily loaded his fork.

'There weren't any girls.'

'Oh, Mark, you don't expect me to believe that! A handsome young fellow
like you, and those French girls. I bet you drove them mad.'

'We were too busy, and besides –' he stopped.

'Besides what?' she insisted, and he looked up at her, silent for a moment,
and then he began to talk. It was suddenly so easy to talk to her, and he
was buoyed up with his new jubilant mood and relaxed with the food and
drink in his belly. He talked to her as he had never talked to another human
being, and she answered him with the frankness of another man.

'Oh, Mark, that's nonsense. Not every woman is sick, it's only the street
girls.'

'Yes, I know. I didn't believe every girl, but well, they are the only ones
that a man can –' he broke off. 'And the others get babies,' he went on lamely.

She laughed and clapped her hands with delight. 'Oh, my darling Mark.
It's not that easy, you know. I have been married for nine years and I've
never had a baby.'

'Well,' Mark hesitated. 'Well, you are different. I didn't mean you, when
I said those things. I meant other girls.'

'I'm not sure if that's meant to be a compliment or an insult,' she teased
again. She had known he was a virgin, of course. There was that transparent
shining innocence that glowed from him, his unpractised and appealing
awkwardness in the presence of women, that peculiar shyness that would pass
so soon but which now heightened her excitement, rousing her in some perverse
way. She knew now why some men paid huge sums of money to despoil

innocence; she touched his bared forearm now, delighting in the smooth hardness of young muscle, unable to keep her hands off him.

'Oh, it was a compliment,' Mark answered her hurriedly.

'Do you like me, Mark?'

'Oh, yes. I like you more than I've ever liked any other girl.'

'You see, Mark,' she leaned closer to him, her voice sinking to a throaty whisper. 'I'm not sick, and I'm not going to have a baby – ever.' She lifted her hand and touched his cheek. 'You are a beautiful man, Mark. I liked you from the first moment I saw you coming up the walk like a stray puppy.'

She stood up slowly and crossed to the kitchen door, deliberately she turned the key and flipped up the light switch. The small room was dark, but for the shaft of light from the hallway.

'Come, Mark.' She took his hand and drew him to his feet. 'We are going to bed now.'

At the door to Mark's bedroom she reached up on tip-toe and kissed his cheek lightly, and then without another word she let his hand drop and glided away from him.

Uncertainly Mark watched her go, wanting to call to her to stay, wanting to run after her – and yet relieved that she had gone, that the headlong rush into the unknown had abruptly halted. She reached the door of her own bedroom and went through without looking back.

Torn by conflicting emotions, he turned away and went through into his own room. He undressed slowly, disappointment now stronger than relief, and while he folded his clothing, he listened to her quiet movements in the room beyond the thin wall.

He climbed at last into the narrow iron bed, and lay rigid until he heard the light switch click next door; then he sighed and picked up the book from the bedside table; he had not yet read it through, but now the dull political text might divert his emotions enough to allow him to sleep.

The latch of his door snapped softly. He had not heard her in the passage, and she stepped into the room. She wore the gown of slippery peach-coloured satin and she had recombed her hair and retouched her cheeks and lips.

Carefully, she closed the door and crossed the room with slow swaying hips under the moving satin.

Neither of them spoke as she stopped by the side of his bed.

'Have you read it, Mark?' she asked softly.

'Not all of it.' He placed the book aside.

'Well, this isn't the time to finish it,' she said, and deliberately opened the gown, slipped it from her shoulders and dropped it over the back of the chair.

She was naked, and Mark gasped. She was so smooth. He had not expected that somehow, and he stared at her as she stood close beside him. Her skin had an olive creaminess, like old porcelain, a sheen that caught the light and glowed. Mark felt his whole body rocked by the exquisite tension of arousal, and he tried feebly to thrust it aside. He tried to think of Fergus, of the trust that had been placed in him.

'Look after Helena, lad, and yourself.'

Her breasts were big for the slimness of her body, already they hung heavily, almost overripe, drooping smooth and round with startlingly large nipples, rosy brown and big as ripe grapes. They swung weightily as she moved closer to him, and he saw that there were sparse dark hairs curling from the puckered aureole around the nipples.

There was hair also curling out in little wisps from under her arms, dark glossy hair – and a huge wild bush of it below the smooth creamy slightly bulging belly.

The hair excited him, so dark and crisp against the pale skin, and he stared at it, transfixed. All thoughts of honour and trust faded, he felt the dam wall inside him creak and strain.

She reached out and touched his bare shoulder, and it convulsed his body like a whip-lash.

'Touch me, Mark,' she whispered, and he reached out slowly, hesitantly, like a man in a trance, and touched with one finger the smooth ivory warmth of her hip, still staring fixedly at her.

'Yes, Mark. That's right.' She took his wrist and slowly drew his hand upwards, so that the tips of his fingers traced featherlike over her flank and the outline of her ribs.

'Here, Mark,' she said, 'and here.' The big dark nipples contracted at the touch of his fingers, changing shape, thrusting out and hardening, swelling and darkening. Mark could not believe it was happening, that woman's flesh could react as swiftly and dramatically as a man's.

He felt the dam break, and the flood came pouring through the breach. Too long contained, too powerful and weighty to resist, it poured through his mind and body, sweeping all restraint before it.

With a choking cry, he seized her around the waist with both arms, and drew her fiercely to him, pressing his face into the smooth soft warmth of her naked belly.

'Oh, Mark!' she cried, and her voice was hoarse and shaking with lust and triumph, as she twisted her fingers into the soft brown hair and stooped over his head.

The days blurred and telescoped together, and the universe shut down to a tiny cottage in a sordid street. Only their bodies marked the passage of time, sleeping and waking to love until exhaustion overtook them and they slept again to wake hungry, ravenous for both food and loving.

At first he was like a bull, charging with a mindless energy and strength. It frightened her, for she had not expected such strength from that slim and graceful body. She rode with his strength, little by little controlling and directing it, changing its course, and then she began gently to teach.

Long afterwards, Mark would think back on those five incredible days and realize his good fortune. So many young men must find their own way into the uncharted realms of physical love-making, without guide, accompanied usually by a partner making her own hesitant first journey into the unknown.

'Did you know that there is a tribe in South America, Mark, that have a rule that every married woman must take one young warrior of the tribe and teach him to do what we are doing?' she asked, as she knelt beside him in one of the intervals of quiet between the storms.

'What a shame,' he smiled lazily. 'I thought we were the first two ever to think of it.' He reached out for the pack of Needlepoint cigarettes on the bedside table and lit two of them.

Helena drew upon hers and her expression was fond and proud. He had changed so swiftly and radically in the last few days, and she was responsible for that. This new assurance, this budding strength of purpose. The shyness and reticence were fading. He spoke now in a way that he had never spoken before, calmly and with authority. Swiftly he was becoming a full man – and she had had a hand in it.

Mark believed that each new delight was the ultimate one, but she proved him wrong a dozen times. There were things that, had he heard them spoken of might have appalled and revolted him, but when they happened the way Helena made them happen, they left only wonder and a sense of awe. She taught him a vast new respect for his own body, as it came at last fully alive, and he became aware of new broad reaches and depths of his own mind.

For five days neither of them left the cottage; then on the sixth day there was a letter brought by a uniformed postman on a bicycle and Mark, who accepted it, recognized immediately Fergus MacDonald's cramped and laboured hand. Guilt hit him like a fist in the stomach; the dream shattered like fragile crystal.

Helena sat at the newspaper-covered table in the kitchen with the now soiled peach gown open to the waist and read the letter aloud, mocking the writer with the inflection of her voice as he reported a string of petty achievements, applause at party meetings where a dozen comrades had gathered in a back room, messages of loyalty and dedication to bring back to the Central Committee, commitment to the cause and promises of action when the time to strike was ripe.

Helena mocked him, rolling her eyes and chuckling when he asked after Mark – was he well and happy, was Helena looking after him properly.

She drew deeply on the stub of the cigarette and then dropped it into the dregs of the coffee cup at her elbow, where it was extinguished with a sharp hiss. This simple action caused in Mark an unnatural reaction of revulsion.

Suddenly he saw her clearly, the sallow skin wrinkled finely in the corners of her eyes as her youth cracked away like old oilpaint; the plum-coloured underlining of the eye sockets, the petulant quirk of her lips and the waspish sting to her voice.

Abruptly, he was aware of the squalid room, with the greasy smell of stale food and unwashed dishes, of the grubby and stained gown and the pendulous droop of the big ivory-coloured breasts beneath the gown.

He stood up and left the room.

'Mark, where are you going?' she called after him.

'I'm going out for a while.'

He scrubbed himself in the stained enamel bath, running the water as hot as he could bear it so that his body glowed bright pink as he towelled himself down.

At the railway booking office he stood for nearly half an hour, reading the long lists of closely printed timetables pasted to the wall.

Rhodesia. He had heard they needed men on the new copper mines. There was still a wilderness up there, far horizons and the great wild game, lakes and mountains and room to move.

He moved to the window of the booking-office and the clerk looked out at him expectantly.

'One second-class single to Durban,' he said, surprising himself. He was going back to Natal, to Ladyburg. There was unfinished business there, and answers to search for. An unknown enemy to find and confront.

As he paid for the ticket with the old man's sovereigns, he had a vivid mental picture of the old man on the stoep of Andersland – with his great spiky whiskers and the old terai hat pulled low over his pale calm eyes. Mark knew then that this had been only a respite, a hiatus, in which he had found time to heal and gather courage for the task ahead.

He went back to collect his belongings. There was not much to pack, and he was in a consuming hurry now. As he swept his few spare shorts and clean socks into the cardboard suitcase, he was suddenly aware of Helena's presence, and he turned quickly.

She had bathed and dressed and she stood in the doorway watching him, her expression too calm for the loneliness in her voice.

'You are going.' It was a statement, not a question.

'Yes,' he answered simply, turning to snap the catches on the case.

'I'm coming with you.'

'No. I'm going alone.'

'But, Mark, what about me?'

'I'm sorry, Helena. I'm truly sorry.'

'But don't you see, I love you –' her voice rose in a low wail of despair. 'I love you, Mark darling, you can't go.' She spread her arms to block the doorway.

'Please, Helena. We both knew it was madness. We both knew there was nothing for us. Don't make it ugly now, please let me go.'

'No.' She covered her ears with both hands. 'No, don't talk like that. I love you. I love you.'

Gently he tried to move her from the doorway.

'I have to go. My train –'

Suddenly she flew at him, vicious as a wounded leopard. He was unprepared, and her nails raked long bloody lines across his face, narrowly missing his eyes.

'You bastard, you selfish bastard,' she shrieked. 'You're like all of them,' and she struck again, but he caught her wrists.

'You're all the same, you take – you take –'

He turned her, wildly struggling, and tipped her back on to the unmade bed. Abruptly the fight went out of her and she pressed her face into the pillow. Her sobs followed Mark as he ran down the passage, and out of the open front door.

It was more than three hundred miles to the port of Durban on the coast, and slowly the train huffed up the great barrier of the Drakensberg Mountains, worming its way through the passes until at last it plunged joyously over the escarpment and ran lightly down into the deep grassy bowl of the eastern littoral, dropping less steeply as it neared the sea and emerged at last into the lush semi-tropical hot-house of the sea-board with its snowy white beaches and the warm blue waters of the Mozambique current.

Mark had much time to think on the journey down, and he wasted most of it in vain regrets. Helena's cries and accusations echoed through his mind while the cold grey stone of guilt lay heavily in the pit of his stomach, whenever he thought of Fergus MacDonald.

Then, as they passed through the town of Pietermaritzburg and began the last leg of the journey, Mark put aside guilt and regret, and began to think ahead.

His first intention had been to return directly to Ladyburg, but now he realized that this was folly. There was an enemy there, a murderous enemy, a hidden enemy striking from cover, a rich enemy, a powerful enemy, who could command a bunch of armed men who were ready to kill.

Mark thought then of those bloody attacks that he and Fergus had made in France. Always the first move had been to identify and mark the enemy, locate where he was lying, find his stance and assess him. How good was he, was his technique rigid, or was he quick and changeable? Was he sloppy, so that the hunters could take risks, or were risks suicidal?

'We got to try and guess the way the bastard's thinking, lad –' was Fergus's first concern, before they planned the shoot.

'I've got to find who he is,' Mark whispered aloud, 'and guess the way the bastard is thinking.'

One thing at least was clear, a hundred pounds was too high a price in blood money for such an insignificant person as Mark Anders; the only thing that could possibly make him significant in any way was his relation to the old man and to Andersland. He had been seen at Andersland by both the Hindu babu and the white foreman. Then he had brazened into the town asking questions, perusing documents. Only then had they come after him. The land was the centre of the puzzle, and he had the names of all the men who had any interest in the sale.

Mark lifted the suitcase from the luggage rack and, holding it on his lap, hunted for and found his notebook. He read the names: DIRK COURTNEY, RONALD PYE, DENNIS PETERSEN, PIET GREYLING and his son CORNELIUS.

His first concern must be to find out all he could about those men, find out where each was lying, find his stance and assess him, decide which of them was the sniper. While he did this, he must keep his own head well down below the parapet. He must keep clear of enemy country, and enemy country was Ladyburg.

His best base would be Durban city itself; it was big enough to absorb him without comment, and, as the capital of Natal, he would have many sources of information there, libraries, government archives, newspaper offices. He began making a list of all possible sources in the back of the notebook, and immediately found himself regretting bitterly that Ladyburg itself was closed to him. Records in the Lands Office and Company Registers for the district were not duplicated in the capital.

Suddenly he had a thought. 'Damn it, what was her name!' Mark closed his eyes, and he saw again the bright, friendly and cheerful face of the little girl in the Companies office in Ladyburg.

'Mark, that's a strong romantic name –' He could even hear her voice, but the train was sliding into the platform before her name came to him again.

'Marion!' and he scribbled it into the notebook.

He climbed down on to the platform, carrying his case, and joined the jostling throng of travellers and welcomers. Then he set out to find lodgings in the city.

A penny copy of the *Natal Mercury* led him through its small advertisements to a rooming house in Point Road, down by the docks. The room was small, dark and smelled of those gargantuan cockroaches that infest the city, swarming up from the sewers each evening in shiny black hordes, but the rental was only a guinea a week, and he had the use of the lavatory and shower room across the small enclosed yard.

That night he wrote a letter:

Dear Marion,

I don't suppose you remember me, my name is Mark Anders, the same as Mark Antony! I have thought of you often since I was compelled to leave Ladyburg unexpectedly before I had a chance to see you again –'

Tactfully he avoided any mention of the research work he wanted undertaken. That could wait for the next letter. He had learned much about women recently, and he addressed the letter simply to 'Miss Marion, Company Registrar's Office, Ladyburg.'

Mark started the following morning at the City Library, walking up Smith Street to the four-storied edifice of the Municipal Buildings. It looked like a palace flanked by the equally imposing buildings of the Royal Hotel and the cathedral, with the garden square neatly laid out in front of it, bright with spring blooms.

He had another inspiration as he approached the librarian's desk.

'I'm doing research for a book I intend writing –'

Immediately the grey-haired lady who presided over the dim halls and ceiling-high racks of books softened her severe expression. She was a book person, and book people love other book people. Mark had the key to one of the reading rooms given him, and the back copies of all the Natal newspapers, going back to the time of the first British occupation, were put at his disposal.

There was immediately a temptation for Mark, voracious reader that he was, to lose himself in the fascination of history printed as urgent headlines – for history had been one of Mark's favourite subjects both at Ladyburg School and at University College.

He resisted the temptation and went at once to the drawers that contained the copies of the *Ladyburg Lantern and Recorder*. The first copies were already yellowing with age and tore easily, so he handled them with care.

The first mention of the name 'Courtney' leapt at him in thick black headlines on one of the earliest copies from 1879.

Ladyburg Mounted Rifles massacred at Isandhlwana.
Colonel Waite Courtney and his men cut down to a man.
Blood-crazed Impis on the rampage.

Mark guessed that this must refer to the founder of the family in Ladyburg; after that the name cropped up in nearly every issue, there were many Courtneys and all of them lived in the Ladyburg district, but the first mention of Dirk Courtney came in 1900.

Ladyburg welcomes one of its Favourite Sons.
Hero of the Anglo-Boer War Returns.
Colonel Sean Courtney purchases Lion Kop Ranch.
Ladyburg welcomes the return of one of her favourite sons after an absence of many years. There are very few of us who are not acquainted with the exploits of Colonel Sean Courtney, DSO, DCM, and all will recall the major role he played in the establishment of the prosperous gold-mining industry on the Witwatersrand ...

A long recital of the man's deeds and reputation followed, and the report ended,

Colonel Courtney has purchased the ranch Lion Kop from the Ladyburg Farmers Bank. He intends making this his home and will plant the land to timber. Major Courtney is a widower and is accompanied by his ten-year-old son, Dirk.

The ancient report shocked Mark. He had not realized that Dirk Courtney was the son of his old General. The big, bearded, hook-nosed man he had met that snowy night in France, the man whom he had immediately respected and liked – no, more than liked. The man whose vital force and presence, together with his reputation, had roused in him an almost religious awe.

His instant reaction was to wonder if the General himself was in any way involved in the murderous attack he had survived on the escarpment; and the thought disturbed him so that he left the library and went down to the palm-lined esplanade and found a bench overlooking the quiet sheltered waters of the bay, with the great whale-backed mountain of the bluff beyond.

He watched the shipping, as he pondered the tangled web that was centred in Ladyburg, where the hidden spider sat. He knew that his investigations were going to take time. The reading was a slow business and it would be days before he could expect to have a reply to his letter to Marion.

Later, in his dingy room, he counted the remaining sovereigns in his money belt, and knew that living in the city they would not last him long.

He needed a job.

The floor manager had the beer belly and flash clothing that seem always to go with salesmen in the motor industry; Mark answered his questions with extreme politeness and a false cheerfulness, but with despair below the surface.

He had trudged the city for five days, from one faint prospect of work to another.

'Times are hard,' almost every prospective employer told him at the beginning of the interview, 'and we are looking for a man with experience.'

Mark had no time to pursue his quest at the library. Now he sat on the front edge of his chair waiting to thank the man and say goodbye as soon as he was dismissed, but the man went on talking long after he should have closed the interview. He was talking about the salesmen's commission, and how it was so generous that there was plenty for two.

'– if you know what I mean.' The man winked and fitted a cigarette into his ivory holder.

'Yes, of course,' Mark nodded vehemently, having absolutely no idea what the man meant, but eager to please.

'Of course, I'd be looking after you personally. If we came to some sort of arrangement, right?'

'Right,' Mark agreed, and only then did he realize that the manager was soliciting a kick-back off Mark's commission. He was going to get the job.

'Of course, sir.' He wanted to leap up and dance. 'I'd like to think we were equal partners.'

'Good.' Fifty per cent of Mark's commission was more than the manager had expected. 'Start Monday, nine o'clock sharp,' he said quickly, and beamed at Mark.

Mark wrung his hand gratefully, but as he was leaving the little cubicle of the office the manager called after him.

'You do have a decent suit, Anders, don't you?'

'Of course,' Mark lied quickly.

'Wear it.'

He found a Hindu tailor at the Indian market who ran up a grey three-piece suit overnight, and charged him thirty-two shillings.

'You wear clothes beautiful, sir. Like a royal duke,' the tailor told him, as he pointed Mark at the fly-blown mirror in his fitting-room, standing behind him and skilfully holding a fold of surplus material at the small of Mark's back to give the front of the suit a fashionable drape. 'You will be an extremely first class advertisement for my humble skills.'

'You can drive a car, of course?' the manager, whose name was Dicky Lancome, asked him casually as they crossed the showroom floor to the glistening Cadillac.

'Of course,' Mark agreed.

'Of course,' Dicky agreed. 'Otherwise you wouldn't have applied for a job as a car salesman, would you?'

'Of course not.'

'Hop in then,' Dicky invited. 'And whip us around the block.'

Mark reeled mentally, but his tongue was quick enough to rescue him.

'I'd prefer you to point out the special features first. I've never driven a Cadillac before.' Which was for once the literal truth. He had never driven a Cadillac, or any other motor vehicle, before.

'Righty ho,' Dicky agreed, and as they sped down the Marine Parade with Dicky whistling and tipping his hat to the pretty girls on the sidewalk, Mark watched his every action with wheel and pedal avidly.

Back at the showrooms in West Street, Dicky flicked casually through a bunch of forms.

'If you make a sale, you fill in one of these – and make sure you get the money.' Then he pulled out his watch.

'God, it's late. I've got a desperately important lunch date,' it was a little after eleven o'clock, 'very important client.' Then he dropped his voice, 'Blonde, actually. Smasher!' and he winked again. 'See you later.'

'But what about prices, and that sort of thing?' Mark called desperately after him.

'There is a pamphlet on my desk. Gives you all that stuff. Ta-ta!' and Dicky disappeared through the back door.

Mark was circling the Cadillac uncertainly, utterly engrossed with the pamphlet, muttering aloud as he tried to master the operating instructions and identify the various component parts of the vehicle from the line-drawing and numerated list, when there was a tap on his arm.

'Excuse me, young man, but are you the salesman?' Before him stood an elderly couple, the man dressed in beautifully tailored dark cloth, a carnation in his buttonhole and a cane in one hand.

'We would like a drive in the motor vehicle – before we decide,' said the elegant lady beside him, smiling at Mark in a motherly fashion through the light veil that draped down over her eyes from the brimmed hat. The hat was decorated with artificial flowers, and her hair below the brim was washed silver and neatly waved.

Mark felt waves of panic threaten to engulf him. He looked about desperately for an escape, but already the gentleman was handing his wife into the front seat of the Cadillac.

Mark closed the doors on the couple, and ducked behind the machine for one last brief perusal of the operating pamphlet. 'Depress clutch pedal with left foot, engage gear lever up and left, depress accelerator pedal firmly with right foot, release clutch pedal,' he muttered, stuffed the pamphlet into his pocket and hurried to the driver's seat.

The gentleman sat forward in the centre of the back seat, both hands resting on the head of his cane, grave and attentive as a judge.

His wife beamed kindly at Mark. 'How old are you, young man?'

'Twenty, ma'am, almost twenty-one.' Mark pressed the starter and the engine growled, so she had to raise her voice.

'My,' she nodded, 'the same age as my own son.'

Mark gave her a pale and sickly grin, as he silently repeated the instructions in his mind.

'– accelerate firmly.' The engine beat rose to a deafening bellow, and Mark clung to the driving-wheel until the knuckles of both hands blanched with the pressure of his grip.

'Do you live at home?' asked his passenger.

'No, ma'am,' Mark answered and let out the clutch. The back wheels screeched like a wounded stallion, and a blue cloud blew out from behind as the entire machine seemed to rear upwards, and then hurl itself, slewing wildly, towards the street doors, leaving two long black rubber smears across the polished showroom floor.

Mark fought the wheel and the Cadillac swayed and skidded, lined up with the doors at the last possible moment and careered into the street, moving sideways like a crab. A team of horses drawing a passing coach shied out of the path of the roaring machine, and behind Mark the elderly gentleman managed to struggle up into a sitting position again and find his cane.

'Good acceleration!' Mark shouted above the roar of the engine.

'Excellent,' agreed his passenger, his eyes popping in the rear view mirror.

His wife adjusted her flowered hat that had come down over her eyes, and shook her head sadly.

'You young boys! As soon as you leave home you starve yourselves. I could tell you are living on your own – you are as thin as –'

Mark took the intersection of Smith and Aliwal at the charge, but halfway through it a heavily laden lorry lumbered across their front and Mark spun the wheel nimbly. The Cadillac changed direction ninety degrees and ducked into Aliwal on two wheels.

'– as a rake,' said the lady, holding firmly to the door handle with one hand, and with the other to her hat. 'You should come up to the house one Sunday for a decent meal.'

'Thank you, ma'am, that's very kind.'

When Mark stopped the Cadillac against the pavement in front of the show-rooms at last, his hand was shaking so feverishly that he had to make a second effort to earth the magneto. He could feel the damp of nervous sweat soaking through the jacket of his new suit, and he had not the strength to let himself out of the cab.

'Incredible,' said the elderly gentleman in the back seat. 'What control, what mastery – I feel quite young again.'

'It was very nice, dear,' his wife agreed.

'We'll take her,' her husband decided impulsively, and Mark could not believe he had heard right. He had made his first sale.

'Wouldn't it be nice if this young man would come to us as a chauffeur. He is such an excellent driver.'

'No, ma'am,' Mark nearly panicked again. 'I couldn't think of leaving my job here – thank you all the same.'

'Jolly good show, old man.' Dicky Lancome folded the two five-pound notes that were his half-share of Mark's commission on the sale of the Cadillac. 'I can see a great future ahead for you.'

'Oh, I don't know,' Mark demurred modestly.

'A great future,' Dicky predicted sagely. 'But just one thing, old man – that suit,' he shuddered gently, 'let me introduce you to my tailor, now that you can afford it. No offence, of course, but that looks like you are on your way to a fancy-dress ball.'

That evening after close of business Mark hurried back to the library for the first time in a week. The librarian welcomed him with a severe expression like a disapproving school ma'am.

'I thought we had seen the last of you – that you had given up.'

'Oh no, by no means,' Mark assured her, and again she softened and handed him the key to the reading-room.

Mark had mapped out a family tree for the Courtneys in his notebook, for it was confusing. There was a brother to Sean, who was also a colonel at the end of the Boer War, but also a holder of the Victoria Cross for gallantry – a distinguished family indeed. This brother, Colonel Garrick Courtney, had gradually become a noted and then a famous author of military history and of biographies of other successful soldiers – beginning with his *With Roberts to Pretoria* and *Buller, a Fighting Soldier*, and going on to *Battle for the Somme* and *Kitchener. A Life*. The books were all extensively and glowingly reviewed in the *Lantern*. The author had a single son, Michael Courtney. Prior to 1914, there were references to this son's business activities as managing director of the Courtney Saw Mills in the Ladyburg district, and his skills as an athlete and horseman in many local meetings. Then 1917 – LADYBURG HERO DECORATED.

Captain Michael Courtney, son of Colonel Garrick Courtney VC, was awarded the Distinguished Flying Cross for his exploits with the 21st RFC Fighter Squadron in France. Captain Courtney has been credited with five 'kills' of German aircraft, and was described by his commanding officer as a 'courageous and dedicated officer of high flying skills'. Hero, son of a hero.

Then again, within months, a front-page article outlined in a square of heavy black type.

It is with great regret that we report the death in action of CAPTAIN MICHAEL COURTNEY DFC. It is believed that Captain Courtney was shot down in flames behind enemy lines and that his executioner was none other than the notorious Baron von Richthofen of bloody reputation. *The Ladyburg Lantern* extends its deepest and sincerest condolences to his father and family. 'A Rose plucked in full bloom.'

The activities of this branch of the family, its triumphs and tragedies were all reported in detail – and it was the same with the Sean Courtney family for the period from the turn of the century to May of 1910.

Sean Courtney's marriage to Mrs Ruth Friedman in 1903 was described in loving detail, from the bride's dress to the icing on the cake. 'One of the flower girls was Miss Storm Friedman, aged four, who wore an exact replica of her mother's dress. She makes a pretty new sister for Master Dirk Courtney.' Again the mention of the name that truly interested Mark, and he noted it, for it was the last until May 1910.

Colonel Sean Courtney's achievements in politics and business and the more serious fields of recreation filled page after page of subsequent editions; his election to the legislative council of Natal, and later to Prime Minister Louis Botha's Cabinet; he became leader of the South Africa Party in Natal – and was a delegate to Whitehall in London, taking his entire family with him, to negotiate the terms of Union.

Sean Courtney's business interests flourished and multiplied, new sawmills, new plantations, elevation to new offices, the chairman of the first Building Society in Southern Africa, director of Union Castle Shipping Lines, head of the Government Commission on Natural Resources. Chairman of the South African Turf Club, a one hundred and fifty foot luxury yacht built for him by Thesens of Knysna, Commodore of the Royal Natal Yacht Club – but no further mention of Dirk Courtney until May 1910.

The Ladyburg Lantern and Recorder's front page of the edition of 12th May 1910.

The Ladyburg Lantern takes great pleasure in announcing that its entire paid up share capital has been acquired by Mr Dirk Courtney, who recently returned to Ladyburg after an absence of some years.

Mr Courtney tells us that the intervening years have been spent in travel, gaining both experience and capital. Clearly they were not wasted, for immediately on his arrival home, Mr Courtney purchased a controlling interest in the Ladyburg Farmers Bank for a reputed one million pounds sterling in cash.

Ladyburg and all its inhabitants are sure to benefit enormously by the vast energy, wealth and drive that Mr Dirk Courtney brings to the district.

'I intend taking a close day-to-day interest in all aspects of my companies' operations in Ladyburg,' he said, when asked of his future plans. 'Progress, Growth, Prosperity for All, are my watchwords.'

Mr Dirk Courtney, *The Ladyburg Lantern* salutes you and welcomes you as a notable ornament to our fair community.

After that, hardly an edition of *The Lantern* did not contain fawning eulogies of Mr Dirk Courtney – while mention of his father and family was reduced to an occasional small article in the inside pages.

To find news of Sean Courtney, Mark had to turn to the other Natal newspapers. He began with the *Natal Mercury*.

Ladyburg Mounted Rifles Sail for France
General Courtney Takes his Men to War once more.

That jolted Mark, he could remember the sea mist on the bay and the ranks of khaki-clad figures climbing the gangways, each of them burdened by kitbag and rifle. The singing, and the cries of the women, paper streamers and flower petals twisting and falling in gay and gaudy clouds about them, and the sound of the fog horns reverberating mournfully from the bluff. It was so clear in his mind still. How soon he was to follow them, after exaggerating his age to a recruiting sergeant who did not inquire too closely.

Ladyburg Rifles Badly Mauled
Attack Fails at Delville Wood
General Courtney: 'I am proud of them.'

Mark felt sudden stinging tears burn his eyelids as he went slowly down the long casualty lists, pausing as he recognized a name – remembering, remembering – lost again in those terrible seas of mud and blood and suffering.

A hand touched his shoulder arousing him, and he straightened up from the reading table, bewildered at his sudden return to the present.

'We are closing now, it's after nine o'clock,' said the young assistant librarian softly. 'I'm afraid you will have to leave now.' Then she peered more closely at him. 'Are you all right? Have you been crying?'

'No.' Quickly Mark groped for his handkerchief. 'It's just the strain of reading.'

His landlady shouted down the stairs to him as he let himself into the hall. 'I've got a letter for you.'

The letter looked as thick as a complete works of William Shakespeare, but when he opened it there were only twenty-two pages, beginning:

My dear Mark,
    Of course I remember you so clearly, and I was have thought about you often, wondering what ever had become of you – so your welcome letter came as a marvellous surprise –

Mark felt a guilty twinge at the unrestrained joy that her letter voiced.

I realize that we know so little about each other. You did not even know my name!! Well, it is Marion Littlejohn – silly name, isn't it? I wish I could change it (that's not a hint, silly!) and I was born in Ladyburg (I'm not going to tell you when! A lady never reveals her age!) My father was a farmer, but he sold his farm five years ago, and now he works as a foreman at the sugar mill.

The entire family history, Marion's schooling, the names and estates of all her numerous relatives, Marion's hopes, dreams, aspirations – 'I'd love to travel, wouldn't you? Paris, London' – were laid out in daunting detail, much of it in parentheses and liberally punctuated with exclamation and question marks.

Isn't it strange that our names are so similar – Mark and Marion? It does sound rather grand, doesn't it?

Mark had stirrings now of alarm – it seemed he had called the whirlwind when he had merely whistled for a breeze – and yet there was an infectious gaiety and warmth that came through to him strongly, and he regretted that the girl's features were so hazy in his mind. He realized that he might easily pass her in the street without recognizing her.

He replied that night, taking special care with his penmanship. He could not yet blatantly come to the true purpose of his letters, but hinted vaguely that he was considering writing a book, but that it would require much research in the Ladyburg archives, and that as yet he did not have either the time nor the capital to make the journey, and he concluded by wondering if she did not have a photograph of herself that he might have.

Her reply must have been written and posted the same day as his letter was received.

'My dearest Mark –' He had been promoted from 'Dear Mark'.

There was a photograph accompanying the twenty-five pages of closely written text. It was stiffly posed, a young girl in party clothes with a fixed nervous smile on her face, staring into the camera as though it were the muzzle of a loaded howitzer. The focus was slightly misty, but it was good enough to remind him what she looked like, and Mark felt a huge swell of relief.

She was a little plump, but she had a sweet heart-shaped face with a wide friendly mouth and well-spaced intelligent eyes, an alert and lively look about her; and he knew already that she was educated and reasonably well read – and desperately eager to please.

On the back of the photograph he had received further promotion:

> To darling Mark,
> With much love,
> Marion.

Under her name were three neat crosses. The letter was bursting with un-bounded admiration for his success as a Cadillac salesman, and with awe for his aspirations to be a writer.

She was anxious to be of help in his researches, he had only to let her know what information he needed. She herself had access to all the Governmental and Municipal archives ('and I won't charge you a search fee this time!'), her elder sister worked in the editorial office of the *Ladyburg Lantern*, and there was an excellent library in the Town Hall building where Marion was well known and where she loved to browse – please would he let her help?

One other thing, did he have a photograph of himself, she would love to have a reminder of him.

For half a crown Mark had a photograph taken of himself at a beachfront open-air studio, dressed in his new suit, and with a straw boater canted at a rakish angle over one eye and a dare-devil grin on his face.

> My darling Mark,
> How handsome you are!! I have shown all my friends and they are all quite envious.

She had some of the information he requested, and more would follow.

From Adams Booksellers in Smith Street, Mark purchased a bulky leather-bound notebook, three enormous sheets of cardboard, and a large-scale survey map of Natal and Zululand. These he pinned up on the walls of his room, where he could study them while lying in bed.

On one sheet he laid out the family trees of the Courtneys, the Pyes and the Petersens, all three names associated with the purchase of Andersland on the documents he had seen in Ladyburg Deeds Office.

On one other sheet he built up a pyramid of companies and holdings con-trolled by the Ladyburg Farmers Bank, and on another he pyramided in the same way the companies and properties of General Sean Courtney's holding company, Natal Timber and Estates Ltd.

On the map he carefully shaded in the actual land holdings of the two groups, red for General Courtney and blue for those controlled by his son, Dirk Courtney Esquire.

It gave him new resolution and determination to continue his search when he carefully shaded with blue the long irregular shape of Andersland, with its convoluted boundary that followed the south bank of the river; and when he had done so and wiped the crayon from his fingers, he was left with the bitter lees of anger in his mouth, a reaffirmation of his conviction that the old man would never have let it go – they would have had to kill him first.

The anger was with him again whenever he filled in another section of the map, or when he lay in bed each night, smoking a last cigarette and studying the blue and red patchwork of Courtney holdings. He smiled grimly when he thought what Fergus MacDonald would say about such wealth in the hands of a single father and son, and then he wrote in the leather-bound notebook any new information that he had accumulated during the day.

He would switch out the light then and lie long awake, and often, when at last he slept, he dreamed of Chaka's Gate, of the great cliffs guarding the river and the tumbled wilderness beyond the gates, that concealed a lonely grave. A grave unmarked, overgrown now with the lush restless vegetation of Africa – or, perhaps, long ago dug open by hyena or the other scavengers.

One day, when Mark spent his customary evening's study in the library reading-room, he turned first to the recent issues of the *Ladyburg Lantern*, searching through those editions covering the week following his flight from Ladyburg, and he almost missed the few lines on an inside page.

> Yesterday the funeral service was held of Mr Jacob Henry Rossouw at the Methodist Church in Pine Street. Mr Rossouw fell to his death in the gorge of the Baboon Stroom below the new railway bridge while hunting with a party of his friends.
>
> Mr Roussouw was a bachelor employed by the Zululand Sugar Co. Ltd. The funeral service was attended by the Chairman of the Company, Mr Dirk Courtney, who made a short but moving tribute at the graveside, once again illustrating his deep concern for even the humblest of the employees of his many prosperous enterprises. 'Greatness shows itself in small ways.'

The date coincided neatly with his escape from the valley. The man might have been one of his hunters, perhaps the one who had caught his damaged ankle as he hung from the goods truck. If he was, then the connection with Dirk Courtney was direct. Slowly Mark was twisting a rope together, but he needed a head for the noose.

Yet, in one direction, Mark felt easier. There seemed to exist a deep rift between father and son, between General Sean Courtney and Dirk. None of their companies overlapped, none of their directorships interlocked, and each pyramid of companies stood alone and separated. This separation seemed to extend beyond finance or business, and Mark had found no evidence of any contact between the two men at the social level, in fact active hostility between them was indicated by the sudden change in the *Ladyburg Lantern*'s attitude to the father, once the son took control of its editorial policy.

Yet he was not entirely convinced. Fergus MacDonald had repeatedly warned him of the perfidious cunning of the bosses, of all wealthy men. 'They will go to any lengths to hide their guilt, Mark, no trick is too low or despicable to cover the stains of honest workers' blood on their hands.'

Perhaps Mark's first concern must be to establish beyond doubt that he was hunting only one man. Then, of course, the next move must be to go back to Ladyburg, to try and provoke another attack – but this time he would be ready for it and have some idea from which direction it would come. His mind went back to the way in which he and Fergus MacDonald had used Cuthbert, the dummy, to draw fire and force the enemy to reveal himself, and he grinned ruefully at the thought that this time he must do Cuthbert's job himself. He felt for the first time a fear he had not known in France before a shoot, for he must go out against something more formidable and ruthless than he had ever believed possible before, and the time was fast approaching.

He was distracted then by another massive epistle from Ladyburg, one that gave him honest cause for delaying direct action.

My dearest darling,

What great news I have for you!! If the mountain will not come to Mohammed, then he (or she!) must go to the mountain. My sister and her husband are going to Durban for four days' holiday, and they have asked me to join them. We will arrive on the fourteenth – and will be staying at the Marine Hotel on the Marine Parade – won't we be posh!

Mark surprised himself by the strength of his pleasure and anticipation. He had not realized the affection that he had slowly accumulated at such long remove for this willing and friendly creature. He was surprised again when he met her, both of them dressed with obvious pains and attention to detail, both in an agony of shyness and restraint under the surveillance of Marion's sister.

They sat on the hotel veranda and stiffly sipped tea, making small talk with the sister while surreptitiously examining each other over the rim of their cups.

Marion had lost weight, Mark saw immediately, but would never know that the girl had almost starved herself to do so in anticipation of this moment; and she was pretty – much prettier than he remembered or than her photograph suggested. More important was her transparent wholesomeness and warmth. Mark had been a lonely boy for most of his life, but more particularly so in these last weeks, living in his small dingy room with only the cockroaches and his plans for company.

Now he reacted to her like a traveller coming in out of the snow-storm responds to the tavern fire.

The sister took her duties as chaperone seriously at first, but she was only five or six years older than Mark, and perceptive enough to be aware of the younger people's attraction for each other and to recognize the essential decency of the boy. She was also young enough and herself so recently married as to have sympathy for them.

'I would like to take Marion for a drive – we wouldn't be gone very long.' Marion turned eyes as soulful and pleading as those of a dying gazelle on her sister.

'Oh please, Lyn.'

The Cadillac was a demonstration model, and Mark had personally supervised while two of the Zulu employees at Natal Motors had burnished its paintwork to a dazzle.

He drove down as far as the mouth of the Umgeni River, with Marion sitting close and proud and pretty beside him.

Mark felt as good as he ever had in his life; dressed in fashionable style, with gold in his pocket, a big shining automobile under him and a pretty adoring girl beside him.

Adoring was the only word to describe Marion's attitude towards him. She could hardly drag her eyes from his face for a moment, and she glowed every time he glanced across at her.

She had never imagined herself beside such a handsome, sophisticated beau. Not even her most romantic daydreams had ever included a shining Cadillac, and a decorated war hero.

When he parked off the road and they picked a path through the densely overgrown dunes down to the river mouth, she clung to his arm like a drowning sailor.

The river was in spate from some upland rainstorm; half a mile wide and muddy brown as coffee, it surged and swirled down to meet the green thrust of the sea in a leaping ridge of white water. Carried down on the brown water were the debris of the flood, and the carcasses of drowned beasts.

A dozen big black sharks were there to scavenge, pushing high up the river, their dark triangular fins knifing and circling.

Mark and Marion sat side by side on a dune overlooking the estuary.

'Oh,' sighed Marion, as though her heart would break, 'we've only got four days together.'

'Four days is a long time,' Mark laughed at her, 'I don't know what we are going to do with it all.'

They spent nearly every hour of it together. Dicky Lancome was most understanding with his star salesman. 'Just show your face here for a few minutes every morning, to keep the boss happy, then you can slip off. I'll hold the fort for you.'

'What about the demonstration model?' Mark asked boldly.

'I'll tell him you are making a sale to a rich sugar farmer. Take it, old chap, but for God's sake, don't wrap it round a tree.'

'I don't know how I'll ever repay you, Dicky, really I don't.'

'Don't worry, old boy, we'll think of a way.'

'I won't ask again, it's just that this girl is really special.'

'I understand.' Dicky patted his shoulder in a paternal fashion. 'Most important thing in life – a likely bit of crumpet. My heart goes out to you, old son. I'll be cheering you on in spirit every inch of the way.'

'It's not like that, Dicky,' Mark denied, blushing fiercely.

'Of course not, it never is. But enjoy it anyway,' and Dicky winked lasciviously.

Mark and Marion – she was right, it did sound rather grand – spent their days wandering hand in hand through the city. She was delighted by its bustle and energy, enchanted by its sophistication, by its culture, its museums and tropical gardens, by its playground beachfront with myriad fairy lights, the open-air concerts in the gardens of the old fort, by the big departmental stores in West Street, Stuttafords and Ansteys, their windows packed with expensive imported merchandise, by the docks with great merchant ships lining the wharf and the steam cranes huffing and creaking above them.

They watched the Indian fishermen running their surfboats out from the glistening white beach, through the marching lines of green surf to lay their long nets in a wide semi-circle out into deep water. Then Marion hitched up her skirts and Mark rolled his trousers to the knee to help the half-naked fishermen draw in the long lines, until at last a shimmering silver mound of fish lay on the boat, still quivering and twitching and leaping in the sunlight.

They ate strawberry-flavoured icecream out of crisp yellow cones, and they rode in an open rickshaw down the Marine Parade, drawn by a leaping howling Zulu dressed in an incredible costume of feathers and beads and horns.

One night they joined Dicky Lancome and a languid siren to whom he was paying court, and the four of them ate grilled crayfish and danced to a jazz band at the Oyster Box Hotel at Umhlanga Rocks, and came roaring home in a Cadillac, tiddly and happy and singing, with Dicky driving like Nuvorelli, rocketing the big car over the dusty rutted road, and Mark and Marion cuddling blissfully in the back seat.

In the lobby of the hotel, under the watchful eye of the night clerk who was poised to intercept Mark if he tried for the elevator, they whispered goodnight to each other.

'I have never been so happy in all my life,' she told him simply, and stood on tip-toe to kiss him full on the lips.

Dicky Lancome had disappeared with both Cadillac and lady-friend, probably to some dark and secluded parking place along the sea front, and as Mark walked home alone through the deserted midnight streets, he thought about Marion's words and found himself agreeing. He could not remember being so happy either, but then, he grinned ruefully, it hadn't been a life crowded with wild happiness up to then. To a pauper, a shilling is a fortune.

It was their last day together, and the knowledge weighted their pleasure with poignancy. Mark left the Cadillac at the end of a narrow track in the sugar cane fields and they climbed down to the long white curve of snowy sand beach, guarded at each end by rocky headlands.

The sea was so clear that from the tall dunes they could see deep down to the reefs and sculptured sand banks below the surface. Farther out, the water shaded to a deep indigo blue, that met at last a far horizon piled with a mountainous range of cumulus clouds, purple, blue and silver in the brilliant sunlight.

They walked down barefooted through the crunching sand, carrying the picnic basket that Marion's hotel had prepared for them and a threadbare grey blanket from Mark's bed, and it seemed that they were the only two persons in the world.

They changed into swimming costumes, modestly separating to each side of a dense dark green milk-wood bush, and then they ran laughing into the warm clear water at the edge of the beach.

The thin black cotton of Marion's costume clung wetly to her body, so that it seemed that she were naked, although clothed from mid thigh to neck, and when she pulled the red rubber bathing cap from her head and shook out the thick tresses of her hair, Mark found himself physically roused by her for the first time.

Somehow the pleasure he had taken in her up until then had been that of friendship, and companionship. Her patent adoration had filled some void in his soul, and he had felt protective, almost brotherly towards her.

She sensed instantly, with some feminine instinct, the change in him. The laughter died on her lips, and her eyes went grave and there were shades in them of fear or apprehension – but she turned to face him, lifting her face to him, seeming to steel herself with a conscious act of courage.

They lay side by side on the grey blanket, in the heavy shade of the milk bush, and the midday was heavy and languorous with heat and the murmur of insects.

The wet bathing-suits were cool against their hot skins, and when Mark gently peeled hers away, her skin was damp beneath his fingers, and he was surprised to find her body so different from Helena's. Her skin was clear milky white, tipped with palest pink, lightly sugared with white beach sand, and the hair of her body was fine as silk, light golden brown and soft as smoke. Her body was soft also, with the gentle yielding spring of woman's flesh, unlike the lean hard muscle of Helena's, and it had a different feel to it, a plasticity that intrigued and excited him.

Only when she gasped, and bit her lip and then turned her face and hid it against his neck did Mark realize suddenly, through the mists of his own arousal, that all the skills Helena had taught him were not moving Marion, as they were him. Her body was rigid, and her face pale and tensed.

'Marion, are you all right?'

'It's all right, Mark.'

'You don't like this?'

'It's the first time it's ever happened –'

'We can stop –'

'No.'

'We don't have to –'

'No, Mark, go on. It's what you want.'

'But you don't want it.'

'I want what you want, Mark. Go on. It's for you.'

'No –'

'Go on, Mark, please go on.' And now she looked at him and he saw her expression was pitiful, her eyes swimming with bright tears and her lips quivering.

'Oh, Marion, I'm sorry.' He recoiled from her, horrified by the misery he saw reflected in her expression, but immediately she followed him throwing both arms around his neck, lying half on top of him.

'No, Mark – don't be sorry. I want you to be happy.'

'It won't make me happy – if you don't want to.'

'Oh, Mark, don't say that. Please don't say that – all I want in the world is to make you happy.'

She was brave and enduring, holding him tightly over her, both arms locked around his neck, her body rigid but spread compliantly, and for Mark the ordeal was almost as painful; he suffered for her as he felt the tremble of locked nerves and the small sounds of pain and tension that she tried to keep deep in her throat.

Mercifully for both of them, it was swiftly ended, but still she clung to him.

'Was it good for you, Mark my darling?'

'Oh, yes,' he assured her vehemently. 'It was wonderful.'

'I want so much to be good for you in every way, my darling. Always and in every way, I want to be good for you.'

'It was the best thing in my life,' he told her, and she stared into his eyes for a moment, searching for assurance, and finding it because she wanted it so terribly.

'I'm so glad, darling,' she whispered, and drew his head down on to her damp warm bosom, so soft and pink and comforting. Holding him like that, she began to rock him gently, the way a mother rocks her child. 'I'm so glad, Mark, and it will be better and better. I'll learn, you see if I don't, and I'll try so hard for you, darling, always.'

Driving home slowly in the dusk, she sat proudly next to him on the wide leather seat, and there was a new air about her, an air of confidence and achievement, as though she had grown from child to matron in the space of a few short hours.

Mark felt a rush of deep affection for her. He felt that he wanted to protect her, to keep that goodness and sweetness from souring, to protect her from unhappiness and wanton damage. For a fleeting moment he felt regret that she had not been able to feed that raging madness of his body, and regret also that he had not been able to lead her through the storm to the same peace. Perhaps that would come, perhaps they would find the way together – and if they didn't, well it wasn't that important. The important thing was the sense of duty he felt towards this woman, she had given him everything of which she was capable, and it was his duty now to give back in equal measure – to protect and cherish her.

'Marion, will you marry me?' he asked quietly, and she began to cry softly, nodding her head vehemently through the tears, unable to speak.

Marion's sister, Lynette, was married to a young lawyer from Ladyburg and the four of them sat up late that night discussing the betrothal.

'Pa won't give permission for you to marry before you are twenty-one, you know how Peter and I had to wait.'

Peter Botes, a serious young man, nodded wisely and placed his finger tips together carefully. He had thin sandy hair, and was as pompous as a judge in scarlet.

'It won't do any harm to wait a few years –'

'Years?' wailed Marion.

'You're only nineteen,' Peter reminded her. 'And Mark will need to build up some capital before he takes on the responsibility of a family.'

'I can go on working,' Marion came in hotly.

'They all say that.' Peter waggled his head sagely. 'And then two months later there's a baby on the way.'

'Peter!' His wife rebuked him primly, but he went on calmly.

'And now, Mark, what about your prospects? Marion's father will want to know.'

Mark hadn't expected to present an account of his affairs, and on the spur of the moment he could not be certain if his total worth was forty-two pounds twelve shillings – or seven and sixpence.

He saw them off on the Ladyburg train the next morning, with a long lingering embrace and a promise to write every day, while Marion swore she would work at filling her bottom drawer, and at altering her father's prejudice against early marriage. Walking back from the railway, Mark remembered, for no apparent reason, a spring morning in France coming back out of the line to go into reserve, and his shoulders went back and his step quickened and became springy and elastic once more. He was out of the line, and he had survived – that was as far as he could think at that moment.

Dicky Lancome's polished elastic-sided boots were propped on the desk in front of him and fastidiously crossed at the ankles. He looked up from his newspaper, a tea cup held in the other hand with little finger extended delicately.

'Hail the conquering hero comes, his weary weapon slung over his shoulder.'

'Oh come on, Dicky!'

'– weak at the knees, bloodshot eye and fevered brow –'

'Any calls?' Mark asked seriously.

'Ah, the giant mind now turns to the more mundane aspects of life.'

'Play the game, Dicky.' Mark riffled quickly through a small pile of messages that awaited him.

'A surfeit of love, a plethora of passion, an overdose of crumpet, a genital hangover.'

'What's this? I can't read your scrawl.' Mark averted his eyes, concentrating on his reading.

'Mark my words, Mark, that young lady has got the brood lust. If you turn your back on her for ten minutes, she will be up the nearest tree building a nest.'

'Cut it out, Dicky.'

'That's precisely what you should do, old boy, unless you can face the prospect of her dropping your whelps all over the scenery.' Dicky shuddered theatrically. 'Never ride in a saloon if you can drive a sports model, old chap, which reminds me,' he dropped the newspaper, checked the watch from his waistcoat pocket, 'I have this important client.' He inspected his glossy boots a moment, flicked them lightly with the handkerchief from his breast pocket, stood up and adjusted the straw-basher on his head and winked at Mark. 'Her husband's gone up country for a week. Hold the fort, old boy, it's my turn now.'

He disappeared through the office door into the showroom, and then re-appeared instantly, an expression of horror on his face. 'Oh God, customers! Get after them, Mark my boy, I'm taking the back door,' and he was gone, leaving only the faint perfume of brilliantine on the air.

Mark checked his tie in the sliver of broken mirror wedged in the frame of the window, and adjusted his welcoming smile as he hurried to the door – but at the threshold he stopped with the stillness and concentration of a wild gazelle, listening with every fibre and every quivering nerve end to a sound of such aching and penetrating beauty that it seemed to freeze his heart. It lasted only a few seconds, but the sound of it shimmered and thrilled in the air for long seconds afterwards, and only then did Mark's heart beat again, surging heavily against his rib cage.

The sound was the laughter of a girl. It was as though the air around Mark had thickened to honey, for it dragged heavily at his legs as he started forward, and it required a physical effort to draw it down into his lungs.

From the doorway he looked into the showroom. In the centre of the wide floor stood the latest demonstration model Cadillac, and beside it stood a couple.

The man had his back to Mark, and left only the impression of massize size, a towering figure dressed in dark cloth. Beside him, the girl was dainty, almost ethereal, she seemed to float, light and lovely as a humming-bird on invisible wings.

The earth tilted beneath Mark's feet as he gazed at her.

Her head was thrown back to look up at the man. Her throat was long and smooth, balancing the small head with its huge dark eyes and the laughing mouth, small white regular teeth beyond pink lips, a fine bold brow, pale and wide above those haunting eyes – and all of it crowned by a heart-stopping tumble of thick lustrous hair, hair so black that its waves and falls seemed to be sculptured from freshly oiled ebony.

She laughed again, a lovely joyous ripple of sound, and she reached up to touch the man's face. Her hand was narrow, with long tapered fingers, strong capable-looking hands – so that Mark realized that his first impression had been wrong.

The girl was small only in comparison to the man, and her poise heightened the illusion. However, Mark saw now that she was tall, but graceful as a papyrus stem in the wind, supple and slim, with tiny waist and long legs beneath the light floating material of her skirt.

With her fingertips, she traced the jawline of the man; tilting her head on its long swanlike neck, her beauty was almost unbearable, as her huge eyes shone now with love, and the line of the lips was soft with love.

'Oh Daddy, you are an old-fashioned, grumpy old bear.' She spun away from him, lightly as a ballerina, and struck an exaggerated pose beside the huge glistening machine, putting on a comic French accent. '*Regarde! Mon cher papa, c'est très chic –*'

The man growled. 'I don't trust these fancy new machines. Give me a Rolls.'

'Rolls?' cried the girl, pouting dramatically, 'they're so staid! So biblical! Darling Daddy, this is the twentieth century, remember?' Then she drooped like a dying rose in a vase. 'How could I hold my head up among my friends if you force me to ride in one of those great sombre coffins?'

At that instant she noticed Mark standing in the doorway of the sales office, and her entire mien changed, the carriage of head and body, the expression of mouth and eye flowing instantly from clown to lady.

'Pater,' she said softly, the voice cultivated and the eye cool as it flicked over Mark, a steady encompassing sweep from his head to his feet. 'I think the sales person is here.' She turned away, and Mark felt his heart convulse again at the way her hip swung and pushed beneath the skirt – and he saw for the first time the cheeky, challenging roll of her small rounded backside as she walked slowly around the Cadillac, calm and aloof, not glancing in his direction again.

Mark stared at her, with fascination, all his emotions in upheaval. He had never seen anything so beautiful, so completely captivating in all his life.

The man had turned and was glaring at him angrily. He seemed, as the girl had teased him, to be biblical. A gaunt and towering figure with shoulders wide as the gallows tree and the big fierce head exaggerated in size by the slightly twisted hooked nose and the dark thick bush of beard, shot through with grey.

'I know you, dammit!' he growled. The face had been burned almost black by twenty thousand suns, but there were deep white creases in the corners of his eyes and the skin in a line below the thick curls of his silvering hair was white also, protected by the band of a hunter's hat – or a uniform cap.

Mark roused himself, tearing his eyes off the girl, for the fresh shock of recognition. At the time he could only believe it was some monstrous coincidence – but in the years that followed he would know differently. The threads of their lives were plaited, and intertwined. But in this instant the shock, coming so close on the other, unsettled him and his voice croaked.

'Yes, General Courtney, I am –'

'Don't tell me, goddammit,' the General cut in, his voice like the crack of a Mauser shooting from cover, and Mark felt his spirit quail before the expression on his face; it was the most formidable he had ever confronted.

'I know – the name is right there!' he glowered at Mark. 'I never forget a face.' The tremendous force and presence of the man threatened to swamp him.

'It's a sign of old age, Pater,' said the girl coolly, glancing over her shoulder without smile or expression.

'Don't you say that, girl,' the man rumbled like an active volcano. 'Don't you dare say that.' He took a threatening step towards Mark, the dark brow corrugated and the blue eyes cutting into his soul like a surgeon's knives. 'It's the eyes! Those eyes.'

Mark retreated a hurried step before the limping, mountainous advance, not quite sure what to expect, but ready to believe that Sean Courtney might at any moment lunge at him with the heavy ebony cane he carried, so murderous seemed his anger.

'General –'

'Yes!' Sean Courtney snapped his fingers with a crack like a breaking oak branch, and the scowl smoothed away, the blue eyes crinkling into a smile of such charisma, of such infectious and conspiratorial glee, that Mark had to smile back at him.

'Anders,' he said. 'Anders and MacDonald. Martin? Michael? No. Mark Anders!' And he clenched his fist and struck his own thigh. 'Old, is it? Girl – who said old?'

'Pater, you are a marvel.' She rolled her eyes, but Sean Courtney was advancing on Mark, seizing his hand in a grip that made the bones creak until he recovered himself and squeezed back, matching the big man's grip.

'It was the eyes,' laughed Sean. 'You've changed so much from that day, that night –' and the laughter dried, as he remembered the boy in the stretcher, pale and moribund, smeared with mud and thick drying blood, and heard again his own voice, 'He's dead!' He drove back the image.

'How are you now, my boy?'

'I'm fine, sir.'

'I didn't think you were going to pull through.' Sean peered closely at him. 'I'll grant you seem to have made it with all colours flying. How many did you collect, and where?'

'Two, sir, high in the back.'

'Honourable scars, my boy, we'll compare notes one day.' And then he scowled again, horrendously. 'You got the gong, didn't you?'

'Yes, sir.'

'Good, you never know in this man's army. I wrote the citation that night, but you never know. What did they give you?' Sean smiled his relief.

'The MM, sir. I got it at the hospital in England.'

'Excellent. That's good!' he nodded, and he let go of Mark's hand, turning to the girl again.

'Darling, this gentleman was with me in France.'

'How nice.' She touched the design on the radiator of the car with one finger, as she drifted past it, not glancing back at them. 'Do you think we might have a drive now, Pater?'

Mark hurried to the back door to hold it open. 'I'll drive,' she said, and waited for him to jump to the driver's door.

'The starter button is here –' he explained.

'Thank you, I know. Sit in the back, please.'

She drove like a man, very fast but skilfully, picking a tight line into the corners and using the gearbox to brake, double declutching with dancing feet on the pedals, and hitting the shift with a quick sure hand.

Beside her the General sat with the set to his shoulders of a younger man.

'You drive too fast,' he growled, the ferocious tone given the complete lie by the fond smile he turned on her.

'And you're an old fusspot, Daddy,' she laughed again; the thrill of it sang in Mark's ears as she hurled the big powerful machine into the next bend.

'I didn't beat you enough when you were young.'

'Well, it's too late now.' She touched his cheek with her free hand.

'Don't bank on that, young lady – don't ever take bets on that.'

Shaking his head in mock despair, but with the adoration still glowing in his eyes, the General heaved himself around in the seat and subjected Mark to another dark penetrating scrutiny.

'You don't turn out at the weekly parades.'

'No, sir.'

'It's an hour on Friday evenings – half an hour square-bashing and then a lecture.'

'Yes, sir?'

'Good fun, really. Tremendous spirit, even though we have combined with the other peace-time regiments now.'

'Yes, sir.'

'I'm the Colonel-in-Chief,' Sean chuckled. 'They couldn't get rid of me that easily.'

'No, sir.'

'We have a monthly shoot – good prizes, and a barbecue afterwards.'

'Is that so, sir?'

'We are sending a team to shoot for the Africa Cup this year, all expenses paid. Marvellous opportunity for the lucky lads who get chosen.'

'I'm sure, General.'

Sean waited for more, but Mark was silent. He could not meet the big man's fierce, unrelenting gaze, and he shifted his eyes – catching as he did so the girl's face reflected in the rear-view mirror.

She was watching him intently, with an unfathomable expression – contempt perhaps, dry amusement, maybe, or something else – something much more intriguing or dangerous. For the split part of an instant, their eyes met, and then her head turned away on the tall graceful column of her neck. The dark shining hair was brushed away from the nape, and there at the juncture with pale skin, the hair was fine and silky, a tiny whorl of it like a question mark at the back of her small sculptured ear.

Mark had an almost insane desire to lean forward and press his lips to it. The thought struck like a physical blow in his groin, and he felt the nerves along his spine racked out cruelly. He realized suddenly then, with a shock that made his senses tilt again, that he was in love with her.

'I want to win that cup,' said the General softly, watching him. 'The regiment has never won it before.'

'I've rather had enough of uniform and war, General.' Mark forced his eyes back to meet the General's. 'But I do wish you good luck.'

The chauffeur held the rear door of the Rolls Silver Wraith open, and Sean Courtney lowered himself into the seat beside his daughter. He lifted his right hand in a brief, almost military, salute at the young man on the pavement and the car pulled smoothly away.

The instant they were alone, his daughter let out a girlish squeal of delight and threw both arms around his neck, ruffling his beard and his heart with her kisses.

'Oh, Daddy, darling, you spoil me!'

'Yes, I do – don't I?'

'Irene will turn bright green and curl up like an anchovy. I love you, my kind and beautiful Daddy. Her father has never bought her a Cadillac!'

'I like that lad, he's one of the bright ones.'

'The sales person? I hadn't really noticed.' She released her grip and sat back in the seat.

'He's got heart.' He was silent a moment then, remembering the snow falling silently across a shell-ravaged hill in France. 'He's got the guts and brightness for better things than selling motor cars.' Then he grinned mischievously, looking young enough to be her brother. 'And I'd love to see Hamilton's face when we take the Africa Cup away from him.'

Beside him Storm Courtney was silent, her hand still in the crook of her father's arm while she wondered what had disturbed her about Mark Anders. She decided it was his eyes – those serene yellow eyes, calm but watchful, floating like golden moons.

Involuntarily, Mark braked the big car almost to a standstill before the white gates. They were tall twin columns, plastered and white-washed with the Zulu name in raised letters on each: EMOYENI – it was a lovely haunting name, the place of the wind, and on the crest of the hills above Durban town, it would indeed receive the cool blessing of the sea breezes during the sweltering summer months. The swinging portion of the gate was two racks of heavy cast-iron spears, but they stood open now, and Mark crossed the iron grid which would prevent hooved animals entering or escaping and started up the gentle curve of the driveway, butter yellow flint pebbles carefully raked and freshly watered, set on each side with deep beds of cannas which were now in full bloom. They had been arranged in banks of solid colour, scarlet and yellow and white, dazzling in the bright sunshine, and beyond them were lush lawns of deep tropical green, mown carpet-smooth but studded with clumps of indigenous trees which had obviously been spared for their size or beauty or unusual shape. They were festooned with garlands of lianas, the ubiquitous monkey rope plants of Natal, and even as Mark watched, a small blue-grey vervet monkey dropped lithely down one of the living ropes, and, with its back arched like a cat and its long tail held high in mock alarm, bounded across an open stretch of lawn until it reached the next clump of trees where it shot to the highest branches and chattered insolently at the slowly passing car.

Mark knew from his investigation that this was merely the Courtney town house, the main family home was at Ladyburg, and he had not expected anything like this splendour. And yet why not, he grinned wryly, the man had everything in the world, this was a mere pied-à-terre. He twisted his head to look back. The gates were out of sight behind him now, and there was still no sign of the house ahead. He was surrounded by a fantasy landscape, half wild and yet lovingly groomed and tended, and now he saw the reason for the animal grid at the main gates.

Small herds of semi-domesticated game cropped at the short grass of the lawn or stood and watched the passing car with mild curiosity. He saw graceful golden brown impala with snowy bellies and spindly back-curved horns, a dainty blue duiker as big as a fox terrier with pricked-up ears and bright button eyes; an eland bull with hanging dewlap, thick twisted horns arming the short heavy head, and a barrel body heavy as a pedigree Afrikander bull.

He crossed a low bridge over the narrow neck of an artificial lake. The blue water lotus blooms stood high above their huge round green leaves that floated flat on the surface. Their perfume was light and sweet and nostalgic on the bright warm air, and the dark torpedo shapes of bass hung suspended in the clear water below the sheltering lotus leaves.

On the edge of the lake, a black and white spur-winged goose spread its wings, as wide as the reach of a man's arms, and pressed forward with snake-like neck and pink wattled head, threatening flight at the intrusion; then, thinking better of such effort, it furled the great wings again and waggled its tail, satisfied with a single harsh honk of protest as the Cadillac passed.

The roof of the house showed through the trees ahead now, and it was tiled in candy pink, towered and turreted and ridged, like a Spanish palace. The last curve of the driveway brought Mark out into full view of the building. Before it lay an open expanse of blazing flowerbeds. The colour was so vibrant and so concentrated that it daunted the eye, and was relieved only by the tall soft ostrich feathers of spray that poured high into the air from the fountains set in the centre of four round ponds, parapeted in stone. The breeze blew soft wisps of spray like smoke across the flowerbeds, wetting the blooms and enhancing the already dazzling colour.

The house was two stories high, with random towers breaking the solid silhouette and columns, twisted like candy sticks, ornamenting the entrance and supporting the window lintels; it was painted white, and it shone in the sunlight like a block of ice.

It should have given the impression of solid size and ostentatious display, but the design was so cunning that it seemed light as a French pastry – a gay and happy house, built in a spirit of fun and probably of love. A rich man's gift to a lovely woman, for the feminine touch was everywhere evident, and the great masses of flowers, the fountains and peacocks and marble statues seemed right, the only setting for such a structure.

Slowly, awed and enchanted, Mark let the Cadillac roll down the last curve of the driveway, and the light faint cries of female voices caught his attention.

The tennis courts stood at the end of the lawns, and there were women at play, their white dresses sparkling in the sun, their limbs flashing as they ran and swerved and struck at the ball. Their voices and laughter were sweet and melodious in the warm hush of the tropical mid-morning.

Mark left the car, and started across the lawn towards the courts. There were other female figures, also white-clad, that lolled in deck-chairs in the shade of the banyan trees, watching the play and conversing languidly as they sipped at long frosted glasses, waiting their turn on the courts.

None of them noticed Mark until he was on the edge of their group.

'Oh, I say, girls.' One of them turned quickly in her chair, and appraised Mark with eyes suddenly no longer bored, but clear blue and acquisitive. 'A man! We *are* in luck.'

Instantly the other three changed, each reacting differently: one exaggerating her indifferent and indolent loll in the low chair, another tugging at her skirt with one hand and pushing at her hair with the other, smiling brightly and sucking in her tummy.

They were all young and sleek as cats, glossy with youth and health and that elusive but unmistakable aura of wealth and breeding.

'And what is your pleasure, sir?' asked the one with blue eyes. She was the prettiest of the four, with fine pale golden hair in a halo around the small neat head and good white teeth as she smiled.

Mark felt discomforted under their stares, especially when the speaker turned further in her chair, slowly uncrossed and crossed her legs, managing to give Mark a flash of white silk panties under the short skirt.

'I am looking for Miss Storm Courtney.'

'God,' said the smiler. 'They all want Storm – why don't any of them ever want me?'

'Storm!' The blonde called out to the court.

Storm Courtney was about to serve, but the call distracted her and she glanced across. She saw Mark and her expression did not change, her attention switched back to the game. She threw the ball high and swung overhand at it, the stroke was fluid and controlled. The racket twanged sharply, and the movement threw her white cotton skirt high against the back of her thighs. Her legs were beautifully moulded, slim ankles and gently swelling calves, knees marked only by symmetrical dimples.

She spun lightly and caught the return of the ball, a long lightly tanned arm flashing in a full sweep and the ball leapt from the racket in a white blur; again her skirt kicked up and Mark shifted slightly on his feet, for the earth had tilted again.

She ran back to the baseline, short neat steps on those long narrow feet, head thrown back to follow the high parabola of the lobbing ball against the blue of the sky. Her dark hair seemed to glow with the metallic sheen of the sunbird's wing as she judged her stroke, and then her whole body went into it, power uncoiling along those long beautiful legs, driven up from tensed and rounded buttocks under the light cotton skirt, through the narrow waist, along young hard back muscles and exploding down through the swinging right arm.

The ball hummed like an arrow, flashed low across the net and kicked a white puff of dust from the baseline.

'Too good!' wailed her opponent despairingly, and Storm laughed, gay and triumphant, and came back to the high fence to pick up the spare balls from the gutter.

'Oh Storm, there's a gentleman here to see you.' The blonde called again, and Storm flipped up a ball with the tip of her racket and the side of her foot bouncing it once on the turf of the court and then catching it in her free hand.

'Yes, Irene,' she answered lightly. 'I know. He's only a sales person. Ask him to wait by the car until I'm ready to deal with him.'

She had not looked at Mark again, and now she turned away. 'Forty – love,' she called gaily, and ran back to the baseline. Her voice had a music and lilt that did nothing to sweeten the sudden flare of anger which made Mark's jaw set grimly.

'If you are a sales person,' Irene murmured, 'then you can sell me something some time. But right now, darling, I suggest you do what Storm says – otherwise we will all know about it.'

When Storm came to where he waited, she was flanked by the other girls, like maids in waiting attending a princess, he thought, and he felt his resentment fade as he watched her. You could forgive somebody like that, somebody so royal and lovely and heart-achingly beautiful – you could forgive them anything.

He stood attentive, waiting for her, and he realized then how tall she was. The top of that glossy head reached to his chin, almost.

'Good morning, Miss Courtney. I have brought your new Cadillac, and all of us at Natal Motors wish you much joy and enjoyment.' It was a little speech he always used when making a delivery, and he spoke it with all the warmth and charm and sincerity which had made him in so few months the star salesman of Natal Motors.

'Where are the keys?' Storm Courtney asked, and for the first time looked at him directly. Mark realized that her eyes were that dark, almost black, blue like the General's. There was no question who her father was.

She opened them a little wider, and in the sunlight they were the colour of polished sapphires or the blue of the Mozambique current, out in the deep water at noon.

'They are in the car,' he answered, and his voice sounded strange in his own ears, as though it came from a distance.

'Get them,' she said, and he felt himself start to move, to hurry to her bidding. Then something like that sense of danger he had known and developed in France warned him. Her expression was neutral, completely unconcerned, as though she found the effort of talking directly to him was wasted, just one of these tiresome moments in an otherwise important march of events. Yet the warning was clear as the chime of a bell in his head, and only then he saw something else move in her eyes, something dangerous and exciting like the shape of a leopard hunting in the shadows. A challenge, perhaps, a dare – and suddenly he knew clearly that no daughter of Sean Courtney would be reared to such natural arrogance and rudeness. There was a reason, some design in her attitude.

He felt a lightness of mind, that kind of special madness which had driven away fear of consequence so often in moments of peril or desperate enterprise, and he grinned at her. He did not have to force the grin, it was natural and devilish and challenging.

'Certainly, Miss Courtney. Of course I'll get them, just as soon as you say please.'

There was an audible communal gasp from the girls around her, and they stilled with awed delight, their eyes darting to Storm's face and then back to Mark's.

'Say please to the nice man, Stormy.' Irene used the patronizing voice for instructing young children, and there was a delighted burst of giggles from the others.

For one unholy instant something burned in the girl's dark blue eyes, something fierce that was not anger. Mark recognized the importance of that flash; although he did not truly know the exact emotion it betrayed, yet he knew it might affect him. Then it was gone and in its place was true unfeigned anger.

'How dare you!' Storm's voice was low and quivering, but her lips were suddenly frosty white as the blood drained away. The anger was too swift, too strong for the occasion, out of all proportion to the mild exchange, and Mark felt a reckless excitement that he had been able to reach her so deeply. He kept the grin mocking and taunting.

'Hit him, darling,' Irene teased, and for a moment Mark thought she really might.

'You keep your silly mouth shut, Irene Leuchars.'

'Oh la la!' Irene gloated. 'Temper!'

Mark turned casually away, and opened the driver's door of the Cadillac.

'Where are you going!'

'Back to town.' He started the engine, and looked out of the window at her. There was no doubt now that she was the most beautiful creature he had ever seen. Anger had rouged her cheeks, and the fine dark hair at her temples was still damp from her play on the courts. It was plastered against the smooth skin in tiny curls.

'That is my car!'

'They'll send somebody else up with it, Miss Courtney, I'm used to dealing with ladies.'

Again the wondering gasp and burst of giggles.

'Oh, he's a darling!' Irene clapped her hands in applause, but Storm ignored her.

'My father will have you fired.'

'Yes, he probably will,' he agreed. Mark thought about that solemnly for a moment, then he nodded and he let out the clutch. He looked back in the mirror as he took the first bend in the driveway and they were still standing in a group staring after him in their white dresses, like a group of marble statues. 'Nymphs Startled by Satyr' was a fitting title, he thought, and laughed with the reckless mood still on him.

'Jesus,' Dicky Lancome whispered, clutching his brow with horror. 'What made you do it?' He shook his head slowly, wonderingly.

'She was damned rude.'

Dicky dropped his hands and stared at him aghast. '*She* was rude to *you*. Oh my God, I don't think I can stand much more. Don't you realize that if she was rude to you, you should be grateful? Don't you know that there are thousands of peasants like us who go through their entire lives without being insulted by Miss Storm Courtney?'

'I was not going to take that,' Mark explained reasonably, but Dicky cut in.

'Look, old bean, I've taught you all I know, and you still know nothing. Not only do you take it, but if Miss Courtney expresses a desire to kick your fat stupid arse, the correct reply is "Certainly, ma'am, but first let me don fresh bags lest I soil your pretty foot!"'

Mark laughed, the reckless mood still there but fading, and Dicky's expression became more lugubrious.

'That's right, have yourself a good laugh. Do you know what happened?' and before Mark could answer he went on, 'A summons from on high, the ultimate, the Chairman of the Board himself. So the boss and I dash across town – fear, trepidation, cautious optimism – are we to be fired, promoted, congratulated on the month's sales figures? And there is the Board, the full Board mind you, looking like a convention of undertakers who have just been informed of the discovery of Pasteur's vaccine –'

Dicky stopped, the memory was too painful, and he sighed heavily. 'You didn't really tell her to say "please", did you?'

Mark nodded.

'You didn't really tell her she was not a lady?'

'Not directly,' Mark protested. 'But I did imply it.'

Dicky Lancome tried to wipe his face off with one hand, starting at the hairline and drawing the palm of his hand down slowly to his chin.

'I've got to fire you, you know that, don't you?'

Mark nodded again.

'Look,' said Dicky. 'I tried, Mark, I really did. I showed them your sales figures, I told them you were young, impulsive – I made a speech.'

'Thank you, Dicky.'

'At the end of the speech, they almost fired me also.'

'You shouldn't have stuck your neck out for me.'

'Anyone else – you could have picked on anyone else, old chap, you could have punched the mayor, sent abusive letters to the king, but why in the name of all holy things did you have to pick on a Courtney?'

'You know something, Dicky?' and it was Dicky's turn silently to shake his head.

'I loved it – I loved every moment of it.'

Dicky groaned aloud, as he took out his silver cigarette case and offered it to Mark. They lit their cigarettes, and smoked in silence for a few moments.

'So I am fired, then?' Mark asked at last.

'That's what I have been trying to tell you for the last ten minutes,' Dicky agreed.

Mark began to clear out the drawers in his desk, then stopped and asked impulsively, 'Did the General – did General Courtney make the demand for my head?'

'I have no idea, old chap – but sure as hell it was made.'

Mark wanted to believe that it had not been the General. It was too mean a gesture from such a big man. He could imagine the General bursting into the showroom, brandishing a horsewhip.

The man who could take such revenge for a small flash of spirit might be capable of other things – like killing an old man for his land.

The thought sickened Mark, and he tried to thrust it aside.

'Well, then, I suppose I'd better be getting along.'

'I'm sorry, old bean.' Dicky stood up and offered his hand, then looked embarrassed. 'You all right for the filthy lucre? I could let you have a tenner to tide you over.'

'Thanks, Dicky, but I'll be all right.'

'Look,' Dicky blurted out impulsively. 'Give it a month or so, time for the dust to settle, and then if you haven't got yourself fixed, come and see me. I'll try and sneak you in again through the back door – even if we have to write you up on the paysheet under an assumed name.'

'Goodbye, Dick, and thanks for everything. I really mean that.'

'I'm going to miss you, old chap. Keep your head down below the parapet in future, won't you?'

The pawn shop was in Soldiers Way, almost directly opposite the railway station. The front room was small and overcrowded with a vast array of valuables, semi-valuables and rubbish left here by the needy over the years.

There was a melancholy about the racks of yellowing wedding dresses, in the dusty glass cases of old wedding rings, engraved watches, cigarette cases and silver drinking flasks – all given in love or respect, each with its own sad story.

'Two pounds,' said the pawnbroker, after a single glance at the suit.

'It's only three months old,' Mark said softly. 'And I paid fifteen.'

The man shrugged and the steel-framed spectacles slid down his nose.

'Two pounds,' he repeated, and pushed the spectacles up with a thumb that looked grey and dusty as his stock.

'All right – and what about this?'

He opened the small blue case, and showed the bronze disc nestled in a nest of silk, pinned by its gay little ribbon of white and red and blue. The Military Medal for gallantry displayed by non-commissioned officers and other ranks.

'We get a lot of those – not much call for them.' The man pursed thin lips. 'Twelve pounds ten,' he said.

'How long do you keep them before you sell them?' Mark asked, suddenly reluctant to part with the scrap of metal and silk.

'We keep 'em a year.'

The last ten days of constant search for employment had depleted Mark's resources of cash and courage.

'All right,' he agreed.

The pawnbroker wrote the ticket, while Mark wandered into the back reaches of the shop. He found a bundle of old military haversacks and selected one; then there was a rack of rifles, most of them ancient Martinis and Mausers, veterans of the Boer war – but there was one among them that stood out. The woodwork was hardly marked, and the metal shone smooth and oily, no scratches or pitting of rust, and Mark picked the weapon off the rack and the shape and feel of it brought memories crowding back. He thrust them aside. He would need a rifle where he was going, and it was sensible to have one he knew so well. Fate had put a P.14 there for him, and damn the memories, he decided.

He slipped the bolt from the breech and held the barrel to the light from the doorway, peering into the mouth of the breech. The bore of the barrel was unmarked, the rifling described its clean glistening spirals, again without fouling or pitting. Somebody had cared well for the weapon.

'How much?' he asked the pawnbroker, and the man's eyes turned to lifeless pebbles behind his steel-rimmed spectacles.

'That's a very good rifle,' he said, 'and I paid a lot of money for it. There's a hundred rounds of ammunition goes with it also.'

Mark found he had gone soft in the city, his feet ached within the first five miles and the straps of rifle and haversack cut painfully into his shoulders.

The first night he lay down beside the fire and slept as though he had been clubbed. In the morning he groaned at the effort of sitting upright, the stiffness was in his legs and back and shoulders.

The first mile he hobbled like an old man, until his muscles began to ease, and he was going well by the time he reached the rim of the escarpment and started down into the coastal lowlands.

He kept well away from Andersland, crossing the river five miles upstream. His clothing and rifle and pack were balanced on his head as he waded through a shallow place between white sandbanks, and he dried naked in the sun, sprawled out like a lizard on a rock, before he dressed again and headed north.

The third day, he settled into the long swinging hunter's stride, and the pack rode lightly on his back. The going was hard, the undulating folds of the ground forced him to climb and then descend, taxing every muscle, while the thick thorn scrub made him weave constantly to find a way through, wasting time and almost doubling the distance between point and point. Added to this, the grass was dried and seeding. The seeds were sharp as spears and worked easily through his woollen socks into his flesh. He had to stop every half hour or so to dig them out – but still he made thirty miles that day. In the gathering dusk he crossed another of the countless ridges of higher ground. The distant blue loom of Chaka's Gate almost blended with darkening clouds of evening.

He camped there that night, sweeping a bed on the bare ground below an acacia thorn tree and eating bully beef and maize porridge by the light of the fire of acacia wood that burned with its characteristic bright white flame and the smell of incense.

General Sean Courtney stood at the heavy teak sideboard, with its tiers of engraved glass mirrors and displays of silver plate. In one hand he held the ivory-handled carving fork and in the other the long Sheffield knife.

He used the knife to illustrate the point he was making to the guest-of-honour at his table.

'I read it through in a single day, had to stay up until after midnight. Believe me, Jan, it's his best work yet. The amount of research – quite extraordinary.'

'I look forward to reading it,' said the Prime Minister, nodding acknowledgement to the author of the work under discussion.

'It's still in manuscript. I am not entirely satisfied yet, there is still some tidying up to do.'

Sean turned back to the roast and, with a single practised stroke of the blade for each, cut five thin slices of pink beef rimmed with a rind of rich yellow fat.

With the fork he lifted the meat on to the Rosenthal porcelain plate and immediately a Zulu servant in a flowing white kanza robe and red pillbox fez carried the plate to Sean's place at the head of the long table.

Sean laid the carving-knife aside, wiped his hands on a linen cloth, and then followed the servant to the table and took his seat.

'We were wondering if you might write a short foreword for the book,' Sean said, as he raised a cut crystal glass of glowing red wine to the Prime Minister, and Jan Christiaan Smuts inclined his head on narrow shoulders in an almost birdlike gesture. He was a small man, and the hands laid before him on the table were almost fragile; he had the mien of a philosopher, or a scholar, which was not dispelled by the neat pointed beard.

Yet it was hard to believe that he was small. There was a vital force and awesome presence about him that belied the high, rather thin voice in which he replied,

'Few things would give me as much pleasure. You do me honour.'

He seemed to bulk huge in his chair, such was the power of character he commanded.

'I am the one who is honoured,' Colonel Garrick Courtney replied gravely from across the table, bowing slightly – and Sean watched his brother fondly.

'Poor Garry,' he thought, and then felt a guilty stab. Yet it seemed so natural to think of him in those terms. He was frail and old now, bowed and grey and dried out, so that he seemed smaller even than the little man opposite him.

'Have you a title yet?' asked Jan Smuts.

'I have thought to call it *The Young Eagles*. I hope you do not find that too melodramatic for a history of the Royal Flying Corps.'

'By no means,' Smuts contradicted him. 'I think it excellent.'

'Poor Garry,' Sean thought again. Since Michael had been shot down, the book filled the terrible gap that his son's death had left; but it had not prevented him from growing old. The book was a memorial to Michael, of course, an act of great love – 'This book is dedicated to Captain Michael Courtney DFC, one of the Young Eagles who will fly no more.' Sean felt the resuscitation of his own grief, and he made a visible effort to suppress it.

His wife saw the effort, and caught his eye down the length of the table. How well she knew him after all these years, how perfectly she could read his emotions, she thought, as she smiled her sympathy for him, and saw him respond, the wide shoulders squaring up and heavy bearded jaws firming as he smiled back at her.

Deftly she changed the mood. 'General Smuts has promised to walk around the gardens with me this afternoon, Garry, and advise me on planting out the proteas he brought me from Table Mountain. You are also such a knowledgeable botanist. Will you join us?'

'As I warned you, my dear Ruth,' said Jan Smuts in that ready, yet compelling voice, 'I do not give much hope for their survival.'

'Perhaps the Leucadendrons,' ventured Garry, 'if we find a cool, dryish place?'

'Yes,' agreed the General, and immediately they fell into an animated discussion. She had done it so skilfully, that she seemed to have done nothing.

Sean paused in the doorway of his study and ran a long lingering gaze over the room. As always, he felt a glow of pleasure at re-entering this sanctuary.

The glass doors opened now on to the massed banks of flowers, and the smoking plumes of the fountain, yet the thick walls ensured that the room remained cool even in the sleepy hush of midday.

He crossed to the desk of stinkwood – dark and massive and polished, so that it shone even in the cool gloom – and he lowered himself into the swivel chair, feeling the fine leather stretch and give under his weight.

The day's mail was neatly arranged on a silver salver at his right hand, and he sighed when he saw that, despite the careful screening by the senior clerk down at the city Head Office, there were still not much less than a hundred envelopes awaiting him.

He delayed the moment by swinging the chair slowly to look once again about the room. It was hard to believe it had been designed and decorated by a woman – unless it was a woman who loved and understood her man so well that she could anticipate his lightest whim and fancy.

Most of the books were bound in dark green leather, and stamped on their spine in gold leaf with Sean's crest. The exceptions were the three ceiling-high shelves of first editions with African themes. A dealer in London, and another in Amsterdam had *carte blanche* instructions from Sean to search for these treasures. There were autographed first editions by Stanley, Livingstone, Cornwallis Harris, Burchell, Munro and almost every other African explorer or hunter who had ever published.

The dark panelled woodwork between the book shelves was studded with the paintings of the early African artists; the Baines glowed like rich gems in their flamboyant colours and naïve, almost childlike, depiction of animal and countryside. One of these was set in an intricately carved frame of Rhodesian redwood and engraved, 'To my friend David Livingstone, from Thomas Baines.'

These links with history and the past always warmed Sean with pleasure, and he fell into a mild reverie.

The deep carpeting deadened her footsteps, but there was the light perfume on the air that warned Sean of her presence, and he swung his chair back to the desk. She stood beside his chair, slim and straight as a girl still.

'I thought you were walking with Garry and Jan.'

Ruth smiled then, and seemed as young and beautiful as when he had first met her so many years before. The cool gloom of the room disguised the little lines at the corners of her eyes and the light streaking of silver in the dark hair drawn back from her temples and caught with a ribbon at the back of her neck.

'They are waiting for me, but I slipped away for a moment to make certain that you had all you wanted.' She smiled down at him, and then selected a cigar from the silver humidor and began to prepare it.

'I will need an hour or two,' he said, glancing at the pile of mail.

'What you really need, Sean, is an assistant.' She cut the cigar carefully, and he grunted.

'You can't trust any of these young people –' and she laughed lightly as she placed the cigar between his lips.

'You sound as old as the prophets.' She struck a Vesta and waved it to clear the sulphur before she held it to the tip of the cigar. 'It's a sign of old age to mistrust the young.'

'With you beside me, I'll be young for ever,' he told her, still awkward with a compliment after all these years and she felt her heart swell with her love, knowing the effort it had required.

She stooped quickly and kissed his cheek, and with a speed and strength that still astonished her, one of his thickly muscled arms whipped around her waist and she was lifted into his lap.

'You know what happens to forward young ladies – don't you?' He grinned at her, his eyes crinkling wickedly.

'Sean,' she protested, in mock horror. 'The servants! Our guests!' She struggled out of his embrace with the warmth and wetness of his kiss still on her lips, together with the tickle of his whiskers and the taste of his cigar, and rearranged her skirts and her hair.

'I'm a fool.' She shook her head sorrowfully. 'I always trust you.' And then they smiled at each other, lost for a moment in their love.

'My guests,' she remembered suddenly, a hand flying to her mouth. 'May I set the tea for four o'clock? We'll have it down at the lake. It's a lovely day.'

When she had gone, Sean wasted another minute staring after her through the empty doorway into the gardens. Then he sighed again, contentedly, and drew the silver salver of mail towards him.

He worked quickly, but with care, pencilling his instructions at the foot of each page and initialling them with a regal 'S.C.'

'No! – but tell them politely. S.C.'

'Let me have the previous year's figures of purchase – and delay the next shipment against bank guarantee. S.C.'

'Why did this come to me? Send it to Barnes. S.C.'

'Agreed S C.'

'To Atkinson for comment, please. S.C.'

The subjects were as diverse as the writers – politicians, financiers, supplicants, old friends, chancers, beggars – they were all there.

He flicked over a sealed envelope and stared at it for a moment, not recognizing the name or the occasion.

'Mark Anders Esq., Natal Motors, West Street, Durban.'

It was written in the hand that was so bold and flourishing that nobody could mistake it for any other but his own, and he remembered sending the letter.

Somebody had written across the envelope, 'Left – no forwarding address – return to sender.'

Sean clamped the cigar in the corner of his mouth and slit the flap with a Georgian silver paper-knife. The card was embossed with the regimental crest.

The Colonel-in-Chief and the officers of the Natal Mounted Rifles request the pleasure of *MARK ANDERS ESQ.* at a regimental reunion dinner to be held at the Old Fort ...

Sean had written in the boy's name in the blank space, and at the end of the card, 'Do try to come. S.C.'

Now it was returned, and Sean scowled. As always, he was impatient and frustrated by even the slightest check in his plans. Angrily he tossed both card and envelope at the wastepaper bin, and they both missed, fluttering to the carpet.

Surprisingly, even to himself, his mood had altered, and though he worked on, he fumed and gruffed now over his correspondence and his instructions became barbed.

'The man is a fool or a rogue or both – under no circumstances will I recommend him to a post of such importance, *despite* the family connection! S.C.'

After another hour, he had finished and the room was hazed with cigar smoke. He lay back in the chair and stretched voluptuously like an old lion, then glanced at the wall clock. It was five minutes short of four o'clock, and he stood up.

The offending card caught his eye again, and he stooped quickly and picked it up, reading it again as he crossed the room, tapping the stiff cardboard thoughtfully on the open palm of his hand as he limped out heavily into the sunlight and across the wide lawns.

The gazebo was set on a constructed island in the centre of the lake with a narrow causeway joining it to the lawns.

Sean's household and guests were gathered there already, sitting about the table in the shade under the crazily contrived roof of the gazebo with its intricate cast-iron work painted with carnival colours. Already a host of wild duck had gathered about the tiny island, quacking loudly for pieces of biscuit and cake.

Storm Courtney saw her father coming across the lawns, and she let out one small excited squeak, leapt from the tea table and flew down the causeway to meet him before he reached the lake.

He lifted her easily, as though she were still a baby, and when he kissed her, she inhaled the smell of him. It was one of the lovely smells of her existence, like the smell of rain on hot dry earth, or horses, or the sea. He had a special perfume like old polished leather.

When he lowered her, she took his arm and pressed close to him, matching her light quick step to his limp.

'How was your lunch appointment?' he asked, looking down on her shining lovely head, and she rolled her eyes and then squinted ferociously.

'He is a very presentable young man,' Sean told her sternly. 'An excellent young man.'

'Oh, Daddy, from you that means he is a weak-minded bore.'

'Young lady, I would like to remind you that he is a Rhodes scholar, and that his father is the Chief Justice.'

'Oh, I know all that – but, Daddy, he just hasn't got zing!'

Even Sean looked for an instant nonplussed. 'And what, may I ask, is "zing"?'

'Zing is indefinable,' she told him seriously, 'but you've got zing! You're the zingiest man I know.'

And with that statement Sean found all his fatherly advice and disapproving words gone like migrating swallows, and he grinned down at her, shaking his head.

'You don't really believe that I swallow all your soft soap, do you?'

'You'll never believe it, Daddy, but Payne Bros. have got in twelve actual Patou Couture models – they're absolutely exclusive – and Patou is all the rage now –'

'Women in savage, barbaric colours, driven mad by those machiavellian scheming monsters of Paris,' growled Sean, and Storm giggled delightedly.

'You are a scream, Daddy,' she told him. 'Irene's father has told her she may have one of them – and Mr Leuchars is a mere tradesman!'

Sean blinked to hear the head of one of the largest import houses in the country so described.

'If Charles Leuchars is a tradesman – what, pray, am I?' he asked curiously.

'You are landed gentry, a Minister of the Crown, a General, a hero – and the zingiest man in the world.'

'I see,' he could not help but laugh, 'that I have a position to uphold. Ask Mr Payne to send the account to me.'

She hugged him again, ecstatically, and then for the first time noticed the card he still held in his hand.

'Oh,' she exclaimed. 'An invitation!'

'Not for you, my girl,' he warned her, but she had taken it from his hand, and her face changed as she read the name. Suddenly she was quiet and subdued.

'You are sending that to that – sales person.'

He frowned again, his own mood altering also. 'I sent it. It was returned. He has left, without a forwarding address.'

'General Smuts is waiting to talk to you.' With an effort she recaptured the smile and skipped beside him. 'Let's hurry.'

'It's serious, old Sean. They are organized, and there is no question but that they are seeking a direct confrontation.' Jan Christiaan Smuts crumbled a biscuit between his fingers, and tossed it to the ducks. They squabbled noisily, splashing in the clear water and chattering their broad flat bills as they dipped for the scraps.

'How many white workers will they lay off?' Sean asked.

'Two thousand, to begin with,' Smuts told him. 'Probably four thousand, all in all. But the idea is to do it gradually, as the blacks are trained to replace them.'

'Two thousand,' Sean mused, and he could not help but imagine the wives, and the children – the old mothers, the dependants. Two thousand wage-earners out of work represented much suffering and misery.

'You like it as little as I do.' The shrewd little man had read his thoughts; not for nothing did his opponents call him 'slim Jannie', or 'clever Jannie'. 'Two thousand unemployed is a serious business,' he paused significantly. 'But we will find other employment. We need men desperately on the railways and on other projects like the Vaal-Harts irrigation scheme.'

'They will not earn there the way they do in the mines,' Sean pointed out.

'No,' Jan Smuts drew out the negative thoughtfully, 'but should we protect the income of two thousand miners, at the cost of closing the mines themselves?'

'Surely it is not that critical?' Sean frowned quickly.

'The Chairman of the Chamber of Mines assures me that it is – and he has shown me figures to support this view.'

Sean shook his head, half in incredulity and half in anguish. He had been a mine-owner himself once – and he knew the problem of costs, and also the way that figures can be made to speak the language their manipulators taught.

'You know also, old Sean, you especially – how many others depend for life on those gold mines.' It was a hard probing statement, with a point like a stiletto. The previous year, for the first time, the sales of timber pit-props from Sean's sawmills to the gold mines of the Transvaal had exceeded two million pounds sterling. The little General knew it as well as he did.

'How many men are employed by Natal Sawmills, old Sean, twenty thousand?'

'Twenty-four thousand,' Sean answered shortly, one blond eyebrow lifted quizzically, and the Prime Minister smiled softly before going on.

'There are other considerations, old friend – that you and I have discussed before. On those occasions, it was you who told me that to succeed in the long term, our nation must become a partnership of black man and white, that our wealth must be shared according to a man's ability rather than the colour of his skin – not so?'

'Yes,' Sean agreed.

'It was I who said we must make haste slowly in that direction, and now it is you who hesitate and baulk.'

'I also told you that many small steps were surer than a few wild leaps, made under duress, made only with an assegai at your ribs. I said, Jannie, that we should learn to bend so that we might never have to break.'

Jannie Smuts turned his attention back to the ducks, and they both watched them distractedly.

'Come, Jannie,' Sean said at last. 'You mentioned other reasons. Those you have given me so far are good but not deadly urgent and I know you are politician enough to save the best until the end.'

Jannie laughed delightedly, almost a giggle, and leaned across to pat Sean's arm. 'We know each other too well.'

'We should,' Sean smiled back at him. 'We fought each other hard enough.' They both sobered at mention of those terrible days of the civil war. 'And we had the same tutor, God bless him.'

'God bless him,' echoed Jan Smuts, and they remembered for a moment that colossus Louis Botha, warrior and statesman, architect of Union, and first Prime Minister of the new nation.

'Come,' Sean insisted. 'What is your other reason?'

'It is quite simple. We are about to decide who governs. The duly elected representatives of the people, or a small ruthless band of adventurers who call themselves trade union leaders, representatives of organized labour – or quite simply international communism.'

'You put it hard.'

'It is hard, Sean. It is very hard. I have intelligence facts that I shall lay before the first meeting of the Cabinet when Parliament reconvenes. However, I wanted to discuss these with you personally before that meeting. I need your support again, old Sean. I need you with me at that meeting.'

'Tell me,' invited Sean.

'Firstly, we know that they are arming, with modern weapons, and that they are training and organizing the mine-workers into war commandos.' Jan Smuts spoke quickly and urgently for nearly twenty minutes, and when he had finished he looked at Sean.

'Well, old friend, are you behind me?'

Bleakly Sean looked out into the future, seeing with pain the land he loved once more torn by the hatred and misery of civil war. Then he sighed.

'Yes,' he nodded heavily, 'I am with you, and my hand on it.'

'You and your regiment?' Jan Smuts took the big bony hand. 'As a Minister of the Government and as a soldier?'

'Both,' Sean agreed. 'All the way.'

Marion Littlejohn read Mark's letter, sitting on the closed seat of the office toilet, with the door locked, but her love transcended her surroundings, discounted even the hiss and gurgle of water in the cistern suspended on its rusty downpipe above her head.

She read the letter through twice, with eyes misty and a tender-smile tugging uncertainly at her lips, then she kissed his name on the final page and carefully folded it back into its envelope, opened her bodice and nestled the paper between her plump little breasts. It made a considerable lump there when she returned to the main office and the supervisor looked out from his glass cubicle and made a show of consulting his watch. It was an acknowledged, if unwritten, rule in the Registrar's office that calls of nature should be answered expeditiously, and in no circumstances should the answer occupy more than four minutes of a person's working day.

The rest of the day dragged painfully for Marion, and every few minutes, she touched the lump in her bodice and smiled secretively. When at last the hour of release came, she hurried down Main Street and arrived breathless just as Miss Lucy was closing the doors of her shop.

'Oh, am I in time?'

'Come in, Marion dear – and how is your young man?'

'I had a letter from him today,' she announced proudly, and Miss Lucy nodded her silver curls and beamed through the silver steel frames of her spectacles.

'Yes, the postman told me.' Ladyburg was not yet such a large town that it could not take an intimate interest in the affairs of all its sons and daughters. 'How is he?'

Marion prattled on, flushing and shiny-eyed, as she inspected once again the four sets of Irish linen sheets that Miss Lucy was holding for her.

'They are beautiful, dear, you can really be proud of them. You'll have fine sons between them.' Marion blushed again.

'How much do I still owe you, Miss Lucy?'

'Let's see, dear – you've paid off two pounds and sixpence. That leaves thirty shillings balance.'

Marion opened her purse and counted its contents carefully, then after a mental struggle reached a decision and laid a shiny golden half sovereign on the counter.

'That leaves only a pound.' She hesitated, flushed again, then blurted out, 'Do you think I might take one pair with me now? I would like to begin the embroidery work.'

'Of course, child,' Miss Lucy agreed immediately. 'You have paid for three already. I'll open the packet.'

Marion and her sister Lynette sat side by side on the sofa. Each of them had begun at one side of the sheet and their heads were bent together over it, the embroidery needles flicking in the lamplight as busily as their tongues.

'Mark was most interested in the articles I sent him on Mr Dirk Courtney and he says that he feels Mr Courtney will have a prominent place in the book –'

Across the room, Lyn's husband worked head down over a sheath of legal documents spread on the table before him.

He had lately affected a briar pipe, and it gurgled softly with each puff. His hair was brilliantined and brushed down to a polish with a ruler-straight parting of white scalp dividing it down the middle.

'Oh, Peter,' Marion exclaimed suddenly, her hands stilling and her face lighting. 'I have just had a wonderful idea.'

Peter Botes looked up from his papers, a small frown of annoyance crinkling the serious white brow, a man interrupted at his labour by the silly chatter of woman.

'You do so much work for Mr Courtney down at the bank. You've even been up to the big house, haven't you? He even greets you on the streets – I've seen that.'

Peter nodded importantly, puffing at the pipe. 'Yes, Mr Carter has often remarked that Mr Courtney seems to like me. I think I will be handling the account more and more in the future.'

'Oh, darling, won't you speak to Mr Courtney and tell him that Mark is doing all this work for his book on Ladyburg, and that he is ever so interested in Mr Courtney and his family –'

'Oh, come now, Marion.' Peter waved the pipe airily. 'You can't expect a man like Mr Courtney –'

'You might find he is flattered to be in Mark's book – please dear. I know Mr Courtney will listen to you. You might find he likes the idea – and it will reflect credit on you.'

Peter paused thoughtfully, weighing carefully the value of impressing the womenfolk with his importance and influence against the dread prospect of speaking on familiar terms with Mr Dirk Courtney. The thought appalled him. Dirk Courtney terrified him and in his presence he affected a fawning, self-effacing manner which was, he realized, part of the reason why Dirk Courtney liked to work with him; of course, he was also a painstaking meticulous lawyer, but the main reason was his respectful attitude, Mr Courtney liked respect from his underlings.

'Please, Peter, Mark is going to so much trouble over this book. We must try and help him. I was just telling Lynette that Mark has taken a month's leave from his job to go on an expedition up to Chaka's Gate, just to gather facts for the book.'

'He's gone to Chaka's Gate?' Peter looked mystified, and removed the pipe from his mouth. 'What on earth for? There is nothing up there but wilderness.'

'I'm not sure,' admitted Marion, and then quickly, 'but it's important for the book. We must try and help him.'

'What exactly do you want me to ask Mr Courtney?'

'Won't you ask him to meet Mark, and sort of tell him his life story in his own words. Imagine how that would be in the book.'

Peter swallowed once. 'Marion, Mr Courtney is a busy man, he can't –'

'Oh please.' Marion jumped up and crossed the room to kneel beside his chair. 'Pretty please, for my sake!'

'Well,' he mumbled, 'I'll mention it to him.'

Peter Botes stood like a guardsman beside the head seat of the long ormolu table, bending stiffly from the waist only when it was necessary to turn the page.

'– and here please, Mr Courtney.'

The big man in the chair dashed a careless signature across the foot of the document, hardly glancing at it and without interrupting his conversation with the other fashionably dressed men further down the table.

There was a strong perfume hanging about Dirk Courtney, he wore it with the panache of a cavalry officer's cloak, and Peter tried in vain to identify it. It must be terribly expensive, but it was the smell of success, and he made a resolution to acquire a bottle of whatever it was.

'– and here again, please, sir.'

He noticed now at close range how Dirk Courtney's hair was shining and cut longer at the temple, free of brilliantine and allowed to curl into the sideburns. Peter would wash the brilliantine from his own hair tonight, he decided, and let it grow out a little longer.

'That is all, Mr Courtney. I'll have copies delivered tomorrow.'

Dirk Courtney nodded without glancing up at him, and, pushing back his chair, he stood up.

'Well, gentlemen,' he addressed the others at the table, 'we should not keep the ladies waiting,' and they all laughed with that lustful, anticipatory laugh, their eyes gleaming like those of caged lions at feeding time.

Peter had heard in detail of those parties that Dirk Courtney held out at Great Longwood, his big house. There was gaming for high stakes, sometimes dog-fighting – two matched animals in a pit, ripping each other to ribbons of dangling skin and flesh – sometimes cock-fighting, always women – women brought in closed cars from Durban or Johannesburg. Big city women and Peter felt his body stir at the thought. Introductions to the parties were limited to men of importance or influence or wealth, and during the weekend that the revels continued, the grounds were guarded by Dirk Courtney's bully boys.

Peter dreamed sometimes of being invited to one of those parties, of sitting across the green baize table from Dirk Courtney and casually drawing towards him the multi-coloured pile of ivory chips without removing the expensive cigar from his lips, or of sporting among the rustling silks and smooth white limbs – he had heard of the dancers, beautiful women who disrobed as they danced the Seven Veils, and ended mother-naked while the men roared and groped.

Peter roused himself almost too late. Dirk Courtney was across the room, ushering his guests ahead of him, laughing and charming, flashing white teeth from the swarthy handsome face, a servant standing ready with his overcoat, chauffeurs waiting with the limousines in the street below – about to depart into a realm about which Peter could only speculate in disturbing erotic detail.

He hurried after him, stammering nervously.

'Mr Courtney, I have a personal request.'

'Come, Charles,' Dirk Courtney did not look at Peter, but smilingly laid a friendly arm across one of his guests' shoulders, 'I trust you are in better luck than last time, I hate to take a friend's money.'

'My wife's sister has a fiancé, sir,' Peter stumbled on desperately. 'He's writing a book about Ladyburg, and he would like to include an account of your personal experience –'

'Alfred, will you ride with Charles in the first car.' Dirk Courtney buttoned his coat, and adjusted his hat, beginning to turn towards the door, just a slight crease to his brow showing his annoyance at Peter's importunity.

'He is a local man,' Peter was almost in tears of embarrassment, but he went on doggedly, 'with a good war record, you might remember his grandfather John Anders –'

A peculiar expression came over Dirk Courtney's face, and he turned slowly to look directly at Peter for the first time. The expression struck instant terror into him, Peter had never before seen such burning malevolence, such merciless cruelty on a man's face before. It was only for an instant – and then the big man smiled. Such a smile of charm and good fellowship that Peter felt dizzy with relief.

'A book about me?' He took Peter's arm in a friendly grip above the elbow. 'Tell me more about this young man. I presume he is young?'

'Oh yes, sir, quite young.'

'Gentlemen.' Dirk Courtney smiled apologetically at his guests. 'Can I ask you to go ahead of me. I will follow shortly. Your rooms are prepared, and please do not feel you have to await my arrival before sampling the entertainment.'

Still holding Peter's arm, he led him courteously back into the huge board room to a seat in one of the leather chairs by the fireplace. 'Now, young Master Botes, how about a glass of brandy?' and Peter watched bemused as he poured it with his own hands, big strong hands, covered with fine black hair across the back and with a diamond the size of a ripe pea on the little finger.

With each step northwards, it seemed to Mark that the great bastions of Chaka's Gate changed their aspect gradually, from silhouettes smoked blue with distance until the details of the living rock came into focus.

The twin bluffs faced each other in almost mirror image, each towering a thousand sheer feet but deeply divided by the gorge through which the Bubezi River spilled out on to the coastal lowlands of Zululand and then meandered down a hundred and twenty miles into a maze of swamp and lagoon and mangrove forest, before finally escaping through the narrow mouth of the tidal estuary. The mouth sucked and breathed with the tide, and the ebb blew a stain of discoloured water far out into the electric blue of the Mozambique Current, a brown smear that contrasted sharply with the vivid white rind of sandy beaches that stretched for a thousand miles north and south.

If a man followed the course of the Bubezi up through the portals of Chaka's Gate, as Mark and the old man had done so often before, he came out into a wide basin of land below the main escarpment. Here, among the heavy forests, the Bubezi divided into its two tributaries, the White Bubezi that dropped in a series of cataracts and falls down the escarpment of the continental shield – and the Red Bubezi, which swung away northwards following the line of the escarpment up through more heavy forest and open grassy glades until at last it became the border with the Portuguese colony of Mozambique.

In the flood seasons of high summer, this tributary carried down with it the eroding laterite from deposits deep in Mozambique; turning to deep bloody red, it pulsed like a living artery, and well earned its name, the Red Bubezi.

Bubezi was the Zulu name for the lion, and indeed Mark had hunted and killed his first lion on its banks, half a mile below the confluence of the two tributaries.

It was almost noon, when at last Mark reached the river at the point where it emerged from the gorge between the gates. He reached for his watch to check the time and then arrested the gesture. Here time was not measured by metal hands, but by the majestic swing of the sun and the eternal round of the seasons.

He dropped his pack and propped the rifle against a tree trunk; the gesture seemed symbolic. With the weight from his shoulders, the dark weight on his heart seemed to slip away also.

He looked up at the rock cliffs that filled half the sky above him, and was lost in awe as he had been when he looked up at the arched stone lattice-work of the Henry VII chapel in Westminster Abbey.

The columns of rock, sculptured down the ages by wind and sun and water, had that same ethereal grace, yet a freedom of line that was not dictated by the strict rules of man's vision of beauty. The cliffs were painted with lichen growth, brilliant smears of red and yellow and silvery grey.

In cracks and irregularites of rock grew stunted trees; hundreds of feet above their peers, they were deformed and crippled by the contingencies of nature as though by the careful skills of a host of Japanese Bonzai gardeners, and they twisted out at impossible angles from the face of the cliff, holding out their branches as if in supplication to the sun.

The rock below some narrow ledges was darkened by the stain of the urine and faeces of the hyrax, the fluffy rock rabbits, which swarmed from every crack and hole in the cliff. Sitting in sleepy ranks, on the very edge of the drop, sunning their fat little bodies and blinking down at the tiny figure of the man in the depth of the gorge.

Following the floating wide-pinioned flight of a vulture, Mark watched it swing in steeply, planing and volleying its great brown wings to meet the eddy of the wind across the cliff face, reaching forward with its talons for a purchase as it pulled up and dropped on to its nesting ledge a hundred and fifty feet above the river, folding its wings neatly and then crouching in that grotesque vulturine attitude with the bald scaly head thrust forward, as it waddled sideways along the rim of its huge shaggy nest of sticks and small branches built into the rockface.

From this angle Mark could not see the chicks in the nest, but clearly he recognized the heaving motions of the bird as it began to regurgitate its cropful of rotten carrion for its young. Gradually a sense of peace settled like a mantle over Mark, and he sat down, his back against the rough bole of a fever tree, and slowly, without sense of urgency, he selected and lit a cigarette, drawing the smoke with an unhurried breath and then letting it trickle out through his nostrils, watching the pale blue tendrils rise and swirl on the lazy air.

He thought perhaps that the nearest human being was forty miles distant, the nearest white man almost a hundred – and the thought was strangely comforting.

He wondered at the way in which all man's petty striving seemed insignificant in this place, in this vast primeval world – and suddenly he thought that if all men, even those who had known nothing but the crowded ratlike scrambling of the cities, could be set down in this place, even for a brief space of time, then they might return to their lives cleansed and refreshed, their subsequent strivings might become less vicious, more attuned to the eternal groundswell of nature.

Suddenly he grunted, his reverie shattered by the burning needle sting in the soft of his neck below the ear, and he slapped at it with open palm. The small flying insect was stunned, its carapace too tough to be crushed, even by a blow that heavy. It fell spinning and buzzing into Mark's lap, and he picked it up between thumb and forefinger, examining it curiously, for it was many years since last he had seen one.

The tsetse fly is slightly larger than the house fly, but it has a sleeker more steamlined body, with transparent wings veined in brown.

'The saviour of Africa,' the old man had called it once, and Mark repeated the words aloud as he crushed it between his fingers. It burst in a bright liquid red explosion of the blood it had sucked from his neck. He knew the bite would swell and turn angry red, all the subsequent bites would react in the same way, until swiftly his body rebuilt its immunity. Within a week he would not even notice their stings, and the bite would cause less discomfort than that of a mosquito.

'The saviour of Africa,' the old man had told him. 'This little bastard was all that saved the whole country being over-run and over-grazed with domestic animals. Cattle first, and after cattle the plough, and after the plough the towns and the railway tracks.' The old man had chewed slowly, like a ruminating bull in the light of the camp fire, his face shaded by the spread of the terai hat. 'One day they will find some way to kill him, or something to cure the sleeping sickness – the nagana – that he carries. Then the Africa we know will have gone, lad.' He spat a long honey-brown spirt of juice into the fire. 'What will Africa be without its lonely places and its game? A man might as well go back and live in London town.'

Looking with new eyes and new understanding at the majestic indigenous forest around him, Mark saw in his imagination what it might have been like without its tiny brown-winged guardians; the forests chopped out for firewood, and cleared for ox-drawn cultivation, the open land grazed short and the hooves of the cattle opening the ground cover to begin the running ulcers of erosion, the rivers browned and sullied by the bleeding earth and by man's filth.

The game hunted out – for its meat and because it was in direct competition to the domestic animals for grazing. For the Zulu, cattle was wealth, had been for a thousand years, and wherever cattle could thrive, they came with their herds.

Yet it was ironic that this wilderness had had another guardian, apart from the winged legions, and that guardian had been a Zulu. Chaka, the great Zulu king, had come here long ago. Nobody knew when, for the Zulu does not measure time as a white man does, nor record his history in the written word.

The old man had told Mark the story, speaking in Zulu which was fitting for such a story, and his old Zulu gunbearer had listened and nodded approvingly, or grunted a correction of fact; occasionally he spoke at length embroidering a point in the legend.

In those days there had lived here in the basin a small tribe of hunters and gatherers of wild honey, so they called themselves Inyosi, the bees. They were a poor people but proud, and they resisted the mighty king and his insatiable appetite for conquest and power.

Before his swarming impis, they had withdrawn into the natural fortress of the northern bluff. Remembering the story, Mark raised his eyes and looked across the river at the sheer cliffs.

Twelve hundred men and women and children, they had climbed the only narrow and dangerous path to the summit, the women carrying food upon their heads, a long dark moving file against the rock wall, they had gone up into their sanctuary. And from the summit the Chief and his warriors had shouted their defiance at the king.

Chaka had gone out alone and stood below the cliff, a tall and lithe figure, terrible in the strength of his youth and majesty of his presence.

'Come down, oh Chief, receive the king's blessing and be a chief still – under the sunshine of my love.'

The Chief had smiled and called in jest to his warriors around him, 'I heard a baboon bark!' Their laughter rang against the rock cliffs. The king turned and strode back to where his impis squatted in long patient ranks, ten thousand strong.

In the night Chaka picked fifty men, calling each softly by name. Those of great heart and fearsome reputation. And he had told them simply, 'When the moon is down, my children, we will climb the cliff above the river,' and he laughed that low deep laugh, the sound of which so many had heard as their last sound on this earth. 'For did not that wise chief call us baboons – and the baboon climbs where no man dares.'

The old gunbearer had pointed out to Mark in daylight the exact route that Chaka had taken to the top. It needed binoculars to trace the hairline cracks and the finger-wide ledges.

Mark shuddered now, retracing the route with his eyes, and he remembered that Chaka had led that climb without ropes, in the pitch darkness after the moon, and carrying his shield and his broad-bladed stabbing spear strapped on his back.

Sixteen of his warriors had slipped and fallen during the climb, but such was the mettle of the men that Chaka had chosen that not one of them had uttered a sound during that terrible dark plunge, not a whisper of sound to alert the Inyosi sentries until the final soft thud of flesh on rock down below in the gorge.

In the dawn, while his impis diverted the Inyosi by skirmishing on the pathway, Chaka had slipped over the rim of the cliff, regrouped his remaining warriors and – thirty-five against twelve hundred – carried the summit with a single shattering charge, each stab of the great blades crashing through a body from chest to spine, and the withdrawal sucking the life blood out in a gushing burst of scarlet.

'Ngidhla! I have eaten,' roared the king and his men as they worked, and most of the Inyosi threw themselves from the cliff top into the river below, rather than face Chaka's wrath. Those who hesitated to jump were assisted in their decision.

Chaka lifted the chief of the Inyosi with both hands high above his head, and held him easily as he struggled.

'If I am a baboon – then you are a sparrow!'

He roared with savage laughter. 'Fly, little sparrow, fly!' and he hurled the man far out into the void.

For once they spared not even the women nor the children, for among the sixteen Zulus who had fallen from the cliff during the climb were those whom Chaka loved.

The old gunbearer had scratched in the debris of the scree face below the cliff and showed Mark in the palms of his hand chips of old bone that might have been human.

After his victory on the summit, Chaka had ordered a great hunt in the basin of the two rivers.

Ten thousand warriors to drive the game, and the hunt had lasted four days. They said that the king alone with his own hands had slain two hundred buffalo. The sport had been such that afterwards he had made the decree:

'This is a royal hunting ground, no man will hunt here again, no man but the king. From the cliffs over which Chaka threw the Inyosi, cast to the mountain crests, south and north for as far as a man may run in a day, and a night, and another day, this land is for the king's hunt alone. Let all men hear these words, tremble and obey.'

He had left a hundred men under one of his older indunas to police the ground, under the title of 'keeper of the king's hunt', and Chaka returned again and again, perhaps drawn to this well of peace to refresh and rest his tortured soul with its burning crippling craving for power. He had hunted here, even in that period of dark madness while he mourned his mother Nandi, the Sweet One. He had hunted here nearly every year until at last he had died beneath the assassin's blades wielded by his own brothers.

Probably nearly a century later, the legislative council of Natal, sitting in solemn conclave, hundreds of miles distant from the cliffs of Chaka's Gate, had echoed his decree and proclaimed the area reserved against hunting or despoliation, but they had not policed the Royal Hunt as well as had the old

Zulu King. The poachers had been busy over the years, with bow and arrow, with snare and pit, with spear and dog pack, and with high-powered rifled weapons.

Perhaps soon, as the old man had predicted, they would find a cure for the nagana or a means of eradicating tsetse fly. A man-made law would be repealed, and the land given over to the lowing, slow-moving herds of cattle and to the silver-bright blade of the plough. Mark felt a physical sickness of the stomach at the prospect, and he rose and set off along the scree slope to let the sickness pass.

The old man had always been a creature of habit, even to the clothes he wore and his daily rituals of living. He always camped at the same spot when he travelled a familiar road or returned to a place he had visited before.

Mark went directly to the old camp site above the river junction in the elbow of the main river course, where flood waters had cut a steep high bank and the elevated ground above it formed a plateau shaded by a grove of sycamore fig trees, with stems thick as Nelson's column in Trafalgar Square and the cool green shade below them murmurous with the sound of insects and purple doves.

The hearth stones for the camp fire were still there, scattered a little and blackened with soot. Mark built them back into the correct shape.

There was plenty of firewood, dead and fallen trees and branches, driftwood brought down by the floods and cast up on the high watermark on the bank.

Mark drew clear water from the river, put the billy on to boil for tea, and then, from the side pocket of the pack, brought out the sheath of paper, held together by a clasp and already much fingered and a little tattered, that Marion had sent him.

'Transcript of the evidence from the coroners' inquiry into the death of JOHN ANDERS ESQUIRE of the farm ANDERSLAND in the district of LADYBURG.'

Marion Littlejohn had typed it out laboriously during her lunch hours, and her lack of skill with the machine was evident in the many erasures and over-types.

Mark had read it so many times before that he could almost repeat the entire text from memory, even the irrelevant remarks from the bench.

Mr Greyling (Snr): We was camped there by the Bubezi River, Judge –
Magistrate: I am not a judge, sir. The correct form of address to this court is Your Worship.

But now he began again at the beginning, searching carefully for some small clue to what he was seeking that he might have overlooked in his previous readings.

But always he came back to the same exchange.

Magistrate: Will the witness please refer to the deceased as 'the deceased' and not 'the old man'.
Mr Greyling (Snr): Sorry, your worship. The deceased left camp early on the Monday morning, he says like he's going to look for kudu along the ridge. It would be a little before lunchtime we hears a shot and my boy, Cornelius, he says – 'Sounds like the old man got one' – beg your pardon, I mean the deceased.
Magistrate: You were still in camp at that time?

Mr Greyling (Snr): Yes, Your Worship, my boy and me, we was cutting
and hanging biltong – we didn't go out that day.

Mark could imagine the butchering of the game carcasses, the raw red meat
hacked into long strips, soaked in buckets of brine, and then festooned on the
branches of the trees – a scene of carnage he had witnessed so often before.
When the meat had dried to black sticks, like chewing tobacco, it was packed
into jute sacks for later carriage out on the pack donkeys. The wet meat dried
to a quarter of its weight, and the resulting biltong was highly prized through
Africa and commanded such a high price as to make the poaching a lucrative
trade.

Magistrate: When did you become concerned by the deceased's absence?
Mr Greyling: Well, he didn't come into camp that night. But we weren't
worried like. Thought he might have been spooring up a hit one, and
slept up a tree.

Further on in the evidence was the statement:

Mr Greyling (Snr): ... Well, in the end we didn't find him until the fourth
day. It was the assvogels – beg pardon, the vultures – that showed us
where to look. He had tried to climb the ridge at a bad place, we found
where he had slipped and the gun was still under him. It must have been
that shot we heard – we buried him right there, you see he wasn't fit
to carry – what with the birds and the sun. We put up a nice cross,
carved it myself, and I said the Christian words.

Mark refolded the transcript, and slipped it back into the pack. The tea was
brewing and he sweetened it with thick condensed milk and brown sugar.
Blowing on the mug to cool it, and sipping at the sweet liquid, he pondered
what he had gleaned. A rocky ridge, a bad place, within sound of gunshot of
where he now sat, a cairn of stones, probably, and a wooden cross, perhaps long
ago consumed by termites.
He had a month, but he wondered if that was time enough. On such slim
directions it was a search that could take years, if luck ran against him.
Even if he was successful, he wasn't yet sure what he would do next. The main
concern that drove him on was merely to find where the old man lay. After that
he would know what to do.

He worked the ridges and the rocky ground on the south bank first. For ten
days he climbed and descended the rugged rim of the basin, hard going against
the grain of the natural geological formations, and at the end of that time he
was lean as a greyhound, arms and face burned to the colour of a new loaf by
the sun and with a dark crisp pelt of beard covering his jaw. The legs of his
pants were tattered by the coarse, razor-edged grass and by the clumps of aptly
named wait-a-bit thorns, that grabbed at him to delay his progress.
There was a rich treasure of bird life in the basin, even in the heated hush
of midday the air rang with their cries – the fluting mournful whistle of a wood
dove or the high piping chant of a white-headed fish eagle circling high
overhead. In the early morning and again in the cool of the evening, the bush
came alive with the jewelled flash of feathers – the scarlet breast of the

impossibly beautiful narina trogon, named long ago for a Hottentot beauty by one of the old travellers, the metallic flash of a sunbird as it hovered over the pearly fragrant flowers of a buffalo creeper, the little speckled woodpeckers tapping furiously with heads capped in cardinal red, and, in the reeds by the river, the ebony sheen of the long floating tail feathers of the sakabula bird. All this helped to lighten the long weary hours of Mark's search, and a hundred times a day he paused, enchanted, to watch for a few precious moments.

However, of the larger animals he saw very little, although their sign was there. The big shiny pellets of kudu dung scattered along their secret pathways through the forest, the dried faeces of a leopard furry with baboon hair from its kill, the huge midden of a white rhinoceros, a mountain of scattered dung accumulated over the years as this strange animal returned to the same place daily to defecate.

Pausing beside the rhinoceros midden, Mark grinned as he remembered one of the old man's stories, the one that explained why the rhinoceros was so fearful of the porcupine and why he always scattered his own dung.

Once, long ago, he had borrowed from the porcupine a quill to sew up the tear in his skin caused by a red-tipped mimosa thorn. When the job was done the rhinoceros had held the quill between his teeth as he admired his handiwork, but by accident he swallowed the quill.

Now, of course, he runs away to avoid having to face the porcupine's recriminations – and he sifts each load that he drops, to try and recover the missing quill.

The old man had a hundred yarns like that one to delight a small boy, and Mark felt close to him again; his determination to find his grave strengthened, as he shifted the rifle to his other shoulder and turned once more to the rocky ridge of the high ground.

On the tenth day, he was resting in the deep shade at the edge of a clearing of golden grass, when he had his first good sighting of larger game.

A small herd of graceful pale brown impala, led by three impressively horned rams, emerged from the far side of the clearing. They fed cautiously, every few seconds they froze into perfect stillness with only the big scooplike ears moving as they listened for danger, and their wet black noses snuffing silently.

Mark was out of meat, he had eaten the last of the bully the previous day, and he had brought the rifle for just this moment – to relieve a diet of mealie porridge – yet he found himself strangely reluctant to use it now, a reluctance he had never known as a boy. For the first time, he looked with eyes that saw not just meat but rare and unusual beauty.

The three rams moved slowly across the clearing, passing a hundred paces from where Mark sat silently, and then drifted away, pale shadows, into the thorn scrub. The does followed them, trotting to keep up, one with a lamb stumbling on long gawky legs at her flank, and at the rear of the troop was a half-grown doe.

One of her back legs was crippled, it was withered and stunted, swinging free of the ground and the animal was having difficulty keeping up with the herd. It had lost condition badly, bone of rib and spine showed clearly through a hide that lacked the gloss and shine of health.

Mark swung up the P.14 and the flat crack of the shot bounced from the cliffs across the river, and startled a flock of white-faced duck into whistling flight off the river.

Mark stooped over the doe as she lay in the gras and touched the long curled lashes that fringed the dark swimming eye. There was no reflex blink, and the check for life was routine only. He knew the shot had taken her in the centre of the heart, an instantaneous kill.

'Always make the check.' The old man's teachings again. 'Percy Young would tell you that himself if he could, but he was sitting there on a dead lion he had just shot, having a quiet pipe, when it came to life again. That's why he isn't around to tell you himself.'

Mark rolled the carcass and squatted to examine the back limb. The wire noose had cut through the skin, through sinew and flesh, and had come up hard against the bone as the animal struggled to break out of the snare. Below the wire the leg had gangrened and the smell was nauseous, summoning a black moving wad of flies.

Mark made the shallow gutting stroke, deflecting the blade upwards to avoid puncturing the gut. The belly opened like a purse. He freed the anus and vagina with the deft surgeon strokes, and lifted out bladder and bowel and gut in one scoop. He dissected the purple liver out of the mass of viscera, cut away the gall bladder and tossed it aside. Grilled over the coals, the liver would make a feast for his dinner. He cut away the rotten, stinking hind leg, and then he carefully wiped out the stomach cavity with a handful of dry grass. He cut flaps in the skin of the neck. Using the flaps of skin as handles, he hefted the whole carcass and lugged it down to the camp by the river. Cut and salted and dried, he now had meat for the rest of his stay. He hung the strips of meat high in the sycamore fig to save them from the scavengers who would surely visit the camp during his daily absences, and only when he had finished the task, and he was crouching over his fire with the steaming mug in his hand, did he think again of the snaring wire that had crippled the impala doe.

He felt an indirect flash of anger at the person who had set that noose, and then almost immediately he wondered why he should feel particular anger at the trapper, when a dozen times he had come across the old abandoned camps of white hunters. Always there were the bones, and the piles of rotting worm-riddled horns.

The trapper was clearly a black man, and his need was greater than that of the others who came in to butcher and dry and sell.

Thinking about it, Mark felt a despondency slowly overwhelm him. Even in the few short years since he had first visited this wilderness, the game had been reduced to but a small fraction of its original numbers. Soon it would all be gone – as the old man had said, 'The great emptiness is coming.'

Mark sat at his fireside, and he felt deeply saddened at the inevitable. No creature would ever be allowed to compete with man, and he remembered the old man again.

'Some say the lion, others the leopard. But believe me, my boy, when a man looks in the mirror, he sees the most dangerous and merciless killer in all of nature.'

The pit had been built to resemble a sunken water reservoir. It was fifty feet across and ten feet deep, perfectly circular, plastered and floored in smooth cement.

Although there were water pipes installed and its position on the first slope of the escarpment above Ladyburg was perfectly chosen to provide the correct fall to the big gabled house below, yet it had never held water.

The circular walls were white-washed to gleaming purity, and the floor was lightly spread with clean-washed river sand and neatly raked.

Pine trees had been planted to screen the reservoir. A twelve-stranded barbed wire fence enclosed the whole plantation, and there were two guards at the gate this evening, tough, silent men who checked the guests as the cars brought them up from the big house.

There were forty-eight men and women in the excited, laughing stream that flowed through the gate, and followed the path up among the pines to where the pit was already starkly lit by the brilliant glare of the Petromax lanterns suspended on poles above it.

Dirk Courtney led the revellers. He wore black gaberdine riding breeches and polished knee-length boots to protect his legs from slashing fangs, and his white linen shirt was open almost to the navel, exposing the hard bulging muscle of his chest and the coarse black body hair which curled from the vee of the neck. The sleeves of the shirt were cut full to the wrist, and he rolled a long thin cheroot from one corner of his mouth to the other without touching it, for his arms were around the waists of the women who flanked him, young women with bold eyes and laughing painted mouths.

The dogs heard them coming and bayed at them, leaping against the padded bars of their cages, hysterical with excitement as they tried to reach each other through the gaps, snarling and snapping and slavering while the handlers attempted to shout them into silence.

The spectators lined the circular parapet of the pit, hanging over the edge. In the merciless light of the Petromax, the faces were laid bare, every emotion, every stark detail of the blood lust and sadistic anticipation was revealed – the hectic colouring of the women's cheeks, the feverish glitter of the men's eyes, the shrillness of their laughter and the widely exaggerated gesturing.

During the early bouts, the small dark-haired girl beside Dirk screamed and wriggled, holding her clenched fists to her open mouth, moaning and gasping with fascinated, delighted horror. Once she turned and buried her face against Dirk's chest, pressing her body, trembling and shuddering, against him. Dirk laughed and held her around the waist. At the kill she screamed with the rest of them and her back arched; then Dirk half lifted her, as she sobbed breathlessly, and supported her to the refreshment table where there was champagne in silver buckets and sandwiches of brown bread and smoked salmon.

Charles came to where Dirk sat with the girl on his lap, feeding her champagne from a crystal glass, surrounded by a dozen of his sycophants, jovial and expansive, enjoying the rising sense of tension for the final bout of the evening when he would match his own dog, Chaka, against Charles's animal.

'I feel bad, Dirk,' Charles told him. 'They have just told me that your dog is giving almost ten pounds.'

'That mongrel of yours will need every pound, Charles, don't feel bad now – keep it for later, when you'll really need it.' Dirk was suddenly bored with the girl, and he pushed her casually from his lap, so that she almost lost her balance and fell. Piqued, she settled her skirts, pouted at Dirk and when she realized he had already forgotten her existence, she flounced away.

'Here.' Dirk indicated the chair beside him. 'Do have a seat, Charles old boy, and let's discuss your problem.'

The crowd drew closer around them, listening eagerly to their banter, and braying slavishly at each sally.

'My problem is that I should like a small wager on the bout, but it does seem most unsporting to bet against a light dog, like yours.' Charles grinned as he mopped his streaming red face with a silk handkerchief, sweating heavily with champagne and excitement and the closeness of the humid summer evening.

'We all know that you make your living betting on certainties.' Charles was a stock-broker from the Witwatersrand. 'However, the expression of such noble sentiment does you great credit.' Dirk tapped his shoulder with the hilt of his dogwhip, a familiar condescending gesture that made Charles's grin tighten wolfishly.

'You will accommodate me then?' he asked, nodding and winking at his own henchmen in the press of listening men. 'At even money?'

'Of course, as much as you want.'

'My dog Kaiser against your Chaka, to the death. Even money, a wager of –' Charles paused and looked to the ladies, smoothing the crisp little moustache with its lacing of iron grey, drawing out the moment. 'One thousand pounds in gold.' The crowd gasped and exclaimed, and some of the listeners applauded, a smattering of handclaps.

'No! No!' Dirk Courtney held up both hands in protest. 'Not a thousand!' and the listeners groaned, his own claque shocked and crestfallen at this loss of prestige.

'Oh dear,' Charles murmured, 'too strong for your blood? Name the wager then, old boy.'

'Let's have some real interest – say ten thousand in gold.' Dirk tapped Charles's shoulder again, and the man's grin froze over. The colour faded from the scarlet face, leaving it blotched purple and puffy white. The small acquisitive eyes darted quickly around the circle of laughing applauding faces, as if seeking an escape, and then slowly, reluctantly returned to Dirk's face. He tried to say something, but his voice squeaked and broke like a pubescent boy.

'Ah, and what exactly does that mean?' Dirk inquired with elaborate politeness. Charles would not trust his voice again, but he nodded jerkily and tried to resurrect his cheeky grin, but it was crooked and tense and hung awkwardly on his face.

Dirk carried the dog under his right arm, enjoying the hard rubbery feel of the animal's compact body, carrying its fifty-pound weight easily, as he dropped lightly down the steps to the floor of the pit.

Every muscle in the dog's body was strained to a fine tension, and Dirk could feel the jump and flutter of nerves and sinew, every limb was stiff and trembling and the deep crackling snarls kept erupting up the thick throat, shaking the whole body.

He set the dog down on the raked sand, with the leash twisted securely around his left wrist, and as the dog's paws touched ground he lunged forward, coming up short against the leash so hard that Dirk was almost pulled off his feet.

'Hey, you bastard,' he shouted, and pulled the animal back.

Across the pit, Charles and his handler were bringing down Kaiser, and it needed both their strength for he was a big dog, black as hell, and touched with tan at the eyes and chest, a legacy of the Dobermann Pinscher in his breeding.

Chaka saw him, his lunges and struggles became wilder and fiercer, and the snarls sounded like thick canvas ripping in a hurricane.

The timekeeper called from the parapet, lifting his voice above the excited buzz of the watchers.

'Very well, gentlemen, bate them!'

The two owners set them at each other with cries of 'Sick him up, Kaiser!'

and 'Ger him boy. Kill! Kill!' but held them double-handed on the leash, driving them into a madness of frustration and anger.

On the short leash, the Dobermann weaved and ducked, leggy for a fighting dog, with big shoulders dropping back to lower quarters. He had good teeth, however, and a threatening gape, enough to lock the teeth into the killer grip at the throat. He was fast too, swinging and weaving against the leash, barking and thrusting with the long almost snakelike neck.

Chaka did not bark, but the thick barrel of his chest vibrated to the deep rolling snarls and he stood foursquare on his short legs. He was heavy and low in silhouette, Staffordshire bull terrier blood carefully crossed with mastiff, and his coat was coarse and brindled gold on black. The head was short and thick, like that of a viper, and when he snarled, his upper lip lifted back in deep creases revealing the long ivory yellow fangs and the dark pink gums. He watched the other dog with yellow leopard eyes.

'Bate them! Bate them!' yelled the crowd above, and the owners worked the leashes like jockeys pushing for the post, pointing the animals at each other and driving them on.

Dirk slipped a small steel implement from his pocket, and dropped on his knee beside his dog. Instantly the animal swung on him with gaping jaws but the heavy muzzle caged his fangs. His saliva was beginning to froth, and it splattered the spotless linen of Dirk's shirt.

Dirk reached behind the dog and stabbed the short spur of steel into his flesh, a shallow goading wound at the root of his testicles, just enough to break the skin and draw a drop of blood – the animal snarled on a newer higher note, slashing sideways, and Dirk goaded him again, driving him further and further into the black fighting rage. Now at last he barked, a series of almost maniacal surges of sound from his straining throat.

'Ready to slip,' shouted Dirk, struggling to manage his animal.

'Ready here!' Charles panted across the pit, his feet sliding in the sand as Kaiser reared chest high.

'Slip them!' yelled the timekeeper, and at the same instant, both men slipped muzzle and leash and studded collars, leaving both animals free, and unprotected.

Charles turned and scrambled hurriedly out of the pit, but Dirk waited extra seconds, not wanting to miss the moment when they came together.

The Dobermann showed his speed across the pit, meeting Chaka in his own ground, bounding in on those long legs, leaning forward so the sloping back was flattened in his run.

He went for the head, slashing open the skin below the eye in a clean sabre-stroke of white teeth, but not holding.

Chaka did not go for a hold either, but turned at the instant of impact; using his shoulder and the massive strength of his squat frame, he hit the bigger dog off-balance, breaking his charge, so that he spun away and would have gone over but the white-washed wall caught him, and saved him – for Chaka had turned neatly to catch him as he fell.

Now, however, Kaiser was up and with a quick shift of weight he was in balance again – and he cut for the face mask, missing as the smaller brindled dog ducked, catching only the short cropped ear and splitting it, so that blood flew in black droplets to splatter the sand.

Again Chaka hit with the shoulder, blood streaming from cheek to ear, as he put his weight into the charge. The bigger dog reared out, declining to meet shoulder with shoulder and as he came over he went for a hold – but the crowd screamed as they saw his mistake.

'Drop it! Drop it!' howled Charles, his face purple as an over-ripe plum – for his dog had got into that thick loose skin, padded with fat between the shoulder, and he growled as he worried it.

'Work him, Chaka. Work him!' howled Dirk, balancing easily on the narrow parapet above them. 'Now's your chance, boy.'

Locked into his grip the Dobermann was holding too high, his neck and head up and off-balance. As he worried the hold, it gave and pulled like rubber, not affording purchase or leverage to throw his weight across and bring down the brindled terrier.

The smaller dog seemed not even to feel the grip, although a small artery had ruptured, sending a fine spurt of blood dancing into the lantern light like a pink flamingo's feather.

'Drop it,' screamed Charles again in agony, wringing his hands, sweat dripping from his chin.

'Belly him! Belly him!' exhorted Dirk, and his dog twisted under the big dog's chest, forcing him higher so that his front paws were off the ground, and he hit him in the belly, gaping wide and then plunging his yellow eye teeth full into the bare, shiny dark skin below the ribs.

The Dobermann screamed and dropped his shoulder hold, twisting out violently so that Chaka's fangs tore out of his belly hold, ripping out a flap of stomach-lining through which wet purple entrails bulged immediately – but he beat the terrier's try for the throat, jaw clashing into open snarling jaw, and teeth cracked together, before they spun off and circled.

Both heads were masks of blood now, eyelids blinking rapidly, the eyeballs smeared with flying blood from wound and bite, the fur of the faces plastered with black blood, blood filling the mouths and turning the exposed teeth pink, trickling from the corners of the jaw, staining the froth of saliva bright rose red.

Twice more they came together, each charge initiated by the smaller squatter Chaka, but each time the Dobermann avoided the solid contact of chest to chest for which Chaka's instincts dictated that he must keep trying. Instead, Chaka received two more slashes deeply through the brindled skin, into the flesh, down to white bone, so that when his next charge carried him to the wall he left a broad thick smear of red across the whitewash before turning to attack again.

The Dobermann was humped up from the belly wound, arching his back to the agony of it, but fast and lithe still, not trying for another hold since that fool's hold at the shoulder, but cutting hard and deep and keeping off his opponent like a skilled boxer.

Chaka was losing too much blood now, and as he circled again he lolled his tongue for the first time, frothy saliva discoloured with blood dripping from it, and Dirk swore aloud at this sign of weakness and imminent collapse.

Big Kaiser attacked again now, cutting in sharply as though for the throat and then turning in a low dark streak for another weakening flank cut. As he hit, Chaka turned into him steeply, and snapped at his lean belly again, reaching low and with fortune taking a hold on the bulging entrails that showed in the open flap of the wound.

Instantly the terrier went stiff on his forelegs, and hunched his neck, bringing his chin down on to his chest to hold the grip. The Dobermann's charge carried him on and his entrails were pulled out of him, a long thick glistening ribbon in the lantern light – and the women screamed, high with anguished delight, while the men roared.

Chaka crossed the bigger dog's rump now, still holding his guts and tangled his back legs in the slippery rubbery pink tubes that hung out of the stomach cavity, so that he stumbled off-balance – and the terrier lunged forward, hitting him solidly with the chest, knocking him into the air so he dropped on to his back, screaming and kicking.

Chaka's follow-up was so instinctive, so natural to his breed, that it was swift as the flash of a striking adder and he had his killing hold – locked deep and hard into the throat, bearing down with the solid bone of his jaws, snuffing and working his head on the short hunched neck until his long eye teeth met in the Dobermann's windpipe.

Dirk Courtney jumped down lightly from the parapet, his laugh was pitched unnaturally high and his face was darkened to a congested sullen red as he whipped off his dog, and turned the carcass of the Dobermann with the toe of his boot.

'A fair kill?' he laughed up at Charles, and the man glowered down at him a moment before shrugging acknowledgement of defeat and turning away.

Dicky Lancome sat with the voice-piece of the telephone set on the desk in front of him and the ear-piece held loosely to his cheek, trapped there by a hunched shoulder while he trimmed his finger-nails with a gold-plated penknife.

'What can I say, old girl, except that I am desolate, but then Aunty Hortense was rich as that fellow that turned everything to gold, that's right Midas, or was it Croesus, I just cannot give her funeral a miss, you do understand? You don't?' and he sighed dramatically, as he returned the penknife to his waistcoat pocket and began to thumb through the address book for the other girl's number. 'No, old girl, how can you say that? Are you certain? Must have been my sister –'

It was almost noon on Saturday morning and Dicky had the premises of Natal Motors to himself. He was making his domestic arrangements for the weekend on the firm's telephone account before locking up, and finding some wisdom in the admonition against changing mounts in mid-stream.

At that moment he was distracted by the crack of footsteps on the marbled floor of the showroom, and he swivelled his chair for a glimpse through the door of his cubicle.

There was no mistaking the tall figure that strode through the street doors, the wide shoulders and thrusting bearded jaw, the dark glint of eyes like those of an old eagle.

'Oh, Lord preserve us,' Dicky breathed, his guilty conscience delivering a heavy jolt into his belly, 'General Courtney,' and he let the ear-piece of the telephone drop and dangle on its cord, while he slid forward stealthily from his chair and crawled into shelter below his desk, knees drawn up to his chin.

He could imagine exactly why General Courtney was calling. He had come to discuss the insult to his daughter in person, and Dicky Lancome had heard enough about the General's temper to want to avoid joining this discussion.

Now he listened like a night animal for the stalk of the leopard, cocking his head for the sound of further footsteps and bating his breath to a shallow cautious trickle, in order not to disclose his hiding-place.

The ear-piece of the telephone still dangled on its cord, and now it emitted the high-pitched distorted voice of an irate female. Without leaving the cover of the desk, he reached out to try and muffle the ear-piece, but it dangled tantalizing inches beyond his finger-tips.

'Dicky Lancome, I know you are there,' squawked the tinny voice, and Dick wriggled forward another inch.

A hand, in size not unlike that of a bull gorilla, entered Dicky's field of vision, closed on the ear-piece, and placed it in Dicky's outstretched fingers.

'Please allow me,' said a deep gravelly voice from somewhere above the desk.

'Thank you, sir,' whispered Dicky, trying not to draw too much attention to himself even at this stage. For want of anything better to do, he listened respectfully to the ear-piece.

'It is no good pretending not to be listening,' said the female voice. 'I know all about you and that blonde hussy –'

'I expect you need this,' said the deep voice from on high, and the hand passed the mouthpiece of the telephone down into his hiding-place.

'Thank you, sir,' Dicky whispered again, uncertain as to which emotion dominated him at that moment, humiliation or trepidation. He cleared his throat and spoke into the telephone.

'Darling, I have to go now,' he croaked. 'I have an extremely important client in the shop.' He hoped that the touch of flattery might sweeten the coming encounter. He broke the connection and crawled out unwillingly on his hands and knees.

'General Courtney!' He dusted himself down and smoothed his hair, assembled his dignity and salesman's smile. 'We are honoured.'

'I hope I did not interrupt you in anything important?' Only the sapphire twinkle in the heavily browed eyes betrayed the General's amusement.

'By no means,' Dicky assured him, 'I was –' he looked around wildly for inspiration, 'I was merely meditating.'

'Ah!' Sean Courtney nodded. 'That explains it.'

'How can I be of service to you, General?' Dicky went on hurriedly.

'I wanted to find out about a young salesman of yours – Mark Anders.' Dicky's heart was struck by black frost again.

'Don't worry, General, I fired him myself,' Dicky blurted out. 'But I tore a terrible strip off him first. You can be sure of that.' He saw the General's dark beetling brows come together and the forehead crease like an eroded desert landscape, and Dick nearly panicked. 'He won't get another job in this town, count on it, General. I have put the word out – the black mark – he's properly queered around here, he is.'

'What on earth are you talking about, man?' the General rumbled, like an uneasy volcano.

'One word from you, sir, was enough.' Dicky found that the palms of his hands were cold and slippery with sweat.

'From me?' The rumble rose to a roar and Dicky felt like a peasant, looking fearfully up the slopes of Vesuvius. 'What did I have to do with it?'

'Your daughter,' choked Dicky, 'after what he did to your daughter.'

'My daughter?' The huge voice subsided to something that was close to a whisper, but was too cold and intense. It was a fiercer sound than the roar that preceded it. 'He molested my daughter?'

'Oh God no, General,' Dicky moaned weakly. 'No employee of ours would raise a finger to Miss Storm.'

'What happened? Tell me exactly.'

'He was insolent to your daughter, I thought you knew?'

'Insolent? What did he say?'

'He told her she did not conduct herself like a lady. She must have told you?' Dicky gulped, and the General's fearsome expression melted. He looked stunned and bemused.

'Good God. He said that to Storm? What else?'

'He told her to use the word "please" when giving orders.' Dicky couldn't meet the man's eyes and he lowered his head. 'I'm sorry, sir.'

There was a strangled growling sound from the General, and Dicky stepped back quickly, ready to defend himself. It took him seconds to realize that the General was struggling with his mirth, gales of laughter that shook his chest – and when at last he let it come, he threw back his head and opened his mouth wide.

Weak with relief, Dicky essayed a restrained and cautious chuckle – in sympathy with the General.

'It's not funny, man,' roared Sean Courtney, and instantly Dicky scowled.

'You are much to blame – how can you condemn a man on the whim of a child?' It took Dicky a moment to realize that the child in question was the gorgeous, head-strong darling of Natal society.

'I understood that the order came from you,' stammered Dicky.

'From me!' The laughter stopped abruptly, and the General mopped at his eyes. 'You thought I would smash a man because he was man enough to stand up to my daughter's tantrums? You thought that of me?'

'Yes,' said Dicky miserably, and then quickly, 'No,' and then hopelessly, 'I didn't know, sir.'

Sean Courtney took an envelope from his inside pocket, and looked at it thoughtfully for a moment.

'Anders believed, as you did, that I was responsible for his dismissal?' he asked soberly now.

'Yes, sir. He did.'

'Can you contact him? Will you see him again?'

Dicky hesitated, and then steeled himself and took a breath. 'I promised him his job back at the end of the month – after we had gone through the motions of dismissal, General. Like you, I didn't think the crime deserved the punishment.'

And Sean Courtney looked at him with a new light in his eye, and a grin lifting the corner of his mouth and one eyebrow.

'When you see Mark Anders again, tell him of our conversation – and give him this envelope.' Dicky took the envelope, and as the General turned away, he heard him mutter darkly, 'And now for Mademoiselle Storm.' Dicky Lancome felt a comradely pang of sympathy for that young lady.

It was almost noon on a Saturday morning and Ronald Pye sat in the back seat of the limousine, stiffly as an undertaker in his hearse, and his expression was as lugubrious. He wore a three-piece suit of dark grey cloth and a high starched collar with stiff wings; gold-rimmed spectacles glittered on his thin beaky nose.

The chauffeur swung off the main Ladyburg road into the long straight avenue that led up to the glistening white buildings of Great Longwood on the lower slopes of the escarpment. The avenue was lined with cycads that were at least two hundred years old, thick-stemmed palm-like plants each with a golden fruit the size of hogshead, like a monstrous pine cone, nestled in the centre of the graceful fronds. Dirk Courtney's gardeners had scoured the countryside for a hundred miles in each direction to find them, and had lifted them, matched them for size and replanted them here.

The driveway had been smoothed and watered to keep down the dust, and parked in front of the house were twenty or thirty expensive motor cars.

'Wait for me,' said Ronald Pye. 'I won't be long,' and as he alighted, he glanced up at the elegant façade. It was an exact copy of the historic home of

Simon van der Stel, the first Governor of the Cape of Good Hope, which still stood at Constantia. Dirk Courtney had his architects measure and copy faithfully every room, every arch and gable. The cost must have been forbidding.

In the hall, Ronny Pye paused and looked about him impatiently, for there was nobody to welcome him, although he had been specifically invited – perhaps summoned was a better word – for noon.

The house was alive; there were women's voices and the tinkling bells of their laughter from deep in the interior, while closer at hand the deeper growl of men punctuated by bursts of harsh laughter and voices raised to that reckless, raucous pitch induced by heavy drinking.

The house smelled of perfume and cigar smoke and stale alcohol, and Ronny Pye saw empty crystal glasses standing carelessly on the priceless rosewood hall table, leaving rings of damp on the polished surface – and an abandoned pair of pearly rose women's silk cami-knickers were draped suggestively over the door handle that led to the drawing-room.

While he still hesitated, the door across the hall opened and a young woman entered. She had the dazed, detached air of a sleep-walker, gliding silently into the room on neatly slippered feet. Ronny Pye saw that she was a young girl, not much more than a child, although her cosmetics had run and smeared. Dark rings of mascara gave her a haunted consumptive look, and her lipstick was spread so that her mouth looked like a bruised and overblown rose.

Except for the slippers on her small feet, she was stark naked and her breasts were immature and tender, with pale unformed nipples, and snarled dishevelled tresses of pale blonde hair hung on to her shoulders.

Still with slow, drugged movements, she took the knickers from the door handle, and stepped into them. As she pulled them to her waist she saw Ronny Pye standing by the main door, and she grinned at him – a lopsided depraved whore's smile on the smeared and inflamed lips.

'Another one? All right, come along then, love.' She took a step in his direction, tottered suddenly and turned away to grab at the table for support, the painted doll's face suddenly white and translucent as alabaster, then slowly she doubled over and vomited on the thick silken expanse of woven Qum carpet.

With an exclamation of disgust, Ronald Pye turned away, and crossed to the doors that led into the drawing-room.

Nobody looked up as he entered, although there were twenty people or more in the room. They were gathered intently about a solid round gaming-table of ebony with ivory and mosaic inlay. The tabletop was scattered with poker chips, brightly coloured ivory counters, and four men sat at the table, each holding a fan of cards to his chest, watching the figure at the head of the table. The tension crackled in the room like static electricity.

He was not surprised to see that one of the men at the table was his brother-in-law. He knew that Dennis Petersen regularly attended the soirées at Great Longwood, and he thought briefly of his pliant dutiful sister and wondered if she knew.

'The man has drawn us all in,' Ronny thought bitterly, glancing at Dennis and noticing his bleary, inflamed eyes, the nervous drawn white face. 'At least I have withstood this, this final filthy degradation. Whatever other evils he has led me into, I have kept this little shred of my self respect.'

'Well, gentlemen, I have bad news to impart, I'm afraid,' Dirk Courtney smiled urbanely. 'The ladies are with me,' and he spread his cards face up on the green baize. The four queens in their fanciful costume stared up with wooden expressions, and the other players peered at them for a moment, and then one at a time, with expressions of disgust, discarded their own hands.

Dennis Petersen was the last to concede defeat, and his face was stricken, his hand shook. And then with a sound that was almost a sob, he let his cards flutter from his fingers, pushed back his chair and blundered towards the door.

Halfway there, he stopped suddenly as he recognized the gaunt forbidding figure of his brother-in-law. He stared at him for a moment, the lips still trembling, blinking his bloodshot eyes; then he shook his head as though doubting his senses.

'You here?'

'Oh yes,' Dirk called from the table where he was gathering and stacking the ivory chips. 'Did I forget to mention that I had invited Ronald? Forgive me,' he told the other players, 'I will be back in a short while.' He stood from the table, brushed away the clinging hands of one of the women, and came to take the elbows of Ronald Pye and his brother-in-law in a friendly grip, and to guide them out of the drawing-room, down the long flagged passage to his study.

Even at midday, the room was cool and dark, thick stone walls and heavy velvet drapes, dark wooden panelling and deep Persian and Oriental carpeting, sombre smoky-looking oil paintings on the panelling, one of which Ronald Pye knew was a Reynolds, and another a Turner, heavy chunky furniture, with coverings of chocolate-coloured leather – it was a room which always depressed Ronald Pye. He always thought of it as the centre of the web in which he and his family had slowly entangled themselves.

Dennis Petersen slumped into one of the leather chairs, and after a moment's hesitation, Ronald Pye took the one facing him and sat there stiffly, disapprovingly.

Dirk Courtney splashed single malt whisky into the glasses that were set out on a silver tray on the corner of the big mahogany desk, and made a silent offer to Ronald Pye, who shook his head primly.

Instead, he carried a glass of the glowing amber liquor to Dennis who accepted it with trembling hands, gulped a mouthful and then blurted thickly,

'Why did you do it, Dirk? You promised that nobody would know I was here, and you invited –' he glanced across at the grim countenance of his brother-in-law.

Dirk chuckled. 'I always keep my promises – just as long as it pays me to do so.' He lifted his own glass. 'But between the three of us there should be no secrets. Let's drink to that.'

When Dirk lowered his glass, Ronald Pye asked, 'Why did you invite me here today?'

'We have a number of problems to discuss – the first of which is dear Dennis here. As a poker player, he makes a fine blacksmith.'

'How much?' Ronald Pye asked quietly.

'Tell him, Dennis,' Dirk invited him, and they waited while he studied the remaining liquor in his glass.

'Well?' said Ronald Pye again.

'Don't be shy, Dennis, me old cocky diamond,' Dirk encouraged him. Dennis mumbled a figure without looking up.

Ronald Pye shifted his weight in the leather chair, and his mouth quivered. 'It's a gambling debt. We repudiate it.'

'Shall I ask one or two of the young ladies who are my guests here to go down and give your sister a first-hand account of some of the other little tricks Dennis has been up to? Did you know that Dennis likes to have them kneel over –'

'Dirk, you wouldn't,' bleated Dennis. 'You're not going to do that –' and he sank his face into his hands.

'You will have a cheque tomorrow,' said Ronald Pye softly.

'Thank you, Ronny, it really is a pleasure to do business with you.'

'Is that all?'

'Oh no,' Dirk grinned at him. 'By no means.' He carried the crystal decanter across to Dennis and recharged his glass. 'We have another little money matter to discuss.' He filled his own glass with whisky and held it to the light. 'Bank business,' he said, but Ronny Pye cut in swiftly.

'I think you should know that I am about to retire from the Bank. I have received an offer for my remaining shares, I am negotiating for a vineyard down in the Cape. I will be leaving Ladyburg and taking my family with me.'

'No,' Dirk shook his head, smiling lightly. 'You and I are together for ever. We have a bond that is unbreakable. I want you with me always – somebody I can trust, perhaps the only person in the world I can trust. We share so many secrets, old friend. Including murder.'

They both froze at the word, and slowly colour drained from Ronald Pye's face.

'John Anders and his boy,' Dirk reminded them, and they both broke in together.

'The boy got away –'

'He's still alive.'

'Not for much longer,' Dirk assured them. 'My man is on the way to him now. This time there will be no further trouble from him.'

'You can't do it,' Dennis Petersen shook his head vehemently.

'Why, in God's name? Let it be.' Ronald Pye was begging now, suddenly all the stiffness going out of his bearing. 'Let the boy alone, we have enough –'

'No. He has not left us alone,' Dirk explained reasonably. 'He has been actively gathering information on all of us and all our activities. By a stroke of fortune I have learned where he is and he is alone, in a lonely place.'

They were silent now, and while he waited for them to think it out, Dirk flicked the stub of his cheroot on to the fireplace and lit another.

'What more do you want from us, now?' Ronald asked at last.

'Ah, so at last we can discuss the matter in a businesslike fashion?' Dirk propped himself on the edge of the desk and picked up an antique duelling pistol that he used as a paper weight. He spun it on his finger as he talked. 'I am short of liquid funds for the expansion programme that I began five years ago. There has been a decline in sugar prices, a reduction in the Bank's investment flow – but you know all this, of course.'

Ronald Pye nodded cautiously. 'We have already agreed to adapt the land purchases to our cash flow, for the next few years at least. We will be patient.'

'I am not a patient man, Ronny.'

'We are short two hundred thousand a year over the next three years. We have agreed to cut down,' Ronald Pye went on, but Dirk was not listening. He twirled the pistol, aimed at the eye of the portrait above the fireplace and snapped the hammer on the empty cap.

'Two hundred thousand a year for three years is six hundred thousands of sterling,' Dirk mused aloud, and lowered the pistol. 'Which is by chance exactly the amount paid by me to you for your shares, some ten years ago.'

'No,' said Ronald Pye, with an edge of panic in his voice. 'That's mine, that's my personal capital, it has nothing to do with the Bank.'

'You've done very nicely with it too,' Dirk congratulated him. 'Those Crown

Deep shares did you proud, an excellent buy. By my latest calculations, your personal net worth is not much less than eight hundred thousand.'

'In trust for my family, my daughter and my grandchildren,' said Ronny, his voice edged with desperation.

'I need that money now,' Dirk spoke reasonably.

'What about your own personal resources?' Ronald Pye demanded desperately.

'Stretched to their limit, my dear Ronald, all of it invested in land and sugar.'

'You could borrow on –'

'Oh, but why should I borrow from strangers, when a dear and trusted friend will make the loan to the Ladyburg Farmers Bank. What finer security than that offered by that venerable institution? A loan, dear Ronald, merely a loan.'

'No.' Ronald Pye came to his feet. 'That money is not mine. It belongs to my family.' He turned to his brother-in-law. 'Come. I will take you home.'

Smiling that charming, sparkling smile, Dirk aimed the duelling pistol between Dennis Petersen's eyes.

'Stay where you are, Dennis,' he said, and snapped the hammer again.

'It's all right,' said Ronald Pye to Dennis. 'We can break away now. If you stick with me.' Ronald was panting a little, and sweating like a runner. 'If he accuses us of murder, he accuses himself also. We can prove that we were not the planners, not the ones who gave the orders. I think he is bluffing. It's a chance we will have to take to be rid of him.' He turned to face Dirk now, and there was the steel of defiance in his eyes. 'To be rid of this monster. Let him do his worst, and he damns himself as much as he does us.'

'How well conceived a notion!' Dirk laughed delightedly. 'And I do really believe that you are foolish enough to mean what you say.'

'Come Dennis. Let him do his worst.' Without another glance at either of them, Ronald Pye stalked to the door.

'Which of your grandchildren do you cherish most, Ronny. Natalie or Victoria?' Dirk asked, still laughing. 'Or, I imagine, it's the little boy – what's his name? Damn! I should know the brat's name – I am his godfather.' He chuckled again, then snapped his fingers as he remembered. 'Damn me, of course, Ronald, like his granddaddy. Little Ronald.'

Ronald Pye had turned at the door and was staring across the room at him. Dirk grinned back at him, as though at some delicious joke.

'Little Ronald,' he grinned, and aimed the pistol at an imaginary figure in the centre of the open carpet, a diminutive figure it seemed, no higher than a man's knee. 'Goodbye, little Ronald,' he murmured, and clicked the hammer. 'Goodbye, little Natalie.' He swung the pistol to another invisible figure and snapped the action. 'Goodbye, little Victoria.' The pistol clicked again – the metallic sound shockingly loud in the silent room.

'You wouldn't –' Dennis's voice was strangled, 'you wouldn't –'

'I need the money very badly,' Dirk told him.

'But you wouldn't do that –'

'You keep telling me what I wouldn't do. Since when have you been such a fine judge of my behaviour?'

'Not the children?' pleaded Dennis.

'I've done it before,' Dirk pointed out.

'Yes, but not children – not little children.'

Ronald Pye stood at the door still. He seemed to have aged ten years in the last few seconds, his shoulders had sagged and his face was grey and deeply lined, the flesh seemed to have fallen in around his eyes, sagging into loose folds.

'Before you leave, Ronny, let me tell you a story you have been desperate to hear for twelve years. I know you have spent much time and money trying to find out aleady. Return to your chair, please. Listen to my story and then you are free to go – if you still want to do so.'

Ronald Pye's hand fell away from the door handle, and he shambled back and dropped into the leather chair as though his limbs did not belong to him.

Dirk filled a spare glass with whisky and placed it on the arm of his chair, within easy reach – and Ronny did not protest.

'It's the story of how a nineteen-year-old boy made himself a million pounds in cash, and used it to buy a bank. When you have heard it, I want you to ask yourself if there is anything that boy would *not* do.' Dirk stood up and began to pace up and down the thick carpeting between their chairs like a caged feline animal, lithe and graceful, but sinister also, and cruel; and he began to speak in that soft purring voice that wove a hypnotic web about them, and their heads swung to follow his regular measured pacing.

'Shall we call the boy Dirk, it's a good name – a tough name for a lad who was thrown out by a tyrannical father and set out to get the things he wanted his own way, a boy who learned quickly and was frightened of nothing, a boy who by his nineteenth birthday was first mate of a beaten-up old coal-burning tramp steamer running dubious cargoes to the bad spots of the Orient. A boy who could run a ship single-handed and whip work out of a crew of niggers with a rope end, while the skipper wallowed in gin in his cabin.'

He paused beside the desk, refilled his glass with whisky and asked his audience,

'Does the story grip you so far?'

'You are drunk,' said Ronald Pye.

'I am never drunk,' Dirk contradicted him, and resumed his pacing.

'We will call the steamer *L'Oiseau de Nuit* – "The Bird of Night", though, in all truth, it's an unlikely name for a stinking old cow of a boat. Her skipper was Le Doux – the sweet one – again a mild misnomer,' and Dirk chuckled reminiscently, and sipped at his glass. 'This merry crew discharged a midnight cargo in the Yellow River late in the summer of '09 and next day put into the port of Liang Su for a more legitimate return cargo of tea and silks.

'From the roadstead, they could see that the outskirts of the town was in flames, and they could hear the crackle of small arms fire. The basin was empty of shipping, just a few sampans and one or two small junks, and the fear-crazed population of the city was crowding the wharf, screaming for a berth to safety.

'Hundreds of them plunged into the basin and swam out to where "The Bird of Night" was hovering. The mate let two of them come aboard and then turned the hoses on the others, driving them off, while he learned what was happening.' Dirk paused, remembering how the pressure of the solid jets of water had driven the swimmers under the filthy yellow surface of the basin, and how the others had wailed and tried to swim back. He grinned and roused himself. 'The Communist war-lord, Han Wang, was attacking the port and had promised the rich merchants an amusing death in the bamboo cages. Now the mate knew just how rich the merchants of Liang Su really were. After consulting the captain, the mate brought "The Bird of Night" alongside the wharf, clearing it of the peasant scum with steam hoses and a few pistol shots, and he led an armed party of lascars into the city to the guild house where the Chinese tea merchants were gathered, paralyzed with terror and already resigned to their fate. Another whisky, Ronny?'

Ronald Pye shook his head, his eyes had not left Dirk's face since the tale began, and now Dirk smiled at him.

'The mate set the passage money so high that only the very richest could afford to pay it, two thousand sovereign a head – but still ninety-six of them came aboard "The Bird of Night", each staggering under the load of his possessions. Even the children carried their own weight, boxes and bales and sacks – and while we are on the subject of children, there were forty-eight of them in the party, all boys of course, for no sane Chinaman would waste two thousand pounds on a girl child. The little boys ranged from babes to striplings, some of them of an age with your little Ronald.' Dirk paused to let it register, then, 'It was a close run, for as the last of them came aboard, the mate cast off from the wharf and Han Wang's bandits burst out of the city and hacked and bayoneted their way on to the wharf. Their rifle-fire spattered the upper works, and swept "The Bird of Night's" decks, sending her newly boarded passengers screaming down into the empty holds, but she made a clear run of it out of the river and by dark was pushing out into a quiet tropical sea.

'Le Doux, the captain, could not believe his fortune – almost two hundred thousand sovereigns in gold, in four tea chests in his cabin, and he promised young Dirk a thousand for himself. But Dirk knew the value of his captain's promises. Nevertheless, he suggested a further avenue of profit.

'Old Le Doux had been a hard man before the drink got to him. He had run slaves out of Africa, opium out of India, but he was soft now, and he was horrified by what his young mate suggested. He blasphemed by praying to God and he wept. "Les pauvres petits," he slobbered, and poured gin down his throat until after midnight he collapsed into that stupor that Dirk knew would last for forty-eight hours.

'The mate went up on to the bridge and sounded the ship's siren, shouting to his passengers that there was a government gunboat overtaking them, and driving them from the open deck back into the holds. They went like sheep, clutching their possessions. The mate and his lascars battened down the hatches, closing 'em up tight and solid. Can you guess the rest of it?' he asked. 'A guinea for the correct solution.'

Ronald Pye licked his dry grey lips, and shook his head.

'No?' Dirk teased him. 'The easiest guinea you ever missed – why, it was simple. The mate opened the seacocks and flooded the holds.' He watched them curiously, anticipating their reactions. Neither of his listeners could speak, and as Dirk went on, there was a small change in his telling of it. He no longer spoke in the third person. Now it was 'we' and 'I'.

'Of course, we couldn't flood to the top, even in that low sea she might have foundered, and rolled on her back. There must have been a small airspace under the hatch, and they held the children up there. I could hear them through the four-inch timbers of the hatch. For almost half an hour they kept up their howling and screaming until the air went bad and the roll and slosh of the water got them, and when at last it was all over and we opened the hatches, we found that they had torn the woodwork of the underside of the covers with their fingers, ripped and splintered it like a cage full of monkeys.'

Dirk turned to the empty chair nearest the fireplace and sank into it. He swilled the whisky in his right hand and then swallowed it. He threw the crystal glass into the empty fireplace and it exploded into diamond fragments. They were all silent, staring at the glass splinters.

'Why?' whispered Dennis huskily at last. 'In God's name, why did you kill them?'

Dirk did not look at him, he was lost in the past, reliving a high tide in his life. Then he roused himself and went on, 'We pumped out the hold, and I had the lascars carry all the sodden sacks and bales and boxes up into the saloon. God, Ronny, you should have been there. It was a sight to drive a man like you mad with greed. I piled it all up on the saloon table. It was a treasure that had taken fifty cunning men a lifetime to accumulate. There was gold in coin and bar, diamonds like the end of your thumb, rubies to choke a camel, emeralds – well, the merchants of Liang Su were some of the richest in China. Together with the passage money, the loot came to just over a million in sterling –'

'And the captain, Le Doux, his share?' Ronald Pye asked, even in his horror his accountant's mind was working.

'The captain?' Dirk shook his head and smiled that light, boyish smile. 'Poor Le Doux, he must have fallen overboard that night. Drunk as he was, he would not have been able to swim – and the sharks were bad out there in the China Sea. God knows that with the water full of dead Chinese, there was enough to attract them. No, there was only one share, not counting a token to the lascars. Two hundred pounds for each of them was a fortune beyond their wildest dreams of avarice. That left a million pounds for a night's work. A million before the age of twenty.'

'That's the most terrible story I've ever heard.' Ronald Pye's voice shook like the hand that raised the glass to his lips.

'Remember it when next you have naughty thoughts of leaving Ladyburg,' Dirk counselled him, and leaned across to pat his shoulder. 'We are comrades – unto death,' he said.

For Mark the allotted days were running out swiftly. Soon he must leave the valley and return to the world of men, and a quiet desperation came over him. He had searched the south bank and the steep ground above it, now he crossed to the north bank and started there all over again.

Here, for the first time, he had warning that he was not the only human being in the valley. The first day he came across a line of snares laid along the game trails that led down to drinking places on the river. The wire used was the same as that he had found on the gangrened leg of the crippled impala doe, eighteen-gauge galvanized mild steel wire, probably cut from some unsuspecting farmer's fence.

Mark found sixteen snares that day and tore each out, bundled the wire and hurled it into one of the deeper pools of the river.

Two days later, he came across a log deadfall, so cunningly devised and so skilfully set that it had crushed a full-grown otter. Mark used a branch to lever the log clear and drew out the carcass. He stroked the soft, lustrous chocolate fur and felt again the stirring of his anger. Quite unreasonably, he was developing a strange proprietary feeling for the animals of this valley, and a growing hatred for anyone who hunted or molested them.

Now his attention was divided almost equally between his search for his grandfather's grave and for further signs of the illegal trapper. Yet it was almost another week before he had direct sign of the mysterious hunter.

He was crossing the river each morning in the dawn to work the north bank. It might have been easier to abandon the camp under the fig trees, but sentiment kept him there. It was the old man's camp, their old camp together, and in any case he enjoyed the daily crossing and the journey through the swampland formed in the crotch of the two rivers. Although it was only the very edge of this watery world that he moved through, yet he recognized it as the very heart of this wilderness, an endless well of precious water and even more precious life, the last secure refuge of so many creatures of the valley.

He found daily evidence of the big game on the muddy paths through the towering stands of reed and papyrus, which closed overhead to form a cool gloomy tunnel of living green stems. There were Cape buffalo, and twice he heard them crashing away through the papyrus without a glimpse of them. There were hippopotamus and crocodile but they spent the days deep in the dark reed-fringed lakelets and mysterious lily-covered pools. At night he often woke and huddled in his blanket to listen to their harsh grunting bellows resounding through the swampland.

One noonday, sitting on a low promontory of rocky wooded ground that thrust into the swamp, he watched a white rhinoceros bring its calf out of the sheltering reeds to feed on the edge of the bush.

She was a huge old female, her pale grey hide scarred and scratched, folded and wrinkled over the massive prehistoric body that weighed at least four tons, and she fussed over the calf anxiously, guiding it with her long slightly curved nose horn; the calf was hornless and fat as a piglet. Watching the pair, Mark realized suddenly how deeply this place had touched his life, and the possessive love he was developing for it was reaffirmed.

Here he lived as though he was the first man in all the earth, and it touched some deep atavistic need in his spirit. It was on that same day that he came upon recent signs of the other human presence beyond Chaka's Gate.

He was following one of the faint game paths that skirted another ridge, one of those that joined the main run of ground into the slopes of the escarpment, when he came upon the spoor.

It was barefooted, the flat-arched and broad soles of feet that had never been constricted by leather footwear. Mark went down on his knees to examine it carefully. Too big for a woman, he knew at once.

The stride told him the man was tall. The gait was slightly toe-in and the weight was carried on the ball of the foot, the way an athlete walks. There was no scuff or drag of toe on the forward swing, a high lift and a controlled transfer of weight – a strong, quick, alert man, moving fast and silently.

The spoor was so fresh that at the damp patch where the man had paused to urinate, the butterflies still fluttered in a brilliant cloud for the moisture and salt. Mark was very close behind him, and he felt the hunter's thrill as, without hesitation, he picked up and started to run the spoor.

He was closing quickly. The man he was following was unaware. He had paused to cut a green twig from a wild loquat branch, probably to use as a tooth pick, and the shavings were still wet and bleeding.

Then there was the place where the man had paused, turned back on his own spoor a single pace, paused again, almost certainly to listen, then turned abruptly off the path; within ten more paces the spoor ended, as though the man had launched into flight, or been lifted into the sky by a fiery chariot. His disappearance was almost magical, and though Mark worked for another hour, casting and circling, he found no further sign.

He sat down and lit a cigarette, and found he was sweaty and disgruntled. Although he had used all his bushcraft to come up with his quarry, he had been made to look like an infant. The man had become aware of Mark following, probably from a thousand yards off, and he had jinked and covered his spoor, throwing the pursuit with such casual ease that it was a positive insult.

As he sat, Mark felt his ill-humour harden and become positive hard anger. 'I'll get you yet,' he promised the mysterious stranger aloud, and it did not even occur to him what he might do, if he ever did come up with his quarry. All that he knew was that he had been challenged, and he had taken up the challenge.

The man had the cunning of – Mark sought for a simile, a properly disparaging simile – and then grinned as he found a suitable one. The man had the cunning of a jackal, but he was Zulu so Mark used the Zulu word '*Pungushe*'.

'I'll be watching for you, Pungushe. I'll catch you yet, little jackal.'

His mood improved with the insult, and as he crushed out his cigarette, he found himself anticipating the contest of bush skills between himself and Pungushe.

Now whenever Mark moved through the wilderness, part of his attention was alert for the familiar footprints in the soft earthy places or for the glimpse of movement and the figure of a man among trees. Three times more he cut the spoor, but each time it was cold and wind-eroded, not worth following.

The days passed in majestic circle of sky and mountain, of sun and river and swamp, so that time seemed without end until he counted on his fingers and realized that his month was almost run. Then he felt the dread of leaving, a sinking of the spirits such as a child feels when the moment of return to school comes at the end of an idyllic summer holiday.

That night he returned to the camp below the fig tree with the last of the light, and set his rifle against the stem of the tree. He stood a moment, stretching aching muscles and savouring the coming pleasure of hot coffee and a cheerful fire, when suddenly he stooped and then dropped on one knee to examine the earth, soft and fluffy with leaf mould.

Even in the bad light, there was no mistaking the print of broad bare feet. Quickly, Mark looked up and searched the darkening bush about him, feeling an uneasy chill at the knowledge that he might be observed at this very moment. Satisfied at last that he was alone he backtracked the spoor, and found that the mysterious stranger had searched his camp, had found the pack in the tree and examined its contents, then returned them carefully, each item to its exact place and replaced the pack in the tree. Had Mark not seen the spoor in the earth he would never have suspected that his pack had been touched.

It left him disquieted and ill at ease to know that the man he had tracked and followed had been tracking and probably watching him just as carefully – and with considerably greater success rewarding his efforts.

Mark slept badly that night, troubled by weird dreams in which he followed a dark figure that tap-tapped with a staff on the rocky dangerous path ahead of him, drawing slowly away from Mark without looking back, while Mark tried desperately to call to him to wait, but no sound came from his straining throat.

In the morning he slept late, and rose dull and heavy-headed to look up into a sky filled with slowly moving cumbersome ranges of dark bruised cumulus cloud that rolled in on the south-east wind from off the ocean. He knew soon it would rain, and that he should be going. His time had run, but in the end he promised himself a few last days, for the old man's sake and his own.

It rained that morning before noon, a mere taste of what was to come, but still a quick cold grey drenching downpour that caught Mark without shelter. Even though the sun poured through a gap in the clouds immediately afterwards, Mark found that the cold of the rain seemed to have penetrated his bones, and he shivered like a man with palsy in his sodden clothing.

Only when the shivering persisted long after his clothes had dried, did Mark realize that it was exactly twenty-two days since his first night under the fig tree, and his first exposure to the river mosquitoes.

Another violent shivering fit caught him, and he realized that his life probably depended now on the bottle of quinine tablets in the pack high in the branches of the fig tree, and on whether he could reach it before the malaria struck with all its malignance.

It was four miles back to camp and he took a short route through thick thorn and over a rocky ridge, to intersect the path again on the far side.

By the time he cut the path, he was feeling dizzy and light-headed, and he had to rest a moment. The cigarette he lit tasted bitter and stale, and as he ground the stub under his heel he saw the other spoor in the path. In this place it had been protected from the short downpour of rain by the dense spreading branches of a mahoba hoba tree. It overlaid his own outward spoor, moving in the same direction as he had, but the thing that shocked him was that the feet that had followed his had been booted, and shot with hob-nails. They were the narrower elongated feet of a white man. There seemed in that moment of sickness on the threshold of malaria to be something monstrously sinister in those booted tracks.

Another quick fit of shivering caught Mark, and then passed, leaving him momentarily clear-headed and with the illusion of strength, but when he stood to go on, his legs were still leaden. He had gone another five hundred yards back towards the river when a day-flighting owl called on the ridge behind him, at the point where he had just crossed.

Mark stopped abruptly, and tilted his head to listen. A tsetse fly bite at the back of his neck began to itch furiously, but he stood completely still as he listened.

The call of the owl was answered by a mate, the fluting hoot-hoot, skilfully imitated, but without the natural resonance. The second call had come from out on Mark's right, and a new chill that was not malaria rippled up his spine as he remembered the hooting owls on the escarpment above Ladyburg on that night so many months ago.

He began to hurry now, dragging his heavy almost disembodied legs along the winding path. He found that he was panting before he had gone another hundred yards, and that waves of physical nausea flowed upwards from the pit of his belly, gagging in his throat as the fever tightened its grip on him.

His vision began to break up, starring and cracking like shattered mosaic work, irregular patches of darkness edged in bright iridescent colours, with occasional flashes of true vision, as though he looked out through gaps in the mosaic.

He struggled on desperately, expecting at any moment now to feel the spongy swamp grass under his feet and to enter the dark protective tunnels of papyrus which he knew so well, and which would screen him and direct him back to the old camp.

An owl hooted again, much closer this time and from a completely unexpected direction. Confused, and now frightened, Mark sank down at the base of a knob-thorn tree to rest and gather his reserves. His heart was pounding against his ribs, and the nausea was so powerful as almost to force him to retch, but he rode it for a moment longer and miraculously his vision opened as though a dark curtain had been drawn aside, and he realized immediately that in his fever blindness he had lost the path. He had no idea where he was now, or the direction in which he was facing.

Desperately he tried to relate the angle of the sun, or slope of the ground, or find some recognizable landmark, but the branches of the knob-thorn spread overhead and all around him the bush closed in, limiting his vision to about fifty paces.

He dragged himself to his feet and turned up the rocky slope, hoping to reach high ground, and behind him an owl hooted – a mournful, funereal sound.

He was blind and shaking again when he fell, and he knew he had torn his shin for he could feel the slow warm trickle of blood down his ankle, but it seemed unrelated to his present circumstances, and when he lifted his hand to his face, it was shaking so violently that he could not wipe the icy sweat from his eyes.

Out on his left, the owl called again, and his teeth chattered in his head so that the sound was magnified painfully in his ears.

Mark rolled over and peered blindly in the direction of the hooting owl, trying to force back the darkness, blinking the sweat that stung like salt in his eyes.

It was like looking down a long dark tunnel to light at the end, or through the wrong end of a telescope.

Something moved on a field of golden brown grass, and he tried to force his eyes to serve him, but his vision wavered and burned.

There was movement, that was all he was sure of – then silent meteors of light, yellow and red and green, exploded across his mind, and cleared, and suddenly his vision was stark and brilliant, he could see with unnatural almost terrifying clarity.

A man was crossing his flank, a big man, with a head round and heavy as a cannon ball. He had a wrestler's shoulders, and a thick bovine neck. Mark could not see his face. It was turned away from him, yet there was something dreadfully familiar about him.

He wore a bandolier over his shoulder, over the khaki shirt with military-style button-down pockets, and his breeches were tucked into scuffed brown riding-boots. He carried a rifle at high port across his chest, and he moved with a hunter's cautious, exaggerated tread. Mark's vision began to spin and disintegrate again.

He blundered to his feet, dragging himself up the stem of the knob-thorn and one of the sharp curved thorns stabbed deeply into the ball of his thumb; the pain was irrelevant and he began to run.

Behind him there was a shout, the view-halloo of the hunter, and Mark's instinct of survival was just strong enough to direct his feet. He swung away abruptly, changing direction, and he heard the bullet a split second before the sound of the shot. It cracked in the air beside his head like a gigantic bull-whip, and after it, the secondary brittle snapping bark of the shot.

'Mauser,' he thought, and was transported instantly to another time in another land.

Some time-keeping instinct in his head began counting the split instants of combat, tolling them off even in his blindness and sickness, so that without looking back he knew when his hunter had reloaded and taken his next aim. Mark jinked again in his stumbling, unseeing run and again the shot cracked the air beside him, and Mark unslung the P.14 from his shoulder and ran on.

Suddenly he was into trees, and beside him a slap of bark exploded from a trunk, torn loose by the next Mauser bullet in a spray of flying fragments and sap, leaving a white wet wound in the tree. But Mark had reached the ridge, and the instant he dropped over it, he turned at right angles, doubled up from the waist and dogged away, seeking desperately in the gloom for a secure stance from which to defend himself.

Suddenly he was deafened by a sound as though the heavens had cracked open, and the sun had fallen upon him – sound and light so immense and close that he thought for an instant that a Mauser bullet had shattered his brain. He dropped instinctively to his knees.

It was only in the silence that followed that he realized lightning had struck the ironstone ridge close beside him, and the electric stench of it filled the air around him, the rumbling echo of thunder still muttered over the blue wall of the escarpment and the huge bruised masses of cloud had tumbled down out of the endless blue vault of the sky to press close against the earth.

The wind came immediately, cold and swiftly rushing, thrashing the branches of the trees above him, and when Mark dragged himself to his feet again, it billowed his shirt and ruffled his hair, inducing another fit of violent shivering. It seemed the sweat on his face had been turned instantly to hoarfrost; in the rush of the wind, an owl hooted somewhere close at hand, and it began to rain again.

In the rain ahead of Mark, there was the gaunt, tortured shape of a dead tree. To his fever-distorted eyes it had the shape of an angry warlock, with threatening arms and twisted frame, but it offered a stance, the best he could hope for at this exposed moment.

For a few blessed moments, the darknesss behind his eyes lightened and his vision opened to a limited grey circle.

He realized that he had doubled back and come up against the river. The dead tree against which he stood was on the very brink of the sheer high bank. The river had undercut its roots, killing it, and in time would suck it into the flood and carry it away downstream.

At Mark's back, the river was already high and swift and brown with rain water, cutting off any retreat. He was cornered against the bank while the hunters closed in on him. He knew there were more than one, the owl calls had been signals, just as they had on the escarpment of Ladyburg.

Mark realized that perhaps his only hope was to separate them, and lead them unsuspecting on to his stance, but it must be quick, before the fever tightened its hold on his sense.

He cupped one hand to his mouth and imitated the sad, mournful call of the Scops owl. Then he leaned back against the tree and held the rifle low across one hip. Off on the right his call was answered. Mark did not move. He stood frozen against the tree trunk, only his eyes swivelled to the sound and his forehead creased in his effort to see clearly. Long minutes drew out, and then the owl hoot came, even closer at hand.

The rain came now on the wind, driving in at a steep angle, ice-white lances of slanting rain, tearing at the bush and open grassland beneath it, hammering into Mark's face with sharp needles that stung his eyelids, and yet cleared his vision again so that he could see into the swirling white veils of water. Carefully Mark cupped his mouth and hooted the owl call, bringing his man closer.

'Where are you?' a voice called softly. 'Rene, where are you?'

Mark swivelled his eyes to the sound. A human figure loomed out of the sodden trees, half obscured by the sheets of falling rain.

'I heard your shots – did you get him?' He was coming towards Mark, a tall lean man with a very dark brown sun-scorched face, deeply lined and wrinkled around the eyes, with a short scraggy growth of grizzled hair covering his jowls.

He carried a Lee-Metford rifle at the trail in one hand, and a rubber ex-army gas-cape draped over his shoulders, wet and shiny with rain, a man past the prime of his life, with the dull, unintelligent eyes and the coarse almost brutal features of a Russian peasant. The face of one who would kill a man with as little compunction as he would slit a hog's throat.

He had seen Mark against the dead tree trunk, but the swirling rain and the bad light showed him just the dark uncertain shape, and the call of the owl had lulled him.

'Rene?' he called again, and then stopped, for the first time uncertain, and he squinted into the teeming rain with those flat expressionless eyes. Then he swore angrily, and tried to bring up the Lee-Metford, swinging it across his belly and wiping the safety-catch across with one calloused thumb. 'It's him!' He recognized Mark, and the dismay was clear to see on his face.

'No,' Mark warned him urgently, but the rifle barrel was coming up swiftly, and Mark had heard the metallic snick of the safety-catch and knew that in an instant the man would shoot him down.

He fired with the P.14 still held low across his hip, the man was that close, and the shot crashed out with shocking loudness.

The man was lifted off his feet, thrown backwards with the Lee-Metford spinning from his hands, hitting the rocky ground with his shoulder blades, his heels kicking and drumming wildly on the earth and his eyelids fluttering like the wings of trapped butterflies.

The blood that streamed from his chest soaked into the sodden material of his shirt and was diluted immediately to a paler rose pink by the hammering raindrops.

With a final spasm, which arched his back, the man subsided and lay completely still. He seemed to have shrunk in size, looking old and frail, and his lower jaw hung open, revealing the pink rubber gums of a set of tobacco-stained false teeth. The rain beat into the open staring eyes, and Mark felt a familiar sense of dismay. The cold familiar guilt of having inflicted death on another human being. He had an irrational desire to go to the man, to give him succour, though he was far past any human help, to try to explain to him, to justify himself. The impulse was fever-born and carried on wings of rising delirium; he was at the point now where there was no clear dividing line between fantasy and reality.

'You shouldn't have,' he blurted, 'you shouldn't have tried, I warned you, I warned –' He stepped out from the shelter of the dead tree trunk, forgetting the other man, the man that his senses should have warned him was the more dangerous of the two hunters.

He stood over the man he had killed, swaying on his feet, holding the rifle at high port across his chest.

Hobday had missed with his first three shots, but the range had been two hundred or more and it was up-hill shooting, with intervening bush and tree and shrub, snap shooting at a running, jinking target, worse than jump-shooting for kudu in thick cat bush – a slim swift human shape. He had fired the second and third shots in despair, hoping for a lucky hit before his quarry reached the crest of the ridge and disappeared.

Now he could follow only cautiously, for he had seen the rifle strapped on the boy's back, and he might be lying up on the ridge – waiting his chance for a clear shot. He used all the cover there was, and at last the sheets of falling rain, to reach the rocky crest, at any moment expecting retaliatory fire, for he had shown his own hand clearly. He knew the boy was a trained soldier. He was dangerous and Hobday moved with care.

His relief when he reached the crest was immense, and he lay there on his belly in the wet grass with the reloaded Mauser in front peering down the reverse slope for a sign of his quarry.

He heard the owl hoot out on his left, and frowned irritably. 'Stupid old bastard!' he grunted. 'Pissing himself with fright still.' His partner needed constant reassurance, his old nerves too frayed for this work, and he used no judgement in timing his contact calls. The damned fool! He must have heard the shots and known the critical stage of the hunt was on, yet here he was, calling again, like a child whistling in the dark for courage.

He brushed the man from his thoughts and concentrated on searching the rain-swept slope, until he froze with disbelief. The owl call had been answered, from his left, just below the crest.

Hobday came up on his feet. Crouching low, he worked swiftly along the crest.

He saw solid movement in the grey, wind-whipped scrub and dropped into a marksman's squat, drawing swift aim on the indistinct target, blinking the rain out of his eyes, waiting for a clean shot and then grunting with disappointment as he recognized his own partner, bowed under the glistening wet gas-cape, moving heavily as a pregnant woman in the gloom beneath the rain cloud and dense overhead branches.

The man paused to cup his hand over his mouth and call the mournful owl hoot again, and the bearded hunter grinned. 'Decoy duck,' he whispered aloud, 'the stupid old dog!' and he felt no compunction that he was going to let his ally draw fire for him. He watched him carefully, keeping well down on the skyline, the silhouette of his head and shoulders broken by the low bush under which he crouched.

The old man in the gas-cape called again, and then waited listening with his head cocked. The reply called him on, and he hurried forward into the wind and the rain, drawn on to his fate. Hobday grinned as he watched. One share was better than two, he thought, and wiped the clinging raindrops off the rear sight of the Mauser with his thumb.

Suddenly the old man checked and began to swing up the rifle he carried, but the shot crashed out and he went down abruptly in the grass. Hobday swore softly, bitterly, he had missed the moment, had not been able to place the spot from which the shot had been fired. Now he waited with a finger on the trigger, screwing up his eyes against the rain, less certain of himself, feeling a new awe and respect for his quarry, and the first tingle of fear. It had been a good kill, that one, leading the old man right in close, calling him up as though he were a hungry leopard coming to the bleat of a duiker horn.

Then suddenly the bearded hunter's doubts were dispelled, and for an instant he could hardly believe his fortune. Just when he had been steeling himself for a dangerous and long-drawn-out duel, his quarry stepped out into the open from the cover of a twisted dead tree trunk on the bank of the river, a childlike, ridiculously artless act – an almost suicidal act, so ingenuous that for a moment he feared some trap.

The young man stood for a moment over the corpse of the man he had killed. Even at this range, it seemed as though he swayed on his feet, his face very pale in the weak grey light but the khaki of his shirt standing out clearly against the back lighting from the surface of the river.

It needed no fancy shooting, the range was less than a hundred and fifty yards and for an instant Hobday held his aim in the centre of the boy's chest, then he squeezed off the shot with exaggerated care, knowing that it was a heart shot. As the rifle pounded back into his shoulder and the brittle crack of the Mauser stung his eardrums, he watched the boy hurled backwards by the shock of the strike and heard the bullet impact with a jarring solid thud.

Mark never even heard the Mauser shot for the bullet came ahead of the sound. There was only the massive shock in the upper part of his body, and then he was hurled backwards with a violence that drove the air from his lungs.

The earth opened behind him, and as he fell, there was the sensation of being engulfed in a swirling vortex of blackness – and he knew for just a fleeting moment of time that he was dead.

Then the icy plunge into the swirling brown current of the river caught him and shocked him back from the edge of blackness. The water engulfed his head and he had the strength to kick away from the muddy bottom. As his head broke the surface, he dragged precious air into his crushed burning lungs and realized that he held the P.14 in both hands still.

The wooden stock of the rifle was directly in front of his eyes, and he saw where the Mauser bullet had smashed into the wood and then flattened against the solid steel of the breech block.

The bullet was squashed to a misshapen lump, like a pellet of wet clay hurled against a brick wall. The rifle had stopped it dead, but the tremendous energy of impact had driven the P.14 into his chest, expelling the air from both lungs and hurling him backwards over the bank.

With enormous relief, Mark let the rifle drop into the muddy bottom below him, and was swept away by the current into a swirling nightmare of malaria and rain and raging brown water. Slowly the darkness overwhelmed him, and his last conscious thought was the irony of being saved from death by rifle shot to be immediately drowned like an unwanted kitten.

The water came up over his mouth again, he felt it burn in his lungs and then he was gone into nothingness.

There can be few terrors like those of a mind tortured by malaria fever, a mind trapped in an endless nightmare from which there is no escape, never experiencing the relief of waking in the sweat of terror and knowing it was only delirium.

The nightmares of malaria are beyond the creation of the healthy brain, they are unremitting and they are compounded by a consuming thirst. The thirst as the body burns its strength and fluid in the heat of the conflict, a cycle of attack no less terrible for its regular familiar stages: icy chills that begin the cycle, followed by burning Saharan fevers that rocket the body heat to temperatures so high that they can damage the brain, and that are followed by the great sweat, when body fluid streams from every pore of the victim's body, desiccating him and leaving him without the strength to lift head or hand while he awaits the next round of the cycle to begin, the next bout of icy shivering chill.

There were semi-lucid moments for Mark between the periods of heat and cold and nameless terror. Once, when the thirst burned so that every cell of his body shrieked for moisture and his mouth was dry and swollen, it seemed that strong cool hands lifted his head and bitter liquid, bitter but cold and wonderful, flooded his mouth and ran like honey down his throat. At other times in the cold, he pulled his own grey woollen blanket close around his shoulders and the smell of it was familiar and well-beloved – the smell of woodsmoke and cigarette and his own body smell. Often he heard the rain and crash-rumble of thunder, but always he was dry, and then all sound faded and he was swept away on the next cycle of the fever.

He knew it was seventy-two hours after the first chilling onslaught that he came once again fully conscious. The malaria is that predictable in its cycle that he knew when it was to within a few hours.

It was late afternoon and Mark lay wrapped in his blanket on a mattress of fresh-cut grass and aromatic leaves. It was still raining, a steady grey relentless downpouring from the low pregnant cloudbanks that seemed to press against the tree-tops – but Mark was dry.

Above him was a low roof of rock, a roof that had been blackened over the millennium by the wood fires of others who had sought shelter in this shallow cave; the opening of the shelter faced north-west, away from the prevailing rain-bearing winds, and just catching the last glimmerings of light from where the sun was sinking behind the thick cloud-cover.

Mark lifted himself with enormous effort on one elbow and looked about him, bemused. Propped against the rock wall near his head was his pack. He stared at it for a long time, puzzled and completely bewildered. His last coherent memory had been of engulfing icy waters. Closer at hand was a round-bellied beer pot of dark fire-baked clay, and he reached for it immediately, his hands shaking not only from weakness but from the driving need of his thirst.

The liquid was bitter and medicinal, tasting of herbs and sulphur, but he drank it with panting grateful gulps until his belly bulged and ached.

He lowered the pot then and discovered beside it a bowl of stiff cold maize porridge, salted and flavoured with some wild herb that tasted like sage. He ate half of it and then fell asleep, but this time into a deep healing sleep.

When he awoke again, the rain had stopped and the sun was near its zenith, burning down through the gaps and soaring valleys of the towering cloud ranges.

It required an effort, but Mark rose and staggered to the opening of the rock shelter. He looked down into the flooded bed of the Bubezi River, a roaring red-brown torrent in which huge trees swirled and tumbled on their way to the sea, their bared roots lifted like the crooked arthritic fingers of dying beggars.

Mark peered to the north and realized that the whole basin of swamp and bush had been flooded, the papyrus beds were submerged completely under a dull silver sheet of water that dazzled like a vast mirror, even the big trees on the lower ground were covered to their upper branches, and the higher ridges of ground and the low kopjes were islands in the watery waste.

Mark was still too weak to stay long on his feet, and he staggered back to his bed of cut grass. Before he slept again he pondered the attack, and the disquieting problem of how the assassins had known he was here at Chaka's Gate; somehow it was all bound up with Andersland and the death of the old man in the wilderness here. He was still pondering it all when sleep overtook him.

When he awoke, it was morning again, and during the night somebody had replenished the beer pot with the bitter liquid and the food bowl with stiff porridge and a few fragments of some roast flesh, that tasted like chicken but was probably iguana lizard.

The waters had fallen dramatically, the papyrus beds were visible with their long stems flattened and the fluffy heads wadded down by the flood, and the trees were exposed, the lower ground drying out; the Bubezi River in the deep gorge below Mark's shelter had regained some semblance of sanity.

Mark was suddenly aware of his own nudity, and of the stink of fever and body wastes that clung to him. He went down to the water's edge, a long slow journey during which he had to pause often to regain his strength and for the dizziness to stop singing in his ears.

He bathed away the smell and the filth and examined the dark purple bruise where the Mauser bullet had smashed the P.14 into his chest. Then he dried in the fierce glare of the noon sun. It warmed the last chills of the fever from his body – and he climbed back up to the shelter with a spring and lightness in his step.

In the morning he found that the beer pot and food bowl had disappeared, and he sensed somehow that the gesture was deliberate and carried the message that, as far as his mysterious benefactor was concerned, he was able to fend for himself again, and that he had begun to outlive his welcome.

Mark gathered his possessions, finding that all his clothing had been dried out and stuffed into the canvas pack. His bandolier of ammunition was there also and the bone-handled hunting knife was in its sheath, but his food supply was down to one can of baked beans.

He opened it and ate half, saved the rest for his dinner, left the pack in the back of the shelter, and set out for the far side of the basin.

It took him almost two hours to find the killing ground, and he recognized it at last only by the dead tree with its twisted arthritic limbs. The ground here was lower than he had imagined, and had been swept by the flood waters; the grass was flattened against the earth, as though brilliantined and combed down, some of the weaker trees had been uprooted and swept away and, in the lower branches of the larger stronger trees, the flood debris clung to mark the high-water level.

Mark searched for some evidence of the fight, but there was none, no body nor abandoned rifle, it was as though it had never been ... Mark began to doubt his own memory until he slipped his hand into the front of his shirt and fingered the tender bruising.

He searched down the track of the waters, following the direction of the swept grass for half a mile. When he saw vultures sitting in the trees and squabbling noisily in the scrub, he hurried forward, but it was only a rhino calf, too young to have swum against the flood, drowned and already beginning to putrefy.

Mark walked back to the dead tree and sat down to smoke the last cigarette in his tin, relishing every draw, stubbing it out half-finished and carefully returning the butt to the flat tin with its picture of the black cat – and the trade mark 'Craven A'.

He was about to stand when something sparkled in the sunlight at his feet, and he dug it out of the still damp earth with his finger.

It was a brass cartridge case, and when he sniffed at it, there was still the faint trace of burned cordite. Stamped into the base was the lettering 'Mauser Fabriken. 9 mm' and he turned it thoughtfully between his fingers.

The correct thing was to report the whole affair to the nearest police station, but twice already he had learned the folly of calling attention to himself while some remorseless enemy hunted him from cover.

Mark stood up and went down the gentle slope to the edge of the swamp pools. A moment longer he examined the brass cartridge case, then he hurled it far out into the black water.

At the rock shelter he hefted his pack on to his shoulders, bouncing from the knees to settle the straps. Then, as he crossed to the entrance, he saw the footprints in the fine cold ash dust of the fire. Broad, bare-footed, he recognized them instantly.

On an impulse he slipped the sheathed hunting knife off his belt, and laid it carefully exposed in an offertory position at the base of the shelter wall; then, with a stub of charcoal from the dead fire, he traced two ancient symbols on the rock above it – the symbols that old David had told him stood for 'The-bowed-slave-who-bears-gifts'. He hoped Pungushe, the poacher, would come again to the rock shelter and that he could interpret the symbols and accept the gift.

On the slope of the south butt of Chaka's Gate, Mark paused again and looked back into the great sweep of wilderness, and he spoke aloud, softly, because he knew that if the old man were listening, he would hear, no matter how low the voice. All he had learned and experienced here had hardened his resolve to come to the truth and to unravel the mystery and answer the questions that still hid the facts of the old man's death.

'I'll come again – some day.' Then he turned away towards the south, lengthening his stride and swinging into the gait just short of a trot that the Zulus call '*Minza umhlabathi*' – or 'eat the earth greedily'.

The suit felt unfamiliar and confining on his body, and the starched collar was like a slave's ring about Mark's throat, the pavement hard and unyielding to his tread and the clank of the trams and the honk and growl and clash of train and automobile were almost deafening after the great silences of the bush, and yet there was excitement and stimulation in the hurrying tide of human beings that swirled around him, strident and colourful and alive.

The tropical hot-house of Durban town encouraged all growth of life, and the diversity of human beings that thronged her streets never failed to intrigue Mark; the Hindu women in their shimmering saris of gaudy silk with jewels in their pierced nostrils and golden sandals on their feet; the Zulus, moon-faced and tall, their wives with the conical ochre headdresses of mud and plaited hair that they wore for a lifetime, bare-breasted under their cloaks, big stately breasts fruitful and full as those of the earth mother, to which their infants clung like fat little leeches, and the short leather aprons high on their strong glossy dark thighs swinging as they walked; the men in loin-cloths muscled and dignified – or wearing the cast-off rags of Western clothing with the same jaunty panache and self-conscious assurance that the mayor wore his robes of office; the white women, remote and cool and unhurried, followed by a servant as they shopped or encapsuled in their speeding vehicles; their men in dark suits and the starched collars better suited to the climes of their native north, many of them yellowed with fever and fat with rich foods as they hurried about their affairs, their faces set in that small perpetual frown, each creating for himself an isolation of the spirit in the press of human bodies.

It was strange to be back in the city. Half of Mark's soul hated it while the other half welcomed it, and he hurried to find the human company for which he had sometimes hungered these long weeks just past.

'Good God, my dear old sport.' Dicky Lancome, with a red carnation in his button-hole, hurried to meet him across the showroom floor. 'I am delighted to have you back. I was expecting you weeks ago. Business has been deadly slow, the girls have been ugly, tiresome and uncooperative; the weather absolutely frightful – you have missed nothing, old son, absolutely nothing.' He held Mark off at arm's length and surveyed him with a fond and brotherly eye. 'My God, you look as though you've been on the Riviera, brown as a pork sausage but not as fat. God, I do declare you've lost weight again –' and he patted his own waistcoat which was straining its buttons around the growing bulge of his belly. 'I must go on a diet – which reminds me, lunch-time! You will be my guest, old boy, I insist – I absolutely insist.'

Dicky began his diet with a plate piled high with steaming rice, coloured to light gold and flavoured with saffron; over this was poured rich, chunky mutton curry, redolent with Hindu herbs and garnished with mango chutney, ground coconuts, grated Bombay Duck and half a dozen other sauces, and as the turbaned Indian waiter offered him the silver tray of salads, he loaded his side plate enthusiastically without interrupting his questioning.

'God, I envy you, old boy. Often promised myself that. One man against the wilderness, pioneer stuff, hunting and fishing for the pot.' He waved the waiter away and lifted a quart stein of lager beer to salute Mark. 'Cheers, old boy, tell me all about it.'

Dicky was silent at last, although he did the curry full justice, while Mark told him about it – about the beauty and the solitude, about the bushveld dawn and the starry silent nights, and he sighed occasionally and shook his head wistfully.

'Wish I could do it, old boy.'

'You could,' Mark pointed out, and Dicky looked startled. 'It's out there now. It won't go away.'

'But what about my job, old boy? Can't just drop everything and walk away.'

'Do you enjoy your job that much?' Mark asked softly. 'Does peddling motorcars feed your soul?'

'Hey?' Dicky began to look uncomfortable. 'It's not a case of enjoying it. I mean nobody really enjoys having to work, do they? I mean it's just something one does, you know. One is lucky to find something one can do reasonably well where one can earn an honest coin, and one does it.'

'I wonder,' Mark mused. 'Tell me, Dicky, what is most important, the coin or the good feeling down there in your guts?'

Dicky stared at him, his lower jaw sagging slightly, exposing a mouthful of half-masticated rice.

'Out there, I felt clean and tall,' Mark went on, fiddling with his beer stein. 'There were no bosses, no clients, no hustling for a commission. I don't know, Dicky – out there I felt important.'

'Important?' Dicky swallowed the unchewed curry noisily. 'Important? Hey now, old boy, they're selling rakes like you and me on the street corners at ninepence a bunch.' He washed down the rice with a swallow of beer, and then patted the froth from his upper lip with the crisp white handkerchief from his breast pocket. 'Take an old dog's advice, when you say your prayers at night give thanks that you are a good motorcar salesman, and that you have found that out. Just do it, old son, and don't think about it, or it will break your heart.' He spoke with an air of finality that declared the subject closed, and stooped to open his brief case on the floor beside his chair. 'Here, I've something for you.'

There were a dozen thick letters in Marion Littlejohn's neat feminine hand, all in blue envelopes, a colour which she had explained in previous letters indicated undying love; there was also an account for a disputed twelve and sixpence which his tailor insisted Mark had underpaid; and there was another envelope of marbled paper, pale beige and watered expensively, with Mark's name blazoned across it in a peremptory, arrogant hand – and no address.

Mark singled it out and turned it over to examine the crest, thickly crusted in heavy embossing that stood out on the flap.

Dicky watched him open it and then leaned forward to read it unashamedly, but Mark saved him the effort and flipped it across to him.

'Regimental dinner,' he explained.

'You'll just make it,' Dicky pointed out. 'Friday the 16th.' Then his voice changed, imitating a regimental sergeant-major. 'Two oh hundred hours sharpish. Dress formal and RS bloody VP. Take your dressing from the right, you lucky blighter, your guinea has been paid by your Colonel-in-Chief – Lord Muck-a-Muck General Courtney his exalted self. Off you go, my boy, drink his champagne and steal a handful of cigars. Up the workers, say I.'

'I think I'll give it a miss,' murmured Mark, and placed Marion's letters in his inside pocket, to prevent Dicky reading those also.

'You've gone bush-crazy, the sun touched you, old boy,' Dicky declared solemnly. 'Think of those three hundred potential owners of Cadillacs sitting around one table, pissed to the wide, and smoking free cigars. Captive audience. Whip around the table and peddle them a Cadillac each while they are still stunned by the speeches.'

'Were you in France?' Mark asked.

'Not France.' Dicky's expression changed. 'Palestine, Gallipoli and suchlike sunny climes.' The memory darkened his eyes.

'Then you'll know why I don't feel like going up to the old fort to celebrate the experience,' Mark told him, and Dicky Lancome studied him across the loaded table. He had made himself a judge of character, of men and their workings. He had to be a good judge to be a good salesman, so he was surprised that he had not recognized the change in Mark sooner. Looking at him now, Dicky knew that he had acquired something, some new reserve of strength and resolution the likes of which few men gathered about them in a lifetime. Suddenly he felt a humility in Mark's presence, and although it was tinged with envy, the envy was without rancour. Here was a man who was going somewhere, to a place where he would never be able to follow, a path that needed a man with a lion's liver to tread. He wanted to reach across the table and shake Mark's hand and wish him well on the journey, but instead he spoke quietly, dropping the usual light and cavalier façade.

'I wish you'd think about it, Mark. General Courtney came to see me himself –' and he went on to tell him of the visit, of Sean Courtney's anger when he had heard that Mark had been discharged at his daughter's behest. 'He asked for you to be there especially, Mark, and he really meant it.'

Mark showed his invitation at the gates, and was passed through the massive stone outer fortifications.

There were fairy lights strung in the trees along the pathway that led through the gardens of the old fort, giving the evening a frivolous carnival feeling at odds with the usual atmosphere this bastion had known from the earliest British occupation, through siege and war with Dutch and Zulu; many of the Empire's warriors who had paused here on their occasions.

There were other guests ahead of and behind him on the pathway, but Mark avoided them, feeling self-conscious in the dinner-jacket he had hired from the pawnbroker when he retrieved his decorations. The garment had the venerable greenish tinge of age, and was ventilated in places by the ravages of moths. It was too tight across the shoulders and too full in the belly, and it exposed too much cuff and sock, but when he had pointed this out to the pawnbroker, the man had asked him to finger the pure silk lining and had reduced the hire fee to five shillings.

Miserably he joined the file of other dinner-jacketed figures on the steps of the drillhall, and when his turn came, he stepped up to the reception line.

'So!' said General Sean Courtney. 'You came.' The craggy features were suddenly boyish, as he took Mark's hand in a grip that felt like tortoise-shell, cool and hard and calloused. He stood at the head of the reception line like a tower, broad and powerful, resplendent in immaculately cut black and crisp starched white with a gaudy block of silk ribbons and enamel crosses and orders across his chest. With a twitch of an imperial eyebrow, he summoned one of his staff.

'This is Mr Mark Anders,' he said. 'You remember the old firm of Anders and MacDonald, 1st brigade?'

'Indeed, sir.' The officer looked at Mark with a quick interest, his eye dropping from his face to the silk ribbons on his lapel and back to his face.

'Look after him,' said General Courtney, and then to Mark, 'Get yourself a drink, son, and I'll talk to you later.' He released Mark's hand and turned to the next in line, but such was the magnetism and charm of the big man that after the brief contact and the few gruff words, Mark was no longer the gawky stranger, callow and awkward in cast-off clothes, but an honoured guest, worthy of special attention.

The subaltern took his charge seriously and led Mark into the dense crowd of black-clad males, all of them still subdued and self-conscious in their unaccustomed finery, standing in stiff knots, although the waiters moved among them bearing silver trays laden with the regiment's hospitality.

'Whisky, is it?' asked the subaltern, and picked a glass from one of the trays. 'All liquid refreshment tonight is with the General's compliments,' and took another glass for himself. 'Cheers! Now let's see – 1st brigade –' and he looked around. 'You must remember Hooper, or Dennison?'

He remembered them and others, dozens of them, some were vaguely familiar features, just shades at the edge of his memory, but others he knew well, had liked, or disliked, and even hated. With some he had shared food, or passed a cigarette butt back and forth, with others he had shared moments of terror or exquisite boredom; the good ones, the workers, the cowards and the shirkers and the bullies were all there – and the whisky came endlessly on silver trays.

They remembered him also, men he had never seen in his life came up to him. 'You remember me, I was section leader at D'Arcy Wood when you and MacDonald –' And others, 'Are you *the* Anders, I thought you'd be older somehow – your glass is empty,' and the whisky kept coming on the silver trays – and Mark felt tall and clever, for men listened when he talked, and witty, for men laughed when he jested.

They sat at a table that stretched the full length of the hall and was covered with a damask cloth of dazzling white; the regimental silver blinked like heliographs in the candlelight, and now it was champagne cascading into crystal glass in showers of golden bubbles. All around, the comradely uproar of laughter and of raised voices – and each time Mark lowered his glass, there was a turbaned figure at his side and a dark hand poising the green bottle over his glass.

He sagged back in his chair with his thumbs hooked in his armpits and a black cigar sticking a foot out of his mouth, 'Hear! Hearing!' and 'Quite righting!' the after-dinner speakers, as owlish and wise as the best of them, exchanging knowledgeable nods of agreement with his neighbours, while the ruby port smouldered in his glass.

When the General rose from his centre seat at the cross piece of the table, there was an audible stir in the company which had become heavy and almost somnolent with port and long meandering speeches. They grinned at each other now in anticipation, and though Mark had never heard Sean Courtney speak, he sensed the interest and recharged enthusiasm and he sat up in his chair.

The General did not disappoint them, he started with a story that left them stunned for a moment, gasping for breath, before they could bellow with laughter. Then he went at them in a relaxed easy manner that seemed casual and natural, but using words like a master swordsman using a rapier, a jest, an oath, a solid piece of good sense, something they wanted to hear, followed immediately by something that disturbed them, singling out individuals for praise or gentle censure.

'Third this year in the national polo championships, gentlemen, an honour which the regiment carried easily last year – but a certain gentleman seated at this board has chosen to ride for the sugar planters now, a decision which it is his God-given right to make, and which I am certain not one of us here would condemn,' and Sean Courtney paused, grinning evilly and smoothing his whiskers, while the entire company booed raucously and hammered the table with their dessert spoons. The victim flushed to vivid scarlet and squirmed in the cacophony.

'However, good news and great expectations for the Africa Cup this year. By dint of adroit sleuthing, it has been discovered that dwelling in our very midst –' and the next moment the entire hall was slapping palm to palm, a great thunder of sound, and heads were craning down to Mark's end of the table, while the General nodded and beamed at him, and when Mark slumped down quickly in his seat and tried to make his lanky frame fold like a carpenter's ruler, Sean Courtney called, 'Stand up, son, let them get a look at you.'

Mark rose uncertainly and bobbed his head left and right, and not until later did it occur to him that he had been skilfully manoeuvred into accepting their applause, that in doing so, he was committed. It was the first time he witnessed from a front-row seat the General handling the destiny of a man and achieving his object without apparent effort.

He was pondering this, a little muzzily, as he steered for the safe base of the next lamp post. It would, of course, have been wiser and safer to accept the offer made to him by one of the rickshaw drivers at the gates of the fort, when he had reeled out into the street two hours after midnight. However, his recent unemployment and extravagant expenditure on fancy clothing had left him no choice as to his means of transport. He faced now a walk of some three miles in the dark, and his progress was erratic enough to make it a long journey.

He reached the lamp post and braced himself just as a black Rolls-Royce stopped beside him and the back door swung open.

'Get in!' said the General, and as Mark tumbled ungracefully into the soft leather seat, an iron grip steadied him.

'You are not a drinking man.' It was a statement, not a question, and Mark had to agree.

'No, sir.'

'You've got a choice,' said the General. 'Learn, or leave it alone completely.'

Sean had waited for almost half an hour, the Rolls parked under the banyan trees, for Mark to appear through the gates, and he had been on the point of abandoning the evening and giving his driver the order to return to Emoyeni when Mark had tottered out into the street, brushed away the importunate rickshaw drivers and set off like a crab along the pavement, travelling further sideways than forward.

The Rolls had crept silently along behind him with the headlights dark, and Sean Courtney had watched with a benevolent smile the young man's erratic progress. He felt a gentle indulgence for the lad and for himself, for the odd little quirks and whims with which he still surprised himself occasionally. At sixty-two years of age, a man should know himself, know every strength and be able to exploit it, know every weakness, and have built a secure buttress against it.

Yet here he was, for no good reason that he could fathom, becoming more and more emotionally involved with a young stranger. Spending time and thought for he was not sure what end.

Perhaps the boy reminded him of himself at the same age, and now he thought about it, he did detect beneath the warm glow of champagne in his belly the nostalgia for that troubled time of doubt and shining ambition when a boy stood on the threshold of manhood.

Perhaps it was that he admired – no, cherished was a better word – cherished special quality in any animal. A fine horse, a good dog, a young man, that excellence that horsemen might call 'blood', or a dog-handler 'class'. He had detected it in Mark Anders, and as even a blood horse might be damaged by bad handling or a class dog spoiled, so a young man who had the same quality needed advice and direction and opportunity to develop his full capability. There was too much mediocrity and too much dross in this world, Sean thought, so that when he found class, he was drawn strongly to it.

Or perhaps again – and suddenly he felt that terrible black wave of mourning sweep over him – or perhaps it is simply that I do not have a son.

There had been three sons: one had died before he had lived, still-born in the great wilderness beyond the Limpopo River. Another had been borne by a woman who was not his wife and the son had called another man father. Here Sean felt the melancholy deepen, laden with guilt; but this son was dead also, burned to a charred black mass in the flimsy machine of wood and canvas in which he had flown the sky. The words of Garry's dedication to his new book were clear in Sean's mind. 'This book is dedicated to Captain Michael Courtney, DFC, one of the Young Eagles who will fly no more.' Michael had been Sean's natural son, made in the belly of his brother's wife.

The third son lived still, but he was a son in name only and Sean would have changed that name had it been within his power. Those ugly incidents that preceded Dirk Courtney's departure from Ladyburg so many years before, among them casual arson and careless murder, were nothing compared to the evil deeds he had perpetrated since his return. Those close to him knew better than to speak the name 'Dirk Courtney' in his hearing. Now he felt the melancholy change to the old anger, and to forestall it, he leaned forward in his seat and tapped the chauffeur's shoulder.

'Pull up beside him,' he said, pointing to Mark Anders.

'What you need is fresh air,' Sean Courtney told Mark. 'It will sober you up or make you puke, either of which is desirable.'

And by the time the Rolls parked at the foot of West Street pier, Mark had, by dint of enormous mental effort, regained control of his eyes. At first, every time he peered at the General beside him, he had the nauseous certainty that there was a third eye growing in the centre of his forehead, and that he had multiple ears on each side of his head, like ripples on the surface of a pond.

Mark's voice had at first been as uncontrolled, and he had listened with mild disbelief to the odd blurred sounds with which his lips had replied to the General's questions and comments. But when he frowned with the effort, and spoke with exaggerated slowness and articulation, it sounded vaguely intelligible.

However, it was only when they walked side by side down through the loose sand to the edge of the sea where the outgoing tide had left the sand hard and wet and smooth, that he began to listen to what the General was saying and it wasn't tea-party talk.

He was talking of power, and powerful men, he was talking of endeavour and reward, and though his voice was rumbling and relaxed, yet it was like the purr of an old lion who has just killed, and would kill again.

Somehow Mark sensed that what he was hearing was of great value, and he hated himself for the alcohol in his veins that slowed his mind and haltered his tongue. He fought it off actively.

They walked down along the glistening strip of wet smooth sand, that was polished yellow by the sinking glow of the late moon; the sea smelt of salt and iodine, a crisp antiseptic smell, and the little breeze chilled him so that he shivered even in his dinner jacket. But soon his brain was keeping pace with that of the burly figure that limped beside him, and slowly a sense of excitement built up within him as he heard things said that he had only sensed deep in some secret place of his soul, ideas that he recognized but that he had believed were his alone.

His tongue lost its drag and blur and he felt suddenly bright as a blade, and light as the swallow that drinks in flight as it skims the water.

He remembered how he had at one time suspected that this man might have been responsible in some way for the loss of Andersland, and the old man's death. But now those suspicions smacked almost of blasphemy, and he thrust them aside to throw all his mind into the discussion in which he found himself so deeply involved.

He never did suspect until long afterwards how important that single night's talk would be in his life, and if he had known perhaps his tongue would have seized up solid in his mouth and his brain refused to keep pace, for he was undergoing a rigorous examination. Ideas thrown at Mark seemingly at random were for him to pick up and carry forward or to reject and leave lying. Every question raked his conscience and bared his principles, and gradually, skilfully, he was forced to commit himself on every subject from religion to politics, from patriotism to morals. Once or twice the General chuckled, 'You're a radical, did you know that? But I suppose I was at your age – we all want to change the world. Now tell me what do you think about –' and the next question was not related to the one that preceded it. 'There are ten million black men in this country, and a million whites. How do you think they are going to be able to live together for the next thousand years?' Mark gulped at the enormity of the question, and then began to talk.

The moon paled away in the coming of the dawn, and Mark walked on into an enchanted world of flaming ideas and amazing visions. Though he could not know it, his excitement was shared. Louis Botha, the old warrior and statesman, had said to Sean once, 'Even the best of us gets old and tired, Sean, and when that happens, a man should have somebody to whom he can pass the torch, and let him carry it on.'

With a suddenness that took them both by surprise, the night was passed, and the sky flamed with gold and pink. They stood side by side, and watched the rim of the sun rise from the dark green sea and climb swiftly into the sky.

'I have needed an assistant for many years now. My wife hounds me,' Sean chuckled at the hyperbole, 'and I have promised her I will find one, but I need somebody quick and bright and trustworthy. They are hard to find.' Sean's cigar was long dead and horribly chewed. He took it from his mouth and examined it with mild disapproval before tossing it into the creeping wavelets at his feet. 'It would be a hell of a job, no regular hours, no set duties, and, God knows, I'd hate to work for me, because I am a cantankerous, unsympathetic old bastard. But on the other hand one thing I'd guarantee – whoever took the job wouldn't die of boredom, and he'd get to learn a thing or two.'

He turned now, thrusting his head forward and staring into Mark's face. The wind had ruffled his beard, and he had long ago stripped off his black tie and thrust it into a pocket. The golden rays of the rising sun caught his eyes and they were a peculiarly beautiful shade of blue.

'Do you want the job?' he demanded.

'Yes, sir,' Mark answered instantly, dazzled by the prospect of an endless association with this incredible man.

'You haven't asked about the money?' growled Sean.

'Oh, the money isn't important.'

'Lesson one.' Sean cocked a beetling black eyebrow over the amused blue twinkle of his eye. 'The money is always important.'

The next time Mark entered the gates of Emoyeni was to enter a new life, an existence beyond any he had ever imagined; and yet, in all the overpowering new experience, even in the whirl of having to adjust to new ideas, to the daunting procession of visitors and endless new tasks, there was one moment that Mark dreaded constantly. This was his next meeting with Miss Storm Courtney.

However, he would never know if it had not been carefully arranged by General Courtney, but Storm was not at Emoyeni on Mark's first day, nor during the days that followed, although the memory of her presence seemed everywhere in the portraits and photographs in every room, especially the full-length oil in the library where Mark spent much of his time. She was dressed in a full-length ivory-coloured dress, seated at the grand piano in the main drawing-room, and the artist had managed to capture a little of her beauty and spirit. Mark found the tantalizing scrutiny which the portrait directed at him disconcerting.

Quickly a relationship was established between Mark and the General, and during the first few days, the last of Sean's misgivings were set at rest. It was seldom that the close proximity of another human being over an extended period of time did not begin to irritate Sean, and yet with this youngster he found himself seeking his company. His first ideas had been that Mark should be taught to deal with day-to-day correspondence and all the other time-consuming trivia, leaving Sean a little more leisure and time to devote to the important areas of business and politics.

Now he would drift through into the library at odd times to discuss an idea with Mark, enjoying seeing it through younger and fresher eyes. Or he might dismiss his chauffeur and have Mark drive the Rolls out to one of the sawmills, or to a board meeting in the city, sitting up front beside him on the journey and reminiscing about those days in France, or going further back to the time before Mark was born, enjoying Mark's engrossing interest in talks of gold-prospecting, and ivory-hunting in the great wilderness beyond the Limpopo River in the north.

'There will be an interesting debate in the Assembly today, Mark. I am going to give that bastard Hendricks hell on the Railway budget. Drive me down, and you can listen from the visitors' gallery.

'Those letters can wait until tomorrow. There's been a breakdown at the Umvoti Sawmill, we'll take the shotguns and on the way back try and pick up a couple of guineafowl.

'Drillhall at eight o'clock tonight, Mark. If you aren't doing anything important –' which was a command, no matter how delicate the phrasing, and Mark found himself sucked gently back into the ranks of the peace-time regiment. He found it different from France, for he now had powerful patronage. 'You are no use to me as third rank marker. You're getting to know the way I work, son, and I want you at hand even when we are playing at soldiers. Besides,' and here Sean grinned that evil, knowing grin, 'you need a little time for range practice.'

At the next turn-out, still not accustomed to the speed with which things happened in the world ruled by Sean Courtney, Mark found himself in the full fig of Second Lieutenant, including Sam Browne cross-strap and shining single pips on his shoulders. He had expected antagonism, or at least condescension from his brother officers, but found that when he was placed in command of range drill, he was received with universal enthusiasm.

In the household Mark's standing was not at first clear. He was awed by the mistress of Emoyeni, by her mature beauty and cool efficiency. She was remote but courteous for the first two weeks or so, referring to him as 'Mr Anders', and any request was preceded by a meticulous 'please' and followed by an equally punctilious 'thank you'.

When the General and Mark were at Emoyeni for the midday meal, Mark was served by one of the servants from a silver tray in the library, and in the evenings, after he had taken his leave from the General, he climbed on the elderly Ariel Square Four motorcycle he had acquired, and clattered off down the hill into the sweltering basin of the city to his verminous lodgings in Point Road.

Ruth Courtney was watching Mark with an even shrewder eye than her husband had used. Had he in any way fallen short of her standards, she would have had no compunction in immediately bringing all her influence to bear on Sean for his dismissal.

One morning while Mark was at work in the library, Ruth came in from the garden with an armful of cut flowers.

'Don't let me disturb you.' She began to arrange the flowers in the silver bowl on the central table. For the first few minutes she worked in silence, and then in a natural and friendly manner, she began to chat to Mark, quietly drawing from him the details of his domestic arrangements – where he slept and ate, and who did his laundry, and secretly she was appalled.

'You must bring your laundry up here, to be done with the household washing.'

'That's very kind of you, Mrs Courtney. I don't want to be a nuisance.'

'Oh nonsense, there are two dhobi wallahs with nothing else to do but wash and iron.'

Even Ruth Courtney, one of the first ladies of Natal, still a renowned beauty as a matron well past forty years of age, was not immune to Mark's unstudied appeal. To his natural charm was added the beneficial effect his coming had upon her own man.

Sean seemed younger, more lighthearted in these last weeks, and watching it, she realized that it was not only the burden of routine work that had been lifted from him. The boy was giving him back a little of that spirit of youth, that freshness of thought, that energy and enthusiasm for the things of life that had gone slightly stale and seemed no longer quite worth the effort.

It was their custom to spend the hour before bed in Ruth's boudoir, Sean lounging in a quilted dressing-gown, watching her brush out her hair and cream her face, smoking his last cigar, discussing the day's events while he enjoyed her still slim lithe body under the thin silk of her night-dress, feeling the slow awakening of his own body in anticipation of the moment when she would turn from watching him in the mirror and rise, holding out one hand to him, and lead him through into the bedroom, to the huge four-poster bed under the draped and tasselled velvet canopy.

Three or four times in the weeks since Mark's arrival in the household, Sean had made a remark so radical, so unlike his usual old-fashioned conservative self, that Ruth had dropped the silver hairbrush into her lap and turned to stare at him.

Each time he had laughed self-consciously and held up a hand to prevent her teasing. 'All right, I know what you're going to say, but I was discussing it with young Mark.' He would chuckle again. 'That boy talks a lot of good sense.'

Then one evening, after Mark had been with them just over a month, they had sat in companionable silence for a while when Sean said suddenly, 'Young Mark, doesn't he remind you of Michael?'

'I hadn't noticed – no, I don't think so.'

'Oh, I don't mean in looks. It's just something about the way he thinks.'

Ruth felt the old crushing regret welling up within her like a cold dark tide. She had never given Sean a son. It was the only true regret, the only shadow on all their sunlit years together. Her shoulders sagged now, as though under the burden of her regret, and she looked at herself in the mirror, seeing the guilt of her inadequacy in her own eyes.

Sean had not noticed, had gone on blithely, 'Well, I can hardly wait until February. It's going to break Hamilton's heart to hand over that big silver mug. Mark's changed the whole spirit of the team. They know they can win now, with him shooting number one.'

She had listened quietly, hating herself for not being able to give him what he had wanted so badly, and she glanced down at the little carved statue of the God Thor on her dressing-table. It had stood there all these years since Sean had given it to her, a talisman of fertility. Storm had been conceived in the height of a raging electrical thunderstorm, and had been named for it. He had joked that it needed thunder and had given her the little godlet.

'A fat lot of help you were,' she thought bitterly, and looked up at her own body under the silk in the mirror.

'So good to look at, and so damned useless!' She did not usually curse, it was a measure of her distress. Lovely as it was, her body would not bear another child. All it was good for now was to give him pleasure. She stood up abruptly, her nightly ritual incomplete, and she crossed to where he sat and removed the cigar from his lips, crushing it out deliberately in the big glass ashtray.

Surprised, he looked up at her, about to ask a question, but the words never reached his lips. Her eyelids were half hooded, they drooped languorously, and her lips pouted slightly to reveal the white small teeth, and there were spots of hectic colour on her high beautifully moulded cheek-bones.

Sean knew this expression and the mood it heralded. He felt his heart lurch and then begin to pound like an animal in the cage of his ribs. Usually their loving was a thing of depth and mutual compassion, a thing grown strong and good over the years, a complete blending of two persons, symbolic of their lives together – but once in a rare while, Ruth would droop her eyelids and pout that way with the colour in her cheeks, and what followed was so wild and wanton and uncontrolled that it reminded him of some devastating natural phenomenon.

She pushed one slim hand into his gown, and long nails raked lightly across his stomach so that his skin was instantly tingling and alive, and she leaned forward and with the other hand twined her fingers into his beard and twisted his face up to her and kissed him full on the lips, thrusting a sharp pink tongue deep into his mouth.

Sean let out a growl, and seized her, trying to draw her down into his lap and at the same time pulling open the bodice of her nightdress so that her small pointed breasts fell free, but she was quick and strong, twisting out of his grip, the ivory and pink sheen of her skin glowing through the transparent silk of her gown and her bared breasts joggling delightfully as she flew on long shapely legs into the bedroom, her laughter mocking and goading and inviting.

The following morning, Ruth cut an armful of crimson and white carnations and carried them into the library where young Mark Anders was at work. He stood up immediately and as she replied to his greeting, she studied his face. She had not truly realized how handsome he was, and she saw now that it was a face that would age well. There was a good bone structure and a proud strong nose. He was one of those lucky ones who would improve with the addition of a few wrinkles and lines around the eyes, and a little silver in the hair. That was a long way off, however, now it was the eyes that demanded attention.

'Yes,' she thought, looking into his eyes. 'Sean is right. He has the same strength and goodness that Michael had.'

She watched him surreptitiously as she worked at her flower arrangement, deliberately picking the words as she began to chat to him, and when she had completed the flower bowl, she stood back to admire her work and spoke without looking at him.

'Why don't you join us for lunch on the terrace, Mark?' and the use of his name was deliberate, both of them very conscious of it as it was spoken. 'Unless you'd prefer to continue eating here.'

Sean glanced up from his newspaper as Mark came out on to the terrace, but his expression did not change as Ruth waved Mark to the seat opposite him and he immediately plunged back into the paper and angrily read out the editorial to them, mocking the writer by his tone and emphasis before crumpling the news sheet and dropping it beside his chair.

'That man's a raving bloody idiot – they should lock him up.'

'Well, sir,' Mark began delicately.

Ruth sighed a silent breath of relief for she had not consulted Sean on the new luncheon arrangements, but the two of them were instantly in deep discussion, and when the main course was served, Sean growled, 'Take care of the chicken, Mark, and I'll handle the duck,' so that the two of them were carving and arguing at the same time, like members of the same family, and she covered her smile with her table napkin as Sean ungraciously conceded a debating point to his junior.

'I'm not saying you are right, of course, but if you are, then how do you account for the fact that –'

And he was attacking again from a different direction, and Ruth turned to listen as Mark adroitly defended himself again; as she listened, she began to appreciate a little more why Sean had chosen him.

It was over the coffee that Mark learned at last what had become of Storm Courtney.

Sean suddenly turned to Ruth. 'Was there a letter from Storm this morning?' When she shook her head he went on, 'That damned uppity little missy must learn a few manners – there hasn't been a letter in nearly two weeks. Just where are they supposed to be now?'

'Rome,' said Ruth.

'Rome!' grunted Sean. 'With a bunch of Latin lovers pinching her backside.'

'Sean!' Ruth reprimanded him primly.

'Beg your pardon.' He looked a little abashed, and then grinned wickedly. 'But she's probably putting it in the correct position for pinching right at this moment, if I know her.'

That night when Mark sat down to write to Marion Littlejohn, he realized how the mere mention of Storm Courtney's name had altered his whole attitude to the girl he was supposed to marry. Under the enormous work-load which Sean Courtney had dropped casually on his shoulders, Mark's letter to Marion was no longer a daily ritual, and at times there were weeks between them.

On the other hand, her letters to him never faltered in regularity and warmth, but he found that it was not really the pressure of work that made him keep deferring their next meeting. He sat now chewing the end of his pen until the wood splintered, seeking words and inspiration, finding it difficult to write down flowery expressions of undying love on every page; each empty page was as daunting as a Saharan crossing, yet it had to be filled.

'We will be travelling to Johannesburg next weekend to compete in the annual shooting match for the Africa Cup,' he wrote, and then pondered how to get a little more mileage out of that intelligence. It should be good for at least a page.

Marion Littlejohn belonged to a life that he had left behind him when he passed through the gates of Emoyeni. He faced this fact at last, but was none the less dismayed by the sense of guilt the knowledge brought him, and he tried to deny it and continue with the letter but images kept intruding themselves – and the main of these was a picture of Storm Courtney, gay and sleek, glitteringly beautiful and as unobtainable as the stars.

The Africa Cup stood almost as high as a man's chest on a base of polished ebony. The Emoyeni houseboys had polished it for three days before they had achieved the lustre that General Courtney found acceptable, and now the cup formed the centre-piece of the buffet table, elevated on a pyramid of yellow roses.

The buffet was set in the antechamber to the main ballroom, and both rooms overflowed with the hundreds of guests that Sean Courtney had invited to celebrate his triumph. He had even invited Colonel Hamilton of the Cape Town Highlanders to bring his senior officers by Union Castle liner, travelling first class, as the General's guests to attend the ball.

Hamilton had refused by means of a polite thank-you note, four lines long, without counting the address and the closing salutation. The cup had been in the Cape Town Castle since it had been presented by Queen Victoria in the first year of the Boer War, and Hamilton's mortification added not a little to Sean Courtney's expansive mood.

For Mark it had been the busiest period he had known since coming to Emoyeni. Ruth Courtney had come to place more and more trust in Mark, and under her supervision he had done much of the work of preparing the invitations and handling the logistics of food and liquor.

Now she had him dancing with all of the ugly girls who would otherwise have sat disconsolately along the wall, and at the end of each dance, the General summoned him with an imperious wave of his cigar above the heads of his guests to the buffet table where he had taken up a permanent stance close to the cup.

'Councillor, I want you to meet my new assistant – Mark, this is Councillor Evans. That's right, Pussy, this is the young fellow who clinched it for us.'

And while Mark stood, colouring with embarrassment, the General repeated for the fifth or sixth time that evening a shot by shot account of the final day's competition when the two leading regiments had tied in the team events, and the judges had asked for an individual re-shoot to break the deadlock.

'A cross wind gusting up to twenty or thirty miles an hour, and the first shoot at two hundred yards –'

Mark marvelled at the intense pleasure this trinket gave the General. A man whose fortune was almost beyond calculation, whose land could be measured by the hundred square miles, who owned priceless paintings and antique books, jewellery and precious stones, houses and horses and yachts – but none of them at this moment as prized as this glittering trifle.

'Well, I was marking myself,' the General had taken enough of his own good whisky to begin acting out his story, and he made the gesture of crouching down in the bunker and looking up at the targets, 'and I don't mind telling you that it was the worst hour of my life.'

Mark smiled in agreement. The Highlander marksman had matched him shot for shot. Each of them signalled as a bullseye by the flags of the markers.

'They both shot possibles at two hundred yards, and then again at five hundred yards, it was only at the thousand-yard targets that young Mark's uncanny ability to judge the crosswind –' By this time, Sean's audience was cow-eyed with boredom, and there were still ten rounds of deliberate and another ten of rapid fire to hear about. Mark sensed panic signals across the ballroom and he looked up.

Ruth Courtney was beside the main doors of the ballroom and with her was the Zulu butler. A man with warrior blood in his veins and the usual bearing of a chief, now he was grey with some emotion close to fear and his expression was pitiable as he spoke rapidly to his mistress.

Ruth touched his arm in a gesture of comfort and dismissal, and then turned to wait for Mark.

As he hurried to her across the empty dance floor he could not help but notice again how much mother resembled daughter. Ruth Courtney still had the figure of an athletic young woman, kept slim and firm and graceful by hard riding and long walking, and only when he was close to her were the small lines and tiny blemishes in her smooth ivory skin apparent. Her hair was dressed high on her head, scorning the fashionable shorter cut, and her gown had a simple elegance that showed off the lines of her body and the small shapely breasts. One of her guests reached her before Mark did, and she was relaxed and smiling while Mark hovered close at hand until she excused herself and Mark hurried to her.

'Mark.' Her worry showed only in her eyes as she looked up at him towering above her, but her smile was light and steady. 'There is going to be trouble. We have an unwelcome visitor.'

'What do you want me to do?'

'He is in the entrance hall now. Please, take him through to the General's study, and stay with him until I can warn my husband and send him to you. Will you do that?'

'Of course.'

She smiled her thanks, and then as Mark turned away she stopped him with a touch.

'Mark, try to stay with them. I don't want them to be alone together. I'm not sure what might happen.' Then her reserve cracked. 'In God's name why did he have to come here – and tonight when –' She stopped herself then, and the smile firmed on her lips, steady and composed, but they both knew that she had been going to say, 'Tonight when Sean has been drinking.'

Mark now knew the General well enough to share her concern. When Sean Courtney was drinking, he was capable of anything – from genial and expansive bonhomie to dark, violent and undirected rage.

'I'll do what I can,' he agreed, and then, 'Tell me, who is it?'

Ruth bit her lower lip, the strain and worry clear on her face for a moment before she checked herself, and her expression was neutral when she replied.

'It's his son – Dirk – Dirk Courtney.'

Mark's own shock showed so clearly that she frowned at him.

'What's wrong, Mark? Do you know him?'

Mark recovered quickly. 'No. I have heard of him, but I don't know him.'

'There is bad blood, Mark. Very bad. Be careful.' She left him and drifted quietly away across the floor, nodding to a dowager, stopping to exchange a word and a smile, and then drifting on to where Sean Courtney still held court in the buffet room.

Mark paused in the long gallery, and looked at himself in one of the tall gilt-framed mirrors. His face looked pale and strained, and when he smoothed his hair, his fingers were trembling slightly.

Suddenly he realized that he was afraid; dread was like a heavy weight in his bowels, and his breathing was cramped and painful.

He was afraid of the man he was going to meet. The man that he had stalked so long and painstakingly, and who he had come to know so well in his imagination.

In his mind he had built up an awesome figure, a diabolic figure wielding great and malignant power, and now he was consumed by dread at the prospect of meeting him face to face.

He went on down the gallery, his footsteps deadened by the thick pile of the carpet, his eyes not seeing the art treasures that adorned the panelled walls, for a sense of imminent danger blinded him to all else.

At the head of the marble staircase, he paused and leaned out with one hand on the balustrade to look down into the entrance hall.

A man stood alone in the centre of the black and white checkered marble floor. He wore a black overcoat, with a short cape hanging from the shoulders, a garment which enhanced his size.

His hands were clasped behind his back, and he balanced on the balls of his feet with head and jaw thrust forward aggressively, an attitude so like that of his father that Mark blinked in disbelief. His bare head was a magnificent profusion of dark curls which were shot by the overhead candelabra with sparkling chestnut highlights.

Mark started down the wide staircase and the man lifted his head and looked at him.

Mark was struck instantly by the man's fine looks, and then immediately afterwards by his resemblance to the General. He had the same powerful jaw, and the shape of his head, the set of his eyes and the lines of his mouth were identical, yet the son was infinitely more handsome than the father.

It was the noble head of a Michelangelo statue, the beauty of his David and the magnificent strength of his Moses, yet for all his beauty he was human, not the implacable monster of Mark's imagining, and the unreasonable fear released its grip on Mark's chest, and he could smile a small welcoming smile as he came down the steps.

Dirk watched him without blinking or moving, and it was only when Mark reached the checkered marble floor that he realized how tall the man was. He towered three inches over Mark, and yet his body was so well proportioned that its height did not seem excessive.

'Mr Courtney?' Mark asked, and the man inclined his head slightly without bothering to reply. The diamond that clasped the white silk cravat at his throat flashed sullenly.

'Who are you, boy?' Dirk Courtney asked, and his voice had the depth and timbre to match his frame.

'I am the General's personal assistant.' Mark did not let the disparaging form of address ruffle his polite smile, though he knew that Dirk Courtney was his senior by less than ten years. Dirk Courtney ran an unhurried glance from his head to his shoes, taking in the cut of Mark's evening dress and every other detail in one casual sweep before dismissing him as unimportant.

'Where is my father?' He turned to adjust his cravat in the nearest mirror. 'Does he know I've been waiting here for almost twenty minutes?'

'The General is entertaining, but he will see you presently. In the meantime, will you care to wait in the General's study? If you will follow me.'

Dirk Courtney stood in the middle of the study floor and looked about him. 'The old boy is keeping grand style these days.' He smiled with a flash of startlingly white teeth and then crossed to one of the studded leather armchairs by the stone fireplace. 'Get me a brandy and soda, boy.'

Mark swung open the dummy-fronted bookcase, selected a Courvoisier Cognac from the orderly ranks of bottles, poured some into a goblet, squirting soda on top of it, and carried it to Dirk Courtney.

He sipped the drink and nodded, sprawling in the big leather chair with the insolent grace of a resting leopard, and then once again he surveyed the room. His gaze, checking at each of the paintings, at each of the items of value which decorated the room, was calculating and thoughtful, and he asked his next question carelessly, not really interested in the answer.

'What did you say your name was?'

Mark stepped sideways, so that his view of the man's face was uninterrupted, and he watched carefully as he replied.

'My name is Anders – Mark Anders.'

For a second the name had no effect, then it struck Dirk and a remarkable transformation passed over his features. Watching it happen, Mark's fear was regenerated in full strength.

When he had been a lad, the old man had snared a marauding leopard in a heavy steel spring-tooth trap, and when they had walked up to the site the following morning, the leopard had charged them, coming up short against the heavy retaining chain within three feet of Mark and with its eyes almost on a level with his own. He had never forgotten the terrible blazing malevolence in those eyes.

Now he was seeing the same expression, an emotion so murderous and unspeakably evil that he drew back involuntarily.

It lasted only an instant, but it seemed that the entire face changed, from extravagant beauty to grotesque ugliness and back to beauty in the time it takes to draw breath. Dirk's voice, when he spoke, was measured and controlled, the eyes veiled and the expression of polite indifference.

'Anders? I've heard the name before –' He thought for a moment, as though trying to place it, and then dismissed it as unimportant, his attention returning to the Thomas Baines painting above the fireplace – but in that instant Mark had learned with complete certainty that the vague, unformed suspicions he had harboured so long were based on hard cold fact. He knew now beyond any doubt that something evil had happened, that the sale of Andersland and the old man's death and burial in an unmarked grave were the result of deliberate planning, and that the men who had hunted him on the Ladyburg escarpment and again in the wilderness beyond Chaka's Gate were all part of a design engineered by this man.

He knew that at last he had identified his adversary, yet to hunt him down and bring him to retribution was to be a task that might be beyond his capability, for the adversary seemed invincible in his strength and power.

He turned away to tidy the pile of documents on the General's desk, not trusting himself to look again at his enemy, lest he betray himself completely.

Already he had exposed himself dangerously, but it had been necessary, an opportunity too heaven-sent to allow to pass. In exchange for exposing himself he had forced his enemy to do the same, he had forced him into the open, and he counted himself the winner in the exchange.

There was another factor now that had made his exposure less than suicidal. Whereas before he had been friendless and alone, now he was protected by his mere association with Sean Courtney.

If they had succeeded that night on the Ladyburg escarpment or again at Chaka's Gate, it would be the unimportant passing of a rootless vagrant; now his death or disappearance would rouse the immediate attention of General Courtney, and he doubted if even Dirk Courtney could afford that risk.

Mark looked up quickly from the papers, and Dirk Courtney was watching him again, but now his expression was neutral and his eyes were hooded and guarded. He began to speak, but checked himself as they heard the heavy dragging tread in the passage and they both turned expectantly to the door as it was flung open.

Sean Courtney seemed to fill the entire doorway, the top of the great shaggy head almost touching the lintel and the shoulders wide as the cross-trees of a gallows as he leaned both hands on the head of his cane and glared into the room.

His eyes went immediately to the tall elegant figure that rose from the leather armchair, the craggy sun-browned features darkening with blood as he recognized him.

The two men confronted each other silently, and Mark found himself a fascinated spectator, as he followed intuitively the play of emotions, the re-awakening of the memory of ancient wrongs – and of the elemental love and affection of son for father and father for son that had long ago been strangled and buried, but were now exhumed like some loathsome rotting corpse, more horrible for once having lived and been strong.

'Hello, Father,' Dirk Courtney spoke first, and at the sound of his voice, the rigidity went out of Sean's shoulders, and the anger out of his eyes to be replaced by a sense of sadness, of regret for something that had once had value but was lost beyond hope, so his question sounded like a sigh.

'Who do you come here?'

'Can we speak alone – without strangers?' Mark left the desk and crossed to the door, but Sean stopped him with a hand on the shoulder.

'There are no strangers here. Stay, Mark.' It was the kindest thing that anybody had ever said to Mark Anders, and the strength of the affection he felt for Sean Courtney at that moment was greater than he had ever felt for another human being.

Dirk Courtney shrugged, and smiled for the first time, a light faintly mocking smile.

'You were always too trusting, Father.' Sean nodded as he crossed heavily to the chair behind his desk.

'Yes, and who should remember that better than you.'

Dirk's smile faded. 'I came here hoping that we might forget, that we might look for forgiveness from each other.'

'Forgiveness?' Sean asked, looking up quickly. 'You will grant me forgiveness – for what?'

'You bred me, Father. I am what you made me –'

Sean shook his head, denying it, and would have spoken, but Dirk stopped him.

'You believe I have wronged you – but I *know* that you have wronged me.'

Sean scowled. 'You talk in circles. Come to the point. What do you want that brings you uninvited to this house?'

'I am your son. It is unnatural that we should be parted.' Dirk was eloquent and convincing, holding out his hands in a gesture of supplication, moving closer to the massive figure at the desk. 'I believe I have the right to your consideration –' he broke off and glanced at Mark. 'God damn it, can't I speak to you without this gawking audience?'

Sean hesitated a moment, was on the point of asking Mark to leave, and then remembered the promise he had made to Ruth only minutes before. 'Don't let him be alone with you for a moment, Sean. Promise me you will keep Mark with you. I don't trust him, not at all. He is evil, Sean, and he brings trouble and unhappiness – I can smell it on him. Don't be alone with him.'

'No.' He shook his head. 'If you have something to say, get it over with. If not, go, and leave us in peace here.'

'All right, no more sentiment,' Dirk nodded, and the role of the supplicant dropped from him. He turned and began to stride up and down the study floor, hands thrust deep into the pockets of his overcoat. 'I'll talk business, and get it over with. You hate me now, but when we have worked together – when I have shared with you the boldest and most imaginative venture this land has ever known – then we will talk again of sentiment.'

Sean was silent.

'As a business man now and as a son later. Do you agree?'

'I hear you,' said Sean, and Dirk began to talk.

Even Mark could not but stand in admiration of Dirk Courtney's eloquence, and the winning and persuasive manner in which he used his fine deep voice and his magnificent good looks; but these were theatrical tricks, well rehearsed and stagey.

What was spontaneous was the burning, almost fanatical glow of commitment to his own ideas which radiated from him as he talked and gestured. It was easy to believe him, for he so clearly believed himself.

Using his hands and his voice, he conjured up before his father a vast empire, endless expanses of rich land, thousands upon thousands of square miles, a treasure the likes of which few men had ever conceived, planted to cotton and sugar and maize, watered by a gigantic dam that would hold back an inland sea of sweet, fresh water – it was a dream quite breathtaking in its scope and sweep.

'I have half of the land already,' Dirk paused and cupped his hands with fingers stiff and grasping as the talons of an eagle, 'here in my hands. It's mine. No longer a dream.'

'And the rest of it?' Sean asked reluctantly, swept along on the torrent against his will.

'It's there – untouched, ripe, ready.' Dirk paused dramatically. 'It is as though nature had designed it all for just this purpose. The foundations of the dam are there, built by God as though as a blessing.'

'So?' Sean grunted sceptically. 'Now you are an instrument of God's will, are you? And where is this empire he has promised you?'

'I own all the land south of the Umkomo River, that is the half I have already.' He stopped in front of the mahogany desk and leaned forward with his hands on the polished wood, thrusting a face that glowed with the aura of a religious fanatic towards Sean Courtney.

'We will build a dam between the cliffs of Chaka's Gate and dam the whole of the Bubezi Valley, a lake one hundred and sixty miles long and a hundred wide – and we'll open the land between there and the Umkomo River and add it to the land I already own in the south. Two million acres of arable and irrigated land! Think of that!'

Mark stared at Dirk Courtney, utterly appalled by what he had just heard, and then his gaze switched to Sean Courtney, appealingly, wanting to hear him reject the whole monstrous idea.

'That's tsetse belt,' said Sean Courtney at last.

'Father, in Germany three men, Dressel, Kothe and Rochl, have just perfected and tested a drug called Germanin. It's a complete cure for tsetse-borne sleeping-sickness. It's so secret still that only a handful of men know about it,' Dirk told him eagerly, and then went on, 'Then we will wipe out the tsetse fly in the whole valley.'

'How?' Sean asked, and his genuine interest was evident.

'From the air. Flying machines spraying pythagra extract, or other insect-killers.'

It was a staggering concept, and Sean was silent a moment before he asked reluctantly, 'Has it been done before?'

'No,' Dirk smiled at him. 'But we will do it.'

'You've thought it out,' Sean lay back in his chair and groped absently in the humidor for a cigar, 'except for one little detail. The Bubezi Valley is a proclaimed area – has been since the time of Chaka, and most of the other ground between the Bubezi and Nkomo Rivers is either tribal trust land, Crown land or forestry reserve.'

Dirk Courtney lifted a finger at Mark. 'Get me another brandy, boy.' Mark glanced at the General. Sean nodded slightly, and there was silence again while Mark poured the brandy and brought the glass to Dirk.

'You trust him?' Dirk asked his father again, indicating Mark with his head as he accepted the glass.

'Get on with it, man,' snapped Sean irritably, not bothering to answer the question. Dirk saluted his father with the cut-glass tumbler and smiled knowingly.

'You make the laws, Father, you and your friends in the Cabinet and in the Provincial Assembly, and you can change them. That's your end of the bargain.'

Sean had drawn a swelling chestful of cigar smoke as Dirk spoke, and now he let it trickle out so that his head was wreathed in drifting blue smoke as he replied.

'Let's get this clear. You put up the money and I force through Parliament legislation repealing the proclamation of these lands we need between Nkomo and the Bubezi Rivers?'

'And the Bubezi Valley,' Dirk cut in.

'And the Bubezi Valley. Then I arrange that some front company gets control of that land, even if it's only on a thousand year ground rental?'

Dirk nodded. 'Yes, that's it.'

'What about the cost of the dam and the new railroad to the dam – have you got that type of capital?' Mark could hardly believe what he was hearing, that Sean Courtney was haggling over the assets of the nation, treasures that had been entrusted to him as a high representative of the people. He wanted to shout out, to lash out at them as they schemed. The deep affection he had felt moments before turned slowly to a deep sense of outrage and betrayal.

'Nobody has that type of capital,' Dirk told him. 'I've had my people work out a rough estimate, and there will be little change left out of four million pounds. No individual has that sort of money.'

'So?' Sean asked, the wreaths of cigar smoke drifted away from his head and it seemed to Mark that he had aged suddenly. His face was grey and haggard, the deep-set eyes turned by a trick of the light into the dark empty eye-sockets of a skull.

'The Government will build them for us,' and Dick chuckled richly, as he resumed his pacing. 'Or rather, they'll build dam and railway for the nation. To open up valuable natural resources.' Dirk chuckled again. 'And imagine the prestige of the man that shepherds these measures through Parliament, the man who brings progress and civilization into the wilderness.' He picked up the brandy glass and tossed off half the contents. 'It would all be named after him – the Sean Courtney Dam perhaps?'

'It sounds impressive.'

'A fitting monument, Father.' Dirk lifted the glass to his father.

'But what of the tribal lands, Dirk?' Sean used his son's name for the first time, Mark noticed, and glanced sharply at him.

'We'll move the blacks out,' Dirk told him casually. 'Find a place for them in the hills.'

'And the game reserves?'

'Good God, are we going to let a few wild animals stand in the way of a hundred million pounds?' He shook the handsome head of curls in mock dismay. 'Before we flood the valley, you can take a hunting safari there. You always did enjoy the hunt, didn't you? I remember you telling me about the big elephant hunts in the old days.'

'Yes,' Sean nodded heavily. 'I killed a lot of elephant.'

'So, Father, we are agreed then?' Dirk stopped once more before Sean, and there was for the first time an anxious air, a small frown of worry puckering his bold high forehead. 'Do we work together?'

Sean was silent for seconds longer, staring at the blotter on his desk-top, then he raised his head slowly and he looked sick and very old.

'What you have told me – the sheer size of it all – has taken me completely by surprise.' He spoke carefully, measuring each word.

'It's big and it's going to take guts,' Dirk agreed. 'But you have never been frightened before, Father. You told me once, "If you want something, go out and get it – for one thing is sure as all hell, nobody is going to bring it to you."'

'I am older now, Dirk, and a man grows tired, loses the strength of his youth.'

'You're as strong as a bull.'

'I want time to think about it.'

'How long?' Dirk demanded.

'Until,' Sean faltered, and thought a moment, 'until after the next parliamentary sessions. I will need to speak to people, examine the feasibility of the whole idea.'

'It's too long,' Dirk scowled, and suddenly the face was no longer beautiful, the eyes changed, coming together into a mean ferrety look.

'It's the time I need.'

'All right,' Dirk agreed, and thrust the scowl aside, smiling down at the massive seated figure. He began the gesture of putting out his right hand, but Sean did not look up and instead he thrust the hand back into his overcoat pocket.

'I am neglecting my guests,' said Sean softly. 'You must excuse me now. Mark will see you out.'

'You will let me know?' Dirk demanded.

'Yes,' said Sean heavily, still not looking up. 'I will let you know.'

Mark led Dirk Courtney down to the front doors, and he felt feverish with anger and hatred for him. They walked in silence, side by side, and Mark fought the wild, dark and violent impulses that kept sweeping over him. He hated him for having tarnished the man he had respected and worshipped, for having smeared him with his own filth. He hated him for the old man and for Andersland, and for the dreadful but unknown deeds he had ordered, and he hated him for what he was about to do to that beloved land beyond Chaka's Gate.

At the front doors, Dirk Courtney took his hat from the table and adjusted it over his eyes as he studied Mark carefully.

'I am a good friend to have,' he said softly. 'My father trusts you, and I am sure he confides in you. You would find me grateful and generous, and I am sure that, since you overheard our conversation, you will know what small items of information might interest me.'

Mark stared at him. His lips felt numb and cold, and his whole body trembled with the effort it took to control himself. He did not trust his own voice to speak.

Dirk Courtney turned away abruptly, not bothering with his reply and he strode lightly down the front steps into the night.

Mark stared after him long after he disappeared. There was the crackling snarl of a powerful engine, the crunch of gravel under spinning wheels, and the twin beams of headlights swept the garden, and were gone.

Mark's feet kept pace with the furious rush of his anger, and he was almost running when he reached the General's study. Without knocking, he pushed open the door.

Words threatened to explode out of him – bitter condemnation, accusation and rejection – and he looked to the General's desk, but it was empty.

He was going to warn the General that he would use any means to expose the foul bargain that had been proposed that evening, he was going to voice his disillusion – his horror that Sean Courtney had even listened to it, let alone given it serious thought and the half-promise of his support.

The General stood at the window, his back to the room and the wide square shoulders slumped. He seemed to have shrunk in size.

'General,' Mark's voice was harsh, strident with his anger and determination, 'I am leaving now – and I won't be coming back. But before I go, I want to tell you that I will fight you and your son –'

Sean Courtney turned into the room, his shoulders still drooped and his head held at a listening angle, like that of a blind man, and Mark's voice trailed away, his fury evaporating.

'Mark?' Sean Courtney asked, as though he had forgotten his existence, and Mark stared at him, not believing what he was seeing – for Sean Courtney was weeping.

Bright tears had swamped and blinded his eyes and streamed down the lined and sun-seared cheeks, clinging in fat bright droplets to the coarse curls of his beard. It was one of the most distressing sights Mark had ever witnessed, so harrowing that he wanted to turn away from it – but could not.

'Get me a drink, son.' Sean Courtney crossed heavily towards his desk and one of his tears fell to the starched snowy front of his dress shirt, leaving a wet mark on the material.

Mark turned away, and made a show of selecting a glass and pouring whisky from the heavy decanter. He drew the simple act out and when he turned back Sean Courtney was at his desk.

He held a crumpled white handkerchief in his hand that had damp patches on it, but although his cheeks were dry now, the rims of his eyelids were pink and inflamed and the marvellous sparkling blue clarity of his eyes was dulled with swimming liquid.

'Thank you, Mark,' he said as he set the glass on the desk in front of him. Sean did not touch the glass but stared at it, and when he spoke his voice was low and husky.

'I brought him into the world with my own hands, there was no doctor, I caught him in my own hands still wet and warm and slippery – and I was proud. I carried him on my shoulder, and taught him to talk and ride and shoot. There are no words to explain what a man feels for his first-born son,' Sean sighed, a broken gusty sound. 'I mourned for him once before, I mourned him as though he was dead, and that was many years ago.' He drank a little of the whisky and then went on softly, so softly that Mark could hardly hear the words. 'Now he comes back and forces me to mourn him again, all over again.'

'I am sorry, General. I thought – I believed that you were going to – bargain with him.'

'That thought dishonours me.' Sean did not raise his voice nor his eyes. 'Leave me now, please Mark. We'll talk about this again at some other time.'

At the door Mark looked back, but the General was not aware of his presence. His eyes were still misty, and seemed to stare at a far horizon. Mark closed the door very softly.

Despite Sean Courtney's promise to discuss Dirk Courtney's proposition again, long weeks went by without even the mention of his name. However, though the life at Emoyeni seemed to continue in its busy round, yet there were times when Mark entered the panelled and book-lined study to find the General brooding darkly at his desk, beak-nosed and morbid as some roosting bird of prey, and he withdrew quietly, respecting his melancholy, knowing he was still in mourning. Mark realized it would take time before he was ready to talk.

During this period there were small changes in Mark's own circumstances. One night, long after midnight, Sean Courtney had entered his dressing-room, to find the lights were still on in the bedroom and Ruth propped on her pillows and reading.

'You shouldn't have waited up for me,' he told her severely. 'I could have slept on the couch –'

'I prefer you here.' She closed the book.

'What are you reading?' She showed him the title.

'D. H. Lawrence's new novel, *Women in Love*.'

Sean grinned as he unbuttoned his shirt. 'Did he teach you anything?'

'Not yet, but I'm still hoping.' She smiled at him, and he thought how young and lovely she looked in her lace nightdress. 'And you? Did you finish your speech?'

'Yes.' He sat to remove his boots. 'It's a masterpiece – I'm going to tear the bastards to pieces.'

'I heard Mark's motorcycle leaving a few minutes ago. You kept him here until midnight.'

'He was helping me look up some figures and searching Hansard for me.'

'It's awfully late.'

'He's young,' grunted Sean. 'And damned well paid for it.' He picked up his boots and stumped through into the dressing-room, the limp more noticeable now that he was in his stockinged feet. 'And I haven't heard him complain yet.'

He came back in his nightshirt and slipped into bed beside her.

'If you are going to keep the poor boy to these hours, it's not fair to send him back to town every night.'

'What do you suggest?' he asked, as he wound his gold hunter and then placed it on the bedside table.

'I could turn the gatekeeper's cottage into a flat for him. It wouldn't need much, even though it's been deserted for years.'

'Good idea,' Sean agreed casually. 'Keep him on the premises so I can really get some work out of him.'

'You're a hard man, General Courtney.' He rolled over and kissed her lingeringly, then whispered in her ear.

'I am glad you noticed.'

She giggled like a bride and whispered back, 'I didn't mean that.'

'Let's see if we can teach you something that Mr Lawrence could not,' he suggested.

The cottage, once it was repainted and furnished with discards from the big house, was by Mark's standards palatial, and marvellously free of vermin and cockroaches. It was less than half a mile from the main house, and his hours became as irregular as those of his master, his position each day more trusted and naturally integrated into the household. His duties came to cover the entire spectrum from speech-writing and researching, answering all correspondence that was not important enough for the General's own hand, operating the household accounts, to merely sitting quietly sometimes when Sean Courtney needed somebody to talk to, and acting as a sounding board for arguments and ideas.

Yet there was still time for his old love of reading. There were thousands of volumes that made up the library at Emoyeni and Mark took an armful of them down to the cottage each evening and read until the early hours, devouring with omnivorous appetite history, biography, satire, political treatise, Zane Grey, Kipling and Rider Haggard.

Then suddenly there was a new spirit of excitement and upheaval in Emoyeni as the next session of Parliament approached. This meant that the household must uproot itself, and move almost a thousand miles to Cape Town.

Lightly Ruth Courtney referred to this annual political migration as the 'Great Trek', but the description was justified, for it meant moving the family, fifteen of the senior servants, three automobiles, a dozen horses, all the clothing, silver, glassware, papers, books and other incidentals that would be necessary to sustain in the correct style a busy social and political season of many months, while General Courtney and his peers conducted the affairs of the nation. It meant also closing Emoyeni and opening the house in Newlands, below the squat bulk of Table Mountain.

In the middle of all this frantic activity, Storm Courtney arrived home from the grand tour of the British Isles and the Continent on which she and Irene Leuchars had been chaperoned by Irene's mother. In her last letter to Ruth Courtney, Mrs Leuchars had admitted herself to be both physically and mentally exhausted. 'You will never know, my dear, the terrible weight of responsibility I have been under. We have been followed across half the world by droves of eager young men — Americans, Italians, Frenchmen, Counts, Barons, sons of industrialists, and even the son of the dictator of a South American Republic. The strain was such that at one period I could bear it no longer and locked both girls in their room. It was only later that I discovered they had escaped by means of a fire escape and danced until the following morning at some disreputable *boîte de nuit* in Montparnasse.' With the tact of a loving wife, Ruth refrained from showing the letter to Sean Courtney and so he prepared to welcome his daughter with all the enthusiasm of a doting father, unclouded by awareness of her recent escapades.

Mark was for once left out of the family preparations and he watched from the library window when Sean handed his wife into the Rolls. He was dressed like a suitor in crisply starched fly-away collar, a gay silk cravat, dark blue suit with white carnation in the button-hole and a beaver tilted jauntily over one eye; his beard was trimmed and shampooed and there was a merry anticipatory sparkle in his eyes, and he twirled his cane lightly as he went round to his own seat.

The Rolls purred away, almost two hours ahead of the time when the mailship was scheduled to berth at No. 1 wharf. It was followed at a respectful distance by the second Rolls which would be needed for the conveyance of Storm Courtney's baggage.

Mark lunched alone in the study and then worked on, but his concentration was broken by the imminent arrival of the returning cavalcade, and when it came, he hurried to the windows.

He caught only a glimpse of Storm as she left the car and danced up the front steps hand in hand with her mother. They were followed immediately by the General, his cane snapping a staccato beat off the marble as he hurried to match their swiftness; on his face he wore an expression that tried to remain severe and stern but kept breaking into a wide beaming grin.

Mark heard the laughter and the excited murmur of the servants assembled to greet her in the entrance hall, and Storm's voice giving a new sweet lilt to the cadence of the Zulu language as she went to each of them in turn.

Mark returned to his open books, but did not look down at them. Instead he was savouring that one glimpse he had of Storm.

She had grown somehow lovelier, he had not believed it possible, but it had happened. It was as though the divine essence of young womanhood had been distilled in her, all the gaiety and grace, all the warmth and smoothness, the texture of skin and silken hair, the perfect moulding of limb and the delicate sculpturing of feature, the musical lilt of her voice, clear as the ring of crystal, the dancing grace of her movements, the very carriage of the small perfect head on bare brown shoulders.

Mark sat bemused, acutely aware of the way in which the whole huge house had changed its mood since she entered it, had become charged with her spirit, as though it had been waiting for this moment.

Mark had excused himself from dinner that evening, not wanting to intrude on the family's first evening together. He intended going down to the drill-hall for the weekly muster, and afterwards he would dine with some of the other young bachelor officers. At four o'clock, he left the house through a side entrance and went down to the cottage to bath and change into his uniform.

He was thundering out of the gates of Emoyeni on the Ariel Square Four when he remembered that the General had asked for the Railway report to be left on his desk. In the distraction of Storm's arrival, he had forgotten it, and now he swung the heavy machine into a tight turn and tore back up the driveway.

In the paved kitchen yard he pulled the motorcycle up on its stand, and went in through the back door.

He was standing at the library table with the report in his hands, glancing through it quickly to check his own notations, when suddenly the latch on the door clicked. He laid aside the report and turned just as the door swung open.

This close, Storm Courtney was lovelier still. She was three quick light paces into the room before she realized she was not alone, and she paused, startled, poised with the grace of a gazelle on the point of flight.

One hand flew to her mouth, and her fingers were delicately tapered with long nails that gleamed like pink mother of pearl. She touched her lips with the tip of one finger; the lip trembled slightly, wet and smooth and glistening, and her eyes were huge and a dark fearful blue. She looked like a little girl, frightened and alone.

Mark wanted to reassure her, to protect her from her own distress, to say something to comfort her, but he found he could not move or speak.

He need not have worried, her distress lasted only a fleeting beat of time, just long enough for her to realize that the source of her alarm was a tall young man, dashing in the dress uniform he wore, a uniform that set off the slim graceful body, a uniform emblazoned with badges of courage and of responsibility.

Subtly, with barely a shadow of movement, her whole poise changed. The finger on her lip now touched one cheek with an arch gesture, and the trembling lip stilled and parted slightly into a thoughtful pout. The huge eyes, no longer fearful, almost disappeared behind drooping lids, and then examined Mark critically, lifting her chin to look up into his face.

Her stance changed also, one hip thrusting forward an inch, the twin mounds of her breasts lifting and pressing boldly against the gossamer silk of her bodice. The tender taunting line of her lips was enough to make Mark's breath catch in his throat.

'Hello,' she said. Her voice, although low and throaty, bounced the word off Mark's heart, drawing it out into two syllables that seemed to hang in the air seconds later.

'Good evening, Miss Courtney,' he answered her, surprised that his voice came out level and assured. It was the voice that triggered her memory, and the blue eyes flew wide as she stared at him. Slowly her surprise turned to angry outrage. The eyes snapped sparks and two bright scarlet blotches of crimson burned suddenly on the smooth, almost waxy perfection of her cheeks.

'You?' she asked incredulously. 'Here?'

'I'm afraid so,' he agreed, and her consternation was so comical that he grinned at her, his own misgivings evaporating. Suddenly he felt relaxed and at his ease.

'What are you doing in this house?' She drew herself up to her full height, and her manner became frostily dignified. The full effect was spoiled by the fact that she had to look up at him, and that her cheeks still burned with agitation.

'I am your father's personal assistant now,' and he smiled again. 'However, I am sure you will soon become reconciled to my presence.'

'We will see about that,' she snapped. 'I shall speak to my father.'

'Oh, I was led to understand that you and the General had already discussed my employment – or rather my unemployment.'

'I –' said Storm, and then closed her mouth firmly, the colour spreading from her cheeks down her throat as she remembered with sudden acute discomfort the whole episode. The humiliation was still so intense that she felt herself wilting like a rose on a summer's day, and a small choke of self-pity constricted the back of her throat. It was enough that it had happened, that instead of her father's unquestioning support – something she had been accustomed to since her first childhood memories – he had told her angrily that she had acted like a spoiled child, that she had shamed him by misusing his power and influence, and that the shame had been made more intense by the way she had used it without his knowledge, by sneaking behind his back, as he put it.

She had been frightened, as she always was by his anger, but not seriously disturbed. It was almost ten years since he had last lifted a hand to her.

'A true lady shows consideration to all around her, no matter what their colour or creed or station.'

She had heard it often before, and now her fear was turning to irritation.

'Oh, la-di-da, Pater! I'm not a child any more!' she flounced. 'He was insolent, and anyone who is insolent to me will damned well pay for it.'

'You have made two statements there,' the General noted with deceptive calm, 'and both of them need correction. If you are insolent, then you will get back insolence – and you *are* a child still.' He rose from his chair behind the desk, and he was huge, like a forest oak, like a mountain. 'One other little thing, ladies do not swear, and you are going to be a lady when you grow up. Even if I have to beat it into you.'

As he took her wrist, she suddenly realized with a sense of incredulous dismay what was about to happen. It had not happened since she was fourteen years of age, and she had believed it would never happen again.

She tried to pull away, but his strength was enormous, and as he lifted her easily under one arm and carried her to the leather couch, she let out her first squeal of fear and outrage. It changed swiftly to real anguished howls as he positioned her carefully across his lap and swept her skirts up over her head. Her pantaloons were of blue *crêpe de Chine* with little pink roses decorating the target area, and his palm horny and hard, snapped over the tight double bulge of her buttocks with a sharp rubbery crack. He kept it up until the howling and kicking subsided into heart-racking sobs, and then he lowered her skirts and told her quietly, 'If I knew where to find him, I'd send you to apologize to that young man.'

Storm remembered that threat, and felt a moment of panic. She knew her father was still quite capable of making her apologize even now, and she nearly turned and rushed out of the library. It required a supreme effort once more to draw herself up and lift her chin defiantly.

'You are right,' she said coldly. 'The hiring and firing of my father's servants is not a subject with which I should concern myself. Now, if you would kindly stand aside –'

'Of course, forgive me.' Still smiling, Mark bowed extravagantly and made way for her to pass.

She tossed her head and swished her skirts as she passed him and, in her agitation, went to the wrong shelves. It was some little time before she realized that she was studying intently a row of bound copies of ten-year-old parliamentary white papers, but she would not admit her mistake and humiliate herself further.

Furiously she pondered her next sally, picking and discarding half a dozen disparaging remarks before settling on, 'I would be obliged if in future you would address me only when it is absolutely necessary, and right at this moment I should like to be alone.' She spoke without interrupting her perusal of the white papers.

There was no reply, and she turned haughtily. 'Did you hear what I said?' Then she paused.

She was alone, he had gone silently and she had not even heard the click of the latch.

He had not waited to be dismissed, and Storm felt quite dizzy with anger. Now a whole parade of brilliant and biting insults came readily to her lips, and frustration spiced her anger.

She had to do something to vent it, and she looked around for something to break – and then remembered, just in time, that it was Sean Courtney's library, and everything in it was treasured. So instead, she racked her brain for its foulest oath.

'Bloody Hell!' She stamped her foot, and it was entirely inadequate. Suddenly she remembered her father's favourite.

'The bastard,' she added, rolling it thunderously around her tongue as Sean did, and immediately she felt better. She said it again and her anger subsided, leaving an extraordinary new sensation.

There was a disturbing heat in that mysterious area between navel and knees. Flustered and alarmed, she hurried out into the garden. The short glowing tropical dusk gave the familiar lawns and trees an unreal stagelike appearance, and she found herself almost running over the spongy turf, as though to escape from her own sensations.

She stopped beside the lake, and her breathing was quick and shallow, not entirely from her exertions. She leaned on the railing of the bridge and in the rosy light of sunset her reflection was perfectly mirrored in the still pearly waters.

Now that the disturbing new sensation had passed, she found herself regretting that she had fled from it. Something like that was what she had hoped for when –

She found herself thinking again of that awkward and embarrassing episode in Monte Carlo; goaded on by Irene Leuchars, teased and tempted, she had been made to feel inadequate because she lacked the experience of men that Irene boasted of. Chiefly to spite Irene, and to defend herself against her jibes, she had slipped away from the Casino with the young Italian Count and made no protest when he parked the Bugatti among the pine trees on the high-level road above Cap Ferrat.

She had hoped for something wild and beautiful, something to bring the moon crashing out of the sky and to make choirs of angels sing.

It had been quick, painful and messy – and neither she nor the Count had spoken to each other on the winding road down to Nice, except to mutter goodbye on the pavement outside the Negresco Hotel. She had not seen him again.

Why she thought of this now she could not understand, and she thrust the memory aside without effort. It was replaced almost instantly with a picture of a tall young man in a handsome uniform, of a cool mocking smile and calm penetrating gaze. Immediately she was aware of the warmth and glow in her lower belly again, and this time she did not attempt to fly from it, but continued leaning on the bridge, smiling at her darkening image in the water.

'You look like a smug old pussy cat,' she whispered, and chuckled softly.

Sean Courtney rode like a Boer, with long stirrups, sitting well back in the saddle with legs thrust out straight in front of him and the reins held loosely in his left hand, the black quirt of hippo-hide dangling from its thong on his wrist so that the point touched the ground. His favourite mount was a big rawboned stallion of almost eighteen hands with a white blaze and an ugly unpredictable nature that only the General could fathom; but even he had to use an occasional light cut with the quirt to remind the beast of his social obligations.

Mark had an English seat, or, as the General put it, rode like a monkey on a broomstick, and he added darkly, 'After only a hundred miles or so perched up like that, your backside will be so hot you could cook your dinner on it. We rode a thousand miles in two weeks when we were chasing General Leroux.'

They rode almost daily together, when even the huge rooms of Emoyeni became confining, and the General started to fret at the caging of his big body; then he would shout for the horses.

There were thousands of acres of open ground still backing the big urban estates, and then beyond that there were hundreds of miles of red dirt roads criss-crossing the sugar-cane fields.

As they rode, the day's work was continued, with only the occasional interruption for a half mile of hard galloping to charge the blood, and then the General would rein in again and they would amble on over the gently undulating hills, knee to knee. Mark carried a small leather-bound notebook in his inside pocket to make notes of what he must write up on their return, but most of it he carried in his head.

The week before the departure to Cape Town had been filled with the implementation of details and of broad policies, the winding up of the domestic business of the provincial legislative council before beginning on the national business of Parliament, and, deep in this discussion, their daily ride had carried them further than they had ridden together before.

When at last the General reined in, they had reached the crest of a hill, and the view before them spread down to the sea, and away to the far silhouette of the great whale-backed mountain above Durban harbour. Directly below them, a fresh scar had been torn in the earth, like a bold knife stroke through the green carpet of vegetation, into the red fleshy earth.

The steel tracks of the permanent way had reached this far, and as they sat the fidgeting horses, the loco came huffing up to the railhead, pushing the track carrier ahead of it under its heavy load of steel.

Neither of them spoke, as the tracks were dumped with a faint clattering roar, and the tiny antlike figures of the tracklaying gang swarmed over them, man-handling them on to the orderly parallel rows of timber sleepers. The tap of the swinging hammers began then, a quick rhythmic beat as the fishplates were spiked into place.

'A mile a day,' said Sean softly, and Mark saw from his expression that he was thinking once again of another railroad far to the north, and all that it betokened. 'Cecil Rhodes dreamed of a railway from Cairo to Cape Town – and I believed once that it was a grand dream.' He shook his beard heavily. 'God knows, perhaps we were both wrong.'

He turned the stallion's head away and they walked back down the hill in silence except for the jingle of harness and the clip of hooves. They were both thinking of Dirk Courtney, but it was another ten minutes before Sean spoke.

'Do you know the Bubezi Valley, beyond Chaka's Gate?'

'Yes,' said Mark.

'Tell me,' Sean ordered, and then went on, 'It is fifty years since I was last there. During the war with the old Zulu king Cetewayo, we chased the remains of his impis up there, and hunted them along the river.'

'I was there only a few months ago. Just before I came to you.'

Sean turned in the saddle, and his black brows came together sharply.

'What were you doing there?' he demanded harshly.

For an instant Mark was about to blurt out all his suspicions – of Dirk Courtney, of the fate that had overtaken the old man, of his pilgrimage to find the grave and to fathom the mystery beyond Chaka's Gate. Something warned him that to do so would be to alienate Sean Courtney completely. He knew enough about him now to realize that although he might accuse and even reject his own son, he would not listen to nor tolerate those accusations from someone outside the family, particularly if those accusations were without substance or proof. Mark put the temptation aside and instead he explained quietly.

'My grandfather and I went there often when I was a child. I needed to go back – for the silence and the beauty, for the peace.'

'Yes.' The General understood immediately. 'What's the game like there now?'

'Thin,' Mark answered. 'It's been shot out, trapped and hunted. It's thin and very wild.'

'Buffalo?'

'Yes, there are some in the swamps. I think they graze out into the bush in the night but I never saw them.'

'In 1901 old Selous wrote that the Cape buffalo was extinct. That was after the rinderpest plague. My God, Mark, when I was your age there were herds of ten and twenty thousand together, the plains along the Limpopo were black with them,' and he began to reminisce again. It might have been boring, an old man's musty memories, but he told it so vividly that Mark was carried along, fascinated by the tales of a land where a man could ride with his wagons for six months without meeting another white man.

It was with a sick little slide of regret, of something irretrievably lost that he heard the General say,

'It's all gone now. The railway line is right through to the copperbelt in Northern Rhodesia. Rhodes Column has taken the land between the Zambezi and the Limpopo. Where I camped and hunted, there are towns and mines, and they are ploughing up the old elephant grounds.' He shook his head again. 'We thought it would never end, and now it's almost gone.' He was silent and sad again for a while. My grandchildren may never see an elephant or hear the roar of a lion.'

'My grandfather said that when Africa lost its game, he would go back and live in old London town.'

'That's how I feel,' Sean agreed. 'It's strange but perhaps Dirk has done something of great value for Africa and for mankind.' The name seemed to choke in his throat, as though it was an effort to enunciate it – and Mark was silent, respecting that effort. 'He has made me think of all this as never before. One of the things that we are going to do during this session of Parliament, Mark, is to make sure that the sanctuary in the Bubezi Valley is ratified, and we are going to get funds to administer it properly, to make sure that nobody, ever, turns it into a sugar cane or cotton field, or floods it beneath the waters of a dam.' As he spoke, Mark listened with a soaring sense of destiny and commitment. It was as though he had waited all his life to hear these words.

The General went on, working out what was needed in money and men, deciding where he would lobby for support, which others in the Cabinet could be relied on, the form which the legislation must take, and Mark made a note of each point as it came up, his pencil hurrying to keep pace with the General's random and eclectic thoughts.

Suddenly, in full intellectual flight, the General broke off and laughed aloud. 'It's true, you know, Mark. There is nobody so virtuous as a reformed whore. We were the great robber barons – Rhodes and Robertson, Bailey and Barnato, Duff Charleywood and Sean Courtney. We seized the land and then ripped the gold out of the earth, we hunted where we pleased, and burned the finest timber for our camp fires, every man with a rifle in his hand and shoes on his feet was a king – prepared to fight anybody, Boer, Briton or Zulu, for the right of plunder.' He shook his head and groped in his pockets before he found his cigars. He laughed no longer, but frowned as he lit the cigar. The big stallion seemed to sense his mood, and he crabbed and bucked awkwardly. Sean rode him easily and quirted him lightly across the flank. 'Behave yourself!' he growled, and then when he quieted Sean went on. 'The day that I met my first wife, only thirty-two years ago, I hunted with her father and her brother. We rode down a herd of elephant and between the three of us we shot and killed forty-three of them. We cut out the tusks and left the carcasses lying. That's over one hundred and sixty tons of flesh.' Again he shook his head. 'Only now am I coming to realize the enormity of what we did. There were other things – during the Zulu wars, during the war with Kruger, during Bombata's rebellion in 1906. Things I don't even like to remember. And now perhaps it's too late to make amends. Perhaps also it's just the way of growing old that a man regrets the passing of the old ways. He initiates change when he is young and then mourns that change when he grows old.'

Mark was silent, not daring to say a word that might break the mood. He knew that what he was hearing was so important that he could then only guess at the depths of it.

'We must try, Mark, we must try.'

'Yes, sir. We will,' Mark agreed, and something in his tone made the General glance across at him, mildly surprised.

'This really means something to you.' He nodded, confirming his statement. 'Yes, I can see that. Strange, a young fellow like you! When I was your age all I ever thought about was a quick sovereign and a likely piece of–' He caught himself before he finished, and coughed to clear his throat.

'Well, sir, you must remember that I had my full share of destruction at an earlier age than you did. The greatest destruction the world has ever known.' The General's face darkened as he remembered what they had shared together in France. 'When you've seen how easy it is to tear down, it makes the preservation seem worth while.' Mark chuckled ruefully. 'Perhaps I was born too late.'

'No,' said the General softly. 'I think you were born just in time,' and he might have gone on, but high and clear on the heat-hushed air came the musical cry of a girl's voice, and instantly the General's head went up and his expression lightened.

Storm Courtney came at the gallop. She rode with the same light lithe grace which marked all she did. She rode astride, and she wore knee-high boots with baggy gaucho pants tucked into the tops, a hand-embroidered waistcoat in vivid colours over a shirt of white satin with wide sleeves, and a black wide-brimmed vaquero hat hung on her back from a thong around her throat.

She reined in beside her father, laughing and flushed, tossing the hair out of her face, and leaning out of the saddle to kiss him, not even glancing at Mark, and he touched his reins and dropped back tactfully.

'We've been looking for you all over, Pater,' she cried. 'We went as far as the river – what made you come this way?'

Coming up more sedately behind Storm on a bay mare was the blonde girl whom Mark remembered from that fateful day at the tennis courts. She was more conventionally dressed than Storm in dove-grey riding breeches and tailored jacket, and the wind ruffled the pale silken gold of her cropped hair.

While she made her greetings to the General, her eyes kept swivelling in Mark's direction and he searched for her name and remembered she had been called Irene – and realized she must be the girl who had been Storm's companion on the grand continental tour. A pretty, bright little thing with a gay brittle style and calculating eyes.

'Good afternoon, Miss Leuchars.'

'Oh la!' She smiled archly at him now. 'Have we met?' Somehow her mare was kneed away from the leading pair, and dropped back beside Mark's mount.

'Briefly, yes, we have,' Mark admitted, and suddenly the china-blue eyes flew wide and the girl covered her mouth with a gloved hand.

'You are the one –' then she squealed softly with delight, and mimicked him, 'just as soon as you say please!'

Storm Courtney had not looked round, and she was paying exaggerated attention to her father, but Mark watched her small perfect ears turn pink, and she tossed her head again, but this time with an aggressive, angry motion.

'I think we might forget that,' Mark murmured.

'Forget it?' chirruped Irene. 'I'll never forget it. It was absolutely classic.' She leaned over and placed a bold hand on Mark's forearm. At that moment Storm could contain herself no longer; she swivelled in the saddle and was about to speak to Irene, when she saw the hand on Mark's arm.

For a moment Storm's expression was ferocious, and the dark blue eyes snapped with an electric sparkle. Irene held her gaze undaunted, making her own paler blue eyes wide and artless, and deliberately, challengingly, she let her hand linger, squeezing lightly on Mark's sleeve.

The understanding between the two girls was instantaneous. They had played the game before, but this time intuitively Irene realized that she had never been in a stronger position to inflict punishment. She had never seen such a swift and utterly malevolent reaction from Storm – and they knew each other intimately. This time she had Missy Storm in a vice, and she was going to squeeze and squeeze.

She edged her mare in until her knee touched Mark's, and she turned away from Storm, deliberately looking up at the rider beside her.

'I hadn't realized you were so tall,' she murmured. 'How tall are you?'

'Six foot two.' Mark only dimly realized that something mysterious, which promised him many awkward moments, was afoot.

'Oh, I do think height gives a man presence.'

Storm was now laughing gaily with her father, and trying to listen to the conversation behind her at the same time. Anger clawed her cruelly and she clutched the riding-crop until her fingers ached. She was not quite sure what had affected her this way, but she would have delighted in lashing the crop across Irene's silly simpering face.

It was certainly not that she felt anything for Mark Anders. He was, after all, merely a hired servant at Emoyeni. He could make an idiot of himself over Irene Leuchars and she would not even glance aside at any other time or place. It was just that there were some things that were not done, the dignity of her position, of her father, and family – yes, that was it, she realized. It was an insult that Irene Leuchars, as a guest in the Courtney home, should make herself free, should flaunt herself, should make it so blatant that she would like to lead Mark Anders along the well-travelled pathway to her steamy – she could not continue the thought, for the vivid mental image of that pale, deceptively fragile-looking body of Irene's spread out, languid and naked, and Mark about to – another wave of anger made her sway in the saddle, and she dropped the riding-crop she carried and turned quickly.

'Oh Mark, I've dropped my crop. Won't you be a dear and fetch it for me?'

Mark was taken aback, not only by the endearment, but also by the stunning smile and warmth of Storm's voice. He almost fell from the saddle in his haste, and when he came alongside Storm to hand the crop back to her, she detained him with a smile of thanks, and a question.

'Mark, won't you help me label my cases? It's only a few days and we'll all be leaving for Cape Town.'

'I'm so looking forward to it,' Irene agreed as she pushed her mare up on Mark's other side, and Storm smiled sweetly at her.

'It should be fun,' she agreed. 'I love Cape Town.'

'Grand fun,' Irene laughed gaily, and Storm regretted bitterly the invitation that would make her a guest for four months in the Courtney's Cape Town home. Before Storm could find a cutting rejoinder, Irene leaned across to Mark.

'Come on, then,' she said, and turned her mare aside.

'Where are you going?' Storm demanded.

'Mark is taking me down to the river to show me the monument where Dick King crossed on his way to fetch the English troops from Grahamstown.'

'Oh, Irene darling,' Storm dabbed at her eye with the tail of her scarf, 'I seem to have something in my eye. Won't you see to it? No, don't wait for us, Mark. Go on ahead with the General. I know he needs you still.'

And she turned her small perfect head to Irene for her ministrations.

With patent relief, Mark spurred ahead to catch up with the General, and Irene told Storm in honeyed tones,

'There's nothing in your eye, darling, except a touch of green.'

'You bitch,' hissed Storm.

'Darling, I don't know what you mean.'

The *Dunottar Castle* trembled under the thrust of her engines and ran southwards over a starlit sea that seemed to be sculpted from wet black obsidian, each crest marched with such weighty dignity as to seem solid and unmoving. It was only when the ship put her sharp prow into them that they burst into creaming white, and hissed back along the speeding hull.

The General paused and looked at the southern sky, to where the great cross burned among its myriad cohorts, and Orion the hunter brandished his sword.

'That's the way the sky should be,' he nodded his approval. 'I could never get used to the northern skies. It was as though the universe had disintegrated, and the grand designs of nature had been plunged into anarchy.'

They went to the rail and paused there to watch the moon rise out of the dark sea, and as it pushed its golden dome clear of the horizon, the General pulled out the gold hunter watch from his waistcoat pocket and grunted. 'Twenty-one minutes past midnight, the moon is punctual this morning.' Mark smiled at the little joke. Yet he knew that it was part of the General's daily ritual to consult his almanac for sunrise and moonrise, and the moon phases. The man's energy was formidable.

They had worked until just a few minutes previously and had been at it since mid-morning. Mark felt muzzy and woolly headed with mental effort and the pungent incense of the General's cigars which had filled the suite.

'I think we overdid it a little today, my boy,' Sean Courtney admitted, as though he had read the thought. 'But I did want to be up to date before we dock in Table Bay. Thank you, Mark. Now why don't you go down and join the dancing.'

From the boat deck, Mark looked down on to the swirling orderly confusion of dancing couples in the break of the promenade deck. The ship's band was belting out a Strauss waltz and the dancers spun wildly, the women's skirts flaring open like the petals of exotic blooms and their laughing cries a sweet and musical counterpoint to the stirring strains of the waltz.

Mark picked Storm Courtney out of the press, her particular grace making it easy to distinguish her, she lay back in the circle of her partner's arms and spun dizzily, the light catching the dark sparkle of her hair and glowing on the waxy golden perfection of her bare shoulders.

Mark lit a cigarette, and leaned on the rail, watching her. It was strange that he had seldom felt lonely in the great silences and space of the wilderness, and here, surrounded by music and gaiety and the laughter of young people, he knew deep loneliness.

The General's suggestion that he go down and join the dancing had been unwittingly cruel. He would have been out of place there among the rich young clique who had known each other since childhood, a close-knit élite that jealously closed ranks against any intruder, especially one that did not possess the necessary qualifications of wealth and social standing.

He imagined going down and asking Storm Courtney for a waltz, her humiliation at being accosted by her father's secretary, the nudging and the snide exchanges, the patronizing questions. 'Do you actually type letters, old boy?' And he felt himself flushing angrily at the mere thought of it.

Yet he lingered by the rail for another half hour, delighting in each glimpse of Storm, and hating each of her partners with a stony implacable hatred; and when at last he went down to his cabin, he could not sleep. He wrote a letter to Marion Littlejohn, and found himself as warmly disposed towards her as he had been in months. Her gentleness and sincerity, and the genuineness of her affection for him were suddenly very precious assets. On the pages he recalled the visit she had made to Durban just before his departure. The General had been understanding and they had had many hours together during the two days. She had been awed by his new position, and impressed by his surroundings. However, their one further attempt at physical intimacy, even though it had been made in the security and privacy of Mark's cottage, had been, if anything, less successful than the first. There had been no opportunity, nor had Mark had the heart to break off their engagement, and in the end Mark had put her on the train to Ladyburg with relief, but now loneliness and distance had enhanced her memory. He wrote with real affection and sincerity, but when he had sealed the envelope, he found that he still had no desire for sleep.

He had found a copy of *Jock of the Bushveld* in the ship's library and was rereading the adventures of man and dog, and the nostalgic and vivid descriptions of African bush and animals with such pleasure, that his loneliness was forgotten. There was a light tap on the door of his cabin.

'Oh Mark, do let me hide in here for a moment.' Irene Leuchars pushed quickly past him before he could protest, and she ordered, 'Quickly, lock the door.' Her tone made him obey immediately, but when he turned back to her he had immediate misgivings.

She had been drinking. The flush of her cheeks was not all rouge, the glitter in her eyes was feverish, and when she laughed it was unnaturally high.

'What's the trouble?' he asked.

'Oh God, darling, I have had the most dreadful time. That Charlie Eastman is absolutely hounding me. I swear I'm terrified to go back to my cabin.'

'I'll talk to him,' Mark offered, but she stopped him quickly.

'Oh, don't make a scene. He's not worth it.' She flicked the tail of the ostrich feather boa over her shoulder. 'I'll just sit here for a while, if you don't mind.'

Her dress was made of layers of filmy material that floated in a cloud about her as she moved, and her shoulders were bare, the bodice cut so low that her breasts bulged out, very round and smooth and white and deeply divided.

'Do you mind?' she demanded, very aware of the direction of his eyes, and he lifted them quickly to her face. She made a moue of impatience as she waited for his reply. Her lipstick was startling crimson and glossy, so her lips had a full ripe look.

He knew he must get her out of his cabin. He knew that he was in danger. He knew how vulnerable he was, how powerful her family, and he guessed how shallow and callous she could be. But he was lonely, achingly grindingly lonely.

'You can stay, of course,' he told her, and she drooped her eyelids and ran a sharp pink tongue across the painted lips.

'Have you got a drink, darling?'

'No, I'm sorry.'

'Don't be, don't ever be sorry.' She swayed against him and he could smell the liquor on her breath, but it was not offensive and, with her perfume, blended into a spicy fragrance.

'Look,' she told him, holding up the silver evening bag she carried. 'The "It" girl with every home comfort,' and she took a small silver jewelled flask from the bag. 'Every comfort known to man,' she repeated, and parted her lips in a lewd but intensely provocative pout.

'Come and I'll give you a little sample.' Her voice dropped to a husky whisper, and then she laughed and swirled away in a waltzing turn, humming a bar of the Blue Danube and the gossamer of her skirts floated about her thighs. Clad in silk, her limbs gleamed in the soft light and when she dropped carelessly on to Mark's bunk, her skirts ballooned and then settled so high that he could see that the black elastic suspender-belt that held her stocking tops was decorated with embroidered butterflies. The butterflies were spangled with brilliant colour and in exotic contrast to the pale soft skin of her inner thighs.

'Come, Markie, come and have a little itsy bitsy drinkie.' She patted the bunk beside her and then wriggled her bottom across to make room for him. The skirts rucked up higher and exposed the wedge of her panties between her thighs. The material was so sheer that he could see the pale red-gold curls trapped and flattened by the silk.

Mark felt something crack inside him. For another moment he tried to reckon consequence, to force himself back on to the course that was both moral and safe, but he knew that in reality the decision had been made when he had allowed her to stay.

'Come, Mark.' She held the flask like bait, and the light reflected off it in silver splinters that she played into his eyes. The crack opened, and like a bursting dam, all restraint was swept aside. She recognized the moment and her eyes flared with triumph and she welcomed him to the bed with a little animal squeal, and with slim pale arms that wrapped about his neck with startling strength.

She was small and strong, quick and demanding, and as skilled as Helena MacDonald – but she was different, so very different.

Her youth gave her flesh a sweetness and freshness, her skin an unblemished lustre, a luscious plasticity that was made more startling by her pale pigmentation.

When she slipped the strap off one shoulder and popped one of her glossy breasts out of the top of her bodice, offering it to Mark with a sound in her throat which was like the purr of a cat, he gasped aloud. It was white as porcelain and had the same sheen, too large for the slim fragile body but hard and firm and springy to his touch. The nipple was tiny, set like a small jewel in the perfect coin of its aureole, so pale and delicate pink when he remembered Helena, dark and puckered and sprinkled with sparse black hair.

'Wait, Mark. Wait,' she chuckled breathlessly, and stood quickly to drop the boa and dress to the cabin floor in one quick movement, and then to slip the sheer underwear to her ankles and kick it carelessly aside. She lifted her hands above her head and twirled slowly in front of him.

'Yes?' she asked.

'Yes,' he agreed. 'Oh very much yes.'

Her body was hairless and smooth except for that pale red mist that hazed the fat mound at the base of her belly, and her breasts rode high and arrogant.

She came back to him, kneeling over him.

'There,' she whispered. 'There's a good boy,' she crooned, but her hands were busy, unbuckling, unbuttoning, questing, finding – and then it was her turn to gasp.

'Oh, Mark, you clever boy – all by yourself too!'

'No,' he laughed. 'I had a little help.'

'And you are going to get a lot more,' she promised, and dropped her soft, fluffy golden head over him. He thought that her mouth was as red and voracious as one of those low-tide rock-pool anemones that he had fed with such delight as a child, watching it softly enfold each tidbit, sucking it in deeply.

'Oh God,' he croaked, for her mouth was hot – hotter and deeper than any sea animal could ever be.

Irene Leuchars carried her shoes in one hand and the feather boa hung over her other arm and trailed on the floor behind her. Her hair stood out in a soft pale halo around her head, and her eyes were underlined by dark blue smudges of sleeplessness, while the outline of her mouth was smudged and blurred, her lips puffed and inflamed.

'God,' she whispered, 'I'm still tiddly,' and she giggled, and lurched unsteadily to the roll of the ship. Then she pulled up the strap which had slipped from her shoulder.

Behind her in the long passageway, there was a clatter of china and she glanced back, startled. One of the white-jacketed stewards was pushing a trolley of cups and pots towards her. The morning ritual of tea and biscuits was beginning and she had not realized the hour.

Irene hurried away, turning the corner from the steward's sly and knowing grin, and she reached the door of Storm Courtney's cabin without another encounter.

She hammered on the door with the heel of one shoe, but it was a full five minutes before the door swung open and Storm looked out at her, a gown wrapped around her shoulders and her big dark eyes owlish from sleep.

'Irene, are you crazy?' she asked. 'It's still night!' Then she saw Irene's attire and smelled the rich perfume of her breath. 'Where on earth have you been?'

Irene pushed the door open and almost tripped over the threshold.

'You're drunk!' accused Storm resignedly, closing the door behind her.

'No.' Irene shook her head. 'It isn't liquor – it's ecstasy.'

'Where have you been?' Storm asked again. 'I thought you were in bed hours ago.'

'I have flown to the moon,' intoned Irene dramatically. 'I have run barefooted through the stars, I have soared on eagles' wings above the mountain peaks.'

Storm laughed, coming fully awake now, as beautiful even in *déshabillé* as Irene would never be, so graceful and lovely that Irene hated her again. She savoured the moment, drawing out the pleasure of anticipation.

'Where have you been, you mad bad woman?' Storm started to catch the spirit of the moment. 'Tell all!'

'Through the gates of paradise, to the land of never-never on the continent of always –' Irene's smile became sharp, spiteful and venomous, 'in short, darling, Mark Anders has been bouncing me like a rubber ball!'

And the expression on Storm Courtney's face gave her the most intense satisfaction she had known in her life.

'On the third day of January, the Chamber of Mines deliberately tore up the Agreement that it had come to with your Union to maintain the status quo. It tore that agreement to a thousand pieces and flung them in the faces of the workers.' Fergus MacDonald spoke with a controlled icy fury that carried to every corner of the great hall, and it stilled even the rowdies in the back seats who had brought their bottles in brown paper packets. Now they listened with intensity. Big Harry Fisher, sitting beside him on the dais, turned his head slowly to assess the man, peering at him under beetling eyebrows and with the bulldog folds of his face hanging mournfully. He marvelled again at how Fergus MacDonald changed when he stood to speak.

Usually he cut a nondescript figure with the small bulge of a paunch beginning to distort the spare frame, the cheap and ill-fitting suit shiny at the elbows and seat with wear, the collar of the frayed shirt darned, and grease spots on the drab necktie. His hair was thinning, starting up in wispy spikes around the neck, pushing back from the brow and with a pink bare patch in the crown. His face had that grey tone from the embedded filth of the machine shops, but when he stood under the red flag and the emblem of the Amalgamated Mineworkers Union on the raised dais facing the packed hall, he grew in stature, a physical phenomenon that was quite extraordinary. He seemed younger and there was a fierce and smouldering passion which stripped away his shoddy dress and armoured him with presence.

'Brothers!' He raised his voice now. 'When the mines re-opened after the Christmas recess, two thousand of our members were discharged, thrown out into the street, discarded like worn-out pairs of old boots –'

The hall hummed, the warning sound of a beehive on a hot summer's day, but the stillness of thousands of bodies pressed closely together was more menacing than any movement.

'Brothers!' Fergus moved his hands in a slow hypnotic movement. 'Brothers! Beginning at the end of this month, and for every month after that, another six hundred men will be,' he paused again and then spat the official word at them, 'retrenched.'

They seemed to reel with the word, the whole concourse stunned as though by a physical blow, and the silence drew out – until a voice at the back yelled wildly,

'No, brothers. No!'

They roared then, a sound like the surf on a stormy day when it breaks upon a rocky shore.

Fergus let them roar, and he hooked his thumbs into his rumpled waistcoat and watched them, gloating in the feeling of exultation, the euphoria of power. He judged the strength of their reaction, and the moment it began to falter he raised both hands, and almost immediately the silence fell upon the hall again.

'Brothers! Do you know that the wages of a black man are two shillings and two pence a day? Only a black man can live on that wage!' He let it sink in a moment, but not too long before he went on, asking a reasonable question, 'Who will take the place of our brothers who are now out of work? Who will replace the six hundred that will join them at the end of this month, and the next – and the next? Who will take *your* job,' he was picking out individuals, pointing at them with an accuser's finger, 'and *yours*, and *yours*? Who will take the food from your children's mouths?' He waited theatrically for an answer, cocking his head, smiling at them while his eyes smouldered.

'Brothers! I tell you who it will be. Two and tuppenny black kaffirs – that's who it will be!'

They came upon their feet, a bench here and there crashing over backwards and their voices were a blood-roar of anger, clenched fists thrust out in fury.

'No, brothers. No!' Their booted feet stamped in unison and they chanted, their fists punching into empty air.

Fergus MacDonald sat down abruptly and Harry Fisher congratulated him silently, squeezing his shoulder in a bear's paw before lumbering to his feet.

'Your executive has recommended that all members of our Union come out on general strike. I put it to you now, brothers, all those in favour –' he bellowed, and his voice was drowned in a thousand others.

'Out, brothers! We're out! Out! Out!'

Fergus leaned forward in his seat and looked down the length of the trestle table.

Helena's dark head was bowed over the minute book, but she sensed his gaze and looked up. Her expression glowed with a fanatic's ecstasy, and there was open adoration in her eyes that he saw only at moments like this. Harry Fisher had told him once, 'For all women, power is the ultimate aphrodisiac. No matter how puny in body, no matter what he looks like – power makes a man irresistible.'

In the thunder of thousands of voices, the pounding feet and the heady roar of power, Fergus was on his feet again.

'The mine-owners, the bosses have challenged us, they have scorned your executive, they have stated publicly that we are too faint-hearted to rally the workers and come out on general strike! Well, brothers, we are going to show them.' The lion's voice of the crowd rose again and he silenced it only after another minute. 'First, we are going to drive on the scabs, there are going to be no strike-breakers.' When the sound subsided he went on, 'Slim Jannie Smuts has talked of force to beat a strike, he has an army, but we are going to have one also. I think the bosses have forgotten that we fought their bloody war for them in France and East Africa, at Tabora and Delville Wood.' The names sobered them and they were listening again. 'Last time we fought for them, but this time we are fighting for ourselves. Each one of you will report to his area commander – you will be formed into fighting commandos, each man will know his job, and each man will know what is at stake. We will beat them, brothers, the bloody bosses and their greedy grasping minions. We will fight them and beat them!'

'They are organized into military-style commandos,' said the Prime Minister softly, breaking the crisp brown roll of bread with fingers that were surprisingly small, neat and capable as a woman's. 'Of course, we know that George Mason wanted to form labour commandos in 1914. It was the main reason I had him deported.' The other guests at the luncheon table were silent. The deportation of Mason was not an episode that reflected credit on Jannie Smuts. 'But this is a different animal we are dealing with now. Nearly all the younger members of the unions are trained veterans. Five hundred of them paraded outside the Trade Union Hall in Fordsburg last Saturday.' He turned and smiled that impish, irresistible smile at his hostess. 'My dear Ruth, you must forgive my bad manners. This talk detracts from the delicious meal you have provided.'

The table was set under the oak trees on lawns so vivid green that Ruth always thought of them as 'English green'. The house itself had the solid imposing bulk of Georgian England, so different from the frivolous fairy castle at Emoyeni; the illusion of old England was spoiled only by the soaring cliffs of grey rock that rose as a backdrop to the scene. The sheer slopes of Table Mountain were softened by the pine trees that clung precariously for footholds on each ledge and in each tiny pocket of soil.

Ruth smiled at him. 'In this house, General, you may do as you wish.'

'Thank you, my dear.' The smile flickered off his face and the merry twinkle of the pale blue eyes changed to the glint of swords, as he turned back to his listeners. 'They are seeking confrontation, gentlemen, it's a blatant test of our power and resolution.'

Ruth caught Mark's eye at the foot of the table and he rose to refill the glasses with cold pale wine tinged with a touch of green, dry and crisp and refreshing, but as he moved down the board, pausing beside each guest – three Cabinet ministers, a visiting British Earl, the Secretary of the Chamber of Mines – he was listening avidly.

'We can only hope you put it too highly, Prime Minister,' Sean Courtney intervened gruffly. 'They have only broomsticks with which to drill, and bicycles on which to ride into battle...'

And while they laughed, Mark paused behind Sean's chair with the bottle forgotten in his hand. He was remembering the cellars below the Trade Union Hall in Fordsburg, the racks of modern rifles, the gleaming P.14 reserved for him and the sinister squatting Vickers machine gun. When he returned to the present, the conversation had moved on.

Sean Courtney was assuring the company that militant action by the unions was unlikely, and that in the worst circumstances, the army was geared to immediate call-up.

Mark had a small office adjoining the General's study. It had previously been a linen room, but was just large enough to accommodate a desk and several shelves of files. The General had ordered a large window knocked through one wall to give it air and light, and now, with his ankles crossed and propped on the desk-top, Mark was staring thoughtfully out of the window. The view across lawns and through oaks encompassed a sweep of Rhodes Avenue, named after that asthmatic old adventurer who had seized an empire in land and diamonds, and ended up Prime Minister of the first Cape Parliament, before suffocating from his weak lungs and heavy conscience. The Cape home of the Courtneys was named Somerset Lodge after Lord Charles, the nineteenth-century governor, and the great houses on the opposite side of Rhodes Avenue perpetuated the colonial tradition, Newlands House and Hiddingh House, gracious edifices in spacious grounds.

Looking out at them through the new window, Mark was comparing them with the miners' cottages in Fordsburg Dip. He had not thought of Fergus and Helena in many months, but the conversation at lunch had brought them back forcibly, and he felt himself torn by sharply contradictory loyalties.

He had lived in both worlds now, and seen how each opposed the other. He was trying to think without emotion, but always a single image intruded, the cruel shape of weapons in orderly racks, deep in a dark cellar, and the slick smell of gun oil in his throat.

He lit another cigarette, delaying the decision. Through the solid teak door, the sound of voices from the General's study was muted, the higher clearer tones of the Prime Minister, bird-like almost, set against the rumbling of Sean's replies.

The Prime Minister had stayed on after the other luncheon guests had left, as he often did, but Mark wished that he would leave now, thus deferring the decision with which he was wrestling.

He had been trusted by a comrade, somebody who had shared mortal danger with him, and then had unstintingly shared the hospitality of his home, had trusted him like a brother, had not hesitated to give him access to the direst knowledge, had not hesitated to leave him alone with his wife. Mark had betrayed half of that trust – and he stirred restlessly in his seat as he remembered those wicked stolen days and nights with Helena. Now must he betray the rest of the trust that Fergus MacDonald had placed in him?

Once more the image of racked weapons passed before his eyes, they faded only slowly to be replaced with a vivid shocking picture of a face.

It was the face of a marble angel, smooth and white and strangely beautiful, with blue eyes in pale blue sockets, a burst of pale golden curls escaping from under the rim of the steel helmet on to the smooth pale forehead –

Mark dropped his feet from the desk with a crash, fighting away the memory of the young German sniper, forcing it from his mind, and coming to his feet abruptly.

He found that his hands were shaking and he crushed out the cigarette and turned to the door. His knock was over-loud and demanding, and the voice from beyond was gruff with irritation.

'Come in.' He stepped through. 'What do you want, Mark, you know I don't –' Sean Courtney cut himself short and the tone of his voice changed to concern as he saw Mark's face. 'What is it, my boy?'

'I have to tell you something, sir,' he blurted.

They listened with complete attention as he described his involvement with the executive of the Communist Party, and then broke off to steel himself for the final betrayal.

'These men were my friends, sir, they treated me as a comrade. You must understand why I am telling you this, please.'

'Go on, Mark,' Sean Courtney nodded, and the Prime Minister had drawn back in his chair – still and quiet and unobtrusive, sensing the struggle of conscience in which the young man was involved.

'I came to believe that much of what they were striving for was good and just – opportunity and a share of life for every man, but I could not accept the methods they had chosen to bring these about.'

'What do you mean, Mark?'

'They are planning a war, a class war, sir.'

'You have proof of that?' Sean's voice did not rise, and he asked the question carefully.

'Yes. I have.' Mark drew a deep breath before he went on. 'I have seen the rifles and machine guns they have ready for the day.'

The Prime Minister shifted in his chair and then was still again, but now he was leaning forward to listen.

'Go on,' Sean nodded, and Mark told them in detail, stating the unadorned facts, reporting exactly what he had seen and where, accurately estimating the numbers and types of every weapon, and finally ending,

'MacDonald led me to believe that this was only one arsenal, and that there were others, many others, on the Witwatersrand.'

Nobody spoke for many seconds, and then the Prime Minister stood up and went to the telephone on Sean's desk. He wound the crank handle, and the whirr-whirr was loud and obtrusive in the silent room.

'This is the Prime Minister, General Smuts, speaking. I want a maximum priority connection with Commissioner Truter, the Chief of the South African Police in Johannesburg,' he said, and then listened, his expression bleak and his eyes sparkling angrily. 'Get me the Exchange Supervisor,' he snapped and then turned to Sean, still holding the earpiece. 'The line is down. Floods in the Karroo,' he explained, 'indefinite delay.' Then he turned his attention back to the telephone and spoke quietly for many minutes with the Supervisor, before cradling the earpiece. 'They will make the connection as soon as possible.'

He returned to his seat by the window and spoke across the room. 'You have done the right thing, young man.'

'I hope so,' Mark answered quietly, and the doubts were obvious, shadows in his eyes and the strains of misery in his voice.

'I'm proud of you, Mark,' Sean Courtney agreed. 'Once again you have done your duty.'

'Will you excuse me now, please gentlemen?' Mark asked, and without waiting for a reply, crossed to the door of his own office.

The two men stared at the closed teak door long after it had closed, and it was the Prime Minister who spoke first.

'A remarkable young man,' he mused aloud. 'Compassion and a sense of duty.'

'He has qualities that could carry him to great heights, qualities for which one day we may be grateful,' Sean nodded. 'I sensed them at our first meeting, so strongly that I sought him out.'

'We will need him – and others like him in the years ahead, old Sean,' Jannie Smuts stated and then switched his attention. 'Truter will have a search warrant issued immediately, and with God's help we will crush the head of the snake before it has a chance to strike. We know about this man MacDonald, and of course we have been watching Fisher for years.'

Mark had walked for hours, escaping from the tiny box of his office. He had been driven by his conscience and his fears, striding out under the oaks, following narrow lanes, crossing the little stone bridge over the Liesbeeck stream, torturing himself with thoughts of Judas.

'They hang traitors in Pretoria,' he thought suddenly, and he imaged Fergus MacDonald standing on the trap in the barnlike room while the hangman pinioned his arms and ankles. He shuddered miserably and stopped walking, with his hands thrust deeply into his pockets and shoulders hunched, and he looked up to find himself standing outside the Post Office.

Afterwards he realized that it had probably been his destination all along, but now it seemed an omen. He did not hesitate a moment, but hurried into the office and found a pile of telegram forms on the desk. The nib of the pen was faulty and it spluttered the pale watery ink, and stained his fingers.

'MACDONALD 55 LOVERS WALK FORDSBURG.
THEY KNOW WHAT YOU HAVE GOT IN THE CELLAR
GET RID OF IT.'

He did not sign it.

The Post Office clerk assured him that if he paid the sevenpence for urgent rating, the message would have priority as soon as the northern lines were reinstated.

Mark wandered back into the street, feeling sick and depleted by the crisis of conscience, not certain that he had done the right thing in either circumstance, and he wondered just how futile was his hope that he might have forced Fergus MacDonald to throw that deadly cargo down some disused mine shaft before death and revolution was turned loose upon the land.

It was almost dark as Fergus MacDonald wheeled his bicycle into the shed and paused in the small back yard to slip the clips off the cuffs of his trousers, before going on to the kitchen door.

The smell of cooking cabbage filled the small room with a steamy moist cloud that made him pause and blink.

Helena was sitting at the kitchen table and she hardly glanced up as he entered. A cigarette dangled from her lips with an inch of grey ash clinging hopelessly to the end of it.

She still wore the grubby dressing-gown she had worn at breakfast, and it was clear that she had neither bathed nor changed since then. Her hair had grown longer and now dangled in oily black snakes to her cheeks. She had grown heavier in the last months, the line of her jaw blurring with a padding of fat and the hair on her upper lip darker and denser, breasts bulging and drooping heavily in the open front of her gown.

'Hello then, love.' Fergus shrugged out of his jacket and dropped it across the back of a kitchen chair. She turned the page of the pamphlet she was reading, squinting at the curl of blue smoke that drifted across her eyes.

Fergus opened a black bottle of porter and the gas hissed fiercely. 'Anything happened today?'

'Something for you,' she nodded at the kitchen dresser, and the cigarette ash dropped down the front of her gown, settling in fine grey flakes.

Carrying the bottle, Fergus crossed to the dresser and fingered the buff envelope.

'One of your popsies,' Helena chuckled at the unlikeliness of her sally, and Fergus frowned and tore open the envelope.

He stared at the message for long uncomprehending seconds before he swore bitterly. 'Jesus Christ!' He slammed the bottle down on the kitchen table with a crash.

Even this late in the evening, there were small groups on each street corner. They had that disconsolate and bored air of men with too little to fill their days, even the commando drilling and the nightly meetings were beginning to pall. As Fergus MacDonald pedalled furiously through the darkening streets, his first alarm and fright turned to fierce exultation.

The time was right, they were as ready as they would ever be, if time drifted on without decisive action from either side, the long boring days of strike inactivity would erode their determination. What had seemed like disaster merely minutes before, he now saw was a heaven-sent opportunity. *Let them come, we will be ready for them*, he thought, and braked alongside a group of four loungers on the pavement outside the public bar of the Grand Fordsburg Hotel.

'Get a message to all area commanders, they are to assemble at the Trade Hall immediately. It's an emergency. Brothers, hurry.'

They scattered quickly, and he pedalled on up the rising ground of the dip, calling out his warning as he went.

In the Trade Union offices, there were still a dozen or so members; most of them were eating sandwiches and drinking Thermos tea, while a few worked on the issue of strike relief coupons to Union families, but the relaxed atmosphere changed as Fergus burst in.

'All right, comrades, it's beginning. The ZARPS* are on their way.'

It was classic police tactics. They came in the first light of dawn. The advance guard rode down into the dip of land between Fordsburg and the railway crossing, where the Johannesburg road ran down between sleazy cottages and overgrown plots of open ground, thick with weeds and mounds of rotting refuse.

There was a heavy ground-mist in the dip, and the nine troopers on police chargers waded through it, as though fording the sluggish waters of a river crossing.

They had muted harness and muffled accoutrements, so that it was in ghostly silence that they breasted the softly swirling mists. The light was not yet strong enough to pick out their badges and burnished buttons, it was only the dark silhouette of their helmets that identified them.

Fifty yards behind the leading troopers followed the two police carriages. High four-wheelers with barred windows to hold prisoners, and beside each one of them marched ten constables. They carried their rifles at the slope, and were stepping out sharply to keep up with the carriages. As they entered the dip, the mist engulfed them, chest-high, so that their disembodied trunks bobbed in the white soft surface. They looked like strange dark sea-animals, and the mist muted the tramp of their boots.

Fergus MacDonald's scouts had picked them up before they reached the railway crossing and for three miles had been pacing them, slipping back unseen ahead of the advance, runners reporting every few minutes to the cottage where Fergus had established his advance headquarters.

'All right,' Fergus snapped, as another of the dark figures ducked through the hedge of the sanitary lane behind the cottage and mumbled his report through the open window. 'They are all coming in on the main road. Pull the other pickets out and get them here right away.'

The man grunted an acknowledgement and was gone. Fergus had his pickets on every possible approach to the town centre. The police might have split into a number of columns, but it seemed his precautions were unnecessary. Secure in the certainty of complete surprise and in overwhelming force, they were not bothering with diversion or flanking manoeuvres.

Twenty-nine troopers, Fergus calculated, together with the four drivers, was indeed a formidable force. More than sufficient, if it had not been for the warning from some unknown ally.

Fergus hurried through into the front parlour of the cottage. The family had been moved out before midnight, all the cottages along the road had been cleared. The grumpy squalling children in pyjamas carried on the shoulders of their fathers, the women with white frightened faces in the lamplight, bundling a few precious possessions with them as they hurried away.

Now the cottages seemed deserted, no lights showed, and the only sound was

* Zuid Afrikaanse Republiek Polisie, used as a derogatory term.

the mournful howling of a mongrel dog down in the dip. Yet in each cottage, at the windows that faced on to the road, silent men waited.

Fergus spoke to one of them in a whisper and he pointed down into the misty hollow, then spat and worked a round into the breech of the Lee-Enfield rifle which was propped on the windowsill.

The rifle bolt made a small metallic clash that lit a sparkle of memory and made the hair rise on Fergus's neck. It was all so familiar, the silence, the mist and the night fraught with the menace of coming violence.

'Only on my order,' Fergus warned him softly. 'Easy now, lads. Let them come right in the front door before we slam it on their heads.'

He could see the leading horsemen now, half a mile away but coming on fast in the strengthening light. It wasn't shooting light yet, but the sky beyond the dark hills of the mine dumps was turning to that pale gull's-egg blue that promised shooting light within minutes.

Fergus looked back at the road. The mist was an added bonus. He had not counted on that, but often when you did not call for fortune, she came a-knocking. The mist would persist until the first rays of the morning sun warmed and dispersed it – another half hour at least.

'You all know your orders.' Fergus raised his voice and they glanced at him, distracted for only a moment from their weapons and the oncoming enemy.

They were all good men, veterans, blooded, as the sanguine generals of France would have it. It flashed through Fergus's mind once again how ironical it was that men who had been trained to fight by the bosses were now about to tear down the structure which the bosses had trained them to defend.

'We will tear down and rebuild,' he thought, with exultation tingling in his blood. 'We will destroy them with their own weapons, strangle them with their own dirty loot –' he stopped himself, and pulled the dark grey cloth down over his eyes and turned up the collar of his coat.

'Good luck to all of us, brothers,' he called softly, and slipped out through the front door.

'That old bugger has got guts,' acknowledged one of the soldiers at the window.

'You're right, he ain't afraid of nothing,' agreed another, as they watched him dodge under the cover of the hedge and run forward until he reached the ditch beside the road, and jump down into it.

There were a dozen men lying there below the lip, and as he dropped beside them, one of them handed him a pick handle.

'You strung that wire good and tight?' Fergus asked, and the man grunted.

'Tighter than a monkey's arsehole,' the man grinned wolfishly at him, his teeth glinting in the first soft light of morning. 'And I checked the pegs meself – they'll hold against a charging elephant.'

'Right, brothers,' Fergus told them. 'With me when I give the word.'

And he lifted himself until he could see over the low blanket of mist. The troopers' helmets bobbed in the mist as they came on up the slope, and now he could make out the sparkle of brass cap badges and see the dark sticklike barrels of their carbines rising above each right shoulder.

Fergus had paced out the ranges himself and marked them with pieces of rag tied to the telephone posts on the verge.

As they came up to the one-fifty-yard mark Fergus stood up from the ditch, and stepped into the middle of the road. He held his pick-handle above his head and shouted,

'Halt! Stay where you are!'

His men rose out of the mist behind him and moved swiftly into position like a well-drilled team; dark, ominous figures standing shoulder to shoulder, blocking the road from verge to verge, holding their pick-handles ready across their hips, faces hidden by caps and collars.

The officer in the centre of the squadron of horsemen raised a hand to halt them and they bunched up and sat stolidly while the officer rose in his stirrups.

'Who are you?'

'Strikers' Council,' Fergus shouted back, 'and we'll have no scabs, black-legs or strike-breakers on this property!'

'I am under orders from the Commissioner of Police, empowered by a warrant of the Supreme Court.' The officer was a heavily built man, with a proud erect seat on his horse, and a dark waxed moustache with points that stuck out on each side of his face.

'You're strike-breakers!' Fergus yelled. 'And you'll not set a foot on this property.'

'Stand aside!' warned the officer. The light was good enough now for Fergus to see that he wore the insignia of a Captain, and that his face was ruddy from sun and beer, his eyebrows thick and dark and beetling under the brim of his helmet. 'You are obstructing the police. We will charge if we have to.'

'Charge and be damned, puppets of imperialism, running dogs of capitalism –'

'Troop, extend order,' called the Captain, and the ranks opened for the second file to come up into a solid line. They sat on the restless horses, knee to knee.

'Strike-breakers!' yelled Fergus. 'Your hands will be stained with the blood of innocent workers this day!'

'Batons!' called the Captain sternly, and the troopers drew the long oaken clubs from the scabbards at their knees and held them in the right hand, like cavalry sabres.

'History will remember this atrocity,' screamed Fergus, 'the blood of the lamb –'

'Walk, march! Forward!' The line of dark horsemen waded forward through the mist as it swirled about their booted legs.

'Gallop, charge!' sang out the Captain, and the riders swung forward in their saddles, the batons extended along the horses' necks, and they plunged forward; now the hooves drummed low thunder as they came down upon the line of standing figures.

The Captain was leading by a length in the centre of the line, and he went on to the wires first.

Fergus's men had driven the steel jumper bars deep into the verge, pounding them in with nine-pound hammers, until only two feet of their six-foot length protruded, and they had strung the barbed wire across the road, treble strands pulled up rigid with the fencing strainers.

It cut the forelegs out from under the leading charger, the bone broke with a brittle snap, startlingly loud in the dawn, and the horse dropped, going over on to its shoulder still at full gallop.

An instant later the following wave of horsemen went on to the wire, and were cut down as though by a scythe, only three of them managing to wheel away in time. The cries of the men, and the screaming of the horses, mingled with the exultant yells of Fergus's band as they ran forward, swinging their pick-handles.

One of the horses was up, riderless, its stirrups flapping, but it was pinned on its haunches, the broken forelegs flapping and spinning as it pawed in anguish at the air, its squeals high and pitiful above the cries of fallen men.

Fergus pulled the revolver out of the waist-band of his trousers, dodged around the crazed screaming animals and pulled the police Captain to his knees.

He had hit the ground with his shoulder and the side of his face. The shoulder was smashed, sagging down at a grotesque angle and the arm hanging twisted and lifeless. The flesh had been shaved from his face, ripped off by stone and gravel, so that the bone of his jaw was exposed in the mangled flesh.

'Get up, you bastard,' snarled Fergus, thrusting the pistol into the officer's face, grinding the muzzle into the lacerated wound. 'Get up you bloody black-leg. We'll learn you a lesson.'

The three troopers who had escaped the wire had their mounts under control, and had circled to pick up their downed comrades, calling to them by name.

'Grab a stirrup, Heintjie!'

'Come on, Paul. Get up!'

Horses and men, milling and shouting and screaming in the mist, a savage confused conflict, above which Fergus raised his voice.

'Stop them, don't let the bastards get away,' and his men swung the pick-handles, dodging forward under the police batons to thrust and hack at the horsemen, but they were not quick enough.

With men hanging from each stirrup leather, the horsemen reared and wheeled away, leaving only the badly hurt officer and another inert body lying among the wires and the terribly mutilated animals, while the police escort was doubling forward up the road in two columns.

Fergus saw them and fumed impatiently, trying to force his captive to his feet, but the man was hardly capable of sitting unaided.

The twenty constables stopped at fifty yards and one rank knelt, while the others fell in behind them, rifles at the ready. The command carried clearly.

'One round. Warning fire!'

The volley of musketry crashed out. Aimed purposely high, it hissed and cracked over the heads of the strikers, and they scattered into the ditch.

For one moment, Fergus hesitated and then he pointed the pistol into the air and fired three shots in rapid succession. It was the agreed signal, and instantly a storm of rifle fire crashed from the silent cottages along the road, the muzzle flashes of the hidden rifles dull angry red in the dawn. The fire swept the road.

Fergus hesitated a second only and then he lowered the pistol. It was a Webley ·455, a British officer's sidearm. The police Captain saw his intention in his eyes, the merciless glare of the stooping eagle, and he mumbled a plea through his mangled lips, trying to lift hands to protect his face.

The pistol shot was lost in the storm of rifle fire from the cottages, and the answering police fire as they fell back in confusion into the dip.

The heavy lead bullet smashed into the Captain's open pleading mouth, knocking the two front teeth out of his upper jaw, and then it plunged on into his throat and exited through the back of his skull in a scarlet burst of blood and bone chips, clubbing him down into the dirt of the roadway – while Fergus turned and darted away under the cover of the hedge.

Only at Fordsburg were the police raids repelled, for at the other centres there had been no warning, and the strikers had not taken even the most elementary precautions of placing sentries.

At the Trades Hall in Johannesburg, almost the entire leadership of the strike was assembled, meeting with the other unions who had not yet come out, but were considering sympathetic action. There were representatives of the Boilermakers' Society, the Building and Allied Trades, the Typographical Union and half a dozen others – together with the most dynamic and forceful of the strikers. Harry Fisher was there, Andrews and Ben Caddy, and all the others.

The police were into the building while they were deep in dialectic, debating the strategy of the class struggle, and the first warning they had was the thunderous charge of booted feet on the wooden staircase.

Harry Fisher was at the head of the conference table, slumped down in his chair with his tangled wiry hair hanging on to his forehead and his thumbs hooked in his braces, his sleeves rolled up around the thick hairy arms.

He was the only one to move. He leaned across the table and grabbed the rubber stamp of the High Council of Action and thrust it into his pocket.

As the rifle butts smashed in the lock of the Council Chamber, he leapt to his feet and thrust his shoulder into the shuttered casement. It burst open and, with surprising nimbleness for such a big man, he slipped through it.

The façade of the Trades Hall was heavily encrusted with fancy cast-iron grille work, and it gave him hand-holds. Like a bull gorilla, he swarmed up on to the third-floor ledge and worked his way to the corner.

Below him he heard the crash of overturning furniture, the loud challenges of the arresting officers and the outraged cries of the labour leaders.

With his back pressed to the wall and his hands spread out to balance himself, Harry Fisher peered around the corner into the main street. It swarmed with uniformed police, and more squads were marching up briskly. An officer was directing men to the side alleys to surround the building, and Harry Fisher drew back quickly and looked around him for escape.

It was senseless to re-enter another window, for the whole building was noisy with the tramp of feet and shouted orders.

Fifteen feet below him was the roof of a bottle store and general dealer's shop, but the alleyway between was ten feet wide and the roof of galvanized corrugated iron.

If he jumped, the noise he would make on landing would bring police running from all directions – yet he could not stay where he was. Within minutes the building would be surrounded.

He inched sideways to the nearest downpipe and began to climb. He reached the overhang of the roof and had to lean out to get a grip on the rim of the guttering, then he kicked his feet clear and hung from his arms. The drop of fifty feet below him sucked at his heels, and the guttering creaked and sagged perceptively under his weight – but he drew himself up on his arms, wheezing and straining until he could hook one elbow over the gutter and wriggle the rest of his body up and over the edge.

Still panting from the effort, he crawled slowly round the steeply gabled roof and peered down into the main street, just as the police began hustling the strike leaders out of the front doors.

Fifty helmeted constables with sloped rifles had formed a hollow square in the road, and the strikers were pushed into it; some of them bare-headed and in their shirt-sleeves.

Already a crowd was forming on the sidewalks, and every minute it swelled, as the news was shouted from door to door and the curious hurried from every alleyway.

Harry Fisher counted the prisoners as they were brought out and the total was twenty before the mood of the crowd began changing.

'That's it, comrades,' Harry Fisher grunted, and wished he could have been down there to lead them. They surged angrily up to the police lines, calling to the prisoners and hissing and booing the officer who ordered them, through a speaking trumpet, to disperse.

Mounted police wheeled into line, pushing the crowd back and as the last prisoner was led out, the escort stepped out, maintaining its rigid box-formation which enclosed the dejected huddle of strikers.

Somebody began to sing the 'Red Flag', but the voices that joined in were thin and tuneless, and the escort moved off towards the fort, carrying away not only most of the strike leadership but all of its moderate faction, those who had so far counselled against violence, against criminal activity and bloody revolution.

Harry Fisher watched them go with a rising sense of triumph. In one stroke he had been given a band of martyrs for the cause and had all serious opposition to his extreme views swept away. He had also in his hip pocket the seal of the Action Committee. He smiled a thin, humourless grin and settled down on the canted roof-top to wait for nightfall.

Mark Anders carried the General's heavy crocodile-skin brief case down the steps to the Rolls and placed it on the seat beside the chauffeur while he gave him his instructions.

'To Groote Schuur first, and then to the City Club for lunch.' He stood back as the General came out of the house and paused on the top step to kiss his wife as though he were about to leave on a crusade to far places. He smothered her in a vast bear-hug and when he released her, he whispered something in her ear that made her bridle and slap his shoulder.

'Off with you, sir,' she told him primly, and Sean Courtney came down the steps looking mightily pleased with himself, and grinned at Mark.

'The Prime Minister is making a statement to the House today, Mark. I'll want to see you directly afterwards.'

'Very well, sir,' Mark returned the grin.

'I'll look for you in the visitors' gallery as soon as he's finished, and give you the nod. Then we'll meet in the lobby and I'll see you up to my office.'

Mark helped him into the back seat of the Rolls while he was speaking. He was always clumsy and awkward when moving sideways on to the bad leg, nevertheless he resented the helping hand fiercely, hating any weakness in himself even more than he disliked it in others, and he shrugged Mark's hand away the moment he was comfortably seated.

Mark ignored the gesture and went on levelly,

'Your notes for the Cabinet meeting are in the first folder,' he indicated the crocodile bag on the front seat beside the chauffeur, 'and you are lunching at the Club with Sir Herbert. The House sits at 2.15 and you have three questions from Opposition members, even Hertzog himself has one for you.' Sean growled like an old lion bated by the pack.

'That bastard!'

'I have your replies clipped to your Order Paper. I checked with Erasmus and then I added a few little touches of my own, so please have a look at them before you stand up – you may not approve.'

'I hope you stuck it to them hard!'

'Of course,' Mark smiled again. 'With both barrels.'

'Good boy,' Sean nodded. 'Tell him to drive on.'

Mark watched the Rolls go down the driveway, check at the gates and then swing out into Rhodes Avenue, before he turned back into the house.

Instead of going down the passageway to his own office, Mark paused in the hall and glanced guiltily about him. Ruth Courtney had gone back into the domestic depths of the kitchen area and there were no servants in sight.

Mark took the stairs three at a time, swung through the gallery and down to the solid teak door at the end.

He did not knock but turned the handle and went in, closing the door behind him quietly.

The stench of turpentine was a solid shock that made his eyes water for a few seconds until they adjusted.

Mark knew that he was quite safe. Storm Courtney never emerged before mid-morning from that sacrosanct area beyond the double doors that were painted with gold cherubim and flying doves. Since arriving in Cape Town, Storm Courtney had kept such hours that even her father had grumbled and huffed.

Mark found himself lying awake at night, just as he was sure the General did, listening for the crunch of wheels on the gravel drive, straining his ears for the faint sounds of gay voices and mentally judging the length and passion of each farewell, troubled by feelings to which he could not place a name.

His relations with Storm had retrogressed drastically. In Natal there had been the beginnings of a relaxed acceptance and undertones of warmth. It had begun with a smile and a friendly word from Storm, then he had escorted her on the daily ride, driven with her to South Beach to swim in the warm surf and sat in the sun arguing religion with her instead. Storm was going through a fashionable period of spiritualism and Mark had felt it his duty to dissuade her.

From religion, the next step had been when Storm had announced, 'I need a partner to practise a new dance with.'

Mark had wound the gramophone, changed the needles and danced to Storm's instruction.

'You really are quite good, you know,' she had told him magnanimously, smiling up at him, light and graceful in his arms as they spun around the empty ballroom of Emoyeni.

'You would make a crippled blacksmith look good.'

'Oh la!' she laughed. 'You are the gallant, Mr Anders!'

This had all changed abruptly. Since they had arrived in Cape Town she had neither smiled nor spoken directly to him, and Irene Leuchars, who was to have been a house guest of Storm's for four months, stayed only one night, and then caught the next mailship home.

Her name had not been mentioned again, and Storm's hostility to Mark had been so intense that she could hardly bear to be in the same room with him.

Now Mark felt like a thief in her studio, but he had not been able to resist the temptation to steal a glimpse of the progress she had made on her latest canvas.

Full-length windows had been put into the north wall for the light, and they looked out on the mountain. Storm's easel stood in the centre of the bare uncarpeted floor – and the only other items of furniture were the artist's stool, a carpenter's table cluttered with paint pots and a chair on the raised model's dais.

Framed canvases in all sizes and shapes were stacked against the walls, most of them still blank. At one stage, during the period of friendliness, she had even asked Mark to help with the timber framework. He felt a pang when he remembered; she was a ruthless supervisor, checking every joint and tack with a perfectionist's meticulous care.

The canvas was almost completed, and he wondered when she had found time to do so much work in the last few days, and realized that he had misjudged her. She had been working when he had believed she was lying abed, but now he became absorbed by the picture.

He stood before it with his hands thrust into his pockets and felt a glow of pleasure spread slowly through his body.

It was a picture of trees, a forest glade with sunlight playing on earth and rock and two figures – a woman in a white dress, stooping to gather wild flowers, while a man sat aside, sprawled against a tree trunk and watching her.

Mark was aware that it was a great advance on anything she had painted before, for although it was a simple picture, it evoked in him an emotion so strong that he felt it choke in his throat. He was awed by the peculiar talent which could have produced this work.

He marvelled at how she had taken reality and refined it, captured its essence and made of it an important occasion.

Mark thought how it was possible for an untrained eye to pick out special talent in any field, just as a person who had never watched *épée* used before would recognize a great swordsman after the first exchange; now Mark, who knew nothing of painting, was moved by the discovery of real beauty.

The latch clicked behind him, and he spun to face it. She was well into the studio before she saw him. She stopped abruptly and her expression changed. Her whole body stiffened and her breathing sounded stifled.

'What are you doing here?'

He had no answer for her, but the mood of the picture was still on him. 'I think that you will be a great artist one day.'

She faltered, taken completely off balance by the compliment and its obvious sincerity, and her eyes slipped away to the picture. All the antagonism, all the haughtiness drained from her.

Suddenly she was just a very young girl in a baggy smock, smeared and daubed with oil paint, and with a wash of pleased and modest colour spreading over her cheeks.

He had never seen her like this, so artless – so open and vulnerable. It was as though for a moment she had unveiled the secret compartments of her soul to allow him to see where she kept her real treasures.

'Thank you, Mark,' she said softly, and she was no longer the glittering butterfly, the spoiled flighty little rich girl, but a creature of substance and warmth.

The rush of his own feelings must have been as obvious – he had almost succumbed to the desire he felt to take her in his arms and hold her hard – for she stepped back a pace, looking flustered and uncertain of herself, as though she had read his intention.

'And yet you won't slide out of it that easily.' The curtains were drawn hastily across the secret places, and the old familiar ring was in her voice. 'This is my private place, even my father wouldn't dare come in here – without my permission first obtained.'

The change was extraordinary. It was like a superb actress slipping into a familiar role, she even stamped her foot, a gesture that he found suddenly insupportable.

'It won't happen again,' he assured her brusquely, and he stepped to the doorway, passing her closely. He was so angry he felt himself trembling.

'Mark!' She stopped him imperiously, but it was with an effort he forced himself to turn back; his whole body felt rigid, and his lips were numb and stiff with anger.

'My father asks permission to come in here,' she told him, and then she smiled, a slightly tremulous but utterly enchanting thing. 'Couldn't you just do the same?'

She had him off balance, his anger not fully aroused before she assuaged it with that smile, he felt the rigidity melting out of his body, but she had turned to the bench and was clattering her pots busily and she spoke without looking up.

'Close the door as you leave,' she instructed, a princess tossing an order to a serf. His anger, not yet fully assuaged, flared again brightly and he strode to the door with his heels clashing on the bare boards and he was about to slam it with all of his strength, and hope that it smashed off its hinges, when she stopped him again.

'Mark!'

He stopped, but could not bring himself to answer.

'I will be coming down to Parliament with you this afternoon. We will leave directly after lunch – I want to hear General Smuts's speech, my father says it will be important.'

He thought that if he tried to answer her, his lips might tear, they felt as stiff and brittle as parchment.

'Oh dear,' she murmured. 'I had completely forgotten – when addressing Mark Anders Esquire, one must always say please!'

She crossed her hands demurely in front of her, hung her head in a caricature of contrition and made those dark blue eyes huge and soulful.

'Please may I ride to Parliament with you today? I would be ever so grateful, I really would. And now you can slam the door.'

'You should be on the stage – you're wasted as a painter,' he told her, but he closed the door with studied deliberation and she waited to hear the latch click before she dropped into the model's chair, and began to shake with laughter, hugging herself delightedly.

Gradually the laughter dried up, but she was still smiling as she selected a blank canvas from the stock and placed it on the easel.

Working with charcoal, she blocked in the shape of his head, and it was right at the first attempt.

'The eyes,' she whispered, 'his eyes are the key.' And she smiled again as they appeared miraculously out of the blank canvas, surprised that she had them fixed perfectly in her mind. She began to hum softly as she worked, completely absorbed.

The Assembly Chamber of Parliament House was a high square hall, tiered with the galleries for Press and visitors. It was panelled in dark carved indigenous wood, and the canopy above the Speaker's chair was ornately worked in the same wood.

Softly muted green carpeting set off the richer green leather of the members' benches, and every seat was filled, the galleries crowded, but the silence that gripped that concourse was of extraordinary intensity, a cathedral hush into which the high piping voice of the Prime Minister carried clearly. He made a slight but graceful figure as he stood in his seat below the Speaker's dais.

'The entire Witwatersrand complex is passing slowly into the hands of the red commandos –' He used his hands expressively, and Mark leaned forward to obtain a better view. The movement brought his outer leg against Storm Courtney's, and he was aware of the warmth of her thigh against his during the rest of the speech. 'Three members of the police have been killed in a brutal attack at Fordsburg, and two others have been critically injured in clashes with strikers' commandos. These groups are armed with modern pattern military firearms, and they are marching freely through the streets in quasi-military formations, committing acts of outrage on innocent members of the public, on public officers going about their duties, on all who cross their paths. They have interfered with public services, transport, power and communication, and have attacked and occupied police stations.'

Sean Courtney, who had been slumped in his front bench seat with one hand covering his eyes, lifted his head and said 'Shame!' in a sonorous voice; it was his third-whisky voice, and Mark could not help but grin as he guessed that the club lunch had fortified him for the session.

'Shame indeed,' Smuts agreed. 'Now the strikers have gathered about them all the feckless and dissolute elements in the community, their mood has become ugly and threatening. Legitimate strike action has given way to a reign of terror and criminal violence. Yet the most disturbing aspect of this terrible business is that the management of this labour dispute – or should I say, the stage-managing of the strike – has passed into the hands of the most reckless and lawless men, and these men seek nothing less than the overthrow of civilized government, and a rule of Bolshevik anarchy.'

'Never!' boomed Sean, and the cry was taken up across the assembly.

'This house, and the whole nation is faced by the prospect of bloodshed and violence on a scale which none of us expected or believed possible.'

The silence was unbroken now as Smuts went on carefully.

'If any blame attaches to this Government, it is that we have been too patient and shown too much forbearance for the miners' grievances, we have allowed them too much latitude, too much expression of their demands. This was because we have always been aware of the temper of the nation, and the rights of individuals and groups to free expression.'

'Quite right too,' Sean agreed, and, 'Hear! Hear!' answered, 'Hoor! Hoor!' across the floor.

'Now, however, we have been forced to reckon the cost of further forbearance – and we have found it unacceptable.' He paused and bowed his head for a moment, and when he lifted it again, his expression was bleak and cold. 'Therefore a state of martial law now exists throughout the Union of South Africa.'

The silence persisted for many seconds, and then a roar of comment and question and interjection filled the house. Even the galleries buzzed with confusion and speculation, and the Press reporters jostled and fought each other at the exit doors in the race to reach a telephone.

Martial law was the weapon of the last resort, and had only been used once before, during the 1916 rebellion, when De Wet had raised his commandos again and ridden against Botha and Smuts. Now there were cries of protest and anger from the Opposition benches, Hertzog shaking his fist and his pince-nez glinting, while the Government members were also on their feet voicing their support. The Speaker's vain cries of 'Order! Order!' were almost drowned in the uproar.

Sean Courtney was signalling to Mark in the gallery, and he acknowledged and helped Storm to her feet, shielding her through the excited press of bodies as they left the gallery and went down the passage to the staircase.

The General was waiting for them at the visitors' entrance. He was scowling and dark-faced with concern, a measure of his agitation was the perfunctory kiss he dropped on Storm's uplifted face before turning to Mark.

'A pretty business, my boy.' He seized his elbow. 'Come on, let's go where we can talk,' and he led them to the members' entrance, and up the stairs under the portraits of stern-faced Chief Justices to his own office.

Immediately the door was closed, he waved Storm away to one of the chairs, and told Mark, 'The regiment was called out at ten o'clock this morning. I managed to get Scott on the telephone at his home – and he's got it in hand. He's a good man. They will be fully mobilized by now, and there is a special train being made up. They will entrain and leave for the Witwatersrand at eleven o'clock tonight, in full battle order.'

'What about us?' Mark demanded. Suddenly he was a soldier again and he dropped neatly into the role. His place was with the regiment.

'We'll join there. We leave tonight. We are going up in convoy with the Prime Minister, and we'll travel all night – you will drive one of the cars.' Sean was at his desk now, beginning to pack his briefcase. 'How long will it take us?'

'It's a thousand miles, sir.' Mark pointed out.

'I know that, damn it,' snapped Sean. 'How long?' Sean had never liked nor understood the internal combustion engine, and his dislike showed in his ignorance of their speed and capability whereas he could finely judge a journey by wagon or horseback.

'We won't be there before tomorrow evening – it's a hell of a road.'

'Bloody motorcars,' Sean growled. 'The regiment will be there before us by rail.'

'They've only three hundred miles to go.' Mark felt obliged to come to the defence of the car, and Sean grunted.

'I want you to get on home now. Have my wife pack my campaign bag and get your duffle together. We'll leave immediately I get home.' He turned to Storm. 'Go along with Mark, now, Missy. I'm going to be busy here for a while.'

Mark strapped up his bag, and reflected how his worldly possessions had multiplied since he had joined the Courtney household. There had been a time when he could carry everything he owned in his pockets – the thought was broken by a knock on the door.

'Come in,' he called, expecting a servant. Only Ruth Courtney ever came down this end of the house on her weekly inspection, a determined crusade against dust and cockroaches.

'Please take it down to the car,' he said in Zulu, adjusting his uniform cap in the mirror above the wash-basin.

'All on my own?' Storm asked sweetly in the same language, and he turned startled.

'You shouldn't be here.'

'Why not – am I in danger of violation and ravishment?' She had closed the door and leaned against it, her hands behind her back, but her eyes bold and teasing.

'It would be safer, I should imagine, to attempt to ravish a swarm of hornets.'

'That was merely boorish, coarse and insulting,' she said. 'You really are improving immensely.' And she looked at the strapped case on the bed.

'I was going to offer to help you pack – most men are hopeless at that. But I see you've managed. Is there anything else I can do for you?'

'I am sure I could think of something,' he said with a solemn expression, but something in the tone of his voice made her smile and caution him.

'Not too much improvement in one day, please.' She crossed to the bed and bounced on it experimentally. 'God! Who filled it with bricks? No wonder Irene Leuchars went home! The poor darling must have sprained her back!' Her expression was innocent, but her gaze raked him and Mark felt himself blushing furiously. Suddenly, much that had puzzled him was clear, and as he turned back to the mirror, he wondered how she had found out about Irene. For something to do, he tipped the brim of his cap.

'Beautiful,' she agreed. 'Are you going up there to brutalize those poor strikers – or to bounce on their wives also?' And before he could give expression to the shock he felt she went on, 'Funnily enough, I didn't really come down here to fight with you. I once had another old tomcat and I was really very fond of him, but he got run over by a car. Have you got a cigarette, Mark?'

'You don't smoke.' He had found it difficult to keep up with the conversation.

'I know – but I have decided to learn. It's so suave, don't you think?' Suave was the fashionable word at that moment.

She held the cigarette with an exaggerated vampish pose after he had lit it. 'How do I look?'

'Bloody awful,' he said, and she batted her eyes and took a tentative draw, held it for a moment and then started to cough.

'Here, give it to me.' He took it away from her, and it tasted of her mouth. He felt the ache in his body, the terrible wanting, mingled now with a strange tenderness he had never felt before. She seemed, for once, so tender and young.

'Will it be dangerous?' she asked, suddenly serious.

'I don't think so – we'll be just like policemen.'

'They are killing policemen.' She stood up and walked to the window. 'The view is dreadful, unless you like dustbins. I'd complain, if I were you.' She turned back to face him.

'I've never seen a man off to war before. What should I say?'

'I don't know. Nobody ever saw me off before.'

'What did your mother say?'

'I never knew my mother.'

'Oh Mark. I'm sorry. I didn't mean to –' Her voice trailed off, and he was shocked to see that her eyes were brimming with tears.

'It doesn't matter,' he assured her quickly, and she turned back to the window.

'Actually, you can just see the top of Devil's Peak, if you twist your head.' Her voice was thick and nasal, and it was many seconds before she turned back.

'Well, we're both new to this, so we'll just have to help each other.'

'I suppose you should say, "Come back soon."'

'Yes, I suppose I should – and then what do I do?'

'You kiss me.' It was out before he had thought about it, and he was stunned by his own audacity.

She stood very still, rooted by the words, and when she began to move, it was with the slow deliberation of a sleepwalker, and her eyes were huge and unblinking. She came across the room.

She stopped in front of him, and, as she lifted her arms, she came up on her toes.

The air about her was filled with her fragrance, and her arms were slim and strong about his neck, but it was the softness and the warmth of her lips that amazed him.

Her body swayed against him, and seemed to melt with his own, and the long artistic fingers slowly caressed the nape of his neck.

He passed an arm around her waist, and was again amazed at how narrow and slim it was; but the muscles of her back were firm and pliant as she arched it, pushing forward with her hips.

He heard her gasp as she felt him, and a slow voluptuous shudder shook her. For long moments she lingered, her hips pressed to his and her breasts flattened against his tunic.

He stooped over her, his hands beginning to move up the hard resilient little back, his mouth forcing hers open so the soft lips parted like the fleshy petals of an exotic blooming orchid.

She shuddered again, but then the sound in her throat turned into a panicky moan of protest and she twisted out of his arms, though he tried desperately to hold her. But she was strong and supple and determined.

At the door, she stopped to stare at him. She was trembling, her eyes were wide and dark, as though she had truly only seen him for the first time. 'Oh la! Who was talking about swarms of hornets!' she mocked, but her voice was gusty and unsteady.

She twisted the door open, and tried to smile, but it was a poor lopsided thing, and she did not yet have control of her breathing. 'I'm not so sure of that "Come back soon" any more.' She held the door open to give herself courage, and her next smile was more convincing, 'Don't get run over, you old tomcat,' and she slipped out into the passageway. Her receding footsteps were light and dancing in the silence of the big house, and Mark's own legs were suddenly so weak that he sat down heavily on his bed.

Mark drove fast, concentrating all his attention on the twisting treacherous road through the mountains, driving the big heavily laden Rolls down the path of its own glaring brass-bound headlights, up Baines Kloof where the mountain fell away on his left hand sheer into the valley, past Worcester with its orderly vineyards standing in dark lines in the moonlight, before the final ascent up the Hex River Mountains to the rim of the flat compacted shield of the African interior.

They came out over the top, and the vast land stretched away ahead of them, the dry treeless karroo, where the flat-topped kopjes made strangely symmetrical shapes against the cold starry sky.

Now at last, Mark could relax in the studded leather driver's seat, driving instinctively, the road pouring endlessly towards him, pale and straight out of the darkness, and he could tune his ears to the voice of the two men in the rear seat.

'What they don't understand, old Sean, is that if we do not employ every black man who offers himself for work – no, more than that, if we don't actively recruit all the native labour we can get hold of – it will result not only in fewer jobs for white men, but, in the long run, it will mean, finally, no jobs at all for the white men of Africa.'

A jackal, small and furry as a puppy, lolloped into the path of the headlights with its ears erect, and Mark steered carefully to miss it, his own ears cocked for Sean's reply.

'They think only of today.' His voice was deep and grave. 'We must plan for ten years from now – for thirty, fifty years ahead, for a nation firm and undivided. We cannot afford once again to have Afrikander against Briton, or worse, we dare not have white against black. It is not enough that we are forced to live together, we must learn to work together.'

'Slowly, slowly – old Sean,' the Prime Minister chuckled. 'Don't let dreams run away with reality.'

'I don't deal in dreams, Jannie. You should know that. If we don't want to be torn to pieces by our own people, we must give all of them, black, white and brown, a place and a share.'

They ran on hard into the endless land, and the light of a lonely farm house on a dark ridge emphasized how vast and empty it was.

'Those who clamour so loudly for less work and more pay may find that what benefit they get now will have to be paid for at a thousand per cent interest some day in the future. A payment in misery and hunger and suffering,' Sean Courtney was speaking again. 'If we are to steer off the reef of national disaster, then men will have to learn to work again, and to take seriously once more the demands of a disciplined and orderly society.'

'Have you ever wondered, Sean, at how many people these days depend for their livelihood on nothing else but finding areas of dispute between the employers and the employed, between labour and management?'

Sean nodded, taking it up where Smuts left off. 'As though the two were not shackled to each other with bonds that nothing can break. They travel the same road, to the same goal, bound together irretrievably by destiny. When one stumbles, he brings the other down on bloody knees, when one falls the other comes down with him.'

Slowly, as the stars made their circuit of grandeur across the heavens, the talk in the back seat of the Rolls dwindled into silence.

Mark glanced in the mirror and saw that Sean Courtney was asleep, a travelling rug about his shoulders and his black beard on his chest.

His snores were low and regular and deep, and Mark felt a rush of feeling for the big man. It was a fine mixture of respect and awe, of pride and affection. 'I suppose that is what you would feel, if you had a father,' he thought, and then, embarrassed by the strength and presumption of his feeling, he once again concentrated all his attention on the road.

The night wind had sifted the sky with fine dust, and the dawn was a thing of unbelievable splendour. From horizon to horizon, and right across the vaulted domes of the heavens, vibrant colour throbbed and glowed and flamed, until at last the sun burst clear of the horizon.

'We won't stop in Bloemfontein or any of the big towns, Mark. We don't want anybody to see the Prime Minister.' Sean leaned across the back of the seat.

'We'll need petrol, General.'

'Pick one of the roadside pumps,' Sean instructed. 'Try and find one with no telephone lines.'

It was a tiny iron-roofed general dealer's store set back from the road under two scraggy eucalyptus blue gum trees. There was no other building in sight, and the open empty veld stretched dry and sun-seared to the circle of the horizon. The plaster walls of the store were cracked and in need of whitewash, plastered with advertisement boards for Bovril and Joko tea. The windows were shuttered and the door locked, but there were no telephone lines running from the solitary building to join those that followed the road, and a single red-painted petrol pump stood at rigid attention in the dusty yard below the stoep.

Mark blew a long continuous blast on the Rolls's horn, and while he was doing so, the Prime Minister's black Cadillac that was following turned off the main road and parked behind them. The driver and the three members of the ministerial staff climbed out and stretched their stiff muscles.

When the proprietor of the store emerged at last, unshaven, red-eyed, but cheerfully doing up his breeches, he spoke no English. Mark asked in Afrikaans,

'Can you fill up both cars?'

While the storekeeper swung the handle of the pump back and forth, and the fuel rose alternately into the two one-gallon glass bowls on the top of the pump, his wife came out from the store with a tray of steaming coffee mugs and a platter of crisp golden freshly baked rusks. They ate and drank gratefully, and were ready to go on again within twenty minutes.

The storekeeper stood in the yard, scratching the stubble of his beard and watched the twin columns of red dust billowing into the northern sky. His wife came out on to the stoep and he turned to squint up at her.

'Do you know who that was?' he asked, and she shook her head.

'That was Clever Jannie – and his English gunmen. Didn't you see the uniform the young one wore?' He spat into the red dirt, and his phlegm balled and rolled. 'Khaki! Damned khaki!' He ripped the word out bitterly, and went around the side of the building to the little lean-to stable.

He was clinching the girth on the old sway-backed grey mare, when she followed him into the stall.

'It's none of our business, Hendrick. Let it stand.'

'None of our business?' he demanded indignantly. 'Didn't I fight khaki in the English war, didn't I fight it again in 1916 when we rode with old De Wet – isn't my brother a rock-breaker on the Simmer and Jack mine, and isn't that where Clever Jannie is going with his hangmen?'

He swung up on the mare and put his heels to her. She jumped away, and he pointed her at the ridge. It was eight miles to the railway siding, and there was a telegraph in the ganger's cottage; the ganger was a cousin of his. The Railway Workers' Union was out in sympathy with the miners now. The Action Committee would have the news in Johannesburg by lunch time that Clever Jannie was on his way.

While Mark Anders drank coffee at the wayside store, Fergus MacDonald lay under the hedge at the bottom of a garden ablaze with crimson cannas in orderly beds, and peered through a pair of binoculars down the slope at the Newlands Police Station. They had sand-bagged the windows and doors.

The lady of the house had sat on her veranda the previous evening, drinking coffee and counting forty-seven police constables arriving by motor lorry to reinforce the station. Her son was a shift boss on the Simmer and Jack. Whoever commanded the police at Newlands was no soldier, Fergus decided, and grinned that wolfish wicked grin.

He had seen the dead ground instantly, any soldier would have picked it up at a glance.

'Pass the word for the Mills bombs,' he muttered to the striker beside him, and the man crawled away.

Fergus swung the glasses up along the road where it started to climb the kopjes, and grunted with satisfaction. The telephone wires had been cut, along with the power lines. He could see the loose ends dangling from the poles.

The police station was isolated.

The striker crawled back to Fergus' side, dragging a heavy rucksack. He had a tooth missing from his upper jaw, and he grinned gap-toothed at Fergus.

'Give them hell, comrade.'

Fergus's face was blackened with soot and his eyelashes were singed away. They had burned the Fordsburg Police Station a little before midnight.

'I want covering fire – on my whistle.'

'You'll get it – never fear.'

Fergus opened the rucksack and glanced at the steel globes, with their deeply segmented squares for fragmentation, then he slung the strap over his shoulder and adjusted the burden to hang comfortably on his flank.

'Look after it well.' He handed his Lee-Enfield rifle to the gap-toothed striker. 'We'll need it again today.' He crawled away down the shallow drainage ditch that led to a concrete culvert which crossed under the road.

The culvert was lined with circular tubes of rusty corrugated iron, and Fergus wriggled through it carefully, emerging on the far side of the road.

Lying on his side, he raised himself slightly to peer over the edge of the drainage ditch. The police station was a hundred and fifty yards away. The blue light over the front door, with the white lettered 'POLICE', was dead, and the flag hung limply on its pole in the still windless morning.

It was fifty yards to the slope of dead ground under the eastern windows of the brick building, and Fergus could see the rifle barrels of the defenders poked through the gaps in the sand-bags.

He pulled the silver whistle from his back pocket by its lanyard, and came up on his knees like a sprinter on the blocks.

He drew a deep breath and blew a long shrill ringing blast on the whistle. Immediately a storm of rifle fire crashed out from the hedges and ditches that surrounded the station.

The blue lamp shattered into flying fragments, and red brick dust popped off the walls like dyed cotton pods.

Fergus came out of the ditch at a run. A bullet kicked dust and stone chips stung his ankles, and another jerked like an impatient hand at the tail of his coat, then he was into the dead ground and out of their field of fire.

He still ran doubled over, however, until he reached the police station. Then he flattened himself against the wall between two of the sand-bagged windows while he struggled with his breathing.

A rifle barrel protruded from the left-hand window as it blazed away up the slope of the kopje. Fergus opened the rucksack and took out a grenade with his left hand. He pulled the pin with his teeth, while he groped for the Webley ·455 revolver stuck into the belt of his trousers.

He locked one arm over the barrel of the police rifle, dragging it harmlessly aside, then he stepped into the window, and, still holding the rifle, looked through the narrow hole in the sand-bags.

A young, beardless face stared back at him, the eyes wide with amazement, the mouth hanging open slightly and the police helmet pulled down low over the eyes.

Fergus shot him in the bridge of the nose, between the startled staring eyes, and the head was smashed backwards out of view.

Fergus hurled the grenade through the gap and ducked down. The explosion in the confined space was vicious and ear-numbing, Fergus bobbed up and tossed in another grenade.

Glass and smoke blew from the windows, and from within there were the screams and cries of the trapped police constables, the groans and gasping wails of the wounded.

Fergus threw in a third grenade, and screamed, 'Chew on that you bloody strike-breakers.' The bomb exploded, shattering out a panel from the front door, and smoke billowed from all windows.

Inside a single voice started screaming. 'Stop it! Oh God, stop it! We surrender!'

'Come out with your hands in the air, you bastards!'

A police sergeant staggered out of the shattered doorway. He held one hand above his head, the other hung at his side in a torn and blood-soaked sleeve.

The last call that went out from Newlands Police Station before the strikers cut the lines was a call for help. The relieving column coming over the ridge from Johannesburg in a convoy of three trucks got as far as the Hotel in Main Street where it was halted by rifle fire, and the moment it stopped, strikers ran out into the roadway behind it and set all the trucks ablaze with petrol bombs.

The police abandoned their vehicles and raced for cover in a cottage beside the road. It was a strong defensive position and they looked set to hold out against even the most determined attacks, but they left three dead constables lying in the road beside the burning trucks, and another two of their number lying near them, so badly wounded they could only cry out for succour.

A white flag waved from across the road, and the police commander stepped out on to the veranda of the cottage.

'What do you want?' he called across.

Fergus MacDonald walked out into the road, still waving the flag, a slight unwarlike figure in shabby suit and cloth cap.

'You can't leave these men out here,' he shouted back, pointing at the bodies.

The commander came out with twenty unarmed police into the road to carry away the dead and wounded, and while they worked, strikers under Fergus's orders slipped in through the back of the cottages.

Suddenly Fergus whipped the Webley out from under his coat and pressed it to the commander's head.

'Tell your men to put their hands up – or I'll blow your bloody brains all over the road.'

In the cottage, Fergus's men knocked the weapons out of the hands of the police, and in the roadway armed strikers were among them.

'You were under a flag of truce,' protested the commander bitterly.

'We aren't playing games, you bloody black-leg,' snarled Fergus. 'We're fighting for a new world.' The commander opened his mouth to protest again and Fergus swung the revolver sideways, slashing the barrel into his face, snapping out the front teeth from his upper jaw, and crushing the lip into a red wet smear. The man dropped to his knees, and Fergus strode among his men.

'We'll siege the Brixton ridge now – and after that Johannesburg. By tonight, we'll have the red flag flying on every public building in town. Onward, comrades, nothing will stop us now.'

The Transvaal Scottish detrained at Dunswart Station that same morning to march in and seize the mining town of Benoni, which was under full control of the Action Committee's commandos, but the strikers were waiting for them.

The advancing troops were caught in flank and rear by the cross-fire from hundreds of prepared positions, and fought hard all that day to extricate themselves, but it was late afternoon when, still under sniping fire, they were able to retrain at Dunswart.

They carried with them three dead officers and nine dead other rankers. Another thirty were suffering from gunshot wounds, from which many would later die.

From one end to the other of the Witwatersrand, the strikers were on the rampage. The Action Committee controlled that great complex of mining towns and mining properties that follows the sweep of the gold-bearing reef across the bleak African veld, sixty miles from Krugersdorp to Ventersdorp, with the city of Johannesburg at its centre.

It is the richest gold-bearing formation yet discovered by man, a glittering treasure house, the foundation stone of the prosperity of a nation – and now the strikers carried the red flag across it at will, and at every point the force of law and order reeled back.

Every police commander was loath to initiate fire, and every constable loath to act upon the order when it did come. They were firing upon friends, countrymen, brothers.

In the cellars of the Fordsburg Trade Union Hall they were holding a kangaroo court; a traitor was on trial for his life.

Harry Fisher's huge bulk was clad now in a military style bushjacket, with buttoned patch-pockets, over which he wore a bandolier of ammunition. On his right arm was a plain band of red cloth, but his unkempt black hair was uncovered, and his eyes were fierce.

His desk was a packing case, and Helena MacDonald stood behind his stool. She had cropped her hair as short as a man's, and she wore breeches tucked into her boots, and the red armband on her tunic. Her face was pale and gaunt, her eyes in deep plum-coloured sockets were invisible in the bad light, but her body was tensed with the nervous energy of a leashed greyhound with the smell of the hare in its nostrils.

The accused was a storekeeper of the town, with pale watery eyes behind the steel-rimmed spectacles which he blinked rapidly as he watched his accuser.

'He asked to be connected with police headquarters in Marshall Square.'

'Just a minute,' Helena interrupted. 'You are on the local telephone exchange, is that right?'

'Yes, that's right. I am Exchange Supervisor.' The woman looked like a schoolteacher, iron-haired, neatly dressed, unsmiling.

'Go on.'

'I thought I'd better listen in, you know, see what he was up to.'

The storekeeper was wringing white bony hands, and chewing nervously on his lower lip. He looked at least sixty years old with the the pale silver fluff of hair standing up comically from his bald pink pate.

'Well, when he started giving them the details of what was happening here, I broke the connection.'

'What exactly did he say?' Fisher demanded.

'He said that there was a machine gun here.'

'He said that?' Fisher's expression was thunderous. He transferred his glare to the storekeeper, and the man quailed.

'My boy is in the police – he's my only boy,' he whispered, and then blinked back the tears from the pale eyes.

'That's as good as a confession,' said Helena coldly, and Fisher glanced over his shoulder at her and nodded.

'Take him out and shoot him,' he said.

The light delivery van bumped along the overgrown track and stopped beside the old abandoned No. 1 shaft on the Crown Mine's property. It had not been used for twelve years, and concrete machinery slabs and the collar of the shaft were thick with rank grass that grew out of the cracks in the concrete and covered the rusted machinery.

Two men dragged the storekeeper to the dilapidated barbed-wire fence that protected the dark black hole of the shaft. No. 1 shaft was fifteen hundred feet deep, but had flooded back to the five-hundred-foot level. The warning notices on the barbed-wire fence were embellished with the skull and cross-bones device.

Helena MacDonald stayed at the wheel of the delivery van. She lit a cigarette and stared ahead, waiting without visible emotion for the executioner's shot.

The minutes passed, while the cigarette burned down between her fingers, and she snapped impatiently when one of the armed strikers came to the side window of the van,

'What's keeping you?'

'Begging your pardon, missus, neither of us can do it.'

'What do you mean?' Helena demanded.

'Well,' the man dropped his eyes. 'Old Cohen's been selling me my groceries for ten years now. He always gives the kids a candy bar when they go in –'

With an impatient exclamation, Helena opened the van door and stepped out.

'Give me your revolver,' she said, and as she strode to where the second striker guarded the old storekeeper she checked the load and spun the chamber of the pistol.

Cohen started to smile, a mild ingratiating smile as he peered at her face myopically, then he saw her expression and the pistol in her hand.

He dropped to his knees, and he began to urinate in terrified spurts down the front of his baggy grey flannel trousers.

When Helena parked the van in the street behind the market building, she was aware immediately of a new charge of excitement in the air. The men at the sand-bagged windows called out to her,

'Your old man's back, missus. He's down in the cellar with the boss!'

Fergus looked up from the large-scale map of the East Rand over which he and Harry Fisher were poring. She hardly recognized him.

He was sooty and grimed as a chimney sweep, and his eyelashes had been burned away, giving him a bland startled look. His eyes were bloodshot and there were little wet beads of dirty mucus in the corners.

'Hello, luv,' he grinned wearily at her.

'What are you doing here, comrade?' she demanded. 'You are supposed to be at Brixton ridge.'

Harry Fisher intervened, 'Fergus has taken the ridge. He's done fine work, really fine work. But now we have been granted a stroke of really good fortune.'

'What is it?' Helena demanded.

'Slim Jannie Smuts is on his way from Cape Town.'

'That's bad news,' Helena contradicted coolly.

'He's coming by road – and he's got no escort with him,' Harry Fisher explained.

'Like a lover – right into our arms,' grinned Fergus, and spread his own arms wide. There were dark splotches of dried blood on his sleeves.

*   *   *

The Prime Minister's aide-de-camp had spelled Mark at the wheel of the Rolls on the long stretch northwards from Bloemfontein. Mark had been able to sleep, hunched up on the front seat, oblivious of the lurching and shaking over the bad stretches of road, so that he woke refreshed when Sean Courtney stopped the little convoy on a deserted hilltop fifteen miles south of the built-up complex of mines and towns of the Witwatersrand.

It was late afternoon and the lowering sun turned the banks of low false cloud in the north to a sombre purple hue. It was not cloud but the discharge from the hundreds of chimneys of the power stations and refineries, of the coal-burning locomotives and the open fires of tens of thousands of African labourers in their locations, and of burning buildings and vehicles.

Mark wrinkled his nose as he smelled the acrid taint of the city fouling the clean dry air of the highveld.

The entire party took the opportunity to stretch cramped muscles and to relieve other physical needs. Mark noted wryly that nice social distinctions were observed when those members of the party who had general officer's rank and Cabinet Minister's status used the screened side of the parked cars, while the lesser members stood out in the open road.

While they went about their business, there was an argument in progress. Sean was advocating caution and a round-about approach through the suburbs and outlying areas of Johannesburg.

'We should cut across to Standerton and come in on the Natal road – the rebels are holding all the southern suburbs.'

'They'll not be expecting us, old Sean. We'll go through fast and be at Marshall Square before they know what's happened,' Jannie Smuts decided. 'I can't afford the extra two hours it will take us to circle around.'

And Sean growled at him, 'You always were too damned hot-headed, Jannie. Good God, you were the one who rode into the Cape with a hundred and fifty men in your commando to capture Cape Town from the whole British army.'

'Gave them the fright of their lives,' the Prime Minister chuckled as he came around the back of the Rolls, buttoning his trousers, and Sean, following him, went on with relish.

'That's right, but when you tried the same tricks on Lettow von Vorbeck in German East Africa, you were the one who got the fright. He roasted your arse for you.'

Mark winced at Sean's choice of words, and the Prime Minister's party looked to heaven and earth, anywhere except at their master's suddenly unsmiling countenance.

'We are going into Johannesburg on the Booysens Road,' said Jannie Smuts coldly.

'You'll be no damned good to us dead,' grumbled Sean.

'That's enough, old Sean. We'll do it my way.'

'All right,' Sean agreed lugubriously. 'But you'll ride in the second car. The Cadillac will lead with your pennant flying.' He turned to the Prime Minister's driver, 'Flat out, you understand, stop for nothing.'

'Yes, sir.'

'Have you gentlemen got your music with you?' he demanded, and all of them showed him the sidearms they carried.

'Mark,' Sean turned to him. 'Get the Mannlicher off the roof.' Mark unstrapped the leather case from the luggage rack and assembled the 9·3 mm sporting rifle, the only effective weapon they had been able to find at short notice in Somerset House before leaving. He loaded the magazine and handed the weapon to Sean, then slipped two yellow packets of Eley Kynoch ammunition into his own pockets.

'Good boy,' Sean grunted, and peered at him closely. 'How are you feeling? Did you get some sleep?'

'I'm fine, sir.'

'Take the wheel.'

Darkness fell swiftly, smearing the silhouettes of the blue gum trees along the low crests of the rolling open ground, crowding in the circle of their vision.

There were the flickering pinpoints of open cooking fires from a few of the native shacks among the hills, but these were the only signs of life. The road was deserted, and even when they began to speed past the first brick-built buildings, there were no lights, and the stillness was unnatural and disquieting.

'The main power station has shut down. The coal-miners were limiting supply to fifty tons a day for essential services, but now they've stopped even that,' the Prime Minister mused aloud, and neither of them answered him. Mark followed the twinkling red rear-lights of the Cadillac, and the darkness pressed closer. He switched on the main beams of his headlights, and suddenly they were into the narrow streets of Booysens, the southernmost suburb of Johannesburg.

The miners' cottages crowded the road like living and menacing presences. On the left, against the last faint glimmer of the day, Mark could make out the skeletal shape of the steel headgear at Crown Mines' main haulage, and ahead, the low table-like hillocks of the mine dumps gave him a nostalgic twinge.

He thought suddenly of Fergus MacDonald, and Helena, and glanced once again to his left, lifting his eyes from the road for a moment.

Just beyond the Crown Deep headgear, not more than a mile away, was the cottage on Lover's Walk where she had taught him he was a man.

The memory was too wrapped around with pain and guilt, and he thrust it aside and turned his full attention back to the road just as the first rifle shots sparkled from the darkened cottage windows on the right side of the road ahead.

Instantly, he was judging the angle and field of the enemy fire, noticing how they had chosen the curve of the road where the vehicles must slow. 'Good,' he thought dispassionately, applauding the choice, and he hit the gear lever of the Rolls, double declutching into a lower gear to build up revolutions for the turn.

'Get down!' he shouted at his illustrious passengers.

Ahead the Cadillac swerved wildly at the volley and then recovered, and went roaring into the turn.

'Six or seven rifles,' Mark estimated, and then saw the high hedge and the open pavement below the cottage windows. He would give them a changing closing target, he decided, and used the power and rush of the Rolls to broadside up on to the pavement, under the cover of the hedge.

Foliage brushed with a light rushing whisper against the side of the roaring vehicle and behind him a service revolver banged lustily as Sean Courtney fired through the open window.

Mark hit the brakes and fanned the back of the Rolls through the turn, bounded off the pavement and let her sway out across the road, to further confuse the riflemen in the cottages. Then he tramped down hard on the accelerator, gunned her through the turn and went howling down into the dark deserted commercial area of Booysens, leaving the stupefied riflemen staring into the deserted bend, and listening to the receding note of the Rolls-Royce engine.

Only two miles and they would be through the danger area, over the ridge and into Johannesburg proper.

Ahead of him, the Cadillac was running through the area of shops and warehouses and small factories, its headlights blazing harshly on the buildings that lined the road, carving a tunnel of light down their avenue to safety.

In the back seat of the Rolls, the two Generals had not taken Mark's advice to seek cover, and were both sitting bolt upright, discussing the situation objectively in cool measured tones.

'That was quick thinking,' Smuts said. 'They weren't expecting that turn.'

'He's a good lad,' Sean agreed.

'But you are wasting your time with that pistol.'

'Gives me something to do,' Sean explained, as he reloaded the chambers of his revolver.

'You should have ridden with my commando, old Sean, I would have taught you to save ammunition.' Smuts sought revenge for Sean's earlier remarks.

The headlights of the Cadillac tipped slightly upwards as it charged through the dip and reached the first rising ground. They all saw the road-block at the same moment.

It was flung up crudely across the road, oil drums, baulks of timber, iron bedsteads, sand-bags and household furniture obviously dragged from the cottages.

Sean swore loudly and with ferocity.

'I can turn now,' Mark shouted. 'But they'll get us when we slow down — and we'll have to go back through the ambush.'

'Watch the Cadillac,' Sean shouted back.

The heavy black machine had not hesitated, and it roared up the slope at the barricade, picking the spot which seemed weakest.

'He's going to open a breach! Follow him, Mark.'

The Cadillac smashed into the road-block, and tables and chairs flew high into the night. Even above the roar of wind and engine, Mark could hear the tearing crashing impact, and then the Cadillac was through and going on up the ridge, but its speed was bleeding away and a white cloud of steam plumed from the torn radiator.

However, they had forged a breach in the barricade and Mark steered for it, bumping over a mangled mass of timber and then accelerating away up the slope, gaining rapidly on the leading vehicle.

The Cadillac was losing spee, clearing suffering a mortal injury.

'Shall I stop for them?' Mark demanded.

'No,' said Sean. 'We have to get the Prime Minister —'

'Yes,' said Smuts. 'We can't leave them.'

'Make up your bloody minds,' yelled Mark, and there was a stunned disbelieving silence in the back, and Mark began to brake for the pick up.

The machine gun opened from the scrubby bush at the base of the nearest mine dump. The tracer flailed the night, brilliant white fire sweeping down the road in a blinding storm, the high ripping tearing sound was unmistakable and Mark and Sean exclaimed together in appalled disbelief.

'Vickers!'

The Prime Minister's green and golden pennant on the bonnet of the Cadillac drew the deadly sheet of fire, and in the horrified micro-seconds that Mark watched, he saw the car begin to break up. The windshield and side windows blew away in a sparkling cloud of glass fragments, the figures of the three occupants were plucked to pieces like chickens caught in the blades of a threshing-machine.

The Cadillac slewed off the road and crashed headlong into the blank wall of a timber warehouse on the edge of the road, and still the relentless stream of Vickers fire tore into the carcass, punching neat black holes into the metal-work, holes that were rimmed with bare metal that sparkled in the headlights of the Rolls like newly minted silver dollars.

It would only be seconds before the gunner swivelled his Vickers on to the Rolls, Mark realized, and he searched the road ahead for a bolthole.

Between the timber warehouse and the next building was a narrow alleyway, barely wide enough to admit the Rolls. Mark swung out to make a hay-cart turn for the alley, and the gunner guessed his intention, but was stiff and low on his traverse as he swung the Vickers on to the Rolls.

The sheet of bullets ripped the surface of the road, a boiling teeming play of dust and tarmac that ran down under the side of the car.

Before the gunner could correct his aim, the petrol tank of the ruined Cadillac exploded in a woofing clap of sound and a vivid rolling cloud of scarlet flame and dense black smoke.

Under its cover Mark steered for the alleyway, and slammed the Rolls into it although she was suddenly heavy on the steering, and thumping brutally in her front end.

Fifty feet down, the alley was blocked with a heavy haulage trailer, piled high with newly sawn timber baulks – and Mark skidded to a halt, and jumped out.

He saw that for the moment they were covered by the corner of the warehouse from the Vickers, but the timber trailer cut off their escape down the alley and it would be only minutes before the strikers realized their predicament and moved the Vickers to enfilade the alleyway and shoot them to pieces. One glance showed him that machine-gun fire had shredded the off-side leading wheel. Mark jerked open the rear door and snatched the Mannlicher from Sean, and paused only a moment to snap at the two Generals,

'Get the wheel changed. I'll try and hold them off.' Then he was sprinting back down the alleyway.

'I shall have to insist that in future, when he gives me an order, he calls me sir,' Sean said with thin humour, and turned to Smuts. 'Have you ever changed a wheel, Jannie?'

'Don't be stupid, old Sean. I'm a horse soldier, and your superior officer,' Smuts smiled back at him, with his golden beard looking like a refined Viking in the reflected headlights.

'Bloody hell!' grunted Sean. 'You can work the jack.'

Mark reached the corner of the warehouse and crouched against it, checking the load of the Mannlicher before glancing around.

The Cadillac burned like a huge pyre, and the stink of burning rubber and oil and human flesh was choking. The body of the driver still sat at the wheel, but the smoky red flames rushed and drummed about him so that his head was blackening and charring, and his body twisted and writhed in a slow macabre ballet of death.

There was a wind that Mark had not noticed before, a fitful inconstant wind that gusted and puffed down the ridge, rolling thick clouds of the stinking black smoke across the road and then changing strength and direction so that for a few seconds the smoke pall once again poured straight upwards into the night sky.

Over all blazed the flickering orange wash of the flames, uncertain light which magnified shadow and offered false perspective.

Mark realized that he had to get across the road into the scrub and eroded ground below the mine dump before he could get a chance at the Vickers gunner. He had to cross fifty open yards before he reached the ground where he could turn the clumsiness and relative immobility of the Vickers to his own account. He waited for the wind.

He saw it coming, rustling the grass tops in the firelight and rolling a dirty ball of newspaper down the road, then it picked up the smoke and wafted it in a stinking black pall across the open roadway.

Mark launched himself from the corner of the warehouse and had run twenty paces before he realized that the wind had tricked him. It was merely a gust, passing in seconds and leaving the night still and silent when it had gone, silent except for the snapping, crackling flames of the burning Cadillac.

He was halfway across as the smoke opened again, and the cold weight of dread in his belly seemed to spread down into his legs and slow them as he ran like a man in shackles; but the battle clock in his head was running clearly, tolling off the seconds, judging finely the instant that the Vickers gunner up on the dump spotted his shadowy running figure, judging the time it took for him to swing and resight the heavy weapon.

'Now!' he thought, and rolled forward from the waist without checking his speed, going on to his shoulder and somersaulting, ducking under the solid blast of machine-gun fire that came at the exact second he had expected it.

The momentum of his fall carried him up on to his feet again, and he knew he had seconds before the unsighted gunner picked him up again. He plunged onwards and lances of pain shot through the old bullet wounds in his back, wounds which he had not felt in over a year; the pain was in anticipation, as well as from the wrench of his fall.

The bank of red earth on the far side of the road seemed to loom far off while instinct warned him that the Vickers was on to him again. He launched himself feet first, like a baseball player sliding for the plate, and at the same instant the stream of Vickers's bullets tore a leaping sheet of dust off the lip of the bank, and the ricochets screamed like frustrated banshees and wailed away into the night.

Mark lay under the bank for many seconds with his face cradled in the crook of his arm, sobbing for breath while the pain in his old wounds receded and his heart picked up its normal rhythm. When he lifted his head again, his expression was bleak and his anger was cold and bright and functional.

Fergus MacDonald swore softly with both hands on the firing handles of the Vickers, his forefingers still holding the automatic safety-catch open and his thumbs poised over the firing button. He kept the weapon swinging in short rhythmic traverses back and forth as he peered down the slope, but he was swearing, monotonous profanity in a low tight whisper.

The man beside him was kneeling, ready to feed the belt to the gun, and now he whispered hoarsely, 'I think you got him.'

'The hell I did,' hissed Fergus, and jerked the gun across as something in shadow caught his eye down on the road. He fired a short holding burst, and then muttered.

'Right, let's pull out.'

'Damn it, comrade, we've got him —' protested the loader.

'You bloody fool, didn't you see him?' Fergus asked. 'Didn't you see the way he crossed the road, don't you realize we've got a real ripe one on our hands? Whoever he is, he's a killer.'

'Are we going to let one bastard chase us —'

'You're so right,' snapped Fergus. 'When it's that bucko down there, I'm not going to risk this gun. It's worth a hundred trained men,' he patted the square steel breech block. 'We came here to kill Clever Jannie, and he's down there, cooking in his fancy motorcar. Now, let's get the hell out of here –' and he started the complicated process of unloading the Vickers, cranking it once to clear the chamber of its live round and then cranking again to clear the round in the feed block. 'Tell the boys to cover us when we pull back,' he grunted, as he extracted the ammunition belt from the breech pawls, and then started uncoupling the Vickers from its tripod.

'Come on, work quickly,' he snapped at his loader. 'That bastard is on his way, I can feel him breathing down my neck already.'

There were eight strikers on the slope of the dump, Fergus and two for the Vickers, with five riflemen spread out around the gun to support and cover.

'Right, let's go.' Fergus carried the thick-jacketed barrel over one shoulder and a heavy case of ammunition in his left hand; his number two wrestled with the ungainly fifty-pounds weight of metal tripod and the number three carried the five-gallon can of cooling water and the second case of ammunition.

'We are pulling out,' Fergus called to his riflemen, 'look lively, that's a dangerous bastard coming after us!'

They ran in a group, bowed under their burdens, feet slipping in the loose white cyanided sand of the dump.

The shot was from the left, Fergus had not expected that, and it was impossibly high on the dump. The bastard must have grown wings and flown to get there, Fergus thought.

The report was a heavy booming clap, some sort of sporting rifle, and behind him the number three made a strange grunting sound as though his lungs had been forcibly emptied by a heavy blow. Fergus glanced back and saw him down, a dark untidy shape on the white sand.

'Good Christ,' gasped Fergus. It had to be flukey shooting at that range, and in this impossible light, just the early stars and the ruddy glow of the burning Cadillac.

The rifle boomed again, and he heard one of his riflemen scream and then thrash about wildly in the undergrowth. Fergus knew he had judged his adversary fairly, he was a killer. They were all running now, shouting and firing wildly as they scattered back under the lee of the dump, and Fergus ran with them, only one thought in his mind – he must get his precious Vickers safely away.

The sweat had soaked through his jacket between the shoulders, and had run down from under his cap so that he was blinded, and unable to speak when at last he tumbled into the cover of a deep donga and sat against the earth of the bank, with the machine gun cradled in his arms like an infant.

One after another his riflemen reached the donga and fell thankfully into cover.

'How many were there?' gasped one of them.

'I don't know,' panted another, 'must have been a dozen ZARPS, at least. They got Alfie.'

'And they got Henry also, I saw five of them.'

Fergus had recovered his breath enough to speak now. 'There was only one, only one – but a good 'un.'

'Did we get Slim Jannie?'

'Yes,' said Fergus grimly. 'We got him all right. He was in the first car – I saw his flag and I saw him cooking. We can go home now.'

*   *   *

It was a little before eleven o'clock when the solitary Rolls-Royce was halted at the gates of police headquarters on Marshall Square by the suspicious sentries, but when the occupants were recognized, half a dozen high-ranking police and military officers hurried down the steps to welcome them.

The Prime Minister went directly to the large visitors' drawing-room on the first floor which had been transformed into the headquarters of the military administration, empowered and entrusted by the declaration of martial law with the Government of the nation. The relief on the faces of the assembled officers was undisguised. The situation was a mess, but Smuts was here at last and now they could expect order and direction and sanity to emerge from the chaos.

He listened to their reports quietly, tugging at his little goatee beard, his expression becoming more grim as the full extent of the situation was explained.

He was silent a little longer, brooding over the map, and then he looked up at General van Deventer, an old comrade in arms during two wars, a man who had ridden with him on that historic commando into the Cape in 1901 and who had fought beside him against the wily old German, Lettow von Vorbeck, in German East Africa.

'Jacobus,' he said, 'you command the East Rand.' Van Deventer whispered an acknowledgement, his vocal chords damaged by a British bullet in '01.

'Sean, you have the west. I want the Brixton ridge under our control by noon tomorrow.' Then, as an afterthought, 'Have your lads arrived from Natal yet?'

'I hope so,' said Sean Courtney.

'So do I,' Smuts smiled thinly. 'You will have a merry time taking the ridge single-handed.' The smile flickered off his face. 'I want your battle plans presented by breakfast time, gentlemen. I don't have to remind you that, as always, the watchword is speed. We have to cauterize this ulcer and bind it up swiftly.'

In early autumn, the highveld sun has a peculiar brilliance, pouring down through an atmosphere thinned by altitude out of a sky of purest gayest blue.

It was weather for picnicking and for lovers in quiet gardens, but on 14th March 1922 it was not calm, but a stillness of a menacing and ominous intensity which hung over the city of Johannesburg and its satellite towns.

In just two days van Deventer had swept through the East Rand, stunning the strikers with his Boer Commando tactics, rolling up all resistance in Benoni and Dunswart, recapturing Brakpan and the mine, while the Brits column under his command drove through the Modder and Geduld mines and linked with van Deventer at Springs. In two days, they had crushed the revolt on the East Rand, and thousands of strikers came in under the white flag to be marched away to captivity and eventual trial.

But Fordsburg was the heart and the Brixton ridge which commanded it was the key to the revolt.

Now at last, Sean Courtney had the ridge, but it had been two days of hard and bitter fighting. With artillery and air support, they had swept the rocky kopjes, the school buildings, brickfields, the cemetery, the public buildings and the cottages, each of which the strikers had turned into a strongpoint; and in the night they had carried in the dead of both sides, and buried them in the Milner Park cemetery, each with his own comrades, soldier with soldier and striker with striker.

Now Sean was ready for the thrust to the heart, and below them the iron roofs of Fordsburg blinked in the fine clear sunlight.

'Here he comes now,' said Mark Anders, and they all lifted their binoculars and searched for the tiny fleck of black in the immense tall sky.

The DH.9 sailed in sedately, banking slowly in from the south and levelling for the run over the cowering cottages of Fordsburg.

Through the lens of his glasses, Mark could make out the head and shoulders of the navigator in the forward cockpit as he hoisted each stack of pamphlets on to the edge of the cockpit, cut the strings and then pushed them over the side. They flurried out in a white storm behind the slow-moving machine, caught in the slipstream, spreading and spinning and drifting like flocks of white doves.

A push of the breeze spread some of the papers towards the ridge, and Mark caught one out of the air and glanced at the crude printing on cheap thick paper.

MARTIAL LAW
NOTICE

Women and children and all persons well disposed towards the Government are advised to leave before 11 a.m. today that part of Fordsburg and vicinity where the authority of the Government is defied and where military operations are about to take place. No immunity from punishment or arrest is guaranteed to any person coming in under this notice who has broken the law.

SEAN COURTNEY
CONTROL OFFICER

It was clumsy syntax. Mark wondered who had composed it as he crumpled the notice and dropped it into the grass at his feet.

'What if the pickets won't let them come out, sir?' he asked quietly.

'I don't pay you to be my conscience, young man,' Sean growled warningly, and they stood on in silence for a minute. Then Sean sighed and took the cigar from his breast pocket and offered one to Mark as a conciliatory gesture.

'What can I do, Mark? Must I send my lads into those streets without artillery support?' He bit the tip off his cigar and spat it into the grass. 'Whose lives are more important – the strikers and their families or men who trust me and honour me with their loyalty?'

'It's much easier to fight people you hate,' Mark said softly, and Sean glanced at him sharply.

'Where did you read that?' he demanded, and Mark shook his head.

'At least there are no blacks caught up in this,' he said. Mark had personally been in charge of sending disguised black policemen through the lines to warn all tribesmen to evacuate the area.

'Poor blighters,' Sean agreed. 'I wonder what they make of this white men's madness.' Mark strode to the edge of the shallow cliff, ignoring the danger of sniping fire from the buildings below, and glassed the town carefully. Suddenly he exclaimed with relief,

'They're coming out!'

Far below where they stood, the first tiny figures straggled out of the entrance of the Vrededorp subway. The women carried infants and dragged reluctant children at arm's length. Some were burdened with their personal treasures, others brought their pets, canaries in wire cages, dogs on leashes. The first small groups and individuals became a trickle and then a sorry, toiling stream, pushing laden bicycles and hand carts, or simply carrying all the possessions they could lift.

'Send a platoon down to guide them, and give them a hand,' Sean ordered quietly, and brooded heavily with his beard on his chest. 'I'm glad to see the women out of it,' he growled. 'But I'm sad for what it means.'

'The men are going to fight,' Mark said.

'Yes,' Sean nodded. 'They're going to fight. I had hoped we had had enough slaughter – but they are going to make a bitter ending to a tragic tale.' He crushed the stub of his cigar under his heel. 'All right, Mark. Go down and tell Molyneux that it's on. Eleven hundred hours we'll open the barrage. Good luck, son.'

Mark saluted, and Sean Courtney left him and limped back from the crest to join General Smuts and his staff who had come out to watch the final sweep of the battle.

The first shrapnel bursts clanged across the sky, and burst in bright gleaming cotton pods of smoke above the roofs of Fordsburg, cracking the sky and the waiting silence, with startling violence.

They were fired by the horse artillery batteries on the ridge, and immediately the other batteries on Sauer Street joined in.

For twenty minutes, the din was appalling and the brilliant air was sullied by the rising mist of smoke and dust. Mark stood in the hastily dug trench and peered over the parapet. There was something so dreadfully familiar in this moment. He had lived it fifty times before, but now he felt his nerves screwing down too tightly and the heavy indigestible lump of fear in his guts nauseated him.

He wanted to duck down below the parapet, cover his head to protect his ears from the great metallic hammer-blows of sound, and stay there.

It required an immense effort of will to stand where he was and to keep his expression calm and disinterested – but the men of 'A' Company lined the trench on each side of him and, to distract himself, he began to plan his route through the outskirts of the town.

There would be road-blocks at every corner, and every cottage would be held. The artillery barrage would not have affected the strikers under cover, for it was limited to shrapnel bursts. Sean Courtney was concerned with the safety of over a hundred police and military personnel who had been captured by the strikers and were being held somewhere in the town.

'No high explosive,' was the order, and Mark knew his company would be cut to ribbons on the open streets.

He was going to take them through the kitchen yards and down the sanitary lanes to their final objective, the Trades Hall on Commercial and Central Streets.

He checked his watch again, and there were four minutes to go.

'All right, Sergeant,' he said quietly.

The order passed quickly down the trench and the men came to their feet, crouching below the parapet.

'Like old times, sir,' the Sergeant said affably, and Mark glanced at him. He seemed actually to be enjoying this moment – and Mark found himself hating the man for it.

'Let's go,' he said abruptly, as the minute hand of his watch touched the black hair-line division, and the Sergeant blew his whistle shrilly.

Mark put one hand on the parapet and leapt nimbly over the top.

He started to run forward, and from the cottages ahead of him came the harsh crackling of musketry. Suddenly, he realized he was no longer afraid.

He was little more than a youth, with smooth pink cheeks and the lightest golden fluff of a moustache on his upper lip.

They shoved him down the last few steps into the cellars, and he lost his footing and fell.

'Another yellow belly,' called the escort, a strapping bearded fellow with a rifle slung on his shoulder and the red band around his upper arm. 'Caught him trying to sneak out of the subway.'

The boy scrambled to his feet. He had skinned his knees in his fall and he was close to tears as Harry Fisher towered over him. He carried a long black sjambok in his right hand, a vicious tapered whip of cured hippo-hide.

'A traitor,' bellowed Fisher. In the last days of continuous planning and fighting, the strain had started to show. His eyes had taken on a wild fanatical glare, his movements were jerky and exaggerated, and his voice ragged and overloud.

'No, comrade, I swear I'm no traitor,' the youth bleated pitifully.

'A coward, then,' shouted Fisher, and caught the front of the boy's shirt in one big hairy fist and ripped it open to the waist.

'I didn't have a rifle,' protested the boy.

'There'll be rifles for all later – when the first comrades die.'

The lash of the sjambok split the smooth white skin of the boy's back like a razor stroke, and the blood rose in a vivid bright line as he fell to his knees.

Harry Fisher stood over him and swung the sjambok until there were no more screams or groans, and the only sound in the cellar was the hiss and splat of the lash – then he stood back panting and sweating.

'Take him out so the comrades can see what happens to traitors and cowards.'

A striker took each of the boy's arms and as they dragged him up the steps, the flesh of his back hung in ribbons and tatters and the blood ran down over his belt and soaked into the gaberdine of his breeches.

Mark dropped cat-footed over the back wall into the tiny paved yard. Cases of empty beer bottles were piled high along the side walls, and the smell of stale liquor was fruity and heady in the noon heat.

He had reached the bottle store in Mint Road less than an hour after the starting time of the drive, and the route he had led his men, through the backyards and over the roof-tops, had been more successful than he had dared hope.

They had avoided the road-blocks and twice had out-flanked groups of strikers dug into strong positions, surprising them completely, and scattering them with a single volley.

Mark ran across the yard and kicked in the back door of the bottle store, and in the same movement flattened himself against the wall, clear of the gaping doorway and any striker fire from the interior of the building.

The Sergeant and a dozen men followed him over the wall, and spread out to cover the doorway and barred windows. He nodded at Mark, and Mark dived through the doorway sideways with the rifle on his hip, and his eyes screwed up against the gloom after the bright sunlight outside.

The store was deserted, the shutters bolted down over the front windows and shelves of bottles untouched by looters, in testimony of the strikers' discipline. The tiers of bottles stood neatly in their gaily coloured labels, glinting in the dusky light.

The last time Mark had been in here was to buy a dozen bottles of porter for Helena MacDonald, but he pushed the thought aside and went to the shuttered windows just as the Sergeant and his squad burst in through the back door.

The shutters had been pierced by random shrapnel and rifle fire, and Mark used one aperture as a peephole.

Fifty yards across the road was the Trades Hall, and the complex of trenches and defences that the strikers had thrown up around the square.

Even the public lavatories had been turned into a blockhouse, but all the defenders' attention was directed into the streets across the square.

They lined the parapets and were firing frantically at the kilted running figures of the Transvaal Scottish racing towards the square from the station side.

The strikers were dressed in a strange assortment of garb, from greasy working overalls and quasi-military safari jackets, caps and slouch hats and beavers, to Sunday suits, waistcoats and ties. But all of them wore bandoliers of ammunition draped from their shoulders, and their backs were exposed to Mark's attack.

A volley through the bottle-store windows would have done terrible execution among them, and already the Sergeant was directing his men to each of the windows in a fierce and gleeful croak of anticipation.

'I could order up a machine gun,' Mark thought, and something in him shied away from the mental image of a Vickers firing into that exposed and unsuspecting group. 'If only I hated them.'

As he watched, first one and then others of the strikers at the barricades crouched down hopelessly from the withering fire the Highlanders were now pouring on to them.

'Fix bayonets,' Mark called to the men, and the steel scraped from the metal scabbards in the sombre gloom of the store. A stray bullet splintered the shutter above Mark's head and burst a bottle of Scotch whisky on the shelves behind him. The smell of the spirit was sharp and unpleasant, and Mark called again,

'On my order, break open the windows and doors, and we'll show them steel.'

The shutters crashed back, the main doors flew open, and Mark led his company in a howling racing line across the road. Before they reached the first line of sand-bags, the strikers began throwing down their rifles and jumping up with their hands lifted above their heads.

Across the square, the Highlanders poured into the street cheering and shouting and raced for the barricades; Mark felt a surge of relief that he had taken the risk of going with the bayonet, rather than ordering his men to shoot down the exposed strikers.

As his men ran into the square, knocking the weapons out of their hands and pushing the strikers into sullen groups, Mark was racing up the front steps of the Trades Hall.

He paused on the top step, shouted, 'Stand back inside' and fired three rifle bullets into the brass lock.

Harry Fisher leaned against the wall and peered out of the sand-bagged window into the milling yelling chaos of the square.

The madness of unbearable despair shook the huge frame, and he breathed like a wounded bull when it stands to take the matador's final thrust. He watched his men throw down their arms, saw them herded like cattle, with their hands held high, stumbling on weary careless feet, their faces grey with fatigue and sullen in defeat.

He groaned, a low hollow sound of emotional agony stretched to its furthest limits, and the thick shoulders sagged. He seemed to be shrinking in size. The great unkempt head lowered, the blazing vision dimmed in his eyes as he watched the young lieutenant in barathea battle-dress race up the stairs below him, and heard the rifle shots shatter the lock.

He shambled across to his desk and slumped down into the chair facing the closed door, and his hand was shaking as he drew the service revolver from his belt and cocked the hammer. He laid the weapon carefully on the desk in front of him.

He cocked his head and listened to the shouted orders and the trampling confusion in the square below for a minute, then he heard the rush of booted feet up the wooden staircase beyond the door.

He lifted the revolver from the desk, and leaned both elbows on the desk-top to steady himself.

Mark burst in through the main doors of the hall and stopped in surprise and confusion. The floor was covered with prostrate bodies, it seemed there must be hundreds of them.

As he stared, a Captain of Highlanders and half a dozen men burst in behind him. They stopped also.

'Good God,' panted the Captain, and then suddenly Mark realized that the bodies were all uniformed, police khaki, hunting green kilts, barathea.

'They have slaughtered their prisoners,' Mark thought with nightmare horror, staring at the mass of bodies, then suddenly a head lifted cautiously and another.

'Oh thank God,' breathed the Captain beside Mark, as the prisoners began scrambling to their feet, their faces shining with relief, a single voice immediately becoming a hubbub of nervous gaiety.

They surged for the door, some to embrace their liberators and others merely to run out into the sunlight.

Mark avoided a big police Sergeant with rumpled uniform and three days' growth of beard, ducked under his arms and ran for the staircase.

He took the stairs three at a time, and paused on the landing. The doors to five offices on this floor were standing open, the sixth was closed. He moved siwftly down the corridor, checking each of the rooms.

Cupboards and desks had been ransacked, and the floors were ankle-deep in paper, chairs overturned, drawers pulled from desks and dumped into the litter of paper.

The sixth door at the end of the passage was the only one closed. It was the office of the local Union chairman, Mark knew, Fergus MacDonald's office. The man for whom he was searching, driven by some lingering loyalty, by the dictates of shared comradeship and friendship to find him now – and to give him what help and protection he could.

Mark slipped the safety-catch on the rifle as he approached the door. He reached for the handle, and once again that sense of danger warned him. For a moment he stood with his fingers almost touching the brass lock, then he stepped quietly out of the line of the doorway, reaching sideways he rattled the handle softly and then turned it.

The door was unlocked, and the latch snicked and he pushed the door open.

Nothing happened, and Mark grunted with relief and stepped through the doorway.

Harry Fisher sat at the desk facing him, a huge menacing figure, crouching over the desk with the big tousled head lowered on massive shapeless shoulders and the revolver held in both hands, pointing directly at Mark's chest.

Mark knew that to move was death. He could see the rounded leaden noses of the bullets in the loaded chambers of the cylinder and the hammer fully cocked, and he stood frozen.

'It is not defeat,' Harry Fisher spoke with a strangled hoarse voice that Mark did not recognize. 'We are the dragon's teeth. Wherever you bury one of us, a thousand warriors will spring up.'

'It's over, Harry,' Mark spoke carefully, trying to distract him, for he knew he could not lift the rifle and fire in the time Harry Fisher could pull the trigger.

'No.' Fisher shook the coarse tangled locks of his head. 'It is only just beginning.'

Mark did not realize what he was doing, until Harry Fisher had reversed the pistol and thrust the muzzle into his own mouth. The explosion was muffled, and Harry Fisher's head was stretched out of shape, as though it were a rubber ball struck by a bat.

The back of his skull erupted, and a loose mass of bright scarlet and custard yellow splattered the wall behind him.

The impact of the bullet hurled his body backwards and his chair toppled and crashed over.

The stench of burned powder hung in the room on filmy wisps of gunsmoke, and Harry Fisher's booted heels kicked and tapped a jerky, uneven little dance on the bare wooden floor.

'Where is Fergus MacDonald?' Mark asked the question a hundred times of the files of captured strikers. They stared back at him, angry, bitter, some of them still truculent and defiant, but not one of them even deigned to answer.

Mark took three of his men, under the pretext of a mopping-up patrol, down to Lover's Walk as far as the cottage.

The front door was unlocked, and the beds in the front room were unmade. Mark felt a strange repugnance of mind, balanced by a plucking of lust in his loins, when he saw Helena's *crêpe de Chine* dressing-gown thrown across the chair, and a crumpled pair of cotton panties dropped carelessly on the floor beside it.

He turned away quickly, and went through the rest of the house. The dirty dishes in the kitchen had already grown a green fuzz of mould, and the air was stale and disused. Nobody had been in these rooms for days.

A scrap of paper lay on the floor beside the coal-black stove. Mark picked it up and saw the familiar hammer and sickle device on the pamphlet. He screwed it up and hurled it against the wall. His men were waiting for him on the stoep.

The strikers had dynamited the railway lines at Braamfontein station, and at the Church Street level-crossing, so the regiment could not entrain at Fordsburg. Most of the roads were blocked with rubble and the detritus of the final struggle, but most dangerous was the possibility of stubborn strikers still hiding out in the buildings that lined the road through the dip to Johannesburg.

Sean Courtney decided to move his men out up the slope to the open ground of the Crown Deep property.

They marched out of Fordsburg in the darkness, before good shooting light. It had been a long uncomfortable night, and nobody had slept much. Weariness made their packs leaden to carry and shackled their legs. There was less than a mile to go, however.

The motor transport was drawn up in the open ground near the headgear of Crown Mine's main haulage, a towering structure, shaped like the Eiffel Tower, steel girders riveted and herring-boned for strength, rising a hundred feet to the huge wheels of the winching equipment. When the shift was in, these wheels spun back and forth, back and forth, lowering the cages filled with men and equipment, hundreds of feet into the living earth, and raising the millions of tons of gold-bearing rock out of the depths.

Now the great wheels stood motionless, they had been dead for three months now, and the buildings clustered about the tower were gloomy and deserted.

The transport was an assortment of trucks and commercial vans, commandeered under martial law – gravel lorries from the quarries, mining vehicles, even a bakery van, but it was clear that there was not enough to take out six hundred men.

As Mark came up, marching on the flank of 'A' Company, there were half a dozen officers in discussion at the head of the convoy. Mark recognized the familiar bearded figure of General Courtney standing head and shoulders above the others, and his voice was raised in an angry growl.

'I want all these men moved before noon. They've done fine work, they deserve hot food and a place –'

At that moment he saw Mark, and frowned heavily, waving him over and beginning to speak before he had arrived.

'Where the hell have you been?'

'With the company –'

'I sent you to take a message, and expected you back. You know damned well I didn't mean you to get into the fighting. You are on my staff, sir!'

Mark was tired and irritable, still emotionally disturbed by all that he had seen and done that day, and he was in no mood for one of the General's tantrums.

His rebellious expression was unmistakable. 'Sir,' he began, and Sean shouted at him.

'And don't take that tone to me, young man!'

An uncaring, completely irresponsible dark rage descended on Mark. He didn't give a damn for the consequences and he leaned forward, pale with fury, and opened his mouth.

The regiment was bunched up now, halted in the open roadway, neat symmetrical blocks of khaki, six hundred men in ranks three deep.

The shouted orders of the NCOs halted each section, one after the other, and stood them at the easy position.

From the top of the steel headgear, they made an unforgettable sight in the rich yellow light of early morning.

'Ready, luv,' whispered Fergus MacDonald, and Helena nodded silently. Reality had long faded and been replaced by this floating dreamlike state. Her shoulders were raw where the carrying straps of the heavy ammunition boxes had bitten into the flesh, but there was no pain, just a blunting numbness of body. Her hands seemed bloated, and clumsy, the nails broken off raggedly and rinded with black half-moons of dirt, and the harsh canvas of the ammunition belts between her fingers felt smooth as silk, the brass cartridge cases cool, so that she felt like pressing them to her dried cracked lips.

Why was Fergus staring at her that way, she wondered with a prickle of irritation that did not last, once again the dreamy floating sensation.

'You can go down now,' Fergus said quietly. 'You don't have to stay.' He looked like a very old man, his face shrivelled and falling in upon itself. The stubble of beard on his lined and haggard cheeks was silvery as diamond chips, but the skin was stained by smoke and dirt and sweat.

Only the eyes below the peak of the cloth cap still burned with the dark fanatic flames.

Helena shook her head. She wanted him to stop talking, the sound intruded, and she turned her head away.

The men below stood shoulder to shoulder in their orderly ranks. The low sun threw long narrow shadows from their feet across the red dust of the roadway.

A second longer Fergus stared at her. She was a pale, wasted stranger, the bones pushing through the smooth drawn flesh of her face, the scarf wound like a gypsy around her head, covering the black cropped hair.

'All right then,' he murmured, and tapped the breech of the Vickers, once, twice, training it slightly left.

There was a group of officers near the head of the column. One of them was a big powerful man with a dark beard. The sunlight sparkled on his shoulder-tabs, Fergus lowered his head and looked through the rear sight of the Vickers.

There was a younger slimmer officer with the other, and Fergus blinked twice rapidly, as something stirred deep in his memory.

He hooked his fingers into the automatic safety-bar and lifted it, priming the gun, and he brought his thumbs on to the firing button.

He blinked again. The face of the young officer moved something in him, he felt a softening and blurring of his determination and he rejected it violently and thrust down on the button with both thumbs.

The weapon juddered on its tripod, and the long belt was sucked greedily into the breech, Helena's small pale hands guiding it carefully, and the empty brass cases spewed out from under the gun, tinkling and ringing and bouncing off the steel girders of the headgear.

The sound was a deafening tearing roar that seemed to fill Helena's head and beat against her eyes, like the frantic wings of a trapped bird.

Even the most skilled marksman must guard against the tendency to ride up on a downhill shot. The angle from the top of the headgear was acute and the soft yellowish early light further confused Fergus's aim. His first burst carried high – shoulder-high instead of belly-high, which is the killing line for machine-gun fire.

The first bullets struck before Mark heard the gun. One of them hit Sean Courtney high up in the big bulky body. It flung him forward, chest to chest with Mark, and both of them went down, sprawling in the roadway.

Fergus tapped the breech block, dropping his aim a fraction on to the belly line, and traversed in a long unhurried sweep along the ranks of standing soldiers, cutting them with the scythe of the Vickers in the eternal seconds that they still stood in stunned paralysis.

The stream of tracer hosed them, and washed them into crazy heaps, piled them on each other, dead and wounded together, their screams high and thin in the rushing hurricane of Vickers fire.

Sean rolled half off Mark, and his face was contorted, angry and outraged, as he tried to struggle on to his knees, but his one arm was dangling. His blood splattered them both and he flopped helplessly.

Mark wriggled out from under him, and looked up at the headgear. He saw the tracer flickering like fire-flies and darting into the crowded roadway on the triumphant fluttering roar of the gun. Even in his own confusion and despair, he saw that the gunner had picked a good stance. He would be hard to come at.

Then he looked down the road and a cold fist clenched on his guts as he saw the bloody execution. The ranks had broken, men running and stumbling for what little cover the vehicles and ditches offered, but the road was still filled.

They lay in windrows and piles, they crawled and cried and twisted in the dust which their blood was turning to chocolate-red mud – and the gun swivelled and came back, flickering tracer into the carnage, chopping up the road surface into a spray of dust and leaping gravel, running viciously over the piles of wounded, coming back to where they lay.

Mark twisted up into a crouch, and slipped an arm under the General's chest. The weight of the man was enormous, but Mark found strength that he had not known before, goaded on by the fluttering rushing roar of the Vickers. Sean Courtney heaved himself up like a bull caught in quicksand, and Mark got him on to his feet.

Bearing half his weight, Mark steadied him and kept him from falling. He weaved drunkenly, hunched over, bleeding badly, breathing noisily through his mouth, and Mark forced him into an ungainly crouching run.

The gun swept their heels, kicking and smashing into the back of a young lieutenant who was creeping towards the ditch, dragging both useless legs behind him. He dropped face down and lay still.

They reached the drainage ditch and tumbled into it. It was less than eighteen inches deep, not enough to cover the General fully, even when he lay flat on his belly, and the Vickers was still hunting.

After that first long slicing traverse, it was firing short accurate bursts at selected targets, more deadly than random fire, keeping the gun from overheating and preventing a stoppage, conserving ammunition. Mark, weighing it all, realized that there was an old soldier up there in the tower.

'Where are you hit?' he demanded, but Sean struck his hands away irritably, twisting his head to peer up into the tall steel headgear.

'Can you get him, Mark?' he grunted, and pressed his fingers into his shoulder, where the blood welled up thick and dark as molasses.

'Not from here,' Mark answered quickly. It had taken him seconds to assess the shoot. 'He's holed up tight.'

'Merciful Jesus! My poor boys.'

'He's built himself a nest.' Mark studied the steelwork. The platform below the winch wheels was covered with heavy timber, fitted loosely into the framework of steel.

The gunner had pulled these up and built himself four walls of wood, perhaps two feet thick. Mark could see the light glimmering through the open gaps in the floor boards, and make out the shape and size of the fortified nest.

'He can hold us here all day!' Sean looked down at the piles of khaki bodies in the roadway, and they both knew many of the wounded would bleed to death in that time. Nobody dared go out to them.

The gun came back, ripping a flail across the earth near their heads and they ducked their faces to the ground, pressing their bodies into the shallow ditch.

The ground sloped down very gradually towards the steel tower, only when you lay at ground level like this was the gradient apparent.

'Somebody will have to get under him, or behind him,' Mark spoke quietly, thinking it out.

'It's open ground all the way,' Sean grunted.

On the opposite side of the road fifty yards away, a narrow-gauge railway ran down the short open grassy slope to the foot of the tower. It was used to truck the waste material from the shaft-head to the rock dump, half a mile away.

Almost opposite where they lay, half a dozen of the steel cocoa pans had been abandoned at the beginning of the strike. They were small four-wheeled tip-trucks, coupled to each other in a line, each of them heaped high with big chunks of blue rock.

Mark realized he was still wearing his pack and he shrugged out of the straps as he planned his stalk, judging angles and range as he groped for the field-dressing and handed it to Sean.

'Use this.'

Sean tore open the package and wadded the cotton dressing into the front of his tunic. His fingers were sticky with his own blood.

Mark's P.14 rifle lay in the road where he had dropped it, but there were five clips of ammunition in the pouches on his webbing belt.

'Try and give me some covering fire when I start to go up,' he said, and watched the tower for the next burst of tracer.

'You'll never get there,' said Sean. 'We'll bring up a thirteen-pounder and shoot the bastard out of there.'

'That will take until noon, it will be too late for them.' He glanced at the wounded in the road, and at that moment a stream of brilliant white tracer flew from the tower, aimed at the far end of the column, and Mark was up and running hard, stooping to gather the rifle at full run, crossing the road in a dozen flying strides, stumbling in the rough ground beyond, catching his balance and sprinting on.

That stumble had cost him a tenth of a second, the margin of life and death perhaps, while the gunner high up in the tower spotted him, swivelled the gun and lined up. The steel cocoa pans were just ahead, fifteen paces, but he wasn't going to make it – the warning flared in his brain, and he dropped into the short grass and rolled sideways, just as the storm of Vickers fire filled the air about him with the lash of a hundred bullwhips.

Mark kept rolling, like a log, and the gun gouged a furrow out of the dry stony earth inches from his shoulder.

He came up against the wheels of the cocoa pan with a force that bruised his hip and made him cry out involuntarily. Vickers bullets hammered and clanged against the steel body of the truck and howled off in ricochet, but Mark was under cover now.

'Mark, are you all right?' the General's bull-bellow carried across the road.

'Give me covering fire.'

'You heard him, lads,' shouted the General, and one or two rifles began firing spasmodically from the ditches, and from behind the stranded motor lorries.

Mark dragged himself on to his knees, and quickly checked the rifle, brushing the sights with his thumb to make certain they were cleaned of dirt and undamaged in the fall.

Then he worked his way to the coupling of the cocoa pan and threw the release toggle. The brake wheel was stiff and required both his hands to unwind it. The brake chocks squeaked softly as they disengaged, but the slope of the ground was so gentle that the truck did not move until Mark put his shoulder to it.

He strained with all his weight before the steel wheels made a single reluctant revolution, then gravity took her and the cocoa pan began to roll.

'Give the bastard hell!' Sean Courtney yelled, as he realized suddenly what Mark was going to do, and Mark grinned without mirth at that characteristic exhortation, and he trotted along, doubled up behind the heavily-laden steel truck.

A terrible tearing, hammering storm of Vickers broke over the slowly rolling truck, and instinctively Mark ducked lower and steadied himself against the metal side.

He realized that as he came close to the tower, so the gunner's angle would change until he was shooting almost directly down on top of Mark – then the side of the truck would give him no cover, but he was committed. Nothing would stop the slowly accelerating rush of the cocoa pan down the slope, it had the weight of ten tons of rock behind it and its speed was gathering. Soon he would not be able to keep up with it, already he was running – and the Vickers roared again, the bullets screeching and wailing furiously off the steel body.

Twisting as he ran, he slung the rifle on one shoulder and reached up to hook both hands over the side of the truck. He was pulled instantly off his feet, and they dangled without foothold, in danger of being caught up in the spinning steel wheels. He drew his knees up under his chin, hanging all his weight on his arms and taking the intolerable strain in his belly muscles as the truck flew down into the stretching octopus shadow of the headgear.

Still hanging on his arms, Mark flung his head back and looked up. The tower was foreshadowed by perspective, and it crouched over him like some menacing monster, stark against the mellow morning sky, crude black steel and timber baulks pyramiding into the heavens. At its zenith, Mark could see the pale mirrorlike face of the gunner, and the thick water-jacketed barrel of the Vickers trained down at its maximum depression.

The gun flamed, and bullets rang the steel near his head like a great bell. They churned into the blue rock, disintegrating into chips of buzzing metal and shattering the rock into vicious splinters and pellets that cut at his hands so that he screwed his eyes shut and clung helplessly.

Such was the speed of the truck now that he was under fire for only seconds, and the gunner's aim could not follow it, as it raced down on to the concrete loading bank, and slammed into the buffers. The force of the impact was brutal and Mark was hurled from his perch, the rifle-strap snapped and the weapon sailed away, and Mark turned in the air and hit the sloping concrete ramp on his side with a crash that jarred his teeth in his head. The rough concrete ripped away the thick barathea cloth from his hip and leg and shoulder, and seared the flesh beneath with gravel burn.

He came up at last against a stack of yellow-painted oil-drums, and his first concern was to roll on to his back and stare upwards.

He was under the headgear now, protected from the gunner by the legs and intricate steel girders of the tower itself, and he pulled himself to his feet, dreading the give and crippling drag of broken bone. But though his body felt crushed and bruised, he could still move, and he hobbled to where his rifle lay.

The strap was broken, and the butt was cracked and splintered, and as he lifted it, it snapped into two pieces. He could not fire from the shoulder.

The foresight had been knocked off, and the broken metal had a sugary grey crystalline look. He could not aim the weapon. He would have to get close, very close.

There was a deep bright scar in the steel of the breech. He muttered a prayer, 'Please God!' as he tried to work the bolt open. It was jammed solid and he struggled with it fruitlessly for precious seconds.

'All right,' he thought grimly. 'No butt to hold to the shoulder, no foresight with which to aim, and only the one cartridge in the breech – it's going to be interesting.' He looked around him quickly.

Beneath the steel tower, the two square openings to the main shaft were set into the concrete collar, protected by screens of steel mesh. The one cage stood at the surface station, doors open, ready for the next shift. The other was at the bottom station, a thousand feet below ground level.

They had stood that way for months now. On the far side was the small service elevator which would take maintenance teams the hundred feet to the summit of the tower in half a minute. However, there was no power on the shaft head, and the elevator was useless.

The only other way up was the emergency ladder. This was an open steel stairway that spiralled up around the central shaft, protected only by a low handrail of inch piping.

High above Mark's head the Vickers fired again, and Mark heard a scream of agony out there on the roadway. It hastened him, and he limped to the stairway.

The steel-mesh gate was open, the padlock shattered, and Mark knew by what route the sniper had reached his roost.

He stepped on to the stairway and began to climb, following the coils up the casing round and round, and up and up.

Always at his right hand, the open black mouth of the shaft gaped, an obscene dark orifice in the earth's surface, dropping straight and sheer into the very bowels, a thousand dark terrifying feet.

Mark tried to ignore it, dragging his bruised and aching body up by the handrail, carrying the broken weapon in his other hand, and strained his neck backwards for the first glimpse of the gunner above.

The Vickers fired again, and Mark glanced sideways. He was high enough now to see into the road.

One of the trucks was burning, a tall dragon's breath of smoke and sullen flame pouring into the sky – and the drab khaki bodies were still strewn in the open, death's discarded toys.

Even as he watched, the Vickers fire thrashed over them, mangling already dead flesh, and Mark's anger became cold and bright as a dagger's blade.

'Keep firing, luv,' Fergus croaked in that husky stranger's voice. 'Short bursts. Count to twenty slowly, and then a touch on the button. I want him to think that I am still up here.' He pulled the Webley from his belt, and crawled on his belly towards the head of the steep staircase.

'Don't leave me, Fergus.'

'It'll be all right,' he tried to grin, but his face was grey and crumpled. 'Just you keep firing. I'm going down to meet him halfway. He'll not expect that.'

'I don't want to die alone,' she breathed. 'Stay with me.'

'I'll be back, luv. Don't fuss yourself,' and he slid on his belly into the opening of the staircase.

She felt like a child again, in one of those terrible dark nightmares, trapped and enmeshed in her own fate, and she wanted to cry out. The sound reached her lips but died there as a low blubbering moan.

A rifle bullet chunked into the barricade of timber beside her. They were shooting from down below. She could not pick them out, for they were hidden in the ditches and the irregularities of the ground, screened by long purple shadows, and her eyes were blurred with tears and with exhaustion; yet she found the last few grains of her strength and crawled to the gun.

She squatted behind it and her hands were almost too small to reach the firing button. She pressed the barrel downwards, and forced her blearing vision to focus, marvelling at the little toy figures in the field of the sight. The gun juddered in her hands like a living creature.

'A short burst,' she whispered to herself, repeating Fergus's instructions, and lifted her thumbs from the firing button. 'One – two – three,' she began to count to the next burst.

Mark paused at the next burst of firing and stood for a moment staring up. He was over halfway to the top, and now he could make out the floor of the service platform below the winch wheels, the platform on which the Vickers was sited.

There were narrow cracks in the woodwork through which bright lines of open sky showed clearly, and as he watched he saw one of the lines of light interrupted by a dark movement beyond. It was that flicker of movement that caught his attention, and he realized that he was looking at the body of the person who served the gun. He must be squatting directly over one of the narrow joints in the floor of the platform, and his movements blocked out part of that bright line of light.

A bullet through the gap would cripple and pin him, but he glanced at the broken weapon in his hand and knew that he would have to get closer, much closer.

He began to run upwards and though he tried to keep his weight lightly on the balls of his feet, the hobnails in his boots rang on the steel stairs.

Fergus MacDonald heard them and checked his own run, shrinking into the protective lee of one of the steel girders.

'One man only,' he muttered. 'But coming up fast.' He dropped on one knee and peered down through the gaps between the stairs, hoping for sight of the man who he was hunting. The steps overlapped each other like fanned playing-cards, and the lateral supports of the tower formed an impenetrable steel forest below him.

The only way he could hope for a glimpse was to hang out over the handrail and look down the central shaft-well.

The idea of that thousand-foot black hole repelled him, and he had formed an estimate of his opponent high enough to guess that the reward for putting his head over the side would be a bullet between the eyes.

He edged into a better position where he could cover the next spiral of staircase below him.

'I'll let him come up to me,' he decided, and braced his arm against the girder at the level of his chin, and laid the Webley over the crook of his elbow to give the heavy pistol support. He knew that over ten paces it was wildly inaccurate, but the dead rest would give him at least one fair shot.

He cocked his head slightly to listen to the clatter of booted feet on steel, and he judged that the man was very close. One more spiral of the stair would bring him into shot. Carefully, he thumbed back the hammer of the Webley and looked down over the slotted rear-sight.

Above them, the Vickers fired again, and Mark paused to catch his breath and check the situation of the gunner, and to his dismay he realized that he had climbed too high in the tower.

He had changed the angle of sight, and could no longer see through the cracks in the timber platform. He had to retreat carefully down the staircase before once again the bright lines of light opened in the dark underbelly of timber.

A vague blur of movement reassured him that the gunner had not changed his position. He was still squatting over the joint, but the shot was almost impossible.

He was shooting directly upwards, awkward even in the best conditions, but now he had no butt to steady the rifle and no foresight, he was shooting into a single dark mass of timber and had to guess the position of the crack because the gunner's body obscured the light from the far side. The crack itself was only two inches wide, and if he missed by a smallest fraction the bullet would bury itself harmlessly in the thick timber.

He tried not to think that there would be only one shot, the jammed breach made that certain.

He put his hip to the guardrail and leaned out over the open shaft, squinted upwards trying to set the target in his mind as he lifted the broken rifle in an easy natural movement. He knew that he had to make the shot entirely by instinct. He had no chance if he hesitated or tried to hold his aim steadily on the target.

He swept up the shattered weapon and at the moment the long barrel aligned, he pressed the trigger.

In the flash and thunder of the shot a tiny white splinter of wood jumped from the edge of the crack. The bullet had touched wood and Mark felt an instant of utter dismay.

Then the body that had obscured the light was jerked abruptly aside, and the crack was a single uninterrupted line again – and on the platform somebody screamed.

Helena MacDonald had just reached the count of twenty again, and was aiming at a gathering of men she could see grouping beyond one of the lorries. She squatted low over the gun and was on the point of jamming her thumbs down on the firing button, when the bullet came up through the floor timbers.

It had touched one of the hard mahogany baulks, just enough to split the casing of the bullet and alter its shape, mushrooming it slightly, so that it did not enter her body through a neat round puncture.

It tore a ragged entry into the soft flesh at the juncture of her slightly spread thighs and plunged upwards through her lower abdomen, striking and shattering the thick bony girdle of her pelvis, glancing off the bone with still enough impetus to bruise and weaken the lower branch of the descending aorta, the great artery that runs down from the heart, before going on to embed itself in the muscles high in the left side of her back.

It lifted Helena into the air, and hurled her across the platform on to her face.

'Oh God, oh God, help me! Fergus! Fergus! I don't want to die alone,' she screamed, and the sound carried clearly to the two men in the steel tower below her.

Mark recognized the voice instantly. It did not need the name to confirm it.

His mind shied at the enormity of what he had done. The broken rifle almost ripped from his hands, but he saved it and caught at the handrail for support.

Helena cried again, a sound without words – it was exactly that strange wild cry that she had uttered at the zenith of one of their wildest flights of passion together, and for an instant Mark remembered her face shining and triumphant, the dark eyes burning and the open red mouth and the soft pink petal of her tongue aflutter.

Mark started to run, hurling himself upwards.

The screams caught Fergus like a flight of arrows in the heart. A piercing, physical agony, he dropped the pistol to his side and stood irresolute staring upwards, not knowing what had happened, except that Helena was dying. He had heard the death scream too often to have any doubt about that. What he was listening to was mortal agony, and he could not force his body to begin the climb upwards, to the horror he knew waited him there.

While he hesitated, Mark came around the angle of the staircase and Fergus was not ready for him. The pistol was at his side, and he fell back and tried to bring it up, to fire at point-blank range into the chest of the uniformed figure.

Mark was as off balance as he was. He had not expected to run into another enemy, but he saw the pistol and swung the broken rifle at Fergus's head.

Fergus ducked, and the Webley fired wide, the bullet flew inches past Mark's temple and the report slammed against his eardrum and made him flinch his head. The rifle struck the girder behind Fergus and was jerked from Mark's grip, then they came together chest to chest. Mark seized the wrist of his pistol hand and held with all his strength.

Neither of them had recognized the other. Fergus had aged into a grey caricature of himself and his eyes were shaded by the cloth cap. Mark was in unfamiliar uniform, dusty and bloodied, and he had changed also, youth had become man.

Mark was taller, but they were matched in weight and Fergus was endowed with the terrible fighting rage of the berserker which gave him superhuman strength.

He drove Mark back against the guardrail, and bowed his back out over the open shaft, but Mark still had his pistol wrist, and the weapon was pointed up over his head.

Fergus was sobbing wildly, driving with all the wiry uncanny strength of a body tempered by hard physical work, and fired now by the strength of anger and sorrow and despair.

Mark felt his feet slip, the hob-nails of his boots skidding on the steel steps and he went over further, feeling the mesmeric suck of a thousand feet of open space plucking at his back.

Above them, Helena screamed again, and the sound drove like a needle into the base of Fergus's brain, he shuddered, and his body convulsed in one great rigid spasm that Mark could not hope to hold. He went backwards over the guardrail, but still he had his grip on Fergus's gun hand and his other arm he had wound about his shoulders.

They slid into the void, locked together in a horrible parody of a lovers' embrace, but as they started to fall, Mark hooked both legs over the rail, like a trapeze artiste, and jerked to a halt, hanging upside down into the shaft.

Fergus was somersaulted over him by the force of his own thrust; as he turned in the air, the cloth cap flew from his head and he was torn from the arm that Mark had around his shoulder.

He came up with a jerk that almost tore Mark's shoulder from its socket, for some animal instinct had kept Mark's grip locked on the pistol hand, and he dangled from that precarious hold.

The two of them pendulumed out over the black emptiness of the shaft, Mark's legs hooked over the rail, hanging at full stretch, with Fergus's body the next link in the chain.

Fergus's head was thrown back, staring up at Mark, and with the cap gone, his lank sandy hair fell back from his face and Mark felt fresh shock loosen his grip.

'Fergus!' he croaked, but the madman's eyes that stared back at him were devoid of recognition.

'Try and get a grip,' Mark pleaded, swinging Fergus towards the staircase. 'Grab the rail.'

He knew he could not hold many seconds longer, the fall had wrenched and weakened his arm, and the blood was rushing to his head in this inverted position, he could feel his face swelling and suffusing and the pounding ache in his temples – while the black and hungry mouth of the shaft sickened him; with his other hand he groped and got a second hold on Fergus's wrist.

Fergus twisted in his grip, but instead of going for the rail he reached upwards and took the pistol from his own hand, transferring it to his free hand.

'No,' Mark shouted at him. 'Fergus, it's me! It's me, Mark!'

But Fergus was far past all reason, as he juggled with the Webley, getting a firing grip on the hilt with his left hand.

'Kill them,' he muttered. 'Kill all the scabs.'

He lifted the barrel to aim upwards at Mark, dangling over the drop, twisting slowly in that double retaining grip.

'No, Fergus!' screamed Mark, and the muzzle of the revolver pointed into his face. At that range, it would tear half his head away, and he saw Fergus's forefinger tighten on the trigger, the knuckle whitening under pressure.

He opened his hands and Fergus's wrist slipped from his fingers.

He spun away, falling swiftly, and the revolver never fired but Fergus began to scream a high thin wail.

Still hanging upside down Mark watched Fergus's body, limbs spread and turning like the spokes of a wheel, as it dropped away, shrinking rapidly in size, and the despairing wailing cry receding with it, dwindling away to a small pale speck, like a dust mote which was swallowed abruptly into the dark mouth of the shaft far below and the wailing cry with it.

In the silence afterwards, Mark hung batlike, blinking the sweat out of his eyes and for many seconds unable to find strength to move. Then from the platform above him came a long shuddering moan and it roused him.

Forcing his bruised body to respond, he managed to get a grip on the guardrail and drag himself up, until he tumbled on to the staircase, and started up it on rubbery legs.

Helena had dragged herself to the pile of timber, leaving a dark wet smear across the platform. The khaki breeches she wore were sodden with blood and it oozed from her still to form a spreading puddle in which she sat.

She lay back against the timber next to the tripoded Vickers in an attitude of utter weariness, and her eyes were closed.

'Helena,' Mark called her, and she opened her eyes.

'Mark,' she whispered, but she did not seem surprised. It was almost as though she expected him. Her face was completely drained of all colour, the lips seemed rimed with frost, and her skin had an icy sheen to it. 'Why did you leave me?' she asked.

Hesitantly, he crossed to her. He knelt beside her, looked down at her lower body and felt the scalding flood of vomit rise into his throat.

'I truly loved you,' her voice was so light, breathing soft as the dawn wind in the desert, 'and you went away.'

He put out his hand to touch her legs, to spread them and examine the wound, but he could not bring himself to do it.

'You won't go away again, Mark?' she asked, and he could hardly catch the words. 'I knew you'd come back to me.'

'I won't go away again,' he promised, not recognizing his own voice, and the smile flickered on her icy lips.

'Hold me, please Mark. I don't want to die alone.'

Awkwardly, he put an arm around her shoulders and her head lolled sideways against him.

'Did you ever love me, Mark, even a little bit?'

'Yes, I loved you,' he told her, and the lie came easily. Suddenly there was a hissing spurt of brighter redder blood from between her thighs as the damaged artery erupted. She stiffened, her eyes flew wide open, and then her body seemed to melt against him and her head dropped back.

Her eyes were still wide open and dark as a midnight sky. As he stared at it, slowly her face changed. It seemed to melt like white candle wax held too close to the flame, it ran and wavered and reformed – and now it was the face of a marble angel, smooth and white and strangely beautiful, the face of a dead boy in a land far away – and the fabric of Mark's mind pulled and tore.

He began to scream, but no sound came from his throat – the scream was deep down in his soul, and his face was without expression, his eyes dry of tears.

They found him like that an hour later. When the first soldiers climbed cautiously up the iron staircase to the top of the steel tower, he was sitting quietly, holding the woman's dead body in his arms.

'Well,' said Sean Courtney, 'they've hanged Taffy Long!' He folded the newspaper with an angry gesture and dropped it on to the paving beside his chair.

In the dark shiny foliage of the loquat tree that spread above them, the little white-eyes pinkled and twittered as they probed the blossoms with sharp busy beaks and their wings fluttered like moths about the candle.

Nobody at the breakfast table spoke. All of them knew how Sean had fought for leniency for those strikers on whom the death sentence had been passed. He had used all his influence and power, but it had not availed against the vindictive and vengeful who wanted full measure of retribution for all the horrors of the revolt. Sean brooded now at the head of the table, hunched in his chair with his beard on his chest, staring out over the Ladyburg valley. His arm was still supported by the linen sling; it had not healed cleanly and the bullet wound was still open and draining. The doctors were anxious about it, but Sean had told them,

'Leopard, and bullet and shrapnel and knife – I've had them all before. Don't twist a gut for me. Old meat heals slowly, but it heals hard.'

Ruth Courtney watching him now was not worried about the wounds of the flesh. It was the wounds of the mind that concerned her.

Both the men of her household had come back deeply marked by the lash of guilt and sorrow. She was not sure what had happened during those dark days, for neither man had spoken about it, but the horror of it still stalked even here at Lion Kop, even in the bright soft days, on these lovely dreaming hills where she had brought them to heal and rest.

This was the special place, the centre and fortress of their lives, where Sean had brought her as his bride. They owned other great houses, but this was home, and she had brought Sean here now after the strife and the turmoil. But the guilt and the horror had come with them.

'Madness,' muttered Sean. 'Utter raving madness. How they cannot see it, I do not know.' He shook his head, and was silent a moment. Then he sighed. 'We hang them now – and make them live for ever. They'll haunt and hound us all our days.'

'You tried, dear,' said Ruth softly.

'Trying isn't enough,' he growled. 'In the long run, all that counts is succeeding.'

'Oh Pater, they killed hundreds of people,' Storm burst out, shaking her shining head at him, with angry colour in her cheeks. 'They even tried to kill you!'

Mark had not spoken since the meal began, but now he lifted his head and looked at Storm across the table. She checked the other words that sprang to her lips as she saw his expression.

He had changed so much since he had come home. It was as though he had aged a hundred years. Though there was no new line or mark on his face, yet he seemed to have shed all his youth and taken upon himself the full burden of knowledge and earthly experience.

When he looked at her like that, she felt like a child. It was not a feeling she relished. She wanted to pierce this new armour of remoteness that invested him.

'They're just common murderers,' she said, addressing the words not to her father.

'We are all murderers,' Mark answered quietly, and though his face was still remote, the knife clattered against his plate as he put it down.

'Will you excuse me, please, Mrs Courtney –' he turned to Ruth, and she frowned quickly.

'Oh Mark, you've not touched your food.'

'I'm riding into the village this morning.'

'You ate no dinner last night.'

'I want the mail to catch the noon train.' He folded his napkin, rose quickly and strode away across the lawn – and Ruth watched the tall, graceful figure go with a helpless shrug before turning to Sean.

'He's wound up so tight – like a watch spring about to snap,' she said. 'What's happening to him, Sean?'

Sean shook his head. 'It's something that nobody understands,' he explained. 'We had so much of it in the trenches. It's as though a man can stand just so much pressure, and then something breaks inside him. We called it shell-shock, for want of a better name, but it's not just the shelling,' he paused. 'I have never told you about Mark before, about why I picked him, about how and when I first met him –' and he told it to them. Sitting in the cool green shade of the loquat tree, he told them of the mud and the fear and the horror of France. 'It's not just for a single time, or a day or a week – but it goes on for what becomes an eternity. But it is worse for a man who has special talents. We, the Generals, have to use them ruthlessly. Mark was one of those –' And he told them how they had used Mark like a hunting dog, and his two women listened intently, all of them bound up in the life of the young man who had gradually come to mean so much to each of them. 'A man gathers horror and fear like a ship gathers weed. It's below the waterline, you cannot see it, but it is there. Mark carries that burden, and at Fordsburg something happened that brought him close to the breaking-point. He is on the very edge of it now.'

'What can we do for him?' asked Ruth softly, watching his face, happy for him that he had a son at last – for she had long known that was what Sean saw in Mark. She loved her husband enough not to resent that it was not her own womb that had given him what he so desperately wanted, glad only that he had it at last, and that she could share it with him.

Sean shook his head. 'I don't know.' And Storm made an angry hissing sound. They both looked at her.

Sean felt that soft warmth spreading through his chest, a feeling of awe that this lovely child could be part of him. Storm looked so smooth and fragile, yet he knew she had the strength of braided whipcord. He knew also that though she had the innocence of a newly opened bloom, yet she could sting like a serpent; she had the brightness and beauty that dazzled, and yet below that were depths that mystified and awed him; and when her moods changed so swiftly, like this unaccountable spurt of anger, he was enchanted by her, under her fairy spell.

He frowned heavily now to hide his feelings.

'Yes, Missy, what is it now?' he grumped at her.

'He's going away,' she said, and Sean blinked at her, swaying back in his chair.

'What are you talking about?' he demanded.

'Mark. He's going away.'

'How do you know that?' Something deep inside of Sean cringed at the prospect of losing another son.

'I know, I just know,' she said, and came to her feet with a flash of long sleek limbs, like a gazelle rising in alarm from its grassy bed. She stood over him.

'You didn't think he would be your lap dog for ever?' she asked, a biting scorn in her tone that at another time would have brought from him a sharp retort. Now he stared at her speechless.

Then suddenly she was gone, crossing the lawn in the sunlight that gilded her loose dark hair with stark white light and struck through the flimsy stuff of her dress, revealing her long slim body in a stark dark silhouette, surrounding her with a shimmering halo of light, that made her seem like some lovely unearthly vision.

'Don't you see that it's better you cry a little now – than cry for the rest of your life?' Mark asked gently, trying not to let her see how the tears had eroded his resolve.

'Won't you ever come back?' Marion Littlejohn was not one of those women who cried well. Her little round face seemed to smear and lose its shape like unfired clay, and her eyes swelled and puffed pinkly.

'Marion, I don't even know where I am going. How can I know if I'm coming back?'

'I don't understand, Mark, I truly don't understand.' She twisted the damp linen handkerchief in her hands, and she sniffed wetly. 'We were so happy. I did everything I knew to make you happy – even that.'

'It's not you, Marion,' Mark assured her hurriedly. He did not want to be reminded of that which Marion always referred to as 'that'. It was as though she had loaned him a treasure which had to be returned with interest at usurious rates.

'Didn't I make you happy, Mark? I tried so hard.'

'Marion, I keep trying to tell you. You are a fine, pretty girl – you're kind and good and the nicest person I know.'

'Then why don't you want to marry me?' Her voice rose into a wail, and Mark glanced with alarm down the length of the porch. He knew that sisters and brothers-in-law were probably straining their hearing for snatches of the conversation.

'It's that I don't want to marry anybody.'

She made a low moaning sound and then blew her nose loudly on the inadequate scrap of sodden linen. Mark took his own handkerchief from his inside pocket, and she accepted it gratefully.

'I don't want to marry anybody, not yet,' he repeated.

'Not yet,' she seized the words. 'But some day?'

'Some day,' he agreed. 'When I have discovered what it is I want out of my life and how I am going to get it.'

'I will wait for you.' She tried to smile, a brave watery pink smile. 'I'll wait for you, Mark.'

'No!' Mark felt alarm flare through every nerve of his body. It had taken all his courage to tell her, and now it seemed that he had achieved nothing. 'God knows how long it will be, Marion. There will be dozens of other men – you're a kind sweet loving person –'

'I'll wait for you,' she repeated firmly, her features regaining their usual pleasant shape, and her shoulders losing their dejected droop.

'Please, Marion. It's not fair on you,' Mark tried desperately to dissuade her, realizing that he had failed dismally. But she gave one last hearty sniff and swallowed what was left of her misery, as though it were a jagged piece of stone. Then she smiled at him, blinking the last tears from her eyes.

'Oh, it doesn't matter. I am a very patient person. You'll see,' she told him comfortably.

'You don't understand,' Mark shrugged with helpless frustration.

'Oh, I do understand, Mark,' she smiled again, but now it was the indulgent smile of a mother for a naughty child. 'When you are ready, you come back here to me.' She stood up and smoothed down the sensible skirts. 'Now come along, they are waiting lunch for us.'

Storm had taken great care choosing her position. She had wanted to catch the play of afternoon light and the run of the clouds across the escarpment, and yet to be able to see into the gorge, for the white plume of falling spray to be the focus of the painting.

She wanted also to be able to see down along the Ladyburg road, and yet not be overlooked by a casual observer.

She placed her easel on the lip of a small saucer of folded ground near the eastern boundary peg of Lion Kop, positioning both easel and herself with an artist's eye for aesthetic detail. But when she posed on the lip of the saucer, with the palette cradled in the crook of her left arm and the brush in the other, she lifted her chin and looked up at the powerful sweep of land and forest and sky, at the way the light was working and at the golden-tinged turquoise of the sky – and immediately she was intrigued.

The pose was no longer theatrical, and she began to work, tilting her head to appraise a colour mix, moving about the canvas in a slow ritual, like a temple maid making the sacrifice, so completely absorbed that when she heard the faint putter of Mark's motorcycle, it did not penetrate into the silken cocoon of concentration she had woven about herself.

Although her original intention in coming to this place had been to waylay him, now he was almost past before she was aware of him, and she paused with the brush held high in one hand, caught in the soft golden light of late afternoon, a much more striking picture than she could have composed with studied care.

The dusty strip of road snaked five hundred feet below where she stood, making its first big loop on to the slope of the escarpment, and, as he came into the bend, Mark's eyes were drawn naturally to the small delicate figure on the slope.

There were clouds along the summit of the escarpment, and the late sun burned through the gaps, cutting long shimmering beams across the valley, and one of these fell full on Storm.

She stood completely still, staring down the slope at him, making no gesture of recognition or welcome.

He pulled the big machine into the side of the road, and sat astraddle, pushing the goggles on to his forehead.

Still she did not move, and they stared at each other. Mark made a move at last as though to restart the machine, and Storm felt a shock of deprivation, although it did not show either on her face nor in the stillness of her body.

She exerted all her will, trying consciously to reach him with mind, and he paused and looked up at her again.

'Come!' she willed him, and with an impatient, almost defiant gesture, he pulled the goggles off his head and stripped the gloves off his hands.

Serenely, she turned back to the painting, a small secret smile playing like light across her softly parted lips and she did not watch him climbing up through the yellow knee-high grass.

She heard his breathing behind her, and she smelled him. He had a special smell that she had learned to know, a floury smell a little like a suckling puppy or freshly polished leather. It made her skin feel hot and sensitized, and put a painful little catch in her breathing.

'That's beautiful,' he said, and his voice felt like the touch of fingers along the nape of her neck. She felt the fine soft hair there rise, and the flush of blood spread warmly down her chest and turn her nipples into hard little pebbles. They ached with something which was not pain – something more obsessive. She wanted him to touch her there, and at the thought she felt her legs tremble under her and the muscles cramped deeply in the wedge of her thighs.

'It's truly beautiful,' he said again, and he was so close she could feel his breath stir the fine hair of her neck, and another thrill ran down her spine, this time it was like a claw cutting through her flesh and she clenched her buttocks to ride the shock of it as though she was astride a mettlesome horse.

She stared at the painting, and she saw that he was right. It was beautiful, even though it was half-finished. She could see the rest of it in her mind – and it was beautiful and right, but she wanted the touch of his hands now.

It was as though the painting had heightened her emotional response, opened some last forbidden door and now she wanted his touch with a terribly deep physical ache.

She turned to him, and he was so close and tall that she felt her breathing catch again, and she looked up into his face.

'Touch me,' she willed him. 'Touch me,' she commanded silently, but his hands hung at his side and she could not fathom his eyes.

She could not stand still a moment longer, and she stirred her hips in a slow voluptuous gesture, something was melting and burning deep in her lower body.

'Touch me,' she tried to force him silently to her will. 'Touch me there where it hurts so fiercely.'

But he did not heed her, would not respond to all her silent pleas, and suddenly she was angry.

She wanted to lash out at him, to strike him across that solemn handsome face, she had a mental image of ripping his shirt away and sinking her nails deep into the smoothly muscled chest. She stared now at the vee of his open shirt, at the coils of dark hair, and his skin had an oiled gloss gilded by the sun to warm golden brown.

Her anger flared and focused. He had aroused these surging emotions which she could neither understand nor control, these heady terrifying waves of physical arousal, and she wanted to punish him for it, to make him suffer, to have him mauled by his desires as she was; at the same instant in time, she wanted to take that splendid proud head of his and hold it to her bosom like a mother holds her child, she wanted to cherish, and gentle and love him, and claw and ravage and hurt him, and she was confused and giddy and angry and puzzled – but most of all she was racing high on a wave of physical excitement that turned her birdlike and quick and vital.

'I suppose you've been bouncing about on that fat little trollop of yours,' she almost snarled it at him. Immediately the hurt and shock showed in his eyes, and she was pleased and savagely triumphant, but also aching with contrition, wanting to fall at his feet and plead for forgiveness, or to lash out with her nails and raise deep bleeding lines across that smooth brown dearly beloved face.

'Wouldn't it have been wonderful if the providence that gave you your beauty and your talent had thought to make you a nice person at the same time,' he said quietly, almost sadly. 'Instead of a vicious spoiled little brat.'

She gasped with the delicious profane shock of it, the insult gave her cause to discard the last vestige of control. Now she could loose the rein and use lash and spur without restraint.

'Oh you swine!' she flew at him, going for his eyes, knowing he was too quick and strong for her, but forcing violent physical contact on him, forcing him to seize her, and when he held her powerless by both arms, she flung her body against his, driving him back a pace, and she saw the surprise on his face. He had not expected such strength. She turned against him, her body fined and tuned and hardened by physical exercise on the courts and in the saddle, forcing him off balance, and, as he shifted his weight from foot to foot, she hooked one ankle with hers and threw her weight in the opposite direction.

They fell together, tumbling backwards into the grassy saucer of ground, and he released her wrists, using both hands to break their fall and cushion her shock as she landed on her back.

Instantly she was at him with both hands, and her nails stung his neck. He grunted and she saw the first flare of real anger in his eyes. It delighted her, and when he seized her wrist, she twisted and bit him in the hard sinewy muscle of his forearm. Hard enough to break the skin, and leave a double crescent of small neat teeth-marks.

He gasped and his anger mounted as he rolled over her, pinning her lower body with one leg as he fought to hold her flying flailing hands.

She bucked under him, her skirts had pulled up to her waist, one slim smooth thigh thrusting up, natural, untutored, cunning, into his groin, not hard enough to injure him, but enough to make him suddenly conscious of his own arousal.

As he realized what was happening, his grip of her arms slackened and he tried desperately to disengage, but one of her arms slid around his neck and the silken warmth of her cheek was pressed to his.

His hands acted without command, running down the deep groove in the centre of her arched back, following the small hard knuckles of her spine to the rounded divide of her buttocks, felt through the glossy slipperiness of silken underwear.

Her breathing rasped hoarsely as sandpaper, and she shifted her head and her mouth joined his, arching her back and lifting her lower body to let her silk underwear come away freely in his hands.

The waxen fork of her body rose out of the bright disordered petals of her skirts like the stamen of some wondrously exotic orchid; its flowing perfection interrupted only by the deep finely sculptured pit in the centre of the perfect plain of her belly, and below that the shockingly abrupt explosion of dark smoky curls, a fat deep wedge that changed shape as she relaxed in a slow voluptuous movement.

'Oh Mark,' she breathed. 'Oh Mark, I can't stand it.' Her anger had all evaporated, she was soft and breathless, slowly entwining, warm and gentle and loving, but the sound of her voice woke him suddenly to reality. He realized the betrayal of the trust placed in him by Sean Courtney, the abuse of a privileged position, and he pulled away from her, appalled at his own treachery.

'I must be mad,' he gasped with horror, and tried to roll away from her. Her response was instantaneous, the instinctive reaction of a deprived lioness, that uncanny ability to go from soft purring repose to dangerous blazing anger in the smallest part of a second.

Her open hand cracked across his face, in an explosion of brilliant catherine wheels of colour that starred his vision, and she screamed at him.

'What kind of a man are you?'

She tried to strike him again, but he was ready for her and they rolled together chest to chest in the grass.

'You're a nothing, and you'll stay like that because you haven't the guts and the strength to be anything else,' she hissed at him, and the words hurt a thousand times worse than the blow. His own anger flared to match hers and he came up over her.

'Damn you. How dare you say that!'

She shouted back at him. 'At least I dare, you wouldn't dare –' But she broke off then as she felt it happen, then she cried out again but in a different voice.

'Oh God!' Her whole body racked as she locked him to her, enfolding and holding him while she purred and murmured with a voice gone low and husky and victorious.

'Oh Mark, oh darling, darling Mark.'

Sean Courtney sat his horse with the slumping comfortable seat of the African horseman. Long stirrups and legs thrust forward, sitting well back on his mount, sjambok trailing from his left hand and reins held low on the pommel of the saddle.

In the shade of the leadwood tree, his stallion stood with the patience of a trained gun horse, its weight braced on three legs and the fourth cocked at rest, neck stretched against the reins as it reached to crop the fine sweet grass that covered the upper slopes of the escarpment, its teeth making a harsh tearing sound with each mouthful.

Sean looked out across the spreading forests and grassland below him, and realized how much it had all changed since he had run across it barefooted with his hunting dogs and throwing sticks, a small boisterous child.

Four or five miles away, nestled against the protective wall of the escarpment, was the homestead of Theunis Kraal, where he had been born in the old brass bedstead in the front room, both he and Garrick, his twin brother, in the course of a single sweltering summer morning, a double birthing that had killed the mother he had never known. Garrick lived there still, and at last he had found peace and pride among his books and his papers. Sean smiled with affection and sympathy, tinged with ancient guilt – what might his brother have been if one leg had not been shattered by the careless shotgun that Sean had fired? He thrust the thought aside, and instead turned in the saddle to survey his own domain.

The thousands upon thousands of acres that he had planted to timber, and which had given him the foundation of his fortune. From where he sat he could see the sawmills and timber yards adjoining the railway yards down in the town, and once again he felt the warm contentment of a life not thrown to waste, the glow of achievement and endeavour rewarded. He smiled and lit one of the long dark cheroots, striking the match off his boot, adjusting easily to the shifting balance of the horse under him.

A moment longer he indulged this rare moment of self-gratification, almost as though to avoid thinking of the most pressing of his problems.

Then he let his eyes drift away across the spreading roof-tops of Ladyburg to that new ungainly structure of steel and galvanized sheet iron that rose tall enough to dwarf any other structure in the valley, even the massive four-storey block of the new Ladyburg Farmers Bank.

The sugar refinery was like some heathen idol, ugly and voracious, crouching at the edge of the neat blocks of planted sugar which stretched away beyond the limit of the eye, carpeting the low rolling hills with waving, moving green that roiled in the wind like the waves of the ocean, planted to feed that eternally hungry structure.

The frown puckered the skin between Sean's eyes at the bridge of his big beaky nose. Where he counted his land in thousands of acres, the man who had once been his son counted his in tens of thousands.

The horse sensed his change of mood and gathered itself, nodding its head extravagantly and skittering a little in the shade, ready to run.

'Easy, boy,' Sean growled at him, and gentled him with a hand on his shoulder.

He waited now for that man, having come early to the rendezvous as was always his way. He liked to be there first and let the other man come to him. It was an old trick, to let the other seem the interloper in established territory, while the waiting man had time to consider and arrange his thoughts, and to study the other as he approached.

He had chosen the place and the time with care. He had not been able to sanction the thought of Dirk Courtney riding on to his land again, and entering his home. The aura of evil that hung around the man was contagious, and he did not want that evil to sully the inner sanctum of his life which was the homestead of Lion Kop. He did not even want him on his land, so he had chosen the one small section of boundary where his land actually bordered on that of Dirk Courtney. It was the only half mile of any land of Sean's along which he had strung barbed wire.

As a cattleman and horseman, he had an aversion to barbed wire, but still he had strung it between his land and that of Dirk Courtney, and when Dirk had written asking him for this meeting, he had chosen this place where there would be a fence between them.

He had chosen the late afternoon with intent also. The low sun would be behind him and shining into the other man's eyes as he came up the slope of the escarpment.

Now Sean drew the watch from his waistcoat and saw it was one minute before four, the appointed time. He looked down into the valley, and scowled. The slope below him was deserted, and he could follow the full length of the road into town beyond that. Since he had seen young Mark puttering past on his motorcycle half an hour before, the road also had been deserted.

He looked beyond the town to the flash of the white walls of the grand mansion that Dirk Courtney had built when first he returned to the valley. Great Longwood, a pretentious name for a pretentious building.

Sean did not like to look at it. To him it seemed that the same aura of evil shimmered about it, even in the daylight an almost palpable thing, and he had heard the stories – they had been repeated to him with glee by the gossip-mongers – about what happened up there under the cover of night.

He believed those stories, for he knew with the deep instinct which had once been love, the man who had once been his son.

He looked again at the watch in his hand, and scowled at it. It was four o'clock. He shook the watch and held it to his ear. It ticked stolidly, and he slipped it back into his pocket and gathered the reins. He wasn't coming, and Sean felt a sneaking coward's relief, because he found any meeting with Dirk Courtney draining and exhausting.

'Good afternoon, Father.' The voice startled him, so that he gripped the horse with his knees and jerked the reins. The stallion pranced and circled, tossing his head.

Dirk sat easily on a golden red bay. He had come down out of the nearest edge of the forest, walking his mount carefully and silently over the thick mattress of fallen leaves.

'You're late,' growled Sean. 'I was just leaving.' Dirk must have circled out, climbing the escarpment below the falls on to Lion Kop, avoiding the fence and riding up through the plantations to come to the rendezvous from the opposite direction. Probably he had been sitting among the trees watching Sean for the last half hour.

'What did you want to speak to me about?' He must never again underestimate this man. Sean had done so many times before, each time at terrible cost.

'I think you know,' Dirk smiled at him, and Sean was reminded of some beautiful glossy and deadly dangerous animal. He sat his horse with a casual grace, at rest but in complete control – and he was dressed in a hunting-jacket of finely woven thorn-proof tweed, with a yellow silk cravat at the throat; his long powerful legs were encased in polished chocolate leather.

'Remind me,' invited Sean, consciously hardening himself against the fatal mesmeric charm that the man could project at will.

'Oh come now, I know you have been busy thrashing the sweating unwashed hordes back into their places. I read with pride of your efforts, Father. Your butcher's bill at Fordsburg was almost as fearsome as when you put down Bombata's rebellion back in 1906. Magnificent stuff –'

'Get on with it.' Sean found himself hating again. Dirk Courtney had a high skill at finding weakness or guilt, and exploiting it mercilessly. When he spoke like this of the manner in which Sean had been forced to discharge his duty, it shamed him more painfully than ever.

'Of course it was necessary to get the mines operating again. You do sell most of your timber to the gold mines, I have the exact sales figures somewhere.' Dirk laughed lightly. His teeth were perfect and white, and the sunlight played in the shining curls of his big handsome head, back-lighting him and making his looks more theatrically magnificent. 'Good on you, dear Papa. You always had a keen eye for the main chance. No future in letting a bunch of wild-eyed reds put us all out of business. Even I am utterly dependent on the gold mines in the long run.'

Sean could not bring himself to answer, his anger was choking him. He felt dirtied and ashamed.

'It's one of the many things for which I'm indebted to you,' Dirk went on, watching him carefully, smiling and urbane and deadly. 'I am your heir, I have inherited from you the ability to recognize opportunity and to seize it. Do you recall teaching me how to take a snake, how to pin it and hold it with thumb and forefinger at the back of the neck?'

Sean remembered the incident suddenly and vividly. The fearlessness of the child had frightened him even then.

'I see you do remember.' The smile faded from Dirk's face, the lightness of his manner was gone with it. 'So much, so many little things – do you remember when we were lost after the lions stampeded the horses in the night?'

Sean had forgotten that also. Hunting in Mopani country, the child's first overnight away from the security and safety of the wagons. A little adventure that had turned into nightmare, one horse killed by the lions and the other gone, and a fifty-mile walk back through dry sandveld and thick trackless bush.

'You showed me how to find water. The puddle in the hollow tree – I can still taste the stink of it. The bushmen wells in the sand, sucking it up with a hollow straw.'

It all came back, though Sean tried to shut his mind against it. They had gone wrong on the third day, mistaking one small dry stony river bed for another and wandering away into the wilderness to a lingering death.

'I remember you made a sling from your cartridge belt, and carried me on your hip.'

When the child's strength had gone, Sean had carried him, mile after mile, day after day in the thick dragging sand. When finally his own great strength had been expended also, he had crouched down over the child, shielding him from the sun with his shadow, and had worked his swollen tongue painfully for each drop of saliva to inject into Dirk's cracked and blackening mouth, keeping him alive just long enough.

'When Mbejane came at last, you wept.'

The stampeded horse had reached the wagons with the lion claw-marks slashed deeply across its rump. The old Zulu gunbearer, himself sick with malaria, had saddled the grey and taken a pack horse on the lead rein. He had back-tracked the loose horse to the lion camp, and then picked up the spoor of man and child, following them for four days along a cold wind-spoiled spoor.

When he reached them, they were huddled together in the sand, under the sun – waiting for death.

'It was the only time in my life I ever saw you cry,' Dirk said softly. 'But did you ever think how often you made me weep?'

Sean did not want to listen longer. He did not want to be further reminded of that lovely, headstrong, wild and beloved child who he had reared as mother and father together, yet Dirk's quiet insidious voice held him captive in a web of memory from which he could not escape.

'Will you ever know how I worshipped you? How my whole life was based on you, how I mimicked every action, how I tried to become you?'

Sean shook his head, trying to deny it, to reject it.

'Yes, I tried to become you. Perhaps I succeeded –'

'No.' Sean's voice was strangled and thick.

'Perhaps that's why you rejected me,' Dirk told him. 'You saw in me the mirror-image of yourself, and you could not bring yourself to accept that. So you turned me away, and left me to weep.'

'No. God, no – that's not true. It was not that way at all.'

Dirk swung his horse in until his legs touched Sean's.

'Father, we are the same person, we are one – won't you admit that I am you, just as surely as I fell from your loins, just as surely as you trained and moulded me?'

'Dirk,' Sean started, but there were no words now, his whole existence had been touched and shaken at its very core.

'Don't you realize that every thing I have ever done was for you? Not only as a child, but as a youth and a man. Did you never think why I came back here to Ladyburg, when I could have gone to any other place in the world – London, Paris, New York – it was all open to me. Yet I came back here. Why, Father, why did I do that?'

Sean shook his head, unable to answer, staring at this beautiful stranger, with his vital strength and his compelling disturbing presence.

'I came back because you were here.'

They were both silent then, holding each other's eyes in a struggle of wills and a turmoil of conflicting emotions. Sean felt his resolve weakening, felt himself sliding slowly under the spell that Dirk was weaving about him. He heeled his horse, forcing it to wheel and break the physical contact of their legs, but Dirk went on remorselessly.

'As a sign of my love, of this love that has been strong enough to stand against all your abuse, against the denials you have made, against every blow you have dealt it – as a sign of that, I come to you now – and I hold out my hand to you. Be my father again, and let me be your son. Let us put our fortunes together and build an empire. There is a land here, a whole land, ripe and ready for us to take.'

Dirk reached out across the space between the horses with his right hand, palm upwards, fingers outstretched.

'Take my hand on it, Father,' he urged. 'Nothing will stop us. Together we will sweep the world from our path, together we will become gods.'

'Dirk,' Sean found his voice, as he fought himself out of the coils in which he had been trapped. 'I have known many men, and not one of them was all good nor completely evil. They were all combinations of those two elements, good and evil – that is, until I came to know you. You are the only man who was totally evil, evil unrelieved by the slightest shading of good. When at last I was forced to face that fact, then I turned my back on you.'

'Father.'

'Don't call me that. You are not mine, and you never will be again.'

'There is a great fortune, one of the great fortunes of the world.'

'No,' Sean shook his head. 'It is not there for either you or me. It belongs to a people, to many peoples – Zulu, and Englishman and Afrikander – not to me, but especially not to you.'

'When I came to see you last, you gave me cause to believe,' Dirk began to protest.

'I gave you no cause, I made no promise.'

'I told you everything, all my plans.'

'Yes,' said Sean. 'I wanted to hear it, I wanted to know every detail, not so that I could help you – but so that I could stand in your way.'

Sean paused for emphasis, and then leaned across so his face was close to Dirk's and he could look into his eyes.

'You will never get the land beyond the Bubezi River. I swear that to you,' he said it quietly, but with a force that made every word ring like a cathedral bell.

Dirk recoiled, and the high colour drained away from his face.

'I rejected you because you are evil. I will fight you with all my strength, with my life itself.'

Dirk's features changed, the line of the mouth and the set of the jaw altered, the slant and tilt of the eyes became wolfish.

'You deceive yourself, Father. You and I are one. If I am evil, then you are the source and fountain and father of that evil. Don't spout noble words to me, don't strike postures. I know you, remember. I know you perfectly – as I know myself.' He laughed again, but not the bright easy laughter of before. It was a cruel thin sound and the shape of the mouth did not lose its hard line. 'You rejected me for that Jewish whore of yours, and the bastard slut you spawned on her soft white belly.'

Sean bellowed, a low dull roar of anger, and the stallion reared under him, coming up high on his hindquarters and cutting at the air, and the bay mare swung away in alarm, milling and trampling as Dirk sawed at its mouth with the curb.

'You say you will fight me with your life,' Dirk shouted at his father. 'It may just come to that! I warn you.'

He brought the horse under control, barging in on the stallion so he could shout again.

'No man stands in my way. I will destroy you – as I have destroyed the others who have tried it. I will destroy you and your Jewish whore.'

Sean swung back-handed with the sjambok, a polo cut, using the wrist so the thin black lash of hippo-hide fluted like the wing of a flighting goose. He aimed at the face, at the snarling vicious wolf's head of the man who once had been his son.

Dirk threw up his arm and caught the stroke, it split the woven tweed of his sleeve like a sword cut and bright blood sprang to stain the luxurious cloth, as he kneed the bay away in a wide prancing circle.

He held the wound, pressing the lips of the cut together while he glared at Sean, his face contorted with utter malevolence.

'I'll kill you for that,' he said softly, and then he swung the bay away and put her into a dead gallop, straight at the five-stranded, barbed fence.

The bay went up and stretched at the jump, flying free of earth and then landing again on the far side, neatly gathered and fully in hand, reached out again into a run, a superb piece of horsemanship.

Sean walked the stallion, fighting the temptation to lash him into a gallop, following the path over the high ground, a path now almost indiscernible, long overgrown. Only a man who knew it well, who had been along it often before, would know it as a path.

There was nothing left of the huts of Mbejane's kraal, except the outline of building stones, white circles in the grass. They had burned the huts, of course, as is the Zulu custom when a chief is dead.

The wall of the cattle kraal was still intact, the stone carefully and lovingly selected, each piece fitted into the shoulder-high structure.

Sean dismounted and tethered the stallion at the gateway. He saw that his hands were still shaking, as though in high fever, and he felt sick to the gut, the aftermath of that wild storm of emotion.

He found his seat on the stone wall, the same flat rock that seemed moulded to his buttocks, and he lit a cheroot. The fragrant smoke calmed the flutter of his heart, and soothed the tremble in his hands.

He looked down at the floor of the kraal. A Zulu chief is buried in the centre of his cattle kraal, sitting upright facing the rising sun, with his unduna's ring still on his head, wrapped in the wet skin of a freshly killed ox, the symbol of his wealth, and with his food pot and his beer pot and his snuff box, his shield and his spears at his side, in readiness for the journey.

'Hello, old friend,' said Sean softly. 'We reared him, you and I. Yet he killed you. I do not know how, nor can I prove it, but I know he killed you – and now he's vowed to kill me also.' And his voice quivered.

* * *

'Well,' smiled Sean. 'If you have to make an appointment to speak with me, it must be some business of dire consequence.'

Through the merry twinkle of his eye, he was examining Mark with a shrewd assessing gaze. Storm had been right, of course. The lad had been gathering himself to make the break. To go off somewhere on his own, like a wounded animal perhaps, or a cub lion leaving the pride at full growth? Which was it, Sean wondered, and how great a wrench would the parting make on the youngster?

'Yes, sir, you could say that,' Mark agreed, but he could not meet Sean's eyes for once. The usually bright and candid eyes slid past Sean's and went to the books on the shelves, went on to the windows and the sweeping sunlit view across the tops of the plantations and the valley below. He examined it as though he had never seen it before.

'Come on in then.' Sean swivelled his chair away from the desk, and took the steel-rimmed spectacles off his nose and waved with them at the armchair below the window.

'Thank you, sir.'

While he crossed to the chair, Sean rose and went to the stinkwood cabinet.

'If it's something that important, we'd best take a dram to steel ourselves – like going over the top.' He smiled again.

'It's not yet noon,' Mark pointed out. 'That's a rule you taught me yourself.'

'The man who makes the rules is allowed to change them,' said Sean, pouring two huge measures of golden brown spirit, and spurting soda from the siphon. 'That's a rule I've just this moment made,' and he laughed, a fat contented chuckle, before he went on, 'Well, my boy, as it so happens, you have chosen a good day for it.' He carried one glass to Mark, and returned to his desk. 'I also have dire and important business to discuss.'

He took a swallow from his glass, smacked his lips in evident relish, and then wiped his moustaches on the back of his hand.

'As the elder, will it be in order if we discuss my business first?'

'Of course, sir.' Mark looked relieved and sipped cautiously at his glass, while Sean beamed at him with ill-concealed self-satisfaction.

Sean had conceived of a scheme so devious and tailored so fittingly to his need, that he was a little in awe of the divine inspiration which had fostered it. He did not want to lose this young man, and yet he knew that the surest way of doing so was trying to hold him too close.

'While we were in Cape Town I had two long discussions with the Prime Minister,' he began, 'and since then we have exchanged lengthy correspondence. The upshot of all this is that General Smuts has formed a separate portfolio, and placed it under my ministry. It is simply the portfolio of National Parks. There is still legislation to see through Parliament, of course, we will need money and new powers – but I am going ahead right away with a survey and assessment of all proclaimed areas, and we will act on that to develop and protect –' He went on talking for almost fifteen minutes, reading from the Prime Minister's letters and memoranda explaining and expanding, going over the discussions, detailing the planning, while Mark sat forward in his chair, the glass at his side forgotten, listening with a rising sense of destiny at work, hardly daring to breathe as he drank in the great concept that was unfolded for him.

Sean was excited by his own vision, and he sprang up from the desk and paced the yellow wood floor, gesturing, using hands and arms to drive home each point, then stopping suddenly in full flight and turning to stand over Mark.

'General Smuts was impressed with you – that night at Booysens, and before that.' He stopped again, and Mark was so engrossed that he did not see the cunning expression on Sean's face. 'I had no trouble persuading him that you were the man for the job.'

'What job?' Mark demanded eagerly.

'The first area I am concentrating on is Chaka's Gate and the Bubezi valley. Somebody has to go in there and do a survey, so that when we go to Parliament, we know what we are talking about. You know the area well –'

The great silences and peace of the wilderness rushed back to Mark, and he felt himself craving them like a drunkard.

'Of course, once the Bill is through Parliament, I will need a warden to implement the act.'

Mark sank slowly back in his chair. Suddenly the search was over. Like a tall ship that has made its offing, he felt himself come about and settle on true course with the wind standing fair for a fine passage.

'Now, what was it you wanted to talk to me about?' Sean asked genially.

'Nothing,' said Mark softly. 'Nothing at all.' And his face was shining like that of a religious convert at the moment of revelation.

Mark Anders had been a stranger to happiness, true happiness, since his childhood. He was like an innocent discovering strong liquor for the first time, and he was almost entirely unequipped to deal with it.

It induced in him a state of euphoria, a giddy elation that transported him to levels of human experience whose existence he had not previously guessed at.

Sean Courtney had engaged a new secretary to take over Mark's duties from him. He was a prematurely bald, unsmiling little man, who affected a shiny black alpaca jacket, an old-fashioned celluloid butterfly collar, a green eye-shade and cuff-protectors. He was silent, intense and totally efficient, and nobody at Lion Kop dreamed of calling him anything but 'Mr Smathers'.

Mark was to stay on for a further month to instruct Mr Smathers in his new duties, and at the same time Mark was to set his own affairs in order and make the preparations for his move to Chaka's Gate.

Mr Smathers's inhuman efficiency was such that within a week Mark found himself relieved almost completely of his previous duties, and with time to gloat over his new happiness.

Only now that it had been given to him did he realize how those tall stone portals of Chaka's Gate had thrown their shadows across his life, how they had become for him the central towers of his existence, and he longed to be there already, in the silence and the beauty and the peace, building something that would last for ever.

He realized how the recent whirlpool of emotion and action had driven from his mind the duty he had set himself – to find the grave of old Grandfather Anders, and fathom the mystery of his death. It was all now before him, and his life had purpose and direction.

But, this was only the foundation and base of his happiness, from which he could launch himself into the towering heady heights of his love.

True enchantment had sprung from that incredible moment in the grassy saucer on the slopes of the Ladyburg escarpment.

His love, which he had borne secretly, a burden cold and heavy as a stone, had in a single magical instant burst open, flowering like a seed into a growth of such vigour and colour and beauty and excitement, that he could not yet grasp it all.

He and Storm cherished it so dearly that no other must even guess at its existence. They made elaborate plans and pacts, weaved marvellously involved subterfuges about themselves to protect this wondrous treasure of theirs.

They neither spoke to each other, nor even looked at the other in the presence of a third party and the restraint taxed each of them so that the moment they were alone together they fell ravenously each upon the other.

When they were not alone together, they spent most of their time planning and scheming how to be so.

They wrote each other flaming notes which were passed under the table in the presence of Sean and Ruth and should have seared the fingers that touched them. They developed codes and signs, they found secret places, and they took hideous chances. Danger spiced their already piquant banquet of love and delight, and they were both insatiable.

At first, they rode to hidden places in the forest along separate and convoluted pathways and galloped the last mile, arriving breathless and laughing, embracing, still in the saddle while the horses stamped and snorted. The first time they were still locked together when they tumbled from the saddles to the forest bed of dead leaves and ferns, and they left their horses loose. It had been a long walk home, especially as they clung to each other like drunkards, laughing and giggling all the way. Luckily their horses had found a field of lucerne before they reached the homestead, and their riderless return had not alerted the grooms. Their secret remained intact, and after that they wasted a few seconds of their precious time together while Mark hobbled the horses.

Soon it was not enough to have only a stolen hour in the day and they met in Storm's studio. Mark climbed the banyan tree, crawling out along the branch, while Storm held the window open and squealed softly with horror when his foot slipped, or hissed a warning when a servant passed, then clapped her hands and flung her arms around his neck as he came in over the sill.

The studio was furnished with a single wooden chair, the floor was bare and hard, and the danger of sudden intrusion too great for even them to ignore. However, they were undaunted and inventive, and they found almost immediately that Mark was strong enough and she was light enough and that all things are possible.

Once Mark became unsteady at the scorching noonday of their loving and backed her into one of her own unfinished masterpieces. Afterwards, she knelt on the wooden chair holding her skirts to her waist and elevated her perfect little round stern while Mark removed the smudges of burnt umber and prussian blue with a rag moistened with turpentine. Storm was shaking so violently with suppressed laughter that Mark's task was much complicated. She was also blushing so furiously that even her bottom glowed a divine ethereal pink, and for ever afterwards, the smell of turpentine acted on Mark as a powerful aphrodisiac.

On another terrifying occasion, there was the heavy tramp, and the unmistakable limping drag in the passageway beyond the studio door, and they were frozen and ashen-faced, unable to breathe as they listened to its approach.

The peremptory knock on the door almost panicked her and she stared into Mark's face with huge terrified eyes. He took control instantly, realizing just how terrible was the danger. Sean Courtney, faced with the sight of somebody actually tupping his ewe lamb, was fully capable of destroying both them and himself.

The knock came again, impatient, demanding, and Mark whispered quickly as they adjusted their clothing with frantic hands. She responded bravely, though her voice caught and quavered.

'One moment, Daddy.'

Mark seized her paint-stained smock and slipped it over her head, grabbed a brush from the pot and put it in her right hand, squeezed her shoulders to brace her, and then pushed her gently towards the door.

There was just enough space between the wall and a canvas for him to crawl in and crouch, trying to still his breathing, while he listened to Storm shoot the door-bolt and greet her father.

'Locking the door now, Missy?' Sean growled at her, throwing a suspicious glance around the bare studio. 'Intruding, am I?'

'Never, Pater, not you!'

And they were into the room, Storm following meekly, while Sean gave critical judgement of her work.

'There isn't a tree on Wagon Hill.'

'I'm not taking photographs, Daddy. There should be a tree there. It balances the composition. Don't you see?' She had recovered like a champion and Mark loved her to the point of pain.

Mark was emboldened enough to take a cautious glance around the edge of the canvas, and the first thing he saw was a five-guinea pair of cami-knickers in sheer oyster silk, the wide legs cuffed with ivory cambrai lace, lying crumpled and abandoned on the studio floor where Storm had dropped them earlier.

He felt a cold sheen of sweat break out afresh across his brow; on the bare floor, the lovely silk was as conspicuous as a battle ensign. He tried to reach that blatantly sinful little pile, but it was beyond his finger-tips.

Storm was hanging on to her father's arm, probably because her legs were too weak to support her, and she saw what Mark's desperate arm and groping hand protruding from behind the canvas was trying to reach. Her panic flooded back again at high spring tide.

She gabbled meaningless replies to her father's questions and tried to lead him towards the door, but it was like trying to divert a bull elephant from his set purpose. Inexorably Sean bore down upon the discarded knickers and the canvas where Mark cowered.

At his next step, the silk wrapped itself around the toe of his boot. The material was so filmy and light that he did not notice it, and he limped on happily, one foot draped in an exotic piece of feminine underwear, while two young people watched in abject terror the knickers' slow circuit of the room.

At the door, Storm flung her arms around his neck and kissed him, managing to anchor the knickers with the toe of her shoe, and then propelling her father into the passage with indecent despatch and slamming the door behind him.

Weak with terror and laughter, they clung together in the middle of the studio, and Mark was so chastened that, when he regained his voice, he told her sternly,

'We are not going to take any more chances, do you understand?'

'Yes, master,' she agreed demurely, but with a wicked sparkle in her eye. Mark was awakened a few minutes after midnight with a wet pointed tongue probing deeply into his ear and he would have let out a great shout but a strong little hand was pressed firmly across his mouth.

'Are you mad?' he whispered, as he saw her bending over him in the moonlight from the open window, and realized that she had made the journey across the full length of the house, down cavernous passageways and creaking staircases, in pitch darkness and clad only in a gossamer pair of pyjamas.

'Yes,' she laughed at him. 'I'm mad, completely wonderfully insane, a magnificent noble rage of the mind.'

He was only half awake or he would not have asked the next question. 'What are you doing here?'

'I have come to ravish you,' she said, as she slipped into the bed beside him.

'My feet are cold,' she announced regally. 'Warm them for me.'

'For God's sake, don't make so much noise,' he pleaded, which was a ridiculous request in the circumstances, for only minutes later they were both raising such a chorus of cries that should have woken the entire household.

Long afterwards, she murmured in that special purry feline voice of hers that he had come to know so well.

'You really are an amazingly talented man, Mr Anders. Where ever did you learn to be so utterly depraved?' And then she chuckled sleepily, 'If you tell me, I shall probably claw your eyes out of your head.'

'You mustn't come here again.'

'Why not? It's so much better in bed.'

'What will your father do if he finds out?'

'He'll murder you,' she said comfortably. 'But what on earth has that got to do with it?'

One of the ancillary benefits which accrued to Storm from this relationship was that she had at last a fine male figure model for her work, something which she had always needed but had never found the courage even to ask her father to give her. She knew exactly what his reaction would be.

Mark was not gushing with enthusiasm for the idea either, and it took all her wheedling and cooing to have him disrobe in cold blood. She had picked one of their secret places in the forest for her figure studio, and Mark perched self-consciously on a fallen log.

'Relax,' she pleaded. 'Think beautiful thoughts.'

'I feel such an ass,' he protested, wearing only a pair of striped cotton underpants, at which he had drawn the line, despite her entreaties.

'Anyway, there's nothing under there you could paint on canvas,' he pointed out.

'But that's not the point, you're supposed to be an ancient Greek, and who ever saw an Olympic athlete –'

'No,' Mark cut her short. 'They stay on. That's final.' She sighed at the intransigence of men, and applied herself to her paints and canvas. Slowly he did relax, and even began to enjoy the freedom and the feel of the sunlight and the air on his skin.

He enjoyed watching her work also, the little frown of total concentration, the half-closed eyes, the porcelain white teeth nibbling thoughtfully at her lower lip, the almost dancing ritual of movement she performed around the canvas, and while he watched her he fantasized a future in which they walked hand in hand through the garden wilderness beyond Chaka's Gate. A future bright with happiness, and radiant with shared labour and achievement, and he began to tell her about it, letting his thoughts find expression in words, that Storm did not hear. Her ears were closed, her whole existence transferred into eyes and hands, seeing only colour and form, sensitive only to mood.

She saw the awkwardness and rigidity of his body flowing into a pose of natural grace such as she could never have composed; she saw the rapture dawning on his features, and she nodded and murmured agreement softly, not wanting to spoil it or break the mood; her fingers racing to capture the moment, all her mind and art concentrated on that single task; her own rapture rising to complement and buoy his even higher, seemingly bound close and fast by the silken traces of love and common purpose, but in reality as far from each other as earth is from moon.

'I'll be studying the ground for the exact place to site the homestead,' he told her, 'and it will take a full year to see it all in every season. Good water in the dry, but safe from flood in the rains. The cool sea breeze in summer and protected from the cold weather in winter.'

'Oh yes,' she murmured, 'that's marvellous.' But she was looking at his eyes.

'If only I can capture that fleck of light that makes them shine so,' she thought, and dabbed a touch of blue to the white to mix the shade.

'Two rooms to start. One to sleep and one to live. Of course a wide veranda looking out across the valley.'

'That's wonderful,' she exulted softly, as she touched the eye with the tip of the brush and it came instantly alive, gazing back at her from the canvas with an expression that squeezed her heart.

'I'll quarry the stone from the cliff, but away from the river so there'll be no scar to spoil it, and we'll cut the thatch from the edge of the swamp, and the roof poles from the forest.'

The sun had swung to the west and it filtered down through the forest roof with a cool greenish light that touched the smooth hard muscles of his arm and the sculptured marble of his back, and she saw that he was beautiful.

'We can build on slowly, as we need new rooms, I'll design it that way. When the children come, we can change the living room to a nursery and add a new wing.'

He could almost smell the aromatic shavings of the wit-els poles, and the sweet perfume of new cut thatch, and in his mind he saw the bright new roof mellowing and darkening in the weather, feel the cool of the high deep rooms at midday, and hear the crackle of the fiercely burning mimosa thorn in the stone fireplace on the cold and starry nights.

'We'll be happy, Storm, I promise you that.' They were the only words she heard – and she lifted her head and looked at him.

'Oh yes. We'll be happy,' she echoed, and they smiled at each other in total misunderstanding.

When Sean had told Ruth Courtney that Mark was leaving, her dismay had alarmed him. Sean had not realized that he had taken such a place in her affections also.

'Oh, no, Sean,' she had protested.

'It's not as bad as it might have been,' he assured her quickly. 'We'll not lose him altogether, it's just that he'll be on a longer rein, that's all. He'll still be working for me, but now only in my official capacity.' And he explained it all to her. She was silent for a long time when he had finished, considering it from every angle before she gave her opinion.

'He'll be good at that, I think,' she nodded at last. 'But I had rather got used to having him around us. I'll miss him.'

Sean grunted what could have been agreement, not able to make such a sentimental admission outright.

'Well,' Ruth went on immediately, her whole attitude becoming businesslike, 'I'll have to get on with it,' which meant that Mark Anders was to be fitted out for his move to Chaka's Gate by one of the world's leading experts. She had sent her man on campaign or on safari so often, that she knew exactly what was necessary, the absolute bare necessity for survival and comfort in the African bush. She knew that anything more than that would not be used, bundles of luxuries would come home untouched, or be abandoned along the way. Yet everything she selected was of the finest quality, for she raided Sean's campaign bag blatantly, justifying each theft with the firm utterance,

'Sean won't be using that again.'

The sleeping roll needed darning, and she made the repair a little work of art. Then she applied herself to the one luxury the pack would contain, books. This choice she and Mark discussed at length, for weight and space made it essential that each book must be able to withstand numerous rereadings. They had a wide selection from which to make their choice, hundreds of battered old volumes, stained by rain and mud, spilled tea and, in more than one case, by splotches of dried blood, and faded by sunlight and age, all of them having been carried great distances in Sean's old canvas book-bag.

Macaulay and Gibbon, Kipling and Tennyson, Shakespeare and even a small leather-bound Bible were given place, after being carefully screened by the selection committee, and Mark, whose previous camping equipment had been limited to a blanket, a pot and a spoon, felt as though he had been given a permanent suite at the Dorchester.

Sean provided the other essentials for the expedition. The 9.3 Mannlicher in its leather case and two mules. They were big rangy animals, both hard workers and of equitable temper, both salted by having been deliberately exposed to the bite of the tsetse fly and surviving the onslaught of the disease that resulted. They had cost Sean dearly for this immunity, but then the nagana had an almost ninety per cent mortality rate. Salted animals were essential. It would have been less trouble and had the same end result to shoot them between the eyes, rather than take unsalted animals into the fly belt beyond Chaka's Gate.

Each day, Sean set aside an hour or so to discuss with Mark the objects and the priorities of the expedition. They drew up a list, which was added to daily and, as it grew, so did Sean Courtney's enthusiasm. More than once he broke off to shake his head and grumble. 'You lucky blighter, what I wouldn't give to be your age again – and to be going back into the bush.'

'You could come and visit me,' Mark smiled.

'I might just do that,' Sean agreed, and then resettled his spectacles on his nose to bring up the next point for discussion.

The first of Mark's tasks was to compile an estimate of what species of wild animal still existed in the proclaimed area, and how many of each there were. Clearly this was of the utmost importance to any attempt at protection and conservation. All would depend on there being sufficient wild-life surviving to make their efforts worthwhile.

'It may already be too late in the afternoon,' Sean pointed out.

'No.' Mark would not even listen to the suggestion. 'There is game there. Just enough to give us a chance. I'm sure of it.'

Next important was for him to contact the people living in the area of Chaka's Gate, the Zulus grazing cattle along the edge of the tsetse fly belt, the native hunters and gatherers living within the belt, each wandering group, each village, each headman, each chief, and hold discussions with them; gauging the attitude of the Zulu peoples to the stricter administration of the proclaimed area, and warning them that what for many years they and their ancestors had looked upon as commonage and tribal hunting-ground was under new control.

Men were no longer free to cut timber and thatch, to gather and hunt at will. Mark's intimate knowledge of the Zulu language would serve him well here.

He was to build temporary accommodation for himself, and conduct a survey to choose the final site for a permanent warden's post. There were fifty other tasks less important, but no less demanding.

It was a programme to excite and intrigue Mark, and make him want to begin, and as the day drew nearer, only one cloud lay dark and heavy on the splendid horizon ahead of him. He would be parting from Storm, but he consoled himself with the sure knowledge that it would not be for long. He was going ahead into Eden to prepare a place for his Eve.

As Storm watched him sleep flat on his back, spread like a crucifix on the forest floor, without even the cotton underpants between him and nature, the possessive smile of a mother watching over the child at her breast warmed and softened Storm's lips.

She was naked also, her clothing scattered around them like the petals of an overblown rose, thrown there by the storm winds of passions which were now spent and quiescent. She sat over him cross-legged on the corner of the plaid rug, and she studied his face, wondering at how young he looked in sleep, feeling a choking of tenderness in her throat, and the soft melting after-glow of loving deep in her body where he had been.

She leaned over him, and her breasts swung forward with a new weightiness, the tips darker and wrinkled like small pinky brown raisins. She dipped her shoulders and let the nipples brush lightly across his face, and smiled again as he screwed up his nose and pursed his lips in his sleep, snorting as if to blow away a bothersome fly.

He came awake suddenly and as he reached for her, she squealed softly and plucked her breasts away from him, slapping at his hands.

'Unhand me, sir, this instant!' she commanded, and he caught her and pulled her down on to his chest, so that she could hear his heart beating under her ear.

She snuggled down, making throaty little sounds of comfort. He sighed deeply, and his chest swelled and expanded under her cheek and she heard the air rush into his lungs.

'Mark?' she said.

'I'm here.'

'You're not going. You know that, don't you?'

The air in his lungs stayed there as he held his breath, and the hand that was stroking lightly up from the small of her back to the nape of her neck stilled. She could feel the tension in his fingers.

They stayed like that for many seconds and then he let the air out of his lungs with an explosive grunt.

'What do you mean?' he asked. 'Where am I not going?'

'This place up there in the bush,' she said.

'Chaka's Gate?'

'Yes. You're not going.'

'Why not?'

'Because I forbid it.'

He sat up abruptly, joggling her roughly off his chest.

They sat facing each other, and he was staring at her with such an expression that she ran her fingers through her hair and then folded her arms across her breasts, covering them protectively.

'Storm, what on earth are you talking about?' he demanded.

'I don't want you to waste any more time,' she told him. 'You must start making your way now, if you're ever going to amount to anything.'

'This is my way – our way,' he said, bewildered. 'We agreed on it. I will go up there to Chaka's Gate and build our home.'

'Home!' She was truly appalled. 'Up there in the bush – me in a grass hut? Mark, are you out of your mind?'

'I thought –'

'What you're going to do is start making some money,' she told him fiercely, and, picking up her blouse, she pulled it over her head, and as her tousled head emerged she went on, 'and forget about little boys' games.'

'I'll be making money.' His expression was stiff, and becoming hostile.

'What money?' she asked, just as frostily.

'I'll have a salary.'

'A salary!' She flung back her head and gave a high peal of scornful laughter. 'A salary, forsooth! How much?'

'I don't know,' he admitted. 'It isn't really all that important.'

'You're a child, Mark. Do you know that? A salary, twenty pounds a week? Can you really and truly imagine me living on your salary?' She gave the word a world of contempt. 'Do you know who earns salaries? Mr Smathers earns a salary,' she was on her feet now, hopping furiously on one leg as she drew on her knickers, 'Daddy's foremen at the saw-mills earn salaries. The servants that wait on the table, the stable-grooms earn salaries.'

She was pulling up her riding breeches, and with them all her dignity.

'Real men don't earn salaries, Mark.' Her voice was high and shrill. 'You know what real men do, don't you?'

He was buttoning the fly of his breeches also, forced to follow her example, and he shook his head silently.

'Real men pay salaries – not take them,' she said. 'Do you know that when my father was your age he was already a millionaire!'

Mark was never able to fathom what it was that triggered him, perhaps the mention of Sean at that particular moment, but suddenly he lost his temper. He felt it like a hot red fog behind his eyes.

'I'm not your bloody father,' he shouted.

'Don't you swear at my father,' she shouted back. 'He's five times the man you'll ever be.'

They were both panting and flushed, clothing rumpled, half-clad, with wild hair and wilder eyes glaring at each other like animals, speechless with hurt and anger.

Storm made the effort. She swallowed painfully, and held out her hands palms upwards.

'Listen, Mark. I've got it all planned. If you went into timber, selling to the mines, Daddy would give you the agency and we could live in Johannesburg.'

But Mark's anger was still on him, and his voice was rough and scaly with it.

'Thank you,' he said. 'Then I could spend my life grubbing money for you to buy those ridiculous clothes and –'

'Don't you insult me, Mark Anders,' she blazed.

'I'm me,' Mark told her. 'And that's what I'm going to be the rest of my life. If you loved me, you'd respect that.'

'And if you loved me, you wouldn't want me to live in a grass hut.'

'I love you,' he shouted her down. 'But you'll be my wife and you'll do what I decide.'

'Don't challenge me, Mark Anders. I warn you. Don't ever do that!'

'I'll be your husband,' he began, but she snatched up her boots and ran to her horse, stooping to loose the hobble and then flinging herself on to its back bare-footed and looked down at him. She was breathless with anger, but she struggled to make her voice icy and cutting.

'Don't take any bets on that!' And she dragged the horse's head around and kicked him into a run.

'Where is Missy?' Sean demanded as he unfolded his napkin and tucked the corner into his waistcoat, glancing at Storm's empty place at the table.

'She's not feeling very well, dear,' Ruth told him, as she began serving the soup, ladling it out of the fat-bellied tureen in a cloud of fragrant steam. 'I allowed her to have her dinner sent up to her room.'

'What's wrong with her?' Sean looked up with concern creasing his forehead.

'It's nothing serious,' said Ruth firmly, closing the door on further discussion. Sean stared at her for a moment, and then understanding dawned.

'Oh!' he said. The functions of the female body had always been shrouded for Sean Courtney in deepest mystery, and awakened in him an abiding awe.

'Oh!' he said again, and leaned forward to blow noisily on a spoonful of soup to cover his embarrassment, and the niggling resentment that his beloved child was a child no longer.

Across the table, Mark applied himself to his spoon with equal determination, but with an empty aching feeling below his ribs.

'Where is Missy tonight?' Sean asked, with what was for him a certain diffidence. 'Still not well?'

'She telephoned Irene Leuchars this morning. Apparently the Leuchars are having a huge party tonight and she wanted to go. She left after lunch. She's driving herself back to Durban in the Cadillac.'

'Where will she stay?' Sean demanded.

'With the Leuchars, naturally.'

'She should have asked me,' Sean frowned.

'You were down at the saw-mills all day, dear. The decision had to be made immediately, or she would have missed the party. I knew you wouldn't mind.'

Sean minded everything that took his daughter away from him, but he could not say so now. 'I thought she hated Irene Leuchars,' he complained.

'That was last month,' said Ruth.

'I thought she was sick,' Sean persisted.

'That was last night.'

'When is she coming home?'

'She may stay in town for the race-meeting at Greyville on Saturday.'

Mark Anders listened with the empty space in his chest turning to a great bottomless void. Storm had gone back to join that close group of rich, indolent and privileged young people, to their endless games and their eternal round of extravagant partying, and on Saturday Mark was leaving with two mules for the wilderness beyond Chaka's Gate.

* * *

Mark would never fathom how Dirk Courtney knew. To him it seemed further evidence of the man's power, the tentacles of his influence that reached into every corner and crevice.

'I understand you are to make the survey for the Government, to decide whether it's worth developing the proclaimed area beyond Chaka's Gate?' he asked Mark.

Mark could still hardly believe the fact that he stood unarmed and completely unprotected here at Great Longwood. His skin tingled with warning of deadly danger, his nerves were drawn like bow-strings, and he walked with exaggerated care, one hand clenched in the hip-pocket of his breeches.

Beside him, Dirk Courtney was tall and courteous and affable. When he turned to make that statement, he smiled, a warm spread of the wide and handsome mouth – and he laid a hand on Mark's upper arm. A light but friendly touch, which shocked Mark as though a mamba had kissed him with its little flickering black tongue.

'How does he know it?' Mark stared at him, his feet slowing, so that he pulled gently away from Dirk's touch.

If Dirk noticed the withdrawal, it did not show in his smile, and he let his hand fall naturally to his side and took the flat silver cigarette-case from his jacket pocket.

'Try one,' he murmured. 'They are made especially for me.'

Mark tasted the incense of the sweetish Turkish tobacco, using the act of lighting the cigarette to cover his uncertainty and surprise. Only Sean Courtney and his close family knew, and of course the Prime Minister's office – the Prime Minister's office, if that was it, as it seemed it must be, then Dirk Courtney's tentacles stretched far indeed.

'Your silence I must take as confirmation,' Dirk told him, as they came down the paved alleyway between two lines of white-washed loose boxes. From over the half-doors, the horses stretched out their necks to Dirk and he paused now and then to caress a velvety muzzle with surprisingly gentle fingers, and to murmur an endearment.

'You are a very silent young man.' Dirk smiled that warm endearing smile again. 'I like a man who can keep his own counsel and respect the privacy of others.' He turned to confront Mark, forcing him to meet his eyes.

Dirk reminded Mark of some glossy cat, one of the big predators, not the tabby domestic variety. The leopard, golden and beautiful and cruel. He wondered at his own courage, or foolhardiness, in coming here right into the leopard's lair. A year ago it might have been suicidal to put himself in this man's hands. Even now, without Sean Courtney's protection, he would never have dared. Yet although it was logical to believe that nobody, not even Dirk Courtney, would dare touch him, now that he was Sean Courtney's protégé with all that that implied, yet prickles of apprehension nettled his spine as he looked into those leopard's eyes.

Dirk took his elbow, not giving him opportunity to avoid the touch, and led him through a gateway to the stud pens.

The two pens were enclosed with ten-foot high pole fences, carefully padded to prevent damage to the expensive animals that would be confined here. The earth within the rectangular enclosures was ankle-deep with fresh sawdust, and though one was empty, there was a group of four grooms busy in the nearest pen.

Two of them had the mare on a double lead rein. She was a young animal, a deep red bay in colour, and she had the beautiful balanced head of the Arab, wide nostrils which promised great heart and stamina, and strong but delicate bones.

Dirk Courtney placed a booted foot on the bottom rail of the pen, and leaned forward to look at her with a gloating pride.

'She cost me a thousand guineas,' he said, 'and it was a bargain.'

The two other grooms had the stallion in check. An old, heavily built animal, with grey dappling his muzzle. He wore a girdle, strapped under his belly, and up between the hindlegs, a cage like an old-fashioned chastity belt of woven light chain that was called the teaser. It would prevent him effectively covering the mare.

The grooms gave him rein to approach the mare, but the instant she felt his gentle nuzzling touch under her tail, she put her head down and lashed out with both back legs, a murderous hissing cut of hooves that flew within inches of the stallion's head.

He snorted and backed away. Then, undeterred, he closed with her once more, reaching out to touch her flank, running his nose with a gentle lover's touch across the glossy hide, but the mare made her skin shudder wildly, as though she were beset by bees, and she let out a screaming whinny of outrage at the importunate touch on her maidenly virtue. One of the grooms was dragged down on his knees as she flashed at the stallion with terrible yellow teeth, catching him in the neck and ripping open his old dappled hide in a shallow bloody cut before they pulled her off.

'Poor old beggar,' murmured Mark, although the injury was superficial; it was the indignity of the whole business that aroused Mark's sympathy. The old stallion must endure the kicks and bites, until at last the temperamental filly was wooed and willing. Then he would be led away, his work done.

'Never waste sympathy for the losers in this world,' Dirk advised him. 'There are too many of them.'

In the sawdust-covered arena, the filly lifted her tail, the long glossy hairs forming a soft waving plume, and she urinated a sharp spurt that was evidence of her arousal.

The stallion circled her, rolling back his upper lip, exposing his teeth, and his shoulder muscles spasmed violently as he nodded his head vigorously and reached out to her again.

She stood quietly now, with her tail still raised, and trembled at the soft loving touch of his muzzle, ready at last to accept him.

'All right,' Dirk shouted. 'Take him out.' But it required the strength of both grooms to drag his head around and lead him out of the tall gate that Dirk swung open.

'Strangely enough, I don't believe that you are one of this life's losers,' Dirk told Mark easily, as they waited by the gate. 'That is why you are here at this moment. I only trouble myself with a certain type of man. Men with either talent, or strength or vision – or all of those virtues. I believe you may be of that type.'

Mark knew then that all this had been carefully arranged, the meeting with Peter Botes, Marion Littlejohn's brother-in-law, outside the post office in Ladyburg, the urgent summons to Dirk Courtney's estate he had delivered, so there was no opportunity to report to Sean Courtney and discuss the invitation, and now this erotic show of mating horses – all of it planned to confuse and unsettle Mark, to keep him unbalanced.

'I think you are more like this,' Dirk went on, as the grooms led in the stud stallion, an animal too valued to risk damaging by putting to an unwilling female, a tall horse, black as a rook's wing, high-stepping and proud, kicking the soft sawdust with polished hooves, and then coming up hard and trembling on stiff legs as he smelt the waiting mare, and the great black root grew out of his belly, long as a man's arm and as thick, arrogant, and with a flaring head that pulsed with a life of its own and beat impatiently against the stallion's chest.

'The losers toil, and the winners take the spoil,' said Dirk, as the huge beast reared up over the mare. One of the grooms darted forward to guide him, and the mare hunched her back to receive the long gliding penetration.

'The winners and the losers,' he repeated, watching the stallion work with glistening bulging quarters, and Dirk's handsome face was flushed with high colour, and his hands gripped the poles of the fence until the knuckles blanched like marble.

When at last the stallion dropped back off the mare on to four legs, Dirk sighed, took Mark's elbow again and led him away.

'You were present when I spoke with my father of my dream.'

'I was there,' Mark agreed.

'Oh good,' Dirk laughed genially. 'You have a voice – I was beginning to doubt it. But my information is that you have a good brain also.'

Mark glanced at him sharply and Dirk assured him, 'Naturally, I have made it my business to find out all about you. You know certain details of my plans. I must be in a position to protect myself.'

They skirted the ornamental pond, below the homestead, the surface covered with flat lily pads and the smell of their blooms light and sugary in the afternoon heat, and they went on through the formal rose garden, neither of them speaking again until they had entered the high-ceilinged and overfurnished study; Dirk had closed the wooden shutters against the heat, making the room cool and gloomy, and somehow forbidding.

He waved Mark to a chair across from the fireplace and went to the table on which stood a silver tray of bottles and crystal.

'Drink?' he asked, and Mark shook his head and watched Dirk pour from a black bottle.

'You know my dream,' Dirk spoke, still concentrating on his task. 'What did you think of it?'

'It's a large concept,' Mark said cautiously.

'Large?' Dirk laughed. 'It's not the word I would have chosen.' He saluted Mark with the glass and sipped at it, watching him over the rim.

'Strange how the fates work,' Dirk thought, watching the slim graceful figure. 'Twice I tried to be rid of the nuisance he could have caused me. If I had succeeded, I would not be able to use him now.'

He hitched one leg over the corner of his desk and set the glass aside carefully to leave both hands free, and he gesticulated as he talked.

'We are talking of opening a whole new frontier, a huge step forward for our nation, work for tens of thousands of people, new towns, new harbours, railways – progress.' He spread his hands, a gesture of growth and limitless opportunity. 'That one wonderful word that describes it all – progress! And anybody who tries to stop that is worse than a fool, he's a criminal, a traitor to his country, and should be treated as one. He should be brushed mercilessly aside, by any means that comes to hand.'

He paused now and glowered at Mark. The threat was barely concealed, and Mark stirred restlessly in his chair.

'On the other hand,' Dirk smiled suddenly, like a flooding beam of sunlight bursting through the grey overcast of a storm sky. 'Every man who works towards the fulfilment of this huge concept will be fully entitled to a share of the rewards.'

'What do you want from me?' Mark asked, and the abrupt question caught Dirk with his hands poised and the next flight of oratory on his lips. He let the hands drop to his sides, and watched Mark's face expectantly, as though there was something still to come. 'And what are the rewards you speak of?' Mark went on, and Dirk laughed delightedly, those were the words for which he had been waiting – each man has a coin for which he will work.

'You know what I want from you,' he said.

'Yes, I think I do,' Mark agreed.

'Tell me what I want,' Dirk laughed again.

'You want a report that recommends that the development of the Chaka's Gate proclaimed area as a National Park is not practical.'

'You said it, not me,' Dirk picked up his glass again and lifted it to Mark. 'But, none the less, I'll drink to it.'

'And the rewards?' Mark went on.

'The satisfaction of knowing that you are doing your patriotic duty for the peoples of this nation,' Dirk told him solemnly.

'I had all the satisfaction I need for a lifetime in France,' Mark said softly. 'But I found out you can't eat or drink it,' and Dirk laughed delightedly. 'That really is choice, I must remember it. Are you certain you won't have a drink?'

Mark smiled for the first time. 'Yes, I'll change my mind.'

'Whisky?'

'Please.'

Dirk stood up and went to the silver tray, and he realized that he felt a sneaking relief. If it had proved that this man had no price, as he had started to believe possible, it would have destroyed one of the headstones on which he had based his whole philosophy of life. But it was all right again now. The man had a price, and he felt a sudden contempt and scorn – it would be money, and a paltry sum at that. There was nothing different about this fellow.

He turned back to Mark.

'Here is something you can drink.' He gave him the crystal glass. 'Now let's discuss something you can eat.'

He went back to the desk, slid open one of the drawers, and took out of it a brown manilla envelope, sealed with red wax.

He laid it on the desk-top, and picked up his own glass. 'That contains an earnest of my good will,' he said.

'How earnest?'

'One thousand pounds,' Dirk said. 'Enough to buy a mountain of bread.'

'One of your companies bought a farm from my grandfather,' Mark spoke carefully. 'He had promised that farm to me, and he died without leaving any of the money.'

Dirk's expression had closed suddenly and his eyes were wary and watchful. For a moment he played with the idea of feigning ignorance, but already he had admitted he had investigated Mark thoroughly.

'Yes,' he nodded. 'I know about that. The old man wasted it all away.'

'The price of that farm was three thousand pounds,' Mark went on. 'I feel that I am still owed that money.'

Dirk dropped his hand into the drawer again, and brought out two identical sealed envelopes. He laid them carefully on top of the first envelope.

'By a strange coincidence,' he said. 'I just happen to have that exact amount with me.'

A paltry sum indeed, he smiled his contempt. What had made him suspect that there was something unusual about this man, he wondered. In the desk drawer were seven other identical manilla envelopes, each containing one hundred ten pound notes. He had been prepared to go that high for the report – no, he corrected himself, I would have been prepared to go further, much further.

'Come,' he smiled. 'Here it is.' And he watched Mark Anders rise from the chair and cross the room, pick up the envelopes and slip them into his pocket.

Sean Courtney's beard bristled like the quills on the back of an angry porcupine, and his face turned slowly to the colour of a badly fired brick.

'Good God!' he growled, as he stared at the three envelopes on his desk top. The seals had been carefully split and the contents arranged in three purple blue fans of crisp treasury bills. 'You took his money?'

'Yes, sir,' Mark agreed, standing in front of the desk like a wayward pupil before the head pedagogue.

'Then you have the brass to come to me with it?' Sean made a gesture as though to sweep the piles of bills on to the floor. 'Take the filthy stuff away from me.'

'Your first lesson, General. The money is always important,' Mark said quietly.

'Yes, but what must I do with this?'

'As patron of the Society for the Protection of African Wildlife, your duty would be to send the donor a letter of acceptance and thanks for his generous donation –'

'What on earth are you talking about?' Sean stared at him. 'What society is this?'

'I have just formed it, sir, and elected you patron. I am sure we will be able to draw up a suitable memorandum of objects and rules of membership, but what it boils down to is a campaign to make people aware of what we are going to do, to gather public support –' Mark spoke rapidly, pouring it all out, and Sean listened with the brick colour of his face slowly returning to normal, and a slow but delighted grin pulling his beard out of shape. 'We'll use this money for advertisements in the press to make people aware of their heritage,' Mark raced on, ideas tumbling out of him, and immediately spawning new ideas, while Sean listened, his grin becoming a spasmodic chuckle that shook his shoulders, and then finally a great peal of laughter, that went on for many minutes.

'Enough!' at last he bellowed delightedly. 'Sit down, Mark, that's enough for now.' And he groped for a handkerchief to mop his eyes and blow the great hooked beak of a nose like a trumpet, while he recovered his self-control. 'It's indecent,' he chortled. 'Positively sacrilegious! You have no respect for money at all. It's unnatural.'

'Oh, yes, I have – but money is only a means, not an end, sir,' Mark laughed also, for the General's mirth was contagious.

'My God, Mark. You are a prize, you really are. Where ever did I find you?' He gave one last chuckle, and then grew serious. He drew a clean sheet of paper from the side-drawer and began to make notes. 'As though I haven't enough work already,' he growled. 'Now let's draw up a list of objects for this bloody society of yours.'

They worked for nearly three hours, and Ruth Courtney had to come and call them to the dinner table.

'In a minute, dear,' Sean told her, and placed a paper-weight on the thick pile of notes he had made; he was about to rise when he frowned at Mark.

'You have chosen a dangerous enemy for yourself, young man,' he warned him.

'Yes, I know,' Mark nodded soberly.

'You say that with feeling.' He stared at Mark questioningly. Mark hesitated a moment and then he began.

'You know my grandfather, John Anders, you spoke of him once before.' Sean nodded, and sank back into the padded leather chair. 'He had land, eight thousand acres, he called it Andersland –'

Sean nodded again, and Mark went on carefully, telling it all without embellishment, stating the facts, and when he had to guess or make conjecture, stating that it was so. Again Ruth came to call them to dinner, just when Mark was describing the night on the escarpment when the gunmen had come to his camp. She was about to insist they come before the meal spoiled, but then she saw their faces and came silently to stand behind Sean's chair and listen, her face becoming paler and more set.

He told them about Chaka's Gate, how he had searched for his grandfather's grave and the men who had come to hunt him, and when he had finished the story they were all silent, until at last Sean roused himself, sighed – a gusty, sorrowful sound – before he spoke.

'Why didn't you report this?'

'Report what? Who would have believed me?'

'You could have gone to the police.'

'I have not a shred of evidence that points to Dirk Courtney, except my own absolute certainty.' And he dropped his eyes. 'It's such a wild, unlikely story that I was afraid to tell even you, until this moment.'

'Yes,' Sean nodded. 'I can see that. Even now I don't want to believe it is true.'

'I'm sorry,' said Mark simply.

'I know it's true – but I don't want to believe it.' Sean shook his head, and lowered his chin on to his chest. Ruth, standing behind him, placed a comforting hand on his shoulder. 'Oh God, how much more must I suffer for him?' he whispered, then lifted his head again.

'You will be in even greater danger now, Mark.'

'I don't think so, General. I am under your protection, and he knows it.'

'God grant that is enough,' Sean muttered, 'but what can we do against him? How can we stop this –' Sean paused, seeking the word, and then hissed it savagely, 'this monster?'

'There is no evidence,' Mark said. 'Nothing to use against him. He has been too clever for that by far.'

'There is evidence,' said Sean with complete certainty. 'If all this is true, then there is evidence – somewhere.'

Trojan the mule's broad back felt like a barrel under Mark, and the sun beat through his shirt so that his sweat rose in dark damp patches between his shoulder blades and at his armpits, as he jogged down the bank of the Bubezi with Spartan, the second heavily burdened mule, following him on a lead rein.

In the river bed on one of the sugary white sandbanks, he let the mules wade in knee-deep and begin to drink, sucking up the clear water noisily so that he could feel the animal's belly swelling between his knees.

He pushed his hat on to the back of his head and wiped away the drops from his brow with one thumb as he looked up at the portals of Chaka's Gate. They seemed to fall out of the sky like cascades of stone, sheer and eternal, so vast and solid that they dwarfed the land and the river at their feet.

The double pannier on the back of the lead mule was the less onerous of the burdens that he had brought with him from the teeming reaches of civilization. He had brought also a load of guilt and remorse, the sorrow of a lost love, and the galling of duty left unperformed. But now, beneath the cliffs of Chaka's Gate, he felt his burden lightening, and his shoulders gathering strength.

Something indefinable seemed to reach out to him from across the Bubezi River, a feeling of destiny running its appointed course, or more a sense of home-coming. Yes, he thought, with sudden joy, I am coming home at last.

Abruptly Mark was in a hurry. He pulled up Trojan's reluctant head, with water still pouring from his loose rubbery lips, and kicked him forward into the swirling green eddy of the river, slipping from the saddle to swim beside him when he lost his footing.

As the big soup-plate hooves touched bottom, he threw his leg back across the saddle and rode up the far bank, his breeches clinging to his thighs and his sodden shirt streaming water.

Suddenly, for the first time in a week, and for no good reason, he laughed, a light unstrained burst of laughter that hung about him like a shimmering halo long afterwards.

The sound was so low, and the hooves of Trojan the grey mule were plugging into the soft earth along the river with a rhythmic chuffing sound, so that Mark was not sure of what he had heard.

He reined Trojan to a stop and listened. The silence was so complete that it seemed to hiss like static, and when a wood dove gave its melodious and melancholy whistle a mile along the river, it seemed close enough to touch.

Mark shook his head, and flicked the reins. At the first hoof fall, the sound came again – and this time there was no mistaking it. The hair down the nape of Mark's neck prickled, and he straightened quickly out of his comfortable saddle slouch. He had heard that sound only once before, but in circumstances that made certain he would never forget it.

It was close, very close, coming from the patch of thick green riverine bush between him and the river, a tangled thicket of wild loquat and hanging lianas, typical cover for the animal that had called.

It was a weird unearthly sound, a fluid sound, almost like liquor poured from the neck of a stone jug – and only one who had heard it before would recognize the distress and warning call of a fully grown leopard.

Mark swung the mule away, and set him lumbering up the rising ground until he reached the spreading shade of a leadwood, where he tethered him and loosened his girth. Then he slipped the Mannlicher out of its scabbard, and quickly checked the loaded magazine, the fat brass cartridges with their copper-jacketed noses were still bright and slick with wax, and he snapped the bolt closed.

He carried the rifle casually in his left hand, for he had no intention at all of using it. Instead he was aware of a pleasurable glow of excitement and anticipation. In the two months of hard riding and walking since his return to Chaka's Gate, this was the first chance he had been given of sighting a leopard.

There were many leopard along the Bubezi, he had seen their sign almost daily, and heard them sawing and coughing in the night. Always the leopard and the kudu are the last to give way before man and his civilization. Their superior cunning and natural stealth protect them long after the other species have succumbed.

Now he had a chance at a sighting. The patch of riverine bush, though dense, was small, and he longed for a sighting, even if just a flash of yellow in deep shade, something concrete, a firm entry in his logbook, another species to add to the growing list of his head count. He circled out cautiously, his eyes flickering from the thick green wall of bush to soft ground at his feet, checking for spoor as well as for actual sight of the yellow cat.

Just above the steep river bank he stopped abruptly, and stared down before going on to one knee to touch the earth.

They weren't leopard tracks, but others he had grown to know and recognize. There was no special distinguishing characteristic, no missing toes, no scarring or deformity, but Mark's trained eye recognized the shape and size, the slight splaying toe-in way the man walked, the length of his stride and a toe-heavy impression, that of a quick alert tread. The distress call of the animal in the thicket made sense now. 'Pungushe,' said Mark quietly. 'The jackal at work again.' The tracks were doubled, entering the thicket and returning. The inward tracks seemed deeper, less extended, as though the man carried a burden, but the outward tracks were lighter, the man walked freely.

Slowly, Mark edged in towards the thicket, following the man's prints. Pausing for long minutes to examine the undergrowth carefully every few paces, or squatting down to give himself better vision along the ground under the hanging lianas and branches.

Now that he knew what he was going to find, the pleasurable glow of excitement had given way to the chill of anger and the cold knowledge of mortal danger.

Something white caught his eye in the gloomy depths of the thicket. He stared at it moments before he saw the white, bleeding pith of a tree trunk, where it had been ripped by the claws of an anguished beast, long raking marks deep through the dark woody bark. His anger slid in his belly like an uncoiling serpent.

He moved sideways and slowly forward, the rifle held ready now, low across his hips, three paces before he stopped again. On the edge of the thicket there was an area of flattened grass and scrub; the soft black leaf-mould earth had been churned and disturbed, something heavy had been dragged back and forth, and there was a fleck of wet red lit by a single beam of falling sunlight that might have been the petal of a wild flower – or a drop of blood.

He heard another sound then, the clink of metal on metal, link on link, steel chain moved stealthily in the dark depths of the thicket and it sighted him. He knew where the animal was lying now, and he moved out sideways, crabbing step after step, slipping the safety-catch of the rifle, and holding it at high port across his chest.

White again, unnatural white, a round blob of it against dark foliage and he froze staring at it. Long seconds passed before he realized that it was the raw wood of a cut log, a short fork-shaped log as thick as a young girl's waist, so freshly cut that the gum was still bleeding from it in sticky wine-coloured drops. He saw also the twist of stolen fencing wire that held the chain to the log. The log was the anchor, a sliding drag weight which would hold the trapped animal without giving it a solid pull against which to pit itself and tear itself free.

The chain clinked again.

The leopard was within twenty paces of him. He knew exactly where it was but he could not see it, and as he stared, his mind was racing, remembering everything he had heard about the animal, the old man's stories.

'You won't see him until he comes, and even then he will only be a yellow flash of light, like a sunbeam. He won't warn you with a grunt, not like a lion. He comes absolutely silently, and he won't chew your arm or grab you in the shoulder. He'll go for your head. He knows all about two-legged animals, he feeds mostly on baboon, so he knows where your head is. He'll take the top off your skull quicker than you open your breakfast egg, and for good measure his back legs will be busy on your belly. You've seen a cat lie on his back and hook with his back legs when you scratch his belly. He'll cat you the same way, but he'll strip your guts out of you just like a chicken, and he'll do it so quickly that if there are four of you in the hunting-party he'll kill three of them before the fourth man gets his gun to his shoulder.'

Mark stood absolutely still and waited. He could not see the animal, but he could feel it, could feel its eyes, they stung his skin like the feet of poisonous crawling insects, and he remembered the shiny marble white scar tissue that Sean Courtney had shown him once in one of those mellow moments after the fourth whisky, pulling up his shirt and flexing muscle, so the cicatrice bulged with the gloss of satin.

'Leopard,' he had said. 'Devil cat – the worst bastard in all the bush.'

He felt his feet pulling back slowly, and the dead leaves rustled. He could walk away and leave it, come back when the vultures told him the animal was dead or too weak to be a danger. Then he imagined the terror and anguish of the animal – and suddenly it was not the animal, but his animal, his charge, his sacred charge, and he stepped forward.

The chain clinked again and the leopard came. It came with a terrible silent rush, and in the blurring streaming charge, only the eyes blazed, they blazed yellow with hatred and fear and agony. The chain flailed out behind it, spinning and snapping, and as Mark brought the rifle up the last six inches to his shoulder he saw the trap hanging on its fore-leg like a sinister grey metallic crab. The heavy steel trap slowed the charge just that fraction.

Time seemed to pass with a dreamlike slowness, each microsecond falling heavily as drops of thick oil, so that he saw that the leopard's foreleg above the grip of the steel jaws was eaten through. He felt his stomach turn over as he realized that the frenzied animal had gnawed through its own bone and flesh and sinew in its desperate try for freedom. The leg was held by only a thread of bloody ragged skin, and that last thread snapped at the heavy jerk of the steel trap.

The leopard was free, mad with pain and fear, as it launched itself at Mark's head.

The muzzle of the Mannlicher almost touched the broad flat forehead; he was so close that he could see the long white whiskers bristling from the puckered snarling lips like grass stalks stiff with the morning frost, and the yellow fangs behind wet black lips, the furry pink tongue arched across the open throat, and the eyes. The terrible hating yellow eyes.

Mark fired and the bullet clubbed the skull open, the yellow eyes blinked tightly at the jarring shock, and the head was wrenched backwards, twisted on the snakelike neck, while the lithe body lost its grace and lightness and turned heavy and shapeless in mid-air.

It fell like a sack at Mark's feet, and tiny droplets of brilliant red blood spattered the scuffed toe cap of Mark's boot, and glittered there like cut rubies.

Mark touched the open staring eye, but the fierce yellow light was fading and there was no blinking reflex of the eyelids with their long beautiful fans of dark lashes. The leopard was dead, and Mark sat down heavily in the leaf-mould beside the carcass and groped for his cigarette tin. The hand that held the match shook so violently that the flame fluttered like a moth's wing. He shook out the flame, threw the match away, and then stroked his open palm across the soft thick fur, the amber gold dabbed with the distinctive rosettes of black, as though touched by the five bunched fingertips of an angel's right hand.

'Pungushe – you bastard!' he whispered again. The animal had died for that golden dappled hide, for the few silver shillings that it would bring when sold in the village market, at a country railway halt, or on the side of a dusty road. A death in unspeakable agony and terror to make a rug, or a coat for a lady. Mark stroked the glowing fur again, and felt his own fear give way to anger for the man who had saved his life once, and who he had hunted these two months.

He stood up and went to the steel trap, lying at the end of its chain. The severed leg was still held between the relentless jaws, and Mark squatted to examine it. The trap was the type they call a 'Slag Yster', a killing iron, and the spikes of the jaws had been carefully filed to bite but not sever. It weighed at least thirty pounds and it would take a thick branch to lever those jaws open, and reset the mechanism.

The steel was dark and sooty where the poacher had scorched it with a torch of dry grass to kill the man-smell on the metal. Lying at the edge of the thicket was the half decomposed carcass of a baboon, the odoriferous bait which had been irresistible to the big yellow cat.

Mark reloaded the Mannlicher, and his anger was so intense that he would have shot down the man who had done this thing, if he had come across him in that moment, despite the fact that he owed him his life.

He walked back up the slope and unsaddled Trojan, hobbled him with the leather straps, and hung his saddle-bags in the branches of the leadwood out of the way of a questing hyena or badger.

Then he went back and picked up the poacher's spoor at the edge of the thicket. He knew it would be useless to follow on the mule. The poacher would be alerted at a mile range by that big clumsy animal, but he had a chance on foot.

The spoor was fresh and the poacher's camp would be close, he would not stray far from such a valuable asset as his steel trap. Mark had a very good chance.

He would be cagey, of course, sly and cunning, for he would know that it was now forbidden to hunt in the valley. Mark had visited each village, spoken with each tribal headman and drank his beer while he explained to him the new order.

The poacher knew that he was outside the law. Mark had followed his spoor so often, and the precautions Pungushe took, the elaborate ruses to throw any pursuit, made it clear that he was in guilt, but now Mark had a good chance at him.

The spoor crossed the river half a mile down-stream, and then started to zig-zag back and forth among the scrub and forest and brush as the poacher visited his trap line.

The leopard trap was clearly the centre of his line, but he was noosing for small game, using light galvanized baling wire, probably purchased for a few shillings at a country general dealer's store. He was also using copper telegraph wire, probably obtained by blatantly scaling a telegraph pole in some lonely place.

He was trapping for jackal, baiting with offal, and he was trapping indiscriminately at salt licks and mud wallows, any place that might attract small game.

Following the trap line diligently, Mark sprang every wire noose and ripped it out. He closed rapidly with his quarry, but it was three hours before he found the poacher's camp.

It was under the swollen, bloated reptilian grey branches of a baobab tree. The tree was old and rotten, its huge trunk cleaved by a deep hollow, a cave that the poacher had used to shield his small smokeless cooking fire. The fire was dead now, carefully smothered with sand – but the smell of dead smoke led Mark to it. The ashes were cold.

Tucked away in the deepest recess of the hollow tree were two bundles tied with plaited bark string. One bundle held a greasy grey blanket, a carved wooden head-rest, a small black three-legged pot and a pouch of impala skin which contained two or three pounds of yellow maize and strips of dried meat. The poacher travelled light, and moved fast.

The other bundle contained fifteen jackal skins, sun-dried and crackling stiff, beautiful furs of silver and black and red, and two leopard skins, a big dark golden tom and a smaller half-grown female.

Mark relit the fire and threw the blanket, the head-rest and the bag upon it, deriving a thin vindictive satisfaction as they smouldered and blackened. He smashed the iron pot with a rock and then he slung the roll of dried skins on his shoulder and started back.

It was almost dark when he got back to the leopard thicket beside the river.

He dropped the heavy bundle of dried skin, which by this time felt like a hundredweight sack of coal on his shoulder, and he stared uncomprehendingly at the leopard's carcass.

It swarmed with big green metallic shiny flies. They were laying their eggs on the dead flesh, like bunches of white boiled rice, but what astonished Mark was that the carcass was naked. It had been expertly stripped of its golden fur, and now it was a raw pink, laced with yellow fat and the white tracery of muscle ligaments. The head was bare, the mask stripped away so that dull startled eyes started out of the skull like marbles, and tufts of black hair sprang from the open ear holes, the fangs were exposed in a fixed yellow grin.

Quickly Mark ran to the anchor log. The chain and trap were gone.

It was fully a minute before the next logical step occurred to him. He ran up the slope to the leadwood tree. Trojan was gone. The hobbling straps had been cut with a razor-sharp blade and laid out neatly under the leadwood tree.

Trojan, unexpectedly relieved of his hobble, had reacted gratefully in a fully predictable manner. He had set off, arrow-straight through the forest, back home to his rude stable, his nightly ration of grain, and the congenial company of his old buddy Spartan.

It was a fifteen-mile walk back to main camp, and it would be dark in fifteen minutes.

The saddle-bags had been taken down from the tree, and the contents meticulously picked over. What Pungushe had rejected, he had folded and stacked neatly on a flat rock. He clearly did not think much of William Shakespeare, his tragedies had been put aside, and he had left Mark his chamois hunting-jacket, a last minute gift from Ruth Courtney.

He had taken the gentleman's sleeping bag, which had once belonged to General Courtney, with its built-in ground sheet and genuine eider filling, twenty-five guineas' worth from Harrods of London, good exchange for a threadbare greasy blanket and wooden head-rest.

He had taken the cooking pot, pannikin and cutlery, the salt and flour and bully beef, but had left a single tin of beans.

He had taken the clean shirt and khaki trousers, but had left the spare woollen socks and rubber-soled boots. Perhaps it was chance that the boots pointed down-stream to Mark's camp – or was it mockery? A can of beans and boots to carry Mark home.

Through the red mists of his humiliation and mounting rage, Mark glimpsed suddenly a whimsical sense of humour at work. The man had been watching him. Mark was sure of that now, his selection from the saddle-bags echoed too faithfully what Mark had burned of his.

In his imagination, Mark heard the deep bell of Zulu laughter, and he snatched up the Mannlicher and picked up Pungushe's outgoing spoor.

He followed it for only a hundred yards and then stopped. Pungushe was heavily laden with trap, wet skin, and booty, but he had hit the Zulu's stride '*Minza umhlabathi*', and he was eating ground to the north at a pace which Mark knew was pointless to try and imitate.

He walked back to the leadwood tree and sank down beside the trunk. His rage turned to acute discomfort at the thought of the fifteen-mile walk home, carrying the saddle-bags, and the roll of dried skins, for honour dictated he did not abandon his meagre spoils.

Suddenly he began to laugh, a helpless, hopeless shaking of his shoulders, and he laughed until tears ran down his cheeks and his belly ached.

'Pungushe, I'll get even for this,' he promised weakly, through his laughter.

It rained after midnight, a quick hard downpour, just enough to soak Mark and to bow the grass with clinging drops.

Then a small chill wind came nagging like an old wife, and the wet grass soaked his boots until they squelched and chafed with each step, and his cigarettes had disintegrated into a yellow porridge of mangled tobacco and limp rice paper, and the roll of skin and the saddle and the bags cut into his shoulders, and he did not laugh again that night.

In the pre-dawn, the cliffs of Chaka's Gate were purple and milky smooth, flaming suddenly with the sun's ardent kiss in vivid rose and bronze, but Mark plodded on under his burden, tired beyond any appreciation of beauty, beyond feeling or even caring, until he came out of the forest on to the bank of the Bubezi River and stopped in mid-stride.

He sniffed in total disbelief, and was immediately assailed by the demands of his body, the quick flood of saliva from under his tongue and the cramping of his empty belly. It was the most beautiful odour he had ever smelled, bacon frying and eggs in the pan, slowly gelling and firming in the sizzling fat. He knew it was only a figment of his exhaustion, for he had eaten his last bacon six weeks before.

Then his ears played tricks also, he heard the ring of an axe-blade on wood and the faint melody of Zulu voices, and he lifted his head and stared ahead through the forest into his old camp below the wild figs.

There was a cone of pristine white canvas, an officer's bell tent, recently pitched beside his own rudely thatched lean-to shelter. The camp fire had been built up, and Hlubi, the old Zulu cook, was busy with his pans over it, while, beyond the flames, in a collapsible canvas camp chair, sitting comfortably, was the burly figure of General Courtney, watching his breakfast cook with a critical eye.

He looked up and saw Mark, bedraggled and dirty as an urchin at the edge of the camp, and his grin was wide and boyish.

'Hlubi,' he said in Zulu. 'Another four eggs and a pound of bacon.'

Sean Courtney's vast energy and enthusiasm were the beacon flames that made the next week one of the memorable interludes in Mark's life. He would always remember him as he was in those days, belly-laughing at Mark's tale of woe and frustration with Pungushe, and then still chuckling, calling to his servants and repeating the story to them, with his own comments and embellishments, until they rocked and reeled with mirth and old fat Hlubi overturned a pan of eggs, his great paunch bouncing like a ball and his cannon-ball of a head, with its hoar-frosting of pure white wool, rolling uncontrollably from side to side.

Mark, half-starved on a diet of bully and beans, gorged himself on the miraculous food that flowed from Hlubi's spade-sized, pink-palmed hands. He was amazed at the style in which Sean Courtney braved the hardships of the African bush, from his full sized hip-bath to the portable kerosene-burning ice-box that delivered endless streams of frothing cold beer against the stunning heat of midday.

'Why travel in steerage, when you can go first class?' Sean asked, and winked at Mark as he spread a large-scale map of northern Zululand on the camp table. 'Now, what have you got to tell me?'

Their discussions lasted late into each night, with a Petromax hissing in the tree overhead and the jackals yipping and piping along the river, and in the days they rode the ground. Sean Courtney up on Spartan, so clearly enjoying every moment of it, with the vitality of a man half his age, keeping going without a check even in the numbing heat of noon, inspecting the site that Mark had chosen for the main camp, arguing as to where the Bubezi bridge should be built, following the road through the forest where Mark had blazed the trees, exulting at the sight of a big black nyala ram with his heavy mane and ghostly stripes, as it raced away panic-stricken by the approach of man, sitting in his hip-bath under the fig trees, up to his waist in creaming white suds, with a cigar in his mouth and a long glass of beer in his hand, bellowing for Hlubi to top up with boiling water from the big kettle when his bath cooled. Big and scarred and hairy – and Mark realized then what a wide space this man had filled in his life.

As the day drew closer when he must leave again, Sean's mood changed, and in the evenings he brooded over the list of animals that Mark had compiled.

'Fifty zebra,' he read Mark's estimate, and poured the last few inches of whisky from the pinch-bottle into his glass. 'On the Sabi River in '95 a single herd crossed in front of my wagons. It took forty minutes at the gallop to go by, and the leaders were over the horizon when the tail passed us. There were thirty thousand animals in that one herd.'

'No elephant?' he asked, looking up from the list, and when Mark shook his head, he went on softly, 'We thought it would last for ever. In '99 when I rode into Pretoria from the north, I had ten tons of ivory on board. Ten tons, twenty thousand pounds of ivory.'

'No lions there?' and again Mark shook his head.

'I don't think so, General. I've seen no sign of them, nor heard them in the night, but when I was a boy I shot one near here. I was with my grandfather.'

'Yes,' Sean nodded. 'When *you* were a boy – but, what about your son, Mark? Will he ever see a lion in the wild?'

Mark did not answer, and Sean grunted.

'No lions on the Bubezi River, God! What have we done to this land?' He stared into the fire. 'I wonder if it was mere chance that you and I met, Mark. You have opened my eyes and conscience. It was I, and men like me, that did this –'

He shook that great shaggy head and groped in the side-pocket of his baggy hunting-jacket, and produced a leather-bound pocket-size book, a thick little volume well-thumbed and shiny with the grease of grubby hands.

Mark did not recognize it for a moment, but when he did, he was startled.

'I did not know you read the Book,' he exclaimed, and Sean glanced up at him from under beetling brows.

'I read it,' he said gruffly. 'The older I get, the more I read it. There is a lot of solace here.'

'But, sir,' Mark persisted, 'you never go to church.'

This time Sean frowned as though he resented the prying questions. 'I live my religion,' he said. 'I don't go singing about it on Sunday, and drop it for the rest of the week, like some I know.' His tone was final, forbidding further discussion, and he turned his attention to the battered volume.

He had marked his place with a pressed wild flower, and the Bible fell open at the right page.

'I found it last night,' he told Mark, as he propped the steel-rimmed spectacles on his nose. 'It seemed like an omen, and I marked it to read to you. Matthew x.' He cleared his throat and read slowly;

'Are not two sparrows sold for a farthing?

And one of them shall not fall on the ground without your Father.'

When he had finished, he tucked the Bible away in his pocket, and they were both silent, thinking about it and watching the shapes in the ashes of the fire.

'Then perhaps he will help us to save the sparrow from its fall, here at Chaka's Gate,' said Sean, and he leaned forward to take a burning twig from the fire. He lit a fresh cigar with it and puffed deeply, savouring the taste of wood smoke and tobacco before speaking again.

'It is just unfortunate that it all comes at a time like this. It will be the end of the next year before we can make an official move to have the proclamation ratified and budget for full development here.'

Mark was instantly alert, and his voice sharp as he demanded,

'Next year?'

'I'm afraid so.'

'But why so long?'

'The grim reality of politics, son,' Sean growled. 'We have just received a shattering blow, and all else must wait while we play the game of power.'

'What has happened?' Mark asked with real concern now. 'I haven't read a newspaper in two months.'

'I wish I were that lucky.' Sean smiled without humour. 'There was a by-election in a little place up in the Transvaal. It's a seat that has always been ours, a good safe seat, in the hands of a respected backbencher of great loyalty and little intellect. He had a heart attack in the dining-room of the House, expiring between the soup and the fish. We went to our safe little constituency to elect a new member,' here Sean paused, and his expression went bleak, 'and we got the trouncing of our lives. A fifteen per cent swing to the Hertzog Party. They fought us on our handling of the strike last year – and it was a disaster.'

'I didn't know. I'm sorry.'

'If that swing, fifteen per cent, carries for the whole country, then we will be in opposition after the next election. Everything else is of no significance. General Smuts has decided to go to the country next year in March, and we will be fighting for our existence. Until then, we cannot introduce this type of legislation, or ask for funds.'

Mark felt cold despair spread out to numb his very fingertips. 'What happens here?' he asked. 'In the meantime must we stop what I am doing? Do we just leave it? Another year of poaching and hunting, another year without protection or development?'

Sean shook his head. 'I've had my people studying the existing proclamation. We have powers there that we can enforce, but no money to do it.'

'You can't do anything without money,' said Mark miserably.

'Ah, so at last a little respect for the power of money.' Sean shot him a thin smile across the fire, and then went on seriously. 'I've decided to finance the development and running of the proclaimed area until I get a budget allocation for it. I'll foot the bill from my own pocket. Perhaps I'll get reimbursed from the budget later, but if I don't,' he shrugged, 'I reckon I owe that much at least. I've had a pretty good run.'

'It won't need much,' Mark rushed in eagerly but Sean quieted him irritably.

'You'll get the same salary as before, and we'll make a start on the main camp. I'm going to give you four men to do the work,' he went on, speaking quietly. 'We'll have to make do without a bridge across the river, and only a wagon track for our first road, but it'll be a start – and let's just hope like hell we win our election.'

On the last day at breakfast, Sean laid a folder in front of Mark.

'I talked Caldwell, the man who did the drawings for *Jock of the Bushveld*, into designing the layout,' he smiled, as Mark opened the folder. 'I wanted you to get the best for your three thousand pounds.'

In the folder was a mock-up of the full-page Press announcement which would launch the 'Friends of African Wildlife'.

The margin contained magnificent line-drawings of wild animals, and under the heavy typed announcement was set out the objects of the Society, and an eloquent plea for support and membership.

'I had my lawyers draft the articles and draw up the wording. We'll run it in every newspaper in the country. The Society's address is the Head Office of Courtney Holdings and I have taken on a full-time clerk to handle all the paper work. I've also got a young journalist to edit the Society's newspaper. He's full of ideas and caught up in the whole thing. With luck, we'll get huge public support behind us.'

'It's going to cost more than three thousand pounds.' Mark was torn between delight, and concern for the size to which his simple idea had grown.

'Yes,' Sean laughed. 'It's going to cost more than three thousand pounds, which reminds me. I sent Dirk Courtney a receipt for his money – and a life membership of the Society!' The joke carried them over the awkwardness of the last moments before departure.

Sean's bearers disappeared among the trees, carrying head loads of equipment to where the motor lorry had been left on the nearest road twenty miles beyond the cliffs of Chaka's Gate, and Sean lingered regretfully.

'I'm sad to go,' he admitted. 'It's been a good time, but I feel stronger now – ready to face whatever the bastards have got to throw at me.' He looked about him, taking farewell of river and mountain and wilderness. 'There is magic here.' He nodded. 'Look after it well, son,' and he held out his hand.

It was Mark's last opportunity to ask the question which he had tried to ask a dozen times already, but each time Sean had turned it aside, or simply ignored it. But now he had to have an answer, and he took Sean's big gnarled bony fist in a grip that would not be denied.

'You haven't told me how Storm is, sir. How is she? Is she well? How is her painting?' he blurted.

It seemed even then that Sean would not be drawn. He stiffened angrily, made as if to pull his hand away, and then the anger faded before it reached his eyes. For a moment there showed in the deep-set eyes a dark unfathomable grief, and his grip tightened on Mark's hand like a steel trap.

'Storm was married a month ago. But I have not seen her since you left Lion Kop,' he said, and he dropped Mark's hand. Without another word, he turned and walked away. For the first time he went slowly and heavily, swaying against the drag of his bad leg, shuffling like an old man – a very tired old man.

Mark wanted to run after him, but his own heart was breaking and his legs would not carry him.

He stood forlornly and watched Sean Courtney limp away into the trees.

The Natal Number Two came in along the line, his pony's hooves kicking up little spurts of white marking-lime like a machine gun traversing, and he caught the ball two feet before it dribbled out of play.

He leaned low out of the saddle and took it backhanded under his pony's neck, a full-blooded stroke that finished with the mallet high above his head, and the ball rose in a floating arc, a white blur against the stark blue of summer sky.

From the club house veranda, and the deck-chairs beneath the coloured umbrellas, applause splattered above the drum of hooves, and then rose into a swelling hum as they saw that Derek Hunt had anticipated.

He was coming down in a hard canter with Saladin not yet asked to extend. Saladin was a big pony, with a mean and ugly head that he cocked to watch the flight of the white ball, his over-large nostrils flaring so the shiny red mucous membrane flashed like a flag. The eye that watched the ball rolled in the gaunt skull, giving the horse a wild and half-crazed air. He was of that raggedy roan and grey that no amount of currying would ever brighten into a gloss, and his hooves looked like those of a cart-horse. He had to lift them high in the ungainly action that was quickly carrying him ahead of the hard-running Argentinian pony at his shoulder.

Derek sat him as though he were an armchair, idly penduluming his stick from his wrist, his pith helmet hard down over his ears and strapped up tightly under the chin. His belly bulged out over the belt of his breeches, his arms were long and thick as those of a chimpanzee, covered in a thick fuzz of ginger hair. The skin was heavily freckled and had a raw red look between the freckles, as though it had been scalded with boiling water. His face was the same raw painful looking red, tinged by the purplish glaze of the very heavy drinker, and he was sweating.

The sweat glistened like early dew on his face and dripped from his chin. His short-sleeved cotton singlet looked as though he had been caught in a tropical downpour. It clung to the thick bearlike shoulders, and was stretched so tightly over his bulging paunch and so transparent with wetness, that you could see the deep dark pit of his belly button from the sidelines.

At each jar, as Saladin's hooves struck the hard-baked earth, Derek Hunt's great backside in the tight-fitting white breeches quivered like a jelly in the saddle.

Two Argentinian ponies were cutting across field to cover, their handsome riders olive-skinned and dashing as cavalry officers, riding with huge verve and excited Spanish cries, and Derek grinned under his bristling ginger moustache, as the ball started its long plummeting curve back to earth.

'Christ,' drawled one of the members on the club house steps. 'The ugliest horse in Christendom.' And he raised his pink gin to salute Saladin.

'And the ugliest four-goal handicapper in the entire world on his back,' agreed the masher beside him. 'Poor bloody dagoes should turn to stone just looking at them.'

Saladin and the Argentinian Number One arrived at the drop of the ball at exactly the same moment. The Argentinian rose in the saddle to trap the fall, his white teeth sparkling under the trim black pencil-line of his moustache, the smooth darkly tanned muscles of his arm bulging as he prepared to go on to the forehand drive, his sleekly beautiful pony wheeling into line for the shot, nimble and quick as a ferret.

Then an extraordinary thing happened. Derek Hunt sat fat-gutted and heavy in the saddle and nobody could see the touch of rein and heel that made Saladin switch his quarters. The Argentinian pony cannoned off him as though she had hit a granite kopje, and the rider went over her head, going in an instant from balanced perfection to sprawling windmilling confusion, falling heavily in a cloud of red dust, and rolling to his knees to scream hysterical protest to the umpire and the skies.

Derek leaned slightly and there was the tap of mallet against bamboo root, a gentle almost self-effacing little tap, and the ball dropped meekly ahead of Saladin's slugging, hammering head.

It bounced once, twice, and then came up obediently for the next light tap that kept it hopping down the field. The Argentinian Number Four swept in from the right, with all the smooth-running grace of a charging lioness – and the roar of the crowd carried across the open field, spurring him on to make the challenge. He shouted a wild Spanish oath, his eyes flashing with excitement.

Smoothly, Derek changed the mallet from his right hand to his left, and tapped the bouncing white ball on to his off-side, forcing the Argentinian to increase the angle of his interception.

The instant he was drawn, Derek cropped hard, lofting the ball in an easy lob high over the Argentinian's head.

He said, 'Ha!' but not loudly, and touched Saladin with his heels. The big ugly roan stretched out his neck and extended, with Derek moving now to help him push.

They ran past the Argentinian as though he had indeed turned to stone, they left him floundering in their wake and picked up the ball beyond him. Tap! Tap! And tap again, he ran it down through the exact centre of the stubby goal-posts and then turned and trotted back to the pony lines.

Chuckling so that his belly bounced, Derek swung one leg forward over Saladin's neck and slid down to the ground, letting him go free to the grooms.

'I'll take Satan for the next chukka,' he shouted in that beery throaty voice.

Storm Courtney saw him coming, and knew what was going to happen. She tried to rise, but she was slow and clumsy, the child in her womb anchored her like a stone.

'One for the poor, what!' shouted Derek, and caught her with one long, ginger-fuzzed, boiled red arm.

The sweat on his face was icy cold and smeared down her own cheek, and he smelled of sour beer and horse. He kissed her with an open mouth, in front of Irene Leuchars and the four other girls, and their husbands, and all the grinning grooms, and the members on the veranda.

She thought desperately that she was going to be ill. The acid vomit rose into her throat, and she thought she was going to throw up in front of them all.

'Derek, my condition!' she whispered desperately, but he held her under his one arm as he took the bottle of beer that one of the white-jacketed club servants brought on a silver tray, and, scorning the glass, he drank straight from the bottle.

She struggled to be free, but he held her easily with immense and careless strength – and he belched, a ripping explosion of gas. 'One for the poor,' he shouted again, and they all laughed – like courtiers at the king's jest. Good old Derek. Law unto himself, old Derek.

He dropped the empty bottle. 'Keep it until I get back, wifey!' he laughed, and took one of her swollen breasts in his huge raw-knuckled, red-boiled hand and squeezed it painfully. She felt cold and trembly and weak with humiliation and hatred.

She had missed a month many times before, so Storm did not begin to worry until the second blank came up on her pocket diary. She had been about to tell Mark then, but that had been the time they had parted. Still, she had expected it all to resolve itself, but as the weeks passed, the enormity of it all began to reach her in her gold and ivory castle. This sort of thing happened to other girls, common working girls, ordinary girls – it did not happen to Storm Courtney. There were special rules for young ladies like Storm.

When it was certain, beyond all doubt, the first person she thought of was Mark Anders. As the panic caught at her heart with fiery little barbs, she wanted to rush to him and throw her arms about his neck. Then that stubborn and completely uncontrollable pride of the Courtneys smothered the impulse. He must come to her. She had decided, he must come on her terms – and she could not bring herself to change the rules she had laid down. Though still, even in her distress, her chest felt tight and her legs shaky and weak, whenever she thought of Mark.

She had wept, silently in the night, when she had first left Mark – and now she wept again. She longed for him even more now, with his child growing in the secret depths of her body. But that perverse and distorted pride would not release its bulldog hold on her, would not allow her even to let him know of her predicament.

'Don't challenge me, Mark Anders,' she had warned him, and he had done it. She hated him, and loved him for that. But now she could not bend.

The next person she thought of was her mother. She and Ruth Courtney had always been close, she had always been able to rely on her mother's loyalty and shrewdly practical hard sense. Then she was stopped dead by the knowledge that if Ruth were told, then her father would know within hours. Ruth Courtney kept nothing from Sean, or he from her.

Storm's soul quailed at the thought of what would happen once her father knew that she carried a bastard. The immense indulgent love he had for her would make his anger and retribution more terrible.

She knew also Mark would be destroyed by it. Her father was too strong, too persistent and single-minded for her to believe she would be able to keep Mark's name from him. He would squeeze it out of her.

She knew of her father's affection for Mark Anders, it had been apparent for anyone to see, but that affection would not have been sufficient to save either of them.

Sean Courtney's attitude to his daughter was bound by iron laws of conduct, the old-fashioned view of the father that left no latitude for manoeuvre. Mark Anders had contravened those iron laws and Sean would destroy him, despite the fact he had come to love him, and in doing so, he would destroy a part of himself. He would reject and drive out his own daughter, even though it left him ruined and broken with grief.

So, for her father's sake and for Mark Anders's sake, she could not go for comfort and help to her mother.

She went instead to Irene Leuchars, who listened to Storm's hesitant explanations with rising glee and anticipation.

'But you silly darling, didn't you take precautions?'

Storm shook her head glumly, not quite certain what Irene meant by precautions, but certain only that she hadn't taken them.

'Who was it, darling?' was the next question, and Storm shook her head again, this time fiercely.

'Oh dear,' Irene rolled her eyes. 'That many candidates for the daddy? You are a dark horse, Storm darling.'

'Can't one – well, can't one actually do something?' Storm asked miserably.

'You mean an abortion, darling?' Irene asked brutally, and smiled a sly spiteful smile when Storm nodded.

He was a tall pale man, very grey and stooped, with a reedy voice and hands so white as to be almost transparent. Storm could see the blue veins and the fragile ivory bones through the skin. She tried not to think of those pale transparent hands as they pried and probed, but they were cold and cruelly painful.

Afterwards, he had washed those pale hands at the kitchen sink of his small grey apartment with such exaggerated care that Storm had felt her pain and embarrassment enhanced by a sense of affront. The cleansing seemed to be a personal insult.

'I imagine you indulge in a great deal of physical activity – horse-riding, tennis?' he asked primly, and when Storm nodded he made a little sucking and clucking sound of disapproval. 'The female body was not designed for such endeavour. You are very narrow, and your musculature is highly developed. Furthermore, you are at least ten weeks pregnant.' At last he had finished washing, and now he began to dry his hands on a threadbare, but clinically white towel.

'Can you help me?' Storm demanded irritably, and he shook his pale grey head slowly from side to side.

'If you had come a little earlier –' and he spread the white transparent hands in a helpless gesture.

They had drawn up a list of names, she and Irene, and each of the men on the list had two things in common. They were in love, or had professed to be in love with Storm, and they were all men of fortune.

There were six names on the list, and Storm had written cards to two of them and received vague replies, polite good wishes, and no definite suggestion for a meeting.

The third man on the list she had contrived to meet at the Umgeni Country Club. She could still wear tennis clothes, and the pregnancy had given her skin a new bloom and lustre, her breasts a fuller ripeness.

She had chatted lightly, flirtatiously, with him, confident and poised, giving him encouragement he had never received from her before. She had not noticed the sly, gloating look in his eyes, until he leaned close to her and asked confidentially,

'Should you be playing tennis – now?'

She had only been able to keep herself from breaking down until she reached the Cadillac parked in the lot behind the courts. She was weeping when she drove out through the gates, and she had to park in the dunes above the ocean.

After the first storm of humiliation had passed, she could think clearly.

It had been Irene Leuchars, of course. She must have been blind and stupid not to realize it sooner. Everybody, every single person, would know by now, Irene would have seen to that.

Loneliness and desolation overwhelmed her.

Derek Hunt had not been on the list of six, not because he was not rich, not because he had never shown interest in Storm.

Derek Hunt had shown interest in most pretty girls. He had even married two of them, and both of them had divorced him in separate blazes of notoriety, not before they had, between them, presented him with seven offspring.

Derek Hunt's reputation was every bit as vast and flamboyant as his fortune.

'Look, old girl,' he had told Storm reasonably. 'You and I have both got a problem. I want you, have always wanted you. Can't sleep at night, strewth!' and his ginger whiskers twitched lasciviously. 'And you need me. The word's out about you, old girl. Mark of the beast, condemnation of society, and all that rot, I'm afraid.

'Your loss, my gain. I've never given a stuff for the condemnation of society. I've got seven little bastards already. Another one won't make any difference. What about it, then? One for the poor, what?'

They had driven up to Swaziland, and Derek had been able to get a special licence, lying about her age.

There had been nobody she knew at the ceremony, only five of Derek's cronies – and she had not told her father, nor her mother, nor Mark Anders.

She heard him coming home, like a Le Mans Grand Prix winner, a long cortege of motor cars roaring up the driveway, then the squeal of brakes, the cannonade of slamming doors, the loud comradely shouts and the snatches of wild song.

Derek's voice, louder and hoarser than the rest. 'Caramba, me hearties! Whipped your pants off on the field, going to drink you blind now. This way, the pride of the Argentine –' the stamping and shouting, as they trooped up the front staircase.

Storm lay flat on her back and stared at the plaster cupids on the ceiling. She wanted to run, this senseless panicky urge to get up and run. But there was no place to run to.

She had spoken to her mother three times since the wedding, and each time had been agony for both of them.

'If only you had told us. Daddy might have been able to understand, to forgive –'

'Oh darling, if you only knew the plans he used to make for your wedding. He was so proud of you – and then not to be at your wedding. Not even invited –'

'Give him time, please, Storm. I am trying for you. Believe me darling. I think it might have been better, if it was anybody in the world but Derek Hunt. You know what Daddy thinks of him.'

There was nowhere to run, and she lay quietly, dreading, until at last the heavy unsteady boots came clumping up the staircase, and the door was thrown open.

He had not changed, and he still wore riding-boots. The backside of his breeches was brown with dubbin from the saddle, and the crotch dropped almost to his knees, like a baby's soiled napkin; the sweat had dried in salty white circles on the cotton singlet.

'Wake up, old girl. Time for every good man and true to perform his duty.' He let his clothing lie where it fell.

His bulging belly was fish white, and fuzzed with ginger curls. The heavy shoulders were pitted and scarred purple with the old cicatrices of myriad carbuncles and small boils, and he was massively virile, thick and hard and callous as the branch of a pine tree.

'One for the poor, what?' he chuckled hoarsely, as he came to the bed.

Suddenly and clearly, she had an image of Mark Anders's slim and graceful body, with the clean shape of young muscle, as he sat in the dappled sunlight of the glade.

She remembered with a terrible pang of loss the lovely head with the fine strong lines of mouth and brow, and the serene poet's eyes.

As the bed dipped beneath the solid weight of her husband, she wanted to scream with despair and the knowledge of coming pain.

For breakfast Derek Hunt liked a little Black Velvet, mixing the Guinness stout and champagne in a special crystal punch bowl. He always used a Bollinger Vintage 1911 and drank it out of a pewter tankard.

He believed in a substantial breakfast, and this morning it was scrambled eggs, Scotch kippers, devilled kidneys, mushrooms and a large well-done fillet steak – all of it on the same plate.

Although his eyes were watery and pink-rimmed with the previous night's revelry, and his face blazed crimson as the rising sun, he was cheerful and loudly friendly, guffawing at his own jokes, and leaning across the table to prod her with a thick red thumb like a boiled langouste to emphasize a point.

She waited until he had picked up the bowl and tilted the last of the Black Velvet into his tankard, and then she said quietly,

'Derek, I want a divorce.'

The grin did not leave his face, and he watched the last drops fall into the tankard.

'Damn stuff evaporates – or the dish has got a hole in it,' he wheezed, and then chuckled merrily. 'Get it? A hole in it! Good, what?'

'Did you hear what I said? Aren't you going to answer?'

'Needs no answer, old girl. Bargain is a bargain, you've got a name for your bastard – I've still got my share coming.'

'You've had that, as many times as you could wish,' Storm answered quietly, with a whole world of resignation in her voice. 'Won't you let me go now?'

'Good God!' Derek stared at her over the rim of his tankard, his moustache bristling and the pink eyes wide with genuine amazement. 'You don't think I was really interested in the crumpet, do you? Can get that anywhere, all of it looks the same in the dark.' He snorted with real laughter now. 'Good God, old girl – you didn't really think I fancied your lily-white titties that much?'

'Why?' she asked.

'Ten million good reasons, old girl.' He gulped a mouthful of scrambled eggs and kidney, 'and every single one of them in General Sean Courtney's bank account.'

She stared at him. 'Daddy's money?'

'Right first time,' he grinned. 'Up you go to the head of the class.'

'But – but –' she made fluttery little gestures of incomprehension with both hands. 'I don't understand. You are so rich yourself.'

'Was, old girl, used to be – past tense.' And he let out another delighted guffaw. 'Two loving wives, two unsympathetic divorce judges, seven brats, forty polo ponies, friends with big right hands, rocks that shouldn't have been where the road was going, a mine with no diamonds, a building that fell down, a dam that burst, a reef that pinched out, cattle that got sick and myopic lawyers who don't read the small print, that's the way the money goes, pop goes the weasel!'

'I don't believe it.' She was aghast.

'Would never joke about that,' he grinned. 'Never joke about money, one of my principles. Probably my only principle.' And he prodded her. 'My only principle – get it? Skunked, absolutely flatters, I assure you. Daddy is the last resort, old girl – you'll have to speak to him, I'm afraid. Last resort, what? One for the poor, don't you know?'

There was no answer to the front door and Mark almost turned away and went back into the village, feeling a touch of relief and a lightening of heart that he recognized as cowardice. So instead, he jumped down off the veranda and went around the side of the house.

The stiff collar and tie chafed his throat and the jacket felt unnatural and constricting, so that he shrugged his shoulders and ran a finger around inside his collar as he came into the kitchen yard of the cottage. It was five months since last he had worn clothes or trodden on a paved sidewalk – even the sound of women's voices was unfamiliar. He paused and listened to them.

Marion Littlejohn was in the kitchen with her sister, and their merry prattle had a lilt and cadence to which he listened with new ears and fresh pleasure.

The chatter ceased abruptly at his knock, and Marion came to the door.

She wore a gaily striped apron, and her bare arms were floury to the elbows. She had her hair up in a ribbon but tendrils of it had come down in little wisps on to her neck and forehead.

The kitchen was filled with the smell of baking bread, and her cheeks were rosy from the heat of the oven.

'Mark,' she said calmly. 'How nice,' and tried to push the curl of hair off her forehead, leaving a smudge of white flour on the bridge of her nose. It was a strangely appealing gesture, and Mark felt his heart swell.

'Come in.' She stood aside, and held the door open for him.

Her sister greeted Mark frostily, much more aware of the jilting than Marion herself.

'Doesn't he look well?' Marion asked, and they both looked Mark over carefully, as he stood in the centre of the kitchen floor.

'He's too thin,' her sister judged him waspishly, and began untying her apron-strings.

'Perhaps,' Marion agreed comfortably, 'he just needs the proper food.' And she smiled and nodded as she saw how brown and lean he was, but she recognized also, with eyes as fond as a mother's, the growing weight of maturity in his features. She saw also the sorrow and the loneliness, and she wanted to take him in her arms and hold his head against her bosom.

'There is some lovely butter-milk,' she said instead. 'Sit down, here where I can see you.'

While she poured from the jug, her sister hung the apron behind the door and without looking at Mark said primly,

'We need more eggs. I'll go into the village.'

When they were alone, Marion picked up the roller, and stood over the table, leaning and dipping as the pastry spead and rolled out paper thin.

'Tell me what you have been doing,' she invited, and he began, hesitantly at first, but with blossoming sureness and enthusiasm, to tell her about Chaka's Gate, about the work and the life he had found there.

'That's nice.' She punctuated his glowing account every few minutes, her mind running busily ahead, already making lists and planning supplies, adapting pragmatically to the contingencies of a life lived far from the comforts of civilization, where even the small comforts become luxuries – a glass of fresh milk, a light in the night – all of it has to be planned for and carefully arranged.

Characteristically she felt neither excitement nor dismay at the prospect. She was of pioneer stock. Where a man goes, the woman follows. It was merely work that must be done.

'The site for the homestead is up in the first fold of the hills, but you can see right down the valley, and the cliffs of Chaka's Gate are right above it. It's beautiful, especially in the evenings.'

'I'm sure it is.'

'I have designed the house so it can be added on to, a room at a time. To begin with there will only be two rooms –'

'Two rooms will be enough to begin with,' she agreed, frowning thoughtfully. 'But we'll need a separate room for the children.'

He broke off and stared at her, not quite certain that he had heard correctly. She paused with the rolling-pin held in both hands and smiled at him.

'Well, that's why you came here today, isn't it?' she asked sweetly.

He dropped his eyes from hers and nodded. 'Yes.' He sounded bemused. 'I suppose it is.'

She lost her aplomb only briefly during the ceremony, and that was when she saw General Sean Courtney sitting in the front pew with his wife beside him, Sean in morning suit and with a diamond pin in his cravat, Ruth cool and elegant in a huge wagon-wheel sized hat, the brim thick with white roses.

'He came!' Marion whispered ecstatically, and could not restrain the triumphant glance she threw to her own friends and relatives, like a lady tossing a coin to a beggar. Her social standing had rocketed to dizzying heights.

Afterwards the General had bussed her tenderly on each cheek, before turning to Mark. 'You've picked the prettiest girl in the village, my boy.' And she had glowed with pleasure, pink and happy and truly as lovely as she had ever been in her life.

With the help of the four Zulu labourers Sean had given him, Mark had opened a rough track in as far as the Bubezi River. He brought his bride to Chaka's Gate on the pillion of the motorcycle, with the side-car piled high with part of her dowry.

Far behind them, the Zulus led Trojan and Spartan under heavy packs, the rest of Marion's baggage.

In the early morning the mist lay dense along the river, still and flat as the surface of a lake, touched to shades of delicate pink and mauve by the fresh new light of coming day.

The great headlands of Chaka's Gate rose sheer out of the mist, dark and mysterious, each wreathed in laurels of golden cloud.

Mark had chosen the hour of return so that she might have the best of it for her first glimpse of her new home. He pulled the cycle and side-car off the narrow, stony track and switched off the motor.

In the silence they sat and watched the sun strike upon the crests of the cliffs, burning like the beacons that the mariner looks for in the watery deserts of the ocean, the lights that beckon him on to his landfall and the quiet anchorage.

'It's very nice, dear,' she murmured. 'Now show me where the house will be.'

She worked with the Zulus, muddy to the elbows as they puddled the clay for the unburned Kimberley bricks, joshing them in their own language and bullying them cheerfully to effort beyond the usual pace of Africa.

She worked behind the mules, handling the traces, dragging up the logs from the valley, her sleeves rolled high on brown smooth arms and a scarf knotted around her head.

She worked over the clay oven, bringing out the fat golden brown loaves on the blade of a long handled spade, and watched with deep contentment as Mark wiped up the last of the stew with the crust.

'Was that good, then, dear?'

In the evenings she sat close to the lantern, with her head bowed over the sewing in her lap, and nodded brightly as he told her of the day's adventures, each little triumph and disappointment.

'What a shame, dear.' Or, 'How nice for you, dear.'

He took her, one bright, cloudless day, up the ancient pathway to the crest of Chaka's Gate. Holding her hand as he led her over the narrow places, where the river flowed six hundred sheer feet below their feet. She tucked her skirts into her bloomers, took a firm hold on the basket she carried and never faltered once on the long climb.

On the summit, he showed her the tumbled stone walls and overgrown caves of the old tribesmen who had defied Chaka, and he told her the story of the old king's climb, pointing out the fearsome path up which he had led his warriors – and finally he described the massacre and pictured for her the rain of human bodies hurled down into the river below.

'How interesting, dear,' she murmured, as she spread a cloth from the basket she had carried. 'I brought scones and some of that apricot jam you like so much.'

Something caught Mark's eye, unusual movement far down in the valley below, and he reached for his binoculars. In the golden grass at the edge of the tall reed beds they looked like a line of fat black bugs on a clean sheet. He knew what they were immediately, and with a surging uplift of excitement he counted them.

'Eighteen!' he shouted aloud. 'It's a new herd.'

'What is it, dear?' She looked up from the scone she was spreading with jam.

'It's a new herd of buffalo,' he exulted. 'They must have come in from the north. It's beginning to work already.'

In the field of the binoculars he saw one of the great bovine animals emerge into a clearing in the long grass. He could see not only its wide black back, but the heavy head and spreading ears beneath the mournfully drooping horns. The sunlight caught the bosses of the polished black horns so that they glittered like gunmetal.

He felt an enormous proprietary pride. They were his own. The first to come into the sanctuary he was building for them.

'Look.' He offered her the binoculars, and she wiped her hands carefully and pointed the glasses over the cliff. 'There on the edge of the swamp.' He pointed, with the pride and joy shining on his face.

'I can see them,' she agreed smiling happily for him. 'How nice, dear.'

Then she swung the binoculars in a wide sweep across the river to where the roof of the homestead showed above the trees.

'Doesn't it look so nice with its new thatch?' she said proudly. 'I just can't wait to move in.'

The following day they moved up from the shack of crude thatch and canvas at the old camp under the sycamore fig trees, and a pair of swallows moved in with them. The swiftly darting birds began to build their neat nest with little shiny globs of mud under the eaves of the new yellow thatch against the crisply white-washed wall of Kimberley brick.

'That's the best of all possible luck,' Mark laughed.

'They make such a mess,' said Marion doubtfully, but that night, for the first time ever, she initiated their love-making; rolling comfortably on to her back in the double-bed, drawing up her nightdress to her waist, and spreading her warm womanly thighs.

'It's all right, if you want to, dear.' And because she was kind and loved him so, he was as quick and as considerate as he could be.

'Was that good, then, dear?'

'It was wonderful,' he told her, and he had a sudden vivid image of a lovely vital woman, with a body that was lithe and swift and – and his guilt was brutal like a fist below the heart. He tried to thrust the image away, but it ran ahead of him through his dreams, laughing and dancing and teasing, so that in the morning there were dark blue smears beneath his eyes and he felt fretful and restless.

'I'm going up the valley on patrol.' He did not look up from his coffee.

'You only came back last Friday.' She was surprised.

'I want to look for those buffalo again,' he said.

'Very well, dear. I'll pack your bag – how long will you be gone – I'll put in your sweater and the jacket, it's cool in the evenings – it's a good thing I baked yesterday –' she prattled on cheerfully, and he had a sudden terrible urge to shout at her to be silent. 'It will give me a chance to plant out the garden. It will be nice to have fresh vegetables again, and I haven't written a letter for ages. They'll be wondering about us at home.' He rose from the table and went out to saddle Trojan.

The flogging explosion of heavy wings roused Mark from his reverie and he straightened in the saddle just as a dozen of the big birds rose from the edge of the reed-beds.

They were those dirty buff-coloured vultures, powering upwards as they were disturbed by Mark's approach, and undergoing that almost magical transformation from gross ugliness into beautiful planing flight.

Mark tethered Trojan and slipped the Mannlicher from its scabbard as a precaution. He felt a tickle of excitement, hopes high that he had come upon a kill by one of the big predatory cats. Perhaps even a lion, one of the animals for which he still searched the valley in vain.

The buffalo lay at the edge of the damp soft ground, half hidden by the reeds and it was so freshly dead that the vultures had not yet managed to penetrate the thick black hide, nor to spoil the sign which was deeply trodden and torn into the damp earth. They had only gouged out the uppermost eye and, with their beaks, scratched the softer skin around the bull's anus, for that was always their access point to a big thick-skinned carcass.

The buffalo was a big mature bull, the great boss of his horns grown solidly together across the crown of his skull, a huge head of horn, forty-eight inches from tip to tip. He was big in the body also, bigger than a prize Hereford stud bull, and he was bald across the shoulders, the scarred grey hide scabbed with dried mud and bunches of bush ticks.

Mark thrust his hand into the crease of skin between the back legs and felt the residual body warmth.

'He's been dead less than three hours,' he decided, and squatted down beside the huge body to determine the cause of death. The bull seemed unmarked until Mark managed to roll him over, exerting all his strength and using the stiffly out-thrust limbs to move the ton and a half of dead weight.

He saw immediately the death wounds, one was behind the shoulder, through the ribs, and Mark's hunter's eye saw instantly that it was a heart-stroke, a wide-lipped wound, driven home deeply; the clotted heart blood that poured from it had jellied on the damp earth.

If there was any doubt at all as to the cause of that injury, it was dispelled instantly when he looked to the second wound. This was a frontal stroke, at the base of the neck, angled in skilfully between bone, to reach the heart again, and the weapon had not been withdrawn, it was still plunged in to the hilt and the shaft was snapped short where the bull had fallen upon it.

Mark grasped the broken shaft, placed one booted foot against the bull's shoulder and grunted with the effort it required to withdraw the blade against the reluctant suck of clinging flesh.

He examined it with interest. It was one of those broad-bladed stabbing spears, the assegai which had been designed by the old king Chaka himself. Mark remembered Sean Courtney reminiscing about the Zulu wars, Isandhlwana, and Morma Gorge.

'They can put one of those assegais into a man's chest and send the point two feet out between his shoulder blades, and when they clear the blade, the withdrawal seems to suck a man as white as though he had his life blood pumped out of him by a machine.' Sean had paused for a moment to stare into the camp fire. 'As they clear, they shout *"Ngidhla!"* I have eaten! Once you have heard it, you'll not forget it. Forty years later, the memory still makes the hair come up on the back of my neck.'

Now still holding the short heavy assegai, Mark remembered that Chaka himself had hunted the buffalo with a similar weapon. A casual diversion between campaigns – and as Mark glanced from the blade to the great black beast, he felt his anger tempered with reluctant admiration. His anger was for the wanton destruction of one of his precious animals, and his admiration was for the special type of courage that had done the deed.

Thinking of the man, Mark realized that there must have been special circumstances for that man to abandon such a valuable, skilfully and lovingly wrought weapon together with the prize he had risked his life to hunt.

Mark began to back-track the sign in the soft black earth, and he found where the bull had come up one of the tunnel-like pathways through the reeds after drinking. He found where the huntsman had waited in thick cover beside the path, and his bare footprints were unmistakable.

'Pungushe!' exclaimed Mark.

Pungushe had lain upwind and, as the bull passed, he had put the steel behind his shoulder, deeply into the heart.

The bull had leapt forward, crashing into a ponderous gallop as Pungushe cleared his point, and the blood had sprayed from the wide wound as though the standing reeds had been hosed by a careless gardener.

The buffalo is one of the few wild animals which will turn and actively hunt its tormentor. Although the bull was dead on his feet, spurting blood with every lunging stride, he had swung wide into the wind to take Pungushe's scent and when he had it, he had steadied into that terrible crabbing, nose up, wide-horned, relentless charge that only death itself will stop.

Pungushe had stood to meet him as he came thundering down through the reeds, and he had picked the point at the base of the neck for his second stroke and put the steel in cleanly to the heart, but the bull had hit him also, before blundering on a dozen paces and falling to his knees with that characteristic death bellow.

Mark found where Pungushe had fallen, his body marks etched clearly in the soft clay.

Mark followed where he had dragged himself out of the edge of the reed beds and shakily regained his feet.

Slowly Pungushe had turned northwards, but his stride was cramped, he was heeling heavily, not up on his toes, not extended into his normal gait.

He stopped once where he had left his steel-jawed spring trap, and he hid it in an ant bear hole and kicked sand over it, obviously too sick and weak to carry it or to cache the valuable trap more securely. Mark retrieved the trap and, as he tied it on to Trojan's saddle, he wondered briefly to how many of his animals it had dealt hideous death.

A mile further on, Pungushe paused to gather leaves from one of the little turpentine bushes, a medicinal shrub, and then he had gone on slowly, not using the rocky ridges, not covering or back-tracking as he usually did.

At the sandy crossing of one of the steep narrow dry water courses, Pungushe had dropped on one knee, and had used both hands to push himself upright.

Mark stared at the sign for there was blood now for the first time, black droplets that had formed little pellets of loose sand, and in his anger and jubilation, Mark felt a prick of real concern.

The man was hard hit, and he had once saved Mark's life. Mark could still remember the blessed taste of the bitter medicine in the black baked pot cutting through the terrible thirsts of malaria.

He had been leading Trojan up to this point, to keep down, to show a low silhouette, so as not to telegraph heavy hoof-beats ahead to his quarry.

Now he swung up into the saddle, and kicked the mule into a plunging sway-backed canter.

Pungushe was down. He had gone down heavily at last, dropping to the sandy earth. He had crawled off the game path, under a low bush out of the sun, and he had pulled the light kaross of monkey-skins over his head, the way a man settles down to sleep – or to die.

He lay so still that Mark thought he was indeed dead. He slipped down off Trojan's back and went up cautiously to the prostrate body. The flies were buzzing and swarming gleefully over the bloody bundle of green turpentine leaves that were bound with strips of bark around the man's flank and across the small of his back.

Mark imagined clearly how he had received that wound, Pungushe standing to meet the charging buffalo, going for the neck with the short heavy-bladed assegai, putting the steel in cleanly and then jumping clear, but the bull pivoting hard on his stubby front legs and hooking with the massive bossed and wickedly curved horns.

Pungushe had taken the hook low in the side, far back behind the hip-bone of the pelvis. The shock would have hurled him clear, giving him time to crawl away while the bull staggered on, fighting the deep steel in his chest, until at last he had gone down on his fore-legs with that last defiant death bellow.

Mark shuddered in the harsh sunlight at the wound that bundle of leaves covered, and went down on one knee to brush the flies away.

Now for the first time, he became aware of the man's physique. The kaross covered his head and shoulders only, the great chest was exposed. A loin-cloth of softly tanned leather embroidered with blue beads was drawn up between his legs, leaving free the solid bulge of his buttocks, and the sinewy thews of his thighs and the flat hard plain of the belly.

Each separate muscle was clearly defined, and the ropey veins below the surface of the skin were like bunches of serpents, testimony to the man's tremendous physical development and fitness. The skin itself was lighter than that of the average Zulu. It had the smooth dark buttery colour and lustre of a woman's skin, but tight dark curls covered the chest.

'I baited for a jackal,' Mark thought wonderingly, 'and I caught myself a lion, a big old black-maned lion.' And now he felt real concern that Pungushe was dead. For such a splendid animal, death was a shabby bargain.

Then he saw the gentle, almost imperceptible rise and fall of the deep muscled chest, and he reached out and touched the shoulder through the kaross.

The man stirred, and then painfully lifted himself on one elbow, letting the kaross fall back, and he looked at Mark.

He was a man in the full noon of his strength and pride and dignity, perhaps forty years of age, with just the first frosts of wisdom touching the short cap of dark wool at his temples.

The agony did not show in his face, the broad forehead was smooth as polished amber, the mouth was in repose, and the eyes were dark and fierce and proud. It was the handsome moon face of the high-bred Zulu.

'Sakubona, Pungushe,' said Mark. 'I see you, O Jackal.'

The man looked at him for a moment, thinking about the name and the style of greeting, the language and the accent in which it was spoken. The calm expression did not change, no smile nor snarl on the thick sculptured lips, only a new light in the dark eyes.

'Sakubona, Jamela. I see you, O Seeker.' His voice was deep and low, yet it rang on the still air with the timbre of a bronze gong, and then he went on immediately, 'Sakubona, Ngaga.'

Mark blinked. It had never occurred to him that the jackal might think of him by a name every bit as derogatory. Ngaga is the pangolin, the scaly ant-eater, a small creature that resembles an armadillo, a nocturnal creature, which if caught out in daylight, scurries around like a bent and wizened old man pausing to peer shortsightedly at any small object in its path, then hurrying on again.

The two names 'Jamela' and 'Ngaga' used together described with embarrassing clarity somebody who ran in small circles, peering at everything and yet blindly seeing nothing.

Suddenly Mark saw himself through the eyes of a hidden observer, riding a seemingly pointless patrol through the valley, dismounting to peer at anything that caught his interest, then riding on again – just like an ngaga. It was not a flattering thought.

He felt with sudden discomfort that despite Pungushe's wounds, and Mark's position of superiority, so far he had had the worst of the exchange.

'It seems the ngaga has at last found what he seeks,' he pointed out grimly, and went to the mule for his blanket roll.

Under the bloody bunch of leaves there was a deep dark hole where the point of the buffalo horn had driven in. It might have gone in as far as the kidneys, in which case the man was as good as dead. Mark thrust the thought aside, and swabbed out the wound as gently as he could with a solution of acriflavine.

His spare shirt was snowy white and still crisp from Marion's meticulous laundering and ironing. He ripped off the sleeves, folded the body into a wad and placed it over the gaping hole, binding it up with the torn sleeves.

Pungushe said nothing as he worked, made no protest nor showed any distress as Mark lifted him into a sitting position to work more easily. But when Mark ripped the shirt he murmured regretfully,

'It is a good shirt.'

'There was once a young and handsome ngaga who might have died from the fever,' Mark reminded him, 'but a scavenging old jackal carried him to a safe place and gave him drink and food.'

'Ah,' Pungushe nodded. 'But he was not such a stupid jackal as to tear a good shirt.'

'The ngaga is much concerned that the jackal is in good health, so that he will be able to labour mightily at the breaking of rocks and other manly tasks when he is an honoured guest at the kraal of King Georgey.' Mark ended that subject, and repacked his blanket roll. 'Can you make water, O Jackal? It is necessary to see how deep the buffalo has speared you.'

The urine was tinged pinky brown, but there were no strings of bright blood. It seemed that the kidneys may merely have been badly bruised, and that the thick pad of iron muscle across the Zulu's back had absorbed much of the brutal driving thrust. Mark found himself praying silently that it was so, although he could not imagine why he was so concerned.

Working quickly, he cut two long straight saplings, and plaited a drag litter from strips of wet bark. Then he padded the litter with his own blankets and Pungushe's kaross, before hitching it up to Trojan.

He helped the big Zulu into the litter, surprised to find how tall he was, and how hard was the arm he placed around Mark's shoulder to support himself.

With Pungushe flat in the litter, he led the mule back along the game trail, and the ends of two saplings left a long snaking drag mark in the soft earth.

It was almost dark when they passed the scene of the buffalo hunt. Looking across the reed banks, Mark could make out the obscene black shapes of the vultures in the trees, waiting their turn at the carcass.

'Why did you kill my buffalo?' he asked, not certain that Pungushe was still conscious. 'All men know the new laws. I have travelled to every village, I have spoken with every induna, every chief – all men have heard. All men know the penalty for hunting in this valley.'

'If he was your buffalo, why did he not carry the mark of your iron? Surely it is the custom of the *Abelungu* – the white men – to burn their mark upon their cattle?' Pungushe asked from the litter, without a smile nor with any trace of mockery, yet mockery Mark knew it was. He felt his anger stir.

'This place was declared sacred, even by the old king, Chaka.'

'No,' said Pungushe. 'It was declared a royal hunt, and,' his voice took a sterner ring, 'I am Zulu, of the royal blood. I hunt here by my birthright – it is a man's thing to do.'

'No man has the right to hunt here.'

'Then what of the white men who have come here with their *isibamu* – their rifles – these past hundred seasons?' asked Pungushe.

'They are evil-doers, even as you are.'

'Then why were they not taken to be guests at the kraal of King Georgey, as I am so honoured?'

'They will be in future,' Mark assured him.

'Ho!' said Pungushe, and this time his voice was thick with contempt and mockery.

'When I catch them, they will go also,' Mark repeated doggedly, but the Zulu made a weary gesture of dismissal with one expressive pink-palmed hand, a hand that said clearly that there were many laws – some for rich, some for poor, some for white and some for black. They were silent again until after dark when Mark had camped for the night, and put Trojan to graze on a head-rope.

As he squatted over the fire, cooking the evening meal for both of them, Pungushe spoke again from his litter in the darkness beyond the firelight.

'For whom do you keep the *silwane* – the wild animals of the valley? Will King Georgey come here to hunt?'

'Nobody will ever hunt here again, no king nor common man.'

'Then why do you keep the *silwane*?'

'Because if we do not, then the day will dawn when there will be no more left in this land. No buffalo, no lion, no kudu, nothing. A great emptiness.'

Pungushe was silent for the time it took Mark to spoon a slop of maize porridge and bully beef into the lid of the pannikin and take it to the Zulu.

'Eat,' he commanded, and sat cross-legged opposite him with his own plate in his lap.

'What you say is true,' Pungushe spoke thoughtfully. 'When I was a child – of your age,' Mark noted the barb but let it pass, 'there were elephant in this valley, great bulls with teeth as long as a throwing-spear, and there were many lions, herds of buffalo like the great king's cattle,' he broke off. 'They have gone, soon what is left will go also.'

'Is that a good thing?' Mark asked.

'It is neither a good thing nor a bad thing.' Pungushe shrugged and began to eat. 'It is merely the way of the world – and there is little profit in pondering it.'

They finished eating in silence and Mark cleared the plates and brought coffee, which Pungushe waved away.

'Drink it,' snapped Mark. 'You must have it to cleanse the blood from your water.'

He gave Pungushe one of his cigarettes, and the Zulu carefully broke off the brown cork tip before putting it between his lips. He wrinkled his broad flat nose at the insipid taste, for he was accustomed to the ropey black native tobacco, but he would not belittle a man's hospitality by making comment.

'When it is all gone, when the great emptiness comes here to this valley, what will become of you, O Jackal?' Mark asked.

'I do not understand your question.'

'You are a man of the *silwane*. You are a great hunter. Your life is yoked to the *silwane*, as the herdsman is yoked to his cattle. What will become of you, O mighty hunter, when all your cattle are gone?'

Mark realized that he had reached the Zulu. He saw his nostrils flare, and something burn up brightly within him, but he waited while Pungushe considered the proposition at great length and in every detail.

'I will go to *Igoldi*,' said Pungushe at last. 'I will go to the gold mines, and become rich.'

'They will put you to work deep in the earth, where you cannot see the sun nor feel the wind, and you will break rocks, just as you go now to do at the kraal of King Georgey.'

Mark saw the repugnance flit across the Zulu's face.

'I will go to *Tekweni*,' Pungushe changed his mind. 'I will go to Durban and become a man of much consequence.'

'In *Tekweni* you will breathe the smoke of the cane mills into your lungs, and when the fat babu overseer speaks to you, you will reply, *yehbo*, Nkosi – yes, master!'

This time the repugnance on the Zulu's face was deeper still and he smoked his cigarette down to a tiny sliver of paper and ash which he pinched out between thumb and forefinger.

'Jamela,' he said sternly. 'You speak words that trouble a man.'

Mark knew well that the big Zulu's injury was more serious than his stoic acceptance of it would indicate. It was womanly to show pain.

It would be a long time before he was ready to make the journey by side-car over the rough tracks and rutted dusty roads to the police station and magistrate's court at Ladyburg.

Mark put him into the small lean-to tool-shed that he had built on to the far wall of the mule stables. It was dry and cool, and had a sturdy door with a Yale padlock. He used blankets from Marion's chest and the mattress she had been saving for the children's room, despite her protests. 'But he's a native, dear!'

Every evening, he took the prisoner's meal down to him in the pannikin, inspected the wound and dressed it afresh.

Then while he waited for Pungushe to eat, he sat on the top step in the doorway to the shed and they smoked a cigarette while they talked.

'If the valley belongs now to King Georgey, how is it that you build your house here, plant your gardens and graze your mules?'

'I am the king's man,' Mark explained.

'You are an induna?' Pungushe paused with a spoon of food halfway to his mouth, and stared at Mark incredulously. 'You are one of the king's counsellors?'

'I am the keeper of the royal hunt,' Mark used the old Zulu title, and Pungushe shook his head sadly.

'My father's father was once the keeper of the royal hunt – but he was a man of great consequence, with two dozen wives, a man who had fought in a dozen wars, and killed so many enemies that his shield was as thick with oxtails as there is grass on the hills in springtime.' The oxtail was the decoration which the king grants a warrior to adorn his shield when he has distinguished himself in battle. Pungushe finished his meal and added simply,

'King Chaka knew better than to send a child to do man's work.'

The next evening Mark saw that the wound was healing cleanly and swiftly. The man's tremendous fitness and strength were responsible for that. He was able to sit cross-legged now, and there was a new jauntiness in the way he held his head. It would be sooner than Mark had thought that Pungushe would be fit enough to make the journey to Ladyburg, and Mark felt an odd sinking feeling of regret.

'King Georgey is doubtlessly a great, wise and all-seeing king,' Pungushe opened the evening's debate. 'Why then does he wait until sundown to begin work that should have been started at dawn? If he wanted to avoid the great emptiness in this valley, his father should have begun the work.'

'The king's affairs are many, in far countries. He must rely on indunas to advise him who are not as wise or all-seeing,' Mark explained.

'The *Abelungu* – the white men – are like greedy children, grabbing up handfuls of food they cannot eat. Instead they smear it over their faces.'

'There are greedy and ignorant black men also,' Mark pointed out. 'Some who even kill leopards with steel traps for their fur.'

'To sell to the greedy white men, to dress their ignorant women,' Pungushe agreed, and that makes the score deuce, Mark thought as he gathered up the empty pannikins.

The next evening Pungushe seemed sad, as at the time of leave-taking.

'You have given me much on which I must think heavily,' he said.

'You will have much time to do so,' Mark agreed. 'In between the breaking of rocks.' And Pungushe ignored the reference.

'There is weight in your words, for one who is still young enough to be herding the cattle,' he qualified the compliment.

'Out of the mouths of babes and sucklings,' Mark translated into Zulu and Pungushe nodded solemnly, and in the morning he was gone.

He had opened the thatch at the back of the roof, and wriggled through the small hole. He had taken his kaross and left Marion's blankets neatly folded on the mattress. He had tried for the steel spring-trap, but Mark had locked it in the kitchen, so he had left it and gone northwards in the night.

Mark was furious for so misjudging his prisoner's recovery, and he muttered darkly as he plunged along after him on Trojan.

'This time I'm going to shoot the bastard on sight,' he promised, and realized at that moment that Pungushe had back-tracked on him. He had to dismount and laboriously unravel the confused trail.

Half an hour later, Pungushe led him into the river, and it was well after noon when he at last found where the Zulu had left the water, stepping lightly on a fallen log.

He finally lost the cold spoor in the rocky ground on the far rim of the valley, and it was almost midnight when he rode wearily back to the thatched cottage. Marion had his dinner ready and ten gallons of hot water bubbling on the fire.

Six weeks later, Pungushe returned to the valley. Mark sat astounded on the stoep of the cottage, and watched him come.

He walked with the long gliding stride that showed he was fully recovered from his wound. He wore the beaded loin-cloth and the jackal-skin cloak over his shoulders. He carried two of the short-shafted stabbing assegai, with the broad steel blades, and his wives followed at a respectable distance behind him.

There were three of them. They were bare-breasted, with the tall clay headdress of the Zulu matron. The senior was of the same age as her husband, but her dugs were flat and empty as leather pouches and she had lost her front teeth. The youngest wife was a child still in her teens, a pretty plump little thing with jolly melon breasts, and a fat brown infant on her hip.

Every wife carried an enormous bundle on her head, balancing it easily without use of hands, and they were followed by a gaggle of naked and half-naked children. Like their mothers, the little girls each carried a headload, the size of it directly proportional to the age and stature of the bearer. The smallest, perhaps four years of age, carried a beer gourd the size of a grapefruit, echoing faithfully the straight erect carriage and swaying buttocks of her seniors.

Mark counted seven sons and six daughters.

'I see you, Jamela.' Pungushe paused below the stoep.

'I see you also, Pungushe,' Mark acknowledged cautiously, and the Zulu squatted down comfortably on the lowest step. His wives settled down at the edge of Marion's garden – politely out of earshot. The youngest wife gave one of her fat breasts to the infant and he suckled lustily.

'It will rain tomorrow,' said Pungushe. 'Unless the wind goes into the north. In which case it will not rain again until the full moon.'

'That is so,' Mark agreed.

'Rain now would be good for the grazing. It will bring the *silwane* down from the Portuguese territory beyond the Pongola.'

Mark's astonishment had now given way to lively curiosity.

'There is talk in the villages, common word among all the people that has only recently come to my ears,' Pungushe went on airily. 'It is said that Jamela, the new keeper of the royal hunt of King Georgey, is a mighty warrior who has slain great multitudes of the king's enemies in the war beyond the sea.' The Jackal paused and then went on, 'Albeit, he is still unbearded and green as the first flush of the spring-time grass.'

'Is that the word?' Mark inquired politely.

'It is said that King Georgey has granted Jamela a black oxtail to wear on his shield.' A black oxtail is the highest honour, and might loosely be considered the equivalent of a MM.

'I am also a warrior,' Pungushe pointed out. 'I fought with Bombata at the gorge, and afterwards the soldiers came and took away my cattle. This is how I became a man of *silwane*, and a mighty hunter.'

'We are brothers of the spear,' Mark conceded. 'But now I will make ready my *isi-du-du-du*, my motorcycle, so that we may ride to Ladyburg and speak with the magistrate there of matters of great interest to all of us.'

'Jamela!' The Zulu shook his head grievingly, like a father with an obtuse son. 'You aspire to be a man of the *silwane*, you aspire to fill the great emptiness – and yet who will there be to teach you, who will open your eyes to see and your ears to hear, if I am in the kraal of King Georgey breaking his rocks?'

'You have come to help me?' Mark asked. 'You and your beautiful fat wives, your brave sons and nubile daughters?'

'It is even so.'

'This is a noble thought,' Mark conceded.

'I am Zulu of royal blood,' Pungushe agreed. 'Also my fine steel trap was stolen from me, even as my cattle were stolen, thus making me a poor man once more.'

'I see,' Mark nodded. 'It remains only for me to put out of my mind the business of leopard skins and dead buffalo?'

'It is even so.'

'Doubtless I will also find it in my heart, to pay you for this help and advice.'

'That also is so.'

'What size is the coin in which you will be paid?'

Pungushe shrugged with disinterest. 'I am royal Zulu, not a Hindu trader haggling in the market-place. The coin will be just and fair,' he paused delicately, 'always bearing in mind the multitude of my beautiful wives, my many brave sons and the host of nubile daughters. All of whom have unbelievable appetites.'

Mark had to remain silent, not trusting himself to speak until he controlled the violent urge to burst out laughing. He spoke again, solemnly, but with laughter rippling his belly muscles.

'In what style will you address me, Pungushe? When I speak, will you answer "*Yehbo*, Nkosi – Yes, Master."?'

Pungushe stirred restlessly, and an expression flitted across the broad smooth features like a fastidious eater who had just discovered a large fat worm on his plate. 'I will call you Jamela,' he said. 'And when you speak as you have just spoken, I will answer "Jamela, that is a great stupidity."'

'In what style will I address you?' Mark inquired politely, fighting his mirth.

'You will call me Pungushe. For the jackal is the cleverest and most cunning of all the *silwane*, and it is necessary for you to be reminded of this from time to time.'

Then something happened that Mark had not seen before. Pungushe smiled. It was like the break-through of the sun on a grey overcast day. His teeth were big and perfect and white, and the smile stretched so wide that it seemed his face might tear.

Mark could no longer contain it. He laughed out loud, beginning with a strangled chuckle. Hearing it, Pungushe laughed also, a great ringing bell of laughter.

The two of them laughed so long and hard, that the wives fell silent and watched in amazement, and Marion came out on to the stoep.

'What is it, dear?'

He could not answer her, and she went away shaking her head at the craziness of men.

At last they both fell silent, exhausted with mirth, and Mark gave Pungushe a cigarette from which he carefully broke the corked tip. They smoked in silence for nearly a minute, then suddenly without warning Mark let out another uncontrolled guffaw, and it started them off again.

The cords of sinew stood out on Pungushe's neck, like columns of carved ebony, and his mouth was a deep pink cavern lined with perfect white teeth. He laughed until the tears ran down his face and dripped from his chin, and when he lost his breath, he let out a great whistling snort like a bull hippo breaking surface, and he wiped the tears away with his thumb and said, 'Ee – hee!' and slapped his thigh like a pistol shot, between each fresh paroxysm of laughter.

Mark ended it by reaching out his shaking right hand, and Pungushe took it in a reverse grip, panting and heaving still.

'Pungushe, I am your man,' Mark sobbed.

'And I, Jamela, am yours.'

There were four men sitting in a semi-circle around the wall of the hotel suite. They were all dressed in such fashion that it seemed a uniform. The dark high-buttoned suits, the glazed celluloid collars and sober neckties. Although their ages were spread over thirty years, although one of them was bald with grey wisps around his ears and another had a fiery red bush of hair, although one wore a prim gold pince-nez pinched on to a thin aquiline nose while another had the open far-seeing gaze of the farmer, yet all of them had those solid hewn calvinistic faces, indomitable, unrelenting and strong as granite.

Dirk Courtney spoke to them in the young language which had only recently received recognition as a separate entity from its parent Dutch, and had been given the name of Afrikaans.

He spoke it with an elegance and precision that softened the reserve in their expressions, and eased the set of jaw and the stiffness in their backs.

'It's a Jingo area,' Dirk told them. 'There is a Union Jack flying on every roof-top. It's a rich constituency, land-owners, professional men – your party has no appeal there.' He was talking of the parliamentary constituency of Ladyburg. 'In the last elections you did not even present a candidate, nobody fool enough to lose his deposit, and the Smuts Party returned General Courtney unopposed.'

The eldest of his listeners nodded over his gold pince-nez, inviting him to continue.

'If you are to fight the Ladyburg seat, you will need a candidate with a different approach, an English speaker, a man of property, somebody with whom the voters can identify –'

It was a beautiful performance. Dirk Courtney, handsome, debonair, articulate in either language, striding back and forth across the carpeted lounge, holding all their attention, stopping dramatically to make a point with a graceful gesture of strong brown hands, then striding on again. He talked for half an hour, and he was watching his audience, noting the reaction of each, judging their weaknesses, their strengths.

At the end of that half hour, he had decided that all four of them were dedicated, completely committed to their political faith. They stirred only at appeals to patriotism, to national interest, at reference to the aspirations of their people.

'So,' Dirk Courtney thought comfortably. 'It's cheaper to buy honest men. Rogues cost good bright gold – while honest men can be had with a few fine words and noble sentiments. Give me an honest man every time.'

One of the older men leaned forward and asked quietly,

'General Courtney has had the seat since 1910. He is a member of the Smuts Cabinet, a war hero, and a man of huge popular appeal. He is also your father. Do you think the voters will take the young dog when they can have the sire?'

Dirk answered: 'I am prepared not only to risk my deposit if I achieve the National Party nomination, but I am confident enough of my eventual success to make a substantial earnest of my serious intentions to the campaign funds of the party.' He named a sum of money that made them exchange quick glances of surprise.

'In exchange for all this?' the elder politician asked.

'Nothing that is not in the best interest of the nation, and of my constituency,' Dirk told them soberly, and he pulled down the map that hung on the far wall facing them.

Again he began to speak, but now with the contagious fervour of the zealot. In burning words, he built up a vision of ploughed fields stretching to the horizon, and sweet clean water running deep in endless irrigation furrows. The listeners were all men who had farmed and ploughed the rich but hostile soil of Africa, and all of them had searched blue and cloudless skies with hopeless eyes for the rain clouds that never came. The image of deeply turned furrows and slaking water was irresistible.

'Of course, we will have to repeal the proclamation on the Bubezi Valley,' Dirk said it glibly, and not one of them showed shock or concern at the statement. Already they could see the inland sea of sweet limpid water ruffling in the breeze.

'If we win at this election,' the eldest politician began.

'No, Menheer,' Dirk interrupted gently, '*when* we win.'

The man smiled for the first time. 'When we win,' he agreed.

*   *   *

Dirk Courtney stood high on the platform, with thumbs hooked into his waistcoat. When he smiled and tilted that noble lion head with the shining mane of curls, the women in the audience that packed the church hall rustled like flowers in the breeze.

'The Butcher,' said Dirk Courtney, and his voice rang with a depth and resonance that thrilled them all, man and woman, young and old. 'The Butcher of Fordsburg, his hands red with blood of our countrymen.'

The applause began with the men that Dirk Courtney had in the audience, but it spread quickly.

'I rode with Sean Courtney against Bombata –' one man was on his feet, near the back of the hall. 'I went to France with him,' he was shouting to be heard above the applause. 'And where were you, Mr Dirk Courtney, when the drums were beating?'

The smile never left Dirk's face, but two little spots of hectic colour rose in his cheeks.

'Ah!' He faced the man across the craning heads of the audience. 'One of the gallant General's gunmen. How many women did you shoot down at Fordsburg?'

'That doesn't answer my question,' the man shouted back, and Dirk caught the eye of one of the two big men who had risen and were closing in quietly on the questioner.

'Four thousand casualties,' said Dirk. 'The Government would like to hide that fact from you, but four thousand men, women and children –'

The two big men had closed in on their quarry, and Dirk Courtney drew all eyes with a broad theatrical gesture.

'A Government that has that contempt for the life, property and freedom of its people.'

There was a brief scuffle, a yelp of pain and the man was hustled out of the side door into the night.

The newspapers started picking it up almost immediately, the same editorials which had ranted against the 'Red Cabal' and the 'Bolshevik threat', which had praised Smuts's 'direct and timely action', were now remembering 'a high-handed and brutal solution'.

Across the nation, begun by Dirk Courtney and picked up by all the Hertzoglites, the balance of public feeling was swinging back, like a pendulum, or the curved blade of the executioner's axe.

Dirk Courtney spoke in the Town Hall of Durban, to three thousand, in the Church Hall of Ladyburg to three hundred. He spoke at every country church in the constituency, at little crossroad general-dealer shops where a dozen voters assembled for an evening's entertainment, but always the Press was represented.

Dirk Courtney worked slowly northwards, during the day visiting all his land holdings, each of his new cane mills, and each evening he spoke to the little assemblies of voters. Always he was vibrant and compelling, handsome and articulate, and he painted a picture for them of a land crossed with railways and fine roads, of prosperous towns, and busy markets. They listened avidly.

'There are two,' said Pungushe. 'One is an old lion. I know him well. He stayed last year in Portuguese territory along the north bank of the Usutu River. He was alone then, but now he has found a mate.'

'Where did they cross?' Mark asked.

'They crossed below Ndumu, and came south between the swamp and the river.'

The lion was five years old, and very cunning, a lean tom, tall at the shoulder and with a short ruff of reddish mane. There was an ugly bald scar across his forehead, and he favoured his right foreleg where a piece of hammered pot-leg fired from a Tower musket two years previously had lodged against the shoulder joint. He had been hunted by man almost without remission since he was a cub, and he was getting old now, and tired.

He crossed the river in the dark, swimming his lioness ahead of him, going south from the hunters who had assembled to drive the bush along the river the next morning. He could hear the drums still beating, and smell the smoke of their fires. He could hear also the yapping clamour of the dog packs. They had assembled, two or three hundred tribesmen with their hunting dogs and a dozen Portuguese half-breeds with breech-loading rifles, for the lions had killed two trek oxen on the outskirts of one of the river villages. In the morning the hunt would begin, and the lion took his mate south.

She was also a big animal, and though she was still very young and not as experienced, yet she was quick and strong, and she learned from him each day. Her hide was still clean and unscarred by claw or thorn. Across the back she was a sleek olive tan shading down to a lovely buttery yellow at the throat and fluffy cream on the belly.

She still had traces of her kitten spots dappling her quarters, but the night they swam the Usutu, she came into season for the first time.

On the south bank, they shook the water from their bodies, with fierce shuddering spasms, and then the lion snuffed at her, drumming softly in his throat and then lifting his snout to the bright white stars, his back arching reflexively at the tantalizing musk of her pale blood-tinged oestrous discharge.

She led him half a mile up one of the thickly wooded tributary valleys, and then she crept into the heart of the thicket of tangled bush, a stronghold guarded by the fierce two-inch, wickedly hooked thorns, tipped in red as though they had already drawn blood.

Here in the dawn, he covered her for the first time. She crouched low against the earth, hissing and crackling with angry snarls, while he came over her, biting at her ears and neck, forcing her to submit. Afterwards, she lay close against him, licking at his ears, nuzzling his throat and belly, turning half away from him and nudging him flirtatiously with her hind quarters, until he rose and she crouched down submissively and snarled at him while he mounted her briefly once again.

They mated twenty-three times that day, and in the night they left the thorn thicket and wandered southwards again.

A half hour before the set of the moon, they reached the edge of the ploughed land, and the lion stopped and growled softly at the smell of man and cattle.

Tentatively he reached out one paw and tested the freshly turned earth, then he drew his leg back and made a little troubled mewing sound of indecision. The lioness brushed herself lovingly against him, but he turned aside and led her along the edge of the ploughed land.

'Will they reach the valley, Pungushe?' Mark asked, leaning out of the saddle to speak to the Zulu as he trotted at Trojan's shoulder.

Pungushe spoke easily, despite the fact he had run without rest for nearly three hours. 'They must cross almost half a day's march of land where men are working, where the ploughs of the new sugar-growers are busy. Besides, Jamela, they know nothing of your valley, and the mad Ngaga who would welcome them.' Mark straightened in the saddle and rode on grimly. He knew that this pair, this mating pair, would be his last chance to have lions in his valley. Yet there was twenty miles of danger to cross such as these animals, coming out of the wilderness of Portuguese Mozambique, would never have experienced before, ploughlands, declared cattle area, where lions were vermin. An area devoid of wild prey, but heavily populated with domestic animals. An area where the cry of 'Lion' would send fifty men running eagerly for a rifle, fifty white men competing fiercely for the trophy, hating the big predatory cats with a blind unthinking hatred, welcoming what was probably their only chance at one of them, safe in the knowledge that they were fair game, unprotected by law in the cattle areas.

The lions came to the camp downwind, and they lay flat in the short grass in the darkness at the edge of the camp.

They listened to the drowsy voices of the men at the fire, and smelled the myriad strange smells, of tobacco smoke, of cooking maize meal and the sour tang of Zulu beer, and they lay very flat and tense against the earth, only their round black-tipped ears cocked and their nostrils flaring and sucking the air.

The oxen were kraaled with a low circular enclosure of felled thorn trees, arranged with their trunks inward and the bushy thorny tangle outwards. The smell of the cattle was strong and tempting.

There were seventy-two oxen in the kraal, two full spans. They belonged to Ladyburg Sugar Company and they were ploughing the new lands east of Chaka's Gate, after the labour teams had stumped out the standing timber and burned it in long windrows.

The lion waited, patient, but alert and tensed and silent, while the silver moon went down below the trees and the men's voices dwindled into silence. He waited while the fires died down into puddles of dull ruddy ash. Then he rose silently.

The lioness did not move, except that the great muscles in her chest and limbs swelled, rigid with tension, and her ears cocked fractionally forward.

The lion circled cautiously upwind of the camp. There was a soft cool wash of breeze coming steadily out of the east and he used it skilfully.

The oxen caught the whiff of lion as he moved into the wind, and he heard them coming up, rising in that awkward plunging leap from where they had settled.

Horns clashed together as they swung into a tight group facing upwind, and one of them let out a soft mournful lowing. Immediately it was taken up, and their low bellows woke the men at the fires. Somebody shouted, and threw a log on the fire. A torrent of sparks rose into the dark branches of the mimosa and the log caught, lighting the camp with a yellow leaping dancing light. The ploughmen and the lead boys were gathered fearfully around the fire, still with skin karosses draped around their shoulders, owl-eyed with sleep and alarm.

The lion slipped like a shadow, dark and flat against the earth towards the kraal, and the cattle bunched and bellowed wildly at the sharp rank cat smell.

Against the thorny windward side of the kraal, the lion crouched, arched his back and ejected a stream of urine.

The pungent, biting ammoniac stink was too much for the mass of cattle. In a single solid bunch, they swung away downwind and charged the thorny wall of the temporary kraal, crashing through it without check, and they thundered free, quickly spreading, losing the solid formation and scattering away into the night.

The lioness was ready for them, and she streaked in across the flank of the panicking plunging formation, selecting a single victim, a heavy young beast. She drove him onwards, chivvying him like a sheep dog, crossing and recrossing his frantic driving quarters, running him far from the fires and the ploughmen before coming snaking up alongside and hooking expertly at one of his powerfully driving forelegs, and the curved yellow claws biting in just above the hock until they grated against the bone. Then she went back on her own bunched quarters and dragged the leg to cross the other.

The ox dropped as though he had been shot through the brain, and he somersaulted haunch over head, and slid against the earth on his back, all four legs kicking to the starry sky.

In a rubbery flash of supple speed, the cat closed, judging finely the massive hooves that could have crushed her skull and the wide straight horns which could have impaled her rib to rib.

She bit in hard at the base of the skull, driving the long ivory yellow eye teeth into the first and second vertebrae, so they crunched sharply like a walnut in the jaws of the cracker.

When the lion came padding hurriedly out of the night, she had already opened the belly cavity of the ox and her whole head was red and toffee sticky with blood as she went for liver and spleen and kidneys.

She flattened her ears against her bloody skull and snarled murderously at him, but he put his shoulder to her flank and pushed her aside, she snarled again and he cuffed her with a lordly paw and began to feed in the hole she had made.

She glared at him for a second, then her ears came erect and she began to lick his shoulder with long pink voluptuous strokes, purring with a deep soft rattle in her throat, pressing her long sleek body against him. The lion tried to ignore her and fed with snuffling grunts and wet tearing ripping sounds.

But she became bolder, the eternal female taking advantage of her new highly attractive condition, liberties which before would have brought swift and stern disciplinary action.

Desperately the lion tried to restrain her by placing a huge paw on her head, claws carefully retracted, and gulped furiously, trying to eat the entire ox before she could join in, but she wriggled out from under the paw and licked his ear. He growled half-heartedly, flickered the ear. She inched forward and licked his eyes, so he had to close them tightly, furrowing his brow and trying to feed blind, but finally he surrendered to the inevitable and allowed her to force her head into the bloody crater.

Side by side, purring and growling softly, they fed.

There were eighteen of them, gathered on the wide mosquito-screened veranda of the foreman's cottage under the hissing Petromax lamps. The brandy bottle had been out since sundown, and most of the men were red-faced and bright-eyed as they listened to Dirk Courtney.

'There will be schools and hospitals within a twenty mile ride of everybody,' he promised, and the women looked up from their knitting. They knew what it was like to raise a young family out here. 'This is the beginning only,' he promised the men. 'And those of you who were first in will be the first to profit. Once I am in Parliament, you'll have a strong voice speaking up for you. You'll see improvement here you couldn't imagine possible – and quickly.'

'You're a rich man, Mr Courtney,' one of them said. He was a small trader, not directly employed by Ladyburg Sugar, but sufficiently reliant on it to phrase his question with respect. 'One of the bosses. How come you speak out for the working man?'

'I'm rich because I worked hard, but I know that without you men, I won't be rich much longer. We are linked together like a team.'

They nodded and murmured and Dirk went on quickly. 'One thing I promise you. When I can hire a white man at a decent wage, I won't push in coolie or nigger labour!'

They cheered him then, and filled their glasses to toast him.

'Your present Government, the Smuts men, tried that on the gold mines. Two and tuppence a day for black men, and white men out on the street. When the workers protested, they sent the bloody Butcher of Fordsburg, a man who I am ashamed to call my father –'

There was an urgent hammering on the kitchen door, and the foreman excused himself quietly and hurried out. He was back within a minute and whispered to Dirk Courtney. Dirk grinned and nodded, and turned back to his audience.

'Well, gentlemen, a fine bit of sport in the offing – a lion has killed one of my oxen, down on the new Buli block. The plough boy has just come in to report it. It happened only an hour ago, so we will have an excellent sporting chance at him. May I move closure of this meeting, and we'll meet here again at,' he glanced at his watch, 'at five o'clock tomorrow morning, every man with a horse and rifle!'

Mark and Pungushe slept, each under a single blanket, on the sunbaked earth, with Trojan cropping the scraggy dry yellow grass nearby. There was a cold little breeze out of the east, and they woke in the total dark of not-yet dawn and sat over the fire drinking coffee and smoking silently until Pungushe could take the spoor again.

From the back of Trojan it was still too dark to see the ground, but Pungushe ran confidently ahead, forcing the mule into a reluctant lumbering trot to keep pace.

At the edge of the ploughed land, he had to cast, but he cut the lion spoor on its new track almost immediately. They went off again, with the sunrise outlining the upper branches of the trees, turning them black and spiky against the ruddy gold.

The soft amber rays were without warmth, and threw long distorted shadows of mule and men on the hard red earth. Mark marvelled once again that the Zulu could run a spoor in this light over such ground, where he could see no mark or sign of the lions' passing.

There was a single gun shot, so faint that Mark thought he might have imagined it, but Pungushe stopped instantly and signalled him to rein in the mule.

They stood and listened intently, and suddenly there was a distant popping fusillade, ten, eleven rifle-shots and then silence again.

Pungushe turned and looked at Mark expressionlessly. The silence was complete, even the morning bird chorus was stilled by the gunfire for a moment. Then as the silence persisted, a troop of little brown francolin started chirruping again on the edge of the ploughed lands.

'Go on!' Mark nodded to Pungushe, trying to keep his face as expressionless, but his voice shook with outrage. They were too late. The last lions south of the Usutu were dead. He felt sick with helpless anger.

They did not notice Mark until he was right up to them. They were too excited, too intent on their work.

There were eight white men, all heavily armed and dressed in rough hunting clothes, with two Zulu grooms holding the horses.

In a trampled opening among the mimosa trees lay the half-eaten carcass of a red and white ox. However, this was not what was engaging their attention. They were grouped in a tight circle beyond the ox, and their voices were raucous, raised in rough jest and cheerful oath.

Mark dismounted and handed the reins to Pungushe. He walked slowly towards the group, dreading what he would find, but he stopped again as one of the men looked up and saw him. He recognized Mark instantly.

'Ah, warden!' Dirk Courtney laughed, tossing that splendid head of glossy curls. 'We are doing your job for you.' The laughter was sly and spiteful, the malice so apparent that Mark knew he was thinking of the bribe that Mark had accepted and then turned against him.

'Here is one that you can cross off your report,' Dirk chuckled again, and gestured for his men to stand aside. The circle opened and Mark stepped into the opening. The men around him were still red-faced and garrulous, and he could smell the stale liquor on them.

'Gentlemen, may I present the newly appointed warden of Chaka's Gate proclaimed area.' Dirk stood opposite him, across the circle, with one hand thrust carelessly into the pocket of his chamois-leather jacket, a hand-made double barrelled .450 elephant rifle by Gibbs of London tucked into the crook of his elbow.

The lion lay on its side with all four legs extended. He was an old, scarred tom, so lean and rangy that each rib showed clearly through the short tan hair. There were four bullet-holes in the body, the one behind the shoulder would have raked both lungs, but another heavy bullet had shattered the skull. The mouth hung open slackly and a little blood-stained saliva still oozed out on to the lolling pink tongue.

'Congratulations, gentlemen,' Mark nodded, and only Dirk Courtney caught the irony in his voice.

'Yes,' he agreed. 'The sooner we clear this area and make it safe for settlement – the better for all.'

There was a hearty chorus of agreement and one of them produced a brown bottle from his back pocket, and passed it from hand to hand, each in turn pointing its base briefly heavenwards, then exclaiming appreciatively and smacking their lips.

'What about the lioness?' Mark asked quietly, refusing his turn at the bottle.

'Don't worry about her,' one of them assured him. 'She's down already. I hit her clean in the shoulder. We are just giving her a chance to stiffen up, before we go after her to finish her off.' And he drew his sheath knife and began to skin out the carcass of the lion, while his comrades passed loud comment and advice.

Mark walked back to Pungushe who squatted patiently at Trojan's head.

'The lioness is wounded, but has run.'

'I have seen the spoor,' Pungushe nodded, and pointed it out with his eyes, not moving his head.

'How bad is she hit?'

'I do not know yet. I must see how she settles to run before judging.'

'Take the spoor,' said Mark. 'Let us go quietly, without alerting these mighty hunters.'

They drifted away from the clearing, leading the mule casually, Mark following a dozen paces behind the Zulu.

Five hundred yards further on, Pungushe stopped and spoke quietly.

'She is hit in the right shoulder or leg, but I do not think the bone has gone, for she touches with every second pace. She goes well on three legs, and at first there was a little blood, but it dries quickly.'

'Perhaps she bleeds inside?' Mark asked.

'If that is so, we will find her within a short while – dead,' Pungushe shrugged.

'All right.' Mark swung up into the saddle. 'Let us go swiftly, that we may outrun these others, none of them will be able to follow across such hard ground.'

He was too late.

'Anders!' Dirk Courtney shouted, riding up at the head of his band. 'What the hell do you think you are doing?'

'My job,' Mark answered. 'I'm following a wounded beast.'

'We are coming with you.'

Mark glanced at Pungushe, and a silent accord flashed between them, then he turned back to the group.

'You all realize the danger involved? These animals have probably been hunted before, and my tracker thinks the lioness is only lightly hit.'

There was a little sobering and hesitation, but all eight of them rode on after Pungushe. He went hard, loping away, *minza umhlabathi*, stretching the horses into an easy canter and after the first hour Dirk Courtney swore bad-temperedly.

'I don't see any blood.'

'The blood has dried,' Mark told him. 'The wound has closed.'

The contents of the brown bottle were long ago exhausted. Red faces were sweating heavily in the rising heat, eyes were bloodshot and high good humour turning to headaches and woolly tongues; none of them had remembered to bring a water-bottle.

Two of them turned back.

An hour later Dirk Courtney snarled suspiciously, 'This bloody nigger is giving us a bum run. Tell him I'll take the horse-whip to him.'

'The lioness is going strongly –'

'I don't believe it. I can't see any spoor.'

Pungushe stopped abruptly, motioned them to stay and went forward cautiously into a low thicket of waterbuck scrub.

'I've had a guts full of this,' muttered one of the hunters miserably.

'Me too.'

'I've got work to do.'

Three more of them turned back, and those that remained sat their restless horses until Pungushe emerged from the thicket and beckoned them forward.

In the heart of the thicket, impressed deeply into the soft mound of a mole heap he showed them the unmistakable pad of a lioness. It headed relentlessly southward.

'All right,' Dirk Courtney acknowledged. 'He's still on the spoor. Tell him to keep going.'

An hour after noon, the lioness led them on to a low unbroken cap of solid grey granite, and Pungushe sat down wearily. His muscles shone in the sunlight with sweat, as though they had been oiled. He looked up at Mark on the mule and shrugged with an expressive gesture of helplessness.

'Dead spoor,' said Mark. 'Gone away.'

Dirk Courtney pulled up his horse's head with a cruel jerk of the curb, and snapped at Mark.

'Anders. I want to speak to you.' He trotted away out of earshot of the group, and Mark followed him.

They stopped and faced each other, and Dirk's mouth was twisted into a pinched and bitter line.

'This is the second time you have been clever at my expense,' he started grimly. 'You could have had me as an ally – but instead you had my father send me a receipt for my gift. Now you and your savage have pulled another trick. I don't know how you did it, but it's the last time it will happen.'

He stared at Mark, and the slant of the eyes altered, once again that mad malevolent light burned in their depths.

'A powerful friend I would have been – but a much more powerful enemy I am now. So far only my father's protection has saved you. That will change. No man stands in my way, I swear that to you.'

He wheeled his horse, put spurs to it and galloped away. The other two disconsolate hunters trailed away after him.

Mark rode back to Pungushe, and they drank from the water-bottle and smoked a little before Mark asked, 'Where is the lioness?'

'We left her spoor two hours back.'

Mark glanced sharply at him, and Pungushe stood up and walked to another mole heap at the edge of the granite. He squatted beside it, and with a roll of his open palm outlined the fleshy pad of a lion paw, then he bunched his knuckles and rolled them for the toe marks.

Miraculously, the spoor of a full-grown lion appeared in the soft earth, and Pungushe looked up at Mark's startled unbelieving expression and let out one of those whistling hippo-snorts of laughter, rocking back on his heels delightedly. 'For two hours we followed the Tokoloshe,'* he hooted.

'I cannot see her,' said Mark, carefully glassing the shallow wooded valley below them.

'Oh! Jamela, who cannot see.'

'Where is she, Pungushe?'

'Do you see the forked tree, beyond the three round rocks –' A step at a time he directed Mark's gaze, until suddenly he made out just the two dark round blobs of her ears above the short yellow grass, about six hundred yards from where they sat. She was lying close in under the spread of a thorn thicket, and even as he watched, she lowered her head and the ears vanished.

'Not that she is alone, she wishes to return to the place she knows well, beyond the Usutu. That is why she moves always that way, when the pain of the wound allows.'

Before they had come up with her, they had found three places where she had lain to rest, and at one such place there had been a smear of blood and a dozen yellow hairs glued into the clot. Pungushe had inspected the hairs, minutely; by colour and texture he could tell from which part of the lioness's body they had come.

'High in the right shoulder – and if she was bleeding inside she would be down already. But she is in great pain, for she walks short. The wound has stiffened. She cannot go far.'

Now Mark swung the glasses towards the west, and longingly stared through

---

* A Tokoloshe is a mythical creature from Zulu magical legend.

them at the blue misty loom of the cliffs of Chaka's Gate, half a dozen miles away.

'So close,' he murmured, 'so close.' But the exhausted cat was dragging herself painfully away from sanctuary, back towards the ploughed lands, towards cattle and men and the dog packs.

Instinctively he turned in that direction now, swinging the binoculars in a long slow traverse across the north and east.

From the low ridge he had a good field of sight, across miles of light forest to the open chocolate expanse of ploughed land.

Something moved in the field of the binoculars and he blinked his eyes and refocused carefully. Three horsemen were coming slowly in their direction, and even at this range Mark could see the dogs running ahead of them.

Quickly he looked back at the leading rider. There was no mistaking that arrogantly erect figure. Dirk Courtney had not given up the hunt. He had merely returned to assemble a hunting-pack, and now the dogs were coming down fast on the smell of the wounded cat.

Mark laid a hand on the hard muscle of Pungushe's shoulder, and with his free hand he pointed. The Zulu stood up and stared for a full minute at the oncoming horsemen, then he began to speak quickly.

'Jamela, I will try to call the lioness, and lead her –'

Mark started to ask a question, but Pungushe stopped him harshly. 'Can you pull the dogs away, or stop them?'

Mark thought for a moment, then nodded. 'Give me your snuff, Pungushe.'

He took the snuff horn that hung on a thong around his neck and handed it to Mark without question.

'Go,' said Mark. 'Call my lioness for me.'

Pungushe slipped away down the ridge and left Mark to hurry to Trojan.

There were three sticks of black dried meat left in Mark's food bag. He found two flat stones and pounded the dry meat into a fine powder between them, glancing up every few seconds to see the huntsmen coming on rapidly.

Once the meat was powdered he scooped it into his pannikin and added an ounce of native snuff from the horn, mixing the two powders with his fingers as he ran back down the ridge to intersect the lioness trail at the point they had left it.

When he reached the shoulder of the ridge where the wounded cat had skirted a rocky outcrop, he knelt and made three neat piles of the mixed powder directly in the path of the oncoming dogs.

The dried meat would be irresistible when they reached it, the dogs would sniff at it greedily.

He could hear them already, baying excitedly, coming on swiftly, leading the hunters at a canter. As he ran back up the ridge to where Trojan stood, Mark smiled bleakly. A hound with a good suck of fiery native snuff up his nose wasn't going to smell anything else for at least twelve hours.

The lioness lay on her side, with her mouth open. She panted for air, and her chest pumped like a blacksmith's bellows, and her eyes were tightly closed.

The bullet had been fired from her right quarter. It was a soft lead slug from a .455 Martini Hendry and it had taken her high in the shoulder, but far forward, cutting in through the heavy muscle and grazing the big joint of the shoulder, lacerating sinew and shattering that extraordinary small floating bone, found only in the shoulder of a lion, the lucky bone so prized as a hunter's talisman.

The bullet had missed the artery as it plunged into the neck and lodged there beneath the skin, a lump the size of the top joint of a man's thumb.

The flies swarmed joyously into the mouth of the wound, and she lifted her head and snapped at them, and then mewing softly at the agony that movement had caused, she began to lick the bullet hole carefully, the long tongue rasping roughly against her hide, curling pink and dextrous as it cleansed the fresh little trickle of watery blood that had sprung from it. Then she sank back wearily and closed her eyes again.

Pungushe was aware of the wind in the same way as the helmsman of a tall ship is, for it was as important to him as it is to a mariner. He knew exactly at each moment of the day its force and direction, anticipated any change before it occurred and he did not have to carry an ash bag nor wet a finger, the knowledge was instinctive.

Now he moved carefully into a downwind position from the wounded animal. It did not occur to him to thank any providence for the constant easterly breeze that put him fairly between the cat and the near boundary of Chaka's Gate.

Silent as the cloud shadow moves across the earth, he moved in on the cat, judging the extreme limit of her acute hearing before kneeling facing where she lay three hundred yards away.

He filled and deflated his lungs rapidly a dozen times, the great muscled chest swelling and subsiding as he built up reserves of oxygen in his blood. Then he caught a full breath and stretched out his neck at a peculiar angle, cupping his hands to his gaping mouth to act as a sounding board.

From the depths of the straining chest issued a low drumming rattle, that rose and sank to a natural rhythm and ended with an abrupt little cough.

The lioness's head came up in a single flash of movement, her ears erect, her eyes alight with yellow lights, for in her pain and fear and confusion she had heard the old tom calling to her, that low, far-carrying assembly call with which he had directed her hunting so often, and which he had used to bring her to him when separated in thick bush.

The pain of rising was almost too much for her, the wound had stiffened and her neck and shoulder and chest were crushed under a granite boulder of agony, but at that moment she heard for the first time the distant yelping chorus of the dog pack. She and the old tom had been hunted by dogs before, and the sound gave her strength.

She came up and stood for a moment on three legs, favouring the right fore, panting heavily and then she went forward, whining softly at the pain, carrying the bad leg high, lunging for balance at each stride.

Mark watched from the ridge, saw the yellow cat start to move again, hobbling slowly westwards at last. Far ahead of her, keeping out of sight, the big Zulu trotted, pausing whenever she faltered to kneel and repeat the assembly call of a dominant male lion, and each time the lioness answered him with eager little mewling grunts and hobbled after him, westward towards the dreaming blue hills that guarded the Bubezi Valley.

Mark had heard the old hunters' stories before; old man Anders had always claimed that his gunbearer, who had been killed by an elephant on the Sabi River in '84, could call lions. However, Mark had never seen it done, and secretly had put the story into the category of the picturesque but apocryphal.

Now he saw it happening, and still wanted to doubt it. He watched fascinated from his grandstand upon the ridge, and only a change in the clamour of the dog pack made him swing his binoculars back towards the east.

At the rocky shoulder of the ridge, where he had set his bait of powdered biltong and snuff, the pack milled confusedly. There were eight or nine dogs, a mongrel pack of terriers and boer hounds and ridgebacks.

The determined hunting chorus had disintegrated into a cacophony of whines and yelps, while Dirk Courtney over-rode them, standing in his stirrups to lay about them furiously with the horse-whip.

Mark took Trojan's reins and led him down off the ridge, using what little cover there was, but confident that the huntsmen were too involved with their own problems to look ahead and see him.

When he reached the place beside the thorn thicket where the lioness had last lain, he cut a branch with his clasp knife, and used it like a broom to brush away any sign the cat had left.

He followed slowly westwards towards Chaka's Gate, pausing every few minutes to listen for the drumming lion call, watching the ground as he moved, and using the branch to brush away all lion sign, covering for his lioness, until in the dusk they climbed a low saddle through the hills and in slow, drawn-out procession, went down to the Bubezi River.

Pngushe made his last call in darkness, and then ran out in a wide circle, leaving the lioness within a hundred yards of the river, knowing how she would be burned up by the heat of the wound and crazed for water.

He found Mark by the glow of his cigarette.

'Get up,' said Mark, and gave him an arm. Pungushe did not argue. He had run almost without a pause since before dawn, and he swung up behind Mark.

They rode home, two up on Trojan's broad sway back, and neither of them spoke until they saw the lantern light in the cottage window.

'Jamela,' said Pungushe. 'I feel the way I did the day my first son was born.' And there was a tone of wonder in his voice. 'I did not believe a man could feel thus for a devil that kills cattle and men.'

Lying in the darkness, with Marion beside him in the double bed, Mark told her about it. Trying to convey the wonder and the sense of achievement. He told her what Pungushe had said, and stumbled for words to describe his own feelings, to come haltingly at last into silence.

'That's very nice, dear. When are you going into town again? I want to buy some curtains for the kitchen. I thought a checked gingham would look pretty, what do you think, dear?'

The lioness gave birth to her cubs in the thick jessie bushes that choked one of the narrow tributary valleys which came down off the escarpment.

There were six cubs, but they were almost three weeks old when Mark first saw them. He and Pungushe lay belly down on the edge of the cliff that overlooked the valley when she led them back from the river in the dawn. The cubs followed her in an untidy straggle spread over a hundred yards. The sinew in her right fore had healed crooked and slightly shorter, which gave her a heaviness in her gait, a roll like a sailor's, as she came up the draw. One of the cubs, more persistent than the rest was trying to suckle from her pendulant, heavy, multiple dugs as she walked. He kept making clumsy flying leaps at them as they swung above his head, mostly he fell on his head and got trodden on by his mother's back feet, but once he succeeded and hung like a fat brown tick on one nipple. The lioness whirled about and cuffed him left and right, then began to lick him with a tongue that wrapped around his head entirely and knocked him on his back again.

One of the other cubs was stalking his siblings, crouching in ambush behind a single blade of grass, with flattened ears and viciously slitted eyes. When he leapt out on his brothers and sisters and they totally ignored his warlike manoeuvres, he covered his embarrassment by turning back and sniffing the grass blade with such attention that it seemed this had been his original intention.

Three of the others were hunting butterflies. There had been a new hatching of *colotis ione*. On white and purple wings they fluttered close to the earth and the cubs reared on their hind legs and boxed at them with more gusto than skill, over-balancing at the end of each attack and collapsing in a fluffy tangle of outsized paws.

The sixth cub was hunting the tails of the butterfly-hunters. Every time they slashed their little tufted tails in the feverish excitement of the chase, he pounced upon them with savage growls and they were forced to turn and defend themselves against the sting of his needle-sharp baby teeth.

The progress of the family from river to jessie thicket was a long drawn out series of unseemly brawls, which the lioness finally broke up. She turned back and gave that drumming cough which promised imminent retribution if not obeyed instantly. The cubs abandoned their play, formed an Indian file and trotted after the lioness into the shelter of the jessie.

'I would like to know how many females there are in the litter,' Mark whispered, grinning fondly like a new father as he watched them go.

'If you wish, Jamela, I will go down and look under their tails,' Pungushe offered solemnly. 'And you will treat my widows generously.'

Mark chuckled and led the way back down the side of the hill.

They had almost reached the tree where Mark had left Trojan, when something caught his eyes. He turned aside and kicked hopefully at the little heap of stones, before he realized that they had not been erected by human hands, but had been pushed up by the surface roots of a siringa tree.

He gave a grunt of disappointment and turned away. Pungushe watched him speculatively, but made no comment. He had seen Mark perform that strange little ritual a hundred times before, whenever an unusual rock or pile caught his attention.

It had become a custom that every few evenings Mark would wander across from the thatched cottage at main camp, half a mile to where Pungushe's wives had erected the cluster of huts that was the family home.

Each hut was shaped in the perfect cone of a beehive, long whippy saplings bent in to form the framework and the thatch bound in place by the plaited string of bark stripped from the saplings.

The earth between the huts was smoothed and brushed, and Pungushe's carved wooden stool set before the low doorway of his personal sleeping hut. After Mark's fourth visit another, newly carved stool appeared beside it. Though it was never spoken of, it was immediately apparent that this had been reserved exclusively for Mark's visits.

Once Mark was seated, one of the wives would bring him a bowl to wash his hands. The water had been carried laboriously all the way from the river, and Mark merely damped his fingertips so that it would not be wasted.

Then the youngest wife knelt in front of him, smiling shyly, and offered with both hands a pot of the delicious sour utshwala, the Zulu millet beer, thick as gruel and mildly alcoholic.

Only when Mark had swallowed the first mouthful would Pungushe look up and greet him.

'I see you, Jamela.'

Then they could talk in the relaxed desultory fashion of men totally at ease in each other's company.

'Today, when we came down off the hill after watching the lions, you turned off the path and kicked at some stones. It was for this strange custom I named you, this endless seeking, this looking and never finding.'

Pungushe would never ask the direct question, it would have been the grossest bad manners to ask outright what Mark was looking for; only a child or an umlungu, a white man, would be so callow. It had taken him many months to ask the question, and now he framed it in the form of a state- ment.

Mark took another pull at his beer pot and offered Pungushe his cigarette case. The Zulu declined with an open hand, and instead began to roll his own smoke, coarse tarry black tobacco in a thick roll of brown paper, the size of a Havana cigar. Watching his hands Mark replied:

'My father and my mother died of the white sore throat, diphtheria, when I was a child, and an old man became both father and mother to me.' He started to answer the question in as devious a manner as it had been asked, and Pungushe listened, nodding and smoking quietly.

'So this man, my grandfather whom I loved, is buried somewhere in this valley. It is his grave I seek,' he ended simply, and realized suddenly that Pungushe was staring at him with a peculiar sombre expression.

'What is it?' Mark asked.

'When did this happen?'

'Six seasons ago.'

'Would this old man have camped beneath the wild figs?' Pungushe pointed down the valley. 'Where first you camped?'

'Yes,' Mark agreed. 'He always camped there.' He felt the surge of something in his chest, foreknowledge of something momentous about to happen.

'There was a man,' said Pungushe, 'who wore a hat, a hat under which an impi could have camped –' and he made a circle of his arms, exaggerating only a little the size of a double terai brim, 'and who had a beard, shaped thus like the wings of a white egret –' An image of the old man's forked beard, snowy and stained only around the mouth with tobacco juice, leapt in Mark's mind. 'An old man who walked like the secretary bird when it hunts for locusts in the grass.' The long thin legs, the stooped arthritic shoulders, the measured stride, the description was perfect.

'Pungushe!' Mark exploded with excitement. 'You know him!'

'Nothing moves in this valley, no bird flies, no baboon barks, but the jackal hears and sees.'

Mark stared at him, appalled at his own oversight. Of course Pungushe knew everything. Pungushe the silent watcher, why in God's name had he not thought to ask him before?

'He followed this path.' Pungushe walked ahead of Mark, and with the natural skill of the born actor he mimicked John Anders, the halting gait, and stooped shoulders of an old man. If Mark half closed his eyes, he could see his grandfather as he had seen him so many times before.

'Here he turned off the path,' Pungushe left the game trail and started up one of the narrow dried-out water-courses. Their feet crunched in the sugary sand. Half a mile further, Pungushe stopped and pointed at one of the shiny water-polished black boulders.

'Here he sat and set his rifle aside. He lit his pipe and smoked.'

Pungushe turned and scrambled up the steep bank of the water-course.

'While the old man smoked, the fourth man came up the valley. He came as a hunter, silently, following the easy spoor of the old man.' He used the Zulu word of respect for an elder, *ixhegu*.

'Wait, Pungushe,' Mark frowned. 'You say the fourth man? I am confused. Count the men for me.'

They squatted down on the bank and Pungushe took a little snuff, offered the horn to Mark who refused, then sniffed the red powder out of his palm, closing one nostril at a time with his thumb. He screwed his eyes closed and sneezed deliciously before going on.

'There was the old man, your grandfather, *ixhegu*.'

'That is one.'

'Then there was another old man. Without hair on his head nor on his chin.'

'That is two,' Mark agreed.

'Then there was a young man with very black hair, a man who laughed all the time and walked with the noise of a buffalo herd.'

'Yes. That is three.'

'These three came together to the valley. They hunted together and camped together below the wild figs.'

Pungushe must be describing the Greylings, the father and son who had made the sworn deposition to the Ladyburg magistrate. That was as he had expected, but now he asked, 'What of the fourth man, Pungushe?'

'The fourth man followed them secretly and *ixhegu*, your grandfather, did not know of him. He had always the manner of the hunter of men, watching from cover and moving silently. But once when your grandfather, *ixhegu*, had left camp to hunt alone for birds along the river, this secret man came to the camp below the wild figs and all three of them spoke together, quietly but with closed faces and wary eyes of men who discuss affairs of deadly moment. Then the silent man left them again and went to hide in the bush before *ixhegu* returned.'

'You saw all this, Pungushe?' Mark asked.

'What I did not see, I read in the spoor.'

'Now I understand about the fourth man. Tell me what happened that day.'

'*Ixhegu* was sitting there, smoking his pipe,' Pungushe pointed down into the water-course. 'And the silent one came and stood here, even where we now sit, and he looked down at your grandfather without speaking, holding his *isibamu*, his rifle, thus.'

'What did *ixhegu* do then?' Mark asked. He felt nauseous with the horror of it.

'He looked up and asked a question in a loud voice, as a man does when he is afraid, but the silent one did not reply.'

'Then?'

'I am sorry, Jamela, knowing that *ixhegu* was of your blood, the telling of it gives me pain.'

'Go on,' said Mark.

'Then the silent one fired once with his rifle, and *ixhegu* fell face down in the sand.'

'He was dead?' Mark asked, and Pungushe was silent a moment.

'He was not dead. He was shot here, in the belly. He moved, he cried out.'

'The silent one fired again?' Mark felt the acid bite of vomit in the back of his throat.

Pungushe shook his head.

'What did he do?'

'He sat down on the bank, here where we sit, and he smoked silently, watching the old man *ixhegu* lying down there in the sand, until he died.'

'How long did he take to die?' Mark asked in a choked, angry voice.

Pungushe swept a segment of the sky to indicate two hours of the sun's course. 'At the end *ixhegu* was calling out in Zulu as well as his own language.'

'What did he say, Pungushe?'

'He asked for water, and he called to God and to a woman who might have been his mother or his wife. Then he died.'

Mark thought about it with surges of nausea alternating with flashes of bitter hating anger, and racking grief. He tried to imagine why the killer had let his victim die so slowly, and it was many minutes before he remembered that the story must have already been arranged that the old man was to die in a hunting accident. No man accidentally shoots himself twice. The body was to have only one gunshot wound. But, the stomach was always the most agonizing wound. Mark remembered how the gut-wounded screamed in the trenches as they were being carried back by the stretcher-bearers.

'I grieve with you, Jamela.'

Mark roused himself at Pungushe's words.

'What happened after *ixhegu* died?'

'The other two men, the old bald one and the young loud one, came from the camp. All three of them talked here, beside the body. They talked for a long time, with shouting and red angry faces, and they waved their hands thus, and thus.' Pungushe imitated men in heated argument. 'One pointed here, another pointed there, but in the end the silent one spoke and the other two listened.'

'Where did they take him?'

'First they opened his pockets, and took from them some papers and a pouch. They argued again, and the silent one took the papers and put them back in the dead man's pockets –' Mark realized the wisdom of this. An honest man does not rob the corpse of an accident victim. 'Then they carried him up the bank, and this way –' Pungushe stood and led Mark four hundred yards into the forest, below the first steep gradient of the escarpment. 'Here they found a deep ant-bear hole, and they pushed the old man's body down into it.'

'Here?' Mark asked. There was short rank grass and no sign of a cairn nor a mound. 'I see nothing.'

'They collected rocks from the cliff there and placed them in the hole on top of the body, so that the hyena would not dig it out. Then they covered the rocks with earth, and they smoothed it with a tree branch.'

Mark went down on one knee and inspected the ground.

'Yes,' he exclaimed. There was a very shallow depression in the earth, as though it had subsided a little over an excavation.

Mark drew his sheath-knife and blazed four of the nearest trees, making it easier to return to this place, and he built a small pyramid of rocks on the depressed saucer of earth.

When he had finished, he asked Pungushe, 'Why did you not tell anybody of this before? Why did you not go to the police in Ladyburg?'

'Jamela, the madness of white men does not concern me. Also it is a very long journey to Ladyburg, to the policeman who would say, "Ho, kaffir, and what were you doing in the Bubezi Valley to see such strange events?"' Pungushe shook his head. 'No, Jamela, sometimes it better for a man to be blind and deaf.'

'Tell me truly, Pungushe. If you saw these men again, would you remember them?'

'All white men have faces like boiled yams, red, lumpy and without shape.' Then Pungushe remembered his manners. 'Except you, Jamela, who are not so ugly as all that.'

'Thank you, Pungushe. So you would not know them again?'

'The old bald one and the young loud one I might know.' Pungushe furrowed his brow in thought.

'And the silent one?' Mark asked.

'Ho.' Pungushe's brow cleared. 'Does one forget what a leopard looks like? Does one forget the killer of men? The silent one I would remember at any time and in any place.'

'Good!' Mark nodded. 'Go back home now, Pungushe.'

He waited until the big Zulu was out of sight among the trees, then Mark went down on his knees and removed his hat.

'Well, Pops,' he said, 'I'm not very good at this. But I know you'd have liked to have the words said.' His voice was so hoarse and low that he had to clear his throat loudly before he went on.

The house on Lion Kop was shuttered, and the furniture all under white dust sheets, but the head servant met Mark in the kitchen yard.

'Nkosi has gone to *Tekweni*. He left two weeks ago.'

He gave Mark a breakfast of grilled bacon and fried eggs. Then Mark went out and mounted his motorcycle again. It was a long hard run down to the coast, and Mark had plenty of time to think as the dusty miles spun away under the wheels of the Ariel Square Four.

He had left Chaka's Gate within hours of finding the old man's grave, going instinctively to one man for advice and guidance.

He had wanted Marion to come with him, at least as far as Ladyburg where she could have stayed with her sister. However Marion had refused to leave her home or her garden, and Mark had felt secure in the knowledge that Pungushe would be sleeping in the toolshed behind the stables to guard the homestead in Mark's absence.

Mark had waded the river and trudged up the slope below to the beginning of the track where he kept the motorcycle in its thatched shelter.

It had been a slow, bumpy journey in the dark, and he had reached Lion Kop in the dawn to find Sean Courtney had moved his household to Durban.

Mark rode through the gates of Emoyeni in the late afternoon, and it was like coming home again.

Ruth Courtney was in the rose garden, but she dropped the basket of cut flowers and lifted her skirts to her knees as she ran to meet him, the wide-brimmed straw hat flying from her head and hanging by its ribbon around her throat and her delighted spontaneous laughter ringing like a young girl's.

'Oh Mark – we've missed you so.' She took him in a motherly embrace, kissing both his cheeks. 'How brown and hard you look, and you've filled out beautifully.' She held him at arm's length and felt his biceps in mock admiration before embracing him again. 'The General will be delighted to see you.' She took Mark's arm and led him towards the house. 'He hasn't been well, Mark, but seeing you again will be a tonic to him.'

Mark stopped involuntarily in the doorway and felt the shock dry the saliva under his tongue.

General Sean Courtney was an old man. He sat at the bay windows of the bedroom suite. He wore a plaid dressing-gown and a mohair rug was tucked around his legs. On the table beside him was a pile of files and reports, Parliamentary White Papers and a sheath of letters, all the documentation of his life that Mark remembered so well, but the General had fallen asleep, and the metal-rimmed spectacles had slid down on to the tip of his nose. He snored softly, his lips fluttering at each breath. His face seemed to have wasted so that the bones of cheek and brow stood out gauntly. His eyes receded into deep plum purple cavities, and his skin had a greyish lifeless tinge to it.

But the truly shocking thing was the colour of his beard and the once thick bush of his hair. On Sean Courtney the late snows were falling. His beard had turned into a silver cascade, and his hair was as white and as thin as the fine sun-bleached grasses of the Kalahari desert.

Ruth crossed to his chair and lifted the spectacles off his nose, then gently, with a loving wife's concern, she touched his shoulder.

'Sean, darling. There is somebody here to see you.'

He woke the way an old man wakes, blinking and mumbling, with small inconclusive movements of his hands. Then he saw Mark and his expression firmed, suddenly there was a little of the old sparkle in the dark eyes and the warmth in his smile.

'My boy!' he said, lifting his hands, and Mark stepped forward quite naturally. Then for the first time they embraced like father and son, and afterwards Sean beamed at him fondly.

'I was beginning to believe we had lost you for ever to the ways of the wild.' Then he looked up at Ruth beside his chair. 'In celebration I think we can advance the hour a little, my dear. Won't you have Joseph bring up the tray?'

'Sean, you know what the doctor said yesterday.' But Sean snorted with disgust.

'For fifty years, man and boy, my stomach has got used to its evening dash of John Haig pinch bottle. Lack of it will kill me more swiftly and surely than Doctor Henderson and all his pills and potions and blatant quackeries.' He placed one arm about her waist and squeezed her winningly, 'There's a bonnie girl!'

When Ruth had gone, smiling and shaking her head disapprovingly, Sean waved Mark to the chair opposite him.

'What does the doctor say is wrong with you, sir?'

'Doctor!' Sean blew through his lips. 'The older I get, the less faith I have in the whole sorry bunch.' He reached for the cigar box, 'They even wanted me to stop these. What on earth is the use of living, if you have to give up all the processes of life – I ask you.' He lit the cigar with a flourish and drew on it with relish.

'I'll tell you what's wrong with me, son. Too many years of running hard, of fighting and riding and working. That's all it is. Now I'm having a nice little rest, and in a week or so I'll be chipper and fly as I ever was.'

Ruth brought the silver tray and they sat until it was dark, talking and laughing. Mark told them of the life at Chaka's Gate, about each little triumph, describing the cottage and the work done on the roads; he told them of the buffalo and the lioness and the cubs, and Sean told him of the progress made by their Wildlife Society.

'It's disappointing, Mark, nothing like I had hoped for. It's extraordinary just how little people care about things that don't affect their daily lives directly.'

'I never expected instant success. How can people care about something they have never seen? Once we have made the wilderness accessible, once people can have the experience, like seeing these cubs, it will begin then.'

'Yes,' Sean agreed thoughtfully. 'That's what the true object of the Society is. To educate them.'

They talked on while darkness fell and Ruth closed the shutters and drew the curtains. Mark waited for an opportunity to speak of the true reason for his coming to Emoyeni, but he was uncertain of how it might affect a man who was already sick.

At last he could wait no longer. He drew a deep breath, hoped for grace, and told it quickly and without trimmings, repeating Pungushe's story exactly and describing what he had seen himself.

When he finished, Sean was silent for a long time, staring into his glass. At last he roused himself and began asking questions, shrewd cutting questions that showed his mind was as quick and crisp as it had been before.

'Have you opened the grave?' and Mark shook his head.

'Good,' said Sean and went on. 'This Zulu, Pungushe, was the only witness. How reliable is he?'

They discussed it for another half hour, before Sean asked the one question he had obviously been avoiding.

'You think Dirk Courtney is responsible for this?'

'Yes,' Mark nodded.

'What proof is there?'

'He is the only one who could have profited by my grandfather's murder, and the style is his.'

'I asked what proof there is, Mark.'

'There is none,' he admitted, and Sean was silent again while he weighed it all.

'Mark, I understand just how you feel – and I think you know how I feel. However, there is nothing we can do now that will have any effect, beyond alerting the murderer, whoever he is.' He leaned forward in his chair and stretched out a hand to grip Mark's forearm in a gesture of comfort. 'All we have now is the unsupported testimony of a Zulu poacher who speaks no English. A good lawyer would eat him without spitting out the bones, and Dirk Courtney would have the best lawyer, even if we could trace this mysterious "Silent One" to him and get him into court. We need more than this, Mark.'

'I know,' Mark nodded. 'But I thought we might be able to trace the Greyling father and son. They went to Rhodesia, I believe. The foreman at Ladyburg railway station told me that.'

'Yes, I'll get somebody on to that. My lawyers will know a good investigator.' He made a note on the pad at his side. 'But in the meantime, we can only wait.'

They talked on, but it was clear that the discussion had tired Sean Courtney, and grey and blue shadows etched the lines and wrinkles on his face. He settled down a little deeper in his chair, his beard lowered on to his chest and suddenly he had fallen asleep again. He sagged slowly sideways, the crystal glass fell from his hand to the carpet with a soft thud and splattered a few drops of whisky, and he snored a soft single snort.

Ruth picked up the glass, arranged the rug carefully around his shoulders and signalled Mark to follow her.

In the passage she chatted brightly. 'I have told Joseph to make up your bed in the blue room, and there is a good hot bath waiting. There will be only the two of us for dinner, Mark. The General will have a tray in his room.'

They had reached the door of the library and Mark could be silent no longer. He caught Ruth's arm.

'Mrs Courtney,' he pleaded. 'What is it? What is wrong with him?'

The bright smile faded slowly, and she swayed slightly on her feet. Now for the first time he noticed how the few strands of white had turned to deep iron grey wings at her temples. He saw also the little lines and creases around her eyes, and the deeper furrows of worry across her brow.

'His heart is broken,' she said simply, and then she was weeping. No hysterical sobs or wild cries of grief, but a slow deep welling up of tears that was more harrowing, more poignant than any theatrical display.

'They have broken his heart,' she repeated, and swayed again, so that Mark caught and steadied her.

She clung to him, her face pressed to his shoulder.

'First the estrangement from Dirk and then Michael's death,' she whispered. 'He never let it show, but they destroyed some part of him. Now the whole world has turned against him. The people to whom he has devoted his life in peace and war. The newspapers call him the Butcher of Fordsburg, Dirk Courtney has whipped them upon him like a pack of wild dogs.'

He led her into the library and made her sit on the low buttoned sofa while he knelt beside her and found a crumpled handkerchief in his jacket pocket.

'On top of it all, there is Storm. The way she ran off and married that man. He was a horrible man, Mark. He even came here asking for money, and there was a terrible scene. That's when Sean had his first attack, that night. Then finally there was further shame, further heartbreak when Storm was divorced. It was all too much, even for a man like Sean.'

Mark stared at her. 'Storm is divorced?' he asked softly.

'Yes,' Ruth nodded, and then her expression lightened. 'Oh Mark, I know you and Storm were becoming such good friends. I am sure she is fond of you. Can't you go to her? It might be the cure for which we all pray.'

Umhlanga Rocks was one of those little seaside villages that were scattered along the sandy coast line on each side of the main port of Durban. Mark crossed the low bridge over the Umgeni River, and headed north.

The road cut through the thick jungly coastal bush, dense as an equatorial forest, and hung with ropes of lianas from which the little blue vervet monkeys swung and chattered.

The road ran parallel with the white beaches, but at the twelfth milestone Mark reached the turn-off and went directly down to the coast.

The village was clustered around the iron-roofed Oyster Box Hotel where Mark and Dicky Lancome had danced and dined with Marion and that other nameless girl so long ago.

The only other buildings were twenty or thirty cottages set in large gardens, over-run by the rampant jungle, and overlooking the sea with its rowdy frothing surf and rocky points jutting out from the smooth white beaches.

Ruth had given him accurate directions and Mark parked the motorcycle on the narrow dusty lane and followed the pathway that wound without apparent direction through a wild garden of purple bougainvillaea and brilliant poinsettia.

The cottage was small, and the bougainvillaea had climbed up the pillars of the veranda and spread in brilliant, almost blinding display across the thatched roof.

Mark knew at once that he had the right place, for Storm's Cadillac was parked in the open under the trees. It looked neglected and in careless disrepair. The tread was worn from the tyres, there was a long deep scratch down one side. A side window was cracked, and the paintwork was dull with dust and splattered with the dung of the fruit bats hanging in the tree above.

Mark stopped and stared at the Cadllac for a full minute. The Storm he had known would have stamped her foot and screamed for her father if anybody had tried to make her ride in that.

Mark climbed the veranda steps, and paused to look about him. It was a peaceful and lovely spot, such as an artist might choose, but in its remoteness and its neglected and untrimmed profusion hardly suitable for one of the elegant young ornaments of society.

Mark knocked on the front door, and heard somebody moving about inside for some minutes before the door was opened.

Storm was more beautiful by far than he had remembered. Her hair was long and bleached at the ends by salt water and sun. Her feet were bare, her arms and legs were tanned and slim and supple as ever, but it was her face that had changed.

Although she wore no cosmetics, the skin had the shine of vibrant youth like the lustre inside a sea shell, and her eyes were clear and bright with health, yet there were new depths to them, the petulant set of her mouth had softened, her arrogance had become dignity.

In that moment as they stared at each other he knew that she had indeed grown from girl to woman in the time since he had last seen her. And he sensed that the process had been agonizing, but that from it all was emerging a new value, a new strength, and the love which had been in him all this time spread out to fill his soul.

'Storm,' he said, and her eyes opened wide as she stared at him.

'You!' Her voice was a little cry of pain, and she tried to drag the door closed. Mark jumped forward and held it.

'Storm, I must speak with you.'

She tugged desperately at the door handle.

'Go away, Mark. Please go away.' All the new dignity and poise seemed to crumble and she looked at him with the wide frightened eyes of a child waking from nightmare. At last she knew that she could not force the door against his strength, and she turned away and walked slowly back into the house.

'You shouldn't have come,' she said miserably, and the child seemed to sense the changed air. It squalled.

'Oh hush, baby,' Storm called softly, but her voice goaded it into a fresh outburst, and she crossed the room on bare feet with the long veil of hair hanging down her back.

The room was starkly furnished, the cement floor bare and cool, no rugs to soften them, but along the walls were stacked her canvases, many of them blank, but others half-finished, or completed, and the familiar evocative smell of turpentine was heavy and pungent.

The child lay belly down on a kaross of monkey skins laid out on the cement floor. Legs and arms were spread in that froglike baby attitude, and except for a towelling napkin around the hips, it was naked and sun-tanned. The head was thrown back angrily, and the face flushed with the force of its yells.

Mark stepped into the room, and stared with sickly fascination at the child. He knew nothing of babies, but he could see that this was a sturdy and aggressively healthy small animal. The limbs were strong, kicking and working with a violent swimming motion, and the back was broad and robust.

'Hush now, darling,' cooed Storm, as she knelt beside him, and lifted him under the armpits. The napkin slid down to the child's knees and there was no doubting that he was a boy. His tiny penis stuck out at half mast, like a white finger with its little floppy chef's cap of loose wrinkled skin.

Mark found himself hating this other man's child, with a sudden frightening hatred. Yet he went forward involuntarily to where Storm knelt with the baby in her lap.

Mother's touch had quelled the shouts of anger, and now the boy was smacking his lips and making little anticipatory hunger grunts and pawing demandingly at Storm's bosom.

The child had a fine golden cap of hair, through which Mark could see the perfect round of his skull and the little blue veins under the almost translucent skin. Now that the furious crimson tide of anger had receded from his face, Mark saw how beautiful was the child, as beautiful as the mother – and he hated it, he hated it with a bitter sickening feeling in his stomach, and a corrosive taste in his mouth.

He moved closer, watching Storm wipe a dribble of saliva from the child's chin and hoist up his napkin to his waist.

The child became aware of a stranger. He started and lifted his head to stare at Mark, and there was something hauntingly familiar in that face. The eyes that looked at him had looked at him before, he knew them so well.

'You should not have come,' said Storm, busy with her baby, not able to lift her eyes to him. 'Oh God, Mark, why did you come?'

Mark went down on one knee and stared into the child's face, and it reached out towards him with a pair of plump hands, dimpled and pink and damp with spit.

'What is his name?' Mark asked. Where had he seen those eyes? Involuntarily, he extended his forefinger and the child grabbed it with a fat little chuckle and tried to stuff it into his mouth.

'John,' Storm answered, still not looking at him.

'John was my grandfather's name,' Mark said huskily.

'Yes,' whispered Storm. 'You told me.'

The words meant nothing for a moment, all he was aware of was that the hatred he felt for this little scrap of humanity slowly faded. In its place there grew something else.

Then suddenly he knew where he had seen those eyes.

'Storm?' he asked.

Now she lifted her head, and stared into his face. When she replied she was half proud and half defiant.

'Yes!' she said, and nodded once.

He reached for her clumsily. They knelt facing each other on the monkey-skin kaross, and they embraced fiercely, the child held awkwardly between them, gurgling and hiccuping and drooling merrily as it chewed Mark's finger with greedy toothless gums.

'Oh God, Mark, what have I done to us?' whispered Storm brokenly.

Baby John woke them in the silvery slippery-grey light of before dawn. Mark was grateful to him, for he did not want to miss a minute of that coming day. He watched Storm light the candle and then work over the cradle.

She made small soothing sounds as she changed the baby, and the candlelight glowed on the sweet clean lines of her naked back. Dark silky hair hung over her shoulders, and he saw that childbirth had not thickened her waist, it still had the flared graceful line, like the neck of a wine bottle above the tight round double bulge of her buttocks.

At last she turned and carried the baby to the bed, smiling at Mark as he lifted the blankets for her.

'Breakfast time,' she explained. 'Will you excuse us, please?' She sat cross-legged in the bed, and she took one of her nipples between thumb and forefinger and directed it into the open questing mouth.

Mark drew as close as he could and placed one arm around Storm's shoulders. He watched with total fascination. Her breasts were big now, and heavy, jutting out into rounded cones. There was a pale blue dappling of active veins deep below the skin, and the nipples were the colour of almost ripe mulberries, with the same rough shiny texture. The child's tugging induced a sympathetic blue-white drop of milk to well from the tip of her other breast. It glistened there like a pearl in the candlelight.

John fed with tightly closed eyes and piglet grunts and snuffles. The milk ran from the corners of his mouth, and after the first pangs of his hunger were appeased, Storm had to prod him to keep him from falling asleep again.

At each prod, his jaw worked busily for a minute or so, and then the level of activity slowly declined until the next prod.

Storm changed him from one breast to the other and laid her own cheek gratefully against the hard lean muscle of Mark's chest.

'I think I am happy,' she murmured. 'But I've been unhappy for so long that I am not quite sure.'

John lay in a puddle of sea water two inches deep. He was stark naked and brown all over to prove this was no unusual state. He slapped at the water with both hands, and it splashed into his face so that he gasped and blinked his eyes and licked his lips, uncertain whether to be angry or to cry. Instead he repeated the experiment with exactly the same consequences, and he spluttered sand and sea water.

'Poor little devil,' Storm watched him. 'He has inherited the Courtney pride and stubbornness. He won't give up until he drowns himself.'

She lifted him from the puddle and there was instantly such a howl of protest that she had to return him hurriedly.

'I am sure if you went to the General – with John,' Mark persevered.

'You don't really understand us Courtneys.' Storm sat back and began to plait her hair over one shoulder. 'We don't forget or forgive that easily.'

'Storm, won't you try it? Please go to him.'

'I know exactly how he is, Mark. Better than you, better than Daddy knows himself. I know him so well as I do myself, because we are one person. I am he, and he is me. If I go to him now, having done what I did – having insulted him, having destroyed all the dreams he wove about me – if I go now, when I am destitute of pride and honour, if I go as a beggar, he will despise me for ever.'

'No, Storm, you are wrong.'

'On this I am never wrong, Mark darling. He would not want to despise me, just as he does not want to hate me now, but he would not be able to help himself. He is Sean Courtney, and he is trapped in the steel jaws of his own honour.'

'He is a sick man – you must give him the chance.'

'No, Mark. It would kill him. I know that – and it would destroy me. For both our sakes, I dare not go to him now.'

'You don't know how much he cares for you.'

'Oh I do, Mark. I also know how much I care for him – and one day, when I am proud again, I will go to him. I promise you that. When I know he can be proud of me, I will take him that as a gift –'

'Oh damn you and your stiff cruel pride, you nearly destroyed us with it also.'

'Come, Mark,' she stood up. 'Take John's other hand.'

They walked the child between them along the firm wet sand at the edge of the surf. He hung on their hands, leaning forward to watch his own feet appear and disappear magically below him, and he let out great shouts of triumph at his accomplishment.

The day was bright and clean, and the gulls caught the wind and rode above them on smoky white wings, answering the child's shouts with their own harsh cries.

'Oh, I had so many fine clothes and fancy friends.' Storm watched the gulls. 'I sold the clothes and lost the friends, and found how little any of it really meant to me. Look at the gulls!' she said, head thrown back. 'See the sunlight through the spread feathers. I was so busy that I never had time to see clearly before. I never saw myself, nor those around me. But now I am learning to look.'

'I saw that in your painting,' Mark said, and lifted John to his chest, delighting in the hot restless little body. 'You are painting different subjects.'

'I want to be a great artist.'

'I think you will be. That Courtney stubbornness again.'

'We don't always get what we want,' she told him, and the spent surf came sliding up the beach and creamed around their ankles.

The child slept face down on the monkey-skin kaross, exhausted with sun and sea and play, his belly bulging with food.

Storm worked at the easel under the window with narrowed eyes and cocked head.

'You are my favourite model,' she said.

'That's just because I'm so cheap.' And she laughed lightly.

'With what I pay you, I could be rich,' she pointed out.

'You know what they call ladies who do it for money?' Mark asked lazily and relapsed into silence, giving himself up to the full pleasure of watching her and they were silent for nearly an hour – silent but close and spiritually in tune.

Mark spoke at last. 'I know what you mean by seeing more clearly now. That one,' he pointed at one of the larger canvases against the wall, 'that's probably the best thing you've ever done.'

'I hated to sell it – the man who bought it is coming tomorrow.'

'You've sold some of your paintings?' he was startled.

'How do you think John and I live?'

'I don't know.' He hadn't thought about that. 'I supposed your husband.'

Her expression changed, darkening swiftly. 'I want nothing from him.' And she tossed her head so that the braid of hair flicked like the tail of an angry lioness. 'I want nothing from him, and his friends, and my loving friends, all those nice loyal people who stay away from me in droves now that I am the scarlet divorcée. I've learned a lot since last I saw you, and especially I have learned about that kind of person.'

'They are rich,' Mark pointed out. 'You once told me how important that is.'

The dark anger went out of her, and she drooped a little, the brush falling to her side.

'Oh Mark, please don't be bitter with me. I don't think I could stand that.'

He felt something tear in his chest, and he rose swiftly and went to her, picked her up with a swing of his shoulders and carried her high, through the curtained doorway into the small cool dark bedroom.

It was strange, but their love-making was never the same, always there were new wonders, new accords of desire, the discovery of some little things that excited them both beyond all relation to its apparent significance.

Repetition could not weary nor dull the appetite they had for each other, and even as that appetite was totally satiated, so the endless well of their mutual desire began to fill again.

It would start again immediately with the lazy touch of fingers as they lay curled together like sleepy puppies, the sweat of their loving cooling on their skin, raising little goose bumps around the dark rosy aureoles of her nipples.

A finger drawn lightly down his cheek, rasping on the sandpaper of his beard, and then pushing lightly between his lips, making him turn his head for another kiss, a mere touch of lips and the mingling of their breath so that he could smell that peculiar perfume of passion from her mouth, a smell like newly dug truffles, a mushroomy exciting smell.

She saw the new spark of interest in his eyes and drew softly away to chuckle at him, a throaty sensuous sound, and she drew one sharp fingernail swiftly down his spine so that little sparks of fire flew along his nerves and his back arched.

'I am going to claw you because you deserve it, you randy old tomcat.' She made a growly sound in her throat and curled her nails into a lion's claw, drawing it lightly across his shoulder, and then hard down his belly, so that her nails left red lines against the skin.

She studied the red lines, with her lips parted and the tip of her pink tongue touching her small white teeth. The nipples of her breast swelled as she watched, growing like new buds, as though they were about to burst. She saw the direction of his eyes, and she put her hand behind his head, drawing him down gently, pulling back her shoulder so that the heavy rounded bosom was offered like a sacrifice.

Mark took some of the big scaly crayfish from the low-tide pools, and they smelled of kelp and iodine, thumping their tails furiously in his grip, snapping their legs and bubbling at the small mouths with their multiple mandibles.

Mark rose, streaming salt water, from the depths of the pool and handed them up to Storm, who squealed with excitement on the rocky edge of the pool and took them gingerly, using her straw hat as a glove against the spiky carapace and waving legs.

Mark built a fire in a scooped fireplace in the sand, while Storm held John on her lap and fed him through a discreetly unbuttoned blouse, offering advice and ribald comment as he worked.

Mark threw wet seaweed over the coals, put the crayfish on top of that and covered them with another layer of seaweed, topping it off with a final layer of sand, and while they waited for the crayfish to cook and John to finish his noisy guzzling, they drank wine and watched the setting sun turn the sea clouds into a brilliant display.

'God, Nature's an old ham. If I painted like that, they'd say I had no sense of colour, and I could go work for a chocolate company painting boxes.'

Afterwards, Storm lay John in the apple basket that served as a portable cradle and they ate crayfish, pulling the long luscious sticks of white meat from the horny legs and washing it down with the tart white Cape wine.

In the darkness the stars were stark pricks of brilliant white, and the surf boomed in long soft phosphorescent lines.

'It's so wonderfully romantic.' Storm watched it, sitting hugging her knees, and then turned her head and smiled wickedly. 'And you can take that as a hint, if you want to.'

On the rug together she said, 'Do you know what some people do?'

'No, what do some people do?' Mark seemed more interested in what he was doing than the actions of the nameless somebodies.

'You don't expect me just to say it out like that.'

'Why not?'

'It's rude.'

'All right, so whisper it.'

So she whispered it, but she was giggling so much that he was not sure he had heard right.

She repeated it, and he had heard right. He was truly stunned, so that he found himself blushing in the dark.

'That's terrible,' he answered huskily. 'You would never do that!' However, he was over the first shock, and the idea intrigued him.

'Of course not,' she whispered, and then after a silence, 'Unless of course you want to.'

There was another long silence during which Storm made some investigations. 'If I'm any judge, and I should be by now, you want to,' she stated flatly.

Long afterwards, naked in the dark, they swam together out beyond the first line of breakers. The water was warm as fresh milk and they trod water to kiss with wet salty lips.

On the beach Mark built up the fire and they sat close to it, cuddled together in the yellow light of the flames, and they drank the rest of the wine.

'Mark,' she said at last, and there was a sadness in her voice that he had never heard before. 'You have been with us two days now, which is two days too much. Tomorrow I want you to go. Go early before John and I are awake, so we don't have to watch you.'

Her words struck like a lash so that he writhed at the sting. He turned to her with a stricken face in the firelight.

'What are you saying? You and John are mine. We belong together the three of us, always.'

'You didn't understand a word of what I was saying, did you?' she asked softly. 'You didn't understand when I said I must rebuild my pride, refashion my honour?'

'I love you, Storm. I have always loved you.'

'You are married to somebody else, Mark.'

'That doesn't mean anything,' he pleaded.

'Oh yes, it does.' She shook her head. 'And you know it does.'

'I will leave Marion.'

'Divorce, Mark?'

'Yes.' He was desperate. 'I'll ask her for a divorce.'

'That way we can both be truly proud. That will be a fine way for me to go to my father. Think how proud we will make him. His daughter, and the son he never had, for that's the way he thinks of you, both of them divorced. Think of baby John. How high he will hold his head. Think of us – what a noble life we can build on the misery of the girl who was your wife.' Looking into her eyes in the firelight, he saw that her pride was iron and her stubbornness was steel.

Mark dressed quietly in the dark, and when he was ready he groped his way to the cradle and kissed his son. The child made a little whimpering sound in his sleep, and he smelt warm and milky, like a new-born kitten.

He thought that Storm was sleeping also as he stooped over her, but then he realized that she was lying rigidly with her face pressed into the pillow to stifle the harsh silent sobs that convulsed her.

She did not lift her face to him and he kissed her hair and her neck, then he straightened up and walked out into the dark. The motorcycle started at the first kick and he wheeled it out into the lane.

Storm lay in the dark and listened to the sound of the engine die away into the night, and afterwards there was only the lonely mournful sound of the surf and the clink of the tree frogs outside the window.

Mark sat on the carved wooden stool in the sunset, in front of Pungushe's hut, and he asked for the first time something that had been in his mind since their first meeting.

'Pungushe, tell me of the time when the Jackal pulled the Ngaga from the flooding river.'

And the Zulu shrugged. 'What is there to tell? I found you caught in the branches of a flooded tree on the edge of the river – and if I had sense, I would have walked away, for you were clearly a very dead Ngaga and the brown water was washing over your head.'

'Did you see how it was that I fell into the river?'

There was a pause, while Pungushe steeled himself to admit ignorance. 'It seemed to me that you had been blinded with fever and fallen into the river.'

'You did not see the man I killed, nor the man that fired at me with a rifle?'

Pungushe covered his amazement nobly, but shook his head. 'A little time before I found you in the river I heard the sound of guns, four, perhaps five shots, from up the valley. This must have been you and the one who hunted you, but I saw no man and the rain washed away all sign, before the next morning. The flood waters would have washed the dead man away and the crocodiles eaten him.'

They were silent again while the beer pot passed between them.

'Did you see the man who fired at you?' Pungushe asked.

'Yes,' said Mark. 'But my eyes were weak with fever, and as you say, it was raining. I did not see him clearly.'

Hobday stood within the hall, against the wall, out of the crush of excited bodies. He stood like a rock, solid and immovable, his head lowered on the thick wrestler's neck. His eyes were hooded, as though he were able like a great bird of prey to draw an opaque nictitating membrance across them. Only his jaw made an almost imperceptible chewing motion, grinding the big flat teeth together so that the muscle in the points of his jaw bulged slightly.

He was watching Dirk Courtney across the crowded hall, the way a faithful mastiff watches its master.

Tall and urbane, Dirk Courtney had a warm double handshake for each of those who crowded forward to assure him of support and to wish him luck. His gaze was straight and calm, but it kept flicking back to the long counting tables.

They were trestle tables that had done duty at a thousand church socials, and as many weddings.

Now the scrutineers sat along them, and the last ballot boxes from the outlying areas were carried in through the front doors of the Ladyburg Church Hall.

The sprawling shape of the constituency of Ladyburg meant that some of the boxes had come in sixty miles, and although the voting had closed the previous evening, it was now an hour before noon and no result had yet been announced.

Mark crossed slowly towards where General Sean Courtney sat, pushing his way gently through the throng that lined the roped-off area around the counting tables.

Mark and Marion had come in from Chaka's Gate three days before, especially to assist at the elections. There were never enough helpers, and Marion had been completely at home, cutting sandwiches and dispensing coffee, working with twenty other women under Ruth Courtney's supervision in the kitchens behind the hall.

Mark had scoured the village district with other party organizers. Like a press gang, they had hunted down missing or recalcitrant voters and brought them into the ballot stations.

It had been hard work, and then none of them had slept much the previous night. The dancing and barbecue had lasted until four in the morning – and after that the anticipation of the announcement of the result had kept most of them from sleep.

For Mark it all had a special significance. He knew now with complete certainty, that if Dirk Courtney was returned as the member of Parliament for Ladyburg, then his dreams for Chaka's Gate were doomed.

As the voters had come in during the day, their hopes had see-sawed up and down. Often it seemed that the end of the hall where Dirk Courtney's organizers sat under huge posters of their candidate was as crowded as Sean Courtney's end of the hall was deserted.

When this happened, Marion's brother-in-law, Peter Botes, removed his pipe from his mouth and smirked comfortably at Mark across the length of the hall. He had become an enthusiastic supporter of Dirk Courtney's, and his circumstances had altered remarkably in the last six months. He had opened offices of his own on the first floor of the Ladyburg Farmers Bank. He drove a new Packard and had moved from the cottage to a fine rambling house in three acres of garden and orchard, where he had insisted that Marion and Mark dine with him the previous night.

'The evening star sets, the morning star rises, my dear Mark. The wise man recognizes that,' he had sermonized as he carved the roast.

'General Courtney's star has not set yet,' said Mark stubbornly.

'Not yet,' agreed Peter. 'But when it does, you will need new friends. Powerful friends.'

'You can always rely on us,' said Marion's sister kindly. 'You don't always have to live out there in the bush.'

'You don't understand,' Mark interrupted quietly. 'My life's work is out there – in the bush.'

'Oh, I wouldn't bank on that.' Peter heaped slices of roast beef on to Mark's plate. 'There are going to be changes in the Ladyburg district when Mr Dirk Courtney takes over. Big changes!'

'Besides, it isn't fair on poor Marion. No woman wants to live out there –'

'Oh, I am quite happy wherever Mark wants to go,' Marion murmured.

'Don't worry,' Peter assured them. 'We'll look after you.' And he patted Mark's shoulder in a brotherly fashion.

'Mr Dirk Courtney thinks the world of Peter,' said his wife proudly.

Now as Mark crossed the hall towards General Sean Courtney, he felt the heavy doughy feeling of dread in his guts. He did not want to bear the tidings he had for the General, yet he knew it was better that they came gently from a friend, rather than in gloating triumph from an enemy.

He paused to watch Sean Courtney from a distance, feeling both pity and anger. Sean had rallied strongly since those low days at Emoyeni. His shoulders had regained some of that wide rakish set, and his face had filled out. Some of the gaunt shadows had smoothed away, and he had been in the sun again. The skin was tanned brown against the silver of his beard and his hair.

Yet he was seated now. The strain of the last few days had taxed him sorely. He sat erect on a hard-backed chair, both hands resting on the silver head of his cane. With him were many of his old friends who had gathered to give him support, and he listened seriously to his brother Garrick who sat in the chair beside him, nodding his agreement.

Mark did not want to go to him, he wanted to delay the moment, but then there was a stir across the hall. Mark saw Peter Botes scurrying across to where Dirk Courtney stood, and his face was bright scarlet with excitement. He spoke rapidly, gesticulating widely, and Dirk Courtney leaned forward to listen eagerly.

Mark could not delay a moment longer. He hurried forward and Sean saw him coming.

'Well, my boy, come and sit a while. They tell me the voting is extremely close so far, but we'll have the result before noon.' Then he saw Mark's face. 'What is it?' He demanded harshly.

Mark stooped over him, his mouth almost touching the General's ear, and his voice croaked in his own ears.

'It's just come in on the telegraph, General. We have lost Johannesburg Central, Doornfontein and Jeppe –' They were all solid safe Smuts seats, they had been South Africa Party since Union in 1910, and now they were gone. It was a disaster, a stunning catastrophe. Sean gripped Mark's forearm as if to take strength from him, and his hand shook in a gentle palsy.

Across the hall they heard the wild gloating cheers start ringing out, and Mark had to hurry.

'That's not all, sir. General Smuts himself has lost his seat.' The nation had rejected them, the coalition of the Labour and the National Party under Hertzog were sweeping into power.

'My God,' muttered Sean. 'It's come. I didn't believe it possible.'

Still gripping Mark's arm, he pulled himself to his feet. 'Help me out to the car, my boy. I don't think I can bring myself to congratulate the new member for Ladyburg.'

But they were too late. The announcement came before they reached the door. It was shouted in a stentorian voice, by the chief scrutineer from the platform at the end of the hall.

'Mr Dirk Courtney, National Labour Party: 2683 votes. General Sean Courtney, South Africa Party: 2441 votes. I give you the new member for Ladyburg –' And Dirk Courtney leapt lightly on to the platform, clasping both hands above his head like a prize-fighter.

'Well.' There was a twisted grin on Sean's face, the skin had that greyish tone again and his shoulders had slumped. 'So, exit the Butcher of Fordsburg –' and Mark took him out to where the Rolls waited in the street.

*   *   *

The champagne was a Dom Perignon of that superb 1904 vintage, and Sean poured it with his own hands, limping from guest to guest.

'I had hoped to toast victory with it,' he smiled. 'But it will do as well to drown our sorrows.'

There was only a small gathering in the drawing-room of Lion Kop homestead, and the few attempts at joviality were lost in the huge room. The guests left early. Only the family sat down to dinner, with Marion in Storm's old seat and Mark between her and Ruth Courtney.

'Well, my boy, what are your plans now?' Sean abruptly asked in one of the silences, and Mark looked up with genuine astonishment.

'We'll be going back to Chaka's Gate, of course.'

'Of course.' Sean smiled with the first spontaneous warmth of that dark day. 'How foolish of me to think otherwise. But you do realize what this,' Sean made a gesture with one hand, unable to say the word defeat, 'what this could mean for you?'

'Yes, sir. But you still have enormous influence. There is our Wildlife Society – we can fight. We have to fight to keep Chaka's Gate.'

'Yes,' Sean nodded, and there was a little sparkle in his eyes again. 'We'll fight, but my guess is it will be a hard, dirty fight.'

At first there was no sign of the gathering clouds to darken the tall blue sky above Chaka's Gate. The only change was that Mark was submitting his monthly report, not to Sean Courtney, but to the new Minister of Lands, Peter Grobler, a staunch Hertzog man. His reports were acknowledged formally, but although his salary was still paid regularly by the Department, in a short official letter Mark was informed that the whole question of the proclaimed areas was now under consideration at Cabinet level, and that new legislation would be promulgated at the next session of Parliament. His appointment as game warden was to be considered a temporary post, without pension benefits, and subject to monthly notice.

Mark worked on doggedly, but many nights he sat late in the lantern light writing to General Courtney. The two of them were planning at long distance their campaign to awaken public interest in Chaka's Gate, but when Marion had gone off to bed in the next room, he would take a fresh page and cover it with the small cramped lines to Storm, pouring out to her all his thoughts and dreams and love.

Storm never replied to his letters, he was not even certain that she was still in that thatched cottage above the beach, but he imagined her there, thinking of her at odd hours of the day and the night, seeing her working at her easel, or walking the beach with baby John tottering at her side. One particular night he lay awake and imagined her in the tiny shuttered bedroom with the child at her breast, and the image was too vivid, too painful to allow him sleep.

He rose quietly, left a note for Marion as she slept heavily, and, with Pungushe trotting at Trojan's head, set off up the valley.

Marion woke an hour after he had gone, and her first waking thought was that if there was still no show on this morning then it was certain. She had waited all these weeks for that absolute certainty, before telling Mark. Somehow she had been afraid that if she had spoken of it too soon, it would have been bad luck.

She slipped from the bed and crossed the still dark room to the bathroom. When she returned minutes later she was hugging herself with suppressed joy, and she lit the candle by her bedside, eager to see Mark's face when she woke him to tell him.

Her disappointment when she saw the empty rumpled bed and the note propped on the pillow was intense, but lasted only a short while before her usual gentle placid nature reasserted itself.

'It will give me more time to enjoy it by myself,' she said aloud, and then she spoke again. 'Harold – Harold Anders? No, that's too common. I will have to think of a really fine-sounding name.'

She hummed happily to herself as she dressed, and then went out into the kitchen yard.

It was a cool still morning with a milky pink sky. A baboon called from the cliffs of Chaka's Gate, the short explosive bark ringing across the valley, a salute to the sunrise that was turning the heights to brazen splendour.

It was good to be alive and to have a child growing on such a day, Marion thought, and she wanted to do something to celebrate it. Mark's note had told her that he would be home by nightfall.

'I'll bake a new batch of bread, and –' She wanted something very special for this day. Then she remembered that it had rained five days previously. There might be wild mushrooms coming up from the rains, those rounded buds with sticky brown tops; the rich meaty flesh was a favourite of Mark's and he had taught her when and where to find them.

She ate her breakfast absent-mindedly with Mark's copy of *The Home Doctor* propped against the jam jar, re-reading the section on 'The Expectant Mother'. Then she began on her housework, taking a comfortable pride in the slippery glaze of the cement floors and the burnish which she had worked on to the wood of the simple furniture, in the neatness and order, the smell of polish, the wild flowers in their vases. She sang as she worked and once laughed out loud for no reason.

It was mid-morning before she tied her sun bonnet under her chin, put a bottle of 'Chamberlain's Superior Diarrhoea Remedy' into her basket, and set off up the valley.

She stopped at Pungushe's kraal and the youngest wife brought the baby to her. Marion was relieved to see that he was much improved, and Pungushe's wife assured her that she had given him much liquid to drink. Marion took him in her lap and fed him a spoonful of the diluted remedy, despite his violent protests, and afterwards the five women sat in the sun and talked of children and men and childbirth, of sickness and food and clothing, and all the things that absorb a woman's life.

It was almost an hour later that she left the four Zulu women and went down towards the river.

The downpour of rain had disquieted the lioness. Some deep instinct warned her that it was but the harbinger of the great storms to come.

The jessie thickets in the valley were a suitable retreat for her litter no longer. Heavy rain on the escarpment would soon turn the steep narrow valley into a cascading torrent.

Twice already she had tried to lead the cubs away, but they were older now and had developed a stubbornness and tenacity. They clung to the haven of the thick thorny jessie, and her efforts had failed. Within half a mile, one or two of the faint-hearts would turn and scurry back to what they considered home. Immediately the lioness turned back to seize the deserter, it precipitated an undignified rush by the others in the same direction, and within five minutes they were all back in the jessie.

The lioness was distracted. This was her first litter, but she was governed by instinct. She knew that it was time to wean her cubs, to take them out of the trap of the narrow valley, to begin their hunting lessons, but she was frustrated by the size of her litter, six-cub litters were a rarity in the wilderness and so far there had been no casualties among the cubs; her family was becoming too ungainly for her to handle.

However, instinct drove her and in the middle of a cool bright morning in which she could smell the rain coming, she tried again. The cubs gambolled along behind her, falling over each other and sparring amicably, as far as the river. This was familiar ground and they went along happily.

When the lioness started out across the open white sandbanks towards the far side, there was immediately the usual crisis in confidence. Three cubs followed her willingly, two stood undecidedly on the high bank and whined and mewled with concern, while the sixth turned and bolted straight back up the valley for the ebony.

The lioness went after him at a gallop and bowled him on his back. Then she took the scruff of his neck and lifted him. The cubs were big now, and although she lifted him to the full stretch of her neck, his backside still bumped on every irregularity of the ground. He curled up his legs, wrapped his tail tightly up under his quarters and closed his eyes, hanging from her mouth as she carried him down into the bed of the Bubezi River.

The river was five hundred yards wide at this point, and almost completely empty at the end of the dry season. There were still deep green pools of water between the snowy-white sand-banks, and the pools were connected by a slow trickle of warm clear water only a few inches deep. While five cubs watched in an agony of indecision from the near bank, the lioness carried the cub through the shallows, soaking his dragging backside so he hissed and wriggled indignantly, then she trotted up the far bank and found a clump of dense wit-els where she placed him.

She turned back to fetch another cub, and he followed her with a panicky rush. She had to stop and box him about the ears, snarling until he squealed and fell on his back. She grabbed him by the neck and dragged him back into the wit-els. She started back across the river to find the cub stumbling along on her heels again. This time she nipped hard enough to really hurt, and bundled him back into the thicket. She nipped again at his hindquarters until he cowered flat on the earth, so subdued and chastened that he could not gather the courage to follow again. He lay under the bush and made distraught little sounds of anguish.

Marion had never been this far from the cottage alone, but it was such a lovely warm clear morning, peaceful and still, that she wandered on in a mood of enchantment and happiness such as she had seldom known before.

She knew that if she followed the river bank, she could not lose herself, and Mark had taught her that the African bush is a safer place in which to wander abroad than the streets of a city – as long as one followed a few simple rules of the road.

At the branch of the two rivers she stopped for a few minutes to watch a pair of fish eagles on top of their shaggy nest in the main fork of a tall leadwood tree. The white heads of the two birds shone like beacons in contrast to the dark russet plumage, and she thought she could just make out the chirruping sound of the chicks in the cup of the hay-stack nest.

The sound of the young heightened the awareness of the life in her own belly, and she laughed and went on down the branch of the Red Bubezi.

Once a heavy body crashed in the undergrowth nearby, and there was a clatter of hooves on stony earth. She froze with a fleeting chill of fear, and then when the silence returned she regained her courage and laughed a little breathlessly and went on.

There was a perfume on the warm still air, sweet as full-blooming roses, and she followed it, twice going wrong but at last coming on a spreading creeper hanging over a gaunt dead tree. The leaves were dark shiny green and the dense bunches of flowers were pale butter yellow. She had never seen the plant before, nor the swarm of sunbirds that fluttered about it. They were tiny restless darting birds, with bright, metallic, shiny plumage like the little humming-birds of America, and they dipped into the perfumed flowers with long slim curved beaks. Their colours were unbelievable in the sunlight, emerald greens and sapphire blue, black like wet anthracite and reds like the blood of kings. They thrust their beaks deep into the open throats of the yellow blooms to sip out the thick clear drops of nectar through their hollow tubular tongues.

Watching them, Marion felt a deep pervading delight, and it was a long time before she moved on again.

She found the first batch of mushrooms a little further on, and she knelt to snap the stems off at the level of the earth and then hold the umbrella-shaped fleshy plant to her face and inhale the delicious musty odour, before laying it carefully, cap uppermost, in the basket so that grit and dirt would not lodge in the delicately fluted gills. She took two dozen mushrooms from this one patch, but she knew they would cook down to a fraction of their bulk.

She went on, following the lip of the steep bank.

Something hissed close by and her heart skipped again. Her first thought was of a snake, one of those thick bloated reptiles, with the chocolate and yellow markings and flat scaly heads, which blew so loudly that they were called puff-adders.

She began moving backwards carefully staring into the clump of first growth wit-els from which the sound had come. She saw small movement, but it was some seconds before she realized what she was seeing.

The lion cub was flat on its belly in the dappled shadow of the thicket, and its own dappled baby spots blended beautifully against the bed of dried leaves and leaf mould on which it lay.

The cub had learned already the first lesson of concealment, absolute stillness; except for his two round fluffy ears. The ears flicked back and forth, signalling clearly every emotion and intention. He stared at Marion with wide round eyes that had not yet turned the ferocious yellow of full growth, but were still hazed with the bluish glaze of kittenhood. His whiskers bristled stiffly, and his ears signalled wildly conflicting messages.

Flattening against the skull: 'One step nearer and I'll tear you to pieces.'

Shooting out sideways: 'One step nearer and I'll die of fright.'

Coming up and cupping forward: 'What the hell are you anyway?'

'Oh,' exclaimed Marion. 'You darling little thing.' She set down the basket, and squatted. She extended one hand and made soft cooing noises.

'There's a darling. Are you all alone then, poor baby?'

She moved forward slowly, still talking and cooing.

'Nobody's going to hurt you, baby.'

The cub was uncertain, its ears rising into an attitude of curiosity and indecision as it stared at her.

'Are you all alone then? You'll make a lovely pet for my own baby, won't you?'

Closer and closer she edged, and the cub warned her with a half-hearted apologetic hiss.

'What a cheeky darling we are,' Marion smiled and squatted three feet from the cub.

'How are we going to take you home?' Marion asked. 'Will you fit in the basket?'

In the river bed, the lioness carried the second cub through the shallows, and was followed by one of the heroes of the litter, struggling along gamely through the thick white sand. However, when he reached the edge of the shallow stream and tested it with one paw, his new-found courage deserted him at the cold wet touch, and he sat down and wept bitterly.

The lioness, by this time almost wild with distraction and frustration, turned back, and dropped her burden which immediately set off in clumsy gallop for the jessie thicket again, then she seized the weeping hero instead and trotted back through the stream and set off determinedly for the far bank.

Her huge round pads made no sound in the soft earth as she came up the bank, carrying the cub.

Marion heard the crackling spluttering explosion of sound behind her, and she whirled to her feet in one movement.

The lioness crouched on the lip of the bank fifty yards away. It warned her again with that terrible sound.

All that Marion saw were the eyes. They were a blazing yellow, a ferocious terrifying yellow – and she screamed, a wild high ringing, rising sound.

The sound launched the lioness into her charge, and it came with an unbelievably fluid flowing speed that turned into a yellow rushing blur. She snaked in low, and the sand spurted beneath her paws, all claws fully extended, the lips drawn back in a fixed silent snarl, the teeth exposed, long and white and pointed.

Marion turned to run, and had gone five paces when the lioness took her. She pulled her down with a swipe of a forepaw across the small of her back and five curved yellow claws cut deeply – four inches through skin and muscle, opening the abdominal cavity like a sabre cut, crushing the vertebrae and bursting both kidneys instantaneously.

It was a blow that would have killed even a full-grown ox, and it hurled Marion twenty feet forward, but as she fell on her back, the lioness was on her again.

The jaws were wide open, the long white fangs framed the deep wet pink cavern of tongue and throat. In an instant of incredibly heightened perception, Marion saw the smooth ridges of firm pink flesh that covered the arched roof of the lioness's mouth in regular patterns, and she smelt the meaty stink of her breath.

Marion lay twisted under the great yellow cat, she was still screaming and her lower body lay at an odd angle from the shattered spine, but she lifted both arms to protect her face.

The lioness bit into the forearms, just below the elbows and the bone crunched sharply, shattering into slivers and splinters in the mangled flesh, both arms were severed almost through.

Then the lioness seized Marion's shoulder, and worried it until the long eye teeth meshed through broken bone and fat and tissue – and Marion kept screaming, twisting and writhing under the cat.

The lioness took a long time to kill her, confused by her own anger and the unfamiliar taste and shape of the victim. She tore and bit and ripped for almost a minute before she found the throat.

When the lioness stood up at last, her head and neck were a gory mask, her fur sticky and sodden with blood.

Her tail still lashed from side to side in residual anger, but she licked her face with a long dextrous tongue and her lip curled at the sweet unfamiliar flavour. She wiped her face carefully with her paws before trotting back to her cub, and licking him also with long pink protective strokes.

Marion's broken torn body lay where she left it, until Pungushe's wives came, a little before sundown.

Mark and Pungushe crossed the river in darkness with the moonlight turning the sand-banks to ghostly grey, and the round white moon itself reflected perfectly in the still mirror-surface of the pool below the main camp. The turbulence of their fording shattered the image into a thousand points of light, like a crystal glass flung on to a stone floor.

As they rode up the bank, they heard the death wail in the night, that terrible keening, the mourning of Zulu women. The men halted involuntarily, the sound striking dread into both of them.

'Come!' shouted Mark and kicked one foot from the stirrup. Pungushe grabbed the leather and swung off his feet as Mark lashed Trojan into a gallop and they tore up the hill.

The fire that the women had lit threw a grotesque yellow wavering glow, and weird dancing shadows.

The four women sat in a group around the long, kaross-wrapped bundle. None of them looked up as the men ran forward into the firelight.

'Who is it?' Mark demanded. 'What has happened?'

Pungushe seized his eldest wife by the shoulders, and shook her, trying to interrupt the hysteria of mourning, but Mark strode forward impatiently and lifted one end of the kaross.

He stared for a moment, not understanding, not recognizing, then suddenly all colour fled from his face and he turned and ran into the darkness. There he fell to his knees and leaned forward to retch up the bitter bile of horror.

Mark took Marion into Ladyburg, wrapped in a canvas buck-sheet, and strapped into the side-car of the Ariel.

He stayed for the funeral and for the grief and recriminations of her family.

'If only you hadn't taken her out there into the bush —'

'If only you had stayed with her —'

'If only —'

On the third day he went back to Chaka's Gate. Pungushe was waiting for him at the ford of the river.

They sat together in the sunlight under the cliffs, and when Mark gave Pungushe a cigarette, he broke off the cork tip carefully and they smoked in silence until Mark asked,

'Have you read the sign, Pungushe?'

'I have, Jamela.'

'Tell me what happened.'

'The lioness was moving her little ones, taking them one at a time across the river from the jessie bush.' Slowly, accurately, Pungushe reconstructed the tragedy from the marks left in the earth which he had studied in Mark's absence, and when he was finished speaking, they were silent again.

'Where is she now?' Mark asked quietly.

'She has taken the little ones north, but slowly, and three days ago, the day after,' Pungushe hesitated, 'the day after the thing was done, she killed an impala ram, and the cubs ate a little with her. She begins now to wean them.'

Mark stood up and they forded the river, climbing together slowly up through the forest to the cottage.

While Pungushe waited on the front stoep, Mark went into the small deserted home. The wild flowers had died and wilted in their vases, giving the room a sad and dejected feeling. Mark began to gather up all Marion's personal possessions, her clothing, and cheap but treasured jewellery, her combs and brushes, and the few hoarded pots of cosmetics. He packed them carefully into her largest suitcase to take to her sister, and when he was finished he carried the case out and locked it in the tool shed. It was too painful a reminder to keep in the house with him.

Then he went back and changed out of his town clothes. He took the Mannlicher down from the rack and loaded it with brass cartridges from a fresh package. The casings of the cartridges were glistening yellow under their film of wax, the bullets soft-nosed for maximum shock at impact.

When he went out on to the stoep carrying the rifle, Pungushe was still waiting.

'Pungushe,' he said. 'We have work to do now.'

The Zulu stood up slowly, and for a moment they stared at each other. Then Pungushe dropped his eyes and nodded.

'Take the spoor,' Mark commanded softly.

They found where the lioness had killed the impala, but the scavengers of the bush had cleaned the area effectively. There were a few splinters of bone that had fallen out of the crushing jaws of the hyena, a little hair, pulled out in tufts, a shred of dried skin, and part of the skull with the twisted black horns still intact. But the spoor was cold. Wind and the trampling feet of the scavengers, the jackals, and hyena, the vultures and marabou storks, had wiped sign.

'She will keep going north,' said Pungushe, and Mark did not ask how he knew that, for the Zulu could not have answered. He simply knew.

They went slowly on up the valley, Pungushe scouting ahead of the mule, making wide tracks back and forth, casting carefully for the sign, and on the second day he cut the spoor.

'She has turned now.' Pungushe squatted over the pug marks, the big saucer-sized pads and the smaller myriad prints of the cubs.

'I think she was going back towards the Usutu.' He nodded over the spoor, touching it with the thin reed wand he carried as a tracking stick. 'She was taking the little ones back, but now she has changed her mind. She has turned southwards, she must have passed close to where we camped last night. She is staying in the valley. It is her valley now, and she will not leave it.'

'No,' Mark nodded grimly. 'She will not leave the valley again. Follow, Pungushe.'

The lioness was moving slowly and the spoor ran hotter every hour. They found where she had hunted without success. Pungushe pointed out where she had stalked, and then the deep driving back claws had raked the earth as she leapt to the back of a full-grown zebra. Twenty paces further, she had fallen heavily, dislodged by the stallion's plunging. She had struck shoulder first, Pungushe said, and the zebra had run free but bleeding from the long slash of her claws. The lioness had limped away, and lain under a thorn tree for a long time before rising and going back slowly to where she had left her cubs. Probably she had torn muscle and sinew in that fall.

'When will we come up with her?' Mark asked, his face a stony mask of vengeance.

'Perhaps before sunset.' But they lost two hours on a rocky ridge, and Pungushe had to cast widely and work with all his skill to cut the spoor again at the point where it doubled sharply and turned west towards the escarpment.

Pungushe and Mark camped on her spoor with only a tiny fire for comfort and they lay directly on the earth. Mark did not sleep. He lay and watched the waning moon come up over the tree tops, but it was only when Pungushe spoke quietly that he realized that the Zulu also was sleepless.

'The cubs are not weaned,' he said. 'But they will take a long time to die.'

'No,' Mark replied. 'I will shoot them also.'

Pungushe roused himself and took a little snuff, leaning on one elbow and staring into the coals of the fire.

'She has tasted human blood,' Mark said at last. Even in his grief and anger, he sensed Pungushe's quiet disapproval and wanted to justify what he was about to do.

'She did not feed,' Pungushe stated. Mark felt his gorge rise and the bitter taste of it again as he remembered the terrible mutilation, but Pungushe was right, the lioness had not eaten any of that poor torn flesh.

'Pungushe, she was my wife.'

'Yes,' Pungushe nodded. 'That is so. Also it was her cub.'

Mark considered the words, and felt for the first time a confusion of his own objects. The lioness had acted out of one of the oldest instincts of life, the urge to protect her young – but what were his motives?

'I have to kill her, Pungushe,' he said flatly, and there was some slimy obscene thing in his belly; it moved there for the first time, and he tried to deny its existence.

Marion was dead. Sweet, loyal, dutiful Marion, who had been all that a man could ask for in a wife. She had died an unspeakable death – and now Mark was alone, or did the word 'free' come too readily to his tongue?

Suddenly he had an image of a slim, dark lovely girl and a lusty naked little boy walking in the sunset at the edge of the sea.

Guilt, that slimy thing, uncoiled in his belly and began to ripple and undulate like a serpent, and he could not crush it down.

'She has to die,' Mark repeated, and perhaps his own guilt could die in that same purging.

'Very well,' Pungushe agreed. 'We will find her before noon tomorrow.' He lay back and pulled his kaross over his head and his voice was muffled, the words almost lost. 'Let us hurry now towards the great emptiness.'

They found the lioness early the next morning. She had moved in close under the hills of the escarpment, and when the first heat of the day made the cubs flag and begin to trail disconsolately along behind her, she had selected an umbrella thorn with a flat-topped mass of foliage spreading from the straight trunk and she had lain in the shade on her side, exposing the soft creamy fur of her belly and the double row of flat black nipples.

Now the cubs were alost satiated, only two of the greediest still suckled valiantly, their bellies bulging and the effort of swallowing almost too much.

The indefatigable hunter of tails was now concentrating all his prowess on his mother's long whip-lash with its fine black tuft of hair which she jerked out from under his nose at the very instant of each attack.

The other three were fighting off sleep, with violent outbursts of undirected energy, succumbing slowly to drooping eyelids and strained bellies, until at last they lay in an untidy heap of fluff and fur.

Mark was one hundred and twenty yards downwind. He lay belly down behind a small ant-heap, and it had taken almost an hour to work in this close. The umbrella thorn was set in an area of short open grassland, and he had been forced to stalk flat, tortoising forward on his elbows with the rifle held across the crook.

'Can we get closer?' Mark asked, his whisper merely a soft breath. The short stiff yellow grass was just high enough to screen the cat when she lay flat on her side.

'Jamela, I could get close enough to touch her.' He put the emphasis on the word 'I' and left the rest of it unstated.

So they waited in the sun, another twenty minutes until at last the lioness lifted her head.

Perhaps some deep sense of survival had warned her of the presence of the hunters. Her head came up in a flash of yellow movement, the extraordinary swiftness so characteristic of all the big cats, and she stared fixedly downwind, the sector of maximum danger.

For long seconds she watched, and the wide yellow eyes were steady and unblinking. Sensing her concern, two of the cubs sat up sleepily and waited with her.

Mark felt the lioness was looking directly at him, but he obeyed the law of absolute stillness. The first movement of lifting the Mannlicher would send her away in a blur of speed. So Mark waited while the seconds spun out. Then suddenly the lioness dropped her head and stretched out flat once again.

'She is restless,' warned Pungushe. 'We can get no closer.'

'I cannot shoot from here'

'We will wait,' said Pungushe.

All the cubs slept now, and the lioness dozed, but always all her senses were working, nostrils tasting carefully each breath of the wind for the taint of danger, the big round ears never still, flicking to the slightest sound of wind or branch, bird or animal.

Mark lay in the direct sunlight, and the sweat rose to stain his shirt. A tsetse fly settled behind his ear and bit into the softness of his neck, but he did not make the movement of brushing it away. It was an hour before his chance came.

The lioness rose suddenly to her full height, and swung her tail from side to side. She was too restless to stay here under the thorn tree any longer. The cubs sat up groggily, and looked to her with puzzled furrowed faces.

The lioness was standing broadside to where Mark lay. She held her head low, and her jaws were a little open as she panted softly in the heat. Mark was close enough to see the dark specks of the tsetse fly sitting on her flanks.

She was still in shadow but now she was backlit by the pale yellow grass beyond her. It was a perfect shot – the point of the elbow the hunter's aiming mark; the span of a hand back from there, and the bullet would rake both lungs, the span of a hand lower would take the heart cleanly.

The lungs were certain, but the heart was swift. Mark chose the heart and lifted the rifle to his shoulder. The safety-catch had long before been set at the firing position.

Mark took up the slack in the trigger and felt the final resistance before the mechanism tripped.

The bullet was 230 grains in weight, and the bronze jacket of the slug was tipped with a grey blob of lead so that it would mushroom on impact and open massive damage through the lioness's chest cavity.

The lioness called her cubs with a soft moaning grunt, and they scrambled obediently to their feet, still a little unsteady from sleep.

She walked out into the sunlight, with that loose feline gait, her head swinging from side to side at each pace, the long back slightly swayed and the heavy droop of her full dugs thickening the graceful line of her body.

'No,' thought Mark. 'I will take the lungs.' He lifted his aim a fraction, holding steady and true four inches behind the point of the elbow, swinging the rifle to follow her as she went into a short restless trot.

The cubs tumbled along behind her in disorder.

Mark held his aim until she reached the edge of the bush, and then she was gone with the insubstantial blurred movement of a wisp of brown smoke on the wind.

When she was gone, he lowered the rifle and stared after her.

Pungushe saw the thing break in him at last. The cold stillness of hatred and guilt and horror broke, and Mark began to cry, hacking tearing sobs that scoured and purged.

It is a difficult thing for a man to watch another weep, especially if that man is your friend.

Pungushe stood up quietly and walked back to where they had tethered the mule. He sat alone in the sun and took a little snuff and waited for Mark.

GOVERNMENT MINISTER SPEAKS ON DUTY TO HUMANITY

The newly appointed Deputy Minister of Lands, Mr Dirk Courtney, expressed concern today at the mauling of a young woman in the proclaimed area of Northern Zululand.

The woman, Mrs Marion Anders, was the wife of the Government Ranger in the area. She was mauled to death by a lioness last Friday.

This unfortunate incident underlines the grave danger of allowing wild animals to exist in proximity to settled areas of human habitation.

Residents in these areas will be in constant danger of animal attack, of crop depredation and game-borne diseases of domestic animals as long as this position is allowed to continue.

Mr Dirk Courtney said that the rinderpest epidemic at the turn of the century had accounted for a loss of domestic cattle estimated to exceed two million head. Rinderpest was a game-borne disease. The minister pointed out, 'We cannot risk a repetition of such a calamity.'

The proclaimed area of Northern Zululand encompasses both highly valuable arable land, and a major watershed vital to proper conservation of our natural resources. If the full potential of our national assets is to be exploited, these areas must be turned over to properly controlled development. The minister went on, 'Your Government has placed priority on this issue, and we will be placing legislation before Parliament at the next sitting.'

Mark read the article through carefully. It was placed prominently on the leader page of the *Natal Witness*.

'There are more,' General Sean Courtney thumbed open a slim folder with half a dozen other cuttings, 'take them with you. You'll see it's all the same general purport. Dirk Courtney is beating the drum with a very big stick, I'm afraid.'

'He's in such a position of power now. I never dreamed he would be a Deputy Minister.'

'Yes,' Sean nodded. 'He has rushed to power, but on the other hand we still have a voice. One of our members in a solid seat has stood down for Jannie Smuts, even I have been offered a seat in a safer constituency.'

'Will you take it, sir?'

Sean shook his silver beard slowly. 'I've had a long time in public life, my boy – and anything you do too long becomes a bore.' He nodded as he thought about his words. 'Of course, that's not strictly true. I am tired, let the younger ones with more energy pick up the reins now. Jannie Smuts will keep in close touch, he knows he can call on me, but I feel like an old Zulu chief. I just want to sit in the sun, drink beer, grow fat and count my cattle.'

'What about Chaka's Gate, sir?' Mark pleaded.

'I have spoken to Jannie Smuts and some of the others, on both sides of the house. We have a lot of support in the new Government as well. I don't want to make it a party issue, I'd like to see it as an issue of each man's own conscience.'

They went on talking until Ruth intervened reluctantly. 'It's after midnight, dear. You can finish your talk in the morning. When are you leaving, Mark?'

'I should be back at Chaka's Gate tomorrow night.' Mark felt a prick of guilt as he lied. He knew damned well he was not going home just yet a while.

'But you'll stay for lunch tomorrow?'

'Yes, I'd like that. Thank you.'

As Mark rose he picked up the file of newspaper clippings from Sean's desk. 'I'll let you have them back tomorrow, sir.'

However, the moment Mark was alone in his room, he dropped into an easy chair and turned avidly to the reverse side of the newspaper cutting he had brought with him. He had not dared to turn over the cutting and read the words that had caught his eyes in the General's presence, but now he lingered over them, re-reading and savouring. Part of the article was missing, scissored away when the Deputy Minister's speech had been trimmed, but there was enough.

EXCEPTIONAL EXHIBITION BY YOUNG ARTIST

Presently showing at the sample rooms of the Marine Hotel on the Marine Parade is an exhibition of thirty paintings by a young lady artist.

For Miss Storm Courtney, it is her first public exhibition and even a much older and more established artist could have been justly gratified with such a reception by the art-lovers of our fair city. After the first five days, twenty-one of her paintings had found enthusiastic purchasers at prices as high as fifty guineas each. Miss Courtney has a classical conception of form, combined with both a sure sense of colour and a mature and confident execution rare in an artist of such tender years.

Worthy of special mention is Number 16, 'Greek athlete at rest'. This painting, property of the artist and not for sale, is a lyrical composition that would perhaps raise the eyebrows of the more old-fashioned. It is an unashamedly sensual ode to –

Here the scissors had cut through, leaving Mark with a disturbing unfinished feeling. He read it once more, inordinately pleased that Storm had reverted to her maiden name with which to sign her work. Then carefully he folded the cutting into his wallet, and he sat in the chair staring at the wall, until he fell asleep, still fully dressed.

A young Zulu lass, no more than sixteen years of age, opened the door of the cottage. She was dressed in the traditional white cotton dustcoat of the nanny and she carried baby John on her hip.

Both nanny and child regarded Mark with huge solemn eyes, but the nanny's relief was patent when Mark addressed her in fluent Zulu.

At the sound of Mark's voice John let out an excited squawk that could have been recognition, but was probably merely a friendly greeting. He began to leap up and down on the nanny's hip with such force that she had to grab to prevent him taking off like a sky rocket.

He reached out both hands towards Mark, burbling and laughing and shouting, and Mark took him, all warm and wriggling and baby-smelling, from the maid. John immediately seized a handful of Mark's hair and tried to remove it by the roots.

Half an hour later when Mark handed him back to the little moon-faced maid, and went down the steep pathway to the beach, John's indignant howls of protest followed him, only fading with distance.

Mark kicked off his shoes and left them and his shirt above the high-tide mark, then he turned northwards and followed the white sweep of sand, his bare feet leaving wet prints on the smooth firm edge of the seashore.

He had walked a mile, and there was no sign of any other person. The beach sand was rippled by static wind-blown wavelets, and dappled with the webbed prints of sea-birds.

On his right hand, the surf rose in long glassy lines, curling green and then dropping over in a crash of white water that shook the sand beneath his feet. On his left hand, the dense, dark green bush rose above the white beach, and again beyond that, the far blue hills and taller bluer sky.

He was alone – until he saw, perhaps a mile ahead, another solitary figure, also following the edge of the sea, a far small and lonely figure, coming towards him, still too distant to tell whether it was man or woman, friend or stranger.

Mark lengthened his stride, and the figure drew nearer, clearer.

Mark began to run, and the figure ahead of him stopped suddenly, and stood with that stillness poised on the edge of flight.

Then suddenly the stillness exploded, and the figure was racing to him.

It was a woman, a woman with dark silky hair streaming in the wind, a woman with outstretched arms and flying bare brown feet, and white teeth and blue, very blue eyes.

*   *   *

They were alone in the bedroom. Baby John's cot had been removed to the small dining-room next door, since he had begun to show an interest in everything that looked like a good romp, hanging on the edge of his cot with shouts of applause and approbation, and then trying his utmost to scale the wooden railings and join the play.

Now they were enjoying those contented minutes between love and sleep, talking softly in the candlelight under a single sheet, lying on their sides facing each other, holding close, with their lips almost touching as they murmured together.

'But darling Mark, it is still a thatched hut, and it is still wild bush.'

'It's a big thatched hut,' he pointed out.

'I don't know. I just don't know if I have changed that much.'

'There is only one way to find out. Come with me.'

'But what will people say?'

'The same as they'd say if they could see us now.'

She chuckled easily, and snuggled a little closer. 'That was a silly question. The old Storm speaking. People have said all there is to say about me, and none of it really mattered a damn.'

'There aren't a lot of people out there to sit in judgement. Only Pungushe, and he's a very broad-minded gentleman.'

She laughed again sleepily. 'Only one person I care about – Daddy mustn't know. I've hurt him enough already.'

So Storm came at last to Chaka's Gate. She came in the beaten and neglected Cadillac, with John on the seat beside her, her worldly possessions crammed into the cab or strapped on the roof and Mark riding his motorcycle escort ahead of her over the rude and bumpy track.

Where the track ended above the Bubezi River, she climbed out and looked around her.

'Well,' she decided after a long thoughtful survey of the towering cliffs, and the river in its bed of green water and white banks, framed by the tall nodding strands of fluffy-headed reeds and great spreading sycamore figs, 'at least it's picturesque.'

Mark put John on his shoulder. 'Pungushe and I will come back with the mules for the rest of your gear.' And he led her down the footpath to the river.

Pungushe was waiting for them under the trees on the far bank, tall and black and imposing in his beaded loin cloth.

'Pungushe, this is my lady and her name is Vungu Vungu – the Storm.'

'I see you, Vungu Vungu, I see also that you are misnamed,' said Pungushe quietly, 'for a storm is an ugly thing which kills and destroys. And you are a lady of beauty.'

'Thank you, Pungushe,' Storm smiled at him. 'But you are also misnamed, for a jackal is a small mean creature.'

'But clever,' said Mark solemnly, and John let out a shout of greeting and bounced on Mark's shoulder, reaching out with both hands for Pungushe.

'And this is my son.'

Pungushe looked at John. There are two things a Zulu loves dearly, cattle and children. Of the two, he prefers children, preferably boy-children. Of all boy-children, he likes best those that are robust, and bold and aggressive.

'Jamela, I should like to hold your son,' he said, and Mark gave John to him.

'I see you Phimbo,' Pungushe greeted the child. 'I see you little man with a great voice.' And then Pungushe smiled that great beaming radiant smile, and John shouted again with joy and thrust his hand in Pungushe's mouth to grab those white shining teeth, but Pungushe swung him up on to his shoulder and laughed with a great hippo-snort and carried him up the hill.

So they came to Chaka's Gate, and there was never any doubt, right from that first day.

Within an hour, there was a polite tap on the screen-door of the kitchen and when Mark opened it there stood in a row on the covered stoep all of Pungushe's daughters, from the eldest who was fourteen to the youngest of four.

'We have come,' announced the eldest, 'to greet Phimbo.'

Mark looked at Storm inquiringly, and she nodded. The eldest daughter swung John up on to her back with a practised action, and strapped him there with a strip of cotton limbo. She had played nurse-maid to all her brothers and sisters, probably knew more about small children than both Storm and Mark combined, and John took to the froglike position on her back as though he had been born Zulu. Then the little girl bobbed a curtsey to Storm and trotted away, with all her sisters in procession, bearing John off to a wonderland peopled entirely with playmates of endless variety and fascination.

On the third day, Storm began sketching, and by the end of the first week she had taken over the household management on a system that Mark referred to as comfortable chaos, alternating with brief periods of pandemonium.

Comfortable chaos was when everybody ate what they wanted, perhaps chocolate biscuits and coffee for dinner one night and a feast of barbecued meat the next. They ate it where they felt like it, perhaps sitting up in bed or lying on a rug on the sand-bank of the river. They ate when they wanted, breakfast at noon or dinner at midnight, if talking and laughing delayed it that long.

Comfortable chaos was when the dusting of furniture or polishing of floors were forgotten in the excitement of living, when clothes that needed mending were tossed into the bottom of the cupboard, when Mark's hair was allowed to grow in points over the back of his collar. Comfortable chaos ended unpredictably and abruptly to be replaced by pandemonium.

Pandemonium began when Storm suddenly got a steely look in her eye and announced, 'This place is a pig sty!' followed by the snipping of scissors, buckets of steaming water, clouds of flying dust, banging pots, and flashing needles. Mark was shorn and clad in refurbished clothing, the cottage gleamed and sparkled, and Storm's housekeeping instincts were exhausted for another indefinite period. And the next day she would be up on Spartan's back, John strapped Zulu-fashion behind her, following Mark on patrol up the valley.

The first time John had been taken on patrol, Mark had asked anxiously, 'Do you think it's wise to take him, he's still very small?'

And Storm had replied, 'I am older and more important than Master John. He fits into my life, not me into his.'

So John rode patrol on muleback, slept in his apple basket under the stars at night, and took his daily bath in the cool green pools of the Bubezi River, quickly developed an immunity to the occasional tsetse bite, and flourished.

They climbed the steep pathway to the summit of Chaka's Gate, sat with their feet dangling over that fearful drop, and they looked across the whole valley, the far blue hills and the plains and swamps and the wide winding rivers.

'When I first met you, you were poor,' Storm said quietly, leaning against Mark's shoulder with her eyes filled with the peace and wonder of it, 'but now you are the richest man in the world, for you are the owner of paradise.'

*   *   *

He took her up the river to the lonely grave below the escarpment. Storm helped him to build a pile of rocks, and to set the cross that Mark had made over it. He told her Pungushe's story of how the old man had been killed, and she cried openly and unashamedly, holding John on her lap, sitting on the gravestone, listening and living every word.

'I have looked – but never truly seen before,' she said, as he showed her the nest of a sunbird, cunningly woven of lichen and spider web, turning it carefully so she could peer into the funnel entrance and see the tiny speckled eggs.

'I never knew what true peace was until I came to this place,' she said, as they sat on the bank of the Bubezi in the yellow light of fading day, and watched a kudu bull with long spiral corkscrew horns and chalk-striped shoulders lead his big-eared cows down to the water.

'I did not know what happiness was before,' she whispered, when they had woken together a little after midnight for no reason and reached for each other in the darkness.

Then one morning she sat up in the rumpled bed, over which John was rampaging unchecked and sowing crumbles of lightly chewed biscuit, and she looked at Mark seriously.

'You once asked me to marry you,' she said. 'Would you like to repeat that question, sir?'

And it was later that same day they heard the axeman at work up the valley.

The blade of a two-handed axe, swung against the bole of a standing hardwood tree, rings like a gunshot, and the sound of it bounced against the cliffs of Chaka's Gate and was flung back to break in dying echoes down the valley, each stroke still lingering on the air while the next cracked off the grey cliffs. There was more than one axeman at work, so that the din was continuous, like the sounds of battle.

Storm had never before seen such a passion of anger on Mark's face. His skin was drained of blood so that the tan of the sun was fever-yellow and his lips seemed frost-bitten and pinched by the force of it. Yet his eyes blazed, and she had to run to match his angry stride as they went up the scree slope from the river beneath the cliffs, and the sound of the axes broke over them, each separate stroke as brutal and shocking as the ones that preceded it.

Ahead of them, one of the lofty leadwoods quivered as though in agony and moved against the sky. Mark stopped in mid-stride to watch it, with his head thrown back and the same agony twisting his own lips. It was a tree of extraordinary symmetry, the silvery trunk rising with such grace as to seem as slim as a young girl's waist. It had taken two hundred years to reach its towering height. Seventy feet above the ground, it spread into a dark green dome of foliage.

As they watched, the tree shuddered again and the axes fell silent. Slowly, majestically, the leadwood swung into a downward arc, gathering ponderous momentum, and the partially severed trunk groaned and popped as the fibres tore; faster and faster still she fell, crashing through the tops of the lesser vegetation below her, the twisting tearing wood shrieking like a living thing until she struck solid earth with a jarring impact they could feel in their guts.

The silence lasted many seconds, and then there was the sound of men's voices, awed voices, as though intimidated by the magnitude of the destruction they had wrought. Then almost immediately after that, the axes started again, fragmenting the great silences of the valley – and Mark began to run. Storm could not keep pace with him.

He came out in an area of devastation, a growing swathe of fallen trees where fifty black men worked like ants, half-naked and burnished with their own sweat, as they stripped the branches and piled them in windrows for burning. The wood chips shone white as bone in the sunlight and the sap that oozed from the axe cuts had the sweetish smell of newly spilled blood.

At the head of the long narrow clearing, a single white man crouched to the eyepiece of a theodolite set on its squat tripod. He was aiming the instrument down the clearing and directing with hand signals the setting of brightly painted markers.

He straightened from the instrument to face Mark – a young man with a mild friendly face, thick spectacles in silver wire frames, lank sandy hair flopping on to his forehead.

'Oh, hello there,' he smiled, and then the smile froze as Mark hissed at him. 'Are you in charge here?'

'Well, yes, I suppose I am,' the young surveyor stuttered.

'You are under arrest.'

'I don't understand.'

'It's quite simple,' Mark blazed at him. 'You are cutting standing timber in a proclaimed area. I am the Government Ranger, and I am placing you under arrest.'

'Now look here,' the surveyor began placatingly, spreading his open hands in a demonstration of his friendly intentions. 'I'm just doing my job.'

In his blind wholesale rage, Mark had not noticed the approach of another man, a heavy broad-shouldered man who moved silently out of the uncut brush along the edge of the clearing. However, the thick north-country accent was instantly familiar, and struck sparks along the surface of Mark's skin. He remembered Hobday from that day when first he had returned to Andersland to find his world turned upside down.

'That's all right, chummy. I'll talk to Mister Anders.' Hobday touched the young surveyor's shoulder placatingly and smiled at Mark, a smile that exposed the short evenly ground teeth, but was completely lacking in any warmth or humour.

'There is nothing you can tell me,' Mark started, and Hobday lifted one hand to stop him.

'I am here in my official capacity as a Provincial Inspector for the Ministry of Lands, Anders. You'd better listen.'

The angry words died and Mark stared at him, while Hobday calmly unfolded a letter from his wallet and proffered it to Mark. It was typewritten on Government paper and signed by the Deputy Minister of Lands. The signature was bold and black – Dirk Courtney. Mark read through the letter slowly, with a plunging sense of despair, and when he finished, he handed it back to Hobday. It gave him unlimited powers in the valley, powers backed by all the authority and weight of Government.

'You are going up in the world,' he said, 'but still working for the same master.' And the man nodded complacently, and then his eyes switched away from Mark's face as Storm came up. The expression on his face changed, as he looked at her.

Storm had her hair in thick twin braids, dangling forward on to each breast. The sun had turned her skin to a rich reddish brown, against which her eyes were startlingly blue and clear. Except for the eyes, she looked like a Sioux princess from some romantic novel.

Hobday dropped his eyes slowly over her body, with such intimate lingring insolence that she reached instinctively for Mark's arm and drew closer to him, as though to bring herself under his direct protection.

'What is it, Mark?' She was still breathless from her climb up the slope, and high colour lit her cheeks. 'What are they doing here?'

'They're Government men,' said Mark heavily. 'From the Ministry of Lands.'

'But they can't cut our trees,' she protested, her voice rising. 'You've got to stop them, Mark.'

'They're cutting survey lines,' Mark explained. 'They are surveying the valley.'

'But those trees –'

'It don't really matter, ma'am,' Hobday told her. His voice was lower now with a thick gloating tone, and his eyes were still busy on her body, like insects crawling greedily to the scent of honey, moving over the thin sun-bleached cotton that covered her breasts. 'It don't matter a damn,' he repeated. 'They are all going to be under water anyway, cut or standing – it's all going under.' He turned away from her at last, and swept one hand down the rude clearing. 'From that side to this,' he said, indicating the gap between the towering grey cliffs of Chaka's Gate, 'right across it, we're going to build the biggest bloody dam in the whole world.'

They sat together in darkness, close together as though for comfort, and Mark had not lit the lantern. The reflected glow of stars was thrown in under the thatched veranda of the cottage, giving them just enough light to make out each other's faces.

'We knew it was coming,' whispered Storm. 'And yet somehow I did not believe it. Just as though wishing could make it stop.'

'I'm going through early tomorrow to see your father,' Mark told her. 'He has to know.'

She nodded, 'Yes, we must be ready to confront them.'

'What will you do? I can't leave you here with John.'

'And you can't take me with you. Not to my father,' she agreed. 'It's all right, Mark, I'll take John back to the cottage. We'll wait for you.'

'I'll come for you there, and next time we return here, you'll be my wife.'

She leaned against him 'If there is anything to return to,' she whispered. 'Oh Mark, Mark – they can't do it! They can't drown all this – this –' The words eluded her and she fell silent, clinging to him.

They did not speak again, until minutes later a low polite cough roused them, and Mark straightened to see the dark familiar bulk of Pungushe standing below the veranda in the starlight.

'Pungushe,' he said. 'I see you.'

'Jamela,' the Zulu replied, and there was a tone and tightness in his voice that Mark had never heard before. 'I have been to the camp of the strangers. The cutters of wood, the men with painted poles, and bright axes.'

He turned his head to look down the valley, and they followed his gaze. The ruddy glow of many camp fires flickered against the lower slopes of the cliffs and on the still night air, the sounds of laughter and men's voices carried faintly.

'Yes?' Mark asked.

'There are two white men there. One of them is young and blind and of no importance – while the other is a square thick man, who stands solid on his feet like a bull buffalo, and yet moves silently, and speaks little and quietly.'

'Yes?' Mark asked again.

'I have seen this man before in the valley,' Pungushe paused. 'He is the silent one of whom we have spoken. He is the one who shot *ixhegu*, your grandfather – and smoked as he watched him die.'

Hobday moved quietly, solidly, along the edge of the slash line of the trees. The axes were silent, now, but the end of the noon break would be enforced to the minute. At the stroke of the hour they would be back at work. He was driving them hard, he always worked his gangs hard, took a pride in his ability to extract from each man effort beyond his wage. It was one of the qualities that Dirk Courtney valued in him – that and his loyalty, a fierce unswerving loyalty that baulked at no demand upon it. There was no squeamishness, no hesitating. When Dirk Courtney ordered it, there was no question asked. Hobday's reward was every day more apparent, already he was a man of substance, and when the new land was apportioned, that red sweet well-watered soil, rich as newly butchered beef, then his reward would be complete.

He paused at the spot where the slope increased sharply, angling into its plunge to the river bed below, and he looked out across the land. Involuntarily he licked his lips, like a glutton smelling rich food.

They had worked so long for this, each of them in his own way, led and inspired by Dirk Courtney, and although Hobday's personal share of the spoil would be a minute fraction of a single per cent, yet it was riches such as most other men only dream of.

He licked his lips again, standing very still and silent in the shadows and he looked to the sky. The clouds were piled to the very heavens, mountains of silver, blinding in the sunlight, and as he watched they moved ponderously down on the light wind. He could feel the closeness, and he stirred impatiently. Rain would delay them seriously, and rain was coming, the big torrential summer rains.

Then he was distracted again. Something moved on the far side of the slash line, and his eye darted to the movement. It was a flash of bright colour like the flick of a sunbird's wing, and his veiled eyes jumped to it instantly, his body without moving became charged with tension.

The girl came out of the brush line, and paused thirty paces away. She had not seen him, and she stood poised, listening, head cocked like a forest animal.

She stood lightly, gracefully, and her limbs were slim and brown, the flesh so firm and young and sweet that he felt the quick bright rush of lust again as he had when, the previous day, he had seen her for the first time.

She wore a loose, wide peasant skirt of gay colour, and a thin cotton bodice pulled low at the front and drawn loosely with a string that left the bulge of bosom pushing free, the fine skin shading from dark ruddy brown to pale cream. She was dressed like a girl going to meet a lover, and there was a deliciously fearful tenseness in the way she took a step forward and stopped again uncertainly. He felt the lust fuelled in his groin, and he was suddenly aware of his own hoarse breathing.

The girl turned her head and looked directly at him, and as she saw him, she started visibly, dropping back a pace with one hand flying to her mouth.

She stared at him for fully five seconds, and then slowly a transformation came over her.

The fingers dropped away from her face and she put both hands behind her back, a movement that thrust the pert breasts against the cotton of her bodice so he could see the rosy dark buttons of her nipples through the material. She thrust out one hip at a saucy angle, and lifted her chin boldly. Deliberately she let her eyes slide down his body, let them linger on his groin, and then rise again to his face. It was an invitation as clear as the spoken word, and Hobday heard the blood roaring in his ears.

She tossed her head, flicking the thick braid of hair over her shoulder, and she turned away, walking deliberately back to the tree-line, exaggerating the roll of tight round buttocks under the skirt.

She looked back over her shoulder, and as he started forward to follow, she let out a tingling flirt of laughter and ran lightly on sandalled feet, turning at an angle down the slope and Hobday began to run.

Within fifty yards Storm had lost sight of him in the heavy underbrush, and she stopped to listen, fearful that he might have given up the pursuit. Then there was movement above her, at the crest of the slope, and she realized with the first pang of real alarm that he had moved more swiftly than she had anticipated, and he had not followed her down, but had stayed above her in a position of command.

She went off again, running, and almost immediately she realized that he was ahead of her, moving fast along the crest. From up there, he could trap her by a swift turn directly down the slope.

She felt panic spur her, and started to run in earnest. Immediately the loose scree betrayed her and slipped away under her feet. She fell and rolled, flailing her arms for support and coming up on to her knees the moment her fall was broken.

She let out a little sob of fear. The man had seen her fall and had come down the slope. He was so close that she could see the square white teeth in the brown smooth face. He was grinning, a keen excited grimace, and he was steady and quick, moving down directly into the path along which she must run to safety, cutting her off squarely from where Mark waited.

She jumped to her feet and swirled away, doubling the slope, instinctively turning directly away from her pursuer – and from all help. Suddenly, she was completely alone, fleeing on frantic feet into the lonely spaces of the bush, beyond earshot of succour. Mark had been right, she realized, he had not wanted her to act as the bait. He had known just how dangerous a game she had set out to play, but in her stubborn arrogant way she had insisted, laughing at his protests, belittling his fears, until he had reluctantly agreed. Now she was running, terrified, the terror making her heart pound and squeezing her lungs so that her legs felt weak and rubbery under her.

Once she tried to turn back, but like an old and wily hound coursing a hare, he had anticipated and was there to block her, again she ran and suddenly the river was in front of her. The up-country rains had spated the course of the Bubezi and it rolled past in wide green majesty. She had to turn again along the bank, and was immediately into the area of thick jessie bush. The heavy thorn crowded her closely, leaving only narrow passages, a labyrinth of dark and secret twists and turns in which almost immediately she lost direction. She stopped and stood, trying to listen over the rush of her own breathing, trying to see through the wavering mist of her tears, tears of fear and of helplessness.

Her hair had come down in little wisps over her forehead, her cheeks blazed with high colour, and the tears made her eyes glitter with a feverish sheen.

She heard nothing, and the brown thorn encircled her. She turned slowly, almost like a blind woman, and now she was sobbing softly in her terror; she chose one of the narrow passages for escape and dived into it.

He was waiting for her. She came round the first twist of the pathway and ran almost directly into his chest.

Only at the very last instant she saw the outstretched arms, thick and brown and smooth, with the fingers of both hands hooked to seize her.

She screamed, high and shrill, and spun away, back along the path she had come, but his fingers caught in the thin cotton of her blouse. It tore like paper, and as she ran, the smooth creamy flesh of her back shone through the rent, flashing with a pearly promise that spurred his lust even higher, and when he laughed, it was a hoarse breathless blurt of sound that launched Storm into a fresh paroxysm of terror.

He hunted her through the jessie, and twice when he could have taken her, he deliberately let her slip through his fingers, drawing out the excruciating pleasure of it, cat with mouse, delighting at the way she shrieked at his touch, and at the fresh outburst of frantic terror with which she tried to escape him.

But at last she was finished, and she backed up into a corner of solid impenetrable thorn wall, and crouched there, clutching the shreds of her torn blouse about her, trembling with the wild uncontrollable shudders of a patient in high fever, her face smeared with tears and her sweat, staring at him with huge dark blue eyes.

He came slowly to her. He stooped and she was unresisting as he placed his big square brown hands on her shoulders.

He was still chuckling, but his own breath was unsteady, and his lips were drawn back from the square white teeth in a grimace of lust and excitement.

He pressed his mouth down over hers, and it was like one of those nightmares in which she could not move nor scream. His teeth crushed painfully against her lips, and she tasted her own blood, a slick metallic salt on her tongue and she felt herself suffocating, his hands were hard and rough as granite on the soft silk of her breasts and she came to life again, tugging unavailingly at his wrists, trying to drag them away.

'Yes,' he grunted, in the soft thick choked voice. 'Fight. Keep fighting me. Yes. Yes. That's right – struggle – don't stop.'

His voice roused her from the hypnotic spell of terror, and she screamed again.

'Yes,' he said. 'Do that. Scream again.' And he turned her across his body, forcing her down until his knee caught her in the small of the back, and her body bent backwards like a drawn bow, her hair sweeping the ground and the curve of her throat was soft and white and vulnerable, he placed his open mouth on her throat.

She was pinned helplessly as with one hand he swept the wide peasant skirt up above her waist.

'Scream!' he whispered gutturally. 'Scream again.' And with complete and horrified disbelief she felt those thick brown fingers, calloused and deliberately cruel, begin to prise open her body. They seemed to tear her tenderest, most secret flesh, like the talons of an eagle – and she screamed and screamed.

Mark had lost them in the labyrinthine maze of the jessie bush, and there had been silence now for many minutes.

He stood bareheaded and panting, listening with every fibre of his being in the aching silence of the jessie thorn, his eyes were wild, and he hated himself with bitter venom for letting himself be persuaded by Storm.

He had known how dangerous this man was, he was a killer, a coldly competent killer, and he had sent a girl, a young and tender girl, to bait him.

Then Storm screamed, close by in the jessie, and with a violent lift of savage relief, Mark began to run again.

At the last moment Hobday heard him coming, and he dropped Storm's slim abused body and turned with unbelievable speed, dropping into the crouch of a heavyweight prize-fighter, solid and low behind lifted arms and hunched shoulders, thick and rubbery with muscle.

Mark swung the weapon he had made the night before, a long sausage of raw-hide, the seams double sewn, and then filled with lead buckshot. It weighed two pounds, and it made a sound through the air like the wings of a wild duck and he swung full-armed, the blow given power and weight by his terrible anger and hatred.

Hobday threw up his right arm to catch the blow. The bones of his forearm broke cleanly, with a sharp crackle, but still the force of the blow was not fully expended and the leaded bag flew on, directly into Hobday's face.

Had he not caught the full weight of it on his arm, the blow would have killed him. As it was, his face seemed to collapse and his head snapped backwards to the full stretch of his neck.

Hobday crashed backwards into the wall of jessie and the curved, red-tipped thorns caught in his clothing and flesh and held him there, sprawling like a boneless doll, arms outspread, legs dangling, his face hanging forward on his chest and the thick dark droplets of blood beginning to fall on to his shirt and roll softly downwards across his belly, leaving wet crimson lines down the khaki drill.

The rain began as they carried Hobday up the track to where the two vehicles were kept under the lee of the cliffs of Chaka's Gate, on the south bank of the Bubezi. It came with the first splattering of fat warm drops, that stung exposed skin with their weight and momentum. It fell heavily and still more heavily, turning the surface of the track to a glaze like melting chocolate, so they slipped under their burden.

Hobday was chained at his ankles with the manacles that Mark used for holding arrested poachers. His good arm was cuffed to the leather belt at his waist, the other arm was crudely splinted and strapped down to the same belt.

Mark had tried to force him to walk, but either he was shamming or he was really too weak. His face was grotesquely distorted, the nose was swollen and pushed to one side, both eyes almost closed and leaden blue with bruises, his lips also were swollen and thickly scabbed with black dried blood where they had been mashed against his teeth, and through the mangled flesh were the dark gaps where five of the big square teeth had been torn out or snapped off level with the gum by the murderous force of Mark's blow.

Pungushe and Mark carried him between them, laboriously up the steep path in the teeming, stinging rain, and behind them trailed Storm with baby John on her hip, her hair melting in long black shiny smears down her face in the rain. She was shivering violently, in sudden uncontrollable spasms, either from the cold or from lingering shock. The child on her hip squalled petulantly, and she covered him with a fold of oilskin and tried to hush him distractedly.

They reached the two vehicles under the crude thatched shelter Pungushe had built to protect them from the elements. They put Hobday into the side-car of the Ariel, and Mark buttoned the canvas screen over him to protect him from the rain and to hold him secure. He lay like a corpse.

Then Mark crossed to where Storm sat, shivering, and sodden and miserable, behind the wheel of the battered old Cadillac.

'I'm sending Pungushe with you,' he said, as he took her in his arms and held her briefly. She did not have the strength or will to argue, and she leaned heavily against Mark's chest for comfort.

'Go to the cottage – and stay there,' he instructed. 'Don't move out of it until I come for you.'

'Yes, Mark,' she whispered, and shuddered again.

'Are you strong enough to drive?' he asked with sudden gentleness, and she roused herself and nodded gamely.

'I love you,' he said. 'More than anything or anybody in this world.'

Mark led on the motorcycle over the slippery, muddy track, and it was almost dark when they reached the main road, itself hardly better than a track with deeply churned double ruts in the glutinous mud, and all the time the rain fell.

At the crossroads, Mark pulled the motorcycle off the road, and hurried back to talk to Storm through the open window of the Cadillac.

'It's six hours from here to Umhlanga Rocks in this mud, don't try and push it,' he told her, and reached through the window. They embraced awkwardly but fiercely, and then she rolled up the window and the Cadillac pulled away, the rear end sliding and skidding in the mud.

Mark watched it over a rise in the land, and when the rear lights winked out over the ridge, he went back to the motorcycle and kicked the engine to life.

In the side-car the man stirred, and his voice was mushy and distorted through the mangled lips.

'I'm going to kill you for this,' he said.

'Like you killed my grandfather?' Mark asked softly, and wheeled the cycle into the road. He took the fork to Ladyburg, thirty miles away through the darkness and the mud and the rain, and his hatred and anger warmed him all the way like a bonfire in his belly, and he marvelled at his own restraint in resisting the temptation to kill Hobday with the bludgeon when he had the chance.

The man who had tortured and murdered the old man, and who had abused the desecrated Storm was in his power – and still the temptation to avenge himself was fierce. Mark pushed it aside and drove on grimly into the night.

The motorcycle slipped and slid from one verge of the road to the other as he took it up the steep ascent of the Ladyburg escarpment, and below him the lights of the town were blanketed by the falling white fog of rain.

Mark was uncertain as to whether or not the General was in residence at Lion Kop, but as he gunned the machine into the walled kitchen yard he saw lights in the windows, and a clamorous pack of the General's hunting dogs rushed out into the night followed by three Zulu servants with lanterns. Mark shouted at them.

'Is the Nkosi here?'

Their answers were superfluous, for as Mark dismounted, he looked up and saw the bulky familiar beloved shape step into the lighted window of the study, head held low on broad shoulders, as Sean Courtney peered down at him.

Mark ran into the house, stripping off his streaming oilskins, and he burst into the General's study.

'My boy.' Sean Courtney hurried to meet him across the huge room. 'What is it?' Mark's whole being was charged with a fierce and triumphant purpose.

'I have the man who killed my grandfather,' he exulted, and halfway across the study Sean stopped dead and stared at him.

'Is it –' he stopped, and the dread was plain on his face, 'is it Dirk Courtney, is it my son?'

The servants carried Hobday's heavy inert body into the study and laid him on the buttoned leather sofa in front of the fire.

'Who put those chains on him?' growled Sean, studying the man, and then without waiting for a reply, 'Take them off him. My God, what happened to his face?'

Ruth Courtney came then, awakened by the uproar and excitement, dressed in a long dressing-gown with her night cap still knotted under her chin.

'Good Lord,' she stared at Hobday. 'His arm is broken, and perhaps his jaw also.'

'How did it happen?' Sean demanded.

'I hit him,' Mark explained, and Sean was silent for a long moment staring at him, before he spoke again.

'I think you had better tell me the whole story,' he said. 'From the beginning.'

While Ruth Courtney worked quietly over Hobday's broken face, Mark began his explanation to the General.

'His name is Hobday, he works for Dirk Courtney – has done so for years. One of his right-hand men.'

'Of course,' Sean nodded. 'I should have recognized him. It was the swollen face. I've seen him before.'

Quietly, quickly, Mark told everything he knew about the man, starting from his first meeting with Hobday at the deserted homestead on Andersland.

'He told you he was working for Dirk Courtney then?' Sean demanded.

'For Ladyburg Sugar,' Mark qualified, and Sean nodded his white beard on to his chest.

'Go on.'

Mark repeated Pungushe's story of the old man's death, how the three men had come with him to the valley, and how 'the silent one' had shot him and waited for him to die, and how they had buried him in an unmarked grave.

However, Sean shook his head, frowning, and Hobday on the couch stirred and tried to sit up. His swollen, distorted jaw worked and the words were blurred.

'It's a bloody nigger lie,' he said. 'First time I've ever been to Chaka's Gate was three days ago.'

Sean Courtney's worry showed clearly on his gaunt features as he turned back to Mark.

'You say you hit this man, that you are responsible for his injuries. How did it happen?'

'When he came to the valley, Pungushe recognized him as the man who killed John Anders. I lured him out of his camp, and Pungushe and I captured him and brought him here.'

'After half killing him?' Sean asked, heavily, and did not wait for Mark's reply. 'My boy, I think you've put yourself into a very serious position. I cannot see a shred of evidence to support all this, evidence that would convict a man in a court of law – while on the other hand you have assaulted somebody, grievous bodily harm and abduction at the least –'

'Oh, I do have proof,' Mark cut in quickly.

'What is it?' Sean asked gruffly.

The man on the couch turned his battered face to Sean, and his voice rose confidently.

'He's a bloody liar. It's all lies –'

'Quiet!' Sean waved him to silence, and looked to Mark again. 'Proof?' he asked.

'My proof will be in the fact that Dirk Courtney kills this man, or has him killed, the moment we turn him free.'

They all stared at Mark in stunned silence, and Mark went on seriously.

'We all know how Dirk Courtney works. He destroys anything that stands in his way, or that is a danger to him.'

Hobday was watching him, and for once the eyes were no longer veiled and cold. His mangled lips quivered and gaped slightly, showing the black gaps where the teeth were missing from his jaw.

'It isn't necessary for this man to confess anything to us. The fact that he has been here, in this house, with the General and myself, in the camp of Dirk Courtney's enemies, the fact that his face bears the marks of heavy persuasion – that will be enough for Dirk Courtney. Then one phone call is all it would take. Something like this.' Mark paused, then went on. '"Hobday was with us, he is ready to make a sworn statement – about the killing of John Anders." Then we take Hobday down to the village and leave him there. Dirk Courtney kills him, but this time we are ready. For once we can trace the murder directly to him.'

'God damn you,' snarled Hobday, struggling into a sitting position. 'It's a lie. I haven't confessed anything.'

'You can tell that to Dirk Courtney. He might believe you,' Mark told him quietly. 'On the other hand, if you turned king's evidence and did confess, you'd have the protection of the General and the law, all the force of the law – and we would not turn you loose.'

Hobday looked around him wildly, as though some avenue of escape might open miraculously for him, but Mark went on remorselessly.

'You know Dirk Courtney better than any of us, don't you, Hobday? You know how his mind works. Do you think he will take the chance that you didn't confess? Just how useful are you going to be to him in the future? Can you trust his loyalty, now that the shadow of doubt is on you? You know what he is going to do, don't you? If you think about it, you'll realize that your only chance of survival will be to have Dirk Courtney locked up safely, or dancing at the end of a rope.'

Hobday glared at him. 'You bastard,' he hissed through his broken lips, and it was as though a cork had been drawn; a steady stream of obscenity poured from him, vicious filth, the ugly meaningless words repeated over and over again, while his naked eyes glittered with helpless hatred.

Mark stood up and cranked the handset of the telephone on Sean's desk.

'Exchange,' he said into the mouthpiece. 'Please connect me with the residence of Mister Dirk Courtney.'

'No!' choked Hobday. 'Don't do that!' and now terror had replaced hatred, and his face seemed to collapse around the ruined nose and mouth.

Mark made no effort to obey, and clearly everybody in the room heard the click of a connection being made, and then the squawk of a voice distorted by the wires and distance.

'This is the residence of the Honourable Deputy Minister for Lands, Mr Dirk Courtney –'

Hobday lumbered off the couch, and staggered to the desk, he snatched the earpiece from Mark's hand and slammed it back on to its bracket of the telephone.

'No,' he panted, with pain and fear. 'Please don't do that.'

He hung on to the corner of the desk, hunched up with the pain, clutching his broken arm to his chest, his mashed features working convulsively. They waited quietly, Mark and Ruth and Sean, waiting for him to reach his decision.

Hobday turned and staggered heavily back to the sofa. He collapsed upon it with his head hanging forward, almost touching his knees, and his breathing hissed and sobbed in the silence.

'All right,' he whispered hoarsely. 'What do you want to know?'

General Sean Courtney shook himself as though awaking from a nightmare, but his voice was decisive and brisk.

'Mark, take the Rolls. Go down into town and get me a lawyer. I want this statement drawn up in proper form – I'm still a Justice of the Peace and Commissioner of Oaths. I will witness the document.'

Mark parked the Rolls in Peter Botes's gravel driveway of the big new house on the outskirts of town.

The house was dark and silent, but to Mark's heavy knocking on the carved teak front door, a dog began to bark in the house somewhere, and at last a light bloomed in an upstairs window and the sash slid up with a squeal.

'Who is it? What do you want?' Peter's voice was querulous and fuddled with sleep.

'It's Mark,' he shouted up at the window. 'You've got to come with me, now!'

'My God, Mark, it's after eleven o'clock. Can't it wait until morning?'

'General Courtney wants you, now.'

The name had its effect. There was a mumble of voices within the bedroom, Marion's sister protesting sleepily, and then Peter called down again.

'All right, give me a minute to dress, Mark.'

As he waited in the driver's seat of the Rolls with the rain slashing down on the roof, and rippling in wavering lines down across the windshield, Mark pondered briefly why he had chosen Peter Botes. It was not only that he knew exactly where to find him so late at night. He realized that he wanted Peter to be there when they tore down his idol, he wanted to rub his nose in it when they proved Dirk Courtney a thief and a murderer. He wanted that satisfaction, and he smiled bleakly without humour in the darkened Rolls.

'I deserve at least that,' he whispered to himself, and the front door of the house opened. Peter hurried out, ducking his head against the slanting rain.

'What is it?' he demanded, through the window of the Rolls. 'It had better be important – getting me out at this time of night.'

'It's important enough,' Mark told him, and started the engine. 'Get in!'

'I'll follow you in my Packard,' Peter told him and ran to the garage.

Peter Botes sat at General Courtney's big desk. Hurriedly dressed, he was without a necktie and his small prosperous paunch bulged the white shirt, pulling it free of his trousers' waistband. His sandy hair was thinning and ruffled, so that pink scalp showed through as he bowed over the foolscap sheet of paper.

He wrote swiftly, a neat regular script, his features betraying each new shock at the words he was transcribing, his cheeks pale and his mouth set and thin.

Every few minutes he would pause incredulously and stare at Hobday across the room, breathing heavily at some new and terrible admission.

'Have you got that?' the General demanded, and Peter nodded jerkily and began to write again.

The others listened intently. The General slumped in his chair by the fire. His eyes were closed, as though he slept, but the questions he rapped out every few minutes were bright and penetrating as a rapier blade.

Mark stood behind his chair, quiet and intent, his face expressionless, although his anger and his hatred cramped in his guts.

Hobday sat forward on the sofa and his voice was a muffled drone in his thick north-country accent, muted in contrast to the terrible words he spoke.

It was not only the killing of John Anders. There was more, much more. Forgery of State documents, bribery of high officials, direct abuse of public office, and Mark started and leaned forward with shock as Hobday recounted how he had tried on two occasions, following Dirk Courtney's orders, to kill him.

Mark had not realized nor recognized him, but now Hobday's stocky shape tied in his memory with the shadowy faceless hunter in the night on the escarpment – and with the other figure seen through the rain and the fever mists. Hobday did not look up as he told it, and Mark had no questions to ask. It was as though once Hobday had started, he must purge himself of all this filth, as though he were now deriving some perverse satisfaction from the horror his words struck into his audience.

They listened, appalled by the magnitude of it all. Every few minutes, Ruth exclaimed involuntarily, and Sean would open his eyes briefly to stare at her, before closing them again and covering them with one hand.

At last Hobday came to the murder of John Anders, and each detail was exactly as Pungushe had described it. Mark felt sickened and wretched as he listened, but he asked only one question.

'Why did you let him die so slowly – why didn't you finish him?'

'It had to look like an accident.' Hobday did not look up. 'One bullet only. A man does not shoot himself twice by accident. I had to let him die in his own time.'

There was no breadth nor horizon to Mark's anger, and this time Ruth Courtney caught her breath with a sound like a sob. Again Sean Courtney opened his eyes. 'Are you all right, my dear?'

She nodded silently, and Sean turned back to Hobday. 'Go on,' he said.

At the end, Peter Botes read the statement back, his voice quivering and fading at the more horrendous passages, so that Sean had to gruff at him fiercely.

'Speak up, man.' He had made two fair copies, and Hobday signed each page with an illiterate scrawl, and then each of them signed below him, and Sean pressed his wax seal of office on to the final page of each copy.

'All right,' he said, as he carried the top document to the iron safe built into the wall behind his desk. 'I want you to keep and file the other copy,' he said to Peter. 'Thank you for your help, Mr Botes.' He locked the safe and turned back into the room. 'Mark, will you telephone Doctor Acheson now, please? We've got to take care of our witness, I suppose. Though, for my money, I'd just as soon see him suffer.'

When Doctor Acheson arrived at Lion Kop, it was almost two in the morning, and Ruth Courtney took him up to the guest room where Hobday lay.

Neither Sean Courtney nor Mark went up; they stayed in the study, sitting quietly together across the fire which a servant had built. Against the windows, the wind bumped and the rain spattered. Sean was drinking whisky, and Mark had filled his glass twice for him in the last hour. He was slumped down in his favourite chair now, tired and old and bowed with grief, holding the glass with both hands.

'If I had the courage, I would take the rifle to him myself – like a rabid dog. But he is still my son, no matter how often I deny it, he is still of my blood, of my loins.'

Mark was silent, and Ruth came into the room.

'Doctor Acheson is setting that man's arm,' she said. 'He will be another hour, but I think you should come up to bed now, my dear.' She crossed to Sean's chair and laid a gentle hand on his shoulder. 'We have all had more than enough for one day.'

The telephone rang on the desk, a tinny irritant sound that startled them all. They stared at it for a full five seconds, until it rang again demandingly and Ruth crossed to it and lifted the earpiece.

'Mrs Ruth Courtney,' she said softly, almost fearfully.

'Mrs Courtney, are you the mother of Mrs Storm Hunt?'

'Yes, this is correct.'

'I am afraid we have very bad news. This is the Superintendent of Addington Hospital in Durban. Your daughter has been involved in a motor accident. The rain and the mud, I am afraid. Her son, your grandchild, has been killed outright. Thankfully he suffered no pain, but your daughter is in a critical condition. Can you come to her, as soon as you possibly can? We don't know if she will last the night, I'm afraid.'

The telephone dropped from Ruth's hand, and she swayed on her feet, the colour flying from her face, leaving it frosted with icy white.

'Oh God!' she whispered, and she started to fall, her legs collapsed and she crumpled forward. Mark caught her before she hit the floor and lowered her on to the sofa.

Sean crossed to the dangling earpiece and lifted it. 'This is General Courtney,' he barked angrily. 'What is it?'

Mark took the big Rolls down the long slanting right hand turn towards the bridge very fast. The woman he loved, the mother of his dead child, was dying – and Mark's heart was breaking. The road was deep with chocolate mud, and other vehicles had rutted it deeply, churning the mud to a thick ugly porridge. The Rolls flared and kicked in the ruts, but Mark fought the wheel grimly.

The bridge over the Baboon Stroom was five hundred yards ahead of them, still invisible in the endless driving rain. The headlights faded fifty feet ahead, overwhelmed by the flights of white raindrops, thick as javelins.

In the rear seat, Ruth Courtney sat quietly, staring ahead with eyes that did not see. The collar of her fur coat was pulled up around her ears, so she looked small and frail as a child.

General Sean Courtney sat beside Mark, and he was talking quietly, as though to himself.

'I've left it too late. I've been a stubborn old fool. I wanted too much from her – I wanted her to be better than human, and I was too harsh on her when she did not meet the standards I set for her. I should have gone to her long ago, and now perhaps it's too late.'

'It's not too late,' Mark denied. 'She will live, she must live.'

'It's too late for my grandson,' whispered Sean. 'I never saw him – and only now I realize how much I wanted to –'

At the mention of baby John, Mark felt the sickening jolt of despair in his stomach again and he wanted to shout.

'He was my son. My first born!' But beside him, Sean was talking again.

'I've been a spiteful and unforgiving old man. God have mercy on me, but I even cut my own daughter out of my will. I disowned her, and now I hate myself for that. If only we can reach her, if only I can talk to her once more. Please, God, grant me that.'

Ahead of them the steel guard railings of the bridge loomed out of the torrential darkness, and lightning bounced off the belly of the clouds. For an instant Mark saw the spidery steel tracery of the railway bridge spanning the chasm two hundred yards downstream. Under it, the rocky sides of the gorge dropped almost sheer a hundred and fifty feet to the swollen racing brown flood waters of the Baboon Stroom.

Mark touched the brakes, and then double-declutched the gears, bringing the Rolls under tighter control as he lined up for the entrance to the road bridge.

Suddenly, dazzling light flared from the darkness on the right hand side of the road, and Mark threw up one hand to protect his eyes.

Out of the darkness rushed a great dark shape, with two blazing headlights glaring like malevolent eyes as it came.

With sudden clarity of mind, Mark realized that the Rolls was trapped helplessly on the approach ramp to the bridge, and that on his left hand, only a frail railing of iron pipes screened them from the drop and that the monstrous vehicle racing down from the right would come into a collision which would hurl the Rolls through the railing as though it were a child's toy.

'Hold on!' he screamed, and swung the wheel to meet the roaring towering monster of steel, and the blinding white light cut into his eyes.

Peter Botes pulled off the road into the pine trees and switched off the engine of the Packard. In the silence he could hear the pine branches thrashing restlessly on the wind, and the dislodged rain-drops tapped on the roof.

Peter lit a cigarette and the match danced in his cupped hands. He inhaled deeply, waiting for the calming effect of the tobacco smoke, and he stared ahead up the straight roadway that led to Great Longwood, the homestead of Dirk Courtney.

He sensed that the decision he must make now was the most vital of his entire life. Whichever way he decided, his life was already changed for ever.

When Dirk Courtney fell, he would bring down all those close to him, even the innocent, as he was innocent. The scandal and the guilt would sully him, and he had worked so hard for it. The prestige, the blooming career and all the sweets that he was just now starting to enjoy. All of it would be gone, and he would have to begin again, perhaps in another town, another land, to begin again right at the very bottom. The thought appalled him, he had become used to being a man of substance and importance. He did not know if he could face a new beginning.

On the other hand, if Dirk Courtney did not come down, if he were saved from death and disaster – just how grateful would he be to the man who worked his salvation? He knew the extent of Dirk Courtney's present fortune and power, and it was conceivable that some of that, perhaps a large slice of that might come to him, to Peter Botes, the man who had saved Dirk Courtney, and yet still retained the instrument of his destruction.

It was one of those moments of destiny, Peter realized, that come only occasionally to a chosen few. On one hand, dishonour and obscurity – on the other, power and riches, tens of thousands, perhaps even millions.

He started the engine of the Packard and the rear wheels spun in the slimy mud, and then he swerved back on to the driveway, and put the big machine to the hill.

Dirk Courtney sat on the corner of his desk, one foot swinging idly. He wore a dressing-gown of patterned silk, and the lustrous material caught the lamplight as he moved. There was a white silk scarf at his throat, and his eyes were clear and alert in the handsome tanned face, as though he had not just risen from deep sleep.

He spun the duelling pistol on his forefinger as he listened intently.

Peter Botes sat nervously on the edge of the chair, and though there was a fire in the grate that Dirk had poked and fed to a fierce blaze, still he shivered every few moments and rubbed his hands together. The cold was in his soul, he realized, and his voice rose a little as he gabbled on.

Dirk Courtney did not speak, made no comment nor exclamation, asked no question until he was done. He spun the pistol, two turns and the butt snapped into the palm of his hand. Two turns, and snap.

When Peter Botes finished, Dirk cocked the hammer of the pistol and the click of the mechanism was unreasonably loud in the silent room.

'Hobday, my father, his wife, young Anders – and yourself. The only ones that know.'

'And the Zulu.'

'And the Zulu,' Dirk agreed, and dry-fired the pistol. The hammer cracked against the pan.

'How many copies of the statement?'

'One,' lied Peter. 'In the iron safe of the General's study.'

Dirk nodded and re-cocked the pistol. 'All right. If there is another copy, you have it,' he said. 'But we don't lie to each other, do we, Peter?'

It was the first time he had used his given name, there was a familiarity and a threat in it, and Peter could only nod with a dryness in his throat.

Again Dirk dry-fired the pistol, and smiled. It was that warm and charming smile, that frank and friendly smile that Peter knew so well.

'We love each other too much for that, don't we ?' He kept smiling.

'That's why you came to tell me this, isn't it? Because we love each other?'

Peter said nothing, and Dirk went on, still smiling, 'And of course you are going to be a rich man, Peter – if you do as I ask. A very rich man. You will do as I ask, won't you, Peter?'

And Peter nodded again. 'Yes, of course,' he blurted.

'I want you to make a phone call,' said Dirk. 'If you speak through a handkerchief, it will sound as though it's long distance, and it will muffle your voice. Nobody will recognize it. Will you do that?'

'Of course,' Peter nodded.

'You will phone my father's house, speak either to him or his wife. I want you to pretend that you are the Superintendent of Addington Hospital, and here is what you will tell them –'

* * *

Dirk Courtney sat in the darkened cab of the truck, and listened to the rain as he reviewed his plans and preparations carefully.

He did not like having to move in a hurry, without time for careful planning. It was too easy to overlook some vital detail.

He did not like having to do this type of work himself. It was best to send another. He did not take personal risks, not any more, not unless there was no other way.

Regrets and misgivings were vain and wasted the moments which still remained before action. He turned all his attention back to his planning.

They would use the Rolls, and there would be three of them, the General and his Jewish whore, and that arrogant scheming puppy Anders.

Dirk had picked the spot with care, and the farmyard truck was loaded with fifty sacks of horse-feed. Three tons of dead weight. It would give it irresistible momentum.

Afterwards he must do two things, firstly he must make sure of them. He had a length of lead piping wrapped in hessian packing. It would crack a skull without breaking skin. Then he must take the General's keys. The key of the safe was on the bunch, and it was on his watch chain. The thought of plundering his father's dead body did not cause him even a tremor. His only concern was that the keys were retrievable, that there was no fire and that the Rolls was not submerged in the roaring torrent of the Baboon Stroom.

If that did happen, he must rely then on the General not having changed his habits of twenty years before. The spare key had been kept in the wine cellar then, on the rack above the champagne bottles. Dirk had discovered it there when he had used the cellar in a boyhood game, and he had taken the key twice for his own ends, and returned it secretly. The General was an old dog, a creature of habit. It would still be there. Dirk was certain.

All right, then, the safe. Two keys. If neither was available, then it was an old safe, but he did not want to use force on it. He must hope for the keys. Anyway, he was content that he could open it one way or another.

The statement was his, to be carefully burned, and that left Hobday. Probably in one of the guest rooms, sedated, helpless. The lead pipe again, and then an overturned paraffin lamp. It was a big house of old dry wooden beams and thick thatch. It would burn as a pyre, with Hobday lying in it like a Viking chieftain.

That left only Peter Botes, Dirk glanced sideways at him. The situation was containable, it was no worse than fifty others he had survived. It needed only swift, direct action. He spoke encouragingly to Peter.

'Don't worry,' he said. 'After tonight, a new life awaits you, I'm going to take you with me along the paths of wealth and power, Peter. You'll never regret this night, I swear it to you.'

He squeezed Peter's upper arm, a comradely gesture in the darkness. Of course, he had a copy of the statement, Dirk thought, but afterwards there would be time – plenty of time to find it and to be rid of the pompous little prig. In a year or so, when the excitement had died down, another little accident, and it would all be over.

'Have you got the pistol?' he asked, and Peter gulped nervously, clutching the bulky military model Smith Wesson with both hands between his knees.

'You are not to use it,' Dirk warned again. 'Except as the very last resort. We don't want bullet holes to explain. You do understand?'

'Yes, I understand.'

'You are insurance, that's all. Final insurance.' And out in the darkness, through the slanting arrows of rain a light glowed and faded and grew again higher up the slope.

'Here they come,' said Dirk, and started the engine of the truck.

Mark spun the wheel hard right, and thrust the accelerator pedal against the floor-boards, trying to ride off the collision and beat the great roaring vehicle to the threshold of the bridge.

Behind him Ruth Courtney screamed shrilly, but Mark thought he had made it, he thought for an instant that the sudden acceleration had forged the Rolls ahead, but the truck slewed hard, swinging viciously, and he felt the crack of impact in every bone of his body.

It struck at the level of the rear wheels of the Rolls, and the big heavy car snapped sideways, tearing his hands from the steering-wheel and hurling Mark against the door. He felt bones break in his chest like dry twigs, and then the world turned end over end as the Rolls cartwheeled. A shower of bright white sparks flamed like the tail of a meteor in the darkness as steel brushed murderously against steel. There was another jerk as the Rolls crashed through the guardrail of the bridge and then they were dropping free, plunging silently into black space.

In the rear seat, Ruth Courtney was still screaming, and the Rolls struck, a glancing shuddering blow, bounding off the rock wall of the gorge, and leaping out into space once more.

Mark was pressed against the side door, held there by the accelerating dropping force of the plunging Rolls, but at the next impact the door burst open, and Mark was hurled like a stone from a slingshot, out into resounding swirling darkness.

He saw the burning headlights of the Rolls, spinning in a great vortex of blinding white, below him, and the gorge rang with the iron echoes of steel on rock, and the crazy bellowing roar of the Rolls-Royce engine jammed at full power.

He seemed to fall for ever, through darkness, and then suddenly he struck with a force that drove the air from his lungs. The hard, unyielding impact convinced him for a moment that his body was crushed to boneless pulp on the rocky floor of the gorge, but then the cold, tumultuous torrent of racing water overwhelmed him. He had been thrown far enough to fall into the river itself.

Clinging to his last shreds of consciousness, he fought for breath, fought to keep his head above the surface, as the torrent swept him away. Glistening black boulders leapt like predators out of the dark, clawing at his legs, pummelling his injured chest, barging into him with numbing bruising power in the flood, and icy water gushed down his straining throat – burning his lungs, and making him choke and retch for each breath.

He slid down a racing spill of white rapids, feeling skin stripped from his hip and shoulder at the contact of harsh rock and then, at the bottom, he struck again, jammed solid between two monumental rocks. In the darkness, they stood over him like gravestones.

He was held in their jaws, and the water tore furiously at him, as though denied of its prey, trying to pluck him away.

There was light, just enough to make out shapes and distances, and Mark marvelled at that with a brain jellied by pounding and starved of oxygen. Then he looked up, and through streaming eyes saw that the truck was parked on the threshold of the bridge high above the gorge, its headlights struck the ironwork and the light was broken up and diffused by the rain. It cast a vague uncertain glow into the gorge.

Added to this was a closer, more powerful light source. The smashed carapace of the Rolls-Royce lay at the foot of the cliff, half in the water, half upon the rocky ledge. It lay on its back, with all four wheels spiralling idly, but both headlights still burned fiercely, striking the uneven rock walls, providing a dramatic stage lighting.

Mark looked around him, and saw that the current had swept him in under the cliff, and that a ledge of glistening black rock extended out over his head. He reached up with his right hand, and then cried out as his fingers touched the ledge, and bright agony flared in his wrist.

Something was broken there, he realized, as he clung desperately to the slippery boulders, and tried to force the fingers of his right hand to open or close.

The torrent was too strong to resist much longer, and he felt himself starting to slide, dragging over the boulders, on the point of being swept away once more. He knew that less than a hundred yards downstream, the first waterfall plunged, frothing and thundering, down the sheer side of the escarpment.

He released his grip with the left hand, and threw himself upwards with all his strength. His fingers caught on the sharp lip of the ledge above his head, and his body swung like a pendulum, the hungry waters slashing at his knees, testing the strength of his grip, trying to drag him away, trying to break the hooked fingers, tearing the finger-nails loose so that droplets of blood squeezed out from under them.

Slowly, achingly, Mark bent the arm at the elbow, lifting his knees, drawing his feet clear of the water and its murderous drag.

He hung another moment, gathering what was left of his strength and resolve, and then, with one last convulsive heave, he threw his right arm upwards and hooked his elbow over the ledge, and followed it immediately with his left elbow.

Another moment of rest, and then he wriggled painfully out on the ledge and lay face down. He thought he was blind now, or that the lights had been doused, but the darkness was in his head only.

Slowly the darkness cleared, and he lifted his head. The thunder of the river drowned out all other sound, he could not hear the scrabble of loose stone and the slide of booted feet as Dirk Courtney came down the almost vertical pathway below the bridge. It did not surprise Mark that it was him – it seemed only natural that Dirk Courtney should be here, at the scene of disaster. He was dressed in hunting breeches and calf-length boots, a thick navy pea jacket and a woollen cap pulled low over his face.

He slid down the last ten feet of the cliff, keeping his balance, light as a dancer on his feet, and he paused on the ledge beside the shattered Rolls. Carefully he looked about him, flashing a lantern into the shadows and crevices.

Mark flattened himself down on the rock, but he was beyond the range of the lantern beam.

Dirk turned the beam on to the Rolls, and Mark groaned with the shock of it.

General Sean Courtney had been thrown halfway through the windscreen, and then the full weight of the machine had rolled on to his upper torso. His head was almost severed, and the thick white beard was sodden with bright blood, that shone like rubies in the lantern light.

Dirk Courtney stooped over him, and felt for the carotid pulse in the throat. Despite the fearful mutilation, he must have detected some flutter of stubborn life there. Dirk rolled the head sideways, and the eyes were open and startled.

Dirk lifted the short thick club he carried in his right hand. It was wrapped in coarse brown hessian, but its weight and heft were obvious, by the way he handled it.

Mark tried to cry out, but his hoarse croak was lost in the roar of waters. Dirk struck his father across the temple, above the right ear, where the wet grey curls were plastered against the skull, and Mark seemed to feel the thud of the blow in his own soul.

Then with one exploring forefinger, Dirk pressed the temple and felt the give of mortal damage, the grating of the rough edges of shattered bone shard deep in his father's head.

Dirk's features were expressionless, cold and remote, but then he did something which seemed to Mark more dreadful, more shocking than the killing blow. With a tender touch of his fingertips, he closed the eyelids over Sean Courtney's dead staring eyes. Then he went down on one knee and kissed his father's bloodied lips lightly, without a change of expression. It was the act of an unhinged mind. It was only at that moment that Mark realized that Dirk Courtney was insane.

Almost immediately, Dirk's manner changed and his hands lost the gentle touch, becoming once again businesslike and precise. He rolled the body, unbuttoned the camel-hair overcoat and searched swiftly through Sean's clothing. Then he drew out a gold watch chain with the keys and gold hunter attached.

He examined the keys briefly and then pushed them into his pocket. He stood and went to the rear door of the Rolls and struggled with the handle. The door burst open at last, and Ruth Courtney's body spilled out sideways and lay at his feet. He took a handful of her thick dark hair and drew her head back. Again he swung the short thick club against her temple, and again he felt the skull like a doctor making his diagnosis, prodding to feel the soft spot of crushed bone.

Satisfied, he lifted Ruth Courtney's limp, childlike body in his arms and carried her to the edge of the water. He dropped her over the side, and she was gone instantly, dashed away on the dark current, down to where the plunging waterfalls would tumble her body into the Ladyburg valley, and the cruel rocks would leave no doubt in a coroner's mind as to how she had died.

Helpless with his injuries and exhaustion, his body battered and strained beyond its natural limits, Mark could not move, could hardly breathe as he watched Dirk Courtney stoop and grasp his father's ankles. He dragged the General's heavy body to the edge of the torrent, straining backwards, against the dead weight.

Mark dropped his face into his hands and found that he was weeping, great racking dry sobs that probed the injuries deep in his chest.

When he looked up again, Sean Courtney's body was gone, and Dirk Courtney was coming towards where he lay, cautiously following the narrow ledge, searching the darkness with the lantern beam, sweeping the dark tumbling waters, examining each foot of the ledge, looking for him – looking for Mark, knowing he had been in the Rolls. The headlights of the truck had struck full into Mark's face in that fatal instant of collision. Dirk Courtney knew he was here – somewhere.

Mark rolled on to his side and tried to unfasten the buttons of his coat, but in his haste he had tried with the right hand, and he whimpered with the pain. With his left hand now, he ripped the buttons away and struggled out of the garment, its wet folds resisting each movement so that when he at last was free of it, Dirk Courtney was only fifty feet away, coming steadily, carefully along the ledge, the lantern in one hand, the short heavy club dangling in the other.

Lying on the edge of the river, Mark flipped the jacket sideways, trying to make it fall on to the rocks in the torrent below, but he had no time to see if he had succeeded. Dirk Courtney was too close.

Mark rolled in towards the foot of the cliff, stifling the cry of pain as his damaged ribs and broken wrist came in rude contact with the rock.

In the lee of the cliff there was a dark shallow chimney, screened from the light of the headlights and lantern. Mark came to his feet. Dirk Courtney was out of sight beyond the angle of the cliff, but the beam of his lantern jumped and swept and swung, bobbing with each pace as he came on.

Mark turned his face to the cliff, gathered himself, and found that some of his dissipated strength was returning, and his anger was still alive, like a small warm flame in his chest. He did not know if it was enough strength, or anger, to carry him through, but he began to climb, slowly, clumsily, like a maimed insect he clung to the cold wet rock and dragged himself upwards.

He was twenty feet up when Dirk Courtney stopped on the ledge directly below him. Mark froze into stillness, the last defence of the helpless animal, but he knew that the instant Dirk lifted the beam, he was discovered. He waited for it, with the numbed resignation of the beast waiting in the abattoir chute.

Dirk made another careful search, swinging the lantern in a full slow traverse of both sides of the river, and he was on the point of lifting the beam to play it on to the cliff where Mark hung, when something caught his attention.

He took two hurried paces to the edge of the rocky ledge and shone the lantern downwards.

Mark's jacket was caught on one of the boulders, and Dirk went down on one knee to try and reach it with one outstretched arm.

It was the respite that Mark needed. Dirk's full attention was on the stranded jacket and the rush and roar of water covered the noise of Mark's scrabbling feet and hands on the cliff.

He did not look down again until he had dragged himself fifty feet higher, and then he saw that the jacket had succeeded as a decoy. Dirk Courtney was a hundred feet downstream, standing on the lip of the first steep waterfall, on the very edge of the escarpment. He had the sodden jacket in his hands and he was peering over the fearsome drop. In the lantern light, the water was black and smooth as oil, as it streamed into the abyss, turning slowly to thick white spume as it fell.

Dirk Courtney threw the jacket out into black space and stood back from the drop. He settled down comfortably on his haunches, sheltered by the cliff from rain and wind, and quite calmly he selected and lit a cigar, like a workman taking a break after performing satisfactorily a difficult task.

That casual little act, the flare of a sulphur match, and the contented puff of blue tobacco smoke in the lantern light, probably saved Mark's life. It stoked his anger to the point when it could overcome his agony and bodily exhaustion. It provided him with the will to go on, and he began to climb again.

Sometimes during the climb, reality faded away from Mark. Once a sense of warmth and well-being began to suffuse his whole body, a wonderful feeling, floating as though on the very frontiers of sleep, but he caught himself before he fell, and deliberately punched his right hand against the rock face. He screamed with the pain of it, but with the pain came new resolve.

But resolve faded slowly in the cold and the pain, and fantasy grew again. He believed that he was one of King Chaka's chosen, following the old king up that terrible cliff to the summit of Chaka's Gate, and he found himself talking gibberish in broken Zulu, and in his head he heard the deep resonant voice of the old king calling him on, giving him encouragement, and he knew if he climbed faster he might catch a glimpse of the king's face. He lost his grip in his impatience, and slid away, gathering momentum down the incline, until he crashed into one of the stunted dwarf trees that grew from the cliff face. It broke his fall, but he screamed again at the pain of broken ribs.

He climbed on, and then he heard Storm's voice. It was so clear and close that he stopped, and turned his face up into the rain and darkness. She was there, floating above his head, so beautiful and pale and graceful.

'Come, Mark,' she said, and her voice echoed and rang like a silver bell in his head. 'Come, my darling.'

He knew then that she was alive, that she was not dying in a cold hospital bed, that she was here, come to him in his pain and exhaustion.

'Storm,' he cried, and threw himself upwards, falling forward, and lying face down in the short wet grass at the top of the cliff.

He just wanted to lie there, for ever. He was not even sure that he had reached the top, was not sure if this was not yet another fantasy, perhaps he was dead already and this was all there was to it.

Then slowly he was aware of the raindrops on his cheek, and the sound of the little tree frogs clinking in the rain, and the cold breath of the wind, and he realized with regret that he was still alive.

The pain began returning then. It started in his wrist first, and began to spread, and he did not think he had the strength left to ride it.

Then suddenly he had the image, clearly formed in his mind, of Dirk Courtney stooped over his father's body, with the club raised in his hand to strike – and Mark's anger came to save him again.

Mark pushed himself to his knees and looked about him. A hundred yards away, the truck was parked on the threshold of the iron bridge, and in its headlights, he could make out the shape of a man.

With one more huge, draining effort, Mark came to his feet, and stood swaying, gathering himself for his next lumbering step.

Peter Botes stood in the rain, holding the heavy pistol hanging in his right hand. The rain had soaked his fine sandy hair, and it ran down his cheeks and forehead, so he kept wiping it away with his left hand.

The rain had soaked through the shoulders of his overcoat also, and he shivered spasmodically, as much from fear as from cold.

He was caught up in the great swirl of events over which he had no control, an encircling web from which he could see no escape, even though his lawyer's mind twisted and turned.

'Accessory to murder – before and after the fact.' He did not want to know what was going on down there at the foot of the cliff, and yet he felt the sick fascination and dread of it.

This was not what he had imagined when he had made the decision to go to Dirk Courtney. He had thought it would be a few words, and he could walk away, pretending it had not happened, crawling back into his wife's warm bed and pulling the blankets over his head.

He had not been prepared for this horror and violence, for a gun in his hand, and this ugly bloody business in the gorge.

'The penalty is death,' he thought, and shivered again. He wanted to run, but there was no place to run now.

'Oh God, why did I do it?' he whispered aloud. 'I wish, oh God, I wish –' the age-old cry of the weakling, but he did not finish the wish. There was a sound behind him and he began to turn, lifting the pistol and beginning to point it with both arms at full stretch in front of him.

A figure came towards him out of the darkness, and Peter opened his mouth to cry out. The figure was an apparition of blood and mud, with a distorted pale face, and it came so swiftly that the cry never reached his lips.

Peter Botes was a man of words and ideas, a soft little man of desks and rich foods, and the man who came out of the darkness was a soldier.

Mark knelt over him in the mud, panting and holding his ribs, waiting for the pain of movement to recede, and for his starred vision to clear.

He looked down at the man under him. His face was pressed into the mud, and Mark took a handful of his hair and rolled the head on its narrow shoulders to prevent the man drowning; it was only then that Mark recognized him.

'Peter!' he whispered hoarsely, and felt his senses reel again, uncertain if this was another fantasy.

He touched the unconscious man's lips, and they were warm and soft as a girl's.

'Peter!' he repeated stupidly, and suddenly he knew it all. It did not have to be thought out a step at a time. He understood how Dirk Courtney had known where to set his ambush. He knew that Peter was the traitor, and he knew that the decoy had been Storm and baby John, he knew it was all a lie then. He knew that Storm and her child were safe and sleeping in the tiny bedroom above the beach – and the knowledge buoyed him.

He picked the Smith Wesson revolver out of the mud with his left hand and wiped it carefully on his shirt.

Dirk Courtney paused at the head of the pathway. He was only slightly breathless from the climb, but his boots were thick with mud and raindrops dewed his shoulders, glittering in the burning headlights of the truck.

The headlights dazzled him, and there was an area of unfathomable darkness behind them.

'Peter?' he called, and lifted one arm to shield his eyes. He saw the shadowy figure of the waiting man leaning against the cab of the truck, and he walked forward.

'It's done,' he said. 'You have nothing to worry about now. I have the key to the safe, it's just the cleaning up left to do.'

He stopped abruptly, and peered again at the waiting figure. The man had not moved.

'Peter,' his voice cracked. 'Come on, man! Pull yourself together. There is still work to do.'

And he started forward again, stepping out of the beam of the headlights.

'What time is it?' he asked. 'It must be getting late.'

'Yes.' Mark's voice was thick and slurred. 'For you, it's very late.' And Dirk stopped again, staring at him. The silence seemed to last for all of eternity, but it was only the instant that it took Dirk to see the revolver and the pale mud-smeared face. He knew that the bullet would come now, and he sought to delay it, just long enough.

'Listen to me,' said Dirk urgently. 'Wait just one second.'

He changed his grip on the lantern in his right hand, and his voice was compelling, the tone quick and persuasive, just enough to hold Mark's finger on the trigger.

'There is something you must know.' Dirk made a disarming gesture, swinging the lantern back, and then hurling it forward in a wide arc of his long powerful arm, and, at the same instant, hurling himself forward.

The lantern struck Mark on the shoulder, a glancing blow, just enough to deflect his gun hand as he fired.

But he heard the bullet strike, that muffled thumping sound of soft lead expanding into living flesh, and he heard the grunt of air driven forcibly from Dirk Courtney's lungs by the strike.

Then the man's big hard body crashed into Mark, and as they reeled sideways, supported by the chassis of the truck, he felt one arm lock around his chest and hard fingers close over his gun hand.

In that first moment of direct encounter, Mark knew instantly that Dirk Courtney's strength and weight were far greater than his own. Even if he had been uninjured, it would have been no contest, he was so out-matched that he felt as though he had been caught up in the cogs of a powerful piece of machinery. Dirk Courtney's body seemed not to be made of flesh and bone, but of brutal iron.

Mark's broken ribs moved in the vast encircling grip, and he cried out as the sharp edges of splintered bone lanced into his flesh. He felt his gun hand being forced back, the muzzle of the pistol training up into his own face, and Dirk Courtney swung him off his feet, both of them spinning into a turn like a pair of waltzing dancers, so that only the wildest effort and a lucky trick of balance allowed Mark to come down on his feet again. But now he no longer had the support of the truck chassis and the next effort would throw him headlong into the mud.

He felt Dirk Courtney gather himself for the next effort, the hard athlete's muscles moving him into perfect balance. Mark tried desperately to meet it, but it came with a smooth surge of power as irresistible as a huge comber rushing towards the beach. Then miraculously, at the moment when he was going, Mark felt the big body hit with a tremor, heard the sobbing outrush of Dirk Courtney's breath, and almost instantly Mark's stomach was drenched with a copious rush of warm liquid as it poured from his adversary.

The strength melted out of Dirk Courtney's body, Mark could feel his balance go, the grip on his pistol hand relaxed slightly – and Mark realized that his bullet had done damage, and that that last effort had torn something open in Dirk's chest. His life blood was expelled from the wound in thick hissing jets by the powerful pump of his heart, and Mark found he was able, by a supreme effort, to reverse the direction of the pistol barrel, swinging it in a slow arc back, back until pointed into Dirk Courtney's face.

Mark did not believe that he had the strength left to pull the trigger. The weapon seemed to fire of its own accord, and the muzzle flash almost blinded him.

Dirk Courtney's head snapped back as though he had been hit in the mouth with the full swing of a baseball bat. He was hurled backwards, out of the beam of the headlights into the darkness, and Mark heard his body sliding and tumbling down the steep side of the gorge.

The pistol dropped from Mark's hand, and he fell, first on to his knees, and then slowly toppled forward on to his face in the mud.

This is the last Will and Testament of SEAN COURTNEY, married out of community of property to RUTH COURTNEY, (formerly FRIEDMAN, born COHEN), and presently residing at Lion Kop Ranch in the district of Ladyburg.
.... *I give and bequeath my entire estate and effects, movable or immovable, whether in possession, reversion, expectancy or contingency, wherever situate and of whatever description nothing excepted, to my wife the said RUTH COURTNEY.*

At first light the next morning, Mark led the search party down the steep river banks. His right arm was in a sling, his ribs were strapped tightly under his shirt, and he hobbled painfully with his injuries.

They found Sean Courtney half a mile below the last cataract, where the Baboon Stroom debouched into the valley.

He lay on his back, and there was no blood, the waters had cleansed every drop of it, and even his wounds were clean and washed pale blue. Except for the dent in his temple, his features were almost unmarked, and the white bush of his beard had dried in the early morning sun. It curled proudly on his chest. He looked like a carved stone effigy of a medieval knight laid out with his armour and sword on a sarcophagus in the dim depths of an ancient cathedral.

In the event of my wife predeceasing me, or dying simultaneously, or within six months of each other —

The river had been kind and carried her down to the same sand-bank. She was lying face down, half buried in the soft white sand. One slim naked arm was outflung, and on the third finger was the simple band of bright gold. The fingers almost, but not quite, touched her husband's arm.

They buried them together, side by side, in the same deep excavation on the slope of the escarpment, a little way beyond the big house of Lion Kop.

.... I direct that the following shall apply in regard to the rest and residue of my estate.

There followed almost five hundred separate bequests which covered fifty pages, and totalled almost five millions of sterling. Sean Courtney had forgotten nobody. Beginning with the humblest grooms and domestic servants — enough for a piece of ground, a small herd, the equivalent of a life pension.

To those with a lifetime of service and loyalty, the gift was greater, in proportion.

To those who had laboured to build up the various prosperous companies and enterprises, there was a share of those companies, a large share.

He had not forgotten a single friend nor relative — not one of them.

I acknowledge that I have one legitimate man-child, though I hesitate to employ the word son — one DIRK COURTNEY, presently residing at Great Longwood in the district of Ladyburg. However, God or the devil has already provided for him so abundantly, that anything I could add would be superfluous. Therefore I leave him nothing — not even my blessing.

They buried Dirk Courtney in the pine forest, below the dog ring. No priest could be found to recite the office of burial, and the undertaker closed the grave under the curious eyes of a few members of the Press and a throng of sensation-seekers. Though there were many to stare, there was nobody to weep.

To my daughter STORM HUNT (born COURTNEY), who took lightly her filial duties, I, in turn, discharge my paternal duties with the bequest of a single guinea.

'He did not mean it,' Mark whispered to her. 'He was talking about you that night — as it happened, he was remembering you.'

'I had his love,' she said softly. 'Even though — at the end — he tried to deny it, I will have it always. That is riches enough. I don't need his money as well.'

To MARK ANDERS, for whom I have conceived the affection a man usually accords only to his natural son, I leave no money, as I am well aware of the contempt he holds for that commodity. I bequeath to him, in lieu of cash, all my books, paintings, guns, pistols and rifles, personal jewellery, and all my domestic animals, including dogs, horses and cattle.

The paintings in themselves made up a considerable fortune, and many of the books were unique in rarity and condition.

Mark sold only the cattle and the horses, for they were many and there was no place for them all in the tsetse-infested valley of the Bubezi.

The rest and residue of my Estate I bequeath to the said MARK ANDERS in his capacity as the Trustee of the Wild Life Protection Society. The bequest to be used to further the aims of the Society, particularly to the development and extension of the proclaimed lands presently known as Chaka's Gate, into a Wild Life Reservation.

'No one in Government will want to touch a Bill that was drawn up and piloted by the former Deputy Minister of Lands,' General Jannie Smuts prophesied to Mark, as they stood talking quietly together after the funeral. 'The man's name will leave a pungent stink on anything he ever touched. Political reputations are too fragile to risk like that – I foresee a stampede by the new Government to dissociate themselves from his memory. We can confidently expect a new Bill being introduced, confirming and upgrading the status of the proclaimed lands of Chaka's Gate, and I can assure you, my boy, that the Bill will have the full support of my party.'

As General Smuts had foreseen, the Bill passed through the House at the following Session, becoming law on 31st May 1926, as Act No. 56 of 1926 of the Parliament of the Union of South Africa. Five days later, the telegram from the Minister of Lands arrived at Ladyburg confirming Mark's appointment as first Warden of Chaka's Gate National Park.

There was no trial at which Hobday could turn king's evidence and claim immunity from the crime of murder; so at Hobday's own trial, the Public Prosecutor asked for the death sentence. In his summing up, the Chief Justice mentioned the evidence given by Sithole Zama, alias Pungushe. 'He made an excellent impression on this Court. His answers were clear and precise At no time did the defence shake his transparent honesty and powers of total recall.'

On Christmas Eve in the white-washed room at Pretoria Central Gaol, with his arms and legs pinioned by leather straps, and his head covered by a black cotton bag, Hobday dropped to eternity through the crashing wooden trap.

Peter Botes, cleared of any implication in the crimes of murder and attempted murder by the testimony of Mark Anders, was not placed on trial.

'His crimes were weakness and greed,' Mark tried to explain to Storm. 'If there were punishment for those, then there would be a gallows waiting for each of us. Besides, there has been enough vengeance and death already.'

Peter Botes left Ladyburg immediately after the hearings, and Mark never learned where he went or what became of him.

*　　*　　*

Now, when you cross the Bubezi River by the low concrete bridge, where Dirk Courtney's dam wall and hydro-electric station might have stood, you will come to the barrier on the far bank.

A Zulu ranger in smart suntans and a slouch hat will salute you, and give you a smile that sparkles like the Parks Board badge on his hat brim.

When you leave your vehicle and go into the office building of hewn stone and neat thatch to sign the register, look then to the left wall beyond the reception desk. In a glass case there is a permanent display of photographs and memorabilia from the park's early days. The centre-piece of this collection is a large photograph of a sprightly old gentleman, lean and tanned and tough as a strip of raw-hide, with a shock of pure white hair and a marvellous pair of spiky moustaches.

His cotton jacket is a little rumpled and fits him as though it was made for his elder brother, the knot of his tie has slipped down an inch and one tab of his shirt collar is slightly awry. Although his smile is impish, his jaw is firm and determined. However, it is the eyes that arrest attention. They are serene and direct, the eyes of a visionary or a prophet.

Under the photograph is the legend: 'Colonel Mark Anders, First Warden of Chaka's Gate National Park.' And below that again in smaller letters, 'Because of this man's energy and farsightedness, Chaka's Gate National Park has come down to posterity. Colonel Anders served on the Board of the National Parks Trust from its inception in 1926. In 1935, he was elected Chairman. He fought with distinction in two world wars, was severely wounded in one, and commanded his battalion in North Africa and Italy in the second. He is the author of many books on wildlife, including *Sanctuary* and *Vanishing Africa*. He has travelled the world to lecture and to gain support for the work of conservation. He has been honoured by monarchs and governments and universities.'

In the photograph, a tall slim woman stands beside the Colonel. Her hair is streaked with grey and drawn back severely from her face, and although there are crow's-feet at the corners of her eyes and deep lines around her mouth, yet they are the lines of laughter and the planes and angles of her face still show traces of what must once have been great beauty. She leans half protectively, half possessively against the Colonel's right arm and below the photograph the legend continues:

'His wife and life-long companion in his work was the internationally celebrated artist, who painted her memorable African landscapes and wildlife studies under her maiden name of Storm Courtney.

'In 1973, Colonel Anders retired from his position of Chairman of the Parks Board, and went with his lady to live in a cottage overlooking the sea at Umhlanga Rocks on the Natal Coast.'

When you have read the legend you may go back to your motorcar. The Zulu ranger will salute you again and raise the barrier. Then you too can go, for a short time, into Eden.

The Courtney Novels:

WHEN THE LION FEEDS

'Mr Smith is a natural story-teller . . .'
(The Scotsman)

THE SOUND OF THUNDER

'A violent sage-type story set in Boer War Africa and told with vigour and enthusiasm.'
(The London Standard)

A SPARROW FALLS

'He packs humanity into a bag already overflowing with adventure, excitement, and realism.'
(Yorkshire Post)

THE BURNING SHORE

'. . . Courage, drama, love and revenge on land, sea and in the air towards the end of the first world war are blended in fine style. Mr Smith's research into events and places is spot-on, as usual.'
(Bolton Evening News)

POWER OF THE SWORD

'. . . A stupendous story, written in the grand old manner, from the master of thoroughgoing adventure.'
(David Hughes, *The Mail on Sunday*)

Also by Wilbur Smith:

THE DARK OF THE SUN

'If the phrase "a man's book" has any meaning, it describes this powerful savage story.'
(Books & Bookmen)

SHOUT AT THE DEVIL

'A fast and thrilling adventure.'   *(Northern Echo)*

GOLD MINE

'. . . violent action and informed technical detail . . . Mr Smith is at his liveliest and best.'
(The London Standard)

THE DIAMOND HUNTERS

'A gem of a suspense/adventure novel.'   *(Mirror)*

THE SUNBIRD

'A splendid panoramic piece of writing, with colourful characters woven into an enthralling plot.'
(Oxford Times)

EAGLE IN THE SKY

'Wilbur Smith . . . rarely misses a trick . . . Terribly competent.'   *(Sunday Times)*

THE EYE OF THE TIGER

'... Supreme professionalism, vividness, and attention to detail.'

(*Sunday Express*)

CRY WOLF

'A rattling good adventure yarn ...'

(*The London Standard*)

HUNGRY AS THE SEA

'Hardly time to draw a breath. You can see at once why this is a bestseller.'

(*The London Standard*)

WILD JUSTICE

'... a gold-plated guarantee of pace, tension, and a thoroughly satisfying plot.'

(*Morning Telegraph*)